PENGUIN BOOKS

STRANGERS AND BROTHERS

VOLUME ONE

To Her
Who After The First Volume Was Part Of It
This Work
With Gratitude And Love

C. P. SNOW

STRANGERS

AND

BROTHERS

Volume One

Time of Hope (1914–33)
George Passant (1925–33)
The Conscience of the Rich (1927–37)
The Light and the Dark (1935–43)

PENGUIN BOOKS

Penguin Books Ltd, Harmondsworth, Middlesex, England
Penguin Books, 40 West 23rd Street, New York, New York 10010, U.S.A.
Penguin Books Australia Ltd, Ringwood, Victoria, Australia
Penguin Books Canada Ltd, 2801 John Street, Markham, Ontario, Canada L3R 1B4
Penguin Books (N.Z.) Ltd, 182–190 Wairau Road, Auckland 10, New Zealand

Reproduced, printed and bound in Great Britain by
Hazell Watson & Viney Limited,
Member of the BPCC Group,
Aylesbury, Bucks

CONTENTS

INDEX OF CHARACTERS

KEY

GODFREY AILWYN: Anglo-Catholic priest. Friend of Maurice Hollis. 11

VERA ALLEN: Secretary to Lewis Eliot in Whitehall. In love with Norman Lacey. 6, 7

SIR LAURENCE ASTILL: Scientist and member of Roger Quaife's advisory committee on nuclear armaments. 9

— BEDDOW: Member of the committee of the Technical College and School of Art, Labour councillor 2

TED BENSKIN: Leading counsel for Cora Ross. 10

GORDON BESTWICK: Cambridge undergraduate, friend of Charles Eliot. Involved in student protest. 11

HUMPHREY BEVILL: Son of Lord and Lady Boscastle. 4

THOMAS BEVILL: Second cousin of Lord Boscastle. M.P. and Minister responsible for the Atomic Energy Establishment at Barford. A predecessor of Roger Quaife. Shortly before death, goes to the House of Lords as Lord Grampound. 6, 7

BIDWELL: Servant at the Cambridge college, looks after Lewis Eliot and Roy Calvert. 4, 5

MYRA BOLT: Student at the university in the provincial town. Brought before the university's court for disciplinary action. Defended by Lewis Eliot. 10

LADY BOSCASTLE (Countess of): Wife of Lord Boscastle and mother of Humphrey Bevill. 4

LORD BOSCASTLE (Earl of): Brother of Lady Muriel Royce. Husband of Lady Boscastle and father of Humphrey Bevill. 4

CLIVE BOSANQUET: Leading prosecution counsel in the trial of Cora Ross and Kitty Pateman. 10

VISCOUNT BRIDGEWATER see SIR HORACE TIMBERLAKE

MICHAEL BRODZINSKI: Polish refugee scientist. Member of Roger Quaife's advisory committee on nuclear armaments and in favour of their manufacture. 9

ARTHUR BROWN: Fellow of the Cambridge college. Junior and later Senior Tutor. Elder statesman of college politics. 4, 5, 8, 11

IRENE BRUNSKILL see IRENE ELIOT

— CALVERT: Father of Roy Calvert. Owner of the local evening newspaper in the provincial town. 2

MURIEL CALVERT: Daughter of Rosalind and Roy Calvert. First wife of Pat Eliot: divorced. Reverted to maiden name. Mistress of Charles Eliot. 10, 11

OLIVE CALVERT: Cousin of Roy Calvert and a member of George Passant's group. Accused with George Passant and Jack Cotery of fraud. Mistress and later wife of Jack Cotery: divorced. Married Juckson-Smith. 2, 10

ROSALIND CALVERT see ROSALIND SCHIFF

ROY CALVERT: Friend of Lewis Eliot. Marries Rosalind Wykes. Brilliant oriental scholar and fellow of the Cambridge college. 1, 2, 4, 5

— CAMERON: Principal of the Technical College and School of Art. 2

MONTY CAVE: Conservative M.P., later Cabinet Minister. 9, 10

C. P. CHRYSTAL: Fellow of the Cambridge

PREFACE
TO THE OMNIBUS EDITION

THE sequence of novels called *Strangers and Brothers* was, from the beginning, conceived as one work: and, throughout the writing, it has been my hope that it would ultimately be read as one. As soon as I finished the last volume, I spent nearly a year producing a final recension designed for that purpose. This edition – granted the slips which are the chagrin of all writers – contains the text which I should like to be read. The arrangement of the volumes is different from that in which they have been separately published, and there is a fair amount of amendment both in structural detail and in words. I should prefer it if readers now forgot about the earlier text of the individual volumes, and accepted these. But, for anyone who is curious about the changes I have made, perhaps I should add a note.

I began by saying that *Strangers and Brothers* was conceived as one work. That is true, but it needs explaining. As I have written elsewhere, the conception came to me at a specific time – to be precise, on 1 January 1935, in Marseilles. The autobiographical history of the writing wouldn't be in place here: I shall probably include it in a collection of personal and literary pieces to be called *Private Affairs*. What may be in place here, though, is to qualify what the initial conception actually was.

It would be silly, and false, to leave the impression that the entire structure suddenly sprang into the light, clear in my mind, that evening. That would be demonstrably absurd, for a work intended to cover a large slice of a man's life, part of it stretching into the future. Even with that reserve, there is a danger that memory is liable to cheat, and to become altogether sharper and more codified than the original concept. To the best of my belief, however – and this is partially confirmed by notes and letters written shortly afterwards – I started with a defined idea of where I was going to end. In fact, no one would commit himself to this kind of project without a sense of the total shape. I also knew, in part in actualised novelist's terms, elsewhere more vague, some of the steps along the way – the first half of *Time of Hope*, the whole of *George Passant* (originally called by the series title) and *The Masters*, most of *The Conscience of the Rich*, the personal relations of *The New Men* (though not, of course, the scientific side, since I wasn't a prophet), and the germ of *The*

Sleep of Reason, which ran me into a lot of trouble later. So I had a tenuous intimation of the general curve. I also had, for that was implicit in the people and scenes I was imagining, a certainty of the major themes – in shorthand terms, possessive love, man-in-society (including politics, but somewhat more than that), man-alone. To me the first and third of those three carried the greatest emotional weight.

If one allows for the over-clarification of memory, that, or something like it, was the inception. Between the beginning and the end, I had naturally to let improvisation, chance and life play with me. This was a gamble. During the war, and in one or two physical accidents, it sometimes seemed a poor gamble. I hadn't for some years any assurance about how many volumes I should require for the complete structure. Five? Eight? Certainly I didn't warn publishers what I had in mind: I was more or less unknown, and it wouldn't have encouraged them. Recently an acquaintance, the former head of an English university, said that he remembered me saying, in Cambridge in the late thirties, that I was writing a nine-volume sequence. He didn't believe it, he now tells me. During the war, I was otherwise occupied, and for five years couldn't write at all. But I was able to brood, and by 1945 the scale of the sequence had pretty well settled itself.

The individual volumes were not published either in the order of writing, or in their proper place in the design. That was due to non-literary reasons, which are of no consequence to anyone but myself. I should like to think that, if they had appeared in the order I planned them (which was not always the order of writing), some of the thematic structure might have been more obvious. Anyway, the order of this edition is that in which they have existed in my mind. With one half-exception, and one note about a discarded volume.

The half-exception is that for some time I was undecided whether the sequence should begin with *George Passant* or *Time of Hope*. *George Passant* is, as it were, a long insert in *Time of Hope*. It has a significance in Lewis Eliot's experience which is eventually resolved in the final volumes. It caused me more difficulty to write than any of the others, except one. There were various drafts, four or five, all lost, and all much longer than the published version. I am now inclined to think that I cut it too much. The character of Arthur Morcom, for instance, was originally designed to foreshadow some aspects of Charles March and of Lewis Eliot himself: in the published text he plays a very minor part. Paring to the bone is usually a sign of lack of confidence, and this was probably a mistake. In the end, though the central figure of George Passant is something like what I intended, the volume doesn't throw all the shadows before it as it should, if it is to introduce the work. So I came to the decision that *Time of Hope* was the more natural and satisfactory beginning.

That has been the one major internal argument. There was a lesser one, half-way through, about the discarded volume. Lewis Eliot is sometimes thought of as a rational man. In fact, reason seems to him very weak as opposed to unreason. He is not romantic about unreason, though, and he knows from his own self-knowledge that the surface of human civility is very fragile. He doesn't believe for an instant that uncontrolled natural impulse leads men towards whatever hope there may be of the good. To him, reason is the only equipment, however poor, for exploring and coming to terms with the irrational. It was essential, accordingly, to represent somewhere in the sequence an extreme form of unreason. Right from the inception, there was to be a volume about utterly irrational actions, almost certainly a crime, human beings with the controls discarded, cut off, or nonexistent.

I made an attempt at this in the fifties. It was called 'The Devoted', and the central incident was a murder. By itself, it wasn't an entirely unsuccessful novel. But, in the sequence, it didn't do what was required of it. It was too neat, and too light-weight. As a result, I scrapped it (this sounds easy, but it wasn't quite so easy at the time) and set myself to wait for a while. I found something nearer what I was looking for in *The Sleep of Reason*. 'The Devoted' will not be published at any time in the future: it would now be a distraction from the rest of the work. I managed to use one or two episodes from it, and one character, in *The Sleep of Reason*.

The suppression of 'The Devoted' meant some changes in this final text. The intention underlying it, expressed in *The Sleep of Reason*, is hinted at in several of the volumes, and apart from minor adjustments there was nothing ill-fitting about that. But in the original text (compare *Homecomings*) there occur explicit references to what is clearly 'The Devoted' and to a story which is never told. Two people are introduced, Vera Allen and Norman Lacey, in order to be involved in that story as innocent participants in an extreme situation. In this recension the foreboding is removed, the story is no longer suggested and the characters' significance is diminished.

Changes of a similar form, though not so obvious, have been made at several points throughout the work. There were, not volumes completed and abandoned, like 'The Devoted', but possibilities which at one time or another attracted me. Preparations were laid down – fairly tentatively, since the possibilities hadn't crystallised – for some of these putative developments. I needn't specify these thoughts that came to nothing: they are now of no interest. I might mention, however, that for a while I seriously contemplated adding a twelfth volume, in which the theme of man-in-society was given another variation, this time showing the decline and loss of power in the ambience of industrial tycoons. It was partly for this reason that Sir Horace Timberlake and Lord Lufkin were drawn into the work. The possibility of this volume of decline had faded before I did much with them: it didn't seem to add enough which couldn't be shown implicitly. But it left certain emphases which, in the final text, have been diminished or wiped away.

At a more intimate level – that is, not of volumes but of individual people – there were characters whom I thought could be developed later in the work, whom I found it interesting to play round, and then, some-times reluctantly, left in their minor roles. Again, I won't specify many of these, though there are quite a number – Martineau was one, and Betty Vane another. This kind of intrusion of interest was, I think, bound to happen in a work stretching over a long period. Anyway, in the recension, certain pointers and promises have been eliminated, not drastically, but I hope enough.

Another much more prosaic and practical problem occurred because of the publication of the volumes as independent and self-sufficient novels. It seemed to me from the beginning, and still does, that there were only two ways open. Either one said that the volumes were unintelligible unless the reader is familiar with all that has gone before: or, alternatively, one used all appropriate means to make them effectively independent, or at the very least capable of being read on their own account. The latter choice was really the only one practicable, and I did what I could to meet the obligation. Within limits, I think I succeeded. Some of the volumes are more independent than others: but, until the final one, *Last Things*, I fancy any of them can be read, granted a degree of forbearance, as self-contained novels. This, however, meant, and couldn't help but mean, a certain amount of repetitive explanation (what was Lewis Eliot doing? where had he come from?) and, above all, of repetitive introduction of characters. In particular, a number of characters run through much of the work, not often in the foreground, but as plinths of continuity in the whole structure – such as Francis Getliffe, Martin Eliot, Arthur Brown, and (in the second half of the work) Hector Rose. In the original individual volumes, they had to be introduced afresh and in full each time.

In this edition, designed to be read as one, all of that would be irritating or worse, destructive of the unity of the whole. It has been eliminated, though a few devices for keeping memory alive are, as in any long work, occasionally necessary and have been quietly inserted. Apart from those, I have to assume that, with the work complete and seen as one, anyone who starts to read will have some idea of what he is in for, and won't need artificial props along the way.

That, as I said, was a practical adjustment: but there was another which I thought twice, or more than twice, before making. Lewis Eliot is describing events in his life, external and internal, over more than fifty years. During that time some of his attitudes change. That doesn't need saying: but they change in a not entirely orthodox fashion. He becomes, in middle age and later, less morally relativistic than as a young man. For the purposes of human behaviour, he finds that he has to make some assumptions *as if* they were fixed and true. This development, which is usually left implicit, but towards the end occasionally stated, is important to the essence of the work. He writes in his younger experience as though it had recently happened, through his young man's mind. After some hesitation, I thought that that immediacy wouldn't be affected if, on some significant occasions, I added comments in retrospect, made by his older self. These are intended to suggest the curve of change and also to help bind the work together.

Just as Eliot's attitude to moral experience changes, not dramatically but perceptibly, so does his attitude to individual people. He has learned more and seen more, but it isn't that his sympathies have widened (in some ways the reverse is true). It is more that his taste in personality has altered. It is unlikely, for instance, that as a young man he would have been deeply interested in someone like Hector Rose. On the other hand, when older, he becomes more easily tired of excessively fluid characters, such as Jack Cotery or Herbert Getliffe. At any time of his life, he would have recognised that George Passant was a person of unusual power and depth: but, of George Passant in particular, since he embodies one of the meanings of the whole work, it seemed desirable to see him through an old man's qualifications as well as the young one's enthusiasm.

The young one gives him a transcendent value. The old one, if he met George Passant for the first time, wouldn't. The old man wouldn't assume that he was wiser, just that these are the kind of judgments that differ qualitatively with age. The same would apply to other figures who capture Eliot's imagination in his youth, notably Roy Calvert. Not to Sheila, for he knows clearly enough that he surrounds her with the aura of romantic love. Since the major characters in *Strangers and Brothers* aren't symbols, but occupy some of the places that symbols might, I have in the final version included suggestions of how Lewis Eliot might reconsider them if he met them first at various stages of his life.

Finally the words of the text. This was the main objective of the recension, by far the most delicate part of the whole exercise, and the reason why it took so long. The writing of *Strangers and Brothers* extended over thirty-five years. In that kind of duration, the manner (or, if you like, the tone of voice, the rhythm, the predilection for individual words) in which anyone writes isn't likely to stay quite still. That happened with me. The effect was to an extent masked, because the volumes, as I mentioned before, weren't published in the order of writing, and because two or three of them were written simultaneously. But still it happened, and there were incongruities and disparities in language too marked to be acceptable in the final text. The counsel of perfection would be, of course, to write the whole thing again, in one continuous effort, from beginning to end. But that would be a somewhat fatuous counsel of perfection. There are a million and a half words in the sequence: to write a million and a half words would take three years, and once more one's language at the end wouldn't be quite the same as at the beginning.

It is apparent that one isn't going to achieve, there is no method of achieving, anything like uniformity of texture. Maybe it isn't worth wishing for. Anyway, it certainly isn't possible. The best one can do is to bring off a compromise. Line by line, one can eliminate tones and turns of phrase which jar. Inaccuracies can go, and bits of unsuitable rhetoric. In some volumes, individual words seem to have hypnotised me – as they do most writers. They have been grossly over-used, and sometimes shouldn't have been used at all. That can be dealt with. In one volume, I was overcome by a verbal extravagance, in particular an adverbial extravagance, which is entirely out of tune with anything I wrote before or since. That can be brought to order.

This verbal scrutiny was duly conducted. There haven't been many pages in any volume which were left untouched. As I have said, I can't pretend that the language of *Time of Hope* has been made indistinguishable from that of *Last Things*. The aim has been to see that the differences were unobtrusive, or in the nature of what happens with the passage of time.

A chronological note. The first words of *George Passant* were written in the summer of 1935. The last words of *Last Things* were written in January 1970. The recension of the text was carried out in 1970: a good deal of preparatory work had been done in 1967. I have written this preface in November 1971.

C.P.S.

Time of Hope

1914–33

CONTENTS

PART ONE. SON AND MOTHER

PART TWO. TOWARDS A GAMBLE

PART THREE. THE END OF INNOCENCE

Contents

PART FOUR. THE FIRST SURRENDER

PART FIVE. THE HARD WAY

PART SIX. A SINGLE ACT

PART SEVEN. THE DECISION

SON AND MOTHER

CHAPTER I

CHIME OF A CLOCK

THE midges were dancing over the water. Close to our hands the reeds were high and lush, and on the other side of the stream the bank ran up steeply, so that we seemed alone, alone in the hot, still, endless afternoon. We had been there all day, the whole party of us; the ground was littered with our picnic; now as the sun began to dip we had become quiet, for a party of children. We lay lazily, looking through the reeds at the glassy water. I stretched to pluck a blade of grass, the turf was rough and warm beneath the knees.

It was one of the long afternoons of childhood. I was nearly nine years old, and it was the June of 1914. It was an afternoon I should not have remembered, except for what happened to me on the way home.

It was getting late when we left the stream, climbed the bank, found ourselves back in the suburb, beside the tramlines. Down in the reeds we could make believe that we were isolated, camping in the wilds; but in fact, the tramlines ran by, parallel to the stream, for another mile. I went home alone, tired and happy after the day in the sun. I was not in a hurry, and walked along, basking in the warm evening. The scent of the lime trees hung over the suburban street; lights were coming on in some of the houses; the red brick of the new church was roseate in the sunset glow.

At the church the street forked; to the right past the butcher's, past a row of little houses whose front doors opened on to the pavement; to the left past the public library along the familiar road towards home. There were the houses with 'entries' leading to their back doors, and the neat, minute gardens in front. There was my aunt's house, with the BUILDER AND CONTRACTOR sign over the side gate. Then came ours: one of a pair, older than the rest of this road, three storeys instead of two, red brick like the church, shambling and in need of a coat of paint to cover the sun-blisters. Round the bend from the library I could already see the laburnum in the summer twilight. I was in sight of home. Then it happened.

Without warning, without any kind of reason, I was seized with a sense of overwhelming dread. I was terrified that some disaster was waiting for me. In an instant, dread had pounced on me out of the dark. I was too young to have any defences. I was a child, and all misery was eternal. I could not believe that this terror would pass.

Tired as I was, I began to run frantically home. I had to find out what the premonition meant. It seemed to have come from nowhere; I could not realise that there might be anxiety in the air at home, that I might have picked it up. Had I heard more than I knew? As I ran, as I left behind 'good nights' from neighbours watering their flowers, I felt nothing but terror. I thought that my mother must be dead.

When I arrived, all looked as it always did. From the road I could see there was no light in the front-room window; that was usual, until I got back home. I went in by the back door. The blinds were drawn in the other sitting-room, and a band of light shone into the back garden; in the kitchen there was a faint radiance from the gas mantle, ready for me to turn it up. My supper was waiting on the table. I rushed through the passage in search of my mother. I burst into the lighted sitting-room. There she was. I cried out with perfect relief.

She was embarrassed to see me. Her face was handsome, anxious, vain and imperious; that night her cheeks were flushed, her eyes bright and excited instead of, as I knew them best, keen, bold and troubled. She was sitting at a table with two women, friends of hers who came often to the house. On the table lay three rows of cards, face upwards, and one of my mother's friends had her finger pointing to the king of spades. But they were not playing a game – they were telling fortunes.

These séances happened whenever my mother could get her friends together. When these two, Maud and Cissie, came to tea, there would be whispers and glances of understanding. My mother would give me some pennies to buy sweets or a magazine, and they left to find a room by themselves. I was not told what they did there. My mother, proud in all ways, did not like me to know that she was extremely superstitious.

'Have you had your supper, dear?' she said that night. 'It's all ready for you on the table.'

'I'm just showing your mother some tricks,' said Maud, who was portly and good-natured.

'Never mind,' said my mother. 'You go and have your supper. Then it'll be your bed-time, won't it?'

But as a fact I had no particular 'bed-time'. My mother was capable but preoccupied, my father took it for granted that she was the stronger character and never made more than a comic pretence of interfering at home; I received nothing but kindness from them: they had large, vague hopes of me, but from a very early age I was left to do much as I wanted. So after I had finished supper I came back along the passage to the empty dark front room; from the other sitting-room gleamed a chink of light beneath the door, and the sound of whispers from my mother and her friends – their fortune-telling was always conducted in the lowest of voices.

I found some matches, climbed on the table, lit the gas lamp, then settled down to read. Since I had arrived at the house, found all serene, seen my mother, I was completely reassured. I was wrapped in the security of childhood. Just as the misery had been eternal, so was this. The dread had vanished. For those moments, which I remembered all my life, had already passed out of mind the day they happened. I curled up on the sofa and lost myself in *The Captain*.

I read on for some time. I was beginning to blink with sleepiness, the day's sun had made my forehead burn; perhaps I should soon have gone to bed. But then, through the open window, I heard a well-known voice.

'Lewis! What are you doing up at this time of night?'

It was my Aunt Milly, who lived two houses down the road. Her voice was always full and assertive; it swelled through any room; in any group, hers was the voice one heard.

'I never heard of such a thing,' said Aunt Milly from the street.

'Well, since you are up – instead of being in bed a couple of hours ago,' she added indignantly, 'you'd better let me in the front door.'

She followed me into the front room and looked down at me with hot-headed, vigorous reprobation.

'Boys of your age ought to be in bed by eight,' she said. 'No wonder you're tired in the morning.' I argued that I was not, but Aunt Milly did not listen.

'No wonder you're skinny,' she said. 'Boys of your age need to sleep the clock round. It's another thing that I shall have to speak to your mother about.'

Aunt Milly was my father's sister. She was a big woman, as tall as my mother and much more heavily built. She had a large, blunt, knobbly nose, and her eyes protruded: they were light blue, staring, and slightly puzzled. She wore her hair in a knob above the back of her head, which gave her a certain resemblance to Britannia. She had strong opinions on all subjects. She believed in speaking the truth, particularly when it was unpleasant.

She thought I was both spoilt and neglected, and was the only person who tried to govern my movements. She had no children of her own.

'Where is your mother?' said Aunt Milly. 'I came along to see her. I'm hoping that she might have something to tell me.'

She spoke in an accusing tone that I did not understand. I told her that mother was in the other room, busy with Maud and Cissie – 'playing cards,' I fabricated.

'Playing cards,' said Aunt Milly indignantly. 'I'd better see how much longer they think they're going on.'

Through two closed doors I heard Aunt Milly's voice, loud in altercation. I even caught some of her words: she was wondering how grown-up people could believe in such nonsense. Then followed a pause of quiet, in which I imagined my mother must be replying, though I could hear nothing. Then Aunt Milly again. Then a clash of doors, and Aunt Milly rejoined me.

'Playing cards!' she cried. 'I don't think much of cards, but I wouldn't say a word against it. If that was all it was!'

'Aunt Milly, you have—' I said, defending my mother. Aunt Milly had reproved her resonantly for suggesting whist last Boxing Day. I was going to remind her of it.

'Seeing the future!' said Aunt Milly with scorn, as though I had not made a sound. 'It's a pity she hasn't something better to do. No wonder things get left in this house. I suppose I oughtn't to tell you, but someone ought to be thinking of the future for your father and mother. I've said so often enough, but do you think they would listen?'

Outside, in the hall, my mother was saying goodbye to Maud and Cissie. The door swung slowly open and she entered the room. She entered very deliberately, with her head high and her feet turned out at each step; it was a carriage she used when she was calling up all her dignity. She had in fact great dignity, though she invented her own style for expressing it.

She did not speak until she had reached the middle of the room. She faced Aunt Milly, and said:

'Please to wait till we are alone, Milly. The next time you want to tell me what I ought to do, I'll thank you to keep quiet in front of visitors.'

They were both tall, they both had presence, they both had strong wills. They were in every other way unlike. My mother's thin beak of a nose contrasted itself to Aunt Milly's bulbous one. My mother's eyes were set deep in well-arched orbits, and were bold, grey, handsome and shrewd. Aunt Milly's were opaque and protruding. My mother was romantic, snobbish, perceptive and intensely proud. Aunt Milly was quite unself-conscious, a busybody, given to causes and good works, impervious to people, surprised and hurt when they resisted her proposals, but still continuing active, indelicate and undeterred. She had no vestige of humour at all. My mother had a good deal – but she showed none as she confronted Aunt Milly in front of the mantelpiece.

They had been much together since my parents' marriage. They maddened each other: they lived in a state of sustained mutual mis-understanding; but they never seemed able to keep long apart.

'Please to let my visitors come here in peace,' said my mother.

'Visitors!' said Aunt Milly. 'I've known Maud Taylor longer than you have. It's a pity she didn't get married when we did. No wonder she wants the cards to tell her that she's going to catch a husband after all.'

'When she's in my house, she's my visitor. I'll thank you not to thrust your opinions down her throat.'

'It's not my opinions,' said Aunt Milly, loudly even for her. 'It's nothing but common sense. Lena, you ought to be ashamed of yourself.'

'I'm not in the least ashamed of myself,' said my mother. She kept her haughtiness; but she would have liked to choose a different ground.

'Reading the cards and looking at each other's silly hands and – ' Aunt Milly paused triumphantly, ' – and gaping at some dirty tea-leaves. I've got no patience with you.'

'No one's asked you to have patience,' said my mother stiffly. 'If ever I ask you to join us, then's the time for you to grumble. Everyone's got a right to their own opinions.'

'Not if they're against common sense. Tea-leaves!' Aunt Milly snorted. 'In the twentieth century!' She brought out those last words like the ace of trumps.

My mother hesitated. She said:

'There's plenty we don't know yet.'

'We know as much as we want to about tea-leaves,' said Aunt Milly. She roared with laughter. It was her idea of a joke. She went on, ominously: 'Yes, there's plenty we don't know yet. That's why I can't understand how you've got time for this rubbish. One of the things we don't know is how you and Bertie and this boy here are going to live. There's plenty we don't know yet. I was telling the boy—'

'What have you told Lewis?' My mother was fierce and on the offensive again. When Aunt Milly had jostled her away from propriety and etiquette and made her justify her superstitions, she had been secretly abashed. Now she flared out with anxious authority.

9

'I told him that you've let things slide for long enough. No wonder you're seeing it all go from bad to worse. You never ought to have let—'

'Milly, you're not to talk in front of Lewis.'

'It won't hurt him. He's bound to know sooner or later.'

'That's as may be. I won't have you talk in front of Lewis.'

I knew by now that there was great trouble. I asked my mother:

'Please, what is the matter?'

'Don't you worry,' said my mother, her face lined with care, defiant, protective and loving. 'Perhaps it will blow over.'

'Your father's making a mess of things,' said Aunt Milly.

But my mother said: 'I tell you, you're not to talk in front of the child.'

She spoke with such quiet anger, such reserve of will, that even Aunt Milly flinched. Neither of them said another word for some moments, and one could hear the tick of the clock on the mantelpiece. I could not imagine what the trouble was, but it frightened me. I knew that I could not ask again. This time it was real; I could not run home and be reassured.

Just then the latch of the front door clicked, and my father came in. There was no mystery why he had been out of the house that night. He was an enthusiastic singer, and organised a local male-voice choir. It was a passion that absorbed many of his nights. He came in, batting short-sighted eyes in the bright room.

'We were talking about you, Bertie,' said Aunt Milly.

'I expect you were,' said my father. 'I expect I've done wrong as usual.'

His expression was mock-repentant. It was his manner to pretend to comic guilt, in order to exaggerate his already comic gentleness and lack of assertion. If there was clowning to be done, he could never resist it. He was a very small man, several inches shorter than his wife or sister. His head was disproportionately large, built on the same lines as Aunt Milly's but with finer features. His eyes popped out like hers, but, when he was not clowning, looked reflective, and usually happy and amused. Like his sister's his hair was on the light side of brown (my mother's was very dark), and he had a big, reddish, drooping moustache. His spectacles had a knack of running askew, above the level of one eye and below the other. Habitually he wore a bowler hat, and while grinning at his sister he placed it on the sideboard.

'I wish you'd show signs of ever doing anything,' said Aunt Milly.

'Don't set on the man as soon as he gets inside the door,' said my mother.

'I expect it, Lena. I expect it.' My father grinned. 'She always puts the blame on me. I have to bear it. I have to bear it.'

'I wish you'd stand up for yourself,' said my mother irritably.

My father looked somewhat pale. He had looked pale all that year, though even now his face was relaxed by the side of my mother's. And he made his inevitable comment when the clock struck the hour. It was a marble clock, presented to him by the choir when he had scored his tenth year as secretary. It had miniature Doric columns on each side of the face, and a deep reverberating chime. Each time my father heard it he made the same remark. Now it struck eleven.

'Solemn-faced clock,' said my father appreciatively. 'Solemn-toned clock.'

'Confound the clock,' said my mother with strain and bitterness.

As I lay awake in the attic, my face was hot against the pillow, hot with sunburn, hot with frightened thoughts. I had added some codicils to my prayers, but they did not ease me. I could not imagine what the trouble was.

CHAPTER II

MR ELIOT'S FIRST MATCH

FOR a fortnight I was told nothing. My mother was absent-minded with worry, but if she and my father were talking when I came in they would fall uncomfortably quiet. Aunt Milly was in the house more often than I had ever seen her; most nights after supper there boomed a vigorous voice from the street outside; whenever she arrived I was sent into the garden. I got used to it. Often I forgot altogether the anxiety in the house. I liked reading in the garden, which was several steps below the level of the yard; there was a patch of longish grass, bordered by a flower-bed, a rockery and some raspberry canes; I was specially fond of the trees – three pear trees by the side wall and two apple trees in the middle of the grass. I used to take out a deck-chair, sit under one of the apple trees, and read until the summer sky had darkened and I could only just make out the print on the shimmering page.

Then I would look up at the house. The sitting-room window was a square of light. Sometimes I felt anxious about what was being said in there.

Apart from those conferences, I did not see any change in the routine of our days.

I went as usual to school, and found my mother at midday silent and absorbed. My father went, also as usual, to his business. He took to any routine with his habitual mild cheerfulness, and even Aunt Milly could not complain of the hours he worked. We had a servant-girl of about sixteen, and my father got up when she did, in the early morning, had left for work long before I came down to breakfast, and did not return for his high tea until half-past six or seven.

For three years past he had been in business on his own. Previously he had been employed in a small boot factory; he had looked after the books, been a kind of utility man and second-in-command, and earned £250 a year. On that we had lived comfortably enough, servant-girl and all. But he knew the trade, he knew the profits, he reported that Mr Stapleton, his employer, was drawing twelve hundred a year out of the business. To both my parents, to Aunt Milly, to Aunt Milly's husband, that income seemed riches, almost unimaginable riches. My father thought vaguely that he would like to run his own factory. My mother urged him on. Aunt Milly prophesied that he would fail and reproached him for not having the enterprise to try.

My mother impelled him to it. She chafed against the limits of her sex. If she had been a man she would have driven ahead, she would have been a success. She lent him her savings, a hundred and fifty pounds or so. She helped borrow some more money. Aunt Milly, whose husband in a quiet inarticulate fashion was a good jobbing builder and appreciably more prosperous than we were, lent the rest. My father found himself in charge of a factory. It was very small. His total staff was never more than a dozen. But there he was, established on his own. There he had spent his long days for the past three years. At night I had often watched my mother look over the accounts, have an idea, ask why something had not been done, say that he ought to get a new traveller. That had not happened recently in my hearing, but my father was still spending his long days at the factory. He never referred to it as 'my business' or 'my factory' – always by a neutral, geographical term, 'Myrtle Road'.

One Friday night early in July my mother and father talked for a long time alone. When I came in from the garden I noticed that he was upset. 'Lena's got a headache. She's gone to bed,' he said. He gazed miserably at me, and I did not know what to say. Then, to my astonishment, he asked me to go with him to the county cricket match next day. I thought he had been going to tell me something painful: I did not understand it at all.

Myself, I went regularly to the 'county' whenever I could beg sixpence, but my father had not been to a cricket match in his life. And he said also that he would meet me outside the ground at half-past eleven. He was going to leave Myrtle Road early. That was also astonishing. Even for a singing practice, even to get back to an evening with a travel book, he had never left the factory before his fixed time. On Saturdays he always reached home at half-past one.

'We'll have the whole day at the match, shall we?' he said. 'We'll get our money's worth, shall we?'

His voice was flat, he could not even begin to clown.

Next morning, however, he was more himself. He liked going to new places; he never minded being innocent, not knowing his way about. 'Fancy!' he said, as he paid for us both and we pushed through the turnstiles. 'So that's where they play, is it?' But he was looking at the practice nets. He was quite unembarrassed as I led him to seats on the popular side, just by the edge of the sight screen.

Soon I had no time to attend to my father. I was immersed, tense with the breath-taking freshness of the first minutes of play. The wickets gleamed in the sun, the ball flashed, the batsmen played cautious strokes; I swallowed with excitement at each ball. I was a passionate partisan. Leicestershire were playing Sussex. For years I thought I remembered each detail of that day; I should have said that my father and I had watched the first balls of the Leicestershire innings. But my memory happened to have tricked me. Long afterwards I looked up the score. The match had begun on the Thursday, and Sussex had made over two hundred, and got two of our wickets for a few that night. Friday was washed out by rain, and we actually saw (despite my false remembrance) Leicestershire continue their innings.

All my being, soul included, was set on their getting a big score. And I was passionately partisan among the Leicestershire side itself. I had to find a hero. I had not so much choice as I should have had, if I had been luckier in my county; and I did not glow with many dashing vicarious triumphs. My hero was C. J. B. Wood. Even I, in disloyal moments, admitted that he was not so spectacular as Jessop or Tyldesley. But, I told myself, he was much sounder. In actual fact, my hero did not often let me down. On the occasions when he failed completely, I wanted to cry.

That morning he cost me a gasp of fright. He kept playing – I think it must have been Relf – with an awkward-looking, clumsy, stumbling shot that usually patted the ball safely to midoff. But once, as he did so, the ball found the edge of the bat and flew knee high between first and second slip. It was four all the way. People round me clapped and said fatuously: 'Pretty shot.' I was contemptuous of them and concerned for my hero, who was thoughtfully slapping the pitch with the back of his bat.

After a quarter of an hour I could relax a little. My father was watching with mild blue-eyed interest. Seeing that I was not leaning forward with such desperate concentration, he began asking questions.

'Lewis,' he said, 'do they have to be very strong to play this game?'

'Some batsmen,' I said confidently, having read a lot of misleading books, 'score all their runs by wristwork.' I demonstrated the principle of the leg-glance.

'Just turn their wrists, do they?' said my father. He studied the players in the field. 'But they seem to be pretty big chaps, most of these? Do they have to be big chaps?'

'Quaife is ever such a little man. Quaife of Warwickshire.'

'How little is he? Is he shorter than me?'

'Oh yes.'

I was not sure of the facts, but I knew that somehow the answer would please my father. He received it with obvious satisfaction.

He pursued his chain of thought.

'How old do they go on playing?'

'Very old,' I said.

'Older than me?'

My father was not yet forty, though to me he seemed old. I assured him that W. G. Grace went on playing till he was fifty-eight. My father smiled reflectively.

'How old can they be when they play for the first time? Who is the oldest man to play here for the first time?'

For all my Wisden, it was beyond me to tell him the record age of a first appearance in first-class cricket. I could only give my father general encouragement.

He was given to romantic day-dreams, and that morning he was indulging one of them. He was dreaming that all of a sudden he had become miraculously skilled at cricket; he was brought into the middle, everyone acclaimed him, he won instantaneous fame. It would not have done for the dream to be absolutely fantastic. It had to take him as he was, getting on for forty and five feet four in height. He would not imagine himself taken back to youth and transformed into a man strong, tall and glorious. No, he accepted himself in the flesh. He grinned at himself – and then dreamed about all that could happen.

For the same reason he read all the travel books he could lay his hands on. He went down the road to the library and came home with a new book about the headwaters of the Amazon. In his imagination he was still middle-aged, still uncomfortably short in the leg, but he was also paddling up the rain-forests where no white man had ever been.

I used, both at that age and when I was a little older, to pretend to myself that he read these books for the sake of knowledge. I liked to pretend that he was very learned about the tropics. But I knew it was not true. It hurt me, it hurt me with bitter twisted indignation, to hear Aunt Milly accuse him of being ineffectual, or my mother of being superstitious and a snob. It roused me to blind, savage, tearful love. It was a long time before I could harden myself to hear such things from her. Yet I could think them to myself and not be hurt at all.

My father treated me to ginger-beer and a pork pie in the lunch interval, and later we had some tea. Otherwise there was nothing to occupy him, after his romantic speculations had died down. He sat there patiently, peering at the game, not understanding it, not seeing the ball. I was not to know that he had a duty to perform.

After the last over the crowd round us drifted over the ground.

'Let's wait until they've gone,' said my father.

So we sat on the emptying ground. The pavilion windows glinted in the evening sun, and the scoreboard threw a shadow half way to the wicket.

'Lena thinks there's something I ought to tell you,' said my father.

I stared at him.

'I didn't want to tell you before. I was afraid it might spoil your day.'

He looked at me, and added:

'You see, Lewis, it isn't very good news.'

'Oh!' I cried.

My father pushed up his spectacles.

'Things aren't going very well at Myrtle Road. That's the trouble,' he said. 'I can't say things are going as we should like.'

'Why not?' I asked.

'Milly says that it's my fault,' said my father uncomplainingly. 'But I don't know about that.'

He began to talk about 'bigger people turning out a cheaper line'. Then he saw that he was puzzling me. 'Anyway,' he said, 'I'm afraid we may be done for. I may have to file my petition.'

The phrase sounded ominous, deadly ominous, to me, but I did not understand.

'That means,' said my father, 'that I'm afraid we shan't have much money to spare. I don't like to think that I can't find you a sovereign now and then, Lewis. I should like to give you a few sovereigns when you get a bit older.'

For a time, that explanation took the edge off my fears. But my father sat there without speaking again. The seats round us were all empty, we were alone on that side of the ground; scraps of paper blew along the grass. My father pulled his bowler hat down over his ears. At last he said, unwillingly:

'I suppose we've got to go home some time.'

The gates of the ground stood wide open, and we walked along the road, under the chestnut trees. Trams kept passing us, but my father was not inclined to take one. He was quiet, except that once he remarked:

'The trouble is, Lena takes it all to heart.'

He said it as though he was asking me for support.

As soon as he got inside the house and saw my mother, he said:

'Well, I've seen my first match! There can't be many people who haven't seen a cricket match until they're my age—'

'Bertie,' said my mother in a cold angry voice. Usually she let him display his simplicity, pretend to be simpler than he was. That night she could not bear it.

'You'd better have your supper,' she said. 'I expect Lewis can do with it.'

'I expect he can,' said my father. Nine times out of ten, for he never got tired of the same repartee, he would have said 'I expect I can too'. But he felt the weight of my mother's suffering.

We sat round the table in the kitchen. There was cold meat, cheese, a bowl of tinned pears, jam-tarts and a jug of cream.

'I don't suppose you've had much to eat all day,' said my mother. 'You'll want something now.'

My father munched away. I was ashamed to be so hungry, in sight of my mother's face that night, but I was famished. My mother said she had eaten, but it was more likely that she had no appetite for food. From the back kitchen (the house sprawled about without any plan) came the singing of a kettle on the stove.

'I'll have a cup of tea with you,' said my mother. Neither of them had spoken since we began the meal. As my father pushed up his moustache and took his first sip of tea, he remarked, as though casually:

'I did what you told me, Lena.'

'What, Bertie?'

'I told Lewis that we're worried about Myrtle Road.'

'Worried,' said my mother. 'I hope you told him more than that.'

'I did what you told me.'

'I'd have kept it from you if I could,' my mother said to me. 'But I wasn't going to have you hear it first from Aunt Milly or someone else. If you've got to hear it, I couldn't abide it coming from anybody else. It had to be from us.'

She had spoken with affection, but most of all with shame and bitter pride.

Yet she had not given up all hope. She was too active for that. The late sun streamed across the kitchen, and a patch of light, reflected from my mother's cup of tea, danced on the wall. She was sitting half-in, half-out of the shadow, and she seldom looked at my father as she spoke. She spoke in a tight voice, higher than usual but unbroken.

Most of it swept round me. All I gathered was the sound of calamity, pain, disgrace, threats to the three of us. The word 'petition' kept hissing in the room, and she spoke of someone called the 'receiver'. 'How long can we leave it before he's called in?' asked my mother urgently. My father did not know; he was not struggling as she was, he could not take her lead.

She still had plans for raising money. She was ready to borrow from the doctor, to sell her 'bits of jewellery', to go to a money lender. But she did not know enough. She had the spirit and the wits, but she had never had the chance to pick up the knowledge. Despite her courage, she was helpless and tied.

It seemed that Aunt Milly had offered help, had been the only relative to offer practical help. 'We're always being beholden to her,' said my mother. I was baffled, since I was used to taking it for granted that Aunt Milly was a natural enemy.

My father shook his head. He looked cowed, miserable, but calm.

'It's no good, Lena. It'll only make things worse.'

'You always give up,' cried my mother. 'You always have.'

'It's no good going on,' he said with a kind of obstinacy.

'You can say that,' she said with contempt. 'How do you think I'm going to live?'

'You needn't worry about that, Lena,' said my father, in a furtive attempt to comfort her. 'I ought to be able to find a job if you give me a bit of time. I'll bring home enough to keep you and Lewis.'

'Do you think that is worrying me?' my mother cried out.

'It's been worrying me,' said my father.

'We shall make do somehow. I'm not afraid of that,' said my mother. 'But I shall be ashamed to let people see me in the streets. I shan't be able to hold up my head.'

She spoke with an anguish that overawed my father. He sat humbly by, not daring to console her.

Watching their faces in the darkening kitchen, I craved for a distress that would equal my mother's. I was on the point of acting one, of imitating her suffering, so that she would forget it all and speak to me.

CHAPTER III

AN APPEARANCE AT CHURCH

THAT night, when I went to bed, I took the family dictionary with me. It was not long since I had discovered it, and already I liked not having to be importunate. Now I had a serious use for the dictionary. It was a time not to worry my mother: I had to be independent of her. Through the tiny window of the attic a stretch of sky shone faintly as I entered the room. I could see a few faint stars in the clear night. There was no other light in the attic, except a candle by my bed. I lit it, and before I undressed held the dictionary a foot away, found the word 'petition', tried to make sense of what the book said.

The breeze blew the candle wax into a runnel down one side, and I moulded it between my fingers. I repeated the definitions to myself, and compared them with what I remembered my father saying, but I was left more perplexed.

It was still the month of July when I knew that the trouble had swept upon us. My father's hours became more irregular; sometimes he stayed in the house in the morning and sometimes both he and my mother were out all day. It was on one of these occasions that Aunt Milly found me alone in the garden.

'I came to see what they were doing with you,' she said.

I had been playing French cricket with some of the neighbouring children. Now I was sitting in the deck-chair under my favourite apple tree. My aunt looked down at me critically.

'I hope they leave you something to eat,' she said.

Yes, I said, resenting her kindness. Then I offered her my chair: my mother had strong views on etiquette, some of them invented by herself. Aunt Milly rebuffed me.

'I'm old enough to stand,' she said. She stared at me with an expression that made me uncomfortable.

'Have they told you the news?' she asked.

I prevaricated. She cross-questioned me. I said, feeling wretched, that I knew there was trouble with my father's business.

'I don't believe you know. No wonder everything goes wrong in this house,' said Aunt Milly. 'I suppose I oughtn't to tell you, but it's better for you to hear it straight out.'

I wanted to beg her not to tell me; I looked up at her with fear and hatred.

Aunt Milly said firmly:

'Your father has gone bankrupt.'

I was silent. Aunt Milly stood, large, formidable, noisy, in the middle of the garden. In the sunlight her hair took on a sandy sheen. A bee buzzed among the flowers.

'Yes, Aunt Milly,' I said, 'I've heard about his – petition.'

Inexorably Aunt Milly went on:

'It means that he isn't able to pay his debts. He owes six hundred pounds – and I suppose I oughtn't to tell you, but he won't be able to pay more than two hundred.'

Those sounded great sums.

'When you grow up,' said Aunt Milly, 'you ought to feel obliged to pay every penny he owes. You ought to make a resolution now. You oughtn't to rest until you've got him discharged and your family can be honest and above board again. Your father will never be able to do it. He'll have his work cut out to earn your bread and butter.'

As a rule at that age I should have promised anything that was expected of me. But this time I did not speak.

'There won't be any money to send you to the secondary school,' said Aunt Milly. 'Your father wouldn't be able to manage the fees. But I've told your mother that we can see after that.'

I scarcely realised that Aunt Milly was being kind. I had no idea that she was being imaginative in thinking three years ahead. I hated her and I was hurt. Somewhere deep within the pain there was anger growing inside me. Yet, obeying my mother's regard for style, I produced a word or two of thanks.

'Mind you,' said Aunt Milly, 'you mustn't expect to run away with things at the secondary school. After all, it doesn't take much to be top of that old-fashioned place your mother sends you to. No wonder you seem bright among that lot. But you'll find it a different kettle of fish at a big school. I shouldn't wonder if you're no better than the average. Still, you'll have to do as well as you can.'

'I shall do well, Aunt Milly,' I said, bursting out from wretchedness. I said it politely, boastingly, confidently – and also with fury and extreme rudeness.

Just then my mother came down to join us. 'So you've got back, Lena,' said Aunt Milly.

'Yes, I've got back,' said my mother, in a brittle tone. She was pale and exhausted, and for once seemed spiritless. She asked Aunt Milly if she would like a cup of tea in the open air.

Aunt Milly said that she had been telling me that she would help with my education.

'It's very good of you, I'm sure, Milly,' said my mother, without a flicker of her usual pride. 'I shouldn't like Lewis not to have his chance.'

'Aunt Milly doesn't think I shall do well at the secondary school,' I broke in. 'I've told her that I shall.'

My mother gave a faint grin, wan but amused. She must have been able to imagine the conversation; and, that afternoon of all afternoons, it heartened her to hear me brag.

Aunt Milly did not exhort my mother, and did not find it necessary to tell her any home truths. Aunt Milly, in fact, made a galumphing attempt to distract my mother's mind by saying that the news looked bad but that she did not believe for a single instant in the possibility of war.

'After all,' she said, 'it's the twentieth century.'

My mother sipped her tea. She was too tired to be drawn. Often they quarrelled on these subjects, as on all others: Aunt Milly was an enthusiastic liberal, my mother a patriotic, jingoistic, true-blue conservative.

Aunt Milly tried to cheer her up. Many people were asking after her, said Aunt Milly.

'I'm sure they are,' said my mother, with bitter self-consciousness.

Some of her women friends at the church were anxious to call on her, Aunt Milly continued.

'I don't want to see any of them,' said my mother. 'I want to be left alone, Milly. Please to keep them away.'

For several days my mother did not go outside the house. She had collapsed in a helpless, petrified, silent gloom. She could not bear the sight of her neighbours' eyes. She could guess only too acutely what they were saying, and she was seared by each turn of her imagination. She knew they thought that she was vain and haughty, and that she put on airs. Now they had her at their mercy. She even put off her fortune-telling friends from their weekly conclave. She was too far gone to seek such hope.

I went about quietly, as though she were ill. In fact she was often ill; for, despite her vigour and strength of will, her zest in anything she did, her dignified confidence that, through the grand scale of her nature, she could expect always to take the lead – despite all the power of her personality, she could never trust her nerves. She had much stamina – in the long run she was tough in body as well as in spirit – but some of my earliest recollections were of her darkened bedroom, a brittle voice, a cup of tea on a little table in the twilight, a faint aroma of brandy in the air.

She never drank, except in those periods of nervous exhaustion, but in my childish memory that smell lingered, partly because of the heights of denunciation to which it raised Aunt Milly.

After the bankruptcy, my mother hid away from anything they were saying about us. She was not ill so much as limp and heartbrokenly despondent. It was a week before she took herself in hand.

She came down to breakfast on the first Sunday in August (it was actually Sunday, 3 August 1914). She carried her head high, and her eyes were bold.

'Bertie,' she said to my father, 'I shall go to church this morning.'

'Well, I declare,' said my father.

'I want you to come with me, dear,' my mother said to me. She took it for granted that my father did not attend church.

It was a blazing hot August morning, and I tried to beg myself off.

'No, Lewis,' she said in her most masterful tone. 'I want you to come with me. I intend to show them that they can say what they like. I'm not going to demean myself by taking any notice.'

'You might leave it a week or two, Lena,' suggested my father mildly.

'If I don't go today, people might think we had something to be ashamed of,' said my mother, without logic but with some magnificence.

She had made her decision on her way down to breakfast, and, buoyed up by defiance and the thought of action, she looked a different woman. Almost with exhilaration, she went back to the bedroom to put on her best dress, and when she came down again she wheeled round before me in a movement that was, at the same time, stately and coquettishly vain.

'Does mother look nice?' she said. 'Will you be proud of me? Shall I do?'

Her dress was cream-coloured, with leg-of-mutton sleeves and an hour-glass waist. She picked up the skirt now and then, for she took pleasure in her ankles. She was putting on a large straw hat and admiring herself in the mirror over the sideboard, when the church bell began to ring. 'We're coming,' said my mother, as the bell clanged on insistently. 'There's no need to ring. We're coming.'

She was excited, flushed and handsome. She gave me the prayer books to carry, opened a white parasol, stepped out into the brilliant street. She walked with the slow, stylised step that had become first nature to her in moments of extreme dignity. She took my hand: her fingers were trembling.

Outside the church we met several neighbours, who said 'Good morning, Mrs Eliot'. My mother replied in a full, an almost patronising tone, 'Good morning Mrs——' (Corby or Berry or Goodman, the familiar names of the suburb). There was not time to stop and talk, for the bell was ringing twice as fast, in its final agitated minute.

My mother swept down the aisle, me behind her, to her usual seat. The church, as I have said, was quite new. It was panelled in pitch-pine, and had chairs, painted a startling yellow, instead of pews; but already the more important members of the parish, led by the doctor and his sister, had staked out their places, which were left empty at any service to which they did not come. My mother had not been far behind. She had established her right to three seats, just behind the churchwardens'. One was always empty, since my father was obstinately determined never to enter the church.

To the right of the altar stood a small organ with very bright blue pipes. They were vibrating with the last notes of the 'voluntary' as my mother knelt on the hassock before her chair. The windows were polychromatic with new stained glass, and the bright morning light was diffused and curiously coloured before it got inside.

The service began. Usually it was a source of interest, of slightly shocking interest, to my mother, for the vicar was an earnest ritualist, and she was constantly ou edge to see how 'high' he would dare to go. 'He's higher than I ever thought,' she would say, and the word 'higher' was isolated in a hushed, shocked, thrilling voice. My mother was religious as well as superstitious, romantic and nostalgic as well as a snob; and she had a pious tenderness and veneration for the old church where she had worshipped as a child, the grey gothic, the comely, even ritual of the broad church. She was disappointed in this new edifice, and somehow expressed her piety in her Sunday-by-Sunday scrutiny of the vicar's progress away from all she loved.

At that morning service, however, she was too much occupied to notice the vicar's vestments. She believed that everyone was watching her. She could not forget herself, and, if she prayed at all, it was for the effrontery to carry it off. She had still to meet the congregation coming out after service. That was the time, each Sunday, when my mother and her acquaintances exchanged gossip. In the churchyard they met and lingered before going off to their Sunday meals, and they created there a kind of village centre. It was that assembly my mother had come out to face.

She chanted the responses and psalms, sang the hymns, so that all those round could hear her. She sat with her head back through the sermon, in which the vicar warned us in an aside that we ought to be prepared for grave events. But it was no more than an aside: to most people there, not only to my mother, the 'failure' of Mr Eliot was something more interesting to talk about than the prospect of a war. Their country had been at peace so long: even when they thought, they could not imagine what a war might mean, or that their lives would change.

The vicar made his dedication to the Trinity, the after-sermon hymn blared out, my mother sang clearly, the sidesmen went round with the collection bags. When the sidesman came to our row, my mother slipped me sixpence, and herself put in half a crown, holding the bag for several instants and dropping the coin from on high. Those near us could see what she had done. It was a gesture of sheer extravagance. In the ordinary way she gave a shilling night and morning, and Aunt Milly told her that that was more than she could afford.

At last came the benediction. My mother rose from her knees, pulled on her long white gloves, and took my hand in a tight grip. Then she went deliberately past the font towards the door. Outside, in the churchyard, the sunlight was dazzling. People were standing about on the gravel paths. There was not a cloud in the sky.

The first person to speak to my mother was very kind. She was the wife of one of the local tradesmen.

'I'm sorry you've had a bit of trouble,' she said. 'Never mind, my dear. Worse things happen at sea.'

I knew that her voice was kind. Yet my mother's mouth was working – she was, in fact, at once disarmed by kindness. She only managed to mutter a word or two of thanks.

Another woman was coming our way. At the sight of her my mother's neck stiffened. She called on all her will and pride, and her mouth became firm. Indeed, she put on a smile of greeting, a distinctly sarcastic smile.

'Mrs Eliot, I was wondering whether you will be able to take your meeting this year.'

'I hope I shall, Mrs Lewin,' said my mother with condescension. 'I shouldn't like to upset your arrangements.'

'I know you're having your difficulties—'

'I don't see what that has to do with it, Mrs Lewin. I've promised to take a meeting as usual, I think. Please to tell Mrs Hughes [the vicar's wife] that you needn't worry to find anyone else.'

My mother's eyes were bright and bold. Now that the first test was over, she was keyed up by the ordeal. She walked about the churchyard, pointing her toes, pointing also her parasol; she took the initiative, and herself spoke to everyone she knew. She had specially elaborate manners for use on state occasions, and she used them now.

Her hand was still quivering and had become very hot against mine, but she outfaced them all. No one dared to confront her with a direct reference to the bankruptcy, though one woman, apparently more in curiosity than malice, asked how my father was.

'Mr Eliot has never had much wrong with his health, I'm glad to say,' my mother replied.

'Is he at home?'

'Certainly,' my mother said. 'He's spending a nice quiet morning with his books.'

'What will he do now – in the way of work, Mrs Eliot?'

My mother stared down at her questioner.

'He's considering,' said my mother, with such authority that the other woman could not meet her glance. 'He's weighing up the pros and cons. He's going to do the best for himself.'

CHAPTER IV

MY MOTHER'S HOPES

AT home my mother could not rest until my father got a job. She pored with anxious concentration through the advertisement columns of the local papers; she humbled herself and went to ask the advice of the vicar and the doctor. But my father was out of work for several weeks. His acquaintances in the boot and shoe trade were, so he tried to apologise, 'drawing in their horns' because of the war. The hours of that sunlit August were burning away; somehow my mother spared me sixpence on Saturdays to go to the county; the matches went on, the crowds sat there, though outside the ground flared great placards that often I did not understand. The one word MOBILISATION stood blackly out, on a morning just after my father's bankruptcy; it puzzled me as 'petition' had done, and carried a heavier threat than to my elders.

It was not till the end of August that my father's case was published. He had gone bankrupt to the amount of six hundred pounds; his chief creditors were various leather merchants and Aunt Milly's husband; he was paying eight shillings in the pound. That news was tucked away in the local papers on a night when the British Army was still going back from Mons. For all her patriotism, my mother wished in an agony of pride and passion that a catastrophe might devour us all – her neighbours, the town, the whole country – so that in wreckage, ruin and disaster her disgrace would just be swept away.

October came, the flag-pins on my mother's newspaper map were ceasing to move much day by day, before my father got a job. He returned home one evening and whispered to my mother. He was looking subdued; and, for the first time, I saw her shed a tear. It was not in gratitude or relief; it was a tear so bitterly forced out that I was terrified of some new and paralysing danger. All this time I had had a fear, acute but never mentioned, that my father might have to go to prison. Perhaps this infected me because my mother had warned me, one evening when we were having tea alone, that he must never contract a debt, and that we had from now on always to take care that we paid in the shop for every single article we bought. As I saw the tears in my mother's eyes, the harsh grimace that she made, I was terrified that he might have forgotten. I was surprised to hear my mother say, in a dull and toneless voice:

'Father will be going to work next week, dear.'

I heard the details from Aunt Milly, when she next came into our house.

'Well, your father's got a job,' she said.

'Yes, Aunt Milly.'

'I can't see him doing much good as a traveller. If they say no, he'll just grin and go away. No wonder they're only paying him enough to keep body and soul together.'

My father's former employer, always known as 'Mr Stapleton', had persuaded a leather merchant to take him on as traveller, so that he could go the rounds of his old competitors.

'I suppose I oughtn't to tell you,' said Aunt Milly, 'but they're giving him three pounds a week. I don't know how you're going to manage. Of course, it's better than nothing. I suppose he wouldn't get more anywhere else.'

It must have been almost exactly that time when my mother realised that she was pregnant again. I knew nothing of it; I saw that she was ill, and moved slowly, but I was used to her being ill; I knew nothing of it, all through that winter and spring, but I knew that she was constantly needing to talk to me.

I used to arrive back from school on an autumn afternoon and find her sitting by the fire in the front room. Outside, the rain fell gently in the wistful dusk, and the flames of the blazing coal began to be reflected in the window-panes. My tea was ready, a good tea, for our standard of eating had not been much reduced; we did not have so much meat, we had to go without the occasional 'bird' which had once given my mother a lively social pleasure, but she would have still felt it beneath her to provide me with margarine instead of butter. So I tucked into my boiled egg, had some rounds of bread and butter and jam, finished off with a piece of home-made cake. There was no Vera to take away the tea-things, but we left them on the table, for Aunt Milly used to send her own maid round for an hour in the morning and an hour at night.

My mother liked to wait until it was quite dark before we lit the gas and drew the blinds, so that we sat and watched the lavish, glowing fire. In one of the lumps of coal, remote from the red-hot centre, a jet of gas would catch alight and make my mother exclaim with pleasure; she used to want me to imagine the same pictures in the fire.

On those afternoons, as we sat in the dark, the fire casting a flickering glow upon the ceiling, my mother talked to me about the hopes of her youth, her family, her snobbish ambitions, her feeling for my father, her need that I should rectify all that had gone wrong in her life.

The child she was carrying – of which I was innocently ignorant, although she turned to me with an insistence I had never seen before – was to her a mistake, unwanted, conceived after a nine years' interval in defeat and bitterness of heart. Possibly she had never loved my father, though for a long time she must have felt an indulgent half-amused affection for his good nature, his amiable mildness, his singular lack of self-regard. Although she was realistic in her fashion, she may have had her surprises; for he was one of those little men who, unassertive in everything else, are anything but unassertive in their hunger for women. That would have made her love him more, if she had loved him at all. But, without love, with only a shaky affection to rest on, it meant that she was always on the fringe of feeling something like contempt. After failing, after exposing her to a humiliation which she could not forgive, he had lost nothing of his ardour – he had given her another child. She told me, much later, that it was done against her will. It rankled to the depth of her proud soul.

'I married the wrong man,' said my mother as we sat by the fire. She said it with naked intensity. She was nearly forty; and she could scarcely believe that all she longed for as a girl should have come to this.

Her hopes had been brilliant. She had a romantic, surging, passionate imagination, even then, when a middle-aged woman beaten down by misfortune. As a girl she had expected – expected as of right – a husband who would give her love and luxury and state. She thought of herself in her girlhood, and as she spoke to me she magnified the past, enhanced all that she could glory in, cherished her life with her own family now that she looked back with an experienced and a disappointed heart.

Her family had been different in a good many ways from my father's. The Eliots, apart from my father, who was unlike the rest, were an intelligent, capable lot without much sensitivity or intuition, whose intelligence was usually higher than their worldly sense; they were a typical artisan, lower-middle-class family thrown up in their present form by the industrial revolution, who should, but for a certain obtuseness, have done much better for themselves. My grandfather Eliot, my father's and Aunt Milly's father, was a man of force and intellect, who had mastered the nineteenth-century artisan culture, who knew his 'penny magazines' backwards, read Bradlaugh and William Morris, picked up some mathematics at a mechanics' institute. He had died early in the year of my father's bankruptcy. He had never climbed farther than maintenance foreman at the local tramway depot.

He had quarrelled with my mother whenever they argued, for he was a serious nineteenth-century agnostic, she devout; he voted radical and she was a vehement tory; and they were both strong characters. Their temperaments clashed, my mother had no more in common with him than with his daughter Milly; and my mother's family, and all the background of her childhood, had roots quite different from theirs.

Her family, unlike the Eliots, had never lived in the little industrial towns that proliferated in the nineteenth century, the Redditches and Walsalls where my grandfather had spent his early years. My mother's family had had nothing to do with factories and machines; they were still living, those that were left, in an older, agricultural, more feudal England, in the market towns of Lincolnshire or, as gamekeepers and superior servants and the like, on the big estates. They were not more prosperous than the Eliots, as my mother admitted. She was entirely truthful and had a penetrating regard for fact, despite her nostalgia and imagination. She did not even allow herself to pretend, although she would have dearly loved to, that they were noticeably more genteel. No, she told me the truth, though she had a knack of making it shimmer a little at the edges. Her father's name was Sercombe, and he had been employed, like his father and grandfather before him, in the grounds of Burghley Park: to my mother, for ever after, that mansion signified the height of all worldly ambition. The Sercombe men often ran true to a physical type. Like my mother, they were dark as gypsies; they were dashing, physically active, fond of the open air, naturally good at games but too careless to learn them properly, gay, completely unbookish – men who loved all the joys of young manhood and were lost when youth ended. Almost all were born with an air of command, and stood out in a crowd. They won much love from women, but had not as a rule the steadiness or warmth of nature to make them good friends to other men. Sometimes they used their boldness, dash and charm to marry above themselves.

It was these marriages that gave my mother her best chance to stick to the truth, and yet to glorify it. Her own father had married as his second wife someone from a Stamford family which had known better days. My mother was a child of that second marriage; and in her girlhood there were Wigmore cousins, who lived in solid middle-class comfort, who had a 'position' in the town and with whom occasionally she was invited to stay. Those visits stayed in her mind with a miraculous radiance. To me, to herself, she could not help embellishing the wonder. She did not know that she was romanticising – for to her nothing could be more romantic than those visits in girlhood, when she felt transported to her own proper place, when she dreamed of love and marriage, when she dreamed that one day she would find her way to her proper place again.

She could never quite convey the marvel of those Wigmore households. The skating in the bitter winter of 1894, when she was nineteen! The braziers on the ice, a handsome cousin teaching her to cut figures (my mother, like her Sercombe brothers, was adept at dancing and games), music afterwards in the drawing-room! The gigs clattering up the street to her cousin's office – he was a solicitor – and the clients having a glass of sherry at eleven in the morning! How he drove out to 'late dinner' with one or two of the minor gentry! The young officers at a new year's ball! The hushed confidences afterwards with the other girls!

'You never know what's going to happen to you,' said my mother, with the curious realistic humour that came out when one least expected it. 'I didn't bargain on finding myself here.'

Often she felt that she had been deprived of her birthright. She did not ask for pity, she was sarcastic and angry in her frustration, and would have answered with pride if anyone condoled too facilely. She wanted it taken for granted that life had not dealt with her in a fitting fashion; that she was cut out to remain in the houses of those elysian visits; that she was not designed to stay among the humble of the world. And, with her romantic, surging, passionate spirit she believed – in the midst of heartbreak and disgrace – that there was still time for her luck to change.

I was marked out as the instrument of fortune. Since the bankruptcy, she had invested all her hopes in me. She thought that I was clever; she believed that I was bone of her bone, with the same will and the same pride.

'I want you to remember,' said my mother, as the flames danced on the ceiling, 'that you haven't got to stay in this road. I want you not to be content with anything you can find round here. I expect big things from you, dear.'

She looked at me with her keen, luminous eyes.

'You're not the sort of boy to be satisfied, are you, Lewis? You're like me in that. Remember, I've seen the things that would just suit your lordship. Please to remember that. I don't want you to be satisfied until you've got there.'

My mother was thinking still of a solicitor's house in Stamford, with the carriages outside, snug and prosperous at the turn of the century – but all seen through the lens of her brilliant imagination.

'You're not going to sit down and let them do what they like with you, are you, dear? I know you. You're going to have your own way. You needn't look as though butter wouldn't melt in your mouth. Your eyes are a lot too sharp. You've just come out of the knife-box, haven't you?'

She grinned. I always enjoyed her mocking, observant grin. Then she spoke with passion again:

'I want to live long enough to see you get there, Lewis. You'll take me with you, won't you? You'll want me to share it, won't you? Remember, I know all about you. I know just what you want. You're not going to be satisfied until you've done everything I've told you, are you, my son?'

I was quick to say yes, to weave fantasies with her, to build houses and furnish them and give her motor cars and furs. Already I loved to compete, I revelled in her pictures of success. Yet I was not easy with her that evening. I was not often easy with my mother.

She meant much to me, much more than any other human being. It was her anxiety and pain that I most dreaded. I always felt threatened by her illnesses. I waited on her, I asked many times a day how she was; and, when in the dark room I heard her answer 'not very well, dear', I wanted to reproach her for being ill, for making the days heavy, for worrying me so much. It was her death that I feared as the ultimate gulf of disaster. She meant far more to me than my father; yet with him I never felt a minute's awkwardness. He was amiable, absorbed in his own daydreams; he liked me to give him a kind of reassurance, and otherwise made no claims. He did not invade my feelings, and only wished for a response that it was innate in me to give, to him and to others, and which I began giving almost as soon as I could talk.

For I was not shy with people. Apart from Aunt Milly, whom at times I hated, I liked those I came into contact with; I liked pleasing them and seeing them pleased. And I liked being praised, and at that age I was eager to have my own say, show off, cut a dash. I had nothing to check my spontaneity, and, despite the calamities of my parents, I was very happy.

I could make the response that others wished for, except to my mother. I was less spontaneous with her than with anyone else, either at this time or later in my boyhood. It was long before I tried to understand it. She needed me more than any of the others needed me. She needed me with all the power of her nature – and she was built to a larger scale than the other figures of my childhood. Built to a larger scale, for all her frailties; most of those frailties I did not see when I was a child; when I did see them, I knew that I too was frail. She needed me. She needed me as an adult man, her son, her like, her equal. She made her demands: without knowing it, I resisted. All I knew was that, sitting with her by the fire or at her bedside when she was ill, my quick light speech fled from me. I was often curt, as I should never have been to a stranger. I was often hard. Yet, away from her presence, I used to pray elaborately and passionately that she might become well, be happy, and gain all her desires. Of all the prayers of my childhood, those were the ones that I urged most desperately to God.

CHAPTER V

A TEN-SHILLING NOTE IN FRONT OF THE CLASS

WHEN I was eleven, it was time that I was sent to the secondary school, if ever I were to go. There was no free place open for me, since my mother had not budged from her determination not to let me enter a council school. The fees at the secondary school were three guineas a term.

My mother sat at the table, moistening a pencil against her lip, writing down the household expenses in a bold heavy hand; she kept the bills on a skewer, and none of the shopkeepers was allowed to wait an hour for his money; she had developed an obsession, almost an obsession in the technical sense, about debt. My father's salary had only gone up by ten shillings a week since the war began. It was now 1917, the cost of living was climbing, and my mother was poor to an extent she had never known. Later I believed that she welcomed rationing and all the privations of war, because they helped to conceal what we had really come to.

She could invent no way of squeezing another nine guineas out of her budget. She had to turn it into shillings a week, for those were the terms in which she was continually thinking. 'Three and eightpence about, it comes out to,' she said. 'I can't manage it, Lewis. It means cutting out the Hearts of Oak, and then I don't know what would happen to us if Bertie goes. And there will be other things to pay for beside your fees. There'll be your cap, and you'll want a schoolbag and – I don't know. I'm not going to have you suffer by the side of the other boys.'

My mother submerged her pride, as she could just bring herself to do for my sake, and went to remind Aunt Milly of her promise to pay for my schooling. Aunt Milly promptly redeemed it. Her husband was doing modestly well out of the war, and with the obscure comradeship that linked her to my mother she was concerned about each new sign of penury. But Aunt Milly found it hard to understand the etiquette my mother had elaborated for herself or borrowed from the shabby genteel. My mother would accept the loan of the maid, or 'presents', or 'treats' at my aunt's house; she would have accepted more if Aunt Milly had been careful, but she could not take blunt outright undisguised charity. This 'bit of begging' – as she called it – for my fees was the first she had descended to since she was faced with the expenses of my brother Martin's birth and her illness afterwards. Those would have crippled us entirely, and she let Aunt Milly pay.

Aunt Milly even spared my mother any exhortation when she agreed to find my fees. She saved that for me an hour or two later. She was never worried about repeating herself, and so she gave me the same warning as on the afternoon of my father's bankruptcy, three years before. I was not to expect success. It was likely that I should have a most undistinguished career at this new school.

'You've got too good an opinion of yourself,' said Aunt Milly firmly and enthusiastically, with her usual lack of facial expression. 'I don't blame you for it altogether. It's your mother's fault for letting you think you're something out of the ordinary. No wonder you're getting too big for your boots.'

To the best of Aunt Milly's belief, I should find myself behind all other boys of my age. I should, in all probability, find it impossible to catch up. Aunt Milly would consider that her money had been well invested if I contrived to scrape through my years at school without drawing unfavourable attention to myself. And once more I was to listen to her message. My first duty, if ever my education provided me with a livelihood, was to save enough money to pay twenty shillings in the pound on my father's liabilities, and so get him discharged from bank-ruptcy.

I was practised in listening silently to Aunt Milly. Sometimes she discouraged me, but for most purposes I had toughened my skin. My skin was not, however, tough enough for an incident which took place in my first term at the new school.

Several of the boys there knew that my father had 'failed in business'. They came from the same part of the town, they had heard it gossiped about; my father might have passed unnoticed, but my mother was a conspicuous figure in the parish. One of them twitted me with it, saying each time he saw me, 'Why did your dad go bust?' in the nagging, inde-fatigable, imbecile, repetitious fashion of very small boys. I flushed at first, but soon got used to him, and it did not hurt me much.

Curiously enough, until the incident of the subscription list, I was more embarrassed by the notoriety of no less a person than Aunt Milly. Her vigour in the cause of temperance was well known all over the town. During the summer she had organised a vast teetotal procession through the streets: it consisted of carts in which each of the Rechabite tents staged its own tableau, usually of an historical nature and in fancy dress, followed by the Templar lodges on foot and carrying banners. My aunt, and the other high officers, made up the end of the procession; wearing their 'regalia' of red, blue, or green, according to the order, with various signs of rank, something like horses' halters round their necks, they sat on small chairs on a very large cart.

Like all Aunt Milly's activities, the procession had been organised with extraordinary thoroughness and staff-officer precision. But some of my form-mates who had seen it – perhaps some had even taken part – dis-covered that she was my aunt and decided that to have such an aunt was preposterously funny. I then found out that shame is an unpredictable thing. For I should have said that I could take any conceivable joke against Aunt Milly without a pang: in fact, I was painfully ashamed.

The incident of the subscription list took place in November, a couple of months after I first attended the school. Each boy in each form had been asked to make a donation to the school munitions fund. The headmaster had explained how, if we could give only sixpence, we should be doing our bit; all the money would go straight to buy shells for what the headmaster called 'the 1918 offensive – the next big push'.

I reported it all to my mother. I asked her what we could afford to give.

'We can't afford much really, dear,' said my mother, looking upset, preoccupied, wounded. 'We haven't got much to spare at the end of the week. I know that you've got to give something.'

It added to her worries. As she had said before, she was not going 'to have me suffer by the side of the other boys'.

'How much do you think they'll give, Lewis?' she enquired. 'I mean, the boys from nice homes.'

I made some discreet investigations, and told her that most of my form would be giving half a crown or five shillings.

She pursed her lips.

'You needn't bother yourself, dear,' she said. 'I'm not going to have you feel out of it. We can do as well as other people.'

She was not content with doing 'as well as other people'. Her imagination had been fired. She wanted me to give more than anyone in the form. She told herself that it would establish a position for me, it would give me a good start. She liked to feel that we could 'still show we were someone'. And she was patriotic and war-like, and had a strong sense of war-time duty; though most of all she wanted me to win favour and notice, she also got satisfaction from 'buying shells', from taking part in the war at second-hand.

She skimped my father's food and her own, particularly hers, for several weeks. After a day or two my father noticed, and mildly grumbled. He asked if the rations were reduced so low as this. No, said my mother, she was saving up for the subscription list at school.

'I hope you don't have many subscriptions,' said my father to me. 'Or I expect she'll starve me to death.'

He clowned away, pretending that his trousers had inches to spare round his middle.

'Don't be such a donkey, Bertie,' said my mother irritably.

She kept to her intention. They went without the small luxuries that she had managed to preserve, through war, through the slow grind of growing poverty – the glass of stout on Saturday night, the supper of fish and chips (fetched, for propriety's sake, by Aunt Milly's maid), the jam at breakfast. On the morning when we had to deliver our subscriptions, my mother handed me a new ten-shilling note. I exclaimed with delight and pressed the crisp paper against the tablecloth. I had never had one in my possession before.

'Not many of them will do better than that,' said my mother contentedly. 'Remember that before the war I should have given you a sovereign. I want you to show them that we've still got our heads above water.'

Under the gaslight, in the early morning, the shadow of my cup was blue on the white cloth. I admired the ten-shilling note, I admired the blue shadows, I watched the shadows of my own hands. I was thanking my mother: I was flooded with happiness and triumph.

'I shall want to hear everything they say,' said my mother. 'They'll be a bit flabbergasted, won't they? They won't expect anyone to give what you're giving. Please to remember everything they say.'

I was lit up with anticipation as the tramcar clanged and swayed into the town. Mist hung over the county ground, softened the red brick of the little houses by the jail: in the mist – not fog, but the clean autumnal mist – the red brick, though softened, seemed at moments to leap freshly on the eye. It was a morning nostalgic, tangy and full of well-being.

In the playground, when we went out for the eleven-o'clock break, the sun was shining. Our subscriptions were to be collected immediately afterwards: as the bell jangled, my companions and I made our way chattering through the press of boys to the room where we spent most of our lessons.

Mr Peck came in. He taught us algebra and geometry; he was a man about fifty-five who had spent his whole life at the school; he was bald, fresh-skinned, small-featured, constantly smiling. He lived in the next suburb beyond ours, and occasionally he was sitting in the tramcar when I got on.

Some boy had written a facetious word on the blackboard. Peck smiled deprecatingly, a little threateningly, and rubbed out the chalkmarks. He turned to us, still smiling.

'Well,' he said, 'the first item on the programme is to see how much this form is going to contribute to make the world safe for democracy.' There was a titter; he had won his place long ago as a humorist.

'If any lad gives enough,' he said, 'I dare say we shall be prepared to let him off all penalties for the rest of the term. That is known as saving your bacon.'

Another titter.

'Well,' he went on, 'I don't suppose for a moment that you want to turn what you are pleased to call your minds to the problems of elementary geometry. However, it is my unfortunate duty to make you do so without unnecessary delay. So we will dispose of this financial tribute as soon as we decently can. I will call out your names from the register. Each lad will stand up to answer his name, announce his widow's mite, and bring the cash up here for me to receive. Then the last on the list can add up the total and sign it, so as to certify that I haven't run away with the money.'

Peck smiled more broadly, and we all grinned in return. He began to read out the names. The new boys were divided into forms by alphabetical order, and ours ran from A to H.

'Adnitt.' 'Two shillings, sir.' The routine began, Adnitt walked to the front of the class and put his money on the desk. I was cherishing my note under the lid of the desk; my heart thudded with joyful excitement. 'Aldwinckle.' 'Two and sixpence.' 'Brookman.' 'Nothing.'

Brookman was a surly, untidy boy, who lived in the town's one genuine slum. Peck stared at him, still smiling. 'You're not interested in our little efforts, my friend?' said Peck.

Brookman did not reply. Peck stared at him, began another question, then shrugged his shoulders and passed on.

'Buckley.' 'A shilling.' 'Cann.' 'Five shillings.' The form cheerfully applauded. 'Coe.' 'A shilling.' 'Cotery.' 'Three shillings and two pence.' There was laughter; Jack Cotery was an original; one could trust him not to behave like anyone else. 'Dawson.' 'Half a crown.' There were several other D's, all giving between a shilling and three shillings. 'Eames.' 'Five shillings.' Applause. 'Edridge.' 'Five shillings.' Applause. My name came next. As soon as Peck called it out, I was on my feet. 'Ten shillings, sir.' I could not damp a little stress upon the ten. The class stamped their feet, as I went between the desks and laid the note among the coins in front of Peck.

I had just laid the note down, when Peck said:

'That's quite a lot of money, friend Eliot.' I smiled at him, full of pleasure, utterly unguarded; but at his next remark the smile froze behind my lips and eyes.

'I wonder you can afford it,' said Peck. 'I wonder you don't feel obliged to put it by towards your father's debts.'

It was cruel, casual and motiveless. It was a motiveless malice as terrifying for a child to know as his first knowledge of adult lust. It ravaged me with sickening shameful agony – and, more violently, I was shaken with anger, so that I was on the point of seizing the note and tearing it in pieces before his eyes.

'Let me give you a piece of advice, my friend,' said Peck, complacently. 'It will be to your own advantage in the long run. You're a bright lad, aren't you? I'm thinking of your future, you know. That's why I'm giving you a piece of advice. It isn't the showy things that are most difficult to do, Eliot. It's just plodding away and doing your duty and never getting thanked for it – that's the test for bright lads like you. You just bear my words in mind.'

Somewhere in the back of consciousness I knew that the class had been joining in with sycophantic giggles. As I turned and met their eyes on my way back, they were a little quieter. But they giggled again when Peck said:

'Well, I shall soon have to follow my own advice and plod away and do my duty and never get thanked for it – by teaching a class of dolts some geometrical propositions they won't manage to get into their thick heads as long as they live. But I must finish the collection first. All contributions thankfully received. 'Fingleton.' 'Two shillings, sir.' 'Frere.' 'A shilling.'

I watched and listened through a sheen of rage and misery.

At the end of the morning, Jack Cotery spoke to me in the playground. He was a lively, active boy, short but muscular, with the eyes of a comedian, large, humorous, and sad.

'Don't mind about Pecky,' he said with good nature and without care. 'I don't mind a scrap.'

'You were as white as a sheet. I thought you were going to howl.'

I did not swear as some of the boys in the form habitually did; I had been too finically brought up. But at that moment all my pain, anger and temper exploded in a screaming oath.

Jack Cotery was taken aback. 'Keep your shirt on,' he said.

On the way to the tram stop, where we travelled in different directions, he could not resist asking me: 'Is you old man in debt, really?'

'In a way,' I said, trying to shield the facts, not to tell an actual lie – wanting both to mystify and to hide my own misery. 'In a way. It's all very complicated, it's a matter of – petitions.' I added, as impressively as I could, 'It's been in the solicitor's hands.'

'I'm glad mine's all right,' said Jack Cotery, impressive in his turn. 'Of course, I could have brought a lot more money this morning. My old man is making plenty, though he doesn't always let on. He'd have given me a *pound* if I'd asked him. But' – Jack Cotery whispered and his eyes glowed – 'I'm keeping it in reserve for something else.'

When I arrived home, my mother was waiting for me with an eager question.

'What did they think of your subscription, dear?'

'All right,' I said.

'Did anyone give more than ten shillings?'

'No. Not in our form.'

My mother drew herself up and nodded her head: 'Was ours the highest?'

'Oh yes.'

'What was the next highest?'

'Five shillings,' I said.

'Twice as much,' said my mother, smiling and gratified. But she was perceptive; she had an inkling of something wrong.

"What did they *say*, though, dear?'

'They thanked me, of course.'

'Who was the master who took it?' she asked.

'Mr Peck.'

'Was he pleased with you?'

'Of course he was,' I said flatly.

'I want to hear everything he said,' said my mother, half in vanity, half trying to reach my trouble.

'I can't now, Mother. I want to get back early. I'll tell you everything tonight.'

'I don't think that's very grateful of you,' said my mother. 'Considering what I did to find you all that money. Don't you think I deserve to be told all about it now?'

'I'll tell you everything tonight.'

'Please not to worry yourself if it's too much trouble,' she said haughtily, feeling that I was denying her love.

'It's not too much trouble, Mother. I'll tell you tonight,' I said, not knowing which way to turn.

I did not go straight home from school that evening. Instead, I walked by myself a long way round by the canal; the mist was rising, as fresh and clean as that morning's mist; but as it swirled round the bridges and warehouses and the trees by the waterside, it no longer exalted me. I was inventing a story, walking that long way home through the mist, which would content my mother. Of how Mr Peck had said my contribution was an example to the form, of how he had told other masters, of how someone said that my parents were public-spirited. I composed suitable speeches. I had enough sense of reality to make them sound plausible, and to add one or two disparaging remarks from envious form-mates.

I duly repeated that fiction to my mother. Nothing could remove her disappointment. She had thought me inconsiderate and heartless, and now, if she believed at all, she felt puzzled, cast-off and only a little flattered. I thought that I was romancing simply to save her from a bitter degradation. Yet I should have brought her more love if I had told her the truth. It would have been more loving to let her take an equal share in that day's suffering. That lie showed the flaw between us.

There were nights that autumn, however, when my mother and I were closer than we had ever been. They were the nights when she tried to learn French. She saw me with my first French grammar, and she was seized with a desire to follow my lessons. French to her was romantic, genteel, emblem and symbol of the existence she had so much coveted. Her bold, handsome eyes were bright each time we spread the books on the front-room table. Her health was getting worse, she was having frightening fits of giddiness, but her interest and nervous gusto and hope pressed her on as when she was a girl.

'Time for my French lesson,' she said eagerly when Saturday evening came round. We started after tea and she was downcast if I would not persevere for a couple of hours. Often on those Saturday nights the autumn gales lashed rain against the windows; to that accompaniment, my mother tried to repeat my secondary school phonetics.

Actually, she found my attempts to retail the phonetic lessons quite impossible to imitate. She learned entirely by eye, and was comfortable when she could pronounce the words exactly as in English. But she learned quickly and accurately by eye, as I did myself. Soon she could translate the simple sentences in my reader. It gave her a transfiguring pleasure; she held my hand, and translated one sentence after another. 'Is that right? Is that right?' she cried wildly and happily, and laughed at me. 'You're not ashamed of your pupil, are you, dear?'

CHAPTER VI

THE FIRST START

I BURIED deep the claims my mother made of me and which I could not meet. I could forget them more easily because, in my successes at school, I provided her, for the only time for years, with something actual for her hopes to feed on. She still read the cards and teacups, she had taken to entering for several competitions a week in *Answers* and *John Bull*; but when she studied my end-of-term reports, she felt this was her solitary promise for the future. As soon as she had received one and read it through, she put it in her bag, changed into her best dress, and, pointing her toes, set off in dignity for Aunt Milly, the doctor and the vicar.

When I took the Senior Oxford, I gave her something more to flaunt. My last term at school was over and I waited for the result. It was the brilliant summer of 1921, and one night I came home after baking all day at the county ground. As I came up our street in the hot and thundery evening, I saw my mother and brother waving to me from the window.

My mother opened the door herself. She was displaying the evening paper. She looked flushed and well, her eyes were flashing, although she had had a heart attack that summer.

'Do you know, dear?' she cried.

'No. Is it—?'

'Then let me be the first to congratulate you,' she said with a grand gesture. 'You couldn't have done better. It's impossible for you to have done better!'

It was her way, her romantic and superb way, of saying that my name appeared in the first class. She was exultant. My name was alone! – she was light-headed with triumph. I was recklessly joyful myself, but each time I caught my mother's eye I felt I had never seen such triumph. She had none of the depression, or the drop into anti-climax that chases after a success; she had looked forward to this moment, one of many moments to come, and her spirit was strong enough to exult without a single qualm.

My mother at once sent my young brother out for foods that we could not usually afford. She intended to have a glorious supper – not that she could eat much nowadays, but for the sake of style and for my sake. My father had, a year past, ceased to be a traveller and had moved back to 'Mr Stapleton's' as a cashier at four pounds a week. He was competent at paper-work, but my mother ground the aching tooth and told herself that it was shameful to return to such a job in a place where he had once been second-in-command, that the job was just a bone thrown in contemptuous friendliness and charity. Thus, with the fall in the value of money, our meals were not as lavish as they had been even immediately after my father's bankruptcy. Even so, my mother never lost her taste for the extravagant. She still paid each bill on Saturday morning; but if luxuries were required for a state occasion, such as that night, luxuries were bought, though it meant going hungry for the rest of the week.

That night we ate a melon and some boiled salmon and éclairs and meringues and mille feuilles. My mother's triumph would have been increased if she could have had Aunt Milly there to gloat over; but she could not have Aunt Milly as well as a glass of wine, and my mother's sense of fitness would not be satisfied without wine on the table; she wanted to fill the wine-glasses which she had received as a wedding present and which were not used more than once a year. So young Martin had been sent on another errand to the grocer, and the glasses were filled with tawny port.

My father, who had changed not at all in the last seven years, kept saying, 'Well, I didn't pass the examination. But I can dispose of the supper as well as anyone,' and ate away with his usual mild but hearty content. My mother was too borne up to say more than, 'Bertie, don't be such a donkey'. She took her share of the meal, which nowadays she rarely did, and several glasses of wine. More than once she put up her spectacles to her long-sighted eyes and read the announcement again. 'No one in the same division!' she cried. 'It will give them all something to think about!' She decided that she must have two dozen copies of the paper to send to friends and relatives, and ordered Martin to make sure and go to the newsagents first thing next morning.

My mother talked to me across the supper-table.

'I always told you to make your way,' she said. The room was gilded in the sunset, and she raised a hand to shield her eyes. 'I want you to remember that. No one else told you that, did they?'

She was illuminated with triumph and her glasses of wine, but she asked insistently.

'No,' I said.

'No one else at all, did they?'

'Of course not, Mother,' I said.

'I don't expect you to be satisfied now,' she said. 'There's a lot to do. You've got a long way to go. You remember all you've promised me, don't you?'

It turned out, almost at once, very easy not to be satisfied. For I was faced with the choice of my first job. When the examination result came out, I had actually left school, although we had put off the question of my job. And now my mother and I conferred. What was I to do? We had no one to give us accurate information, let alone advice. No boy at the school had ever taken a scholarship to the university; those masters who had degrees had taken them externally through London and Dublin. None of them knew his way about. One or two, wanting to help me, suggested that I might stay at school and then go to a teacher's training college. It meant real hardship to my mother unless I earned some money at once; not that she would have minded such hardship – she would have cherished it, if her imagination had been caught – but she resented stinting us all for years so that I might in the end become an elementary school teacher.

My mother found no more help in the parish. This was the *vie de province*, the life of an unnoticed and suburban province. The new vicar, though even 'higher', was less cultivated than the old one. The doctor had lived in the district all his life, except when he was struggling his way through a London hospital and the conjoint; from his excessive awe at my passing an examination, I suspected that he had had trouble with his own. He knew the parish house by house, person by person, but he was quite ignorant of the world outside. He could suggest nothing for me. Perhaps he was anxious to take no responsibility, for my mother, given the slightest lead, would not have refused to let him set me going. My mother had always believed that if I showed promise Dr Francis would interest himself practically in my career. But Dr Francis was a wary old man.

Aunt Milly took it into her head that I ought to become an engineer. She first of all pointed out that, though I might have done better than anyone from the local schools, no doubt plenty of boys in other places had achieved the same result. Then, in her energetic fashion, she went off, without getting my mother's agreement or mine, and plunged into discussions with some of her father's acquaintances at the tram depot. She obtained some opinions which later I realised were entirely sensible. It would be necessary for me to become a trade apprentice: that meant five years on the shop-floor, and working at the technical college at night; it would be easy to get taken as an apprentice by one of the town's big engineering firms. Aunt Milly produced these views with vigorous satisfaction. She felt, as usual, confident that she had done the right thing and that this was the only conceivable course for me. She overlooked two factors. One, that my mother was shocked, not only in her nerves, but deeper, by the thought that I should become for years what seemed to her nothing but a manual worker. Two, that there was almost no occupation which I should have liked less or been more completely unfitted for. Aunt Milly left the house in a huff, and it was apparent that we could expect no further aid from her.

That aggravated our distress, for up to now my mother had always known that she had Aunt Milly as an ultimate reserve, in the very long run. It was only a few days afterwards, when I had begun answering advertisements in the local paper, that I received a letter from my headmaster. If I was not fitted with what he called a 'post', would I go to see him? At once my mother's romantic hope surged up. Perhaps the school had some funds to give me a grant, perhaps after all they would manage to send me to a university – for, learning from the handbooks on careers that I had discovered, my mother now saw a university as our Promised Land.

In brutal fact, the offer was a different one. The education office in the town hall had asked the school to recommend someone as a junior clerk. It was the kind of job much coveted among my companions – the headmaster was giving me first refusal, as a kind of prize. The pay was a pound a week until seventeen and then went up by five shillings a week each year, until one reached three pounds, the top of the scale. It was a perfectly safe job; there were prospects of going reasonably high in the local government offices, perhaps to a divisional chief at £450 a year. There was, of course, a pension. The headmaster strongly advised me to take it. He had himself begun as an elementary schoolteacher in the town, had acquired a Dublin degree, and when our school had been promoted to secondary status he had had his one great piece of luck. He was a full-blooded and virile man, but he was hardened to his pupils having to cut down their expectations.

I thanked him, and took the job. There seemed nothing else to do.

When I told my mother her face on the instant was open with disappointment.

'Oh,' she said. Then she added, trying to make her voice come full and unconcerned: 'Well, dear, it's better than nothing.'

'Oh yes,' I said.

'It's better than nothing,' said my mother. She was recovering herself. It was only another of her many disappointments. They had taught her to be stoical. And she still kept, which was part of her stoicism, her unquenched appetite for the future; for an appetite for the future was, with her, another name for hope.

She enquired about the job, the work, where it would lead. She liked the phrase 'local government'; she would use that to the doctor and the vicar, for it took some of the chill away, it made my doings seem much grander.

'How do you feel about it, dear?' she asked, after she had been imagining how I could turn it all to profit.

'It's better than nothing.' With a sarcastic flick, I returned her phrase.

'You know I only want the best for you,' she said.

'Of course I know.'

'We can't have everything. I haven't had everything I should like, have I? You'll manage as well as you can, won't you?'

'Of course.'

She looked at me with trouble in her eyes, with guilt and with reproach.

'There's still time if you can see anything else to do, dear. Please to tell me. Please – if there's any mortal person I can talk to for you—'

'It's all right, Mother,' I said, and let it stop at that.

My feelings were mixed. I was, in part, relieved and glad, absurd though it seemed only a few months later; but I was glad to be earning a living, and to know that next week I should have a little money in my pocket. I was nearly sixteen, it was irksome to be so often without a shilling, and that trivial relief lightened me more than I could believe.

I disliked the sound of the job – I felt it was nothing like good enough. Yet I was interested, just as I was in any new prospect or change. I had spasms of rancour that I had been so helpless. If I had known more, if I had moved among different people, I could have looked after myself and this would never have happened. But that rancour was not going to cripple me. I was not a good son to my mother, but I was very much her son: I had the same surgent hope. Other disasters might wound me beyond repair, but not anything like this, not anything outside myself that I could learn to master. I knew, with the certainty that comes when one is in touch with a deep part of one's nature, that this setback was not going to matter much. My hope was like my mother's, but more stubborn and untiring. I believed I could find a way out.

CHAPTER VII

THE EFFECT OF A FEUD

AUNT MILLY was violently opposed to my 'white-collar job'. 'That's all it is,' said Aunt Milly in her loudest voice to my mother. 'He's just going off to be a wretched little clerk in a white-collar job. I never did believe all that people told me about your son, but he seems to have more brains than some of them. Now he's content to go off to the first white-collar job he sees. Don't complain to me when he finds himself in the same office when he's forty. No wonder they say that the present generation hasn't got a scrap of enterprise.'

My mother recounted the scene, and her own dignified retort, with the humorous haughty expression that she wore when she had been most upset. For, particularly as the months went on, and I had been catching the eight-forty tram for a year, for a year and a half, she wondered painfully if we had made a mistake. She was a little better off, since I paid her ten shillings a week for my keep – but she could not see any sign of the dramatic transformation scene she had always longed for, always in her heart expected, as I came to manhood. She would have been content with the slightest tangible sign for her indomitable spirit to fasten on. If, for example, I had been working for a university scholarship, she would have foreseen fantastic, visible, miraculous success at the university, herself joining me there, all her expectations realised at a stroke. She did not mind how many years ahead the transformation scene took place, so long as there was just one real sign for her imagination to refresh itself upon. As she saw me go to the office, day following day, the months lengthening into a year, she could not find that one real sign.

She had to come to earth now and again, if her excursions into the future were to keep her going. In her fashion, she was both shrewd and realistic, though with a minimum of encouragement she could draw wonderful pictures of how her life might yet be changed. She was too shrewd and realistic to derive any encouragement from my days at the office. She took to filling in more of her competition coupons. Her health became worse, and one heart attack made her spend a whole spring as an invalid, lying all day on a sofa. She stood it all, hope deferred, illness, pride once more wounded, with the fierce steady endurance that did not seem in any way affected by her own quivering nerves.

I used to work through the long, tedious hours in a room which over-looked the tramlines. The trams ran past the office windows in Bowling Green Street; our room, three storeys up, looked down on the tram tops and the solicitors' and insurance offices on the other side of the street. I shared the room with six other clerks and one more senior man, Mr Vesey, who was called a departmental head and paid £250 a year. The work was one long monotony for me, interspersed by Mr Vesey's slowly growing enmity. He was in charge of the branch, which was part of the secondary school department; I made lists of the children from elementary schools who won free places, and passed the names on to the accountant's room. I also made lists of pupils at each secondary school who left before taking the General Schools or Senior Oxford examinations. I compiled a good deal of miscellaneous statistical information of that kind, which Mr Vesey signed and sent up to the director. Our room did little but accumulate such facts, pass records of names to other departments, and occasionally draw up a chart. Very few decisions were ever taken there. The most onerous decision with which Mr Vesey was faced was whether to allow a child to leave school before the age of fifteen without paying a penalty of five pounds. He was allowed the responsibility of omitting the penalty; if he wished it imposed, the case had to go before the director.

That suited Mr Vesey very well. He had no desire to take decisions, but an insatiable passion for attracting the notice of his superiors. When I first went into the office, I rather liked the look of him. He was a spruce, small man of about forty, who must have spent a large fraction of his income on clothes. His shirts were always spotless, he had a great variety of ties, all quiet and carefully selected. His eyes, which were full and exophthalmic, were magnified still further because of the convex lenses which he wore, so that one's first impression, after seeing his trim suit, was of enormous and somewhat baffled and sorrowful eyes. He told me my duties in a manner which was friendly, if a little fussed, and I was young enough, and enough of a stranger, to be grateful for any kindness and not over-critical of its origin.

It took me some time to realise that Mr Vesey spent fifty-nine minutes in the hour tormenting himself about his prospects of promotion. He was a departmental officer grade one, salary scale £225 to £315; his entire activity was spent in mounting to the next grade. As I came to know him, I heard of nothing else. A contemporary of his in another office got promoted. 'Why don't they do something about me?' sounded Mr Vesey's *cri du cœur*. His technique for achieving his aim was, in principle, very simple. It consisted of keeping in the public eye. If ever he could invent an excuse for calling on the director, he did so. So that every child who left school before the age of fifteen secured a visit to the director's room; a trim, spectacled figure, holding a file, knocked briskly on the door, the director was entangled in an earnest consultation, found himself faced with enormous exophthalmic eyes. The director soon became maddened, and sent down minutes about types of case which it was unnecessary for him to see. Mr Vesey went to see him to discuss each minute.

When any senior person came into our room to inspect the work, a trim spectacled figure stood beside him, on the alert, agog and on tenterhooks to seize the chance. The visitor asked one of the clerks a question. Mr Vesey leapt in to answer it. The visitor asked me to describe some of the statistics. Mr Vesey was quicker than ever off the mark.

All lists, charts, notes of any kind going out from our room had to be initialled N.C.W.V. For a time he experimented with hyphenating the

W and V, possibly in the hope that it would make the initials impossible to miss. There were rumours that his wife wanted to be called Mrs Wilson-Vesey. However, the assistant director asked him brusquely what the hyphen was put in for. All superiors were important to Mr Vesey, though some were more important than others. The hyphen disappeared overnight.

His worst moments were when, as occasionally happened, the assistant director – instead of asking for information through Mr Vesey as head of the branch – demanded a clerk by name. Mr Vesey's enmity towards me first showed itself after a few such calls. The assistant director found I knew my lists inside out (which was a simple game to anyone with a good memory), took a fancy to me, said maddeningly once that if I were still at school the department would make a grant to help me go to a university. Meanwhile, Mr Vesey was raising cries to heaven: how could he organise his branch if people did not go through the proper channels? How could he secure discipline and smooth working if people went over his head? Junior clerks did not understand the whole scope of his responsibilities – they might give a wrong impression and that meant his promotion would never come. There was such a thing, said Mr Vesey in a tone full of meaning, as junior clerks trying to draw attention to themselves.

So it went on, a blend of monotony and Mr Vesey. So it went on, from nine to one, from two to five-thirty, from my sixteenth birthday to my seventeenth and beyond. Often, during those tedious days, I dreamed the ambitious dreams of very young men. Walking past the lighted shops in the lunch hour on a winter's day, I dreamed of fame – any kind of fame that would put my name in men's mouths, in the newspapers, make people recognise me in the streets. Sometimes I was a great politician, eloquent, powerful, venerated. Sometimes I was a writer as well known as Shaw. Sometimes I was extraordinarily rich. Always I had the power to make my own terms, to move through the world as one who owned it, to be waited on and give largesse.

The harsh streets were lit by my fancies, and I was drunk with them – and yet they were altogether vague. There was a good deal of ambition, I knew later, innate within me; and I had listened since I was a child to my mother's prompting. But those dreams of mine had not much in common with the ambition which drives a man, which in time drove me, to action. These were just the lazy and grandiose dreams of youth. They were far more like the times when, lying awake on windy autumn nights or sitting under the apple tree in the garden after my parents had gone to bed, I first luxuriously longed, through a veil of innocence, for women's love.

Even at sixteen, however, I felt sometimes guilty, because I was only dreaming. The pictures in my mind were so heady, so magnificent – they made all practical steps that I could take seem puny. Puny they seemed, as I took the opportunity one day to talk to my acquaintance, the assistant director. He had sent for me again, inflaming Mr Vesey to transports of injured dignity. Darby was a decent pale man with a furrowed forehead, sitting in his small, plain office. He gave me prosaic but sensible advice. It might be worth while thinking of the possibility of an external Londo degree. It might be worth while picking up some law, which would be useful if I stayed in the office. I ought to consult the people at the College of Art and Technology.

I did so, and enrolled in the law class at the college – which everyone called 'the School', and which was at that time the only place of higher education in the town – in the summer of 1922, when I was not yet seventeen. The School was the lineal descendant of the mechanics' institute, where my grandfather had learned his mathematics; it was housed in a red-brick building, a building of remarkable Victorian baroque. There was a principal and a small permanent staff, but most of the lecturers had other jobs in the town, were secondary schoolmasters and the like, and gave their school lectures in the evening. The first law class I attended was given by a solicitor from the town clerk's department. It was a course on a dull subject, dully taught. It lasted through the autumn: I used to walk down the Newarke on Tuesday and Friday evenings after the office, wondering whether I was not wasting my time.

I was still wondering, towards the end of the year, whether to give up the law courses, when I happened to see a notice in the School, announcing a new course in the spring term – 'Fundamentals of Law, I. Criminal, by G. Passant'. I thought I would give him a trial. Before I had listened for ten minutes to the first lecture, I knew this was something of a different class, in sheer force, in intellectual competence and power, from anything I had yet heard.

George Passant's voice was loud, strained, irascible and passionate. He gave the entire lecture at a breakneck speed, as though he were irritated with the stupidity of his class and wanted to get it over. His voice and manner, I thought, were in curious contrast to his face, which wore an amiable, an almost diffident smile. His head was large and powerful, set on thick, heavy shoulders; and under the amiable smile, the full amiable flesh, his cheekbones, the bones of his forehead and chin were made on the same big scale. He was not much over middle height, but he was obviously built to put on weight. His hair was fair: he was a full blond, with light blue eyes, which had a knack of looking past the class, past the far wall, focusing on infinity.

After that night, I made enquiries about George Passant. No one could tell me much: he had only come to the town in the previous autumn, was a qualified solicitor, was working as managing clerk in the solid, respectable firm of Eden & Martineau. He was very young, not more than twenty-three or four, as indeed one could see at a glance. Someone had heard a rumour that he led a 'wild' life.

Meeting George Passant was the first piece of pure chance which affected all that I did later. The second piece of chance in my youth happened within a fortnight.

My mother was one of a very large family – or rather of two families, for, as I mentioned previously, her father had married twice, having four children by his first wife, and seven, of whom my mother was one of the youngest, by his second. For many years she had been on bad terms with her half-brothers and sisters: within her own mother's family there was great affection, and they saw and wrote to each other frequently their whole lives long, but none of them visited their seniors or spoke of them without a note of anger and injury.

I had first heard the story in those talks by the fireside, when my mother let her imagination return to the winter of 1894. It was then that she told me of the intrigues of Will and Za. For a long time I thought she had exaggerated in order to paint the wonder of the Wigmores. In her version, the villain of the piece was my Uncle Will. He was the eldest son of the first family, and my mother described him with hushed indignation and respect. His villainy had consisted of diverting money intended for the younger family to himself and his sisters. My mother never succeeded in making the details clear, but she believed something like this: her mother had brought some money with her when she married (was she not a Wigmore?) How much it was my mother could not be sure, but she said in a fierce whisper that it might have been over fifteen hundred pounds. This money her mother had 'intended' to be divided among the younger family at her death. But Uncle Will had intervened with their father, to whom the money was left and who was then a very old man. Through Uncle Will's influence, every penny had gone to himself and his two sisters (the fourth of the first family had died young).

I never knew the truth of it. My mother believed her story implicitly, and she was an honest woman, honest in the midst of her temptation to glorify all that happened to her. It was certainly true that Aunt Za, the oldest sister of all, Uncle Will and Aunt Florrie all had a little money, while none of the other family had inherited so much as a pound. It was also true that all my mother's brothers and sisters bore the same grievance.

After twenty years of the quarrel, my mother tried to make peace. She did it partly for my sake, since Aunt Za was the widow of an auctioneer and thought to have 'more than she needs for herself'. She had, since her husband died, gone to live near her brother Will, who ran a small estate agency in Market Harborough. My mother wanted also to repair the breach in order to show me off; but the chief reason was that she had deep instinctive loyalties, and though she told herself that she was making an approach purely for my sake, as a piece of calculation, it was really that she did not want any of them to die unreconciled.

Her move went about halfway to success. She visited Market Harborough and was welcomed by Za and Will. After that visit, birthday and Christmas correspondence was resumed. But neither Za nor Will returned her visit, nor would they, as she tried to persuade them, write a word to any others of the younger family. My mother, however, secured one positive point. She talked about me; it was easy to imagine her magnifying my promise, and being met in kind, for Za and Will had exactly her sort of stately, haughty manner. I was about fourteen at the time, and was invited over to Will's for a week in the summer holidays. Since then I had gone to Harborough often, as an emissary between the two families, as a sign that the quarrel was at least formally healed.

On these visits to Harborough, I did not see much of Aunt Za (her name, an abbreviation of Thirza, was pronounced Zay). Her whole life, since her husband died, was lived in and round the church. She taught a Sunday-school class, helped with mothers' meetings, attended the sick in the parish, but most of all she lived for her devotions, going to church morning and night each day of the year. I used to have tea with her, once and only once, each time I stayed with Uncle Will. She was an ageing woman, stately and sombre, with a prow-like nose and sunken mouth. She had little to say to me, except to ask after my mother's health and to tell me to go regularly to church. She always gave me seedcake with the tea, so that the taste of caraway years later brought back, like a Proustian moment, the narrow street, the dark house, the taciturn and stiff old woman burdened with piety and the dreadful prospect of the grave.

I did not entertain her, as sometimes I managed to entertain Uncle Will. Yet apparently she liked me well enough – or else there was justice in my mother's story, and Aunt Za felt a wound of conscience throbbing as she became old. Whatever her motive, she wrote to my mother in the autumn I entered the office, said that she was making a new will, and proposed in doing so to leave me 'a small remembrance'.

My mother was resplendent with pleasure. It gratified her that she had brought off something for me, that her schemes had for once not been blocked. It gratified her specially that it should come through her family, and so prove something of past glories. As she thought of it, however, she was filled with anxiety. 'I hope Za doesn't tell Will what she intends to do,' said my mother. 'He'll find a way to put it in his own pocket, you can bet your boots. You're not going to tell me that Will has stopped looking after himself.'

My mother's suspicion of Uncle Will flared up acutely eighteen months afterwards – in the spring of 1923, when I was seventeen and a half. My mother had been ill, and was only just coming down again to breakfast. There was a letter for her, addressed in a hand that could belong to no one but Uncle Will, a fine affected flowing Italian hand, developed as an outward mark of superiority, with dashes everywhere instead of full stops. As she read it, my mother's face was pallid with anger.

'He didn't mean us to get near her,' she said. 'Za's gone. She went yesterday morning. He says that it was very sudden. Of course, he was too upset to send us a wire,' she added with savage sarcasm.

However, this latest hope of hers was not snatched away. My father and I attended the funeral, and afterwards heard the will read in Uncle Will's house. I received £300. Three hundred pounds. It was much more than I expected, or my mother in her warmest flush of optimism. Cheerfully, my heart thumped.

My father ruminated with content as we walked to the station:

'Three hundred of the best, Lewis. Think of that! Three hundred of the best. Why, there's no knowing what you'll be able to do with it. Three blooming hundred.'

Almost for the first time in my experience, he was impelled to assert himself. 'I hope you won't think of spending it without consulting me,' he said. 'I know what money is, you realise. Why, every week at Mr Stapleton's I pay out twice as much as your three hundred pounds. I can keep you on the right track, as long as you never commit yourself without consulting me.'

I assured him – in the light, familiar, companionable tone that had always existed naturally between us – that we would have long and exacting conferences. My father chuckled. A trifle puffed out by his success, he produced a singular piece of practical advice.

'I always tell people,' he said, as though he were in the habit of being deferred to on every kind of financial business, 'never to go about without five pounds sewn in a place where no one can find it. You never know when you'll need it badly, Lewis. It's a reserve. Think of that! If I were you, I should get Lena to sew five of your pound notes into the seat of your trousers. You never know when you'll want them. One of these days you'll thank me for the idea, you mark my words.'

In the train, we found an empty third-class carriage. My father stretched his short legs, I my long ones, and we looked out of the window at the sodden fields, sepia and emerald in the drizzle of the March afternoon.

'I don't like funerals, Lewis,' said my father meditatively in the dark carriage. 'When they put me away, I wish they wouldn't make all this fuss about it. Lena would insist on it, though, wouldn't she?'

His thoughts turned to more cheerful themes.

'I've got to say this for Will, they did give us some nice things to eat,' said my father, as naturally and simply as ever. 'Did you try the cheese cakes?'

'No,' I said with a smile.

'You made a mistake there, Lewis,' said my father. 'They were the best I've tasted for a very long time.'

We did not go straight home, but instead crossed the road from the station and called at the old Victoria, which later became, for George Passant and me and the circle of friends we called the 'group', our habitual public house. My father suggested, feeling a very gay dog, that we should celebrate the legacy. I drank two or three pints of beer; my father did not like beer, but put away several glasses of port and lemon. He became gay without making any effort to control himself. Once he lifted his voice in a song, his surprisingly loud and tuneful voice. 'No singing, please,' called the barmaid sourly. 'Don't be such a donkey, Bertie,' my father muttered to himself, mildly and cheerfully, imitating my mother's constant reproof.

Their relation, I knew, had deteriorated with the years. It was held together now only by habit, law, the acquiescence of his temperament, the pride of hers, and most of all the difficulty of keeping two *ménages* for those as poor as they were. He did not mind very much. So much of his life was lived inside himself; in his own comical fashion he was far better protected than most men; his inner life went on, whatever events took place outside – failure, humiliation, the disharmony of his marriage. That day, for example, he had experienced happy moments as the accomplished financier and, later in the Victoria, as the hard-bitten man of the world.

He was simple, he did not mind being laughed at, he was quite happy, the happiest member of the family, all the years of his life.

I got on with him as I had always done, on the same level, with little change since my childhood. He asked for nothing. He was grateful for a little banter and just a little flattery. It would not have occurred to him, now that I was in his eyes grown-up, to ask me to spend a day with him. If one came by accident, such as this outing to Market Harborough, he placidly enjoyed it, and so did I.

At last we went home. We got off at the tram-stop and walked by the elementary school, the library, Aunt Milly's house, just the same way as I had run in sudden trepidation that night before the war, when I was a child of eight. Returning from Za's funeral, however, I was, like my father, comfortable with a little drink inside me. A cold drizzle was falling, but we scarcely noticed it. My father was humming to himself, then talking, as I teased him. He hummed away, zum, zoo, zum, zoo, zoo, zoo, pleased because I was inventing reasons for his choice of tune.

We were almost outside our house before I took in that something was not right. The gas in the front room was alight, but the blinds were not drawn. That was strange, different from all the times I had walked that road and seen the light behind the blinds.

I looked straight into the empty, familiar room. Above, in my mother's bedroom, the light was also burning, but there the blinds were drawn.

Aunt Milly let us in. In her flat energetic way she said that my mother had had another attack that afternoon, and was gravely ill.

CHAPTER VIII

A SUNDAY MORNING

I WENT to see my mother late that night. Her voice was faint and thick, the lids fell heavy over her eyes, but she was quite lucid. I only stayed a moment, and left the bedroom with the weight of anxiety lightened. She seemed no worse than I had often seen her. None of us knew how ill she was, that night or the next day. We were so much in ignorance that, on the next evening, Aunt Milly set about attacking me on how I should dispose of my legacy.

I was sitting in the front room, below my mother's bedroom, when Aunt Milly came downstairs.

'How is she?' I said. I had not been inside my mother's room since early that morning, before I departed for the office.

'About the same,' said Aunt Milly. With no change of expression at all, she went on, her voice loud and vigorous: 'Now you'll be able to start making an honest man of your father. It's high time.'

'What do you mean, Aunt Milly?'

'You know very well what I mean.' Which, though she had moment-arily startled me, was true. 'You can pay off another ten shillings in the pound.'

I met her stare.

'It's the honest thing to do,' she said. 'You needn't pay Tom's share yet awhile. You can keep that in the bank for yourself. But you'll be able to pay the other creditors.'

An obstinate resolve had formed, when she bullied me as a child, that I would never pay those debts, however much money I made and however long I lived. Now I liked her better, saw her as a woman by herself, not just as a big impassive intruding face, an angry threatening voice, that filled the space around and wounded me. I liked her better; but the resolve had stayed intact since I was eight. However much Za had left me, I should not have used a penny as Aunt Milly wanted.

But I could deal with Aunt Milly by now. Once she used to hurt me, then I had toughened my skin and listened in silence; now that I was growing up, I had become comfortable with her.

'Do you want to ruin me, Aunt Milly? I might take to drink, you know.'

'I shouldn't be surprised. Anyone who doesn't pay his debts,' said Aunt Milly unrelentingly, 'is weak enough for anything.'

'I might be able to get qualified in something with this money. You tried hard enough to get me qualified as an engineer, didn't you? You ought to approve if I tag some letters after my name.'

I said it frivolously, but it was a thought that was going through my mind. That too made me hang on to the money, perhaps it determined me more than the resolution of years past.

Aunt Milly had no humour at all, but she could vaguely detect when she was being teased, and she did not dislike it. But she was obdurate.

'You can always fix up reasons for not doing the right thing,' she said at the top of her voice.

Soon I went upstairs to my mother. I expected to find her asleep, for the room was dark except for a night-light; but, in the shadowy bedroom, redolent with eau-de-Cologne, brandy, the warm smell of an invalid's bedroom, my mother's voice came, slurred but distinct:

'Is that you, dear?'

'Yes.'

'What was Milly shouting about?'

'Could you hear?'

'I'm not quite deaf yet,' said my mother, smiling in the flickering light, smiling with affronted humour, as she did when, at nearly fifty, she heard herself described as middle-aged. Her physical vanity and her instinctive hold on youth had not abandoned her. 'What was she shouting about?'

'Nothing to worry you,' I said.

'Please to tell me,' said my mother. She sounded exhausted, but she was still imperious.

'Really, it's nothing, Mother.'

'Was it about Za's money?' Her intuition stayed quick, realistic, suspicious. She knew she had guessed right. 'Please to tell me, dear.'

I told her, as lightly as I could. My mother smiled, angry but half-amused.

'Milly is a donkey,' she said. 'You're to do nothing of the sort.'

'Of course, I shouldn't think of it.'

'Remember, it's some of the money I ought to have had. Please think of it as money I've given you. You're to use it to make your way. I hope I see you do it.' Her tone was firm, quiet, unshaken, and yet worried. I noticed, with discomfort, how easily she became out of breath. After saying those words to me, she had to breathe hard.

'It's a great comfort to me,' she went on, 'to see the money come to you, dear. It's your chance. We shall have to think how you're going to take it. You mustn't waste it. Remember that you're not to waste it.'

'We won't do anything till you get better,' I said.

'I hope it won't be too long,' said my mother, and I caught the tone again, unshaken but apprehensive.

'How are you feeling?' I asked.

'I'm not getting on as fast as I should like,' said my mother.

As I said good night, she told me:

'I'm angry with myself. I don't like lying here. It's time I made myself get well.'

She was undaunted enough to tell Aunt Milly, on each of the next two days, that I was on no account to spend any of the legacy in getting my father's discharge. My mother stated haughtily that it was not to happen.

She explained to Aunt Milly that it was only right and just for her son to possess 'my money', and that that money must be used to give him a start. In a few years, Lewis would be able to settle Bertie's affairs without thinking twice.

Aunt Milly had to restrain herself, and listen without protest. For by this time she, like all of us, realised that my mother might not live.

She seemed to have, Dr Francis explained to me, the kind of heart failure that comes to much older people. If she recovered, she would have to spend much of her time lying down, so as to rest the heart. At present it was only working strongly enough just to keep her going without any drain of energy whatever.

From our expressions, from the silences in the house, my mother knew that she was in danger. Her hope was still fierce and courageous. She insisted that she was 'better in myself'. Impatiently she dismissed what she called 'minor symptoms', such as the swelling of her ankles; her ankles had swollen even though she lay in bed and had not set foot on the floor for three weeks.

One Sunday morning Dr Francis spent a long time upstairs. Aunt Milly, my father and I sat without speaking in the front room.

Dr Francis had come early that morning, so as not to miss the service. The church bell was already ringing when he joined us in the front room. He had left his hat on the table, the tall hat in which he always went to church, the only one in the congregation. I thought he had come to take it, and would not stay with us. Instead, he sat down by the table and ran his white, plump fingers over the cloth. The skin of his face was pink, and the pink flush seemed to shade up to the top of his bald dome. His expression was stern, resentful and commanding.

'Mr Eliot, I must tell you now,' he said. His voice was hoarse as well as high.

'Yes, doctor?' said my father.

'I'm afraid she isn't going to get over it,' said Dr Francis.

The church bell had just stopped and the room was so quiet that it seemed to have gone darker.

'Isn't she, doctor?' said my father helplessly. Dr Francis shook his head with a heavy frown.

'How long has she got?' said Aunt Milly, in a tone subdued for her but still instinct with action.

'I can't tell you, Mrs Riddington,' said Dr Francis. 'She won't let herself go easily. Yes, she'll fight to the last.'

'How long do you think?' Aunt Milly insisted.

'I don't think it can be many weeks,' said Dr Francis slowly. 'I don't think any of us ought to wish it to be long, for her sake.'

'Does she know?' I cried.

'Yes, Lewis, she knows.' He was gentler to me than to Aunt Milly; his resentment, his almost sulky sense of defeat, he put away.

'You've told her this morning?'

'Yes. She asked me to tell her the truth. She's a brave soul. I don't tell some people, but I thought I had to, with your mother.'

'How did she take it?' I said, trying to seem controlled.

'I hope I do as well,' said Dr Francis. 'If it happens to me like this.'

Dr Francis had deposited his gloves within his tall hat. Now he took them out, and gradually pulled on the left-hand one, concentrating on each fold in the leather.

'She asked me to give you a message,' he said as though casually to my father. 'She would like to see Lewis before anyone else.'

My father nodded, submissively.

'I should give her a few minutes, if I were you,' said Dr Francis to me. 'I expect she'll want to get ready for you. She doesn't like being seen when she's upset, does she?'

He was thinking of me too. I could not reply. He gazed at me sharply, and clicked his tongue against his teeth in baffled sympathy. He pulled on the other glove and said that, though it was late, he would run along to church. He would get in before the first lesson. He said good morning to Aunt Milly, good morning to my father, put his hand on my arm. We saw him pass the window in short, quick, precise steps, his top hat gleaming, his plump cushioned body braced and erect.

'Well,' said Aunt Milly, 'when the time comes, you will have to leave this house.'

'I suppose we shall, Milly,' my father said.

'You'll have to come to me. I can manage the three of you.'

'It's very good of you, Milly, I'm sure.'

'You two might have to share a room. I'll set about moving things,' said my aunt, satisfied that there was a practical step to take.

Then the clock struck the half-hour. My father did not repeat his ritual phrase. Instead he said:

'Lena didn't use to like the clock, did she? She used to say "Confound the clock. Confound the clock, Bertie." That's what she used to say. "Confound the clock." I've always liked it myself, but she never did.'

CHAPTER IX

AT A BEDSIDE

My mother's head and shoulders had been propped up by pillows, in order to make her breathing easier – so that, asleep or awake, she was half-sitting, and when I drew up a chair that Sunday morning, her eyes looked down into mine.

They were very bright, her eyes, and the whites clear. The skin of her face was a waxy ochreous cream, and the small veins were visible upon her cheeks, as they sometimes are on the tough and weatherbeaten. She gave me the haughty humorous smile which she used so often to pass off a remark which had upset her.

Outside, it was a windy April day, changing often from sunlight to shade. When I went in the room was dark; but, before my mother spoke, the houses opposite the window, the patch of ground between them, stood brilliant in the spring sunshine, and the light was reflected on to my mother's face.

'When it's your time, it's your time,' said my mother. She was speaking with difficulty, as though she had to think hard about each word, and then could not trust her lips and tongue to frame it. I knew – with the tight, constrained, dreadful feeling which overcame me when she called out for my love, for in her presence I could not let the tears start, un-bidden, spontaneously, as they did when Dr Francis spoke of her courage – that she had rehearsed the remark to greet me with.

'When it's your time, it's your time,' she repeated. But she could not maintain her resignation. Her real feeling was anger, grievance and astonishment. 'It's all happened through a completely unexpected symptom,' said my mother. 'Completely unexpected. No one could have expected it. Dr Francis says he didn't. It's a completely unexpected symptom,' she kept saying with amazement and anger. Then she said, heavily: 'I don't want to stay like this. Just like an old sack. It wouldn't do for me, would it?'

For once, I found my tongue. I told her that she was looking handsome. She was delighted. She preened herself like a girl, and said:

'I'm glad of that, dear.'

She glanced round the bedroom, which was covered with photographs on all the walls – photographs of all the family, Martin, me, but most of all herself. She had always had a passion for photographic records: she had always been majestically vain.

'But I shouldn't like you to think of me like this,' she said. 'Think of me as I am in the garden photograph, will you, dear?'

'If you want, Mother,' I said. The 'garden' photograph was her favourite, taken when she was thirty, in the more prosperous days just after I was born. She was in one of the long dresses that I remembered from my earliest childhood. She had made the photographer pose her under the apple tree, and she was dressed for an Edwardian afternoon.

She saw herself as she had been that day. She rejected pity, she would have rejected it even if she had found what she had sought in me, one to whose heart her heart could speak. She would have thrown pity back even now, even if I could have given it with spontaneous love. But she saw herself as she had been in her pride; and she wished me eternally to see her so.

We were silent; the room was dark, then sunny, then dark again.

'I've been wondering what you'll do with Za's money,' said my mother.

'I'm not sure yet,' I said.

'If it had come to me as it ought to have done,' she said, 'you should have had it before this. Then I should have seen you started, anyway.'

'Never mind,' I replied. 'I'll do something with it.'

'I know you will. You'll do the things I hoped for you.' She raised her voice. '*I shan't be there to see.*'

I gasped, said something without meaning.

'I didn't want just the pleasure of it,' said my mother fiercely. 'I didn't want you to buy me presents. You know I didn't want that.'

'I know,' I said, but she did not hear me.

'I wanted to go along with you,' she cried. 'I wanted to be part of you. That's all I wanted.'

I tried to console her. I told her that, whatever I did, I should carry my childhood with me: always I should hear her speaking, I should remember the evenings by the front-room fire, when she urged me on as a little boy. Yet afterwards I never believed that I brought her comfort. She was the proudest of women, and she was vain, but in the end she had an eye for truth. She knew as well as I, that if one's heart is invaded by another, one will either assist the invasion or repel it – and if one repels it, even though one may long, as I did with my mother, that one might do otherwise, even though one admires and cherishes and assumes the attitude of love, yet still, if one repels it, no words or acting can for long disguise the lie. That was how I thought of it, when I had learned more myself. Later still, as I listened to my own son, I fancied I might have been making the phrases too magniloquent: the facts of life were sometimes simpler, less easy to dress up, untidier than that.

My mother was exhausted by her outburst. She found it harder to keep her speech clear, and once or twice her attention did not stay steady, she began talking of something else. She was acutely ashamed to be 'muddle-headed', as she called it; she screwed up all her will.

'Don't forget,' she said, sounding stern with her effort of will, 'that Za's money ought to have been mine. I should like to have given it to you. It was Wigmore money to start with. Don't forget that.'

Her lips took on the grand smile which I used to see when she told me of her girlhood. She lay there, the room in a bright phase of light, with her grand haughty smile.

I noticed that a Sunday paper rested on the bed, unopened. It was strange to see, for she had always had the greatest zest for printed news. After a time, I said:

'Are you going to read it later on today?'

'I don't think so, dear,' she said, and the anger and astonishment had returned to her voice. 'What's the use of me reading the paper? I shall give it up now. What's the use? I shall never know what happens.'

For her, more than for most people, everything in the future had been interesting. Now it could interest her no longer. She would never know the answers.

'Perhaps I shall learn about what's going on here,' she said, but in a formal, hesitating tone, 'in another place.'

That morning, such was the only flicker of comfort from her faith.

We were quiet; I could hear her breathing; it was not laboured, but just heavy enough to hear.

'Look!' said my mother suddenly, with a genuine, happy laugh. 'Look at the ducks, dear!'

For a second I thought it was an hallucination. But I followed her glance; her long-sighted eyes had seen something real, and she was enjoying what she saw. I went to the window, for at a distance her sight was still much better than mine.

Between the houses opposite, there was a space not yet built over. It had been left as rough hillocky grass, with a couple of small ponds; on it one of our neighbours kept a few chickens and ducks. It was a duck and her brood of seven or eight ducklings that had made my mother laugh. They had been paddling in the fringe of one pond. All of a sudden they fled, as though in panic, to the other, in precise Indian file, the duck in the lead.

Then, as though they had met an invisible obstacle, they wheeled round, and, again in file, raced back to their starting point.

'Oh dear,' said my mother, wiping her eyes. 'They are silly. I've always got something to watch.'

She was calmed, invigorated, made joyful by the sight. She had been so ambitious, she had hoped so fiercely, she had never found what she needed to make her happy – yet she had had abounding capacity for happiness. Now, when her vision was foreshortened, she showed it still. Perhaps it was purer, now her hopes were gone. She was simple with laughter, just as I remembered her when I was five years old, when she took me for a walk and a squirrel came quarrelling down a tree.

I came back to the bedside and took her hand. It occurred to her at that moment to tell me not to underestimate my brother Martin. She insisted on his merits. In fact, it was an exhortation I did not need, for I was extremely fond of him. My mother was arguing with her own injustice, for she had never forgiven his birth, she had never wanted to find her match and fulfilment in him, as she had in me.

There was a flash of irony here – for he was less at ease with others than I was, but more so with her.

Then she got tired. She tried to hide it, she did not choose to admit it. Her thoughts rambled; her speech was thicker and hard to follow; Martin Francis (my brother's names) took her by free association to Dr Francis, and how he had come specially to see her that morning, which he would not do for his ordinary patients. She was tired out. With perfect lucidity, she said once:

'I should like to go in my sleep.'

Her thoughts rambled again. With a last effort of will, she said in a clear, dignified manner:

'I didn't have a very good night. That's what it is. Perhaps I'd better have a nap now. Please to come and see me after tea, dear. I shan't be a bother to you then. I like to talk to you properly, you know.'

CHAPTER X

THE VIEW OVER THE ROOFS

MY mother died in May. From the cemetery, my father and I returned to the empty house. I drew up the blind, in the front room; after three days of darkness, the pictures, the china on the sideboard, leaped out, desolatingly bright.

'Milly keeps on at me about living with her,' said my father.

'I know,' I said.

'I suppose we shall have to,' said my father.

'I'm not sure what I shall do,' I said.

My father looked taken aback, mournfully dazed, with his black tie and the armlet round his sleeve.

I had been thinking what I should do, when I sat in the house and my mother lay dying. I had been making up my mind while in the familiar bedroom her body rested dead. I was too near her dying and her death to acknowledge my own bereavement. I did not know that I should feel remorse, because I had not given her what she asked of me. I was utterly ignorant of the flaw within, which crept to the open in the way I failed my mother.

At the time of my mother's death I was as absorbed in the future, as bent upon my plans, as she might have been. My first decision, in fact, was more in my mother's line than my own of later years. For it was a bit of a gesture. I had decided that I would not go to live with Aunt Milly.

When I told my father that I was 'not sure' of my intentions, that was not true. The decision was already made, embedded in a core of obstinacy. What I said about it, however much I prevaricated or delayed, did not matter. On this occasion, I had already, in the days between my mother's death and the funeral, been looking for lodgings. I had found a room in Lower Hastings Street, and told the landlady that I would let her know definitely by the end of the week.

I should have to pay twelve and six a week for that room and breakfast. I was getting twenty-five shillings from the education office. I calculated that I could just live, though it would mean one sandwich at lunch-time and not much of a meal at night. Clothes would have to come out of Za's money; that was my standby, that made this manœuvre possible; but I resolved not to take more than ten pounds out of the pool within the next year. In due time I should make another choice – and then that money meant my way out.

I knew clearly why I was making the gesture. I had suffered some shame through my father's bankruptcy. This was an atonement, a device for setting myself free. It meant I was not counting every penny – and to smile off the last winces of shame, I had to throw away a little money too. I had to act as though I did not care too much about money. And this gesture meant also that I was defying Aunt Milly, the voice of conscience from my childhood, the voice that had driven the shame into me and had, at moments since, trumpeted it awake. If it had been anyone else but Aunt Milly who had offered to take us in, I believed that I should have said yes gratefully and saved my money.

I was fairly adroit, however, in explaining myself to her – more adroit, I thought later with remorse, than I had often been with my mother, and then I thought once more that adroitness would have been no good, neither adroitness nor the tenderest consideration. With Aunt Milly, it was not so difficult. I did not want to hurt her; I had become fond enough of her to be considerate. It would hurt her a little, I knew. For, in her staring blank-faced dynamic fashion, Aunt Milly had always been starved of children. She had felt maternally towards me and my brother, though it sometimes struck me that she used a curious method for expressing it. And she could not understand that she put people off, most of all young children, whom she desired most for her own.

She left my father alone with me after we came back from the cemetery; Martin had stayed at her house since before my mother's death. Aunt Milly did not let us alone all day, however; she came in that night, and discovered us in the kitchen eating bread and cheese. She examined the shelves, note-book in hand. She was marking down the crockery which was to be transferred. It was then that I put in a word.

'I don't know, Aunt Milly,' I said, 'but it might be better if I went off by myself.'

'I never heard of such a thing,' said Aunt Milly.

'I don't want to be in the way,' I said.

'That's for me to settle,' she said.

She had turned round, her face impassive and pop-eyed, but tinged with indignation. My father was watching with mild interest.

'I know you'll put yourself out and never tell us.' I laughed at her. 'And take it out of us because you've done so.'

'I don't know what you're talking about.'

'I should like to come –'

'Of course you would. Anyone in his senses would,' said Aunt Milly. 'You don't get your board and lodging free everywhere.'

'As well as a few home truths now and again. It would be very good for us both, wouldn't it?'

'It would be very good for you.'

'I've looked forward to it.'

'I expect you have. Well, I'm ready to have you. I don't know what all the palaver is about.'

Aunt Milly took words at their face value; to cheek and compliments she returned the same flat, uncompromising rebuff; but sometimes they had just a little effect.

'Listen, Aunt Milly, I'll tell you. I expect I shall want to study—'

'I should think you will,' she said.

'That does mean I ought to be on my own, you know.'

'You can study in my house.'

'Could you study,' I said, 'if you had to share a room with my father – or your brother?'

Aunt Milly was the least humorous of women, and rarely smiled. But she was capable of an enormous hooting laugh. She had also been conditioned to think, all her life, that my father ought to evoke laughter. So she burst into a humourless roar that echoed round the kitchen. My father obligingly burst into a snatch of song, then pretended to snore.

'One of the two,' he said with his clowning grin. 'One of the two. That's me, that is.'

'Stop it, Bertie,' said Aunt Milly implacably.

My father, still clowning, shrank into a corner.

The argument went on. Well, Martin could share my room instead, said Aunt Milly. I was ready to stick it out all night. I was as obstinate as she was, but that she did not know. I played all the tricks I could: I flattered her, I was impertinent, I stood up to denunciation, I gave vague hints of how I thought of living.

Those hints made her voice grow louder, her eyes more staring and glazed. I proposed to go into lodgings, did I – and how was I going to pay for them out of a clerk's earnings? I described what I thought my budget would be.

'You're not leaving yourself any margin,' she retorted.

'I've got a little money in the bank now, you know,' I said.

I had been careless to speak so. It might have provoked a storm, about bankruptcy, my father's debts, my duty. She would not have been restrained because my father was present. But it happened that my mother, before she died, had made her promise not to deter me from 'taking my chance'. Aunt Milly prided herself on having dispensed with 'superstitious nonsense' – for after all this was the twentieth century, as she asserted in every quarrel with my mother. She would have said that she paid no special reverence to deathbed promises. If she kept this one, she would have said, it was because she always kept her word.

'I won't say what I think of that,' said Aunt Milly, with a thunderous exertion of self-control. Then she indulged in one, but only one, loud cry of rage: 'No wonder this family will come to a bad end.'

The evening became night. To say that she gave in would not be true; but she acknowledged my intention, though with a very bad grace. To say that I had got so far without hurting her would be nonsense. We were set on aims that contradicted each other; they could not be reconciled, and no gloss on earth could make them so. But at least in Aunt Milly's understanding we had not split or parted. She did not consider it a break. I had promised to go and have tea at her house each Sunday afternoon.

It was a warm, wet evening late in May when I first went as a lodger to my room in Lower Hastings Street. The room was at the top of the house, and was no larger than my attic at home. From the window I looked over slate roofs, the roofs of outhouses and sheds, glistening in the rain. Beyond, there was a cloud of sulphurous smoke, where a train was disappearing through a tunnel into the station yard.

I had brought all my possessions in two old suitcases – another suit, two pairs of flannels, some underclothes, a few books and school photographs. I left them on the floor, and stood by the window, looking over the roofs, my heart quickening with a tumult of emotions. I felt despondent in the strange, cheerless room, and yet hopeful with the hope that I saw so often in my mother; anxious, desperately anxious that I might have chosen wrong, and at the same time ultimately confident; lonely and also free.

There was everything in the world to do. There was everything in front of me, everything to do – yet what was I to do that moment, with an evening stretching emptily ahead? Should I lie on my bed and read? Or should I walk the streets of the town, alone, in the warm wet night?

PART TWO

TOWARDS A GAMBLE

CHAPTER XI

DISCONTENT AND TALKS OF LOVE

DURING the summer after my mother's death I used to walk to the office in the warm and misty mornings; there was a smell of rain freshening the dusty street, and freshening my hopes as well, as I walked along, chafing at another wasted day ahead.

I ticked off names, names written in violet ink that glared on the squared paper. I read each date of birth, and underlined in red those born before 31 August 1908. I gazed down into the sunlit street, and my mind was filled with plans and fancies, with hope and the first twist of savage discontent. My plans were half-fancies still, not much grown up since my first days in the office, when I walked round the town hall square at lunch-time and dreamed that I had suddenly come into a fortune. I still made resolutions about what to read, or what prospectus to write for next, with an elation and sense of purpose that continued to outshine the unromantic act of carrying the resolution out. But there was some change. I had my legacy. I was angry that I could not see my way clear, I was angry that no one gave advice that sounded ambitious enough. Gazing down, watching the tramcars glitter in the sun, waiting with half an ear for Mr Vesey's cry of complaint, I began to suffer the ache and burn of discontent.

Yet I was side-tracked and impeded by that same discontent. There were days when the office walls hemmed me in, when Mr Vesey became an incarnate insult, when I was choking with hurt pride, when Darby in all kindness gave me grey and cautious advice. Those were the days when I felt I must be myself, break out, not in the planned-for distant future, but now, before I rusted away, now, while my temper was hot.

It was a temptation then to show off, get an audience by any means I could, and at that age I could not resist the temptation. I scarcely even thought of trying, it seemed so natural and I got so fierce a pleasure. I had a quick, cruel tongue, and I enjoyed using it. It seemed natural to find myself at the I.L.P., getting myself elected on to committees, making inflammatory speeches in lecture halls all over the town. Only the zealots attended in the height of summer, but I was ready to burst out, even before a handful of the converted, and still be elated and warm-tempered as we left the dingy room at ten o'clock on a midsummer evening and found ourselves blinking in the broad daylight. The town was not large enough for one to stay quite anonymous, and some of my exploits got round. A bit of gossip reached even Aunt Milly, and the next Sunday, when I visited her house for tea, she was not backward in expressing her disapproval.

To myself, I could not laugh that attack away as cheerfully as I did most of Aunt Milly's. I was practical enough to know that I was doing nothing 'useful'. As I strolled to my lodgings ('my rooms', I used to call them to my acquaintances, with a distinct echo of my mother, despite my speeches on the equality of man) late on those summer nights, I had moments of bleak lucidity. Where was I getting to? What was I doing with my luck? Was I so devoid of will, was I just going to drift? Those moments struck cold, after the applause I had won a few hours earlier with some sarcastic joke.

But once on my feet again, with faces in front of me, or distracted in a different fashion by Jack Cotery and his talk of girls, I was swept away. My own chilling questions were just insistent enough to keep me going regularly to the law classes at the School, and that was all. I intended to get to know George Passant, and I may have had some half-thought that his advice would be grander than that of Darby and the rest; but my first expectations were forgotten for ever, in the light of what actually happened. I had not, however, forced myself into his notice before the School closed for the summer holidays. Occasionally I saw him from my office window, for the firm of Eden & Martineau occupied a floor on the other side of Bowling Green Street. On many mornings I watched George Passant cross over the tramlines, wearing a bowler hat tilted back on his head, carrying a briefcase, swinging a heavy walking-stick. I was due at nine, and he used to cross the street with extreme punctuality half an hour later.

All that summer, when I was not what Aunt Milly denounced as 'gassing', I spent lazy lotos-eating evenings in the company of Jack Cotery. At school he had been too precocious for me; now he was a clerk in the accounts branch of a local newspaper, he ate his sandwiches at midday in the same places as I did, and we drifted together. He had become a powerfully built young man, still short but over-muscled; he had the comedian's face that I remembered, fresh, lively, impudent, wistful. His large ardent eyes shone out of his comedian's face, and his voice was soft and modulated, surprisingly soft to come from that massive chest and throat. He was eighteen, a few months my senior; and he was intoxicated by anything that could come under the name of love. In that soft and modulated voice he talked of girls, women, romance, passion, the delights of the flesh, the incredible attraction of a woman he had seen in the tram that morning, the wonderful prospect of tracking her down, the delights not only of the flesh but of first hearing her voice, the delight that the world was so made that, as long as we lived, the perfume of love would be scattered through the air.

It was talk that I was ready and eager to hear. Not primarily because of the interest of Jack himself, though, when I could break through the dreams his talk induced, he was fun in his own right. In his fashion, he was kind and imaginative. It had been like him, even as a boy, to try to console me on that shameful morning of the ten-shilling note. When one was in his company, he lavished all his good nature, flattering and sweet.

But he was the most unreliable of friends.

He was also a natural romancer. It came to him, as easy as breathing, to add to, to enhance, to transmogrify the truth. As a boy he had boasted – utterly untruthfully – how his father had plenty of money. And now 'I'm on the evening paper,' he could not resist saying, when someone asked his job, and proceeded – from the nucleus of fact that he worked in the newspaper office – to draw a picture of his daily life, as a hard-drinking, dashing, unstoppable journalist. He had enough of a romancer's tact to point out that the glamour of the journalist's occupation had been grossly over-drawn. He shrugged his shoulders like a disillusioned professional.

It was the same with his stories of his conquests. He had much success with women, even while he was still a boy. If he had stuck to the facts, he would have evoked the admiration, the envious admiration, of all his companions, me among them. But the facts were too prosaic for Jack. He was impelled to elaborate stories of how a young woman, obviously desirable, obviously rich and well-born, had come into the office and caught his eye; how she had come in, on one pretext after another, morning after morning; how in the end she had stopped beside his desk, and dropped a note asking him to meet her in the town; how she had driven him in her own car into the country, where they had enjoyed a night of perfect bliss under the stars. 'Uncomfortable at times, clearly,' said Jack, with his romancer's knack of adding a note of comic realism.

He knew that I did not believe a word of it. I was amused by him and fond of him, and I envied his impudence and confidence with women, and of course his success. Chiefly, though, he carried with him a climate in which, just at that time, I wanted to bask; because he was so amorous, because everything he said was full of hints, revelations, advice, fantasies, reminiscences, forecasts, all of love, he brought out and magnified much that I was ready to feel.

For at this stage in our youth we can hold two kinds of anticipation of love, which seem contradictory and yet co-exist and reinforce each other. We can dream, delicately because even to imagine it is to touch one of the most sacred of our hopes, of searching for the other part of ourselves, of the other being who will make us whole, of the ultimate and transfiguring union. (At least this was true of us, when I was young. Later on, seeing my son and his friends breathing fresher air, I wondered how far it was still true for them. How much romantic hope was left, when sex came easier? More, perhaps, than most of them told one another.) At the same time we can gloat over any woman, become insatiably curious about the brute facts of the pleasures which we are then learning or which are just to come. In that phase we are coarse and naked, and anyone who has forgotten his youth will judge that we are too tangled with the flesh ever to forget ourselves in the ecstasy of romantic love. But in fact, at this stage in one's youth, the coarseness and nakedness, the sexual preoccupations, the gloating over delights to come, are – in the reveries where they take place – themselves romantic. They are a promise of joy. Much that Jack Cotery and I said to each other would have been repulsive to a listener who forgot that we were eighteen. Yet at the time they drove from my mind both the discontents and the ambitions. They enriched me as much as my hope, my anticipation, of transfiguring love.

CHAPTER XII

PRIDE AT A FOOTBALL MATCH

AUTUMN came, and I was restless, full of expectation. The School reopened. In the bright September nights I walked down the Newarke to George Passant's classes, full of a kind of new-year elation and resolve. Going back to my lodgings under the misty autumn moon, I wondered about the group that Passant was collecting round him. They were all students at the School, some of whom I knew by name; young women who attended an occasional class, one or two youths who were studying full-time for an external London degree. They gathered round him at the end of the evening, and moved noisily back into the town.

Their laughter rang provocatively loud as they jostled along, a compact group, on the other side of the road. I felt left out. I was chagrined that George Passant had never asked me to join them. I felt very lonely.

Not long afterwards I took my chance and forced myself upon him. It happened in October, a week after my eighteenth birthday. I had come out of the office late. There, on the pavement ten yards ahead, George Passant was walking deliberately with his heavy tread, whistling and swinging his stick.

I caught him up and fell into step beside him. He said good evening with amiable, impersonal cordiality. I said that it was curious we had not met before, since we worked on opposite sides of the street. George agreed that it was. He was half-abstracted, half-shy; I was too intent to mind. He knew my name, he knew that I attended his class. That was not enough. I was going to cut a dash. We passed the reference library, and I referred airily to the hours I spent there, the amount of reading I had done in the last few months; I expounded on Freud, Jung, Adler, Tolstoi, Marx, Shaw. We came to a little bookshop at the corner of Belvoir Street. The lights in the shop window shone on glossy jackets, the jackets of the best sellers of the day, A. S. M. Hutchinson and P. C. Wren and Michael Arlen, with some copies of *The Forsyte Saga* in an honourable position on the right.

'What can you do?' I demanded of George Passant. 'If that's what you give people to read?' I waved my arm at the window. 'If that's what they're willing to take? I don't suppose there's a volume of poetry in the shop. Yeats is one of the greatest poets of the age, and you couldn't go into that shop and buy a single word of his.'

'I'm afraid I don't know anything about poetry,' said George Passant, quickly and defensively, in the tone of a man without an ounce of blague in his whole nature. 'I'm afraid it's no use expecting me to give an opinion about poetry.' Then he said: 'We ought to have a drink on it, anyway. I take it you know the pubs of this town better than I do. Let's go somewhere we shan't be cluttered up with the local bellwethers.'

I was bragging, determined to make an impression, roaring ahead without much care of what he thought. George Passant was five years older, and many men of his age would have been put off. But George's nerves were not grated by raw youth. In a sense, he was perpetually raw and young himself. Partly because of his own diffidence, partly because of his warm, strong fellow-feeling, he took to me as we stood outside the bookshop. Shamelessly I lavished myself in a firework display of boasting, and he still took to me.

We sat by the fire at the Victoria. When we arrived, it was early enough for us to have the room to ourselves: later it filled, but we still kept the table by the fire. George sat opposite me, his face flushed by the heat, his voice, always loud, growing in volume with each pint he drank. He paid for all the beer, stood the barmaids a drink and several of the customers. 'I believe in establishing friendly relations. We shall want to come back here. This is a splendid place,' George confided to me, with preternatural worldly wisdom and a look of extreme cunning: while in fact he was standing treat because he was happy, relaxed, off his guard, exhilarated and at home.

It was a long time that night before I stopped prating on with my own self-advertisement. The meeting mattered to me – I knew that while living in it, though I did not know how much. I was impelled to go on making an impression. It was a long time before I paid any attention to George.

At close quarters, his face had one or two surprises. The massive head was as impressive as in the lecture-room. The great forehead, the bones of the jaw under the blanket of heavy flesh – they were all as I expected. But I was surprised, having only seen him tense and concentrated, to realise that he could look so exuberantly relaxed. As he drank, he softened into sensual content. And I was more surprised to catch his eyes, just for a moment, in repose. His whole being that night exuded power, and happiness, and excitement at having someone with whom to match his wits. He smacked his lips after each tankard, and billowed with contented laughter. But there was one interval, perhaps only a minute long, when each of us was quiet. It was the only silent time between us, all that night. George had put his tankard down, and was staring past me, down the room and into vacant space. His eyes were large, blue, set in deep orbits: in excitement they flashed, but for that moment they were mournful and lost.

In the same way, I heard occasional tones in his speech that seemed to come from different levels from the rest. I listened with all my attention, as I was to go on listening for a good many years. He was more articulate than anyone I had heard, the words often a little stiff and formal, his turns of phrase rigid by contrast to the loud hearty voice with its under-tone of a Suffolk accent. He described his career to me in that articulate fashion, each bit of explanation organised and clear. He was the son of a small-town postmaster, had been articled to an Ipswich firm, had done well in his solicitors' examinations. George did not conceal his satisfaction; everything he said of his training was cheerful, abounding in force, rational, full of his own brimming optimism. Then he came to the end of his articles, and there was a change in tone that I was to hear so often. 'I hadn't any influence, of *course*,' said George Passant, his voice still firm, articulate, but sharp with shrinking diffidence. I recognised that trick in the first hour we talked, but there were others that puzzled me for years, to which I listened often enough but never found the key.

At Eden & Martineau's, George was called the assistant solicitor, but this meant no more than that he was qualified. He was in fact a qualified managing clerk on a regular salary. I could not be sure how much he earned, but I guessed about £300 a year. Yet he thought himself lucky to get the job. He still seemed a little incredulous that they should have appointed him, though it had happened nearly a year before. He told me how he had expected them to reject him after the interview. He believed robustly enough that he was a competent lawyer, but that was something apart. 'I couldn't expect to be much good at an interview, of course,' said George. He was naïf, strangely naïf, in speculating as to why they had chosen him. He fancied that Martineau, the junior partner, must have 'worked it'. George had complete faith and trust in Martineau.

'He's the one real spot of light,' cried George, ramming down his tankard, 'among the Babbitts and bellwethers in this wretched town!'

But we did not talk for long that night of our own stories. We wanted to argue. We had come together, struck sparks, and there was no time to lose. We were at an age when ideas were precious, and we started with different casts of mind and different counters to throw into the pool. Such knowledge as I had picked up was human and literary; George's was legal and political. But it was not just knowledge with which he bore me down; his way of thinking might be abstract, but it was full of passion, and he made tremendous ardent plans for the betterment of man. 'I'm a socialist, of course,' he said vehemently. 'What else could I be?' I burst in that so was I. 'I assumed that,' said George, with finality. He added, still more loudly:

'I should like someone to suggest an alternative for a reasonable man today. I should welcome the opportunity of asking some of our confounded clients how I could reconcile it with my conscience if I wasn't a socialist. God love me, there are only two defensible positions for a reasonable man. One is to be a philosophical anarchist – and I'm not prepared to indulge in that kind of frivolity; the other,' said George, with crushing and conclusive violence, 'is to be exactly what I am.'

As the evening passed he assaulted me with constitutional law, political history, how the common man had won his political freedom, how it was for us and our contemporaries to take the next step. He made my politics look childish. George had bills for nationalisation ready in his head, clear, systematic, detailed, thought out with the concentration and mental horsepower that I had admired from a distance. 'The next few years,' said George, having sandbagged all of my criticisms, 'are going to be a wonderful time to be alive. Eliot, my boy, have you ever thought how lucky you and I are – to be our age at this time of all conceivable times?'

Giddy with drink, with the argument and comradeship, I walked with him through the town. We ate some sandwiches in a frowsty café by the station, and then strolled, still arguing, down the streets near our offices, deserted now until next morning, the streets that had once been the centre of the old market town – Horsefair Street, Millstone Lane, Pocklington's Walk. George's voice rang thunderously in the deserted streets, echoed between the offices and the dark warehouses. At the corner of Pocklington's Walk there shone the lighted windows of a club. We stood beneath them, on the dark and empty pavement. George's hat was tilted back, and I saw his face, which had been open and happy in the heat of argument all night long, turn rebellious, angry and defiant. The curtains were not drawn, and we watched a few elderly men, prosperously dressed, sitting with glasses at their side in the comfortable room. It was a scene of somnolent and well-to-do repose.

'The sunkets!' cried George fiercely. 'The sunkets!' He added: 'What right do they think they've got to sit there as though they owned the world?'

In the next days I thought over that first meeting. From the beginning, I believed that I could enlist George's help. His fellow-feeling was so strong, one could not doubt it, and he knew much more than I. Yet I found it painfully hard to explain my position outright and put the question. Not from scruple, but from pride. I was seeing George regularly now. He took me as an equal: I was more direct than he, I could meet him on something like equal terms; it was wounding to upset the companionship in its first days and confess that I was lost.

While George, for all his good will, made it more awkward because of his own heavy-footed delicacy. He was not the man to take a hint or breathe in a situation through his pores. He needed an explicit statement. But he was too deliberately delicate to ask. It was not for a fortnight that he discovered exactly what I did for a living. Even then, his approach was elaborate and oblique, and he seemed to disbelieve my answers.

It happened, George's first attempt to help me, on a Saturday afternoon, on our way to a league football match. George had a hearty taste for the mass pastimes, chiefly because he enjoyed them, and a little out of defiance. We were jostling among the crowd, the cloth-capped crowd that hustled down the back streets towards the ground; and George, looking straight in front of him, asked a labyrinthine question.

'I take it that when you've got to the top in the education office – which I assume will be in about ten years' time – you won't find it necessary to make the schools in this town change over to the more gentlemanly sport of rugger?'

I was already accustomed to George's outbursts of anti-snobbery, of social hatred. I grinned, and assured him that he could sleep easy; but I knew that I was evading the real question.

'By the way,' George persisted, 'I take it that my assumption is correct?'

'What assumption, George?'

'You will be properly recognised at the education office in ten years' time?'

I made myself speak plainly.

'In ten years' time,' I said, 'if I stay there – I might have gone up a step or two. As a clerk.'

'I'm not prepared to accept that,' said George. 'You're underestimating yourself.'

We came to the ground. As we passed through the turnstiles, I asked: 'Do you realise what my job is?'

'I've got a general impression,' said George uncomfortably, 'but I'm not entirely clear.'

We clambered up the terrace, and there I began to tell him. But George was not inclined to believe it. He proceeded to speak as though my job were considerably grander and had more future than I had ever, in all my wishes, dared to imagine.

'It may be difficult now,' said George, 'but it's obvious that you're marked down for promotion. It's perfectly clear that they must have some machinery for pulling people like you to the top. Otherwise, I don't see how local government is going to function.'

That was a typical piece of George's optimism. I was tempted to leave him with it. Like my mother, I had to struggle to admit the humble truth – even though I managed to keep a hold on it, sometimes a precarious one. It was bitter. Yet, again like my mother, I felt that I must swallow the bitterness in order not to miss a chance – to impress on George that I was nothing but a clerk.

'I'm a very junior clerk, George. I'm getting twenty-five shillings a week. I shall be ticking off names for the next five years. Just as I'm doing now.'

George was both angry and abashed. He swore, and the violence of his curse made some youths in white mufflers turn and gape at him. He hesitated to ask me more, and then did so. Awkwardly he tried to pretend that things were not as bad as I painted them. Then he swore again, and he was near one of his storms of rage.

He said brusquely:

'Something will have to be done about it.'

He was brusque with embarrassment. I too was speaking harshly.

'That's easy to say,' I replied.

'I shall have to take a hand myself,' said George, still in a rough and off-hand tone.

Now I had only to ask for help. I wanted it acutely; I had been playing for it; now it was mine for the asking, I was too proud to move. I turned as awkward as George.

'I expect I shall be able to manage,' I said.

George was abashed again. He stared fixedly at the empty field, where the turf gleamed brilliantly under the sullen sky.

'It's time these teams came out,' he said.

CHAPTER XIII

THE HOPES OF OUR YOUTH

GEORGE was embarrassed at having his interest repulsed. For days and weeks he made no reference to my career or even to my daily life. He did not see so much of me alone. Cross with myself, incensed at my own involuntary stiffness, I tried half-heartedly to open the conversation again. But George went by rule, not by shades of feeling. He had made a mistake which caused him to feel inept. More than most men, he was paralysed when he felt inept. So he studied his mistake, so as to teach himself not to repeat it.

Without any embarrassment at all, however, he plunged me into the centre of the 'group'. That was our name, then and always, for the young men and women who gathered round George and whose leader he became. Theirs was the laughter I had envied, walking on the other side of the road, before George took me up. In the future, although we had no foresight of it then, he was to devote to them a greater and a greater share of his vigour; until in the end he lived altogether in them and for them. Until in the end, through living in them and for them, he destroyed his own blazing promise – and, for me and others, destroyed more than that.

But George's is a story by itself. When I first knew him, the crises of his life were years ahead, and he was assembling the 'group' round him, heartening and melting everyone within it, so brimful of hope for each one of us that no one could stay cold. All the group were students at the School, and, though the number increased later, in my time it was never larger than ten. Most of them were girls – some from the prosperous middle class, who went to the School to pass their time before they got married, and saw in George an escape from the restrictions of their homes. Most of the group, however, were poor and aspiring – young women working in the town, secretaries and clerks or elementary school-teachers like my friend Marion Gladwell. They went to the School to better themselves professionally, or because they were hungry for culture, or because they might there find a man. They were always the backbone of George's group, together with one or two eager and ambitious young men, such as I was then.

That was the material George had to work on. We sat hour after hour at night or on Sunday afternoons in dingy cafés up and down the town, the cafés of cinemas or, late at night, the lorry drivers' 'caff' beside the railway station. In those first years, George did not find it easy to collect the group together, but soon we developed the practice of all going to spend weekends in a farmhouse ten miles away, where we could cook our own food, pay a shilling a night for a bed, and talk until daybreak.

Under the pink-shaded lights at the picture-house café, round the oil lamp on the table at the farm, we sat while George made prophecies of our future, shouted us down for false arguments, enlarged us with hope. He gave us credit for having all his own qualities and more. I knew he was overestimating the others, and sometimes, even with the conceit of eighteen, I did not recognise myself in his descriptions, and wished uncomfortably that they were nearer to the truth. He endowed me with all varieties of courage, revolutionary and altruistic zeal, aggressive force, leadership, unbreakable resolution and power of will. He used to regret, with his naïve and surprising modesty, that he was not blessed with the same equipment. I was inflated, and acted for a time as though George's picture of my character were accurate; but I had a suspicion lurking underneath – for I was already more suspicious of myself and other human beings than George would be at fifty – that I was quite unlike George's noble picture, and that so also were all living men.

Yet George gave us such glowing hope just because he was utterly unsuspicious of men's nature and the human condition. As a child I had been used to my mother's roseate hopes for a transformation in her life, but by those she meant nothing more nor less than a fulfilment for herself – sometimes that she might find love, always that she might live like a lady. George's hopes were as passionate as hers, and more violent, but they were different in kind. He believed, with absolute sincerity and with each beat of his heart, that men could become better; that the whole world could become better; that the restraints of the past, the shackles of guilt, could fall off and set us all free to live happily in a free world; that we could create a society in which men could live in peace, in decent comfort, and cease to be power-craving, avaricious, censorious and cruel. George believed, with absolute sincerity and with each beat of his heart, that all this would happen before we were old.

It was the first time, for Jack Cotery and me and the rest, that we had been near a cosmic faith. But these were the middle twenties, and the whole spirit of the time was behind George Passant. It was a time when political hope, international hope, was charging the air we breathed. Not only George Passant was full of faith as we cheered the Labour gains in the town hall square on the election night in 1923. And it was a time of other modes of hope. Freud, D. H. Lawrence, Rutherford – messages were in the air, and in our society we did not listen to the warnings. It was a great climacteric of hope, and George embodied it in his flesh and bone.

At another period he would have thrown himself into a religion. As it was, he made a creed out of every free idea that spurted up in those last days of radical and rootless freedom. He believed that it was better to be alive in 1923 than at any other moment in the world's history. He believed – with great simplicity, despite his wild and complex nature – in the perfectibility of man.

That faith of his did not really fit me at all – though for a time it coloured many of my thoughts. In due course I parted from George on almost all of the profound human questions. For all his massive intelligence, his vision of life was so different from mine that we could not for long speak the same mental language. And yet, despite that foreignness, despite much that was to happen, I was grateful that, for those years in my youth, I came under his influence. Our lives were to take us divergent ways. As I have said, we parted on all the profound human questions – except one. Though I could not for long think happily as he did of the human condition, I also could not forget the strength of his fellow feeling. I could not forget how robustly he stood by the side of his human brothers against the dark and cold. Human beings were brothers to him – not only brothers to love, but brothers to hate with violence. When he hated them, they were still men, men of flesh and bone – and he was one among them, in their sweat and bewilderment and folly. He hoped for so much from them – but if he had hoped for nothing, he would still have felt them as his brothers and struggled as robustly by their side. He took his place among them. By choice he would not move a step away from the odour of man.

There I did not want to part from him. His fellow feeling had strengthened mine.

Later, when I was an ageing man, I had to know that I had sentimentalised his influence. It was what I should have liked, and what in part I tried to invent. Yet I did not invent it all.

Quite soon after George took me into the group, our difference began to show. Yet I too was full of hope. I might attack George's utopian visions, but then at times George provoked all my destructive edge. There were other times I remembered afterwards, in which I was as unshielded as my mother used to be, in which I had learned nothing of disappointment.

I remembered the first time that Marion Gladwell asked me to call on her at school. She had been promising to lend me a book, but whenever we met in the group she had forgotten it; I could have it, she said, if I went round to her school in the lunch-hour.

The school was in Albion Street, near to the middle of the town, a diminutive red-brick barracks drawing in the children from the rows of red-brick houses in the mean streets near. Marion had only taught there a year, since she came out of her training college. She was twenty-one, and engrossed in her work. She often talked to us about the children, laughed at herself for being 'earnest', and then told us some more.

When I arrived in her classroom that afternoon she was just opening a window. The room was dark and small, and there was a faint, vestigial, milky smell of small children. Marion said, in her energetic, over-emphatic, nervous fashion, that she must let some oxygen in before the next lesson. She moved rapidly to the next window, opened it, returned to the blackboard, shook the duster so that a cloud of chalk hung in the air.

'Sit down, Lewis,' she said. 'I want to talk to you.'

She stood by the blackboard, twisting the duster. At the group she was over-emphatic, over-decisive, but no one minded it much from her, since she was so clearly nervous and anxious to be liked and praised. She was tallish and strong, very quick and active physically, but a little clumsy, and either her figure was shapeless or she dressed so sloppily that one could not see she had a waist. But she had an open, oval, comely face, and her eyes were striking. They were not large, but bright and continually interested. Despite her earnestness, they were humorous and gay.

That afternoon she wrung out the duster, unusually restless and nervous even for her.

'I'm worried about you,' she said.

'What's the matter?'

'You mustn't burn the candle at both ends.'

I asked what she meant, but I had a very good idea. Marion, like most of the girls in the group, came from a respectable lower-middle-class home, and their emancipation had still not gone far. So Marion and the others were shocked, some of them pleasantly shocked, at the gossip they heard of our drinking parties and visits to Nottingham. The gossip became far more lurid than the facts – Jack saw to that, who was himself a most temperate man – and George and the rest of us acquired an aura of sustained dissipation.

I was not displeased. It was flattering to hear oneself being rescued from sin. I tried to pare off the more extravagant edges of the stories, but Marion wanted to believe them, and I should have had to be much more whole-hearted to persuade her.

'You mustn't wear yourself out,' said Marion obstinately.

'I'm pretty good at looking after myself,' I said.

'I don't believe it,' said Marion. 'Anyway, you mustn't waste yourself. Think of all you've got to do.'

She was watching me with her clear, bright eyes. She must have seen a change in my expression. She knew that I was softened and receptive now. She gave up twisting the duster and put it in its box. In doing so she knocked down a piece of chalk, and cried 'Oh, why do I always upset everything?' Her eyes were lit up with gaiety, and she leaned against the desk. Her voice was still decisive, but it was easy to confide.

'Tell me what you want to do. Tell me what you want.'

My first reply was:

'Of course, I want to see a better world.'

Marion nodded her head, as though she would have given the same answer. We were sufficiently under George Passant's influence to make such an answer quite un-selfconsciously. We were children of our class and time, and took that hope as unchallengeable. That afternoon in Marion's schoolroom in 1923, both she and I expected it to be fulfilled.

'What do you want for yourself?' asked Marion.

'I want success.'

She seemed startled by the force with which I had spoken. She said: 'What do you call success?'

'I don't mean to spend my life unknown.'

'Do you want to make money, Lewis?'

'I want everything that people call success. Plus a few requirements of my own.'

'You mustn't expect too much,' said Marion.

'I expect everything there is,' I said. I went on: 'And if I fail, I shan't make any excuses. I shall say that it is my own fault.'

'Lewis!' she cried. There was a strange expression on her face. After a silence, she asked: 'Is there anything else you want?'

This time I hesitated. Then I said:

'I think I want love.'

Marion said, her voice emphatic and decisive, but her face still soft with pain:

'Oh, I haven't had time for that. There's too much else to do. I wonder if *you'll* have time.'

I was too rapt to attend to her. Just then, I was living in my imagination. Marion contradicted herself, and said:

'Oh, I suppose you're right. I suppose we all want – love. But, Lewis, I wonder if we mean the same thing by love?'

I was living in my imagination, and I could not tell her the essence of my own hope, let alone come near perceiving hers. I had confessed myself to her with ardour. I began to enquire about what she would teach that afternoon.

CHAPTER XIV

AN ACT OF KINDNESS

THAT winter I found the days in the office harder than ever to bear. At night I drank with George, stood at coffee-stalls, sat in his room or my attic, tirelessly walked the streets until the small hours, while we stimulated each other's answers to the infinite questions of young men – man's destiny, the existence of God, the organisation of the world, the nature of love. It was hard to wake up, with the echoes of the infinite questions still running through my head, to get to the office by nine and to stare with heavy eyes at the names of fee-paying children at one of the secondary schools.

Mr Vesey did not make it easier. He considered that I was living above my station, and he disapproved intensely. He had heard that I was seen in the London Road one night, excessively cheerful with drink. He had heard also of my political speeches. Mr Vesey was outraged that I should presume to do things he dared not do. He said ominously that the life of his clerks out of hours was part of his business, whatever we might think. He addressed the office in characteristically dark and cryptic hints: how some people deliberately drew attention to themselves, either by 'sucking up to authority' or by 'painting the town red', with only one intention, which was to discredit their superior and obstruct his promotion.

He was watching for a chance to report me. But here his mania for promotion made him cautious. He knew that I was in favour higher up. He realised he must have a solid case, unless he were to lose his reputation for 'knowing his men'. He would rather sacrifice his moral indignation, let me go unpunished for a time, than make a false move. 'One doesn't want to drop a brick,' said Mr Vesey cryptically to the office, 'just when *they* must be realising that certain things are overdue.'

Of course, it made him dislike me more. The story of my relation with Mr Vesey became a good one with which to entertain the group; but it was not so funny during the monotonous, drab, humiliating days. Dislike at close quarters can be very wearing, and it does not console one much if the dislike shows on a comic face. I used to look up from my desk and see the enormous spectacled eyes of Mr Vesey fixed upon me. I could not make myself impervious to the thought that I had become an obsession within him, part of his web of persecution. When I described him to George and the rest, he was a trim spectacled figure, crazed with promotion-fever, keeping in the public eye; but in the office, where I spent so many desert hours, he became a man, a feeling and breathing man, who loathed me, every action I performed and every word I spoke.

Sitting in the office on winter afternoons, looking out into the murk of Bowling Green Street, I was angry that I had delayed taking George's help, even by a week. I was paying for my pride. Very soon I was ready to humble myself, apologise, and ask his advice. It was early in '24, not more than a couple of months after his first approach. But I was spared: George had been considering his 'mistake', and he was not prepared to let me waste more time. He got in first. Stiffly he said, one night, with the formality that came over him when he was feeling diffident about expressing concern or affection:

'I propose that we adjourn to my place. I want to make some points about your career. I don't feel justified in respecting your privacy any longer. I have certain suggestions to make.'

This time I was in a hurry to accept.

It was not until we had reached his lodgings, and settled ourselves by the fire, that George began with his 'suggestions'. It surprised people that he, one of the most turbulent of men, should sometimes behave so punctiliously and formally, as though he were undertaking a piece of delicate official diplomacy. That night he propitiated his landlady into making us a pot of tea, propitiated her because she was truculent and did nothing for him. George lived among the furniture of an artisan's front room; all he contributed were pipes, a jar of tobacco, a few books, documents from the office and sheaf upon sheaf of foolscap.

We drank our tea. At last George thought it was a fitting time to begin.

'Well,' he said, firmly and yet uncomfortably, 'I propose to start on the basis of your legacy. I assume that I should have been told if the position had altered to any material extent.'

Aunt Za's will had taken a long time to prove, and I had often thought how inevitably my mother would have seen the sinister hand of Uncle Will. But in fact I had actually received the three hundred pounds a few weeks before.

'Of course you would have been told,' I said. 'It's still there.'

'The sum is three hundred pounds?' asked George unnecessarily, for his memory was perfect.

'Less what I owe you,' I said.

'I don't intend to consider that,' said George, for the first time hearty and comfortable. With money, he was lavish, easy, warm-hearted and prodigal. At the end of each month, when he received his pay, he had taken to asking if he could lend me a pound or two. 'I don't intend to consider that for a minute. Three hundred pounds is your basis. You've got to use it to establish yourself in a profession. That's the only serious question, and everything else is entirely irrelevant.'

'I'm not going to disagree.' I smiled. I was on tenterhooks, excited, vigilant.

'Excellent,' said George. 'Well, I expect other people have made suggestions, but unless you stop me I propose to present you with mine.'

'If other people had made suggestions,' I said, 'I should probably have got a move on by now. You don't realise how you've altered the look of things,' I went on, with spontaneous feeling—and with a hint of something he wanted to hear mixed in the feeling, for that too came just as naturally.

'I don't know about that,' said George, and hurried on with his speech. 'I can't see that there is any alternative to my case. (*a*) You've got to establish yourself in a profession; (*b*) You insist that you haven't any reasonable contacts anywhere, and (*c*) I haven't any influence, *of course*. With one exception that I regard as important, and that is obviously Martineau. Which brings up the possibility of my own profession and my own firm. (*d*) It goes without saying that you'd become an incomparably better solicitor than most of the bellwethers and sunkets who disfigure what I still consider a decent profession for a reasonable man. I can tell you here and now, from what I've seen of your work, that you would pass the examinations on your head, if you only follow my old maxim and work when there is nothing else to do. If you manage three hours' work a night before you come out for a drink, there will be nothing to stop you. (*e*) Your basic sum of three hundred pounds is enough to pay the cost of your articles, even if Martineau can't manage to get you in free. I can't be expected to answer for other professions, but I haven't been able to think of another where you won't have financial difficulties. (*f*) Martineau can be persuaded to let you serve your articles in our firm, which would be very convenient for all concerned.' George leant back in his chair with an expression seraphic and complacent. 'I'm afraid I can't see any alternative,' he said contentedly. 'Everything points to your becoming articled to the old firm of Eden & Martineau. I propose you give the egregious Vesey a parting kick, and get your articles arranged in time for the spring. That's my case.' He stared challengingly at me. 'I should like to hear if you can find any objections.'

'How much would it need? What would it cost?'

George answered with mechanical accuracy. No one was ever more conversant with regulations.

'If there's any snag,' said George, 'I should expect you to look on me as your banker. I don't see how you can possibly need more than a hundred pounds on top of your basic sum. Somehow or other, that will have to be found. I insist that you don't let a trivial sum affect your decision.'

I tried to speak, but George stopped me with a crashing, final shout: 'I regard it as settled,' he cried.

But I did not. I was touched and affected and my heart was thumping, just as I was affected all my life by any kindness. For another to take a step on one's behalf – it was one of the most difficult things to become hardened to. And I was attracted by George's proposal. It was a way of escape, a goodish way compared with my meaningless and servile days in the education office. With George's praise to bolster me up, I did not doubt that I should make a competent solicitor. As my mother would have said, it would be 'better than nothing' – and, sitting in George's room, excited, touched by his comradeship, avid with the drawing near of my first leap, I thought for a moment how gratified my mother would have been, if she had seen me accept his suggestion, become a solicitor, set up in a country town, make some money and re-establish the glory of her Wigmore uncle when she was a girl.

I was softened and mellow with emotion. In the haze of George's tobacco my head was swimming. Through the haze, George's face, the mantelpiece, the framed diploma hanging over the whatnot, all shone out, ecstatically bright. For the first time, as though my sight had sharpened, I read some words in the diploma. Suddenly I was seized by laughter. George looked astonished, then followed my finger, stared across the room at the diploma, and himself roared until the tears came. For it was a certificate, belonging presumably to his landlady's husband, which testified to a record of ten years' total abstinence – it was issued by one of Aunt Milly's organisations.

Yet, all the time, I was wondering. At bottom I was warier than George, shrewder, far more ambitious and more of a gambler. If I was going to take this jump, why not jump further? – that question was half-formed inside me. George was not a worldly man, I realised already. Outside the place where chance had brought him, he did not instinctively know his way about. I never forgot the first night we talked, when George stood in the dark street and cursed up at the club windows; for him, it was always others who sat in the comfortable places, in the warm and lighted rooms.

With delight I accepted his invitation to take me to the next of Martineau's 'Friday nights' – 'To carry out our plan which I regard as settled in principle,' said George complacently. Yet there might be other ways for me. Even that evening, with the excitement still hot upon me, I found time to ask some questions about a barrister's career. Not that I was contemplating it for a moment myself, I said. Becoming a solicitor might be practicable: this was not. But, just as a matter of interest, how well should I cope with the Bar examinations? George thought the question trivial and irrelevant, but said again that, with three or four years' work, I should sail through them.

He might not be worldly, but he was a fine lawyer, whose own record in examinations was of the highest class. Decisions are taken before we realise them ourselves: above all, perhaps, those that matter to us most.

I did not know it, but my mind may have been made up from that moment.

CHAPTER XV

AN INTENTION AND A NAME

I set out to win the support of Martineau and Eden. Whichever way I moved, I should need them. I could not afford to fail. When George took me, first to Martineau's house, then to Eden's office, I was nervous; but it was a pleasurable nervousness that sharpened my attention and my wits. Unlike George, who was embarrassed at any social occasion, I was enjoying myself.

I got airy encouragement from Martineau, but no more. Although none of us realised it then, he was losing all interest in his profession. He welcomed me to his 'Friday night' parties; it was the first salon I had ever attended, and knowing no others I did not realise how eccentric it was. I enjoyed being inside a comfortable middle-class house for the first time. I could not persuade him to attend to my career, though he made half-promises, chiefly I thought because he was so fond of George.

It was quite different with Eden. Before George introduced me, I knew that the meeting was critical, for Eden was the senior partner. I guessed that I had disadvantages to overcome. Before I had been in Eden's office three minutes, I felt with an extra tightening of the nerves that I had more than a disadvantage against me: I was struggling with Eden's unshakeable dislike of George.

The office was warm and comfortable, with a fire in an old-fashioned grate, leather-covered armchairs, sets of heavy volumes round the walls. Eden sat back in his chair, smoking a pipe, when George awkwardly presented me; and then George stood for a time, not knowing whether to leave us or stay, with me still standing also. Eden was just going to speak, but George chose that moment to say that he did not agree with Eden's general line of instructions about a new case.

Eden was bald and frog-faced, substantial in body, comfortably and pleasantly ugly. His manner was amiable, but he ceased to be so bland when he replied to George. They had a short altercation, each of them trying hard to be courteous, Eden repressing his irritation, George insisting on his opinion and his rights. Soon Eden said:

'Well, well, Passant, this isn't the best time to discuss it. Perhaps you might leave me with this young man.'

'If you prefer it, Mr Eden,' said George, and backed away.

Eden might have been designed to extract the last ounce of misunderstanding out of George. He was a solid, indolent, equable, good-humoured man, modest about everything but his judgment. He was often pleased with his own tolerance and moderation. He respected George's intellect and professional competence – it was comfortable for him to respect the latter, for Eden was not overfond of work, and, having once assured himself of George's skill, was content to let that dynamo-like energy dispose of most of the firm's business. But everything else about George repelled him. George's 'wildness', formality, passion for argument, lack of ease – they infuriated Eden. Before he spoke to me, when George at last left us alone, I knew that I was under the same suspicion. Some of George's aura surrounded me also, in Eden's eyes. I had to please right in the teeth of a prejudice.

'Well, young man,' said Eden with a stiff, courteous but not over-amiable smile, 'what can I do for you?' I replied that above all things I needed the guidance of a man of judgment. And I continued in that vein.

My brashness and spasms of pride with George were not much like me, or at least not like the self that in years to come got on easily with various kinds of men and women. Even in the months between my meetings with George and Eden, I was learning. In casual human contacts, I was already more practised than George, who stayed all his life something like most of us at eighteen. I was much more confident than George that I should get along with Eden or with anyone that I met; and that confidence made me more ready to please, more unashamed about pleasing. It was not until later, when my character had hardened, that I distrusted in myself that particular art.

Eden became much less suspicious. He went out of his way to be affable. He did not make up his mind quickly about people, but he was very genial, pleased with himself for being so impartial, satisfied that one of Passant's friends could – unlike that man Passant – make so favourable an impression. Eden liked being fair. Passant made it so difficult to be fair – it was one of his major sins.

Eden did not promise anything on the spot, as Martineau had done. He told me indulgently enough that I should have to 'sober down', whatever career I took up. In a local paper he had noticed a few violent words from a speech of mine. The identical words would have damned George in Eden's mind, but did not damn me. At first sight he felt he could advise me, as he could never have advised George. 'Ah well! Young men can't help making nuisances of themselves,' he said amiably. 'As long as you know where to draw the line.'

It would have offended Eden's sense of decorum to form an impression in haste, or to make a promise without weighing it. He believed in taking his time, in gathering other people's opinions, in distrusting impulse and first impressions, and in ruminating over his own preliminary judgment. He spoke, so I heard, to Darby and the director. He had a word with my old headmaster. It was a fortnight or more before he sent across to the education office a note asking me if I would make it convenient to call on him.

When I did so, he still took his time. He sat solidly back in his chair. He was satisfied now that the investigation was complete and the ceremony of forming a judgment properly performed. He was satisfied to have me there, waiting on his words. 'I don't believe in jumping to conclusions, Eliot,' he said. 'I'm not clever enough to hurry. But I've thought round your position long enough now to feel at home.' Methodically he filled his pipe. At last he came to the point.

'Do you know, young man,' said Eden, 'I don't see why you shouldn't make a job of it.'

Unlike Martineau, he made a definite offer. If I wanted to serve my articles as a solicitor, he would accept me on the usual footing, I paying my fee of two hundred and fifty guineas. It was entirely fair: it was exactly as he had treated any other of the articled clerks who had gone through the firm. He explained that he was not making any concessions to partiality or to the fact that I was so poor. 'If we started that, young man, we should never know when to stop. Pay your way like everyone else, and we shall all be better friends,' said Eden, with the broad judgment-exuding smile that lapped up the corners of his mouth. But he knew that, when I had paid the fee, I should not have enough to live on. So he was prepared to allow me thirty shillings a week while I served my time. With his usual temperateness he warned me that, before I took articles in the firm, I ought to be reminded that there was not likely to be a future for me there 'when you become qualified, all being well'. For George Passant was not, so far as Eden knew, likely to move, and the firm did not need another qualified assistant.

I thanked him with triumph, with relief. I said that I ought to think it over, and Eden approved. He had no doubt that I was going to accept. I said that I might have other problems to raise, and Eden again approved. He still had no doubt that I was going to accept.

How much doubt had I myself, that day in Eden's room? Or back at my desk, under Mr Vesey's enormous and persecuted eyes, on those spring afternoons, waiting for the day's release at half-past five? There is no doubt that, on the days after Eden's offer, I often steadied myself with the thought that I need not stand it. I had a safe escape now. I could end the servitude tomorrow. If I did not, it was of my own volition.

I assuaged each morning's heaviness with the prospect of that escape. Yet I had a subterranean knowledge that I should never take it. The nerves flutter and dither, and make us delay recognising a choice to ourselves; we honour that process by the title of 'making up our minds'. But the will knows.

I had rejected George's proposition the minute it was uttered – and before I set out to work for Martineau's and for Eden's help. I wanted that help, but for another reason. I was going – there was at bottom no residue of doubt, however much I might waver on the surface – to choose the wilder gamble, and read for the Bar.

I had not yet admitted the intention to the naked light, even in secret; but it was forcing its way through, flooding me with a sense of champagne-like risk and power. It was hard to defend, which I knew better than all those I should have to argue with, for I felt the prickle of anxiety even before I admitted the intention to myself. If all went perfectly, I should have spent my 'basic sum' by the time I took Bar Finals. There was no living to look forward to immediately, nor probably for several years; it meant borrowing money or winning a studentship. It left no margin for any kind of illness or failure. I should have to spend two-thirds of the three hundred pounds on becoming admitted to an Inn. If anything went wrong, I had lost that stake altogether, and so had no second chance.

I did not even escape the office. For·I should leave myself so little money, after the fees were paid, that my office wages would be needed to pay for food and board. Instead of crossing Bowling Green Street and working alongside of George, I should have to discipline myself to endure the tedium, the hours without end of clerking, Mr Vesey. All my study for the Bar examinations I should have to do at night; and on those examinations my whole future rested.

In favour of the gamble, there was just one thing to say. If my luck held at every point and I came through, there were rewards, not only money, though I wanted that. It gave me a chance, so I thought then, of the paraphernalia of success, luxury and a name and, yes, the admiration of women.

There was nothing more lofty about my ambition at that time, nothing at all. It had none of the complexity or aspiration of a mature man's ambition – and also none of the moral vanity. Ten years later, and I could not have felt so simply. Yet I made my calculations, I reckoned the odds, I knew they were against me, almost as clear-sightedly as if I had been grown-up.

When I knew, with full lucidity, that the decision was irrevocably taken, I still cherished it to myself for days and weeks.

I was intensely happy, in that spring and summer of my nineteenth year. The days were wet; rain streamed down the office window; I was full of well-being, of a joyful expectancy, now that I knew what I had to do. I was anxious and had some of my first sleepless nights. But it was a happy sleeplessness, so that I looked with expectation on the first light of a summer dawn. Once I got up with the sun and walked the streets that were so familiar to George and me at the beginning of the night. Now in the dawn the road was pallid, the houses smaller, all blank and washed after the enchantment of the dark. I thought of what lay just ahead. There would be some trouble with Eden, which I must surmount, for it was imperative to keep his backing. Perhaps George might not be altogether pleased. I should have to persuade them. That would be the first step.

It was in those happy days that, attuned so that my imagination stirred to the sound of a girl's name, I first heard the name of Sheila Knight. I was attuned so that an unknown name invited me, as I had never been invited before, attuned because of my own gamble and the well-being which made the blood course through my veins, attuned too because of the amorous climate which lapped round our whole group on those summer evenings. For George's pleasures could not be long concealed from us at our age, thinking of love, talking of love, swept off our feet by imagined joys. In Jack's soft voice there came stories of delight, his conquests and adventures and the whispered words of girls. We were at an age when we were deafened by the pounding of our blood. We began to flirt, and that was the first fashion. Jack's voice murmured the names of girls, girls he had known or whom he was pursuing. I flirted a little with Marion, but it was the unknown that invited me. Sheila's name was not the first nor only one that plucked at my imagination. But each word about her gave her name a clearer note.

'She goes about by herself, looking exceedingly glum,' said Jack. 'She's rather beautiful, in a chiselled, soulful way,' said Jack. 'She'd be too much trouble for me. It isn't the pretty ones who are most fun,' said Jack. 'I advise you to keep off. She'll only make you miserable,' said Jack.

None of the group knew her, though Jack claimed to have spoken to her at the School. It was said that she lived in the country, and came to an art class one night a week.

One warm and cloudy midsummer evening, I had met Jack out of the newspaper office, and we were walking slowly up the London Road. A car drove by close to the pavement, and I had a moment's sight, blurred and confused, of a young woman's face, a smile, a wave. The car passed us, and I turned my head, but could see no more. Jack was smiling. He said:

'Sheila Knight.'

CHAPTER XVI

DENUNCIATION

For weeks no one knew that, instead of taking articles, I was determined to try reading for the Bar. I delayed breaking the news longer than was decent, even to George, most of all to George. I was apprehensive of his criticisms; I did not want my resolution shaken too early. The facts were harsh: I could face them realistically in secret, but it was different to hear them from another, just as it had been different to hear Aunt Milly's criticisms of my parents, though I could make those same criticisms to myself. Also I was uneasy. Could I still keep Eden's goodwill? Could I secure my own way without loss? I screwed myself up to breaking the news one afternoon in September. I thought I would get it over quickly, tell them all within an hour.

I took the half-day off, incidentally raising Mr Vesey's suspicions to snapping-point. I went into the reference library, so as to pass the time before Eden returned from lunch. I meant to tell George first, but not to give myself long. The library was cool, aquarium-like after the bright day outside. Instead of bringing calm, the chill, the smell of books, the familiar smell of that room only made me more uneasy, and I wished more than ever that I had this afternoon behind me.

Just before my appointment with Eden I looked into George's office and told him what I was going to say. I saw his face become heavy. He said nothing. There was no time for either of us to argue, for we could hear Eden's deliberate footsteps outside the open door.

Eden settled himself in his armchair. Now that the hesitation was over, now that I was actually in the room to make the best of it, I plunged into placating him. I told him how his support had stimulated and encouraged me. If I was attempting too much, I said with the mixture of deference and cheek that I knew would please him, it was really his fault – for giving me too much support. I liked him more, because I was seeing him with all my nerves alive with excitement – with the excitement that, when plunged into it, I really loved. I saw him with great clarity, from the pleased, reluctant, admonishing smile to the peel of sunburn on the top of his bald head.

He was pleased. There was no doubt about that. But he was too solid a man to have his judgments shaken, to give way all at once, just because he was pleased. He was severe, reflective, minatory, shocked, and yet touched with a sneaking respect. 'These things will happen,' he said, putting his finger-tips together. 'Young men will take the bit between their teeth. But I shouldn't be doing my duty, Eliot, if I didn't tell you that you were being extremely foolish. I thought you were a bit more level-headed. I'm afraid you've been listening to some of your rackety friends.'

I told him that it was my own free choice. He shook his head. He had obstinately decided that it must be Passant's fault, and the more I protested, the more obstinate he became.

'Remember that some of your friends have got through their own examinations,' he said. 'They may not be the best company for you, even if they seem about the same age. Still, you'll make your own mistakes. I know how you feel about things, Eliot. We've all been young once, you know. I can remember when I wanted to throw my cap over the windmill. Nothing venture, nothing win, that's how you feel, isn't it? We've all felt it, Eliot, we've all felt it. But you've got to have a bit of sense.'

He was certain that I must have made up my mind in a hurry, and he asked me to promise that I would do nothing irrevocable without thinking it over for another fortnight. If I did not consent to that delay, he would not be prepared to introduce me to an acquaintance at the Bar, whose signature I needed to support me in some of the formalities of getting admitted to an Inn.

'I'm not sure, young man,' said Eden, 'that I oughtn't to refuse straight out – in your own best interests. In your own best interests, perhaps I should put a spoke in your wheel. But I expect you'll think better of it anyway, after you've cooled your heels for another fortnight.'

In one's 'own best interests' – this was the first time I heard that ominous phrase, which later I heard roll sonorously and self-righteously round college meetings, round committees in Whitehall, round the most eminent of boards, and which meant inevitably that some unfortunate person was to be dished. But Eden had not said it with full conviction. Underneath his admonishing tone, he was still pleased. He felt for me a warm and comfortable patronage, which was not going to be weakened. I left his room, gay, relieved, with my spirits at their highest.

Then, along the corridor, I saw George standing outside his own room, waiting for me.

'You'd better come out for a cup of tea,' he said in a tone full of rage and hurt.

The rage I could stand, and in the picture-house café I was denounced as a fool, an incompetent, a half-baked dilettante, an airy-fairy muddler who was too arrogant to keep his feet on the ground. But I was used to his temper, and could let it slide by. That afternoon I was prepared for some hot words, for I had behaved without manners and without consideration, in not disclosing my plans to him until so late.

I had imagined vividly enough for myself what he was shouting in the café, oblivious of the customers sitting by, shouting with the rage I had bargained on and a distress which I had not for a minute expected. The figures of 'this egregious nonsense' went exploding all over the café, as George became more outraged. He extracted them from me by angry questions and then crashed them out in his tremendous voice. Two hundred and eight pounds down! At the best, even if I stayed at that 'wretched boy's job' (cried George, rubbing it in brutally), which was ridiculous if I were to stand any chance in the whole insane venture – even if nothing unexpected happened and my luck was perfect, I should be left with eighty pounds. 'What about your fees as a pupil? In this blasted gentlemanly profession in which you're so anxious to be a hanger-on, isn't it obligatory to be rooked and go and sit in some nitwit's chambers and pay some sunket a handsome packet for the privilege?' George, as usual, had his facts right. I wanted another hundred pounds for my pupil's fees, and support for whatever time it was, a time which would certainly be measured in years, before I began earning. Against that I had my contemptible eighty pounds, and any money I could win in studentships. 'Which you can't count on, if you retain any shred of sanity at all, which I'm beginning to doubt. What other possible source of money have you got in the whole wide world?'

'Only what I can borrow.'

'How in God's name do you expect anyone to lend you money? For a piece of sheer fantastic criminal lunacy—'

He and Aunt Milly were, in fact, the only living persons from whom I had any serious hope of borrowing money. When he was first persuading me to become articled as a solicitor, George had, of course, specifically offered to be my 'banker'. How he thought of managing it, I could not imagine; for his total income, as I now knew, was under £300 a year, he had no capital at all, and made an allowance to his parents. Yet he had promised to find a hundred pounds for me and, even that afternoon, he was conscience-stricken at having to take the offer back. As well as being a generous man, George had the strictest regard for his word. That afternoon he was abandoned to anger and distress. He said that he washed his hands of my future, as though he were dismissing it once for all. But even then he felt obliged to add:

'I am sorry that any promise of mine may have helped to encourage you in this piece of lunacy. I took it for granted that you'd realise it was only intended for purposes within the confines of reason. I'm sorry.'

He went away from the cafe abruptly. I sat alone, troubled, guilty, anxious. I needed someone to confide in. There was a pall of trouble between me and the faces in the streets, as I walked up the London Road, my steps leading me, almost like a sleepwalker, to Marion. I sometimes talked to her about my plans, and she scolded me for not telling her more. Now I found myself walking towards her lodgings. I was voraciously anxious for myself; and mixed with the anxiety (how could I set it right?) I felt sheer guilt – guilt at causing George a disappointment I could not comprehend. I had been to blame; I had been secretive, my secrecy seemed like a denial of friendship and affection. But secrecy could not have wounded George so bitterly.

His emotion had been far more violent than disappointment, it had been furious distress, coming from a depth that I found bafflingly hard to understand. Very few people, it did not need George's response to teach me, could give one absolutely selfless help. They were obliged to help on their own terms, and were pained when one struggled free. That was the pattern, the eternally unsatisfactory pattern, of help and gratitude. But George's distress was far more mysterious than that.

On the plane of reason, of course, every criticism he made was accurate. It was only years later, after the gamble was decided, that I admitted how reasonable his objections were. But no one, not even George, could become so beside himself because of a disagreement on the plane of reason. He had been affected almost as though I had performed an act of treachery. Perhaps that was it. Perhaps I seemed like a deserter.

In his urge to befriend, George was stronger than any man. But he needed something back. On his side he would give money, time, thought, all the energy of his nature, all more than he could afford or anyone else could have imagined giving: in return he needed an ally. He needed an ally close beside him, in the familiar places. I should have been a good ally, working at his side in the office, continuing to be his right-hand man in the group, sharing his pleasures and enough of his utopian hopes. In fact, if I had accepted his plan, become articled to Eden & Martineau's, and stayed in the town, it might have made a difference to George's life. As it was, I went off on my own. And, from the beginning, from that violent altercation in the picture-house café, George felt that I had, without caring, left him isolated to carry on alone.

But that evening, as I told Marion, I could not see my way through. I could not understand George's violence; I was wrapped in my own anxiety. As soon as I went into her sitting-room, Marion had looked at me, first with a smile, then with eyes sharp in concern.

'What's the matter, Lewis?' she said abruptly.

'I've run into some trouble,' I said.

'Serious?'

'I exepect I'll get out of it.'

'You're looking drawn,' said Marion. 'Sit down and I'll make you some tea.'

She lodged in the front room of a semi-detached house, in a neat privet-hedged street just at the beginning of the suburbs. The hedge was fresh-clipped, the patch of grass carefully mown. She had only just returned from her holidays, and on her sofa there was a note-book open, in which she was preparing her lessons for the term. Outside in the sun, a butterfly was flitting over the privet-hedge.

'Why haven't I seen you before?' said Marion, kneeling by the gas-ring. 'Oh, never mind. I know you're worried. Tell me what the trouble is.'

I did not need to explain it all, for she had written to me during her holiday and I had replied. On paper she was less brisk and nervous, much softer and more articulate. She had asked when I was going to 'take the plunge', assuming like everyone else that I was following George's plan. In my reply I had told her, with jauntiness and confidence, that I had made up my mind to do something more difficult. She was the first person to whom I told as much. Even so, she complained in another letter about 'your cryptic hints', and as she gave me my cup of tea, and I was at last explicit about my intention, she complaıned again.

'Why do you keep things to yourself?' she cried. 'You might have known that you could trust me, mightn't you?'

'Of course I trust you.'

'I hope you do.' She was sitting on the sofa, with the light from the window falling on her face, so that her eyes shone excessively bright. Her hair had fallen untidily over her forehead; she pushed it back

impatiently, and impatiently said: 'Never mind me. Is it a good idea?'
(She meant my reading for the Bar.)

'Yes.'

'No one else thinks so – is that the trouble?' she said with startling
speed.

'Not quite.' I would not admit my inner hesitations, the times that
afternoon when my doubts were set vibrating by the others. Instead,
I told her of the scene with George. I described it as objectively as I could,
telling her of George's shouts which still rang word for word in my ears.
I left out nothing of his fury and distress, speculated about it, asked
Marion if she could understand it.

'That doesn't matter,' said Marion. 'George will get over it. I want to
know about you. How much does it mean to you?'

Though she was devoted to George, she would not let me talk about
him. Single-mindedly, with an intense single-mindedness that invaded
my thoughts, she demanded to know how much I was dependent on
George's help. I answered that, without his coaching, I should find the
work much more difficult, but not impossible; without a loan from him,
I did not see how I could raise money even for my pupil's year.

Marion was frowning.

'I think you'll get his help,' she said.

She looked at me.

'And if you don't,' she said, 'shall you have to call it off?'

'I shan't do that.'

Still frowning, Marion enquired about George's objections. How much
was there in them? A great deal, I told her. She insisted that I should
explain them; she knew so little of a career at the Bar. I did so, dispassionately and sensibly enough. It was easy at times to face objection
after objection, to lay them down in public view like so many playing-cards
upon the table. It was some kind of comfort to put them down and inspect
them, as though they were not part of oneself.

Marion asked sharply how I expected to manage. I said that there were
one or two studentships and prizes, though very few, if I came out high
in the Bar Finals. 'Of course, you're clever,' said Marion dubiously.
'But there must be lots of competition. From men who've had every
advantage that you haven't, Lewis.'

I said that I knew it. I mentioned Aunt Milly: with luck, I could
conceivably borrow a hundred or two from her. That was all.

From across the little room, Marion was looking at me – not at my face,
but looking me up and down, from head to foot.

'How strong are you, Lewis?' she said suddenly.

'I shall survive,' I said.

'I'm sure you're highly strung.'

'I'm tougher than you think.'

'You're packed full of vitality, I've told you that. But, unless you're careful, aren't you going to burn yourself out?'

She got up from the sofa and sat on a chair near mine.

'Listen to me,' she said urgently, gazing into my eyes. 'I wish you well. I wish you very well. Is it worth it? It's no use killing yourself. Why not swallow your pride and do what they want you to do? It's the sensible thing after all. And it isn't such a bad alternative, Lewis. It will give you a comfortable life – you might even make another start from there. It won't take anything like so much out of you. You'll have time for everything else you like.'

My hand was resting on the arm of my chair. She pressed hers upon it: her palm was very warm.

I met her gaze, and said:

'Do you think that I'm cut out to be a lawyer in a provincial town?'

She left her hand on mine, but her eyes shrank away.

'All I meant was – you mustn't damage yourself.'

Wretched after my day, I wanted to leave her. But before I went she made me promise that I would report what Eden said next, and whether George came round. 'You must tell me,' said Marion. 'I want to know. You mustn't let me think I shouldn't have spoken. I couldn't help it – but I want everything you want, you know that, don't you?'

CHAPTER XVII

THE LETTER ON THE CHEST-OF-DRAWERS

IN fact, I soon had good news to tell Marion – and I did so at once, to make amends for having been angry with her. This time she did not stop me describing both George's words and Eden's.

George had spoken to me, only three or four days after our quarrel, stiffly, still half-furiously, in great embarrassment. He could not withdraw any single part of his criticisms. He regarded me as lost to reason; but, having once encouraged me to choose a career and offered his help, he felt obliged to honour his word. He would be behind me, so far as lay in his power. If I wanted money, he would do his best, though I must not count on much. He would, naturally, coach me in private for the Bar examinations. 'I refuse to listen to any suggestion that you won't find the blasted examinations child's play,' said George robustly. 'That's the one item in the whole insane project that I'm not worrying about. As for the rest, you've heard my opinions. I propose from now on to keep them to myself.'

He spoke with a curious mixture of stubborn irritation, diffidence, rancour, magnanimity, and warmth. I was disarmed and overjoyed.

As for Eden, when I told him that I had not changed my mind, he shook his head, and said: 'Well, I suppose young men must have their fling. If you are absolutely determined to run your head against a brick wall, I shan't be able to stop you.' That did not prevent him from giving me a series of leisurely sensible homilies; but he was willing to sign my certificates of character and to introduce me to a barrister. He wrote the letter of introduction on the spot (there were one or two technical difficulties about my getting admitted to an Inn). The name on the envelope was Herbert Getliffe.

All that was left, I said to Marion, was to pay my fee.

It was a few days later, in the October of 1924, on a beautiful day of Indian summer – I was just nineteen – that I announced that my admission was settled and the fee paid. Now it was irrevocable. I went to Aunt Milly's house on Friday evening, and proclaimed it first to Aunt Milly and my father. On recent visits there for tea, I had hinted that I might spend the legacy to train myself for a profession. Aunt Milly had vigorously remonstrated; but now I told them that I had paid two hundred pounds in order to start reading for the Bar, she showed, to my complete surprise, something that bore a faint resemblance to approval.

'Well, I declare,' said my father, equably, on hearing the news.

Aunt Milly rounded on him. 'Is that all you've got to say, Bertie?' she said. Having dismissed him, she turned to me with a glimmer of welcome. 'I shan't be surprised if it's just throwing good money after bad,' said Aunt Milly, automatically choosing to begin with her less encouraging reflections. 'It's your mother's fault that you want a job where you won't dirty your hands. Still, I'd rather you threw away your money failing in those examinations than see you putting it in the tills of the public houses.'

'I don't put it in the tills, Aunt Milly,' I said. 'Only the barman does that. I've never thought of being a barman, you know.'

Aunt Milly was not diverted.

'I'd rather you threw your money away failing in those examinations,' she repeated, 'than see you do several things that I won't mention.

I suppose I oughtn't to say so, but I always thought your mother might get above herself and put you in to be a parson.'

Aunt Milly seemed to be experiencing what for her was the unfamiliar emotion of relief.

I had arranged to meet George in the town that evening; he liked to have a snack before we made our usual Friday night call at Martineau's. 'Drop in for coffee – *or whatever*'s *going*,' George remarked, chuckling, munching a sandwich. He was repeating Martineau's phrase of invitation, which never varied. 'I'd been to half a dozen Friday nights before it dawned on me that coffee was always going – by itself.'

I broke in:

'This is a special occasion. The deed's done.'

'What deed?'

'I sent off the money this afternoon.'

'Did you, by God?' said George. He gazed at me with a heavy pre-occupied stare, and then said:

'Good luck to you. You'll manage it, of course. I refuse to admit any other possibility.'

The street lamps shimmered through the blue autumnal haze. As we strolled up the New Walk George said, in a tone that was firm, resigned and yet curiously sad:

'I accept the fact that you'll manage it. But don't expect me to forget that you've been as big a firebrand as I ever have. Some of the entries in my diary may embarrass you later – when you get out of my sight.'

Very rarely – but they stood out stark against his blazing hopes – George had moments of foresight, bleak and without comfort. In the midst of all his hope, he never pictured any concrete success for himself.

Then he went on heartily:

'It's essential to have a drink on it tonight. This calls for a celebration.'

We left Martineau's before the public-houses closed. George, as always, was glad of the excuse to escape a 'social occasion': even in that familiar drawing-room, he felt that there were certain rules of behaviour which had paralysingly been withheld from him; even that night, when I was proclaiming my news to Martineau, I noticed George making a conscious decision before he felt able to sit down. But once outside the house, he drank to my action with everyone we met. There was nothing he liked more than a 'celebration', and he stood me a great and noisy one.

Arriving at my room after midnight, I saw something on the chest-of-drawers which I knew to be there, which I had remembered intermittently several times that evening, but which would have astonished all those who had greeted my 'drastic' step, George most of all. It was a letter addressed in my own handwriting. After midnight, I was still drunk enough from the celebration, despite our noisy procession through the streets, to find the envelope glaring under the light. I saw it with guilt. It was a letter addressed in my own handwriting to my prospective Inn. Inside was the money. It was the letter, which, for all my boasts, I had not yet had the courage to send off. I had been lying. There was still time to back out.

They thought of me as confident. Perhaps they were right in a sense, and I had a confidence of the fibres. In the very long run, I did not doubt that I should struggle through. But they, who heard me boast, were taken in when they thought I took this risk as lightly as I pretended. They did not see the interminable waverings, the attacks of nerves, the withdrawals, the evenings staring out in nervous despondency over the roofs, the dread of tomorrow so strong that I wished time would stand still. They did not detect the lies which I told myself as well as them. They did not know that I changed my mind from mood to mood; I used an uprush of confidence to hearten myself on to impress Eden that I was absolutely firm. But a few hours later that mood had seeped away and I was left with another night of procrastination. That had gone on for weeks. My natural spirits were high, and my tongue very quick, or else the others would have known. But in fact I concealed from them the humiliating anxieties, the subterfuges, the desperate attempts to find an excuse, and then another, for not committing myself without any chance of return. They could not guess how many times I had shrunk back from paying the fee, so that I could still feel safe till another day. At last, that Friday, I had brought myself to sign the letter and the cheque; in ebullient spirits I had told them all, Aunt Milly, my father, George, Martineau, all the rest, that the choice was made, and that I was looking ahead without a qualm; but in the small hours of Saturday the letter was still glaring under the light, on the top of the chest-of-drawers.

It was Monday before I posted it.

PART THREE

THE END OF INNOCENCE

CHAPTER XVIII

WALKING ALONE

MY first meeting with Sheila became blotted from my memory. The first sight of her, as Jack and I walked up the London Road and she waved from her car, stayed clear always; so did the sound of her name, echoing in my mind before I had so much as seen her face. But there was a time when we first spoke, and that became buried or lost, irretrievably lost, so that I was never able to recapture it.

It must have been in the summer of 1925, when we were each nearly twenty. During the winter I had heard a rumour that she was abroad – being finished, said someone, for her health, said another. Her name dropped out of the gossip of the group; Jack forgot all about her and talked with his salesman's pleasure, persuading himself as well as his audience, of the charms of other girls. It was the winter after I had made the choice, when I was trying to assuage my doubts by long nights of work: days at the office, evenings with George and the group, then nights in my cold room, working like a medieval student with blankets round my knees, in order to save shillings in the gas-fire. There were times when, at two or three o'clock, I went for a walk to get my feet warm before I went to bed.

Sheila and I must have met a few months later, in the summer. I did not remember our first calling each other by name. But, with extreme distinctness, a few words came back whenever I tried to force my memory. They had been spoken not at our first meeting, but on an occasion soon after, probably the first or second time I took her out. They were entirely trivial, and concerned who should pay the bill.

We were sitting in a kind of cubicle in an old-fashioned café. From the next cubicle to ours sounded the slide and patter of draughts, for this was a room where boxes of chessmen and draughts stood on a table, and people came in for a late tea and stayed several hours.

Through the tobacco smoke, Sheila was staring at me. Her eyes were large and disconcertingly steady. At the corner of her mouth, there was a twitch that looked like a secret smile, that was in fact a nervous tic.

'I want to pay my share,' she said.

'No, you can't. I asked you to come out.'

'I can. I shall.'

I said no. I was insecure, not knowing how far to insist.

'Look. I've got some. You need it more than I do.'

We stared at each other across the table.

'You're here. In this town. I'm not far away.' Her voice was high, and sometimes had a brittle tone. 'We want to see each other, don't we?'

'Of course,' I said in sudden joy.

'I can't unless I pay for myself. I shouldn't mind you paying – but you can't afford it. Can you?'

'I can manage.'

'You can't. You know you can't. I've got some money.'

I was still insecure. Our wills had crossed. Already I was enraptured by her.

'Unless you let me pay for myself I shan't come again.' She added: 'I want to.'

If I had met her when I was older, and she had spoken so, I should have wondered how much it was an exercise of her will, how much due to her curious kindness. But that afternoon, after we had parted, I simply said to myself that I was in love. I had no room to think of anything but that.

I said to myself that I was in love. It was different from all I had imagined. I had read my Donne, I had listened to Jack Cotery, that cheerful amorist, and had agreed, out of the certainty of my inexperience, that the root of love was sensual desire, and that all that mattered was the bed. Yet it did not seem so, now that I was in love. Even though each moment had become enhanced, so that I saw faces in the evening light with a tenderness that I had never felt before. The faces of young men and women strolling in the late sunlight – I saw the bloom on the girls' cheeks, I saw them feature by feature, as though my eyesight had suddenly become ten times as acute. As I watched the steam rising from my teacup the next morning, I felt that I was seeing it for the first time, as though I had just been born with each sense fresh and preternaturally strong. Each moment was sensually enhanced because of the love inside me. Yet for her who inspired that love I had not in those first days a sensual thought.

I did not make dreams of her, as I had done of many other girls. That first state of love was delectable beyond my expectation; in its delight I did not stop to wonder that I had often imagined love, and imagined it quite wrong. I breathed in the delight with every breath, those first mornings. I did not stop to wonder why my thoughts of her were vague, why I was content to let her image – unlike those of everyone else I knew – lie vague underneath my mind.

It was the same when I pictured her face. I was used already to studying the bones and skin and flesh of those I met, and I could, as a matter of form and habit, have described Sheila much as I should have described Marion or even George or Jack. I could have specified the thin, fine nose; great eyes, which had not the lemur-like sadness of most large eyes, but were grey, steady, caught and held the light; front teeth which only the grace of God saved from protruding, and which sometimes rested on her lower lip. She was fair, and her skin was even, pale, and of the consistency that most easily takes lines – so that one could see, before she was twenty, somes of the traces which would deepen in ten years. She was tallish for a woman, strong-boned and erect, with an arrogant toss to her head.

I should have described her in those terms, just as I might have described the others, but to myself I did not see her as I did them. For I thought of her as beautiful. It was an objective fact that others did so too. Few of my friends liked her for long, and almost none was easy with her; yet even George admitted that she was a handsome bitch, and the women in the group did not deny that she was good looking. They criticised each feature, they were scornful of her figure, and it was all true; but they knew that she had the gift of beauty. At that time I believed it was a great gift – and so did she, proud in her looks and her youth. Neither of us could have credited that there would come a day when I was to see her curse her beauty and deliberately, madly, neglect it.

To me she was especially beautiful. And, in the first astonishment of love, I saw her, and thought of her, just like that. I did not see her, as I was to see her in the future, with the detailed fondness of an experienced love, in which I came to delight in her imperfections, the front teeth, the nervous, secret-smiling tic. No, I saw her as beautiful, and I was filled with love.

I did not mind, I noticed as it were without regarding, how in company she was apt to fall constrained and silent, pallid-faced, the smile working her mouth as though she were inwardly amused. The first time Jack Cotery saw her and me together, we were alone, and she was laughing; afterwards, Jack proceeded to congratulate me. 'You're getting on,' he said good-naturedly. He was glad to witness me at last a captive. He was glad that I was sharing in his human frailty. He had always been half-envious that I was less distracted than he. And he was also glad that I was happy: like most carnal men, he was sorry if his friends were fools enough not to enjoy the fun. 'She's not my cup of tea.' He grinned. 'And I'm not hers. She'd just look through me with those searchlight eyes. But clearly she's the best-looking girl round here. And you seem to have made a hit. Just let yourself go, Lewis, just let yourself go.'

One day, however, she came with me to the group. She greeted them all high-spiritedly enough, and then, though they were talking of books which she and I had discussed together, she fell into an inhibited silence and scarcely spoke a word. Jack cross-questioned me about her. 'Is she often like that? Remember, they sometimes give themselves away when they're not trying. It's easy to shine when someone's falling in love with you.' He shook his head. 'I hope she isn't going to be too much of a handful. If she is, the best thing you can do is cut your losses and get out of it straight away.'

I smiled.

'It's all very well to laugh. I know it would be a wrench. But it might be worse than a wrench if you get too much involved – and you can't trust the girl to behave.'

I paid no attention. Nor did I to the curious incidents which I noticed soon after we met, when, instead of seeing her silent and pallid in company, I found her sitting on the area-steps of my lodging-house, chatting like a sister to the landlady. The landlady was a slattern, who came to life when she broke into ruminations about her late husband or the Royal Family. Sheila listened and answered, relaxed, utterly at ease. And she did the same with the little waitress in the café, who liked her and took her for granted as she did no other customer. Somehow Sheila could make friends, throw her self-consciousness away, if she was allowed to choose for herself and go where no one watched her.

But I did not try, or even want, to think what she was truly like. If Marion had performed those antics, I should have been asking myself, what kind of nature was this? In the first weeks of my love for Sheila, I was less curious about her than about any other person. It even took me some time to discover the simple facts, such as that she was my own age within a month, that she was an only child, the daughter of a clergyman, that her mother had money, that they lived in a village twelve miles outside the town.

Walking in the windy autumn nights, I thought of her with the self-absorption of young love. I chose to be alone on those nights, so that I could cherish my thoughts, with the lights twinkling and quivering in the wind.

I was self-absorbed, yet with the paradox of such a love I had not begun to ask, even in my thoughts, anything for myself. I had not kissed her. It was enough just then that she should exist. It was enough that she should exist, who had brought me to this bliss, who had transformed the streets I walked in so that, looking down the hill at the string of lights, I felt my throat catch with joy.

I thought of her as though she alone were living in the world. I had never seen her house, but I imagined her within it, in her own room, high and light. She sat with a reading-lamp at her side, and for a time she was still. Then she crossed the room and knelt by the bookshelves: her hair was radiant in the shadow. She went back to her chair, and her fingers turned the page.

I saw her so, and that was all I asked, just then.

CHAPTER XIX

THE CALM OF A SEPTEMBER AFTERNOON

I WAS diffident in making the first approach of love. It was not only that the magic was too delicate to touch. I was afraid that I had no charm for her. I had none of Jack's casual confidence that he could captivate nine women out of ten; and I had not that other confidence which underlay George's awkwardness and which was rooted in his own certainty of his great sensual power. At twenty I did not know whether any woman would love me. Most of all I doubted it with Sheila.

I tried to dazzle her, not with what I was, but with what I could do. I boasted of my plans. I told her that I should be a success. I held out the lure of the prizes I should win by my wits. She was quite unimpressed. She was clever enough to know that it was not just a young man's fantasy. She believed that I might do as I said. But she believed it half with amusement, half with envy.

'You ought to bring off something,' she teased me. 'With your automatic competence.'

It amused her that I could work in the office all day, talk to her at the café over pot after pot of tea until she caught her train, and then go off and apply my mind for hours to the law of torts. But it was an envious amusement. She had played with music and painting, but she had nothing to do. She felt that she too should have been driven to work.

'Of course you'll get somewhere,' she said. 'What happens when you've got there? You won't be content. What then?'

She would not show more than that faint interest in my workaday hopes. She had none of Marion's robust and comradely concern for each detail of what I had to achieve. Marion had learned the syllabuses, knew the dates of the examinations, had a shrewd idea of when I must begin to earn money unless I was to fail. Sheila had faith in my 'automatic competence', but her tone turned brittle as I tried to dazzle her, and it hurt me, in the uncertainty of love.

She was still amused, not much more than that, when I brought her a piece of good news. In September that year, just after I began to meet her regularly, I had a stroke of fortune, the kind of practical fortune which was a bonus I did not count on and had no right to expect. It happened through the juxtaposition, the juxtaposition which became a most peculiar alliance, of Aunt Milly and George Passant. The solicitor who dealt with Aunt Milly's 'bit of property' (as my mother used to describe it, in a humorous resentful fashion) had not long since died.

By various chances, Aunt Milly found her way to the firm of Eden & Martineau, and so into George's office; and there she kept on going.

Aunt Milly was aware that I knew him. It did not soften her judgment. As a matter of course, it was her custom to express disapproval after her first meeting with any new acquaintance. Since she knew George was my closest friend, she felt morally impelled to double the pungency of her expression.

'I suppose I oughtn't to tell you,' said Aunt Milly, 'but that young fellow Passant was smelling of beer. At half-past two in the afternoon. It might be doing everyone a service if I told his employers what I thought of it.' She went on to give a brief sketch of George's character.

To my surprise, it did not take long before her indignation moderated. After a visit or two, she was saying darkly and grudgingly: 'Well, I can't say that he's as hopeless as that other jackass – which is a wonder, considering everything.'

Nevertheless, it came as though from outer space when George told me, as though it were nothing particularly odd, that they had been discussing me and my future. 'I found her very reasonable,' said George. 'Very reasonable indeed.' And again it did not strike him as particularly odd, though he was looking discreet and what my mother would have called chuff, with the self-satisfaction of one holding a pleasant secret, when he summoned me to meet her one lunch-time.

'She's asked me to attend, as a matter of fact,' said George complacently, swinging his stick.

Our meeting-place was the committee-room of one of Aunt Milly's temperance organisations. It was in the middle of the town, on the third floor above a vegetarian café; Aunt Milly was not a vegetarian, but she did not notice what she ate, and when she was working in that room she always sent down for a meal. Our lunch that morning was nut cutlets, and Aunt Milly munched away impassively.

Eating that lunch, we sat, all three of us, at a long committee-table at the end of the room, Aunt Milly in the chair, George at her right hand like a secretary, and me opposite to them. The room was dark and filled with small tables, each covered with brochures, pamphlets, charts, handbills, and maps. Near our end of the room was a special stand, on which were displayed medical exhibits. The one most visible, a yard or so from our lunch, was a cirrhosed liver. I caught sight of Aunt Milly's gaze fixed upon it, and then on George and me. She went on eating steadily.

On the walls were flaunted placards and posters; one of them proclaimed that temperance was winning. George noticed it, and asked Aunt Milly how many people had signed the pledge in 1924.

'Not enough,' said Aunt Milly. She added, surprisingly, in her loud voice: 'That poster's a lie. Don't you believe it. The movement is going through a bad time. We've gone downhill ever since the war, and we shan't do much better till those people stop running away from the facts.'

'You made the best of your position in the war,' said George, with an abstract pleasure in political chess. 'You couldn't possibly have hoped to keep your advantage.'

'That is as may be,' said Aunt Milly.

George argued with her. She was completely realistic and matter of fact about details. She did not shut her eyes to any setback, and yet maintained an absolute and unqualified faith that the cause would triumph in the end.

She broke off brusquely:

'This isn't what I wanted you for. I haven't got all the afternoon to waste. It's time we got down to brass tacks.'

Aunt Milly was offering to make me a loan. Presumably at George's instigation, certainly after consulting him about my chances in the Bar examinations, she had decided to help. George sat by her side, in solid if subdued triumph. I began to thank her, with real spontaneous delight, but she stopped me.

'You wait till I've finished,' she said. 'You may not like my conditions as much as all that. You can take it or leave it.'

The 'conditions' referred to the date of the loan. Aunt Milly would, if she got her own way, lend me two hundred pounds. When would it be most useful to me? She had her view, I had mine: they were, as usual, different. And they were the opposite of what one might have expected. Aunt Milly had taken it into her head that I did not stand 'a dog's chance' in Bar Finals unless I could give up the office and spend the next eighteen months reading law 'as though you were at college, like your mother wanted for you'. I could never understand how Aunt Milly became fixed in this opinion; her whole family had picked up their education at night classes, and she was the last woman to be moved by the claims of social pretension. Perhaps it was through some faint memory of my mother's longings, for Aunt Milly was capable of a certain buried sentiment. Perhaps it was that I was looking overtired: she was always affected by physical evidence, about which there was no doubt or nonsense, which she could see with her own eyes. Anyway, for whatever reason, she had taken the idea into her head, and held it as obstinately as all her other ideas.

My view was the exact opposite. I could, I said, survive my present life until Bar Finals. I would take care, however much sleep I lost, that it would make no difference to the result. Whereas two hundred pounds, once I was in chambers, would keep me going for two years and might turn the balance between failure and success.

George took up the argument with both of us. He was himself a very strong man physically, and he had no patience with the wear and tear that the effort might cost me. That was one against Aunt Milly. On the other hand, he told me flatly that I was underestimating the sheer time that I needed for work. If I did not leave the office now and have my days clear, I could not conceivably come out high in the list. That was a decisive one against me. On the other hand, he fired a broadside against Aunt Milly – it was ridiculous to insist that the whole loan should be used on getting me through the Bar Finals, when a little capital afterwards would be of incalculable value.

Aunt Milly liked to be argued with by George, powerfully, loudly and not too politely. It was a contrast to the meek silences of her husband and her brother. Maybe, I thought, she would have been more placid married to such a man. Was that why, against all the rules, they got on so well?

But, despite her gratification at meeting her match, she remained immovably obstinate. Either I left the office within a month, or the loan was off. Aunt Milly had the power of the purse, and she made the most of it.

At last George hammered out a solution, although Aunt Milly emerged victoriously with her point. I was to leave the office at once: Aunt Milly nodded her head, her eyes protruding without expression, as though it were merely a recognition of her common sense. Aunt Milly would lend me a hundred pounds. 'At three per cent, repayments to begin in five years,' said Aunt Milly promptly.

'On any terms you like,' said George irascibly. The hundred pounds would just carry me through, doing nothing but study law, until Bar Finals. Then, if I secured a first in the examination, she would lend me the other hundred pounds to help towards my first year in chambers.

George chuckled as we walked back to Bowling Green Street. 'I call that a good morning's work,' he said. 'She's a wonderful woman.'

He hinted that I need not worry about taking the money. Even if all went wrong, it would not cripple her. She and her husband were among those of the unpretentious lower middle-class who had, as George archly called it, their nest-eggs tucked away. George would not tell me how much. He was always professionally discreet, in a fashion that surprised some who knew him only at night. But I gathered that they were worth two or three thousand. I also gathered that I was not to expect anything from her will. That did not depress me – two hundred pounds now was worth two thousand pounds in ten years' time. But I should have liked to know how she was leaving her money.

I wanted Sheila to rejoice with me when I told her the news. I did not write to her; I saved it up for our next meeting. She came into the town on a Saturday afternoon, a warm and beautiful afternoon in late September. We met outside the park not far from Martineau's house, walked by the pavilion, and found a couple of chairs near the hard tennis courts. The park was full of people. All round the tennis courts there were children playing on the grass, women sitting on the seats with perambulators in front of them, men in their shirt-sleeves. On the asphalt court there were two games of mixed doubles, youths in grey flannels, girls in cotton dresses.

Sheila sat back with the sunshine on her face, watching the play.

'I'm about as good as she is,' she said. 'I'm no good at tennis. But I can run quite fast.'

She spoke with a secret pleasure, far away, as though she were gazing at herself in a mirror, as though she were admiring her reflection in a pool.

I looked at her – and, in the crowded park, for me we were alone, under the milk-blue sky.

Then I told her that I was leaving the office. She smiled at me, a friendly, sarcastic smile.

'Gentleman of leisure, are you?' she said.

'Not quite,' I said.

'What in the world will you do with yourself? Even you can't work all day.'

I could not leave it, I could not bear that she was not impressed. I told her, I exaggerated, the difference it ought to make to my chances.

'You'll do well anyway,' she said lightly.

'It's not quite as easy as all that.'

'It is for you.' She smiled again. 'But I still don't see what you're going to do with yourself all day. I'm sure you're not good at doing nothing. I'm much better at that than you are. I'm quite good at sitting in the sun.'

She shut her eyes. She looked so beautiful that my heart turned over.

Still I could not leave it. My tongue ran away, and I said that it was a transformation, it was a new beginning. She looked at me; her smile was still friendly, sarcastic and cool.

'You're very excited about it, aren't you?'

'Yes, I am.'

'Then so am I,' she said.

But she responded in a different tone to another story that I told her, as we sat there in the sun. It concerned a piece of trouble of Jack's, which had sprung up almost overnight. It arose because Jack, not for the first time, had evoked an infatuation; but this time he was guiltless, and ironically this was the only time that might do him an injury. For the one who loved him was not a young woman, but a boy of fifteen. The boy's passion had sprung up that summer, it was glowing and innocent, but the more extravagant because it was so innocent. He had just given Jack an expensive present, a silver cigarette-case; and by accident his family had intercepted a letter of devotion that was coming with it. There were various kinds of practical repercussion, which worried us and against which we were trying to act: Jack's future in his firm was threatened; there were other consequences for him, and, in the long run, most of all for George, who had thrown himself, with his whole force, into Jack's support.

Sheila listened with her eyes alight. She was not interested in the consequences, she brushed them impatiently aside. To her the core of the story, its entire significance, lay in the emotion of the boy himself.

'It must be wonderful to be swept away. He must have felt that he had no control over himself at all. I wonder what it was like,' she said. She was deeply moved, and our eyes met.

'He won't regret it.' She added, gently, 'I wish it had happened to me at his age.'

We fell into silence: a silence so charged that I could hear my heart beating. Between her fingers a cigarette was smouldering blue into the still air.

'Who is he, Lewis?' she said.

I hesitated for a fraction of a second. She was very quick.

'Tell me. If I know him, I might help. I shall go and say that I envy him.'

'He's a boy called Roy Calvert,' I said.

I had only met him for a few minutes in the middle of this crisis. What struck me most was that he seemed quite unembarrassed and direct. He was more natural and at ease than the rest of us, five years older and more, who questioned him.

Sheila shook her head, as though she were disappointed.

'He must be a cousin of your friend Olive's, mustn't he?' (Olive was a member of the group.)

I told her yes, and that Olive was involved in the trouble.

'I can't get on with her,' said Sheila. 'She pretends not to think much of herself. It isn't true.'

Suddenly Sheila's mood had changed. Talking of Roy, she had been gentle, delicate, self-forgetful. Now, at the mention of Olive, whom she scarcely knew, but who mixed gaily and could forget herself in any company, Sheila turned angry and constrained.

'I once went to a dance at Olive's,' she said. 'We didn't stay long. We went by ourselves to the palais. That was a lot better.'

For the first time, I was learning the language of a beloved. I was learning the tension, the hyperaesthesia, with which one listens to the tone of every word. And I was learning too, in the calm of that September afternoon, the first stab of jealousy. That 'we', said so clearly, that re-iterated 'we': was it deliberate, was her companion a casual acquaintance, was she threatening me with someone for whom she cared?

She looked at me. At the sight of my face, her tone changed again.

'I'm glad you told me about Roy,' she said.

'Why are you glad?'

'I don't know.'

'Sheila, why are you glad?'

'If I knew, I shouldn't tell you.' Her voice was high. Then she smiled, and said with all simplicity and purity: 'No, I should tell you. I should want to. It would mean I had found something important, wouldn't it?'

CHAPTER XX

IN THE RAIN

WHEN she was not there, I was happy in my thoughts. They were pierced, it is true, by the first thrusts of jealousy, the sound of that clear 'we' in the calm air, not so much a memory but as though the sound stayed in my ears. They were troubled by the diffidence of my love, so that now I could not often think of her alone in her room, without needing some sign of love to calm me. But the rapture was so strong, it swept back after those intrusions; she existed, she walked the same earth, and I should see her in three days' time.

Once, meeting her after a week's absence, I felt incredulous, all the excitement deflated, all the enchantment dead. Her face seemed, at the first glance, not different in kind from other faces – pale, frigid, beaky, ill-tempered. Her voice was brittle, and grated on my nerves. Everything she thought was staccato. There was no flow or warmth about her, or about anything she said or did. I was, for a few minutes, nothing but bored. Nothing deeper than that, just bored. Then she gazed at me – not with a smile, but with her eyes steady and her face quite still; on the instant, the dead minutes were annihilated and I was once more possessed.

Later that day, I happened to tell her that the group were spending the following weekend out at the farm. She always took a curious, half-envious, half-mocking interest in the group's affairs. That afternoon she was speculating, like one left outside a party, about how she should pass the weekend. I knew her house was only two or three miles from the farm, and I begged her to drop in.

'I can't stand crowds,' she said. Then, as though covering herself, she retorted: 'Why shouldn't you come and see me? It's no further one way than the other.'

I was overjoyed.

She added:

'You'll have to meet my parents. You can study them, if you like.'

We arranged that I should walk over for tea on the Saturday afternoon. That Saturday, in the middle of October, was my last day in the office;

and I was thinking of the afternoon as I said all my goodbyes. Mr Vesey reminded me that I was under his control until one o'clock; he told me three times not to be careless about leaving my papers in order, then he shook my hand, and said that he had not yet been provided with my successor, and that some people had never realised his difficulties. How could he be expected to run his section well if his one good clerk went and left him? Why did he never get a chance himself? 'Never mind, Eliot,' he said bravely, shaking my hand again. 'I don't expect to be in the lime-light. I just carry on.'

I was thinking of the afternoon to come; but, stepping out of the office on to the wet pavement, leaving for the last time a place which for years had been a prison, I felt an ache of nostalgia, of loss and of regret.

George and I went out by bus, through a steady drizzle. At half-past three, when I started out from the farm, the rain was heavier; I was getting wet as I cut across the fields, down the country lanes, to Sheila's house. I was happy and apprehensive, happy because she had asked me, apprehensive because I was sensible enough to know that I could not possibly be welcome. She had asked me in innocence: that I took for granted. She would not care what her parents thought, if she wanted to see me. Through her actions there shone so often a wild and wilful innocence. And I, far more realistic than she in all other ways, had for her and with her the innocence of romantic love. So that, tramping through the mud that afternoon, I was happy whatever awaited me. I wanted nothing but the sight of her; I knew it, she knew it, and in that state of love there were no others.

But I assumed that her parents would see it differently. I might not have given a conscious thought to marrying her – and that, strange as it later seemed, was true. Her parents would never believe it. To them, I must appear as a suitor – possibly a suitor with an extremely dim outside chance, but nevertheless a suitor, and a most undesirable one. For they were rich, Sheila had both looks and brains; they were bound to expect her to make a brilliant marriage. They were not likely to encourage me. I had nothing whatever with which to mollify them. Some parents might have endured me because I was not a fool, but I guessed that even my wits were suspect. Sheila was capable of recounting my opinions, and then saying that she shared them. I did not know how I was going to carry it off. Yet I was joyful, walking those two miles through the rain.

The vicarage was a handsome Georgian house, lying back behind the trees at the end of the village. I was not far wrong about my welcome. But before Mrs Knight could start expressing herself there was a faintly farcical delay. For I arrived wet through. The maid who let me in did not know how to proceed; Sheila and her mother came out into the hall. Mrs Knight at once took charge. She was prepared to greet me coldly, but she became solicitous about my health. She was a heavily built woman, bigger than Sheila, but much more busy and fussy. She took me into the bathroom, sent the maid for some of the vicar's clothes, arranged to have mine dried. At last I entered the drawing-room dressed in a cricket shirt, grey flannels, pullover, dressing-gown and slippers, all belonging to Sheila's father, all the clothes much too wide for me and the slippers two sizes too big.

'I hope you won't take cold,' Mrs Knight rattled on busily. 'You ought to have had a good hot bath. I think you ought to have a nice stiff whisky. Yes, that ought to keep out the cold.'

She had none of her daughter's fine, chiselled features. She was broad-faced, pug-nosed, with a loud quacking voice; she was coarse-grained and greatly given to moral indignation; yet her eyes were wide-open and child-like, and one felt, as with other coarse-grained women, that often she was lost and did not know her way about the world.

However, she was very far from lost when it came to details of practical administration. I was made to put down a couple of fingers of neat whisky. She decided that I was not wearing enough clothes, and Sheila was sent for one of the vicar's sports-coats.

'He's upstairs in his study,' said Mrs Knight, talking of her husband with a rapt, child-like devotion, accentuating the 'he' in her worship. 'He's just polishing a sermon for tomorrow. He always likes to have them polished. He'll join us later for his tea, if he finishes in time. I should never think of disturbing him, of course.'

We sat down by the fire and began our tea, a very good one, for Mrs Knight liked her food. She expected everyone round her to eat as heartily as she did, and scolded Sheila for not getting on with the toast and honey. I watched Sheila, as her mother jockeyed her into eating. It was strangely comfortable to see her so, by the fireside. But she was silent in her mother's presence – as indeed it was hard not to be, since Mrs Knight talked without interruption and loud enough to fill any room. Yet Sheila's silence meant more than that; it was not the humorous silence of a looker-on.

The more I could keep Mrs Knight on the theme of physical comfort, the better, I thought to myself; and so I praised the house, the sight of it from the village, the drawing-room in which we sat. Mrs Knight forcefully agreed.

'It's perfect for our small family,' she said. 'As I was obliged to explain to my neighbour, Mrs Lacy, only yesterday. Do you know what she had been saying, Sheila? I shouldn't have believed my ears, if I hadn't heard Doris Lacy talk and talk and talk for the last twenty years. Of course, she's a great friend of mine and I'm devoted to her and I know she'd say the same of me' – Mrs Knight put in this explanation for my benefit – 'but the trouble is that she will talk without thinking. And she can't have been thinking at all – even she couldn't have said it if she'd thought for a single moment – she can't have been thinking at all when she talked about this house. She actually said' – Mrs Knight's voice was mounting louder as her indignation grew – 'that this house was *dark*. She said that this house was *dark. She* who doesn't get a ray of sun till half-past three!'

She got fairly started on the misdeeds, the preposterous errors of judgment, the dubious gentility and mercenary marriage, of Mrs Lacy. She kept asking Sheila for her support and then rushing off into another burst of indignation. It was some time before she turned on me. She collected herself, regarded me with open eyes, said how gallant it was for me to visit them on such an afternoon. Then, with elaborate diplomacy, she said:

'Of course, it doesn't feel like living in the country, now Sheila is growing up. She brings people to see us who are doing all kinds of interesting things. Why, it was only the other day we saw one of her friends who they say has a great future in his firm—'

The knife of jealousy twisted. Then I felt a flood of absolute relief, for Sheila said clearly:

'He's dense.'

'I don't think you can say that, Sheila.'

'I can.'

'You mustn't be too hard on your friends,' said Mrs Knight busily. 'You'll be telling me next that Tom Devitt isn't interesting. He's a specialist at the infirmary,' said Mrs Knight to me, and continued with enthusiasm, 'and they say he's the coming man. Sheila will be telling us that he's dense too. Or—'

The involuntary smile had come to Sheila's mouth, and on her forehead I could see the lines. The jealous spasm had returned, with Tom Devitt's name, with the other names (for Mrs Knight had by no means finished), but it merged, as I watched Sheila, into a storm of something that had no place in romantic love, something so unfamiliar in my feeling for her that I did not recognise it then. It lasted only for a moment, but it left me off my balance for Mrs Knight's next charge.

'I think I remember Sheila saying that you were kept very busy,' she remarked. 'Of course, I know we can't all choose exactly what we want, can we? Some of us have got to be content—'

'I've chosen what I want, Mrs Knight,' I said, a little too firmly.

'Have you?' She seemed puzzled.

'I'm a law student. That's what I've chosen to do.'

'In your spare time, I suppose?'

'No,' I said. 'I'm reading for the Bar. Full-time. I shan't do anything else until I'm called.' It was technically true. It had been true since one o'clock that day. 'I shan't earn a penny till I'm called.'

Mrs Knight was not specially quick in the uptake. She had to pause, so as to readjust her ideas.

'I do my reading in the town,' I said. 'Then I go up to my Inn once a term, and get through my dinners in a row. It saves money – and I shall need it until I get a practice going, you know.'

It was the kind of career-talk she was used to hearing; but she was baffled at hearing it from me.

'All the barristers I've known,' she said, 'have eaten their dinners while they were at college. I remember my cousin used to go up when he was at Trinity –'

'Did he ever get through an examination?' asked Sheila.

'Perhaps he wasn't clever at his books,' said Mrs Knight, becoming more cross, 'but he was a good man, and everyone respected him in the county.'

'My friends at the Inn,' I put in, 'nearly all come from Cambridge.' Here I was stretching the truth. I had made one or two friendly acquaintances there, such as Charles March, who were undergraduates, but I often dined with excessively argumentative Indians.

Mrs Knight was very cross. She did not like being baffled and confused – yet somehow I had automatically to be promoted a step. She had to say, as though Sheila had met me at the house of one of their friends:

'I've always heard that a barrister has to wait years for his briefs. Of course, I suppose you don't mind waiting—'

I admitted that it would take time. Mrs Knight gave an appeased and comforted sigh, happy to hear something that she recognised.

Soon after, there was a footfall outside the room, a slow footfall. Mrs Knight's eyes widened. 'He's coming!' she said. 'He must have finished!'

Mr Knight entered with an exaggeratedly drooping, an exaggeratedly languid step. He was tall, massive, with a bay-window of a stomach that began as far up as his lower chest. He was wearing a lounge suit without a dog-collar, and he carried a sheaf of manuscript in his hand. His voice was exaggeratedly faint. He was, at first glance, a good deal of an actor, and he was indicating that the virtue had gone out of him.

He said faintly to his wife: 'I'm sorry I had to be late, darling,' sat in the armchair which had been preserved for him, and half-closed his eyes.

Mrs Knight asked with quacking concern whether he would like a cup of tea. It was plain that she adored him.

'Perhaps a cup,' he whispered. 'Perhaps just a cup.'

The toast had been kept warm on the hot-plate, she said anxiously. Or she could have some fresh made in three minutes.

'I *can't* eat it, darling,' he said. 'I can't *eat* it. I can't eat *anything*.'

The faintness with which he spoke was bogus. Actually his voice was rich, and very flexible in its range of tone. He had a curious trick of repeating a phrase, and at the second turn completely altering the stress. Throughout his entry, which he enjoyed to the full, he had paid no attention to me, had not thrown me an open glance, but as he lay back with heavy lids drawn down he was observing me from the corner of an eye that was disturbingly sly and shrewd.

When at last he admitted to a partial recovery, Mrs Knight introduced me. She explained volubly the reason for my eccentric attire, taking credit for her speed of action. Then, since they seemed still to be worrying her, she repeated my statements about doing nothing but read for the Bar, as though trusting him to solve the problem.

Unlike his wife, Mr Knight was indirect. He gazed at Sheila, not at me.

'You never tell me anything, do you, my dear girl,' he said. 'You never tell me anything.'

Then slyly, still looking at her, he questioned me. His voice stayed carefully fatigued, he appeared to be taking a remote interest in these ephemeral things. In fact, he was astute. If he had been present, I should never have succeeded for a moment in putting up my bluff with Mrs Knight. Without asking me outright, he soon got near the truth. He took a malicious pleasure in talking round the point, letting me see that he had guessed, not giving me away to his wife.

'Isn't there a regulation,' he inquired, his voice diminishing softly, 'by which you can't read for the Bar if you're following certain occupations? Does that mean one has to break away? I take it, you may have had to select your time to break away – from some other occupation?'

It was not the reason, but it was a very good shot. We talked for a few minutes about legal careers. He was proud of his ability to 'place' people and he was now observing me with attention. Sometimes he asked a question edged with malice. And I was learning something about him.

He and his wife were each snobbish, but in quite different fashions. Mrs Knight had been born into the comfortable moneyed middle class; she was a robust woman without much perception, and accepted those who seemed to arrive at the same level; just as uncritically, she patronised those who did not. Mr Knight's interest was far more subtle and pervading. To begin with, he was no more gently born than I was. I could hear the remains of a northern dialect in that faint and modulated voice. Mr Knight had met his wife, and captured her for good, when he was a young curate. She had brought him money, he had moved through the social strata, he had dined in the places he had longed for as a young man – in the heart of the county families and the dignitaries of the Church. The odd thing was that, having arrived there, he still retained his romantic regard for those very places. All this shrewdness and suspicion went to examine the channels by which others got there. On that subject he was accurate, penetrating, and merciless.

He was a most interesting man. The time was getting on; I was wondering whether I ought to leave, when I witnessed another scene which, though I did not know it, was a regular feature of the vicarage Saturday teas. Mrs Knight looked busily, lovingly, at her husband.

'Please, darling, would you mind giving us the sermon?' she said.

'I *can't* do it, darling. I can't *do* it. I'm too exhausted.'

'Please. Just give us the beginning. You know Sheila always likes to hear the sermon. I'm sure you'd like to hear the sermon.' Mrs Knight rallied me. 'It will give you something to think over on the way home. I'm sure you want to hear it.'

I said that I did.

'I believe he's a heathen,' said Mr Knight maliciously, but his fingers were playing with the manuscript.

'You heard what he said, darling,' urged Mrs Knight. 'He'll be disappointed if you don't give us a good long piece.'

'Oh well.' Mr Knight sighed. 'If you insist. If you insist.'

Mrs Knight began to alter the position of the reading lamp. She made her husband impatient. He was eager to get to it.

The faintness disappeared from his voice on the instant. It filled the room more effortlessly than Mrs Knight's. He read magnificently. I had never heard such command of tone, such control, such loving articulation. And I had never seen anyone enjoy more his own reading; occasionally he peered over the page to make sure that we were not neglecting to enjoy it too. I was so much impressed with the whole performance that I could not spare much notice for the argument.

He gave us a good long piece. In fact, he gave us the whole sermon, twenty-four minutes by the clock. At the end, he leaned back in the chair and closed his eyes. Mrs Knight broke into enthusiastic, worshipping praise. I added my bit.

'Water, please, darling,' said Mr Knight very faintly, without opening his eyes. 'I should like a glass of water. Just water.'

As I changed into my own clothes in the bathroom, I was wondering how I could say goodbye to Sheila alone. In the general haze of excitement, I was thinking also of her father. He was vain, preposterously and superlatively vain, and yet astute; at the same time theatrical and shrewd; malicious, hypochondriac, and subtle; easy to laugh at, and yet exuding, through it all, a formidable power. He was a man whom no one would feel negligible. I believed that it was not impossible I could get on with him. I should have to suffer his malice, he would be a more effective enemy than his wife. But I felt one thing for certain, while I hummed tunelessly in the bathroom: he was worried about Sheila, and not because she had brought me there that afternoon; he was worried about her, as she sat silently by the fire; and there had been a spark, not of liking, but of sympathy, between him and me.

On my way downstairs I heard Mrs Knight's voice raised in indignation.

'It's much too wet to think of such a thing,' came through the drawing-room door. When I opened it, Mrs Knight was continuing: 'It's just asking to get yourself laid up. I don't know when you'll begin to have a scrap of sense. And even if it were a nice night—'

'I'm walking back with you,' said Sheila to me.

'I want you to tell her that it's quite out of the question. It's utterly absurd,' said Mrs Knight.

'I don't know what it's like outside,' I said half-heartedly. 'It does sound rather wild.'

The wind had been howling round the house.

'If it doesn't hurt you, it won't hurt me,' said Sheila.

Mr Knight was still lying back with his eyes closed.

'She *oughtn't* to do it,' a whisper came across the room. 'She oughtn't to *do* it.'

'Are you ready?' said Sheila.

Her will was too strong for them. It suddenly flashed across my mind, as she put on a mackintosh in the hall, that I had no idea, no idea in the world, how she felt towards either of them.

The wind blew stormily in our faces; Sheila laughed aloud. It was not raining hard, for the gale was too strong, but one could taste the driven rain. Down the village street we were quiet; I felt rapturously at ease, she had never been so near. As we turned down a lane, our fingers laced, and hers were pressing mine.

We had not spoken since we left the house. Her first words were accusatory, but her tone was soft:

'Why did you play my mother's game?'

'What do you mean?'

'Pretending to be better off than you are.'

'All I said was true.'

'You gave her a wrong impression,' she said. 'You know you did.'

'I thought it was called for.' I was smiling.

'Stupid of you,' she said. 'I'd rather you said you were a clerk.'

'It would have shocked her.'

'It would have been good for her,' said Sheila.

The gale was howling, the trees clashed overhead, and we walked on in silence, in silence deep with joy.

'Lewis,' she said at last. 'I want to ask you something.'

'Darling?'

'Weren't you terribly embarrassed—?'

'Whatever at?'

'At coming in wet. And meeting strangers for the first time in that fancy dress.'

She laughed.

'You did look a bit absurd,' she added.

'I didn't think about it,' I said.

'Didn't you really mind?'

'No.'

'I can't understand you,' she said. 'I should have curled up inside.' Then she said: 'You are rather wonderful.'

I laughed at her. I said that, if she were going to admire me for anything, she might choose something more sensible to admire. But she was utterly serious. To her self-conscious nerves, it was incredible that anyone should be able to master such a farce.

'I curled up a bit myself this afternoon,' she said, a little later.

'When?'

'When they were making fools of themselves in front of you.'

'Good God, girl,' I said roughly, lovingly, 'they're human.'

She tightened her grip on my hand.

At the end of a lane we came in sight of the farm. There was one more field to cross, and the lights blazed out in the windy darkness. I asked her to come in.

'I couldn't,' she said. I had an arm round her shoulders as we stood. Suddenly she hid her face against my coat. I asked her again.

'I must go,' she said. She looked up at me, and for the first time I kissed her, while the wind and my own blood sang and pounded in my ears. She drew away, then threw her arms round my neck, and I felt her mouth on mine.

'I must go,' she said. I touched her cheek, wet in the rain, and she pressed my hand. Then she walked down the lane, dark that night as a tunnel-mouth, her strong, erect stride soon losing her to sight against the black hedges. I waited there until I could hear nothing, no footsteps, nothing but the sound of the wind.

I returned to the group, who were revelling in a celebration. Jack was starting on his new business, and after supper George sat in our midst, predicting success for us all, for me most of all, complacent with hope about all our futures. It was not until the next, Sunday, night that I spoke to George alone. The others had gone back by the last bus; I was staying till the morning, in order to have the first comfort of my emancipation. That night, when we were left alone, George confided more of his own strange, violent, inner life than he had ever done before. He gave me part of his diary, and there I sat, reading by the light of the oil-lamp, while George smoked his pipe by my side.

When I had finished, George made an enquiry about my love affair. He had only two attitudes towards his friends' attachments. First, he responded with boisterous amusement. Then, when he decided that one was truly in love, he adopted an entirely different manner, circumlocutory, obscure, packed with innuendo, which he seemed to have decided was the height of consideration and tact. In the summer he had jovially referred to Sheila as that 'handsome bitch', but for some time past he had spoken of her, with infinite consideration, in his second manner. On that Sunday night his actual opening was:

'I hope you reached your destination safely yesterday afternoon?'

I said that I had.

'I hope that it all turned out to be' – George pulled down his waistcoat and cleared his throat – 'reasonably satisfactory?'

I said that it did.

'Perhaps I can assume,' said George, 'that you're not completely dissatisfied with your progress?'

I could not keep back a smile – and it gave me right away.

CHAPTER XXI

DECEIVING AND PLEASING

EVEN after that visit to Sheila's house I still did not tell her simply how much I loved her. Her own style seemed to keep my tongue playful and sarcastic; I made jokes about joy and hope and anguish, as though it were all a game. I was not yet myself released.

Once or twice she kept me waiting at a meeting place. The minutes passed, the quarters; I performed all the tricks that a lover does to cheat time, to make it stand still, to pretend not to notice, so as suddenly to see her there. It was an anguish like jealousy, and, like jealousy, when at last she came, it was drowned in the flood of relief.

I complained. But still my words were light; I did not speak from the angry pain of five minutes before. I scolded her, I asked her not to expose me to looks of *Schadenfreude* in the café – but I did it with the playful sarcasm that had become our favourite way of speaking to one another. Nevertheless, it was my first demand. She obeyed. At our next meeting, she was ten minutes early. She was trying to behave, and I was gay; but she was also strained and ill-tempered, as though it were an effort to subdue her pride even by so little.

During my next visit to eat dinners at the Inn, I was waiting for a letter. It was the beginning of December, I was in London for my usual five nights, and I had made Sheila promise to write to me. Hopefully I looked for a letter on the hall-table the morning after I arrived. I used to stay in a boarding-house in Judd Street, rather as though, with a provincial's diffidence, I did not want to be separated too far from my railhead at St Pancras. The dining-room, the hall, the bedroom, all smelt heavily of beeswax and food; the dining-room was dark, and we used to sit down to breakfast at eight o'clock in the winter gloom; there were twelve or so round the table – maiden ladies living there on a pittance, clerks, transients like myself. Through having students pass through the house, the landlady had acquired the patter of examinations. With a booming heartless heartiness, she used to encourage them, and me in my turn, by giving them postcards on the day of their last paper. On the postcard she had already written 'I got through, Mrs Reed'; she exhorted one to post it to her as soon as the result was known.

After each breakfast on that stay, I went quickly to the hall-table. There lay the letters, pale blue in the half-dark – not many in that house: none for me, on the first morning, the second, the third. It was the first time I had been menaced by the post.

Just as when I waited for her, I went through all the calculations of a lover. She could not have written before Monday night, it was more likely she would wait till Tuesday, there was no collection in the village after tea, it was impossible that I could get the letter by Wednesday morning. I was beginning to learn, in those few days, the arithmetic of anxiety and hope.

So, carrying with me that faint ache of worry, knowing that when I returned to the boarding-house my eyes would fly to the hall-table, I went out to eat my dinners at the Inn. On two of the nights I joined a party of my Cambridge acquaintances, Charles March among them; we went away from dinner to drink and talk, before they caught their train from Liverpool Street.

They were the kind of acquaintances on whom I should have sharpened my wits, if I had gone to a university. I had not yet spoken to Charles March alone, but him I felt kinship with, and wanted for a friend. The others I liked well enough, but no better than many of my friendly acquaintances in the town. I was soon easy among them, and we talked with undergraduate zest. When I was alone I compared their luck and mine. Some of them would be rivals. Now that I knew something of them, how did my prospects look?

I thought that, for intellectual machinery, between me and Charles March there was not much in it. I had no doubt that George Passant, both in mental equipment and in horsepower, was superior to both of us – but Charles March and I had a great deal more sense.

At that time I did not see, as I should have done later, that George's intellect was directed inwards, and gave him no creativity outside himself. Of those other Cambridge acquaintances, I did not believe that any of them, for force and precision combined, could compete with either Charles March or me, much less George Passant.

I was reassured to find it so. And I went on, once or twice, to envy them their luck. One of these young men was the son of an eminent K.C., and another of a headmaster: Charles March's family I guessed to be very rich. With that start, what could I not have done? I should have given any of them more than a race, I thought. By their standards, by the standards of the successful world from which they came, it would have been long odds on my being a success. Whereas now I had, in my young manhood, to make an effort and endure a strain that they did not even realise. I felt a certain rancour.

I was capable, however, of a more detached reflection. In one way I had a priceless advantage over these new acquaintances of mine. They had known, at first hand, successful men; and it often took away their confidence. They had lived in a critical climate. Their families had been bound to compare them, say, to an uncle who had 'come off'. There were times, even to a man as vigorous as Charles March, when all achievement seemed already over, all the great things done, all the books written. That was the penalty, and to many of them a crippling penalty, of being born into an old country and an established class. It was incomparably more easy for me to venture on my own. They were held back by the critical voices – or, if they moved at all, they tended to move, not freely, but as though they could only escape the critical voices by the deafening noise of their own rebellion.

I was far luckier. For I was, in that matter, free. From their tradition I could choose what I wanted. I needed neither to follow it completely, nor completely to rebel. I had never lived in a critical climate. There was nothing to hold me back. Far from it; I was pushed forward by the desires, longings, the inarticulate aspirations, of my mother and all her relatives, my grandfather and his companions arduously picking up their artisan culture, all my connections who had stood so long outside the shop-window staring at the glittering toys inside.

Later in my life I should not have wanted to alter any of that reflection. By twenty, in fact, I had a fair conception of most of my advantages and disadvantages, considered as a candidate in worldly affairs. I knew that I was quick-witted and adaptable – after meeting Charles March and the others, I was sure that I could hold my own intellectually. I could get on easily with a large number of human beings, and by nature I knew something of them. That seemed to me, with a kind of mock modesty, my stock-in-trade. But I left something out. Like most young men of twenty I found it impossible to credit that I had much will. George, for example, who had a will of Cromwellian strength, wrote of himself in his diary as being 'vacillating' and 'weak'. Often he thought, with genuine self-condemnation, that he was the most supine of men. It was much the same with me. I should have been surprised if I had been told that I had a tough, stubborn, deep-rooted will, and that it would probably be more use to me than my other qualities all added together.

A letter came. My heart leapt as I saw the envelope on the hall-table. But it was the wrong letter. Marion wrote to say that she had a half-holiday on the Thursday; she wanted to buy a hat, and she needed an impartial male opinion – she could trust me to be impartial, couldn't she? Could I spare her an hour that afternoon? And perhaps, if I were free, we might go to a play at night. She would have to catch the last train home, so I should get her off my hands in good time.

I knew that she was fond of me, but there my imagination stopped. It was still so when I received this letter. I replied by return, saying that of course I should be glad to see her. That was true; but it was also true that I was full of chagrin at finding her letter instead of another, and that made me hasten to reply.

The other arrived, by a coincidence, on the day that Marion was due. It did not say much, it was like Sheila's speech, shut-in, capricious, gnomic. But she referred, with a curious kind of intimacy, brittle and yet trusting, to one or two of our private jokes. That was enough to irradiate the dark hall. That was enough to make me happy all day, to keep the stylised phrases running through my mind, to give me delight abounding and overflowing, so that when Marion arrived I lavished some of it on her.

She told me how well and gay I looked. I smiled and said that I was both those things. She took it as a welcome. Her eyes were bright and I suddenly thought how pretty she could be.

She gave the impression, as usual, of being sloppily dressed. Quite why I could not decide, for she was now spending much attention on her appearance. That afternoon she was wearing the Russian boots fashionable that winter, and a long blue coat. She looked fresh, but nothing could stop her looking also eager and in a hurry. No one had less trace of the remote and arctic.

Practically, competently, she had discovered some hat shops in and near the Brompton Road – they were recommended as smart, she said, and not too dear.

Along we went. Neither she nor I knew much of London, and we traipsed up and down Kensington High Street before we found the first of her addresses. There was a slight fog, enough to aureole the lights and make the streets seem cosier; the shops were decked for Christmas, and inside them one felt nothing but the presence of furs, warm air, and women's scent. I was half-irked, because I hated shopping, half-glad to be among the lights and the crowds – cheerful because of the secret pleasure which she did not know, and also cheerful because of her enjoyment. I did not know it then, but I should have felt that second pleasure if I had been a more experienced man and deceiving her less innocently.

Marion tried on hat after hat, while I watched her.

'You must say what you think,' she said. 'My taste is very vulgar. I'm a bit of a slut, you know.'

There was one that I liked.

'I'm afraid it will show up my complexion,' she said. 'My skin isn't too good, is it?'

She was so straightforward. If Sheila had made that remark, I was thinking, I should have seen her skin as *strange*, transcendentally different from all others. While Marion's, when she drew my eyes to it, I saw just as skin, with a friendly familiar indifference, with the observant eye untouched by magic, just as I might have viewed my own.

I told her, as was true, that most women would envy her complexion. At last the hat was bought. It was expensive, and Marion grimaced. 'Still,' she said philosophically, 'a good hat ought to take a girl a bit farther. A bit farther than a deep interest in the arts. I always have had a deep interest in the arts, haven't I? – and look what it's done for me.'

Over tea she tried to find out whether I had been seeing Sheila. But she soon stopped – for she had discovered that I became claustrophobic when she showed a possessive interest in my life. I shied from her just as – I did not realise it then – I shied from the possessive invasion of my mother. That afternoon, she was satisfied that I seemed untroubled and relaxed.

She did not ask a straight question or inquire too hard. We were still natural with each other. She told me stories of an inspector's visit to her school, and how he was terrified that she was chasing him. Marion had developed a self-depreciating mode of humour, and I found it very funny. The earnestness of manner was disappearing fast, now that she had discovered that she could amuse.

We laughed together, until it became time for me to go to my Inn. I had to score my dinner there, or otherwise I should need to stay an extra night; I left straight after and joined Marion at the theatre. She might be losing her earnestness, but she was still in the *avant garde* of the twenties and she had chosen to see a Pirandello. I bought the tickets. I was cross at her letting me do so; for she had a regular salary, and she knew that each shilling mattered to me. But when I saw her sitting by me, waiting for the curtain to go up, I could not grudge her the treat. She was as naïvely expectant, as blissful to be there, as a child at a pantomime. It was not that she was ungenerous with money, or unthoughtful, but that she consumedly loved being given a treat, being taken out. She was never disappointed. Every treat was always a success. She was disappointed if, immediately afterwards, one said it was a hopeless play. She did not like the gilt rubbed off at once, though a week later she would be as critical as any of us. That night, on our way to St Pancras by the tube, she was a little tender-minded because I made fun of Pirandello.

I desisted. I did not want to spoil her pleasure. And, on the foggy platform, I was warmed by affection for her – affection the more glowing (it did not seem shameful as I laughed at her) because of a letter in my pocket whose words I carried before my eyes. At St Pancras we coughed in the sulphurous fog.

'Fancy having to go back tonight,' said Marion. 'I shall be hours late. I pity the children tomorrow. I shall smack them and shout at them.'

'Poor dear, you'll be tired,' I said.

'I shan't get home till four,' she said. 'And I don't mind a bit. And that's as much in the way of thanks as is good for you.'

Instead of going straight from the station to Judd Street, I found a coffee stall along the Euston Road. The fog, thickening every minute, swirled in front of the lamp, and one inhaled it together with the naphtha fumes and the steam. As I drank a cup of tea, I felt the glow of affection with me still. Then I took out Sheila's letter and read it, though I knew it by heart and word for word, in the foggy lamplight. I felt giddy with miraculous content. The name stood out in the dim light, like no other name. I felt giddy, as though the perfection of the miracle would happen now, and I should have her by my side, and we should walk together through the swirling fog.

CHAPTER XXII

CHRISTMAS EVE

WHEN I next met Sheila she was strangely excited. I saw it before she spoke to me, saw it while she made her way through the café towards our table. She was electric with excitement; yet what she had to say, though it filled me with pleasure, did not explain why. Without any preliminary she broke out:

'You know the Edens, don't you?'

'I know him, of course. I've never been to the house.'

'We drink punch there every Christmas Eve,' she said, and added: 'I love punch,' with that narcissistic indrawn satisfaction which took her far away. Then, electric-bright again, she said: 'I can take anyone I like. Will you come with me?'

I was open in my pleasure.

'I want you to,' she said. 'Make a note of it. I shan't let you forget.'

I could not understand, in the days between, why she laid so much stress on it, but I looked forward happily to Christmas Eve. The more happily, perhaps, because it was like an anticipation in childhood; it was like waiting for a present that one knew all the time one was safely going to receive. I imagined beforehand the warmth of a party, Harry Eden's surprise, the flattery of being taken there by the most beautiful young woman in the room – but above all the warmth of a party and the certain joy of her presence by my side.

On the day before Christmas Eve I was having a cup of tea alone in our habitual café. A waitress came up and asked if I was Mr Eliot: a lady wanted me on the telephone.

'Is that you?' It was Sheila's voice, though I had never heard it before at the other end of a wire. It sounded higher than in life, and remote, as though it came from the far side of a river. 'I didn't think they'd recognise you from my description. I didn't think I should find you.'

She sounded strung-up but exhilarated, laughing to herself.

'It's me all right,' I said.

'Of course it's you.' She laughed. 'Who else could it be?'

I grumbled that this was like a conversation in a fairy-tale.

'Right. Business. About tomorrow night.' Her voice was sharp. My heart dropped.

'You're coming, darling?' I pleaded. I could not keep the longing back: she had to hear it. 'You must come. I've been counting on it—'

'I'll come.'

I exclaimed with relief and delight.

'I'll come. But I shall be late. Go to the party by yourself. I'll see you there.'

I was so much relieved that I would have made any concession. As a matter of form, I protested that it would have been nice to go together.

'I can't. I can't manage it. You can make yourself at home. You won't mind. You can make yourself at home anywhere.' She laughed again.

'But you will come?'

'I'll come.'

I was vaguely upset. Why was she keyed-up to a pitch of excitement even higher than when she first invited me? I felt for a moment that she was a stranger. But she had never failed me. I knew that she would come. The promise of love, of romantic love, of love where one's imagination makes the beloved fit all one's hope, enveloped me again. Once more I longed for tomorrow night, the party, for her joining me as I sat among the rest.

The Edens lived outside the middle of the town, in the fashionable suburb. I strolled slowly across the park on Christmas Eve, up the London Road; I heard a clock strike; the party began at nine o'clock, and I was deliberately a little late. A church stood open, light streaming through the doors. Cars rushed by, away from the town, but the pavement was almost empty, apart from an occasional couple standing beneath the trees in the mild night.

I came to where the comfortable middle-class houses stood back from the main road, with their hedges, their lawns, their gravel drives. Through the curtains of the drawing-rooms the lights glowed warm, and I felt curious, as I often did, walking any street at night, about what was going on behind the blinds. That Christmas Eve, the sight of those glowing rooms made me half-envious, even then, going to a rendezvous in my limitless expectancy; here seemed comfort, here seemed repose and a safe resting-place; I envied all behind the blinds, even while, in the flush of youth and drunkenness of love, I despised them also, all those who stayed in the safe places and were not going out that night; I envied them behind the glowing curtains, and I despised them for not being on their way to a beloved.

The Edens' drawing-room was cheerful with noise when I entered. There was a great fire, and the party sitting round. On the hearth stood an enormous bowl, with bottles beside it, glinting in the firelight. All over the drawing-room there wafted a scent of rum, oranges and lemons. Under the holly and mistletoe and tinsel drifted that rich odour.

Eden was sitting, with an air of extreme permanence, in an armchair by the fireplace. He greeted me warmly. 'I'm very glad to see you, Eliot. This is the young man I told you about—' He introduced me to his wife. 'He's a friend of Sheila Knight's – but I've known him on my own account for, let me see, it must be well over a year. When you get to my age, Eliot, you'll find time goes uncomfortably fast.' He went on explaining me to his wife. 'Yes, I gave him some excellent advice which he was much too enterprising to take. Still, there's nothing like being a young man in a hurry.'

Mrs Eden was kneeling on the hearthrug, busy with hieratic earnestness at the mixing of the punch. The liquid itself was steaming in the hearth; she had come to the point of slicing oranges and throwing in the pieces. She was pale-faced, with an immensely energetic, jerky and concentrated manner. She had bright, brown eyes, opaque as a bird's. She fixed them on me as she went on slicing.

'How long have you known Sheila, Mr Eliot?' she asked, as though the period were of the most critical importance.

I told her.

'She has such style,' said Mrs Eden with concentration.

Mrs Eden was enthusiastic about most things, but especially so about Sheila. She was quite unembarrassed by her admiration; it was easy to think of her as a girl, concentrated and intent, unrestrained in a *schwärmerei*, bringing some mistress flowers and gifts. At any rate, I wondered (I might be distorting her remarks through my own emotion) whether she too was not impatient for Sheila's arrival. With hieratic seriousness she went on cutting the oranges, dropping in the peel. It was luxuriously warm by the fire, the punch was smoking, Eden lay back with a sigh of reminiscent well-being, and began to talk to us – 'in those days,' he said, meaning the days of his youth, the turn of the century. I looked at the clock. It was nine-twenty. The others were listening to Eden, watching his wife prepare the punch. They were jolly and relaxed. I could scarcely wait for the minutes to pass and my heart was pounding.

To all of them except to Eden I was someone whom Sheila Knight had picked up, how they did not know. They were a different circle from ours, more prosperous and more comfortably middle-class. The Edens liked entertaining, and they had a weakness for youth, so nearly all the people round the fire were young, the sons and daughters of some of Eden's clients. The young men were beginning in their professions and in the local firms. Before this, Eden had, with his fair-minded sense of etiquette, invited George to join one of their parties, but George, horrified at the prospect, had made a stiff excuse and kept away. So there were no links between us – they had never heard my name. Sheila, however, had visited the house quite often, possibly owing to the enthusiasm of Mrs Eden, and everyone there had either met her or knew her family – for Mrs Knight was prepared to include the prosperous town families in her ambit, as well as her county friends.

One or two of them inspected me inquisitively. I was quiet, apart from keeping Eden's reminiscences going. I was watching the clock. I did not take much part in the circle; the voices round were loud and careless, but as the minutes passed I was not listening to them, only for a ring at the bell outside.

'Punch is ready,' said Mrs Eden, suddenly and with energy.

'Ah well,' said Eden, 'I like the sound of that.'

'Shall we wait for Sheila?' Mrs Eden's eyes darted round the circle. Cheerily, the circle voted against.

'I really don't see why we should,' said Eden. 'Last come, last served. What do you think, Eliot? I fancy your friend Sheila won't mind if we proceed to the business of the meeting. You can explain to her afterwards that it's what happens to young women when they're late.'

The seconds were pounding on, but under Eden's affable badinage I felt proprietorial. I answered that I was sure she would not mind. The circle cheered. Mrs Eden dipped a ladle in the bowl and intently filled each glass but one.

The punch was hot, spiced and strong. After the first round the circle became noisier, Eden's reminiscences had to give way, someone suggested a game. All the time I was listening. It was past ten o'clock. At last I heard, I heard unmistakably after the false hopes, the sound of a car in the drive. On the instant, I felt superlative content.

'Sheila,' said Mrs Eden with bright eyes.

I basked in well-being. I could sit back now that she would soon be here, and not stare each moment at the door. I did not even need to listen too hard to the sounds outside.

The door opened. Sheila came in, radiant. Behind her followed a man.

Sheila came up to Mrs Eden, her voice sharp with excitement. 'I'm being extremely rude,' she said. 'Will you let me stay if I bring someone else? We've been having dinner, and I thought you wouldn't mind giving him some punch too. This is Doctor Devitt. He works at the infirmary.'

I heard Mrs Eden saying:

'We need another glass. That's all. Sit down, Dr Devitt. I'll get a glass for you.'

Her first response was always action. Perhaps she had not given a thought to what was happening. In any case, she could not resist Sheila, who only had to ask.

Through the haze I watched Eden smile politely, not his full, bland, melon-lipped smile, at Sheila and the other man. Eden looked at me. Was he puzzled? Did he understand? Was he looking at me with pity?

I had known, from the instant I saw her enter. It was not a chance. It was deliberate. It was planned.

The room swam, faces came larger than life out of the mist, receded, voices were far away, then crashingly near. Somehow I managed to speak to Eden, to ask him some meaningless question.

The circle was being expanded, to bring in two more chairs. Sheila and Devitt sat down, Sheila between him and me. As Mrs Eden filled two glasses, Sheila said: 'Can Lewis have another one? Let me pass it.' She took my tumbler without a word between us. Intently, Mrs Eden filled it and gave it back to Sheila, who turned and put it into my hand.

'There,' she said.

Her face was smoother than I had ever seen it. It was open before me, and there seemed no trace or warning of her lines. Until her eyes swept up from the glass, which she watched into my fingers as though anxious not to spill a drop, until her eyes swept up and I could see nothing else, I watched (as if it had nothing to do with the mounting tides of pain, the sickness of misery, the rage of desire) her face – open, grave, pure and illuminated.

The circle went on with a game. It was a game in which one had to guess words. The minutes went by, they might have been hours, while I heard Sheila shouting her guesses from my side. Sometimes I shouted myself. And afterwards I remembered Eden, sitting quietly in his arm-chair, a little put out because the party chose to play this game instead of listening to him, Eden sitting quietly because he was not quick at guessing and so withdrew.

Midnight struck.

'Christmas Day,' said Mrs Eden; and, with her usual promptness, went on: 'Merry Christmas to you all.'

I heard Sheila, at my side, return the greeting.

Soon after, people began to stand up, for the party was ending. At once Sheila went to the other side of the hearth, and started to talk to Mrs Eden. Tom Devitt and I were standing close together – and, through the curious intimacy of rivals, we were drawn to speak.

He was much older than I was, and to me looked middle-aged. He was, I later found, in the middle thirties. His face was heavy, furrowed, kind, and intelligent. We were both tall, and our eyes met at the same level, but already he was getting fat, and his hair was going.

Awkwardly, with kindness, he asked about my studies. He said that Sheila had told him how I was working. He said, with professional concern, that I looked as though I might be overdoing it. Was I short of sleep? Had I anything to help me through a bad night?

I replied that it did not matter, and retaliated by telling him that there was a crack in one of his spectacles: oughtn't he to have it mended?

'It's too near the eye to affect vision,' said Tom Devitt. 'But I do need another pair.'

In the clairvoyance of misery, I knew some vital things about him. I knew that he was in love with Sheila. I knew that he was triumphant to be taking her out that night. He was concerned for me because of his own triumph at being the preferred one. But I knew too that he was a kind, decent man, not at all unperceptive; he realised the purpose for which she had used him, and was angry; he had had no warning until he arrived in that room, and saw that I had already been invited as her partner.

We stood there, talking awkwardly – and we felt sorry for each other. We felt that, with different luck, we should have been friends.

Sheila beckoned to him. I followed them out of the room: at all costs I must speak to her. Any quarrel, any bitterness, was better than this silence.

But they were putting on their coats, and she stayed by Tom Devitt.

'I'm driving him to the infirmary,' she said to me. 'Can we give you a lift?'

I shook my head.

'Oh well.' She gazed at me. 'I'll see you soon.'

They went out of the door together. Just as they got to the car, I saw Devitt turn towards her, as though asking a question. His face was frowning, but at her reply it lightened with a smile.

The hum of the car died at last away. While I could hear it, she was not quite gone. Then I went home the way I had come, four hours before. I was blind with misery; yet as I crossed the park under the dark, low, starless sky, there were moments when I could not believe it, when absurdly I was invaded by the hope that had uplifted me on the outward journey. It was like those times in misery when one is cheated by a happy dream.

Blindly I came home to my room. Under the one bare light the chair and table and bed stood blank before my eyes. They were blank as the darkness into which I stared for hours, lying awake that night. I stared into the darkness while mood after mood took hold of me, as changeable as the fever and chill of an illness, as ravaging and as much beyond my control.

I could have cried, if only the tears would come. I twisted about in a paroxysm of longing. I was seized by a passion of temper, and I could have strangled her.

I had been humiliated once before – on that morning as a child, the memory of which possessed me for a moment in the night, when I offered my mother's ten-shilling note. As a rule, I did not look for or find humiliation. I was no George Passant, going through the world expecting affronts and feeling them right through to his viscera. For my age, I got off lightly, in being free from most of the minor shames. But when humiliation came, it seared me, so that all my hidden pride shrieked out, and in bitterness I vowed that this must be the end, that I would make sure that I never so much as saw her again, that I would act as though she had never been.

Yet, turning over on to the other side, praying for sleep, I hoped, hoped for a word that would put it right. It had been an accident, I thought; she was remote, she lived in a world of her own; she had just happened to see him that night. There must be a simple explanation. With the foolish detailed precision of love, I recalled each word between us since she invited me to go to the Edens'; and I proved to myself, in that armistice of hope, that it was a series of coincidences, and none of it was meant. Tomorrow, no, the day after, I should receive a letter which would resolve it all. She might not know how I had been hurt. At the Edens' she had been light and friendly to me, as though we should meet soon after on our usual terms. Her manner had been the same to both of us. She had not looked at him lovingly.

Then I knew jealousy. Where had they gone after the car drove away? Had he kissed her? Had he slept with her? Were they, at this moment when I was lying sleepless, in each other's arms? For the first time in my thoughts of Sheila, my sensual imagination was active, merciless, gave me no rest.

The night ticked by, slower than my racing heart. Again I knew that it was all planned. Again with detailed precision, but with another purpose, I went over each word that she had spoken since her invitation – her excitement when she first asked me to go, her tense exaltation, the tone in which she had telephoned at the café. It was the edge of cruelty. I had been hurt by motiveless cruelty on that morning of childish humiliation – but this was the first time I had felt cruelty in love. Did I know that night that it was the end of innocence? I felt much that I had imagined of love stripped from me by her outrage, and in the darkness, I saw in her and in myself a depth which was black with hate, and from which, even in misery, I shrank back appalled. I had always known it in myself, but kept my eyes away; now her outrage made me look.

In the creeping winter dawn, my thoughts had become just two. The first was, I must dismiss her from my mind, I must forget her name – and, as I got more tired, I kept holding to that resolve. The second was, how soon would she write to me, so that I could see her again?

CHAPTER XXIII

THE LIGHTS OF A HOUSE

THE days passed; and, working in my room, a veil kept coming between my eyes and the page. When the veil came, I would hear some phrase of

Sheila's, and that set my thoughts racing as on the sleepless night. I sat there at my books, but I could not force my eyes to clear.

I heard nothing, I saw no one, I received no letter, for day after day. George and Jack and I had arranged to meet to see the new year in; but after one drink George went off to an 'important engagement', and Jack and I were left alone.

'He must have found somebody,' said Jack. 'Good luck to him.'

We argued about how we should spend the night. Jack's idea was that there could be no better way than by going to the local palais-de-danse and picking up two girls; but, at the mention of the word, I re-heard Sheila saying 'we went to the palais', and I could not face the faintest chance, the one chance in ten thousand, of seeing her there.

I wanted to stay in the public-house, drinking. Jack was discontented, but, in his good-natured way, agreed. For him, it was a sacrifice. It was only to be convivial, and because he liked us, that he endured long drinking sessions with George and me.

Amiably he sipped at his whisky, and made a slight face. He was so accommodating that I wanted to explain why I could not go to the palais; I was also longing to confide, and I knew that I should get sympathy and some kind of understanding. Yet when I began, my pride clutched me, and the story came out, thin, half-humorous, so garbled that he could get no inkling either of my humiliation or my aching emptiness as each day passed. Even so, I got some relief, perhaps more than if I had exposed the truth.

'We all have lovers' quarrels,' said Jack.

'I suppose so,' I said.

'It's sweet when you make it up,' said Jack.

He smiled at me.

'You'll have to be a bit firm,' he said. 'See that she apologises. Box her ears and make her feel a little girl. Then be specially nice to her.' He went on: 'It's all right as long as you don't take it too tragically. You watch yourself, Lewis. Mind you don't get all the anguish and none of the fun. You'd better get her where you want her this time. I'll tell you how I managed it last week—'

Thus I spent the last hours of 1925 listening to Jack Cotery on the predicaments and tactics of a love affair; of how he had changed a reverse into a victory; of comic misfortune, of tears that were part of the game, of tears that turned into luxurious sighs. And, listening to his eloquence, I was solaced, I half-believed that things would go that way for me.

The first days of January. Not a word. The voice of sense gave way, and

I began to write a letter. Then my pride held me on the edge, and I tore it up. When I could not sleep, I dragged myself out of bed to work. I did not know how long such a state could last. I had nothing to compare it with. I went on – with 'automatic competence', a clear high voice taunted me, more piercing than any voice of those I met. I worked to tire myself, so that I should sleep late into the morning. I was living always for the next day.

Before Christmas the group had arranged to go out to the farm for the first weekend of the year. I had promised to join the party. But now I recoiled from company, I told George that I could not go. 'You're forgetting your responsibilities,' he said stiffly. There were other times when I craved for any kind of human touch. I went the round of pubs, talking to barmaids and prostitutes, anything for a smile. It was in one of those storms that I changed my mind again. On the Friday night I sought George out, and told him that I should like to come after all. 'I'm glad to see you're back in your right mind,' said George. Then he asked formally: 'Nothing seriously wrong with your private affairs, I hope?'

For George, it was a great weekend. Everyone was there, and he could bask right in the heart of his 'little world', surrounded by people whom he loved and looked after, where all his diffidence, prickles, suspiciousness and angry defiance were swept away, where he felt utterly serene. At the farm, surrounded by his group, one saw George at his best. He was a natural leader, though, because of the quirks of his nature, it had to be a leader in obscurity, a leader of a revolt that never came off. He was a strange character – many people thought him so bizarre as to be almost mad: yet to some who weren't hero-worshippers by nature (and that was true of me) there were times when he seemed to be built on the lines of a great man.

Seated at the supper table, outside the golden circle of the oil-lamp, George was at his best. Each word he spoke was listened to, even in the gossip, chatter and argument of the group. That night he talked to us of freedom – how, if we had the will (and that it would never have occurred to him to doubt) we could make our children's lives the best there had ever been in the world. Not only by making a better society, in which they would stand a fair chance, but also by bringing them up free and happy. 'The good in men is incomparably more important than the evil,' said George. 'Whatever happens, we've always got to remember that.'

The whole group was moved, for he had spoken from a great depth. That was his message, and it came from a man who struggled with himself. When Jack, the most impudent person there, twitted him and said the evil could be very delectable, George shouted: 'I don't call *that* evil. It's half the trouble that for hundreds of years all the priests and parents and pundits have tried to make us miserable by a load of guilt.'

I had not said much at supper-time, for my mind was absent, thinking of a recent supper at that table, when I came in wet, alight with a secret happiness. For a moment I shook off my preoccupation, my own load, and looked at George. For I knew that he, more than most of us, was burdened by a sense of guilt – and so he demanded that we should all be free.

After supper, we broke into twos and threes, and Marion and I began to talk out in the window-bay. She had just returned from her Christmas holidays, and it was three weeks since we had met.

'I need your help,' she said at once.

'What about?'

'I've got a problem for you.' Then she added: 'What were you thinking about just now?'

'What's your problem, Marion?' I said, wanting to evade the question.

'Never mind for a minute. What were you thinking about? I've never seen you look so far away.'

'I was thinking about George.'

'Were you?' she said doubtfully. 'When you're thinking of someone, you usually watch them – with those damned piercing eyes of yours, don't you? You weren't watching George. You weren't watching any of us.'

I had had time to collect myself, and I told her that I had been thinking of George's message of freedom compared with the doctrine of original sin. Often she would have been interested, for she tried to get me to talk about people; but just then she did not believe a word of it, she was angry at being put off. Impatiently, as though irrelevantly, she burst out:

'Why in heaven's name don't you learn to keep your tie straight? You're a disgrace.'

It was really a bitter cry, because I would not confide. I felt ashamed of myself, because I was fond of her – but also I felt the more wretched, the more strained, because she was pressing me. It was by an effort that I kept back a cold answer. Instead, I said, as though we were both joking about our untidiness:

'I must say, that doesn't come too well from you.'

Jack was close by, talking to another girl, with an ear alert in our direction. He moved away, as though he had not overheard anything of meaning in our words.

Again I asked about her problem.

'You won't be very interested,' said Marion.

'Of course I'm interested,' I said.

She hesitated about telling me; but she wanted to, she had it ready. She had been offered a job in her own town. It was a slightly better job, in a central school. If she were to make a career of teaching, it would be sensible to take it. She could live with her sister, and save a good deal of money.

She wanted me to say, without weighing any of her arguments, just: you're not to go. Increasingly I felt myself constrained, the offender (increasingly I longed for the lightness that came over me as I talked to Sheila), because I could not. I was tongue-tied, and all I had to say came heavily. My spontaneity had deserted me quite. Yet I should miss her, miss her with an ache of affection, if she went. I knew that somehow I relied on her, even as I tried to speak fairly and she watched me with mutinous eyes and gave me curt, rude answers. I tried to think only of what was best for her – and for that she could not listen to me or forgive me.

George called out heartily:

'Lewis, are you coming for a constitutional?'

This was a code invitation, devised to meet the need of his curious sense of etiquette in front of the young women: a 'constitutional' meant going down the road to the public-house, sitting there for an hour or so, and then coming back, ready to talk until the next morning. That night I was glad to escape from the house; no one else stirred, and George and I went across the field together.

Suddenly, on an impulse that I could not drive down, I said: 'George, I'm going to leave you for an hour. I'm going for a walk.'

At first George was puzzled. Then, with extreme quickness, with massive tact, he said:

'I quite understand, old chap. I quite understand.' He gave a faint, sympathetic, contented chuckle. He proceeded to go through one of his elaborate wind-ups: 'I take it you might prefer me to practise a little judicious prevarication? If we walk back from the pub together, there's no reason why our friends should realise that you've been engaged on – other activities.'

In fact, I had no thought of seeing Sheila. Alone in the dark, I made my way through the lanes, drawn as though by instinct towards her house. I could not have said why I was going – except that each yard I covered gave me some surcease. I knew that I should not see her; with the relic of reason and pride, I knew that it would have been disastrous to see her.

Yet on the way, across the same fields that I had first seen in a downpour with so much joy, surrendered to the impulse that drew me across the fields, down the lanes, towards her house, I felt a peace, such as I had not known since Christmas Eve. It was a precarious peace, it might break at any moment; but I was closer to her, and my whole body melted into the mirage of well-being.

In the village, I drew up my coat-collar. I could not bear the risk of being recognised, if one of the family happened to be out that night. I kept in the shadow, away from the lights of the cottage windows. From the bar parlour came loud and raucous singing. I went past the lych-gate: the spire was dark against the star. I could see the serene lights of the vicarage. I stopped before the drive, huddled myself against a tree, hidden in case anyone should drive out: there I stood, without moving, without any thought or plan. The drawing-room windows were lit up, and so was one on the next floor. I did not even know her room. Was that her room? – the real room, instead of that which, in the first rapture, I had pictured to myself. Was she there, away from anyone who pried, away from anyone who troubled her? Was she there, at that moment, writing to me?

No shadow crossed the window. I did not feel the cold. I could not have said how many minutes passed, before I went back again, keeping to the dark side, down the village street.

CHAPTER XXIV

THE KEY IN THE LOCK

BACK in my room, I slept through broken nights and worked and gazed over the roofs, and all my longings had become one longing – just to be in touch again. The shock of Christmas Eve had been softened by now, and the pain dulled: pride alone was not much of a restraint to keep my hand from the pen, from the comfort of writing Dearest Sheila. Yet I did not write.

Monday went by, after the weekend when I stood outside her house. Tuesday. Wednesday. I longed that we could have some friend in common, so that I could hear of her and drop a remark, as though casually, that I was waiting. A friend could help us both, I thought, could put in a word for me. Apart from our meetings – I was glad to think so, for it shifted the blame outside ourselves, gave me something which could be altered and so a scrap of hope – we had none of the reminders of each other, the everyday gossip, of people who lived in the same circle. My friends inhabited a different world: so far as they knew her, they hated her, while hers I did not know at all.

I was impelled to discover what I could about Tom Devitt. I dug my nails into the flesh, and willed that I must put him out of my mind, together with the scene at the Edens' – together with Sheila and what I felt for her. On the Monday after I returned from the farm, however, I found myself making an excuse to go to the reference library. There was some point not covered by my textbook. In the library I looked it up, but I could safely have left it; it was of no significance at all, and for such a point I should never have troubled to come. I browsed aimlessly by the shelves which contained *Who's Who*, Whitaker, Crockford (where I had already long since looked up the Reverend Laurence Knight) and the rest. Almost without looking, I was pulling out the *Medical Directory*. Devitt A. T. N.; the letters seemed embossed. It did not say when he was born, but he had been a medical student at Leeds and qualified in 1914 (when she and I were nine years old, I thought with envy). In the war, he had been in the R.A.M.C., and had been given a Military Cross (again I was stabbed with envy). Then he had held various jobs in hospitals: in 1924 he had become registrar at the infirmary; I did not know then what the hospital jobs meant, nor the title registrar. I should have liked to know how good a career it had been, and what his future was.

The Thursday of that week was a bright cold sunny day of early January. In the afternoon I was working in my overcoat, with a blanket round my legs. When I looked up from my note-book I could see, for the table stood close to the window, the pale sunlight silvering the tiles.

Someone was climbing up the attic stairs. There was a sharp knock, and my door was thrown open. Sheila came into the room. With one hand she shut the door behind her, but she was looking at me with a gaze expressionless and fixed. She took two steps into the room, then stopped quite still. Her face was pale, hard, without a smile. Her arms were at her sides. I had jumped up, forgetting everything but that she was here, my arms open for her; but when she stayed still, so did I, frozen.

'I've come to see you,' she said.

'Yes,' I said.

'I haven't seen you since that night. You're thinking about that night.' Her voice was louder than usual.

'I'm bound to think of it.'

'Listen to this: I did it on purpose.'

'Why did you do it?'

'Because you made me angry.' Her eyes were steady, hypnotic in their glitter. 'I've not come to tell you that I'm sorry.'

'You ought to be,' I said.

'I'm not sorry.' Her voice had risen. 'I'm glad I did it.'

'What do you mean?' I said in anger.

'I tell you, I'm glad I did it.'

We were standing a yard apart. Her arms were still at her sides, and she had not moved. She said:

'You can hit me across the face.'

I looked at her, and her eyes flickered.

'You should,' she said.

As I looked at her, in the bright light from the window behind my back, I saw the whites of her eyes turn bloodshot. Then tears formed, and slowly trickled down her cheeks. She did not raise a hand to touch them. As she cried, dreadfully still, the hard fierce poise of her face was dissolved away, and her beauty, and everything I recognised.

I took her by the shoulders, and led her, very gently, to sit on the bed. She came without resistance, as though she were a robot. I kissed her on the lips, told her for the first time in words that I loved her, and wiped away the tears.

'I love you,' I said.

'I don't love you, but I trust you,' cried Sheila, in a tone that tore me open both for myself and her. She kissed me with a sudden desperate energy, with her mouth forced on to mine; her arms were convulsively tight; then she let go, pressed her face into the counterpane, and began to cry again. But this time she cried with her shoulders heaving, with relief; I sat on the bed beside her, holding her hand, waiting till she was exhausted; and in those moments I was possessed by the certainty that no love of innocence, no love in which she had been only the idol of my imagination, could reach as deep as that which I now knew.

For now I had seen something frightening, and I loved her, seeing something of what she was. I felt for her a curious detached pity in the midst of the surge of love – and I realised that it was the first ignorant forerunner of pity that I had felt for her in her mother's drawing-room. I felt a sense of appalling danger for her, and, yes, for me: of a life so splintered and remote that I might never reach it; of cruelty and suffering that I could not soften. Yet I had never felt so transcendentally free. Holding her hand as she cried, I loved her, I believed that she in part loved me, and that we should be happy.

She raised her head, sniffed, blew her nose, and smiled. We kissed again. She said:

'Turn your head. I want to see you.'

She smiled, half-sarcastically, half-tearfully, as she inspected me. She said:

'You look rather sweet with lipstick on.'

I told her that her face, foreshortened as I saw it when I kissed her, was different from the face that others saw: its proportions quite changed, its classical lines destroyed, much more squashed, imperfect, and human.

I asked her again about Christmas Eve.

'Why did you do it?'

She said:

'I'm hateful. I thought you were too possessive.'

'Possessive?' I cried.

'You wanted me too much,' said Sheila.

I enquired about Tom. We were sitting side by side, with arms round each other. In the same heartbeat I was jealous and reassured.

'Do you love him?' I said.

'No,' said Sheila. She exclaimed in a high voice: 'I wish I did. He's a good man. He's too good for me. He's a better man than you are.'

'He loves you,' I said.

'I think he wants to marry me,' she said. 'I can't. I don't love him.' Then she said: 'Sometimes I think I shall never love anyone.'

She pulled down my face and kissed me.

'I don't love you, but I trust you. Get me out of this. I trust you to get me out of this.'

I heard her say once more:

'I don't love you, but I trust you.'

I told her that I loved her, the words set free and pouring over: I was forced to speak, able to speak, deliriously happy to speak, as I had never yet spoken to a human being. 'Get me out of this' – that cry turned the key in the lock. I did not know what she meant, and yet it lured me on. I was utterly released; there was no pride, no reserve left, as there was when my mother, when Marion, invaded me with love. Seeing her at last as a person, not just an image in a dream, I threw aside my own burden of self. I told her, the words came bursting out, of every feeling that had possessed me since we first met. In this other nature, remote from anything I knew, I could abandon all, except my passion for her. In her arms, hearing that mysterious and remote cry, I lost myself.

PART FOUR

THE FIRST SURRENDER

CHAPTER XXV

A PIECE OF ADVICE

I HAD thought, when Marion took me shopping in London and talked of her complexion, of how the same words spoken by Sheila would have taken their special place, would have been touched by the enchantment of strangeness: so that I should remember them, as I remembered everything about her, as though they were illuminated. For everything she did, when I was first in love, was separated from all else that I heard or saw or touched; the magic was there, and the magic laid an aura round her; she might have been a creature from another species. For me, that was the overmastering transformation of romantic love. And in part it stayed so – until in middle age, a generation after I first met her, years after she was dead, there were still moments when she possessed my mind, different from all others.

It stayed so, after that January afternoon in my attic. There were nights when we had walked hand in hand through the bitter deserted streets, and I went back alone, re-hearing the words spoken half an hour before, but hearing them as though they were magic words. The slightest touch – not a kiss, but the tap of her fingers on my pocket, asking for matches to light a cigarette – I could feel as though there had never been any other hands.

Yet that January afternoon had added much. That I knew even as she stood there, her face dissolved by tears. I could no longer shape her according to my own image of desire. I was forced to try to know her now. She was no longer just my beloved, she was a separate person whose life had crashed head-on into mine. And I was forced to feel for her something quite separate from love, a strange pity, affection, compassion, inexplicable to me then as it was at the first intimation in her mother's drawing-room.

I began to learn the depth and acuteness of her self-consciousness. She could not believe that I was not tormented likewise. She wondered at it. Whereas she – she smiled sarcastically and harshly, and said: 'It would be hard to be more so. You can't deny it. You can't pretend I'm not.'

She was angry about it. She blamed her parents. Once she said not angrily, but as a matter of fact: 'They've destroyed my self-confidence for ever.' She wanted ease at all costs, and used all her will to get it. If I could give her ease, she never thought twice about visiting me in my room. People might think she was my mistress; she knew now that I hungered for her; her parents would stop her if they could; she dismissed each of those thoughts with contempt, when the mood was on her and she felt that I alone could soothe her. Nothing else mattered, when her will was set.

I knew something else, something so difficult for a lover to accept that I could not face it steadily. Yet I knew that she was going round like a sleepwalker. She was looking for someone with whom to fall in love.

I knew that she was desperately anxious, so anxious that the lines deepened and the skin darkened beneath her eyes, that she would never manage it. She did not love me, but I gave her a kind of hope, an illusory warmth, as though through me she might break out into release – either with me or another, for as to that, in her ruthlessness, innocence and cruelty, she would not give a second's thought.

Such was the little power I had over her.

She was afraid that she would never love a man as I loved her. It was from that root that came her acts of Christmas Eve, her deliberate cruelty.

For she was cruel, not only through indifference, but also as though in being cruel she could find release. In such a scene as that on Christmas Eve, she could bring herself to the emotional temperature in which most of us naturally lived.

It was hard to take, at that age. The more so, as she played on a nerve of cruelty within myself – which I had long known, which except with her I could forget. Once or twice she provoked my temper, which nowadays I had as a rule under control. She made me quarrel: quarrels were an excitement to her, a time in which to immerse herself, to swear like a cheated whore; to me, except in the height of rage, they were – because I had so little power over her – like death.

It was harder for me, because now I longed for her completely. The time was past when I could be satisfied, thinking of her alone in her room; each scrap of understanding, each wave either of compassion or anger, and the more I wanted her. On that January afternoon, when I had the first sight of her as a living creature, driven by her nature, I felt not only the birth of affection, as something distinct from love – but also I was trembling with desire. And that was the first of many occasions when she felt my hand shake, when she felt in me a passion which left her unmoved, which made her uneasy and cruel. For now I wanted her in the flesh.

Although everything I knew made nonsense of the thought, I wanted her as my wife.

I had not enough confidence to tell her so. I had always been afraid that I had no charm for her. Sometimes, now that I wanted her so much, I hoped I had a little; sometimes, I thought, none at all. Occasionally she was warm and active and laughing in my arms; then, at our next meeting, irritated by my need for her, she would smoke cigarette after cigarette in an endless chain so as to give me no excuse to kiss her. I could not face the cold truth she might tell me if I took the cigarette away.

She caused me intense jealousy. Not only with Tom Devitt; in fact she quarrelled with him early in the year. I told her that I was suspicious of her quarrels. 'You needn't be this time,' she said. 'Poor Tom. It's a pity. He couldn't turn me into a doctor's wife.' She reflected, with a frown. 'The more helpless they are, the worse one treats them.' She looked at me. 'I know I'm unpleasant. You can tell me so if you like. But I'm telling the truth. It's also true of less unpleasant women. Isn't it so?'

'I expect it's true of us all,' I said.

'I've never found a man who made me helpless yet,' she said. 'I don't know what it would be like.'

'I've found you,' I said.

She shook her head.

'No,' she said. 'You're not so helpless. I shouldn't come to see you if you were.'

I ceased to be jealous of Tom Devitt, but there were others. They were nearly all misfits, waifs and strays, often – like Devitt – much older than she was. For the smart comely young businessmen who pursued her she had no use whatsoever. But she would find some teacher at the School timid with women or unhappily married, and I should hear a threatening, excited 'we' again. She had a very alert and hopeful eye for men whom she thought might fascinate her. In getting to know them, she rid herself of her self-consciousness; instead of shrinking into a corner, as she did in company, she was ready to take the initiative herself, exactly as though she were a middle-aged woman on the prowl for lovers. I could see nothing in common between those who pleased her. I knew that she herself imagined some implacably strong character, some Heathcliff of a lover who would break her will – but they were all weaker and gentler than she was.

Each of those sparks of interest guttered away, and she came back, sometimes pallid, ill-tempered, more divided than before, sometimes sarcastic and gay.

I was beyond minding in what state she came back. For each time I was bathed in the overwhelming reassurance of the jealous. After days spent in the degrading detective work of jealousy, I saw her in front of me, and the calculations were washed away. It was only the jealous, I thought later, who could be so ecstatically reassured. She had said that she went home by the eight-ten last night. Where had she been between tea-time and the train, with whom had she been? Then she said that her mother had been shopping in the town, and they had gone to the pictures. Only the suspicious could be as simple and wholehearted in delight as I was then.

I did not spend much time with the group during those months. My first Bar examination happened in the summer, and whenever I could not see Sheila I was trying to concentrate upon my work. I went out at night with George and Jack, I still went to Martineau's on Fridays, but the long weekends at the farm I could no longer spare. There was, I knew, a good deal of gossip; by now it was common knowledge that I was, as they called it, head over heels in love with Sheila. Marion also began to keep away from the group, and we never met at all.

There was one pair of curious, observant eyes that did not let me keep my secrets unperceived. Jack Cotery was interested in me, and love was his special subject. He watched the vicissitudes in my spirits as day followed day. He went out of his way to meet Sheila once or twice. Then, in the summer, not long before I set off to London to take the examination, he exerted himself. He came up one night and said, in his soft voice:

'Lewis, I want to talk to you.'

I tried to put him off, but he shook his head.

'No. Clearly, it's time someone gave you a bit of advice.'

He was oddly obstinate. It was the only time I had known him make a determined stand about someone else's concerns. He insisted on taking me to the picture-house café. 'I'm more at home there.' He grinned. 'I'm tired of your wretched pubs.' There, under the pink-shaded lights, with girls at the tables close by, whispering, giggling, he was indeed at home. But that night he was keeping his eyes from girls. With his rolling muscular gait he led the way into the corner, where there was a table separate from the rest. The night was warm; we drank tea, and got warmer; Jack Cotery, in complete seriousness, began to talk to me.

Then I realised that this was an act of pure friendliness. It was the more pure, because I had recently been busy trying to stop one of his dubious projects. In the autumn he had borrowed money from George, in order to start a small wireless business. Since then he had launched out on a speculation that was, if one took the most charitable view, somewhere near the edge of the shady. He was pestering George for more money with which to extricate himself. I had used my influence with George to stop it. My motives were not all disinterested; I might still want to borrow from George myself, and so Jack and I were rivals there; but still, I had a keen nose for a rogue, I had no doubt that to Jack commercial honesty was without meaning, and thus early I smelt danger, most of all, of course, for George.

Jack was a good deal of a rogue, but he bore no grudges. No doubt he enjoyed advising me, showing off his expertness, parading himself where he was so much more knowledgeable, so much less vulnerable, than I. But he had a genuine wish, earthy and kind, to get me fitted up with a suitable bed-mate, to be sure that I was enjoying myself, with all this nonsensical anguish thrown away. He had taken much trouble to time his advice right. With consideration, with experienced eyes, he had been watching until I seemed temporarily light-hearted. It was then, when he felt sure that I was not worrying about Sheila, that he took me off to the picture-house café. He actually began, over the steaming tea:

'Lewis, things aren't so bad with your girl just now, are they?'

I said that they were not.

'That's the time to give her up,' said Jack, with emphasis and conviction. 'When you're not chasing her. It won't hurt your pride so much. You can get out of it of your own free will. It's better for you yourself to have made the break. Lewis, it will hurt you less.'

He spoke so warmly that I had to answer in kind.

'I can't give her up,' I said. 'I love her.'

'I've noticed that,' said Jack, smiling good-naturedly. 'Though why you didn't tell me earlier I just can't imagine. We might have dangled a few distractions before your eyes. Why in God's name should you fall for that – horror?'

'She's not a horror.'

'You know very well she is. In everything that matters. Lewis, you're healthy enough. Why in God's name should you choose someone who'll only bring you misery?'

'Once or twice,' I said, 'I've been happier with her than I've ever imagined being.'

'Don't be silly,' said Jack. 'If you didn't get a spot of happiness when you're first in love, it'd be a damned poor look-out for all of us. Look here. I know more about women than you do. Or if I don't,' he grinned, 'I must have been wasting my time. I tell you, she's a horror. Perhaps she's a bit crazy. Anyway, she'll only bring you misery. Now why did you choose her?'

'Has one any choice?' I said.

'With someone impossible,' said Jack, 'you ought to be able to escape.'

'I don't think I can,' I said.

'You've got to,' said Jack, with more vigorous purpose than I had ever heard from him. 'She'll do you harm. She'll make a mess of your life.' He added: 'I believe she's done you a lot of harm already.'

'Nonsense,' I said.

'I bet you don't know when to make love to her.'

The hit was so shrewd that I blushed.

'Damn the bitch,' said Jack. 'I'd like to have her in a bedroom with no questions asked. I'd teach her a thing or two.'

He looked at me.

'Lewis,' he said, 'it's the cold ones who can do you harm. I expect you wonder if any woman will ever want you.'

'Yes,' I said. 'Sometimes I do.'

'It's absurd,' said Jack, in his flattering, easy, soothing fashion. 'If you'd run across someone warm, you'd know how absurd it is. Why, with just a bit of difference, you'd have a better time than I do. You're sympathetic. You're very clever. You're going to be a success. And – you've got a gleam in your eye. . . . It's like everything else,' he went on. 'You've got to believe in yourself. If she's ruined that for you, I shall never forgive her. I tell you, it's absurd for you to doubt yourself. There are hundreds of nicer girls than Miss Sheila who'd say yes before you'd had time to ask.'

When he cared, he was more skilful than anyone I knew at binding up the wounds, though in himself he had never known that specific wound, the wound in the flesh.

Jack looked across the table. I was certain that he had something else to say, and was working his way towards it. He was using all his cunning, as well as his good nature.

'Now Marion,' he said, as though casually, and I understood, 'would be a hundred times better – for any purpose that you can possibly imagine. I don't mind telling you, I've thought of her myself. I just can't understand why you've done nothing about it.'

'I've been pretty occupied,' I said. 'And I wasn't—'

'I should have thought,' said Jack, 'that you might have found time to think of her. After all, she's been pining for you long enough.'

I was forced on to the defensive. I said, in confusion, that I knew she was rather fond of me, but he was exaggerating it beyond all reason.

'You bloody fool,' said Jack, 'she worships the ground you walk on.'

I still protested, Jack went on attacking me. If I did not realise it, he said roughly, it must be because I was blinded by Sheila. The sooner I got rid of her the better, if I could not notice what was going on round me. 'Remember too,' said Jack, 'if anyone falls in love with you, it is partly your own fault. It's not all innocence on your side. It never is. There's always a bit of encouragement. You've smiled at her, you've been sympathetic, and you've led her on.'

I felt guilty: that was another stab of truth. I argued, I protested again that he was exaggerating. I was confused: I half-wanted to credit what he said, just for the sake of my own vanity; I half-wanted to be guiltless.

'I don't care about the rights and wrongs,' said Jack. 'All I care about is that the young woman is aching for you. Just as much as you ache for your girl. And without any nonsense about it. She wants you, she knows she wants you. But remember she can't wait for ever. If I never advise you again, Lewis, I'm doing so now. Get free – not next week, tonight, go home and write the letter – and take Marion on. It will make all the difference to you. . . . I'm not at all sure,' he said surprisingly, 'that you wouldn't be wise to marry her.'

CHAPTER XXVI

MEETING BY ACCIDENT

The examination did not trouble me overmuch. It was not a decisive one; my acquaintances who were taking law degrees, like Charles March, were exempt from it; unless I did egregiously badly, nothing hung upon the result. Once I got started, I felt a cheerful, savage contempt for those who tried to keep me in my proper station. I had taken only one examination in my life, the Oxford, but I found again that, after the first half-hour, I enjoyed the game. In the first lunch interval, certain that I was not going to disgrace myself, I reflected realistically, as I had done before, that my performance this year would be a guide to my chances twelve months hence in the Bar Finals – on which, in my circumstances, all depended.

I stayed at Mrs Reed's, for no better reason than habit, but this time I did not have to look in entreaty at the hall-table each time I entered the house. Sheila's letter arrived on my second morning, according to her promise. For I had seen her before I left town, not listening to Jack Cotery, despite the comfort he had given me. The letter was in her usual allusive style, but contained a passage which made me smile: 'My father has lost his voice, which is exceedingly just. He croaks pathetically. I have offered to nurse him – would you expect me to be good at the healing word?' And, a little further on, she wrote: 'Curiously enough, he inquired about you the other day. He is probably thinking you might be useful some time for free legal consultations. My family are remarkably avaricious. I don't know whether I shall inherit it. Poor Tom used to have to prescribe for my father. But Tom was a moral coward. You are evasive and cagey, but you're not that.'

Evasive and cagey, I thought, in the luxury of considering a beloved's judgment, in the conceit of youth. Was it true? No one else had ever said so. So far as I knew, no one had thought so. She had seen me get on, in harmony, with all kinds of people – while she shrank into a corner. And she alone had seen me quite free.

She wrote in the same vein about her father, her mother, herself. She was unsparing; equally remote from moral vanity or visceral warmth; she saw no reason to give herself or anyone else the benefit of the doubt. Sometimes her judgments were lunatic, and sometimes they went painfully deep. Those judgments were her revenge. People got through life with their lies and pretences, with their spontaneity, with their gluey warmth denied to her. She was left out of the party. So she told them that the party was false and the goodfellowship just a sham, and in telling them so she was sometimes no truer than a hurt child; but sometimes she tore the façade off the human condition, and made us wince at the truth.

Her letter brought her near, and I went undisturbed through the rest of the papers. I saw Charles March at dinner, with his usual party of Cambridge friends. He undertook to find out my marks in detail; he had no idea why I was so curious, nor that next year's examination was a crisis in my career, but he was a sensitive, quick-witted man, pleased to be of help. I envied his assumption that it was easy to discover what was going on behind the scenes. Some day, I thought, I too must be as sure of myself, as much able to move by instinct among the sources of information and power. Twenty years ahead, and it was ironical to meet Charles March and for us to be reminded that I had once resolved to emulate him.

I remained in London for an extra afternoon, in order to go to Lord's and watch some cricket. There, in the sunshine, I felt peace seep over me like a drug, steadying my heart, slowing my pulse. The examination was safe. Soon I should be seeing Sheila. There was not even the shadow of care, as there had been that day – it suddenly came back to memory and made me smile – when my father watched his first and only cricket match and I sat beside him, eight years old.

But that evening, as the train rushed through the midland fields and in half an hour I should be home, the mood of peace seemed separated from me by years or an ocean. I was fretted by anxiety, as though my mind were a vacuum, and immediately one ominous thought left it, another bored in. I had an irresistible sense that I was returning into trouble, every kind of trouble; I struggled with each item of anxiety, but the future was full of pain. I was angry with myself for being the prey of nerves. It was time to remember that I was strained by this kind of apprehension whenever I came home from a journey. I had just to accept it, like a minor disease. If I did not, I should become as superstitious as my mother. But as I stepped on to the station platform I was looking round in dread, expecting some news of Sheila that would break me. I bought an evening paper, dreading against all reason that she might have chosen this day to become engaged. I rang her up from the station; she sounded surprised, amused and friendly, and had no news at all.

For a moment I was reassured, as though in a fit of jealousy. Then I felt anxious about George, and went to see him; in his case, there had been some faint cause for worry, though neither he nor I had taken it seriously; that night, it still seemed faint, though he did produce some mystifying information about Martineau.

My nerve-storm dropped away; and for weeks after my examination all was smooth. George had a piece of professional success, the alarm over Martineau began to seem unreal; Jack Cotery had begun, by luck or daring, to make some money. Sheila was uncapricious and gay, and had set herself the task of teaching me to take an interest in painting. My examination result appeared in *The Times*, and had gone according to plan. It reappeared in the local papers, having been sent there by Aunt Milly, who had now finally decided to admit that I was less foolish than most young men. Their curious alliance still operating, George impressed on her that I was fulfilling my share of the bargain. He went on 'to gain considerable satisfaction', as he said himself, by ramming the fact of my performance in front of anyone who had ever seemed to doubt me.

I received a few letters of congratulation, a bland one from Eden, an affectionate and generous one from Marion, a fantastically florid one from Mr Vesey – and a note from Tom Devitt. My father professed a comic gratification; and Sheila said: 'I didn't expect anything else. But if you make me celebrate, I shall quite like it.' It was my first taste of success, and it was sweet.

Nevertheless, I had returned into trouble. As the summer went on, some of the ominous thoughts of the journey came back; but this time they were not a trick of the nerves, they were real. The first trouble – the first sign that the luck had changed, I found myself thinking, in the superstitious way of which I was ashamed – was a mild one, but it harassed me. It followed close behind the congratulations, and was a disappointment about my examination. Charles March had kept his word. Somehow or other he had obtained the marks on my individual papers. They were not bad, but I was not high up the list of the first class. They were nothing like good enough if I were to win a studentship or prize next year.

There was no option. Next year I had to do spectacularly well. It was an unfair test, I thought, forgetting that I had once faced these brutal facts – when I first made my choice. But it was different facing facts from a long way off: and then meeting them in one's nerves and flesh. It was very hard to imagine a risk, until one had to live with it.

There was nothing for it. Next year I had to do better. I had to improve half a class.

I consulted George. At first, he was unwilling to accept that anything was wrong. I was exaggerating, as usual, said George stormily; I was losing my sense of proportion just because this man March, whom George had never heard of, reported that I had not done superlatively well in a couple of papers. No one was less ready than George to see the dangerous sign. He had to be persuaded against his will, in the teeth of his violent temper, that a disquieting fact could conceivably exist, particularly in a protégé's career. He denounced Charles March. 'I see no reason,' shouted George, 'why I should be expected to kowtow to the opinions of your fashionable friends.' He denounced me for being an alarmist. I had to be rough and lose my own temper and tell him that, however much he deceived himself about others, he must not do it about me. These were the official marks, never mind how they were obtained. Brusquely I told him that it was just a problem of cramming; the facts were clear, and I was not going to argue about them: I wanted to know one thing – how could I pull up half a class?

Immediately, without the slightest rancour, George became calm and competent. He proceeded to analyse the marks with his customary pleasure in any kind of puzzle. Neither George nor I had been certain that I should need such a degree of detailed knowledge. 'Though,' said George, 'I was under the impression that you had got hold of most of the classical cases. They didn't ask you much that was really out of the way. I imagined that you'd conquered most of this stuff months ago.'

It was too much of a temptation for George to resist saying tactfully: 'Of course, I realise there have been certain complications in your private life.'

'What's to be done?' I said.

'Your memory is first class,' said George. 'So you simply can't have read enough, that's all. We'd better invent a new reading programme for you. We'd better do it now.'

Without needing to look up a single authority, without asking me one question about the syllabus of the Bar examinations (which he had, of course, never taken himself) or what books I had already read, George drew up a working timetable for me for each week between that day and the date of the finals. 'Nine months to go,' said George with bellicose content, and wrote down the first week's schedule. He forgot nothing; the programme was well ordered, feasible, allowed time for a fortnight's revision at the end, and then three days free from work. I preserved that sensible document, so neat and orderly, in George's tidy legal hand-writing. It might have been the work of one of nature's burgesses.

But there were many days in the months ahead when George did not speak or act in the slightest respect like one of nature's burgesses; and that was the second trouble into which we were plunged. It seemed grave then. In retrospect it seemed more than grave, it seemed to mark the point where the curve of George's life began to dip. At this point, I need only say a few words about it. The upheaval in our circle began with Martineau. We had always known that he was restless and eccentric; but we expected him to continue his ordinary way of life, entertaining us on Friday nights, and safeguarding George's future in the firm. Suddenly he went through a kind of religious conversion. That autumn he relinquished his share in the practice. It was a few months later, early in 1927, that he completed his abnegation; then he sold all his remaining possessions, gave the money away, and at fifty-one began to wander round the country, begging his way, penniless and devout.

It was now left to Eden to decide whether George should become a partner. We all urged George at least to establish a working relation with Eden. George, dogged by ill-fortune and his own temperament, promptly performed a series of actions which made Eden, who already disliked him, put him out of consideration, not only then, but always. And so at twenty-seven George was condemned to be a managing clerk for the rest of his life. There were many consequences that none of us could have foreseen; a practical one was that George began to co-operate in Jack Cotery's business.

To me, that trouble was light, though, compared to a quarrel with Sheila – a quarrel which I said to myself must be the last. It came with blinding suddenness, after a summer in which most of our meetings had been happy, happier than any since the days of innocence a year before. We amused each other with the same kind of joke, youthful, reckless and sarcastic. I had discovered that I could often coax and bully her out of her indrawn, icy temper. It was the serene hours that counted. I was not much worried when, in the early autumn, days followed each other when she sat abnormally still, her eyes fixed in a long-sighted stare, when if I took her hand it stayed immobile and I seemed to be kissing a dead cheek. I had been through it before, and that removed the warning. She would emerge. Meanwhile, she was not giving me any excuse for jealousy. For weeks she had not mentioned any other man. And, in those fits of painful still-ness, she saw no one but me.

One day in September we had been walking in the country, and were resting on the grass beside the road. She had been quiet, wrapped deep in herself, all afternoon. Suddenly she announced:

'I'm going shooting.'

I laughed aloud, and asked her when and where. She said she was travelling to Scotland, the next week.

'I'm going shooting,' she repeated.

Again I laughed.

'What's funny about that?'

Her tone was sharp.

'It is funny,' I said.

'You'd better tell me why.'

Her tone was so sharp that I took her shoulders and began to shake her. But she broke loose and said:

'I suppose you mean that I only know these people because my father married for money. I suppose it is a wonderfully good joke that my mother was such a fool.'

With bewilderment I saw that she was crying. She was staring at me in enmity and hate. She turned aside, and dried the tears herself.

On the way back, I made one effort to tell her that nothing had been further from my mind. 'It doesn't matter,' she said, and we went along in silence. Intolerably slowly (and yet I could not bear to part), the miles went by. We came to the suburbs and walked in silence under the chestnut trees.

At the station entrance, she spoke.

'Don't see me off.' She added, as though she was forced to: 'I shall be away a month. I shan't write much. I'm too prickly. I'll tell you when I get back.'

In the days that followed, I was angry as well as wretched. It would be easy to cease to love her, I thought, making myself remember her cold inimical face. Then I cherished those unwilling words at the station. 'Prickly' – was she not trying to soften it for me, in the midst of her own bitterness? Why hadn't I made her speak? This was not a separation, I comforted myself, and wrote to her, as lightly as though that afternoon had not existed. As I wrote, I had the habitual glow, as if she must, through my scribble on the paper, be compelled at that moment to think of me. No answer came.

A fortnight after that walk in the country, I was strolling aimlessly through the market-place. I was on edge, and sleeping badly; it was hard to steer myself through a day's work; I had come out that afternoon, hoping to freshen myself for another two hours later on. It was nearly tea-time on a dark autumn day, with the clouds low, but bright and comforting in the streets, the shops already lighted. Smells poured out into the crowded streets, as the shop doors swung open – smells of bacon, ham, cheese, fruit – and, at the end of the market-place, the aroma of roast coffee beans, which mastered them all, and for a moment dissolved all my anxiety and took me back to afternoons of childhood. In our less penurious days, before the bankruptcy, my mother used to take me shopping in the town, when I was a small child; and I smelt the coffee then, and watched the grinding-machine in the window, and heard my mother assert that this was the only shop she could think of patronising.

I watched the grinding-machine again, sixteen years later (for I could not have been more than five when I accompanied my mother). I would have sworn that she had actually used the word 'patronising'; and indeed it gave me a curious pleasure to think of her so – for few women could the word have been more apt, at that period, before she had been cast down.

At last I turned away. On the pavement, walking towards me, was Sheila. She was wearing a fur coat which made her look a matron, and her head was bent, staring at the ground, so that she had not seen me. At that instant it occurred to me we had never met by accident before.

I called her name. She looked up. Her face was cold and set.

'I didn't know you were back,' I said.

'I am,' said Sheila.

'You said you'd be away a month.'

'I changed my mind,' she said. She added fiercely: 'If you want to know, I hated it.'

'Why didn't you tell me?'

'I might have done in time.'

'I don't mean in time,' I said. 'You ought to have told me before today.'

'Try to remember this,' said Sheila. 'You don't own me. If I wanted you to own me, I should be glad to tell you everything. I don't want it.'

'You let me just run into you like this—' I cried.

'I don't propose to send you word every time I come into the town,' she said. 'I'll let you know when I want to see you.'

'Will you have some tea?'

'No,' she said. 'I'm going home.'

We moved away from each other. I looked back, but not she.

That was all. That was the end, I thought.

I too was full of anger and hate, as I made my resolve that night. I could have stood jealousy, I could have stood her madnesses and cruelty, but this I could no longer stand. I had had too much. I strengthened myself by the pictures of her indrawn face, in which there was no regard for me. There were hours when I hoped that love itself had died.

I must cut her out of my being, I thought. Jack was right; Jack had been right all along. I must cut her out of my being; and I knew by instinct that, to do it, I must not see her again, speak to her, receive a word from her or write to her, even hear of her at second-hand. That was my resolve; and this time, unlike last Christmas Eve, I felt the wild satisfaction that I could carry it out.

I worked with a harsh gusto, staying in my attic when she might be in the town, going to the reference library only when there was no chance that we could meet. I took precautions to avoid her as elaborate as those I had once used to pin down each minute of her day. And then I wanted to distract myself. Jack was right. She had done me harm; she had left me lonely and unsure. I thought (as I had often done since that night in the café, as I had done after meetings where Sheila did not give me a smile) of the bait Jack had laid for me. I thought of Marion. Would she have me, if I went to her now?

I had wondered many times whether Jack was right about her too. Had she really been in love with me? I wanted it to be true. Just then, I was voracious for any kind of woman's love.

I believed that Marion had been fond of me. I believed that if I had wooed her, I could probably have persuaded her to love me. That was as far as I trusted Jack's propaganda. Yet now, unsure of myself, I wanted to meet Marion again. I had not seen her, except to wave to in the streets, for months. She was the most active of us, and it would have been right out of character for her to sit and mope. She had gone off and attached herself to the town's best amateur theatrical company. There she found a new circle: to my surprise, people spoke highly of her as a comic actress. I wished that we could be brought together again, without any contrivance of mine. I had, of course, a furtive, fugitive hope that Jack might not after all have been exaggerating, and that she would fall into my arms.

Strangely enough, it was through Martineau that I caught a glimpse of her at the theatre. It was a Friday night in November. Although we did not know it, Martineau was within a few days of renouncing his share in the firm, and we were to go to the house for only one more Friday night. Unconcerned, amiable, and lighthearted, Martineau mentioned that *The Way of the World* was being acted the following week, and invited me to go with him to see it.

It was a singular choice of entertainment, I thought later, for a man who was on the point of trying to live like St Francis; but Martineau enjoyed every minute of it. He appeared in his wing-collar, frock coat and grey trousers, for, until he actually left the firm, he never relaxed in his dress. We sat near to the stage, and Martineau roared with laughter, more audibly than anyone in the house, at each bawdy joke. And he was particularly taken by Marion. She was playing Millamant, the biggest part she had had with this company, and she won the triumph of the evening. Her bright eyes flashed and cajoled and hinted; on the stage her clumsiness disappeared, she stood up straight, she had presence and a rakish air, and her voice lilted and allured. Despite her reputation, I had not expected anything like it. I felt very proud of her.

Martineau was captivated entirely.

'She's a stunner,' he said, using enthusiastically, as he often did, the slang of years ago. 'She's a perfect stunner.'

I told him that I knew her fairly well.

'Lucky old dog,' said Martineau. 'Lucky old dog, Lewis.'

At the end of the play, Martineau was reluctant to leave the theatre. 'Lewis,' he said, 'what do you say to our paying respects to your young friend? Going round to the stage door, we used to call it.'

We had to wait, along with other friends of the cast, for the theatre was a makeshift one, and all the women dressed in one large room. At last we were allowed in. Marion was still shining in her grease-paint, surrounded by people praising her. She was lapping it up, from all quarters, both sexes, from anyone who had a word of praise, whatever its quality. She caught my eye, looked surprised, smiled, cried out 'Lewis, my dear', then turned to listen, her whole face open to receive applause, to a man who was telling her how wonderful she had been. The air was humming with endearments and congratulations. I took Martineau to Marion, and he added his share, and it was clear that she could not have enough of it.

A couple of young men were competing for her attention, but Martineau held her for a time. Apart from a smile of recognition, and a question upon how I liked the show, she had been too ecstatic in her triumph to come aside to me. She was glad I was there; but she was glad Martineau was there, she was glad everyone in the room was there; she was ready to embrace all of us.

The company were holding a party, and we had to leave. Marion called goodbyes after Martineau, after me, after others who had been praising her.

Martineau and I went out into the cold night air.

'What a stunning girl,' said Martineau. 'I say, Lewis, your friend is something to write home about.'

I agreed. But I was lonely and dispirited. I wished I had not gone.

CHAPTER XXVII

'I BELIEVE IN JOY'

On winter afternoons, when I could not work any longer, I gazed from my attic window over the roofs. This time last year – the thoughts crept treacherously in – I might have been at tea with Sheila. Now the evening ahead was safe, quite safe. I was keeping my resolve. I had abstained from all the forbidden actions, in order to cut her out of my existence. Yet why – I could not help crying to myself – had she of all women the power to set me free?

I was not well that winter, and night after night slept badly and woke in a mysterious malaise. There was nothing I could be definite about, but I was worried, for the Bar Finals and the future, as I lay awake listening to the thudding of my heart. It was necessary, I knew, to take no notice. And I had to do my best to see that George was not too much damaged, now that Martineau had left the firm in November. Often, when I felt like lying in bed, I had to struggle through some work, and then drag myself off to an argument with George or Eden. There were other lives besides one's own; it was a discipline hard to learn, when one was young, ill, and empty with unrequited love.

Perversely, as I later knew, it was a discipline just about as hard to learn when one was ageing and serene.

Sometimes those discussions were a relief, simply because they took away from my loneliness. I had not the spirit to seek for Marion, away from her stage properties. That night at the theatre had been a fiasco when I did not want another. It was out of loneliness that I returned to the group, for there I could find without effort the company of some young women. They welcomed me back. George began by saying:

'I take it that you're slightly reducing the extent of your other commitments.'

'It's over,' I said. I did not wish to speak of it.

'Thank God for that,' said George. 'I'm glad you've come to your senses.' And automatically, from that moment, George demoted Sheila in his speech. After being cloaked in euphemisms for a year, she was referred to once more as 'that damned countyfied bitch'.

Jack was listening, attentively and shrewdly. 'Good,' he said, but he looked troubled. I wondered if he noticed that, when I went out to the farm, I did not stir from the house for fear of the remote chance of meeting Sheila. I wondered too if he would pass any word to Marion.

With a considerateness that touched me, the Edens asked me to their Christmas Eve party, in my own right, telling me to bring a partner if I felt inclined. Eden went out of his way to drop the hint that they had 'rather lost touch with Sheila Knight'. I went alone. Just as last year, the drawing-room was redolent of rum and spice and orange; most of last year's party were there; all was safe, I listened to Eden, the fire blazed, Mrs Eden did not mention Sheila. In the early morning, when I left the house, it was colder than that last warm Christmas morning, and no car outside.

It was on a January morning, returning home from the reference library (I had changed my routine, so as never to be in the main shopping streets in the afternoon), that I found a telegram waiting at my lodgings. Before I opened it, I knew from whom it came. It read: YOU ONCE WANTED TO BORROW A BOOK FROM ME IT IS NOT A GOOD BOOK I SHALL BRING IT TO THE USUAL CAFÉ TOMORROW AT FOUR. It was signed SHEILA, and, luxuriating in the details, I noticed that it had been despatched from her village that morning at nine-five. It gave me the pleasure of intimacy, silly and caressing, to think of her going to the post-office straight after breakfast.

I made no struggle. I had two weapons to keep me out of danger – pain and pride. But I dismissed the pain, and thought only of my emptiness. As for pride, she had appeased that, for it was she who asked. I was infused by hope so sanguine that I felt the well-being pour through me to the finger-tips. I watched motes dancing in the winter sunlight. Just as when I was first in love, it seemed that I had never seen things so fresh before.

The clock was striking four when I went through the café, past a pair of chess players already settled in for the evening, down to the last alcove. She was there, reading an evening paper, holding it as usual a long way from her eyes. She heard my footstep, and watched me as I sat down beside her.

She said: 'I've missed you.' She added: 'I've brought the book. You won't like it much.'

She set herself to talk as though there had been no interval. I was irritated, in one of those spells I had previously known. Was this she whose absence made each hour seem pointless? Yes, she was good-looking, but was that hard beauty really in my style? Yes, she was clever enough, but she had no stamina in anything she thought or did.

At the same instant I was chafing with impatience for reassurances and pledges. I did not want to listen to her, but to take her in my arms.

She saw that something was wrong. She frowned, and then tried to make me laugh. We exchanged jokes, and she worked at a curious awkward attempt to coax me. Once or twice the air was electric, but through my fault there were gaps of silence.

'When shall I see you again?' said Sheila, and we arranged a meeting.

I went away to drink with George, impatient with her, compelled by the habit of love to count the hours until I saw her next – but incredulous that I had not broken away. Perhaps it would have been like that, I thought, if our rôles had been reversed and she had done the loving. There might have been many such tea-times. Perhaps it would have been better for us both. But when I drank with George there was no jubilation in my tone to betray that afternoon, even if he had been a more perceptive man.

By the first post of the day I was expecting her, I received a letter. My heart quickened, but as I read it I chuckled.

'I can't appear tomorrow afternoon,' she wrote, 'because I have a shocking cold. I always get shocking colds. Come and see me, if you'd like to, and can face it. My mother will be out of the way, visiting the sick. If I were a parishioner, she would be visiting me, which would be the last straw.'

When I was shown into the drawing-room, I saw that Sheila was not exaggerating. She was sitting by the fire with her eyes moist, her lids swollen, her nostrils and upper lip all red; on the little table by her side were some books, an inhaler, and half a dozen handkerchiefs. She gave me a weak grin. 'I told you it was a shocking cold. Every cold I have is like this.' Her voice was unrecognisably low, as well as thick and muffled.

'You can laugh if you want to,' she said. 'I know it's comic.'

'I'm sorry, dear,' I said, 'but it is a bit comic.' I was feeling both affectionate and amused; she was so immaculate that this misadventure seemed like a practical joke.

'My father doesn't think so,' she said with another grin. 'He's terrified of catching anything. He refuses to see me. He stays in his study all day.'

We had tea, or rather I ate the food and Sheila thirstily drank several cups. She told the maid that she would not eat anything, and the maid reproached her: 'Feed a cold and starve a fever, Miss Sheila. You're hungrier than you think.'

'That's all you know,' Sheila retorted. In her mother's absence the maid and Sheila were on the most companionable terms.

While I was eating, Sheila watched me closely.

'You were cross with me the other day.'

'A little,' I said.

'Why?'

'It doesn't matter now.'

'I'm trying to behave,' she said. 'What have I done?'

'Nothing.' It was true. Not once had she been cruel, or indifferent, or dropped a hint to rouse my jealousy.

'Wasn't it a good idea to make it up?'

I smiled.

'Then what was the matter?'

I told her that I loved her totally, that no one could be more in love than I was, that no one could ever love her more. I had not seen her for three months and I had tried to forget her – three bitter months; then we met, and she expected me to talk amiably over the tea cups as though nothing had happened.

Sheila blew her nose, wiped her eyes, and considered.

'If you want to kiss me now, you can,' she said. 'But I warn you, I don't feel much like it.'

She pressed my hand. I laughed. Cold or no cold, her spirits were further from the earth than mine could ever be, and I could not resist her.

She was considering again.

'Come to a ball,' she said suddenly. She had been searching, I knew, for some way to make amends. With her odd streak of practicality, it had to be a tangible treat.

'I hate balls,' she said. 'But I'll go to this one if you'll take me.'

'This one' was a charity ball in the town; Mrs Knight was insisting that her husband and Sheila should go; it would annoy Mrs Knight considerably if I made up the party, Sheila said, getting a double-edged pleasure.

'My mother thinks you're a fortune-hunter,' said Sheila with a smile. For a moment I was amused. But then I was seized by another thought, and felt ashamed and helpless.

'I can't come,' I said.

'Why can't you? You must come. I'm looking forward to it.'

I shook my head. 'I can't.'

'Why not?'

I was too much ashamed to prevaricate.

'Why not? It isn't because of Mother, is it? You never mind what people think.'

'No, it's not that,' I said.

'I believe my father doesn't dislike you. He dislikes nearly everyone.'

She unfolded a new handkerchief.

'I'm getting angry,' she said nasally, but she was still good-tempered. 'Why can't you come?'

'I haven't got the clothes,' I said.

Sheila sneezed several times and then gave a broad smile.

'Well!' she said. 'For you of all men to worry about that. I give you up. I just don't understand it.'

Nor did I; it was years since I had been so preposterously ashamed.

'It has worried you, hasn't it?'

'I don't know why, but it has,' I confessed.

Sheila said, with acid gentleness:

'It's made me remember how young you are.'

Our eyes met. She was in some way moved. After a moment she said, in the same tone:

'Look. I want to go to this ball. They don't give me much money, but I can always get plenty. Let me give you a present. Let me buy you a suit.'

'I can't do that.'

'Are you too proud?'

'I suppose so,' I said.

She took my hand.

'If I'd made you happier,' she said, 'and then asked if I could give you a present – would you still be too proud?'

'Perhaps not,' I said.

'Darling,' she said. It was rare for her to use the word. 'I can't be articulate like you when you let yourself go. But if I ask you to let me do it – because of what's happened between us?'

In a brand-new dinner jacket, I arrived with the Knights at the charity ball. It was held in the large hall, close by the park, a few hundred yards away from where Martineau used to live. Perhaps that induced me at supper to tell the story of Martineau, so far as I then knew it; I had seen him leave the town on foot, with a knapsack on his back, only a few days before.

I told the story because someone had to talk. The supper tables were arranged in the corridors all round the main hall, and the meal was served before the dance began. As a party of four, we were not ideally chosen. Sheila was looking tired; she was boldly made up, much to her mother's indignation, but the powder did not hide the rings under her eyes, and the painted lips were held in her involuntary smile. She was strained in the presence of her parents, and some of her nervousness infected me, the more so as I was still not well. With her usual directness and simplicity, Mrs Knight resented my presence. She produced a list of young men who, in her view, would have been valuable additions – some of whom Sheila had been seeing in the last few months, though she had resisted the temptation to let fall their names. As for Mr Knight, he was miserable to be there at all, and he was not the man to conceal his misery.

He was miserable for several reasons. He refused to dance, and he hated others enjoying fun which he was not going to share. His wife and Sheila were active, strong women, who loved using their muscles (Sheila, once set on a dance-floor, forgot she had not wanted to come, and danced for hours); Mr Knight was an excessively lazy man, who preferred sitting down. He also hated to be at any kind of disadvantage. In his own house, backed by everything Mrs Knight could buy for him, he was playing on his home ground. He did not like going out, where people might not recognise him or offer the flattery which sustained him.

I picked up an example right at the beginning of supper. Mrs Knight announced that the bishop had brought a party to the hall. Shouldn't they call on him during the evening? I could feel that she had not abandoned hope of getting her husband some preferment.

'Not unless he asks us, darling,' said Mr Knight faintly.

'You can't expect him to remember everyone,' said Mrs Knight, with brisk common sense.

'He ought to have *remembered* me,' said Mr Knight. 'He *ought* to have.'

I guessed that conversation had been repeated often. She had always planned for him to go far in the Church; he was much more gifted than many who had climbed to the top. When she married him, she was prepared to find ways of getting all the bishops on the bench to meet him. But he would not do his share. As he grew older, he could not humble himself at all. He had too much arrogance, too much diffidence, to play the world's game. Later on, I ran across a good many men who had real gifts but who, in the worldly sense, were failures; and in some of them there was a trace of Mr Knight; like him, they were so arrogant and so diffident that they dared not try.

Mr Knight was miserable; Mrs Knight indignant; Sheila strained. We did not talk much for the first half of supper, and then, in desperation, I brought out the story of Martineau.

'He must be a crank,' said Mrs Knight as soon as I finished.

'Well, Mrs Knight,' I said, 'no one could call him an ordinary man.'

'Harry Eden,' she decided, 'must be glad to see the back of him.'

'I don't think so,' I said. 'Mr Eden is devoted to him.'

'Harry Eden was always a loyal person,' said Mrs Knight.

Sheila broke in, clearly, as though she were thinking aloud:

'He'll enjoy himself!'

'Who will?' her mother asked obtusely.

'Your Martineau.' Sheila was looking at me. 'He'll enjoy every minute of it! It's not a sacrifice.'

'Of course,' said Mr Knight, in his most beautifully modulated voice, 'many religions have sprung up from sources such as this. We must remember that there are hundreds of men like Martineau in every century. Those are the people who start false religions, but I admit that many of them have felt something true.' Mr Knight was theologically fair-minded; but he was disgruntled. If anyone was to act as raconteur to that party, he should do so. He proceeded to tell a long story about the Oneida community. He told it with art, far better than I had told mine, and as we chuckled, he became less sulky. I thought (for I was irritated at not being allowed to shine in front of Sheila) that his story had every advantage, but that mine was at any rate first-hand.

After supper I danced with Sheila and Mrs Knight alternately. They had many acquaintances there, who kept coming up to claim Sheila. As I watched her round the hall, my jealous inquisitiveness flew back, like a detective summoned to an unpleasant duty: was this one with whom she had threatened me last year? But, when I danced with her, she did not mention any of her partners. Her father was behaving atrociously, she said with her usual ruthlessness. And she had to talk to all these other people; she wanted to be quiet with me. So, much of the night, we danced in a silence that to me was languorous.

It was far otherwise in my alternate dances. Mrs Knight disapproved of me, but she demanded her exercise, and dancing with her became vigorous and conversational. She took it heartily, for she had a real capacity for pleasure. I was an unsatisfactory young man, but I was better than no one to whirl her round. She got hot and merry, and as we passed her friends on the floor she greeted them in her loud horsey voice. And she surprised me by issuing instructions that I was to take care of myself.

'You're not looking so well as you did,' she said, in a brusque maternal stand-no-nonsense manner.

I explained that I had been working hard.

'You're not keeping fit. You're pale,' she said. 'How long is it to your exam?'

I knew that exactly. 'Ten weeks.'

'You mustn't crock up, you know.'

I knew that too. Yet, though I wished she was not Sheila's mother, I was coming to like her. And, dancing with her at that ball early in 1927, I had a curious thought. George and I and thoughtful persons round us used to predict that our lives were going to see violent changes in the world. At the ball, inside the Knights' house, those predictions seemed infinitely remote, a bubble no more real than others that George blew. Yet if they came true, if Mrs Knight lost all, lost servants and house and had to work with her hands and cook for her husband, I could imagine her doing it as heartily as she was dancing now. I should not like to be within the range of her indignation, but she would survive.

For one dance, both she and Sheila were taken off by others and I was left at our table with Mr Knight. Out of the corner of his eye, he must have noticed that my own glance was drawn time and again to follow Sheila. He was still bad-tempered at being ignored so much that night, and he did not intend to let me sit and dream. He required me as an audience and I had to listen to the main points of a letter that he thought of writing to *The Times*. Then, half-maliciously, he made me look at a dark-haired girl in a red dress, just dancing by our corner of the hall.

'I'm not certain of your standards, Eliot,' he said, 'but should you say that she was pretty?'

'Very,' I said.

'They live in my parish, but they don't attend. I'm afraid that she's broken a good many hearts.'

He was being deliberately oblique, I knew. He did not appear to be watching me, but he was making sure that I concentrated on the girl in the red dress.

'She ought to get married,' he said. 'She ought to get married. It's bad for anyone to break too many hearts. It shows there's something' – he paused – 'shall I say torn? inside their own.'

He was, of course, talking in code. That was the nearest he would come to mentioning Sheila. But he was so subtle and oblique that I could not be certain what he was telling me. Was he giving me a warning? Was he trying to share a worry, knowing that I loved her, feeling that I too was lost and concerned for what might happen to her? Was he, incredibly, encouraging me? Or was he just being malicious at my expense? I had no idea. In his serious moments, when he gave up acting, I never knew where I was with Mr Knight.

Soon after, Sheila said that she wanted some air. Instead of dancing, we walked outside the hall. There was nowhere to sit out, except in the colonnades which looked over the park. She took my arm, and we stood there. Couples were strolling behind us, though the March night was sharp. Right round the other side of the park, the tram-standards make a necklace of lights (we were looking in the direction that I walked, feet light with hope, the last Christmas Eve but one).

'Rather pretty,' said Sheila. Then she asked, unexpectedly: 'What does Martineau believe?'

I had to collect myself before I replied.

I said: 'I'm not sure that he knows himself. I think he'd say that the only way to live a Christian life was to live like Christ. But—'

'He's doing it because he wants to do it,' said Sheila. From the lights of the hall behind, I could see her face. She was lined, harassed, concentrated and rapt. Her beauty was haggard; she was speaking with absolute certainty. 'All people are selfish. Though they make a better show of it than I do. He'll go about humbly helping his fellow men – because it makes him feel good to do it.'

Looking into the dark stretches of the park, she said:

'What do you believe?'

I gripped her arm, but she said, in the same tone:

'I don't want to hear anything nice. What do you believe?'

I told her – and anything I said seemed flat after the rapt question – that I had no faith in any of the faiths. For me, there was something which took their place; I wanted to find some of the truths about human beings.

'Yes,' said Sheila. In a moment, she said: 'I believe in something.'

'What?'

She said:

'I believe in joy.'

We did not speak again before we returned to the Knights' table. The dance that we had left was not yet ended, and Mrs Knight looked gratified that we had come back so soon. Mr Knight reclined heavily in his chair, spreading himself in the company of his womenfolk. I had just heard an affirmation which sounded in my mind throughout Sheila's life and after, as clear, as thrilling, as vulnerable and as full of hope, as when she stared over the park and spoke into the darkness. Yet that evening it vanished as quickly as a childhood dread. Just then it seemed only a remark, past and already half-forgotten, as, tired and subdued, she took her place by her father. Mr Knight's splendid voice rose, and we all listened to him.

CHAPTER XXVIII

RESULTS OF A PROPOSAL

THERE were nights when it was a pleasure to lie awake. Outside, a train would rattle and roar over the bridge (I remembered, in the Zeppelin raids, my mother saying: 'The trains are our friends. When you can hear them, you feel that everything is going on all right'). I had finished another textbook, and lay there, with a triumphant surge of mastery, because I knew it with something like photographic memory; I would ask myself a question, answer it as though I were already in the examination hall, and then switch on the light to see if I had any detail wrong.

And, night after night, I did not want to sleep until I had re-cherished, like a collector going over his prints, each moment and each word of that absurd scene in the Knights' drawing-room, with Sheila snuffling her m's and n's, and saying 'I wadt you to cub to the ball.'

As I thought of her so, my prayers were cut in two, and my longings contradicted each other. On the one side, I begged: let me stay here, having known that comical delight, having known loving peace; let me stay cherishing it, for that afternoon was so delicate that it would perish at a touch. On the other, I wanted all, not just the tantalising promise: I wanted to be sure of her, to fight my way past the jealousies, to rely on such afternoons for the staple of my life, to risk any kind of pain until I had her for my own.

The first time we met after the ball, neither of us said a word that was not trivial. I was happy; it was an hour in a private world, in which we lived inside a crystal shell, so fragile that either of us could speak and shatter it.

At our next meeting, she did speak. Although she was 'trying to behave', she had to let slip, for the first time since our reconciliation, that a new admirer was what she called 'rushing' her. After one dinner he was demanding some fixture for each day of the next week.

'Shall you go?'

'I shall go once,' Sheila said.

'Shall you go more than once?'

'It depends on how much I like him.' She was getting restive, and there was a harsh glint in her eyes.

There and then I knew I must settle it. I could not go on in this suspense. Even though, before we parted, Sheila said awkwardly: 'He's probably not a very useful young man.'

I must settle it, I thought. I decided how I must talk to her. We had arranged our next assignation in the usual place. I copied her action when she had her cold, and wrote to say that I was laid up. I could borrow some crockery from my landlady – would Sheila come and make tea for me?

The March afternoon was cloudy; I turned the gas-fire full on, and it snored away, brilliant in the dark room. I had tried to work, but gave it up, and was sitting on the bed, listening for each footstep on the stairs.

At last I heard her. At last, but it was only a minute past the hour. The nerves at my elbows seemed stretched like piano-strings. Sheila entered, statuesque in the light from the gas-fire.

'You needn't have asked me to make tea,' she began without any preliminary. 'I should have done it without asking.'

We kissed. I hoped that she did not notice that my hands were shaking. She patted my shoulder.

'Well,' she said, 'what's the matter with you?'

'Nothing much,' I said. 'I'm a bit strung up, that's all.'

She switched on the light.

'I shall never have a bedside manner,' she said. 'Look, if you're worried, you ought to see poor Tom Devitt. He was a sensible doctor.'

I thought it was not meant to be cruel. In her innocence, that was over long ago.

'You rest,' she said. 'I'll make the tea. You needn't have asked me.'

She had brought some cakes, though she never ate them, some books, and, eccentrically, a tie. There was something random about her kindness: it was like a child trying to be kind. She was gay, putting the kettle on the gas-ring, making tea, giving me my cup. She switched off the light again, and sat on the other side of the fire, upright on the hard chair. She talked on, light and friendly. The suspense was raging inside me. I answered absently, sometimes after a delay, sometimes not at all. She looked inquiringly:

'Are you all right?'

'Yes.'

I was quivering, so that I took hold of the bedrail.

She asked another question, about some book or person, which I did not hear. The blood was throbbing in my neck, and I could wait no longer.

'Sheila,' I said. 'Marry me.'

She gazed at me, and did not speak. The seconds spread themselves so that I could not tell how long a time had passed; I could hear the fire, whose noise was a roar in my ears, and my own heart.

'How ever would you manage,' she asked, 'to keep us both?'

I had anticipated any response but that. I was so much astonished that I smiled. My hands were steadier, and for the first time that day I felt a respite.

'We might have to wait,' I said. 'Or I'd find a way.'

'I suppose you could. Yes, you've got plenty of resource.'

'But it's not important,' I cried. 'With you—'

'It might be important,' said Sheila. 'You never give me credit for any common sense.'

'It's not the point,' I said. 'And you know it's not.'

'Perhaps you're right,' she said, as though reluctantly.

'If you'll marry me,' I said, 'I'll find a way.'

'Do you mean it?'

'Do you think I'm playing?'

'No.' She was frowning. 'You know me better than anyone else does, don't you?'

'I hope so.'

'Yes, you do,' she said. 'That's why I came back. And you still want to marry me?'

'More than anything that I shall ever want.'

'Lewis, if I married you I should like to be a good wife. But I couldn't help it – I should injure you. I might injure you appallingly.'

'That is for me to face,' I said. 'I want you to marry me.'

'Oh,' she cried. She stood up, rested an elbow on the mantelpiece, arched her back, and warmed her calves in front of the fire. I watched the glow upon her stockings; she was silent, looking not at me but straight down the room. Then she spoke: 'If I marry, I shall hope to be in love.'

'Yes.'

'I'm not in love with you,' she said. 'You know that, and I've told you.' She was still not looking at me. 'I'm not in love with you,' she repeated. 'Sometimes I ask myself why I'm not. I ask myself what's the matter with me – or what's missing in me, if you like.'

A few times in my life, there came moments I could not escape. This was one. I could not escape the moment in which I heard her voice, high, violent, edged with regret and yet with no pity for herself or me.

In time, I asked:

'Must it always be so?'

'How do I know?' She shrugged her shoulders. 'You can answer that – maybe better than I can.'

'Tell me what you feel.'

'If you must hear,' she said, 'I think I shall never love you.' She added: 'You may as well hear the rest. I've been hoping I should love you – for a long time now. I'd rather love you than any of the others. I don't know why. You're not as nice as people think.'

At that, having heard the bitterest news of my young manhood, I burst out laughing, and pulled her down on to my knee to kiss her. That final piece of ruthless observation took away my recognition of what I had just heard; and suddenly she was glad to be caressed and to caress. For now she was radiant. Anyone watching us then, without having heard the conversation, would have guessed that she had just received a proposal she was avid to accept – or, more likely, that she was out to win someone of whom she was almost but not quite sure. She was attentive, sleek, and shining. She was anxious to stroke my face when I looked downcast. She wanted to rub away the lines until I appeared as radiant as she did. She was reproachful if, for a moment, I fell into silence. She made me lie on the bed, sat by me, and then went out to buy supper. About that we had what to all appearance was a mild, enjoyable lovers' quarrel. She proposed to fetch fish and chips: I told her that, despite her lack of snobbery, she was enough a child of the upper middle class to feel that the pastimes and diet of the poor were really glamorous. The romance of slumming, I said. You're all prostrating yourselves before the millions, I said. And I had a reasonable argument: I had to live in that room; her sense of smell was weak, but mine acute. She pouted, and I said that classical faces were not designed for pouting. We ended in an embrace, and I got my way.

She left late in the evening, so late that I wondered how she would get home. Wondering about her, suddenly I felt the lack of her physical presence in the room. Then – it came like a grip on the throat – I realised what had happened to me. The last few hours had been make-believe. She had spoken the truth. That was all.

It was no use going to bed. I sat unseeing, just where I sat while she answered my proposal. She had spoken with her own integrity. She was as much alone as I was – more, for she had none of the compensations that my surface nature gave me as I moved about the world. She had spoken out of loneliness, and out of her craving for joy. If my heart broke, it broke. If I could make her love me, well and good. It was *sauve qui peut*. In her ruthlessness, she had no space for the sentimentalities of compassion, or the comforting lie. She could take the truth herself, and so must I.

Had I a chance? Would she ever love me? I heard her final voice – 'if you must hear' – and then I thought, why had she been so happy afterwards? Was it simply that she was triumphant at hearing a proposal? There was a trace of that. It brought back my mocking affection for her, which was strongest when I could see her as much chained to the earth as I was myself. She could behave, in fact, like an ordinary young woman of considerable attractions, and sit back to count her conquests. There was something predatory about her, and something vulgar. Yes, she had relished being proposed to. Yet, I believed, with a residue of hope, that that did not explain the richness of her delight. She was happy because I had proposed to her. There was a bond between us, though on her side it was not the bond of love.

But that – I heard her final voice – was the only bond she craved.

I did not know how to endure it. Sitting on my bed, staring blindly at where she had stood, I thought what marriage with her would be like. It would only be liveable if she were subjugated by love. Otherwise she would tear my heart in pieces. Yet, my senses and my memories tore me enough as I sat there, even my memories of that night, and I did not know how to endure losing her.

I did not know on what terms we could go on. I had played my last card. I had tried to cut my suspense, and I had only increased it. Would she sustain the loving make-believe of the last few hours? If she did not, I could not stand jealousy again. I was not strong enough to endure the same torments, with no light at the end. Now it rested with her.

I had not long to wait. The first time we met after my proposal, she was gay and airy, and I could not match her spirits. The second time, she told me, quite casually, that she had visited the town the day before.

'Why didn't you let me know?' The cry forced itself out.

She frowned, and said:

'I thought we'd cleared the air.'

'Not in that way.'

She said:

'I thought now we knew where we stood.'

I had no intention then. But, unknown to me, one was forming.

Three days later, we met again, in the usual alcove in the usual café. She had come from her hairdresser's, and looked immaculately beautiful. I thought, with resentment, with passion, that I had seen her dishevelled in my arms. Through tea we kept up a busy conversation. She made some sarcastic jokes, to which I replied in kind. She said that she was going to a dance. I did not say a word, but went back to the previous conversation. We were talking about books, as though we were high-spirited, literary-minded students, who had met by accident.

She went on trying to reach me – but she knew that I was not there. Her face had taken on an expression of puzzled, almost humorous distress. Her eyes were quizzically narrowed.

She asked the time, and I told her five o'clock.

'I've got lots of time. I needn't go home for hours,' she said.

I did not speak.

'What shall we do?' she persisted.

'Anything you like,' I said, indifferently.

'That's useless.' She looked angry now.

Automatically I said, as I used to:

'Come to my room.'

'Yes,' said Sheila, and began powdering her face.

Then my intention, which up to then I had not known, broke out.

'No,' I said. 'I can't bear it.'

'What?' She looked up from her mirror.

'Sheila,' I said, 'I am going to send you away.'

'Why?' she cried.

'You ought to know.'

She was gazing at me, steadily, frankly, unrelentingly. She said:

'If you send me away now, I shall go.'

'That's want I want.'

'Once I shouldn't have. I should have come back and apologised. I shan't do that now, if you get rid of me.'

'I don't expect you to,' I said.

'If I do go, I shall keep away. I shall take it that you don't want to see me. This time I shan't move a single step.'

'That's all I ask,' I replied.

'Are you sure? Are you sure?'

'Yes,' I said. 'I am sure.'

Without another word, Sheila pulled on her coat. We walked through the smoky café. I noticed our reflections in a steam-filmed mirror. We were both white.

At the door we said the bare word, goodbye. It was raining hard, and she ran for a taxi. I saw her go.

CHAPTER XXIX

SECOND MEETING WITH A DOCTOR

ONE day, between my proposal to Sheila and our parting, I met Marion. I was refreshed to see her. I found time to speculate whether Jack had, in fact, slipped in a word. She was much more certain of herself than she used to be. Of us all, owing to her acting, she had become most of a figure in the town. She threw her head back and laughed, confidently and with a rich lilt. I had no doubt that she had found admirers, and perhaps a lover. Her old earnestness had vanished, though she would always stay the least cynical of women.

With me she was friendly, irritated, protective. Like many others at that time, like Mrs Knight at the ball, she noticed at once that I was looking physically strained. It was easy to perceive, for I had a face on which wear and tear painted itself. The lines, as with Sheila, were etching themselves while I was young.

Marion was perturbed and cross.

'We've got to deliver you in London on the—' It was like her to have remembered the exact date of Bar Finals. 'We don't want to send you there on a stretcher, Lewis.'

She scolded George.

'You mustn't let him drink,' she said. 'Really, you're like a lot of children. I think I'm the only grown-up person among the lot of you.'

Against my will, she made me promise that, if I did not feel better, I would go to a doctor.

I was afraid to go. Partly I had the apprehension of any young man who does not know much of his physical make-up. There might be something bad to learn, and I was frightened of it.

But also I had a short-term fear, a gambler's fear. Come what may, I could not stop working. It was imperative to drive myself on until the examination. Nothing should stop that; a doctor might try to. After the examination I could afford to drop, not now.

I parted from Sheila on a Friday afternoon. The next morning, as I got out of bed, I reeled with giddiness. The room turned and heaved; I shut my eyes and clutched the mantelpiece. The fit seemed to last, wheeling the room round outside my closed eyelids, for minutes. I sat back on the bed, frightened and shaken. What in God's name was this? Nevertheless, I got through my day's quota of reading. If I broke the programme now, I was defeated. I felt well enough to remember what I worked at. But the next morning I had another attack, and so on for two days afterwards, usually in the morning, once at night.

I was afraid: and above all I was savagely angry. It would be intolerable to be cheated at this stage. Despite Sheila, despite all that had happened to me, I had got myself well prepared. That I knew. It was something I had to know; I should suffer too much if I deceived myself this time. George was speaking not with his cosmic optimism, but as a technical expert, when he encouraged me. Recently I had asked him the chances. George did not think naturally in terms of odds, but I pressed him. What was the betting on my coming out high in the first class? In the end, George had answered that he thought the chances were better than even.

It would be bitter beyond bearing to be cheated now. My mind was black with rage. But I was also ignorant and frightened. I had no idea what these fits meant. My fortitude had cracked. I had to turn to someone for help.

I thought of calling on old Dr Francis – but, almost involuntarily one evening, after struggling through another day's work, I began walking down the hill to the infirmary. I was going to ask for Tom Devitt. The infirmary was very near, I told myself, I should get it over quicker; Tom was a modern doctor, and the old man's knowledge must have become obsolete; but those were excuses. She had spoken of him the afternoon that I proposed, and I went to him because of that.

At the infirmary I explained to a nurse that I was an acquaintance of Devitt's, and would like to see him in private. She said, suspiciously, formidably, that the doctor was busy. At last I coerced her into telephoning him. She gave him my name. With a bad grace she told me that he was free at once.

I was taken to his private sitting-room. It overlooked the garden, from which, in the April sunshine, patients were being wheeled. Devitt looked at me with a sharp, open, apprehensive stare. He greeted me with a question in his voice. I was sure that he expected some dramatic news of Sheila.

'I'm here under false pretences,' I had to say. 'I'm presuming on your good nature – because we met once. I'm not well, and I wondered if you'd look me over.'

Devitt's expression showed disappointment, relief, a little anger.

'You ought to have arranged an appointment,' he said irritably. But he was a kind man, and he could no more forget my name than I could his.

'I'm supposed to be off duty,' he said. 'Oh well. You'd better sit down and tell me about yourself.'

We had met just the once. Now I saw him again, either my first impression had been gilded, or else he had aged and softened in between. He was very bald, his cheeks were flabby and his neck thickening. His eyes wore the kind of fixed, lost look that I had noticed in men, who, designed for a happy, relaxed, comfortable life, had run into ill-luck and given up the struggle. I should not have been surprised to hear that Devitt could not bear an hour alone, and went each night for comfort to his club.

There was also a certain grumbling quality which overlaid his kindness. He was much more a tired, querulous, professional man than I had imagined him. But he was, I felt, genuinely kind. In addition, he was business-like and competent, and, as I discovered when I finished telling him my medical history, had an edge to his tongue.

'Well,' said Tom Devitt, 'how many diseases do you think you've got?'

I smiled. I had not expected such a sharp question.

'I expect you must have diagnosed t.b. for yourself. It's a romantic disease of the young, isn't it?'

He sounded my lungs, said: 'Nothing there. They can X-ray you to make sure, but I should be surprised.' Then he set to work. He listened to my heart, took a sample of blood, went through a whole clinical routine. I was sent into the hospital to be photographed. When I came back to his room Devitt gave me a cigarette. He seemed to be choosing his words before he began to speak.

'Well, old chap,' he said, 'I don't think there's anything organically wrong with you. You've got a very slight mitral murmur—' He explained what it was, said that he had one himself and that it meant he had to pay an extra percentage on his insurance premium. 'You needn't get alarmed about that, it might well disappear as you get older. You've got a certain degree of anaemia. That's all I can find. I shall be very annoyed if the X-rays tell us anything more. So the general picture isn't too bad, you know.'

I felt great comfort.

'But still,' went on Tom Devitt, 'it doesn't seem to account for the fact that you're obviously pretty shaky. You are extremely run down, of course. I'm not sure that I oughtn't to tell you that you're dangerously run down.' He looked at me, simply and directly: 'I suppose you've been having a great deal of worry?'

'A great deal,' I said.

'You ought to get rid of it, you know. You need at least six months doing absolutely nothing, and feeding as well as you can – you're definitely under-nourished – and without a worry in your head.'

'Instead of which,' I said, 'in a month's time I take the most important examination of my career.'

'I should advise you not to.'

At that point I had to take him into my confidence. I was not ready to discuss Sheila, even though he desired it and gave me an opening. 'Some men can have their health break down – through something like a broken engagement,' said Tom Devitt naïvely.

'I can believe that,' I said, and left it there. But I was quite open about my circumstances, how I was placed for money, what this examination meant. For every reason I had to take it this year. If my health let me down, I had lost.

'Yes,' said Devitt. 'Yes. I see.' He seemed taken aback, discomfited.

'Well,' he added, 'it's a pity, but I don't think there's a way out. I agree, you must try to keep going. Good luck to you, that's all I can say. Perhaps we can help you just a bit. I should think the most important thing is to see that you manage to sleep.'

I smiled to myself; on our only other meeting, he had been concerned whether I got enough sleep. He gave me a couple of prescriptions, and then, before I went, a lecture.

He told me, in an uncomfortable, grumbling fashion, that I was taking risks with my health; probably I was not unhealthy, but I was liable to over-respond; I was sympathetotonic; I might live to be eighty if I took care of myself. 'It's no use telling you to take care of yourself,' said Tom Devitt. 'I know that. You'll be lucky if you have a comfortable life physically, old chap.'

I thanked him. I was feeling both grateful and relieved, and I wanted him to have a drink with me. He hesitated. 'No. Not now,' he said. Then he clapped me on the shoulder. 'I'm very glad you came. I hope you pull it off. It would be nice to have been some good to you.'

I rejoiced that night, and, though I had another bout of giddiness next day, I felt much better. Perhaps because of Devitt's reassurance, the bouts themselves seemed to become less frequent. I read and wrote with the most complete attention that I could screw out of myself. I was confident now that I should last until the examination.

On the Saturday I travelled out to the farm later than the rest, because I could not spare the afternoon. I had not said much to George about my health. To the little I told him, he was formally sympathetic; but in secret he thought it all inexplicable and somewhat effeminate.

I was so much heartened that I needed to tell someone the truth, and as soon as I saw Marion among the group I took her aside and asked her to come for a walk. We struck across the fields – in defiance, I headed in the direction of the vicarage – and I remarked that I had kept my promise and gone to a doctor. Then I confessed about my symptoms, and what Devitt had said.

'I'm very much relieved, I really am,' cried Marion. 'Now you must show some sense.'

'I shall arrive at that damned hall in six weeks' time,' I said. 'That's the main thing.'

'That's one thing. But you mustn't think you can get away with it for ever.' She nagged me as no one else would have done: I was too wilful, I tried to ride over my illnesses, I was incorrigibly careless of myself.

'Anyone else would have gone to a doctor months ago,' she said. 'That would have spared you a lot of worry – and some of your friends too, I may say. I'm very glad I made you go.'

I could hear those I's, a little stressed, assertive in the middle of her yearning to heal and soothe and cherish. In all tenderness such as hers, there was the grasp of an ego beneath the balm. I had never romanticised Marion. People said she was good, full of loving-kindness, so free from sentimentality in her unselfish actions that one took from her what one could not from another. Much of that was true. Some of us had generous impulses, but she carried hers out. She never paraded her virtues, nor sacrificed herself unduly. If she enjoyed acting, then she spent her time at it, took the applause and revelled in it. She was no hypocrite, and of all of us she did most practical good. And so Jack Cotery and the rest admired her more than any of our friends.

I was very fond of her, and flattered because she was fond of me. Yet I knew that in a sense she was vainer than Sheila, more grasping than myself. I think I liked her more because she needed applause for her tender actions. In my eyes, she was warm, tenacious, tough in her appetite for life, and deep down surprisingly self-centred. It was her lively, self-centred strength that I drew most refreshment from, that and her feeling for me. There was no war inside her, her body and soul were fused and would in the end find fulfilment and happiness. As a result, her company often brought me peace.

She brought me peace that evening (in the lanes I had once walked wet through) in a cool twilight when, behind the lacework of the trees, the sky shone a translucent apple-green. There I confided to her, far more than I had to anyone, of what had happened between me and Sheila. I was too secretive to reveal the depth of my ecstasy, torments, and hope; some of it I wrapped up in mockery and sarcasm; but I gave her a history which, so far as it went, was true. She received it with an interest that was affectionate, greedy, and matter-of-fact. Perversely, so it seemed to me, she did not regard Sheila's behaviour as particularly out of the ordinary. She domesticated it with a curious quasi-physical freemasonry, as though she or any woman might have done the same. She did not consider Sheila either excessively beautiful or strange, just a young woman who was 'not quite certain what she wanted'. Marion's concern was directly for me. 'Yes, it was a pity you ran across her,' she said. 'Mind you, I expect you puzzled her as much as she did you – that is, if I know anything about you.'

I was wondering.

'Still, it's better for you that it's over. I'm glad.'

We had turned towards home. The green of the sky was darkening to purple.

'So you sent her away?' she said.

'Yes, I sent her away.'

'I don't expect she liked that. But I believe it was right for you.'

In the half-dark I put my arm round her waist. She leaned back, warm and solid, against me. Then, with a recoil of energy, she sprang away.

'No, my lad. Not yet. Not yet.' She was laughing.

I protested.

'Oh no,' said Marion. 'I've got something to say first. Are you free of Sheila?'

'Yes,' I said. 'I've told you. I've parted from her.'

'That's not the same,' said Marion. 'My dear, I'm serious. You ought to know I'm not a capricious girl. And,' she said, firmly, confidently, reproachfully, 'you must think of me for once. I've given you no reason to treat me badly.'

'Less than anyone,' I said.

'So I want you to be honest. Answer my question again. Are you free of Sheila?'

The first stars were coming out. I saw Marion's eyes, bright, not sad but vigilant.

I wanted to know her love. But she forced me not to lie. I thought of how I had gone, as though hypnotised, to Tom Devitt, because his life was linked to Sheila's; I thought of my memories, and of waking at nights from dreams that taunted me. I said:

'Perhaps not quite. But I shall be soon.'

'That's honest, anyway,' Marion said, with anger in her voice. Then she laughed again. 'Don't be too long. Then take me out. I'm not risking you on the rebound.'

Decorously, she slipped an arm through mine.

'We're going to be late for supper, my lad. Let's move. We'll talk of something sensible – like your exam.'

In the late spring, in April and early May, even the harsh red brick of the town seemed softened. The chestnuts flowered along the road to Eden's house, the lilacs in the gardens outside Martineau's. I was near the end of my reading, George's calculations had not been fallible, and I had only two more authorities to master. In the mild spring days I used to take my books to the park, and work there.

But there were times when, sitting on a bench with my note-book, I was distracted. On the breeze, the odour of the blossom reached me; I ached with longing; I was full of restlessness, of an unnamed hope. Those were the days when I went into the town in the afternoon; I looked into shop windows, stood in bookshops, went up and down the streets, searched among the faces in the crowd; I never visited our usual café, for she did not go there alone, but I had tea in turn in all those where I had known her meet her mother. I did not see her, neither there, nor at the station (I remembered her trains as I did my last page of notes). Was it just chance? Was she deliberately staying at home? Was she helping me to see her no more? I told myself that it was better. In the spring sunshine, I told myself that it was better.

On the day before I left for London and the examination, George, to whom formal occasions were sacred, had insisted that there must be a drinking party to wish me success. I had to go, it would have wounded George not to; but I, more superstitious and less formal, did not like celebrations before an event. So I was grateful when Marion gave me an excuse to cut the party short.

'I'll cook you a meal first,' she said. 'I'd like to be certain that you have one square meal before your first paper.'

I ate the supper in her lodgings before I joined George at our public-house. Marion was an excellent cook in the hearty English country style, the style of the small farmers and poor-to-middling yeomen stock from which she came. She gave me roast beef and Yorkshire pudding, an apple pie with cheese, a great welsh rarebit. Eating as I did in snacks and pieces, being at my landlady's mercy for breakfast, and having to count the pennies even for my snacks, I had not tasted such a meal for long enough.

'Lewis,' said Marion, 'you're hungry.' She added: 'I'm glad I thought of it. Cooking's a bore, whatever anyone tells you, so I nearly didn't. Shall I tell you why I decided to feed you?'

Comfortably, I nodded my head.

'It's just laying a bait for large returns to come. When you're getting rich and successful, I shall come to London and expect the best dinners that money can buy.'

'You shall have them.' I was touched: this meal had been her method of encouraging me, practical, energetic, half-humorous.

'You see, Lewis, I think you're a pretty good bet.' Soon after, she said: 'You've not told me. Have you seen Sheila again?'

'No.'

'How much have you thought of her?'

I wished that she would not disturb the well-being in the room. Again I had to force myself to answer truly.

I said: 'Now and then – I see ghosts.'

She frowned and laughed.

'You are tiresome, aren't you? No, I mustn't be cross with you. I asked for it.' Her eyes were flashing. 'Go and polish off this exam. Then you must have a holiday. And then – ghosts don't live for ever.'

She smiled luxuriously, as though the smile spread over her whole skin.

'I'm afraid,' she said, 'that I was meant to be moist and jealous and adoring.'

I smiled back. It was not an invitation at that moment. We sat and smoked in silence, in a thunderous comfort, until it was time for my parting drink with George.

CHAPTER XXX

THE EXAMINATION

JUST as George, on the subject of how to prepare for an examination, advised me as though he were one of nature's burgesses, so I behaved like one. I went to London two days before the first paper; I obeyed the maxims that were impressed upon all students, and I slammed the last note-book shut with a night and a day to spare. Slammed it so that I could hear the noise in the poky, varnish-smelling bedroom at Mrs Reed's. Now I was ready. One way or the other, I thought, challenging the luck, I should not have to stay in that house again.

I spent a whole day at the Oval, with all my worries shut away but one. I did not think about the papers, but I was anxious that, at the last moment, I might be knocked out by another turn of sickness. I had been feeling better in the past weeks, and I was well enough as I lolled on the benches for a day, and as I meandered back to Judd Street in the evening. I walked part of the way, over Vauxhall Bridge and along the river, slowly and with an illusion of calm. I stopped to gaze at a mirage-like sight of St Paul's and the city roofs mounted above the evening mist. Confidence seeped through me in the calm – except that, even now, I might be ill.

I slept that night, but I slept lightly. I had been half-awake many times, and it was early when I knew that it was impossible to sleep longer. I looked at the watch I had borrowed for the examination: it was not yet half-past six. This was the day. I lay in bed, having wakened with the fear of the night before. Should I get up and test it? If I were going to be wrecked by giddiness that day, I might as well know now. Carefully I rose, trying not to move my head. I took three steps to the window, and threw up the blind. In streamed the morning sunlight. I was steady enough. Recklessly, I exclaimed aloud. I was steady enough.

I did not return to bed, but read until breakfast-time, a novel I had borrowed from Marion; and at breakfast I was not put off either by Mrs Reed's abominable food or the threat of her abominable postcards. 'I've got one ready for you to take away,' she told me, with her ferocious *bonhomie*. 'I'll send you a bouquet,' I said jauntily, for that was the only way to cope with her. I sometimes wondered if she had a nerve in her body; if she knew young men were nervous at examinations; if she had ever been nervous herself, and how she had borne it.

In good time, I caught a bus down to the Strand. Russell Square and Southampton Row and Kingsway shimmered in the clean morning light. My breath caught, in something between anticipation and fear, between pleasure and pain. Streams of people were crossing the streets towards their offices; the women were wearing summer dresses, for the sky was cloudless, there were all the signs of a lovely day.

The examination was to be held in the dining-hall of an Inn. I was one of the first to arrive outside the doors, although there was already a small knot of candidates, mainly Indians. There I waited by myself, watching a gardener cut the lawn, smelling the new-mown grass. Now the nervousness was needle-sharp. I could not resist stealing glances at my watch, though it was only two minutes since I had last looked. A quarter of an hour to go. It was intolerably long, it was a no-man's-land of time, neither mine nor inimical fate's. Charles March came up with a couple of acquaintances, discussing, in his carrying voice, in his first-hand, candid, concentrated fashion, why he should be 'in a state' before an examination which mattered nothing and which even he, despite his idleness, presumably would manage to scrape through. I smiled. Later I explained to him why I smiled. As the doors creaked open, he wished me good luck.

I said: 'I shall need it.'

The odour of the hall struck me as I went quickly in. It made my heart jump in this intense expectancy, in this final moment. I found my place, at the end of a gangway. The question-paper rested, white, shining, undisturbed, in the middle of the desk. I was reading it, tearing my way through it, before others had sat down.

At first I felt I had never seen these words before. It was like opening an innings, when one is conscious of the paint on the crease, of the bowler rubbing the ball, as though it were all unprecedented, happening for the first time. The rubrics to the questions themselves seemed sinister in their unfamiliarity: 'Give reasons why . . .', 'Justify the opinion that . . .'. Although I had read such formulas in each examination paper for years past, the words stared out, dazzling, black on the white sheet, as if they were shapes unknown.

That horror, that blank in my faculties, lasted only a moment. I wiped the sweat from my temples; it seemed that a switch had been touched. The first question might have been designed for me, if George had been setting the paper. I read on. I had been lucky – astonishingly lucky I thought later, but in the hall I was simply filled by a throbbing, combative zest. There was no question I could not touch. It was a paper without options, and eight out of ten I had waiting in my head, ready to be set down. The other two I should have to dig back for and contrive.

I took off my wristwatch and put it at the top of the desk, within sight as I wrote. I had at my fingers' end the devices which made an answer easy to read. My memory was working with something like the precision of George's. I had a trick, when going so fast, of leaving out occasional words: I must leave five minutes, prosaically I reminded myself, to read over what I had written. Several times, as though I had a photograph in front of me, I remembered in visual detail, in the position they occupied in a textbook, some lines that I had studied. In they went to my answer, with a little lead-up and gloss. I was hot, I had scarcely lifted my eyes, obscurely I knew that Charles March was further up the hall, on the other side of the gangway. This was the chance to try everything I possessed: and I gloried in it.

The luck remained with me throughout. Of all the past papers I had worked over, none had suited me as well as the set this year. Nearly all the specialised knowledge I had acquired from George came in useful (not the academic law he had taught me, but the actual cases that went through a provincial solicitor's office). On the afternoon of the first day I was half-incredulous when I saw my opportunities. Then I forgot everything, fatigue, the beating of my heart, the sweat on my face, as for three hours I made the most of them.

I was jubilant that first night. Jubilant but still guarded and in training, telling myself that it was too early to shout. In the warm May evening, though, I walked at leisure down Park Lane and through the great squares. Some of the houses were brilliant with lights, and through the open doors I saw staircases curving down to the wide halls. Cars drove up, and women swept past me on the pavement into those halls, leaving their scent on the hot still air. In my youth, in my covetousness and pride and excitement, I thought that my time would come and that I too should entertain in such a house.

Curiously, though often I exaggerated the changes that would happen in my own country (which was less affected than most) in my life-time, that night I seemed to think that this rich life would go on for ever.

The last afternoon arrived, and the last paper. The spell had not broken. It suited me as well as the first. Except that by now I was tired, I had spun out my energies so that I was near the end of my stretch. I wrote on, noticing my tiredness not much more than the extreme heat. But my timing was less automatic; I had finished the paper, read it through, and still had five minutes to spare.

Ah well, I was thinking, it has been pretty good. Each paper up to the standard of the first, and one distinctly better. One better than I could have hoped. Then the room went round, sickeningly round, and I clutched the desk. It was not a long attack; when I opened my eyes, the hall stood hazily there. I smiled to myself, a little uneasily. The timing had been close, too close to relish.

I was still sick and giddy as Charles March came down the aisle; but he joined me, we left the hall together, and after the civilities of enquiring about each other's performances we went to get some tea. I was glad of the chance. I had often wished to talk to him alone. We sat in a tea-shop and did post mortems on the papers.

He was an active, rangily built young man with hair as fair as mine and excessively intelligent, inquiring eyes. At a glance, one could tell that he was a man of force and brains. He was also argumentative, which was in George's style rather than mine, and had a talent, more sophisticated than Aunt Milly's, for telling one home-truths. But he was capable of a most concentrated sympathy. Somehow he had divined that this examination was of cardinal importance to me. That afternoon at tea, seeing me delighted with what I had done, yet still strained and limp, he asked me to tell him. Why did it matter seriously? I had obviously done far better than he had, or than any sane person would consider necessary. Why did it matter? Did I feel like telling him?

Yes, I felt like it. In the clammy tea-shop, with the papers spread on the table, I explained my position, under Charles March's keen, hard and appreciative eyes. It was out of my control now, and I talked realistically and recklessly, frankly and with bravado. Until the result came out, I should have no idea what was to become of me.

'Yes,' said Charles March. 'It's too much to invest in one chance. Of course it is. You've done pretty well, of course.' He pointed to the papers. 'Whether you've done well enough – I don't see that anyone can say.'

He was understanding. He knew that I could not have stood extravagant rosy prophecies just then.

Charles had refrained from any kind of roseate encouragement; and he was right, for I could not have received it. Yet, in the theatre that night, listening to the orchestra, I was all of a sudden carried on a wave of joy, certain that all I wanted was not a phantom in the future but already in my hands. I was not musical, but in the melody I possessed all I craved for. A name was mine; I was transferred from an unknown, struggling, apprehensive young man; a name was mine. Riches were mine; all the jewels of the imagination glittered for me, the houses, the Mediterranean, Venice, all I had pictured in my attic, looking down to the red brick houses and the slate; I was one of the lords of this world.

Yes, and love was mine. In the music, I remembered the serene hours with Sheila, her beautiful face, her sarcastic humour, the times when her spirit made mine lighter than a mortal's, the circle of her arms round me and her skin close to.

I had not to struggle for her love. It was mine. I had the certainty of never-ending bliss. As I listened to the music, her love was mine.

CHAPTER XXXI

TRIUMPH AND SURRENDER

WHEN I returned to the town I had four weeks to wait for the result. And I hid from everyone I knew. I paid my duty call on George, to show him the papers and be cross-questioned about my answers: he, less perceptive than Charles March, shouted in all his insatiable optimism that I must have done superbly well. Then I hid, to get out of sight, out of reach of any question.

I was half-tempted to visit Marion. But our understanding was clear – and also, and this kept me away for certain, I was not fit to be watched by affectionate, shrewd eyes. I did not want to be seen by anyone who knew me at all, much less one who, like my mother, would claim the right of affection to know me well. Just as I had never shared my troubles with my mother, so I could not share this suspense now.

Could I have shared it with Sheila, I thought once? I could have talked to her; yet such troubles were so foreign to her, so earth-bound beside her own, that she would not touch them.

Since the night at the theatre, she had been constantly present in my mind. Not in the forefront, not like the shadow of the result. I was not harassed about her. Even with my days quite empty, I never once walked the streets where I might meet her, and in my prowls at night I was not looking for her face. Underneath, maybe, I knew what was to come, what my next act must be.

Yet, one evening in June, my first thought was of her when my landlady bawled up the stairs that a telegram had arrived. I had only received one telegram in my life, and that from Sheila. The examination result, I assumed, would come by the morning post. I ran down, ripped the telegram open just inside the front door. It was not from Sheila, but the blood rushed to my face. I read: CONGRATULATIONS AND HOMAGE STUDENTSHIP PRIZE ACCORDING TO PLAN SEE YOU SOON MARCH.

I threw it in the air and hugged my landlady.

'Here it is,' I cried.

I only half-realised that the waiting was over – just as I had only half-realised it when my mother proclaimed the news of my first examination, that solitary piece of good news in her hopeful life. I was practising the gestures of triumph before I felt it. On my way to George's, telegram in hand, I was still stupefied. Not so George. 'Naturally,' he called out in a tremendous voice. 'Naturally you've defeated the sunkets. This calls for a celebration.'

It got it. George and I called on our friends and we packed into the lounge of the Victoria. George was soon fierce with drink. 'Drink up! Drink up!' he cried, like an angry lion, to astonished salesmen who were sitting quietly over their evening pint. 'Can you comprehend that this is the climacteric of our society?' That extraordinary phrase kept recurring through the mists of drink, the faces, the speeches and the songs. Drunkenly, happily, I impressed upon a commercial traveller and his woman-friend how essential it was to do not only well, but competitively and superlatively well, in certain professional examinations. I had known, I said in an ominous tone, many good men ruined through the lack of this precaution. I was so grave that they listened to me, and the traveller added his contribution upon the general increase in educational standards.

'Toasts,' cried George, in furious cheerfulness, and at the end of each threw his glass into the fireplace. The barmaids clacked and threatened, but we had been customers for years, we were the youngest of their regulars, they had a soft spot for us, and finally George, with formidable logic, demonstrated to them that this was, and nothing else could possibly be, the climacteric of our society.

It went on late. At midnight there was a crowd of us shouting in the empty streets. It was the last of my student nights in the town. George and I walked between the tramlines up to the park, with an occasional lorry hooting at us as it passed. There, in the middle of the road, I expressed my eternal debt to George. 'I take some credit,' said George magnificently. 'Yes, I take some credit.'

I watched him walk away between the tramlines, massive under the arc lights, setting down his feet heavily, carefully, and yet still with a precarious steadiness, whistling and swinging his stick.

All the congratulations poured in except the one I wanted. There was no letter from Sheila. Yet, though that made me sad, I knew with perfect certainty what I was going to do.

I went to London to arrange my new existence. I arranged my interview with Herbert Getliffe, whose chambers I was entering, on Eden's advice; I found a couple of rooms in Conway Street, near the Tottenham Court Road. The rooms were only a little less bleak than my attic, for I was still cripplingly short of money, and might be so for years.

In something of the same spirit in which I had abandoned Aunt Milly's and spent money living on my own, I treated myself to a week in a South Kensington hotel. Then, since it was the long vacation, I should return to the attic for my last weeks in the town – and in October I was ready for another test of frugality in Conway Street. But in this visit, when I was arranging the new life, I deserted Mrs Reed's and indulged myself in comfort – just to prove that I was not frightened, that I was not always touching wood.

It was from that hotel that I wrote to Sheila, asking her to meet me.

I wrote to Sheila. Since the examination I had known that if she did not break the silence, I should. Despite the rebellion of my pride. Despite Jack Cotery's cautionary voice, saying: 'Why must you fall in love with someone who can only make you miserable? She'll do you harm. She can only do you harm.' Despite my sense of self-preservation. Despite any part of me that was sensible and controlled. From within myself and without, I was told the consequences. Yet, as I took a sheet of the hotel note-paper and began to write, I felt as though I were coming home.

It was surrender to her, unconditional surrender. I had sent her away, and now I was crawling back. She would be certain in the future that I could not live without her. She would have nothing to restrain her. She would have me on her own terms. That I knew with absolute lucidity.

Was it also another surrender, a surrender within myself? I was writing that letter as a man in love. That was the imperative I should have found, however thoroughly I searched into myself. I should have declared myself ready to take the chances of unrequited love. And all that was passionately true. Yet was it also a surrender within myself?

I did not hear that question. If I had heard it, writing to Sheila when I was not yet twenty-two, I should have laughed it away. I had tasted the promise of success. I was carving my destiny. Compared with the ordinary run of men, I felt so free. I was ardent and sanguine and certain of happiness. It would have seemed incredible to hear that, in the deepest recess of my nature, I could still stay my own prisoner.

I wrote the letter. I addressed it to the vicarage. There was a moment looking down at it upon the writing-table, when I revolted. I was on the point of tearing it up. Then I was swept on another surge, rushed outside the hotel, found a pillar-box, heard the flop of the letter as it dropped.

I had written the first night of that week in London, asking Sheila to meet me in five days' time at Stewart's in Piccadilly. I was not anxious whether she would come. Of that, as though with a telepathic certainty, I had no doubt. I arrived at the café before four, and captured window seats which gave on to Piccadilly. I had scarcely looked out before I saw her striding with her poised, arrogant step, on the other side of the road. She too had time to spare; she glanced at the windows of Hatchard's before she crossed. Waiting for her, I was alight with hope.

PART FIVE

THE HARD WAY

CHAPTER XXXII

TWO CONTROLLERS

I WAS early for my first interview with Herbert Getliffe. It was raining, and so I could not spin out the minutes in the Temple gardens; I arrived at the foot of the staircase, and it was still too wet to stay there studying the names. Yet I gave them a glance.

LORD WATERFIELD
MR. H. GETLIFFE
MR. W. ALLEN

and then a column of names, meaningless to me, some faded, some with the paint shining and black. As I rushed into the shelter of the staircase, I wondered how they would find room for my name at the bottom, and whether Waterfield ever visited the chambers, now that he had been in the cabinet for years.

The rain pelted down outside, and my feet clanged on the stone stairs. The set of chambers was three flights up, there was no one on the staircase, the doors were shut, there was no noise except the sound of rain. On the third floor the door was open, a light shone in the little hall; even there, though, there was no one moving, I could hear no voices from the rooms around.

Then I did hear a voice, a voice outwardly deferential, firm, smooth, but neither gentle nor genteel.

'Can I help you, sir?'

I said that I had an appointment with Getliffe.

'I'm the clerk here. Percy Hall.' He was looking at me with an appraising eye, but in the dim hall, preoccupied with the meeting to come, I did not notice much about him.

'I suppose,' he said, 'you wouldn't happen to be the young gentleman who wants to come here as a pupil, would you?'

I said that I was.

'I thought as much,' said Percy. He told me that Getliffe was expecting me, but was not yet back from lunch; meanwhile I had better wait in Getliffe's room. Percy led the way to the door at the end of the hall. As he left me, he said: 'When you've finished with Mr Getliffe, sir, I hope you'll call in for a word with me.'

It sounded like an order.

I looked round the room. It was high, with panelled walls, and it had, so Percy had told me, been Waterfield's. When Waterfield went into politics, so Percy again had told me, Getliffe had moved into the room with extreme alacrity. It smelt strongly that afternoon of a peculiar brand of tobacco. I was not specially nervous, but that smell made me more alert; this meeting mattered; I had to get on with Getliffe. I thought of the photograph that Eden had shown me, of himself and Getliffe, after a successful case. Getliffe had appeared large, impassive and stern.

I was impatient now. It was a quarter of an hour past the time he had given me. I got up from the chair, looked at the briefs on the table, the picture over the fireplace, the books on the shelves. I stared out of the windows, high and wide and with their shutters folded back. Alert, I stared down at the gardens, empty in the dark, rainy, summer afternoon. And beyond was the river.

As I was standing by the window, there was a bustle outside the room, and Getliffe came in. My first sight of him was a surprise. In the photograph he had appeared large, impassive and stern. In the flesh, as he came bustling in, late and flustered, he was only of middle height, and seemed scarcely that because of the way he dragged his feet. He had his underlip thrust out in an affable grin, so that there was something at the same time gay and shamefaced about his expression. He suddenly confronted me with a fixed gaze from brown, opaque and lively eyes.

'Don't tell me your name,' he began, in a slightly strident, breathless voice. 'You're Ellis—'

I corrected him.

With almost instantaneous quickness, he was saying:

'You're Eliot.' He repeated: 'You're Eliot,' with an intonation of reproof, as though the mistake had been my fault.

He sat down, lit his pipe, grinned, and puffed out smoke. He talked matily, perfunctorily, about Eden. Then he switched on his fixed gaze. His eyes confronted me. He said:

'So you want to come in here, do you?'

I said that I did.

'I needn't tell you, Eliot, that I have to refuse more pupils than I can take. It's one of the penalties of being on the way up. Not that one wants to boast. This isn't a very steady trade that you and I have chosen, Eliot. Sometimes I think we should have done better to go into the Civil Service and become deputy-under-principal secretaries and get two thousand per annum at fifty-five and our Y.M.C.A. or X.Y.Z. some bright new year.'

At this time I was not familiar with Getliffe's allusive style, and I was slow to realise that he was referring to the orders of knighthood.

'Still, one might be doing worse. And people seem to pass the word round that the work is coming in. I want to impress on you, Eliot, that I've turned down ten young men who wanted to be pupils – and that's only in the last year. It's not fair to take them unless one has the time to look after them and bring them up in the way they should go. I hope you'll always remember that.'

Getliffe was full of responsibility, statesmanship, and moral weight. His face was as stern as in the photograph. He was enjoying his own seriousness and uprightness, even though he had grossly exaggerated the number of pupils he refused. Then he said. 'Well, Eliot, I wanted you to understand that it's not easy for me to take you. But I shall. I make it a matter of principle to take people like you, who've started with nothing but their brains. I make it a matter of principle.'

Then he gave his shamefaced, affable chuckle.

'Also,' he said, 'it keeps the others up to it.'

He grinned at me: his mood had changed, his face was transformed, he was guying all serious persons.

'So I shall take you,' said Getliffe, serious and responsible again, fixing me with his gaze. 'If our clerk can fit you in. I'm going to stretch a point and take you.'

'I'm very grateful,' I said. I knew that, as soon as the examination result was published, he had insisted to Eden that I was to be steered towards his chambers.

'I'm very grateful,' I said, and he had the power of making me feel so.

'We've got a duty towards you,' said Getliffe, shaking me by the hand. 'One's got to look at it like that.' His eyes stared steadily into mine.

Just then there was a knock on the door, and Percy entered. He came across the room and laid papers in front of Getliffe.

'I shouldn't have interrupted you, sir,' said Percy. 'But I've promised to give an answer. Whether you'll take this. They're pressing me about it.'

Getliffe looked even more responsible and grave.

'Is one justified in accepting any more work?' he said. 'I'd like to see my wife and family one of these evenings. And some day I shall begin neglecting one of these jobs.' He tapped the brief with the bowl of his pipe and looked from Percy to me. 'If ever you think that is beginning to happen, I want you to tell me straight. I'm glad to think that I've never neglected one yet.' He gazed at me. 'I shouldn't be so happy if I didn't think so.'

'Shall I do it?' Getliffe asked us loudly.

'It's heavily marked,' said Percy.

'What's money?' said Getliffe.

'They think you're the only man for it,' said Percy.

'That's more like talking,' said Getliffe. 'Perhaps it is one's duty. Perhaps I ought to do it. Perhaps you'd better tell them that I will do it – just as a matter of duty.'

When Percy had gone out, Getliffe regarded me.

'I'm not sorry you heard that,' he said. 'You can see why one has to turn away so many pupils? They follow the work, you know. It's no credit to me, of course, but you're lucky to come here, Eliot. I should like you to tell yourself that.'

What I should have liked to tell myself was whether or not that scene with Percy was rehearsed.

Then Getliffe began to exhort me: his voice became brisk and strident, he took the pipe out of his mouth and waved the stem at me.

'Well, Eliot,' he said. 'You've got a year here as a pupil. After that we can see whether you're ever going to earn your bread and butter. Not to speak of a little piece of cake. Mind you, we may have to tell you that it's not your vocation. One mustn't shirk one's responsibilities. Not even the painful ones. One may have to tell you to move a bit farther up the street.'

'Of course,' I said, in anger and pride.

'Still,' said Getliffe, 'you're not going to sink if you can help it. You needn't tell me that. You've got a year as a pupil. And a year's a long time. Your job is to be as useful as you can to both of us. Start whenever you like. The sooner the better. Start tomorrow.'

Breathlessly, with immense zest, Getliffe produced a list of cases and references, happy with all the paraphernalia of the law, reeling out the names of cases very quickly, waving his pipe as I copied them down.

'As for the root of all evil,' said Getliffe, 'I shall have to charge you the ordinary pupil's fees. You see, Eliot, one's obliged to think of the others. Hundred guineas for the year. October to October. If you start early, you don't have to pay extra,' said Getliffe with a chuckle. 'That's thrown in with the service. Like plain vans. A hundred guineas is your contribution to the collection plate. You can pay in quarters. The advantage of the instalment system,' he added, 'is that we can reconsider the arrangement for the third and fourth quarters. You may have saved me a few days' slogging before then. You may have earned a bit of bread and butter. The labourer is worthy of his hire.' He smiled, affably, brazenly, and said: 'Yes! The labourer is worthy of his hire.'

I think I had some idea, even then, of the part Herbert Getliffe was going to play in my career. He warmed me, as he did everyone else. He took me in often, as he did everyone else. He made me feel restrained, by the side of the extravagant and shameless way in which he exhibited his soul. On the way from his room to the clerk's, I was half-aware that this was a tricky character to meet, when one was struggling for a living. I should not have been astonished to be told in advance the part he was going to play. But Percy Hall's I should not have guessed.

Percy's room was a box of an office, which had no space for any furniture but a table and a chair; Percy gave me the chair and braced his haunches against the edge of the table. He was, I noticed now, a squat powerful man, with the back of his head rising vertically from his stiff collar. No one ever bore a more incongruous Christian name; and it was perverse that he had a job where, according to custom, everyone called him by it.

'I want to explain one or two points to you, sir. If you enter these chambers, there are things I can do for you. I could persuade someone to give you a case before you've been here very long. But' – Percy gave a friendly, brutal, good-natured smile – 'I'm not going to until I know what you're like. I've got a reputation to lose myself. The sooner we understand each other, the better.'

With a craftsman's satisfaction, Percy described how he kept the trust of the solicitors; how he never over-praised a young man, but how he reminded them of a minor success; how he watched over a man who looked like training into a winner, and how he gradually fed him with work; how it was no use being sentimental and finding cases for someone who was not fitted to survive.

Percy was able, I was thinking. He liked power and he liked his job – and he liked himself. It was a pleasure to him to be hard and shrewd, not to succumb to facile pity, to be esteemed as a clear-headed man. And he cherished a certain resentment at his luck. He had not had the chances of the men for whose work he foraged; yet he was certain that most of them were weaklings beside himself.

'I want to know what strings you can pull, sir,' said Percy. 'Some of our young gentlemen have uncles or connections who are solicitors.

It turns out very useful sometimes. It's wonderful how the jobs come in.'

'I can't pull any strings,' I said. He was not a man to fence with. He was rough under the smooth words, and it was wiser to be rough in return.

'That's a pity,' said Percy.

'I was born poor,' I said. 'I've got no useful friends. Apart from my studentship – you knew I'd got one?'

'I see Mr Getliffe's correspondence, sir,' said Percy complacently.

'Apart from that, I'm living on borrowed money. If I can't earn my keep within three years, I'm finished – so far as this game goes.'

'That's a pity,' said Percy. Our eyes met. His face was expressionless.

He said nothing for some moments. He seemed to be assessing the odds. He did not indulge in encouragement. He had, however, read Eden's letters and, with his usual competence, remembered them in detail. He reminded me that here was one solicitor with whom I had some credit. I said that Eden's was a conservative old firm in a provincial town.

'Never mind. They've paid Mr Getliffe some nice little fees.'

'Eden's got a very high opinion of him.'

'I suppose so, sir,' said Percy.

I was fishing for his own opinion, but did not get a flicker of response. He had asked enough questions for that afternoon, and looked content. He banished my future from the conversation, and told me that he bred goldfish and won prizes for them. Then he decided to show me the place where I should sit for the next year. It was in a room close to Getliffe's, and the same size. There were already four people in it – Allen, a man well into middle age, who was writing at a roll-top desk, and three young men, one reading at a small table and two others playing chess. Percy introduced me, and I was offered a small table of my own, under one of the windows. The view was different from that in Getliffe's room: this one looked across the gardens to another court, where an occasional light was shining, though it was tea-time on a summer afternoon. The river was not visible from this window, but, as I turned away and talked to Allen and the others, I heard a boat hoot twice.

CHAPTER XXXIII

MANŒUVRES

I CAME to know the view from that window in chambers very well. I spent weeks in the long vacation there, though it was not realistic to do so.

I learned little, and the others had gone away. Getliffe had asked me to produce some notes for him, but I could have taken my books anywhere. Yet I was restless, away from my place: it was as though I had to catch a train.

I was restless through that autumn and winter, through days when, with nothing to do, I gazed down over the gardens and watched the lights come on in the far court. There was nothing to do. Though Getliffe was good at filling in one's time, though I marked down every case in London that was not sheer routine, still there were days, stretches of days, when all I could do was read as though I were still a student and, instead of gazing from my garret over the roofs, look out instead over the Temple gardens. Some days, in that first year, that seemed the only change: I had substituted a different view, that was all.

I was too restless to enjoy knowing the others in Getliffe's chambers. At any other time I should have got more out of them. I struck up an acquaintance, it was true, with Salisbury, who worked in the other room; he had three years' start on me and was beginning to get a practice together. He boasted that he was earning seven hundred a year, but I guessed that five hundred was nearer the truth. Our acquaintance was a sparring and mistrustful one; he was a protégé of Getliffe's, which made me envy him, and in turn he saw me as a rival. I half-knew that he was a kind, insecure, ambitious man who craved affection and did not expect to be liked; but I was distracted by the sight of his vulpine pitted face bent over his table, as I speculated how he described me to Getliffe behind my back.

Quite often we had a meal together, which was more than I did with any of the others. Of the three in my room, Allen was a precise spinster of a man, curiously happy, who said with simple detachment that he had none of the physical force and vitality of a successful barrister; he lived at his club, marked thousands of examination papers, edited volumes of trials, and for ten years past had averaged eight hundred or nine hundred a year; he had a hope, at forty-five, of some modest permanent job, and made subfusc, malicious, aunt-like jokes at Getliffe's expense; they were cruel, happy jokes, all the happier because they made Salisbury sad. The other two were both pupils, only a term senior to me. One, Snedding, was hard-working and so dense that Percy erased him from serious consideration in his first month. The other, Paget, was a rich and well-connected young man who was spending a year or two at the Bar before managing the family estates. He was civil and deferential to us all in chambers, and played an adequate game of chess; but outside he lived a smart social life, and politely evaded all invitations from professional acquaintances, much to the chagrin of Salisbury, who was a headmaster's son and longed for *chic*.

Paget was no fool, but he was not a menace. I was lucky, I told myself, that neither of those two was a competitor, for it meant that I might get more than my share of the minor pickings. I told myself that I was lucky. But all the luck was put off till tomorrow, and I fretted, lost to reason in my impatience, because tomorrow would not come.

No one was better than Getliffe at keeping his pupils occupied. So Salisbury said, who was fervently loyal to Getliffe and tried to counter all the gossip of the Inn dining-table. There were plenty of times when I was too rancorous to hear a word in Getliffe's favour; yet in fact this one was true. From the day I entered the chambers, he called me into his room each afternoon that he was not in court. 'How are tricks?' he used to say; and, when I mentioned a case, he would expound on it with enthusiasm. It was an enthusiasm that he blew out like his tobacco smoke; it was vitalising even when, expounding impromptu on any note I wrote for him, he performed his maddening trick of getting every second detail slightly wrong. Usually not wrong enough to matter, but just wrong enough to irritate. He had a memory like an untidy magpie; he knew a lot of law, but if he could remember a name slightly wrong he – almost as though on purpose – managed to. That first slip with my surname was just like him; and afterwards, particularly when he was annoyed, apprehensive or guilty because of me, he frequently called me Ellis.

So, in the smell of Getliffe's tobacco, I listened to him as he produced case after case, sometimes incomprehensibly, because of his allusive slang, often inaccurately. He loved the law. He loved parading his knowledge and giving me 'a tip or two'. When I was too impatient to let a false date pass, he would look shamefaced, and then say: 'You're coming on! You're coming on!'

Then he got into the habit, at the end of such an afternoon, of asking me to 'try a draft' – 'Just write me a note to keep your hand in,' said Getliffe. 'Don't be afraid to spread yourself. You can manage three or four pages. Just to keep you from rusting.'

The first time it happened I read for several afternoons in the Inn library, wrote my 'opinion' with care, saw Getliffe flicker his eyes over it and say 'You're coming on!' and then heard nothing more about it. But the second time I did hear something more. Again I had presented the opinion as professionally as I could. Then one morning Getliffe, according to his custom, invited all three of us pupils to attend a conference. The solicitors and clients sat round his table; Getliffe, his pipe put away, serious and responsible, faced them. He began the conference with his usual zest. 'I hope you don't think that I'm a man to raise false hopes,' he said earnestly. 'One would rather shout the winners out in the street up there. But frankly I've put in some time on this literature, and I'm ready to tell you that we should be just a little bit over-cautious if we didn't go to court.' To my astonishment, he proceeded firmly to give the substance of my note. In most places he had not troubled to alter the words.

At the end of that conference, Getliffe gave me what my mother would have called an 'old-fashioned' look.

He repeated this manœuvre two or three times, before, during one of our afternoon *tête-à-têtes*, he said:

'You're doing some nice odd jobs for me, aren't you?'

I was delighted. He was so fresh and open that one had to respond.

'I wanted to tell you that,' said Getliffe. 'I wanted to tell you something else,' he added with great seriousness, 'It's not fair that you shouldn't get any credit. One must tell people that you're doing some of the thinking. One's under an obligation to push your name before the public.'

I was more delighted still. I expected a handsome acknowledgement at the next conference.

I noticed that, just before the conference, Getliffe looked at the other pupils and not at me. But I still had high hopes. I still had them, while he recounted a long stretch from my latest piece of devilling. He had muddled some of it, I thought. Then he stared at the table, and said:

'Perhaps one ought to mention the help one sometimes gets from one's pupils. Of course one suggests a line of investigation, one reads their *billets-doux*, one advises them how to express themselves. But you know as well as I do, gentlemen, that sometimes these young men do some of the digging for us. Why, there's one minor line of argument in this opinion – it's going too far to say that I shouldn't have discovered it, in fact I had already got my observations in black and white, but I was very glad indeed, I don't mind telling you, when my Mr Ellis hit upon it for himself.'

Getliffe hurried on.

I was enraged. That night, with Charles March, I thrashed over Getliffe's character and my injuries. This was the first time he had taken me in completely. I was too much inflamed, too frightened of the future, to concede that Getliffe took himself in too. Actually, he was a man of generous impulses, and of devious, cunning, cautious afterthoughts. In practice, the afterthoughts usually won. I had not yet found a way to handle him. The weeks and months were running on. I did not know whether he would keep any of his promises, or how he could be forced.

He could not resist making promises – any more than he could resist sliding out of them. Charles March, who was a pupil in another set of chambers, often went with me to hear him plead: one day, in King's Bench 4, it was all according to the usual pattern. Getliffe was only just in time. In he hurried, dragging his feet, slightly untidy and flurried – looking hunted as always, his wig not quite clean nor straight, carrying papers in his hand. As soon as he began to speak, he produced the impression of being both nervous and at ease. He was not a good speaker, nothing like so good as his opponent in this case; the strident note stayed in his voice, but it sounded thin even in that little court; yet he was capturing the sympathy of most people there.

At lunch-time, walking in the gardens, Charles March and I were scornful of his incompetence, envious of his success, incredulously angry that he got away with it.

That night in his room I was able to congratulate him on winning the case. He looked at me with his most responsible air.

'One is glad to pull off something for the clients' sakes,' he said. 'It's the easiest fault to forget that they're the people most concerned. One has to be careful.'

'Still, it's very nice to win,' I said.

Getliffe's face broke into a grin.

'Of course it's nice,' he said. 'It gives me a bigger kick than anything in the world.'

'I expect I shall find it the same,' I said. 'If ever I manage it.'

Getliffe laughed merrily.

'You will, my boy, you will. You've got to remember that this ancient Inn wasn't born yesterday It was born before H.M. Edward Three. No one's ever been in a hurry since. You've just got to kick your heels and look as though you like it. We've all been through it. It's good for us in the end. But I'll tell you this, Eliot' – he said confidentially – 'though I don't often tell it to people in your position, that I don't see why next year you shouldn't be able to keep yourself in cigarettes. And even a very very occasional cigar.' He smiled happily at me. 'When all's said and done, it's a good life,' he said.

Years afterwards, I realised that, when I was his pupil, I crassly underestimated Getliffe as a lawyer. It was natural for me and Charles March to hold our indignation meetings in the Temple gardens; but, though it was hard for young men to accept, some of Getliffe's gifts were far more viable than ours. We overvalued power and clarity of mind, of which we each had a share, and we dismissed Getliffe because of his muddiness. We had not seen enough to know that, for most kinds of success, intelligence is a very minor gift, Getliffe's mind was muddy, but he was a more effective lawyer than men far cleverer, because he was tricky and resilient, because he was expansive with all men, because nothing restrained his emotions, and because he had a simple, humble, tenacious love for his job.

It was too difficult, however, for Charles March and me, in the intellectual arrogance of our youth, to see that truth, much less accept it. And I had a good deal to put up with. I had just discovered Getliffe's comic and pathological meanness with money. He had a physical aversion from signing a cheque or parting with a coin. In the evening, after a case, we occasionally went to the Feathers for a pint of beer. His income was at least four thousand a year, and mine two hundred, but somehow I always paid.

My pupil's year was a harassing one. I was restless. Often I was unhappy. Those nights with Charles March were my only respite from anxiety. They were also much more. Charles became one of the closest friends of my life, and he introduced me into a society, opulent, settled, different from anything I had known. His story, like George Passant's, took such a hold on my imagination that I have chosen to tell it in full, separated from my own. All that I need say here is that, during my first year in London, I began to dine with Charles's family in Bryanston Square and his relatives in great houses near. It seemed my one piece of luck in all those months.

I had to return from those dinner parties to my bleak flat. Apart from the evenings with Charles, I had no comfort at all. On other nights I used to stay late in chambers, and then walk up Kingsway and across Bloomsbury, round Bedford Square under the peeling plane trees, past the restaurants of Charlotte Street, up Conway Street to number thirty-seven, where there was a barber's shop on the ground floor and my flat on the third. Whenever I threw open the door, I looked at the table. The light from the landing fell across it, before I could reach the switch. There might be a letter or telegram from Sheila.

The sitting-room struck cold each night when I returned. I could not afford to have a fire all day, and my landlady, amiable but scatter-brained, could never remember which nights I was coming home. Most evenings the table was empty, there was no letter, my hopes dropped and the room turned darker. I knelt on the hearth and lit a firelighter, before going out to make my supper off a sandwich at the nearest bar. Even when the fire had caught, it was a desolate room. There were two high-backed arm-chairs, covered with satin which was wearing through; an old hard sofa which stood just off the hearthrug and on which I kept papers and books; the table, with two chairs beside it; and an empty sideboard. My bedroom attained the same standard of discomfort, and to reach it I had to walk across the landing. The tenants of the fourth floor also walked across the same landing on their way upstairs.

I need not have lived so harshly. For an extra twenty pounds a year, I could have softened things for myself; and, by the scale of my debts, another twenty pounds paid out meant nothing at all, as I well knew. But, as though compelled by a profound instinct, I paid no attention to the voice of sense. Somehow I must live so as constantly to remind myself that I had nowhere near arrived. The more uncomfortable I was, the more will I could bend to my career. This was no resting place. When I had satisfied myself, it would be time to indulge.

I sat by the fire on winter nights, working on one of Getliffe's 'points', forcing back the daydreams, forcing back the anxious hope that tomorrow there would be a letter from Sheila. For I was waiting for letters more abjectly than for briefs. When I asked her to come back, I had surrendered. I had asked for her on her own terms, which were no terms at all. I had no power over her. I could only wait for what she did and gave.

It suited her. She came to see me quite often, at least once a month. With her nostalgia for the dingy, she used to take a room at a shabby Greek hotel a couple of streets away. And she came, out of her own caprices and because of her own needs. Her caprices had her usual acid tone, which I could not help but like. A telegram arrived: CANNOT BEAR MY FATHER'S VOICE PREFER YOURS FOR TWO DAYS SHALL APPEAR THIS EVENING. Once, without any warning, I found her sitting in my room when I got back late at night.

Occasionally we were happy, as though she were on the edge of falling in love with me. But she was flirting with man after man, lit up each time with the familiar hope that here at last was someone who could hypnotise her into complete love. I had to listen to that string of adventures, for she used her power over me to compel me into the rôle of confidant. She trusted me, she thought I understood her better than the others, she found me soothing. Sometimes I could smooth her forehead and lift the dread away. In part she relished playing on my jealousy, hearing me in torment as I questioned her, seeing me driven to another masochistic search.

One morning in February there was a postcard on my breakfast-tray. At the sight of the handwriting my heart leaped. Then I read: 'I want you to dine with me at the Mars tomorrow (Tuesday). I may have a man with me I should like you to meet.'

I went as though I had no will.

The glass of the restaurant door was steamed over in the cold. Inside, I stared frenziedly round. She was sitting alone, her face pallid and scornful.

Still in my hat and coat, I went to her.

'Where is this man?' I said.

She said:

'He was useless.'

We talked little over the meal. But I could not rest without asking some questions. He was another of her lame dogs: she thought he was deep and mysterious, and then that he was empty. She was dejected. I tried to console her. I was stifling the rest, and fell silent.

Afterwards we walked into Soho Square, on the way home. Abruptly she said:

'Why don't you get rid of me?'

'It's too late.'

'You'd like to, wouldn't you?'

'Don't you think I should?' I said flatly, in utter tiredness. She pressed my fingers, and there was no more to say.

All through those months when I was struggling to get started, I could not talk to her about my worries. It was to Charles March that I had to trace and retrace the problems, boring to anyone else, acutely real to me. Was Percy giving me my share of the guinea and two-guinea cases? Would Getliffe let me off the last instalments of my pupil's fees? Had I won any kind of backing yet? Would Getliffe give me a hand, if it cost him nothing, or would he stand in my way?

Sheila could not imagine that daily life of trivial manœuvre, contrivance, petty gains and setbacks. She concerned herself about my need for money, and she bought presents which saved me from taking five pounds one month, ten pounds another, out of my scholarship. In that way she was generous, for, since Mr Knight parted with money only a little more easily than Getliffe, she had to go without dresses, which she did not mind, and beg her father for an extra allowance, which she minded painfully. But the frets and intrigues – those she could not enter. Since we first met, she had taken it for granted that I should prevail. As for my struggles with Getliffe, they did not matter. She could not believe that I cared so much.

CHAPTER XXXIV

A FRIEND'S CASE

PERCY did me no favours in my first year. But he did me no disfavours either. He was neutral, as though I were still under supervision, might be worth backing or might have to be written off. I received my share of the 'running down' cases, the insignificant defences of motoring prosecutions that came Percy's way. Percy also advised me how to pick up more at the police courts. I used to attend several, on the off-chance of a guinea. Those courts were only a few miles apart, but in society the distance was vast – from the smart businessmen showing off their cars on the way home from the tennis court, to the baffled, stupid, foreign prostitutes, the ponces and bullies, the street bookmakers, the blousy landladies of the Pimlico back-streets.

From that police court work, in the year from October '27 to July '28, I earned just under twenty-five pounds. And that was my total professional income for the year. I mentioned the fact to Percy.

'Yes, sir,' he said impassively. 'It's just about what I should have expected.'

He took pleasure in being discreet. But he relented to the extent of telling me that many men, perhaps the majority of men, did worse. And he said, by way of aside, that I ought not to start lecturing or marking papers; I had plenty of energy, but I might need it all; this was a long-distance race, not a sprint, said Percy. It was then I realised that Percy was judiciously, cold-bloodedly, watching my health.

I intended to press Getliffe about my last instalment of fees. He had promised to remit it if I had earned my keep; I had done more than that, I had saved him weeks of work, and he must not be allowed to think that I was over-soft. I knew more of him now. The only way to make him honour a bargain, I thought, was to play on his generous impulse and at the same moment to threaten: to meet expansiveness with expansiveness, to say that he was a fine fellow who could never break his word – but that he would be a low confidence trickster if he did.

The trouble was, as the time came near I found it impossible to get an undisturbed half hour with him. He could smell danger from afar, or see it in one's walk. Somehow he became busier than ever. When, for want of any other opportunity, I caught him on the stairs, he said reprovingly and matily: 'Don't let's talk shop out of hours, Ellis. It can wait. Tomorrow is also a day.'

At the beginning of the long vacation he went abroad for a holiday; the first I knew of it was a genial wave from the door of our room and a breathless, strident shout: 'Taxi's waiting! Taxi's waiting!' He left with nothing settled, I still had not edged in a word. He also left me with a piece of work, arduous and complex, on a case down for October.

Two days after his return, at last I seized the chance to talk.

'I've not paid you my last quarter's fees,' I said. 'But—'

'All contributions thankfully received,' said Getliffe.

'I'd like to discuss my position,' I said. 'I've done some work for you, you know, and you said—'

Getliffe met my eyes with his straightforward gaze.

'I'm going to let you pay that quarter, Eliot,' he said. 'I know what you're going to say. I know you've done things for me, I know that better than you do. But I'm thinking of my future pupils, Eliot. I've tried to give you more experience than you'd have got in the chambers of most of our learned friends. I make it a matter of principle to give my pupils experience, and I hope I always shall. But if I start letting them off their fees when they take advantage of their opportunities – well, I know myself too well, Eliot, I shall just stop putting things in their way. So I'm going to accept your cheque. Of course this next year we must have a business arrangement. This just wipes the slate clean.'

Before I could reply, he told me jollyingly that soon he would be inviting me to a party.

That party was dangled in front of me in many conversations afterwards. Now that my pupil's year was over, I was not called so often into Getliffe's room. For his minor devilling, he was using a new pupil called Parry. But for several cases he relied on me, for I was quick and had the knack of writing an opinion so that he could master its headings in the midst of his hurrying magpie-like raids among his papers. In return, I wanted to be paid – or better, recommended to a solicitor to take a case for which Getliffe had no time. Some days he promised one reward, some days another. When I was exigent, he said with his genial, humble smile that soon I should be receiving an invitation from his wife. 'We want you to come to our party,' he said. 'We're both looking forward to it no end, L.S.' (He was the only person alive who called me by my initials.)

It was nearly Christmas before at last I was asked to their house in Holland Park. I found my way through the Bayswater streets, vexed and rebellious. I was being used, I was being cheated shamelessly – no, not shamelessly, I thought with a glimmer of amusement, for each of Getliffe's bits of sharp practice melted him into a blush of shame. But repentance never had the slightest effect on his actions. He grieved sincerely for what he had done, and then did it again. He was exploiting me, he was taking the maximum advantage of being my only conceivable patron. And now he fobbed me off with a treat like a schoolboy. Did he know the first thing about me? Was it all unconsidered, had he the faintest conception of the mood in which I was going to my treat?

Their drawing-room was large and bright and light. Getliffe himself looked out of place, dishevelled, boyishly noisy, his white tie not clean and a little bedraggled. His wife was elegantly dressed; she clung to my hand, fixed me with warm spaniel-like eyes, close to mine, and said: 'It is nice to see you. Herbert has said such a lot about you. He's always saying how much he wishes I had the chance of seeing you. I do wish I could see more of you all—'

Watching her later at the dinner-table, I thought she was almost a lovely woman, if only she had another expression beside that of eager, cooing fidelity. She was quite young: Getliffe at that time was just over forty, and she was a few years less. They were very happy. He had, as usual, done himself well. They talked enthusiastically about children's books, Getliffe protruding his under-lip and comparing Kenneth Grahame and A. A. Milne, his wife regarding him with an eager loving stare, their warmth for each other fanned by the baby-talk.

Once Mrs Getliffe prattled:

'Herbert always says you people do most of his work for him.' We laughed together.

They talked of pantomimes: they had two children, to what show should they be taken? Getliffe remarked innocently how, when he was an undergraduate, he had schemed to take his half-brother Francis to the pantomime – not for young Francis's enjoyment, but for his own.

That was the party. I said goodbye, in a long-hand clasp with Mrs Getliffe. Getliffe took me into the hall. 'I hope you've enjoyed yourself, L.S.,' he said.

When I thanked him, he went on:

'We may not be the best chambers in London – but we do have fun!'

His face was merry. On the way home, grinning at my own expense, I could not be certain whether his eyes were innocent, or wore their brazen, defiant stare.

In that bitterly cold winter of '28–'29 I reached a depth of discontent. I ached, even more than before, for this suspense to end. In my memory it remained one of the periods I would least have chosen to live through again. And yet there must have been good times. I was being entertained by the Marches, I was making friends in a new society. Long afterwards Charles March told me that I seemed brimming with interest, and even he had not perceived how hungry and despondent I became. That is how I remembered the time, without relief – I remembered myself dark with my love for Sheila, fretting for a sign of recognition in my job, poor, seeing no sign of a break. It was worse because Charles himself, in that December, was given his first important case. It was nothing wonderful – the brief was marked at twenty-five guineas – but it was a chance to shine, and for such a chance just then I would have begged or stolen.

Charles was working in the chambers of a relation by marriage, and the case was arranged through other connections of his family. Nothing could be more natural as a start for a favourably born young man. As he told me, I was devoured by envy. Sheer rancorous envy, the envy of the poor for the rich, the unlucky for the lucky, the wallflower for the courted. I tried to rejoice in his luck, and I felt nothing but envy.

I hated feeling so. I had been jealous in love, but this envy was more degrading. In jealousy there was at least the demand for another's love, the sustenance of passion – while in such envy as I felt for Charles there was nothing but the sick mean stab. I hated that I should be so possessed. But I was hating the human condition. For as I saw more of men in society I thought in the jet-black moments that envy was the most powerful single force in human affairs – that, and the obstinate desire of the flesh to persist. Given just those two components to build with, one could construct too much of the human scene.

I tried to make conscious amends. I offered to help him on the brief; the case was a breach of contract, and I knew the subject well. Charles let me help, and I did a good share of the work. He was himself awkward and conscience-stricken. Once, as we were studying the case, he said:

'I'm just realising how true it is – that it's not so easy to forgive someone, when you're taking a monstrously unfair advantage over him.'

The case was down to be heard in January. I sat by the side of Charles's father and did not miss a word. The judge had only recently gone to the bench, and was very alert and sharp-witted, sitting alone against the red upholstery of the Lord Chief Justice's court. Mr March and I placed ourselves for a day and a half near the door, so as not to catch Charles's eye. Charles's loud voice resounded in the narrow room; his face looked thinner under his new, immaculate wig. The case was a hopeless one from the start. Yet I thought that he was doing well. He impressed all in court by his cross-examination of an expert witness. In the end he lost the case, but the judge went out of his way to pay a compliment: the losing side might, the judge hoped, take consolation from the fact that their case could not have been more lucidly presented.

It was a handsome compliment. It should have been mine, I felt again. Men stood round Charles, congratulating him, taking his luck for granted. I went to join them, to add my own congratulations. Partly I meant them, partly I was pleased – but I would not have dared to look deep into what I felt.

I went back to chambers and told Getliffe the result. It happened that his half-brother, Francis, had been a contemporary and friend of Charles's at Cambridge. Getliffe scarcely knew Charles, but he had a healthy respect for the powerful, and he assured me earnestly:

'Mark my words, Eliot, that young friend of ours will go a long way.'

'Of course he will.'

'Mind you,' said Getliffe, 'he's got some pull. He is old Philip March's nephew, isn't he? It helps in our game, Eliot, one can't pretend it doesn't help.'

Getliffe gazed at me, man to man.

'Don't you wish you were in that racket, Eliot?'

I explained, clearly and with some force, how the brief had arrived at Charles. As a pupil, he had not done much work for his master, Albert Hart, who stood to Charles as Getliffe did to me; but Hart had used much contrivance to divert this case to Charles.

'I've been thinking,' said Getliffe, his mood changing like lightning, 'that you ought to do some shooting yourself before very long. Would you like to, L.S.?'

'Wouldn't you in my place? Wouldn't you?'

'Well, one's roping in quite a bit of paper nowadays. I must look through them and see if there's one you could tackle. I should advise you not to start if you can help it with anything too ambitious. If you drop too big a brick, it means there's one firm of solicitors who won't leave their cards on you again.'

Then he looked at his most worried, and his voice took on a strident edge.

'I must see if I can find you a snippet for yourself one of these days. The trouble is, one owes a duty to one's clients. One can't forget that, much as one would like to.'

He pointed his pipe at me.

'You see my point, Eliot,' he said defiantly. 'One would like to distribute one's briefs to one's young friends. Why shouldn't one? What's the use of money if one never has time to enjoy it? I'd like to give you a share of my work tomorrow. But one can't help feeling a responsibility to one's clients. One can't help one's conscience.'

CHAPTER XXXV

THE FREEZING NIGHT

SOON after Charles's case, the temperature stayed below freezing-point for days on end. For the first time since I went to London, I stayed away from chambers. There was nothing to force me there. During two whole days I went out into the iron frost only for my evening meal, and came back to lie, as I had done all the afternoon, on my sofa in front of the fire.

The cold was at its most intense when Sheila visited me. It was nine o'clock on a bitter February night. She came and sat on the hearth-rug, close to the fire; I lay still on the sofa.

We were quiet. For a moment there was noise, as she rattled the shovel in the coal-scuttle. 'Don't get up. I'll do it,' she said, and knelt, shovelling the coals. Then she stared at the fire again, the darkened fire, cherry-red between the bars, with spurts of gas from the new coal.

We were quiet in the room, and outside the street was silent in the extreme cold.

I watched. She was kneeling, sitting back on her heels, her back straight; I could see her face in profile, softer than when she met me with her full gaze. The curve of her cheek was smooth and young, and a smile pulled on the edge of her mouth.

The fire was burning through, tinting her skin, reminding me of evenings in childhood. She took the poker, stoked through the bars, then left it there. She studied the cave that formed as the poker began to glow.

'Queer,' she said.

The cave enlarged, radiant, like a landscape on the sun.

'Oh, handsome,' she said.

She was sitting upright. I saw the swell of her breast, I saw only that.

I gripped her by the shoulders and kissed her on the mouth. She kissed me back. For a moment we pressed together; then, as I became more violent, she struggled and shrank away.

In the firelight she stared up at me.

'Why are you looking at me like that?' she cried. 'No.'

I said:

'I want you.'

I seized her, forced her towards me, forced my lips upon hers. She fought. She was strong, but I was possessed. 'I can't,' she cried. I tore her dress at the neck. 'I can't,' she cried, and burst into a scream of tears.

That sound reached me at last. Appalled, I let her go. She threw herself face downwards on the rug and sobbed and then became silent.

We were quiet in the room again. She sat up and looked at me. Her brow was lined. It was a long time before she spoke.

'Am I absolutely frigid?' she said.

I shook my head.

'Shall I always be?'

'I shouldn't think so. No.'

'I'm afraid of it. You know that.'

Then suddenly she rose to her feet.

'Take me for a walk,' she said. 'It will do me good.'

I said that it was intolerably cold. I did not want to walk: I had injured my heel that morning.

'Please take me,' she said. And then I could not refuse.

Before we went out she asked for a safety-pin to hold her dress together. She smiled, quite placidly, as she asked, and as she inspected a bruise on her arm.

'You have strong hands,' she said.

Outside my room the cold made us catch our breath. On the stairs, where usually there wafted rich waves of perfume from the barber's shop, all scent seemed frozen out. In the streets the lights sparkled diamond-sharp.

We walked apart, down the back streets, along Tottenham Court Road. My heel was painful, and on that foot I only trod upon the sole. She was not looking at me, she was staring in front of her, but on the resonant pavement she heard me limping.

'I'm sorry,' she said, and took my arm.

In snatches she began to talk. She was a little released because I had tried to ravish her. She could not talk consecutively – so much of her life was locked within her; especially she could not bring out the secret dread and daydream in which she was obsessed by physical love. Yet, after her horror by the fireside, she was impelled to speak, flash out some fragment from her past, in the trust that I would understand. How she had, more ignorant than most girls, wondered about the act of love. How she dreaded it. There was nothing startling in what she said. But, for her, it was a secret she could only let out in a flash of words, then silence, then another flash. For what to another woman would have been matter-of-fact, for her was becoming an obsession, so that often, in her solitary thoughts, she believed that she was incapable of taking a man's love.

Trafalgar Square was almost empty to the bitter night, as she and I walked arm in arm.

I did not know enough of the region where flesh and spirit touch. I did not know enough of the aberrations of the flesh, nor how, the more so because they are ridiculous except to the sufferer, they can corrode a life. If I had been older, I could perhaps have soothed her just a little. If I had been older and not loved her; for all my thoughts of love, all my sensual hopes and images of desire, belonged to her alone. My libido could find no other home; I had got myself seduced by a young married woman, but it had not deflected my imagination an inch from the girl walking at my side, had not diluted by a drop that total of desire, erotic and amorous, playful and passionate, which she alone invoked. Hers was the only body I wanted beside me at night. And so I was the wrong man to listen to her. If I had been twice my age, and not loved her, I could have told her of other lives like her own; I should have been both coarser and tenderer; and I should have told her that, at worst, it is wonderful how people can come to terms and make friends of the flesh. But I was twenty-three, I loved her to madness, I was defeated and hungry with longing.

So she walked, silent again, down Whitehall and I limped beside her. Yet it seemed that she was soothed. It was strange after that night, but she held my hand. Somehow we were together, and she did not want to part. We stood on Westminster Bridge, gazing at the black water; it was black and oily, except at the banks, where slivers of ice split and danced in the light.

'Too cold to jump,' she said. She was laughing. Big Ben struck twelve. 'How's the foot?' she said. 'Strong enough to walk home?'

I could scarcely put it to the ground, but I would have walked with her all night. She shook her head. 'No. I'm going to buy us a taxi.'

She came back to my room, where the fire was nearly out. She built it up again, and made tea. I lay on the sofa, and she sat on the hearth-rug, just as we had done two hours before, and between us there was a kind of peace.

CHAPTER XXXVI

A STROKE OF LUCK

IN the early summer of 1929 I had my first great stroke of luck. Charles March intervened on my behalf. He was a proud man: for himself he could not have done what he did for me. No man was more sensitive to affronts, but for me he risked them. He was importunate with some of his connections. I was invited to a garden party and scrutinised by men anxious to oblige Sir Philip March's nephew. I was asked to dinner, and met Henriques, one of the most prosperous of Jewish solicitors. Charles sat by as impresario, anxious to show me at my best. As it happened, I was less constrained than he. The Harts and Henriques were shrewd, guarded, professional men, but I was soon at my ease, as I had been with Eden. I had everything in my favour; they wished to please Charles, and I had only to pass muster.

In June the first case arrived. It lay on my table, in the shadow. Outside the window the gardens were brilliant in the sunlight, and a whirr came from a lawn-mower cutting grass down below. I was so joyful that for a second I left the papers there, in the shadow. Then it all seemed a matter of everyday, something to act upon, no longer a novelty. The brief came from Henriques, bore the figures 20 + 1. The case was a libel action brought by a man called Chapman. It looked at a first reading straightforward and easy to win.

But there was little time to prepare. It was down for hearing in three days' time. Percy explained that the man to whom the case had first gone was taken suddenly ill; and Henriques had remembered me. It got him out of a difficulty, did me a good turn, and after all I was certain to have three days completely free.

I was sent a few notes from the barrister who had thrown up the case, and worked night and day. My four or five hours' sleep was broken, as I woke up with a question on my mind. I switched on the light, read through a page, made a jotting, just as I used to when preparing for an examination. I was strung-up, light-headed as well as lucid, and excessively cheerful.

Henriques behaved with a consideration that he did not parade, though it came from a middle-aged and extremely rich solicitor to a young and penniless member of the Bar. He called for a conference in person, instead of sending one of his staff; he acted as though this were a weighty brief being studied by the most eminent of silks. Getliffe was so much impressed by Henriques's attention that he found it necessary to take a hand himself, and with overflowing cordiality pressed me to use his room for the conference.

Henriques made it plain that we were expected to win. Unless I were hopelessly incompetent, I knew that we must. The knowledge made me more nervous: when I got on my feet in court, the judge's face was a blur, so were the jurors'; I was uncertain of my voice. But, as though a record was playing, my arguments came out. Soon the judge's face came clear through the haze, bland, cleft-chinned. I saw a juror, freckled, attentive, frowning. I made a faint joke. I was beginning to enjoy myself.

Our witnesses did all I wanted of them. I had one main fact to prove: that the defendant knew Chapman well, not merely as an acquaintance. As I finished with our last witness, I thought, though still anxious, still touching wood, that our central point was unshakeable. The defence's only hope was to smear it over and suggest a coincidence. Actually my opponent tried that tack, but so tangled himself that he never made it clear. He seemed to have given up hope before the case began, and his speech was muddled and ill-arranged. He was a man of Allen's standing, with more force and a larger practice, but nothing like so clever. He called only three witnesses, and by the time two had been heard I was aglow. It was as good as over.

Their last witness came to the box. All I had to do was to make him admit that he and Chapman and the defendant had often met together. It was obviously so – he could not deny it; it left our main point unassailable, and the case was clear. But I made a silly mistake. I could not let well alone; I thought the witness was malicious and had another interest in attacking Chapman. I began asking him about it. I was right in my human judgment, but it was bad tactics in law. First, it was an unnecessary complication: second, as the witness answered, his malice emerged – but so also did his view that Chapman was lying. I was sweating beneath my wig. I perceived what he was longing for the chance to say. I pulled up sharp. It was better to leave that line untidy, and bolt to the safe one; sweating, flustered, discomfited, I found my tongue was not forsaking me, was inventing a bridge that took me smoothly back. It happened slickly. I was cool enough to wonder how many people had noticed the break.

With the jury out, I sat back, uneasy. I went over the case: surely it stood, surely to anyone it must have appeared sound? Foolishly I had done it harm, but surely that had affected nothing?

The jury were very quick. Before I heard the verdict, I knew all was well. I did not want to shout: I just wanted to sink down in relief.

'Very nice,' said Henriques, who had, with his usual courtesy, made another personal appearance. 'My best thanks. If I may say so, you had it in hand all the way. I apologise again for giving you such short notice. Next time we shan't hurry you so much.'

Charles took my hand, and, as Henriques left, began to speak.

'I'm glad,' he said. 'But whatever possessed you to draw that absurd red-herring?'

Just then, I should have liked to be spared Charles's tongue. No one expressed the unflattering truth more pointedly. I thought that I had recovered well, I should have liked some praise.

'I'm very glad,' said Charles. 'But you realise that it might have been a serious mistake? You missed the point completely, don't you agree?'

On the other hand, Getliffe assumed responsibility for my success. He came into my room in chambers (I still had my table in Allen's room) and spoke at large as though he had done it himself. He decided to organise a celebration. While I was writing to Sheila, Getliffe booked a table at the Savoy for dinner and telephoned round to make the party. They were gathered in Getliffe's haphazard manner – some were friends of mine, some I scarcely knew, some, like Salisbury, were acquaintances none too well pleased that at last I should begin to compete. That did not worry Getliffe. Incidentally, though the members of the party were invited haphazard, there was nothing haphazard about the arrangements for payment: Getliffe made sure that each of the guests came ready to pay for himself.

Charles did not come. He was already booked for a dinner-party, but Getliffe expressed strong disapproval. 'He ought to have put anything else off on a night like this! Still,' said Getliffe, 'it's his loss, not ours. We're going to have a good time!' Then Getliffe added, in his most heartfelt tone: 'And while we're talking, L.S., I've always thought young March might have done a bit more for you. He might have pulled a rope or two to get you started. Instead of leaving everything to your own devices – plus, of course, the bits and pieces I've been able to do for you myself.'

I wondered if I had heard aright. It was colossal. Yet, as he spoke, Getliffe was believing every word. That was one of his gifts.

At the party I was seated next to a good-looking girl. Tired, attracted to her, half-drunk, triumphant, I spread myself in boasting, as I had not boasted since my teens.

'I feel extremely jubilant,' I said.

'You look it,' she replied.

'I've often wished that I'd chosen a different line,' I went on. 'I mean, something where one got started quicker. But this is going to be worth waiting for when it comes.'

Provocatively, she talked about friends at the Bar.

'I could have done other things,' I went on bragging. 'I'd have backed myself to come off in several different jobs!'

The irony of the party made me laugh aloud. My first victory – and here I was being drunk to by Getliffe, his smile merry, wily, and open. My first victory – not an intimate friend there, but a good many rivals instead. My first victory – instead of having Sheila in my arms, I was boasting wildly to this cool and pretty girl.

Within three days I received something more than congratulations. Percy spoke to me one morning in the hall, in his usual manner, authoritative under the servility:

'I should like a word with you, Mr Eliot.'

I went into his cubby-hole.

'I've got something for you,' he said.

As I thanked him, Percy's smile was firm but gratified, the smile of power, the smile of a conferrer of benefits.

'Well, sir,' said Percy, 'you've given me a bit to go on now. I can tell them that you won the Chapman case for Henriques. It's not much, but it's better than nothing.'

In fact, Percy had decided that it was safe to give me a minor recommendation. He had been watching me for two years, with interest, never letting his sympathy – though whether he had sympathy I was not sure – interfere with his judgment. He had eked out the driblets, the guineas and the two guineas, to keep me from despair, but he would go no further. Now someone else had taken the risk, Percy was ready to speak in my favour just as much as the facts justified.

This case came from solicitors who had no contact at all with my Jewish friends. It was a case which happened to be rather like Charles's first. It would bring me thirty guineas.

Between July '28 and July '29, I had earned eighty-eight pounds. But of this sum, fifty-two pounds ten had arrived since June, on those two cases. It was more promising than it looked. I dared not tell myself so, but the hope was there. I hoped I was coming through.

CHAPTER XXXVII

VALUE IN OTHERS' EYES

I BEGAN to see how luck attracts luck. Before the long vacation, I received my biggest case so far, from one of Charles March's connections, and at the same time heard that another was coming from Henriques. In high spirits, I felt the trend ought to be encouraged, and so I set to work playing on Getliffe's nature. I was determined not to let him wriggle out of every promise; now the stream was running with me, I intended to make Getliffe help. We had several most moving and heartfelt conversations. I told him that I could not afford a holiday, unless I was certain of earning three hundred pounds next year.

Getliffe said:

'You know, L.S., it's an uncertain life for all of us. How much do you think I'm certain of myself? Only a few hundred. That's the meal-ticket, you understand. I manage to rake in a bit more by way of extras. But as a steady income I can't count on as much as the gentleman who reads my income-tax return.' He was grave with emotion at this thought. 'Then I think of taking silk!' he said. 'It'd be just throwing the steady bread and butter out of the window. I expect I shall some day. One never counts one's blessings. And I can't tell you this,' he added, 'if and when I do take silk, there'll be plenty of confetti coming into the chambers for chaps like you.'

'I'd like a bit more now,' I said.

'So should we all, L.S.,' said Getliffe reprovingly.

But I was becoming more practised with him.

'Look,' I said. 'I'm getting a few briefs now. Charles March has done more than his share. So has Henriques. I think you should do yours now. You've promised to find me some work. I think this would be a good time.'

Getliffe looked at me with a sudden, earnest smile.

'I'm very glad you've spoken like that, L.S. I believe you've spoken like a friend. People sometimes tell me I'm selfish. I get worried. You see, I'm not conscious of it. I should hate to think of myself like that. I want my friends to pull me up if ever they think I'm doing wrong.'

Next day, though, he might think better of it. There was a very strong rumour – I never knew whether it was true – that whenever he took a holiday he tried to divert any cases which might be on the way. He did not divert them to bright young men, but to a middle-aged and indifferently competent figure who came so seldom into chambers that I scarcely knew him. That rumour might be true, I thought: Getliffe did not welcome the sound of youth knocking at the door. Still, I should make him keep his promise.

As I told Getliffe, I could not afford a holiday, but I spent a week that summer with my old friends in the town. I had not been in close touch with them since I came to London. George Passant visited me regularly once a quarter, but I had only returned myself for odd days, when Eden sent me a two-guinea brief on the Midland Circuit. To many people it seemed strange, and they thought me heartless.

That was not accurate. When I stayed in London and avoided the town, it was for a complex of reasons – partly I had to think of the railway fare, partly I was shy of dogging Sheila's tracks, partly I had an instinct to hide until I could come back successful. But the strongest reason was also the simplest: George and the group did not particularly want me. They loved me, they were proud of me, they rejoiced in any victory I won – but I had gone from their intense intimate life, I was no longer in the secrets of the circle, and it was an embarrassment, almost an intrusion, when I returned. So, as the train drew into the station on an August evening, I was unreasonably depressed. From the carriage window I had seen the houses gleam under the clear night sky; the sulphurous smell of the station, confined within the red brick walls, was as it used to be, when I returned home from dining at the Inn; my heart sank.

George greeted me like a conquering hero, and so did the group. In my mood that night, it made me worse to have others over-confident about my future. I explained sharply that I had made an exceptional start for an unknown young man, but that was all. I had been lucky in my friends, I had the advantage in solicitors' eyes of looking older than I was – but the testing-time was the next two years. It was too early to cheer. George would not listen to my disclaimers. Robustly, obtusely, he shouted them away. He was not going to be deprived of his drinking-party. They all drank cheerfully; they were drinking harder than ever, now that they were a little less impoverished; they would rather have been at the farm, without a revenant from earlier days, but nevertheless they were happy to get drunk. But it was sadly that I got drunk that night.

Afterwards, George and I walked by ourselves to his lodgings. I asked about some of our old companions: then I felt the barrier come between us. George was content and comfortable in my presence so long as I left the group alone. I asked about Jack, who had not met me that evening.

'Doing splendidly, of course,' said George, and hurried to another subject.

But it was George who volunteered information on one old friend. Marion was engaged to be married. George did not know the man, or the story, and had scarcely seen her, but he had heard that she was overwhelmingly happy.

I should have wished to be happy for her. But I was not. In the pang with which I heard the news, I learned how unsparingly voracious one is.

Any love that comes one's way – it is bitter to let go. I had not seen Marion for eighteen months, all my love was given to another. Yet it was painful to lose her. It was the final weight on that sad homecoming.

But I was soon cheered up by a ridiculous lunch at the Knights'. Sheila and I had gone through no storms that summer; she had been remotely affectionate, and she had not threatened me with the name of any other man. And she was pleased at my success. In front of her parents she teased me about the income I should soon be earning, about the money and honours on which I had my eye. It seemed to her extremely funny.

It did not seem, however, in the least funny to her father and mother. It seemed to them a very serious subject. At that lunch I found myself being regarded as a distinctly more estimable character.

They were beginning to be worried about Sheila. Mrs Knight was a woman devoid of intuition, and she could not begin to guess what was wrong. All Mrs Knight observed were the rough-and-ready facts of the marriage-market. Sheila was already twenty-four and, like me, often passed for thirty. For all her flirtations, she had given no sign of getting married. Lately she had brought no one home, except me for this lunch. To Mrs Knight, those were ominous facts. Whereas her husband had been uneasy about Sheila's state of mind since her adolescence, and had suppressed his uneasiness simply because in his selfish and self-indulgent fashion he did not choose to be disturbed.

Thus they were each prepared, if not to welcome me, at least to modify their discouragement. Mr Knight went further. He took me into the rose garden, lit a cigar, and, as we both sat in deckchairs, talked about the careers of famous counsel. It was all done at two removes from me, with Mr Knight occasionally giving me a sideways glance from under his eyelids. He showed remarkable knowledge, and an almost Getliffian enthusiasm, about the pricing of briefs. I had never met a man with more grasp of the financial details of another profession. Without ever asking a straightforward question he was guessing the probable curve of my own income. He was interested in its distribution – what proportion would one earn in High Court work, in London outside the High Court, on the Midland Circuit? Mr Knight was moving surreptitiously to his point.

'I suppose you will be appearing now and then on circuit?'

'If I get some work.'

'Ah. It will *come*. It *will* come. I take it,' said Mr Knight, looking in the opposite direction and thoughtfully studying a rose, 'that you might conceivably appear some time at the local assizes?'

I agreed that it was possible.

'If that should happen,' said Mr Knight casually, 'and if ever you want a quiet place to run over your documents, it would give no trouble to slip you into this house.'

I supposed that was his point. I hoped it was. But I was left half-mystified, for Mr Knight glanced at me under his eyelids, and went on:

'You won't be disturbed. You won't be. My wife and daughter might be staying with their relations. I shan't disturb you. I'm always tired. I sleep night and day.'

Whatever did he mean by Sheila and her mother staying with relations, I thought, as we joined them. Was he just taking away with one hand what he gave with the other? Or was there any meaning at all?

I was very happy. Sheila was both lively and docile, and walked along the lanes with me before I left. It was my only taste of respectable courtship.

The Michaelmas Term of 1929 was even more prosperous than I hoped. I lost the case Percy had brought me, but I made them struggle for the verdict, and the damages were low. Percy went so far as to admit that the damages were lower than he expected, and that we could not have done much better in this kind of breach of contract. Henriques's second case was, like the first, straightforward, and I won it. I earned most money, however, from a case in which I did nothing but paper work: this was the case which had come from connections of Charles March just before the vacation. It took some time to settle, and in the end we brought in a K.C. as a threat. The engineering firm of Howard & Hazlehurst were being sued by one of their agents for commission to which he might be entitled in law though not in common sense. The case never reached the courts, for we made a compromise: the K.C.'s brief was marked at one hundred and fifty guineas, and according to custom I was paid two-thirds that fee.

After those events, and before the end of term, at last I scored a point in my long struggle of attrition with Getliffe. I kept reminding him of his promise to unload some of his cases; I kept telling him, firmly, affectionately, reproachfully, in all the tones I could command, that I still had not made a pound through his help. As a rule, I disliked being pertinacious, but with Getliffe it was fun. The struggle swayed to and fro. He promised again; then he was too busy; then he thought, almost tearfully, of his clients; then he offered to pay me a very small fee to devil a very large case. At last, on a December afternoon, his face suddenly became beatific. 'Old H.-J. (a solicitor named Hurton-Jones) is coming in soon! That means work for Herbert. Well, L.S., I'm going to do something for you. I'm going to say to H.-J. that there's a man in these chambers who'll do that job as well as I should. L.S., I can't tell you how glad I am to do something for you. You deserve it, L.S., you deserve it.'

He looked me firmly in the eyes and warmly clasped my hand.

It happened. A ten-guinea brief in the West London County Court came to me from Hurton-Jones: and it had, unquestionably, been offered to Getliffe. Later on, I became friendly with Hurton-Jones, and his recollection was that the conversation with Getliffe went something like this: 'H.-J., do you really want me to do this? Don't get me wrong. Don't think I'm too high-hat to take the county court stuff. It's all grist that comes to the mill, and you know as well as I do, H.-J., that I'm a poor man. But I have got a young chap here – well, I don't say he could do this job, but he might scrape through. Mind you, I like Eliot. Of course, he hasn't proved himself. I don't say that he's ripe for this job –'

Hurton-Jones knew something of Getliffe, and diverted the brief to me. I argued for a day in court, and then we reached a settlement. I had saved our clients a fair sum of money. Getliffe congratulated me, as man to man.

It was a long time before another of his cases found its way to me, but now, by the spring of 1930, I was well under way. Percy judged that he could back me a little farther; Henriques and the Harts were speaking approvingly of me in March circles; Hurton-Jones was trying me on some criminal work, legally dull but shot through with human interest. I was becoming busy. I even knew what it was, as summer approached, to have to refuse invitations to dinner because I was occupied with my briefs.

Just about that time a letter came from Marion. I had written to congratulate her on her engagement, and I had heard that she was married. Now she said that she would much like to visit me. I had a fleeting notion, flattering to my vanity, that she might be in distress and had turned to me for help. But the first sight of her, as she entered my sitting-room, was enough to sweep that daydream right away. She looked sleek, her eyes were shining, she had become much prettier, and she was expensively dressed: though, just as I remembered, she had managed to leave a patch of white powder or scurf on the shoulder of her jacket.

'Not that you can talk,' she grumbled, as I dusted it off.

'I needn't ask whether you're happy,' I said.

'I don't think you really need,' she said.

She was all set to tell me her story. Before we went out to dinner she had to describe exactly how it all happened. She had met Eric at a drama festival and had fallen romantically in love with him, body and soul, she said. And he with her. They fell passionately in love, and decided to get married. According to her account, he was modest, shy, very active physically. It was only after they were engaged that she discovered that he was also extremely rich.

'That's the best example of feminine realism I've ever heard,' I said. Marion threw a book at me.

They were living in a country house in Suffolk. It was all perfect, she said. She was already pregnant.

'What's the use of waiting?' said Marion briskly.

'I must say, I envy you.'

She smiled. 'You ought to get married yourself, my boy.'

'Perhaps,' I said.

She asked suddenly:

'Are you going to marry that woman?'

I was slow to answer. At last I said:

'I hope so.'

Marion sighed.

'It will be a tragedy,' she said. 'You must realise that. You're much too sensible not to see what it would be like. She'll ruin you. Believe me, Lewis, this isn't sour grapes now.'

I shook my head.

'I hate her,' Marion burst out. 'If I could poison her and get away with it, I'd do it like a shot.'

'You don't know all of her,' I said.

'I know the effect she's had on you. No, I don't want you for myself, my dear. I shall love Eric for ever. But there's a corner in my heart for you.' She looked at me, half-maternally. 'Eric's a much better husband than you'd ever have been,' she said. 'Still, I suppose I shan't meet another man like you.'

As we parted she gave me an affectionate kiss.

She had come to show off her happiness, I thought. It was no more than her right. I did not begrudge it. I felt somewhat desolate. It made me think of my own marriage.

For, as I told Marion, I had never stopped hoping to marry Sheila. Since my first proposal I had not asked her again. But she knew, of course, that, whether I was too proud to pester her or not, she had only to show the slightest wish. In fact, we had lately played sometimes with the future. For months past she had seemed to think more of me; her letters were sometimes intimate and content. She had told me, in one of the phrases that broke out from her locked heart: 'With you I don't find joy. But you give me so much hope that I don't want to go away.'

That exalted me more than the most explicit word of love from another woman. I hoped, I believed as well as hoped, that the bond between us was too strong for her to escape, and that she would marry me.

And marriage was at last a practical possibility. I did my usual accounting at the beginning of July 1930. In the last year I had made nearly four hundred and fifty pounds. The cases were coming in. Without touching wood, I reckoned that a comfortable income was secure. More likely than not, I should earn a large one.

Just a week after I went through my accounts I woke in the morning with an attack of giddiness. It was like those I used to have, at the time of the Bar Finals. I was a little worried, but did not think much of it. It took me a day or two to accept the fact that I was unwell. I was forced to remember that I had often felt exhausted in the last months. I had gone home from court, stretched myself on the sofa, been too worn out to do anything but watch the window darken. I tried to pretend it was nothing but fatigue. But the morning giddiness lasted, my limbs were heavy; as I walked, the pavement seemed to sink.

By instinct, I concealed my state from everyone round me. I asked Charles March if he could recommend a doctor; I explained that I had not needed one since I came to London, but that now I had a trivial skin complaint.

I went to Charles's doctor, half anxious, half expecting to be reassured as Tom Devitt had reassured me. I got no decision on the first visit. The doctor was waiting for a blood count. When the result came, it was not clear-cut. I explained to the doctor, whose name was Morris, that I had just established my practice, and could not leave it. I explained that I was hoping to get married. He was kindly and worried. He tried to steady me. 'It's shocking bad luck,' he said. 'But I've got to tell you. You may be rather ill.'

CHAPTER XXXVIII

SOME KINDS OF SUFFERING

In the surgery, my first concern was to put on a stoical front. Alone in my room, I stared out at the summer sky. The doctor had been vague, he was sending me to a specialist. How serious was it? I was enraged that no one should know, that the disaster should be so nebulous, that instead of having mastered the future I could no longer think a month ahead. Sometimes, for moments together, I could not believe it – just as, after Sheila's first cruel act, I walked across the park as though it had not happened. Then I was chilled with dread. How gravely was I ill? I was afraid to die.

Already that afternoon, however, and all the time I was visiting the specialist, there was one direction in which my judgment was clear. No one must know. It would destroy my practice if the truth were known. No one would persevere with a sick young man. That might not matter, I thought grimly. But it was necessary to act as though I should recover. So no one must know, not even my intimates.

I kept that resolve throughout the doctors' tests. Fortunately, it was the long vacation, and Getliffe was away; his inquisitive eyes might have noticed too much. Fortunately also, although I was very pale, I did not look particularly ill; in fact, having had more money and so eating better, I had put on some weight in the past year. I forced myself to crawl tiredly to chambers, sit there for some hours, make an effort to work upon a brief. I thought that Percy had his suspicions, and I tried to deceive him about my spirits and my energy. I mentioned casually that I felt jaded after a hard year and that I might go away for a holiday and miss the first few days of next term.

'Don't be away too long, sir,' said Percy impassively. 'It's easy to get yourself forgotten. It's easy to do that.'

From the beginning the doctors guessed that I had pernicious anaemia. They stuck to the diagnosis even when – as I afterwards realised – they should have been more sceptical. There was some evidence for it. There was no doubt about the anaemia; my blood counts were low and getting lower; but that could have happened (as Tom Devitt had said years ago) through strain and conflict. But also some of the red cells were pear-shaped instead of round, and some otherwise misshapen; since the doctors were ready to believe in a pernicious anaemia, that convinced them.

But the reason why they originally guessed so puzzled me for a long time. For they were sound, cautious doctors of good reputation. It was much later that Charles March, after he had changed his profession and taken to medicine, told me that my physical type was common among pernicious anaemia cases – grey or blue eyes set wide apart, smooth fine skin, thick chest and ectomorphic limbs. Then at last their diagnosis became easy to understand.

They were soon certain of it, assured me that it ought to be controllable, and fed me on hog's stomach. But my blood did not respond: the count went down; and then they did not know what to do. All they could suggest was that I should go abroad and rest, and continue, for want of any other treatment, to eat another protein extract.

This was at the beginning of August. I could leave, as though it were an ordinary holiday. I still kept my secret, although there were times when my nerve nearly broke, or when I was beyond caring. For my resistance was weakening now. Charles March, who knew that I was ill, but not what the doctors had told me, bought my tickets, and booked me a room in Mentone. I was tired out, and glad to go.

I had not seen Sheila since I went to be examined. Now I wrote to her. I was not well, I said, and was being sent abroad for a rest. I was travelling the day after she would receive this letter. I was anxious to see her before I left.

It was my last afternoon in England, and I waited in my room. I knew her trains by heart. That afternoon I did not have long to wait. Within ten minutes of the time that she could theoretically arrive, I heard her step on the stairs.

She came and kissed me. Then she stood back and studied my face.

'You don't look so bad,' she said.

'That's just as well,' I said.

'Why is it?'

I told her it was necessary to go on being hearty in chambers. It was the kind of sarcastic joke that she usually enjoyed, but now her eyes were strained.

'It's not funny,' she said harshly.

She was restless. Her movements were stiff and awkward. She sat down, pulled out a cigarette, then put in back in her case. Timidly she laid a hand on mine.

'I'd no idea there was anything wrong,' she said.

I looked at her.

'It must have been going on for some time,' she said.

'I think it has.'

'I'm usually fairly perceptive,' she said in a tone aggrieved, conceited and remorseful. 'But I didn't notice a thing.'

'I expect you were busy,' I said.

She lost her temper. 'That's the most unpleasant thing you've ever told me.'

She was white with anger, right at the flashpoint of one of her outbursts of acid rage. Then, with an effort, she calmed herself.

'I'm sorry,' she cried. 'I don't know—'

In the lull we talked for a few minutes, neutrally, of where we should dine that night.

Sheila broke away from the conversation, and asked:

'Are you ill?'

I did not reply.

'You must be, or you wouldn't let them send you away. That's true, isn't it?'

'I suppose it is,' I said.

'How badly are you ill?' she asked.

'I don't know. The doctors don't know either.'

'It may be serious?'

'Yes, it may be.'

She was staring full at me.

'I don't think you'll die in obscurity,' she said in a high, level voice, with a curious prophetic certainty. She went on: 'You wouldn't like that, would you?'

'No,' I said.

Somehow, in her bleak insistence, she made it easier for me. Her eyes were really like searchlights, I thought, picking out things that no one else saw, then swinging past and leaving a gulf of darkness.

She tried to talk of the future. She broke away again:

'You're frightened, aren't you?'

'Yes.'

'I think you're more frightened than I should be.' She considered. 'Yet you can put on a show to fool your lawyer friends. There are times when you make me feel a child.'

The day went on. Once she said, without any preliminary: 'Darling, I wish I were a different woman.'

She knew that I was begging her for comfort.

'Why didn't you love someone else? No decent woman could let you go like this.'

I had said not a word. I had not embraced her that day. She knew that I was begging for the only comfort strong enough to drive out fear. She knew that I craved for the solace of the flesh. She had to let me go without.

At Mentone I sat on the terrace by the sea, happy in the first few days as though I were well again, as though I were sure of Sheila. I had never been abroad before, and I was exhilarated by the sight of the warm sea, the quickening of all the senses which I felt by that shore. Some of my symptoms dropped away overnight, as I basked in the sun. The sea was so calm that it lost its colour. Instead it stretched like a mirror with a soft and luminous sheen to the edge of the horizon, where it darkened to a stratum of grey silk. It stretched like a mirror without colour, except where, in the wake of each boat that was painted on the surface, there was pencilled, heightening the calm, a dark unbroken line.

When the Mediterranean summer broke into storms, I still had a pleasure, a reassurance of physical well-being, as I stood by the bedroom window at night and, through the rain and window, smelt the bougainvillaea and the arbutus. Turning back to see my bed in the light of the reading-lamp, I was ready to forget my fears and sleep.

An old Austrian lady was living in the hotel. Because of her lungs she had spent her last ten years by the Mediterranean; she had a viperine tongue and a sweet smile, and I enjoyed listening to her talk of Viennese society in the days of the Habsburgs. Inside a fortnight we became friends. I used to take her for gentle walks through the gardens, and I confided in her. I told her as much about my career as I had told Charles March; and I told her more of my love for Sheila and my illness than I had told anyone alive.

Slowly that respite ended. Slowly the illness returned, at first by stealth, so that I did not know whether a symptom was a physical fact or just an alarm of the nerves; one day I would be abnormally fatigued, and then, waking refreshed next morning, I could disbelieve it. Gradually but certainly, after the first mirage-like week, the weakness crept back, the giddiness, the sinking of the ground underfoot. I had provided myself with an apparatus so that I could make a rough measure of my blood count. While I felt better, I left it in my trunk. Later, as I became suspicious of my state, I tried to keep away from it. Once I had used the apparatus, quite unrealistically I began going through the process each day, as though in hope or dread I expected a miracle. It was difficult to be accurate with the little pipette, I had not done many scientific experiments, I longed to cheat in my own favour, and then over-compensated in the other direction. By the third week in August I knew that the count was lower than in July. It seemed more likely than not that it was still going down.

I used to wake hour by hour throughout the night. Down below was the sound of the sea, which in my first days had given me such content. I was damp with sweat. I thought of all I had promised to do – instead, I saw nothing but the empty dark. In my schooldays I had seen a master in the last stage of pernicious anaemia – yellow-skinned, exhausted, in despair. I had not heard of the disease then. Now I knew what his history must have been, step by step. I had read about the intermissions which now, reconstructing what I remembered, I realised must have visited him. For six months or a year he had come back to teach, and seemed recovered.

If one were lucky – I thought how brilliant my luck had been, how, despite all my impatience and complaints, no one of my provenance had made a more fortunate start at the Bar – one might have such intermissions for periods of years. Lying awake to the sound of the sea, I felt surges of the fierce hope which used to possess my mother and which was as natural to me. Even if I had this disease, then still I might make time to do something.

Sometimes, in those nights, I was inexplicably calmed, I woke up incredulous that this could be my fate. The doctors were wrong. I was frightened, but still lucid, and they were confused. Apart from the misshapen cells, I had none of the true signs of the disease. There were no sores on my tongue. Each time I woke, I tested my tongue against my teeth. It became a tic, which sometimes, when I felt a pain, made me imagine the worst, which sometimes gave me the illusion of safety.

In those hot summer nights, with the sea slithering and slapping below, I thought of death. With animal fear, once or twice with detachment. I should die hard, I knew. If the time was soon to come, or whenever it came, I was not the kind to slip easily from life. Like my mother, I might manage to put a face on it, while others were watching: but in loneliness, in the extreme loneliness before death, I should, again like her, be cowardly and struggling, begging on my knees for every minute I could wrench out of the final annihilation. At twenty-five, when this blow struck me, I begged more ravenously. It would be bitterly hard to die without knowing, what I had longed for with all the intensity of which I was capable, any kind of achievement or love fulfilled. But once or twice, I thought, with a curious detachment, that I should have held on as fearfully and tenaciously if it came twenty or forty years later. When I had to face the infinite emptiness, I should never be reconciled, and should cry out to enjoy myself alone 'Why must this happen to *me*?'

After such a night, I would get up tired, prick my finger, extract a drop of blood and go through my meaningless test: then I had breakfast on the terrace, looking out at the shining sea. My Austrian friend would come slowly along, resting a hand on the parapet. She used to look at me and ask:

'How is it this morning, my dear friend?'

I said often:

'A little better than yesterday, I think. Not perfect—' For it was difficult to disappoint her. A bright concern came to her eyes, intensely alive in the old face.

'Ah,' she said, 'when autumn is here, perhaps we shall both be better.'

Then each day I had to wait for the post from England. It arrived just before tea-time; and as soon as it arrived I was waiting for the next day. I had written to Sheila on my first mórning there, a long, loving, hopeful letter; the days passed, the days became weeks. August was turning into September, and I had heard nothing. For a time it did not worry me. But suddenly, one afternoon, as I waited while the porter ran through the bundle, it seemed that all depended on the next day – and so through afternoons of waiting, of watching the postman bicycle along the road, of the delay while they were sorted. At last, each afternoon, the sad and violent anger when there was nothing from her.

In cold blood, knowing her, I could not understand it. Was she ill herself? She could have told me. Had she found another man? In all her caprices she had never neglected a kind of formal etiquette towards me. Was it an act of cruelty? Had I thrown myself too abjectly on her mercy, that last day? It seemed incredible, even for her, I thought, with my temper smouldering, on those evenings as the lights came out along the shore. I had loved her for five years. I would not have treated the most casual acquaintance so, let alone one in my state. Whatever she was feeling, she knew my state. I could not forgive her. I wanted her to suffer as I did.

I wrote again, and then again.

There were other letters from England, some disquieting rumours about George's indiscretions in the town; the news of the birth of Marion's child, a girl; a story of Charles March's father; and, surprisingly, a letter from Salisbury, saying that he had thought I was not so tireless as usual last term and that – if this was not just his imagination – I might like to know that he himself had a minor collapse just after he began to make a living at the Bar. Was he probing, I thought? Or was it a generous impulse? Perhaps both.

From all that news I got no more than a few minutes' distraction. I was more self-centred than ever in my life. I had no room for anything but my two concerns – my illness, and my obsession with Sheila. All else was trivial; I was utterly uninterested in the passing scene and, for once, in other human beings. I knew that my two miseries played on each other. I had the sense, which all human beings dread, which I was to see dominate another's existence, Roy Calvert's in years to come, of my life being outside my will. However much we may say and know that we are governed by forces outside our control, and that the semblance of volition is only an illusion to us all, yet that illusion, when it is challenged, is one of the things we fight for most bitterly. If it is threatened, we feel a horror unlike anything else in life.

In its extreme form, this horror is the horror of madness: and most of us know its shadow, for moments anyway, when we are in the grip of an overmastering emotion. The emotion may give us pleasure or not; for most of its duration we can feel ourselves in full control. But there are moments, particularly in love, particularly in such a love as mine for Sheila, when the illusion is shattered and we see ourselves in the hands of ineluctable fate, our voices, our protests, our reasons as irrelevant to what we do as the sea sounding in the night was to my wretchedness, while I lay awake.

It was in such moments that I faced the idea of suicide. Not altogether in despair – but with the glint of a last triumph. And I believed the idea had come in that identical fashion to other men like me, and for the same reason. Not only as a relief from unhappiness, but also a sign, the only one possible, that the horror is not there, and that one's life is, in the last resort, answerable to will. At any rate, it was so with me.

In much the same spirit as I entertained the idea of suicide, I made plans for the future that ignored both physical health and Sheila. I've been unhappy for long enough, I thought. I'm going to forget her and get better. I must settle what steps to take. Framing plans which assumed that the passion was over, that I could make myself well by a resolution, plans of all the things I should never be able to do.

Beyond the horror of having lost my will, there was another, a simpler companion of those days. That was suffering. Suffering unqualified and absolute, so that at times the anger fled, the complaints and assertions became squallings of my own conceit, and there was nothing left but unhappiness. It was a suffering simple, uneventful and complete. It lay upon me as weakness lay on my body. I thought I could never be as unhappy again.

It was the middle of September. I had known this suffering for some weeks, during which it was more constantly with me than any emotion I had known. I was sitting by the rocks, looking over to the mountains, arid in brown and purple, overhung by rotund masses of cloud. The water was as calm as in my first days there, and the clouds threw long reflections towards me – thin strips of white across the burnished sea. Mechanically I puzzled why these lattice-like separate strips should be reflected from clouds which, seen from where I sat, were flocculent masses above the hills.

It was as tranquil a sight as I had seen.

Then, for a moment, I knew that I was crying out against my fate no more. I knew that I was angry with Sheila no more (I was thinking of her protectively, reflecting that she must be restless and distressed); that all my protests and plans and attempts to revive my will were as feeble as a child's crying to drown the storm; that my arrogance and spirit had left me, that I could no longer keep to myself the pretence of self-respect. I knew that I had been broken by unhappiness. In that clear moment – whatever I protested to myself next day – I knew that I had to accept my helplessness, that I had been broken and could do nothing more.

October came. Term would begin in a few days. I had to make a practical decision. Should I return?

In the past weeks letters had arrived from Sheila, one every other day, remotely apologetic, without any reason for her silence, yet intimate with a phrase or two that seemed to ask my help. I tried to dismiss those letters as I made my decision. I had to dismiss all I had felt by that shore or seen within myself.

My physical condition was no better, but not much worse. Or rather my blood count was descending, though the rate of descent seemed to have slowed. In other respects I was probably better. I was deeply sunburned, which caused me to look healthy except to a clinical eye. That would be an advantage, I thought, if I tried to bluff it out.

If I were not going to get better, it did not matter what I did.

For any practical choice, I had to assume that I should get better.

That assumed, was it wiser to return to chambers, persist in concealing that I was ill, and try to carry it off? Or to stay away until I had recovered?

There was no doubt of the answer. If, at my stage, I stayed away long, I should never get back. One term's absence would do me great harm, and two would finish me. I might scrape a living or acquire a minor legal job, but I should have been a failure.

No, I must return. Now, before the beginning of term, as though nothing had happened.

There were grave risks. I was very weak. I might, with discipline and good management, struggle through the paper work adequately; but I was in no physical state to fight any case but the most placid. I might disgrace myself. Instead of losing my practice by absence, I might do so by presence.

That was a risk I must take. I might contrive to save myself exhaustion. To some extent, I could pick and choose my cases; I could eliminate the police courts straight away. I should have to alter the régime of my days, and use my energies for nothing but the cardinal hours in court.

Whatever came of it, I must return.

On my last evening the sun was falling across the terrace, shining in the pools left by the day's rain. The arbutus smelt heavily as my friend and I came to the end of our last walk. 'We shall meet again,' she said. 'If not next year, then some other time.' Neither of us believed it.

When the car drove through the gates, and I looked back at the sea, I felt the same distress which, years before, overcame me when I left the office for the last time. But on that shore I had been more unhappy than ever in my youth, and so was bound more tightly. More than ever in my youth, I did not know what awaited me at the end of my journey. So, looking back at the sea, I felt a stab of painful yearning, as though all I wanted in the world was to stay there and never be torn away.

CHAPTER XXXIX

SHEILA'S ROOM

MY luck in practical affairs was remarkable. Looking back from middle age, I saw how many chances had gone in my favour; and I felt a kind of vertigo, as though I had climbed along a cliff, and was studying the angle from a safe place. How well should I face it, if required to do the same again ?

My luck held that autumn, as, dragging my limbs, I made my way each morning across the Temple gardens. Mist lay on the river, the grass sparkled with dew in the October sunshine. They were mornings that made me catch my breath in exhilaration. I was physically wretched, I was training myself to disguise my weakness, but the sun shone through the fresh mist and I caught my breath. And I got through the days, the weeks, the term, without losing too much credit. I managed to carry off what I had planned by the sea at Mentone; I took defeats, strain, anxiety and foreboding, but, with extraordinary luck, I managed to carry off enough to save my practice.

I met some discouragement. Each time I saw him, Getliffe made a point of asking with frowning man-to-man concern about my health. 'I'm very strong, L.S.,' he told me, as though it were a consolation. 'I've always been very strong.'

What was more disturbing, I had to persuade Percy that it was sensible to cut myself off from the county court work. It was not sensible, of course. My income was not large enough to bring any such step within the confines of sense. My only chance was to persuade Percy that I was arrogantly sure of success, so sure that I proposed to act as though I were already established. It was bad enough to have to convince him that I had not lost my head; it was worse, because I believed that he suspected the true reason. If so, I knew that I could expect no charity. Percy's judgment of my future had been – I had long since guessed – professional ability above average, influence nil, health doubtful; as a general prospect, needs watching for years. He would be gratified to have predicted my bodily collapse. It was more important to be right than to be compassionate.

'If you don't want them, Mr Eliot,' said Percy, 'there are plenty who do. In my opinion, it's a mistake. That is, if you're going on at the Bar.'

'In five years,' I said, 'you'll be able to live on my briefs.'

'I hope so, sir,' said Percy.

Going away that afternoon, so tired that I took a taxi home, I knew that I had handled him badly. All through that Michaelmas Term, although briefs came to me from solicitors whose cases I had previously fought, there was not a single one which Percy had foraged for. He had written me off.

Fortunately, there were a number of solicitors who now sent work to me. I received several cases, and there was only one that autumn where my physical state humiliated me. That was a disgrace. My stamina failed me on the first morning, I could not concentrate, my memory let me down, I was giddy on my feet; I lost a case which any competent junior should have won. Some days afterwards, a busybody of an acquaintance told me there was a whisper circulating that Eliot was ill and finished. In my vanity I preferred them to say that than take this performance as my usual form.

But, as I have said, by good luck I wiped out most of that disaster. The whispers became quieter. First I nursed myself through a case of Henriques's, where, though I lost again, I knew I did pretty well. Charles March said it was my best yet, and Henriques was discreetly satisfied. And then I had two magnificent strokes of fortune. In the same week I received two cases of a similar nature; in each the arguments were intricate and needed much research, and neither of them was likely to come to court. Nothing could have been better designed for my condition. In actual fact, I attracted some backers through one of those cases; the other was uneventful; each was settled out of court, and I earned nearly two hundred and fifty pounds for the two together. They made the autumn prosperous. They hid my illness, or at least they prevented it becoming public. I thought I had lost little ground so far. It was luck unparalleled.

In November, without giving me any warning, Sheila came to live in

London. She had compelled her father, so she wrote, to guarantee her three hundred pounds a year. An aunt had just died and left her some money in trust, and so she was at last independent. She had taken a bed-sitting-room in Worcester Street, off Lupus Street, where I could visit her. It was unexpected and jagged, like so many of her actions – like our last meeting, at Victoria Station on my return from France. The train was hours late; she had sent no word; but there she was, standing patiently outside the barrier.

Fog was whirling round the street lamps on the afternoon that I first went to Worcester Street. The trees of St George's Square loomed out of the white as the bus passed by. From the pavement, it was hard to make out the number of Sheila's house. She was living on the first floor; there was a little cardboard slip against her bell – MISS KNIGHT – for all the world like some of my former clients, prostitutes down on their luck, whom for curiosity's sake I had visited in those decaying streets.

Her room struck warm. It was large, with a substantial mantelpiece and obsolete bell-ropes by the side. In the days of the house's prosperity, this must have been a drawing-room. Now the gas-fire burned under the mantelpiece, and, near the opposite wall, an oil stove was chugging away and throwing a lighted pattern on the ceiling.

'How are you?' said Sheila. 'You're not better yet.'

I had come straight from the courts, and I was exhausted. She put me in a chair with an awkward, comradely kindness, and then opened a cup-board to give me a drink. I had never been in a room of hers before; and I saw that the glasses in the cupboard, the crockery and bottles, were marshalled with geometrical precision, in neat lines and squares. That was true of every piece of furniture; she had been there only three days, but all was tidy, was so ordered that she became worried if a lamp or book was out of its proper line.

I chaffed her: how had she stood my disarray?

'That's you,' she said. 'We're different.' She seemed content, secretively triumphant, to be looking after me in a room of her own. As she knelt by the glasses and poured the whisky, her movements had lost their stylised grace. She looked more fluent, comfortable, matter-of-fact and warm. Perhaps I was seeing what I wanted to see. I was too tired to care, too happy to be sitting there, with her waiting upon me.

'It's time you got better,' said Sheila, as I was drinking. 'I'm waiting for you to get better.'

I took her hand. She held mine, but her eyes were clouded.

'Never mind,' I said.

'I must mind,' she said sharply.

'I may be cheating myself,' I said, 'but some days I feel stronger.'

'Tell me when you're sure.' There was an impatient tone in her voice, but I was soothed and heartened, promised her, and, so as not to spoil the peace of the moment, changed the subject.

I reminded her how often she had talked of breaking away from home and 'doing something'; the times that we had ploughed over it; how I had teased her about the sick conscience of the rich, and how bitterly she had retorted. Like her father, I wanted to keep her as a toy. My attitude to her was islamic, I had no patience with half her life. Now here she was, broken away from home certainly, but not noticeably listening to her sick conscience. Instead, she was living like a tart in Pimlico.

Sheila grinned. It was rarely that she resented my tongue. She answered good-humouredly: 'I wish I'd been thrown out at sixteen, though. And had to earn a living. It would have been good for me.'

I told her, as I had often done before, that the concept of life as a moral gymnasium could be overdone.

'It would have been good for me,' said Sheila obstinately. 'And I should have been quite efficient. I mightn't have had time –' She broke off. That afternoon, as I lay tired out in my chair (too tired to think of making love – she knew that, did it set her free?), she did not mind so much being absurd. She even showed me her collection of coins. I had heard of it before, but she had shied off when I pressed her. Now she produced it, blushing but at ease. It stood under a large glass case by the window: the coins were beautifully mounted, documented, and indexed; she showed me her scales, callipers, microscope, and weights. The collection was restricted to Venetian gold and silver from the fourteenth century to the Napoleonic occupation. Mr Knight, who begrudged her money for most purposes, had been incongruously generous over this one, and she had been able to buy any coin that came into the market. The collection was, she said, getting on towards complete.

When she had mentioned her coins previously, I had found it sinister – to imagine her plunged into such a refuge. But as I studied her catalogue, in the writing that I had so often searched for a word of love, and listened to her explanations, it seemed quite natural. She was so knowledgeable, competent, and curiously professional. She liked teaching me. She was becoming gayer and more intimate. If only her records had arrived, she would have begun educating me in music, as she had long wanted to do. She insisted that she must do it soon. As it was, she said she had better instruct me in the science of numismatics. She drew the curtains and shut out the foggy afternoon. She stood above me, looking into my eyes with a steady gaze, affectionate and troubled; then she said:

'Now I'll show you how to measure a coin.'

After that afternoon, I imagined the time when I could tell her that I was well. Would it come? As soon as I came back to London, my doctors had examined me again. They had no reassurance for me. The blood count was perceptibly worse than when I went to France. The treatment had not worked, and, apart from advising me to rest, they were at a loss. In the weeks that followed I lost all sense of judgment about my physical state. Sometimes I thought the disease was gaining. There were mornings, as I told Sheila, when I woke and stretched myself and dared to hope. I had given up taking any blood counts on my own. It was best to train myself to wait. With Sheila, with my career, I thought, I had had some practice in waiting. In time I was bound to know whether I should recover. It would take time to see the answer, yes or no.

But others were not so willing to watch me being stoical. I had let the truth slip out, bit by bit, to Charles March as well as to Sheila. Charles was a man whose response to misery or danger or anxiety was very active. He could not tolerate my settling down to endure – before he had dragged me in front of any doctor in London who might be useful. I told him it would waste time and money. Either this was a psychosomatic condition, I said, which no doctor could reach and where my insight was probably better than theirs. If that was the explanation, I should recover. If not, and it was some rare form of pernicious anaemia untouched by the ordinary treatments, I should in due course die. Either way, we should know soon enough. It would be only an irritation and distress to have more doctors handling me and trying to make up their minds.

Charles would not agree. His will was strong, and mine was weakened, after that November afternoon, by Sheila's words. And also there were times just then when I wanted someone to lean on. So I gave way. Until the end of term I should keep up my bluff; but I was ready to be examined by any of his doctors during the Christmas vacation.

Charles organised it thoroughly. At the time, December 1930, he was, by a slight irony, a very junior medical student, for he had recently renounced the Bar and started what was to be his real career. He had not yet taken his first M.B. – but his father and uncle were governors of hospitals. It did not take long to present me to a chief physician. I was installed in a ward before Christmas. The hospital had orders to make a job of it: I became acquainted with a whole battery of clinical tests, not only those, such as barium meals, which might be relevant to my disease.

I loathed it all. It was hard to take one's fate, with someone forcing a test-meal plunger down one's throat. I could not sleep with others round me. I had lost my resignation. I spent the nights dreading the result.

On the first day of the new year, the chief physician talked to me.

'You ought to be all right,' he said. 'It's much more likely than not.'

He dropped his eyelids.

'You'd better try to forget the last few months. Forget about this disease. I'm confident you've not got it. Forget what you were told,' he said. 'It must have been a shock. It wasn't a good experience for you.'

'I shall get over it,' I said, in tumultuous relief.

'I've known these things leave their mark.'

Having set me at rest, he went over the evidence. Whatever the past, there were now no signs of pernicious anaemia; no achlorhydria; nothing to support the diagnosis. I had had a moderately severe secondary anaemia, which should improve. That was the optimistic view. No one could be certain, but he would lay money on it. He talked to me much as Tom Devitt had once done – with more knowledge and authority, but less percipience. Much of the history of my disease was mysterious, he said. I had to learn to look after myself. Eat more. Keep off spirits. Find yourself a good wife.

After I had thanked him, I said:

'Can I get up and go?'

'You'll be weak.'

'Not too weak to get out,' I said; and, in fact, so strong was the suggestion of health, that as I walked out of the hospital, the pavement was firm beneath my feet, for the first time in six months.

The morning air was raw. In the city, people passed anonymously in the mist. I watched a bank messenger cross the road in his top hat and carrying a ledger. I was so light-hearted that I wanted to stop a stranger and tell him my escape. I was light-hearted, not only with relief but with a surge of recklessness. Miseries had passed; so would those to come. Somehow I survived. Sheila, my practice, the next years, danced through my thoughts. It was a time to act. She was at home for Christmas – but there was another thing to do. In that mood, reckless, calculating and confident, I went to find Percy in order to have it out.

There was no one else in chambers, but he was sitting in his little room, reading a racing edition. He said 'Good morning, Mr Eliot,' without curiosity, though he must have been surprised to see me. I asked him to come out for a drink. He was not over-willing, but he had nothing to do.

'In any case,' I said, 'I must talk to you, Percy. You may as well have a drink while you listen.'

We walked up to the Devereux, and there in the bar-room Percy and I sat by the window. The room was smoky and noisy, full of people shouting new-year greetings. Percy drank from his tankard, and impassively watched them.

I began curtly:

'I've been lying to you.'

Instead of watching the crowd, he watched me, with no change of expression.

'I've been seriously ill. Or at least they thought I was.'

'I saw you weren't up to the mark, Mr Eliot,' he said.

'Listen,' I said. 'I want us to understand each other. They thought that I might have a fatal disease. It was a mistake. I'm perfectly well. If you need any confirmation,' I smiled at him, 'I can produce evidence. From Sir —' I said that I had that morning come from the hospital. I told him the story without any palaver.

He asked:

'Why didn't you let any of us know?'

'That's a bloody silly question,' I said. 'How much change should I have got – if everyone heard I was a bad life?'

For once, his eyes flickered.

'How much work would you have brought me?' I asked.

He did not answer.

'Come to that – how much work did you bring me last term?'

He did not prevaricate. He could have counted briefs which passed through his hands but which he had done nothing to gain. But he said, as brutally as I had spoken:

'Not a guinea's worth. I thought you were fading out.'

'I don't grumble,' I said. 'It's all in the game. I don't want charity. I don't need it now. But you ought to be careful not to make a fool of yourself.'

I went on. I was well now, I should be strong by the summer, the doctors had no doubt that I should stand the racket of the Bar. I had come through without my practice suffering much. I had my connections, Henriques and the rest. It would be easy for me to move to other chambers. A change from Getliffe, a change from Percy to a clerk who believed in me – I should double my income in a year.

Even at the time, I doubted whether that threat much affected him. But I had already achieved my end. He was a cross-grained man. He despised those who dripped sympathy and who expected a flow of similar honey in return. His native language, though he got no chance to use it, was one of force and violence and temper, and he thought better of me for speaking that morning in the language that he understood. He had never done so before, but he invited me to drink another pint of beer.

'You needn't worry, Mr Eliot,' he said. 'I don't make promises, but I believe you'll be all right.'

He stared at me, and took a long gulp.

'I should like to wish you,' he said, 'a happy and prosperous new year.'

CHAPTER XL

LISTENING TO MUSIC

It was still the first week in January, and I was walking along Worcester Street on my way to Sheila's. She had returned the day before, and I was saving up for the luxury of telling her my news. I could have written, but I had saved it up for the glow of that afternoon. I was still light-hearted and lazy with relief. The road glistened in the drizzle, the basement lights were gleaming, here and there along the street one could gaze into lighted rooms – books, a table, a lamp-shade, a piano, a curtained bed. Why did those sights move one so, was it the hint of unknown lives? It was luxurious to see the lighted rooms, walking down the wet street on the way to Sheila.

I had no plan ready-made for that afternoon. I did not intend to propose immediately, now all was well. There was time enough now. Before the month was over I should speak, but it was luxurious to be lazy that day, and my thoughts flowed round her as they had flowed when I first fell in love. It was strange that she should be lodging in this street. She had always felt a nostalgia for the scruffy; perhaps she had liked me more, when we first met, because I was a shabby young man living in a garret.

I thought of other friends, like her comfortably off, who could not accept their lives. The social climate was overawing them. They could not take their good luck in their stride. If one had a talent for non-acceptance, it was a bad generation into which to be born rich. The callous did not mind, nor did the empty, nor did those who were able not to take life too hard; but among my contemporaries I could count half a dozen who were afflicted by the sick conscience of the rich.

Sheila was not made for harmony, but perhaps her mother's money impeded her search for it. If she had been a man, she might, like Charles March, have insisted on finding a job in which she could feel useful; one of Charles's reasons for becoming a doctor was to throw away the burden of guilt; she was as proud and active as he, and if she had been a man she too might have found a way to live. If she had been a man, I thought idly and lovingly as I came outside her house, she would have been happier. I looked up at her window. The light shone rosy through the curtains. She was there, alone in her room, and in the swell of love my heart sank and rose.

I ran upstairs, threw my arm round her waist, said that it had been a false alarm and that I should soon be quite recovered. 'It makes me feel drunk,' I said, and pressed her to me.

'You're certain of it?' she said, leaning back in the crook of my elbow.

I told her that I was certain.

'You're going to become tough again? You'll be able to go on?'

'Yes, I shall go on.'

'I'm glad, my dear. I'm glad for your sake.' She had slipped from my arms, and was watching me with a strange smile. She added: 'And for mine too.'

I exclaimed. I was already chilled.

She said: 'Now I can ask your advice.'

'What do you mean?'

'I'm in love. Quite honestly. It's very surprising. I want you to tell me what to do.'

She had often tortured me with the names of other men. There had been times when her eye was caught, or when she was making the most of a new hope. But she had never spoken with this authority. On the instant, I believed her. I gasped, as though my lungs were tight. I turned away. The reading-lamp seemed dim, so dim that the current might be failing. I was suddenly drugged by an overwhelming fatigue; I wanted to go to sleep.

'I had to tell you,' she was saying.

'Why didn't you tell me before?'

'You weren't fit to take it,' she said.

'This must be the only time on record,' I said, 'when you've considered me.'

'I may have deserved that,' she replied. She added: 'Believe me. I'm hateful. But this time I tried to think of you. You were going through enough. I couldn't tell you that I was happy.'

'When did it happen?'

'Just after you went to France.'

I was stupefied that I had not guessed.

'You didn't write to me for weeks,' I said.

'That was why. I hoped you'd get well quickly.' She twitched her shoulders. 'I'm no good at deceit.'

I sat down. For a period that may have been minutes – I had lost all sense of time – I stared into the room. I half-knew that she had brought up a chair close to mine. At last I said:

'What do you want me to do?'

Her reply was instantaneous:

'See that I don't lose him.'

'I can't do that,' I said roughly.

'I want you to,' she said. 'You're wiser than I am. You can tell me how not to frighten him away.' She added: 'He's pretty helpless. I've never liked a man who wasn't. Except you. He can't cope very well. He's rather like me. We've got a lot in common.'

I had heard other 'we's' from her, taunting my jealousy, but not in such a tone as this. She dwelt on it with a soft and girlish pleasure. I fell again into silence. Then I asked peremptorily who he was.

She was eager to tell me. She spoke of him as Hugh. It was only some days later, when I decided to meet him, that I learned his surname. He was a year or two older than Sheila and me, and so was at that time about twenty-seven. He had no money, she said, though his origins were genteel. Some of his uncles were well off, and he was a clerk at a stockbroker's, being trained to go into the firm. 'He hates it,' she said. 'He'll never be any good at it. It's ridiculous.' He had no direction or purpose; he did not even know whether he wanted to get married.

'Why is he the answer?' I could not keep the question back.

She answered:

'It's like finding part of myself.'

She was rapt, she wanted me to rejoice with her. 'I must show you his photograph,' she said. 'I've hidden it when you came before. Usually it stands—' She pointed to a shelf at the head of the divan on which she slept. 'I like to wake up and see it in the morning.'

She was more girlish, more delighted to be girlish, than a softer woman might have been. She went to a cupboard, bent over and stayed for a second looking at the photograph before she brought it out. Each action and posture was, as I had observed the first time I visited that room, more flowing and relaxed than a year ago. When I first observed that change, I did not guess that she was in love. Her profile was hard and clear, as she bent over the photograph; her lips were parted, as though she wanted to gush without constraint. 'It's rather a nice face,' she said, handing me the picture. It was a weak and sensitive face. The eyes were large, bewildered, and idealistic. I gave it back without a word. 'You can see,' she said, 'that he's not much good at looking after himself. Much less me. I know it's asking something, but I want you to help. I've never listened to anyone else, but I listen to you. And so will he.'

She tried to make me promise to meet him. I was so much beside myself that I gave an answer and contradicted myself and did not know what I intended. It was so natural to look after her; to shield this vulnerable happiness, to preserve her from danger. At the same time, all my angry heartbreak was pent up. I had not uttered a cry of that destructive rage.

She was satisfied. She felt assured that I should do as she asked. 'Now what shall I do for you?' she cried in her rapture. 'I know,' she said, with a smile half-sarcastic, half-innocent as she brought out her anti-climax. 'I shall continue your musical education.' Since my first visit to Worcester Street, she had played records each time I went – to disguise her love. Yet it had been a pleasure to her. She knew I was unmusical, often she had complained that it was a barrier between us, and she liked to see me listening. She could not believe that the sound meant nothing. She had only to explain, and my deafness would fall away.

That afternoon, after her cry 'What shall I do for you?', she laid out the records of Beethoven's Ninth Symphony. Side by side, we sat and listened. Sheila listened, her eyes luminous, transfigured by her happiness. She listened and was in love.

The noise pounded round me. I too was in love.

The choral movement opened. As each theme came again, Sheila whispered to make me recognise it. 'Dismisses it,' she said, sweeping her hand down, as the first went out. 'Dismisses it,' she said twice more. But at the first sound of the human voice, she sat so still that she might have gone into a trance.

She was in love, and rapt. I sat beside her, possessed by my years of passion and devotion, consumed by tenderness, by desire and by the mania of revenge, possessed by the years whose torments had retraced themselves to breaking point as she stood that night, oblivious to all but her own joy. She was carried away, into the secret contemplation of her love. I sat beside her, stricken and maddened by mine.

PART SIX

A SINGLE ACT

CHAPTER XLI

THE SENSE OF POWER

THAT night, after Sheila told me she was in love, I stayed in the street, my eyes not daring to leave her lighted window. The music had played round me; I had said goodbye; but when I came out into the cold night, I could not go home. Each past storm of jealousy or desire was calm compared to this. The evening when I slipped away from George and stood outside the vicarage, just watching without purpose – that was nothing but a youth's lament. Now I was driven.

I could find no rest until I saw with my own eyes whether or not another man would call on her that night. No rest from the calculations of jealousy: 'I shall want some tea,' she had said, and that light phrase set all my mind to work, as though a great piece of clockwork had been wound up by a turn of the key. When would she make him tea? That night? Next day? No rest from the torments, the insane reminders, of each moment when her body had allured me; so that standing in the street, looking at her window, I was maddened by sensual reveries.

It was late. A drizzle was falling, silver and sleety as it passed the street-lamps. Time upon time I walked as far up the street as I could go, and still see the window. Through the curtains her light shone – orange among the yellow squares of other windows, the softest, the most luxurious, of all the lights in view. Twice a man came down the pavement, and as he approached her house my heart stopped. He passed by. A desolate prostitute, huddled against the raw night, accosted me. Some of the lights went out, but hers still shone.

The street was deserted. At last – in an instant when I turned my eyes away – her window had clicked into darkness. Relief poured through me, inordinate, inexpressible relief. I turned away; and I was drowsing in the taxi before I got home.

For days in chambers I was driven, as violently as I had been that night. Writing an opinion, I could not keep my thoughts still. At a conference,

I heard my leader talk, I heard the clients inquiring – between them and me were images of Sheila, images of the flesh, the images that tormented my senses and turned jealousy into a drill within the brain. And in the January nights I was driven to walk the length of Worcester Street, back and forth, hypnotised by the lighted window; it was an obsession, it was a mania, but I could not keep myself away.

One night, in the tube station at Hyde Park Corner, I imagined that I saw her in the crowd. There was a thin young man, of whom I only saw the back, and a woman beside him. She was singing to herself. Was it she? They mounted a train in the rush, I could not see, the doors slid to.

Soon afterwards – it was inside a week since she broke her news – the telephone rang at my lodgings. The landlady shouted my name, and I went downstairs. The telephone stood out in the open, on a table in the hall. I heard Sheila's voice:

'How are you?'

I muttered.

'I want to know: how are you, physically?'

I had scarcely thought of my health. I had been acting as though I were tireless. I said that I was all right, and asked after her.

'I'm *very* well.' Her voice was unusually full. There was a silence, then she asked: 'When am I going to see you?'

'When you like.'

'Come here tonight. You can take me out if you like.'

Once more an answer broke out.

'Shall you be alone?' I said.

'Yes.' In the telephone the word was clear; I could hear neither gloating nor compassion.

When I entered her room that evening she was dressed to dine out, in a red evening-frock. Since I had begun to earn money, we had taken to an occasional treat. It was the chief difference in my way of life, for I had not changed my flat, and still lived as though in transit. She let me do it; she knew that I had my streak of childish ostentation, and that it flattered me to entertain her as the Marches might have done. For herself, she would have preferred our old places in Soho and round Charlotte Street; but, to indulge me, she would dress up and go to fashionable restaurants, as she had herself proposed that night.

She was bright-eyed and smiling. Before we went out, however, she said in a quiet voice:

'Why did you ask whether I should be alone?'

'You know.'

'You're thinking,' she said, her eyes fixed on me, 'of what I did to you once? At the Edens' that night – with poor Tom Devitt?'

I did not reply.

'I shan't do that again,' she said. She added: 'I've treated you badly. I don't need telling it.'

She walked into the restaurant at the Berkeley with me behind her. Just then, at twenty-five, she was at the peak of her beauty. For a young girl, her face had been too hard, lined, and over-vivid. And I often thought, trying to see the future, that long before she was middle-aged her looks would be ravaged. But now she was at the age which chimed with her style. That night, as she walked across the restaurant, all eyes followed her, and a hush fell. She made the conversation. Each word she said was light with her happiness, more than ever capricious and sarcastic. Sometimes she drew a smile, despite myself. Then, in the middle of the meal, she leaned across the table, her eyes full on me, and said, quietly and simply:

'You can do something for me.'

'What?'

'Will you?' she begged.

I stared at her.

'You can be some good to me,' she said.

'What do you want?'

She said:

'I want you to see Hugh.'

'I can't do it,' I burst out.

'It might help me,' she said.

My eyes could not leave hers.

'You're more realistic than I am,' she said. 'I want you to tell me what he feels about me. I don't know whether he loves me.'

'What do you think I am?' I cried, and violent words were quivering behind my lips.

'I trust you,' she said. 'You're the only human being I've ever trusted.'

There was silence. She said:

'There is no one else to ask. No one else would be worth asking.'

In exhaustion, I replied at last:

'All right. I'll see him.'

She was docile with delight. When could I manage it? She would arrange any time I liked. 'I'm very dutiful to Hugh,' she said, 'but I shall make him come – whenever you can manage it.' What about that very night? She could telephone him, and bring him to her room. Would I mind, that night?

'It's as good as any other,' I said.

She rang up. We drove back to Worcester Street. In the taxi I said little, and I was as sombre while we sat in her room and waited.

'He's highly strung,' she said. 'He may be nervous of you.'

A car passed along the street, coming nearer, and I listened. Sheila shook her head.

'No,' she said. 'He'll come by bus.' She asked: 'Shall I play a record?'

'If you like.'

She grimaced, and began to search in her shelf. As she did so, there pattered a light step down below. 'Here he is,' she said.

He came in with a smile, quick and apologetic. Sheila and I were each standing, and for a second he threw an arm round her. Then he faced me, as she introduced us.

'Lewis, this is Hugh Smith.'

He was as tall as I was, but much slighter. His neck was thin and his chest sunken. He was very fair. His upper lip was petulant and vain, but when he smiled his whole face was merry, boyish and sweet. He looked much younger than his years, much younger than either Sheila or me.

He was taken up with Sheila's dress.

'I've not seen you in that before, have I?' he said. 'Yes, it's very very nice. Let me see. Is it quite right at the back – ?' he went on with couturier's prattle.

Sheila laughed at him.

'You're much more interested than my dress-maker,' she said.

Hugh appealed to me:

'Aren't you interested in clothes?'

His manner was so open that I was disarmed.

He went on talking about clothes, and music, and the plays we had seen. Nothing could have been lighter-hearted, more suited to a polite party. She made fun of him, more gentle fun than I was used to. I asked a question about his job, and he took at once to the defensive; I gave it up, and he got back to concerts again. Nothing could have been more civilised.

I was watching them together. I was watching them with a desperate attention, more concentrated than I had summoned and held in all my life before. Around them there was no breath of the heaviness and violence of a passion. It was too friendly, too airy, too kind, for that. Towards him she showed a playful ease which warmed her voice and set her free. When she turned to him, even the line of her profile seemed less sharp. It was an

ease that was full of teasing, half-kittenish and half-maternal. I had never
seen her so for longer than a flash.

I could not be sure of what he felt for her. He was fond of her, was
captivated by her charm, admired her beauty, liked her high spirits – that
all meant little. I thought that he was flattered by her love. He was conceited as well as vain. He lapped up all the tributes of love. He was selfish;
very amiable; easily frightened, easily overweighted, easily overborne.

Sheila announced that she was going to bed. She wanted Hugh and me,
I knew, to leave together, so that I could talk to him. It was past midnight;
the last buses had gone; he and I started to walk towards Victoria. It was a
crisp frosty night, the black sky glittering with stars.

On the pavement in Lupus Street, he spoke, as though for safety, of
the places we lived in and how much we paid for our flats. He was apprehensive of the enmity not yet brought into the open that night. He was
searching for casual words that would hurry the minutes along. I should
have welcomed it so. But I was too far gone. I interrupted:

'How long have you known her?'

'Six months.'

'I've known her six years.'

'That's a long time,' said Hugh, and once more tried to break on to safe
ground. We had turned into Belgrave Road.

I did not answer his question, but asked:

'Do you understand her?'

His eyes flickered at me, and then away.

'Oh, I don't know about that.'

'Do you understand her?'

'She's intelligent, isn't she? Don't you think she is?' He seemed to be
probing round for answers that would please me.

'Yes,' I said.

'I think she's very sweet. She is sweet in her way, isn't she?'

Our steps rang in the empty frost-bound street.

'She's not much like the other girls I've known!' he ventured. He added
with his merry child-like smile: 'But I expect she wants the same thing
in the end. They all do, don't they?'

'I expect so.'

'They want you to persuade them into bed. Then they want
marry them.'

I said:

'Do you want to marry her?'

'I think I'd like to settle down, wouldn't you?' he said

be very sweet, can't she?' He added: 'I've always got out of it before. I suppose she's a bit of a proposition. Somehow I think it might be a good idea.'

The lights of the empty road stretched ahead, the lights under the black sky.

'By the way,' he said, 'I'm frightfully sorry if I've been poaching. I am sorry if I've got in your way. These things can't be helped, though, can they?'

For minutes the lights, the sky, had seemed shatteringly bright, reelingly dark, as though I were dead drunk.

Suddenly my mind leapt clear.

'I should like to talk about that,' I said. 'Not tonight. Tomorrow or the next day.'

'There isn't much to talk about, is there?' he said, again on the defensive.

'I want to say some things to you.'

'I don't see that it'll do much good, you know,' he replied.

'It's got to be done,' I said.

'I'm rather full up this week—'

'It can't be left,' I said.

'Oh, if you want,' he gave way, with a trace of petulance.

Before we parted, we arranged to meet. He was shy of the place and time, but I made him promise – my flat, not tomorrow but the evening after.

The fire was out when I returned to my room. I did not think of sleep, and I did not notice the cold. Still in my overcoat, I sat on the head of the sofa, smoking.

I stayed without moving for many minutes. My thoughts were clear. They had never seemed so clear. I believed that this man was right for her. Or at least with him she might get an unexacting happiness. Knowing her ˙h the insight of passionate love, I believed that I saw the truth. He was ˙veight, but somehow his presence made her innocent and free. Her ˙nce was to marry him.

˙he marry her? He was wavering. He could be forced either way. ˙sh, but this time he did not know exactly what he wanted for ˙d made love to her, but was not physically bound. She had ˙; yet he was thinking of her as his wife. He was irresolute. ˙ be told what to do.

˙ that night, as I did so often afterwards, I had to ˙ was easy to forget, but in fact many of my thoughts ˙ best chance was to marry him. I thought of how ˙ arguments to use, the feelings to play on. Did he know that she would one day be rich? Would he not be flattered by my desire to have her at any price, would not my competition raise her value? I imagined her married to him, light and playful as she had been that night. It was a sacrificial, tender thought.

If I played it right, my passion to marry her would trigger him on.

Yes. Her best chance was to marry him. I believed that I could decide it. I could bring it off – or destroy it.

With the cruellest sense of power I had ever known, I thought that I could destroy it.

CHAPTER XLII

STEAMING CLOTHES BEFORE THE FIRE

I HAD two days to wait. Throughout that time, wherever I was, whoever I was speaking to, I had my mind fixed, my whole spirit and body, bone and flesh and brain, on the hour to come. The sense of power ran through my bloodstream. As I prepared for the scene, my thoughts stayed clear. Underneath the thoughts, I was exultant. Each memory of the past, each hope and resolve remaining – they were at one.

I went into chambers each of those mornings, but only for an hour. I conferred with Percy. On Thursday we were to hear judgment in an adjourned case: that would be the morning after Hugh's visit, I thought, as Percy and I methodically arranged my timetable. February would be a busy month.

'They're coming in nicely,' said Percy.

Those two days were cold and wet, but I did not stay long in chambers or in my room. I was not impatient, but I was active. It was a pleasure to jostle in the crowds. My mind was planning, and at the same time I breathed in the wet reek of Covent Garden, the whispers of a couple behind me at the cinema, the grotesque play of an enraged and pompous woman's face.

I did not hurry over my tea on the second day. He was due at half-past six; I had to buy a bottle of whisky on the way home, but there was time enough. I had been sitting about in cafés most of that afternoon, drinking tea and reading the evening papers. Before I set off for home, I bought the latest edition and read it through. As people came into the café their coats were heavy with the rain, and at the door men poured trickles of water from their hat-brims.

When I reached my door the rain had slackened, but I was very wet.

I had to change; and as I did so I thought with sarcastic tenderness of the first occasion that I arrived at Sheila's house. In the mirror I saw myself smiling. Then I got ready for Hugh's visit. I made up the fire. I had not yet drawn the blinds, and the reflections of the flames began to dance behind the window-panes. I put the bottle of whisky and a jug of water and glasses on the table, and opened a box of cigarettes. Then at last I pulled down the blinds and shut the room in.

He should be here in ten minutes. I was feeling exalted, braced, active with physical well-being; there was a tremor in my hands.

Hugh was a quarter of an hour late. I was standing up as he came in. He gave his bright, flickering smile. I said that it was a nasty night, and asked if he were soaked. He replied that he had found a taxi, but that his trousers were damp below the knees. Could he dry them by the fire? He sat in a chair with his feet in the fireplace. He remarked, sulkily, that he had to take care of his chest.

I invited him to have a drink. First he said no, then he changed his mind, then he stopped me and asked for a very small one. He sat there with glass in hand while I stood on the other side of the hearth. Steam was rising from his trousers, and he pushed his feet nearer to the grate.

'I'm sorry to have brought you out on a night like this,' I said.

'Oh well, I'm here.' His manner, when he was not defending himself, was easy and gentle.

'If you had to turn out tonight,' I said, 'it's a pity that I've got to tell you unpleasant things.'

He was looking at me, alert for the next words. His face was open.

I said casually:

'I wonder if you'd rather we went out and ate first. If so, I won't begin talking seriously until we come back. I must have you alone for what I've got to say. I don't know what the weather's like now.'

I left the fireplace, went to the window and lifted the bottom of the blind. The rain was tapping steadily. Now that our eyes were not meeting, he raised his voice sharply:

'It can't possibly take long, can it? I haven't the faintest idea what it's all about—'

I turned back.

'You'd rather I spoke now?' I said.

'I suppose so.'

I sat down opposite to him. The steam was still wafted by the draught, and there was a smell of moist clothes. His eyes flickered away, and then were drawn back. He did not know what to expect.

'Sheila wants to marry you,' I said. 'She wants to marry you more than you want to marry her.'

His eyelids blinked. He looked half-surprised that I should begin so. 'Perhaps that's true,' he said.

'You're quite undecided,' I said.

'Oh, I don't know about that.'

'You're absolutely undecided,' I said. 'You can't make up your mind. It's very natural that you shouldn't be able to.'

'I shall make it up.'

'You're not happy about it. You've got a feeling that there's something wrong. That's why you're so undecided.'

'How do you know that I feel there's something wrong?'

'By the same instinct that is warning you,' I said. 'You feel that there are reasons why you shouldn't marry her. You can't place them, but you feel that they exist.'

'Well?'

'If you knew her better,' I said, 'you would know what those reasons are.'

He was leaning back in the chair with his shoulders huddled.

'Of course, you're not unprejudiced,' he said.

'I'm not unprejudiced,' I said. 'But I'm speaking the truth, and you believe that I'm speaking the truth.'

'I'm very fond of her,' he said. 'I don't care what you tell me. I shall make up my mind for myself.'

I waited, I let his eyes dart towards me, before I spoke again.

'Have you any idea,' I said, 'what marriage with her would mean?'

'Of course I've an idea.'

'Let me tell you. She has little physical love for you – or any man.'

'More for me than for anyone.' He had a moment of certainty.

I said:

'You've made love to other women. What do you think of her?'

He did not reply. I repeated the question. He was more obstinate than I had counted on – but I was full of the joy of power, of revenge, of the joy that mine was the cruel will. Power over him, that was nothing, except to get my way. He was an instrument, and nothing else. In those words I took revenge for the humiliation of years, for the love of which I had been deprived. It was she to whom I spoke.

I said:

'She has no other love to give.'

'If I feel like marrying her,' he said, 'I shall.'

'In that case,' I said, and now I knew the extreme of effort, the extreme of release, 'you'll be marrying an abnormal woman.'

He misunderstood me.

'No,' I said: 'I don't mean that. I mean that she is hopelessly unstable. And she'll never be anything else.'

I could feel his hate. He hated me, he hated the force and violence in my voice. He longed to escape, and yet he was fascinated.

'But you'd take her on,' he said. 'If only she'd have you. You can't deny it, can you?'

'It is true,' I said. 'But I love her, which is the bitterest fate in my life. You don't love her, and you know it. I couldn't help myself, and you can. And if I married her, I should do it with my eyes open. I should marry her, but I should know that she was a pathological case.'

He avoided my gaze.

'You've got to know that too,' I said.

'Are you saying that she will go mad?'

'Do you know,' I said, 'when madness begins or ends?' I went on: 'If you ask me whether she'll finish in an asylum, I should say no. But if you ask me what it would be like to go home to her after you were married, I tell you this: you would never know what you would find.'

I asked him if he had ever heard the word schizoid. I asked if he had noticed anything unusual about her actions. I told him stories of her. All the time my exultation was mounting higher still; from his whole bearing, I was certain that I had not misjudged him. He would never marry her. He wanted to escape, as soon as he decently could, from a storm of alien violence. He was out of his depth with both her and me. His feeling for her had always been mild; his desire to marry her not much more than a fancy; now I had destroyed it. He hated me, but I had destroyed it.

I despised him, in the midst of passionate triumph, for not loving her more. At that moment I felt nothing but contempt for him. I was on her side as I watched him begin to extricate himself.

'I shall have to think it over,' he said. 'I suppose that it's time I made up my mind.'

He knew that his decision was already taken. He knew that it was surrender. He knew that he would slip from her, and that I was certain of it.

I demanded that, as soon as he told her, he should tell me too.

'It's only between her and me,' he said with an effort of defiance.

'I must know.'

He hated me, but for the last time he gave way.

Right at the end, he asserted himself. He would not come with me to dinner, but went off on his own.

CHAPTER XLIII

MR KNIGHT TRIES TO BE DIRECT

THE next morning I went into court to hear a judgment. It was in one of the London police courts; the case was a prosecution for assault which I had won the week before; the defendant had been remanded for a medical report. He had been pronounced sane, and now the stipendiary sentenced him. There was a shadow of blackmail in the case, and the magistrate was stern. 'It passes my comprehension how anyone can sink to such behaviour. No words are too strong to express the detestation which we all feel for such men as you—'

It had often seemed to me strange that men should be so brazen with their moral indignation. Were they so utterly cut off from their own experience that they could utter these loud, resounding, moral brays and not be forced to look within? What were their own lives like, that they could denounce so enthusiastically? If baboons learned to talk, the first words they spoke would be stiff with moral indignation. I thought it again, without remorse, as I sat in court that Thursday morning.

Later in my life, I shouldn't have been so much consoled with those reflections. I learned to distrust that kind of moral relativism. Yes, you had to know the worst about yourself: but you also had to accept what behaviour should be.

Just then, I was making excuses for myself. I wasn't feeling either remorse or regret. I was still borne up by my excitement, I was waiting to hear from Hugh, but I had no doubt of the answer. Just then, I had one anxiety about my action, and only one: would Sheila learn of it? If so, should I have lost her for good? How could I get her back?

Hugh called on me early the following Sunday, while I was at my breakfast.

'I said that I'd tell you, didn't I?' he said, in a tone weary and unforgiving. He would not sit down. 'Well,' he went on, 'I've written to tell her that I'm walking out.'

'What have you said?'

'Oh, the usual things. We shouldn't get on for long, and it would be mostly my fault. What else could I say?'

'Have you seen her,' I asked, 'since we talked?'

'Yes.'

'Did she guess what was coming?'

'I didn't tell her.' Then he said, with a flash of shrewdness: 'You needn't worry. I haven't mentioned you. But you've given me some advice, and I'm going to do the same to you. You'd better leave her alone for a few months. If you don't, you're asking for trouble.'

Within two days, I was telephoning her. At first, when I got no answer but the ringing tone, I thought nothing of it. She must be out for the evening. But when I had put through call after call, late into the night, I became alarmed. I had to imagine the bell ringing on and on in her empty room. I tried again the next morning as soon as I woke, and went straight round to Worcester Street. Sheila's landlady opened the door to me in the misty morning twilight. Miss Knight had gone away the day before. She hadn't said where she was going, or left an address. She might come back or she might not, but she had paid three months' rent in advance (my heart leapt and steadied with relief).

I asked if I might glance at Sheila's room. There was a book I had lent her, I went on persuading. The landlady knew me, and was fond of Sheila, like everyone who waited on her; so I was allowed to walk round the room, while the landlady stood at the door, and the smell of frying bacon came blowing up the stairs. The room looked high in the cold light. The coins had gone, the records, her favourite books.

I wrote to her, and sent the letter to the vicarage address. I heard nothing, and within a week wrote again. Then I made enquiries through friends in the town – not George Passant and the group, but others who might have contact with the Knights. Soon one of them, a girl called Rosalind, sent me some news. Sheila was actually living at home. She was never seen outside the house. No one had spoken to her. She would not answer the telephone. No one knew how she was.

I could see no way to reach her. That weighed upon me, it was to that thought that I woke in the night, not to the reproach that this had happened through my act.

Yet I sometimes faced what I had done. Perhaps sometimes I exaggerated it. Many years later I could at last ask fairly: would he really have transformed her life? How much difference had my action made? Perhaps I wanted to believe that I had done the maximum of harm. It took away some of the reproach of staying supine for so long.

Often I remembered that evening with remorse. Perhaps, as I say, I cherished it. But at other times I remembered it with an utterly different.

and very curious, feeling. With a feeling of innocence, puzzled and incredulous.

I had noticed this in others who performed an action which brought evil consequences on others and themselves. But I had to undergo it myself before I understood. The memory came back with the innocence of fact ... an act of the flesh, bare limbs on a bed ... a few words on a sheet of paper ... was it possible that such things could shake a life? So it was with me. Sometimes I remembered that evening, not with remorse, but just as words across the fireplace, steam rising from the other man's trousers, some words spoken as I might have spoken them on any evening. All past and gone. How could such facts hag-ride me now, or hold out threats for the years to come?

The summer began, and quite irrelevantly, I had another stroke of practical luck. Getliffe at last took silk. Inevitably, much of his practice must come to me.

For years he had bombarded us with the arguments for and against. He had threatened us with his own uncertainties; he had taken advice from his most junior pupil as well as his eminent friends at the Bar. He had delayed, raised false hopes, changed his mind, retracted. I had come to think that he would never do it – certainly not that summer, 1931, with a financial crisis upon us and the wise men prophesying that legal work would shrink by half.

He told me on an evening in June. I was alone in chambers, working late; he had spent all the day since lunch-time going from one acquaintance to another. He called me into his room.

It was a thundery overcast evening, the sky black beyond the river, with one long swathe of orange where the clouds had parted. Getliffe sat magisterially at his desk. In the dark room his papers shone white under the lamp. He was wearing a raincoat, the collar half-turned up. His face was serious and also a little rebellious.

'Well,' he said, 'I've torn it now. I'm taking the plunge. If —— is going to be one of His Majesty's counsel, I might as well follow suit. One has to think of one's duty.'

'Is it definite?' I said.

'I never bore my friends with my intentions,' Getliffe reproved me, 'until they're cut and dried.'

Getliffe gave me his fixed man-to-man stare.

'Well, there's the end of a promising junior,' he said. 'Now I start again. It will ruin me, of course. I hope you'll remember that I expect to be ruined.'

'In three years,' I said, 'you'll be making twice what you do now.'
He smiled.

'You know, L.S., you're rather a good sort.' Then his tone grew threatening again. 'It's a big risk I'm taking. It's the biggest risk I've ever had to take.'

He enjoyed his ominous air; he indulged himself in his pictures of sacrifice and his probable disaster. Yet he was not much exaggerating the risk. At that moment, it was a brave step. I was astonished that he should take it. I admired him, half-annoyed with myself for feeling so. In that last year as a junior his income was not less than five thousand. Even if the times were prosperous, his first years as a silk were bound to mean a drop. In 1931, with the depression spreading, he would be fortunate if he made two thousand: he might not climb to his old level for years, perhaps not ever.

It could have deterred many men not overfond of money. Whereas Getliffe was so mean that, having screwed himself to the point of taking one to lunch, he would arrive late so that he need not buy a drink beforehand. It must have been an agony for him to face the loss. He can have endured it only because of a force that I was loth to give him credit for – his delight in his profession, his love of the legal honours not only for their cash value but for themselves. If ever the chance came, I ought to have realised, he would renounce the most lucrative of practices in order to become Getliffe J., to revel in the glory of being a judge.

Whatever the results for Getliffe, his move was certain to do me good, now and henceforward. His work still flowed into our chambers: much of it, as a silk, he could not touch. His habits were too strong to break; he was no more reconciled to youth knocking at the door, and he did his best, in his furtive ingenious fashion, to direct the cases to those too dim to be rivals. But he could not do much obstruction, and Percy took care of me. In the year 1930–1, despite my illness, I had earned seven hundred and fifty pounds. The moment Getliffe took silk I could reckon on at least a thousand for each year thereafter. It was a comfort, for these last months I had half-felt some results of illness and my private grief. I had not thrown myself into my cases with the old absorption. I did not see it clearly then, but I was not improving on my splendid start. I should still have backed my chances for great success, but a shrewd observer would have doubted them. Still, I had gone some distance. I was now certain of a decent income. For the first time since I was a child, I was sure of my livelihood.

Once I imagined that I should be overjoyed, when that rasp of worry was conquered. I had looked forward to the day, ever since I began to struggle. It should have marked an epoch. Now it had come, and it was empty. She was not there. All that I had of her came in the thoughts of sleepless nights. On the white midsummer nights, those thoughts gave me no rest. The days were empty. My bit of success was the emptiest of all. Right to the last I had hoped that when it came she would be with me. This would have been the time for marriage. In fact, I had not the slightest word from her. I tried to accept that I might never see her again.

I went out, on the excuse of any invitation. Through the Marches and acquaintances at the Bar, my name was just finding a place on some hostesses' lists. I was a young man from nowhere, but I was presumably unattached and well thought of at my job. I went to dances and parties, and sometimes a girl there seemed real and my love a nightmare from which I had awakened. I liked being liked; I lapped up women's flattery; often I half-resolved to find myself a wife. But I was not a man who could marry without the magic being there. Leaving someone who should have contented me, I was leaden with the memory of magic. With Sheila, I should have remembered each word and touch, whereas this – this was already gone.

One morning in September, soon after I had returned from a holiday, a letter stared from my breakfast-tray. My heart pounded as I saw the postmark of her village; but the letter had been redirected from my Inn, and the handwriting was a man's. It came from Mr Knight, and read:

'My dear Eliot, Even one who hides himself in the seclusion of a remote life and simple duties cannot always avoid certain financial consultations. Much as I dislike coming to London I shall therefore be obliged to stay at the club for the nights of Monday and Tuesday next week. Owing to increasing age and disinclination, I know few people outside my immediate circle, and shall be free from all engagements during this enforced visit. It is, of course, too much to hope that you can disentangle yourself from your professional connections, but if you should remember me and be available, I should be glad to give you the poor hospitality the club can offer at luncheon on either of those days. Very truly yours.'

The letter was signed with a flamboyant 'Laurence Knight'.

The 'club' was the Athenaeum. I knew that from private jokes with Sheila. He had devoted intense pertinacity to get himself elected. It was like him to pick up the jargon, particularly the arrogant private-world jargon, of any institution, and become a trifle too slick with it.

He must want to talk of Sheila. He must be deeply troubled to get in touch with me – and he had done it without her knowledge, for she would have told him my address. Reading his elaborate approach again, I guessed that he was making a special journey. Was she ill? But if so, surely even he, for all his camouflage, would have told me.

In some ways I was as secretive as Mr Knight, but my instinct in the face of danger was not to lose a second in knowing the worst. When I entered the Athenaeum, I was straining to have my anxieties settled. How was she? What was the matter? Had she spoken of me? But Mr Knight was too adroit for me. I was shown into the smoking-room and he began at once:

'My dear fellow, before we do anything else,' I insist on your drinking a glass of this very indifferent sherry. I *cannot* recommend it. I cannot *recommend* it. I expect you to resolve my ignorance upon the position of our poor old pound—'

He did not speak hurriedly, but he gave me no chance to break in. He appeared intent on not getting to the point. Impatience was gnawing me. Of all the interviews at which I had been kept waiting for news, this was the most baffling. Mr Knight was not at home in the Athenaeum, and it was essential for him to prove that no one could be more so. He called waiters by their names, had our table changed, wondered why he kept up his subscription, described a long talk that morning with the secretary. He proceeded over lunch to speculate intricately about the gold standard. On which – though no talk had ever seemed so meaningless – he was far more detached than most of my acquaintances. 'Of course we shall go off it,' said Mr Knight, with surprising decision and energy. 'They're talking complete nonsense about staying on it. It's an economic impossibility. At least I should have thought so, but I never think about these things. I gave up thinking long ago, Eliot. I'm just a poor simple country parson. No doubt this nonsense about the gold standard was convenient for removing our late lamented government, that is, if one had no high opinion of their merits.'

Mr Knight went on, with one of his sly darts, to wonder how warmly I regarded them. It was remarkable, in his view, how increased prosperity insensibly produced its own little effect, its own almost imperceptible effect, on one's political attitude.... 'But it's not for me to attribute causes,' said Mr Knight.

No talk had ever seemed so far away, as though I were going deaf. At last he took me upstairs for coffee, and we sat outside on one of the small balconies, looking over the corner of Waterloo Place and Pall Mall. The sunshine was hot. Buses gleamed in the afternoon light. The streets smelt of petrol and dust.

Suddenly Mr Knight remarked in an aside:

'I suppose you haven't had any experience of psychiatrists, professional or otherwise? They can't have come your way?'

'No, but—'

'I was only asking because my daughter – you remember that she brought you to my house once or twice, perhaps? – my daughter happened to be treated by one recently.'

I was riven by fear, guilt, sheer animal concern.

'Is she better?' I cried out of it all.

'She wouldn't persevere,' said Mr Knight. 'She said that he was stupider than she was. I am inclined to think that these claims to heal the soul. . . .' He was taking refuge in a disquisition on psychology and medicine, but I had no politeness left.

'How is she?' I said roughly. 'Tell me anything. How is she?'

Mr Knight had been surveying the street. For a moment he looked me in the face. His eyes were self-indulgent but sad.

'I wish I knew,' he said.

'What can I do for her?'

'Tell me,' he said, 'how well do you know my daughter?'

'I have loved her ever since I met her. That is seven years ago. I have loved her without return.'

'I am sorry for you,' he said.

For the first time I had heard him speak without cover.

In an instant he was weaving his circumlocutions, glancing at me only from the corner of his eye.

'I am an elderly man,' he remarked, 'and it is difficult to shoulder responsibility as one did once. There are times when one envies men like you, Eliot, in the prime of your youth. Even though one may seem favoured not to be bearing the heat and burden of the day. If my daughter should happen to live temporarily in London, which I believe she intends to, it would ease my mind that you should be in touch with her. I have heard her speak of you with respect, which is singular for my daughter. If she has no reliable friends here, I should find my responsibility too much of a burden.'

Mr Knight looked down his nose, and very intently, at the passers-by across the place.

'It is just possible,' he said, in an off-hand whisper, 'that my daughter may arrive in London this week. She is apt to carry out her intentions rather quickly. She speaks of returning to a house which she has actually lived in before. Yes, she has lived in London for a few months. I think I should like to give you the address, then perhaps if you ever find yourself near— The address is 68 Worcester Street, S.W.1.'

He wrote it on a piece of club paper which he pulled from his pocket. He wrote it very legibly, realising all the time that I knew that address as well as my own.

CHAPTER XLIV

BESIDE THE WATER

I RANG the familiar number on the day that Mr Knight hinted that it was 'just possible' she might return. She answered. Her voice was friendly. 'Come round,' she said, as she might have done at any previous time. 'How did you guess? I don't believe it was clairvoyance.' But she did not press me when we met. She took it for granted that I should be there, and seemed herself unchanged. She made no reference to Hugh, nor to her visit to the psychiatrist.

We sauntered hand in hand that night. For me, there was no future. This precarious innocent happiness had flickered over us inexplicably for a few days, perhaps adding up to a week in all, in our years together. Now it had chosen to visit us again.

She was sometimes airy, sometimes remote, but that had always been so. I did not want to break the charm.

For several days it seemed like first love. I said no word of her plans or mine. If this were an illusion, then let it shine a little longer. People called me clear-sighted, but if this were an illusion I did not want to see the truth.

On a warm September night we dawdled round St James's Park, and sat by the water at the palace end. It was the calmest and most golden of nights. The lamps threw bars of gold towards us, and other beams swept and passed from cars driving along the Mall. On the quiet water, ducks moved across the golden bars and left a glittering shimmer in their wake.

'Pretty,' she said.

The sky was lit up over the Strand. From the barracks the Irish bag-pipers began to play in the distance, marched round until the music was loud, and receded again.

We were each silent, while the band made several circuits. She was thinking. I was enchanted by the night.

She said:

'Was it you who sent him away?'

I answered:

'It was.'

The skirling came near, died away, came near again. Our silence went on. Her fingers had been laced in mine, and there stayed. Neither of us moved. We had not looked at each other, but were still gazing over the water. A bird alighted close in front of us, and then another.

She said:

'It makes it easier.'

I asked: 'What does it make easier?'

She said:

'I'm no good now. I never shall be. I've played my last cards. You can have me. You can marry me if you like.'

Her tone was not contemptuous, not cruel, not bitter. It was resigned. Hearing her offer in that tone, I was nevertheless as joyful as though, when I first proposed to her in my student's attic, she had said yes. I was as joyful as though we had suffered nothing – like any young man in the park that halcyon night, asking his girl to marry him and hearing her accept. At the same time, I was melted with concern.

'I want you,' I said. 'More than I've ever done. But you mustn't come to me if you could be happier any other way.'

'I've done you great harm,' she said. 'Now you've done the same to me. Perhaps we deserve each other.'

'That is not all of us,' I said. 'I have loved you. You have immeasurably enriched my life.'

'You have done me great harm,' she said, relentlessly, without any malice, speaking from deep inside. 'I might have been happy with him. I shall always think it.'

I cried:

'Let me get him back for you. I'll bring him back myself. If you want him, you must have him.'

'I forbid you,' she said, with all her will.

'If you want him—'

'I might find out that it was not true. That would be worse.'

I exclaimed in miserable pity, and put my arm round her. She leant her head on my shoulder; the band approached; a long ripple ran across the pond, and the reflections quivered. I thought that she was crying. Soon, however, she looked at me with dry eyes. She even had the trace of a sarcastic smile.

'No,' she said. 'We can't escape each other. I suppose it's just.'

She stared at me.

'I know it's useless,' she said. 'But I want to tell you this. You need a wife who will love you. And look after you. And be an ally in your career. I can do none of those things.'

'I know.'

'I'll try to be loyal,' she went on. 'That's all I can promise. I shan't be much good at it.'

A couple, arms round each other's waists, passed very slowly in front of us. When they had gone by, I looked once more at the lights upon the water, and then into her eyes.

'I know all this,' I said. 'I am marrying you because I can do nothing else.'

'Yes.'

'Why are you marrying me?'

I expected a terrible answer – such as that we had damaged each other beyond repair, that, by turning love into a mutual torment, we were unfit for any but ourselves. In fact, she said:

'It's simple. I'm not strong enough to go on alone.'

PART SEVEN

THE DECISION

CHAPTER XLV

AN AUTUMN DAWN

LYING awake in the early morning, I listened to Sheila breathing as she slept. It was a relief that she had gone to sleep at last. There had been many nights since our marriage when I had lain awake, restless because I knew that in the other bed she too was staring into the darkness. It had been so a few hours before, worse because at the end of our party with the Getliffes she had broken down.

The chink in the curtain was growing pale in the first light of day. I could just make out the shape of the room. It was nearly a year since we first slept there, when, after our marriage, we moved into this flat in Mecklenburgh Square. I could make out the shape of the room, and of her bed, and of her body beneath the clothes. I felt for her with tenderness, with familiar tenderness, with pity, and, yes, with irritation, irritation that I was forced to think only of her, that looking after her took each scrap of my attention, that in a few hours I should go to the courts tired out after a night of trying to soothe her.

I had thought that I could imagine what it would be like. One can never imagine the facts as one actually lives them, the moment-by-moment facts of every day. I had known that she dreaded company, and I was ready to give up all but a minimum. It seemed an easy sacrifice. After our marriage, I found it a constant drain upon my tenderness. Each sign of her shrinking away made me less prepared to coax her into another party. She was cutting me off from a world of which I was fond – that did not matter much. She kept me away from the 'useful' dinner tables, and professionally I should suffer for it. I saw another thing. She was not getting more confident, but less. More completely since our marriage, she believed that she could not cope.

Often I wondered whether she would have been healed if she had known physical love. Mine she could tolerate at times: she had no joy herself, though there were occasions, so odd is the flesh, when she showed a playful pleasure, which drew us closer than we had ever been. I tried to shake off the failure and remorse, and tell myself that the pundits are not so wise as they pretend. Many pairs know the magic of the flesh in ways which to others would be just a mockery. In cold blood, I thought that those who write on these topics must have seen very little of life.

In later years, when I had been more fortunate and so become more blunted, I felt that some of those reflections had been over-refined. Anyway, they did not comfort me, when she was too strained for me to touch her.

I hoped for a child, with the unrealistic hope that it might settle all: but of that there was no sign.

She wanted to meet no one – except those she discovered for herself. She had only visited her parents once since we married: that was at Christmas, as she kept some of her sense of formal duty. I myself had seen much more of Mr Knight, for we had struck up a bizarre companionship. Sheila let me go to the vicarage alone, while she hid herself in the flat or else went out in search of some of her nondescript cronies. They were an odd bunch. As in her girlhood, she was more relaxed with the unavailing, the down-and-out, even the pretentious so long as they were getting nowhere. She would sit for hours in a little café talking to the waiter; she became the confidante of typists from decayed upper-class families who were looking for a man to keep them; she went and listened to writers who somehow did not publish, to writers who did not even write.

Some of my friends thought that, among that army of the derelict, she took lovers. I did not believe it. I did not ask; I did not spy any longer; I should have known. I did not doubt that she was faithful to me. No, from them she gained the pleasure of bringing solace. She had her own curious acid sympathy with the lost. She was touched by those, young and old, whose inner lives like her own were comfortless. It was in part that feeling which drew her to my attic in my student days.

I did not spy on her any longer. My obsessive jealousy had died soon after I possessed her. When she told me, as she still did, of some man who had taken her fancy, I could sympathise now, and stroke her hair, and laugh. I was capable of listening without the knife twisting within. I thought I should be capable, if ever I discovered a man who could give her joy, of bringing him to her arms. I thought I could do that; I who had, less than two years before, watched her window for hours in the bitter night – I who had deliberately set out to break her chance of joy.

Since then I had made love to her. Since then I had lain beside her in such dawns as this. Hugh was gone now, married, dismissed further into the past in her mind than in mine (I was still jealous of him when all other jealousy was washed away). If ever she felt with another that promise of joy, I believed that I should scheme for her and watch over her till she was happy.

I did not think it was likely to happen. Her fund of interest seemed to have run low. She had gone farther along life's road than I had, though we were the same age and though my years had been more packed than hers. It was to me she turned, hoping for a new idea to occupy her. At times she turned to me as though to keep her going, as though I had to live for two. It was that condition of blankness and anxiety which I feared most in her, and which most wore me down. Even in perfect love it would be hard to live for another. In this love it was a tax beyond my strength.

She looked after the flat with the same competence that she spent on her coins. She was abler than I had thought, and picked up any technique very quickly. She did more of the housework than she need have done, for we could have afforded another servant; perhaps as an expiation, perhaps to console me, Mr Knight had surprised us with a lavish marriage settlement, and between us our income was about two thousand a year. She spent little of it on herself. Sometimes she helped out her cronies, or bought records or books. That was almost all. I should have welcomed any extravagance. I should have welcomed anything into which she could give herself away.

I had threatened Hugh that if he married her he would never know what to expect when he arrived home. No cruel prophecy had ever recoiled more cruelly. After a year of marriage, I used to stay in chambers in the evening with one care after another piling upon me. My career. I was slipping: if I were to achieve half my ambition, this was the time when I ought to take another jump forward. It was not happening. My practice was growing very slightly, but no more. I could guess too clearly that I was no longer talked about as a coming man.

There was another care which had become darker since the summer. Hints kept reaching me of a scandal breaking round George Passant and the group. I had made inquiries, and they did not reassure me. George would not confide, but I felt there was danger creeping up. Oblivious and obstinate, George shut me out. I was frightened of what might happen to him.

With those cares upon me, I would leave chambers at last, and set out home. I wanted someone to talk to, with the comfort of letting the despondency overflow. 'My girl,' I wanted to say, 'things are going badly. My bit of success may have been a flash in the pan. And there's worse news still.' I wanted someone to talk to, and, in fact, when I got home, I might find a stranger. A stranger to whom I was bound, and with whom I could not rest until I had coaxed her to find a little peace. She might, at the worst, be absolutely still, neither reading nor smoking, just gazing into the room. She might have gone out to one of her down-at-heel friends. I could not sleep until she returned, although she tiptoed into the spare room, there to spend the night on the divan. Once or twice I had found her there in the middle of the night, smoking a chain of cigarettes, playing her records, still fully dressed.

There was not one night that summer of 1932, when I could reckon on going back to content.

My unperceptive friends saw me married to a beautiful and accomplished woman, and envied me. My wiser friends were full of resentment. One or two, guessing rightly that I was less a prisoner than before my marriage, dangled other women in front of me. Not even Charles March, whose temperament was closest to my own, had much good to say of her. No one was wise enough to realise that there was one sure way to please me and to win my gratitude: that was to say not that they loved her – she received enough of that – but simply that they liked her. I wanted to hear someone say that she was sweet, and tried to be kind, and that she was harming only herself. I wanted them to be sorry for her, not for me.

Yet, lying beside her, I did not know how long I could stand it.

I was facing the corrosion of my future.

What idea had she of my other life? It seemed to her empty, and my craving for success vulgar. She did not invade me, she did not possess me, she did not wish to push me on. She had known me as a beseeching lover: she turned to me because I knew her and was not put off. For the rest, she left me inviolate and with my secrets.

Lying beside her in the silver light of the October dawn, I did not know how long I could stand it.

She bore the same sense of formal duty to me as to her parents. Just as she visited them for Christmas, so she offered, once or twice, to entertain some legal acquaintances. 'You want me to. I shall do it,' she said. I did want it, but I knew before her first dinner-party that nothing would be more of an ordeal. It was only recently that I had let her try again: and the result had been our dinner of the previous night.

I had mentioned that it was months since Henriques sent me a case. She made some indifferent response; and then, some days later, she asked if she should invite the Henriques to the flat. I was so touched by the sign of consideration that I said yes with gusto, and told her (for the sake of some minor plan) to ask the Getliffes as well. For forty-eight hours before the dinner, she was wretched with apprehension. It tore open her diffidence, it exposed her as crippled and inept.

Before they arrived, Sheila stood by the mantelpiece; I put an arm round her, tried to tease her into resting, but she was rigid. She drank four or five glasses of sherry standing there. It was rare for her to drink at all. But for a time the party went well. Mrs Getliffe greeted us with long, enthusiastic stares from her dog-like brown eyes, and cooed about the beauties and wonders of the flat. Her husband was the most valuable of guests; he was always ready to please, and he conceived it his job to make the party go. Incidentally, he provided me with a certain amusement, for I had often heard him profess a cheerful anti-semitism. In the presence of one of the most influential of Jewish solicitors, I was happy to see that his anti-semitism was substantially modified.

We gave them a good meal. With her usual technical competence, Sheila was a capable cook, and though I knew little about wine I had learned where to take advice. At any party, Getliffe became half-drunk with his first glass, and stayed in that expansive state however much he drank. He sat by Sheila's side; he had a furtive eye for an attractive woman, and a kindly one for a self-conscious hostess who needed a bit of help. He chatted to her, he drew the table into their talk. He was not the kind of man she liked, but he set her laughing. I had never felt so warm to him.

Henriques was his subdued, courteous and observant self. I hoped that he was approving. With his wife, I exchanged gossip about the March family. I smiled down the table at Sheila, to signal that she was doing admirably, and she returned the smile.

It was Getliffe, in the excess of his *bonhomie*, who brought about the change. We had just finished the sweet, and he looked round the table with his eyes shining and his face open.

'My friends,' he said, 'I'm going to call you my friends at this time of night' – he gazed at Henriques with his frank man-to-man regard – 'I've just had a thought. When I wake up in the night, I sometimes wonder what I should do if I could have my time over again. I expect we all do, don't we?'

Someone said yes, of course we did.

'Well then,' said Getliffe triumphantly, 'I'm going to ask you all what you'd really choose – if God gave you the chance on a plate. If He came to you in the middle of the night and said "Look here, Herbert Getliffe, you've seen round some of this business of life by now. You've done a lot of silly little things. Now you can have your time over again. It's up to you. You choose."'

Getliffe gave a laugh, fresh, happy and innocent.

'I'll set the ball rolling,' he said. 'I should make a clean sweep. I shouldn't want to struggle for the prizes another time. Believe me, I should just want to do a bit of good. I should like to be a country parson – like your father' – he beamed at Sheila: she was still – 'ready to stay there all my life and giving a spot of comfort to a few hundred souls. That's what I should choose. And I bet I should be a happier man.'

He turned to Mrs Henriques, who said firmly that she would devote herself to her co-religionists, instead of trying to forget that she was born a Jewess. I came next, and said that I would chance my luck as a creative writer, in the hope of leaving some sort of memorial behind me.

On my left, Mrs Getliffe gazed adoringly at her husband. 'No, I shouldn't change at all. I should ask for the same again, please. I couldn't ask anything better than to be Herbert's wife.'

Henriques said that he would elect to stay at Oxford as a don.

We were all easy and practised talkers, and the replies had gone clockwise round at a great pace. Now it was Sheila's turn. There was a pause. Her head was sunk on to her chest. She had a wineglass between her fingers; she was not spinning it, but tipping it to and fro. As she did so, drops of wine fell on the table. She did not notice. She went on tipping her glass, and the wine fell.

The pause lasted. The strain was so acute that they turned their eyes from her.

At last:

'I pass.' The words were barely distinguishable, in that strangulated tone.

Quick to cover it up, Getliffe said:

'I expect you're so busy taking care of old L.S. – you can't imagine anything else, either better or worse, can you! For better, for worse,' he said, cheerfully allusive. 'Why, I remember when L.S. first pottered into my chambers –'

The evening was broken. She scarcely spoke again until they said goodbye. Getliffe did his best, the Henriques kept up a steady considerate flow of talk, but they were all conscious of her. I talked back, anything to keep the room from silence; I even told anecdotes; I mentioned with a desperate casualness places and plays to which Sheila and I had been and how we had argued or agreed.

They all went early. As soon as the front-door closed, Sheila went straight into the spare room, without a word.

I waited a few minutes, and then followed her in. She was not crying: she was tense, still, staring-eyed, lying on the divan by her gramophone. She was just replacing a record. I stood beside her. When she was so tense, it did harm to touch her.

'It doesn't matter,' I said.

'Speak for yourself.'

'I tell you, it doesn't matter.'

'I'm no good to you. I'm no good to myself. I never shall be.' She added, ferociously: 'Why did you bring me into it?'

I began to speak, but she interrupted me:

'You should have left me alone. It's all I'm fit for.'

As I had so often done, I set myself to ease her. I had to tell her once again that she was not so strange. It was all that she wanted to hear. At last I persuaded her to come to bed. Then I listened, until she was breathing in her sleep.

She slept better than I did. I dozed off, and woke again, and watched the room lighten as the morning light crept in. Pity, tenderness, morbid annoyance crowded within me, took advantage of my tiredness, as I lay and saw her body under the clothes. The evening would do me harm, and she had not a single thought for that. She turned in her sleep, and my heart stirred.

It was full dawn. By ten o'clock I had to be in court.

CHAPTER XLVI

THE NEW HOUSE

ONE night that autumn I arrived home jaded and beset. I had been thinking all day of the rumours about George Passant which I had tried, with no success, to investigate for myself. One explanation kept obtruding itself: that George had shared with Jack Cotery in a stupid, dangerous fraud. George – in money dealings the most upright of men. Often it seemed like a bad dream. That night I could not laugh it away.

Sheila brought me a drink. It was not one of her light-hearted days, but I had to talk to her.

'I'm really anxious,' I said.

'What have I done?'

'Nothing special.' I could still smile at her. 'I'm seriously anxious about old George.'

She looked at me, as though her thoughts were remote. I had to go on.

'I can hardly believe it,' I said, 'but he and some of the others do seem to have got themselves into a financial mess. I hope to God it's not actionable. There are rumours that they've gone pretty near the edge.'

'Silly of them,' she said.

I was angry with her. My own concerns, the lag in my career, the dwindling of my prospects, those she could be indifferent to, and I was still bound to cherish her. But now at this excuse my temper flared, for the first time except in play since we were married. I cried:

'Will you never have a spark of ordinary feeling? Can't you forget yourself for a single instant? You are the most self-centred woman that I have ever met.'

She stared at me.

'You knew that when you married me.'

'I knew it. And I've been reminded of it every day since.'

'It's your own fault,' she said. 'You shouldn't have married someone who didn't pretend to love you.'

'Anyone who married you,' I said, 'would have found the same. Even if you fancied you loved him. You're so self-centred that you'd be a drag on any man alive.'

She said in a clear, steady voice:

'I suppose you're right.'

For several days she was friendly and subdued. She asked me about one of my cases. Then, after sitting silent through a breakfast-time, she said, just as I was leaving for chambers:

'I'm going away. I might come back. I don't know what I shall do.'

I said little in reply, except that I should always be there. My first emotion was of measureless relief. Walking away from Mecklenburgh Square, I felt free, light-footed, a little sad, above all exhilarated that my energies were my own again.

My sense of relief endured. I wrote an opinion that day with a total concentration such as I had not been capable of for months. I felt a spasm of irritation at the thought of explaining to the maid that Sheila was taking a holiday: I was too busy for that kind of diplomacy. But I was free. I had a long leisurely dinner with a friend that night, and returned late to Mecklenburgh Square. The windows of the flat were dark. I went into each room, and they were empty. I made myself some tea, relaxed and blessed because I need not care.

I did a couple of hours' good work before I went to bed. It was lonely to see her empty bed, lonely but a relief.

So I went on for several days. I missed her, but I should have said, if Charles March had examined me, that I missed her as I missed the sea-shore of my illness, with the nostalgia of the prison. I should have said that I was better off without her. But habits are more obstinate than freedoms: the habits of patience, stamina, desire, protective love. I told myself that the cruel words had driven her away. I could not trust my temper even now. I had made the accusations which would hurt her most; they were true, but I had done her enough harm before. I did not like the thought of her wandering alone.

In much that I thought, I was deceiving myself. She was still dear to me, selfishly dear, and that was truer than tenderness or remorse. Yet even so my relief was so strong that I did not act as I should have done only a few months earlier. I worked steadily in chambers and in the flat at night. I wrote for news of George. I did not walk among the crowds in the imbecile hope of seeing her face. All I did was telephone her father: they had had no word. Mr Knight's sonorous voice came down the wire, self-pitying and massively peevish, reproaching me and fate that his declining years and delicate health should be threatened by such a daughter. Then I inquired of some of her acquaintances, and called at the cafés where she liked to hide. No one had seen her.

I began to be frightened about her. Through my criminal cases I had some contact with the police, and I confided in an inspector at the Yard whom I knew to be sensible. They had no information. I could only go home and wait.

I became angry with her. It was her final outrage not to let me know. I was frightened. She was not fit to be alone. I sat in the flat at night, pretending to work, but once more, and for a different reason, her shadow came between me and the page.

Six days after she left, I was sitting alone. The front door clicked, and I heard a key in the lock. She walked into the room, her face grey and strained, her dress bedraggled. Curiously, my first emotion was again of relief, of tired but comforting relief.

'I've come back,' she said.

She came towards me with a parcel in her hands.

'Look, I've brought something for you,' she said.

Under her eyes, I unwrapped the paper. She had kept a child-like habit of bringing me presents at random. This was a polished, shining, rose-wood box: I threw open the lid, and saw a curious array of apparatus.

There were two fountain-pens lying in their slots, bottles of different coloured inks, writing-pads, a circular thermometer, a paper-weight in the shape of a miniature silver-plated yacht. It was the least austere and the most useless of collections, quite unlike her style.

'Extremely nice,' I said, and drew her on to my knees.

'Moderately nice,' she corrected me, and buried her head in my shoulder.

I never knew exactly where she had spent those days. She had certainly slept two or three nights in a low lodging-house near Paddington Station. It was possible that she tried to find a job. She was not in a state to be questioned. She was miserable and defeated. Once more I had to find something to which she could look forward. Make her look forward – that was all I could do for her. Should we go abroad at Christmas? Should we leave this flat, where, I said, bad luck had dogged us, and start again in a new house?

It astonished me, but that night she caught almost hysterically at the idea. She searched through the newspapers, and would have liked me to telephone one agent without waiting till the morning. Midnight had gone, but she was full of plans. To buy a house – it seemed to her like a solution. She felt the pathetic hope that sets the heartbroken off to travel.

So, on the next few afternoons, I had to get away early from chambers in order to inspect houses along the Chelsea reach. The wind was gusty, and the autumn leaves were being whirled towards the bright cloud-swept sky. I begrudged the time. Once again, it meant a case prepared ten per cent less completely than if I were settled. Yet it was a joy, in those windy evenings, to see her safe. She had decided on Chelsea; she had decided that we must have a view of the river; and we looked at houses all along the Embankment from Antrobus Street to Battersea Bridge. In a few days she discovered what she wanted, at the east end of Cheyne Walk. It was a good-looking early-Victorian house with a balcony and a strip of garden, twenty yards by ten, running down to the pavement. I had to pay for a fifteen-year lease. I borrowed the money from Mr Knight. He agreed with me that, if this house might make her tranquil, she must have it. Avaricious as he was, he would have lent more than that so as not to have her on his conscience.

As I signed the lease, I wondered where she and I would be living in fifteen years.

We moved in by the middle of November. On our first evening the fog rolled up from the river, so thick that, walking together up and down the garden, we could not make out people passing by outside. We heard voices, very clear, from a long way down the Embankment. Now and then the fog was gilded as a car groped past. We were hidden together as we walked in the garden; we might have been utterly alone; and there, in the cold evening, in the dark night, I embraced her.

When we went in to dinner, we left the curtains undrawn, so that the fire shone on the writhing fog behind the panes. On the river a boat's horn gave a long stertorous wail. We were at peace.

That visitation of happiness remained for a few days. Then all became as it had been in the flat. Once more I dreaded to go home, for fear of what awaited me. The familiar routine took charge. Once more the night was not over until I knew she was asleep. In the new house, she sat alone beside her gramophone in a high bright room.

One December evening, I was reading, trying to pluck up the fortitude to go into that room and calm her, when the telephone rang. It was to tell me that the police had begun their inquiries into George Passant's affairs, that I was needed that night and must catch the next train.

CHAPTER XLVII

ANOTHER NIGHT IN EDEN'S DRAWING-ROOM

GEORGE'S friends had sent for me because I was a lawyer. Before I had talked to him for half an hour that night, I thought it more likely than not that he would be prosecuted. I was relieved that I had something to do, that I was forced to think of professional action. It would have been harder just to listen helplessly to his distress.

He was both massive and persecuted. He was guarding his group: sometimes he showed his old unrealistic optimism, and believed that this 'outrage' would blow over. I could not be certain how much he was concealing from me, though he was grateful for my affection. Even in the fear of disgrace, his mind was as precise as ever. It was astonishing to listen to a man so hunted, and hear a table of events, perfectly clear and well ordered, in which he and Jack Cotery had taken part for four years past.

I did not understand it all until near the end of the trial; but from George's account, in that first hour, I could put together most of the case that might be brought against them.

George and Jack had been engaged in two different schemes for making money; and the danger was a charge of obtaining this money by false pretences, and (for technical reasons) of conspiracy to defraud.

The schemes were dissimilar, though they had used the same financial technique. After giving up his partnership with Eden, Martineau had played with some curious irrelevant ventures before he finally made his choice and renounced the world; one of those was a little advertising agency, which had attached to it the kind of small advertising paper common in provincial towns.

Jack Cotery had persuaded George that, if they could raise the money and buy out Martineau's partner, the agency was a good speculation. In fact, it had turned out to be so. They had met their obligations and made a small, steady profit. It looked like a completely honest business, apart from a misleading figure in the statement on which they had raised money. No sensible prosecution, I thought both then and later, would bring a charge against them on that count – if there existed one single clinching fact over the other business.

They had gone on from their first success to a project bigger altogether; they had decided to buy the farm and some other similar places and run them as a chain of youth hostels. In George's mind it was clear that one main purpose had been to possess the farm in private, so as to entertain the group. Jack had ranged about among their acquaintances, given all kinds of stories of attendances and profits, and on the strength of them borrowed considerable sums of money. I could imagine him doing it; I had little doubt that, whatever George knew of those stories, Jack Cotery had not kept within the limits of honesty. From the direction of the first enquiries, there seemed a hope that nothing explicitly damning had come to light. Looking at the two businesses together, however, I was afraid that the prosecution would have enough to go on. I went from George to Eden's house, where I was staying the night; and there, by the fireside in the drawing-room, where I had once waited with joy for Sheila, I told Eden the story to date, and what I feared.

'These things will happen,' said Eden, with his usual impenetrable calm. 'Ah well! These things will happen.'

'What do you think?'

'You're right, of course, we've got to be prepared.'

His only sign of emotion was a slight irritability; I was surprised that he was not more upset about the credit of his firm. 'I must say they've been very foolish. They've been foolish whatever they've been doing. They oughtn't to try these things without experience. It's the sort of foolishness that Passant would go in for. I've told you that before—'

'He's one of the biggest men I've met. That still holds after meeting a few more,' I said, more harshly than I had ever spoken to Eden. For a moment, his composure was broken.

'We won't argue about that. It isn't the time to argue now. I must consider what ought to be done,' he said; his tone, instead of being half-friendly, half-paternal as I was used to, had become the practised cordial one of his profession. He did not like his judgment questioned, especially about George. 'I can't instruct you myself. But I can arrange with some-one else to act for Passant. And I shall tell them that you're to be used from the beginning. That is, if this business develops as we all hope it won't. . . .'

I wanted to take the case. For, above all, I knew what to conceal.

I knew that the case might turn ugly. George was frightened of his legal danger: he was a robust man, and it was the simple danger of prison that frightened him most; but there was another of which he was both terrified and ashamed. The use of the farm; the morals and 'free life' of the group; they might all be dragged through the court. It would not be pretty, for the high thinking and plain living of my time had changed by now. The flirtations which had been the fashion in the idealistic days had not satisfied the group for long. Jack's influence had step by step played on George's passionate nature. Jack had never believed in George's ideals for an instant; and in that relation there could only be one winner. George had his great gift for leadership, but he was weak, a human brother, a human hypocrite, uncertain of the intention of his own desires. With someone like Jack who had no doubt of his desires or George's or any man's, George was in the long run powerless. And so it happened that he, who was born to be a leader, was in peril of being exposed to ridicule and worse than ridicule as the cheapest kind of provincial satyr.

I tried to think of any tactic that would save him. Back in London I sat over the papers night after night. Sheila was in her worst mood, but I could do little for her, and made nothing of an attempt. I could not drag myself to her room, if it meant only the usual routine. For once I prayed for someone who would give me strength, instead of bleeding away such as I had.

For some days Hotchkinson, the solicitor to whom Eden had deputed the case, sent me no news. I had a fugitive hope that the police had found the case too thin. Then a telegram arrived in chambers to say 'clients arrested applying for bail'. It was the middle of December, and term would soon be over. After that morning, the next hearing in the police court was fixed for 29 December. I had no case in London till January; I thought I could be more use if I lived in the town for the next fortnight.

I went home to Chelsea to tell Sheila so. I wondered if she would perceive the true reason – that only away from her could I be free enough to work for them all out. I could suffer no distraction now.

She was quiet and sensible that morning, when I told her of the arrests. 'I'm sorry,' she said. 'I suppose it's been worrying you.'

I smiled a little.

'I did my best to warn you,' I said.

'I've been a bit – caged-in.' It was the word she often used; even she, ruthless about herself, sometimes wanted to domesticate her own behaviour.

I said that I ought to stay at Eden's until the New Year.

'Why?'

'I must win this case.'

'Will it help you? Going away like that?' She was staring at me.

'It's rather a tangled case. Remember, they'll tell me everything they can—'

'Is it more tangled than all the others? You've never been away before.'

She said nothing more, except that she would go to her parents for Christmas Day. 'If you think that my father won't find out that you're staying at Eden's,' she said with her old sarcastic grin, 'you're very much mistaken. I'm not going to make your excuses for you. You'd better come over at Christmas and have a shot yourself.'

In the next fortnight I spent much of my time with George, and I saw Jack whenever he wanted me. Step by step they came to feel secure, as though I were still among them. George learned to believe that I had not altered, and was on his side. So far as I had altered, in fact, it was in a direction that brought me nearer to him in his trouble. When I was younger and he had known me best, I was struggling, but failure was an experience that I neither knew nor admitted as possible for myself. I believed with a hard, whole, confident heart that success was to be my fortune. I had the opaqueness of the successful, and the impatience of the successful with those so feeble and divided that they fell away. Since then, in my weeks of illness, I had acknowledged absolute surrender – and that I could not forget. I had known the depth of failure, and from that time I was bound to anyone who started with gifts and hope, and then felt his nature break him; I was bound not by compassion or detached sympathy, but because I could have been his like, and might still be. So, in those threatening days, I came near to George.

And yet, as I walked from Eden's to George's through the harsh familiar streets, I was often hurt by the changes in his life – not the fraud, but the transformation of his ideal society into a Venusberg. I wished that it had not happened. I was hurt out of proportion, considering the world in which I lived. Did I, who thought I could take the truth about any human being, wish to shut my eyes to half of George? Or was I trying to preserve the days of my young manhood, when George was spinning his innocent, altruistic, Utopian plans, and I was happy and expectant because of the delights to come?

It was that pain, added to George's, which led me into an error in legal tactics. I knew quite well that the prosecution's case was likely to be so strong that we had no chance of getting it dismissed in the police court on the twenty-ninth. The only sane course was to hold our defence and let it go to the assizes; on the other hand, if the lucky chance came off, and we defended and won in the police court, we might keep most of the scandal hidden. It was a false hope, and I was wrong to have permitted it. But George's violence and suffering over-persuaded me: if the prosecution in the police court was weaker than we feared, I might risk going for an acquittal there.

It did no positive harm to hold out such a hope. But I had to explain it to Eden and Hotchkinson. They were cool-headed men, and they strongly disagreed. It was much wiser, they said, to make up our minds at once. The case was bound to go to the assizes. Surely I must see that? Eden was troubled: I was young, but I had a reputation for good legal judgment. Both he and Hotchkinson thought I had been a more brilliant success at the Bar than was the fact. They treated me with an uneasy respect. Nevertheless, they were sound, sensible solicitors. They believed that I was wrong in considering such tactics; they believed that I was wrong, said so with weight, and firmly advised me against it.

That discussion took place on Christmas Eve. During my stay so far, I had not felt like visiting my relations and acquaintances in the town, and after the disagreement I felt less so than ever. But I wanted to avoid attending Eden's party, and so I went off to call on Aunt Milly and my father. I had to tell them about the case, which had already been mentioned in the local papers. Aunt Milly, very loyal when once she had given her approval, was indignant about George. She was sure that he was innocent, and could have been involved only through unscrupulous persons who had presumed on his good nature and what she called his 'softness'. Aunt Milly was now in the sixties, but still capable of vigorous and noisy indignation. 'My word!' said my father, full of simple wonder that I should be appearing in public in the town. 'Well, I'll be blowed!' He was just about to slink out of Aunt Milly's house for a jocular Christmas Eve, going round singing with the waits. Getting me alone for two minutes, he at once asked me to join the party. 'Some of these houses do you proud,' said my father, with an extremely knowing look. 'I know where there's a bottle or two in the kitchen –'

I spent next day at the Knights'. It was the most silent time I had known inside that house. The four of us were alone. I was hag-ridden by the case.

When I looked at Sheila, I saw only an inward gaze. She had not made a single inquiry throughout the day. We walked for a few minutes in the rose-garden. She said that she would have liked to talk to me. Not one word about the case. I was angry with her, angry and tired. I could not rouse myself to say that soon I should have time, soon I should be home refreshed and ready to console her.

All that day I wanted to get her out of my sight.

Mrs Knight was unusually quiet. She knew that something was wrong with our marriage, and, though she blamed me, it was out of her depth. As for Mr Knight, he would scarcely speak to me. Not because his daughter was miserable. Not because I was so beset that my voice was dead. No, Mr Knight would not speak to me for the simple reason that he was huffed. And he was huffed because I had chosen to live in Eden's house and not in his.

No explanation was any good – that I must see George and the others night and day, that I could not drive in and out from the country, that, whatever happened, even if we got them off, Eden was George's employer and it was imperative for me to keep his good will. No explanation appeased Mr Knight. And, to tell the truth, I was too far gone to make many.

'No one bothers to see me,' he said. 'No one bothers to see me. I'm not worth the trouble. I'm not worth the trouble.'

He broke his dignified silence only because his inquisitiveness became too strong. No one more loved a scandal, or had a shrewder eye for one, than Mr Knight. Despite being affronted, he could not rest when he had the chief source of secret information at his dinner-table.

I drank a good deal that night, enough to put me to sleep as soon as we went to bed. When I woke, Sheila was regarding me with a quizzical smile.

'The light's rather strong, isn't it?' she said.

She made me a cup of tea. There were occasions when she enjoyed nursing me. She said:

'You got drunk. You got drunk on purpose.' She stared at me, and said: 'You'll get over it.'

As I kissed her goodbye, I reminded her that the case came up on the twenty-ninth. In a tone flatter and more expressionless than she had used that morning, she wished me luck.

In the police court, I had not listened to the prosecutor's speech for half an hour before I knew that Eden and Hotchkinson had been right. There was no chance of an acquittal that day. There never had been a chance. I should have to reserve our defence until the assizes. At the lunch break I said so, curtly because it was bitter to wound him more, to George.

When I told Eden, he remarked: 'I always thought you'd take the sensible view before it was too late.'

The next night Eden and I had dinner together in his house. He was at his most considerate. He said that I had been 'rushing about' too much; it was true that I was worn by some harrowing scenes in the last twenty-four hours. He took me into the drawing-room, and stoked the fire high in the grate. He gave me a substantial glass of brandy. He warmed his own in his hands, swirled the brandy round, smelt and tasted, with a comfortable, unhurried content. Just as unhurriedly, he said:

'How do you feel about yesterday?'

'It looks none too good.'

'I completely agree. As a matter of fact,' he said, 'I've been talking to Hotchkinson about it during the afternoon. We both consider that we shall be lucky if we can save those young nuisances from what, between ourselves, I'm beginning to think they deserve. But I don't like to think of their getting it through the lack of any possible effort on our part. Don't you agree?'

I knew what was coming.

Eden's voice was grave and cordial. He did not like distressing me, and yet he was enjoying the exercise of his responsibility.

'Well then, that's what Hotchkinson and I have been considering. And we wondered whether you ought to have a little help. You're not to misunderstand us, young man. I'd as soon trust a case to you as anyone of your age, and Hotchkinson believes in you as well. Of course, you were a trifle over-optimistic imagining you might get a dismissal in the police court, but we all make our mistakes, you know. This is going to be a very tricky case, though. It's not going to be just working out the legal defence. If it was only doing that in front of a judge, I'd take the responsibility of leaving you by yourself –'

Eden entered on a disquisition about the unpredictable behaviour of juries, their quirks and obstinacies and prejudices. I wanted to be spared that, in my impatience, in my wounded vanity. Soon I broke in:

'What do you suggest?'

'I want you to stay in the case. You know it better than anyone already, and we can't do without you. But I believe, taking everything into consideration, you ought to have someone to lead you.'

'Who?'

'I was thinking of your old chief – Getliffe.'

Now I was savage.

'It's sensible to get someone,' I said with violence, 'but Getliffe – seriously, he's a bad lawyer.'

'No one's a hero to his pupils, you know,' said Eden. He pointed out, as was true, that Getliffe was already successful as a silk.

'I dare say I'm unfair. But this is important. There are others who'd do it admirably.' I rapped out several names.

'They're clever fellows.' Eden gave a smile, obstinate, displeased, unconvinced. 'But I don't see any reason to go beyond Getliffe. He's always done well with my cases.'

I was ashamed that the disappointment swamped me. I had believed that I was entirely immersed in the danger to my friends. I had lain awake at night, thinking of George's suffering, of how he could be rescued, of plans for his life afterwards. I believed that those cares had driven all others from my mind. In fact they were not false.

Yet, when I heard Eden's decision, I could think of nothing but the setback to myself. It was no use pretending. No one can hide from himself which wound makes him flinch more. This petty setback overwhelmed their disaster. It was a wound in my vanity, it was a wound in my ambition. By its side, my concern for George had been only the vague shadow of an ache.

It lay bare the nerve both of my vanity and of my ambition. Much had happened to me since first in this town they had begun to drive me on; sometimes I had forgotten them; now they were quiveringly alive. They were, of course, inseparable; while one burned, so must the other. In all ambitions, even those much loftier than mine, there lives the nerve of vanity. That I should be thought not fit to handle a second-rate case! That I should be relegated in favour of a man whom I despised! I stood by the fire in Eden's drawing-room after he had gone to bed. If I had gone further, I thought, they would not have considered giving me a leader. I knew, better than anyone, that I had stood still this last year, and longer than that. They had not realised it, they could not have heard the whiffs of depreciation that were beginning to go round. But if I had indisputably arrived, they would not have passed me over.

There was one reason, and one reason only, I told myself that night, why I had not arrived. It was she. The best of my life I had poured out upon her. I had lived for two. I had not been left enough power to throw into my ambition. She not only did not help: she was the greatest weight I carried. She alone could have kept me back. Without her, I should have been invulnerable now. It was she who was to blame.

CHAPTER XLVIII

TWO MEN REBUILD THEIR HOPES

IN the assize court, Getliffe began badly. He took nearly all the examinations himself, he did not allow me much part. Once, when he was leading me, he had said with child-like earnestness: 'It's one of my principles, L.S. – if one wants anything done well, one must do it oneself.' The case went dead against us. Getliffe became careless, and in his usual fashion got a name or figure wrong. It did us harm. At those moments – though once we were in court I was passing him a junior's correcting notes, I was carried along by my anxiety about George's fate – I felt a dart of degrading satisfaction. They might think twice before they passed me over for an inferior again.

But then Getliffe stumbled on to a piece of luck. Martineau was still wandering on his religious tramps, but he had been tracked down, and he attended to give evidence about the advertising agency. In the box he allowed Getliffe to draw from him an explanation of the most damning fact against George – for Martineau took the fault upon himself. It was he who had misled George.

From that point, Getliffe believed that he could win the case. Despite the farm evidence which he could not shift; in fact, he worried less about that evidence than about the revelations of the group's secret lives. The scandals came out, and George's cross-examination was a bitter time. They had raised much prejudice, as Getliffe said. Nevertheless, he thought he could 'pull something out of the bag' in his final speech. If he could smoothe the prejudice down, Martineau's appearance ought to have settled it. It was the one thing the jury were bound to remember, said Getliffe with an impish grin.

In his final speech, Getliffe kept his promise and 'pulled something out of the bag'. Yet he believed what he said; in his facile emotional fashion, he had been moved by the stories both of Martineau and of George, and he just spoke as he felt. It was his gift, naïve, subtle and instinctive, that what he felt happened to be convenient for the case. He let himself go; and as I listened, I felt a kind of envious gratitude. As the verdict came near, I was thankful that he was defending them. He had done far better than I should ever have done.

He dismissed the charge over the agency; and the one over the farm, already vague and complicated enough, he made to sound unutterably mysterious. Then we expected him to sit down; but instead he set out to fight the prejudice that George's life had roused. He did so by admitting the prejudice himself. 'I want to say something about Mr Passant, because I think we all realise he has been the leader. He is the one who set off with this idea of freedom. It's his influence that I'm going to try to explain. You've all seen him. . . . He could have done work for the good of the country and his generation – no one has kept him from it but himself. No one but himself and the ideas he has persuaded himself to believe in: because I'm going a bit further. It may surprise you to hear that I do genuinely credit him with setting out to create a better world.

'I don't pretend he has, mind you. You're entitled to think of him as a man who has wasted every gift he possesses. I'm with you.' Getliffe went on to throw the blame on to George's time. As he said it, he believed it, just as he believed in anything he said. He was so sincere that he affected others. It was one of the most surprising and spontaneous of all his speeches.

The jury were out two hours. Some of the time, Getliffe and I walked about together. He was nervous but confident. At last we were called into court.

The door clicked open, the feet of the jury clattered and drummed across the floor. Nearly all of them looked into the dock.

The clerk read the first charge, conspiracy over the agency. The foreman said, very hurriedly: 'Not guilty.'

After the second charge (there were nine items in the indictment), the 'Not guilty' kept tapping out, mechanically and without any pause.

It was not long before George and I got out of the congratulating crowd, and walked together towards the middle of the town. The sky was low and yellowish-dark. Lights gleamed into the sombre evening. We passed near enough to see the window of the office where I had worked. For a long time we walked in silence.

Then George said, defiantly, that he must go on. 'I've not lost everything,' he said. 'Whatever they did, I couldn't have lost everything.'

Then I heard him rebuild his hopes. He could not forget the scandal;

curiously, it was Getliffe's speech, that perhaps saved him from prison, which brought him the deepest rancour and the deepest shame. From now on, he would often have to struggle to see himself unchanged. Yet he was cheerful, brimming with ideas and modest plans, as first of all he thought of how he would earn a living. He wanted to leave the town, find a firm similar to Eden's, and then work his way through to a partnership.

He developed his plans with zest. I was half-saddened, half-exalted, as I listened. It brought back the nights when he and I had first walked in those streets. Just as he used to be, he was eager for the future, and yet not anxious. He was asking only a minor reward for himself. That had always been so; I remembered evenings similar to this, with the shop-windows blazing and the sky hanging low, when George was brimful of grandiose schemes for the group, of grandiose designs for my future. For himself, he had never asked more than the most improbable of minor rewards, a partnership with Eden. I remembered nights so late that all the windows were dark; there were no lights except on the tram-standards; we had walked together, George's great voice rang out in that modest expectation – and the dark streets were lit with my own ravenous hopes.

Walking by his side that evening, I felt the past strengthen me now. Just as I used to be, I was touched and impatient at his diffidence, heartened by his appetite for all that might come. Yet, even for him, perhaps most of all for him, not given insight into his desires, it would be arduous beyond any imagining to rebuild a life. With the strength and hope he had given me as a young man and which, even in his downfall, he gave me still, I thought of his future – and of mine.

We went into a café, sat by an upstairs window, and looked over the roofs out to the wintry evening sky. As George came to think of his private world, the group that had started as Utopia and ended in scandal, his face was less defiant and sanguine than his words. He could not blind himself to what he must go through, and yet he said: 'I'm going to work for the things I believe in. I still believe that most people are good, if they're given the chance. No one can stop me helping them, if I think another scheme out carefully and then put my energies into it again. I haven't finished. You've got to remember I'm not middle-aged yet. I believe in goodness. I believe in my own intelligence and will. You don't mean to tell me that I'm bound to acquiesce in crippling myself?'

He was so much braver than I was. He was facing self-distrust, which as a young man he had scarcely known at all. He realised that there were to be moments when he would ask what was to become of him. Yet he would cling to some irreducible fragment of his hope. And it strengthened me, sitting by him in the café that evening, as I heard it struggle through, as I heard that defiant voice coming out of his scandal, downfall, and escape.

It strengthened me in my different fashion. I should never be so brave, nor have so many private refuges. My life up to now had been more direct than his. I had to come to terms with a simpler conflict. Listening to George that evening, I was able to think of my ambition and my marriage more steadily than I had ever done.

My ambition was as imperative now as in the days when George first helped me. I did not need proof of that – but if I had, Eden's decision would have made it clear. It was not going to dwindle though it might become subtler or change its course. If I died with it unfulfilled, I should die unreconciled: I should feel that I had wasted my time. I should never be able to comfort myself that I had grown up, that I had gone beyond the vulgarities of success. No, my ambition was part of my flesh and bone. In ten years, the only difference was that now I could judge what my limits were. I could not drive beyond them. They seemed to be laid down in black and white, that evening after George's trial.

Much of what I had once imagined for myself was make-believe. I never should be, and never could have been, a spectacular success at the Bar. That I had to accept. At the very best, I could aim at going about as far as Getliffe. It was an irony, but such was my limit. With good luck I might achieve much the same status – a large junior practice, silk round forty, possibly a judgeship at the end.

That was the maximum I could expect. It would need luck. It would mean that my whole life should change before too late. As it was now, with Sheila unhinging me, I should not come anywhere near. As it was now – steadily I envisaged how I should manage. One could make it too catastrophic, I knew. I should not lose much of my present practice. I might even, as my friends became more influential, increase it here and there. Perhaps, as the years went on, I should harden myself and be able to work at night without caring how she was. At the worst, even if she affected me as in the last months, I could probably earn between one and two thousand a year, and do it for the rest of my life. I should become known as a slightly seedy, mediocre barrister – with the particular seediness of one who has a brilliant future behind him.

Could I leave her? I thought of her more lovingly now than in my anger after Eden's decision. I remembered how she had charmed me. But the violence of my passion had burned out. Yes, I could leave her – with sorrow and with relief. At the thought, I felt the same emancipation as when, that morning at breakfast, she announced that she might not return.

I should be free of the moment-by-moment extortion. I could begin, without George's bravery but with my own brand of determination, to rebuild my hopes – not the ardent hopes of years before, nothing more than those I could retain, now I had come to terms. They were enough for me, once I was free.

There was nothing against it, I thought. She was doing me harm. I had tried to look after her, and had failed. She would be as well off without me. As for the difference to me – it would seem like being made new.

George and I were still sitting by the café window. Outside, the sky had grown quite dark over the town. More and more as I grew older, I had come to hide my deepest resolves. George was always the most diffident of men at receiving a confidence – and that day of all days, he had enough to occupy him.

Yet suddenly I told him that my only course was to separate from Sheila, and that I should do so soon.

CHAPTER XLIX

PARTING

I WAITED. I told myself that I wished to make the break seem unforced: I was waiting for an occasion when, for her as well as me, it would be natural to part. Perhaps I hoped that she would go off again herself. Nothing was much changed. Week after week I went to chambers tired and came home heavy-hearted. All the old habits returned, the exhausted pity, the tenderness that was on the fringe of temper, the reminder of passionate and unrequited love. It was a habit also to let it drift. For my own sake, I thought, I had to fix a date.

In the end, it was the early summer before I acted, and the occasion was much slighter than others I had passed by. I had given up any attempt to entertain at our house, or to accept invitations which meant taking her into company. More and more we had come to live in seclusion, as our friends learned to leave us alone. But I had a few acquaintances from my early days in London, who had been kind to me then. Some of them had little money, and had seen me apparently on the way to success, and would be hurt if I seemed to escape them. Theirs were the invitations I had never yet refused, and since our marriage Sheila had made the effort to go with me. Indeed, of all my various friends, these had been the ones with whom she was least ill at ease.

At the beginning of June we were asked to such a party. It meant travelling out to Muswell Hill, just as I used to when I was penniless and glad of a hearty meal in this same house. I mentioned it to Sheila, and as usual we said yes. The day came round; I arrived home in the evening, an hour before we were due to set out. She was sitting in the drawing-room, thrown against the side of an armchair, one hand dangling down. It was a windy evening, the sky dark over the river, so that I did not see her clearly until I went close to. Of late she had been neglecting her looks. That evening her hair was not combed, she was wearing no make-up; on the hand dangling beside her chair, the nails were dirty. Once she had been proud of her beauty. Once she had been the most fastidious of girls.

I knew what I should hear.

'It's no use,' she said. 'I can't go tonight. You'd better cry off.'

I had long since ceased to persuade and force her. I said nothing, but went at once to the telephone. I was practised in excuses: how many lies had I told, to save her face and mine? This one, though, was not believed. I could hear the disappointment at the other end. It was an affront. We had outgrown them. They did not believe my story that she was ill. They were no more use or interest to us, and without manners we cancelled a date.

I went back to her. I looked out of the window, over the Embankment. It was a grey, warm summer evening, and the trees were swaying wave-like in the wind.

This was the time.

I drew up a chair beside her.

'Sheila,' I said, 'this is becoming difficult for me.'

'I know.'

There was a pause. The wind rustled.

I said slowly:

'I think that we must part.'

She stared at me with her great eyes. Her arm was still hanging down, but slowly her fingers clenched.

She replied:

'If you say so.'

I looked at her. A cherishing word broke out of me, and then I said: 'We must.'

'I thought you mightn't stand it.' Her voice was high, steady, uninflected. 'I suppose you're right.'

'If I were making you happy, I could stand it,' I said. 'But – I'm not. And it's ruining me. I can't even work—'

'I warned you what it would be like,' she said, implacably and harshly.

'That is not the same as living it.' I was harsh in return, for the first time that night.

She said:

'When do you want me to go?'

No, I said, she should stay in the house and I would find somewhere to live.

'You're turning me out,' she replied. 'It's for me to leave.' She asked: 'Where shall I go?'

Then I knew for certain that she was utterly lost. She had taken it without a blench. She had made none of the appeals that even she, for all her pride, could make in lesser scenes. She had not so much as touched my hand. Her courage was cruel, but she was lost.

I said that she might visit her parents.

'Do you think I could?' she flared out with hate. 'Do you think I could listen to them?' She said: 'No, I might as well travel.' She made strange fantasies of places she would like to see. 'I might go to Sardinia. I might go to Mentone. You went there when you were ill, didn't you?' she asked, as though it were infinitely remote. 'I made you unhappy there.' All of a sudden, she said clearly: 'Is this your revenge?'

I was quiet while the seconds passed. I replied:

'I think I took my revenge earlier, as you know.'

Curiously, she smiled.

'You've worried about that, haven't you?'

'Yes, at times.'

'You needn't.'

She looked at me fixedly, with something like pity.

'I've wondered whether that was why you've stood me for so long,' she said. 'If you hadn't done that, you might have thrown me out long ago.'

Again I hesitated, and then tried to tell the truth.

'I don't think so,' I said.

Then she said:

'I shall go tonight.'

I said that it was ridiculous.

She repeated:

'I shall go tonight.'

I said:

'I shan't permit it.'

She said:

'Now it is not for you to permit.'

I was angry, just as I always had been when she was self-willed to her own hurt. I said that she could not leave the house with nowhere to go. She must stay until I had planned her movements. She said the one word, no. My temper was rising, and I went to take hold of her. She did not flinch away, but said:

'You cannot do that, now.'

My hands dropped. It was the last stronghold of her will.

Without speaking, we looked at each other.

She got up from her chair.

'Well, it's over,' she remarked. 'You'd better help me pack.'

Her attention was caught by the wind, as mine had been, and she glanced out of the window. The trees swayed to and fro under the grey sky. They were in full June leaf, and the green was brilliant in the diffuse light. Through the window blew the scent of lime.

'I liked this house,' she said, and with her strong fingers stroked the window-sill.

We went into her sitting-room. It was more dishevelled than I had noticed it; until that evening, I had not fully realised how her finicky tidiness had broken down; just as a husband might not observe her looks deteriorate, when it would leap to the eye of one who had not seen her for a year.

She walked round the room. Though her dress was uncared-for, her step was still active, poised and strong. She asked me to guard her coins. They were too heavy, and too precious, to take with her if she was moving from hotel to hotel. The first thing she packed was her gramophone.

'I shall want that,' she said. Into the trunk she began to pack her library of records. As I handed some to her, she gave a friendly smile, regretful but quite without rancour. 'It's a pity you weren't musical,' she said.

I wanted her to think of clothes.

'I suppose I shall need some,' she said indifferently. 'Fetch me anything you like.'

I put a hand on her shoulder.

'You must take care of yourself.' Despite the parting, I was scolding her as in our occasional light-hearted days.

'Why should I?'

'You're not even troubling about your face.'

'I'm tired of it,' she cried.

'For all you can do, it is still beautiful.' It was true. Her face was haggard, without powder, not washed since that morning or longer, but the structure of the bones showed through; there were dark stains, permanent now, under her eyes, but the eyes themselves were luminous.

'I'm tired of it,' she said again.

'Men will love you more than ever,' I said, 'but you mustn't put them off too much.'

'I don't want it.'

'You know that you've always attracted men—'

'I know. If I had attracted them less, it might have been better for me. And for you as well.'

She went on stacking books in the trunk, but I stopped her.

'Listen to me once more. I hope you will find a man who will make you happy. It is possible, I tell you.'

She looked at me, her face still except for the faint grimace of a smile.

'You must believe that,' I said urgently. 'We've failed. But this isn't the end.'

She said:

'I shan't try again.'

She sat down and began, with the competence that had once surprised me, to discuss the matter-of-fact arrangements. She would finish packing within an hour, and would spend that night at an hotel. I did not argue any more. Her passport was in order, and she could travel tomorrow. I would transfer money to her in Paris. It was summer, too hot for her to go south immediately. I thought it strange that, even now, she should be governed by her dislike of the heat. She would probably spend the summer in Brittany, and wait till October before she made her way to Italy. After that, she had no plans. She assumed that sooner or later I should want to marry again. If so, I could divorce her whenever I wished.

'If you are in trouble,' I said, 'you must send for me.'

She shook her head.

'I shan't do that.'

'I should want you to.'

'No,' she said. 'I might want to, but I shan't. I've done you enough harm.'

She rose and turned her face from me, looking out of the window, away from the room. Her shoulders were rigid, and her back erect.

'You may need—'

'It doesn't matter what I need.'

'Don't say that.'

Quite slowly she turned again to face me.

'It doesn't matter.' She spoke with absolute control. Her head was high.

'For a good reason. You said that this wasn't the end for me, didn't you?'

'Yes.'

'You were wrong.'

She was seeing her future; she was asking for nothing. She did not move an inch towards me. She stood quite straight, with her arms by her sides.

'Leave me alone,' she said in a clear voice. 'I'll call you when I go.'

CHAPTER L

WALK IN THE GARDEN

I WALKED in the garden. As I turned at the bottom, by the street gate, I saw that Sheila had switched on a light, so that her window shone into the premature dusk. Out of doors, in the moist air, the scent of lime was overpoweringly sweet. Sometimes the warm wind carried also a whiff of the river-smell; but over all that night hung the sweet and heavy sent, the scent of a London June.

I could not send her away. I could not manage it. I knew with complete lucidity what it meant. If I were ever to part from her, this was the time. I should not be able to change my mind again. This had been my chance: I could not take it. I was going to call her back, and fall into the old habit. I was about to sentence myself for life.

Yet there was no conflict within me. I was not making a decision. Like all the other decisions, this had been taken before I admitted it – perhaps when I knew that she was lost, certainly when I saw her, upright in her pride, asserting that there was nothing for her. She faced it without pretence. I had never known her pretend. And she would set her will to live accordingly. She would move from hotel to hotel, lonely, more eccentric as each year passed.

I could not bear to let her. There was no more to it than that. Whatever our life was like, it was endurable by the side of what she faced. I must stay by her. I could do no other. I accepted it, as the warm wind blew in my face and I smelt the lime. There was no getting out of it now. Somehow I should have to secure some rest for myself: now it was for life, I must find some way of easing it. In my practical and contriving fashion, I was already casting round – I could bear it better if she did not imprison me quite. But that would be only a relief. It was for life, and I must be there when she wanted me.

I sneezed. Some pollen had touched my nostrils. Perhaps it brought back the sensation of the chalky air in Marion's classroom, ten years before. Anyway, for a second, I remembered how I had challenged the future then. I had longed for a better world, for fame, for love. I had longed for a better world; and this was the summer of 1933. I had longed for fame: and I was a second-rate lawyer. I had longed for love: and I was bound for life to a woman who never had love for me and who had exhausted mine.

As I remembered, I was curiously at one with myself. I smiled. No one could call it a good record. The world's misfortunes, of course, had nothing to do with me – but my own, yes, they were my fault. Another man in my place would not have chosen them. I had not seen enough of my life yet to perceive the full truth of what my nature needed. I could not distinguish the chance from the inevitable. But I already knew that my bondage to Sheila was no chance. Somehow I was so made that up to now – was it irremediable – I had to reject my mother's love and its successors. Some secret caution born of a kind of vanity made me bar my heart to any who forced their way within. I had only been able to lose caution and vanity, bar and heart, the whole of everything I was, in the torment of loving someone like Sheila, who invaded me not at all and made me crave for a spark of feeling, who was so wrapped in herself that only the violence and suffering of such a love as mine brought the slightest glow.

My suffering over Sheila was the release of my vanity. At twenty-eight, walking in the garden on that night after I had tried to escape, they were the deepest parts of myself that I had so far seen. It was not the picture that others saw, for I passed as a man of warm affections, capable of sympathy and self-effacingness. That was not altogether false – one cannot act a part for years; but I knew what lay in reserve. It was not tenderness that was to stop me sending Sheila away, at this time when I knew the cost of keeping her and when my passion was spent. It was simply that she touched the depth of my vanity and suffering, and that this had been my kind of love. Yet, like George after his trial, I was still borne up by hope. More realistic than he was, I had seen something of myself, and something of my fate. In detail, I did not burke the certain truths. I should never be able to shelve my responsibility for her. That was permanent – but did I think that one day I should find true love in another ? I should now never make a success at the Bar – did I think one day I might get a new start ?

I was twenty-eight, and I could still hope. Those random encouragements were blowing in the warm wind, and I felt, as well as the strength of acceptance, a hope of the fibres, a hope of young manhood. That night, I had come to terms with what I must do. But I breathed the scent of the limes, and the half-thought visited me: 'She said that she had come to the end. As for me, I am nowhere near the end.'

I looked up at her window. I had delayed going into her, but I could delay no longer. The house was quiet. I opened the door of her room. She was standing, so still that she might have been frozen, by the trunk.

She said:

'I told you to leave me alone.'

I said:

'I can't let you go.'

For a second her face was smooth as though with shock. Then it hardened again.

'I've told you, I shall go tonight.'

I said:

'I can't let you go at all.'

She asked:

'Do you know what you're saying?'

I said: 'I know very well.' I added: 'I'm saying that I shall never speak to you as I did tonight. Not as long as we live.'

'You know what you'll lose?'

I repeated:

'I know very well.'

'I trust you,' she cried. 'I trust you.' Her control was near to snapping, but suddenly she braced herself again and said harshly: 'It won't be any different. I can't make it any easier for you.'

I nodded my head, and then smiled at her.

In the same harsh tone, she said:

'You're all I've got.' Her face was working. She said again: 'You're all I've got.'

She crumpled up, almost as if she were fainting. I sat on the sofa, and she sank her head into my lap, without another word or sound. Time and time again I stroked her hair. Outside the window, the tops of the trees were swaying in the wind.

George Passant

1925–33

George Passant

CONTENTS

PART ONE

THE TRIUMPH OF GEORGE PASSANT

PART TWO

THE FIRM OF EDEN & MARTINEAU

Contents

PART THREE. THE WARNING

PART FOUR. THE TRIAL

THE TRIUMPH OF GEORGE PASSANT

CHAPTER I

FIRELIGHT ON A SILVER CIGARETTE CASE

THE fire in our habitual public-house spurted and fell. It was a comfortable fire of early autumn, and I basked beside it, not caring how long I waited. At last Jack came in, bustled by the other tables, sat down at mine, and said:

'I'm in trouble, Lewis.'

For an instant I thought he was acting; as he went on, I believed him.

'I'm finished as far as Calvert goes,' he said. 'And I can't see my way out.'

'What have you done?'

'I've done nothing,' said Jack. 'But this morning I received a gift—'

'Who from? Who from?'

'From young Roy.'

I had heard Roy's name often in the past two months. He was a boy of fifteen, the son of the Calvert whom Jack had just mentioned and who owned the local evening paper; Jack worked as a clerk in the newspaper office, and during the school holidays, which had not yet ended, the boy had contrived to get to know him. Jack, in his easy-natured fashion, had lent him books, been ready to talk; and had not discovered until the last few days that the boy was letting himself be carried in a dream, a romantic dream.

With a quick gesture Jack felt in his coat pocket and held a cigarette case in front of the fire. 'Here we are,' he said.

The firelight shone on the new, polished silver. I held out my hand, took the case, looked at the initials J.C. (Jack Cotery) in elaborate Gothic letters, felt the solid weight. Though Jack and I were each five years older than the boy who had given it, it had cost three times as much as we had ever earned in a week.

'I wonder how he managed to buy it,' I said.

'His father is pretty lavish with him,' said Jack. 'But he must have thrown away every penny—'

He was holding the case again, watching the reflected beam of firelight with a worried smile. I looked at him: of all our friends, he was the one to whom these things happened. I had noticed often enough how women's eyes followed him. He was ready to return their interest, it is true; yet sometimes he captured it, from women as from Roy, without taking a step himself. He was not handsome; he was not even specially good-looking, in a man's eyes; he was ruddy-faced, with smooth black hair, shortish and powerfully built. His face, his eyes, his whole expression, changed like quicksilver whenever he talked.

'You haven't seen it all,' said Jack, and turned the case over. On this side there was enamelled a brilliant crest, in gold, red, blue and green; the only quarter I could make out contained a pattern of azure waves. 'He put a chart inside the case to prove these were the arms of the Coterys,' Jack went on, and showed me a piece of foolscap, covered with writing in a neat, firm, boyish hand. One paragraph explained that the azure waves 'are a punning device, Côte for Cotery, used by a family of Dorset Coterys when given arms in 1607 by James I.' I was surprised at the detail, the thoroughness, the genealogical references, the devotion to heraldry as well as to Jack; it must have taken weeks of research.

'It's quite possibly genuine,' said Jack. 'The family must have come down in the world, you know. There's still my father's brother, the Chiswick one—'

I laughed, and he let the fancy drop. He glanced at the chart, folded it, put it carefully away; then he rubbed mist from the case and studied the arms, his eyes harassed and half-smiling.

'You'd better send it back to-night,' I said.

'It's too late,' said Jack. 'Didn't you hear what I said – that I'm finished as far as old Calvert goes?'

'Does he know that Roy's given you a present?'

'He knows more than that. He happened to get hold of a letter that was coming with it.'

It was not till then that I realised Calvert had already spoken to Jack. 'What did the letter say?'

'I don't know. He's never written before. But you can guess, Lewis, you can guess. It horrified Calvert, clearly. And there doesn't seem anything I can do.'

'Did you manage to tell him,' I said, 'that it was an absolute surprise to you, that you knew nothing about it?'

'Do you think that was easy?' said Jack. 'Actually, he didn't give me much of a chance. He couldn't keep still for nerves, as a matter of fact.

He just said that he'd discovered his son writing me an – indiscreet letter. And he was forced to ask me not to reply and not to see the boy. I didn't mind promising that. But he didn't want to listen to anything I said about Roy. He dashed on to my future in the firm. He said that he'd always expected there would be a good vacancy for me on the production side. Now he realised that promotions had gone too fast, and he would be compelled to slow down. So that, though I could stay in my present boy's job for ever, he would advise me in my own interests to be looking round for some other place.'

Jack's face was downcast; we were both sunk in the cul-de-sac hopelessness of our age.

'And to make it clear,' Jack added, 'he feels obliged to cut off paying my fees at the School.'

The School was our name for the combined Technical College and School of Art which gave at that time, 1925, the only kind of higher education in the town. There Jack had been sent by Calvert to learn printing, and there each week I attended a couple of lectures on law: lectures given by George Passant, whom I kept thinking of as soon as I knew Jack's trouble to be real.

'Well, we've got a bit of time,' I said. 'He can't get rid of you altogether – it would bring too much attention to his son.'

'Who'll worry about me?' said Jack.

'He can't do it,' I insisted. 'But what are we to do?'

'I haven't the slightest idea,' said Jack.

Then I mentioned George Passant's name. At once Jack was on his feet. 'I ought to have gone round hours ago,' he said.

We walked up the London Road, crossed by the station, took a short cut down an alley towards the noisy street. Fish and chip shops glared and smelt: tramcars rattled past. Jack was more talkative now that he was going into action. 'What shall I become if Calvert doesn't let me print?' he said. 'I used to have some ideas, I used to be a young man of spirit. But when they threaten to stop you, being a printer seems the only possible job in the whole world. What else could I become, Lewis?' He saw a policeman shining his lantern into a dark shop window. 'Yes,' said Jack, 'I should like to be a policeman. But then I'm not tall enough. They say you can increase your height if you walk like this –' he held both arms vertically above his head, like Moses on the hill in Rephidim, and walked by my side down the street saying: 'I want to be a policeman.'

He stopped short, and looked at me with a rueful, embarrassed smile. I smiled too: more even than he, I was used to the hope and hopelessness, the hopes of twenty, desolately cold half an hour ago, now burning hot. I was used to living on hope. And I too was excited: the Cotery arms on the silver case ceased to be so pathetic, began to go to one's head; the story drifted like wood-smoke through the September evening. It was with expectancy, with elation, that, as we turned down a side street, I saw the light of George Passant's sitting-room shining through an orange blind.

At that time, I had known George for a couple of years. I had met him just through the chance that he gave his law lectures at the School – and that was because he wanted to earn some extra money, since he was only a qualified clerk at Eden & Martineau's, not a member of their solicitors' firm. It had been a lucky encounter for me: and George had already exerted himself on my behalf more than anyone I knew.

This was the only house in the town open to us at any hour of night. Jack knocked: George came to the door himself.

'I'm sorry we're bothering you, George,' said Jack. 'But something's happened '

'Come in,' said George, 'come in.'

His voice was loud and emphatic. He stood just over middle height, an inch or two taller than Jack; his shoulders were heavy, he was becoming a little fat, though he was only twenty-six. But it was his head that captured one's attention, his massive forehead and the powerful structure of chin and cheekbone under his full flesh.

He led the way into his sitting-room. He said: 'Wouldn't you like a cup of tea? I can easily make a cup of tea. Perhaps you'd prefer a glass of beer? I'm sure there's some beer somewhere.'

The invitation was affable and diffident. He began to call us Cotery and Eliot, then corrected himself and used our Christian names. He went clumsily round the room, peering into cupboards, dishevelling his fair hair in surprise when he found nothing. The room was littered with papers; papers on the table and on the floor, a brief-case on the hearth, a pile of books beside an arm-chair. An empty tea-cup stood on a sheet of paper on the mantelpiece, and had left a trail of dark, moist rings. And yet, apart from his débris of work, George had not touched the room; the furniture was all his landlady's; on one wall there remained a text 'The Lord God Watcheth Us', and over the mantelpiece a picture of the Relief of Ladysmith.

At last George shouted, and carried three bottles of beer to the table.

'Now,' said George, sitting back in his arm-chair, 'we can get down to it. What is this problem?'

Jack told the story of Roy and the present. As he had done to me, he kept back this morning's interview with Calvert. He put more colour into the story now that he was telling it to George, though: 'This boy is Olive's cousin, you realise, George. And that whole family seems to live on its nerves.'

'I don't accept that completely about Olive,' said George. Olive was one of what we called the 'group', the collection of young people who had gathered round George.

'Still, I'm very much to blame,' said Jack. 'I ought to have seen what was happening. It's serious for Roy too, that I didn't. I was very blind.'

Then Jack laid the cigarette case on the table.

George smiled, but did not examine it, nor pick it up.

'Well, I'm sorry for the boy,' he said. 'But he doesn't come inside my province, so there's no action I can take. It would give me considerable pleasure, however, to tell his father that, if he sends a son to one of those curious institutions called public schools, he has no right to be surprised at the consequences. I should also like to add that people get on best when they're given freedom – particularly freedom from their damned homes, and their damned parents, and their damned lives.'

He simmered down, and spoke to Jack with a warmth that was transparently genuine, open, and curiously shy. 'I can't tell him most of the things I should like to. But no one can stop me from telling him a few remarks about you.'

'I didn't intend to involve you, George,' said Jack.

'I don't think you could prevent me,' said George, 'if it seemed necessary. But it can't be necessary, of course.'

With his usual active optimism, George seized on the saving point: it was the point that had puzzled me: Calvert would only raise whispers about his son if he penalised Jack.

'Unfortunately,' said Jack, 'he doesn't seem to work that way.'

'What do you mean?'

Jack described his conversation with Calvert that morning. George, flushed and angry, still kept interrupting with his sharp, lawyer's questions: 'It's incredible that he could take that line. Don't you see that he *couldn't* let this letter get mixed up with your position in the firm?'

At last Jack complained:

'I'm not inventing it for fun, George.'

'I'm sorry,' said George. 'Well, what did the sunket tell you in the end?'

George just heard him out: no future in the firm, permission to stay in his present job on sufferance, the School course cut off: then George swore. He swore as though the words were fresh, as though the brute physical facts lay in front of his eyes. It takes a great religion to produce one great oath, in the mouths of most men: but not in George's, once inflamed to indignation. When the outburst had spent itself, he said: 'It's monstrous. It's so monstrous that even these bell-wethers can't get away with it. I refuse to believe that they can amuse themselves with being unjust and stupid at the same time – and at the expense of people like you.'

'People like me don't strike them as quite so important,' said Jack.

'You will before long. Good God alive, in ten years' time you will have made them realise that they've been standing in the road of their betters.'

There was a silence, in which George looked at Jack. Then, with an effort, George said: 'I expect some of your relations are ready to deal with your present situation. But in case you don't want to call on them, I wonder—'

'George, as far as help goes just now,' Jack replied, 'I can't call on a soul in the world.'

'If you feel like that,' said George, 'I wonder if you'd mind letting me see what I can do? I know that I'm not a very suitable person for the present circumstances,' he went on quickly. 'I haven't any influence, of course. And Arthur Morcom and Lewis here always say that I'm not specially tactful in dealing with these people. I think perhaps they exaggerate that: anyway, I should try to surmount it in a good cause. But if you can find anyone else more adequate, you obviously ought to rule me out and let them take it up.'

As George stumbled through this awkward speech, Jack was moved; and at the end he looked chastened, almost ashamed of himself.

'I only came for advice, George,' he said.

'I might not be able to do anything effective,' said George. 'I don't pretend it's easy. But if you feel like letting me—'

'Well, as long as you don't waste too much effort—'

'If I do it,' said George, returning to his loud, cheerful tone, 'I shall do it in my own style. All settled?'

'Thank you, George.'

'Excellent,' said George, 'excellent.'

He refilled our glasses, drank off his own, settled again in his chair, and said:

'I'm very glad you two came round tonight.'

'It was Lewis's idea,' said Jack.

'You were waiting for me to suggest it,' I said.

'No, no,' said Jack. 'I tell you, I never have useful ideas about myself. Perhaps that's the trouble with me. I don't possess a project. All you others manage to get projects; and if you don't George provides one for you. As with you, Lewis, and your examinations. While I'm the only one left—' he was passing off my gibe, and had got his own back: but even so, he brought off his mock pathos so well that he disarmed me – 'I'm the only one left, singing in the cold.'

'We may have to consider that, too.' George was chuckling at Jack; then the chuckles began to bubble again inside him, at a thought of his own. 'Yes, I was a year younger than you, and I hadn't got a project either,' he said. 'I had just been articled to my first firm, the one at Wickham. And one morning the junior partner decided to curse me for my manner of life. He kept saying firmly: if ever you want to become a solicitor, you've got to behave like one beforehand. At that age, I was always prepared to consider reasonable suggestions from people with inside knowledge: I was pleased that he'd given me something to aim at. Though I wasn't very clear how a solicitor ought to behave. However, I gave up playing snooker at the pub, and I gave up going in to Ipswich on Saturday nights to inspect the local talent. I put on my best dark suit and I bought a bowler hat and a brief-case. There it is—' George pointed to the hearth. Tears were being forced to his eyes by inner laughter; he wiped them, and went on: 'Unfortunately, though I didn't realise it then, these manœuvres seem to have irritated the *senior* partner. He stood it for a fortnight, then one day he walked behind me to the office. I was just hanging up my hat when he started to curse me. "I don't know what you're playing at," he said. "It will be time enough to behave like a solicitor if ever you manage to become one." '

George roared with laughter. It was midnight, and soon afterwards we left. Standing in the door, George said, as Jack began to walk down the dark street: 'I'll see you tomorrow night. I shall have thought over your business by then.'

CHAPTER II

CONFERENCE AT NIGHT

THE next night George was lecturing at the School. I attended, and we went out of the room together; Jack was waiting in the corridor.

'We go straight to see Olive,' said George, bustling kindly to the point. 'I've told her to bring news of the Calverts.'

Jack's face lit up: he seemed more uneasy than the night before.

We went to a café which stayed open all night, chiefly for lorry drivers working between London and the north; it was lit by gas mantles without shades, and smelt of gas, paraffin and the steam of tea. The window was opaque with steam, and we could not see Olive until we got inside: but she was there, sitting with Rachel in the corner of the room, behind a table with a linoleum cover.

'I'm sorry you're being got at, Jack,' Olive said.

'I expect I shall get used to it,' said Jack, with the mischievous, ardent smile that was first nature to him when he spoke to a pretty woman.

'I expect you will,' said Olive.

'Come on,' said George. 'I want to hear your report about your family. I oughtn't to raise false hopes' – he turned to Jack – 'I can only think of one way of intervening for you. And the only chance of that depends on whether the Calverts have committed themselves.'

We were close together, round the table. George sat at the end; though he was immersed in the struggle, his hearty appetite went mechanically on; and, while he was speaking intently to Jack, he munched a thick sandwich from which the ham stuck out, and stirred a great cup of tea with a lead spoon.

'Well then,' George asked Olive, 'how is your uncle taking it?'

We looked at her; she smiled. She was wearing a brilliant green dress that gleamed incongruously against the peeling wall. Just by her clothes a stranger could have judged that she was the only one of us born in a secure middle-class home. Secure in money, that is: for her father lived on notoriously bad terms with his brother, Jack's employer; and Olive herself had half-broken away from her own family.

She had taken her hat off, and her fair hair shone against the green. Watching her as she smiled at George's question, I felt for an instant that there was something assertive in her frank, handsome face.

'How are they taking it?' George asked.

'It's fluttered the dove-cotes,' she said. 'I'm not surprised. Father heard about it this morning from one of my aunts. They've all done a good deal of talking to Uncle Frank since then.'

'What's he doing?' said George.

'He's dithering,' said Olive. 'He can't make up his mind what he ought to do next. All day he's been saying that it's a pity the holidays last another week – otherwise the best thing would be to send the boy straight back to school.'

'Good God alive,' said George. 'That's a singularly penetrating observation.'

'Anyway,' said Olive, 'the rest of the family seem to have worn him down. He'd made a decision of sorts just before I came along here. He's sending a wire to Roy's housemaster to ask if he can look after the boy—'

'Has that wire been sent?' George interrupted.

'It must have been, by now,' Olive replied.

'Don't you realise how vital that is?' cried George, impatient that anyone should miss a point in tactics.

Olive did not answer, and went on: 'That's all he's plucked up his courage to do. They couldn't bully him into anything stronger. He tries to talk as though Roy was just a bit overworked and only needed a change of air. If I'd performed any of these antics at his age, I should have been in for the biggest hiding of my life. But his father never could control a daughter, let alone a son.'

George was preoccupied with her news; but at her last remark he roused himself.

'You know it's no use pretending to believe in that sadistic nonsense here.'

'I never have pretended to believe in all your beautiful dreams, have I?' she said.

'You can't take sides with those sunkets against me,' said George.

His voice had risen. We were used to the odd Suffolk words as his temper flamed up. Olive was flushed, her face still apart from her full, excitable mouth. Yet, hot-tempered as they both were, they never quarrelled for long: she understood him by instinct, better than any of us at this time. And George was far more easy with her than with Rachel, who stored away every word he spoke and who said at this moment:

'I agree, oh! of course I agree, George. We must help people to fulfil themselves—'

She was the oldest of us there, a year or more older than George: Olive was the same age as Jack and me. When Rachel gushed, it was disconcerting to notice that, in her plump, moon face, her eyes were bright, twinkling, and shrewd.

'In any case,' George said to Olive, 'there's no time tonight to resurrect matters that I've settled with you long ago. We've got more important things to do: as you'd see yourself, if you realised the meaning of your own words.'

'What do you mean?'

'You've given us a chance,' said George. 'Don't you see, your sunket of an uncle has taken two steps? He's penalised Jack: in the present state of things he can do that with impunity. But he's *also* sent messages to a schoolmaster about his son. The coincidence ought to put him in a distinctly less invulnerable position.'

'He's taking it out of Jack,' she said. 'But how can anyone stop him?'

'It's not impossible,' said George. 'It's no use trying to persuade Calvert, of course: none of us have any standing to protest direct to him. But remember that part of his manœuvre was to cut off Jack's fees at the School—' he reminded us that this step would, as a matter of routine, come before the committee which governed the affairs of students at the School – a committee on which Calvert served, as the originator of the scheme of 'bursaries'. By this scheme, employers picked out bright young men as Calvert had picked out Jack, and contributed half their fees. The School remitted the rest.

'It's a piece of luck, his being on the damned committee,' said George. 'We've only got to present our version of the coincidence. He can't let it be known that he's victimising Jack. And the others on the committee would fight very shy of lending a hand.'

'Would they all mind so much about injustice?' said Rachel.

'They mind being suspected of injustice,' said George, 'if it's pointed out to them. So does any body of men.'

'It can't be pointed out,' said Jack.

'It can,' said George. 'Canon Martineau happens to be on the committee. Though he's not a deeply religious man like his brother,' George burst into laughter. 'I can see that he's supplied with the truth. Our Martineau will make him listen.' ('Our Martineau' was the brother of the Canon and a partner in the firm of Eden & Martineau, where George worked.) 'And also—'

'And also what?' said Olive.

'I've a complete right to appear in front of the committee myself. Owing to my position at the School. It would be better if someone else put them right about Jack. But if necessary, I can do it.'

We were confused. My eyes met Olive's; like me, she was caught up in the struggle now; the excitement had got hold of us, we wanted to see it through. At the same instant, I knew that she too felt sharply nervous for George himself.

There was a moment's silence.

'I don't like it,' Olive broke out. 'You might pull off something for Jack. It sounds convincing: but then you're too good at arguing for me.'

'And you're always too optimistic,' I said. 'I don't believe that the Canon is going to make himself unpleasant for a young man he's never met. Even if you persuaded his brother, and I don't think that's likely either.'

'I'm not so sure,' said George. 'In any case, that doesn't cripple us. The essential point is that I can appear myself.'

'And how are *you* going to come out of it?' Olive cried.

'Are you certain that it won't rebound on you, personally?' asked Jack. He had turned away from Olive, angry that she made him speak against his own interest.

'I don't see how it could,' said George.

From his inside pocket he took out a sheet of notepaper and smoothed it on the table. Olive watched him anxiously.

'Look here,' she said, 'you oughtn't to be satisfied with looking after your protégés much longer. We're not important enough for you to waste all your time on us. You've got to look after yourself instead. That means you'll have to persuade Eden and Martineau to make you a partner. And they just won't do it if you've deliberately made a nuisance of yourself with important people. Don't you see,' she added, with a sudden violence, 'that you may soon curse yourself for ever having been satisfied with looking after us?'

George had begun to write on the sheet of paper. He looked up and said:

'I'm extremely content as I am. I want you to realise that I'd rather spend my time with people I value than balance tea-cups with the local bell-wethers.'

'That's because you're shy with them,' said Olive. 'Why, you've even given up going to Martineau's Friday nights.'

'I intend to go this Friday.' George had coloured. He looked abashed for the first time that night. 'And by the way, if I ever do want to become a partner, I don't think there should be any tremendous difficulty. Whatever happens, I can always count on Martineau's support.' He turned back to writing his letter.

'That's true, clearly. I've heard Martineau talk about George,' said Jack.

'You're not impartial,' said Olive. 'George, is that a letter to the committee?'

'It isn't final. I was just letting the Principal know that I might conceivably have a piece of business to bring before them.'

'I still don't like it. You're—'

Just then Arthur Morcom entered the café and walked across to Olive's side. He had recently started practice as a dentist in the town, and only met our group because he was a friend of Olive's. I knew that he was in love with her. Tonight he had called to take her home; looking at her, he felt at once the disagreement and excitement in the air.

Olive asked George:

'Do you mind if we tell Arthur?'

'Not as far as I am concerned,' said George, a little awkwardly.

Morcom had already heard the story of the boy's gift. I was set to explain what George was planning. I did it rapidly. Morcom's keen blue eyes were bright with interest, and he said 'Yes! yes!' urging me on through the last hour's conference; I watched his thin, fine-featured face, on which an extra crease, engraved far out on each cheek, gave a special dryness and sympathy to his smile. When I had finished, he said:

'I am rather worried, George. I can't help feeling that Olive is right.' He turned to Jack and apologised for coming down in the opposing camp. Jack smiled. When Olive had been trying to persuade George, Jack had been hurt and angry: but, now Morcom did the same thing, Jack said quite spontaneously: 'I bear no malice, Arthur. I dare say you're right.'

Morcom raised both the arguments that Olive and I had tried: would George's intervention really help Jack? and, more strongly, wasn't it an indiscreet, a dangerous move for George himself? Morcom pressed them with more authority than we had been able to. He and George were not close friends; neither was quite at ease with the other; but Morcom was George's own age, and George had a respect for his competence and sense. So George listened, showed flashes of his temper, and defended himself with his elaborate reasonableness.

At last Morcom said:

'I know you want to stop your friends being kept under. But you won't have the power to do it till you're firmly established yourself. Isn't it worth while to wait till then?'

'No,' said George. 'I've seen too much of that sort of waiting. If you wait till then, you forget that anyone is being kept under: or else you decide that he deserves it.'

Morcom was not only a more worldly man than George, he was usually wiser. But later on, I thought of George's statement as an example of when it was the unworldly who were wise.

'I shall soon begin to think,' said Morcom, 'that you're anxious to attack the bell-wethers, George.'

'On the contrary,' George replied, 'I am a very timid man.'

There was a burst of laughter: but Olive, watching him, did not join in. A moment after, she said:

'He's made up his mind.'

'Is it any use my saying any more?' said Morcom.

'Well,' said George, with a shy smile, 'I'm still convinced that we can put them into an impossible position. . . .'

CHAPTER III

VIEW OVER THE GARDENS

OUR meeting in the café took place on a Wednesday; two days later, on the Friday afternoon, Olive rang me up at the office. 'Roy has found something out from his father. George ought to know at once, but I can't get hold of him. It's his day at Melton, isn't it?' (The firm of Eden & Martineau had branches in several market towns: and George regularly spent a day a week in the country.) 'He must know before he goes to Martineau's tonight.'

Her voice sounded brusque but anxious; she wanted someone to see Roy, to examine the news. Jack was the obvious person, but him Roy was forbidden to meet. She asked me to go along to Morcom's as soon as I was free; she would take Roy there.

I walked to Morcom's flat in the early evening. The way led from the centre of the town, and suddenly took one between box-hedges and five-storey, gabled, Victorian houses, whose red brick flared in the sunset with a grotesque and Gothic cosiness. But the cosiness vanished, when one saw their dark windows: once, when the town was smaller, they had been real houses: now they were offices, shut for the night. Only Martineau's, at the end of the New Walk, remained a solid private house. The one next door, which he also owned, had been turned into flats: and there Morcom lived, on the top floor.

When I went into his sitting-room, Olive and Roy had just arrived. Olive had brought Morcom a great bunch of deep red dahlias, and she was arranging them on a table by the window. The red blazed as one looked down over the park, where the New Walk came to an end.

Olive put a flower into place: then, turning away from the bowl, she asked Morcom, 'Will they do?'

Morcom smiled at her. And he, the secretive and restrained, could not prevent the smile giving him completely away – more than a smile by Jack would ever do.

As though recovering himself, Morcom turned to Roy, who had stood quietly by, watching the interplay over the flowers. Morcom at once got him into conversation.

Happy because of Olive, Morcom was more than ever careful and considerate. They talked about books, and Roy's future; he was just beginning to specialise at school. They got on very well. As it happened, Morcom need not have been so careful; for Roy surprised us both by being entirely self-possessed, and himself opened the real topic.

'I'm sorry to give you all so much trouble, Mr Morcom,' he said. 'But I did think someone should know what they're doing about Mr Passant.'

He spoke politely, formally, in a light, musical voice: so politely that sometimes there sounded a ripple of mischief. His face was good-looking, highly strung, and very sad for a boy's: but sad, I felt, as much by nature as by his present trouble. Once or twice he broke into a gay, charming smile.

'I've told Olive already – but last night someone visited my father unexpectedly. I got Mother to tell me about it this morning. It was the Principal of – what Jack used to call the School. He had come to tell Father that a Mr Passant might be trying to make a fuss. Mother didn't mention it, of course, but I guessed it was about Jack. And it was all connected with a committee, which I didn't understand at the time. But Olive explained it this afternoon.'

'I had to tell him what George decided to do on Wednesday,' said Olive.

'I shan't let it out,' said Roy. 'I shouldn't have told Olive what I found out this morning – if these things weren't happening because of me.'

I tried to reassure him, but he shook his head.

'It's my fault,' he said. 'They wouldn't have been talking about Mr Passant last night if it hadn't been for me.'

'Do you know anything they said?' I asked.

'I think the Principal offered to deal with Mr Passant himself. He was sure that he could be stopped from going any further.'

'How.'

'By dropping a hint to Mr Eden and Mr Martineau,' said Roy.

I looked at Morcom: we were both disturbed.

'You think that will soon happen?' I said.

'Mother expected the Principal to see them this morning. You see,' said Roy, 'they all seem more angry with Mr Passant than they were with Jack.'

He saw that our expressions had become grave.

'Is this very serious?' he said.

'It might be a little uncomfortable, that's all,' said Morcom lightly, to ease Roy's mind. But he was still watching us, and said:

'Do you mind if I ask another question, Mr Morcom?'

'Of course not.'

'Are you thinking that it has ruined Jack's chances for good?'

'This can't affect them,' I said quickly, and Morcom agreed.

'You mustn't worry about that, Roy,' Olive said.

Roy half-believed her; her tone was kind, she cared for him more than she had admitted on Wednesday night. He was still doubtful, however, until she added:

'If you want to know, we were thinking whether they can do any harm to George Passant.'

The boy's fears lifted; for a few moments his precocity seemed to leave him, and he teased Olive as though the other three of us were not still harassed.

'Are you fond of Mr Passant, Olive?' he asked, with his lively smile.

'In a way,' she said.

'Are you sweet on him?'

'Not in the least,' she replied. She paused, then said vehemently: 'But I can tell you this: he's worth twenty Jack Coterys.'

A little later, they went away. Before they left, Roy shook hands with us both; and, as Morcom and Olive were talking together, Roy said quietly to me: 'I'm being whisked off tomorrow. I don't suppose I shall see you again for a long time, Mr Eliot. But could you spare a minute to send me word how things turn out?'

From the window, Morcom and I watched them walk across the gardens.

'I wonder what sort of life he'll have,' said Morcom. But he was thinking, hopefully that night, of himself and Olive.

We stayed by the window, eating bread and cheese from his pantry, and keeping a watch on the road below; for we had to warn George before he arrived next door, on his visit to Martineau's at home.

CHAPTER IV

A CUP OF COFFEE SPILT IN A DRAWING-ROOM

THE lamplighter passed up the road; under the lamp by Martineau's gate, the hedge top suddenly shone out of the dusk. Looking down over the gardens, Morcom was content to be quiet.

Just then, thinking how much I liked him, I felt too how he could never have blown so many of us into more richly coloured lives, as

George had done. Where should we have been, if George had not come to Eden & Martineau's?

Where should we have been? We were poor and young. By birth we fell into the ragtag and bobtail of the lower middle classes. Then we fell into our jobs in offices and shops. We lived in our bed-sitting-rooms, as I did since my mother's death, or with our families, lost among the fifty thousand houses in the town. The world seemed on the march, we wanted to join in, but we felt caught.

Myself, but for George, I might still have been earning my two pounds a week as a clerk in the education department, and wondering what to do with a legacy of £300 from an aunt. I should have acted in the end, perhaps, but nineteen is a misty age: while George gave me no rest, bullied and denounced me until I started studying law and reading for the Bar examinations. A month before Jack's crisis I had at last stopped procrastinating, and arranged to leave the office at the end of this September.

And so with the others in George's group – except Jack, who had been the unlucky one. George had set us moving, lent us money: he never seemed to think twice about lending us money, out of his income of £250 from the firm, together with an extra £30 from the School. It was the first time we had been so near to a generous-hearted man.

We became excited over the books he told us to read and the views he stood by, violent, argumentative, four square. We were carried away by his belief in human beings and ourselves. And we speculated, we could not help but speculate, about George himself. Olive certainly soon knew, and Jack and I not long afterwards, that he was not a simple character, unmixed, all of a piece. We felt, though, and nothing could shake us, that he was a man warm with broad, living nature; not good nature or bad nature, but simple nature; he was a man of flesh and bone.

I thought this, as I saw him at last walking in the lamplight, whistling, swinging his stick, his bowler hat (which he punctiliously wore when on professional business) pushed on to the back of his head.

I shouted down. George met us on the stairs: it did not take long to explain the news. He swore.

We went back to Morcom's flat to let him think it out. For minutes he sat, silent and preoccupied. Then he declared, with his extraordinary, combative optimism: 'I expect Martineau will get me to stay behind after we've finished the social flummeries. It will give me a perfect opportunity to provide him with the whole truth. They've probably presented us with the best possible way of getting it home to the Canon.'

But George was nervous as we entered Martineau's drawing-room – though perhaps no more nervous than he always felt when forced to go through the 'social flummeries', even the mild parties of Martineau's Friday nights. He only faced this one tonight because of Olive's nagging; while the rest of us went regularly, enjoyed them, and prized Martineau's traditional form of invitation to 'drop in for coffee, *or whatever's going*' – though after a few visits, we learned that coffee was going by itself.

'Glad to see you all,' cried Martineau. 'It's not a full night tonight.' There were, in fact, only a handful of people in the room; he never knew what numbers to expect, and on the table by the fireplace stood files of shining empty cups and saucers; while in front of the fire two canisters with long handles were keeping warm, still nearly full of coffee and milk, more than we should ever want tonight.

Morcom and I sat down. George walked awkwardly towards the cups and saucers; he felt there was something he should do; he felt there was some mysterious etiquette he had never been taught. He stood by the table and changed his weight from foot to foot: his cheeks were pink.

Then Martineau said:

'It's a long time since you dropped in, George, isn't it? Don't you think it's a bit hard if I only catch sight of my friends in the office? You know it's good to have you here.'

George smiled. In Martineau's company he could not remain uncomfortable for long. Even when Martineau went on:

'Talking of my friends in the office, I think Harry Eden is going to give us a look in tonight.'

George's expression became clouded, stayed clouded until Martineau baited him in his friendly manner. The remark about Eden had revived our warning: more, it made George think of a man with whom he was ill-at-ease; but no one responded to affection more quickly, and, as Martineau talked, George could put away unpleasant thoughts, and be happy with someone he liked.

We all enjoyed listening to Martineau. His conversation was gay, unpredictable and eccentric; he had a passion, an almost *mischievous* passion, for religious controversies, and he loved to tell us on Friday nights that he had been accused of yet another heresy. It did not matter to him in the slightest that none of us was religious, even in any of his senses; he was a spontaneous person, and his 'scrapes', as he called them, had to be told to someone. So he described his latest letter in an obscure theological journal, and the irritated replies. 'They say I'm getting dangerously near Manichaeism now,' he announced cheerfully tonight.

George chuckled. He had accepted all Martineau's oddities: and it seemed in order that Martineau should stand in front of his fire, in his morning coat with the carnation in the buttonhole, and tell us of some plan for puzzling the orthodox. It did not occur to any of us that he was fifty and going through the climacteric which makes some men restless at that age. His wife had died two years before; we did not notice that, in the last twelve months, the eccentricities had been brimming over.

Like George, we expected that he would stay as he was this Friday night, standing on his hearth-rug, pulling his black tie into place over his wing collar. I persuaded him to read a letter from a choleric country parson; Martineau smiled over the abusive references to himself, and read them in a lilting voice with his head on one side and his long nose tip-tilted into the air.

Then George teased him affectionately about his religious observances; which seemed, indeed, as eccentric as his beliefs. He had long ago left the Church of England, and still carried on a running controversy with his brother, the Canon; he now acted as steward in the town's most respectable Methodist congregation. There he went with regularity, with enjoyment, twice each Sunday; but he confessed, with laughter and almost with pride, that he reckoned to 'get off' to sleep before any sermon was under weigh.

'Did you manage to get off last Sunday, Mr Martineau?' said George.

'I did in the morning, George. But at night we had a stranger preaching – and there was something disturbing about his tone of voice.'

George beamed with laughter; he sank back into his armchair, and surveyed the room; it was a pleasant room, lofty, painted cream, with a print of Ingres's 'Source' on the wall opposite the fireplace. For once, he did not want his evening in respectable society to end.

And Jack, who came in for half an hour, guessed that all was well. He had been warned by Olive that pressure might be used upon George; but George was so surprisingly at home that Jack's own spirits became high. He left early: soon afterwards the room thinned out, and only George, Morcom and I stayed with Martineau.

Then Eden came in. He walked across the room to the fireplace.

George had half-risen from his chair as soon as he saw Eden: and now stayed in suspense, his hands on the arms of his chair, uncertain whether to offer it. But Eden, who was apologising to Martineau, did not notice him.

'I'm sorry I'm so late, Howard,' Eden said affably to Martineau. 'My wife has some people in, and I couldn't escape a hand of cards.'

The dome of his head was bald; his face was broad and open, and his lips easily flew up at the corners into an amiable smile. He was a few years older than his partner, and looked more their profession by all signs but one: he dressed in a more modern, informal mode. Tonight he was wearing a comfortable grey lounge suit which rode easily on his substantial figure. Talking to Martineau, he warmed a substantial seat before the fire.

George made a false start, and then said:

'Wouldn't you like to sit down, Mr Eden?'

At last Eden attended.

'I don't see why I should turn you out, Passant,' he said. 'To tell you the truth, I don't really want to leave the fire.'

But George was still half-standing, and Eden went on: 'Still, if you insist on making yourself uncomfortable—'

Eden settled into George's chair. Martineau said: 'Will you be kind, George, and give Harry Eden a cup of coffee?'

Busily George set about the task. He lifted the big canister and filled a cup. The cup in hand, he turned to Eden:

'Will that be all right, Mr Eden?'

'Well, do you know, I think I'd like it white.'

George was in a hurry to apologise. He went to put the cup down on the table: Eden, thinking George was giving him the cup, held out a hand: George could not miss the inside of Eden's forearm, and the coffee flew over Eden's coat and the thigh of his trousers.

For an instant George stood immobile. He blushed from forehead to neck.

When he managed to say that he was sorry, Eden replied in an annoyed tone: 'It was entirely my fault.' He was vigorously rubbing himself with his handkerchief. Breaking out of his stupor, George tried to help, but Eden said: 'I can look after it, Passant, I can look after it perfectly well.'

George went on his knees, and attempted to mop up the pool of coffee on the carpet: then Martineau made him sit down, and gave him a cigarette.

Actually, if it was anyone's fault, it was Eden's. But I knew that George could not believe it.

Martineau set us in conversation again. Eden joined in. After a few minutes, however, I noticed a glance pass between them: and it was Martineau who said to George: 'I was very glad to see your friend Cotery tonight. How is he getting on, by the way, George?'

George had not spoken since he tried to dry Eden down. He hesitated, and said: 'In many ways, he's doing remarkably well. He's just having to get over a certain amount of trouble in his firm. But—'

Eden looked at Martineau, and said:

'Why, do you know, Passant, I meant to have a word with Howard about that very thing tonight. I didn't expect to see you here, of course, but perhaps I might mention it now. We're all friends within these four walls, aren't we? As a matter of fact, Howard and I happened to be told that you were trying to steer this young man through some difficulties.'

Eden was trying to sound casual and friendly: he had taken the chance of speaking in front of Morcom and myself, who had originally been asked to Friday nights as friends of George's. But George's reply was edged with suspicion: I felt sure that he was more suspicious, more ready to be angry, because of the spilt cup.

'I should like to know who happened to tell you, Mr Eden.'

'I scarcely think we're free to disclose that,' said Eden.

'If that is the case,' said George, 'at least I should like to be certain that you were given the correct version.'

'Tell us, George, tell us,' Martineau put in. Eden nodded his head. Hotly, succinctly, George told the story that I had heard several times by now: the story of the gift, the victimisation of Jack.

Martineau looked upset at the account of the boy's infatuation, but Eden leant back in his chair with an acquiescent smile.

'These things will happen,' he said. 'These things will happen.'

George finished by describing the penalties to Jack. 'They are too serious for no one to raise a finger,' said George.

'So you are thinking of protesting on his behalf, are you?'

'I am,' said George.

'As a matter of fact, we heard that you intended to take up the matter – through a committee at the School, is that right?'

'Quite right.'

'I don't want to interfere, Passant.' Eden gave a short smile, and brought his finger-tips together. 'But do you think that this is the most judicious way of going about it? You know, it might still be possible to patch up something behind the scenes.'

'I'm afraid there's no chance of that. It's important to realise, Mr Eden,' George said, 'that Cotery has no influence whatever. I don't mean that he hasn't much influence: I mean that he has no single person to speak for him in the world.'

'That is absolutely true,' Morcom said quietly to Eden in a level, reasonable tone. 'And Passant won't like to bring this out himself, but it puts him in a difficult position: if he didn't try to act, no one would.'

'It's very unfortunate for Cotery, of course,' said Eden. 'I quite see that. But you can't consider, Morcom, can you, that Passant is going the right way about it? It only raises opposition when you try to rush people off their feet.'

'I rather agree,' said Morcom. 'In fact, I told Passant my opinion a couple of nights ago. It was the same as yours.'

'I'm glad of that,' said Eden. 'Because I know that Passant thinks that when we get older we like to take the course of least resistance. There's something in it, I'm afraid, there's something in it. But he can't hold that against you. You see, Passant,' he went on, 'we're all agreed that it's very unfortunate for Cotery. That doesn't mean, though, that we want to see you do something hasty. After all, there's plenty of time. This is a bit of a set-back for him, but he's a bright young chap. With patience, he's bound to make good in the end.'

'He's twenty,' said George. 'He's just the age when a man is desperate without something ahead. You can't tell a man to wait *years* at that age.'

'That's all very well,' said Eden.

'I can't bring myself to recommend patience,' said George, 'when it's someone else who has to exercise it.'

George was straining to keep his temper down, and Eden's smile had become perfunctory.

'So you intend to make a gesture,' said Eden. 'I've always found that most gestures do more harm than good.'

'I'm afraid that I don't regard this as a gesture,' said George.

Eden frowned, paused, and went on:

'There is another point, Passant. I didn't particularly want to make it. And I don't want to lay too much emphasis on it. But if you go ahead, it might conceivably raise some personal difficulties for Howard and myself – since we are, in a way, connected with you.'

'They suggested this morning that you were responsible, I suppose?' George cried.

'I shouldn't say that was actually suggested, should you, Howard?' said Eden.

'In any case,' said George, 'I consider they were using an intolerably unfair weapon in approaching you.'

'I think perhaps they were,' said Eden. 'I think perhaps they were. But that doesn't affect the fact.'

'If we were all strictly fair, George,' said Martineau, 'not much information would get round, would it?'

George asked Eden:

'Did you make these people realise that I was acting as a private person?'

'My dear Passant, you ought to know that one can't draw these distinctions. If you – not to put too fine a point on it – choose to make a fool of yourself among some influential people, then Howard and I will come in for a share of the blame.'

'I can draw these distinctions,' said George, 'and, if you will authorise me, I can make them extremely clear to these – to your sources of information.'

'That would only add to the mischief,' said Eden.

There was quiet for a moment. Then George said:

'I shall have to ask you a definite question. You are not implying, Mr Eden, that this action of mine cuts across my obligations to the firm?'

'I don't intend to discuss it in those terms,' said Eden. 'I've been talking in a purely friendly manner among friends. In my opinion you'd do us all a service by sleeping on it, Passant. That's all I'm prepared to say. And now, if you'll forgive me, Howard, I'm afraid that I must go and get some sleep myself.'

We heard his footsteps down the path and the click of the latch. George stared at the carpet. Without looking up he said to Martineau:

'I'm sorry that I've spoiled your evening.'

'Don't be silly, George. Harry Eden always was clumsy with the china.' Martineau had followed George's eyes to the stain on the carpet, and spoke as though he knew that, in George's mind, the spill was rankling more even than the quarrel. Martineau went on: 'As for your little disagreement, of course you know that Harry was trying to smooth the matter down.'

George did not respond, but in a moment burst out:

'I should like to explain to you, Mr Martineau. I know you believe that I should be careful about doing harm to the firm. I thought it over as thoroughly as I could: I'm capable of deceiving myself occasionally, but I don't think I did this time. I decided that it would cause a whiff of gossip – I admit that, naturally – but it wouldn't lose us a single case. You'd have made the same decision: except that you wouldn't have deliberated quite so long.' George was speaking fervently, naturally, with complete trust. I wished that he could have spoken in that way to Eden – if only for a few words.

'I'm a cautious old creature, George,' said Martineau.

'Cautious! Why, you'd bring the whole town down on our heads if you felt that some clerk, whom you'd never seen, wasn't free to attend the rites of a schismatic branch of the Greek Orthodox Church – in which you yourself, of course, passionately disbelieved.' George gave a friendly roar of laughter. 'Or have you been tempted by some new branch of the Orthodox lately?'

'Not yet,' Martineau chuckled. 'Not yet.'

Then George said:

'I expect you understood my position right from the start, Mr Martineau. After Mr Eden's remarks, though, I should like to hear that you approve.'

Martineau hesitated. Then he smiled, choosing his words:

'I don't consider you a man who needs approval, George. And it's my duty to dissuade you, as Harry did. You mustn't take it that I'm not dissuading you.' He hesitated again. 'But I think I understand what you feel.'

George listened to the evasive reply: he may have heard within it another appeal to stop, subtler than Eden's, because of the liking between himself and Martineau. He replied, seriously and simply:

'You know that I'm not going into this for my own amusement. I'm not searching out an injustice just for the pleasure of trampling on it. I might have done once, but I shouldn't now. You've understood, of course: something needs to be done for Cotery, and I'm the only man who can do it.'

CHAPTER V

GEORGE'S ATTACK

THE meeting of the School committee was summoned for the following Wednesday. I knew before George, since the notice passed through my hands in the education office. And, by asking a parting favour from an acquaintance, I got myself the job of taking the minutes.

On Tuesday night, I thought that I might be wasting the effort: for a strong rumour came from Olive that Jack himself had pleaded with George to go no further. But when I saw George later that night, and asked, 'What about tomorrow?' he replied: 'I'm ready for it. And ready to celebrate afterwards.'

I arrived at the Principal's room at ten minutes to six the next evening.

The gas fire was burning; the Principal was writing at his desk under a shaded light; the room seemed solid and official, though the shelves and chairs were carved in pine, in a firm plain style which the School was now teaching.

The Principal looked up as I laid the minute book on a small table; he was called Cameron, and had reddish hair and jutting eyebrows.

'Good evening. I am sorry that we have to trespass on your time,' he said. He always showed a deliberate consideration to subordinates; but from duty, not from instinct. At this time he probably did not know that I attended lectures at the School.

Then Miss Geary, the vice-principal, entered. 'It was for six o'clock?' she said. They exchanged a few remarks about School business: it was easy to hear that there was no friendliness between them. But the temperature of friendliness in the room mounted rapidly when, by the side of Canon Martineau, Beddow came in. He was a Labour councillor, a brisk, cordial, youngish man, very much on the rise; he had a word for everyone, including an aside for me – 'Minuting a committee means they think well of you up at the office. I know it does.'

'I suppose we're waiting for Calvert as usual,' said Canon Martineau, who had a slight resemblance to his brother, but spoke with a drier and more sardonic tang. 'And can anyone tell me how long this meeting is likely to last?'

'No meeting ever seems likely to last long until you've been in it a few hours,' said Beddow cheerfully. 'But anyway, the sooner we begin this, the sooner we shall get through.'

Ten minutes later, Calvert appeared, a small bald man, pink and panting from hurry. Beddow shook his hand warmly and pulled out a chair for him at the committee table.

'I hope you won't mind sitting by me,' he said. He chatted to Calvert for a few moments about investments; and then briskly, but without any implication that Calvert was late, said: 'Well, gentlemen, we've got a certain amount ahead of us tonight. If you don't object I think we might as well begin.'

The City Education Committee was made up partly from councillors and partly from others, like the Canon: in its turn it appointed this one, *ad hoc*: and so Beddow took the chair. He, with Calvert on his right and the Principal on his left, sat looking towards the door, on the same side of the committee table: the Canon and Miss Geary occupied the ends of it. I worked at the smaller table behind theirs, and within reach of the Principal and Beddow.

The Principal read the minutes (I was there purely to record) and then Miss Geary interrupted.

'Can we take No. 6 first, Mr Chairman?' No. 6 on the agenda read: 'J. Cotery. Termination of Bursary.' 'I believe Mr Passant wishes to make a statement. And I noticed that he was waiting in the staff-room.'

'I suggest that the first three items cannot conveniently wait,' said the Principal promptly. Beddow looked round the table.

'I think the feeling of the meeting is for taking those three items first,' he said. 'I'm sorry, Miss Geary: we shan't waste any unnecessary time.'

The three items were, in fact, mainly routine – fees for a new course in architecture, scholarships for next year. The clock on the Principal's desk was striking the third quarter when Beddow said:

'That polishes off your urgent business, doesn't it? Well, I suppose we're obliged to get No. 6 over some time. Perhaps this would be a convenient opportunity to have Mr Passant in.'

The Principal said nothing. Beddow went on:

'But, before I do ring for him, I should like to say something that we all feel. We are all more than sorry that Mr Calvert should be put in the position of having to listen to criticism – criticism of whether he should continue to pay an employee's fees or not. Perhaps he'll let me assure him, as a political opponent, that he has the reputation of being one of the best employers in this city. We all know that he has originated the very scheme over which he is being forced to listen to – unfortunate criticism. Perhaps I can say that one of the compensations for educational work in the city is the privilege of meeting men like Mr Calvert – political opponents though they may be – round the same friendly table.'

The Principal produced a loud, deliberate 'Hear, hear.' Calvert gave a quick, embarrassed smile, and went on scribbling on the pad of foolscap in front of him.

Beddow rang the bell: George was shown in.

'Ah, sit down there, Mr Passant. I'm sorry we've had to keep you so long,' Beddow, with his brisk, friendly smile. His affability was genuine at the root, but had become practised as he found it useful. He pointed out a small cane-bottomed chair on the other side of the table. George sat down; he was isolated from the others; they all looked at him.

'I'll now ask the Principal,' said Beddow, 'to speak to this business of the bursary.'

'This is really a very ordinary matter, Mr Chairman,' said the Principal. 'The Committee is aware of the conditions on which our bursaries are awarded. Owing to the inspiration of our benefactor, Mr Calvert' – the

Canon smiled across at Calvert – 'various employers in the town have co-operated with us in paying the fees of young men of promise. No one has ever contemplated that this arrangement could not be cancelled in any particular case, if there appeared adequate reason to the employer or ourselves. There are several precedents. The present case is entirely straightforward. Cotery, the man in question, has been sent here by Mr Calvert; his course normally would extend over three years, of which he has completed one. But Mr Calvert has decided that there is no likelihood of his being able to use Cotery in a position for which this course would qualify him; and so, in the man's own best interests, he considers that his bursary here should be discontinued. Several of these cases, as I say, have been reported to the committee in previous years. The committee has always immediately approved the employer's recommendation.'

'As the Principal has told us,' Beddow said, 'we have always taken these cases as a matter of form. . . . But Mr Passant, I believe, is interested in this young man Cotery, and has asked permission to attend this business tonight. After the Principal's statement, Mr Passant, is there anything that you want to say?'

'Yes, Mr Chairman, there are some things that I want to say,' said George. He had nowhere to rest his hands: he pulled down his waistcoat. But he was not resentful and defensive, as he had been with Eden the Friday night before. Four out of these five were against him: always ready to scent enemies, he must have known. Yet, now it had come to the moment, his voice was clear, masterful, and strong.

'First, this committee is responsible for appointing Cotery and it is responsible now if his support is withdrawn. The only consideration which such a committee can act upon is whether a man is making good use of his opportunity. Cotery could not be making better. I sent a request to the Principal that a report from those supervising his work here should be circularised to the committee. If it has not arrived, I can say that they regard his ability as higher than anyone in their department for the last three years. You cannot ask more than that. If the committee allows itself to be coerced by an employer to get rid of such a man, it is showing itself singularly indifferent to merit. And it ought in honesty to declare that its appointments are governed, not partly but entirely, by employers' personal vendettas.'

George's voice rang round the room. Calvert's sounded faint by contrast as he broke in:

'I can't allow – I mean, personal considerations have nothing to do with it.'

'I should like to ask, through you, Mr Chairman,' said George, the instant Calvert finished, 'whether Mr Calvert maintains that personal considerations have not dictated his entire course of action?'

'I protest,' said the Principal.

'It's entirely a matter – the organisation of my firm, I mean, didn't happen to give room for another man of Cotery's age. I let him know – I think he realised during the summer. I certainly let him know.'

In the midst of George, Beddow and the Principal, all fluent in their different manners, Calvert was at a loss for words. His face was chubby and petulant, and quite unlike his handsome son's. His irritation seemed naïve and bewildered; but I felt a streak of intense obstinacy in him.

'I think,' said George, 'that Mr Calvert ought to be allowed to withdraw his last suggestion.'

'I have no intention of— No,' said Calvert.

'Then,' said George, '*who* knew that you wouldn't have room for Cotery? and so intended to cut him off here?'

'No one, except Cotery and myself. I don't – it's not necessary to discuss my business with other people.'

'That is, no one knew of your intention until you wrote to the Principal some days ago?' said George.

'There was no need.'

'No one knew of your intention, in fact, until another incident had happened? Until after you told Cotery that you had forbidden your son—'

Beddow interrupted loudly:

'I can't allow any more, Mr Passant. I've got to apologise again' – he turned to Calvert – 'that you've been compelled to listen to remarks that, giving Mr Passant every shadow of a doubt, are in the worst possible taste.'

'I entirely concur,' said the Principal. It was clear that he and Beddow, at any rate, knew the whole sorry story. 'And, Mr Chairman, since a delicate matter has most regrettably been touched on, I wonder if Miss Geary would not prefer to leave the room?'

'Certainly not,' said Miss Geary; and settled herself squatly and darkly in her chair.

'I take it,' said George, 'that to punish a man without trial is in the best possible taste. And I refuse to make this incident sound ominous by brooding over it in silence. Mr Calvert either knows or ought to know that Cotery is absolutely innocent; that the whole matter has been ridiculously exaggerated; that it was nothing but a romantic gesture.'

'I believe that,' said Calvert. A glance of sympathy passed between them; for a second, they were made intimate by their quarrel. Then Calvert said obstinately: 'But it has nothing to do with it.'

'I am a little surprised,' said Canon Martineau, 'that Mr Passant is able to speak with such authority about this young man Cotery. I confess that his standing in the matter isn't quite so obvious—'

'I have the right to appear here about any student,' said George. Their hostility was gathering round him: but he was as self-forgetful as I had ever seen him.

The Principal seized a cue, and said:

'Mr Passant has, as it happens, a right to appear about students with whom he is not connected. In fact, Cotery never attended any of your classes, Mr Passant?'

'He presumably wouldn't have done so exceptionally well in printing,' George said loudly, 'if he had attended my classes in law.'

'Classes in law,' said the Principal, rising to a cautious, deliberate anger, 'which amount to two a week, this committee may remember. Like those given by twenty other visiting helpers to our regular staff.'

'The committee may also remember,' said George, 'that they can terminate the connection at a month's notice. That, however, does not affect the fact that I know Cotery well: I know him, just as I know a good many other students, better than anyone else in this institution.'

'Why do you go to this *exceptional* trouble?' asked the Canon.

'Because I am attached to an educational institution: I conceive that it is my job to help people to think.'

'Some of your protégés are inclined to think on unorthodox lines?' the Principal said.

'No doubt. I shouldn't consider any other sort of thinking was worth the time of a serious-minded man.'

'Even if it leads them into actions which might do harm to our reputations?' said the Principal.

'I prefer more precise questions. But I might take the opportunity of saying that I know what constitutes a position of trust: and I do not abuse it.'

There was a hush. Calvert's pencil scribbled over the paper.

'Well,' said Beddow, 'perhaps if—'

'I have not quite finished,' said George. 'I am not prepared to let the committee think that I am simply intruding into this affair. I am completely unapologetic. I repeat, I know Cotery well: you have heard my questions: I regard my case as proved. But I don't want to leave the committee under a misapprehension. Cotery is one out of many. You will be judged by what you make of them. They are better human material than we are. They are people who've missed the war. They are people who are young at the most promising time in the world's history. If they don't share in it, then it's because this committee and I and all we represent are simply playing the irresponsible fool with our youngers and betters. You may take the view that it's dangerous to make them think: that it's wiser to leave them in the state of life into which it has pleased God to call them. I refuse to take that view: and I shall not, while I have a foot in this building.'

He stood up to go.

Beddow said:

'If no one has anything more to ask Mr Passant. . . .'

Until the door closed Beddow did not speak again, but his eyes moved from Calvert to the Canon.

'Well, Principal,' said Beddow, but his tone had lost (I was excited to notice) some of its buoyancy, 'I take it that you have made your recommendation.'

'I have, sir,' said Cameron emphatically.

'In that case, if no one has a motion, I suppose we accept the recommendation and pass on.'

Miss Geary leaned forward in her chair. 'Certainly not,' she said. 'We've been listening to a man who believes what he says. And I want to hear some of it answered.'

There was a stir round the table. They were relieved that she had spoken out, given them someone to argue against.

'Haven't we been listening,' said Canon Martineau, with his subtle smile, 'to a man who has a somewhat exaggerated idea of the importance of his mission?'

'No doubt,' said Miss Geary. 'Most people who believe in anything have a somewhat exaggerated idea of its importance. And I don't pretend that he made the best of his case. Nevertheless—'

She was speaking from a double motive, of course; her dislike for the Principal shone out of her: so did her desire to help George.

It was still one against four, if it came to a vote; but there was a curious, hypercharged atmosphere that even the absolute recalcitrants, Calvert and the Principal, felt as they became more angry. Over Beddow and Martineau certainly, the two most receptive people there, had come a jag of apprehension. And when, after Miss Geary had competently put the position of Cotery again, and Calvert merely replied stubbornly:

'He's known for months that I didn't intend to keep him here. Nothing else came into account. Nothing else—' the Canon became restless.

'Of course,' he said, 'there are times when it's not only important that justice should be done. Sometimes it's important that justice should appear to be done. And in this case, unless we're careful, it does seem to me possible that our Mr Passant may make a considerable nuisance of himself.'

'I regret the suggestion,' said the Principal, 'that we should consider giving way to threats.'

'That isn't Canon Martineau's suggestion, if I understand it right,' said Beddow. 'He's saying that we mustn't stand on our dignity, even when we're being taught our business by a man like Passant. Because nothing would take the wind out of his sails like giving way a bit. And, on the other hand, it might do this young fellow Cotery some good if we stretched a point.'

'The Chairman has put my attitude,' said Martineau, 'much more neatly than I could myself.'

'I'm afraid that I still consider it dangerous,' said the Principal.

'Well,' said Beddow, 'if we could meet one condition, I myself would go so far as to stretch a point. But the condition is, of course, that we must satisfy Mr Calvert. We shouldn't think of acting against your wishes,' said Beddow to Calvert, in his most cordial and sincere manner.

Calvert nodded his head.

'I can't alter my own position,' he said. 'There's no future – I can't find a place for Cotery. I decided that in the summer. I don't bear him any ill-will—'

'I wonder,' Canon Martineau looked at Beddow with a sarcastic smile, 'whether this idea would meet the case? Cotery would normally have two more years: we pay half the cost, and Mr Calvert half. Mr Calvert, for reasons we all accept, can't go on with his share. But is there anything to prevent us keeping to our commitment, and remitting – may I suggest – not the half, but all Cotery's fees for just *one* year?'

'Except that it would be no practical use to the man himself,' said Miss Geary.

'No,' said Calvert. 'He needs the whole three years.'

'I'm not so desperately concerned about that,' said the Canon.

'He'd have to get the money from some other source. If he wanted to finish,' said Beddow briskly. 'I agree with the Canon. I think it's a decent compromise.'

Miss Geary saw that it was her best chance.

'If you'll propose it, Canon,' she said, 'I'm ready to second.'

'I deeply regret this idea,' said the Principal. 'And I am sure that Mr. Calvert does.'

Canon Martineau and Beddow had judged Calvert more shrewdly, however, and he shook his head.

'No,' he said, 'I can't support the motion. But I shan't vote against it.'

It was carried by three votes to one, with Calvert abstaining.

CHAPTER VI

RESULTS OF A CELEBRATION

I WENT straight from the committee to the Victoria, our public-house, where George and Jack were waiting.

'Well?' cried George, as soon as I entered. I saw that Morcom was with them, sitting by the fire.

'It's neither one thing nor the other,' I said. I told them the decision.

'It's a pretty remarkable result for any sane collection of men to achieve. I never believed that you'd drive them into it. But it doesn't help Jack, of course.'

'Nonsense,' George shouted. 'You're as cheerful as Balfour giving the news of the Battle of Jutland. Your sane collection of men have been made to realise that they can't treat Jack as though he was someone who just had to be content with their blasted charity. Good God alive, don't you see that that's a triumph? We're going to drink a considerable amount of beer and we're going to Nottingham by the next train to have a proper celebration. In the meantime, I'm going to hear every word that they found themselves obliged to say.'

Jack smiled, raised his glass towards George, and said: 'You're a wonderful man, George.' Jack was shrewd enough to know already that, for himself, the practical value of the triumph was nothing: but it was his nature to rejoice with him who rejoices. (I was soon to see the same quality again in Herbert Getliffe.) He could not bear to spoil George's pleasure.

George lived through my description of the meeting before he confronted them and after he left. He was furiously indignant with Beddow's attempt to propitiate Calvert, more then with the Principal's: 'I suppose Cameron, to do him justice, is out to get benefactions for the institution. It's true that he's quite incapable of administering them, but we can't reasonably expect him to realise that. But what Beddow, who calls himself a socialist, thinks he's doing, when he tries to lick the feet of a confounded business man—' so George went on, drinking his beer, chuckling with delight at Miss Geary's interventions, re-interpreting the Canon's equivocal manœuvres as directly due to the influence of Howard Martineau. 'The Canon must have worked out his technique. To come in on our side without letting it seem obvious,' said George. But he had no explanation of Calvert's naïve defence that he formed his decision about Jack long before the incident with his son.

'That's just incredible,' said George. 'If I'd wanted to invent something improbable, I couldn't have invented anything as improbable as that.'

Morcom said little; but he was amused by the change of sides, the choice of partners, before the vote. As I told the story, Jack illustrated it by moving glasses about the table; two glasses of beer representing the Canon and Beddow, a glass of water the Principal, a small square jug Miss Geary, and for Calvert Jack turned a glass upside down. When he moved them into their final places, George gave a loud satisfied sigh.

'They couldn't do anything else,' he said. 'They couldn't do anything else.'

Morcom looked at him with a curious smile.

'I doubt whether anyone else could have made them do it, George,' he said.

'I don't know about that,' said George.

'But, to come back for a minute to what Lewis said, they've still left Jack in the air, haven't they?'

'They've recognised his position. He's got time to turn round.'

'He's really in very much the same position,' said Morcom. 'It's important you should keep that in mind, for Jack's sake—'

'Arthur,' George cried, angrily and triumphantly, 'you tried to dissuade me from breathing a word to the bell-wethers. You don't deny that, I suppose?'

'No,' said Morcom.

'And now I've done it, you're trying to deprive me of the luxury of having brought it off. I'm not prepared to submit to it. I've listened to you on most things, Arthur, but I'm not prepared to submit to it tonight.'

Half-drunk myself, I laughed. This was his night: I was ready, like Jack, to forget tomorrow. Yet, somewhere beneath my surrender to his victory, there crept a chill of disappointment. An hour ago, I had seen

George in his full power and totally admired him; but now, knowing that
Morcom was right, I was young enough to resent the contradiction
between George in his full power and the same man sitting in this chair
by the fire, shutting his eyes to the truth. He ought not to be sitting there,
flushed, optimistic, triumphant, seeing only what he wanted to see.

'In fact,' shouted George, defiantly, 'you're not going to argue me
out of my celebration. I dare say you don't want to come. But the others
will.'

Jack and I were eager for it. We left Morcom sitting by the fire, and
ran across to the station. The eight-forty was a train to Nottingham that
we all knew; for half an hour the lights of farms, the villages, the dark
fields, rushed by. The carriage was full, but George talked cheerfully
of the pleasures to come and how he first met Connie at the 'club';
he was oblivious, as in all happiness or quarrels, to the presence of
strangers; that night none of us cared.

We had a drink in a public-house at the top of Parliament Street, and
crossed over to another on the other side; it was a windy night, and the
wind seemed very loud and the lights spectacularly bright. Jack, though he
drank less than George and I, began demanding bowls of burning gold and
going behind bars to help the maids: George kept greeting acquaintances,
various men, whores, and girls from the factories out for a good time. He
had met them on other night visits to Nottingham: for he went often,
though he concealed it from Jack and me until we discovered by accident.

He knew the back streets better than those of our own town. He led
us to the club by short cuts between high, ramshackle houses, and through
'entries', partly covered over, where George's voice echoed crashingly.
One such entry led to a narrow street, lit only by a single street lamp
at the mouth. At the door of a tall house at the end remote from the
light, George rapped three times with the brass knocker.

A woman climbed up from the area and recognised George. She told
him to take us upstairs, the top door was unlocked. We went up the four
flights of creaking wooden stairs, and met a new, bright blue door which
cut off the attic storey from the landing.

A gramophone was wailing inside. George marched in before us: the
room was half-full, mainly of women; as soon as he entered, a group of
them gathered round him. He was popular there; they laughed at him,
they were after the money which he threw away carelessly at all times,
fantastically so when drunk; but they genuinely liked him. They did him
good turns, and took their troubles to him for advice. With them, he
showed none of the diffidence of a visit to Martineau's respectable

drawing-room; he was cheerfully, heartily enjoying himself, he liked being with them, he felt at home.

Tonight he burst into extravagance from the start. He saw Connie sitting with Thelma, her regular older friend; George put an arm round each of them, and shouted, 'Thelma's here! Of course, I insist that everyone must have a drink – because Thelma's here!'

Connie told him that he was silly, then whispered in his ear; his eyes brightened, and he took out a couple of notes for Thelma to buy drinks round. George shouted to some women across the room, and in the same breath talked in soft chuckles to Connie. She was fair and quite young, with a pretty, impassive face and a nice body. She pretended to escape from his arm: at once he clutched her, and she came towards him: the contact went through George like an electric current, and he shouted jubilantly: 'Make them have another drink, Thelma. Why shouldn't everyone have two drinks at once?'

Soon George and Connie had gone away. The rest of us drank and danced. The floor was rough; there was nothing polished about the 'club' except the bright blue door on the landing. The furniture was mixed, but all old; the red velvet sofas seemed like the relics of a gay house of the nineties; so did the long mirror with the battered gilding. But there were also some marble-topped tables, picked up in a café, several wicker chairs and even two or three soap boxes. One of the bulbs was draped in frilly pink, and one was naked. Women giggled and shrilled; and among it all, the 'manager' (whose precise function none of us knew) sat in the corner of the room, reading a racing paper with a cloth cap on the back of his head.

Now and then a pair went out. The gramophone wailed on, like all the home-sick, lust-sweet longing in the world. The thudding beat got hold of one, it got mixed with the smell of scent. After one dance, Jack spoke to me for a moment.

'Jesus love me, I can't help it, Lewis,' he said with his fresh open smile. 'I'm going all randy sad.'

It was after one o'clock when the three of us gathered round one of the marble-topped tables. The room was nearly empty by then, though the gramophone still played. We should have liked to go, but there was over an hour before the last train home. So we sat there, sobered and quiet, ordering a last glass of gin to mollify the manager: and, of course, we talked of women.

'The first I ever had,' said George, 'happened on the night before my eighteenth birthday. She told me that she did it for a hobby. Afterwards, when I was walking home, it seemed necessary to shout, "Why don't they all take up a hobby? Why don't they *all* take up a hobby?" ' The words would have resounded boisterously three hours ago, when we entered that room; but now they were subdued. He was not randy sad, as Jack and I had been; this was a different, a deeper sadness. He knew the pleasure he had gained; and turning from it, he - whose pictures of the future usually glowed like a sunrise - felt all that he might miss.

'I should have wanted something better before now,' said Jack, 'if I'd been you.'

'It serves my purpose,' said George. 'I don't know about yours.'

Jack smiled. 'Why don't you try nearer home?'

'What do you mean?'

'I mean that some of the young women in our group would be open to persuasion. You'd get more happiness from one of them, George. Clearly you would.'

'That would destroy everything I want to do,' George said. 'You realise that's what you're suggesting? You'd put me into a position where people like Morcom could say that I was building up an impressive façade of looking after our group at the School. That I was building up an impressive façade - and that my real motive was to cuddle the girls on the quiet.'

Jack looked at George in consternation. For once in a quarrel, he had not raised his voice; yet his face bore all the signs of pain. Affectionately, Jack said: 'I want you to be happy, that's all.'

'I shouldn't be happy that way,' said George. 'I can look after my own happiness.'

'Anyway, for my happiness, I'm afraid I shall need love,' said Jack. 'Love with all the romantic accompaniments, George. The sort of love that makes the air seem a remarkable medium to be moving through. I'm afraid I need it.'

'I don't know whether I need it,' I said. 'But I'm afraid that I've got it.'

'Don't you ever want it, George?' Jack asked.

'Of course I want it,' said George. 'Though I shouldn't be prepared to sacrifice everything for it. But of course I want it: what do you think I am? As a matter of fact, I've been thinking tonight that I'm not very likely to find it.' He looked at me with a sympathetic smile. 'I don't know that I've ever been in love - at least not what you'd call love. I've made myself ridiculous once or twice, but it didn't amount to much. I dare say that it never will.'

It seemed strange that George, not as a rule curious about his friends' feelings, should have recognised from the start that my love for Sheila (which had begun that summer) would hag-ride me for years of my life. Yet that night he envied me. George was a sensual man, often struggling against his senses; Jack an amorous one, revelling in the whole atmosphere of love. In their different ways, they both that night wanted what they had not tasted. Saddened by pleasure, they thought longingly of love.

I said to Jack:

'I think that Roy would have understood what we've been saying. It would have been beyond us at fifteen.'

'I suppose he would,' said Jack doubtfully.

'He's been in love,' I said.

'I still find it a bit hard to credit that,' said Jack.

'No one would believe me,' I said, 'if I told them that you were a very humble creature, would they?'

At the mention of Roy's name, George had become preoccupied; his eyes, heavy-lidded after the evening, looked over the now empty room; but that abstracted gaze saw nothing, it was turned into himself. Jack and I talked on; George sat silently by; until he said suddenly, unexpectedly, as though he was in the middle of a conversation: 'I accept some of the criticisms that were made before we started out.'

I found myself seized by excitement. I knew from his tone that he was going to bring out a surprise.

'I scored a point or two,' George said to Jack. 'But I haven't done much for you.'

'Of course you have,' said Jack. 'Anyway, let's postpone it. I'll see you tomorrow.'

'There's no point in postponing it,' said George. 'I haven't done much for you, as Lewis said before ever Morcom did. And it's got to be attended to. Mind you, I don't accept completely the pessimistic account of the situation. But we ought to be prepared to face it.'

Clearly, rationally, half-angrily, George explained to Jack (as Jack knew, as Morcom and I had already said, though not so precisely) how the committee's decision gave him no future. 'That being so,' said George, 'I suppose you ought to leave Calvert's wretched place.'

'I've got to live,' said Jack.

'Is it possible to go to another printer's?'

'I could get an identical job, George. With identical absence of future.'

'Well, I can't have any more of this fatalistic nonsense,' said George, irascibly, and yet with a disarming kindness. 'What would you do – if we could provide you with a free choice?'

'I could do several things, George. But they're all ruled out. They all depend on having some money – now.'

'Do you agree?' George asked me. 'I expect you know Jack's position better than I do. Do you agree?'

I had to, though I could foresee what was coming. If Jack's fortunes were to be changed immediately, he must have a loan. My little legacy had given me a chance: each pound at our age was worth ten to a man whose life was fixed. Jack was young enough to get into a profession – or 'to have a shot at that business we heard about the other day,' as he said himself.

'Yes,' said George. 'So in fact with a little money now, you're confident that you could laugh at Calvert and his friends?'

'With luck, I should make a job of it,' said Jack. 'But—'

'Then the money will have to be produced. I shall want you to let me contribute.' George's manner became, to stop Jack speaking, bleak and businesslike. 'Mind you, I shall want a certain number of guarantees. I shall want to be certain that I'm making a good investment. And also I ought to warn you straightaway that I may not be able to raise much money myself.' He went on very fast. 'I don't see why I shouldn't put my financial position on the table. It's all a matter of pure business. And I've never been able to understand how people manage to be proud about their finances. Anyway, even people who are proud about their finances couldn't be if they had mine. I collect exactly £285 per year. (Such incomes, because of the fall in the value of money, were to seem tiny within thirty years.) Of that I allow £55 to my father and mother. I'm also insured in their interest. I think if I decreased the £55 a bit, and added to the insurance, they oughtn't to be much upset. And then I could probably raise a fair sum from the bank on the policy – but I warn you, it's a matter of pure business. There may be difficulties.'

Neither Jack nor I fully understood the strange nature of George's 'finances'. But Jack was moved so that he did not recover his ready, flattering tongue until we got up to catch our train. Then he said:

'George, I thought we set out tonight to celebrate a triumph.'

'It was a triumph,' said George. 'I shall always insist that we won at that meeting.'

CHAPTER VII

ARGUMENT UNDER THE GASLIGHT

IT took some days for Jack to settle what he wanted to do (from that night at Nottingham, he never doubted that George would find the money): and it took a little longer to persuade George of it.

Those were still the days of the small-scale wireless business. An acquaintance of ours had just started one; Jack had his imagination caught. He expounded what he could make of it – and I thought how much he liked the touch of anything modern. He would have been a *contemporary* man in any age. But he was inventive, he was shrewd, he had a flair for advertisement; he persuaded us all except George.

George did not like it. He would have preferred to try to article Jack to Eden & Martineau. He asked Morcom and me for our opinions. We gave practically the same answer. Making Jack a solicitor would mean a crippling expense for George; and we could not see Jack settling down to a profession if he started unwillingly. His choice was far more likely to come off.

At last George gave way. Then, though Jack, as I say, never doubted that the money would be found, George faced a last obstacle; he had to tell his father and mother that he was lessening his immediate help to them.

For many men, it would have been easy. He could have equivocated; after all, the insurance provided for their future, and he had been making an extravagantly large contribution. But he never thought of evading the truth. He dreaded telling it, for he knew how it would be taken; their family relations were passionately close. But tell it he did, without any cover, three days after our visit to Nottingham.

A week later, when he took me to supper with them, they were still not reconciled to it. It was only Mr Passant's natural courtesy, his anxiety to make me feel at home, that kept them from an argument the moment we arrived.

Actually, I was not a stranger in their house. Until two years before, Mr Passant had been assistant postmaster at Wickham; then, when George got his job at Eden & Martineau's, Mr Passant transferred to the general post office in the town. For fear of their family ties George insisted on going into lodgings, while they lived in this little house, one of a row of identical little houses, each with a tiny front garden and iron railings, on the other side of the town. But George visited them two or three times every week; he took his friends to spend whole evenings with them; tonight we arrived early and George and his mother kissed each other with an affection open and yet suddenly released. She was a stocky, big-breasted woman, wearing an apron over a greyish dress.

'It's half the week since I saw you, old George,' she said: it was the overtones of her racy Suffolk accent that we noticed in George's speech.

She wanted to talk at once about the question of money. Mr Passant managed to stop her, however, his face lined with concern. In a huff, as hot-tempered as George, she went into the back kitchen, though supper would not be ready for an hour.

Mr Passant sat with us round the table in the kitchen. It was hot from a heaped-up fire, and gave out the rich smell of small living-rooms. Under the gaslight, Mr Passant burst into a breathless, friendly, excited account of how, that morning at the post office, a money order had nearly gone astray. He spoke in a kindly hurry, his voice husky and high-pitched. He said:

'Do you play cards, Mr – er – Lewis? Of course you must play cards. George, we ought to play something with him now.'

It was impossible to resist Mr Passant's enormous zest, to prevent him doing a service. He fetched out a pack of cards from the sideboard, and we played three-handed solo. Mr Passant, who had been brought up in the strictest Puritan discipline, was middle-aged before he touched a card; now he played with tremendous enjoyment, with a gusto that was laughable and warmed us all.

When we finished the game, Mr Passant suddenly got up and brought a book to the table.

'Just a minute, Mr – er – Lewis, there's something I thought of when I was playing. It won't take long, but I mustn't forget.'

The book was a Bible. He moistened a pencil in his lips, drew a circle round a word, and connected it by a long line to another encircled word.

I moved to give him more room at the table, but he protested.

'No, please, no. I just do a little preparation each night to be ready for Sunday, you know. I'm allowed to tell the good news, I go round the villages, I don't suppose George has told you.' (Of course, I knew long since that he devoted his spare hours to local preaching.) 'And it's easier if I do a little work every night. I'm only doing it before supper so that afterwards –'

George and I spread out the evening paper and whispered comments to each other. In a few moments Mr Passant sighed and put a marker into the Bible.

'Ready for Sunday?' said George.

'A little more tomorrow.' Mr Passant smiled.

'I suppose you won't have a big congregation,' George said. His tone was both intimate and constrained. 'As it's a slack time of the year.'

Mr Passant said: 'No, we can't hope for many, but that's not the worst thing. What grieves me is that we don't get as many as we used to. We're losing, we've been losing ever since the war.'

'So has the Church of England,' I observed.

'Yes, you're losing too,' Mr Passant smiled at me. 'It isn't only one of us. Which way are you going to win them back?'

I gained some amusement from being taken as a spokesman of the Church of England. I did not obtrude my real beliefs: we proceeded to discuss on what basis the Christian Churches could unite. There I soon made a mistake; for I suggested that Mr Passant might not find confirmation an insurmountable obstacle.

Mr Passant pushed his face forward. He looked more like George than I had seen him. 'That is the mistake you would have to understand before we could come together,' he said. 'Can't I make you see how dangerous a mistake it is, Mr – Lewis? A man is responsible for his own soul. Religion is the choice of a man's soul before his God. At some time in his life, sooner or later, a man must choose to stay in sin or be converted. That is the most certain fact I know, you see, and I could not bring myself to associate in worship with anyone who doesn't want to know it as I do.'

'I understand what you mean by a man being responsible for his soul.' George rammed tobacco into his pipe. 'That's the basis of protestantism, naturally. And, though you might choose to put it in other words' – he looked at me – 'it's the basis of any human belief that isn't completely trivial or absurdly fatalistic. But I never have been able to see why you should make conversion so definite an act. It doesn't happen like that – irrevocably and once for all.'

'It does,' said Mr Passant.

'I challenge it,' said George.

'My dear,' said Mr Passant, 'you know all sorts of matters that I don't know, and on every one of these I will defer to your judgment or knowledge, and be glad to. But you see, I have been living amongst people for fifty years, for fifty-three years and a half, within a few days, and as a result of that experience I know that their lives change all of a sudden – like this—' he took a piece of paper out of his pocket and moistened his pencil against a lip; then he drew a long straight line – 'a man lives in sin and enjoyment and indulgence for years, until he is brought up against himself; and then, if he chooses right, life changes altogether – *so*.' And he drew a line making a sharp re-entrant angle with the first, and coming back to the edge of the paper. 'That's what I mean by conversion, and I couldn't tell you all the lives I've seen it in.'

'I can't claim the length of your experience,' George's tone had suddenly become hard, near anger, 'but I have been studying people intensively for several years. And all I've seen makes me think their lives are more like this—' he took his father's paper under the gaslight, his hand casting a blue shadow; he drew a rapid zig-zag. 'A part of the time they don't trouble to control their baser selves. Then for a while they do and get on with the most valuable task in sight. Then they relax again. And so on another spurt. For some people the down-strokes are longer than the up, and some the reverse. That's all I'm prepared to admit. That's all you need to hope, it seems to me. And whatever your hopes are, they've got to be founded in something like the truth—'

Mr Passant was breathless and excited:

'Mine is the truth for every life I've seen. It's the truth for my own life, and no one else can speak for that. When I was a young man I did nothing but run after enjoyments and pleasures.' He was staring at the paper on the table. It was quiet; a spurt of rain dashed against the window. 'Sensual pleasures,' said Mr Passant, 'that neither of you will ever hear about, perhaps, much less be tempted with. But they were pleasures to me. Until I was a young man about your age, not quite your age exactly.' He looked at George. 'Then one night I had a sight of the way to go. I can never forget it, and I can never forget the difference between my state before and since. I can answer for the same change in others also. But chiefly I have to speak for myself.'

'I have to do the same,' said George.

They stared at each other, their faces shadowed. George's lips were pressed tightly together.

Then Margaret, George's youngest sister, a girl of fourteen, came in to lay the supper. And Mrs Passant, still unappeased, followed with a great metal tray.

Supper was a meal both heavy and perfunctory. There was a leg of cold overdone beef, from which Mr Passant and George ate large slices: after the potatoes were finished, we continued with the meat alone. Mrs Passant herself was eating little – to draw George's concern, I thought. When her husband tried to persuade her, she merely smiled abruptly. His voice was entreating and anxious; for a moment, the room was pierced by unhappiness, in which, as Mr Passant leaned forward, George and the child suddenly took their share.

Nothing open was said until Margaret had gone to bed. From half-way up the stairs, she called out my christian name. I went up, leaving the three of them alone; Margaret was explaining in her nervous, high-pitched voice that her candle had gone out and she had no matches. She kept me talking for a few moments, proud of her first timid attempt to flirt. As she cried 'Good-night' down the stairs, I heard the clash of voices from below. The staircase led, through a doorway, directly into the kitchen; past the littered table, George's face stood out in a frown of anger and pain. Mr Passant was speaking. I went back to my place; no one gave me a glance.

'You're putting the wrong meaning on to us,' the words panted from Mr Passant. 'Surely you see that isn't our meaning, or not what we tried to mean.'

'I can only understand it one way,' George said. 'You suspect the use I intend to make of my money. And in any case you claim a right to supervise it, whether you suspect me or not.'

'We're trying to help you, that's all. We must try to help you. You can't expect us to forget who you are and see you lose or waste everything.'

'That amounts to claiming a right to interfere in my affairs. I've had this out too many times before. I don't admit it for a single moment. If I make my own judgment and decide to spend every penny I receive on my own pleasures, I'm entitled to do so.'

'We've seen some of your judgment,' said Mrs Passant. George turned to her. His anger grew stronger, but with a new note of pleading:

'Don't you understand I can't give way in this? I can't give way in the life I lead or the money I spend. In the last resort, I insist of being the judge of my own actions. If that's accepted, I'm prepared to justify the present case. I warn you that I've made up my mind, but I'm prepared to justify it.'

'You're prepared to keep other people with your money. That's what you want to do,' said Mrs Passant.

'You must believe what I've told you till I'm tired,' George shouted. 'We're only talking about this particular sum of money I propose to use in a particular way. What I've done in the past and what I may do in the future are utterly beside the point. This particular sum I'm not going to spend on a woman, if that's what you're thinking. If you won't believe me—'

'We believe that, we believe that,' Mr Passant burst out. George stared at his mother.

'Very well. Then the point is this, and nothing but this; that I'm going to spend the money on someone I'm responsible for. That responsibility is the most decent task I'm ever likely to have. So the only question is whether I can afford it or not. Nothing I've ever learned in this house has given me any respect for your opinions on that matter. Your only grumble could be that I shan't be discharging my duty and making my contribution here. I admit that is a duty. I'm not trying to evade it. Have I ever got out of it except for a day or two? Have I ever got out of it since I was qualified?'

'You're making a song about it. By the side of what we've done,' she said.

'I want an answer. Have I ever got out of it?'

She shook her head.

'Do you suggest I shall get out of it now?'

She said, with a sudden bitter and defenceless smile:

'Oh, I expect you'll go on throwing me a few shillings. Just to ease your mind before you go off with the others.'

'Do you want every penny I earn?'

'If you gave me every penny,' she said, 'you'd still only be trying to ease your mind.'

George said in a quietened, contrite tone:

'Of course, it's not the money. You wouldn't worry for a single instant if my salary were cut and I couldn't afford to find any. I ought to know' – his face lightened into an affectionate smile – 'that you're just as bad with money as I am myself.'

'I know that you can afford to find money for these other people. Just as you can afford to give them all your time. You're putting them in the first place—'

'It's easy to give your money without thinking,' said Mr Passant. 'But that's worse than meanness if you neglect your real duties or obligations—'

'To hear you talk of duties,' Mrs Passant turned on him. 'I might have listened to that culch if I hadn't lived with you for thirty years.'

'I've left things I ought not to have left,' said Mr Passant. 'You've got a right to say that.'

'I'm going to say, and for the last time,' George cried, 'that I intend to spend this money on the reallest duty that I'm ever likely to find.'

Mrs Passant said to her husband:

'You've never done a mortal act you didn't want. Neither will he. I pity anyone who has to think twice about either of you.'

CHAPTER VIII

GEORGE AT THE CENTRE OF HIS GROUP

IT was all settled by the beginning of October. Just three weeks had passed since George first heard the news of Jack's trouble. Now George was speaking as if those three weeks were comfortably remote; just as, in these same first days of October, he disregarded my years in the office from the moment I quit it. Even the celebratory week-end at the farm was not his idea.

The farm was already familiar ground to George's group. Without it, in fact, we could not have become so intimate; nowhere in the town could we have made a meeting-place for young men and women, some still watched by anxious families. Rachel had set to work to find a place, and found the farm. It was a great shapeless red-brick house fifteen miles from the town, standing out in remarkable ugliness among the wide rolling fields of High Leicestershire; but we did not think twice of its ugliness, since there was room to be together in our own fashion, at the price of a few shillings for a weekend. The tenants did not make much of a living from the thin soil, and were glad to put up a party of us and let us provision for ourselves.

Rachel managed everything. This Saturday afternoon, welcoming us, she was like a young wife with a new house.

She had tidied up the big, low, cold sitting-room which the family at the farm never used; she had a fire blazing for us as we arrived, in batches of two and three, after the walk from the village through the drizzling rain. She installed George in the best armchair by the fire, and the rest of us gathered round; Jack, Olive and I, Mona, a perky girl for whom George had a fancy, several more of both sexes from the School. The entire party numbered twelve, but did not include Arthur Morcom, for George was happiest when it was kept to his own group.

This afternoon he was filled with a happiness so complete, so unashamedly present in his face, that it seemed a provocation to less contented men. He lay back in his chair, smoking a pipe, being attended to; these were his friends and protégés, in each of us he had complete trust; all the bristles and guards of his defences had dropped away.

Cheerfully he did one of his parlour tricks for me. I had been invited

338

for tea in a neighbouring village; I had lived in the county twenty years to George's two, but it was to him I applied for the shortest cut. He had a singular memory for anything that could be put on paper, so singular that he took it for granted; he proceeded to draw a sketch map of the countryside. We assumed that each detail was exact, for no one was less capable of bluffing. He finished, with immense roars of laughter, by drawing a neat survey sign, a circle surmounted by a cross, to represent my destination; for I was visiting Sheila's home for the first time, and George could not recover from the joke that she was the daughter of a country clergyman.

Then, just as I was going out, a thought struck him. Among this group, he was always prepared to think aloud. 'I'm only just beginning to realise,' said George, 'what a wonderful invention a map is. Geography would be incomprehensible without maps. They've reduced a tremendous muddle of facts into something you can read at a glance. Now I suspect economics is fundamentally no more difficult than geography. Except that it's about things in motion. If only somebody could invent a dynamic map—'

Myself, having a taste for these things, I should have liked to hear him out. But people like Mona (with her sly eyes and soft figure and single-minded curiosity about men) listened also: listened, it occurred to me as I walked over the wet fields, because George enjoyed his own interest and took theirs for granted.

When I returned, the room was not so peaceful. I heard Jack's voice, as I shook out my wet coat in the hall; and as soon as I saw him and Olive sitting together by the table, I felt my attention fix on them just as all the others' were fixed. George, sunk into the background, watched from his chair. It was like one of those primitive Last Suppers, in which from right hand and left eleven pairs of eyes are converging on one focus.

Yet, so far as I could tell, nothing had happened. Jack, some sheets of paper in front of him, was expanding on his first plans for the business: Olive had joined him at the table to read a draft advertisement. They had disagreed over one of his schemes, but now that was pushed aside, and Olive said:

'You know, I envy you! I envy you!'

'So you ought,' said Jack. 'But you haven't so much to grumble at, yourself.'

'I suppose you mean that I needn't work for a living. It's true, I could give up my job tomorrow.'

'You wouldn't get so much fun out of that,' said Jack, 'as I did out of telling your uncle that I had become increasingly dissatisfied with his firm—'

Olive smiled, but there was something on her mind. Suddenly I guessed (recalling his manner at Martineau's the night before) that Morcom had proposed to her.

'It's true,' Olive said, 'that my father wouldn't throw me out. I could live on him if I wanted. He probably expects me to be at home, now his health's breaking up. It's also true, I expect, that I could find someone to marry me. And I could live on him. But I envy you, being forced to look after yourself: do you understand that?'

'I don't think you're being honest,' said Jack.

'I tell you, Jack, it's bad luck to be born a woman. There may be compensations – but I'd change like a shot. Don't you think I'm honest about that?'

'I think you ought to get married,' said Jack.

'Why?'

'You wouldn't have so much time to think.'

Jack then became unexpectedly serious.

'Also you talk about your father wanting you at home. It would be better for you to get free of him altogether.'

'That doesn't matter.'

'It does.'

'I tell you I've got a lot of respect for him. But I've got no love.' She turned towards Jack: the light from the oil-lamp glinted on the brooch on her breast.

'You understand other people better than you do yourself,' said Jack.

'What should you say if I decided – I don't think I ever should, mind you – that I ought to put off thinking of marriage yet awhile, and stay at home?'

'I should say that you did it because you wanted to.'

'You think that I want to stay at home, preserving my virginity and reading the monthly magazines?' she cried.

Jack shrugged his shoulders, and gave his good-natured, impudent, amorous smile. He said:

'Well, part of that could be remedied—'

She slapped his face. The noise cracked through the room. Jack's cheek was crimson. He said: 'I can't reply properly here—' but then Rachel intervened.

'I'll knock your heads together if there's any more of it,' she said. 'Olive, you'd better help me lay the supper.'

The meal gleamed in bright colours on the table – the red of tomatoes, russet of apples, green of lettuce, and the red Leicestershire cheese. George, as always at the farm, made Rachel take the head of the table and placed himself at her right hand. Gusts of wind kept beating against the windows and whining round the house. The oil-lamp smoked in front of us at table, and candles flickered on the mantelpiece. The steam from our tea-cups whirled in the lamplight; we all drank tea at those meals, for George, with an old-fashioned formality that amused us, insisted that our drinking and visits to Nottingham should be concealed from the young women – though naturally they knew all the time.

The circle from the lamp just reached the edge of the table. We were all within it, and the shadow outside, the windy night, brought us together like a family in childhood. Olive's quarrel with Jack lost its sting, and turned into a family quarrel. George basked as contentedly as in the afternoon, and was as much our centre.

With great gusto he brought out ideas for Jack's business; they were a mixture, one entirely unrealistic and another that seemed ingenious and sound. Then he made a remark about me, assuming casually and affectionately that I was bound to do well in my examination in the summer. He cherished our successes to come – as though he had them under his fingers in the circle of lamplight.

Olive looked at him. She forgot herself, and felt anxious for him. She cried sharply:

'Don't forget you can't just watch these people going ahead.'

'I don't think you need worry about that,' said George.

'I shall worry, George. You'll find as they get on' – she indicated us round the table – 'that you *need* recognition for yourself. To be practical, you'll need that partnership in the firm.'

'Do you think I shall ever fret so much about a piece of respectable promotion?'

'It's not just that—' but, though she stuck to it, she could not explain her intuition. Others of us stepped in to persuade him; no one spoke as strongly as Olive, but we were concerned. George, gratified but curiously embarrassed, tried to pass it off as a joke.

'As I told you at the café,' he said to Olive, 'when we were going into action about Jack – it shouldn't be so difficult. After all, even if I did perform actions which they don't entirely approve of, I certainly do most of the work, which they approve of very much: Martineau being given to religious disputation, and Eden preferring pure reflection.'

'That isn't good enough,' said Olive.

'Very well,' said George at last. 'I'll promise not to let it go by default. It will happen in time, of course.'

'We want to see it happen,' said Olive. Her eyes were bright and penetrating while she thought only of George. Now they clouded.

'George,' she said, 'I want you to give me some advice.'

'Yes.'

'You heard what I said to Jack. Things at home aren't getting any easier. Possibly I ought to give up the next two or three years to my father. But you know all about it. I just want an answer to this question – ought I to clear out at any price?'

'This is a bit complicated,' said George. 'You know I don't approve of your parents. We'll take that for granted. If you could bring yourself to get away, I think you would be happier. What exactly are you thinking of doing?'

'I might get a better job,' she said, 'and live away from home. Or I might get married soon.'

George stayed silent for a moment. A good-natured smile had settled on his face. He said:

'Getting a job to make yourself really independent wouldn't be as easy as you imagine. Everyone knows what I think of your capabilities, but the fact is, girls of your class aren't trained to be much use in the world.'

'You're right,' said Olive.

'You're given less chance than anybody. It's a scandal, but it's true. To be honest, I don't think it would happen if women weren't in the main destined for their biological purpose. I dare say you could live on your present job. But living in abject poverty isn't much fun. Anyone who's ever tried would have to tell you that. I'm afraid you might begin to be willing – to get wrapped in your family again.'

Everyone was struck by the caution and the moderate tone of his advice: in fact, George, who could take up any other free idea under heaven, never had an illusion about the position of women. Olive inclined her head.

'I'm glad you're speaking out,' she said. 'And marriage?'

George said slowly: 'Escaping even from a family like yours is no reason for marriage. The only reason for marriage is that you are certain that you're completely in love.'

'Perhaps so,' said Olive, 'perhaps so. I don't know.' She sat silently for an instant. Then she smiled at him. 'Anyway, it's more important for you to get established,' she said, as though there was a link between them.

George did not reply, and Olive fell into silence. The windows rattled in the wind. Rachel sighed opulently, and said: 'We've never had a night here quite like this. George, don't you think we ought to remember this Saturday? We ought to make it a festival, and come over here to keep it in October every year.'

The sentiment welled from her; and she gave the rest of us an excuse to be sentimental.

A few moments later I said:

'Some of us are starting. Where we shall have got to, after a few of Rachel's festivals—'

'Good God alive,' George burst into triumphant laughter, 'you don't expect me to choose this day of all days to lose faith in the future, do you?'

The next night, after supper, George and I were alone in the room. The others had gone into the town by the last bus: George was staying another night in order to call at the Melton office in the morning, and I could stretch myself in my new liberty.

We made another pot of tea. 'There's something I should like to show you,' George said suddenly, with a friendly but secret smile. 'I want you to inspect my exhibit. Just to round off the weekend. It is exactly the right night for that.'

He put a small suitcase on the table. This he unlocked and produced a dozen thick folios, held together in a clip-back case.

'You've heard me mention this,' he said. 'I'm going to let you read a few entries about Jack Cotery's affairs. I assume you'll keep them to yourself, naturally.'

It was his diary, which he had kept for years.

He searched through one of the folios, detached pages and handed them to me. At another, more important, moment in George's life, I was to read much of the diary. The appearance of the pages, years later, altered little from when he began it at eighteen. They were all in his clerkly and legible hand; in a wide left-hand margin he printed in capitals (sometimes after the entries were made, usually when a folio was completed) a sort of sectional heading, and another at the top of the page. Thus:

COMFORT WITH THE GROUP
FRIDAY, AUG. 23

I could not let today pass by without writing. It was a day of hard work in the office; Eden listened to my summary and is well and truly launched

PLEASURES
OF ONE DAY

on the co-operative case. I screwed myself up to spend a couple of hours at Martineau's this evening; it is not long since I left him and, as so often, felt stronger by his influence. But, above all, I passed a memorable evening with my friends. . . .

'That entry is just to acclimatise you,' said George. In fact, there were pages of rhapsody over the group; rhapsody in a florid, elaborate and youthful style, which nevertheless could not keep one from believing his enthusiasm; and mixed with the rhapsody, more self-reproach and doubt than his friends would have expected then.

At first sight much of it seemed unfamiliar; for it was bringing home (what at that age I hadn't seen directly) some of the ways in which he appeared to himself. I read:

For I feel these people (these protégés of mine, if they will let me call them that) are gradually renewing their grip on my affections, my thought, my visions, although I have only visited them occasionally. The last weekend was full of drunken nights, of decrepit nights. I went to Nottingham, finding money drip away as usual. . . . I was still on the hunt and finished at Connie's, as in duty bound. Then I realised once again that no other girl of the past year is fit to take her place. I just had time for a huzzlecoo; then I went back on the last train.

It left me in a mood of headache and despair. . . .

And another day:

THEY ARE
REMOTE

I felt very depressed this evening. I arrived at one of those moods when the world seemed useless – when effort seemed in vain; the impossibility of moving mountains had overwhelmed me with my little faith. A chance remark by Olive on the purposelessness of the group had suddenly awakened me to their lack of response, to the lack of response of all of them; to their utter remoteness from me. . . .

Then there was another entry over which I thought a good deal in the next few months.

MORCOM AND MY WORLD
TUESDAY, SEP. 3

Today Morcom entertained me to lunch. He was charming and considerate – the perfect host. He has so much that I fear I shall never

MORCOM RAISES A PROFOUND QUESTION: WHAT SHOULD THE GROUP MEAN? acquire, taste and polish and *savoir faire*, while I am still uncultivated except in my one or two narrow special regions. If only he would abandon his negative attitude and join my attempts! He and I would be the natural alliance, and there is no limit to what we could achieve among the Philistines in this town. He with his strength and command and certainty. I with my burning hopes. When he went out of his way to be pleasant today and issued this invitation, I could scarcely contain my hopes that he was about to throw in his weight on my side. Yet apparently, if ever he possessed it, he withdrew from any such intention, and, indeed, he dropped one or two hints which made me examine myself anew, distressed me profoundly, and caused me, as before, to distrust his influence on some of my closest friends.

Morcom had criticised, sensibly and much as Olive did later, George's devotion to our group. He had said, in short, that it was not close enough to the earth to satisfy a man of power for long. On paper George answered the criticisms, so elaborately that he showed his own misgivings: and finished:

And what else lies in my powers? The gift of creation, worse luck, was not bestowed on me: except, I dare sometimes think, in the chance to help my protégés, beside whom all the artistic masterpieces of the world seem like bloodless artifices of men who have never discovered what it is to live. I must concentrate on the little world: I shall not get esteem, except the esteem which I value more than any public praise; I shall get no fame, except some gratitude which will soon be forgotten; I shall get no power at all. But I shall do what with all your gifts, Morcom, you may never do: I shall enjoy every moment of every day, and I shall gain my own soul.

In the first pages he showed me, Jack played very little part; there was a word in August:

I am still enjoying the fruitful association with Jack Cotery as much as ever. I have never been so lucky in my friends as I am now.

Then the idea of helping Jack came into the forefront of the diary, and continued there for weeks. There were descriptions of days which I remembered from another side: our first telling him the news, his attack on the committee (written with curious modesty), the visit to Nottingham, his resolve to find money for Jack.

Jack himself is easily disposed of. He is obviously the most gifted person I have a chance of helping. It is a risk, he may fall by the wayside, but it is less risky than with any other of the unfortunates.

ISSUES OF JACK   Morcom mustn't think he is the only person to spot talent. We mustn't forget that I first discovered that in spite of his humorous, lively warmth, there is a keen and accomplished edge to Jack's mind.

Jack's flattery, however, he mentioned, to my surprise:

We must perhaps remember that Jack is not completely impartial just now, though I should repudiate the suggestion if it were made. . . .

And the opposition by his mother, he described a little oddly:

QUIET EVENINGS AT HOME, WITH INTERMISSIONS   There had been little visible sign of misunderstanding or incompatibility, but one or two needless scenes.

But there was one thing which astonished me, more than it should have done, since, when I myself rejected George's advice about becoming a solicitor, there must have been similar entries about me. I knew that he had been angry at Jack preferring to experiment in business instead of accepting George's scheme of the law. Until I read George's entries, though, I could not have realised how he felt deserted, how deeply he had taken it to heart.

Cotery wantonly destroyed all my schemes for him . . . after destroying his feeble case for this fatuous project, I went away to consider closely the reasons for this outburst. It is fairly clear that

COTERY REVEALS FEET OF CLAY   he is not such a strong character as I tried to imagine. He may have been subject to underhand influences. I must not blind myself to that; and no doubt he is reacting to his complete acceptance of all I stand for. But, though understandable, such liability to influence and reaction are the signs of a weak character; and it is abundantly certain that I shall have to revise parts of my opinion of him. He will never seem the same again. . . .

Then, a week later, there came the last entry he showed me that night:

I REACH EQUILIBRIUM ON THE COTERY BUSINESS
FRIDAY, SEP. 28

I have settled the difficulty about Cotery at last. I do not withdraw a word of my criticism, either of the wisdom of his course or the causes behind it. In a long and, on the whole, profitable

KERNEL OF
COTERY'S BEHAVIOUR

conversation with Morcom, I forced him to admit that I had been unfairly treated. Morcom is, no doubt, regretful of using his influence without either thought or knowledge. Apart from that, Jack seems, in short, to be handicapping himself at the outset because of an unworthy reaction against me. But that doesn't dispose of my share in his adventure.

I have decided that I owe it to myself to maintain

PROPER ATTITUDE
UNAFFECTED

my offer ... he must be helped, as though he were acting more sanely. .... I talk about freedom, about helping people to become themselves; I must show the scoffers that I mean what I say, I must show that I want life that functions on its own and not in my hothouse. I have got to learn to help people on *their* terms. I wish I could come to it more easily.

As for the money, I shall cease worrying and

THE PRACTICAL
PROBLEM

hope that finance will arrange itself in the long run. I shall carry through this offer to Jack Cotery; then I shall wait and see, and, somehow, pay.

PART TWO

THE FIRM OF EDEN & MARTINEAU

CHAPTER IX

THE ECHO OF A QUARREL

THE winter was eventful for several of us. Olive, as she had foreshadowed that Saturday night at the farm, told Morcom that she could not marry him; she began to spend most of her time at home, looking after her father. Morcom tried to hide his unhappiness; often, he was so lonely that he fetched me out of my room and we walked for hours on a winter night; but he never talked of his own state. He also tried to conceal something else which tormented him: his jealousy for Jack Cotery. It was the true jealousy of his kind of love; it was irrational, he felt degraded by it, yet it was sharp and unarguable as a disease. Walking through the streets on those bitter nights, he could not keep from fearing that Jack might *that very moment* be at the Calverts' house.

Although Morcom was older than I was, too much so for us to have been intimate friends, I understood something of what he was going through, for it was beginning to happen to me. In time, I lost touch with him, and never knew what happened to him in later life. Yet, though I was closer to the others that year, he taught me more about myself.

Meanwhile, Jack himself had plunged into his business. One bright idea had come off: another, a gamble that people would soon be buying a cheap type of valve set, engrossed him all the winter and by spring still seemed to be about an even chance.

But George remained cheerful and content, in the middle of his friends' concerns. He was sometimes harassed by Jack's business, but no one found it easier to put such doubts aside; the group occupied him more and more; he spent extra hours, outside the School, coaching me for my first examination; he was increasingly busy at Eden & Martineau's.

The rest of us had never envied him so much. He was sure of his roots, and wanted no others, at this time when we were all in flux. It was not until the spring that we realised he too could be threatened by a change.

On the Friday night after Easter, I was late in arriving at Martineau's. Looking at the window as I crossed the road, I was startled by a voice from within. I went in; suddenly the voice stopped, as my feet sounded in the hall. Martineau and George were alone in the drawing-room; George, whose voice I had heard, was deeply flushed.

Martineau welcomed me, smiling.

'I'm glad you've come, Lewis,' he said, after a moment in which we exchanged a little news. George stayed silent.

'Everyone's deserting me,' Martineau smiled. 'Everyone's giving me up.'

'That's not fair, Mr Martineau,' George said, with a staccato laugh.

Martineau walked a few steps backwards and forwards behind the sofa, a curious, restless mannerism of his. 'Oh yes, you are,' Martineau's face had a look at once mischievous and gentle. 'Oh yes, you are, George. You're all deciding I'm a useless old man with bees in his bonnet who's only a nuisance to his friends.'

'That simply is not true,' George burst out.

'Some of my friends haven't joined us on Friday for a long time, you know.'

'That's nothing to do with it,' said George. 'I thought I'd made that clear.'

'Still,' Martineau added inconsequently, 'my brother said he might drop in tonight. And I'm hoping the others won't give us the "go-by" for ever.' He always produced his slang with great gusto; it happened often to be slightly out-moded.

The Canon did not come, but Eden did. He stayed fairly late. George and I left not long afterwards. In the hall George said:

'That was sheer waste of time.'

As we went down the path, I looked back and saw the chink of light through the curtains, darkened for an instant by Martineau crossing the room. I burst out:

'What was happening with Martineau before anyone came in? What's the matter?'

George stared ahead.

'Nothing particular,' he said.

'You're sure? Come on—'

'We were talking over a professional problem,' said George. 'I'm afraid I can't tell you anything else.'

Outside the park, under a lamp which gilded the chestnut-trees, I saw George's chin thrust out: he was swinging his stick as he walked.

A warm wind, smelling of rain and the spring earth, blew in our faces. I was angry, young enough to be ashamed of the snub, still on edge with curiosity.

We walked on silently down to the road where we usually parted. He stopped at the corner, and I could see, just as I was going to say an ill-tempered 'Good night,' that his face was anxious and excited. 'Can't you come to my place?' he said abruptly. 'I know it's a bit late.'

Warmed by the awkward invitation, I crossed the street with him. George broke into a gust of laughter, good-humoured and exuberant. 'Late be damned!' he cried. 'I've got a case that's going to keep me busy, and I want you to help. It'll be a good deal later before you get home tonight.'

When we arrived in his room, the fire contained only a few dull red embers. George, who was now in the highest of spirits after his truculence at Martineau's, hummed to himself, as, clumsily, breathing hard, he held a newspaper across the fireplace; then, as the flames began to roar, he turned his head:

'There's something I've got to impress on you before we begin.'

He was kneeling, he had flung off his overcoat, one or two fair hairs caught the light on the shoulders of his blue jacket; his tone, as whenever he had to go through a formal act, was a trifle sententious and constrained (though he often liked performing one).

'What are you going to tell me?' I said, settling myself in the armchair at the other side of the fire. There was a smell of charring; George's face was tinged with heat as he crumpled the paper in the grate.

'That I'm relying on you to keep this strictly confidential,' he said, putting on a kettle. 'I'm laying you under that definite obligation. It's a friendly contract and it's got to be kept. Because I'm being irregular in telling you this at all.'

I nodded. This was not the first of the firm's cases I had heard discussed, for George was not always rigid on professional etiquette; and indeed his demand for secrecy tonight served as much to show me the magnitude of the case as to make sure that I should not speak. It was their biggest job for some time, apart from the routine of conveyancing and so on in a provincial town. A trade union, through one of its members, was prosecuting an employer under the Truck Act.

Eden had apparently realised that the case would call out all George's fervour. It was its meaning as well as its intricacy that gave George this rush of enthusiasm. It set his eyes alight and sent him rocking with laughter at the slightest joke.

As he developed the case itself, he was more at home even than among his friends at the Farm. There, an unexplained jarring note could suddenly stab through his amiability; or else he would be hurt and defensive, often by a remark which was not intended to bear the meaning he wove into it. But here for hours, he was completely master of his surroundings, uncriticised and at ease; his exposition was a model, clear and taut, embracing all the facts and shirking none of the problems.

George himself, of course, was led by inclination to mix with human beings and find his chief interest there. There is a superstition that men like most the things they do supremely well; in George's case and many others, it is quite untrue. George never set much value on these problems of law, which he handled so easily. But, whatever he chose for himself, there was no doubt that, of all the people I knew in my youth, he was the best at this kind of intellectual game; he had the memory, the ingenuity, the stamina and the orderliness which made watching him arrange a case something near an aesthetic pleasure.

As he finished, he smacked his lips and chuckled. He said:

'Well, that reduces it to three heads. Now let's have some tea and get to work.'

We sat down at the table as George wrote down the problems to which he had to find an answer; his saucer described the first sodden circle on a sheet of foolscap. I fetched down some books from his shelves and looked up references; but I could not help much – he had really insisted on my coming in order to share the excitement, and perhaps to applaud. On the other side of the table George wrote with scarcely a pause.

'God love us,' George burst out. 'If only' – he broke into an argument about technical evidence – 'we should get a perfect case.'

'It'll take weeks,' I said. 'Still—' I smiled. I was beginning to feel tired, and George's eyes were rimmed with red.

'If it's going to take weeks,' said George, 'the more we do tonight the better. We've got to get it perfect. We can't give Eden a chance to make a mess of it. I refuse to think,' he cried, 'that we shan't win.'

In the excitement of the night, I forgot the beginning of the evening and the signs of a quarrel with Martineau. But, as George gathered up his papers after the night's work, he said: 'I can't afford to lose this. I can't afford to lose it personally – in the circumstances,' and then hurried to make the words seem innocuous.

CHAPTER X

ROOFS SEEN FROM AN OFFICE WINDOW

MOST nights in the next week I walked round to George's after my own work was done. Often it was so late (for my examination was very near, and I was reading for long hours) that George's was the only lighted window in the street. His voice sounded very loud when he stood in the little hall and greeted me.

'Isn't it splendid? I've got another argument complete. You'd better read it.'

His anxiety, however, was growing. He did not explain it; I knew that it must be caused by some trouble within the firm. Once, when Martineau was mentioned, he said abruptly: 'I don't know what's come over him. He used to have a sense of proportion.' It was a contrast to his old extravagant eulogies of Martineau, but he soon protested: 'Whatever you say, the man's the only spiritual influence in the whole soulless place.'

Then tired over the case, vexed by this secret worry, he was repeatedly badgered by the crisis in Jack's business. For a time Jack had taken Morcom's advice, and managed to put off an urgent creditor. He did not confide the extent of the danger to George until a promise fell through and he was being threatened. George was hot with anger at being told so late.

'Why am I the last person who hears? I should have assumed I ought to be the first.'

'I didn't want to worry you.'

'I suppose you don't think it's worrying me to tell me now in the middle of as many difficulties as anyone ever had?'

'I couldn't keep it back any longer,' said Jack.

'If you'd come before, I should have stopped you getting into this absurd position.'

'I'm there now, said Jack. 'It's not much comfort holding inquests.'

Several nights in the middle of the case, George switched off to study the figures of the business. They were not over-complicated, but it was a distraction he wanted to be spared: particularly as it soon became clear that Jack was expecting money to 'set it straight'. George discovered that Morcom had heard of this misfortune a week before; he exploded into an outburst that lasted a whole night. 'Do you think I'm the sort of man you can ignore till you can't find anyone else? Why don't you let other people finish up the business? There's no need to come to me at all.' He was half-mollified, however, to be told that Morcom's advice had only delayed the crisis, and that he had volunteered no further help.

Affronted as he was, George did not attempt to throw off the responsibility. To me in private, he said with a trace of irritated triumph: 'If I'd asserted myself in the first place, he'd have been settling down to the law by now.' But he took it for granted that he was bound to set Jack going again. He went through the figures.

'You guaranteed this man—?'

'Yes.'

'What backing did you have?'

'It hasn't come off.'

In the end George worked out that a minimum of fifty pounds had to be provided within a month. 'That will avoid the worst. We want three times as much to consolidate the thing. I don't know how we shall even manage the fifty,' George said. As we knew, he was short of money himself; Mrs Passant was making more demands, his sister was going to a different school; he still lived frugally, and then frittered pounds away on a night's jaunt.

It surprised me how during this transaction Jack's manner towards George became casual and brusque. Towards anyone else Jack would have shown more of his finesse, as well as his mobile good nature. But I felt in him a streak of ruthlessness whenever he was intent on his own way: as he talked to George, it came almost to the surface.

I mentioned this strange relation of theirs to Morcom, the evening before I went to London for my examination: but he drove it out of my head by telling me he was himself worried over Martineau.

There was no time for him to say more. But in the train, returning to the town after the examination, I was seized by the loneliness, the enormous feeling of calamity, which seems lurking for us – or at any rate, all through my life it often did so for me – when we arrive home at the end of a journey. I went straight round to George's. He was not in, although it was already evening. His landlady told me that he was working late in the office; there I found him, in his room on the same floor as those which carried on their doors the neat white letters 'Mr Eden', 'Mr Martineau'. George's room was smaller than the others, and in it one could hear trams grinding below, through the centre of the town.

'How did you get on?' George said. Though I felt he was wishing the inquiries over so that he could pass on to something urgent, he insisted on working through my examination paper.

354

'Ah,' George breathed heavily, for he had been talking fast, 'you must have done well. And now we've got a bit of news for you.'

'What is it? Has anything gone wrong?' I was full of an inexplicable impatience.

'I've got the case absolutely cut and dried,' said George enthusiastically. I heard his explanation, which would have been interesting in itself. When he had finished, I asked:

'Anything new about Martineau?'

'Nothing definite.' George's tone was uncomfortable, as though the question should not have been put. 'By the way,' he added, 'Morcom rang up to ask if he could come in tonight and talk something over. I believe it's the same subject.'

'When?' I said. 'When is he coming?'

'Well, as a matter of fact, quite soon.'

'Do you mind if I stay?' I said.

'There's a slight difficulty,' said George. He added: 'You see, we've got to consider Morcom. He's inclined to be discreet—'

'He's already spoken to me about it,' I said, but George was unwilling until I offered to meet Morcom on his way.

When I brought him back, Morcom began:

'It's rather dull, what I've come to you about.' Then he said, after a question to me: 'But you know a good deal about Martineau, George. And you're better than I am at figures.'

George smiled, gratified: 'If that's what you want, Lewis is your man.'

'All the better,' said Morcom. 'You can both tell me what you think. The position is this. You know that Martineau is my landlord. Well, he says he can't afford to let me keep on my flat. It seemed to me nonsense. So I asked for an account of what he spends on the house. I've got it here. I've also made a note of what I pay. That's in pencil; the rest are Martineau's figures. I want to know what you think of them.'

George was sitting at the table. I got up and stood behind him, and we both gazed for some minutes at the sheet of notepaper. I heard George's breathing.

'Well?' said Morcom.

'It's not very – careful, is it?' said George, after a long hesitation.

'What do you say?' Morcom said to me.

'I should go further,' I said. 'It's either so negligent that one can hardly believe it – or else—' I paused, then hurried on: 'something like dishonesty.'

355

'That's sheer fatuity,' George said. 'He's one of the most honest people alive. As you both ought to know. You can't go flinging about accusations frivolously against a man like Martineau.'

'I didn't mean it like that. I meant, if one didn't know him and saw that account—'

'It's a pity,' said George, 'that you didn't say that.'

'How do you explain the figures?' Morcom asked.

'I reject the idea of dishonesty,' George said. 'Right from the beginning; and if you don't, I'm afraid I can't continue with the discussion.'

'I shouldn't believe it. Unless there turned out nothing else to believe,' Morcom said. George went on:

'I grant it might have been dishonest if Lewis or I had produced an account like that. But we shouldn't have done it with such extraordinary clumsiness. Anyone could see through it at a glance. He's put all sorts of expenses down on the debit side that have got as much to do with his house as they have with me.'

'I saw that,' said Morcom.

'That proves it wasn't dishonesty,' George was suddenly smiling broadly. 'Because, as I say, a competent man couldn't have done it without being dishonest. But on the other hand a competent man wouldn't have done it so egregiously. So the person who did it was probably incompetent and honest. Being Martineau.'

'But is he incompetent?'

'He's not bad at his job,' George admitted slowly. 'Or used to be when he took the trouble. He used to be pretty good at financial things—'

Morcom and I leapt at the same words.

'Took the trouble?' said Morcom. 'When has he stopped? What do you mean?'

'I didn't want to say anything about this.' George looked upset. 'You'll have to regard it as in absolute confidence. But he's been slacking off gradually for a long time. The last month or two I've not been able to get him to show any kind of recognition. I tried to make some real demands on him about the case. He just said there were more important things. He's become careless—'

'That was what you were quarrelling about,' I cried out. 'That Friday night – do you remember? I found the two of you alone.'

'Yes,' said George, with a shy grin. 'I did try to make one or two points clear to him.'

'I heard him,' I said to Morcom, 'before I left the gardens.'

Morcom smiled.

'I don't know what is possessing him,' said George. 'Though, as I told him the night we had our disagreement, I can't imagine working under anyone else.'

'It's a pity for his sake,' I said, 'but the most important thing is – what does it mean to you?'

'Yes,' said Morcom. 'We haven't much to go on yet.'

'You'll tell me if you get any news,' said George.

'Of course.'

They were enjoying this co-operation. They each found that pleasure we all have in being on the same side with someone we have regularly opposed.

George walked to the window. It was almost nine, and the summer night had scarcely begun to darken. George looked over the roofs. The buildings fell away in shadow, the roofs shone in the clear light.

'I'm glad you came round,' said George. 'I've been letting it get on my nerves. It doesn't matter to you so much. But it just possibly might upset all the arrangements I have built up for myself. I've always counted on his being perfectly dependable. He is part of the scheme of things. If he's going to play fast-and-loose – it might be the most serious thing that has happened since I came here.'

CHAPTER XI

A FIRM OF SOLICITORS

THE firm of Eden & Martineau had been established, under the name of G. J. Eden, Solicitor, by Eden's father in the eighties. It was a good time for the town, despite shadows of depression outside; by the pure geographical chance of being just outside the great coal- and iron-fields, it was beginning to collect several light industries instead of a single heavy one. And it was still a country market and a centre for litigious farmers. The elder Eden got together a confortable business almost from the beginning.

His son became junior partner in 1896; Martineau joined when the father died, ten years later. Through the next twenty years, down to the time when George was employed, the firm maintained a solid standing. It never obtained any unusual success in making money: a lack of drive in the Edens seemed to have prevented that. The firm, though well thought of in the town, was not among the most prosperous solicitors'. It is doubtful whether Harry Eden ever touched £3,000 a year.

From the moment he entered it, George bore a deep respect for the firm, and still, nearly three years after, would say how grateful he was to Martineau for 'having somehow got past the opposition and wangled me the job'. His pride in the firm should not have surprised us, though it sometimes did. It seemed strange to notice George identifying himself with a solid firm of solicitors in a provincial town – but of course it is not the Georges, the rebels of the world, who are indifferent to authority and institutions. The Georges cannot be indifferent easily; if they are in an institution, it may have to be changed, but it becomes part of themselves. George in the firm was, on a minor scale, something like George in his family; vehement, fighting for his rights, yet proud to be there and excessively attached.

In the same way, his gratitude to Martineau and his sense of good luck at ever having been appointed both showed how little he could take himself and the firm for granted. As a matter of fact, there was no mystery, almost no manœuvring, and no luck; they appointed him with a couple of minutes' consideration.

The only basis for the story of Martineau's manœuvres seemed to be that Eden said: 'He's not quite a gentleman, of course, Howard. Not that I think he's any the worse for that, necessarily,' and Martineau replied: 'I liked him very much. There's something fresh and honest about him, don't you feel?'

At any rate, George, who was drawn to Martineau at sight, went to the firm with the unshakeable conviction that there was his patron and protector.

Eden, George respected and disliked, more than he admitted to himself. It was dislike without reason. It was an antipathy such as one finds in any firm – or in any body of people brought together by accident and not by mutual liking, as I found later in colleges and government departments.

About the relations of Eden and Martineau themselves, George speculated very little. Their professional capacity, however, he decided early. Martineau was quite good while he was at all interested. Eden was incompetent at any kind of detailed work (George under-valued his judgment and broad sense). Between them, they left a good deal of the firm's work to George, and there is no doubt that, after he had been with them a couple of years, he carried most of their cases at the salary of a solicitor's clerk, £250 a year.

With Martineau to look after his interests George felt secure and happy, and enjoyed the work. He did not want to leave; the group at the School weighed with him most perhaps, but also his comfort in the firm. He was not actively ambitious. He had decided, with his usual certain optimism – by interpreting some remark of Martineau's, and also because he thought it just – that he would fairly soon be taken into partnership. Martineau would 'work it' – George had complete faith. Meanwhile, he was content.

And so the first signs of Martineau's instability menaced everything he counted on.

It was the first time we had seen him anxious for his own sake. We were worried. We tried to see what practical ill could happen. I asked George whether he feared that Martineau would sell his partnership; this he indignantly denied. But I was not reassured, and I could not help wishing that his disagreement with Eden last autumn, the whole episode of the committee, was further behind him.

I talked it over several nights that summer with Morcom and Jack; and also with Rachel who, for all her deep-throated sighs, had as shrewd a judgment as any of us. We occupied ourselves with actions, practical prudent actions, that George might be induced to take. But Olive, her insight sharpened by the lull in her own life, had something else to say.

'Do you remember that night in the café – when we were trying to stop him from interfering about Jack?' she said. 'I had a feeling then that he was unlucky ever to come near us. He'd have done more if he'd have gone somewhere that kept him on the rails. Perhaps that's why the firm is beginning to seem important to him now.'

She went on:

'I admire him,' she said. 'We shall all go on admiring him. It's easy to see it now I'm on the shelf. But he's getting less from us – than we've all got from him. We've just given him an excuse for the things he wanted to do. We've made it pleasant for him to loll about and fancy he's doing good. If he hadn't come across such a crowd, he'd have done something big. I know he's been happy. But don't you think he has his doubts? Don't you think he might like the chance to throw himself into the firm?'

Even at that age, Olive had no use for the great libertarian dreams. Perhaps her suspicions jarred on Rachel, who was, like me, concerned to find something politic that George might do. We suggested that it would do no harm to increase Eden's goodwill. 'Just as an insurance,' Rachel said. We meant nothing subtle or elaborate; but there were one or two obvious steps, such as getting Eden personally interested in the case and asking his advice now and then – and taking part in some of the

Edens' social life, attending the parties which Mrs Eden held each month and which George avoided from his first winter in the town.

George was angry at the suggestions. 'He wants me to do his work for him. He doesn't want to see me anywhere else –' and then, as a second line of defence: 'I'm sorry. I don't see why I should make myself uncomfortable without any better reasons than you're able to give. I am no good at social flummery. As I think I proved, the last time you persuaded me to make a fool of myself. I should have thought I'd knocked over enough cups for everyone's amusement. I tell you I'm no good at social flummery. You can't expect me to be, starting where I did.'

Dinner at the Edens' was an ordeal in which the right dress, the right fork, the proper tone of conversation, presented moments of shame too acute to be faced without an overmastering temptation. As he grew older he was making less effort to conquer these moments.

'You can't expect me to, starting where I did.' That was one motive – I knew – why he built up a group where he was utterly at ease, never going out into the uncomfortable and superior world.

None of us could move George to cultivate Eden's favour. We pressed him several times after he returned from vague but disturbing conversations with Martineau. He said: 'I'd rather do something more useful– ' which meant engross himself in the case. Through the uncertainty, it had come to assume a transcendental importance in his mind. Sensibly, Eden was letting him argue it in the court.

Throughout June and July, George worked at it with extraordinary stamina and concentration. I saw him work till the dawn six nights running, and although I made up sleep in the mornings and he went to the office, he was fresher than I each evening and more ready for the night's work to come.

CHAPTER XII

EVENING BY THE RIVER

UNTIL just before the final hearing of the case, George was searching for money to salvage Jack's business. It was a continual vexation; he did not endure it quietly. 'This is intolerable,' he shouted, as his work was interrupted. 'Intolerable!'

I had, in fact, used it as an argument for getting Eden's interest.

Even in the Calvert trouble, Eden had shown a liking for Jack; and it would have been easy, I argued – if George were on friendly terms with Eden – to explain the position and secure an advance of salary for Jack's sake.

Instead, George was harassed by petty expedients. He borrowed a few pounds from Morcom and Rachel, pawned his only valuable possession, a gold medal won at school, increased his overdraft by ten pounds, up to the limit allowed by his bank.

George managed to raise nearly sixty pounds in all, a few days before Jack's grace expired.

'Well, here it is,' he said to Jack. He was sitting in his room for one of his last nights' work on the case. 'You can thank heaven you didn't need any more. I don't know how I could have scraped another penny.'

'Thank you, George,' Jack said. 'Saved again. It won't happen any more, though.'

'I warn you I'm just helpless now,' George said.

'I'll pay it back by the end of the year. I expect you think that I shan't,' Jack said. 'But, you wouldn't believe it, but I'm more confident after this collapse than I was at the start.'

George stared down at his papers.

'There is one other thing.'

'Yes, George?'

'I don't know whether you realise how near you have been to – considerable danger.'

'I don't know what you mean.'

'I mean something definite. Your methods of getting hold of some of that stock were just on the fringe of the law. You didn't know, I expect, but if you hadn't met your bills and they had sued – you stood an even chance of being prosecuted afterwards.'

'I was afraid you were worrying over those figures,' said Jack. 'You're seeing more than is really there, you know.'

'I don't propose to say another word,' George said. 'The whole thing is over. I want you to know that I don't retract anything I've said about expecting you to make a tremendous success. You were unlucky over this affair. You might just as easily have been gigantically lucky. It was probably a bigger risk than you were justified in taking. Perhaps it's wiser not to attempt long-range prophecies. They're obviously the interesting things in business; but then, you see, I'm still convinced that successful business is devastatingly uninteresting. But if you don't reach quite as far, you'll simply outclass all those bloated stupid competitors of yours.

It's unthinkable that you won't. I refuse to waste time considering it.'
His eyes left Jack, and he began studying one of his tables of notes. 'I'm
afraid I shall have to neglect you now. I've got to make certain of smashing
them on Thursday.'

The last hearing of George's case took up a July afternoon. I sat in the
old Assize Hall, where the Quarter Sessions had been transferred this
year. The hall was small, intimate, and oppressive in the summer heat.
Thunder rolled intermittently as George made his last speech, aggressive,
closely packed with an overwhelming argument. He was more nervous
than in his attack on the School committee.

The judge had been a little short with him, provoked by his manner.
Eden, who allowed George complete charge in the later stages, sat with
his lips in a permanent but uneasy smile. When George was given the
case, in words slightly peremptory and uncordial, Eden shook his hand:
'That was an able piece of work, Passant. I must say you've done very
well.' Then Martineau, who had not attended a hearing throughout the
case, entered, was told the news, and laughed. 'You'll go from strength
to strength, won't you, George? You'll be ashamed of being seen with
your old friends—'

When they had gone, I stayed alone with George while he packed his
papers: he bent his head over the desk and made a neat tick on the final
page; he was smiling to himself. We went together to a café by the river;
when we sat down at the little table by the window, he said, with an
exultant sigh:

'Well, we've pulled that off.' A happy smile spread over his face.
'This is one of the best occasions there have ever been,' he said.

'I've never seen anyone look quite so jubilant,' I said, 'as when you
got the verdict.'

George shook with laughter.

'I don't see why anyone shouldn't look pleased,' he said, 'when you
damned well know you've done something in a different class from the
people round you.' His voice calmed down. 'Not that I ever had any
serious doubts about it.'

'Not last week?' I said. 'Walking round the park?'

'You can't expect me not to have bad moments,' George said. 'I
didn't get a reasonable chance to have any faith in myself until – not
long ago. Being as shy as I am in any respectable society doesn't help.
I've never got over my social handicaps. And you realise that I went
through my childhood without anyone impressing on me that I had
ability – considerable ability, in fact.' He chuckled. 'So you can't expect

me not to have bad moments. But they're not very serious. Fortunately, I've managed to convince myself—'

'What of?'

'That I'm capable of doing something useful in the world and that I've found the way of doing it.'

Contentedly he leaned back against the wall, and looked beyond me through the window. It was a cloudy evening, but the sky was bright towards the west; so that in the stream that ran by the café garden the clouds were reflected, dark and sharply cut.

'It was extremely important that I should be a success in the firm,' George went on. 'I regard that as settled now. They couldn't do without me.'

'Do they realise that?'

'Of course.'

'Are you sure?'

George flushed. 'Of course I am. I'm not dealing with cretins. You heard yourself what Martineau said an hour ago.'

'You can't rely on Martineau.'

'Why not?'

'In his present state, he might do anything. Sell his partnership and go into the Church,' I smiled, stretching my invention for something more fantastic than the future could possibly hold.

'Nonsense,' said George. 'He's a bit unsettled. People of imagination often have these bouts. But he's perfectly stable, of course.'

'You've forgotten what Morcom said the other night?'

'I've got it in its right proportion.'

'You were desperately anxious about him. A few days ago. You were more anxious than I've seen you about anything else.'

'You can exaggerate that.'

'So you expect everything to be always the same?'

'As far as the progress of my affairs goes,' said George, 'yes.'

I burst out: 'I must say it seems to me optimism gone mad.'

But actually, when George was shelving or assimilating the past, or doing what was in effect the same, comfortably forecasting his own future, I was profoundly moved by a difference of temperament: far more than by a disinterested anxiety. At that age, to be honest, I resented George being self-sufficient, as it seemed to me, able to soften any facts into his own optimistic world. He seemed to have a shield, an unfair shield, against the realities and anxieties that I already felt.

Also, for weeks I had been working with him, sympathising with his strain during the case, arguing against the qualms which oddly seemed to afflict him more than they would a less hopeful man. It had been easier to encourage him over the doubtful nights than to sit isolated from him by this acceptance of success, so blandly complete that the case might have been over a year ago and not that afternoon. And so, guiltily aware of the relief it gave me, I heard my voice grow rancorous. 'You're making a dream of it,' I said, 'just to indulge yourself. Like too many of your plans. Do you really think it's obvious that Martineau will stay here for the rest of his life?'

'I don't see what else he's going to do,' said George, smiling. But I could detect, as often when he was argued against, a change in tone. 'In any case,' he said, with his elaborate reasonableness, 'I don't propose to worry about that. He's done almost everything I required of him. He's stayed in the firm long enough for me to establish my position. He's given me the chance, and I've taken advantage of it. It doesn't matter particularly what happens now.'

George's face suddenly became eager and happy.

'You see,' he said, 'I have the right to stay here now. I could always have stayed before. Even Eden would never have seriously tried to get rid of me, whether Martineau was there or not. But I couldn't really be entirely satisfied until I'd established to myself the right to go on as I am. I've never had much confidence, and I knew it would take a triumph to prove to myself that I've a right to do as I please. That's why this is so splendid. I'm perfectly justified in staying, now.'

In my resentful state, I nearly pretended to be mystified. But I thought of Olive's premonition; and I was captured by his pleasure in his own picture of himself. One could not resist his fresh and ebullient happiness.

'The people at the School?' I said.

'Obviously,' said George. 'What would happen to everyone if I went away?'

I replied, as he wanted:

'One or two of us you've affected permanently,' I said. 'But the others – in time they'd become what they would have been – if you'd never come.'

'I won't have it,' said George. 'Good God above, I won't have it.' He laughed wholeheartedly. 'Do you think I'm going to waste my time like that? You're right, it's exactly what would happen. And it's simply inconceivable that it should. I refuse to contemplate it,' he said. 'We must go on as we are. God knows, there isn't much freedom in the world, and I'm damned if we lose what little there is. I've started here, and now after this I can go on. I tell you, that's why this mattered so much to me.'

I looked across the table; his eyes were shining in the twilight, and I was startled by the passionate exultation in his voice. 'You've understood before, I've found the only people to whom my existence is important. How can you expect anything else to count beside that fact?'

His voice quietened, he was smiling; the evening light falling from the window at my back showed his face glowing and at rest.

CHAPTER XIII

AN UNNECESSARY CONFESSION

WITH the success behind him, George remarked more often about a partnership 'being not too far away'. For the first time, he showed some impatience about his own future: but he was no longer worried over Martineau. Both Morcom and I began to think he was right; during July and August, I almost abandoned my fear that Martineau might leave and so endanger George's prospects in the firm.

Martineau's behaviour seemed no more eccentric than we were used to. He was still doing everything we wanted of him; we went to Friday nights, we saw him walking backwards and forwards between the sofa and the window, his shadow leaping jerkily into the summer darkness. It was all as it had been last year; just as with any present reality, it was hard to imagine that it would ever cease.

We smiled as we heard him use a mysterious phrase – 'the little plays'.

'Of course, the man's religion is at the bottom of it all,' said George, back into boisterous spirits which were not damped even when Olive had to leave the town; her father's health had worsened, and she took him to live by the sea. George compensated himself for that gap by his enormous pride in Jack's and my performances; for my examination result was a good one, and Jack at last had achieved a business coup.

It added to Jack's own liveliness. He was warmed by having made a little money and by feeling sure of his flair. And it was like him to signalise it by taking Mrs Passant to the pictures – her who was suspicious of all her son's friends, who had denounced Jack in particular as an unscrupulous sponger. Yet he became the only one of us she liked.

It was also Jack who brought the next news of Martineau. One evening in September, George and I were walking by the station when we saw Jack hurrying in. He seemed embarrassed to meet us.

'As a matter of fact,' he said, 'I can't wait a minute. I'm staying at Chiswick for the week-end – my mother's brother, you know.'

'There's no train to London for an hour, surely,' said George. Jack shook his head, smiled, and ran into the booking-hall.

'Of course there's no train at this time.' George chuckled to me. 'He must be after a woman. I wonder who he's picked up now.'

The following day was a Saturday; at eight George and I were sitting in the Victoria; I mentioned that at exactly this time last year, within three days, Jack had been presented with a cigarette-case. George was still smiling over the story when Jack himself came in.

'I was looking for you,' he said.

'I thought you were staying with your prosperous uncle,' said George. Jack did not answer. Instead, he said:

'I've something important to show you.'

He made us leave the public-house, and walk up the street; it was a warm September night, and we were glad to. He took us into the park at the end of the New Walk. We sat on a bench under one of the chestnut-trees and looked at the lights of the houses across the grass. The moon was not yet up; and the sky, over the cluster of lights, was so dense and blue that it seemed one could handle it. Jack pointed to the lights of Martineau's. 'Yes, it's about him,' he said.

He added:

'George, I want to borrow your knife for a minute.'

With a puzzled look, George brought out the heavy pocket-knife which he always carried. Jack opened it; then took a piece of paper from his pocket, unfolded it, and pinned it to the tree by the knife-blade.

'There,' he said. 'You'd have seen plenty of those last night—' if we had gone with him to a neighbouring village.

It was too dark to read the poster in comfort. George struck a match, and peered in the flickering light.

The sheet was headed '*Players of the Market Place*' and then, in smaller letters, '*will be with you on Thursday night to give their LITTLE PLAYS*. Titles for this evening, The Shirt, Circe. Written by us all. Played by us all. There is no collection,' and in very large letters 'WE WOULD RATHER HAVE YOUR CRITICISM THAN YOUR ABSENCE.'

It was a printed poster, and the proofs had been read with typical Martineau carelessness: so that, for instance, 'evening' appeared as 'evenini', like an odd word from one of the lesser-known Latin tongues, Romanian or Provençal.

The match burnt down to George's fingers. He threw it away with a curse.

Jack explained that the 'little plays' purported to carry a religious moral: that they were presumably written by Martineau himself. Jack had watched part of one – 'painfully bad', he said.

George was embarrassed and distressed.

'We can't let him make a fool of himself in public. We must calm him down,' he said. 'He can't have lost all sense of responsibility.'

'He's just kept enough to hide these antics from us,' said Jack. 'Still, I found him out.' Then he laughed, and to my astonishment added: 'Though in the process, of course, I managed to let you find me out.'

'What do you mean now?' said George, uninterested by the side of his concern for Martineau.

'I made that slip about the train.'

'Oh,' said George.

'And, of course, I remembered as soon as I spoke to you last night. I've always told you that my father's brother lived in Chiswick. Last night I said it was my mother's. After you'd noticed that, I may as well say that I've got no prosperous uncles living in Chiswick at all. I'm afraid that one night – it just seemed necessary to invent them.'

Jack spoke fast, smiling freshly in the dusk. Neither George nor I had noticed the slip: but that did not matter; he wanted to confess. He went on to confess some more romances; how he had wrapped his family in mystery, when really they were poor people living obscurely in the town. I was not much surprised. He was so fluid, I had watched him living one or two lies; and I had guessed about his family since he took pains to keep any of us from going near their house. I still was not sure where he lived.

He went on to tell us that one of his stories of an admiring woman had been imaginary. That seemed strange; for, more than most young men, he had enough conquests that were indisputably real. Perhaps he felt himself that this was an inexplicable invention – for he looked at George. The moon was just rising, and George's face was lit up, but lit up to show a frown of anger and incomprehension.

'I suppose it must seem slightly peculiar to you, George,' said Jack. 'But you don't know what it is to be obliged to make the world a trifle more picturesque. I'm not defending myself, mind. I often wish I were a solid person like you. Still, don't we all lie in our own fashion? You hear Martineau say, "George, I'm sure the firm's always going to need you". You'd never think of departing from the literal truth when you told us the words he'd said. But you're quite capable, aren't you, of interpreting the words in your own mind, and convincing yourself that he's really promised you a partnership? While I'm afraid that I might be obliged to invent an offer, with chapter and verse. Lewis knows what I mean better than you do. But I know it makes life too difficult if one goes on after my fashion.'

He was repentant, but he was high-spirited, exalted. 'Did you know,' he went on, 'that old Calvert told the truth at that committee of yours? He had warned me a month or two before that there wasn't an opening for me in the firm.'

'I didn't know,' said George. 'Otherwise, I shouldn't have acted.'

'I can say this for myself,' said Jack, 'that the Roy affair brought him to the point.'

'But you let me carry through the whole business under false pretences,' George cried. 'You represented it simply to get an advantage for yourself – and make sure that I should win it for you under false pretences?'

'Yes,' said Jack.

'No,' I said. 'That was one motive, of course. But you'd have done it if there'd been nothing George could bring off for you. You'd have done it – because you couldn't help wanting to heighten life.'

'Perhaps so,' said Jack.

'I should never have acted,' said George. He was shocked. He was shocked so much that he spoke quietly and with no outburst of anger. I thought that he sounded, more than anything, desperately lonely.

He stared at Jack in the moonlight. At that moment, their relation could have ended. Jack had been carried away by the need to reveal himself; he knew that many men – I myself, for example – would accept it easily; he had not realised the effect it would have on George. Yet, his intuition must have told him that, whatever happened, they would not part now.

George was seeing someone as different from himself as he would ever see. Here was Jack, who took on the colour of any world he lived in, who, if he remembered his home and felt the prick of a social shame, just invented a new home and believed in it, for the moment with his whole existence.

While George, remembering his home, would have thrust it in the world's face: 'I'm afraid I'm no good in any respectable society. You can't expect me to be, starting where I did.'

That was his excuse for his diffidences and some of his violence, for his constant expectation of patronising treatment and hostility. In that strange instant, as he looked at Jack, I felt that for once he saw that it was only an excuse. Here was someone who 'started' where George did, and who threw it off, with a lie, as lightly as a girl he had picked up for an hour: who never expected to find enemies and felt men easy to get on with and easier to outwit.

George knew then that his 'You can't expect me to, starting where I did' was an excuse. It was an excuse for something which any man finds difficult to recognise in himself: that is, he was by nature uneasy and on the defensive with most of his fellow men. He was only fully assured and comfortable with one or two intimate friends on whose admiration he could count; with his protégés, when he was himself in power: with women when he was making love. His shame at social barriers was an excuse for the hostility he felt in other people; an excuse for remaining where he could be certain that he was liked, and admired, and secure. If there had not been that excuse, there would have been another; the innate uneasiness would have come out in some other kind of shame.

That aspect of George, he shared with many men of characters as powerful as his own. The underlying uneasiness and the cloak of some shame, class shame, race shame, even the shame of deformity, whatever you like – they are a combination which consoles anyone like George to himself. For it is curiously difficult for any human being to recognise that he possesses natural limitations. We all tend to think there is some fundamental 'I' which could do anything, which could get on with all people, which would never meet an obstacle – *'if only I had had the chance'*. It was next to impossible – except in this rare moment of insight – for George to admit that his fundamental 'I' was innately diffident and ill-at-ease with other men. The excuse was more natural, and more comforting – *'if only I had been born in gentler circumstances.'*

George stood up, plucked his knife out of the tree and handed the poster to Jack.

'Thank you for taking that trouble about Martineau,' he said. 'I know you did it on my account. You'll let me know the minute you discover anything fresh, of course. We've got to help one another to keep him from some absolutely irretrievable piece of foolishness.'

CHAPTER XIV

THE LAST 'FRIDAY NIGHT'

FOR some time we heard no further news. Friday nights went on in their usual pattern. But one day in November, when I was having tea with George, I found him heavy and preoccupied. I tried to amuse him. Once or twice he smiled, but in a mechanical and distracted way. Then I asked:

'Is there a case? Can I help?'

'There's nothing on,' said George. He picked up the evening paper and began to read. Abruptly he said, a moment later:

'Martineau's letting his mania run away with him.'

'Has anything happened?'

'I found out yesterday,' George said, 'that he was asking someone to value his share in the firm.'

'You actually think he's going to sell?' I said.

'I shouldn't think even Martineau would get it valued for sheer enjoyment,' said George. 'Unless he's madder than we think.'

His optimism had vanished now.

'I thought he was a bit more settled,' I said. 'After he was headed off the plays.'

'You can't tell with him,' said George.

'Whatever can he be thinking of doing?'

'God knows what he's thinking of.'

'There may be enough to live on,' I suggested. 'He might retire and go in for his plays and things – on a grandiose scale. Or he might take another job.'

'It's demoralising for the firm,' George broke out. 'I never know where I'm going to stand for two days together.'

'You've got to forgive him a lot,' I said.

'I do.'

'After all, he's in a queer state.'

'It's absolute and utter irresponsibility,' said George. 'The man's got a duty towards his friends.'

George's temper was near the surface. He went to the next Friday night at Martineau's; and sat uncomfortably silent while Martineau talked as gaily as ever, without any sign of care. Then, as for a moment Martineau left the room, George came over to Morcom and myself and whispered:

'I'm going to tackle him afterwards. I'm going to ask for an explanation on the spot.'

When, at eleven, the others had gone, George said rapidly:

'I wonder if you could spare us a few minutes, Mr Martineau?'

'George?' Martineau laughed at the stiffness of George's tone. He had been standing up, according to his habit, behind the sofa: now he dropped into an armchair and clasped his fingers round his knee.

'We simply want to be reassured on one or two matters,' George said. 'Sometimes you are an anxiety to your friends, you know.' For a second, a smile, frank and affectionate, broke up the heaviness on George's face. 'Will you allow me to put our questions?'

'If I can answer,' Martineau murmured. 'If I can answer.'

'Well then, do you intend to give up your present position?'

'My position!' said Martineau. 'Do you mean my position in thought? I've had so many,' he smiled, 'that some day I shall have to give some of them up, George.'

'I meant, do you intend to give up your position in the firm?'

'Ah,' said Martineau. Morcom leant forward, half-smiling at the curiously naïve attempt to hedge. 'It'd be easier if you hadn't asked—'

'Can you say no?'

'I'm afraid I can't – not a No like yours, George.' He got up from the chair and began his walk by the window. 'I've asked that question to myself, don't you see, and I can't answer it properly. I can't be sure I've made up my mind for certain. But, perhaps I can tell you, I sometimes don't feel I have any right to remain inside the firm.'

I had a sense of certainty that the hesitation was not there: I felt that he was speaking from an unequivocal heart. Whether he knew it or not. I wondered if he knew it.

'Right,' said George. 'Of course you have a right. According to law and conventional ethics and any conceivable ethics of your own. Why shouldn't you stay?'

'It isn't as straightforward,' Martineau shook his head with a smile. 'We touched on this before, George. I've thought of it so often since. You see, I can't forget I've got some obligations which aren't to the firm at all. I may be wrong, but they come before the firm if one has to choose.'

'So have I,' said George. 'But the choice doesn't arise.'

'I'm afraid it does a little,' Martineau replied. 'I told you, I shouldn't be able to stop the things that I feel I'm called for most. I can't possibly stop them.'

'No one wants you to,' said George.

Martineau rested his hands on the sofa.

'But I haven't been able to see a way to keep on with those – and stay in the firm.'

'Why not?'

'Because I oughtn't to be part of a firm and doing it harm at the same time, surely you agree, George? And these other attempts of mine – that I can't give up, they're damaging it, of course.'

'You mean to say the firm's worse off because of your—' George shouted, stopped and said, 'activities?'

'I'm afraid so.'

'What's the evidence?'

'One or two people have said things.' Martineau stared at the ceiling.

'Have they said, plainly and definitely, that they think the firm's worse off than it was a couple of years ago?'

'They haven't said it in quite so many words, but—'

'They've implied it?'

'Yes.'

'Who are they?'

'I forget their names, except—'

'Except who?'

'Harry Eden said something not long ago.'

'Then Eden's a fool and a liar and I shall have pleasure in telling him so to his face,' George was shouting again. 'He wants to get rid of you and is trying a method that oughtn't to take in a child. It's simply nonsense. This is a straightforward matter of fact. The amount of business we did in the last nine months is bigger than in any other twelve months since I came. And we did more last month than during any similar time. It's only natural, of course. Anyone but Eden would realise that. And even he would if he hadn't a purpose of his own to serve. We're bound to have more cases, considering the success we had not long ago.'

'What do you mean?' Martineau, who had been frowning, inquired.

'It's only reasonable to imagine,' George said in a subdued voice, 'that the case in the summer had something to do with it.'

'Oh yes,' Martineau became passive again.

Morcom said:

'Do you think George is wrong, Howard? Do you really think the firm is suffering?'

His voice sounded cold and clear after the others.

'I think perhaps we're talking of different things,' said Martineau. 'I'm sure George's figures are right. I wasn't thinking of it quite in that way. I mean, I believe, I'm doing – what shall I say? – a kind of impalpable harm – just as the work I'm trying to do outside the firm is impalpable work. Which doesn't prevent it' – he smiled – 'being the most practical in the world, in my opinion.'

'I want to know,' George's voice was raised, 'what do you mean by impalpable harm to the firm?'

They argued again: Martineau became more evasive, and once he showed something like a flash of anger.

'I'm trying to do the best thing,' he said. 'I'm sorry you seem so eager to prevent me.'

'That's quite unfair.'

'I hoped my friends at any rate would give me credit for what I'm trying.' Then he recovered his light temper. 'Ah well, George, when you do something you feel is right, you'll know just what to expect.'

'Have you definitely made up your mind', said Morcom, 'to sell your share in the firm?'

'I can't say that,' said Martineau. 'Just now. I will tell you soon.'

'When?'

'It can't be long, it can't possibly be long,' Martineau replied.

'Next Friday?' I asked.

'No, not then. I shan't be in that night.'

Since any of us knew him, he had never missed being at home on Friday night. He announced it quite casually.

'I'll see you soon, though,' he said. 'I'll tell George when we can arrange one of our chats. It's so friendly of you to be worried. I value that, you don't know how I value that.'

In the street there was a mist which encircled the lamps. For a moment we stood outside the park gate; I felt a shiver of chill, and an anxious tension became mixed with the night's cold. Morcom said:

'We'd better go and have a coffee. We ought to talk this out.'

We walked down the road towards the station, chatting perfunctorily, our footsteps ringing heavily in the dank air. We went – there was nowhere else in this part of the town at night – to the cafe where we held the first conference about Jack.

'Can we do anything?' Morcom asked, as soon as we sat down. 'Have either of you any ideas?'

'He must be stopped,' said George.

'That's easy to say.'

'If only he could be made to recognise the *facts*,' George said.

'That doesn't help.'

'Of course it would help. The man's simply been misled. By the way,' George added with an elaborately indifferent smile, 'I thought you might have taken the opportunity to enlighten him. About the importance of the work I've done for them. Particularly the case.'

I saw a light, a narrowed concentration, in Morcom's eyes; I was on edge. I expected him to be provoked by the insistence and say something like, 'I could have explained, George, how important the case seems to you.' Morcom hesitated, and said:

'I would. But it wouldn't have been useful to you – or to him.'

'That's absurd,' George burst out. 'If he could really see.'

'It wouldn't make the slightest difference.'

'I refuse to accept that.'

'Don't you see', Morcom leaned forward, 'that he's *bound to leave*?'

I knew it too. Yet George sat without replying. He seemed blind: he was a man himself more passionate and uncontrolled than any of us, but now he was not able to see past his own barricade of reasons, he was not able to perceive the passions of another.

'You must recognise that,' Morcom was saying. 'You don't think all these arguments matter to him? Except to bolster up a choice he's already been forced to make. That's all. I expect it pleases him' – he smiled – 'to be told how much he's giving up, and how unnecessary it is. It's just a luxury. As for affecting him, one might as well sing choruses from *The Gondoliers*. He's already made the decision in his mind.' He smiled again. 'As far as that goes,' he added, 'he may already have made it in fact.'

'You mean he's actually sold his share?' George said.

'I don't know,' said Morcom. 'It's possible.'

'To some bastard,' said George, 'who happens to have enough money to make a nuisance of himself to other people. Who'll disapprove of everything I do. Who'll make life intolerable for me.'

CHAPTER XV

MARTINEAU'S INTENTION

I WALKED past Martineau's, the following Friday night. The drawing-room window was dark: Martineau, so George thought, was visiting his brother, the Canon. Next day, when I was having supper with Morcom, George sent a message by Jack: Martineau wanted to see us tomorrow (Sunday) afternoon: we were to meet at George's.

'Martineau's getting more fun out of all this than anyone else,' said Jack. 'Like your girl' – he said to Morcom – 'when she decided to sacrifice herself. Blast them both.' He could speak directly to Morcom about Olive, as no one else could; and he went out of his way to ease Morcom's jealousy. 'How is she, by the way? No one else ever hears a word but you.'

'She seems fairly cheerful,' said Morcom.

'Blast her and Martineau as well. Send them off together,' said Jack. 'They deserve each other. That'd put them right if anything could.' His face melted into a mischievous, kindly grin. I had heard him say the same, with even more mischief, about Sheila.

When I arrived at George's the next day, he was smoking after the midday meal. His shout of greeting had a formal cheerfulness, but I could hear no heart behind it.

'You're the first,' he said.

'Martineau *is* coming?'

'I imagine so,' said George. 'Even Martineau couldn't get us all together and then not turn up himself.'

We sat by the window, looking out into the street. The knocker on the door opposite glistened in the sun.

Soon there were footsteps down the pavement. Martineau looked in and waved his hand. George went to let him in.

'Come in,' I heard George saying, and then, 'Isn't it a beautiful day?'

Martineau sat down in an armchair opposite the window; his face, lit by the clear light from the street, looked tranquil and happy. George pushed the table back against the wall, and placed two chairs in front of the fire.

'Have you seen Morcom lately?' he said to Martineau. 'I sent him word.'

'He may be just a little late,' Martineau said. 'He is having lunch with' – he smiled at George – 'my brother.'

'Why's that?' George's question shot out.

'To talk over my little affair, I'm afraid,' Martineau answered. 'I've never made such a nuisance of myself before—' his laugh was full of pleasure.

'What does your brother think of it?'

'Very much the same as you do, George. He rather took the line that I owe an obligation to my relatives.' Martineau stared at the ceiling. 'I tried to put it to him as a Christian minister. I pointed out that he ought to sympathise with our placing certain duties higher than our duties to relatives. But he didn't seem to agree with my point of view.'

'Nor would any man of any sense,' said George.

'But is sense the most important thing?' Martineau asked 'For myself—'

'I refuse to be bullied by all these attacks on reason. I'm sorry, Mr Martineau,' said George, 'but I spend a great deal of my own time, as you know perfectly well, in activities that don't give me any personal profit whatever; but I'm prepared to justify them by reason, and if I couldn't I should give them up. That isn't true of what you propose to do, and so if you've got any respect for your intellectual honesty you've got no option but to abandon it.'

'I'm afraid I don't see it like that.' Martineau moved restlessly; his eyes met mine and then looked into the fire.

'There is no other way of seeing it,' said George.

(Many years later, near the end of George's life, I had to recall that justification of his.)

Through the uproar of George's voice I thought I had heard a knock at the door; it came again, now. I got up, and brought Morcom in. He spoke directly to Martineau.

'Eden's made a suggestion—'

'Where have you been?' George interrupted.

'Having lunch with Eden and Howard's brother.'

'I'm afraid,' Martineau broke in, 'I've been rather guilty this afternoon. I was trying to break it gently, you see, George. You must forgive me!'

'I'd better be told now.'

'Well, I spent all the early part of last week thinking over everything that had been said,' Martineau began. 'It was very difficult with so many friends that I really respect – you must believe that I respect your opinion, George – with so many friends – disapproving so much. But in the end I felt that I had to let them disapprove. The way I'd come to did really seem to be the only way.' He smiled. 'It does still.'

George had flushed. Morcom was looking at Martineau.

'So I told Harry Eden on Monday afternoon,' Martineau went on. 'He said he'd like to see my brother. That's why I arranged for them to meet.'

'You'd arranged that a week ago. So you'd made up your mind then,' George burst out.

'Not quite made up.' For a moment Martineau looked a little distraught. 'And in any case I felt I should like to have his advice, whether I had decided or not, you see. And Eden thought he'd feel easier if he could talk to one of my relatives, naturally.'

'I was brought in,' Morcom said, 'because Martineau hasn't any close friends of his own age in the town. You were ruled out because you were in the firm yourself, George. So Eden asked me in.'

To me, it was natural enough. Morcom at twenty-eight was a man who seemed made for responsibility; and most people thought of him as older.

'I suppose it's understandable,' George said. 'But if you've made up your mind' – he looked at Martineau – 'however fantastic it seems to everyone else, why should Eden become so officious all of a sudden? It's simply a matter of selling your share. I should have thought even Eden could have done that without family conferences.'

There was a pause. Martineau said, his voice trailing off:

'There is one matter that isn't quite—'

'It's this,' said Morcom. 'Martineau doesn't want to sell his share. He insists on giving it up to Eden.'

We sat in silence.

'It's raving lunacy,' George cried out.

'George! You won't be the last to call it that kind of name.' Martineau laughed.

'I'm sorry,' said George, heavily. 'And yet – what else can you call it?'

'I should like to call it something else.' Martineau was still laughing. 'I should like to call it: part of an attempt to live as I think I ought. It's time, George, it's time, after fifty years.'

'*Why* do you think you ought?'

'The religion I try to believe in—'

'You know you're doubtful whether you can call yourself a Christian.'

'This world of affairs of yours, George,' Martineau was following another thought – 'why, my chief happiness in your socialism is that one ought to give up all one has to the common good. It's always been a little of a puzzle how one can fail to do that in practice and keep the faith.'

George was flaring out, when I said:

' "Give it up to the common good" – but you're not doing that. You're giving it to Eden.'

'Ah, Lewis!' Martineau smiled. 'You think at least I ought to dispose of it myself?'

'I should have thought so.'

'Don't you see,' he said, 'that I can't do that? If I admit I have the power to dispose of it, why then I haven't got rid of the chains. I've got to let it slide. I mustn't allow myself the satisfaction of giving it to a friend' – he looked at George – 'or selling it and giving the money to charity. I'm compelled to forgo even that. I must just stand by as humbly as I can and be glad I haven't got the power.'

I looked at Morcom and George. We were all quiet. It was in a flat, level voice that George said:

'No doubt Eden hasn't raised any objections.'

'That's not fair,' said Morcom. 'He's behaved very well.'

Martineau looked cheerfully at George. He still enjoyed a thrust at his partner's expense.

'He's a good fellow,' he said lightly.

'I prefer to hold to my own opinion.'

'He's behaved well,' said Morcom again. 'Better than you could reasonably expect. He refused to do anything at all until he'd seen Martineau's brother. He said today that he doesn't like it and that he won't sign any transfer for three months. If anything happens to make Martineau change his mind during that time, then Eden wants the firm to go on as before. And if it doesn't, well, he said he was a businessman and not a philanthropist, and so he wasn't going to make gestures. He'll just take the offer. He's very fond of Martineau, he's as sorry as anyone else that this has happened—'

'I wish,' Martineau chuckled, 'everyone wouldn't refer to me as though I were either insane or dead.' We all laughed, George very loudly.

'It's good of him,' said Martineau. 'But I'm afraid he might as well save the time. I consider that it isn't mine any longer, you see. For – it isn't decided by a form of law—'

Soon afterwards Martineau left. When I heard the door click outside, I said:

'Whatever's going to become of him?'

On George's face injury struggled with concern: he shook his head. Morcom said: 'God knows.' But, at that time, even our most fantastic prophecies would not have approached the truth.

'The first thing,' said George, 'is to satisfy ourselves that he can find a living. We can't take any other steps until we're sure of that.'

'Apparently he told his brother he was going to earn enough by various methods. Which he wouldn't give any details of,' said Morcom. 'I simply don't know what he means.'

'Though how he reconciles giving up his share,' said George with an impatient laugh, 'and earning a living in any other way, is just beyond me. I suppose consistency isn't his strong point. Oh God!' he broke out, 'don't you find it hard to realise that this has *happened*?'

'Of course he won't starve,' Morcom said. 'That's one comfort. There is plenty of money in the family. In fact, that's one of his brother's chief anxieties. That they'll have to support him. The Canon's a hard man, by the way. I don't think I like him much.'

'Not so much as you like Eden, I suppose,' George said.

Morcom paused slightly: 'Nothing like,' he said.

The strain between them was showing in every word. I said hastily:

'What's he going to do with the house? Does he own it or not?'

'He's got some scheme for turning it into a boarding-house,' said Morcom. 'With his housekeeper in charge.'

'That means we've had the last "Friday night",' I said. 'I shall miss them,' I added.

'You have to realise,' said Morcom deliberately, 'that he's cutting himself away from his present life. That means cutting himself away from us as much as from the firm. You have to understand that. He doesn't want to see much of us again.'

Suddenly George burst into gusts of laughter. I found myself grow tense, watching him shake, seeing the tears that came so easily.

'I've just thought,' he wiped his eyes, then began to laugh again as helplessly. 'I've just thought,' he said at last in a weak voice: 'Martineau's position is exactly this. He thinks a man couldn't hold his share in the firm if he's either a Christian or a socialist. So he gives it up, being neither a Christian nor a socialist.'

It was a typical George joke, in its symmetry, in the incongruity that would strike no one else. But he had been laughing more for relief than at the joke. Soon he was saying, quite soberly:

'We've been assuming all the time that everything's settled. We haven't given ourselves a chance to do anything in the matter.'

'Of course we can't do anything,' said Morcom.

'I don't know whether I accept that completely,' said George. 'But if so we shall have to set to work in another direction.'

I did not know what those words foreshadowed; I was easier in mind than I had been that afternoon, to see his spirits enlivened again.

CHAPTER XVI

WALK IN THE RAIN

AFTER he went away from George's, none of us saw Martineau for weeks. There were some rumours about him; he was said to have bought a share of a small advertising agency, and also to have been seen in a poor neighbourhood visiting from house to house. Several times at Eden's we talked of him and speculated over his next move. The whole episode often seemed remote, as we sat in the comfortable room, hung with a collection of Chinese prints, and heard Eden say:

'These things will happen.' He said it frequently, with a tolerant and good-humoured smile.

Now that 'Friday nights' no longer existed, he had suggested that we call on him instead. He changed the day to Sunday, explaining that Friday was inconvenient for him, as his wife entertained that night. His real reason, I thought later, was a delicacy we did not appreciate enough. He gave us good food and drink, and the conversation was, more often than not, better than at Martineau's. The liking I had formed for Eden after casual meetings strengthened now. It was difficult to remember that this was the man whom George so much disliked.

Though by this time I knew something of George's antipathies, I tried to argue him out of this, the most practically important. It seemed more than ever urgent for him to gain Eden's approval. He protested angrily, but was less obdurate than in the summer. One Sunday I persuaded him to come to the house, and he was nervously silent apart from a sudden quick-worded argument with Eden upon some matter of political history; it was the first time I had seen that drawing-room disturbed. When Morcom and I disagreed with Eden, it meant only one of his good-humoured aphorisms, followed by a monologue that did not lead to controversy.

George said, as he stopped outside the gate to light a pipe:

'I hope you're satisfied now.'

In the match-light, he was smiling happily. To him, I suddenly realised, for whom most meetings and most people were full of unknown hostility, the night had been a success.

'You must go again,' I said.

'Naturally,' said George. 'After all, I've truckled for three years, in the firm. I must say, though, that he went out of his way to be civil tonight.'

It began to rain heavily, and we got on a tram-car. As it moved towards the town, we pieced together the rumours about Martineau. Often George guffawed: 'Fancy having one's goods advertised by Martineau,' he burst out. 'And fancy giving up,' he chuckled, 'a perfectly respectable profession to take up one more disreputable by any conceivable standards in the world. The only advantage being that it's almost certain to fail.' He laughed and wiped his eyes. 'Oh, Good God in Heaven, whatever is the point? Whatever does he think is the point?'

Suddenly George said, without any introduction:

'I think we've exaggerated this upheaval in the firm.'

I shook my head, and said:

'I am quite certain of one thing.'

'What's that?'

'That, whatever happens, Martineau will never come back to the firm. I'm sure that's true. It's unpleasant for you. But you must resign yourself—'

George said:

'I did that weeks ago. I assumed it as soon as Martineau disappeared.'

'Then what did you mean?' I said. 'About the upheaval in the firm being exaggerated. Whatever could you mean?'

'Oh,' said George. 'I decided, as I said, that Martineau could be ruled out. He obviously wouldn't be any further help. But what I meant was, I couldn't see why Eden shouldn't do as much for me as Martineau ever did. And I began to realise there were reasons why he should do a great deal more.'

'At once?'

'I don't see why he shouldn't be taking steps to make me a partner. Fairly soon.'

'Is that likely?' (I was thinking: this ought to have been foreseen.)

'I don't see why not.'

The tram was rattling to a stop: I rubbed the window with my sleeve. The rain had ceased, though it was dripping from the roofs. We were near the railway bridge, by some old mean streets.

'Look here,' said George. 'I've got a bit of a head. Let's walk from here.'

The gutters were swirling as we got off. George said:

'I don't see why not. After all, he'll be gaining enough by this business. He can afford to take a partner without any capital. He would have to get someone in my place, naturally. But Eden would still be better off by a very decent amount, compared with what he has been. With the advantages of having me as a partner.'

'Those being? I mean, from Eden's point of view?'

We were walking under the bridge. Our footsteps echoed, and I shivered in the cold. George's voice came back.

'The first is one we all tend to forget. That is, there is such a thing as ordinary human justice. Eden can't be too comfortable if I'm doing more work than the rest of the firm put together – which I have been doing for the last two years – and getting the money, which doesn't matter so much, and having the position, which matters a great deal, of a fairly competent clerk.'

'Are you sure he realises that – altogether?'

'If he doesn't,' said George, 'it's simply because he doesn't want to see. But even then – it must be perfectly obvious.' He walked along, looking straight ahead. 'The other reason is what plain blunt practical men would consider a great deal more important. That is, Eden doesn't know anything about half the cases we have to deal with. You know perfectly well, we've got a connection in income tax and property law and other kinds of superior accountancy. Well, Martineau could cope with those before he began to be troubled with doubt' – he chuckled – 'and even lately he could give people the impression that he knew something about it. Well, Eden simply couldn't. He's grotesquely incompetent at any piece of financial detail. In three or four years he'd have ruined our connection. It'd be too ridiculous, he's bound to realise it.' He went on, very quickly, as though to dismiss any argument: 'No, so far as I can see, there's only one possible reason for his not taking me in, and that is, he hasn't much sympathy for my general attitude.

'But I can't believe he'd let that outweigh everything else,' George went on. 'There are limits, you can't deny there are limits. And also he's shown signs recently that he's coming round. I think it'll be all right. Anyway we must see it *is* all right. You realise,' he said, 'that Eden can be influenced nowadays.'

'How?'

'I should have thought it was obvious.'

'How?'

'Morcom, of course,' George said. 'Obviously Eden's very much impressed with him for some reason. You noticed how he sent for him for that rather absurd conference with the Martineaus. And Morcom sees him very often—'

'Only on Sundays.'

'I've seen them in the town.' George frowned. 'It's absolutely patent that Morcom counts for a great deal with him. Well, we've got to take advantage of that.'

'He can't—'

'I know what you're going to say,' said George. 'I know as well as you do that Morcom doesn't approve of most of the things I do. I realise that and I've considered it. And I've decided I've a right to demand that he forgets it. He must talk to Eden about me. It's too important to let minor things stand in the way.' He paused, and then turned to me. Before, he had been looking straight ahead down the dark street. 'You mustn't know anything about this. Not even to Morcom. I'll deal with him myself.' Then his voice suddenly became friendly, and he talked as though he was pleasantly fatigued.

'It's important that Eden should take me in,' he said. 'I don't want to stay there as a subordinate and watch myself getting old.'

'That won't happen,' I said.

'I don't know,' said George. 'Things have never fallen in my lap.'

I had a rush of friendship for him, the warm friendship which sometimes at this period I was provoked into forgetting.

'It's time they began,' I said.

'It isn't that I'm not ambitious,' said George. 'I am, you know, to some extent. I know I'm not as determined as you've turned out to be – but matters never shaped themselves to give ambition a chance. I had to take the job here, there wasn't any alternative to that. When I got here, I couldn't do anything different from what I have done. Of course, I got interested in making something of people at the School. But I couldn't help myself.'

'Yes,' I said.

'It's important from every point of view that I get promoted,' he said quickly. 'For the group as well. If I'm really going to do much for anyone. I haven't got the money. I'm often powerless. I nearly was about Jack. God! how crippled one feels when there's someone who only wants money to give them a start.'

'You'd be worse off than you are now.' I smiled. 'Giving it away.'

George's own smile grew vaguer.

'There's another possibility,' he said. 'I don't know, but I may feel some time that I've done as much as I can with the School. After all, the present people will go away in time. I don't know that I shall want to get interested in any more.'

It was the first time I had heard him permit such a suggestion.

'I may want to do something useful in a wider field,' said George. 'And for that, I must be in with Eden. The group's all very well in its way, but its success is inside oneself, as you've said before now. As one gets older, perhaps one isn't pure enough to be satisfied with that.'

I tried to laugh it off. 'Martineau seems to be satisfied pretty easily,' I said. 'If his success isn't inside himself –'

George laughed. Then he said:

'I may even want to get married.'

Although a wish, it was no clearer than the others. It was one of many wishes springing from the unrest, the hope, that brought to his face a happy and expectant smile.

CHAPTER XVII

A SLIP OF THE TONGUE

I WAS upset by that talk with George.

He was mistaken, I knew, when he suddenly discovered that he was ambitious. If he had been truly ambitious, I should not have been so concerned; for, when this partnership failed him, he would have found something else to drive for. While George valued it more acutely, precisely because he did not usually care – just as a man like Morcom, not easily surrendered to love, may once in his life long for it with a passion dangerous to himself.

George at this moment longed for the place and security to which, for years, he had scarcely given a thought.

But that was nothing like all. I realised that Olive had been right. Months before, by a lucky guess or clairvoyance, she had divined something more important. 'I think he sometimes knows he was unlucky to get amongst us. Sometimes he wants to get away,' she said. He was trying to break from his present life, the School, the little world, the group. Jack's confession might have weakened him – but Olive felt it long before, long before his most vehement declaration of faith, that night in the café by the river. I believed that she was right.

However much he was satisfied by the little world he had built up, he was able to think of breaking free. Perhaps he half realised the danger, the crippling danger to himself. Anyway, he seemed to know that for just these months there was a chance to break loose *from his own satisfaction*. He also seemed to know that, if this failed, he would never bring himself to the point again.

Hearing George express his want for a respectable position, a comfortable middle-class income, the restraints of a junior partner in a firm of solicitors in a provincial town, I could not help being moved. Knowing the improbability, knowing above all this new suspicious faith in Morcom's influence, I was afraid. There was only a short time before Eden's period of grace ran out; it need not be final, but it would deprive George of his hopes.

I heard nothing, until a fortnight later, when Morcom and I were on our way towards Eden's. Abruptly Morcom said:

'George thinks Eden will offer him a partnership.'

I exclaimed.

'He stands exactly as much chance as I do,' said Morcom. He gave a short laugh, and talked about George's unrealistic hopes. Then I said:

'They're quite fantastic, of course. But that doesn't prevent him believing in them. It doesn't prevent him attaching as much importance to them as you might to something reasonable. Surely that's true.'

'I expect it is,' said Morcom. His voice sounded flat, his manner despondent and out of spirits. 'Anyway,' he said, 'I can't do anything. Eden will settle it completely by himself.'

'You might sound him,' I said.

'It's a lot of trouble simply because George believes the world revolves round him,' said Morcom.

'If he knew it had been mentioned—' I said. 'You see,' I added, filled with an inexplicable shame as well as anxiety, 'he's always got a dim feeling that you're antagonistic. If that grows, it's going to make life unpleasant.'

Morcom's face, as we came near a street lamp, looked drawn. I was surprised that the statement should have affected him so much. 'All right,' he said. 'I'd better try tonight.'

For most of the evening I sat listening to Eden's anecdotes, laughing more easily to make up for my impatience. The room was warm, there was a fire blazing, stoked high in the chimney: Eden was sitting by its side in his customary armchair, in front of which stood the little table full of books and pipes and a decanter. He wore a velvet smoking-jacket. Morcom sat opposite to him. I in the middle: behind Morcom, the light picked out the golden lines in one of the Chinese pictures.

At last there was a lull. Eden filled his glass. Morcom was leaning forward, the fingers of one hand tight over his knee.

'By the way, the time you gave Martineau to make up his mind – it'll be over soon, won't it?'

'I hadn't thought of it just lately.' Eden sipped, and put down his glass. 'Why, do you know, I suppose it will.'

'There's no chance of his coming back,' said Morcom.

I added: 'None at all.'

'I'm afraid you're right,' said Eden. It was a comfortable fear, I could not help thinking. 'It's a queer business. It's one of the queerest things I've ever struck.'

'What are you going to do about it? About the firm, I mean?' The questions were sharp. I could feel Morcom, as I was myself, responding to a slight, an amiable unwillingness in Eden's manner.

'I dare say it will go on,' Eden smiled. 'When once you've really started, it's not a difficult proposition to keep going, you know.'

'You're not thinking of filling – Martineau's place?'

'I needn't make any decision yet,' Eden said. 'There isn't any hurry, of course. But my present belief is that I shan't take another partner. I'm an old-fashioned democrat in affairs of state' – he smiled – 'but the older I get, the more I believe smaller things ought to be controlled by one man.'

'I can believe that,' said Morcom. 'But it's a lot of work for one man.'

'There's plenty of responsibility,' said Eden. 'But that's the penalty of being in control. No one wants it, but it's got to be shouldered. As for the detailed work, I shan't do any more than I'm doing now. I can trust the staff for anything in the way of routine. And to some extent I can trust Passant to work on his own.'

'He is very capable?' said Morcom.

'Very capable. Very capable indeed.' Eden was talking affably, but his lips had no tendency towards their smile. 'So long as he's working under someone *level-headed*. I know he's a friend of you two. I'm speaking as I shouldn't, you mustn't let it go beyond these four walls. But Passant's a man who'd have a future in front of him if only he didn't spoil himself. He's got a brilliant scholastic record, and though that isn't the same as being able to take your coat off in an office, he's done some good sound work for the firm. An outsider might think that I ought to give him a chance in a year or two to buy a share in the firm. But unless he takes himself in hand I don't believe I shall be able to do it. I couldn't feel I was doing the right thing.'

'Why not?'

'You'll be sure not to let this go any further?' Eden looked at us. 'Though a hint from you' – he glanced at Morcom – 'on your own account wouldn't be amiss. The trouble about Passant is – he's rackety. He's like a tremendous number of young men of your generation. There's nothing to keep him between the rails.'

I suddenly could hear, among the moderate ordinary words, a dislike as intense as that which George bore him.

'I know you can say that's a matter for the man himself. It's no one else's business how he lives. He's a grown man, he's free to choose his own friends and his own pleasures. If he wants to spend his spare time with these young men and girls he collects together, no one's going to stop him. But' – Eden shook his head – 'it's got to be remembered when you're thinking of his position here. I mightn't mind – except that they take up too much of his time – but the great majority of our clients would. And it's very hard to blame them. When you see a man night after night sitting in cafés with hordes of young girls, and you haven't much doubt that he's pretty loose-living all round; when you hear him laying down the law on every topic under heaven, telling everyone how to run the world: when above all you find him making an officious nuisance of himself in matters that don't concern him, like that affair of Calvert's: then you have to be an unusually tolerant man' – Eden leaned back and smiled – 'to feel very happy when you pay the firm a visit and find he's your family solicitor.'

'Particularly if he insists on telling you that you ought to follow his example,' Morcom said. 'And that you ought to bring your daughter just to show there's no ill-feeling.'

Involuntarily, I smiled myself. Then I stared in dismay at Morcom, while Eden continued to laugh. I was thinking, more bitter in my reproaches because I might have committed it myself, that the gibe was less than deliberate. It was one of those outbursts, triumphantly warm on the tongue, whose echo afterwards makes one wince with remorse. It was one of those outbursts that everyone is impelled to at times, however subtle and astute. In fact, I was to discover, the more subtle and astute one was, the more facilely such indiscretions came. Until, like the politicians I knew later, one disciplined oneself to say nothing spontaneous at all.

But that was not the whole of it, I knew, as I listened to Eden's slow and pleasant voice again. For while we listen to a friend being attacked, there are moments of sick and painful indignation, however untrue the charge: and, at other moments such as those when we make Morcom's joke – however untrue the charge – we find ourselves leaping to agree. We find ourselves, ashamed and eager with the laugh, on Eden's side.

Again, until we have hardened our characters, eliminated the trendiness along with the free-flowing.

'After all,' Eden was saying, 'Martineau can't have done us any good. People might respect him if they understood what he was getting at – but they don't want a saint, they want a sensible solicitor. We've got to win a certain amount of confidence back. We couldn't afford another Martineau. I'm afraid Passant would cause a bigger hostility even that that.'

'He's far more competent,' Morcom insisted.

'I suppose he is,' slowly Eden agreed.

'He's in a different class intellectually,' Morcom leaned forward. 'He's got an astounding mental energy. You ought to remember that when you talk of him wasting time. He's capable of amusing himself till midnight and then concentrating for five or six hours.'

'And be worn out next day.' Eden looked a little disturbed.

'No, he'd be tired. But not too tired to work. He's got a curious loyalty. Which we should naturally see more of than you would. He'd never do anything deliberately to harm the firm. Even for his beliefs – which are very real. That affair of Calvert's: he only did it because of his beliefs. He is rather a remarkable man.'

The sentences were rapped out, jerkily and harshly. Eden's face was calm and kindly as he listened, his head thrown back, his eyes looking down so that one saw a half-closed lid.

'Perhaps he's too remarkable,' Eden said, 'for a solicitor in a provincial town.'

When we left, it was late, the cars had stopped, we had to walk through the cold still night. We were both silent; I looked at the stars, without finding the moment's ease they often gave. As we parted, Morcom spoke:

'It would have done no good, whatever I said.'

CHAPTER XVIII

I APPEAL

I SAW none of them for several days. As it happened, I was sleeping badly and in a state of physical malaise. I stayed in my room, goading myself to work with an apprehension never far from my mind.

At last, on an evening in the week that Eden's period ran out, I was driven to visit Martineau. I had not been out for days.

I had heard that his advertising agency was run under the name of a partner called Exell. It took me some time to find their office; it was a tiny room on the fifth storey of an old block of buildings, at the corner of the market place. Martineau sat there alone, and greeted me with a cheerful cry.

'So nice to see you,' he said. 'This is where we keep body and soul together.'

He was dressed untidily in an old grey suit: but the habitual buttonhole still gleamed white and incongruous on his breast.

'Can we do anything for you, Lewis? There must be something we can do.'

'I'm sorry,' I said. 'I only came to talk.'

'Nearly as good,' said Martineau. 'Nearly as good. But I must show you one or two of our little schemes—'

He was so full of them that nothing could stop him describing them, fervently and happily. There were several: from one or two he did make a small income for some time: one I had cause to remember afterwards. They had bought a local advertising paper, which appeared weekly. It was sold at a penny, circulated among shopkeepers in the town, and carried some surburban news. Martineau had published some religious articles in it; he read them aloud enthusiastically, before asking me:

'Have you come for anything special, Lewis?'

'It's dull and private,' I said.

'Fire away,' said Martineau.

As it was cold in their room, however, I took him out to a café. When I explained that I was not well, Martineau said:

'You do look a bit under the weather!'

And when we went into the café lounge, he looked round with his lively curiosity, and said:

'Do you know, Lewis, I've not been in one of these big cafés for years.'

I was too strung up to pay attention then, but later that remark seemed an odd example of the geographical separations of our lives. For nearly two years I had seen Martineau each week. Yet the territory we covered – in a town a few miles square – was utterly different: draw his paths in blue and mine in red, like underground railways, and the only junction would be at his house.

We sat by a window: in the market-place, as I glanced down, the light of a shop suddenly went out.

'You remember what Saturday is?' I said.

'I don't think I do.' Martineau reflected.

'It's the day Eden said he'd accept your share in the firm – if you didn't change your mind.'

'He's an obstinate old fellow.' Martineau smiled. 'I told him he could have it months ago – and he wouldn't believe me. Ah well, he'll have to now.'

'Yes, I know,' I said quickly. 'There's something important about all this. Which may be a calamity to some of your friends. And you can stop it. Shall I go on?'

'You're trying to persuade me to come back?' He laughed.

'No,' I said. 'Not that now. I want to ask – something a good deal less.'

'Go on, Lewis,' he said. 'Go on.'

'It's about your partnership,' I said. 'George has set his heart on having it himself.'

'Oh,' said Martineau. 'I can see one or two difficulties.' His tone was curiously businesslike. 'He didn't behave very wisely over Calvert, you know.'

'*You* can't hold that against him,' I cried.

'Of course I don't,' said Martineau quickly. 'But he's very young yet, of course.'

'It wouldn't have mattered about his age,' I said. 'If he'd the money to buy a partnership somewhere.'

'I believe that's true,' said Martineau.

'It's entirely a matter of money. Of course, he hasn't any.'

'You're sure he really wants to be tied down like that?'

'More than anything in the world. Just at this minute.'

'He used to put – first things first,' said Martineau.

'He still does, I think,' I said. 'But he's not entirely like you. He wants the second things as well.'

'Well done, well done,' he said. Then as he quietened down into a pleased smile, he said:

'Well, if old George really wants to go in, I do hope Eden asks him. George deserves to be given what he wants – more than most of us.'

The affection was, I had always known, genuine and deeper than for any of us. It was as unquestionable as Eden's dislike of George.

'Except,' said Martineau, 'that perhaps none of us deserves to be given what we want.'

'Eden certainly won't ask him,' I said. 'He's said as much.'

'Such a pity,' said Martineau. 'I'm sorry for George, but it can't be helped.'

I was as diffident as though I were asking for money for myself. Of all men, he seemed the most impossible to plead with for a favour: for no reason that I could understand, except a paralysis of one's own will.

'It can be helped,' I said. 'You can help it.'

'I'm helpless.' Martineau shook his head. 'It's Eden's firm now.'

'You needn't give your share to him. You can give it to George instead.'

Very gently, Martineau said:

'You know how I should like to. I'd like to do that more than most things. But haven't I told you already why I can't? You know I can't—'

'I know you said you were giving up everything – and it's being false to yourself to hold on to your share. Even in this way. Can't you think again about that?'

'I wish I could,' said Martineau.

'I wouldn't ask you if it weren't serious. But it's desperately serious.'

Martineau looked at me.

'It's George I'm asking you for. This matters more for George's well-being than it does for all the rest of us put together. It matters infinitely more to him than it does to you.'

'I don't believe George cares as much for ordinary rewards—'

'No. That is trivial by the side of what I mean. I mean this: that George's life is more complicated than most people's. He may make something of it that most people would approve. Even that you might yourself. Or he may just – squander himself away.'

'Perhaps you're right,' said Martineau.

'I can't explain it all, but I'm convinced this is a turning point. If George doesn't get this partnership, it may do him more harm than anything we could invent against him. I'm only asking you to avert that. Just to take a nominal control for George's sake. Can't you allow yourself an – evasion in order not to harm him more than he's ever been harmed? I tell you, this is critical for George. I think he sometimes knows himself how critical it is.'

There was a silence. Martineau said:

'I'm sorry, Lewis. I can't do it, even for that. I can't even give myself that pleasure.'

'So you won't do it?'

'It's not like that. I can't do it.'

'Of course you could do it,' I burst out, angry and tired. 'You could do it – if only you weren't so proud of your own humility.'

Martineau looked down at the table.

'I'm sorry you should think that.'

I was too much distressed to be silent.

'You're proud of your humility,' I said. 'Don't you realise that? You're enjoying all this unpleasantness you're inflicting on yourself. All this suffering and neglect and squalor and humiliation – they're what you longed for, and you're happy now.'

Martineau's eyes looked, smiling, into mine and then aside.

'No, Lewis, you're a little wild there. You don't really think I relish giving up the things I enjoyed most?'

'In a way, I think you do.'

'No. You know how I used to enjoy things, the ordinary pleasant things. Like a hot bath in the evening – and looking at my pictures – and having a little music. You know how I enjoyed those?'

I nodded.

'I've given them up, you know. Do you really think I don't miss them? Or that I actually enjoy the things I have now in their place?'

'I expect there's a difference.'

'You must try to see.' Martineau was smiling. 'I am happy, I know. I'm happy. I'm happier because I've given up my pleasures. But it's not because of the actual fact of giving them up. It's because of the state it's going to bring me to.'

CHAPTER XIX

GEORGE CALLS ON MORCOM

I SPENT the weekend alone in my room: on Sunday I felt better, though still too tired to stir. I could do no more, I worked all day and at night sat reading with a convalescent luxury. But on Monday, after tea, that false calm dropped away as I heard a tread on the stairs. George came in – a parody of a smile on his lips.

'They've arranged it,' he said. He swore coldly. 'They've managed it very subtly. And insulted me at the same time.'

'What's happened?'

'I went to remind Eden today that the time had lapsed.'

'Was that wise?'

'What does it matter whether it's wise or not? Did the man think he could keep me in suspense for ever? I'd got a perfect right to go and ask him what he had decided about the firm.'

'And he told you—'

'Yes, he told me.' George laughed. 'He was very genial and avuncular. He was quite glad to tell me. He went so far as to reassure me – I wasn't to be afraid the change would make any difference to my position. The swine had the impertinence to hint that I thought of myself like any office boy in danger of being dismissed. That's one of the pleasant features of the whole business: Eden having the kindness to say he wasn't going to dismiss me. He even went so far as to mention that he and Martineau had both had a high opinion of my ability, and that I'd done good work for the firm. That was the second insult. And the third was when he said I might have slightly more work to do under the new arrangement: so he proposed to give me an extra twenty-five pounds a year.'

'He meant it good-naturedly.'

'Nonsense,' George shouted. 'If you say that you're merely associating yourself with the insults. It was completely deliberate. He knew he could go as far as he wanted. And he knew, if he insulted me with an offer like that, I had to accept it. But I don't think I left him under the illusion that I accepted it very gratefully.'

'What did you say?'

'After he'd made it quite clear that he intended to do nothing for me, I didn't see any reason why I shouldn't let him know that he was acting atrociously. So I inquired point blank whether he had considered asking me into the firm. Anyway, I had the satisfaction of making him feel ashamed of himself. He said he had thought about the matter – very carefully – very carefully.' In the middle of George's violence, I saw his eyes were bewildered. 'And although he'd like to very much for many reasons, he thought the present time wasn't very opportune. I told him there would never be a more opportune one. Then he tried to stand on his dignity and said he proposed not to discuss it now. I asked him when there would be an opportune time and when he proposed to discuss it. He hedged. I kept at him. In the end he said it wouldn't be until he saw how I developed in the next few years. I asked him what he was implying. He said it was too embarrassing for us both for him to discuss it with me there and then, but that he'd had a few words about it with a friend of mine. He might be able to give me a fairer idea. You realise who that is?' George's voice filled the room.

'Morcom, I suppose,' I said.

'I shall go and get things straight with Morcom,' George said.

'Wait until tomorrow.'

'Why should I wait? I only want to explain a few things.'

'Look here,' I said. 'I was there one night when Morcom was trying to defend you—'

'I don't believe it,' said George. 'You'd better come. I don't want you to be deluded. In any case, I'm going there now.'

When we had walked through the back streets, I was in one of those states of fatigue, almost like extreme well-being, when one is lighter than the dark streets round one, the rain, and the rushing wind; the glowing windows of the shops by the tramlines at the bottom of the road seemed like the lights scattered round a waterfront.

Across the road from Morcom's new lodgings, the trees smelt mustily in the rain: the window (I hoped to see it in darkness) was a square of tawny light, and Morcom let us in himself.

'Good,' he said, with a smile of pleasure.

'I'm afraid,' said George, following him into the room, 'I've only come for a short talk.'

Morcom turned quickly at the tone. 'Sit down,' he said.

'I should like you to explain,' said George, 'something that Eden said to me this afternoon. I don't expect it's necessary to tell you that he refuses to take me into the firm. He suggested you might be able to tell me the reason better than he could himself.'

'Lewis knows as much as I do,' Morcom said.

'Eden mentioned you by name,' said George.

'He'd no right to throw this on me.'

'That's irrelevant,' George said. 'I'm not interested in Eden's behaviour. I've seen enough of that. I want to know the conversations you've had about me.'

'The only time I've heard him speak of you at any length,' said Morcom, 'was' – he looked at me – 'that Sunday. A fortnight ago. I said what you asked me – and tried to find out what he thought of you. I didn't tell you the result because I thought it would hurt you. If you must have it – he admitted rather reluctantly that you'd got ability, but he didn't think you're reliable enough to be in a responsible position and he's afraid you'd be a danger to the firm.'

'What sort of danger?'

'Roughly that your present way of life would put clients off. It was also pretty clear that it put him off.'

'What does he know of my way of life?'

'A fair amount,' said Morcom.

'He had the impertinence to mention the Calvert incident. I suppose he knows about the people at the School.'

'He couldn't very well help it.'

'I don't see why he should imagine anyone disapproving of that.' George's voice was penetrating and subdued, as though he were keeping it low by will alone.

'Simply because he thinks you get the young women together in order to seduce them.'

'That's the kind of cheap suspicion a man like that would have. I suppose you didn't tell him the truth? Did you deny it?'

Morcom flushed. 'I did what I could.'

'Eden didn't give me that impression.'

'It's certainly true,' I broke in. 'Arthur was as near being rude as I ever heard him.'

As I looked at Morcom, we could not forget one remark in another sense.

'Even if that's true,' said George, 'you gave different impressions on other nights.'

'Do you seriously mean,' Morcom suddenly broke out, 'that I've been blackguarding you in private?'

'Eden said that most people who knew me thought I was good at deceiving myself. Who said that if you didn't? Do you mean to say that you never dropped those *other* hints – to Eden about my behaviour?'

'If you want me to pretend that I've treated you as an entirely sacred subject in conversation with Eden or anyone else,' Morcom said, 'I'm afraid I can't. It isn't so easy for an outsider to believe in your divine inspiration, you realise.'

'You mean I'm a megalomaniac?'

'At times, yes.'

'That's an honest remark at last. It's a relief.'

Morcom raised himself in his chair:

'We oughtn't to quarrel. Let's leave this now.'

There was a silence; then George said:

'No, one honest remark isn't enough. It's time some more were made. This has been going on too long already.

'You don't think I've been completely taken in, do you?' George went on. His voice was getting louder now. 'I've credited you with every doubt I could until now. But it wouldn't be charitable to doubt any more, it would merely be culpable madness. Even when I was giving you the benefit of the doubt, I was all but certain you had been working against me at every single point.'

'This is sheer mania,' Morcom said.

'Mania? I dare say you call it mania to be able to see a connection between some very simple events. Do you call it mania to remember that you discouraged me from taking any steps about Jack Cotery? – one of the few effective things I've managed to do in this town. You wouldn't believe it when I brought it off. You went on to advise him to go into business against my judgment – that might have been disastrous for me. You don't deny that you tried to take Olive away. With slightly more success. Though not quite as much as you set out for. You hung round her as soon as you realised she was valuable to me.'

One side of Morcom's mouth was drawn in.

'Or that you discouraged Jack Cotery and Eliot from everything I believed and wanted to do? You did it very subtly and carefully. The great George joke, the silly amiable old ass, with his fatuous causes, just preaching nonsense that might have been fresh fifty years ago, and then cuddling one of the girls on the quiet. Fortunately they had too much independence to believe you altogether – but still it left its mark—'

'Of course not—' I said.

'I can give you plenty of proof of that. Principally from Jack's behaviour.' George turned on me, then back to Morcom. 'And when you'd finished on my friends you tried to stop my career. You encouraged Martineau in his madness, you didn't stop him when he might have been stopped. You let him go ahead with the little plays, blast them to hell. You made suggestions about them as though they were useful. You let him think it was right to allow the firm to go to Eden, and you carefully kept him away from thinking of giving it over to me. Then you made really certain by this business with Eden. I'll admit you've been thorough. That's about all I will admit for you. It's the meanest deliberate attempt to sin against the human decencies that I've come across so far.'

George stopped suddenly: the shout seemed to leave a noise in the ears when his lips were already still.

'I'm not going to argue with you,' said Morcom. 'It isn't any good telling you that quite a lot of things happen in the world without any reference to yourself. It's possible to talk to someone like Martineau about his life without thinking of you for a single instant. But you're pathologically incapable of realising that. It's out of your control—'

'In that case, the sooner we stop pretending to have human intercourse the better. I don't much like being victimised; I dislike even more being victimised by someone who pretends that I'm not sane.'

'The only thing I should like to know,' Morcom said, 'is why you thought I should flatter you – by all these exertions.'

'Because we've always stood for different things,' George cried. 'And you've known it all the time. Because I stand for the hopeful things, and you for their opposite. You've never forgiven me for that. I'm doing something to create the world I believe in – you're sterile and you know it. I believe in human nature. You – despise it because you think all human nature is as twisted as your own. I believe in progress, I believe that human happiness ought to be attained and that we are attaining it. You're bitter because you couldn't believe in any of those things. The world I want will come and you know it – as for yours, it will be inhabited by people as perverted as yourself.'

Morcom sat with his eyes never leaving George's, his arms limp at his sides.

'Good God above, do I wonder you hate me?' George shouted on. 'You've got everything that I needed to make me any use. You could have done everything – if only you could bear to see someone else's happiness. As it is, you can only use your gifts against those who show you what you've missed. You try to get your satisfaction by injuring people who make you feel ashamed. Well, I hope you're satisfied now. Until you find another victim.'

CHAPTER XX

TWO PROGRESSES

THE winter passed. George spent less time with me than formerly; partly because I was working intensively for my final examination in the summer – but also it was now Jack who had become his most confidential friend.

As soon as Eden's decision was made, George had thrown himself into the interests of the group. Several young men and women from the School had been added to it; George talked of them all more glowingly than ever. On the few occasions I went out to the farm that winter, I felt the change from the group which George first devoted himself to. George and Jack, I know, formed parties there each weekend.

George never visited Eden's house again, after the Sunday night when we walked back in the rain. I scarcely heard him mention Eden or the firm; and at Eden's the entire episode of Martineau and George was merely the subject of comfortable reflections.

It was Eden, however, who told me in the early spring that Martineau was making another move, was giving up the agency. He had found some eccentric brotherhood, not attached to any sect, whose members walked over the country preaching and begging their keep. This he was off to join.

'Ah well,' said Eden, 'religion is a terrible thing.'

We heard that Martineau was due to leave early one Saturday morning. I went along to his house that day and outside met George, who said, with a shamefaced smile:

'I couldn't very well let him go without saying goodbye.'

We had to ring the bell. Since the house had been transformed, we did not know where Martineau would be sleeping. The bell sounded, emptily, far away; it brought a desolation. At last his housekeeper came, her face was hostile, for she blamed us for the catastrophe.

'You'll find him in his old drawing-room,' she said. 'And if things had been right you'd never have had any cause to look for him at all.'

He had been sleeping in the drawing-room, in one corner. A rough screen where the sofa used to be; in the bend of the room, between the fireplace and the window, where we used to sit on the more intimate Friday nights, a bed protruded, and there was an alarm clock on the chair beside it. The Ingres had been taken down, the walls were bare, there was a close and musty smell.

Martineau was standing by the bed, packing a rucksack.

'Hallo,' he cried, 'so glad you've come to see the last appearance. It's specially nice that you managed to find time, George.'

His laugh was wholehearted and full of enjoyment, utterly free from any sort of sad remembrance of the past. He was wearing an old brown shirt and the grey coat and trousers in which I had last seen him; he had no tie, and he had not shaved for days.

'Could I possibly help you to pack that?' said George.

'I've always been better with my hands than with my head,' said Martineau. 'But still, George, you have a shot.'

George studied the articles on the bed. There were a few books, an old flannel suit, a sponge bag and a mackintosh.

'I think the suit obviously goes in first,' said George, and bent over the bed.

'This is a change from the old days in the firm,' said Martineau. 'You used to do the brainwork, and I tried on the quiet to clean up the scripts you'd been selecting as ashtrays.'

George laughed. He could forget everything except their liking: and so (it surprised me more) could Martineau.

'How is the firm, by the way?' asked Martineau.

'As tolerable as one can reasonably expect,' said George.

'Glad to hear it,' said Martineau indifferently, and went off to talk gaily of his own plans. He was going to walk fifteen miles today, he said, down the road towards London, to meet the others coming from the east.

'Will there be any chance of seeing you here? On your travels?' said George.

'Some time,' Martineau smiled. 'You'll see me when you don't expect me. I shall pass through some time.'

He went to the door, called 'Eliz-a-beth,' as he used to when he wanted more coffee on a Friday night. He ran down the stairs and his voice came to us lilting and cheerful: we heard her sobbing. He returned with a buttonhole in his shirt. When we had left the garden and turned the corner, out of sight of the house, he smiled at us and tossed the buttonhole away.

Just before we said goodbye, George hesitated. 'There's one thing I should like to say, Mr Martineau. I don't know what arrangements you are making with your connections here. As you realise, they're not people I should personally choose to rely on in case of difficulties. And you're taking a line that may conceivably get you into difficulties. So I thought I ought to say that if ever you need money or anything of the sort – I might be a more suitable person to turn to. Anyway, I should like you to keep that in mind.'

'I appreciate that, George.' Martineau smiled. 'I really appreciate that.'

He shook our hands. We watched him cross over the road, his knapsack lurching at each stride. Up the road, where the houses rested in the misty sunshine, he went on, dark between the trees, until the long curve took him out of sight.

'Well,' said George.

We walked the other way, towards the town. I asked if I should meet him out of the office at midday, as I often did on Saturdays.

'I'm afraid not,' said George. 'As a matter of fact, I thought of going straight over to the farm. I don't suppose you can allow yourself the time off, can you? But Jack is taking over a crowd by the one o'clock bus. I want to work in a full weekend.'

PART THREE

THE WARNING

CHAPTER XXI

NEWS AT SECOND HAND

I TOOK my final examination in May 1927, two months after Martineau's departure; and went into chambers in London in the following September. For several years it was only at odd times that I saw George and my other friends in the town.

Some of that separation was inevitable, of course. I was making my way; it was then that I entered the chambers of Herbert Getliffe, who turned out to be as lively, complex and tricky as Jack himself; there was the long struggle with him (amusing to look back upon) before I emerged to make a decent living at the Bar. And in the process I formed new friendships, and got to know new worlds. That occupied me for a great part of those years; but still I need not have seen so little of George. It was natural for people as shrewd as Rachel to think that I was forsaking my benefactor and close friend of the past.

It was natural; but it was the opposite of the truth. Not by virtue, but by temperament, I was at that age, when I was still childless, bound by chains to anyone who had ever really touched my life; once they had taken hold of me, they had taken hold for good. While to George, though he enjoyed paying me a visit, I became incidental as soon as I vanished from the group. And before long he was keeping from me any news that mattered deeply to him. Yet I could feel that he was going through the most important time of his life.

From various people I heard gossip, rumours, genuine news of his behaviour. Olive sometimes wrote to me; and she was intimate with George again, when, after her father's death in 1930, she came into some money and returned to live in the town. Her letters were full of her own affairs: how she finally decided not to marry Morcom, though for a few months they lived together; how his old jealousy at last justified itself, for she had fallen in love with Jack and hoped to marry him. In the middle of these pages on herself, frequently muddled and self-deceiving, there occurred every now and then one of her keen, dispassionate observations upon George.

Materially, he was not much better off. Eden paid him £325 a year now; he still lectured at the School. But there was one surprising change – so surprising to me that I disbelieved it long after I ought to have been convinced. He had joined, as a concealed partner, in some of Jack's money-making schemes.

They had actually bought the agency and the advertising paper from Martineau and his partner Exell, a year or so after Martineau joined his brotherhood. When Olive returned, the three of them had invented more ambitious plans, and in 1931 raised money to buy the farm and run it as a youth hostel.

These stories were true enough, I found: and they appeared to be making some money. As Olive wrote: 'Of course, with Jack and me, we're just keen on the money for its own sake. But I still don't think anyone can say that of George. He gets some fun out of working up the schemes – but really all he wants money for is to leave him freer with his group.'

George had come, more thoroughly as each year passed, to live entirely within his group of protégés. He still carried young people off their feet; he still gave them faith in themselves; he was still eager with cheerful, abundant help, thoughtless of the effect on himself. Jack was only one out of many who would still have been clerks if they had not come under his influence. And there were others whom he could not help practically, but who were grateful. Olive quoted Rachel as saying: 'Whatever they say, he showed us what it's like to be alive.'

That went on: but there was a change. This was a change, though, that did not surprise me. It had been foreshadowed by Jack years ago, that night of our celebration in Nottingham. When I heard of it, I knew that it had always been likely; and I was curiously sad.

I heard of it, as it happened, from Roy Calvert, whom I met at a dinner-party in Cambridge. He was then twenty-one, polished and elegantly dressed. He talked of his cousin Olive. He was acute, he already knew his way about the world, he had become fond of women and attractive to them. He mentioned that George was attracting some gossip. George was, in fact, believed to be making love to girls within the group.

Roy had no doubt. Nor had I. As I say, it made me curiously sad. For I knew what, in earlier days, it would have meant to George.

I thought of him often after that piece of news. I had no premonition of danger; that did not reach me until a year later, until Morcom's call in the summer of 1932. But I often wished that George's life had taken a different curve.

During one case which regularly kept me late in chambers, so that I walked home through a succession of moonlit nights, those thoughts of George would not leave me alone. He was a man of more power than any of us: he seemed, as he used to seem, built on the lines of a great man. So I thought with regret, almost with remorse, walking in London under the moon.

I wished that I had been nearer his own age: I might have been more use to him: or that I had met him for the first time now.

Time and time again, I thought of him as I had first known him.

CHAPTER XXII

RETURN FROM A HOLIDAY

IT was one of the last days of the Trinity term of 1932 when Morcom visited me. I had just arrived in my chambers, after an afternoon in court.

'I was passing through on my way back,' he said. 'I thought I'd call—'

He had been sailing, he was tanned from the sea; but his face was thinner, and a suspense seemed to tighten his voice.

We had dinner, and then I asked if anything was wrong.

'Nothing much,' said Morcom. He paused. 'As a matter of fact,' he said, 'I'm worried about the people at——' He used the name of the town.

'Is there any news?' I asked.

'No news,' he replied. 'I've been away from them. I've been able to think. They'll finish themselves with a scandal,' he said, 'unless something is done.'

'What sort of scandal?'

'Money,' he said. 'At least, that seems to be the dangerous part.'

'What do you mean?' I said.

'Rumours have been going round for months,' he said. 'I couldn't help hearing them. As well as – private knowledge. When I got away, I realised what they meant.'

'Well?'

'There's no doubt they've been working up some frauds. I've known that for some time. At least I knew they were pretty near the wind. I've

403

only just begun to think that they've gone outside the law.' He paused again. 'That's why I came in tonight.'

'Tell me what you're going on.'

'I don't think I'm wrong,' said Morcom. 'It's all sordid. They've been spending money. They've invented one or two schemes and persuaded people to invest in them. On a smallish scale, I expect. Nothing very brilliant or impressive. They've done the usual tricks – falsified their expectations and got their capital from a few fools in the town.'

I was invaded by a strange 'professional' anxiety; for, although exact knowledge of a danger removes some fears, it can also sharpen others. A doctor will laugh, when another young man comes to him fearing heart disease – but the same doctor takes an excessive care over the milk his children drink. So I remembered other frauds: quickly I pressed Morcom for the facts.

What had happened? What were their schemes? What had been falsified? What was his evidence? Some of his answers were vague, vague perhaps through lack of knowledge, but I could not be sure. At times he spoke with certainty.

He told me, what I had already heard from Olive, of the purchase of Martineau's advertising agency, and the organisation of the farm and another hostel. But he knew much more; for instance, that Miss Geary – who had taken George's part in the committee meeting years ago – was one of the people who had advanced money.

'You may still be wrong,' I said, as I thought over his news. 'Stupidity's commoner than dishonesty. The number of ways people choose to lose their money is remarkable – when everyone's behaving with perfect honesty.'

Morcom hesitated.

'I can't tell you why I'm certain. But I am certain that they have not behaved with perfect honesty.'

'If you're right – does anyone else know this?'

'Not for certain. As far as I know.' He added: 'You may have gathered that I see very little of any of them – nowadays.'

His manner throughout had been full of insistence and conviction; but it was something else which impressed me. He was angry, scornful, and distressed; that I should have expected: but, more disquieting even than his story, was the extraordinary strain which he could not conceal. At moments – more obvious in him than anyone, because of his usual control – he had been talking with hysterical intensity. At other moments he became placid, serene, even humorous. I felt that state was equally aberrant.

'You haven't told me,' I said, 'who "they" are? Who is mixed up in this?'

'Jack,' he began. I smiled, not in amusement but in recognition, for about the whole story there was a flavour of Jack Cotery – 'and George,' Morcom went on.

I said:

'That's very difficult to believe. I can imagine George being drawn to a good many things – but fraud's about the last of them.'

'I don't know,' said Morcom indifferently. 'He may have wanted the money more than usually himself—'

'He's a man of conscience,' I said.

'He's also loose and self-indulgent,' said Morcom.

I began to protest, that we were both using labels, that we knew George and it was useless to argue as though he could be defined in three words; but then I saw Morcom ready to speak again.

'And there's Olive Calvert,' said Morcom.

I did not reply for a second. The use of her surname (for as long as I remembered, she had been 'Olive' to all our friends) made me want to comfort him.

'I should have thought she was too sensible to be let in.' I made an attempt to be casual. 'She's always had a sturdy business sense.'

Morcom's answer was so quiet that I did not hear the words for certain, and, despite my anxiety, I could not ask him to repeat it.

As we walked away from the restaurant, Morcom tried to talk of indifferent things. I looked at him, when we had gone past the lamp in a narrow street. In the uneven light, faint but full of contrast as a room lit by one high window, his face was over-tired. Yet tonight, just as years before, he would take no pity on his physical state; he insisted on walking the miles back to my flat. I had to invent a pretext to stop on the way, at a night-club; where, after we had drunk some whisky, I asked:

'What's to be done?'

'You've got to come in – and help,' said Morcom.

I paused. 'That's not too easy. I'm very much out of touch,' I said. 'And I don't suppose they'd like to tell me this for themselves. I can't say you've spoken to us—'

'Naturally you can't,' said Morcom. 'It mustn't be known that I've said a word. I don't want that known.'

'In that case,' I said, 'it's difficult for me to act.'

'You understand that anything I've said is completely secret. Whatever happens. You understand that.'

I nodded.

'You've got to stop them yourself. You've done more difficult things,' he said. 'Without as much necessity. You've never had as much necessity. It comes before anything else, you must see that.'

'You're sure you can't take control yourself?'

'I can only sit by,' he said.

He meant, he could do nothing for her now. But I felt that he was shutting himself away from release. With a strain that was growing as acute as his own, I begged him to act.

'It's the natural thing,' I said. 'It would settle it – best. You've every reason to do it—'

He did not move.

'See her when you go back. You can still make yourself do that.'

'No.'

'See George, then. It wouldn't be difficult. You could finish it all in a day or two –'

'I can't. There's no use talking any further. I can't.'

He suddenly controlled his voice, and added in a tone light and half rueful: 'If I did interfere, it would only make things worse. George and I have been nominally reconciled for years, of course. But he would never believe I wasn't acting out of enmity.' He was smiling good-naturedly and mockingly. Then his manner changed again.

'If anything's to be done, you've got to do it,' he said. 'They're going to be ruined unless you come in.'

'I can't help thinking you're being too pessimistic,' I said, after a moment. 'I don't believe it's as inevitable as all that.'

'They've gone a long way,' said Morcom.

'It's possible to go a long way in making dishonest money,' I said, 'without being any the worse for it. Still, if I can be any use—'

Then I made one last effort to persuade him to act himself. I looked into his face, and began to talk in a matter-of-fact, callous manner: 'But I shall be surprised if you're not taking it too tragically. First of all, they probably haven't managed anything criminal. Even if they have, we can either finish it or get them off. It's a hundred to one against anything disastrous happening. And if the hundredth chance came off, which I don't believe for a moment, you'd be taking it too tragically, even then. I mean, it would be disastrous, but it wouldn't be death.'

'That's no comfort.'

'I don't mean it wouldn't be unpleasant. I was thinking of something else. I don't believe that being convicted of swindling would be the end of the world for either of us. It's only ruin – when people crumble up inside, when they're punishing themselves. Don't you agree? You ought to know through yourself just now – in a different way. If you went back and protected them – if you weren't forcing yourself to keep away – you would be happier than you are tonight.'

There was a silence.

'You know perfectly well,' he said, 'that everything you've said applies to George. It would be ruin for him. In his own eyes, I mean, just as you've been saying. And the others – she's not a simple person –' He paused. 'And there's more to it than the offence. You've got to realise that. It means the break-up of George's little world. It also means that the inside of the little world isn't going to be private any longer. You know – that isn't all high thinking nowadays.'

I remembered what Roy had told me, and what I had gathered for myself.

'Yes,' I said.

For a few moments he broke into a bitter outburst unlike anything I had heard from him – against idealists who got tangled up with sensuality in the end. His words became full of the savage obscenity of a reticent man. Then he stopped suddenly.

'I'm never fair to that kind of indulgence,' he said, in his ordinary restrained tone. 'They seem to me to win both ways. They get the best of both worlds.'

Then he said:

'That isn't a reason for leaving them alone.' But he would not let himself help them. I accepted that now, and we discussed the inquiries that I might make. Soon he insisted that he must return to the town by the last train; I remembered that, not long after his arrival, he had agreed to stay the night.

The morning after that visit, I wrote to George, asking if he could stay with me in London: I was too busy to leave. I had no reply for several days: then a letter said that he and 'the usual party' were on holiday in the north. I could do nothing more for the time being, and in August, a fortnight after Morcom called, went with Sheila, now my wife, to our own holiday in France.

There I thought over Morcom's story in cold blood. He had heard something from Olive – that was clear. And still loving her, he could make a trivial fact serve as a flare-up for his own unspent emotion. He wanted to worry about her – and had seized a chance to do it on the grand scale.

That must be true: but I was not satisfied. Then often I consoled myself, as one always would at such a time, by thinking 'these things don't happen'. Often I thought, with genuine composure, 'these things don't happen'.

In the end I cut our holiday short by a few days, telling myself I would go to the town and set my mind at rest. Across the sea, in the mist of the September evening, I felt the slight anxious ache that comes, lightly and remorselessly – as I noticed after an examination no, earlier than that, when I was a child – whenever one has been away and is returning home. I was no more depressed than that, no more than if I had been away for a few days and was now (on a cool evening, the coast in sight) on my way home.

CHAPTER XXIII

SIGHT OF OLD FRIENDS

GEORGE wrote, when I suggested paying him a visit:

'We shall be out at the farm that week-end. If you can come over, I'll organise it immediately. You can meet some of the original party and some of the new blood that we've brought on—'

Neither there not in the rest of the letter was there any symptom of uneasiness. It sounded like George for so long, absorbed and contented in the little world.

On the Saturday afternoon a week after my return, I arrived at Eden's house. About a year previously, just as I was beginning to earn a living at the Bar, he had sent me a couple of cases, and since then several invitations to 'stay in your old haunts'. In the drawing-room, where we had argued over Martineau's renunciation, Eden received me cordially and comfortably. He was in his armchair, lying back in golf suit and slippers after an afternoon walk.

'You've done very well,' he said. 'You've done very well, of course. But I heard you were off colour last year. You must take care of that,' he said. 'You won't get anywhere without your health. And unless you learn to be your own doctor by the time you're thirty, you never will afterwards.'

I had always enjoyed his company; he was hospitable and considerate.

'If you want to talk to your friends while you're staying here, just consider the study upstairs as your private property.' He got talking about 'those days', his formula of invocation of his youth; and it was later after dinner than I intended when I caught the bus to the farm.

As I walked across the fields, lights were shining from several of the farm windows. George came to the door.

'Splendid,' he said, with his hand outstretched. 'I was wondering whether you'd lost your way.' In his busy, elaborate fashion he took my coat. 'I knew you wouldn't stay any longer at Eden's than decency compelled you.' The door of one room was open, and there was a hubbub of voices: a smell of fresh paint hung in the hall, and I noticed that the stand and chairs were new.

George whispered:

'There are one or two people here you don't know. They'll be a bit awkward, of course. You'll be prepared to make allowances.' He led the way, and, as soon as we were inside the room, shouted in his loud voice, full of friendly showmanship:

'I don't think you've all met our guest. He used to come here a few years ago. You've all heard of him—'

The room was fogged with smoke and on the air there floated the smell of spirits; some bottles glistened on the table in the light of the two oil-lamps, and others lay in the cushions near the radio set. There was the first dazzling impression of a group of unknown faces, flat like a picture without perspective. I recognised Rachel in one of the window seats, sitting by Roy Calvert, and a girl whom I remembered meeting once.

'You'll have to be introduced all round,' said George from behind, as I went to talk to Rachel. She had aged more than any of us, I was thinking; lines had become marked under her eyes, in the full pale cheeks. Her voice as she said: 'Well, Lewis!' was still zestfully and theatrically rich.

As George took me round the room, Roy caught my eye for a moment. I wondered what he was doing there.

I was introduced to a couple of youths on the sofa, both under twenty: a girl and young man in the opposite window-seat to Roy.

'Then here's Daphne,' said George. 'Miss Daphne Jordan –' he added a little stiffly; she was quite young, full-breasted, with a shrill and childish voice. George's manner bore out the rumours that she was his present preoccupation. Her face was plump, square at the cheek-bones; her upper lip very short, and eyes an intense brown, sharp and ready to stare up at mine.

'What are you doing, George?' she said. 'Why don't you give the poor man a drink?'

'I'm sorry, won't you have something?' George said to me, and with a gust of laughter for the girl: 'I'm always being nagged,' he said.

I went back to the window, near Roy and Rachel. Roy whispered: 'Don't you think Daphne is rather a gem?' He was a little drunk, in the state when he wanted to exaggerate anyone's beauty. 'She is quite a gem,' he said.

With a deep, cheerful sigh, George sank into the chair opposite the fire. Under the heavy lids, his eyes roamed round, paternal, possessive, happy; Daphne curled up on a hassock by his chair, one of her hands staying on the arm.

'What were you saying about Stephen Dedalus –' George said loudly to the young man in the window, 'before' – he paused – 'Eliot came in?'

George was not concealing his pride, his paternal responsibility, in being able to ask the question. It was his creation, he was saying almost explicitly, that these people had interests of this pattern. Half-smiling, he looked at me as the conversation began; he laughed uproariously at a tiny joke.

Then my attention caught a private phrase that was being thrown across the argument, one of the new private phrases, that, more than anything, made me feel the lapse of time. 'Inside the ring' – it bore no deep significance that I could see, but somehow it set alight again the anxieties and suspicions which had, in the freshness of arrival, vanished altogether. What had been happening? Nothing pointed to any dealings with money – except the actual material changes in the house. The demeanour of the party had changed from my time; then George, with the odd stiffness at which we had always laughed, was worried if the women drank with us. There was a quality of sexual feeling in the atmosphere, between many of the pairs and also, in the diffuse polyvalent way of such a society, between people who would never have any kind of relation; just as Rachel years ago had not loved, but been ready to love George, so I saw some other flashes of desire through the idealist argument. But that too, as it must be in any close society, was always present; I remembered evenings, four or five years ago, with Olive, Jack, George, Rachel and some others, when the air was electric with longing.

Daphne was laughing into George's face, after he finished one of his tirades. Clumsily he ran his fingers through her hair. Of all George's fancies this was the most undisguised. One could not see them without knowing that Roy was right.

I had been there about an hour when there was a noise of feet in the hall, and Olive came in, with Jack Cotery behind her.

At once she came across to my chair and took my hands.

'It must be years since I saw you,' she said. Her eyes were full and excited; she was over twenty-eight now, it crossed my mind. Her face had thinned a little into an expression which I could not define at that first glance. As she turned to bring Jack towards me, the strong curve of her hips was more pronounced than when I last met her, the summer she left the town.

'We didn't think you'd be here so early,' she cried. Then, catching someone's smile, her eyes flew to the clock on the mantelpiece: it was after eleven, and she looked at me before breaking into laughter.

'Good to see you,' Jack began, a little breathless and embarrassed in the greeting, until, in a moment, his old ease returned. He took me to one side, and began chatting humorously, confidentially, as though to emphasise that he had a special claim upon my attention. 'Life's rather crowded,' he chuckled when I asked him about himself. 'I've always got something going to happen, you know. I'm just getting on top of it, though. Clearly I am.'

The room had become noisy again. The others were drinking and talking, leaving us in our corner. Over Jack's shoulder, I saw Olive watching us with a frown as she talked to George. Jack was inquisitive about one of my cases. 'If I'd been on the jury, you'd never have got him off—'

Olive came and took us each by the arm.

'A few of us are going into the other room,' she said. 'We can't talk with everyone about.'

They had been quarrelling. Jack looked displeased, as she led us into the other sitting-room. It struck cold as we entered; she lit the lamp and knelt down to put a match to the fire.

'It won't be warm enough,' said Jack. 'We'd better go back.'

Olive looked up.

'No,' she said violently. Jack turned aside; his cheeks reddened.

George came in, bottles clinking in his hands, and Daphne carried the glasses. Rachel followed them.

'Oh, isn't the fire going?' she said. 'I thought you two had been here all night –' then she broke off abruptly.

George's attention at last became diverted. He gazed at her from the tumblers into which he had been pouring gin.

'It isn't cold,' he said. 'The fire will soon be through.' He was placating the inanimate world, as he always had done, never willing to admit the worst of his surroundings.

Olive stood by the fire. The rest of us brought up chairs, and she whispered a word to Jack. She was restless with excitement; a tension had grown up in the room, a foot tapping on the floor sounded very loud. She broke out, inclining her face to me with a quick smile:

'What are you here for, anyway?'

'To have a look at you.'

'Lewis, is that true?'

'What do you mean?'

'I had a feeling,' she said, 'when I saw you tonight – that there was something else behind it. I don't believe it's just a casual visit, is it now?'

I did not speak for a moment. In the presence of Rachel and Daphne I could not be frank.

'As a matter of fact,' I said, 'I was a little worried about some of you.'

'What about us?'

'I heard something – by accident – that made me think you might be taking some silly risks.' I paused. 'Some silly financial risks.'

I expected George to interpose, but it was Olive who answered. She exclaimed: 'Who told you that?'

'No one,' I said. 'I only had the faintest suspicion. I worked it out from something your cousin Roy happened to say. He said it quite innocently, you realise.'

'He says a good deal that isn't innocent.' Olive laughed, frankly and good-naturedly.

I said: 'Look here, I want you to tell me if there's anything in it. I've seen enough money lost, you know.'

Again it was Olive who answered. 'I'm sorry to disappoint you. There's nothing to tell.'

Jack began to talk of my practice, but in a moment Olive interrupted.

'You're not to worry about us,' she said. 'You understand? You can worry about our souls if you like.'

Suddenly she ceased to be competent and masterful, and her voice went hysterically high.

'We've changed since your time,' she said to me. 'Haven't we changed?'

'We all have,' I said.

'That's no good. That's just playing with me,' she said. 'We've changed, I tell you. We're not the same people. Don't you see that?'

George shifted in his chair.

'There's something in it, but it's an exaggeration put like that,' he said. 'You've all developed—'

'We've all developed!' Olive cried. 'As though you'd nothing to do with it. As though you haven't been more responsible than any of us.'

'I accept that,' said George loudly. 'You don't think I should pretend not to accept it. I'm proud of it. I'm prouder of it than anything else in my life.'

'You mean to say you're proud of having us—'

'I'm proud that you're the human being you are. And the same of Jack. And all the others. As well,' said George, 'as of Lewis, here.'

'I've had more to do with myself than you have, George,' Olive broke out, 'and I should laugh at the idea of being proud.

'Yet I've been complacent enough,' she went on. 'God knows how I found any reason for it. I've never done an unselfish action in my life without feeling complacent for being such a whirl of compassion. Oh, I know I looked after my father for years – don't you think I was smug with myself for doing it?'

'If you're going down to that level,' I said, 'we are all the same. You oughtn't to be savage with yourself – just with all people.'

'Just with life,' said Rachel. 'Good God, girl, you've done more than most. You've had a man madly in love with you.'

'Do you think,' she cried, 'I ought to be glad of that?' She hesitated. 'That was the one time,' she said, 'when I thought I might do something unselfish.'

'When?' cried Rachel.

'When I lived with him,' said Olive.

'Why, you were in love with him,' Daphne said, after a moment's silence.

'I never was,' said Olive. She swept an arm round. 'They know I never was.'

'Why then?' George leaned forward. 'For all those months—'

Olive said: 'I did it out of pity.'

Everyone was quiet; I looked into her eyes, and saw her glance fall away. Suddenly George laughed.

The strain had broken down: Jack was whispering to Olive, his eyes and hands eloquent and humorous; Daphne was sitting on the arm of George's chair. I could feel that only my presence was keeping them from a wilder eirenicon; friend as I was, I was also a foreign influence, unfamiliar enough to keep the balance between decorum and release. My own nerves frayed (for I too had been played on by the undersweep of passion), I was glad when Olive rose to go to bed. Soon George and I were left alone.

We filled our glasses, settled into the easy-chairs by the fire, and talked casually for a few minutes.

'It's a long while,' said George comfortably, 'since we came down here together.' I was touched by the sentimentality, unselfconscious and unashamed; perhaps, I thought, it came the easier to George, for, in spite of all his emotional warmth, he was less bound to the past than any of us, far less than Morcom or myself. Perhaps to those like him, solid in the core of their personalities, four-square in themselves, feeling intensely within the core but not stretching out tentacles to any other life, it is easier to admit the past – because it does not matter much, as he showed in our separation. While to Morcom, tied inseparably to a thousand moments of the past, it came too near the truth to acknowledge its softening hand, except by a smile of pretended sarcasm.

After that remark, we argued amiably; George had lost little of his buoyant appetite for ideas. I enjoyed his mental gusto for its own sake, and also because it was impeding the purpose which brought me there.

'We had some rather good talk tonight,' he said, after a time, with the change of his manner to an elated but uneasy defence that still covered him when he talked of the group: 'Didn't you think so?'

'Yes. I confess—'

'Of course you've got to remember the relevant circumstances,' said George hurriedly. 'The kind of people they would have been if they had been left to their own devices. You've got to remember that. Not that they're not an extremely good collection. They're better than they've ever been, of course. We've had some re-orientations. I've reconsidered some of my opinions.'

'Still,' I said, 'I was glad to see some of the old gang. Particularly Olive. Though I thought she was too much upset—'

'Oh, I don't know,' George replied. 'She's had something to put up with, you know. You can't deny that she was magnificently frank about it – she got the whole affair in its right proportion. There aren't many people who'd do that.'

Obstinately he repeated: 'She was magnificently frank.'

'I could find another name for it,' I said. 'But still, I wasn't thinking of her being upset by a love affair. I thought there might possibly be some other cause.'

A frown, or something less (the fixity with which he would at any time have heard a criticism), came into his face.

'What else could be the matter with her?'

'I didn't know her circumstances, since her father died. I thought – perhaps – money—'

'Ridiculous,' George interrupted. 'Completely ridiculous. Her father left her a hundred and fifty a year of her own – and the reversion of the rest of the money when her mother dies.'

'It can't be that, then,' I said. 'I just felt there might be trouble.'

'With no justification at all.'

'Everything is all right?'

'As a matter of fact,' said George, 'I wondered why you were asking about our affairs.'

'I was worried.'

'I think I should have been approached first.'

I half-expected a burst of anger; but instead his manner was more formal than exasperated.

'If I could have got you alone before she spoke—'

'I was prepared to believe that might be the reason.'

'You understood what I meant to ask?'

'I gathered it.'

'George, I can speak out with you. I meant – it's easy to get into financial tangles that are dangerous. If so, you could trust me to help, couldn't you?'

'I know exactly what you meant.'

'Will you let me ask the same question – now?'

'I've got nothing to add.' Each reply had been stiff and distant.

'I can't do this again, you know.'

'Naturally.'

'Everything's completely well with them? With yourself?'

'I'm happier than I've ever been in my life,' George raised his voice. I put in a question about his position in the firm.

'I've dismissed that business for the time being. I had to make a deliberate choice between the successes I considered important – and the successes' – he laughed – 'that an ordinary man with his little house and his little motor-car would consider important. I decided that I couldn't achieve them both, and so I was prepared to sacrifice the trivial ones. Just as you – have sacrificed some successes that I should consider essential. You've repressed all your social sense – well, I should simply have found it impossible to make a spiritual hermit of myself. Even – if it does give the Edens of this world a chance to humiliate me for ever.'

As I had often done when George was talking, I listened to the different levels of self-explanation. I heard nothing that bore on the apprehension. After we had talked on for a few moments, I said:

'The trouble about these choices – I'm not saying that you oughtn't to have made this one – is that you couldn't help yourself.'

'I could certainly help myself—'

'Anyway it does mean a certain practical inconvenience. Money and so on. How's that treating you?'

George's face opened in a chuckle. 'I'm harassed sometimes, as you might expect. I haven't borrowed from you recently, but you mustn't imagine you're completely immune.' He passed on to stories of the group in the last years. He got up to close the windows for the night: he said in a quiet voice:

'I've gained more from the last year or two than all the rest of my life. I know you all think I'm incapable of any sort of change. You haven't noticed that I'm more suggestible than any of you.' He looked over the fields, in the darkness. 'I've had my effect on these people – and they don't think it, but they've had an effect on me. And I'm better and happier because it's happened that way.'

CHAPTER XXIV

THE FIRST INQUIRIES

Morcom was away that weekend. I asked Roy to tell him that I had been in the town, and had called on George and Olive.

Through the autumn, a busy time for me, I was often uneasy. The visit had not brought anything like reassurance; but there seemed nothing I could do. As the months passed, though, I began to feel that my anxieties had run away with me. I heard nothing more until a Friday night in December.

I was tired after a day's work, lying on my sofa with a novel, which, when those moments came to have a significance they did not then possess (through the memory of action, so to speak, which is half-way between involuntary memory – recalled for instance by a smell – and that which we force back), I remembered as Thomas Wolfe's first book. The telephone bell rang. It was a trunk call, and among the murmurs, clangings, and whispers of the operation, I had the meaningless apprehension that sometimes catches hold as one listens and waits.

Then I heard Roy's voice:

'Is that you, Lewis?'

The words were precise and clear, isolated in sound.

'Yes.'

'You should come down tonight. There's a train in half an hour. It would be good if you caught that.'

'What's the matter?'

'You should come at once. Morcom and I are certain you should come at once. Can you?'

'Can't you tell me? Is it necessary?'

'Yes.'

'Can't you tell—?'

'I'll meet you at the station.'

Through the carriage window the lights of villages moved past. As my anger with Roy for leaving me uncertain became sharper, the lights became circled in mist and passed increasingly slow. We stopped at a station; the fog whirled under its lamps. At last the platform. The red-brick walls shone in the translucency; as I got out, the raw air caught at the throat.

Roy went quickly by, missing me in the crowd. I caught him by the arm. He turned and his face was serious and excited.

'Well?' I said.

'They're inquiring into some of George's and Jack's business. They questioned them this afternoon – and took away the accounts and books.'

It sounded inevitable as I heard it. It sounded unlike news, it seemed something I had known for a long time.

'I couldn't say it on the telephone,' Roy was talking fast, 'my parents were too near.'

We went into the refreshment-room on the platform. Roy's tumbler of whisky rattled in his fingers on the marble table, as he described the last few hours. Morcom heard from Jack, saw Roy immediately and insisted that he let me know. Then Roy called at George's office, a few minutes before he telephoned to me. George had said: 'Yes, they've had the effrontery to ask me questions,' and stormed. 'He was afraid though,' said Roy. 'He was anxious to prove that they parted on civil terms.'

'Morcom didn't know the best thing to do,' he said. 'He had no idea of the legal side. So you had to be fetched.'

'I'd better see George at once,' I said.

'I've arranged for him to meet you in my study,' said Roy. 'It's quicker than his lodgings.'

Actually, George's rooms were nearer. It was a strange trick for Roy to fix this meeting in his father's house. Yet he was as concerned as I.

His study reminded me that he was the only son of a prosperous family. It was a room more luxurious than one expected to find in the town: and then, again unexpectedly, the bookshelves of this spoilt young man were packed with school and college prizes. I was looking at them when George entered. He came from the door and shook hands with a smile that, on the moment, surprised me with its cordiality, its show of pleasure.

When the smile faded, however, the corners of his mouth were pulled down. Our range of expression is small, so that a smile in genuine pleasure photographs indistinguishably from a grimace of pain; they are the same unless we know their history and their future.

'This is an unpleasant business,' he said.

'Yes. But still—'

'One's got to expect attacks. Of course,' George said, 'this happens to be particularly monstrous.'

Roy made an excuse, and left us.

'We ought to go into it,' I said. I added: 'We don't want to leave anything to chance. Don't you think?'

'It's got to be stopped.'

'Yes. Can't you tell me what they wanted? It'd be useful to both of us.'

George sat down by the writing-desk. His fingers pushed tobacco into his pipe, and his eyes gazed across the room.

'It's absurd we should have to waste our time,' he said in an angry tone. 'Well, we may as well get it over. I'll organise the facts as we go along.' He began to speak more slowly than usual, emphasising the words, his tone matter-of-fact and yet deliberate with care.

'Jack Cotery made a suggestion over four years ago—' George thought for a second and produced the year and then the month. 'He'd been considering the advertising firm that Martineau went into. He produced some evidence that if it were run more efficiently it could be made to pay. There was a minor advertising paper attached, you remember, called the *Arrow*. I talked to Martineau when he came back to clear up his affairs. That was the summer of 1928. The paper reached a fairly wide public; some thousands, he convinced me of that. Jack's case was – that if we could raise the money and buy Exell out, we could pay interest on the loan and make an adequate profit. I saw nothing against it – I see nothing to make me change my view' – George suddenly burst out – 'I can't be expected to live on a few pounds a week and not look round for money if I can get it without sacrificing important things. You know well enough that nothing's ever made me take money seriously. I've never given much attention to it. I've never made any concessions for the sake of money. But I'm not an anchorite, there are things I could buy if I had money, and I'm not going to apologise for taking chances when they meant no effort and no interruption to my real activities.'

'Of course,' I said.

'I'm glad you accept that,' George said as his voice quietened. I knew that, at moments, I or anyone must be numbered with the accusers now; it was strange to feel how he was obliged to justify the most ordinary contact with the earth. 'So on that basis I was ready to co-operate. Naturally, I hadn't any capital of my own. I was able to contribute about fifty pounds, chiefly by readjusting all my debts. Anyway, my function was to audit the accountancy side, and see how good a property it was—'

'You did that?' I said.

'There wasn't much evidence, which isn't surprising when you think of the two partners. There were a few books kept incompetently by Exell and the statement by Martineau. The statement was pretty definite, and so we considered it and proceeded to action. Olive raised a little. Her father wasn't dead then, so she couldn't do much. By the way, you might as well understand that this business has been consistently profitable. On a small scale naturally, but still it's brought in a pleasant addition to my income. And we met all our obligations. Even in the worst weeks when our patriotic or national government was doing its best to safeguard the liberties of the British people.'

The habitual sarcasm left him, after months of use, as easily and unthinkingly as a 'Good morning'.

'I had very little to do with the financial backing. Jack undertook the whole responsibility for raising that. I should have been completely useless at getting businessmen to part with their money, of course –' he gave a quick, slightly abject smile. 'On the other hand, I can produce their names and the details of the contracts that Jack made with them. We didn't consider it necessary to form a company; he simply borrowed a number of separate sums from various people, and made definite terms about paying them for the risk.'

'They lent it on the security of the firm, I suppose,' I said.

'Yes. It was a series of private loans for a purpose which everyone understood. It's the sort of arrangement which is made every day. The man who was here this afternoon,' he said, 'pestered me for an hour about the details. Incidentally he was unnecessarily offensive to me. That was before he came to the other scheme. It was a long time before I could make him understand they were slightly different. The position was' – he shifted in his chair – 'that Jack produced another idea when Olive's father died. That meant she had a little surplus capital – I mentioned it to you when I saw you last – and it was easy to see modifications in the technique. We'd acquired a little money and a certain amount of experience. So it was possible to think of something on a larger scale. Particularly in the special circumstances of my having a crowd of people that needed to be together. The idea was to buy the farm and one or two other places; then we could use the farm itself for our own purposes. There was no reason why the money we spent shouldn't come back to ourselves in part – and when we weren't using the place, we could let it out as a youth hostel or whatever people call them who haven't the faintest idea of helping people to enjoy their youth.'

'So you did it?'

'Yes. Jack and Olive were in it. I couldn't appear – but it was understood that I was to advise.'

'Jack brought in the money again?'

'Naturally,' said George. 'He collected some fairly large sums from various quarters. I'll make you a list. He's incredibly good at persuading them to part. He's so good that once I found it inconvenient—'

'How was that?'

'Actually,' George hesitated, 'I had to stop him taking it from some of my people.'

'Some of the group? Rachel and the—'

'Jack tried with this young man – Roy.' George looked round the study. 'But he was too cautious. Jack had persuaded Rachel, though; and someone else.'

I said: 'Why did you stop him?'

'I should have thought it was obvious enough. There's bound to be a certain amount of risk in this sort of project. I wasn't going to have it fall on people I was responsible for and who couldn't afford it.'

'One could bring out the fact – significantly.'

'I'm prepared to account for it.'

His voice was harsh and combative: I paused.

'How's this scheme going?' I asked.

'Not as well as the first,' George said slowly. 'It's not had long yet. It's perfectly healthy.'

'What has started the inquiries, then?' I said.

'It's impossible to say. I've been active enough in this place to make a good many people willing to see me disgraced.'

I wondered: was that true or the voice of the persecuted self? the self that was the other side, the complement, of his devotion and unselfseekingness.

'But did they know of these dealings?'

'We tried to keep them secret,' George said. 'None of the initial arrangements can possibly have got out.'

'What were the police looking for?'

'As far as I gathered from the lout who came this afternoon – the obvious thing for them to imagine. Misleading the people who supplied the money. The charge they're trying for is money by false pretences or conspiracy, I suppose. They might put in conspiracy so as to use all their evidence against each of us.' Though he was wincing as he spoke, I could not help noticing that his thought was clear and competent, as it had been all that night; his summary of their ventures could hardly have been better done; he was not detached at any time, there was no man less detached, he was in distress, afraid and resentful, and yet anyone – without my affection and concern – would have admired the stamina and precision of his mind.

Then to my amazement his face cleared and he laughed, shortly, not from his full heart, but still as though the distress had abated.

'It's scarcely likely they'll ever have the opportunity to make a charge.' It came to me like the fantastic optimism with which he sustained himself years ago, during Martineau's departure. I replied:

'So you're completely confident? You don't think it'll go any further?'

Remorsefully, I saw the half-laugh drain away; his voice was flat, with no pretence or anger left:

'If it does, I don't know how I'm going to face it.'

I said: 'As a matter of fact, have you done it?'

For an instant he sat without moving. Then slowly he shook his head.

CHAPTER XXV

CONVERSATIONS AT NIGHT

Roy, quiet and self-effacing, brought in a tray of drinks and again left us alone.

'By the way,' I said, 'does Eden know about these – inquiries?'

'I've not told him.'

'Oughtn't you to?'

'It's obviously quite unnecessary,' George said. 'If these policemen have the sense to keep quiet, there's no reason why he should know. And if – we have to take other circumstances into account, Eden can be told quickly enough. I see no reason to give him the pleasure until it's compulsory.'

'I think he ought to be told,' I said. 'This isn't too large a town, you know. Eden comes across people in the Chief Constable's office every day.'

'That would be a breach of privilege.'

'Yes,' I said. 'But it happens – and it would be wiser for you to tell Eden than for someone who doesn't know you.'

His face was heavy and indrawn.

'You see,' I tried to persuade him, 'there's a good deal that can be done, if they want to inquire any further. You know that as well as I do. If Eden gives me authority, I could stop quite a few of their tricks. If you heard of anyone in your present position – the first advice you'd give, of course, would be for them to arrange with a solicitor—'

George said:

'I don't propose to discuss the matter with Eden.' He added: 'You can tell him yourself if you're so anxious.'

'You give me permission?' I said.

'I suppose so.'

When Roy rejoined us, I left them talking and telephoned Eden. He said he would expect me before eleven, and pressed me to stay in the 'usual room'.

George showed no curiosity when I said that I should not see him again until the morning.

Sitting in Eden's drawing-room, stretching my hands to the fire, I told him the events of the afternoon. He had begun by saying amiably:

'We had another conference about some of your friends here before.'

Eden nodded his head, his lips together, as I told him of their speculations. I finished by saying:

'It may not come to it, I don't know. But we ought to be prepared for a charge.'

'These things will happen,' he said. 'Ah well! these things will happen.'

'What do you think?' I said.

'You're right, of course we've got to be prepared,' he was speaking without heat, with a slight irritability. 'I must say they've been very foolish. They've been foolish whatever they've been doing. They oughtn't to try these things without experience. It's the sort of foolishness that Passant would go in for. I've told you that before—'

'He's one of the biggest men I've met. That still holds after meeting a few more. He's also one of the ablest,' I said in the only harsh words that had passed between Eden and myself, making a protest wrung from me years too late.

His deliberation broken for a moment, Eden said:

'We won't argue about that. It isn't the time to argue now. I must consider what ought to be done.' He laughed without any warmth. 'I can't instruct you myself,' he said slowly, going back to a leisurely professional manner. 'But I can arrange with someone else to act for Passant. And I shall give instructions that you're to be used from the beginning. That is, if this business develops as we all hope it won't—'

The phrase rolled off smooth with use, as he addressed me with the practised cordiality – different from his ordinary familiar manner – into which the disagreement had driven him. It was not until I spoke of visiting Jack Cotery before I went to bed, that he became fully at ease again.

'I'm sorry he's mixed up in this,' Eden said. 'He ought to have gone a long way. I haven't seen much of him the last few years.' He was genuinely distressed. He went on: 'And you want to find out what's been happening to him? I expect you do.' He gave me a latchkey. 'You can keep it until this is all over. You'll have to be down here pretty frequently, you know.' Then I said good night and he smiled. 'Mind you don't wear yourself out before it properly begins.'

The streets were clearer, but still dank with fog. A tram-car came down the lonely road, going on its last journey to the centre of the town; its light was reddened in the mist. What had happened? Through these stories and suspicions, what had happened? If George was lying (I could not be certain. He might be bound to the others – he might be masking some private guilt) how had he found himself in that kind of dishonesty? – which of all of us, careless as he was of money, self-deceiving as he could be in thought, I should have considered him the least likely to commit. And as well as these doubts, there was a sense, not flickering in questions in the mind, of conflict and fatality; of these lives, the people I had once known best, going as they had to go, each life alone, as it were, walking the dark streets. So, in loneliness, they had come to this.

For a time I could not find the street in which Jack lived. He had given up his flat, George said; he had returned to his parents' house. I had never been there in the past. When I first knew him, it was one of his mysteries to mention that he could not invite us to his house – and then, after his self-revelation that night in the park years ago, I had not expected to be asked.

Now, when at last I discovered it, I smiled, in spite of my errand. For the street, as I made my way down the faces of the houses, peering at the numbers in the diffused lamplight, seemed the perfect jumping-off place for day-dreams of magniloquence: and, on the rebound, when he repented of those, just as good a place to let him imagine himself among the oppressed and squalid.

The houses were a neat row from the beginning of the century. Their front doors gave onto the street and the paint on most smelt fresh as I went close; it was a row of houses such as artisans lived in by thousands throughout the town; it was a frontier line of society, the representative street of the highest of the working class and the lowest of the middle. Few windows were lighted at this time of night.

I came to Jack's number. There was a light in the window, shining thin slats of gold between the venetian blinds. I knocked softly on the door; a movement came from inside. The door opened slowly. A voice, light, querulous, said:

'Who's there?'

I answered, and he flung the door open.

'What on earth are you doing here?'

'I'm afraid I've come to worry you,' I said. 'I expect you've had enough for one day.'

'I was just going to bed.'

'I'm sorry, Jack. I'd better come in.'

Then my eyes, dazzled after the darkness, gradually took in a room full of furniture. A tablecloth, carrying some used plates and a dish, lay half over the table. A saucepan of milk was boiling on the hob.

'I have to live here occasionally. It gives them a bit of pleasure.' Jack pointed upstairs. He was wearing a new, well-cut suit. His eyes were excessively bright. I nodded, then threw my overcoat on a chair, and sat down by the fire.

'And so you're after my blood as well.' A smile, mischievous and wistful, shot through his sullenness. As I replied, telling him I had been with George, it was replaced by an injured frown.

'He must have told you everything,' said Jack. 'It's no use me going over it all again.'

'It may be the greatest use.'

'Then you'll have to wait. I'm tired to death.' He poured out the boiling milk into a tumbler. This, ignoring me, he placed on the hearth. I remembered once laughing at him at the farm, when he went through this ritual of drinking milk last thing at night; he had produced pseudo-scientific reasons for it. He had always shown intense concern for his health. It was strange to see it now.

I pressed him to talk, but for a long time he was obstinate. I told him that I should be George's lawyer, if it came to a trial – and his, if he would have me. He accepted that, but still would not describe his interview in the afternoon. I said once again:

'Look, Jack. I tell you we've got to be ready.'

'There's plenty of time.'

'As I say, they'll be making inquiries while we do nothing.'

Suddenly he looked up.

'Will they have gone to Olive yet?'

'Probably,' I said.

'She was visiting a cousin. She won't get back to the town today. I suppose I ought to see her before they do. Clearly,' said Jack.

Then, for the first time, he was willing to talk of their businesses. He did it sketchily, without George's command. He finished up: 'I can't imagine why they expect to find anything shady. It's – it's quite un-reasonable.' Then he said: 'Incidentally, I told the chap this afternoon, and I don't mind telling you, that if you search any business you'll find something that's perfectly legal but doesn't look too sweet. He took the point.' Jack looked at me. 'I'll show you what I mean, sometime, Lewis. It's all legal, but you'd expect me to try a piece of sharp practice occa-sionally, wouldn't you? I've never been able to resist it, you know. And it's never worth the trouble. One's always jumpy when one's doing it, and it never comes to anything worth while.'

I was certain that the 'sharp practice' had nothing to do with the suspicions: I did not follow it up. We were both silent for a moment: Jack pulled out a case and offered me a cigarette. I thought I recognised the case, and Jack said, with his first smile since I tried to question him:

'Yes. It's the famous present.' His smile stayed as he ran a finger along the initials. 'I like having something permanent to remind me exactly who I am. It gives me a sort of solidity that I've always lacked.'

We both laughed. Then Jack said quietly: 'I simply cannot understand what these people expect to find. It's simply unreasonable for them to think they might pull out a piece of dishonesty. Why, if there'd been anything of the kind, I could have covered it up ten times over. If I'd had to meet every penny a month ago, I could have covered it completely.

I happened to have an extra offer of money to tide me over any difficulty just about that time.'

'Who from?'

'Arthur Morcom.'

I exclaimed.

'Why ever not? Oh, you were thinking of his keeping away because of Olive. I don't see why he should.' He hesitated. 'As a matter of fact,' he said, 'he made the same offer this afternoon.'

'It's not useful now,' I said.

'It might be extremely useful,' said Jack. Then he took back the words, and said: 'Of course you're right. I can't use money until they give up these inquiries.' He broke off: 'You know' – he showed, instead of the fear and resentment I had seen so often in his face that night, a frank, surprised and completely candid look – 'these inquiries seem fantastic. They ask me about something I've said years ago – what I told people about the profits of the agency and so on. I just can't believe that what I said then might ruin everything now. Even if I'd done the dishonest things they believe I've done – which I've not – I'm certain that I still couldn't believe it. All those actions of mine they ask about – they're so remote.'

Yes, that was honest. On a different occasion, I had been through the same myself.

When I left, I walked straight to Morcom's. It was after one o'clock, but I had to speak to him that night. As it happened, he was still up From the first word, his manner was constrained. He asked me to have a drink without any welcome or smile. I said straight away:

'I've just come from Jack's. He tells me that you offered him money this afternoon.'

'Yes.'

'Don't you see it might be dangerous?'

'What do you mean?'

'If Jack skips now, they'll take George for certain. For him, it's inevitable disaster. If you make it possible for Jack to go – and, well, it's crossed his mind. He's no hero.'

'That is true,' said Morcom, still in a cold, disinterested tone.

'I had to warn you tonight,' I said.

'Yes.'

After a silence, I said:

'I'm not too happy about them.'

'I'm not surprised,' said Morcom. 'I told you this was likely to happen.

I thought you wouldn't be able to stop it. I might as well say, though, that I rather resent you considered it necessary to tell people that I was paralysed with worry. I dislike being made to look like a nervous busybody. Even when it turns out to be justified.'

'I said nothing.'

'Jack said that he heard I was very worried. I mentioned it to no one but you.'

Casting back in my mind, I was beginning to reassure myself: then, suddenly. I remembered asking Roy to send word at any sign of trouble – because of Morcom's anxiety.

Morcom said: 'You know?'

'I'm sorry,' I said, 'I mentioned it to Roy Calvert. It was my last chance of getting the whole truth. I made it clear—'

'I told you in confidence,' said Morcom.

I took refuge in being angry with Roy. I knew that he was subtle and astute about human feelings – yet he had been so clumsily indiscreet. But I ought to have known that he, like many others, was in fact, subtle, astute – and indiscreet. The same sensitiveness which made him subtle, which gave him antennae to reach another's feelings, also caused this outburst of indiscretion. For it was from the desire to please in another's company, Jack's or George's, that he produced the news of Morcom's concern – from the same desire to share an emotion with another which is the root of all the deepest subtlety, the subtlety, which, whatever it is used for ultimately, arises from a spontaneous realisation and knowledge of another.

Just as, ironically, Morcom himself had once broken into a graver indiscretion in Eden's drawing-room.

It is one of the myths of character that subtlety and astuteness and discretion go hand in hand by nature – without bleak experience and the caution of age, which takes the edge both from one's sensitiveness and the blunders one used to make. The truth is, if one is impelled to share people's hearts, the person to whom one is speaking, must seem, must be, more vivid for the moment than anyone in the world. And so, even if he is irrelevant to one's serious purpose, if indeed he is the enemy against whom one is working, one still has the temptation to be in a moment's conspiracy with him, for his happiness and one's own against the rest. It is a temptation which would have seemed, even if he troubled to understand it, a frivolous instability to George Passant. But, for many, it is a cause of the petty treasons to which they cannot look back without shame.

Morcom was speaking with a restrained distress. Some of it I should have expected, whatever the circumstances, if he heard that he was being discussed in a way he felt 'undignified'. But tonight that was only the excuse for his anger. He was suffering as obviously as George. His cold manner was held by an effort of self-control; he was trying to shelve the anxiety in a justified outburst. Yet his anxiety was physically patent. With a mannerism that I had never seen him use before, he kept stroking his forehead as though the skin were tight.

We talked over the inquiries. Information must have been laid, I said, a week or two ago. I went on: 'Jack told me that he could easily have raised money just before that time. If there had been any call. He said you made your first offer then – is that true, by the way?'

'I ought to have done it in the summer,' said Morcom. 'I suppose it came too late. But I couldn't resist doing it at last. I've always had a soft spot for Cotery, you know.'

That was true: it had been true in the days of his bitterest jealousy. It was true now. He was filled with remorse for not having tried to help them until too late.

In a moment he asked me: 'What are the chances in this case?'

'It's impossible to say. We don't even know they've got enough to prosecute on.'

'What's your opinion?'

I paused: 'I think they'll prosecute.'

'And then?'

'Again I don't know.'

'I'd like to have your view.'

'Well,' I said, 'if you remember it's worth very little at this stage – I think the chances are against us.'

'Look,' he said, 'I can't do anything in the open. I've got to tell you that again. I insist that nothing I've said shall be repeated to anyone else. For any reason whatever. That's got to be respected.'

'Yes.'

'But if I can help in private –' he said. 'You've got to ask. Whatever it is. Remember, whatever it is. You aren't to be prevented by any sort of delicacy about dragging up my past.'

He had spoken very fast. I answered: 'I shall ask. If there's any possible thing you can do.'

'Good.'

'There may be – practical things. We shall probably want money.'

'I should like to give it.'

CHAPTER XXVI

A GUILTY STORY

WHEN I arrived at George's lodgings the next afternoon, I found his father just on the point of leaving. Mr Passant said, with the old mixture of warmth and hesitation: 'It's not – Lewis?' He had aged more than anyone I knew. His breathing was very heavy.

'I'm glad you're helping us, Lewis,' he said. He began to talk hurriedly, about the inquiries. His eyes were full of puzzled indignation against the people who had instigated them. 'You'll help us deal with them,' he said. 'They've got to learn that they suffer if they let their spite run away with them.' It was not that he did nòt know of the danger of a prosecution. George had been utterly frank. But injured as he was, Mr Passant was driven to attack.

'At the end, when it's the proper time, you'll be able to go for compensation against them,' he said. 'The law must provide for that.'

During these outbursts, George was quiet, once augmenting his father's with an indignation of his own. For a moment they looked at each other, on the same side, the outer anxiety pressing them close. But when Mr Passant said, tired with his anger:

'It's a great pity they were ever given the excuse, Lewis—'

George said:

'We've had all this out before.'

'After it's over,' said Mr Passant, 'I still want to think of you yourself.'

George replied:

'I can't alter anything I've already said.'

Both their faces were strained as they parted. Without a word upon his father's visit, George came to the table and brought out his papers. He sat by me through the afternoon and evening, helping me arrange the facts.

The extraordinary precision of his memory might have been laughable in another context. But now I heard his voice on the edge of shouting, when from time to time he burst out:

'It's ludicrous for them to try to manufacture a case like this. We've got an answer for every single point the swine bring up. Do they think I decided to take over Martineau's paraphernalia simply for the pleasure of cooking the figures? When it was perfectly easy for him to check them? A man who'd been used to figures all his life. The suggestion's simply monstrous. If I'd wished to swindle in that particularly fatuous way, I should have chosen someone else—'

'He'd gone away, though, before you took over—'

'Nonsense. That is simply untrue. We bought Exell out in November '28' – he gave the exact date – 'Martineau had been in the town all July. He came back for a couple of weeks continuously the next January. Settling up his house and his other affairs. He could have investigated at any time. Do they think that a man in his senses – whatever else I may be, I suppose they'd give me credit for that – would take a risk of that kind?'

Yet several times I returned to Martineau's statement, in particular the figures of the *Arrow*.

'It seems such a tremendous lot,' I said.

'I thought it was rather large,' George said.

There was a silence.

'I'd have thought if they could reach as wide a public as that,' I went on, 'they'd have made more of a show of it themselves.'

'Jack's magnificent at making things go,' said George. 'He's full of ideas. I left that side to him. It's probably the explanation.' He stared at the paper. 'In any case, I don't think we shall get very far by speculating on Exell's and Martineau's incompetence.'

We continued through the accounts, on to the other business, the farm and its companions. There was, in fact, little written down. Most of the data were supplied by George, without delay or doubts, almost as though he was reading them from some mental sheet.

When at last I had completed my notes, George said:

'You may as well look at these. They're not strictly relevant, but I suppose you'd better see them. I'm sorry I haven't my proper diary here.' He gave me a twopenny notebook; it contained, in his neat hand, an account of his income and expenses, recorded in detail for several years. It struck me as strange he should keep this record of his money, over which he was so prodigal (I later found out that it was not complete or accurate, in contrast to the minute thoroughness of his diary). And I was mystified by his giving me the book. For a time, the statements told me nothing – a slight increase in expenditure for the last eighteen months, several entries reading – 'by cheque from J.C. £10'. Then my eyes caught an entry: 'D at farm £1'; often, most weekends for some time back, the same words recurred.

'Do you pay for yourself at the farm?' I asked. 'I thought—'

'No.' He turned round from the bookshelves. 'I pay for those I take with me.'

'Of course,' I said. 'I ought to have –'

'Go back a few months.' His voice was unfriendly. At the beginning of the year, I found, as well as the entries about D. (whom I knew to be Daphne), another series with a different letter, occupying other dates, thus:

> D at farm £1 Jan. 17.
> F at farm £1 Jan. 24.
> D at farm £1 Jan. 31.

The two sets D. and F. ran on together over several months. I looked up. His expression was angry, pained, and yet, in some way, relieved.

'I don't expect you to understand,' he said. 'I'm not excusing myself, either. I didn't break the rules I'd constructed for myself until I'd fallen abjectly in love: but I repeat, I'm not making that an excuse. I should have come to it in the end. I should have found my own happiness in my own way. I refuse to be ashamed of it; but there is one impression I shouldn't like you to get. Particularly you, because you saw me at the start. Now things may conceivably crash round me, I don't want to let you think that I retract one single word of what the group has meant to me. I don't want you to think I spoilt it all – because, when the rest of them were enjoying their pleasures, I saw no reason for not taking mine.'

'I shouldn't think so,' I said.

As I spoke, his face lightened and looked grateful. Every word in his self-justification carried its weight of angry shame.

'Do you remember how we compared notes on being in love – after a celebration in Nottingham?' said George. 'I hadn't fallen in love then, and I envied you the experience. Do you know, I still didn't fall in love until I was twenty-eight? That must be late for a man who has never been able to put women out of his mind for long. And I suffered for it. She was a girl called Katherine – you never met her – and she was absolutely unsuitable for a man like me. It was trying to find compensation elsewhere that I started with –' he pointed to the F. on the accounts. Both she and Daphne were members of the School and of George's group. 'But I insist, I don't give that as an excuse. I should simply have taken a little longer, but I should have come to the same point in the end. And I don't expect you to understand, but I'm capable of being fond of two women at once. So I kept on with her after I became attached to Daphne. I expect you to think it sordid – but we're not made in the same way.

'As a matter of fact,' he added, his truculence replaced by an almost timid simplicity, 'I discovered that I was hurting someone by the arrangement, so I had to give it up.'

So Daphne was too strong-willed for him; I could imagine her pleading in her child's voice, her upper lip puckered, pleading jealousy, caring nothing for her pride if she could get her own way, older in a fashion at twenty than George would ever be.

Going back through the figures, I found another set which occurred some time after the other began. 'Not. £1 11s 6d.' The amount was constant, and as I went further back, the entry came frequently, never less often than once a fortnight. The sum baffled me, although I guessed the general meaning. I asked him.

'A return to Nottingham, drinks and a woman,' George said. 'I kept to Connie's crowd for a long time, and it always used to cost the same.'

I laughed.

'I remember you used to spend twice as much on drinks round the club.'

'I suppose I did,' said George. 'I forgot to put those down.'

Then he said:

'It was years before I could imagine that I might find something better.'

'And now?'

'It may surprise you to know that I've been happier with Daphne than I've ever been in my life. I am more in love with her than I was with Katherine: I'm not a man who can worship the unattainable for long. This happens to be love for both of us, and it's the first time I've known it. When I realised it properly, I thought it was worth waiting thirty-three years for this.'

His voice became once more angry and defensive. 'After all that I've thought it necessary to show you,' he said pointing to the pocket-book, 'I expect you to laugh at what I say – but I can't believe that I shall know it again. And I'm compelled to think of the position I shall be in when these inquiries are over. I may not be able to inflict myself on her—'

'I don't think she'd leave you,' I said.

'Perhaps not,' said George, and fell into silence. At last he said:

'Just before you arrived, I told my father exactly what I've told you.'

'Why in God's name?'

'It might have come out in public. I considered that it was better I should tell him myself.'

'When I used the same argument about letting Eden know yesterday—'

'I don't recognise a connection with Eden,' said George. 'This was utterly different. I felt obliged to tell my father two things. He had a right to know that I might be providing malevolent people with a handle against him. I said I found that was the thing I could tolerate least of all.'

'What else did you say?'

'I had to say that, apart from the intolerable effect on him, I wasn't ashamed of anything I'd done. He naturally didn't believe that I had swindled: but he was hurt about my life with women. I had to tell him that I saw no reason to repent for any of my actions.'

CHAPTER XXVII

CONFLICT ON TACTICS

A CASE, down for the next Tuesday, sent me back to London on Sunday night. For some days I heard nothing from the town; I rang up each night, but there was no news; and then, one morning in chambers, a telegram arrived from Hotchkinson, the solicitor who was managing the case for Eden: 'Three clients arrested applying for bail this morning.' It was now the middle of the month. I was not appearing in a London court until January; I decided to stay at Eden's until the first hearing was over.

When I arrived in the town, I was told they had been arrested late the night before. The warrant was issued on information sworn by someone called Iris Ward. The name meant nothing to me; but it added to Rachel's misery as soon as she heard it. 'It will seem to George –' she said. 'You see, she was once a member of the group.'

They had spent the night in prison. That morning they had come before a magistrate: the charges were conspiracy to defraud against the three of them on two counts, the agency and the hostels; and also individual charges of obtaining money by false pretences against each on the two counts again. Nothing had been done except hear evidence of arrest and grant bail. The amount was fixed at £250 for each, and independent sureties of £250. This we had provided for in advance. Eden had arranged for two of his friends to transmit money raised by Morcom, Rachel, Roy Calvert and myself. For George and Jack, we had also been compelled to provide their personal surety; for Olive, a friend of her uncle's had been willing to stand. The next hearing was fixed for 29 December.

I knew it would be good professional judgment to hold our hand in the police court on the twenty-ninth and let the case go for trial. I wanted to persuade them of this course at once; so I arranged to meet them at George's that same night.

When I got there, George was alone. I was shocked by his manner. He was apathetic and numbed; he stared at the fire with his unseeing, inturned gaze. I could not stir him into interest over the tactics.

He was in a state that I could not reach. As he stared at the fire I waited for the others to come. I had scarcely noticed anything in the room but his accounts, the last evening I spent there; now I saw that, while everyone else was living more luxuriously, this sitting-room had scarcely altered since I first set foot in it.

Then Olive came in.

She said:

'I told you not to worry. You see how right I was.'

'It might have been better if you had told me the truth—' I was seeing her for the first time since the inquiries, but I was immediately at ease with her.

'I didn't know –' Then she realised that George was sunk into himself, and she tried to restore his defiance.

'It's nasty finding a traitor, George.' With her usual directness, she went straight into his suffering. 'But a man like you is bound to collect envy. The wonder is, there's not been more.'

She used also a bullying candour.

'We may have weeks of this. We mustn't let each other forget it.'

I felt she had done this before. And, as George was fighting against the despair, her instinct led her to another move.

She said:

'It's not going to be pleasant, is it? The twenty-ninth. You know, I simply couldn't realise what it would be like. Being ashamed and afraid in public. Until this morning. Yet sometimes it seemed perfectly ordinary. I felt that, last night in jail. Of course, it hasn't properly begun to happen yet. I only hope I get through it when it really comes.'

'You'll be better than any of us,' George said.

'I hope I shan't let you down,' she said. 'You see' – she suddenly turned to me – 'you can't believe how childish you find yourself in times like this. This is true, it happened this morning. I could face the thought that the worst might come to the worst. We might get twelve months. Then I felt a lump in my throat. I hadn't been near crying before, since it all began. Do you know why I was now? It had just occurred to me they might have had the decency to put it off until Christmas was over.'

She achieved her purpose; for George, with the curious rough comradeship that he had always shown towards her, made an effort to encourage her.

As soon as Jack entered, I was able to discuss the tactics. I argued that we must keep our defence back: there was no chance of getting the case dismissed in the police court: we should only give our points away.

In fact there was really no alternative: as a lawyer as able as George would have been the first to see. But tonight George broke out: 'You've got to defend it in the police court. It's essential to get it dismissed out of hand.'

Several times he made these outbursts, damning the prosecution as 'ludicrous', attacking it from all angles – as he had done since the alarm began. Some of his attacks were good law, and I had learned from them in my preparation of our case; some were fantastically unreal, the voices of his persecuted imagination. Tonight, however, there seemed another reason in the heart of his violence.

Jack detected the reason before I did. He interrupted George brusquely; I felt, not knowing whether I was right, that some of their meetings had gone like that, when the three of them were actually conducting their business.

Jack asked a few masterful, business-like questions:

'You think there's no option? We've clearly got to let it go for trial?'

'Yes.'

'There's no possible way of arranging it now?'

'It's practically certain to be sent on.'

'Everyone else thinks the same? Eden and the others?'

'Yes.'

'I entirely disagree,' said George.

Jack turned on him.

'We know what you're thinking of,' said Jack. 'You're not concerned about getting us off. You just believe that will happen. What you're frightened of – is that your private life may be dragged out. And your precious group. The whole thing for you is wrapped up with your good intentions. You ought to realise that we haven't got time for those now.'

Jack had spoken freshly, intimately, brutally; George did not reply, and for minutes sat in silence.

Jack walked up and down the room. He talked a good deal, and assumed that the tactics were settled.

'If I'd had the slightest idea the hostels would come back on us – I could have worked it out some other way,' he said. 'It would have been just as easy. There was no earthly reason for choosing the way I did. If anyone had told me there was the faintest chance that I was letting us in for this – *waiting*—'

'You needn't blame yourself. More than us,' said Olive.

'I'm not blaming myself. Except for not looking after everything. Next time I do anything, I shall keep it all in my hands.'

'Next time. We've got a long way to go before then,' said Olive.

'I'm not so sure,' said Jack. He sat down by her side.

She looked at him with the first sign of violent strain she had shown that night. I knew she feared that he was thinking of escape: as I had feared the moment he spoke of Morcom's offer.

'We can make something of it,' she said.

'I suppose we can.'

'You're afraid there's a bad patch to go through first?'

'I shan't be sorry when it's over.' He laid a hand on her knee, with a gesture for him clumsy and grateful. He was dominating the room no longer. He said: 'I always told you I should get into the public eye. But I didn't imagine it on such a grand scale.'

It surprised me that he, as much as George, was full of the fear of disgrace. Often of disgrace in its most limited sense – the questions, the appearance in the dock, the hours of being exposed to the public view. They would be open to all eyes in court. Jack could imagine himself cutting a dash – and yet he showed as great a revulsion as George himself.

'Anyway, we've got some time,' said Jack. 'When are the assizes, actually?'

Then George spoke:

'I can't accept the view that this is bound to go beyond the police court. I have thought over your objections, and I refuse to believe that they hold water.'

'We've told you why you refuse to believe it,' said Jack casually. But there came an unexpected flash of the George of years before. He said loudly:

'I don't regard you as qualified to hold an opinion. This is a point of legal machinery, and Lewis and I are the only people here capable of discussing it. I don't propose to give you the responsibility.'

'Jack is right,' said Olive. 'You're thinking of nothing but the group.'

'I'm thinking of ending this affair with as little danger as possible to all concerned,' said George. 'It's true that I have to take other people into account. But, from every point of view, this ought to be settled in the police court. Of course, wherever it's tried, if they understood the law of evidence, our private lives are utterly irrelevant. But in certain circumstances they might find an excuse to drag them into the court. In the police court they can't go so far. Lewis can make them keep their malice to themselves.'

'Is that true?' said Olive.

I hesitated.

'I don't think they will bring it up there. They will be too busy with the real evidence.'

'You're still quite certain that, even if we show our defence, they'll clearly send us for trial?' said Jack.

'You're exaggerating the case against us,' said George. 'And even if you weren't, it's worth the risk. I admit that I want to save other people from unpleasantness as well as myself. But since you're so concentrated on practical results' – he said to Jack – 'I might remind you that our chances are considerably better if that unpleasantness is never raised.'

Olive asked:

'Do you agree?'

'If there were a decent chance of finishing it in the police court,' I said, 'of course George would be right. But I can't believe—'

'You can't pretend there's no chance of finishing it,' George said. 'I want you to give a categorical answer.'

The others looked at me. I said:

'I can't say there's no chance. There may be one in ten. We can't rule it out for certain.'

'Then I insist that we leave the possibility open. I reject the suggestion that we automatically let it go for trial. If you see a chance, even if it's not absolutely watertight, we shall want you to take it.' George raised his voice, and spoke to the other two in the assertive, protective tone of former days:

'You've got to understand it's important for both of you. As well as myself. You realise that the prejudice against us might decide the case.'

'So long as they get us off the fraud—' Jack said.

'I've got to impress on you that the sort of prejudice they may raise is going to be the greatest obstacle to getting us off the fraud,' George said. 'You can't separate them. That's why I insist on every conceivable step being taken to finish it before they can insult us in the open.'

Olive said to me:

'George is convincing me.'

I said:

'I can't go any further than this: if there's any sign of a chance on the twenty-ninth, I'll go for it. But I warn you, there's not the slightest sign so far.'

Jack said: 'If we let you do that, it isn't for George's reasons. You realise that?' he said to George. 'You can't expect—'

George said: 'I intend to be listened to. I've let you over-ride me too easily before. This time it's too important to allow myself to be treated as you want.'

CHAPTER XXVIII

THE TWENTY-NINTH OF DECEMBER

THEY appeared before the magistrates' court in the town hall on 29 December 1932.

In the week before, I had gone over the whole case with Eden and Hotchkinson. I explained to them that, if the unlikely happened and a chance opened, I might risk going for an acquittal on the spot. They both disagreed; I knew that they were right and that they thought I was losing my judgment; for I could not give them the real reason. I was contemplating a risk which, on the legal merits of the case, I should never have taken.

Eden was puzzled, for he knew that I had the case analysed and mastered. It was not an intricate one, but slightly untidy in a legal sense. It depended on a few points of fact, not at all on points of law.

The substance of the case was this: the evidence of fraud over the agency was slight, apart from one definite fact, the discordant information upon the circulation of the *Arrow*. The evidence over the farm and hostels was much stronger, but with no such definite fact. There were several suspicious indications, but the transactions had been friendly, with no written documents except the receipts. (The largest loans were two sums of £750 each from acquaintances of Jack's, and £500 from Miss Geary.)

There existed no record of the information which was supposed to have been given. This was, so the prosecution were to claim, deliberately untrue in two ways: (1) by the receipts of the hostels being falsely quoted – those of the farm itself, by manipulating the figures of the money spent there by George and his friends from '24 to '31; (2) by Jack pretending to have managed such hostels himself and giving details on that authority.

The prosecution could produce, over the farm business, several consistent and interrelated stories. The total effect was bound to be strong. But they did not possess an indisputable *concrete* piece of evidence.

It was that singularly which threw the story of the *Arrow* into relief. When Jack had approached people to borrow money to buy the agency, George had proved its soundness by showing them a definite figure for the circulation. He had put this figure on paper; and his statement had come into the hands of the prosecution. They were out to show that it was deliberately false.

That figure was the most concrete fact they held. Apart from it, they might have omitted the count of the agency altogether.

I have anticipated a little here. We did not possess the structure of the case so completely when we went into the police court on the twenty-ninth.

Before we had been there an hour, I knew, as any lawyer must have known, that we had no choice. It would go for trial; we were compelled to reserve our defence.

The man opposite built up a case that, although we could have delayed it, was not going to be dismissed. During the morning, everyone began to realise that nothing could be settled; Olive told me later that she felt a release from anxiety – as soon as she was certain that this could not be a decisive day.

The prosecution ran through their witnesses. The first was one of the four whom Jack had induced to lend money to buy the advertising firm, a slow-voiced man with kindly and stupid brown eyes.

'Mr Cotery made a definite statement about the firm's customers?' asked T——, the prosecutor.

'Yes.'

'He mentioned the previous year's turnover?'

'Yes.'

'Also the number of advertisers the firm were agents for?'

'Yes.'

After other questions, he asked whether Jack referred to the circulation of Martineau's advertising paper.

'Yes.'

'Can you reproduce that statement?'

'I made a note of it at the time.'

'Will you give me the figures?'

He read them out. The figure of the circulation sounded unfamilar: I remembered it in George's account as 5300; now it appeared as 6000. I looked up my own papers and found that I was right.

'Didn't those figures strike you as large?'

'They did.'

'What did Mr Cotery say?'

'He said they'd be larger still now Mr Martineau had disappeared and his religious articles would be pushed out of the paper.' There were some chuckles.

'Did you ask for some guarantees?'

'Yes.'

'Will you tell us exactly what you did?'

'I asked Mr Cotery if he could show me what these figures were based on. So he introduced me to Mr Passant, who told me that he was a solicitor and had had a good deal to do with figures and had known the former owner of the agency, Mr Martineau. He said he had received a statement from Mr Martineau giving the actual circulation. It was not 6000. Mr Cotery had been a little too optimistic, it was just over 5000. He offered to show me his notes of this statement. And if I were doubtful he promised to trace Mr Martineau, who had gone away, and get him to write to me.'

'Did you take advantage of that offer?'

'No.'

'Why not?'

'I didn't see any reason to. I had known Mr Cotery for some time, I felt sure it was all above board. I could see Mr Passant knew what he was talking about.'

The other witnesses followed with the information that T—— had foretold in his speech; similar stories to the first, some including Olive. Then an accountant brought out some figures of the agency's business, in particular those of the *Arrow*:

'What was the average circulation in the year 1927?'

'Eleven hundred per week. So far as I can tell. The books are not very complete.'

'What would you say was the maximum possible for that year? Making every allowance you can?'

'Perhaps fifteen hundred.' This had been threatened in the speech.

They brought up witnesses against the farm. It was at this stage we realised for certain the legal structure of the case. Essentially the story was the same. George had taken a less prominent part, Olive substantially more. The information which Jack had given his investors was more complicated, not easy to contradict by a single fact; but several men attacked it piece by piece. Jack had asked advice about the business from a man who ran a hostel himself in another part of the country; the accounts he had given second-hand of this interview were different from the other's remembrance of it. The statistics of visitors to the farm before 1929 were compared – though here there were some uncertainties – with those given by George and Jack to several witnesses.

At lunch time I said to George:

'If we defend it today – it is bound to go for trial.'

He argued bitterly, but his reason was too strong in the end.

'You'd better play for safety,' he said. 'Though I still insist there are overwhelming advantages in getting it wiped off now.'

'If we try that,' I said, 'there'll be a remand for a week or two. We shall have to show our hand. And they'll still send the case on.'

'If these magistrates were trained as they ought to be,' said George, 'instead of amateurs who are feeling proud of themselves for doing their civic duty, we could fight it out.'

He turned away. 'As it is, you'd better play for safety.'

I told Eden and Hotchkinson. Eden said: 'I always thought you'd take the sensible view before it was too late.'

When the prosecution's case was finished I made the formal statement that there was no case to go before the jury, but that the nature of the defence could not be disclosed.

The three were committed for trial at the next assizes; bail was renewed for each of them in the same amounts.

CHAPTER XXIX

NEWSPAPERS UNDER A READING-LAMP

THE local papers were lying on a chair in Eden's dining-room when I got back from the court. Under the bright reading-lamp, their difference of colour disappeared – though I remembered from childhood the faint grey sheen of one, the yellow tinge in the other. On both of the front pages, the police court charge flared up.

There was a photograph of Olive. 'Miss Calvert, a well-known figure in town social circles, the daughter of the late James Calvert, J.P.' ... 'Mr Passant, a qualified solicitor and a lecturer in the Technical College and School of Art' ... a paragraph about myself. The reports were fair enough.

Everything in them would inevitably have been recorded in any newspaper of a scandal in any town. They were a highest common factor of interest; they were what any acquaintance, not particularly friendly or malign, would tell his friends, when he heard of the event. But it was because of that, because I could find nothing in the reports themselves to expend my anger on, that they brought a more hopeless sense of loneliness and enmity.

'Allegations against Solicitor.' The pitiful inadequacy of it all! The timorous way in which the news, the reporters, the people round us, we ourselves (for the news is merely our own voice) need to make shapes and counters out of human beings in order not to endanger anything in ourselves. George Passant is not George Passant; he is not the man rooted in as many complexities as we are ourselves, as bewildering in action and yet taking himself as much for granted as we do ourselves; he is not the man with his own private history, desires, mannerisms, perversities like our own, cowardice and braveries, odd habits of mind different from ours but of the same family, delights and, like us all, private oddities in love – a man of flesh and bone, as real as ourselves. He is not that; if he were, our own identity and uniqueness would have gone.

To most of the town tonight George is 'a solicitor accused of fraud'. 'I hope they get him'; a good many men, as kind-hearted as any of us can ever be, said at the time that I was reading. We are none of us men of flesh and bone except to ourselves.

Should I have had that reflection later in my life? Maybe I should have thought it over-indulgent. For in time behaviour took on a significance to me at least as great as inner nature. It was a change in me: not necessarily an increase in wisdom, but certainly in severity: a hardening: not a justification, but a change.

Excusing myself from dinner, I went to George's. He was alone listening to the wireless by the fire. 'Hallo,' he said. His cheeks were pale, and the day's beard was showing. He seemed tired and lifeless.

'I didn't know whether anyone would come round,' he said.

Jack and Olive entered as we were sitting in silence. Although there was a strained note in his laugh, Jack came as a relief.

'We'd better do something,' he said. 'It isn't every day one's sent for trial—'

'You fool,' cried Olive and put her arm round his waist.

Soon the room was crowded. Roy came in, Daphne, several of those I had seen at the farm in September. They had made a point of collecting here tonight. George whispered to Daphne for a while, and then, as the others addressed him with a pretence of casualness, he said:

'I didn't expect you all.' He was embarrassed, uncontrollably grateful for the show of loyalty.

Jack laughed at him. 'Never mind that. We've got to amuse them now they're here. This has got to be a night.'

A girl replied with a sly, hungry joke. There was a thundery uneasiness. The air was full of the hysteria of respite from strain, friendliness mixed with the fear of persecution and the sting of desire. We left the room, and packed into Olive's car and Roy's and another young man's. In the early days none of us thought of owning a car. We were poorer then; but now even the younger members of the group were not willing to take their poverty so cheerfully for granted.

We drove to a public-house outside the town. The streets were still shining with the lights of Christmas week; a bitterly cold wind blew clouds across the sky; the stars were pale. As Olive drove us past the last tram lines, she took a corner very fast, swerved across the road, so that for a second we were blinded in a headlight, and then brought us away by a foot – a flash of light and the road again.

'Silly,' Olive cried.

In this mood, I thought, she could kill herself without it being an accident. Once or twice in our lives, we all know times when some part of ourselves desires to turn the wheel into a crash; just as we shiver on a height, feel the death-wish, force ourselves from the edge.

At the public-house they were quickly drunk, helped by their excitement; Olive and Jack danced on the bar floor, a rough whirling apache dance. Everyone was restless. As the night passed, some of them drove to another town, but before midnight almost the entire party had gathered in Rachel's flat.

'They can't do much harm now,' said Rachel. 'It's a good job there's somewhere safe for them to come.' The flat took up the top storey of an unoccupied house near the station. Rachel had become secretary of her firm, and it was her luxury to entertain George's friends, while she watched them with good-natured self-indulgence.

Olive and I stayed in the inner room. Through the half-open sliding doors we saw some of the girls and heard George's voice throwing out drunken and passionate praise. Jack came to Olive.

'When are we going home?'

'Not yet,' she said. She was smiling at him. Her words were as full of excitement as George's. 'You want to stay, don't you?'

He laughed – but suddenly I felt that he had become dependent on her. He went back, and from our sofa she could see him caressing a girl, and at the same time attracting the attention of the room.

Olive's eyes followed him.

'I don't mind that as much as I did once,' she said to me. She added: 'He isn't as drunk as the rest of us. He never has liked drinking, you know. He's as – temperate as Arthur. It's queer they both should be.' She went on talking quickly about Morcom, among the noise of the other room.

'You know,' she went on, 'I never felt he was such a strong man as the others did. I liked him, of course.' Then she said: 'He wasn't my first lover, perhaps you don't know that. You knew me best when I was still frightened of my virginity, didn't you? Strange how strong that was. But it wasn't strong enough—' She looked into the room with a half-smile. 'Jack seduced me one night—'

'When?' I had not known.

'Before my father died.'

'Were you attached to Jack, then? I didn't think—'

'I was always fond of him, of course. But not in the way that's got hold of me since,' she said. 'No, it just happened – we met in London somehow. He never was a man to fail for want of trying. I had one or two weekends with him, afterwards. At odd times. You know how erratic he used to be. It didn't matter much, just for once he'd think it might be a good idea.'

'And you?'

'Sometimes I refused. In the end, I was driven back, though. I suppose one's always driven back. Then I didn't see him for a long time.'

'What about Arthur, then?'

'I'd thought a lot of him. I'd heard from him all the time we were away. Then when I came back, he wanted me more than ever. Just then I didn't see why not.'

She paused. 'You've no idea how hard a time it was. He was jealous, madly jealous at times. Of anyone I seemed to like. And I couldn't help it, I kept playing on it. There were times when he was so jealous that he only got any rest when we were sleeping together. I drove him to that. He wanted me not really to make love – just to be sure of me. And I couldn't help the little hints, that would set him off tearing himself with suspicion—'

'I know,' I said.

She said: 'He used to treat me rough now and then. I didn't mind that, sometimes I want it. You've guessed that, haven't you? But even then I couldn't believe the will was there.' She went on: 'We didn't reach happiness. We both deteriorated, we were both worse people. Counting it all up, I don't know who got hurt more. I can't bear to think of his life just then; jealousy going on and on. It was like that in the old days, of course. Funny that he was always more jealous of Jack than anyone else. Even when there was no reason for it in the world.'

'And so you left him and went to Jack?' I said.

'It was bound to hurt him – more than if I had gone to anyone else,' she said. 'But that had nothing to do with it. I tell you, I was really in love for the first time in my life.' She added: 'You've seen me with Jack. I want you to tell me that I'm not deceiving myself.'

'I know you love him—'

'But you think it isn't simple – even now?' She broke out. 'I'll confess something. When I went to Jack – I was certain that I belonged to him – I *still* wondered whether it was because of Arthur. That kept coming back. You imagine, it came back when Jack was after a new girl, when I wanted him and felt ashamed of myself. But I'm certain that I belong to him more than ever. It would have happened, if I'd never let Arthur come near me. I know it isn't simple, it isn't just a love affair. I expect he would prefer to have picked up one of those girls in there. I've had too many nights when I've wanted to break it off – and still been making plans for keeping him. But neither of us had any choice—'

Olive's nerves were tightened with fatigue, fear, the laughs of hysterical enjoyment from the outer room. But she was exhilarated by putting Jack off, sitting within a few yards of his drunken party, and then confiding how much she needed him. She had thrown off any covering of self-pity, however. She seemed stronger than any of us. She was still cherishing some petty sufferings, as she had always done. Her longing for humility was real, but it sprang from the depth of her intense spiritual pride. No one could have mistaken – under the surface of her restless nervousness, full of the day's degradation – still warmed and roused by Jack's voice, tired as she was – that she was speaking from an inner certainty of herself.

'If he quits before the trial, mind you, Lewis—' she began.

I exclaimed.

'You know that he's thought of that?'

'Of course I know,' said Olive. 'I'm not blind when I love. He's thought of getting abroad. On the whole, I don't think he'll try.'

'If he did?'

'I should run after him. As soon as he cricked his finger. Whether he cricked his finger or not.'

I thought of George's safety: when she asked, 'How easy is it – for us to get abroad?' I kept the details out of my answer.

Just then I heard George's voice above the rest. The partition had slid further back, and from our room we could see him; he was half-lying on a sofa with Daphne on his knee, one arm round her; in the other hand he held a glass. He had begun to sing at the top of his voice, so violently that his hand shook and the spirit kept spurting out.

Daphne jumped from his knee, and stood behind the sofa, trying to quieten him. He sang on: the words were so loud that I could not disentangle them, but it sounded like one of his father's hymns.

'There's George,' said Olive.

She watched him.

'Some people once thought there might be something between us. They were stupid. We've never had the slightest feeling for each other.'

She went on:

'I know what you were afraid of a minute ago. If Jack flew, I should be ready to desert George. That's true. Yet he's been close to me – in a way I've never understood.'

She got up, and walked into the other room. Some of them looked in Jack's direction, expecting her to go there. But she went and stood by George. I had not seen her touch him, not once in those years. Now she dropped on her knees by the sofa, and took his hand in hers.

CHAPTER XXX

GEORGE'S DIARY

I LEFT them at three o'clock. Some hours later, when I was still in bed, a telephone message came from the hospital: would I go to the children's clinic at once? Morcom was on duty there, he urgently wanted to see me. The streets were filling up as I went out; out of the shops, women bustled by, their cheeks pink in the frost. The indifference of the scene, the comfort, like a Breughel picture, only brought out my anxiety. It was an actual relief to see Morcom's face, meeting me with a look of question and acute strain.

He could ask nothing; a nurse was in the room, and a batch of boys, round the age of twelve or so. As I watched, it was his gentleness which fascinated me. They responded to him immediately, with shrill, high, squealing laughs. With the nurse he was sharply efficient: but, as he talked to the boys, his manner became natural and self-effacing, so that they gathered round him, their nervousness gone, chaffing him. Some of them had noticed his pallor:

'Have you got a headache, Mr Morcom?'

'Were you out on the spree last night, Mr Morcom?'

Then, as he took me into his office, his expression changed.

'Were you with them last night?'

I nodded.

'What do they think?'

'They've a good idea what the chances are.'

'Has George?' asked Morcom.

'Yes.'

'You talked of Jack escaping, the first night this began. Why don't you suggest it to George?'

I hesitated.

'It wouldn't be easy,' I said.

'Easy! You of all people talk of it not being easy – when you know what the alternative is.'

'I know—'

'But you won't go to George.'

'I can't,' I said.

'It's his fault,' said Morcom. 'It's that madman's fault.'

'It's no use blaming anyone now.'

'What do you mean?'

'It's too late to talk about George's fault. Or yours. Or mine for not stopping it,' I said.

'Yes,' said Morcom.

'If you had gone back that night and taken care of them, this might never have happened. That night you warned me, and I begged you to go back. If you had only been able to forget your self-respect,' I said.

My voice had gone harsh like his; he heard me say what he was continually thinking; he was relieved. His face became softened. He said, in a casual, almost light-hearted tone:

'That wouldn't have been so easy, either.' He paused, then said: 'The only thing is, what's to be done? There's still some time.'

'I don't think there's anything you can do,' I said. 'They will have to wait for the trial.'

'You'll be busy with the case?'

'Yes.'

'You're lucky.' Then he said: 'I've not asked you before. But are you as likely to get them off – as anyone we could find?'

'No,' I said. 'If we could afford to pay.'

'I ought to have been told that. I'll give the money—'

'I've thought it out – as dispassionately as I can,' I said. 'I don't think the difference is worth the money. For one reason. Money may be more important afterwards. If we've spent every penny—'

'You mean, if they're convicted—'

'We've got to be ready,' I said.

That afternoon, when I was sitting alone in the drawing-room at Eden's, Daphne visited me. She talked of the previous night.

'It was rather an orgy, wasn't it?' she said. 'Of course, you didn't see it after it really began –' She mentioned a common acquaintance, and said: 'Of course, it would have sent her away for good, wouldn't it? But then she's "upright". I can't help respecting her, you know, when I'm not relapsing like last night.' Then she said: 'But I'm being silly, wasting your time. In the middle of this horror. It's as bad as going mad last night. But that happened because we were in this mess, didn't it?'

The shrewdness shot through the prattle of her talk, and her eyes, often flirtatious, were steady and sensible. 'That's just why I've come up to see you now. I'm getting a bit worked up.'

'Go on.'

'You're easy to talk to, aren't you?' she said (coquettishness returned for a second; her upper lip puckered). 'I shan't be terribly helpful, you know. It's just to get it off my chest. But anyway, it's like this. When George first thought of making passes at me he wanted me to know the awful secrets of his life. He was certain that I should be shocked,' she went on. 'I oughtn't to laugh at him, poor dear. He was serious about it. It must have been a struggle. When he decided it was the right thing to do, he went ahead – though he fancied he was taking a risk. He really believed he might lose me.' She smiled.

'Well, do you know what he did?' she said. 'He insisted on giving me his diary. It's a staggering document. I expect I enjoyed the pieces he thought I'd mind. But there are some I can't always laugh away. I've brought it along.' (She had placed a small despatch case on the floor.) 'I want you to look at it for me –' She sat on the arm of my chair; the arrangement of the first page, as her finger pointed out an entry, seemed identical with those George himself showed me years ago.

First she made me read a series of passages about the agency; quite soon after they bought it, it seemed that George was troubled about the circulation of the *Arrow* – 'it cannot conceivably have reached the figure that Martineau gave me in good faith'. The set of entries went on for several pages: neither of us spoke as I read it.

'That's all about that business,' said Daphne. 'I don't know what it means. But I couldn't rest till you'd seen it. I thought you might need it for the case –' then she broke off. 'Will you read some more? While I'm here?'

There was little else directly bearing on the case in the entries Daphne selected. I saw only a few perfunctory references to his job at Eden's, and little more about the 'enterprises' with Jack and Olive. On the whole, I was surprised that they had seemed to matter so little.

Daphne, in fact, had not brought the diary only to ask about the case. I was not even certain what she inferred from the first entries she had pointed out. Sensibly, she had determined to reveal them to me as his lawyer. Whether she thought George guilty, I did not know. But she was obviously affected by other parts of his confessions.

She was deeply fond of him, and in a youthful, shrewd and managing way she was trying to plan their future life. She felt lost, as she read some passages which a more completely experienced woman might have found alien. Actually Daphne, though lively and sensual, was also sentimental and full of conventional dreams. In imagination, she was contriving a happy marriage with George.

I hesitated. Then I thought she had enough natural insight to stand something of the truth. I tried to explain some of the contradictions in his life as honestly as I could. I regretted it, for I hurt her; and she said goodbye, still convinced that she knew him better than I.

She left the entire diary with me, from 1922 to the month before the preliminary inquiries. I went on reading it for hours. To any intimate of George's, who accepted by habit the strange appearance of his life, it would have been moving. To me, it carried the irretrievability of the past, along with a life close to one's own in affection and pity – and so far away that it brought a desolation of loneliness.

I looked back for the first reference to the group, and read again the early 'justification' which he had shown me that night at the farm, in 1925. There was much more about the School and his friends in that tone, for years afterwards. In 1927, soon after his disappointment in the firm, he was writing:

The family have at last partially got rid of their conception of me as selfish – and he in particular appreciates my care and devotion, in his eagerness to give the world its due. Olive has gone, Mona has just become engaged, many of them have gone: but there are others, there are some closer to me than there have ever been. I find I have been writing of them all this holiday. If anything can be inferred from these expressions of my feelings, I have been useful to these people at the School. There are signs that freedom is life. And three years ago I was groaning inwardly at my distance from my friends. I was watching them from afar.

Then, still explaining to himself the divisions of his emotional life, he returned to the town, and for several weekends in Nottingham and London passed an 'equinox' of sensuality.

This randy fit is going on too long. Last night I could not resist taking the train to London. I was inflamed by the vision of one of our prettiest s—f——s, I found my little girl of 1921, older and more dilapidated, but with the same touching curve of the lips.

Tonight it was still on me. I took the familiar train to Nottingham. I found a pair of old friends in the first pub and spent a half-hour of pleasure looking at Pauline's face; but they were booked, and I was not in a mood to award free sherry for ever, so I moved on. I have hazy recollections of hordes of women that I kissed. I finished up drunk in the train three or four hours ago. And as we came to the scattered lights outside the town, I thought that everything worth while in my life I had invested in this place.

It was in the following autumn that they bought the agency. George's references to the group in the next two years became far more varied: at times impatient, moved by Jack, 'urging me on to his own freedom. Wanting me to destroy the only thing I have ever made. Yet he is a lover of life, he has given me his warm companionship for years, he looks into the odd corners of living' (17 November 1928).

During that autumn, also, a girl called Katherine Faulkner entered the society – usually referred to in the diary as K. For some time she was only mentioned casually.

A New Venture
16 October 1928

Today Jack, Olive and I took over the agency, that curious stage in Martineau's mad progress. It is to be hoped it does well. Money is a
CONTRACT SIGNED
perpetual nuisance: why should I, who care so little for it, have it always dragging round my neck? I have hopes that Jack will win us new comforts. Of course, I am not as optimistic as they all think. I remember his bad luck and bad management with that absurd first attempt of his. But he is still capable of success: it is time we had the luck on our side.

2 December 1928

Jack is busy and active and full of ideas. A little money has come in already. Today it struck me as strange that Jack, of all my friends, should
JACK AGAIN
have been close at my side for the longest time. He was indulging in one of his new attacks on the group. 'Why don't you see what people really want?' He does not

trouble to conceal that he includes me among them. He does not pretend to share my hopes nowadays: he would like me to follow him with his surburban girls. Yet all this sadistic nonsense of his does not seem to interrupt our alliance.

4 DECEMBER 1928

Jack brought in a friend tonight who made a fierce emotional case for immortality. Lewis, in the old days, would have shrugged his shoulders, but I enjoyed the talk. On the train afterwards, going to ARGUMENT this petty little case – I'm tired of being foisted off with Eden's drudgery – I remember that it was the first argument with a stranger for many months. The group is taking up all my energy – more even than it did in the first flush of youthful zeal, religious years that are not quite repeated now. If Jack were not obsessed with his own pleasures, he would see how that answers his attacks.

6 DECEMBER 1928

I thought it was perhaps a mistake not to keep a tiny fraction of my interests away from the 'little world'. I sometimes wish that Lewis were here for a day of two. So on the train I read some A FEW HOURS calculus with immense excitement. Why wasn't I told SNATCHED about these things at school? Also 'Clissold'; Wells is FOR MYSELF childish in politics, but there are moments when he feels for the whole common soul of man.

Yet I have found little time for anything outside the group now.

During the next few weeks, he wrote those entries about the circulation which Daphne had showed me at first. I put them aside to think over again.

22 FEBRUARY 1929

I appeared before the School Committee, asking for money for the brightest man since Lewis's day. It was a horrible fiasco. Cameron was unnecessarily offensive. The cleric Martineau COLLAPSE scored at my expense. I am not so effective as I used to be. I can still hear that grotesque display, and I feel like blinding all the damned night through.

1 MARCH 1929
I COME TO GRIPS AGAIN

Things have not been perfect. I have not quite the usual satisfaction of work well done. The débâcle of my appearance before the committee,

TOO EASILY
DOWNCAST

another storm of lust, Jack's contempt for the 'hole-and-corner' way in which I indulge my passions, have all played their part. Jack hints also that Olive has begun an affair with Morcom of all people, to whom I have scarcely spoken a private word for months. It may take her away from our little business venture, and it's a piece of wanton irritation. However, I ought to be able to ignore it. The sight of K., smiling at the farm, a different person from what she was three months ago, is enough to remove any memories of Olive as anything more than a friendly, competent person, who is some help to Jack and myself.

After a walk in the beautiful rain-sodden evening, I have felt again the essential urge to live among these people. My course is set and my mind made up. Jack's friendship is valuable, but his influence must be despised. I see it clearly now.

2 MARCH 1929

K. and the others made this the most perfect weekend I have ever known. They were alive, we were all on terms of absolute confidence. I was overwhelmed with happiness, unqualified happiness, such happiness as comes unawares and only in rare moments. I was bathed in the warmth of joyous living, so that any trouble seemed incredible.

18 APRIL 1929

Next weekend, so I have just heard, some clod has rented the farm and we cannot be accommodated. Why in heaven should I be denied what is my food and life by the sheer inconsequent whim of some unknown fool?

Although he did not admit it for some months, it was probably about this time that he became engrossed in Katherine – in love with her, perhaps. Never before, at any rate, had any girl in the group meant as much: Mona, now married to an acquaintance of Jack's, had only been one of many 'fancies'. In the diary about this date he dismissed her: 'She was a bright little thing. I could have slept with her if my theory had permitted it – I suppose Jack did not feel any scruples'. There had been another girl, Phyllis, who had by this time finished her training as an elementary schoolmistress, and taken a job in the county; George had toyed half-heartedly with the idea of marrying her, a couple of years back.

But Katherine moved him far more deeply: she came upon him when he was trying to maintain all his ideals over the 'little world'.

I never met her, or knew much of her, except that she was very poor and possessed the delicate and virginal beauty which most excited George. He struggled against recognising the passion. After that outburst over the farm, he tried to miss the group's meetings there. He found himself in one of his whirls of womanising, unusually long drawn out.

RELAPSES
7 MAY

Somehow I have not got the School and the group in my bones as I used to have. This is strange after the promise of a month ago. I am in a tangle of desires, scattering money more frantically than I ever did. I met Winnie in Oxford Street: she is one of the nicest girls I have managed to know. Curious – her face comes and goes. Why? (Peggy's went long since. Dorothy's went, also the Cambridge girl, and the Bear Street one. It needs some effort to recall Hilda.)

FACES IN LONDON

(The names were all of women he had picked up on the streets.)

21 MAY

I am still a libido, though I get some joy from life. No moralising; things happen well when they do happen. Last night it was the old crowd in Nottingham. Some of the old hands are in trouble. Connie owes to a money lender, poor soul. Thelma sees financial ruin coming. I told her that the 'good wife and mother stunt' is off. Why am I so attracted by prostitutes? I finished up with Pat, Connie's successor and the best of all.

3 JUNE

I have wrestled with repentance. Late though it be, I am wholly in love with the group again. I came back to a weekend at the farm – my first for a month – with extraordinary gratitude that they should receive me with a show of happiness and admiration. Jack was not there, and I am ashamed to say that made me easier in mind. They seem to respect me. Little do they know that I am really the prodigal son.

RETURN TO THE GROUP

4 JUNE

I think I am in love with K. I cannot write until I have thought it out.

6 JUNE

I still cannot see my way clear. For hours I have rehearsed renunciatory speeches to myself. Yet I know I shall never make them. About one thing

I must be certain, now and whatever happens in the future; nothing must impair any single person near me. I am beginning to think I have never been in love before – in my purely selfish life, it is the greatest thing that has happened. But that is a trifle beside the people I can still look after. If I neglect that work, there is nothing left of me except an ordinary man and a handful of sensations.

10 JUNE

I met K. by accident tonight. She shook hands as we parted. Her touch is like no other touch. In the whispering air I rode home to a quiet house.

From the diary one gained no clear impression of K. She was probably a complex and sensitive person, easily hurt and full of self-distrust. Her relation with George was strained and unhappy, almost from the beginning: 'the only time I have been utterly miserable over a woman,' he wrote. With the odd humour that came less often in his diary than in speech, he added on 24 July: 'K. let me hold her hand: but that may have been because there was no feeling in her arm'.

His distress and 'longing' (a word which entered frequently that summer) drove him more completely into the group. He resigned from the one or two organisations in the town to which he still belonged – five years before, he had taken part in many. He kept protesting against 'extra work for Eden'. 'I am a solicitor's clerk. I do not consider I am under any obligation to do more than a competent solicitor's clerk usually does. He has no call on me outside office hours.'

He ceased to mention his law lectures, in which he used to take so great a pride.

The same summer – Daphne, who was then nineteen, and Freda (the F. of the accounts which George showed me early in the investigation) joined the group.

8 SEPTEMBER 1929

Last night saw what may be – what ought to be – the concluding stage in the K. business. She let everyone see what she thought of me. Perhaps she will not come near us again. Jack, Rachel and Olive came to see me tonight. Rachel was all sympathy, and Olive did not disguise her own affair. When Rachel had gone, however, Olive got down to some of the agency's accounts. They are rather good, though the trickle of money does not relieve my financial doldrums. It gives Jack a living, though. He was fine and high-handed about K. Either I ought to make love to her, he insisted, or she ought to be thrown out. I think that he was being genuinely warm-hearted, he was thinking only of my peace of mind.

But it is all very well for them to brandish their freedom. They have got to realise that I am in a different position. They say I have created the position and difficulty for myself. That makes it all the more essential.

14 SEPTEMBER

The meek don't want the earth. Yet I have thought of her all day. Is it possible that she is anxious not to give herself away too cheaply? Or does she simply hate and despise me?

If I am not to have her, let me clear the lumber out of my heart and regain the old freedom. If I could only fall in love with Rachel – but this K. business spoils every other relation.

17 SEPTEMBER

Martineau called in for an hour or two. He still wanders on his lonely, meaningless crusade, and remains his gentle self. I told him the agency was going adequately on. He did not seem interested. In the circumstances, I thought it unnecessary to say more. The family this evening asked me for more money: finance will soon be disastrous again.

28 SEPTEMBER

Perhaps K. has gone for good. I have never been in so many troubles. I am baying at the moon. Sometimes the group itself seems like a futile little invention of my own. I am thoroughly despondent. The root of the trouble is a discontent which is not confined to me. There is money, which still harasses me. Apart from K., I begin to think the major cause of my present discontent lies in ambition. It will not be so easy to die in obscurity as I once thought.

3 OCTOBER

K. is in a state of semi-return. Last night was the second weekend running in Nottingham, but if K. comes back I need not go again. Pat's face is too often a disembodied smile, wickedly turned up, saying 'all right' or 'whisky'.

11 OCTOBER

We have had a good weekend at the farm. The people there were all living more abundantly than if I had never happened. I have despaired too easily. I still believe in them and myself, in spite of occasional tremors. In any case, what else could there be in life?

13 OCTOBER

K.'s essence still comes between me and everything. Yet tonight I was infuriated by a blasted business acquaintance of Olive's disregarding my presence and ignoring my intelligence. I cannot admit inferiority. It is an essential to my present poise that I should be supreme in intellect over anyone I meet.

17 OCTOBER

K. is hardly apologetic over her refusal to attend another farm party. She would not explain, and now avoids me. I transferred a little of my affection to Freda, whose smile is sometimes like a faint reflection.

23 OCTOBER

K. looked through me with cold eyes. I can't pretend that I still have any hope.

(later the same night)

I shook myself out of this absurd and humiliating affair and took the train to Nottingham. Pat was as delightful as ever a girl of this kind could be – and, damn it, I like these girls better than any others.

30 OCTOBER

One of the best parties we have had, and sometimes I have managed to put K. out of mind. The group is far better, I am afraid, with Jack not present.

Freda told me that my 'half-closed' eyes were (*a*) concerning K. and Jack,* and (*b*) to Rachel's feeling about me. As for Rachel, she chose her way and I am sure she likes it best.

*This seems to have been quite baseless.

3 NOVEMBER

I find myself longing, as I never longed before. For all my fantasies, I do not suppose I should take her as a mistress, even if she would let me near her. I could not help walking the streets round her house, in the hope of seeing her by accident. I walked through a gathering fog, getting for a moment a feeling of exultation as I sped through the mist, weaving my dreams. Of course I did not see her: I went back to the old café, played four games of draughts, then came home and raved.

That was a couple of hours ago. Since then I have been reading some of the diaries of recent years. It has brought back some of the pleasure and hope I have gathered from these people. Some of them have gone before now, without being helped. But others are free people, a nucleus of friends, thinking and acting and living as no other group I am likely to know again.

That is my achievement, and nothing can take it from me. Jack and Olive, for all their faults and defections: Lewis Eliot, away in London – Phyllis and – and – and –: they're all different for having known me and from my being able to spend my devotion. Well, that must go on – whatever distracts me by the way. Are there many men who have twenty better lives to their credit?

So let us not be sad. Personal misery is grotesque: and who am I to complain of losing one when there are so many to occupy my life? Really, I do not often worry about myself at all.

But the passion lasted – different from any in his life, and nearer to others' experience. The same pattern of unhappiness, desire for freedom and return to K., ran through the diary for months.

13 DECEMBER

I take too little notice of people about me. By this wretched affair, I have hurt Rachel. Apart from business I scarcely ever see Olive. I am vexed with ever-absent money, tension about K., no fame. But K. seems to have hinted to Jack that she would like to be reconciled: which news filled me with wild joy, though I was intensely annoyed by Jack's remark – 'She may think you too mad and dangerous.'

I am a little afraid of Jack at times.

This afternoon Freda said of K. and me:

'When you take a dislike to a person, imagination does the rest.'

5 JANUARY 1930

I wish I could feel for Freda instead of K. Sometimes I think I could: at least I could get comfort from her. But there again I should have other problems to face. I cannot control myself all these years, resist being laughed at by Jack, only to crash all my aspirations by my own deliberate action.

Anyway the question does not arise. With K. it is an ache, a slow corroding pain.

I went off to see Pat, sick at heart. I had quite a pleasant time with her.

14 JANUARY

Tonight K. broke her silence. I saw her quite by chance in Rachel's flat – who, good soul, made a sarcastic remark and then went out. K. began to talk. She did not apologise. After making myself incredibly late for everything else that evening, I went. But not before I had seen her smile, and felt a happiness that seemed unsensuous and perfect.

At times, by the way, she was wearisome and showed signs of being shallow – but I could hardly think of that.

The after effect has been to make me dream of Freda.

MY HAPPIEST DAY
15 JANUARY

REALISING IT It is very difficult to think of her as tangible.

The reconciliation and their 'ethereal' relations continued all that spring. It occupied much of the diary; for the rest he wrote far less of the constructive side of the group – with occasional reiterations that it was still 'my major interest'.

Instead, he became more explicit about his 'sensations' – to begin with, the nights in Nottingham and London were minutely described. Then: 'Jack and I are narrowing our attention to the libido. It is a long time since we talked of our friends in any other way. For myself, I still cannot limit my interest as he does in his frank fashion. Yet no man has lived more freely than Jack. I know they have often thought him a superficial person by the side of some of us. Perhaps that is not just.'

24 MARCH

Tonight Jack told me some of the stories of his conquests. Some I knew, of course; Mona, in the old days, and ——. But Olive! I was astonished at that – though now it makes her Morcom adventure (which is probably ending) more explicable. And he made other hints – I was angry, I told him he had betrayed any decent code of friendship. But I cannot only be jealous. Haven't I inveighed, time after time, against irrational conventions? I must think of his behaviour in the light of reason.

4 APRIL

Last night at the farm I arranged that Freda and I be left alone. And, of course, I made love to her. I felt an altogether marvellous delight – more of the mind than the flesh perhaps, but that was to be expected.

Today I am still in a state of joy – but sometimes now quite easy. I must reassure myself once for all. No one is a penny the worse. It will not interfere with my influence with them, for none of them will know. I am prepared to believe that I could not bring them on as in the past, if this were common property. For many of them, the news would be altogether bad. But for Freda, by herself, it can have done nothing but good. She was longing for the substance of freedom, not only the words. She is older than twenty, in everything that matters: she wanted to begin a life that will be different from all that I have tried to rescue her out of. I am now a completer means of escape. That is all.

Yet tonight I am not altogether tranquil. The years of the group, the continual presence of K. – it all seems strange and not entirely real. I used to think I should not stay in this town for long. Now I am past thirty. I have been at Eden's nearly nine years. Sometimes it seems too long a time.

1 JUNE

It has proved unnecessary to keep my change of attitude secret from the group. I must readjust some of my old values – founded probably on the family and my early upbringing. I am now convinced that it is easy to combine the greatest mental activity with a general view more like Jack's than mine. We are all the better for real freedom. No unnecessary internal restraints – and one has more appetite for constructive good. Of course there are times when I cannot always live up to what seems intellectually established: then I have hankerings after the old days.

4 JUNE

Daphne was at a Whitsun party at the farm, which was remarkable for the afterglow it left.

30 JUNE

Money is desperately short again. The trickle from the agency is lessening. I shall have to borrow. What does that matter in this *fin-de-siècle* time?

15 JULY

The high meridian of freedom is on us now. In our nucleus of free people, anyway – and sometimes I think on the world.

7 AUGUST

I tried uselessly to explain to the family some indication of my changed views. With no result, except great fatigue and bitter distress – though they could not understand all my statements. I am more worn than I have been for years. Old habits are the strongest: and still, at my age, nothing tires me to the heart so much as a family quarrel.

2 SEPTEMBER

K. came unexpected to the farm this Saturday. After tea – Daphne, Iris R. (Mona's half-sister, who used to be a 'regular' and has now come back) and several others were there – K. began to talk to me, then stopped. Suddenly I saw tears running down her face. It upset me a little, though not as much as a possible absence of Daphne or Freda.

DAPHNE ALONE
9 SEPTEMBER

This makes a pale shadow of all the others. Words are too soft for some delights . . . coloured seas and ten million gramophones.

23 SEPTEMBER

There is sometimes too much indiscretion. In a hostile world, a scandal would be dangerous. We cannot ignore it. The raking danger I can sometimes forget, but it returned with an unpleasant scare last week. A fool of a girl thought she might be pregnant. Fortunately it has passed over, but we cannot be too careful.

On the practical issue, Jack insisted that we think of buying the farm. There would be great advantages from every point of view. Jack is certain it could be made to pay. It would make discretion easier. And I insist we have a right to our own world, unspied on and in peace of mind.

Also we must have money. Perhaps I have neglected it too long.

1 OCTOBER

Last night I crawled the pubs in the town. I don't remember ever doing this before. I have always kept these steam-blowing episodes for Nottingham. But what obligations do I owe Eden, after all? After my nine years' servitude.

Anyway, Roy Calvert and I and — (a young man in the group) got drunk and started home. By the post office we saw K. She hurried cringing down a side street. I stopped her. 'Yes – I know, you're drunk,' she said. The vision passed; and I was walking wildly, yelling with Roy, cheering – as we ran round the lamp-posts and crossed the streets.

Through 1931 the diary showed him more and more engrossed with Daphne, although it was not till the middle of the year that he broke off finally from Freda. The references to the purchase of the farm were continued: 'We have to go ahead. I have no alternative.' ... 'I propose to leave the whole business in Jack's charge, far more than I did the agency. There is no reason to occupy myself unnecessarily with it, now it is started, I have better things to do.' These entries both occurred in the autumn of 1931; after that time, during the nine months down to the last entry in my hands, he did not mention the farm business again.

I was forced to compare this silence with the long arguments to himself about the agency; I turned back to those pages which had given Daphne a reason for coming:

16 DECEMBER 1928

Tonight I went over the figures of the first month's business under the new regime (i.e. of the agency). They are satisfactory, and we shall be able to pay our way – but I still find the difficulty which has puzzled me before.*

*There was no previous reference in the diary to this 'difficulty'.

16 JANUARY 1929

The agency is going well. Our profits are up by 10 per cent in the first month. At last Jack is justifying my faith in him (how it would have changed things if he had followed my advice four years ago and entered a profession. Even now I still feel I was right. I should not be fretted by this uneasiness which I cannot quite put aside).

17 JANUARY 1929

I cannot bear this difficulty any longer. There is no doubt that Martineau's statement of the circulation was fantastically exaggerated. On seeing our own figures there is no doubt at all. We are doing better business than they ever did; and we have not disposed of 1,100 copies of the wretched rag. This puts me in a false position. It devolves upon me to consider what is right for the three of us to do.

If I were to be censorious with myself, I should regret not acting on my earlier suspicions. I was amazed by the figure when Martineau first told me. But after all, I had his authority. What reasons could possess him, of all men, to deceive me? There was no justification for inquiring further. I was within every conceivable right in using his statement to help raise our money. There was one period when I came near to investigating the entire matter – that night, a fortnight before we actually completed the purchase, when I mentioned the circulation to Jack and Olive. Jack laughed, and would not explain himself. Olive said nothing. I began to take steps that night; but then it seemed unnecessary, and I decided to go ahead. I can still feel justified that I was right.

After all, what is the present position? We have borrowed money for a business. We have placed information about the business in front of those we persuaded to lend. All that information was given us on the best of authority; we transmitted it, having every rational ground to consider it true. Most of it was true; on one rather inconsiderable fact, it turns out that we were misled ourselves.

It would be an untenable position, of course, if this accidental misrepresentation had been a cause of loss to our creditors. That providentially is the converse of the actual state of affairs. Our creditors are safely receiving their money, more safely than through any similar investment I can imagine. They have done pretty well for themselves.

So what is to be done? There seems only one answer. No one is losing; for everyone's sake we must go on as we are. I do not consider it necessary to raise the subject with Jack. I have disposed of the moments of uneasiness. My mind is at rest.

18 JANUARY 1929

I am now able to feel that the difficulty is resolved. But there is one problem which I cannot settle. Why ever should Martineau have made a false statement in the first place? Can it have been deliberate? It seems unthinkable. I remember his curious manœuvres about Morcom's flat just before he left the firm. But I could not believe that was done from selfish motives; still more I cannot believe anything so ridiculous of him now. After all, he did not touch a penny of the price we paid. He went straight off to his incredible settlement. Since then he has scarcely had a shilling in his pocket.

I suppose he was simply losing his grip on the world, and it is useless to speculate as though he were a rational being.

As soon as I read George's words, I did not doubt that his account of Martineau's statement was true. I wondered what Martineau had really meant; whatever underlay it all, his evidence might be essential now. On the whole, though, I was more distressed than before I knew as much.

Two things struck me most. George had certainly suspected the statement while they were still borrowing money; he had managed to shelve his misgivings for a time. Then at last he put his 'mind at rest'. I was not altogether surprised by his self-explanation; but it became full of meaning when we compared it to his silence over the farm.

He believed himself caught accidentally in a fog of misrepresentation over the agency – what about the other business? I could not help but imagine – was it something he could not reconcile himself to? Something he tried to dismiss from his thoughts?

And I knew what George's feeling for Jack had now become. The mention of the circulation, and Jack's laughter; George afraid, when struggling with his doubt, to speak to Jack again – those hints endowed some of George's words with an ironic, an almost intolerable pathos:

'It devolves on me to consider what is right for the three of us to do.'

CHAPTER XXXI

CONFIDENTIAL TALK IN EDEN'S DRAWING-ROOM

I READ the diary all evening. At dinner Eden and I were alone, and he was kindly and cordial. We went into the drawing-room afterwards; he built up the fire as high as it had been the night of Morcom's slip; he pressed me to a glass of brandy.

Here I have to enter into a conversation which I reported, more subjectively, in a part of my own story.

'How do you feel about yesterday?' he said at length.

'It looks none too good,' I said.

'I completely agree,' he said deliberately, with a friendly smile to mark my judgment and to recognise bad news. 'As a matter of fact, I've been talking to Hotchkinson about it during the afternoon. We both consider we shall be lucky if we can save those young nuisances from what, between ourselves, I'm beginning to think they deserve. But I don't like to think of their getting it through the lack of any possible effort on our part. Don't you agree?'

'Of course,' I said. He was sitting back comfortably now, his voice smooth and friendly, as though I was a client he liked, but to whom he had to break bad news. He was sorry, and yet buoyed up by the subdued pleasure of his own activity.

'Well then, that's what Hotchkinson and I have been considering. And we wondered whether you ought to have a little help. You're not to misunderstand us, young man. I'd as soon trust a case to you as anyone of your age, and Hotchkinson believes in you as well. Of course, you were a trifle over-optimistic imagining you might get a dismissal in the police court, but we all make our mistakes, you know. This is going to be a very tricky case, though. It's not going to be just working out the legal defence. If it was only doing that in front of a judge, I'd take the responsibility of leaving you by yourself, if they were my own son and daughter. But this looks like being one of those cases where the legal side isn't so important –' he chuckled – 'and it'll be a matter of making the best of a bad job with the jury. That's the snag.'

'Almost all my work's been in front of juries.'

'Of course it has. You'll have plenty more. But you know, as we all know, that they're very funny things. And in this case I should say from my experience of them that they'll be prejudiced against your people – simply because they're of the younger generation and one or two stories will slip out that they've gone the pace at times—'

'That's obviously true.'

'Well, I put it to Hotchkinson that they'd be even more prejudiced, if their counsel was the same kind of age and a brilliant young man. They'd resent all the brilliance right from the start, Eliot. You'd only have to make a clever suggestion, and they'd distrust you. They'd be jibbing from all the good qualities of your generation – as well as the bad, but they'd find the bad all right. The racketiness that's been the curse of these days – they'd find that and they'd count it against them in spite of anything you said. Anything you could say would only make it worse.'

'What do you suggest?' I said.

'I want you to stay in the case. You know it better than anyone already, and we can't do without you. But I believe, taking everything into consideration, you ought to have someone to lead you.'

'Who?'

'I was thinking of your old chief – Getliffe.'

'It's sensible to get someone,' I broke out, 'but Getliffe – seriously, he's a bad lawyer.'

'No one's a hero to his pupils, you know,' said Eden.

I persisted:

'I dare say I'm unfair. But this is important. There are others who'd do it admirably.' I gave some names of senior counsel.

'They're clever fellows,' said Eden, smiling as when we argued about George. 'But I don't see any reason to go beyond Getliffe. He's always done well with by cases.'

When I was alone, I was surprised that my disappointment should be so sharp. There was little of my own at stake, a brief in a minor case – for which, of course, I had already refused to be paid. Yet, when it was tested through Eden's decision, I knew – there is no denying the edge of one's unhappiness – that I was more wounded by the petty rebuff than by the danger to my friends.

I was ashamed that it should be so. But for some hours I could think of little else. Despite the anxieties of the case, the chances of Jack running, their immediate fate: despite being present at a time when George needed all the strength of a friend. Often, in the last days, I had lain awake, thinking of what would happen to him. But tonight I was preoccupied with my own vanity.

I went to London next morning and saw Getliffe. He said, alert, bright-eyed and glib after skimming through the documents:

'You worked with Eden once, of course.'

'I know him well,' I said.

'You've seen this case he's sent us?'

'I've watched it through the police court,' I answered.

'Well, L.S.,' his voice rose, 'it'll be good fun working together again. It's been too long since we had a duet, I'm looking forward to this.'

The preparation of the case gave me a chance to be more thorough than if I had been left alone. For there was the need to sit with Getliffe, to bully him, to ignore his complaints that he would get it up in time, to make him aggrieved and patronising. At any cost, he must not go into court in the way I had seen him so often, flustered, with no more than a skipped reading, a half-memory behind him, relying in a badgered and uncomfortable way on his inventive wits, completely determined to work thoroughly in his next case, fidgeting and yet getting sympathy with the court – somehow, despite the mistakes, harassment, carelessness, sweating forehead and nervous eyes, keeping his spirits and miraculously coming through.

I kept the case before him. He was harder-working than most, but he could not bear any kind of continuity. An afternoon's work after his own pattern meant going restlessly through several briefs, picking up a recognition-symbol here and there, so that, when a solicitor came in and mentioned a name, Getliffe's eyes would be bright and intelligent – 'You mean the man who—'

He left me to collect the witnesses. One of my tasks was to trace Martineau; it took a good deal of time. At last I found a workhouse master in the North Riding, who guffawed as I began to inquire over the telephone.

'You mean Old Jesus,' he said. 'He's often been in here.' He added: 'He doesn't seem mad. But he must be right off his head.'

He was able to tell me where 'that crowd' had settled now.

I returned to the town at the weekend. I had not been back an hour before Roy rang up to say that Jack seemed to have disappeared. For a day or two he had been talking of a 'temporary expedition' to Birmingham, to survey the 'prospects' for a new business as soon as the trial was over. Today no one could find him.

A few minutes after the call, Roy brought Olive and Rachel to Eden's house. For the whole afternoon Eden left us to ourselves.

Rachel was desperately worried. Roy also believed that Jack had flown. Of us all, Olive alone was unshaken.

'If you knew him better,' she said, 'you'd know that he fooled himself with his excuses – as well as you. He's really planning a new business. And he also thinks it's a good dodge for getting a few miles away.'

'He needn't stop there,' said Roy.

'I don't believe he's gone near Birmingham,' said Rachel.

'I think you'll find he has,' said Olive.

'I know I'm thinking of George all the time,' cried Rachel. 'We've got to sit by and watch Jack ruin him. And Olive, it's wretched to see you—'

'Go on.'

'I must speak now. I know it's hopeless,' Rachel went on. 'But if only you could see Jack for a minute just as we do—'

'You think he's a scoundrel. That he doesn't care a rap for me. And that he'll marry me because he can't get money some other way. Is that what you mean?' Before Rachel replied Olive added: 'Some of it's quite true.'

'You don't know what a relief it would be – to get you free of him,' Rachel said. 'Is there any chance? When this is over?'

'None,' said Olive. After a moment, she said: 'I don't care what you think of how much he's attached to me. But I'll tell you this. He knows he can live on my money. He may be forced to marry me in the end. But I shall be happier about the arrangement than he will. There'll be times when he's bound to think that I'm dragging him down. He's got more illusions than I have. You've got to persuade yourselves of that.'

Rachel tried to argue with her. She did not resent the obvious pretences and attempts to console her. She said, with a genuine smile: 'It's no use talking. You'll never believe a word I say.'

Rachel once more begged her to trace Jack – 'we can't let George be thrown away,' she cried.

Then the maid announced another visitor for me and Morcom came in. First he caught sight of Roy, and said:

'I can't find any news.'

At that moment, he saw Olive.

'I'm sorry. They didn't tell me—'

'Come and sit by the fire,' she said.

He sat down and spread out his hands. His face looked ill with care. We all knew that this was the first time they had met for months.

In her presence he would not say what he had come for. Roy talked more easily for a few minutes than anyone there could manage: then he took Rachel away.

Olive said to Morcom:

'You're not looking well, Arthur. You must take care of yourself.'

'I'm all right.'

'Promise me you'll look after yourself.'

'If I can,' said Morcom. Their manner to each other was still sometimes tender. Some casual remark made them smile together, and their faces, in that moment, rested in peace.

Soon Olive could not control her restlessness. She crossed to the window, and looked out into the dark; she returned to her chair again, and then got up to go. Her eyes caught the brief lying on the writing-desk. She pointed to the words on the first page – Rex *v.* Passant and Ors.

'Is that us?' She was laughing without any pretence. 'I've never seen anything that looked – so far away.'

She stood still for a moment, and said goodbye. She put her hand on the back of Morcom's chair:

'Goodbye,' she said again.

As soon as the door closed, Morcom said:

'I came to say – you must force George to escape.'

'You think Jack has really gone?'

'I don't know. I advised him to.'

I broke out in angry recriminations, though as he spoke his face was torn with pain. I reminded him of my warning the night of the first inquiries: and how, after the police court, we agreed that I could not tell George to go.

'It's criminal to take the responsibility of persuading Jack – unless George was ready too,' I said.

'I had to speak,' said Morcom.

'You could not face telling me first.'

'Don't you understand that I was bound to speak to Jack?' Morcom said. 'You said I ought to have taken care of them before it happened. Do you think this was any more bearable? It means they will marry. They will stay abroad for years. They will be left with nothing but their own resources. That's what she longs for, isn't it? I've had to try to help it on.'

I looked at him.

'Will you tell George to go now?' he said at last.

'I shall have to try,' I said.

CHAPTER XXXII

VISIT TO GEORGE

I TOOK a taxi to George's lodgings. He was alone, sitting in the same chair, the same position, as in the evening after the police court. He must have heard the taxi drive up outside, but he did not inquire why I had hurried.

He tried to stir himself for my benefit, however. Though his voice was flat, he asked after Sheila with his old friendly diffident politeness; he talked a little of a case that I had just finished in London.

Then I said:

'What do you think of our case, George?'

'It's gone more or less as I expected.'

'Has it?'

George nodded without any protest.

I hesitated.

'Look, George,' I said. 'I'm going to offend you. You'll have to forgive me. I don't care what has actually happened in this business. You know that perfectly well. I can't imagine any action you could do which would make the slightest difference to me. It wouldn't either make me think worse of you or better – it works both ways. Well, I don't know what's happened, you may be technically guilty or you may not, I don't know and, apart from curiosity, I don't care. You've told me you're not.' I met his eyes. 'I know you tell the literal truth more than most of us – but even so, I can imagine all sorts of reasons why you should lie here.'

He gave a resentful, awkward laugh.

'So I've got nothing to do with what really happened,' I said. 'The essential thing is what other people will think happened. That's all. I'm just talking as a lawyer about the probabilities in this case. You know them, you're a better lawyer than I am, of course, whenever you care. What should you say the probabilities are?'

'So far, they're not much in our favour.'

'If you came to me as a client,' I said, 'I shouldn't be as optimistic as that.'

I went on: 'Anyway, supposing you're right, supposing the chances were even or a bit better – ought you to risk it? If it comes down the wrong side—'

'We get a few months. And the consequences—'

'Is the risk worth taking?'

'What do you mean?'

'Jump your bail. I've spoken to the others who put up money. We all want you to please yourself.'

'What should I do?'

'You could be in South America in a fortnight. Nothing will touch you there, in this sort of case.'

There was a silence.

'I don't see how I'm going to live.'

'We can provide a bit. It won't be much, God knows – but it'd help you in a place where living's cheap. And in time it would be possible to make a little money.'

'It would be difficult.'

'Not impossible. You could get qualified there – if there's nothing else.'

'I should never have any security.'

'Think of the alternative.'

'No,' George burst out, in a loud, harsh, emphatic tone. 'I'm afraid it's completely impracticable. I appreciate the offer, of course.' (That 'of course' of George's which, as so often, was loaded with resentment.) 'But it's ludicrous to consider it. Apart from the practical obstacles – I should have to live in discomfort all my life, it isn't pleasant to condemn oneself to squalid exile.'

He added:

'And there's the question of the others.'

'I was coming to that.'

'Well?'

'Olive could go with a clear conscience. Her uncle's wealthy, she has enough to live on.'

He did not reply.

'I'll promise to readjust things with the others so that you won't have any responsibility,' I said. 'You come first. It's more serious for you. You stand to lose most. For me – I needn't tell you – you count very much the most.'

There was a silence before George replied:

'I appreciate the offer. But I can't take it.'

'There is one other thing,' I said.

'What?' His voice had returned to the lifeless tone with which he welcomed me.

'Jack may have gone already.'

'Are you inventing that to get rid of me?'

'I didn't want to tell you,' I said. 'But you've seen some indications, surely?'

'I didn't take them seriously.'

'This you must,' I said.

'I want to know exactly what basis you're going on.'

I told him the facts – that Olive believed Jack would return to stand his trial: that no one else did.

'If he doesn't,' I said, 'you recognise what your chances are?'

'Yes,' said George.

His face was heavy as he thought.

'I don't necessarily accept the view that he won't come back,' he said. 'But if he doesn't – I can't alter my position. I shan't go.'

'For God's sake think it over,' I said. 'We'll make it as easy for you as we humanly can.'

He was silent.

'I've a right to ask you to think it over tonight,' I said. 'I beg you to.'

'I'm sorry. There is no point in that,' George said. 'I shall stay here and let them try me.'

PART FOUR

THE TRIAL

CHAPTER XXXIII

COURTROOM LIT BY A CHANDELIER

THE morning of the trial was dark, and all over the town lights shone in the shop-windows. In front of the old Assize Hall, a few people had gathered on the pavement, staring at the policemen on the steps.

It was still too early. I walked into the entrance hall, which was filling up. George came in: when, after a moment, he saw me in the crowd of strangers, his face became suddenly open and bewildered.

'There are plenty of people here,' he said.

We stood silently, then began to talk about the news in the morning papers. In a few minutes we heard a call from inside which became louder and was repeated from the door.

'Surrender of George Passant! Surrender of George Passant!'

George stared past me, buttoned his jacket, smoothed down the folds.

'Well, I'll see you later,' he said.

In the robing-room Getliffe was sitting in his overcoat taking a glance at his brief. As I came in, he stood up hurriedly.

'Time's getting on,' he said. 'We must be moving.'

I helped him on with his gown; he chatted about Eden.

'Pleasant old chap, isn't he? Not that he's as old as all that. He must be this side of sixty. You know, L.S., I was thinking last night. First of all I was surprised he has been contented to sit in a second-rate provincial town all his life – and then I realised one could be very happy here. Just limiting yourself, knowing what you've got to do, knowing you're doing a useful job which doesn't take too much out of you. And then going away from it and remembering you're a human being. Clocking in and clocking out.'

He was speaking more breathlessly than in normal times. This nervousness before a case – which he had never lost – was mainly a physical malaise, a flutter of the hands, a catch in the voice: perhaps it had once been more, but now it was worn down by habit. He was putting on his wig, which, although it was faintly soiled, at once gave his face a greater distinction. He stared at himself in the mirror; his bands were awry, he was still a little dishevelled, but he turned away with a furtive, satisfied smile.

'All aboard,' he said.

He led the way into court. Olive and George were in the dock, looking towards the empty seats on the bench, which spread in a wide semi-circle round the small, high, dome-shaped room. It had been re-painted since the July afternoon when George won a verdict in it; otherwise I noticed no change.

We came to our places, two or three steps beyond the dock; I turned and glanced at it. Jack was not there. I heard Porson, the leader for the prosecution, in court ten minutes early, greet Getliffe, in a rich, chuckling voice: I found myself anxious about nothing except that Jack should appear for the trial.

The gallery was nearly full. The case had already become a scandal in the town. Suddenly, I heard the last call for Jack and saw him walk quickly towards the dock. The judge entered, the indictment was read, they pleaded. George's voice sounded loud and harsh, the others' quiet.

'You may sit down, of course,' the judge said. His eyes were dark, bright and inquisitive in a jowled, broad face. There was only a small bench in the dock, barely enough for three. 'Why are there no chairs for them? Please fetch chairs.' His voice was kindly but precise.

The voice of the clerk swearing the jury fell distantly on my ears, deafened by habit. I looked round the courtroom. Eden was sitting upstairs, near the benches set aside for the Grand Jury; Cameron, the Principal of the School, had a place close by. Beddow, the chairman of that meeting over seven years before, bustled in, fresh and cheerful, to an alderman's seat. In the small public space behind the dock, several of George's friends were sitting, Mr Passant among them; Roy Calvert was looking after Mr Passant, and stayed at his side throughout the trial.

Just before Porson opened, a note was brought to me from Morcom. 'They say I've just missed rheumatic fever. There is nothing to worry about, but I can't come.' That was all. I kept looking at it; the oath had reached the last man on the jury. In the diffused light of the winter morning, added to by the single chandelier of bulbs hanging over our table, our fingers made shadows with a complex pattern of penumbra, and faces in the court were softened.

The case for the prosecution took up the first two days. It went worse for us than we feared.

Porson's opening was strong. From the beginning he threatened us with George's statement over the circulation of the *Arrow*.

'We possess a piece of evidence that no one can deny,' he said. He drew everyone's attention to a sheet of notepaper which was to be produced at the proper time. He concentrated much of his attack on the agency; then he pointed out how, when they had 'obtained some practice' in their methods, George and the others had gone 'after bigger game'. The Farm business needed larger sums, but they had found it easy to misrepresent what its true position was. 'They didn't trouble to change their methods,' said Porson. 'They had learned after their little experience with the *Arrow* that it was child's play to give false figures. This time they needed larger sums, and you will hear how they obtained them from Miss Geary, Mrs Stuart and—'

He finished by telling the jury that he would produce a witness, Mrs Iris Ward, who would describe an actual meeting at the farm when the three of them decided they must buy it – 'decided they must buy it not only as a business, but because they had reasons of their own for needing somewhere to live in private, out of reach of inquisitive eyes'.

Porson did as he threatened.

The only point which Getliffe scored was made before lunch on the first morning. One of the witnesses over the agency, a man called Attock, said that, before he lent Jack money, he had looked over all the figures of the firm with an accountant's eye. He was a masterful, warm-voiced man, with a genial, violent laugh: Getliffe saw through him, and brought off an ingenious cross-examination. In the end, Getliffe revealed him as a man always priding himself on his shrewdness and losing money in unlikely ventures: and as one who had never managed to finish his accountant's examinations.

At lunch on that first day, Jack and Olive were more composed than before the trial. Even George, sunk in a despondency which surprised those who remembered his optimism but did not know him well, referred to Getliffe's handling of Attock.

It was, however, a false start. First thing in the afternoon, Porson produced the quiet kindly witness of the police court, who told the same story without a deviation. Then two more followed him, with the same account of the acquaintanceship with Jack, the meetings with George, the statement of the circulation of the *Arrow*. They testified to a statement written by George, which now, for the first time, Porson produced in court. It read:

'We are not in a position to give full figures of the Agency's business.

So far as we have examined the position they do not seem to exist. One important indication, however, we can state exactly. The advertising paper run by the Agency – *The Advertisers' Arrow* – has had an average circulation of five thousand per issue. This figure is given on the authority of Mr Martineau, now retiring from the firm.'

Porson gave the sheet of paper to the jury. They passed it round: at last it came to Getliffe and myself. It was as neatly written as a page from the diary. We knew there was no hope of challenging it.

Pertinaciously, good-temperedly, Getliffe worked hard. Questions tapped out in the room as the sky darkened through the lowering afternoon. The illuminated zone from the chandelier left the judge half in darkness. Getliffe did not shake any of the three witnesses. He tried to test their memory of figures by a set of numerical questions which he often used as a last resource. Several times, still good-tempered but harassed, he became entangled in names, that odd but familiar laxness of his – 'Mr Pass*more*,' he said, 'you say you were met by Mr Pass*more*.'

Then Porson called Exell, Martineau's partner in the agency. Getliffe, breathing hard, sweat running down the temples from under his wig, asked me to take him.

'You know, of course, the state of your business just before it was sold?' Porson was asking.

'Yes,' said Exell. He had grown almost bald since I last saw him, at the time of Martineau's departure.

'Was it at its most prosperous just then?'

'Nothing like it. Times had got worse,' said Exell.

'When was it at its most prosperous?'

'Just about the time that Mr Martineau entered it.'

'You would regard the circulation of your paper, the *Arrow*, as some indication of the state of the firm?'

'I'm not certain.' A series of questions followed, in which Porson tried to persuade him. He gave at last a rather unwilling and qualified assent.

'Now you have accepted that figure as an indication, I want to ask you – when did it reach its highest point?'

'At the time I told you. Seven years ago, nearly.'

'What was the circulation at the highest point?'

'Twelve hundred.'

'I should like you to repeat that. I should like the jury to hear you say that again. What was the circulation at the highest point?'

Exell repeated the words.

'There is just one thing else you might tell us, Mr Exell. The jury may find this important. We have been told this afternoon that the circulation at some time – never mind who told us or what the reason was – was estimated at five thousand. Was that ever a conceivable figure?'

'Never. I have told you the highest.'

'And just before the end it didn't rise for any reason?'

'It must have been lower.'

I tried everything I could invent. I asked him about the agency's books. Weren't they singularly carelessly kept? Hadn't he neglected them for years before Martineau joined him? Wasn't it Martineau's task to supervise the books during the months he was a partner? Wasn't it true that Exell could only have a vague knowledge of the agency's finances in general, this circulation in particular, during Martineau's time? Wasn't it true that he was always concerned – and his partner also – with activities outside the ordinary run of business? That Martineau was entirely preoccupied with religion? That Exell himself gave much time to eccentric causes – such as spiritualism and social credit? Wasn't it possible his estimate of the figure was simply a guess without any exact information? He was uneasy, but we gained nothing. His tone grew thinner and more precise. Once his eyes dropped in that mannerism of hampered truculence which in some men is like a child beginning to cry. He would not budge from his figure. 'Twelve hundred's correct,' he said.

When I had finished, Porson said: 'I want the jury to be certain of the figure, Mr Exell. First of all, you have no doubts whatever, despite anything that has been hinted?'

'No.'

'That's right. You have been telling us, with expert authority, the largest figure that the circulation can ever have reached. Now will you let the jury hear it again – for the last time?'

'Twelve hundred.'

As I left the court on that first night, Porson threw me a word, friendly, triumphant and assertive. I saw George hesitate in front of me; then Jack called him, and he walked away with the other two. Having dinner with acquaintances, I heard speculations going on, coolly and disinterestedly, over George and the others: I kept thinking of their evening together. It made me escape early, back to useless work on the case.

The farm evidence took up all the next day. It was heavy and suspicious, as Porson had promised, though there was nothing as clear as George's statement of the circulation. It was a story of Jack mixing in odd company, making friends, inspiring trust: meetings of his new friends with Olive and George: talk of the farm as a business, mention of accounts, figures on the table.

The stories fitted each other: Getliffe could not break any of them: it only needed those figures to be preserved for our last hope to go. But no one possessed a copy. Miss Geary, the witness who gave the sharpest impression of accuracy, said that in her presence no written figures had ever been produced; the whole transaction had been verbal. She obviously blamed herself for a fool, she was bitterly angry with Jack in particular, and she showed herself overfond of money. Yet I thought she inclined, even now, to the side of George and Jack when she was not entirely sure. Once or twice, certainly, she seemed pleased to put Porson off with a doubt.

Her very fairness, though, acted against us. And she was followed by Iris Ward, whom Porson kept to the last.

As her name was called 'Mrs Iris Ward! Mrs Iris Ward!' I caught sight of George's face. She had once been, before her marriage, an obscure member of his group; she was Mona's half-sister, but George had never paid much attention to her. Now he showed an anxiety and suffering so acute that it was noticed by many people in the court.

Her face was pleasant-looking, a little worn and tired. She was a year or two from thirty. She smiled involuntarily in a frank and almost naïve manner when Porson addressed her.

'Mrs Ward,' he began, 'did you hear Mr Passant and his friends talk about buying the farm?'

'I did.'

'When was this?'

'The last year I ever went there. I mean, to the farm itself. Nearly three years ago.'

'That is,' Porson remarked to the jury, 'ten months before the farm was actually bought. Can you describe the occasion for us?'

'I went over one Saturday evening.'

'Who was there?'

'Mr Passant, Mr Cotery, Miss Sands (Rachel)—' She gave several other names.

'Was Miss Calvert there?'

'No.'

'Can you tell us anything that was said at that meeting – about the transaction?'

'We were sitting round after supper. They were all excited. I think they had been talking before I arrived. Mr Cotery said: "It would be a good idea if we ran this place. So that we could have it to ourselves whenever we wanted it. We shan't be safe until we do." '

Porson stopped her for a moment: then he asked:

'What was said then?'

'Mr Passant said it would be useful if we could, but he didn't see how it could conceivably be managed. Mr Cotery laughed at him and called him a good old respectable member of the professional classes. "Haven't I got you out of that after all this time?" he said. "Of course it can be managed. Do you think I can't raise a bit of money for a good cause?" and he went on arguing with Mr Passant, saying it was for an absolutely essential cause. He said: "It takes all the pleasure away. And it's dangerous. I don't propose to stand the strain if you do. Just for the sake of a little money." '

Her voice was quiet, clear and monotonous. Everyone was believing her story. It sounded nothing like an invention: she seemed to draw on one of those minutely accurate memories, common among many people with an outwardly drab and uneventful life.

'What did Mr Passant say?'

'He argued for a while – he talked about the difficulties of raising the money. He said he didn't propose to find himself the wrong side of the law.'

Getliffe made a note. She continued:

'Mr Cotery said how easy it would be to raise the money. "You see," he said, "as soon as we own the place we can kill two birds with one stone. We can make a good deal of money out of it ourselves. It would be a good investment for the people we borrow from. And it's child's play persuading them. We've got all the cards in our hands. We've been here more often than everyone else put together. No one else knows how many people might use a hostel like this. We can tell people what it's possibilities are." '

'From that remark,' Porson said, 'you gathered Mr Cotery was suggesting they should give false information?'

'I can't say.'

'That's what you understood at the time, isn't it?'

'I'd rather not say. I may have got a wrong impression. I'm certain of what was said, though.'

'Very well. What happened afterwards?'

'Mr Cotery went on at Mr Passant. No one else said much. At last Mr

Passant said: "It would be magnificent! It will have to be done! I've respected my obligations long enough and they go on ignoring me. Besides, the suspense is wearing us down." '

'We are hearing about this suspense again. What suspense did they both mean?'

Getliffe objected. He was getting on better with the judge than Porson was, and had begun to play on Porson's truculence. He also knew that the case was important in Porson's career, which hadn't been a lucky one.

Porson turned to the judge. 'I have just supplied what the jury will consider a discussion of a future conspiracy. I wish to carry this line further.'

The judge smiled perfunctorily. 'You may ask the question.'

'What suspense did they mean?'

'He meant – they were afraid.'

'What of?'

'Some of their relations being discovered.'

'You had no doubt of that at the time?'

'None at all.'

Porson's tone was comradely and casual: 'You mean some of them had immoral relations with each other?'

'Is this necessary?' put in the judge. 'I take it you only want to demonstrate that they had a strong reason for attempting to get this farm to themselves? Surely you have asked enough to make the position clear.'

'I consider it's desirable to ask one or two more questions,' Porson said.

'I don't think I can let you proceed any further along this line,' the judge said.

'I wish to make the jury aware of certain reasons.'

'They will have gathered enough.'

'Under protest, I should like to ask one or two relevant questions.'

'Go on,' said the judge.

'Well, Mrs Ward. I shan't keep you long in the circumstances. Can you just tell us whether there was any change in the attitude of Mr Passant and his friends – the attitude of these people whom we have learned to call the *group* – when strangers came to the farm?'

The judge was frowning. Getliffe looked at him, half-rose, then did not object.

'There was a great deal of talk about discretion after the scares began.'

'What were these scares?'

'You may not ask that,' said the judge.

'I should like—'

'You may not ask that.'

Porson turned round to the witness-box.

'I hope the jury will have understood how afraid these people were of any discovery of their activities. Although I haven't been permitted to establish the point to my own satisfaction. However, perhaps I'm allowed to ask you whether you thought any of them, Mr Passant for example, were afraid of having their careers damaged if their activities came out?'

'I thought so.'

'Would you say any of them felt an even more compelling fear?'

'I can't answer that,' she said.

'Why can't you?'

'I'm not certain.'

All of a sudden, Porson was back in his seat, leaning against the bench, his legs crossed and his lids half over his eyes.

Getliffe cross-examined at length. She had left the School and George's company months before the farm was bought. This conversation was long before they made any attempt to raise money? She had not been in their confidence at the critical time? The conversation might have been utterly at random? Obviously this danger which had been so much stressed could not have been urgent – as they went on for months without acting on it?

She answered the questions as straightforwardly as Porson's; she did not seem either malicious or burdened by her responsibility. I had learned only a few random facts about her; she had become a Catholic since she married, the marriage was apparently happy, she now lived in the school house of a country grammar school. She had always been intimate with her half-sister, Mona. None of us understood her part in the trial.

Getliffe finished by a number of questions on the after-supper conversation. Had she never heard people making plans for the fun of it? Had she never made plans herself of how to get rich quick? Had she never even heard people speculating on how to commit the ideal murder? For a moment, her answers were less composed than at the direct and critical points. Then Getliffe asked her about George's remark: 'I don't propose to find myself the wrong side of the law.' 'You are quite certain that was said?' Getliffe said.

'Yes.'

'You believed it at the time?'

'It struck me as a curious remark to make.'

She replied to Porson's re-examination just as equably. Now, however, with people excited by the scandal, he raised several bursts of laughter: it was, for the first time, laughter wholly on Porson's side. It was a sound which George could not escape. A wind had sprung up, the windows rattled, and at times the sun shone in beams across the room; in that rich, mellow, domestic light the court grew more hostile through the afternoon.

CHAPTER XXXIV

DINNER PARTY AFTER A BAD DAY

As soon as the court adjourned, we heard a great deal of talk upon Iris Ward's evidence. Everyone who spoke to us seemed to have believed her account; there was a continuous stir of gossip and curiosity about the lives of George and his friends. They were disapproved of with laughter and excitement: people thought that Porson had been right to force a scandal into notice. 'He's won the case and shown them up at the same time,' someone said in my hearing.

Getliffe himself was unusually grave. He kept talking of Iris's evidence, and seemed both moved and despondent. He was anxious over the result, of course – but something else was taking hold of him.

Though we were to meet at Eden's house for dinner, he kept on talking in the robing-room long after the court had cleared. Then I went straight to George's and stayed for a couple of hours. The three of them were there alone; they had eaten every meal together since the trial began; only my presence tonight prevented an outburst of reproaches – my presence, and the state into which George had fallen.

He scarcely spoke or protested; yet, as his eyes saw nothing but his own thoughts, his face was torn with suffering – just as when he heard the call for Iris Ward.

When Jack spoke now, he assumed that George would obey. Only once did George make an effort to show himself their leader still. He heard me say that Martineau, who had promised to be in the town by that afternoon, had still not arrived. George stirred himself: 'I insist on your tracing him at once. I tried to make Getliffe realise that it was essential to keep in touch with Martineau – on the one occasion when Getliffe spared me a quarter of an hour. He didn't trouble to recognise that my opinion was more valuable than theirs.' He looked at the other two.

When I returned to Eden's house, I rang up Canon Martineau, to ask if he had any news of his brother: and also Martineau's housekeeper in his old house in the New Walk. Neither had heard from him.

As I hurried downstairs to Eden's drawing-room, there came a jolly and whole-hearted peal of laughter. Eden and Getliffe were waiting for me, glasses of sherry standing by their chairs on the broad rail by the fireside. I was five minutes late for dinner, and Eden was a little put out; though, when I said that I had been trying to find Martineau, he smiled at Getliffe's jokes at my expense.

Getliffe, so dejected at the end of the afternoon, was in high spirits now, and as we sat down to dinner Eden looked at him with a broad and happy smile. He enjoyed entertaining him. He liked the reflection of the busy and successful world, and also the glow that Getliffe brought to so many people. With an aftertaste of envy, not unpleasant or bitter, Eden at times insisted on his own travels and tastes.

'I want you to try another wine,' he said, 'I brought it from a place just behind Dijon when I was there – why! it must be five or six years ago.'

Getliffe said: 'One doesn't ask any better than this, you know.' He took a gulp at his glass.

'I don't want you to miss the other,' said Eden. 'I can't let you leave without having something a little unusual.'

'Yours to command,' Getliffe answered.

Getliffe held his glass up to the light.

'I could go on drinking that,' he said. Then he chuckled. 'When I think of all the wine in my ancient Inn I always think it's a shame that there are chaps like me – who could drink any of it and not be much the wiser. But as for this you've given us – well, L.S., you and I can tell our host that if he gives us nothing worse we don't care who's getting amongst the bottles at out respective ancient halls.'

'I've got up another bottle,' Eden said. 'We must finish it before the night's over.' He talked contentedly on, though he looked at me once with kindly concern. 'Those days' came in often, he told stories of counsel he had met at the Assizes, men of the generation in front of Getliffe's. They listened to each other with enjoyment; Getliffe began telling anecdotes about judges. 'That reminds me,' he said, in a few minutes. 'It reminds me of the best remark ever made by a judicial authority within the Empire of His Britannic Majesty. It was actually made by the

Chief Justice of a not unimportant Colony, you understand. He was delivering judgment. You must guess the sort of case for yourself when you've heard the remark. He said, "*However* inclement the weather, His Majesty's police stations must in no circumstances be used for the purpose of fornication".'

Getliffe was still contented with the joke when we returned to the drawing-room. Then he and Eden found another pleasure in talking of London streets, dark during the war.

'I remember going across to the Inn one night when I was home on leave,' said Getliffe.

'I had to go up to see one of your men in the Temple,' Eden replied, 'it must have been the same year.'

'We might have run across each other,' said Getliffe. 'Perhaps we did for all you know.'

At last I could not help coming back to the trial.

On the instant Getliffe's face was clouded.

'I'm worried,' he said. 'I don't mind saying I'm worried—'

Eden broke in:

'Of course we've noticed that it's on Eliot's mind. But I'm afraid I am going to forbid you to discuss it now. We are all exercised about it. I dare say it's specially so with Eliot, because he's been friendly with the three of them for a few years now—'

'I'm worried on their account,' said Getliffe. 'Of course, one likes to win one's cases – but they count more –' He looked at me. 'I'm asking you to believe that,' he said.

'You mustn't begin discussing it,' Eden continued. 'You must keep your minds off it tonight. I can't give either of you much advice, but I'm going to make sure that you follow this.'

His mouth was curved in a firm, kindly, gratified smile. But circumstances were too strong for him. He was himself rung up twice within half an hour. The second call was from Martineau, saying that he had arrived and would come round to Eden's house at ten o'clock. Seeing my relief, Eden said:

'Well, I didn't mean to let you worry tonight. I decided to guard you from some depressing news. But perhaps you'd better hear it now. That first conversation over the phone – it was with Cameron, the Principal at the School.'

'Yes?'

'He was just informing me, as a matter of courtesy, that if Passant couldn't deny the immorality stories, they would be obliged to dismiss him from the School. That applies, of course, whatever the result of the case.'

'I suppose you'd expect them to,' said Getliffe.

'You can't blame them,' said Eden. 'After all they're running an educational institution. They can't be too careful. They're entitled to say that Passant has abused a position of trust.'

I remembered George using exactly those words before the committee years ago: I remembered how he repudiated a suggestion by Jack in Nottingham that same night.

'Shall you get rid of him yourself?' said Getliffe.

Eden considered, and answered deliberately:

'I don't regard that as quite on the same footing. If he's convicted, of course, the question doesn't arise. But if you get them off, I don't think I should feel entitled to dismiss someone who's been found innocent in a court of law. It's true that his private life will have damaged the firm; but I set off against that the good solid work he's done for me in the past. I think, taking everything into account, I shall have to let him stay. Though naturally I shouldn't be able to give him so much responsibility. It would mean harder work than I want until I retire.'

'I must say, you're more tolerant than most of us would be,' said Getliffe. 'I respect you for it.' He broke off: 'As for getting them off, I don't know. We may as well try to find out what Martineau has to say.'

'He'll be here in half an hour,' said Eden.

'Can I get a word with him?' said Getliffe.

'It's not exactly correct, is it?' Eden was frowning.

'But if you're there? I've done it before, believe me.'

'I'd rather Hotchkinson was here too. But maybe in the circumstances there'll be no harm done.'

'Not that I hope for much,' Getliffe said.

'I'm beginning to be sorry I inflicted it on you,' said Eden.

'Never mind that. One's got to do one's job,' Getliffe said. Then he added: 'I wish one of you would tell me what those three were trying to do. It's getting me down.'

'I'm afraid it isn't very difficult. They wanted money to go the pace,' said Eden. 'They weren't the sort to keep within their means. It's a pity.'

'I should have thought they could have made it like the rest of us. If they were as keen on it as all that. Or do you mean, they didn't care a cherub's apron for the way the money comes? With all due respect, I don't see them quite that way. God knows, I don't think much of them—'

'I've sometimes thought,' said Eden, 'that the greatest single difference between our generation and theirs is the way we look at money. It doesn't mean anything like the same as it did when we were starting. You can't altogether blame them, when you look at the world that's coming.'

'That's not true,' I said, 'of two of them at least. George Passant always had strict views about financial honesty, though he throws his own money about. And Olive – she would be perfectly sensible and orthodox about it.'

'I've generally found that people who are loose morally – are loose the other way too,' said Eden.

'You're meaning Cotery was the centre of the piece?' Getliffe said to me.

'I've always rather taken to him,' Eden put in. 'He's a bit weak, that's all. He's the sort of man who'd have done well in different company. Somehow I can't see him just sweeping the other two along.'

'Can you, L.S.?' Getliffe said.

'As for Passant,' Eden went on, 'you've always had too high an opinion of him, you know. As you get older, you'll lose your illusions about human nature. I dare say he did have strict views about financial honesty – when people he disliked were making the money.'

'I believe,' I said, 'that he's been as ashamed of the money part as you would have been yourself.'

'I must say,' said Getliffe, 'that it makes more sense if you take our host's line. It looks as though Passant went in up to the neck right at the beginning. He had no sooner talked to this man Martineau than he was ready to cook his figures. It doesn't leave you much to stand on, L.S.'

I told him, as I had done before, that I believed George's own account; somehow Martineau had let him take away the idea of a large circulation. We had already arranged for him to press this story of George's when Martineau gave evidence. At first Getliffe had welcomed it as a glimmer of hope: tonight he did not pretend to accept it.

'There's only one chance of excusing them that I've been able to believe in,' said Eden. 'That is, Martineau may have been vague when Passant approached him. You must remember he was slightly eccentric at the time. You'll see for yourself soon. You'll find him a very likeable fellow, of course. But, you know, I've been trying to keep that doubt in their favour – and, between ourselves, I can't credit it for a minute. Martineau was always a bit queer – but he was the sharpest man on money matters I ever knew. It's very peculiar, but there – there's nowt as odd as fowk. I don't believe he had it in him not to know exactly what the paper was doing – even if he was going to give it away.'

'And if he was vague – you can't really console yourself with that,' said Getliffe. 'There's too much difference altogether. Passant would have to misunderstand on purpose.'

For a time they talked about the farm. 'If I'd been Porson, I should have given us more of that little business. Just our friends raising money, that's all,' said Getliffe.

Just before ten, I went up to my room. I heard Martineau being received below a few minutes afterwards. Getliffe had told me to be ready to join the interview; nearly an hour passed, but they did not send for me. At last footsteps sounded on the stairs. I opened my door, and from below heard Eden saying: 'Good-bye, Howard. We shall see you tomorrow, then.'

I went back into my room, and walked up and down, unable to keep still. On his way to bed, Getliffe looked in.

'It wasn't worth while bringing you down. I didn't get anywhere,' he said. He looked jaded and downcast.

'What happened?'

'I couldn't get anything out of him.'

'Did you tell him Passant's story? Did you let him see that some of us believe it?'

'I went as far as anyone could,' said Getliffe.

'Shall I see him?'

'I told him you'd satisfied yourself about Passant's version. I tried to make him believe I had too. But' – Getliffe's voice was tired – 'he simply didn't seem interested. He didn't remember it very well. It was all hazy. He couldn't have told Passant anything but the real figures. Even though he didn't have any recollection of it now.'

'You mean, he's going to deny Passant's story?'

'As near as makes no matter,' said Getliffe. 'All I can do is try to make him say that he's forgotten.' He added: 'I never thought Passant's side of it would hold water for a minute.'

CHAPTER XXXV

THE PARK REVISITED

AFTER Getliffe left me, I tried to read. Then I heard the front-door bell ring below: it was just before midnight. There was a long delay: the bell rang again. A maid scampered down the stairs. In a moment a heavy tread ascended towards my door. George came in.

'Has Martineau been?'

'Yes.'

'What did he say?'

'I didn't meet him.'

'Why not?'

'He saw Getliffe,' I said. 'Getliffe couldn't get anything out of him. It seems – unpromising.'

'I must see him tonight,' said George. 'I should like you to come too.'

It was the first time George had visited me since the inquiries began. For weeks before the trial he had scarcely left his lodgings. Now his angry questions seemed like life stirring in him again – but a frightening, persecuted life. As we walked from Eden's house into the town, he said twice: 'I tell you I must see him tonight.' He said it with an intensity such as I had never heard from him before.

Since the preliminary inquiries he had shown only rare moments of anything like open fear. Instead, he had been sunk into the apathetic despair which many of us had noticed. For much of the time, he was shut away from any other person. He had been living with his own thoughts; often with reveries of the past, the meetings of the group at the farm; 'justifications' still came to his mind, and even sensual memories. In his thoughts he sometimes did not escape quite trivial shames, of 'looking a fool' to himself.

But tonight he could no longer look inwards. His thoughts had broken open, and exposed him to nothing but fear.

George made for Martineau's old house. There was a light in what used to be the drawing-room: the housekeeper opened the door.

'I want to see Mr Martineau,' said George.

'He's not in yet. I'm waiting up for him,' she said.

'I'm afraid that it's essential for us to see him tonight,' said George. 'I shall have to wait.'

Then she recognised him. She had not seen him since the morning we came to bid Martineau good-bye.

'It's you,' she said. 'When I heard of your goings-on, I said that I always knew you'd driven him away.'

'I shall have to wait,' said George.

She kept her hand on the latch. She would not ask him into the drawing-room. 'I'm alone,' she said, 'and until he tells me, I can please myself who I let in—'

We argued; I tried to calm her, but she had brooded on losing Martineau all these years; she took her farcical revenge, and we had to wait outside in the raw night.

We walked up and down the end of the New Walk. From the park we could see the gate of Martineau's and the light in the drawing-room, just as we had done that night of Jack's confession.

George, his eyes never leaving the path to the house, began to talk. He had heard, not many minutes after Eden, of the intention to dismiss him from the School. It had leaked out through an acquaintance on the staff; his friends at the School already knew. Then I told him what Eden had said about his position in the firm. He hardly listened.

'You might as well see something. Another sheet of paper,' he said.

I had to light a match to read it. As the flame smoked, I thought of the other sheet of paper, the bill of the little plays which Jack had produced beside these trees. But he did not mean that. He meant the sheet of paper on which he had written down his statement on the circulation – the sheet of paper which lay before the court.

In the matchlight, I read some of this letter.

Dear George,

We are writing in the name of twelve people who have known you at the School, and who are indignant at the news tonight. We wish there was something we could do to help, but at least we feel that we cannot let another day go by without saying how much you have meant to us all. Whatever happens or is said, that cannot be taken away. We shall always remember it with gratitude. We shall always think of you as someone we were lucky to know. . . .

There were four signatures, including those of a young man I had met at the farm in September.

'They meant it,' I said.

'It's too late to be written to now,' said George. With desperate attention he still watched for Martineau. 'Though I don't entirely accept Jack's remarks on the letter.'

'What were they?'

'That the people who wrote it didn't realise that he and I weren't so very different nowadays—'

Without interest, George mentioned a quarrel over the letter. Jack had laughed at George's devotion to his protégés; he took it for granted, he expected George to take it for granted also, that it was just a camouflage to get closer to the women.

George was listening only for footsteps: he had no more thought for

Jack's remark. Yet he had resented it little – suddenly, in this park where he might have finished with Jack, I saw their relation more closely than I had ever done.

Jack's power over George had grown each year. It was not the result of ordinary affection or admiration. It did not owe much to the charm which Jack exercised over many people. At times, George actively disliked him. But now, in the middle of this night of fear, George submitted to having his aspirations mocked.

The fact was, from the beginning Jack had never believed in George's altruistic dreams. For a time – until he had been an intimate friend for years – Jack entered into them, and in George's company talked George's language. But it was always with a wink to himself; he judged George by the standard of his own pleasures; by instinct and very soon by experience he knew a good deal about the erotic life. He saw the sensual side of George's devotion long before George would admit it to himself. Jack thought none the worse of George, he took it as completely natural – but he was often irritated, sometimes morbidly provoked, by the barricade of aspirations. He had spoken of them tonight as 'camouflage'; he had never believed they could be anything else. As soon as George 'got down to business' – his affair with Freda – Jack showed that he both knew and had suspected it all along.

From then onwards, in their curious intimacy, George seemed to be almost eager to accept Jack's valuation – to throw away all 'pretence' and to share his pleasures with someone who was a rake, gay, frank, and unashamed.

That mixture of intimacy and profound disbelief was at the root of Jack's power over George. George was paying a sort of spiritual black-mail. He was, in a fashion, glad to pay it. Very few men, the Georges least of all, are secure in their aspirations; it takes someone both intimate and unsympathetic to touch one's own doubts – to give one, for part of one's life at least, the comfort of taking oneself on the lowest terms. At times we all want someone to destroy our own 'ideals'. We are ready to put ourselves in the power of a destructive, clear-eyed and degrading friend.

The light in the drawing-room went out. Immediately George ran to the house, rang the bell, hammered on the door.

'Where is Mr Martineau? I've got to see him,' he shouted. His voice echoed round the road.

A light was switched on in the hall. The housekeeper opened a crack of door, and said:

'He's not coming home tonight.'

'Let me in,' George shouted.

'He's rung up to say he's sleeping somewhere else.'

She did not know where, or would not say. I thought she was speaking the truth, and did not know.

George and I were left outside the dark house.

'Why didn't you see Martineau? Why wasn't I sent for myself?' George cried.

Afraid also, I tried to give him reasonable answers.

'Getliffe was absolutely clear on the importance. We were talking about it at dinner.'

'With Eden?'

'Yes.'

'Do you think I'm going to be deluded for ever? You can't expect me to believe that Eden is devoted to my welfare. I tell you, I insist on being certain that Getliffe is aware of the point at issue. And that someone whom I can trust must be present with Getliffe and Martineau when this point is being made. You ought to see that I'm right to insist on that. Are *you* going to desert me now?'

'You don't believe we've missed anything so obvious,' I said 'I know Getliffe was going to ask Martineau about the figure. He's very good at persuading people to say what he wants them to say. It's his chief—'

'And he doesn't think that he's persuaded Martineau?'

'No.'

'Don't you admit he would if there had been any serious attempt on my behalf? You come to me saying he's so good – and then apparently he wasn't interested enough to get the one essential piece of information. And then you think I ought not to insist that he's taken every step to get it.'

'It's no use—'

'You know what depends on it,' George cried. 'Do you think I don't know what depends on it?'

'We all know that.'

'But none of you will lift a finger,' he said. 'I'm beginning to realise why Eden imported Getliffe—'

'That's nonsense.'

'I'm not going to listen to that sort of defence. There's one thing more precious than all your feelings,' he shouted. 'It's got to be settled tonight.'

'What do you want to do?'

'I want to hear Getliffe and Martineau discuss the figure of the circulation. With you and myself present.'

I repeated the arguments: it had all been done. We did not know where Martineau was. He attacked me with bitterness and violence. At last, he said:

'I knew you would do nothing. I can't expect any help.'

We argued again. He began to repeat himself. He accused me of taking everyone's side against him. Nothing I said could bring him even a moment's relief.

CHAPTER XXXVI

MARTINEAU'S DAY IN TOWN

When I turned out of —— Street towards the court next morning, George and Martineau were standing on the pavement, outside a newspaper shop. Martineau cried:

'Ah, Lewis! You see I've come! I ran up against old George two minutes ago!' His cheeks were sunburnt and half-hidden by a rich brown beard. His skin was wrinkled with laughter, and his eyes looked clear and bright. In George's presence his gaiety was oppressive; I began a question about his evidence, but he would not reply; I asked quickly about the journey, how did he travel, how was the 'settlement'?

'They're shaking down,' he said. 'Soon they will be able to do without me. I might be justified in making a move—'

To my astonishment, George laughed; not easily – by the sound alone, one would have known him to be in distress – and yet with a note of genuine amusement.

'You don't mean that you are going to start again?'

'I'm beginning to feel I ought, after all.'

'What ought you to do? What more can you do along those lines? There's simply nothing left for you to give up—'

'It doesn't seem to me quite like that—' Martineau began.

I had to leave them, as I saw Getliffe climbing the hall steps.

The court was not so full as the afternoon before. Getliffe opened, and from his first words everyone felt that he was worried and dispirited. He told the jury more than once that 'it may be difficult for you to see your way through all the details. We all feel like that. Even if you've been forced to learn a bit of law, you often can't see the wood for the trees.

You've got to remember that a few pieces of suspicion don't make a proof.'

Much of his speech was in that dejected tone.

The first witnesses before lunch were customers of the advertising agency. Getliffe's questions did not go beyond matters of fact; he was untidy and restless; several times he took off his wig and the forelock fell over his brows. Porson, resting back with his eyes half-closed, did not cross-examine.

As I met the three at lunch, Jack said:

'How was that?'

'He's trying to begin quietly, and go all out in the last speech. It's his common-man technique,' I said.

Olive looked into my face.

'Why are you lying?' she cried. 'Is it as bad as that?'

Jack said:

'It's got no worse. What do you expect him to say?'

'It's your own examination that matters most,' I said. 'Not anything he says. You've got to be at your best tomorrow—'

'We can put a face on it. If you tell us the truth,' she said.

'You've got to be at your best,' I said to George, 'you above all.'

He had not spoken to the others. Once he looked at a stranger with a flash of last night's fear. On the outside, his manner had become more indrawn than before. It was seconds before he replied to me:

'It's scarcely worth while him putting me on view.'

After lunch there was one other witness, and then Martineau was called.

'Howard Ernest Martineau!' The call echoed in the court, and was caught up outside: it occured to me inconsequently that we had never before heard anyone use his second name. When he mounted into the box he apologised with a smile to the judge for being late. He took the oath and stood with his head a little inclined; he was wearing a suit, now creased, dirty, and old-fashioned, that I thought I had seen in the past.

'Mr Martineau, you are a qualified solicitor?'

'Yes.'

'You've practised in this town?'

'Yes.'

'How long were you in practice here?'

'Quite a long time.' Martineau's voice made a contrast to the quick, breathless question; he seemed less self-conscious than anyone who had spoken in the court. 'Let me see, I must think it out. It must have been over twenty – nearly twenty-five years.'

'And you gave it up a few years ago? How long ago, exactly?'

There was a pause.

'Just over six years ago.'

'And you joined Mr Exell in his advertising agency?'

'Yes.'

'What were the arrangements, the business arrangements, I mean, you understand, Mr Martineau – when you joined that firm?'

'I think we worked out the value of the business roughly, and I bought half of it from Mr Exell.'

'How much did you pay?'

'Five hundred pounds.'

Getliffe had asked the question at random. The answer went directly against us: George and Jack had borrowed half as much again.

'You ran the business yourself for a time?'

'I helped, I can only say that. I was also interested in – other fields.'

'You remember the little paper, *The Advertisers' Arrow*, which the agency used to publish?'

'Yes, I do.'

'Your other interests didn't leave you much time to keep acquainted with it, I suppose?'

Martineau hesitated for a moment.

'I think they did, on the whole. I think I knew more about it than anyone else.'

Many people noticed the dejection and carelessness that Getliffe had shown at the beginning of the examination; only a few realised the point at which his manner changed. Actually, it was when he heard this answer. He immediately became nervous but alert, pertinacious, ready to smile at Martineau and the jury. No one understood completely at the time; myself, I suddenly felt that he must be getting a different response from his last night's talk with Martineau.

'How long were you busy with the agency?'

'Not quite a year, not quite a year.'

'And towards the end of that time you received suggestions that you might sell again?'

'Not quite, not quite. It was after I had already got on the move once more. We talked over the possibility of other people buying it. You must forgive me if my memory isn't perfect – but it's some time ago and my life has changed a little since.' He turned to the judge, who smiled back. 'I think that was the first step, though.'

'Whom did you talk over the matter with?'

'Mr Passant, chiefly.'

'What kind of conversation did you have with Mr Passant?'

Martineau laughed.

'That's rather a tall order, I'm afraid. I talked to him a great deal then,' he looked in a friendly way at George, 'and I have talked a good deal since of different things, you know. I can't guarantee to remember very exactly. But I think we discussed the natural things – that is, whether Mr Passant ought to try to buy this business, and the state it was in, and its prospects in the future. My impression is, we touched on all those things –'

'You touched on the *Arrow*, did you?'

'Yes, we certainly did that.'

'Did you come to the conclusion that Mr Passant ought to try to buy the agency?'

'I think we did.'

'Can you recall what you said about its state just then?'

'That's a little difficult.'

'You stated that you did discuss the – condition at that time?'

'Naturally he was interested in those matters, I told him all I could.'

'You must have discussed profits and the turnover and the expenses – and the circulation of the *Arrow*, I expect?' Getliffe was still eager and excited.

'I think so, I think we did.'

'I'm afraid I've got to push on about the circulation. We should all be clearer if you could remember, do you think you can remember? – if you gave him a definite figure?'

'I may have done, but I can't be certain.'

'Is it likely you did?'

'I should have thought I told him in general terms, so that he could make an estimate of the possibilities for himself. I should have thought that was the most likely thing.'

'You think you told him that the circulation was, say, large – or in the thousands, or very small?'

'That was the way. I'm sure that was the way.'

'Now, Mr Martineau, can you think what indication you actually gave him? Did you say that it was very small?'

'No, no.'

'That it was reasonably large?'

Martineau smiled.

'I think I said – something of that nature.'

'If you put it in numbers?'

'I don't believe we were absolutely exact.'

'But if you had to, what would "reasonably large" have meant? More than a thousand?'

'Yes, surely.'

'Several thousand?'

'Something like that, perhaps.'

'You don't mind repeating that, Mr Martineau?'

'Of course not.'

'You're fairly certain that was the kind of number Mr Passant gathered from your discussions?'

'Yes, yes.'

'Thank you very much, Mr Martineau,' Getliffe said. He sat down, and as he took up a pencil to write a note his fingers were trembling. He leaned close to me: 'That's something, anyway,' he whispered.

Porson began in a level voice, spacing the words out:

'You said you gave up your profession as a solicitor six years ago?'

'Yes.'

'How are you earning your living at present?'

'I'm scarcely doing so at all.'

'You mean, you've retired?'

'No, no, I mean almost the opposite. It's only since I've left that I've become active – but that hasn't helped me much to make a living.' Martineau smiled.

'Come, Mr Martineau, where are you living now?'

'I've been living in a little settlement. We try to support ourselves and earn our luxuries by selling what we have left over. But, as I said, that doesn't always do so well.'

'You've been there for long?'

'Nearly two years. But perhaps I may not stay much longer.'

'I think the jury will understand your *temporary* association with the agency if you will tell us something about your movements. From the time you gave up your profession – first of all, you had a short period with the agency, and then—?'

Martineau mentioned his changes: the 'Brotherhood of the Road', the solitary vagrancy, some of his humiliations and adventures (someone in the gallery laughed as he mentioned that he slept in casual wards; Martineau turned towards him and laughed more loudly), the settlement. He did not say any word about his future. As the story went on Getliffe stiffened into attention. The whole court was tense.

'Very well,' said Porson, 'I suppose we can take it for granted you performed this very eccentric behaviour on religious grounds?'

Martineau nodded his head. 'Myself, I should call it trying to find a way of life.'

'Well – you were already trying to do that when you bought part of Mr Exell's business?'

'I think I was.'

'You weren't entirely interested in it as a business?'

'Not entirely.'

'Scarcely at all, in fact?'

'I couldn't say that.'

'You had every reason not to trouble to get any accurate knowledge of it at all?'

'I'm afraid that isn't true,' said Martineau. 'I knew it – pretty well.'

'You won't pretend you seriously thought of this paper, for instance – as a business proposition? You don't deny that you wrote religious articles for it?'

'I thought perhaps I should find others – well, who were trying to find the way too.'

'I'm glad you admit that. You'll also admit, won't you, that you weren't in touch with more prosaic things – like its circulation?'

Martineau shook his head. 'No. I was in touch with them. They were still very close.'

'I hope you'll admit, though, that Mr Exell still had something to do with it?'

'Yes.' Martineau smiled again.

'Perhaps even more than yourself?'

'Very likely he had.'

'Well, then, Mr Martineau, will it surprise you to know that Mr Exell has given the court exact information upon the circulation of this paper, and his information was very different from that which you remember – you vaguely remember – giving to Mr Passant?'

'It doesn't surprise me so very much,' Martineau said.

'So I put it to you that you were incorrect in your recollection of your talk to Mr Passant? You told him a figure very much less than you suggested a few minutes ago?'

'That's not true. Not true.'

'You realise you are contradicting yourself? You have told us you were thoroughly acquainted with the state of the firm.'

'Yes.'

'You've also agreed that Mr Exell knew it well, as well and better than yourself? I've told you that he gave evidence that the *Arrow* at no time had a circulation of more than twelve hundred.'

'Yes.'

'Then, Mr Martineau, I put it to you that either your recollection of your talks with Mr Passant is untrustworthy or—'

Martineau broke in:

'No, no, no. Those talks are returning more and more.'

'In that case, you were never acquainted with the real figures? You've been misleading us?'

'No. I knew them not so badly, not so badly.'

'How can you possibly justify what you have just said?'

Martineau replied: 'Because I should have agreed with Mr Exell.'

There was an instant of silence.

'Yet you said you remembered telling Mr Passant an absolutely different state of affairs? Is it true that you gave Mr Passant to understand that the paper had a large circulation?'

'That is also true.'

'While you yourself knew, with Mr Exell, that it was quite otherwise?'

'That's true as well. As well.'

'You're now saying, Mr Martineau, that you were responsible for telling a dangerous lie. You realise you're saying this?'

'I do.' He smiled. 'Naturally I do.'

The judge coughed, and said quietly: 'Would you mind telling us whether you actually knew the position of your paper in detail at this time?'

'Yes.'

'On the other hand, you gave Mr Passant a different estimate, a very much larger figure?'

'I think I never gave him a figure exactly. I've said before, I don't remember too well. But I let him get an impression of something much larger. I certainly let him get that impression.'

'Can you explain why you did that?'

'I think so. I've already said, m'lord, that the little paper contained some of my plans to find others on the same – well, "exploration" as myself, and it wasn't always easy in those days to confess how unsuccessful I had been.'

The judge pursed his lips into a smile of recognition (not his friendly smile), inclined his head, and made a note.

Porson kept on, his tone angrier and more hectoring.

'Was there any reason why a man who had apparently given up something for his beliefs should go in for indiscriminate lying?'

Martineau said: 'I'm afraid I found there was.'

Could he expect the jury to believe this 'extraordinary thing'? It was not part of his 'new religion' to damage and mislead his friends? The lie might make it more possible to obtain money from his friends, but that was scarcely likely to enter his thoughts? Was the only explanation that Martineau could offer for his 'completely pointless lie' simply his own 'vanity and conceit'?

It was commented on as the bitterest cross-examination which the trial had so far seen; Porson seemed full of personal antipathy. Many people in the court felt pleased at the tranquillity with which Martineau answered. He was still calm when Porson asked his last questions.

'In fact, your *way of life* has made you a person with no respect for the truth in a sense which the jury and all honest men must understand it?'

'I don't feel that's true.'

'You're aware, of course, that if the jury believe this story of your lie it may be of some slight advantage to your friend, Mr Passant?'

'Yes.'

'There's no more reason for them to trust you now than Mr Passant had – according to your story?'

'I hope they will trust me now.'

When Porson sat down, Martineau rested a hand on the box. Getliffe asked him the one question:

'You can say for certain, Mr Martineau, that you gave Mr Passant to understand that the circulation was a largish number, in the thousands?'

'I'm certain,' said Martineau, in a full, confident and happy voice.

CHAPTER XXXVII

NIGHT WITH THE PASSANTS

Two more witnesses were called before the judge rose. I stayed with Getliffe in the robing-room after Porson had gone out, leaving us with a loud laugh and a good night. Getliffe sat on the edge of the table.

'Old Martineau did us proud,' he said.

I nodded.

'You're lucky to have known him,' he said with a warm, friendly smile. 'He's the sort of man who sometimes makes me want to do something different. You can understand my wanting that, can't you?' He was speaking with great eagerness.

'I knew you would,' Getliffe said. We took up our cases and walked through the empty hall. Suddenly Getliffe took my arm. 'I knew you'd understand,' he said. 'You pretend not to be religious, I know that, of course. But you can't get away from your own nature, whatever you like to call it. You can't pull the wool over my eyes. It's something we've got in common, isn't it?

'I don't mean we're better people in one way,' he went on. 'You know I'm not. You've seen enough of me. I can do – things I'm ashamed of afterwards. You can too, can't you? I expect we can both do more bad things than people who've not got the sense of – "religion". In many ways I'm a worse man than they are. But somehow I think there are times when I get a bit further than they manage to. Because I want to, that's all, L.S.'

He laughed. 'Take Porson, for instance. I know what they say about his morals; I'm not taking any notice of them. If you rule that out, he's a better man than I am. He's more honest, he wouldn't have to watch himself as I do. Yet there isn't a scrap of anything deep in him. I'll swear there isn't. He's never prayed. He's never wept at night.'

As we walked on through the street, crowded with the first rush of the evening, Getliffe said: 'What happened to old Martineau, anyway? Did he lie to Passant or did he think of that later?'

'I think he lied to Passant,' I said. I told him of the entry in George's diary: and of that inexplicable chicanery over Morcom's flat years ago – when George had protested, angrily and loyally, that Martineau could never do a dishonest act.

Getliffe said:

'I don't know. He's not got much to lose now, of course – and Passant might gain a good deal. He liked Passant, I could tell that. Anyway, it's given us a chance. With our friend Porson going all out after that set of figures on paper. He never ought to have made so much of it. But as for Martineau – you know, he might have invented it for Passant's sake.'

'It's difficult to believe,' I said. 'He was always fond of George Passant – but personal affections mattered less to him than anyone I've ever met. His own story—'

'What about it?'

'You believed him last night?'

'I fancy I did,' said Getliffe. 'It went just as I told you. It was all a long time ago, he said. He did just remember talking to Passant, but he hadn't any recollection of what they said. He never knew much about the agency or the paper. He had forgotten the little he ever knew. He obviously wasn't going to make any effort to remember, either.'

'Was that all?'

'That was all I got him to say. Once or twice I did wonder whether he really had forgotten. He seemed to be making it too vague altogether. But I tell you, L.S., I'm certain of one thing. *Last night he hadn't the slightest intention of saying what he did today.* I don't believe he had any intention of doing it – until he got into the box. It just came to him on the spur of the moment. I should like to know whether he invented it.'

'I'm certain he lied to Passant,' I said. 'Of course, if he did, Passant would believe him. He would never be suspicious of a friend, particularly of Martineau—'

'I don't think I should have been,' said Getliffe. He smiled at me. Because of these last hours, we were on better terms than we had ever been.

'I don't know,' I said. 'You might have believed him for the moment, but as soon as he went away you'd have taken care to find out.'

'We've got to remember,' said Getliffe, 'that Passant himself must have had his suspicions. He's too able a man not to have seen some snags and – they must all have *known* for certain there was something wrong. Very soon—'

'When?'

'We can both make our own guess, can't we?'

Before the money was borrowed, he was thinking. But his imagination had been caught by Martineau.

'The old chap must have gone through a good deal,' he said, 'getting no one to believe in his faith, at that time. I know you will say this is all too cut and dried, L.S. – but I fancy there is one thing he held on to longer than most. That's his self-respect. And I fancy his performance today had something to do with that.'

'You mean, he might have been trying to free himself – even from self-respect?'

'At times – I can imagine doing it myself.'

'But still,' I thought aloud, 'it's stronger with him than most men – even after today. There's part of it he never will lose. He would be the last man to be able to get free.'

Getliffe laughed affectionately.

'Anyhow, he got rid of a dash of it today.'

At Eden's Olive and Jack were waiting: their solicitor had sent for them, to have a last word before their examination the next day. Olive told me that Martineau was leaving the town within the hour.

Soon I left them, and took a taxi to the omnibus station. George, his father and Roy were standing close to a notice of the services to the North.

Martineau was on the steps by the conductor, and as I hurried towards them he went inside. The engine burred, they lurched off; Martineau was still standing up, waving.

'It's a pity he had to go away tonight,' Mr Passant said. Then he burst out: 'He never ought to go without an overcoat, going right up there in this weather. He ought to know it isn't doing any good—'

We were all sad that he could leave so casually, before the end of the trial. They were angry that he was free of their sorrows. Mr Passant said several times on the way to the Passants' house:

'I should have thought he might have stayed another day or two.'

He repeated it to Mrs Passant, who was waiting in her front room.

'I didn't expect much of him,' she said.

'He used to flatter you very nicely, though,' said Roy, who had replaced Jack in her favour. For one instant her face softened in a pleased, girlish smile.

'He couldn't have made any difference—' Mr Passant began.

'If he had been a decent, sensible man everything would have been different. I shall always say it was his fault. He ought to have looked after you properly,' she said to George. She got up and put a kettle on the fire; since I last saw her, her movements had grown stiff, although her face had aged less than her husband's.

'But he wasn't worried by them this afternoon,' said Mr Passant. 'They couldn't get him to say anything he didn't mean.'

Mrs Passant was saying something in an undertone to George. Mr Passant looked at them, then said to me:

'I couldn't follow what Mr Martineau had been doing himself. I'm not pretending I could help him because I haven't fallen into the same mistakes or misunderstandings. It isn't that, Lewis.'

'No one followed what he'd been doing,' said Roy. 'Believe me. That is so.'

'The main thing is, we ought to be grateful to him,' said Mr Passant. 'When I heard them getting at him this afternoon—'

'I suppose we ought to be grateful to him,' George broke in.

'Of course we ought,' said Mr Passant. 'It's contradicted all they were saying.'

'It's very easy to exaggerate the effect of that.' George turned round to face his father. 'You mustn't let it raise false hopes. There are a great many things you must take into account. First of all, even if they believe him, this is only one part of the case. It isn't the chief part, and if they hadn't been wanting to raise every insinuation against me, they could have missed it out altogether.'

Mr Passant questioned me with a glance. I replied:

'It'll have some effect on the other, of course. But perhaps George is right to—'

'What's more important,' George went on, 'is whether they believe him or not. You can't expect them to believe a man who has left his comfort and thrown his money away, and who would sooner sleep in a workhouse than fritter away an evening at one of their houses. You can't expect them to take him seriously. You've got to realise that they'll think it their duty to put him and me in the same class – and feel proud of themselves for doing it.'

'No, that's not quite right,' Mr Passant said.

'You don't know.'

'I've been watching and listening—'

'You don't know what to listen to. I've had to learn. I've been fairly competent at my profession. If you want anyone to tell you whether my opinion is worth having, you had better ask Eliot.'

'I know it, you can't think I don't know it—'

'It can't be much of a consolation for you,' George said.

He was hoping more from Martineau's evidence than he could let his father see. During their argument, I felt it was one of the few occasions on which I had seen George deliberately dissimulate. Perhaps he had to destroy his own hopes. I wondered if he also consciously wanted to keep up the pretence that there was nothing in the case; and so told Mr Passant that his persecutors would disregard favourable evidence, just as they had invented the whole story of the fraud.

Yet, listening to him, we had all been brought to a pitch of inordinate strain. He had started out to dissimulate, but his own passion filled the words, and he did not know himself how much was acted. Before he stopped, he could not conceal an emotion as violent as that of the night before.

We all looked at him. No one spoke for a time. Then George said:

'Where are you preaching on Sunday?'

'I don't know for certain.'

'The trial will be over,' said George. 'Whatever happens, I want you to preach. Where's the circuit this week?'

Mr Passant mentioned the name of a village.

George said:

'It's grotesque that they always give you the furthest places. You've got to insist on fair treatment.'

'It doesn't matter, going a few miles more,' said Mr Passant.

'It matters to them and it ought to matter to you. But anyway, this place is presumably fixed for Sunday. I want you to go.'

Mrs Passant suddenly tried to stop their pain.

'That's the place old Mr Martineau started his acting tricks, isn't it?' she said. 'I should like to know what culch he's getting up to now.'

'I don't know,' said George.

Mrs Passant said: 'He ought to have looked after you. He used to think you would do big things. When you went to Mr Eden's, he used to think you wouldn't stay there very long.'

'If I had wanted, I could have moved.'

'I never thought you would, somehow,' she said.

'Because I found something valuable to do,' George said.

'You found something you liked doing more. I always knew you would. Even when I told people how well you were getting on.' She spoke in a matter-of-fact tone, with acceptance and without reproach. George looked at her with something like gratitude. At that moment, one felt how close she had been all his life. She understood him in the way Jack did; she, too, did not believe in the purpose and aspirations, she had always seen the weaknesses and self-deceit. Like Jack, she had discounted the other sides of his nature, and possessed a similar power, the greater because of the love between them.

CHAPTER XXXVIII

IMPRESSIONS IN THE COURT

FOR a time the next morning, the feeling of the court was less hostile. Martineau's evidence had raised doubts in some onlookers; and they responded to Getliffe's new zest. Jack's examination went smoothly and he soon made a good impression. The touch of genuine diffidence in his manner seemed to warm people, even in court, to his frank, spontaneous, fluent words. As he answered Getliffe, I thought again how there was a resemblance between them.

He gave an account of his positions in the years before they bought the agency – he was twenty-nine, a year older than he used to tell us in the past, a fact which I should have known if I had studied the register of our old school. He said of the transaction over the agency:

'I wanted money very badly, I'm not going to pretend anything else.'

'About the information you gave to people when you were borrowing money,' said Getliffe, 'that was never false?'

'No. I'd got a good thing to sell, and I was selling it for all I was worth.'

'You told them what you believed to be the truth?'

'Yes. Naturally I was as enthusiastic as I could honestly be.'

'You were certain it was a good thing, weren't you?'

'I put every penny I had got into it, and I spent every working hour of my time improving it for months.'

'You felt like that yourself after you had received Mr Martineau's information?'

'Yes,' said Jack. 'If I'd heard – for instance, that the circulation of the *Arrow* was much smaller – I shouldn't have become as keen. But even so, I should have known there were possibilities.'

'It was a perfectly ordinary business venture, wasn't it? That is how you would look at it?'

'It was a good deal sounder than most. It did quite well, of course. There's a tendency to forget that.'

Once or twice he drew sympathetic laughter. He kept to the same tone, responsible and yet not overburdened, through most of Porson's cross-examination. He denied that he had known the real state of the agency.

'I was a bit puzzled later, but all sorts of factors had to be taken into account. I set to work to put it right.' About the farm he would not admit anything of the stories of Miss Geary and the others. It was noticed on all sides that Porson did not press him. But after several replies from Jack, Porson said:

'The jury will observe there are two accounts of those interviews. One was given by several witnesses. The other was given by you, Mr Cotery.' He added: 'Incidentally, will you tell us why you gave different people so many different accounts of yourself?'

Getliffe objected. Porson said:

'I consider it essential to cross-examine this witness as to credit.'

The judge said: 'In the circumstances, I must allow the question.'

Porson asked whether Jack had not invented several fictitious stories of his life – one, that he had been to a good school and university, another that he had been an officer in the army? Jack, shaken for the first time, denied both.

'It will be easy to prove,' said Porson. He looked at the jury. He had given no warning of this surprise. 'Do you deny that—'

'Oh, I don't deny that I've sometimes got tired of my ordinary self. But that had nothing to do with raising money.' Jack had recovered himself. He replied easily to Porson's questions about his stories: some he just admitted.

At last Porson said:

'Well, I put it to you, Mr Cotery, that you've been living by your wits for a good many years?'

'I think that's true.'

'You've never settled down to a serious occupation? If you like, I can take you through a list of things you've done—'

'You needn't trouble. It's perfectly clear.'

'You've spent your entire time trying to get rich quick?'

'I've spent my time trying to make a living. If I'd been luckier, it wouldn't have been necessary.'

Porson asked a number of questions about the ways in which he had made a living. To many, there was something seedy and repellent in those indications of a life continuously wary, looking for a weakness or a generosity – they were identical when one was selling an idea. But most people actually in court still felt some sympathy with Jack; he was self-possessed, after the moment of anger about his romances, and he answered without either assertiveness or apology. Once he said, with his old half-comic ruefulness:

'It's harder work living by your wits than you seem to think.'

Porson said, after a time: 'You don't in the least regret anything you've done? You don't regret persuading people to lose their money?'

'I'm sorry they've lost it – just as I'm sorry I lost my own. But that's business. I expect to get mine back some day, and I hope they will.'

Porson finished by a reference to Olive's part in the transactions; she had been trying to raise money for the purchase, he suggested, at a time when Jack was taking other women to the farm.

'She was already your mistress as well, wasn't she?'

'Need I answer that?'

As Jack asked the question, several people noticed the distress and anger in his face, but they nearly all thought it was simulated. The general view was that he had chosen his moment to 'act the gentleman'; curiously enough, some felt it the most unprepossessing thing he had done that morning.

'I don't think you need,' said the judge.

Jack's reputation with women was well known in the town, and it was expected that Porson would make a good deal of it. To everyone's surprise, Porson let him go without another question.

Olive entered the box: Getliffe kept to the same lines as with Jack. All through she was abrupt and matter-of-fact; she made one reply, however, which Porson later taxed her with at length. It happened while Getliffe was rattling through his questions over the agency.

'You had considered buying other businesses?'

'Several.'

'Why didn't you go further with them?'

'We wanted a run for our money.'

'But you became satisfied that this one was sound?'

'It was a long way the best we had heard of.'

'Can you tell me how you worked out the possibilities?'

'On the result of Mr Passant's talk with Mr Martineau.'

'You didn't actually see Mr Martineau yourself, I suppose?'

'I didn't want to know any more about it.'

Very quickly, Getliffe asked:

'You mean, of course, that you were completely satisfied by the accounts Mr Passant brought? Obviously they convinced all three of you?'

'Of course. There seemed no need to ask any further.'

Many people doubted whether there had been a moment of tension at all. But when Porson cross-examined her, he began on it at once.

'I want to go back to one of your answers. Why did you say that "I didn't want to know any more about it"?'

'I explained – because I was perfectly well satisfied as it was.'

'Do you think that's a really satisfactory explanation of your answer?'

'It is the only one.'

'It isn't, you know. You can think of something very different. Just listen to what you said again: "I didn't want to know any more about it." Doesn't that suggest another phrase to you?'

'Nothing at all.'

'Doesn't it suggest – "I didn't want to know too much about it"?'

'I should have said that if I meant it.'

'I suggest you meant exactly that, though – before you had your second thoughts?'

'I meant the opposite. I knew enough already.'

Porson kept her an inordinately long time. His questions had become more slowly and truculently delivered since Martineau's evidence, his manner more domineering. It was his way of responding to the crisis of the case, of showing how much he needed to win it: but that would have been hard to guess.

He left no time to begin George's examination before lunch. Irritating the judge, he involved Olive's relations with Jack into his questions over the farm. He brought in a suggestion, so over-elaborate that it was commonly misunderstood, about her raising money in secret, without Jack's knowledge; Porson's insinuation being that she was trying to win Jack back from other women, and using her money as the bait.

But, though he had confused everyone by his legal argument and annoyed the judge, Porson had not entirely wasted his time. Olive was often admired at first sight, but seldom liked: and it had been so in court. Porson had been able to whip up this animosity.

As we went out for lunch, the crowd was full of murmurs about her evidence. Rachel met me, her face full of pity. She said several times – 'If only she'd thrown herself on their mercy.' Her pride had made many people glad to hear Porson's attack. And the impassiveness with which she had received the questions about 'running after a man who didn't want her' had added to their resentment.

Olive and Jack walked slowly together into lunch; they were not speaking when they arrived. George stared at her.

'What did you think of that?'

'Not much. They're waiting for you now.'

We tried to keep up a conversation, but no one made the effort for long. About us all, there hung the minute restlessness of extreme fatigue. Before the meal was finished Jack pushed his chair back.

'I want some air before this afternoon. I'm going for a walk,' he said to Olive. She replied:

'It'll be better if I stay here.'

Without smiling, they looked at each other. Their faces were harassed and grave, but full of intimacy.

'You'd better stay too,' Jack said to George. 'You'll want to get ready.'

George inclined his head, and Jack asked me to go with him into the street.

We found people already on the pavements, waiting for the afternoon's sitting to begin. Jack walked past them, his head back. He was wearing neither overcoat nor hat, and many of them recognised him.

'We gave them something to listen to,' he said. ·

'You did pretty well.'

'You would expect me to, wouldn't you?'

'Yes, I should.'

'Do you know,' he said, 'when I was in the box and saw them looking at me – I felt they were *envying* me, just like these people who're staring now?'

Even then, he was drawing some enjoyment from the eyes of the crowd. But a little later he said:

'There isn't so much to envy, is there? I still don't know why I have never pulled things off. I ought to have done. A good many others would have done in my place. I might have done, of course I might –' He began speaking very fast, as though he were puzzled and astonished.

'Lewis, if I'd been the man everyone thinks, this would never have happened. Do you realise that? I know that I've done things most men wouldn't, clearly I have. But I could have saved myself the trouble if I had lived on Olive from the start. She would have kept me if I'd let her. The man Porson struck something there. But I just couldn't. Why, Lewis, a man like you would have found it infinitely easier to let her than I did!'

'Yes, I should have taken her help,' I said.

'I couldn't,' said Jack. 'I suppose I was too proud. Have you ever known me to be too proud in any other conceivable circumstances before? It's incredible: but I couldn't take the help she wanted to give.'

Jack was reflecting. I recalled how Olive knew that he was struggling against being dependent on her – when we were afraid that he might run. We turned back towards the steps. He again felt curious eyes watching him, and casually smoothed back his hair.

'They think I'm a man who lives on women,' he said. 'It's true that I haven't lost by their company, in my time. The curious thing is – the one occasion when I ought to have let a woman help me, I couldn't manage it.

'I'm not the man they think,' said Jack. 'I've always envied people who've got the power of going straight ahead. I don't think there's much chance I shall learn it now.'

CHAPTER XXXIX

THE LAST CROSS-EXAMINATION

WHEN George walked from the dock to the witness-box, the court was full. There were acquaintances whom he had made at the School and through Eden's firm; as well as close friends, there were several present whom he had quarrelled with and denounced. Canon Martineau, who had not attended to hear his brother, was in court this afternoon, by the Principal's side; Beddow and Miss Geary were also there, of that committee which George once attacked. Roy's father was the only one of the five who had not come to watch. Roy himself stood at the back of the court, making a policeman fetch chairs for Mr and Mrs Passant. Daphne and Rachel stood near to Roy. Eden sat in the place he had occupied throughout the trial. And there were others who had come under George's influence – many of them not ready to believe what they heard against him.

As he waited in the box, the court was strained to a pitch it had not reached before. There was dislike, envy and contempt ready for him; others listened apprehensively for each word, and were moved for him so that their nerves were tense.

At that moment, just as Getliffe was beginning his first question, the judge intervened with a business-like discussion of the timetable of the case. 'Unless you finish by tomorrow lunchtime,' (Saturday) he said to Porson, 'I shall have to leave it over until Monday. I particularly want to have next week clear for other work. If you could cut anything superfluous out of your cross-examination this afternoon – then perhaps you' (he turned to Getliffe) 'could begin your final speech today.'

Getliffe agreed in a word; he felt the suspense in the court, tightened by this unexpected delay. But Porson argued for some minutes, and said that he could not offer to omit essential questions. In fact, George's evidence took up the whole afternoon.

Throughout the hours in the box George was nervous in a way which altered very little, whether it was Getliffe who questioned him or Porson. Yet he was, in many ways, the best witness the trial had seen. His hands strained at the lapels of his coat and his voice kept breaking out in anger; but even here, the rapidity and coherence of his mind, the ease with which his thoughts formed themselves into words, made the answers come clear, definite and undelayed.

In the examination, George gave a more elaborate account of their businesses, and one far more self-consistent and complete than either of the others or Getliffe himself in the opening speech. The answers explained that he and Jack heard of Martineau's leaving the town and wanting to sell the agency. He, as an old friend, undertook the task of asking Martineau about it, in particular whether it was an investment they would be justified in inviting others to join. Martineau told him the agency was in a particularly healthy state – and that the *Arrow* had a circulation of about five thousand. His memory was absolutely precise.

There were no vague impressions. He had not thought of any misrepresentation ('It would have been fantastic,' George broke out, 'to inquire further'). Jack and Olive had approached Attock and the others; the firm was bought; it had brought in a reasonable profit, not as large as they expected. He had been puzzled for some months at the small circulation of the *Arrow* after they took it over. They had not been able to repay more than a fraction of the loan, but had regularly raised the interest. The disorganisation of industry in the town during the economic crisis had also diminished the business, just as it was becoming established. But still, they had maintained some profit and paid the interest regularly. The agency would still have been flourishing, if, in George's words, 'I had not been attacked'.

After the steady results of the agency, they had thought of other ventures. The farm, which he knew through visits with his friends from the School, struck him as a possibility, and he examined its finances together with Jack. They decided that, running it with one or two smaller hostels, and finally a chain, they could make it give profits on a scale different from their first attempt with the agency. They were anxious to make money, George said vehemently, in answer to Getliffe's question: it was also a convenience to manage the farm, as he and a group of friends spent much of their time there. Essentially, however, it was a business step. He gave a precise account of the meeting with Miss Geary and others.

In the middle of the afternoon, when the windows were already becoming dark, Porson rose for the last cross-examination of the trial. He wrapped his fingers in his gown and waited a moment. Then he said:

'In your professional career, haven't you done a good deal of work on financial transactions, Mr Passant?'

'Yes.'

'You would consider yourself less likely than most to make a mistake through ignorance – or vagueness – or any incompetence that a man can fall into out of inexperience?'

'I should.'

'Thank you for admitting that. I don't want to take up the court's time questioning you about the financial cases – very much more complicated than the ones you engaged in yourself – which you handled for Mr Eden during the last five or six years. So, with your knowledge of financial matters, what was your first impression when Mr Martineau described the state of the agency?'

'I accepted it as the truth.'

'You didn't think it remarkable that an agency of that kind – at that time – should be flourishing so excessively?'

'I was interested that it should be doing well.'

'With your experience and knowledge, it didn't occur to you that it might be said to be doing too well?'

'I was told it on the best of authority.'

'I suggest to you, Mr Passant, that if you had been told anything so remarkable, even by Mr Martineau, you would naturally, as a result of your knowledge of these matters, immediately have investigated the facts?'

'I might have done if I hadn't known Mr Martineau well.'

Porson continued with questions on George's knowledge of the agency. He kept emphasising George's competence; several times he seemed deliberately to invite one of the methodical and lucid explanations. Many, however, were now noticing the contrast between the words and the defensive, bitter note in George's voice.

'Obviously, Mr Passant,' Porson said, 'you would never have believed such a story. Whoever told it to you. I put it to you that this tale of Mr Martineau telling you the circulation as a large figure – actually never took place?'

'You've no grounds for suggesting that.'

At last, as George's tired and angry answer was still echoing in the court, Porson left the agency and said:

'Well, I'll put that aside for the present. Now about your other speculation. You gave some explanation of why you embarked on that. Will you repeat it?'

'I wanted money. This looked a safe and convenient method.'

'That's what you said. You also admitted it had some connection with your work at the Technical College and School of Art' – he gave the full title, and then added – 'the institution that seems to be referred to as the School? You admitted this speculation had some connection with your work there?'

'It had.'

'Let us see what your work at the School really amounted to. You are not a regular member of the staff, of course?'

'I've been a part-time lecturer—'

'For the last nine years your status, such as it is, hasn't altered? You've given occasional classes in law which amount to two a week?' By chance, he exactly repeated the Principal's phrase of over seven years before.

'That is true.'

'That is, you've just been a casual visitor at the School. Now can you explain your statement that one reason for buying the farm was this – itinerant connection?'

'I have made many friends among pupils there. I wanted to be useful to them. It was an advantage to have a place to entertain them – entirely at my disposal.'

'Surely that isn't a very important advantage?'

'It's a considerable one.'

'I suggest there were others a good deal more urgent, Mr Passant. Wasn't it more important to keep the activities of your friends secret at this time?'

'It was not important in the sense you appear to be insinuating.'

'Do you deny,' Porson asked, 'after all that's been said – that you wanted to keep your activities secret?'

'I saw no reason to welcome intrusion.'

'Exactly. That is, you admit you had a particularly urgent reason for buying the farm at this time?'

'It was no more urgent than – since I really became interested in a group of people from the School.'

'You know – you've just admitted that you were afraid of intrusion?'

'I knew that if strangers got inside the group, then I should run a risk of being attacked. That was also true since the first days that I began to take them up.'

'You are trying to maintain that that was the same several years ago as in the summer when you bought the farm?'

'Naturally.'

'There is no "naturally", Mr Passant. Haven't you heard something of these scares among your friends – the fear of a scandal just at the psychological moment?'

'I've heard it. Of course. I believe they've all missed something essential out of the idea of that danger.'

Porson laughed.

'So you admit there was a danger, do you?'

'I never had any intention of pretending there wasn't.'

'But you're pretending it was no greater the summer when you wanted very urgently to buy the farm than it was years before?'

'It was very little greater.'

'Mr Passant: the jury has already heard something of the scandals your friends were afraid of when you were buying the farm. What do you expect us to believe, when you say there was no greater danger then?'

George cried loudly:

'I said the danger was very little greater. And the reason for it was that the scandals were only the excuse to destroy everything I had tried to do. Some excuse could easily have been found at any time.' His outburst seemed for a moment to exhaust and satisfy him. He was left spent and listless, while Porson asked his next question.

'I shall have to ask you to explain what you mean by that. Do you really believe anyone threatened your safety for any length of time?'

'I should have thought that events have left little doubt of that.'

'No. You had good and sufficient reasons for fear at the time you wanted to buy the farm. What could you have had before?'

'I was doing something which most people would disapprove of. I didn't deceive myself that I should escape the consequences if ever I gave an excuse. And I wasn't fool enough to think that there were no excuses during a number of years. I was vulnerable through other people long before Mr Martineau himself acquired the agency.'

'You say you were doing something most people would disapprove of. That' – Porson said – 'is apparent at the time I am bringing you to. The time the scandals among your friends were finding their way out. But what were you doing before, what are you referring to?'

'I mean that I was helping a number of people to freedom in their lives.'

'You'd better explain what you mean by helping people to "freedom in their lives".'

'I don't hope for it to be understood. But I believe that while people are young they have a chance to become themselves only if they're preserved from all the conspiracy that crushes them down.'

Porson interrupted, but George did not stop.

'They're crushed into thinking and feeling just as the world outside wants them to think and feel. I was trying to make a society where they would have the chance of being free.'

'But you're asking us to regard that – as the work which would bring you into disrepute? That was the work you seemed to consider important?'

'I consider it more important than any work I could possibly have done.'

'We're not concerned with your own estimate, you know. We want to see how you could possibly think your work a danger – until it had developed into something which people outside your somewhat un-important group would notice?'

'Work of that kind can't be completely ignored.'

'I suggest to you that it would have remained completely unknown – if it hadn't just one external result. That is, this series of scandals.'

'I do not admit those as results. But there are others which people would have been compelled to notice.'

'Now, Mr Passant, what could you imagine those to be?'

'The lives and successes of some of my friends.'

'Do you pretend you ever thought that those would be very easy to show?'

'Perhaps,' George cried loudly again, 'I never credited completely enough how blind people can be. Except when they have a chance to destroy something.'

'That's more like it. You're beginning to admit that you couldn't possibly have attracted any attention, either favourable or unfavourable? Until something was really wrong –'

'I've admitted nothing of the kind.'

'I'll leave it to the jury. In any case, there was no serious scandal threatened until somewhere about the time you considered buying the farm? For several years you had been giving them the chance of what you choose to call "freedom in their lives" – but nothing had resulted until about the time you all got alarmed?'

'There were plenty of admirable results.'

'The more obvious ones, however, were that a good many of your friends began to have immoral relations?'

'You've heard the evidence.'

'Most of them had immoral relations?'

George stood silent.

'You don't deny it?'

George shook his head.

'Your group became, in fact, a haunt of promiscuity?'

George was silent again.

Porson said:

'You admit, I suppose, that this was the main result of your effort to give them "freedom in their lives"?'

'I knew from the beginning that it was a possibility I had to face. The important thing was to secure the real gains.'

'You don't regret that you brought it about? You don't feel any responsibility for what you have done to your – protégés?'

'I accept complete responsibility.'

'Despite all this scandal?'

'I believe it's the final example of the stupid hostility I'd taught them to expect and to dismiss.'

'You have no regrets for these scandals?'

'They are an inconvenience. They should not have happened.'

'But – the happenings themselves?'

'I'm not ashamed of them,' George shouted. 'If there's to be any freedom in men's lives, they have got to work out their behaviour for themselves.'

'So your only objection to this promiscuity was when it became a danger? The danger that suddenly became acute at the time you said, in Mrs Ward's hearing: "If we don't get secrecy soon, we shall lose everything".'

'I should feel justified if much more had happened.'

'You also felt justified in practising what you preach?'

George did not answer. Porson referred to Iris Ward's evidence, the hints of Daphne and other girls. There was a soft, jeering laugh from the court.

George said: 'There's no point in denying those stories.'

'And so all this,' Porson said, 'is the work of which you were so proud? Which you told us you considered the most important activity you could perform?'

There was another laugh. With a flushed face, the judge ordered silence. 'You needn't answer that if you don't want,' he said to George, a kindly curious look in his eyes.

'I prefer to answer it,' said George. 'I've already described what I've tried to do. I can't be expected to give much significance to these incidents you are bringing up – when you compare them with the real meaning they mattered very little one way or the other.'

Porson drank some water. When he spoke again, his voice was a little husky, but still full of energy and assertion.

'You've told us, Mr Passant, that *work* with your group of friends was a very important thing in your life?'

'Yes.'

'And you always realised it might involve you in a certain danger? Shall we say in social disapproval?'

'Yes.'

'You still repeat, however, that the danger at the time of these alarms – just before you considered buying the farm – seemed to you little greater than in previous years?'

'It was an excuse presented to anyone wishing to be hostile. Before, they would have been compelled to invent one. That was all the difference.'

'I'm asking you again. You still deny that the danger really was desperate enough to affect your actions? To force you to make an attempt to buy the farm at all costs?'

'I deny it, naturally.'

Porson paused.

'How then do you explain that you were willing – just about that time – to give up your group of friends altogether? To have nothing more to do with work that you've told us was the most important thing in your life?'

'It's not true.'

'I can recall a witness to prove you said *these words also* at the farm.'

There was a silence. George began speaking fast.

'In a sense I grant it. It was the only course left for me to take. I'd finished as much as I could do. I'd tried to help a fair number of my friends from the School. I'd given them as much chance of freedom as I could. Doing it again with other people would merely mean repeating the same process. I was willing to do that – but if it was going to involve me in continual hostility with everyone round me, I wasn't prepared to feel it a duty to go on. I'd done the pioneer work. I was satisfied to let it go at that.'

As he spoke, George had a helpless and suffering look. This last answer scarcely anyone understood, even those of us who knew something of his language, and the barrier between his appetite for living and his picture of his own soul. He was alone, more than at any time in the trial – more than he had ever been.

For a moment, I found myself angry with him. Despite the situation, I was swept with anger; I was without understanding, as though I were suddenly much younger, as though I were taken back to the night of his triumph years before. For all his eagerness for life – I felt in a moment so powerful that no shame could obscure it – for all the warmth of his heart and his 'vision of God', he was less honest than his attackers, than the Beddows, Camerons, and Canon Martineaus, the Porsons, Edens and Iris Wards. He was less honest than those who saw in his aspirations only the devices of a carnally obsessed and self-indulgent man. He was corrupt within himself. So at the time when the scandal first hung over him, he was afraid, and already dissatisfied, tired of the 'little world'. But this answer which he made to Porson was the manner in which he explained it to himself.

At that moment, he suddenly seemed as alien to me, who had been intimate with him for so many years, as to those who laughed in court the instant before. I was blinded to the fire and devotion which accompanied this struggle with himself; through that struggle, he had deceived himself; yet it had also at moments given him intimations such as the rest of us might never know.

Even our indignations and ideals tend to be made in our own image. For me, to whom a kind of frankness with myself came more naturally than to George, it was a temptation to make that insight and 'honesty' a test by which to judge everyone else – just as an examiner, setting his papers and marking his questions, is always searching to give marks to minds built on the same pattern as his own.

I was blinded also to something as true and more simple. His words sounded less certain to him than to any of his listeners; they were more than anything an attempt to reason away his own misgivings. I ought to have known that he, too, had lain awake at night, seeing his aspirations fallen, bitterly aware of his own fear and guilt, full of the reproach of failure, remorse and the loss of hope. He too had 'wept at night', in a suffering harsher than Getliffe would ever feel, with all excuse seeming useless and remote; he had felt only degrading fear and the downfall of everything he had tried to do.

Yes, there had been self-reproach. I did not know, I couldn't foresee the future, whether it would last, or for how long.

Porson passed on to the money transactions over the farm. Nothing unexpected happened in the rest of the cross-examination, which ended in the early evening.

CHAPTER XL

CONFESSION WHILE GETLIFFE PREPARES HIS SPEECH

I WENT from the court to some friends who had invited me to drink sherry; a crowd of people were already gathered in the drawing-room. Many of them asked questions about the trial. No one there, as it happened, knew that I was so intimate with George. They were all eager to talk of the evidence of the day, discussing Olive's infatuation for Jack, the kind of life they had both led. Several of them agreed that 'she had done it because he was involved already'. It was strange to hear the guesses, some as superficial as that, some penetrating and shrewd. The majority believed them guilty. There was a good-humoured and malicious delight in their exposure, and the gossip was warm with the contact of human life.

From the point of view of the case, they were exaggerating the day's significance. People there felt that George's cross-examination 'had settled the business. He can't get away with that'; just as, in the street, I had overheard two men reading the evening paper and giving the same opinion in almost the same words. Yet, for all the talk of his 'hypocrisy', 'the good time he had managed for himself', there were some ready to defend him in this room. 'I can believe it of the other two easier than I can of him,' one of them said. 'I shouldn't have thought swindling was in his line.' But no one believed that he had ever devoted himself to help his friends.

I returned to dinner at Eden's. Getliffe told Eden that he thought it was 'all right'. He added: 'I'd be certain if it weren't for this prejudice they've raised. I must try to smooth that down.' Yet he was not so cheerfully professional as he sounded; something still weighed on him. As soon as he had finished eating, he said:

'I had better retire now. I must get down to it. I've got to pull something out of the bag tomorrow.'

'I've heard people wondering what you will say,' said Eden.

'One must take a line,' said Getliffe. Soon afterwards, without drinking any wine, he left us. Eden looked at me and said:

'It's no use worrying yourself now. You can't do any more, you know.'

I went to my room, and lay down on the sofa in front of the fire. After a time, footsteps sounded on the stairs, then a knock at the door. The maid came in, and after her Olive. At once I felt sure of what she was going to say. She stood between me and the fire.

'You've worn yourself out,' she said. Then she burst out: 'But you've finished now, it doesn't matter if I talk to you?'

She threw cushions from the chair on to the hearth-rug, and sat there.

'There's something – I shall feel better if I tell you. No one else must know. But I've got to tell you, I don't know why. It can't affect things now.'

'It couldn't at any time,' I replied.

She laughed, not loudly but with the utter abandonment that overtook her at times; the impassiveness of her face was broken, her eyes shone, her arms rested on the sofa head.

'Well, I may as well say it,' she went on in a quiet voice. 'This business isn't all a mistake. We're not as – spotless as we made out.'

'Will you tell me what happened?'

Without answering, she asked abruptly:

'What are our chances?'

'Getliffe still thinks they're pretty good.'

'It oughtn't to make much difference,' she said. 'I keep telling myself it doesn't matter.' She gave a sudden sarcastic laugh, and said: 'It does. More than you'd think. When I heard you say there was still a chance I was more shaken – than if I suddenly knew I'd never done it at all.'

She was silent for a moment. Then she said:

'I'm going to tell you some more. I can't help it.' She broke into a confession of what had happened between the three of them. She was forced on, degraded and yet relieved, just as Jack had been that night in the park years ago. Often she evaded my questions, and more than once she concealed a fact that she clearly knew. There were still places where I was left baffled, but, from what she said and what I already knew, their story seemed to have gone on these lines:

They actually did begin to raise money for the agency in complete innocence. George believed Martineau's account, and Olive took George's opinion; so probably did Jack, for a time. Jack had suggested the idea of taking over the agency – for him it was a commonplace 'flutter', and it was easy to understand George catching at the new interest. He was genuinely in need of money, compelled to see that he had no future in the firm, and, though he would not yet admit it to himself, tired of the group in its original form.

Olive, less clear-sighted on herself than on any other person, gave confused reasons for joining in. I thought that, even so early, she had wanted to control Jack – and that also, as she half-saw, she had been dissatisfied with herself for going back to her father and reverting to the childish, dependent state. This business seemed a 'hand-hold on real things'.

They borrowed their first amount, still believing in their own statements. George and Jack seemed to have realised the true position at about the same time. Neither said anything to the other. All through the transactions, the pretence of ignorance was kept up. Jack only made one hint to Olive (this happened, of course, some time before they were lovers): 'You might get some interesting information if you called on Exell. But it's always safer to wait until we've got the money in.'

As soon as he knew the truth, George passed through a time of misery and indecision. He thought for weeks that he alone had discovered it. He still wanted to consider himself responsible for the other two. At times he came near to stopping the entire business. He went so far as to call a meeting of the others and two of their creditors: and then made an excuse to cancel it. No doubt he was justifying himself: 'after all, we still have Martineau's authority' . . . 'anyway, we have raised most of the money now. The harm's done, whatever we do.' He could also tell himself that, despite the false statement, they would make a success of it and bring money to their creditors. Most of all, perhaps, he was afraid of disclosing his knowledge to the others: because he dreaded that Jack's influence would be too strong – and that Jack would force him through it with *both of them knowing everything*.

George had few illusions about Jack. He remembered Jack's early attempt at something like fraud over the wireless company. But he could not escape from the power which Jack had obtained over him, as their relation slowly developed through the years.

As George went through this period, Jack looked on with a mixture of contempt, anxiety, and even amusement. Himself, he was enjoying the excitement of raising the money and 'putting it across'. He found the same kind of exhilaration that a business deal had always given him – but now far more intense. Often he seemed little more affected than when he first invoked George's help. He told Attock the false story with the same single-mindedness, the same sense both of anxiety and of life beating faster, that he had once experienced when going round, Roy's present in his pocket, to call at George's house.

'He enjoyed it. It was part of the game,' said Olive. She did not talk, however, of the pleasure and authority which Jack now felt completely in George's presence. At last he had become the real leader. Though George still talked as though they all accepted his control, each of them in secret knew what the position was.

Olive said that, about this time, she hated Jack and found herself on George's side. She wanted to break up the whole business. She told Arthur Morcom something of it; she wondered how she could withdraw without throwing suspicion on the others. 'Arthur tried everything he knew to get me out of it. But I couldn't trust him then. If I had been on my own, I should have had more chance of escaping.'

At that time she was not yet living with Arthur, and it was a few months before Jack seduced her. Throughout the confession, her tendency was to see her immersion in the business as a result of her relations with these two. I thought she always undervalued how much she needed to influence and manage and control. As she watched Jack at the drunken party after the police court, she had seen herself more clearly and tonight, with a flash of penetration, she said:

'You used to tell me that I insisted too much on how I liked being someone else's slave, didn't you? I used to say how I wanted someone to make me feel small and dependent. Yet that's always been true. At least it's seemed true. But as soon as I looked at what I'd done, I had to see myself trying to get the exact opposite. I still wanted him to order me about. But in all the big things I was trying to make sure that I should have him in my hands.'

For all her passions of subjection, she actually – in another aspect of her nature – was a strong and masterful person. Perhaps stronger than either George or Jack. Those passions were so important to her that they often obscured her insight. She did not realise how violently she wanted her own kind of power.

Neither she nor George could face easily the actual thought of fraud. All three were often seized by anxiety and almost physical fear – from their first realisation of Martineau's lie down to tonight. But there was something different in Olive and George; they were sometimes conscience-stricken in a way which Jack did not know. They could not excuse themselves for these dishonesties over money. They felt cheapened in their own eyes. They did not even possess a 'rational' excuse to themselves. It was different from their sexual lives; for there, when they acted in an 'irregular' fashion, they had at least a complete rationale to console them. Many of the people whom they had known for long talked and acted against the sexual conventions. On the surface, George, Olive and Morcom would, each of them, recognise them only 'out of convenience'. On the levels of reason and conscience, they were completely at ease about the way they had managed their sexual lives; one had to penetrate beyond reason and conscience, before one realised how misleading George's 'justifications' were.

Over their affairs with money, however, they possessed nothing like these justifications. Even superficially, they had not been accustomed to reason away the conventions. In particular, Olive had been brought up to a strict moral code in money matters – in a circle where openly confessing one's income was improper and brought a hush into the room. As I told

Eden and Getliffe, George, though himself prodigal, had always 'recognised obligations over money', and felt a genuine and simple contempt for dishonesty. I remembered in the past hearing him say, after looking through one of Eden's cases: 'Bell-wethers on the make again! And I'm supposed to see they do it safely.' Once or twice, years ago, he was shocked and angry when the waitress came up after tea in a café and asked: 'How many cakes?' – and Jack looked at her and deliberately undercounted.

And so, as they went on borrowing money on Martineau's statement, there were times when they winced at their own thoughts.

However, the agency was bought and Jack worked hard to make it a success. It was the best continuous work of his life, and Olive said: 'It shows what he could have done if he had had the chance. Or a scrap of luck.' In a small way, it was a remarkable achievement, only possible to a man of unusual personal gifts. He was glad to be doing 'something solid at last', Olive said. 'He kept telling me that.'

George and Olive were overcome with relief as they watched the interest steadily paid off. They were reminded less and less often of what had happened. It had still never been mentioned between the three of them.

After their first perfunctory affair, Olive saw little of Jack. Yet her attitude to him was changing during the months she lived with Arthur. From Arthur she had expected more than their relation ever gave her. If he had been described without her knowing him, she would have thought 'that's the man who'll give me everything I've longed for'. While actually she found herself half-pitying and half-despising him, and her imagination began to fill itself with Jack again. It was not, as one might have thought, Jack the adept lover that she missed. As a matter of fact, she was excitable in love, and, perhaps as a consequence, she did not feel for either Jack or Arthur the kind of exclusive passion which can overwhelm less nervous temperaments. She missed something different. For now she realised or imagined that in Jack she had found what she would never have believed: someone who satisfied two needs of her nature: someone who made her feel utterly submissive and dependent, and yet whom – she thought this less consciously, but it helped to fill her with a glow of anticipation – she could control. She had seen what he could do; she was quite realistic about his character. And yet, he was the only man she had ever known who could imbue her with passionate respect.

In the end she went to Jack. For a long time he would not 'accept her terms', as they both told me. It was on this point that Jack had been provoked to his outburst today. She had tried, not once but several times, to make him live on her. He had to defend himself there: his romantic attitude represented his one streak of aspiration, his one 'spiritual attempt', and was precious in his own eyes on that account.

Meanwhile, George had given way to Jack's influence and had become engrossed in Daphne; in the autumn of 1930 they all wanted to buy the farm. The 'scares' deeply affected George, and the scene recounted by Iris Ward took place; but, although at that gathering Jack spoke as if frightened of a scandal himself, he probably only acted the part to play on George's fears. Himself, he wanted the farm as another business venture, and this was a way to bring George in. He was also exercising his power over George for its own sake.

When George said that he did not propose to get on the wrong side of the law, he was referring to the agency and half-excusing the way it had developed. But the remark bore for himself, and Jack and Olive, a deeper significance. He meant that, if they adopted Jack's suggestions, they would be acting with full knowledge from the beginning. Each would be going into fraud with his eyes open and *knowing the others were aware of it*.

From the moment that remark was made, they all three knew this business could not be done like the other. Iris Ward's evidence suggested that they decided to proceed the same night. That must have been a mistaken impression. George said the words when she remembered, but she did not realise how violently he would retract them the next day.

For weeks Jack kept the fear of scandal in front of him – and all the time suggested that he knew George's objections were sham fighting. He said that he knew George wanted the farm for his own pleasures. He assumed in Olive's presence that George felt no deeper objections than he felt himself. He often took the line that they were in complete agreement.

Olive said: 'I made myself argue for George. But I began to see him just as he looked this afternoon.' (She meant, when he answered Porson's question on why he was willing to give up the group.) 'I knew Jack was the better man. I knew I should always think that.'

This was the time when she tried most strenuously to finance and marry Jack. She found him obstinate. From her account, she went through a mood of complete mistrustfulness of her own intentions. 'I knew there had been sharp practice over the agency, so I told myself I was saving him from trying some more. But it wasn't that. If he had been trying the most creditable object in the world, I should have wanted to buy him out just then. I didn't want him to get on top of the world – and then marry me on his own terms.' Uncertain of herself, she withdrew her opposition to the farm scheme. Then George gave way.

That night, George said, apathetically after the bitter arguments: 'We may as well follow your plan, I suppose.' As soon as he spoke, they were all three plunged for hours into an extraordinary sense of intimacy. They felt exhausted, relieved, and full of complete understanding. They made schemes for Jack to bring in the 'victims'. They discussed the methods by which they could alter the farm's record of visitors. They laughed, 'as though it were an old joke', about the way they had borrowed money for the agency. 'I never felt three people so close together – before or since,' said Olive. 'We forgot we were separate people.'

The mood of that night did not visit them again. They went ahead with the plans, but for days and months their relations were shifting and suspicious. At times, in those days, Olive was overtaken by 'morbid waves' of dislike for Jack. She repeated to herself that she had always admired George, and that he was now not much to blame. George did not once try to withdraw from the arrangement; but he broke into violent personal quarrels with Jack. 'I insist on being treated with respect,' he complained to Olive one night. He needed that she herself should behave towards him as she had done in earlier days.

They did not take long to gather in their money. Jack found most of the investors, but he never settled down to manage the farm. He treated it differently from the agency. He did not make the same effort towards an honest business: he was thinking of extending their hostels into a chain and raising more capital. With a mixture of triumph and pity, he used to talk to George of the 'bigger schemes ahead'.

Now – with the admitted fraud behind them – their relations advanced to the state which I had noticed during the trial. George felt himself undermined and despised, half with his own consent. He obtained moments of more complete naturalness in Jack's company than anywhere else. But much of his nature was driven to protest. As in his cross-examination, he broke out in private and claimed his predominance.

It seemed possible that he would be able to cut away from Jack in the future. Since there was no affection left on George's side, I could imagine that after the trial he might suddenly put Jack out of his mind.

Olive had already shown a similar change of feeling towards George. Or rather, her cold and contemptuous words tonight indicated openly something which had been latent for long. She already felt it that orgiastic night after they had been committed for trial: when, with a gesture that was disturbing to watch, she went to his side as he lay drunk on the sofa.

523

She was thrusting her loyal comradeship in our faces – insisting on it, as one insists on a state which has irrecoverably passed. Just as George himself had most insisted on his devotion to his protégés when, in its true form, it was already dead.

During the first days of the fraud, when Olive felt repelled by Jack, she tried to restore her former admiration and half-dependence on George. But that had gone; and when she could not help still loving and respecting Jack, she transferred to George a good deal of hate and blame. He should have stopped it all. If he had been equal to his responsibilities, this would never have happened. He had made great pretensions to guide her life and Jack's, and he had proved himself to be unavailing and rotten. When she compared him with Jack, frank and spontaneous despite all they were doing, she felt that the one quality which she once admired in George now seemed only a sham. The aspirations which he still talked of appeared to her, as they did to Jack, simply a piece of self-deceit. She had no more use for him.

While Getliffe prepared his speech in his room close by, I defended George against her. This night of all nights, I had to defend him, who had lost the most, against those who had helped to bring him where he was. She was not moved by his fall. At last I said, angry and desolated, 'Whatever happens, Jack won't be much harmed. But George – he will never be able to endure looking back to what he once was. Do you remember telling Roy one afternoon years ago – "he is worth twenty Jack Coterys"? Even if this was inevitable, I believe what you said then. Do you think that such a man will forget this afternoon?'

'You're being sentimental,' she said, and was not even interested. She now thought only of her future with Jack. She realised that, if they got off, he would not be much scarred. If they could move to another town, he would soon put it all behind him. She knew he would become restless with ideas again. Left to himself, he might in time break the law in some similar fashion. She would keep him from that, now.

He would have to marry her. His gratitude and immediate respect for her – they would soon disappear. She talked about the prospect, forcing herself to sound matter-of-fact. She knew that she desired it. In a way, she believed that the life she wanted was only just beginning.

CHAPTER XLI

GETLIFFE'S SPEECH

GETLIFFE'S final speech, which lasted for two hours on Saturday morning, surprised us all. It was in his usual style, spasmodic, still bearing the appearance of nervousness, interjected with jerky asides, ill at ease and yet familiar; he was showing all the touch which made men comfortable with him. He was showing also the fresh enjoyment which seldom left him when he was on his feet in court.

But there was another note which made many of us feel that he was deeply moved. For those, like Eden and myself, who had been close to him through the week, there could be no doubt that something had affected him personally; and as we heard him reiterate a phrase – 'the way in which Mr Passant's freedom has worked out' – we knew at last what it was. He kept using these words, slurring them in his quick voice. Last night, we had heard him promise 'to pull something out of the bag'. We knew that he had chosen this line to divert the jury's prejudice. Yet – I was certain – it was not only as an advocate he was speaking. I had never seen him so possessed by seriousness in court.

He began, in his simple, emphatic, salesman's way, hammering home the division of the case to the jury. The three of them were being tried for a financial offence, and, on the other hand, their manner of life was being used against them. 'First of all,' said Getliffe, 'I'm going to put the financial business out of our way.' He went over the transactions again, quickly, full of impatient liveliness, once or twice forgetting a figure; he described the agency and came to George's buying it from Martineau. 'A lot of this is dull stuff to you and me,' Getliffe smiled at the jury, 'but about that incident we had what I at any rate found an unforgettable experience. I mean, the evidence of Mr Martineau. Now we have all knocked about the world. We know that there are reasons why we're all capable of telling lies and even giving false evidence in a court of law. We all know that, though sometimes we pretend we don't. I'm going to admit to you now that some of the witnesses for the defence, in this case, have had *reasons* which would explain their telling lies. You would know that even if I hadn't told you. You're able to judge for yourselves. But in Mr Martineau we had someone – I think more than any witness I've ever had the privilege of calling – who is completely removed from all the pettiness that we are ashamed of and that we never manage to sweep out of our lives. You can't imagine Mr Martineau lying to us. You heard all about his story, didn't you? He's *done* something that most of us, if we are ordinary, decent, sinful men' – he laughed again – 'with one foot in the mud and one eye on the stars – have thought of at least once in our lives. That is, just cutting away from it all and trying to live the things we think we believe. Of course, we never manage it, you and I. It isn't our line of business. I'm not sure it would be a good thing for the world if we could. But that isn't to prevent us recognising something beyond us when we do see it – in a life like Mr Martineau's, for instance. I don't mind saying – whatever you think of me – that there's something saintly about a life like his. Renouncing, deliberately renouncing, all the things you and I worry about from the time we are young men until we die. I'm not going to persuade you that his evidence is true. It would be insulting you and me and all we hope for if it wasn't true.'

Some thought that this was an example of the craft, apparently naïve but really subtle, which made him, for all his deficiencies, a success at his profession. But they had not heard his confidence on the night of Martineau's examination. If this was subtle, it was all instinctive. He believed what he was saying; he did not need to persuade himself.

He spent a long time over the details of the agency and the farm. Martineau's evidence, he repeated again and again, acquitted them on the first. On the second – this was far vaguer than the agency; if it had not been for 'that curious definite figure of the circulation', then the second charge could never have been brought. He dealt with the figures of the farm, sometimes wrapping them round and complicating them.

All this, both the complication and the air of authority, was not much different from an ordinary defence. It was done with greater life and was less well ordered than most speeches at the end of such a case; but, if he had finished at that point, he would have done all that was expected of him. Instead, he began his last appeal, and for a quarter of an hour we listened in astonishment.

'I submit that you would never think of convicting these three on the evidence that has been put forward, neither you nor I would think they were guilty for a moment – if it were not for something else we have all had in our minds this week. I mean, the way Mr Passant's freedom has worked out. That is, you've heard of some people who have been breaking a good many of the laws that are important to decent men. I don't mean the laws of this country, I mean the laws which lie behind our ordinary family way of life. I won't try to conceal it from you. They haven't shown any shame. I don't know whether it's to their credit that they haven't. They have been living what some would call "a free life". Well, that's bound to prejudice them in your eyes, in the eyes of anyone older who doesn't believe a thing is good just because it is new. I don't mind confessing that it upset me when I discovered the pleasures they took for granted – as though there was nothing else for them to do. I think – I'm positive we think alike – that they are all three people of gifts. But chiefly I want to say something about Mr Passant, because I think we all realise that he has been the leader. He is the one who set off with this idea of freedom. It's his influence that I'm going to try to explain.

'You've all seen him. You can't help recognising that he's a man who actually made his way up to a point, who might have gone as far as he wanted. He could have done work for the good of the country and his generation – no one has kept him from it but himself. No one but himself and the ideas he has persuaded himself to believe in: because I'm going a bit further. It may surprise you to hear that I do genuinely credit him with setting out to create a better world.

'I don't pretend he has, mind you. You're entitled to think of him as a man who has wasted every gift he possesses. I'm with you. I look on him like that myself. He's chased his own pleasures. I'll go as far as any of you in accusing him. I'll say this: he's broken every standard of moral conduct we've tried to keep up, and he's put up nothing in their place. He is a man who has wasted himself.

'I know you're feeling this, and you know I am. I'm reminding you what one has to remind oneself – that he is not on trial, nor are the others, for having wasted himself. But if he was? But if he was? I should say to you what I have thought on and off since I first took on the case. I should say: he started off with a fatal idea. He wanted to build a better world on the basis of this freedom of his: but it's fatal to build better worlds until you know what human beings are like and what you're like yourself. If you don't, you're liable to build, not a better world, but a worse one; in fact you're liable to build a world for one purpose and one only, that is just to suit your own private weaknesses. I'm certain that is exactly what Mr Passant has done. And I'm certain that is exactly what all progressively minded people, if you'll let me call them that, are always likely to do unless they watch themselves. They usually happen to be much too arrogant to watch themselves. I don't think we should be far wrong to regard Mr Passant as a representative of people who like to call themselves progressive. He's been too arrogant to doubt his idea of freedom: or to find out what human beings are really like. He's never realised – though he's a clever man – that freedom without faith is fatal for sinful human beings. Freedom without faith means nothing but self-indulgence. Freedom without faith has been fatal for Mr Passant himself. Sometimes it seems to me that it will be fatal to most of his kind in this country and the world. Their idea of progress isn't just sterile: it carries the seed of its own decay.

'Well, that's how I think of Mr Passant and progress or liberalism or anarchy or whatever you like. I believe that's why he's wasted himself. But you can say – it's still his own fault. After all, he chose this fatal idea. He adopted it for himself. To that, I just want to say one thing more.

'He's a man on his own. I've admitted that. But he's also a child of his time. And that's more important for the way in which he has thrown himself into freedom without faith. You see, he represents a time and generation that is wretchedly lost by the side of ours. It was easy to believe in order and decency when we were brought up. We might have been useless and wild and against everything round us – but our world was going on, and it seemed to be going on for ever. We had something to take our places in. We had got our bearings, most of us had got some sort of religion, some sort of society to believe in and a decent hope for the future.' Eagerly, he laughed. 'We'd got something to stick ourselves on to. It didn't matter so much to us when the war – and everything the war's meant since – came along. We had something inside us too solid to shift. But look at Mr Passant, and all the generation who are like him. He was fifteen when the war began. He had four years of chaos round him just at that time in his life, just at the time when we had quietness and discipline and hope all round us. It's what we used to call "the uncounted cost". You remember that, don't you? And I'm not sure those four years were the worst. Think of everything that has happened in the years, it's nearly nineteen years now, since the war began. Imagine people, alive and full of vitality and impressionable, growing up without control, without anyone believing in control, without any hope for the future except in the violence of extremes. Imagine all that, and think what you would have become yourself if you'd been young during this – I've heard men who believe in youth at any price call it an "orchard time". I should say it was one of the swampy patches. Anyway, imagine you were brought up among these young people wasting themselves. That is, if you're one of us, if you are a normal person who could go either way, who might go either Martineau's or Passant's. Well, if you were young, don't you think you could have found yourself with Passant?

'That's what I should have said. I've let it out because it's something that has been pressing inside me all through this trial, and I couldn't be fair to Mr Passant and his friends unless I – shared it with you. You see, we're not trying them for being wasted. Unless we're careful we shall be. The temptation is to feel they're pretty cheap specimens anyway, to give the benefit of doubt against them. We've got to be careful of our own prejudice. Even when the prejudice happens to be absolutely right, as right as anything we're likely to meet on this earth. But we're not trying them for their sins and their waste of themselves. We're not trying them for a fatal idea of freedom. We're not trying them for their generation. We are trying them for an offence of which there is scarcely a pennyworth of evidence, and which, if it were not for all this rottenness we have raised, you would have dismissed and we should all have been home long ago. You've got to discount the prejudice you and I are bound to feel. . . .'

CHAPTER XLII

FOG OUTSIDE BEDROOM WINDOWS

As soon as Getliffe finished his speech, the court rose for the weekend. He had created an impression upon many there, particularly the strangers and casual spectators. Even some who knew George well were more disturbed than they would admit. Someone told me that he thought the whole speech 'shoddy to the core'; but by far the greater number were affected by Getliffe's outburst of feeling. They were not considering whether it was right or wrong; he was reflecting something which had been in the air the whole week, and which they had felt themselves. Whatever words he used, even if they disagreed with his 'ideas', they knew that he was moved by the same emotions as themselves. They were certain that he was completely sincere.

I went to George's house after lunch. We did not mention the speech. For a time, George talked in a manner despondent and yet uncontrollably nervous and agitated. He had received that morning from the Principal the formal notice of dismissal from the School.

He took a piece of paper and began drawing a pattern like a spider's web with small letters beside each intersection. Some time later, Roy arrived. George did not look up from his paper for a moment. At last he raised his head slowly.

'What is it now?' he said.

'I just called in,' said Roy. He turned his head away, and hesitated. Then he said:

'Yes, there is something. It can't be kept quiet, They've gone for Rachel.'

'What?'

'They've asked her to leave her job.'

'Because she was connected with me?'

'It's bad,' said Roy.

'How is she going to live?' I said.

'I can't think. But she mustn't sit down under it. What move do you suggest?' He looked at George.

'I've done enough damage to her,' said George. 'I'm not likely to do any better in the present situation.'

Roy was sad, but not over-anxious: melancholy he already fought against, even at that age, but anxiety was foreign to him. He and I talked of the practical steps that we could take; she was competent, but over thirty-five. It would be difficult to find another job. In the town, after the trial, it might be impossible.

'If necessary,' said Roy, 'my father must make her a niche. He can afford to unbelt another salary.'

We thought of some people whose advice might be useful; one he knew well enough to call on that afternoon. George did not speak during this discussion, and when Roy left, made no remark on his visit. I turned on the light, and drew my chair closer to the fire.

'How is Morcom?' George asked suddenly. 'Someone said he was ill, didn't they?'

'I've not heard today. I don't think he's much better.'

'We ought to go and see him.'

For a moment I tried to put him off. I suggested that Morcom was not well enough to want visitors, but George was stubborn.

We walked towards Morcom's; a fog had thickened during the day, and the streets were cold and dark.

Morcom's eyes were bright with illness, as he caught sight of George.

'How are things going?' George said, in a tone strangely and uncomfortably gentle.

'It's nothing.'

I walked round to the other side of the bed. Morcom lay back on the pillow after the effort to shake hands. Beyond the two faces, the fog was shining through the window; it seemed to illuminate the room with a white glare.

George made Morcom tell him of the illness. Unwillingly, Morcom said that when he had last seen me at tea with Olive, he had not been well:

a chill had been followed by a day of acute neuritic pain; then the pain lessened, and during the trial he had been lying with a slight temperature.

George sympathised, with his awkward kindness. Their quarrels of the past had been patched up long since; they had met as casual acquaintances in the last few years. Yet, with an inexplicable strain, I remembered the days when Morcom played a special part in George's imagination – the part of the disapproving, persecuting world outside. Now George sat by his bed.

It was strange to see: and to remember how George had once invented Morcom's enmity. Still, more or less by chance, Morcom had done him some bad turns. George did not know that if Morcom had conquered his pride and intervened, the trial might never have happened. Perhaps – I suddenly thought – George, whose understanding sometimes flashed out at random, felt that Morcom also was preyed on, was broken down by remorse.

'This illness is a nasty business,' George was saying. 'You'll have to be careful of yourself. It's a shame having you laid up.'

'You're worrying too much. Your trouble isn't over yet?'

George's face was, for a moment, swept clear of concern and kindness; he was young-looking, as many are at a spasm of fear.

'The last words have been spoken from my side,' he said. 'They've said all they could in my favour. It's a pity they couldn't have found something more.'

'Will he save it –?'

'He told them,' George said, 'that I probably didn't do the frauds they were charging me with. He told them that. He said they weren't to be prejudiced because I was one of the hypocrites who make opportunities for their pleasures, while persuading themselves and other people that they had the highest of motives. I've been used to that attack since you began it years ago. It's suitable it should come in now—'

'I meant nothing like that.'

'He said I believed in freedom because it would ultimately lead me to self-indulgence. You never quite went to the lengths of saying that was the only object in my life. You didn't need to tell me I wanted my sexual pleasures. I've known that since I was a boy. I kept them out of my other happiness for longer than most men would have done. With all the temptations for sexuality for years, I know they have – encroached. You don't think there haven't been times when I regretted that?' He paused, then went on:

'Not that I feel I have hurt anyone or damaged the aims I started out with. But this man who was defending me, you understand, who was saying all that could be said in my favour against everyone there trying to get rid of me – he suggested that I have never wanted anything but sexuality, from the time I began till now. He said I thought I wanted a better world: but a better world for me meant a place to indulge my weaknesses. I was just someone shiftless and rootless, chasing his own pleasures. He used the pleasant phrase – a man who has wasted himself.'

'He was wrong,' said Morcom. He was staring at the ceiling; I felt that the interjection was quite spontaneous.

'He suggested I was "a child of my time".' George went on, 'and not really guilty of my actions because of that. As though he wanted to go to the limit of insulting nonsense. There are a lot of accusations they can make against me, but being a helpless unit in the contemporary stream – that is the last they can make. He said it. He meant it. He meant – running after my own amusement, living in a haze of sexual selfishness, because there's nothing else I wanted to do, because I have lost my beliefs, because there's no purpose in my life. I tell you, Arthur, that's what he said of me. It would be a joke if it had happened anywhere else. With that offensive insult, he dared to put up the last conceivable defence I should ever make for myself. That I had been guilty of a good many sins, that I had been a hypocritical sensualist, but that I wasn't responsible for it because I was "a child of my time". He dared to say that I wasn't responsible for it. Whatever I have done in my life, I claim to be responsible for it all. No one else and nothing else was responsible for what I have done. I won't have it taken away. I am utterly prepared to answer for my own soul.'

The echo died away in the room. Then George said to Morcom:

'Don't you agree? Don't you accept responsibility for anything you may have done?'

There was a silence. Morcom said:

'Not in your way.'

He turned towards George. I listened to the rustle of the bedclothes. He said:

'But after a fashion I do.'

'There are times when it's not easy,' George said. 'When you've got to accept a responsibility that you never intended. This afternoon I heard of the last thing they've done to me. They've dismissed Rachel from her job. Just for being a supporter of mine. You remember her, don't you? Whatever they say against me, they can't say anything against her. But she's going to be disgraced and ruined. I can't lift a finger to help. And I'm responsible. I tell you, I'm responsible. If they want to attack me any more they can say that's the worst thing I've done. I ought not to have exposed anyone to persecution. It's my own doing. There's no way out.'

Morcom lay still without replying. George got up suddenly from his chair.

'I'm sorry I've been tiring you,' he said. 'I didn't think –' He was speaking with embarrassment, but there was also a flicker of affection. 'Is there anything I can do before we go?'

Morcom shook his head, and his fingers rattled with the switch by the bedside. The light flashed back from the windows.

'Are you sure there's nothing I can do?' George asked. 'There's nothing I can fetch? Shall I send you some books? Or is there anything else you'd like sent in?'

'Nothing,' Morcom replied, and added a whisper of thanks.

That night I woke after being an hour or two asleep. The road outside was quiet. I listened for the chimes of a clock. The quarters rang out; I could not get to sleep again.

The central fear kept filling itself with new thoughts. Beyond reach, beyond the mechanical working of the mind, there was not a thought but the shapeless fear. I was afraid of the verdict on Monday.

Sometimes, in a wave of hope, memory would bring back a word, a scrap of evidence, a juror's expression, a remark overheard in court. The fear ebbed and returned. One part of the trial returned with a distress that I could not keep from my mind for long; it was that morning, Getliffe's final speech for the defence.

I could look back on it lucidly and hopelessly, now. There might have been no better way to save them. He had done well for them in the trial; he had done better than I should ever have done; I was thankful now that he had defended them.

And yet – he believed in his description of George, and his excuse. He believed that George had wanted to build a 'better world': a better world designed for George's 'private weaknesses'. As I heard those words again, I knew he was not altogether wrong. His insight was not the shallowest kind, which is that of the intellect alone; he saw with the emotions alone. Yet what he saw was half-true.

George, of all men, however, could not be seen in half-truths. It was more tolerable to hear him dismissed with enmity and contempt. He could not be generalised into a sample of the self-deluded radicalism of his day. He was George, who contained more living nature than the rest of us; whom to see as he was meant an effort from which I, his oldest friend, had flinched only the day before. For in the dock, as he answered that question of Porson's, I flinched from the man who was larger than life, and yet capable of any self-deception; who was the most unselfseeking and generous of men, and yet sacrificed everything for his own pleasures; who possessed formidable powers and yet was so far from reality that they were never used; whose aims were noble, and yet whose appetite for degradation was as great as his appetite for life; who, in the depth of his heart, was ill-at-ease, lonely, a diffident stranger in the hostile world of men. How would it seem when George was older, I thought once or twice that night. Was this a time when one didn't wish to look into the future?

Through that sleepless night, I could not bear to have him explained by Getliffe's half-truth. And, with a renewed distress, I heard also Getliffe's excuse – 'a child of his time'. I knew that excuse was part of Getliffe himself. It was not invented for the occasion. It was the working out of his own salvation. Thus he praised Martineau passionately: in order to feel that, while most aspirations are a hypocrite's or a sensualist's excuse, there are still some we can look towards, which some day we – 'with our feet in the mud' – may achieve.

But there was more to it. 'A child of his time.' It was an excuse for George's downfall and suffering: as though it reassured us to think that with better luck, with a change in the world, his life would have been different to the root. For Getliffe, it was a comfort to blame George through his time. It may be to most of us, as we talk of generations, or the effects of war, or the decline of a civilisation. If one could accept it, it made his guilt and suffering (not only the crime, but the whole story of his creation and its corruption) as impermanent, as easy to dismiss, as the accident of time in which it took place.

In the future, Getliffe was saying, the gentle, the friendly, the noble part of us will survive alone. Yet at times he knew that it was not true. Sometimes he knew that the depths of harshness and suffering will go along with the gentle, corruption and decadence along with the noble, as long as we are men. They are as innate in the George Passants, in ourselves, as the securities and warmth upon which we build our hopes.

That had always appeared true, to anyone like myself. Tonight, I knew it without any relief, that was all.

CHAPTER XLIII

THE LAST DAY

PORSON's closing speech lasted until after twelve on the Monday morning, and the judge's summing up was not quite finished when the court rose for lunch. The fog still lay over the town, and every light in the room was on all through the morning.

Porson's tone was angry and aggrieved. He tried to develop the farm business more elaborately now. 'He ought to know it's too late'; Getliffe scribbled this note on a piece of paper and passed it to me. The feature that stood out of his speech was, however, his violent attack on Martineau.

'His character has been described to you as, I think I remember, a saint. So far as I can see, Mr Martineau's main claim to the title is that he threw up his profession and took an extended holiday – which he has no doubt enjoyed – at someone else's expense. Mr Martineau told you he wasn't above deceiving someone who regarded him as a friend. In a way that might damage the friend seriously, just for the sake of flattering Mr Martineau's own powers as a religious leader. Either that story is true – which I don't for a moment believe, which you on the weight of all the other evidence can't believe either – or else he's perjuring himself in this court. I am not certain which is regarded by my learned friend as the more complete proof of saintliness. From everything Mr Martineau said, from the story of his life both in this town and since he found an easier way of living, it's incredible that anyone should put any faith in his declaration before this court.'

From his bitterness, one or two spectators guessed that the case was important to him. Towards the end of his speech, which was ill-proportioned, he made an attempt to reply to Getliffe's excursion over 'a child of his time'. He returned to the farm evidence before he sat down, and analysed it again.

As we went out to lunch, Getliffe said with a cheerful, slightly shame-faced chuckle: 'He thought because I could run off the rails, he could too.'

Outside the court, most of those who spoke to me were full of the attack on Martineau. Some laughed, others were resentful. As I listened, one impression strengthened. For several Porson had spoken their minds, and yet, at the same time, distressed them.

The judge's face was flushed as he began his summing up.

'A great deal of our time has been spent over this case,' he said, the words spread out with the trace of sententiousness which made him seem never quite at ease. Despite the slow words, his tone held a smothered impatience, as it had throughout the last days of the trial. 'Some of you may think rather more time than was necessary; but you must remember that no time is wasted if it has helped you, however slightly, to bring a correct verdict. I propose to make my instructions to you as brief as possible; but I should be remiss if I did not clear up some positions which have arisen during this trial. First of all, the defendants are being tried for conspiracy to defraud and for obtaining money by false pretences—' he explained, carefully and slowly, the law relating to these crimes. There was a flavour of pleasure in his speech, like a teacher who is confident and precise upon some difficulty his class has raised. 'That is the law upon which they are being tried. The only task which you are asked to undertake is to decide whether or not they are guilty under that law. The only considerations you are to take into account are those which bear directly on these charges. I will lay the considerations before you –' At this point he broke off for lunch.

In the afternoon he gave them a competent, tabulated account of the evidence over the business. It was legally fair, it was tidy and compressed. It went definitely in our favour.

He came to Martineau: 'One witness has attracted more attention than any other. That is Mr Martineau, whom you may consider as the most important witness for the defence and whom the counsel for the prosecution wishes you to neglect as utterly untrustworthy. This is a matter where I cannot give you direct guidance. It is a plain question of whether you believe or disbelieve a witness speaking on oath. There is no possibility, you will have decided for yourselves, that the witness can be mistaken. It is a direct conflict of fact. If you believe Mr Martineau you will naturally see that a considerable portion of the prosecution's case about the agency is no longer tenable. If you disbelieve him, it will no doubt go a long way in your minds towards making you regard the defendants as guilty on that particular charge. If you believe him, you will also no doubt reflect that the most definite part of the prosecution's case has been completely disposed of.

'In such a question, you would naturally be led by your judgment of a witness's character. Here, if I may say so, you are considering the evidence of a witness of unusual character – against whom the leader for the prosecution was able to bring nothing positive but eccentricity and who has certainly undertaken, we must believe, a life of singular self-abnega-tion. I must ask you to consider his evidence in the light of all the connected evidence. But in the end you must settle whether you accept it by asking yourselves two questions: first, whether such a man would not estimate the truth above all other claims; second, whether even a good man – whom you may think eccentric and unbalanced – might not consider himself justified in breaking an oath to save a friend from disgrace.

'I think it necessary to remind you that, according to his own account, you are required to believe him capable of an irresponsible lie.'

One of the jury moistened his lips. The judge paused, passed a finger over his notes, continued:

'That is all I wish to direct your attention towards. But there is one matter which makes me detain you a little longer: and that is to require you to forget, while you consider your verdict, much that you have heard during the conduct of this case. You have been presented with more than a little talk about the private lives of these three young people. You heard it in evidence; both counsel have referred to it with feeling in their closing speeches. I ask you to forget as much of it as is humanly possible. You may thing they have behaved very foolishly; you may think they have behaved very wrongly, as far as our moral standards allow us to judge. But you will remember that they are not being tried for this behaviour; and you must not allow your condemnation of it to affect your deliberations on the real charge against them. You must be as uninfluenced as though you accepted the eloquent plea of Mr Getliffe and believed that the world is in flux, and that these actions have a different value from what they had when most of us were young.' For a moment he smiled.

'That is not to say, though, because you are to assume what may be an effort of charity towards some of the evidence which you have heard, that you are to regard the case itself with lightness. Nothing I have said must lead you to such a course. If you are not entirely convinced by the evidence for the prosecution you will, of course, return, according to the practice of our law, a verdict of not guilty. But if you are convinced by the relevant evidence, beyond any reasonable shade of doubt in your own minds, then you will let nothing stand between you and a verdict of guilty. Whatever you feel about some elements in their lives, whether you pity or blame them, must have no part in that decision. All you must remember is that they are charged with what is in itself a serious offence against the law. It is the probity of transactions such as theirs which is the foundation of more of the structure of our lives than we often think. I need not tell you that, and I only do so because the importance of the offence with which they are charged must not become submerged.'

Several people later mentioned their surprise on hearing, after the tolerant advice and stiff benevolence of his caution upon the sexual aspect of the case, this last sternness over money.

As the jury went out, the court burst into a murmur of noise. One could distinguish no words, but nothing could shut out the sound. It rose and fell in waves, like the drone of bees swarming.

The light from the chandelier touched the varnish on the deserted box.

Getliffe and I walked together outside the court. He said to one of the solicitors, in his breathless confidential whisper: 'I want to get back to the house tonight. One deserves a night to oneself—'

My watch had jerked infinitesimally on. 'They can't be back for an hour,' we were trying to reassure ourselves. At last (though it was only forty minutes since they went out) we heard something: the jury wanted to ask a question. When we got back to our places, the judge had already returned; his spectacles stood before him on his pad, their side arms standing up like antennae; his eyes were dark and bright as he peered steadily into the court.

Through the sough of noise there came Porson's voice, unrestrained and full. 'It's inconceivable that he shouldn't send it before Easter,' he was saying to his junior. His face was high-coloured, but carried heavy purplish pouches under the eyes. He was sitting, one leg over the bench, a hand behind his head, his voice unsubdued, with a bravura greater than anyone's there. He laughed, loud enough to draw the eyes of Mr Passant, who was standing between his wife and Roy, at the back of the court.

The door clicked open. Then we did not hear the shuffle of a dozen people. It was the foreman alone who had come into court.

'We should like to ask a question. We are not certain about a point of law,' he said, nervously brusque.

'It is my place to help you if I can,' said the judge.

'I've been asked to inquire whether we can find one of them definitely had nothing to do with – with any of the charges. If we do that, can we leave out that person and consider the others by themselves?'

The judge said: 'I tried to give you instructions about the law under which they are charged. Perhaps I did not make myself sufficiently clear.' Again he explained. His kindness held a shade of patronage. Two of them could be guilty of conspiracy without a third. It was possible for any of them to be guilty of conspiracy and not guilty of obtaining money by false pretences. (If the jury considered that any of them had not, in fact, profited after joining in a conspiracy.) If they were not guilty of conspiracy, in the circumstances they could not be guilty of obtaining money under false pretences. Unless the jury considered only one person to be responsible – in which case there was no conspiracy, but one person alone could be found guilty of obtaining money by false pretences.

'You are certain you understand?' the judge went on. 'Perhaps you had better write it down. Yes, it would remove any uncertainties if you wrote it down and showed it to me.'

Many found this interruption the most intolerable moment of the trial. Someone said the most sinister – meaning perhaps the confusion, the sudden flash of other lives, of human puzzlement and incompetence.

Through the hour of waiting which still remained, it shot new fragments of thought to many of our minds. Whom did they mean? What were they disagreeing on? But none of us could go on thinking for long: we were wrapped in the emptiness of waiting. The apprehension engrossed us like an illness of the body.

The message came. The jury were coming back. The three were brought up, and took their seats in the dock again. George's arms were folded on his chest. His face was curiously expressionless: but his hands were as livid as though he had been hours in the cold.

The jury came in. Automatically I looked at the clock; it was after half-past four. Their walk was an interminable, drumming sound. The clerk read out the first charge – conspiracy over the agency – with a meaningless emphasis on the name of the town. 'Do you find them guilty or not guilty?'

The foreman said quickly and in a low voice, 'Not guilty.'

Then the second charge – conspiracy over the farm. Again the name of the town started out.

'Guilty or not guilty?' There was a pause. In the silence someone coughed. Suddenly – 'Not guilty.'

Then the individual charges of obtaining money by false pretences. There was a string of 'Not guilty' for Jack and Olive, and finally the charges against George were read out for the last time; the foreman replied 'Not guilty' twice again, in a manner by this time repetitive and without hesitation.

The judge pressed his lips together, and spoke to them with a stiff formal smile:

'You are free to go now.'

CHAPTER XLIV

WALK INTO THE TOWN

THE court seethed with whispers. The three were surrounded by friends and walked to the door. I waited, with Porson and Getliffe, until we could leave ourselves, watching Mr Passant come out of the crowd and take George's hand. Gossip was already in the air. 'They didn't expect –' someone said as I went out with Getliffe. People were laughing with excitement, face after face suddenly leapt to the eyes, vivid and alive.

Getliffe talked in the robing-room until Eden fetched him.

'It's been nice to be together again.' And then: 'Well, one's pulled it off for your people. It was a good case to win.' He smiled. 'We'll have a crack about it in the train tonight. I've learned from it, L.S., I've learned from it.'

When he had shaken hands with Porson and followed Eden out, we heard his voice, cheerful and a little strident, down the corridor. I went across the room to say good-bye to Porson myself. His eyes were narrow with unhappiness.

'I ought not to say it to you, I suppose,' he said, 'but it's incredible these clods of juries should—' then he stopped and laughed. 'Still, good-bye, my boy. We'll run together again one of these days. I hope the job goes well. Let me know if I can be of any use, I expect I can.'

On the pavement outside the court, George and the others were being congratulated by a large party. Olive and Jack had their arms round each other's waists. Soon I was shaking Mr Passant's hand, listening to Olive and Jack and their friends, being invited to visit them later, saying good-bye. In the crowd, someone had put an arm through mine, our voices were raised, there was a great deal of laughter; simply by being together, we were filled with intimacy and excitement. We were careless with the relief, greater and unmixed because others were there to share it. It was only for a few minutes: then Olive took Jack to her car, and Daphne followed after making a sign to George.

The others scattered. I was leaving the town that night, and George told his mother that he would join them in an hour. Roy took the Passants home, and George and I walked up the street alone. The fog had cleared but the sky was low and heavy. Lights were shining in the windows. Neither of us spoke for a few minutes, and then George said:

'This mustn't prevent me doing the essential things.' His voice was sad and defiant. 'I've not lost everything. Whatever they did, I couldn't have lost everything.'

We walked on; he began to talk of his plans for the future, the practical necessities of making a living.

'I shall have to stay with Eden for a few months, of course,' he said. 'Unless they're going through with their persecution. After that –' He became cheerful as he invented schemes for the years afterward: how he would leave Eden's, and get a job at some similar firm where he could work his way through to a partnership. 'I'm ready to leave this place,' he said. 'You used to try to persuade me against my will. I'm prepared to go anywhere. You won't find me so enthusiastic to spend myself without any return.'

It was strange to hear how he enjoyed developing the details of these plans, and the gusto with which he worked them out.

'I've still got time to bring it off. I mustn't leave anything to chance. I can work it out beforehand.'

It reminded me curiously of some of Martineau's happiness as he gave up his career, except that George's hopes were not wild, but modest and within his powers. He was inventive and happy, walking under a sky which seemed darker now we were in the middle of the town. He was in the mood, full of the future, and yet not anxious, which I had not seen since the nights when we first walked in these streets; years before, when he was delighted with the idea of his group of friends, luxuriously thinking of their lives to come and the minor, vaguer, pleasant plans for success in his own life.

After one bitter remark, when we were first alone, everything he said was hopeful and full of zest; several times he laughed, hilariously and without resentment. Just as we were passing a shop, a bicycle, which had been propped up by its pedal against the kerb, toppled over on to the pavement. At the same moment, we happened to notice a man with an unconcealed, satisfied, and cunning smile.

'I wonder,' said George, 'if he's smiling because that bicycle fell over?' Then he broke into a shout of laughter. 'No, it's not that, of course it isn't. He's smiling with relief because there was no one on it.'

We ended the walk at the café near the station, where we held our first conference over Jack. But the café had been respectabilised since then. There were now two floors, and neat waitresses. We went upstairs and sat by the window. We looked down the hill, over the roofs below, out to the grey, even sky.

George elaborated his plans, laughed, drank cup after cup of tea. Then, when I spoke to him, I found his face grown pre-occupied. He replied absently several times. At last he said:

'I've got to show them that I've not lost everything. They've got to realise that I've not lost anything. Not anything that I put a value on. They mustn't think they've dispensed with me as easily as that. I shall keep the essentials. Whatever happened, I couldn't be myself without them. I mean, one way or another. I'm going to work for the things I believe in. I still believe that most people are good, if they're given the chance. No one can stop me helping them, if I think another scheme out carefully and then put my energies into it again. I haven't finished. You've got to remember I'm not middle-aged yet. I believe in other people. I believe in goodness. I believe in my own intelligence and will. You don't mean to tell me that I'm bound to acquiesce in crippling myself?'

His expression was strained and haggard, the opposite of his words. By contrast to the trial, when often he looked young with fear, now his face was older than I had ever seen it.

'I don't deny that I've made mistakes. I gave too much opportunity for jealousy. It's natural they should be jealous, of course. But I shan't leave so many loopholes this time. I didn't make enough concessions. Perhaps I oughtn't to have confined myself to a few people. That was bound to make my enemies hate me more. Whatever I do, it won't have the same completeness this has had for me. But we've got to accept that this is finished. I'm willing to make some concessions now. The main thing is, I shall be keeping on. Everyone would like me to live as they do – shut up in their blasted homes. I'm not going to give them the satisfaction.'

He had not said a word about the substance of the case; he seemed to have dismissed the transactions and charges from his mind.

After a time, feeling he had spoken himself out, I asked about Daphne. As he replied, his voice was quieter.

'I hope she'll marry me,' he said. He smiled in a friendly, almost bantering way. 'It's a pity I didn't find her when you found Sheila'. (He didn't know it, he hadn't guessed it, but that night, as we talked, I was thinking how I could break my marriage.) 'I didn't expect to find everything I wanted in one person then, did I? Still, I ought to have married someone by now, I ought to have made myself.'

'As a result of this trouble—'

George broke out again: 'They've tried to insinuate that everything I've done was because I was sex-crazy. They've tried to explain away the best years of my life – by saying I spent them doing nothing but plot to get a few minutes of pleasure. I ought to have known they would do it.

I trusted them too much. It's senseless letting your faith in goodness run away with you. It would have been easy to shape things differently. I shall profit by it now. Marriage with Daphne will leave me free. As it was, I shan't blame myself. It was bad luck things went the way they did. It wasn't my fault – but when they did, well, they were all round me, I'm not a celibate, my taste is pretty wide. And so I gave them the chance to destroy everything I'd spent all these years in building.'

He paused, then said, in a flat voice, with all the bitterness gone: 'That's why, you see, I've got to show them that it hasn't affected me. I've got to show them for certain that I'm keeping on.'

I could not help but feel that he meant something different and more tormenting. It was himself in whose sight he needed to be seen unchanged. In his heart a voice was saying: 'You can't devote yourself again. You never have. Your enemies are right. You've deceived yourself all this time. And now you know it, you can't begin deceiving yourself again.'

There were to be times – I felt at this moment – when he would want to give up struggling against that voice. There were to be times, darker than now, when he would have to see himself and ask what was to become of him. Yet, in those dark moments, would he – as he was now – be drawing a new strength from his own self-searching, even from his own self-distrust?

After his last remark, both he and I were still eager for what life would bring him. He could still warm himself and everyone round him with his own hope.

The Conscience of the Rich

1927–37

The Conscience of the Rich

The Conscience of the Rich

CONTENTS

PART ONE. INSIDE A FAMILY

PART TWO. FATHER AND SON

PART THREE. THE MARRIAGES

Contents

PART FOUR. THE DANGERS

PART FIVE. ALONE

INSIDE A FAMILY

CHAPTER I

CONFIDENCES ON A SUMMER EVENING

IT was a summer afternoon, the last day of the Bar final examinations. The doors had just swung open; I walked to my place as fast as I could without breaking into a run. For an instant I was touched again by the odour of the old Hall, blended from wooden panels, floor polish, and the after-smell of food; it was as musty as a boarding house, and yet the smell, during those days, became as powerful in making one's heart lift up and sink as that of the sea itself.

As I stared at the question-paper, I went through an initial moment in which the words, even the rubric 'Candidates are required to answer...' appeared glaring but utterly unfamiliar. At the beginning of each examination I was possessed in this way: as though by a magnified version of one of those amnesias in which a single word – for example TAKE – looks as though we have never seen it before, and in which we have to reassure ourselves, staring at the word, that it occurs in the language and that we have used it, spelt exactly in that fashion, every day of our lives.

Then, all of a sudden, the strangeness vanished. I was reading, deciding, watching myself begin to write. The afternoon became a fervent, flushed, pulsing and exuberant time. This I could do; I was immersed in a craftsman's pleasure. In the middle of the excitement I was at home.

Towards the end of the afternoon, the sunlight fell in a swathe across the room, picking out the motes like the beam from a cinema projector. I was cramped, tired, and the sweat was running down my temples; my hand shook as I stopped writing.

In that moment, I noticed Charles March sitting a little further up the hall, across the gangway. His fair hair, just touching the beam of sunlight, set it into a blaze. His head was half-turned, and I could see the clear profile of his clever, thin, fine-drawn face. As he wrote, hunched over his desk, his mouth was working.

I turned back to my paper, for the last spurt.

I had been a little disappointed at not meeting Charles during the course of the examination. We had only talked to one another a few times, when we happened to be eating dinners at the Inn on the same night; but I thought that at first sight we had found something like kinship in each other's company.

I knew little of the actual circumstances of his life, and the little I knew made the feeling of kinship seem distinctly out of place. He came from Cambridge to eat his dinner at the Inn, I from a bed-sitting-room in a drab street in a provincial town. His family was rich, I had gathered: I was spending the last pounds of a tiny legacy on this gamble at the Bar.

We had never met anywhere else but at the Inn dining-table. When I last saw him, we had half-arranged to go out together one night during the examination. All I had heard from him, however, was a 'good luck' on the first morning, as we stood watching for the doors to open.

At last the invigilator called for our papers, and I stayed in the gangway, wringing the cramp out of my fingers and waiting for Charles to come along.

'How did you get on?' he said.

'It might have been worse, I suppose.' I asked about himself as we reached the door. He answered:

'Well, I'm afraid the man next to me is the real victim.'

'What's the matter?'

'He was trying to get a look at my paper most of the afternoon,' said Charles. 'If the poor devil managed it, I should think he'd probably fail.'

I laughed at him for touching wood. He began protesting, and then broke off:

'Look here, would it be a bore for you if we had tea somewhere? I mean, could you possibly bear it?'

I was already used to his anxious, repetitious, emphatic politeness; when I first heard it, it sounded sarcastic, not polite.

We went to a tea-shop close by. We were both very hot, and I was giddy with fatigue and the release from strain. We drank tea, spread the examination paper on the table and compared what we had done. Charles returned to my remark about touching wood:

'It's rather monstrous accusing me of that. If I'd shown the slightest sign of ordinary human competence—' Then he looked at me. 'But I don't know why we should talk about my performances. They're fairly dingy and they're not over-important. While yours must matter to you, mustn't they? I mean, matter seriously?'

'Yes, very much,' I said.

'Just how much? Can you tell me?'

In the light of his interest, which had become both kind and astringer I was able to tell the truth: that I had spent the hundred-or-two pounds (the amount had been actually £300) I had been left in order to read for the Bar; that I had been compelled to borrow some more, and was already in debt. There was no one, literally no one, I had to make it clear, to whom I could turn for either money or influence. So it rested upon this examination. If I did exceptionally well, and won a studentship that would help me over the first years at the Bar, I might pull through; if not, I did not know what was to become of me.

'I see,' said Charles. 'Yes, it's too much to invest in one chance. Of course it is.' He paused. 'You've done pretty well, of course, you know that, don't you? I'm sure you have.' He pointed to the examination paper, still lying on the tablecloth. 'You're pretty confident up to a point, aren't you? Whether you've done well enough – I don't see that anyone can say.'

He gave me no more assurance that I could stand. It was exactly what I wanted to hear said. The tea-shop had grown darker as the sun dipped behind the buildings across the street. We both felt very much at ease. Charles suggested that we should have a meal and go to a theatre; he hesitated for a moment. Then he said:

'I should like you to be my guest tonight.' I demurred: because of the flicker, just for an instant, of some social shame. I remembered the things I usually forgot, that he was rich, elegantly dressed, with an accent, a manner in ordering tea, different from mine. Hurriedly Charles said:

'All right. I'll pay for the meal and you can buy the tickets. Do you agree? Will that be fair?' For a few minutes we were uncomfortable. Then Charles went to telephone his father's house, and came back with a friendly smile. Our ease returned. We walked through the streets towards the west, tired, relaxed, talkative. We talked about books. Charles had just finished the last volume of Proust. We talked about politics; we made harsh forecasts full of anger and hope. It was 1927, and we were each twenty-one.

He took me to a restaurant in Soho. Carefully, he studied the menu card; he looked up from it with a frown; he asked if his choice would suit me and ordered a modest dinner for us both. I knew that he had not forgotten my reluctance to be treated. But now, as we sat by the window (below, the first lights were springing up in the warm evening), his meticulous care seemed familiar, a private joke.

An hour later, we were walking down Shaftesbury Avenue to the theatre. When we arrived at the box office, Charles said:

'Just a minute.' He spoke to the girl inside: 'We asked you to keep seats for Mr Lewis Eliot. Have you got them ready?'

He turned to me, and said in an apologetic tone: 'I thought of it when I was ringing up my father. I decided we might as well be safe. You don't mind too much, do you?'

He stood aside from the grille in order that I could pay for the tickets. The girl gave them to me in an envelope. They were for the pit.

I could not help smiling as I joined him; his manœuvres seemed now even more of a joke. They had made it impossible for me to be extravagant, that was all. As he caught my eye he also began to smile. As we stood in the foyer people passed us, one couple breaking into grins at the sight of ours.

We took our places as the house was filling up. The orchestra was playing something sweet, melancholy and facile. I did not make an attempt to listen, but suddenly the music took me in charge. As I sat down, I had begun to think again of the examination – but on the instant all anxieties were washed away. Not listening as a musician would, but simply basking in the sound, I let myself sink into the sensation that all I wanted had come to pass. The day's apprehension disappeared within this trance; luxury and fame were drifting through my hands.

Then, just before the curtain went up, I glanced at Charles. Soon the play started, and his face was alive with attention; but for a second I thought that he, whom I had so much envied a few hours before, looked careworn and sad.

CHAPTER II

INVITATION TO BRYANSTON SQUARE

THE results of the examination were published about a month later. I had done just well enough to be given a studentship; Charles was lower in the list but still in the first class, which, in view of the amount of work he had done, was a more distinguished achievement than mine.

In September we began our year as pupils and at once saw a good deal of each other. Charles met me the first day I came to London, and our friendship seemed to have been established a long time. He continued to ask about my affairs from where we left off on the night of the examination.

'You're settled for this year, anyway? You've got £150? You can just live on that, can't you?'

He got me to tell him stories of my family; he soon formed a picture of my mother and chuckled over her. 'She must have been an admirable character,' said Charles. But he volunteered nothing about his own family or childhood. When I asked one night, his manner became stiff. 'There's nothing that you'd find particularly interesting,' he said.

He kept entertaining me at restaurants and clubs. One evening he had to give me his telephone number; only then did he admit that he had been living since the summer in his father's house in Bryanston Square. It was strange to feel so intimate with a friend of one's own age, and yet be shut out.

We entered different chambers: I went to Herbert Getliffe and he to someone called Hart, whom I knew by reputation as one of the ablest men at the Common Law Bar. The first weeks in chambers, for me at least, were lonely and pointless; there was nothing to do, and I was grateful when Getliffe appeared and with great gusto recommended some irrelevant book, saying, 'You never know when it will come in handy.' I was under-worked and over-anxious. I had taken two small rooms at the top of a lodging-house in Conway Street, near the Tottenham Court Road. Charles, guessing my state, drove round and fetched me out several nights a week. I wanted to discover why he, too, was harassed.

We each knew that the other was troubled when alone: we each knew that his secretiveness hurt me: yet those first nights in London and in Charles's company were in some ways the most exhilarating I had spent. For a young provincial, the life in London took on, of course, a glamour of its own. Restaurants and theatres and clubs were invested with a warm, romantic haze. And we saw them in a style different from anything I had experienced. The prickliness of the examination evening did not last; it was not much like me, anyway. If we were to go out at all, Charles had to pay.

I noticed that, after he had stopped protecting my feelings, he was not extravagant nor anything approaching it. At bottom, I thought, his tastes were simpler than mine. We ate and went out at night in a decent but not excessive comfort: Soho restaurants, the Carlton Grill, a couple of clubs, the circle and the back row of the stalls. It was decent and not luxurious; it was a scale of living that I had not yet seen.

All that helped. I liked pleasure and good things: and it meant more to me than just the good things themselves; it meant one side, a subsidiary but not negligible side, of the life I wanted to win. Like most young men on the rise, I was a bit of a snob at heart.

In fact, however, I should have gained almost as much exhilaration if I had been walking with Charles through the streets of my own town. There, in the past years as a student, I had made other intimate friends. But George Passant, the closest of them, was a very different person from myself; he saw the world, the people round him, his own passions, in a way which seemed strange to my temperament and which I had to learn step by step. While with Charles, right from our first meeting, I felt that he saw himself and other people much as I did; and he never exhausted his fund of interest.

That was the real excitement, during the first months of our friendship. The picture of those early nights which remained in my memory bore no reference to the dinners and shows, much as I gloated in them; instead, I remembered walking together down Regent Street late one night.

We had just left a coffee stall. Charles carried a mackintosh over his arm; he was stooping a little. He had begun to talk about the characters of Alyosha and Father Zozzima. Didn't I think that no other writer but Dostoevsky could have conveyed goodness in people as one feels it in them? That this was almost the only writer who had an immediate perception of goodness? Why could we accept it from him and doubt it from anybody else?

I could feel the fascination goodness held for him. I recognised what he meant: but at that age I should not have thought of it for myself. We began to argue, with a mixture of exasperation and understanding that often flared up between us. On the one side: isn't it just sentimentality carried out with such touch and such psychological imagination that we swallow it whole? On the other: aren't people like that, even if we choose to see their motives differently, even if we are sceptical about what goodness really means? Then Charles turned to me: his eyes were brighter than ever. They were dark grey, very sharp and intelligent.

'We're each feeling the other's right,' he said. 'The next time I talk about this, I shall appropriate most of what you're saying now – if you're safely out of the way. And you'll do the same, don't you admit it?'

As each day passed in chambers, I looked forward to the evening; but slowly I was managing to occupy myself, and I discovered several odd jobs to do for Getliffe, who soon began to keep me busy. It became clear that Charles was still idle. He seemed to be reading scarcely any law, and I knew quite early that he was unhappy about his career. He spoke of

Hart with a kind of lukewarm respect, but was far more eager to hear my stories of Getliffe.

During those months, I still did not know when to expect Charles's concealments. His family, childhood – yes, as we spoke the blank came between us. About women and love and sex, he was franker than I was and knew more. He was not in love, I was: but we talked without any guards at all. When I spoke about my future, my hopes, he listened; if I asked him his, the secretiveness came back as though I had switched off a light. As an evasion he threw himself with intense vicarious interest into my relations with Herbert Getliffe.

As it happened, Getliffe was a tempting person to gossip about. It was hard not to be captivated by him occasionally: it was even harder not to speculate about his intentions, particularly if they had any effect on one's livelihood. I knew that, the first time he interviewed me in chambers, after I had already arranged to become his pupil. He was late for the appointment, and I waited in his room; it was a rainy summer afternoon, and looking down from the window I saw the empty gardens and the river. Getliffe hurried in, dragging his feet, his lip pushed out in an apologetic grin. Suddenly his expression changed into a fixed gaze from brown and lively eyes.

'Don't tell me your name,' he said. His voice was a little strident, he was short of breath. 'You're Ellis—' I corrected him. As though he had not heard my correction at all, he was saying: 'You're Eliot.' Soon he was telling me:

'I make it a matter of principle to take people like you. Who've started with nothing but their brains.'

He chuckled, suddenly, as though we were jointly doing someone down: 'It keeps the others up to it.'

'And' – his moods were quick, he was serious and full of responsibility again – 'we've got a duty towards you. One's got to look at it like that.'

Inside a quarter of an hour he had exhorted, advised, warned and encouraged me. He finished up: 'As for the root of all evil – I shall have to charge you the ordinary pupil's fees. Hundred pounds for the year. October to October.' He threw out the inducement that he might 're-consider the arrangement' for the last two quarters. If I had done some useful work and 'earned a bit of bread and butter'. He smiled, protruding his lip and saying: 'Yes! The labourer is worthy of his hire.'

I told Charles of this conversation in my first week in London. He said: 'His brother was a friend of mine at Cambridge. By the way, he's singularly unlike him. I was taken to dinner with your Herbert once, last year. Of course, he was the life and soul of the party. The point is, when he was talking to you I'm sure he believed every word he said. That's his strength. Don't you feel that's his strength?'

He added a few minutes later: 'I wish I'd known you were going to him, though.'

Then he knew he had made me more anxious: for the unreliability of Getliffe's temperament was one of those disagreeable truths which I could admit equably enough to myself but was hurt to hear from anyone else. Just as a child I was ravaged by Aunt Milly's strictures about my parents, though I was ready to make them to myself. He said quickly: 'I really meant you might have done better at the Chancery Bar. But it'll make no difference. He'll be better in some ways than a solid cautious man could possibly be. It'll even itself out. It won't affect you too much, you agree, don't you?'

If I had mentioned it to Charles in the summer, he would have sent me to some other chambers, and I should have been spared a good deal. For this year, however, there were certain advantages in being with Getliffe. Quite early in the autumn, he began fetching me into his room two or three times each week. 'How's it going?' he would say, and when I mentioned a case, he would expound with a cheerful, invigorating enthusiasm, more often that not getting the details a trifle wrong (that first slip with my name was typical of his compendious but fuzzy memory). Then he would produce some papers for me: 'I'd like a note on that by the end of the week. Just to keep you from rusting.'

Often there were several days' work in one of those notes, and it was only by not meeting Charles and sitting up late that I could deliver it in time. Getliffe would glance through the pages, take them in with his quick, sparkling eyes, and say affably: 'You're getting on! You're getting on!'

The second time it happened, I was surprised to find the substance of one of those drafts of mine appearing in the course of an opinion of his own. In most places he had not even altered the words.

The weeks went by, the new year arrived: and still Charles had told me little about himself. He had said no more about his family; he had never suggested that I should visit them. He offered no explanation, not even an excuse to save my face. It seemed strange, after he had taken such subtle pains over the most trivial things. It could not be reconciled with all the kind, warm-hearted, patient friendliness I had received at his hands.

At last he asked me. We were having tea in my room on a January afternoon. He spoke in a tone different from any I had heard him use: not diffident or anxious, but cold, as though angry that I was there to receive the invitation.

'I wonder if you would care to dine at my father's house next week?'

I looked at him. Neither of us spoke for a moment. Then he said: 'It might interest you to see the inside of a Jewish family.'

CHAPTER III

MR MARCH WITH HIS CHILDREN

AT the time, Charles was so distressed that I hurried to accept and then turn the conversation away. It was later before I could think over my surprise. For I had been surprised: although as soon as I heard him speak, I thought myself a fool for not having guessed months before.

I remembered hearing Getliffe chat about 'the real Jewish upper deck. They're too aristocratic for the likes of us, Eliot' – and now I realised that he was referring to Charles. As it happened, however, I had known scarcely a single Jew up to the time I came to London. In the midland town where I was born, there had been a few shops with Jewish names over them; but I could not remember my parents and their friends even so much as mention a Jewish person. There were none living in the suburban backstreets; nor, when I got my first invitations from professional families, were there any there.

I could think of just one exception. It was a boy in my form at the grammar school. He stayed at the school only a year or two: he was not clever, and left early: but for the first term, before we were arranged in order of examination results, we shared the same desk because our names came next to each other in the list.

He was a knowing, cheerful little boy who brought large packets of curious boiled sweets to school every Monday morning and gave me a share in the midday break. In Scripture lessons he retired to the back of the class, and studied a primer on Hebrew. He assumed sometimes an air of mystery about the secrets written in the Hebrew tongue; it was only as a great treat, and under solemn promises never to divulge it, that I gained permission to borrow the primer in order to learn the alphabet.

I remembered him with affection. He was small, dark, hook-nosed, his face already set in more adult lines than most of ours in the form. It was an ugly, amiable, precocious face; and on that one acquaintance, so it seemed, I had built up in my mind a standard of Jewish looks.

When I met Charles, it never occurred to me to compare him. He was tall and fair; his face was thin, with strong cheekbones; many people thought him handsome. After one knew that he was a Jew, it became not too difficult to pick out features that might conceivably be 'typical'. For a face so fine-drawn his nostrils spread a little more than one would expect, and his under-lip stood out more fully. But that was like water-divining, I thought, the difficulties of which were substantially reduced if one knew where the water was. After mixing with the Marches and their friends and knowing them for years, I still sometimes wondered whether I should recognise Charles as a Jew if I now saw him for the first time.

I paid my first visit to Bryanston Square on a clear cold February night. I walked the mile and a half from my lodgings: along Wigmore Street the shops were locked, their windows shining: in the side-streets, the great houses stood dark, unlived-in now. Then streets and squares, cars by the kerb, lighted windows: at last I was walking round the square, staring up at numbers, working out how many houses before the Marches'.

I arrived at the corner house; over the portico there was engraved the inscription, in large plain letters, 17, BRYANSTON SQUARE.

A footman opened the door, and the butler took my overcoat. With a twinge of self-consciousness, I thought it was probably the cheapest he had received for years. He led the way to the drawing-room, and Charles was at once introducing me to his sister Katherine, who was about four years younger than himself. As she looked at me, her eyes were as bright as his; in both of them, they were the feature one noticed first. Her expression was eager, her skin fresh. At a first sight, it looked as though Charles's good looks had been transferred to a fuller, more placid face.

'I've been trying to bully Charles into taking me out to meet you,' she said after a few moments. 'You were becoming rather a legend, you know.'

'You're under-estimating your own powers,' Charles said to her.

'What do you mean?'

'You've cross-questioned me about Lewis. You've done everything but trick me. I never realised you had so much character.'

'It was the same with his Cambridge friends,' said Katherine. 'He was just as secretive. It's absolutely monstrous having him for a brother – if one happens to be an inquisitive person.'

She had picked up some of his tricks of speech. One could not miss the play of sympathy and affection between them. Charles was laughing, although he stood about restlessly waiting for their father to come in.

Katherine answered questions before I had asked them, as she saw my eyes looking curiously round the room. It was large and dazzlingly bright, very full of furniture, the sidetables and the far wall cluttered with photographs; opposite the window stood a full-length painting of Charles as a small boy. He was dressed for riding, and was standing against a background of the Row. The colouring was the reverse of timid – the hair bright gold, cheeks pink and white, eyes grey.

'He was rather a beautiful little boy, wasn't he?' she said. 'No one ever thought of painting me at that age. Or at any other, as far as that goes. I was a useful sensible shape from the start.'

Charles said:

'The reason they didn't paint you was that Mr L.' – (their father's first name was Leonard and I had already heard them call him by his nickname) – 'decided that there wasn't much chance of your surviving childhood anyway. And if he tempted fortune by having you painted, he was certain that you'd be absolutely condemned to death.'

I inspected the photographs on the far wall. They were mostly nineteenth century, some going back to daguerreotype days.

'I can't help about those,' said Katherine. 'I don't know anything about them. I'm no good at ancestor worship.' She said it sharply, decisively.

Then she returned, with the repetitiveness that I was used to in Charles, to the reasons why she had not been painted – anxious to leave nothing to doubt, anxious not to be misunderstood.

It was now about a minute to eight, and Mr March came in. He came in very quickly, his arms swinging and his head lowered. As we shook hands, he smiled at me shyly and with warmth. He was bald, but the hair over his ears was much darker than his children's; his features were not so clearcut as theirs. His nose was larger, spread-out, snub, with a thick black moustache under it. When he spoke, he produced gestures that were lively, active and peculiarly clumsy. They helped make his whole manner simple and direct – to my surprise, for I had expected him to seem formidable at once. But I had only to watch his eyes, even though the skin round them was reddened and wrinkled, to see they had once looked like Charles's and Katherine's and were still as sharp.

He was wearing a dinner jacket, though none of the rest of us had dressed. Charles had several times told me not to. Mr March noticed my glance.

'You mustn't mind my appearance,' he said. 'I'm too old to change my ways. You're all too bohemian for me. But when my children refuse to bring any of their friends to see their aged parent if they have to make themselves uncomfortable, I'm compelled to stretch a point. I'd rather have you not looking like a penguin than not at all.'

The butler opened the door; we followed Katherine in to dinner. After blinking under the mass of candelabras in the drawing-room, I blinked again, for the opposite reason: for we might have been going into the shadows of a billiard-hall. The entire room, bigger even than the one we had just left, was lit only at the table and by a few wall-lights. On the walls I dimly saw paintings of generations of the family; later I discovered that the earliest, a picture of a dark full-bearded man, was finished in the 1730s, just after the family settled in England.

I sat on Mr March's left opposite Katherine, with Charles at my side; we took up only a segment of the table. A menu card lay by Mr March's place; he read it out to us with gusto and satisfaction: '*clear* soup, fillets of sole, lamb cutlets, caramel mousse, mushrooms on toast.'

The food was very good. Mr March began talking to me about Herbert Getliffe and the Bar; he already knew something of my career.

'My nephew Robert used to be extremely miserable when he was in your position,' said Mr March. 'My brother-in-law warned him he'd got to wait for his briefs, but Robert always was impatient, and I used to see him being disgorged from theatres every time I took my wife out for a spree. One night I met him on the steps of the St James's—'

'What's going to theatres got to do with his being impatient, Mr L.?' Katherine was beginning to laugh.

Mr March, getting into his stride, charged into a kind of anecdote that I was not ready for. I had read descriptions of total recall: Mr March got nearer to it than anyone I had heard. Each incident that he remembered seemed as important as any other incident (this meeting with his nephew Robert was completely casual and happened over twenty years before): and he remembered them all with extravagant vividness. Time did not matter; something which happened fifty years ago suggested something which happened yesterday.

I was not ready for that kind of anecdote, but his children were. They set him after false hares, they interrupted, sometimes all three were talking at once. I found myself infected with Mr March's excitement, even anxious in case he should not get back to his starting-point.

Listening to the three of them for the first time, I felt dazed. Mr March's anecdotes were packed with references to his relatives and members of their large inter-married families. Occasionally these were explained, but usually taken for granted. He and his children had naturally loud voices, and in each other's presence they became louder still. Between Mr March and Charles I could feel a current of strain; perhaps between Mr March and Katherine also, I did not know; but the relations of all three were very close.

I kept looking from one to another of the clever, energetic, mobile faces. I knew that Charles had regretted inviting me; that, as we waited for his father to come in, he wished the evening were already over; yet now he was more alive than I had ever seen him.

'Yes, what has going to theatres to do with Robert being impatient?' asked Charles.

'If he hadn't been impatient, he wouldn't have gone to theatres,' said Mr March. 'You know he doesn't go now. And if his uncle Philip hadn't been so impatient, he wouldn't have made such a frightful ass of himself last Tuesday. That's my eldest brother, Philip' – he suddenly turned to me – 'I've never known him make such a frightful ass of himself since that night in 1899. The key was lost—'

'When, Mr L.? In 1899?' asked Katherine.

'What key?'

'Last Tuesday, of course. The key of my confounded case. I didn't possess a case in 1899. I used the bag that Hannah gave me. She never liked me passing it on to my then butler. So I told Philip the key was lost when I saw him in my club. They'd just made us trustees of this so-called charity, though why they want to add to my labours and give me enormous worry and shorten my life, I've never been able to understand.' (At this time Mr March was nearly sixty-three. He had retired thirty years before, when the family bank was sold.) 'Philip ought to expect it. They used to call him the longest-headed man on the Stock Exchange. Though since he levelled up on those Brazilian Railways, I have always doubted it.'

'Didn't you level up yourself, Mr L.?' said Katherine. 'Wasn't that the excuse you gave for not buying a car when they first came out?'

'While really he's always been terrified of them. You've never bought a car yet, have you?' said Charles.

'It depends what you mean by buying,' Mr March said hurriedly.

'That's trying to hedge,' said Charles. 'He can't escape, though. He's always hired them from year to year,' he explained to me. 'It must have cost ten times as much, but he felt that if he never really committed himself, he might find some excuse to stop. Incidentally, Mr L., it's exactly your idea of economy.'

'No! No!' Mr March was roaring with laughter, shouting, pointing his finger. 'I refused to accept responsibility for moving vehicles, that's all. I also told Philip that I refused to accept responsibility if he took action before we considered the documents—'

'The documents in the case?'

'He stood me some tea – extremely bad teas they've taken to giving you in the club: they didn't even provide my special buns that afternoon – and I said we ought to consider the documents and then call at the banks. "When are you going to meet me at these various banks?" I said. He said I was worrying unnecessarily. My married daughter said exactly the same thing before her children went down with chicken-pox. So I told Philip that if he took action without sleeping on it, I refused to be a party to any foolishness that might ensue. I splashed off negotiations.'

'What did you do,' said Katherine.

'I *splashed* off negotiations,' said Mr March, as though it was the obvious, indeed the only word.

'Did Uncle Philip mind?'

'He was enormously relieved. Wasn't he enormously relieved?' Charles asked.

Mr March went on:

'Apart from his initial madheadedness, he took it very well. So I departed from the club. Owing to all these controversies, I was five minutes later than usual passing the clock at the corner; or it may have been fast, you can't trust the authorities to keep them properly. Then I got engaged in another controversy with the newsboy under the clock. I took a paper and he insisted I'd paid, but I told him I hadn't. I thought he was a stupid fellow. He must have mixed me up with a parson who was buying a paper at the same time. I tossed him double or quits, and I unfortunately lost. Then I arrived outside the house, and, just as I was thinking of a letter to Philip dissociating myself from his impulsive methods – I saw a light on in my dressing-room. So I ascended the stairs and found no one present in the room. John – that is my butler,' he remarked to me – 'came with me and I asked for an explanation. No one could offer anything satisfactory. We went into my bedroom and I asked the footman. Not that I've ever known him explain anything. He was under the window on all fours—'

'Oh God, Mr L.,' Katherine broke out. 'I've lost my grip. *Why* was the footman on all fours?'

'*Looking for the key*, of course,' Mr March shouted victoriously. 'It was still lost. John discovered it late that night—'

Mr March crashed home, completed the diachronic course, by describing how the documents were read and showed Philip to have assumed one erroneous datum. But, as Mr March admitted, the datum was quite irrelevant to their transaction, and it was only in method that he had scored a decisive point of judgment.

We went back to the drawing-room for coffee. Mr March sat by the fire, radiant, bursting out into another piece of total recall. Nothing prevented him – I was thinking – from saying what he felt impelled to say; the only decorum he obeyed seemed to rest in purely formal things; he was an uncontrollably natural man, and yet when the coffee was two minutes late he felt a pang, as though something improper had happened.

We had not been sitting long in the drawing-room before Mr March was arranging a timetable for the next day. He visited his chauffeur first thing each morning, with written instructions of the times he and Katherine wanted the car; he felt the next day slipping out of his control unless he could compile the list the previous night.

'I suppose you're really going to the dance at last?' he said to Katherine.

'I'm not absolutely certain,' she said.

'I wish you'd make up your mind one way or the other. How can I keep Taylor in a suitable frame of mind tomorrow if he doesn't know whether he's on duty at eight o'clock or not?'

'Look. I can easily take her if she wants to go,' said Charles.

'I refuse to accept responsibility for my son's car,' said Mr March.

'But I'm pretty certain she'd definitely rather not,' said Charles. 'That's true, Katherine, isn't it?'

'I shan't get any pleasure from it myself. If I go it's only to oblige you, Mr L.,' said Katherine.

I glanced at her. For an instant I thought she was frightened of being a failure at the dance. It did not make much sense – she had pleasant looks, she was so fresh and warm. But she was only eighteen, there were the traces of a schoolgirl left in her: I imagined she could be shy of men, or dread they would have no use for her.

Suddenly, I knew that was not the reason. This dance must have a special meaning.

In fact, as I soon gathered, it was one of the regular dances arranged for the young men and girls of Jewish society in London; a means, as Mr March accepted with his usual realism, of helping to marry them off within their proper circle.

'I'll only go to oblige you,' said Katherine.

'I don't want you to oblige me, but I want you to go.'

'I'll promise to get myself there once before the end of the winter,' said Katherine.

'It's no use attending as though you were paying a visit to a mausoleum,' Mr March shouted.

'I'm certain I can't possibly like it,' she said.

'How do you know you won't like it? Florence thought she wouldn't like it till she tried.'

Florence was not, as I thought at the time, the other daughter – but merely a second cousin of Mr March's.

'I'll try to be unprejudiced when I do go,' she said. 'If you don't press me until I just want to get it over.'

'I'm not pressing you. Except that there are certain actions I require of my daughter—'

Charles broke in:

'That's putting her in a false position.' At once Katherine was left out of the quarrel. Mr March's temper flared against his son. He said:

'It's a position you ought to have adopted on your own account. You've only been there once or twice yourself. Though you knew what I required—'

'Don't you see it is for exactly the same reason that I only went once myself? You're asking her to spend her time with totally uncongenial people—'

'What do you mean, uncongenial?'

Charles said:

'She'll only be miserable if you insist.'

Mr March shouted:

'I don't know why you're specially competent to judge.'

'I'm afraid I know,' said Charles.

'I refuse to recognise it for a minute.'

Katherine was flushed and worried, as he looked from one to the other. Now that the anger was concentrated between them, with her left out, it had taken on a different tone.

Charles began to speak quietly to Mr March. I said to Katherine, to take her attention away:

'Don't you think any mass of people sounds rather forbidding? But one can usually find a few who make it tolerable, when one actually arrives.'

She gave an uncomfortable smile. The quarrel, however, seemed to have died down. Soon Mr March said, with no sign that he had been shouting angrily a few minutes before:

'The chief feature of these dances occurred one night when I escorted your mother. I was feeling festive, because we'd recently become engaged. It was 1898, though my sister Caroline always said we were as good as engaged after seder night in '96. She wasn't at this dance, but your mother's sister Nellie was, unfortunately as it turned out. We'd been dancing very vigorously, proper old-fashioned dancing that you're all too degenerate to approve of. So I went outside to mop my brow. When I came back into the room your mother and her sister were sitting down on the other side. Someone stopped me and said: "Mr March, I must felicitate you on your engagement." I didn't like him, but I said "Thank you very much"; I thought I might as well be civil. Then he said: "Isn't your fiancée sitting over there?" And I agreed. He went on – he was a talkative fellow – and said: "I suppose she's the pretty one on the left."' Mr March simmered with laughter. 'Of course, he'd fallen into the trap. That was her sister. No one ever thought my wife was the prettier one. But I liked her more.'

At exactly 10.40 Mr March started to his feet and said good-night. 'You'll visit us again, I hope,' he said, in a manner so simple and natural that it seemed more than a form. Then, with equal attention to the task in hand, he set off on a tour of inspection round the room; he pulled aside each curtain to make sure that the window behind it was latched for the night. His final words were to Charles:

'Don't forget to lock this door. When you decide to retire.'

When he had left, Charles explained:

'The idea is, you imagine a burglar getting through the windows. In spite of the fact that Mr L. has seen they're locked and bolted. Then, having got through the window, the burglar discovers with amazement that the door is locked on the other side.'

Katherine smiled.

'But he was more tolerable than I expected tonight, I must say,' she said. 'I thought there might be a scene. I was afraid it might be embarrassing for you,' she said to me.

'Yes,' said Charles. Then he asked her: 'You are satisfied, aren't you? You do feel that things are coming out better?'

'Thanks to the way you coped,' she said.

In a few minutes she went to bed, and soon Charles and I walked out into the square. I told him how much I liked them both.

'I'm enormously glad,' he said. His face was lit up with a blaze of pleasure; for a second, he looked boyish and happy.

We talked about Mr March. Charles pointed back to the house: several windows were still lighted. 'He's waiting to hear me come in,' he said.

'Then he'll trot downstairs to see that the door is properly fastened.'
Charles was speaking with fondness; but I noticed that he found it easier
to talk of Mr March's eccentric side. He was using this joke, this legend
of Mr March, to distract first my eyes, and then his own.

When I mentioned Katherine again, he broke out without any reserve:

'I'm devoted to her, of course. As it happened, we were bound to have
a lot in common. It was exciting when I suddenly discovered that she was
growing up.' Then he said: 'I couldn't let her be sent to this dance –
without trying to stop it. You could see it wasn't just ordinary diffidence,
couldn't you?'

I said: 'As soon as she spoke.'

'If a man she liked wanted to take her to a dance, she might be nervous,
and then I'd definitely bully her into going,' said Charles. 'It would do her
good to be flirted with. But this is different. It means something important
to her. If she goes, she's accepting—' He hesitated. He had suddenly
begun to speak with obsessive force. He said: 'If she goes, she'll find it
harder to keep on terms with everything she wants to be.'

CHAPTER IV

A SIGN OF WEALTH

CHARLES seemed to be afraid that, during our conversation about
Katherine, he had given himself away. He did not refer to it again until,
in curious circumstances, he made a confession. That happened some
months later than my introduction to his family, on the night after his
first case.

Meanwhile, Mr March and Katherine welcomed me at Bryanston
Square, and I went there often.

On the surface, of course, we were novelties to each other – I as much
to them as they to me. They had never known a poor young man. Mr
March once or twice took an opportunity to put me at my ease; on one
occasion, I had written to him apologising for having caused some
trouble (my rooms became uninhabitable owing to a burst gas-pipe, and
I stayed a couple of nights at Bryanston Square). He replied in a letter
which covered two sheets of writing paper; his handwriting was firm,
his style rather like his speech, but sometimes both eloquent and stately;
he said '. . . as you know, no one deplores more than I the indifference to

manners and common decency displayed by the younger generation. But I am glad to make an exception of yourself, who are always the height of punctiliousness and good form. . . .' It was untrue, by any conceivable standard. It delighted me to read it; it gave me the special pleasure of being flattered on a vulnerable spot.

On my side, I was often fascinated by the sheer machinery of their lives. They were the first rich family I had known; in those first months, it was their wealth that took my attention more, not their Jewishness. It was the signs of wealth that I kept absorbing – yes, with a kind of romantic inflation, as though I had been one of Balzac's young men.

I should have done the same if they had not been Jews at all; yet I had already seen the meaning which being Jews had for both Charles and Katherine. They had not spoken of it. I dared not hurt them by saying a word. I could not forget Charles's invitation to 'see the inside of a Jewish family' nor Katherine's face as they quarrelled about the dance. This silence, which got in the way of our intimacy, had the minor result of misleading me. I did not appreciate for a long time how eminent the family was. I picked up some facts, that Mr March's brother Philip was the second baronet, that both Philip and his father had sat as Conservative members: but no one mentioned, or let me infer, that the Marches were one of the greatest of Anglo-Jewish houses.

About their luxuries, however, they were as amused as I was. Both Charles and Katherine were quick at seeing their everyday actions through fresh eyes.

She said one night as she came down to dinner: 'I thought of you in my bath, Lewis. I just remembered that I've never run one single bath for myself in the whole of my life.'

One afternoon at Bryanston Square, I made another discovery. Charles and I were alone in the drawing-room. There came a tap on the door, and a small elderly man entered the room, wearing a cloth cap. I thought he could scarcely be a servant: Charles took no notice, and went on talking. The man walked up to the clock over the fireplace, opened it, wound it up, and went away.

'Whoever is that?' I asked.

'Oh,' said Charles, 'that's the clock man.'

Charles looked surprised, then began to smile as I asked more questions. The clock man had no other connection with the house: he was appointed to come in on one afternoon a week, and wind up and supervise all the clocks. He was engaged on the same terms by other houses in the square; like many of the Marches' servants, he would be recommended from one relative to another – their butlers and chief parlourmaids usually began as junior servants in another March household. Charles claimed to have heard one of his aunts ask: 'I wonder if you can tell me of a good reliable clock man ?'

It seemed bizarre, more so than any of the open signs of wealth. As Charles said: 'I suppose it is the sort of thing anyone would expect Mr L. to do himself. Putting on his deerstalker hat for the purpose.'

But there was one sign of wealth that neither Charles nor I could face so easily.

Our year as pupils ended in September; at the end of it, Charles remained in Hart's chambers, scarcely mentioning the fact; Getliffe let me stay on in his 'paying a nominal rent. Just as a matter of principle.' He had not referred again to any remission of pupil's fees; he promised to find me some work, and several times I heard the phrase 'the labourer is worthy of his hire'.

In fact, I was doing the same work that winter as when I was still a pupil. I told myself that nothing worth having could possibly come yet. Just as I had done the year before, I attended many cases, as though it were better to be in court as a spectator than not at all. Charles, just as he had done the year before, came with me to hear Getliffe in the King's Bench Courts. One day, it was all according to the usual pattern. Getliffe for once was not late, but he was no less flurried-looking. His wig was grimy, and he pushed it askew. As usual, when he spoke he gave the impression of being both nervous and at home. He used short and breathless sentences and occasionally broke into his impudent shame-faced smile. The case was merely a matter of disentangling some intricate precedent and he was doing it clumsily and at length. Yet the judge was kind to him, most people were on his side.

When they went in to lunch, Charles and I walked in the Temple gardens, just as we had often done the year before.

'One thing about him,' said Charles, 'he does enjoy what he's doing. Don't you agree? He thoroughly enjoys coming into court and wearing his wig. Even though he's a bit nervous. Of course he enjoys being a bit nervous. He's completely happy playing at being a lawyer.'

Then he smiled, and his eyes shone.

'But still, I refuse to let him take me in altogether. It will be monstrous if he wins this case. It will be absolutely monstrous.'

Charles began to argue, at his most incisive, what Getliffe's case should have been. He could not forget what he called the 'muddiness' of Getliffe's mind: even though he felt humorously tender to him as he heard him speak, even though he could not escape the envy that a care-free spontaneous nature evokes in one more constrained.

'Ah well,' I said, 'I wouldn't mind putting up a bit of muddiness myself – if I could get a foot in first.'

Charles was intent on the pure argument; for him, usually so quick, it took moments to realise that I had spoken bitterly. We were further apart than usual; here, more than anywhere, each felt estranged from the other; as our careers came nearer, we began to know for the first time that we were being driven different ways. Then he said:

'I suppose you feel that you're wasting months of your life.'

'Don't you? Don't you?'

'I might waste more than months.' He paused, and went on: 'Don't you think that even Getliffe sometimes wonders whether he's been such a success after all?'

'I'd prefer it to none at all.'

'That's over-simple,' said Charles. 'Or else I'm making excuses in advance. Do you mean that?'

'How much are you looking forward to your first case?' I said.

'Not very much,' said Charles. 'Not in your fashion. I don't know. I may be glad when it comes.'

Within a month of that conversation, his first case came. Something different, that is, from the guinea visits to the police courts, which we both made: instead, a breach of contract, legally interesting although the amounts involved were small, arrived in Hart's chambers. The plaintiff knew one of Charles's uncles, and Hart himself; Hart, who had married a March cousin, suggested that young March was the most brilliant of the family and only needed some encouragement. So the case came to Charles. There was nothing sensational about it; it was a chance for which, that winter, I would have given an ear.

Charles could see the depth, the rancour, of my envy. One of the nights we studied the papers together, he looked at me with eyes dark and hard.

'I'm just realising how true it is,' he said, 'that it's not so easy to forgive someone, when you're taking a monstrously unfair advantage over him.' Trying to compensate for my envy, I spent evenings with him over the case. He was so restless, so anxious, that it was uncomfortable to be near: to begin with, I envied him even that. To have a real event to be anxious about! Then I suspected that this was not just ordinary anxiety.

He worked hard, but he was tense all the time, getting out of bed at night to make sure he had written a point down. If and when my first case came, I thought, I should do the same. But I should still be in high spirits – while one had only to listen to Charles's voice to hear something inexplicably harsh, not only anxious but abnormally strained.

As the hearing drew nearer (it was fixed for the middle of January) he seemed to find a little relief in violent, trivial worries about the case; 'I shall put up the dimmest opening,' he said, 'that's ever been heard in a court of law. Can't you imagine the heights of dimness that I shall manage to reach?'

Several times, as I heard him reiterate these anxieties, I thought how they would have deceived me only a short time before. Charles was the most restrained of his family; but, like Mr March and Katherine, he did not try to be stoical in little things. Many acquaintances felt that their worries (over, for instance, this opening speech, or catching a train, or whether someone had overheard an indiscreet remark) could only be indulged in by weak and unavailing people. It was tempting to regard them as part of the sapping process of luxury. It was tempting: it seemed sociologically just: but in fact, when affliction came, not petty worry, each of the three Marches was stoical in the end.

Katherine knew this, although on those nights at Bryanston Square, while Charles was waiting for his case to come on, she watched him with pain. I wondered if she understood better than I why he was so tense. Whether she understood or not, her own nerves were strung up. But she could still tease him about the symptoms of fuss; as she did so one evening, she repeated in my presence the latest story of Mr March's fussing, which was only a few months old.

As I knew, Mr March always expressed gloomy concern if one of his children had a sore throat: he would enquire after it repeatedly, with the most lugubrious expression: 'Wouldn't it be better if I sent for a practitioner? Not that I pretend to have much faith in any of them. Wouldn't it be better if I sent for one tonight?' In the same way, he profoundly doubted anyone's ability to get to the correct station in time to catch an appropriate train: travelling could only be achieved by a kind of battle against the railways, in which he sat like a general surrounded by maps and timetables, drawing up days before any journey an elaborate chart of possible contingencies.

In the past summer, he had spent himself prodigiously over a journey of Katherine's. She had never been away alone up to this time; even now, it was scarcely alone in any but Mr March's sense of the word, as she was going on a cruise down the Adriatic, in a party organised by her young women's club. Mr March opposed on principle; and, when she got her way, occupied a good part of a night in making certain what would happen if she missed the party at Victoria on the first morning.

Three days after the party started, Mr March received a telegram. It reached him half an hour after breakfast and read: *Regret Katherine ill in —— hospital Venice food poisoning suspected urgent you should join her*. It was signed by the secretary of the club. Mr March said in a business-like tone to Charles: 'Your sister's ill. I may be away some time,' and caught the eleven o'clock boat train.

He arrived at the hospital the following midday; he interviewed the doctors, decided it was nothing grave, and then began to grumble at the heat. He was wearing his black coat and striped trousers, and he had arrived in a Venetian July.

He saw Katherine, said: 'I refuse to believe there's anything wrong,' and walked off to find an English doctor. He had all his life expressed distrust of 'those foreign practitioners'. When he talked to an English one, however, he decided that he was probably incompetent and that the Italians 'seemed level-headed fellows'. So Mr March accepted the position; he could do nothing more; he retired to his hotel and sat in his shirt sleeves looking at the Grand Canal.

In a couple of days Mr March and the Italian doctors agreed that Katherine could be safely moved to the hotel. Mr March arranged everything with competence; as soon as Katherine began to walk about, he said, with an air of conviction and scorn:

'I knew there was never anything wrong.'

They stayed in Venice for a fortnight. From the moment of his arrival, he had behaved with equanimity. When she recovered, however, the air of sensible friendliness suddenly broke: and it broke in a characteristic way. Katherine slept in the room next to Mr March's: like his, its windows gave on to the Canal: to Mr March's horror, she wanted to leave them open all night. Mr March angrily protested. Katherine pointed out that no gondolier could get in without climbing from the balcony beneath: and that, in any case, her jewellery had been deposited in the manager's safe and there was nothing valuable to steal.

Mr March stamped up and down the room. 'My dear girl,' he shouted, 'it's not your valuables I'm thinking of, it's your virtue.' Katherine stuck to her point. An hour later, when they were both in bed, she heard his voice come loudly through the wall:

'How sharper than a serpent's tooth. . . .' The last words sounded, at first hearing, as though they were an invention of her own. But like most of the March stories, this was discussed in Mr March's presence: he protested, chuckled, added to it, and it must have been substantially true. In fact, if Mr March felt like King Lear, he acted upon it, even if the occasion seemed to others inadequate.

The story must have been true, except for what they each left out. They left out what none of us would find it necessary to tell in a family story: the fact that there was deep feeling in the quarrel, though the occasion was so absurd: that Katherine, arguing with her father, felt more over-awed and frightened than she could admit: that Mr March felt a moment of anxiety, such as we all know as we see someone beginning to slip from the power of our possessive love.

CHAPTER V

CONFESSION

CHARLES'S case lasted for a day and a half. From the beginning, lawyers thought it impossible that anyone could win it: at times, particularly on the second morning, I found my judgment wavering – was he going to prove us wrong after all? His manner was restless, sometimes diffident, sometimes sharp and ruthless: I knew – it was not an unqualified pleasure for me to know – that I did not often hear a case argued with such drive and clarity.

Mr March sat through every word. As he watched his son, his face lost its expression of lively, fluid interest, and became tightened into one that was nervous, preoccupied and rigid. He took me out to lunch on the first day; his mood was quieter than usual, and he was glad to have someone to talk to.

'My daughter Katherine has mysteriously refused to put in an appearance,' he said. 'She did not account for her actions, but the reason is, of course, that she couldn't bear to watch my son making a frightful ass of himself in public. I must say that I can sympathise with her attitude. When he contrived to get himself into the team at school, I used to feel that propriety demanded that I should be represented in person: but invariably I wished that I could take a long walk behind the pavilion when he came out to bat.'

Mr March went on:

'I also considered today that propriety demanded that I should be present in person. Even though it might entail seeing my son make a frightful ass of himself upon an important occasion. So far as I can

574

gather with my ignorance of your profession, however, he appears to have avoided disaster so far. Hannah might not think so, but I fail to see why she is specially competent to judge.'

I told him how well Charles had done; Mr March gave a delighted and curiously humble smile.

'I'm extremely glad to have your opinion,' he said. 'This is the first time that I've been able to consider the prospect of any of my family emerging into the public eye.' He added, in a matter-of-fact tone: 'I could never have cut anything of a dash myself. My son may conceivably find it easier.'

We walked back to the court, Mr March still nervous and proud. For the first time I had seen how much he was living again in his son.

In the last hours of the case, Charles's cross-examination of an expert witness secured most attention. Several people later commented on how formidable a cross-examiner he would become. Actually, his own strain gave him an added edge; but still, he enjoyed those minutes. He loved argument: he was sometimes ashamed of the harshness that leapt to his tongue, but when he let himself go, argument made him fierce, cheerful, quite spontaneous and self-forgetful. The court had just admired him in one of those moods.

In the end, Charles lost the case, but the judge paid a compliment to 'the able manner, if I may say so, in which the case has been handled by the plaintiff's counsel'.

As we left the court, men collected round Charles, congratulating him. I joined them and did the same, before I went back to chambers.

'I want to see you rather specially. I'll come round tomorrow night,' said Charles. 'Can you manage to stay in?'

On my way to the Inn, I wondered what he was coming for. He had looked flushed and smiling: perhaps his success – my envy kept gnawing, as sharp, as dominating as neuralgia – had settled him at last. I walked along the back streets down from the Strand; it was a grey afternoon, and a mizzle of rain was greasing the pavement. I thought about Charles's future, compared with mine. In natural gifts there was not much in it. He was at least as clever, and had a better legal mind; perhaps I was the more speculative. In strength of character we were about the same. In everything but natural gifts, he had so much start that, as I had often done before, I didn't like to think of it.

I had one advantage, though. Neither of us was the kind of man whom this career would completely satisfy. Charles had read for the Bar because he could not find a vocation; I had always known that, in the very long run, I wanted other things. The difference was, I had to behave as though the doubt did not exist. To earn a living, I had to work as though I was single-minded. Until I made some money and some sort of name, I could not even let myself look round. Charles often envied that simplification, that compulsory simplification, which being poor imposed upon my life.

Nevertheless, anyone in his senses would put his money on Charles, I told myself that afternoon. As Herbert Getliffe remarked when I arrived and told him of the result: 'Mark my words, Eliot, that young friend of ours will go a long way.' He went on: 'He was lucky to get the job, of course. The boys on the Jewish upper deck are doing a bit of pulling together. Don't you wish you were in that racket, Eliot?'

He looked harassed, responsible, sincere.

'I must see if I can find you a snippet for yourself one of these days. The trouble is, one owes a duty to one's clients. One can't forget that, much as one would like to—'

The next night, I waited in my room for Charles. It was a room which bore only a remote resemblance to Mr March's drawing-room. The satin was wearing through on the two armchairs; the room was unheated all day, and even by the fire at night it struck empty and chill, with the vestige of a smell of hair-lotion drifting up from the barber's shop down below. Charles was late: at last I heard his car draw up in the street beneath, and his footsteps on the stairs. As soon as he entered, I was struck by the expression on his face. The strain had left him. He apologised for keeping me; I knew that he was tired, relaxed and content.

He sat in the other chair, at the opposite side of the fireplace. Nothing had been said except for his apologies. He stretched himself in the chair, and smiled. He said:

'Lewis, I shan't go on with the Bar.'

I exclaimed. After a moment, I said: 'You've not settled anything, have you?'

'What do you think?' He was still smiling.

'You know you'd do well at it,' I began. 'Better than any of us—'

'I'm sure that's nonsense,' he said. 'But in any case, it isn't the point. You know it isn't the point, don't you?'

He had not come for advice. His mind was made up. There was no anxiety or hesitation left in his manner. He was speaking more calmly, with more strength and authority, than I had heard him speak.

'I was very glad that I didn't disgrace myself yesterday,' he said. 'Because one of the reasons for giving up the law wasn't exactly pleasing to one's self-respect. I knew it all along: I wanted to escape because I was frightened. I was frightened that I shouldn't succeed.'

'I don't believe much in that,' I said.

'You mustn't minimise it.' He smiled at me. 'Remember, I'm a much more diffident person than you are. As well as being much more spiritually arrogant. I hate competing unless I'm certain that I'm going to win. The pastime I really enjoy most is dominoes, right hand against left. So I wanted to slip out: but I should have felt cheap doing it.'

I nodded.

'What would have happened if you hadn't done so well yesterday?'

'Do you think I've enough character to go on until I'd satisfied myself?' He chuckled. 'I wonder if I or anyone else could really have stuck on doggedly at the Bar until they felt sufficiently justified. It would have been rather heroic: but it would also have been slightly mad. Don't you agree it would have been mad? No, I'm sure I should have given it up whatever had happened. But if I'd been a complete failure yesterday, I should have felt pretty inferior because I was escaping. Now I don't, at any rate to the same extent.' He went on: 'Of course, you know what I think about the law.'

He meant the law as an occupation: for a time we went over our past arguments: I knew as well as he did how he found the law sterile, how he could not feel value in such a life. Then Charles said:

'Well, those were two reasons I've thought about for months. You can't dismiss them altogether. I shall always have a slight suspicion that I ran away. But, like all the other reasons one thinks about for months, they had just about as much effect on my actions as Mr L.'s patent medicines have on his superb health. It was something quite different – that I didn't need or want to think about – that made it certain I should have to break away.'

He looked straight at me.

'I think you've realised it for long enough,' he said. 'You remember the first time I talked to you about Katherine?'

'Yes.'

'I was afraid afterwards that you must have noticed something,' he said, with a grim smile. 'It was the first time you came to our house, of course. I was very much upset because she was being sent to that dance against her will. I was pretending to be concerned only about her welfare. I was talking about her, and trying to believe that I was being detached and dispassionate. You've done the same thing yourself, haven't you? It was the sort of occasion when one sits with a furrowed brow trying to work out someone else's salvation – and knows all the time that one's talking about oneself.'

'Yes,' I said.

'Probably you understand,' said Charles, 'without my saying any more. But I want to explain myself. It's curiously difficult to speak, still. Even tonight, when I'm extremely happy, I'm still not quite free.'

He said, slowly:

'The Bar represented part of an environment that I can't accept for myself. You see, I can't say it simply. If I stayed at the Bar, I should be admitting that I belonged to the world' – he hesitated – 'of rich and influential Jews. That is the world in which most people want to keep me. Most people, both inside it and outside. If I stayed at the Bar, I should get cases from Jewish solicitors, I should become one of the gang. And people outside would dismiss me, not that they need so much excuse, as another bright young Jew. Do you think it's tolerable to be set aside like that?'

There was a silence. He went on:

'I haven't enjoyed being a Jew. Since I was a child, I haven't been allowed to forget – that other people see me through different eyes. They label me with a difference that I can't accept. I know that I sometimes make myself feel a stranger, I know that very well. But still, other people have made me feel a stranger far more often than I have myself. It isn't their fault. It's simply a fact. But it's a fact that interferes with your spirits and nags at you. Sometimes it torments you – particularly when you're young. I went to Cambridge desperately anxious to make friends who would be so intimate that I could forget it. I was aching for that kind of personal success – to be liked for the person I believed myself to be. I thought, if I couldn't be liked in that way, there was nothing for it: I might as well go straight back to the ghetto.'

He stopped suddenly, and smiled. He looked very tired, but full of relief.

As I listened, I was swept on by his feeling, and at the same time surprised. I had noticed something, but nothing like all he had credited me with. I had seen him wince before, but took it to be the kind of wound I had known in myself through being born poor; I too had sometimes been looking out for snubs. In me, that was not much of a wound, though: it had never triggered off a passion. Now I was swept along by his, moved and yet with a tinge of astonishment or doubt.

'What shall you do?' I said, after a silence. 'Do you know what your career's to be?'

'Most people will assume that I intend to drift round and become completely idle.'

Then I asked if anyone else knew of his abandoning the Bar. He shook his head.

'Mr L. will be disappointed, of course,' he said.

'He was talking to me yesterday,' I said. 'He was delighted about the case. He's set his heart on your being a success in the world.'

For a moment, Charles was angry.

'You're exaggerating that,' he said. 'You forget that he'd get equally excited if any of his relations made a public appearance of any kind.' Then he added, in a different tone:

'I hope you're not right.'

I was startled by the concern which had suddenly entered his voice: he seemed affected more strongly than either of us could explain that night.

CHAPTER VI

FULL DINNER PARTY

WITHIN a few days of Charles's visit, he told me that he had broken the news to Mr March. He also told me how Mr March had responded: he wanted to convince me that his father had accepted the position without distress. In fact, Mr March's behaviour seemed to have been odd in the extreme.

His first reply was: 'I don't believe a word of it.' This was said in a flat, dejected tone, so Charles admitted: but at once Mr March began to grumble, almost as though he were parodying himself: 'You ought to have chosen a more suitable time to tell me. You might have known that hearing this would put me out of step for the day.' Then he added again: 'In any case, I don't believe a word of it.'

For several days he refused to discuss the matter. He seemed to be pretending that he had forgotten it. At the same time, he kept asking with concern about his son's health and spirits; one day at lunch, without any preamble, he offered Charles a handsome increase of his allowance to pay for a holiday.

Mr March still went about the house as though he had not so much as heard Charles's intention. It was not until the next full family dinner party that he had to face it.

Each Friday night, when they were in London, Mr March and his brothers took it in turn to give a dinner party to the entire family: the entire family in its widest sense, their wives, their sisters and their sisters' husbands, the children of them all, remoter relations. When I first knew the Marches, it was rare for a 'Friday night' to be attended by less than thirty, and fifty had been reached at least once since 1918.

The tradition of these parties went back continuously to the eighteenth century; for the past hundred years they had been held according to the same pattern, every week from September to the end of the London season.

As luck would have it, I was invited for that night. As a rule, friends of the family were asked only if they were staying in the house; it was by a slight extension of the principle that Mr March invited me.

Getliffe's brother Francis, whose friendship with Charles began in their undergraduate days, had been living at Bryanston Square for the week. When I arrived there for tea on the Thursday, the drawing-room was empty. It was Francis who was the first to join me. He came in with long, plunging, masterful strides, strides too long for a shortish man. His face was clearly drawn, fastidious, quixotic, with no kind of family resemblance to Herbert's, who was his father's son by a first marriage. He had not a trace of Herbert's clowning tricky matiness. Indeed, that afternoon he was nervous in the Marches' house, though he often stayed there.

He disliked being diffident; he had trained himself into a commanding impatient manner; and yet most people at that time felt him to be delicate underneath. He was two years older than Charles; he was a scientist, and the year before had been elected a fellow of their college.

'Will you dine with me tomorrow, Lewis?' he asked. 'They've got their usual party on here, and it'd be less trouble if I got out of the way.'

'Of course,' I said.

'Good work,' said Francis. Then he asked, a little awkwardly, how I was getting on with his brother.

'He's very stimulating,' I said.

'I can believe that,' said Francis. 'But has he put you in the way of any briefs?'

'No,' I said.

Francis cursed, and flushed under his dark sunburnt skin. He was both a scrupulous and a kind-hearted man.

Just then Charles and Katherine came in. As we began tea, Francis said, with an exaggerated casualness: 'By the way, I've arranged to dine out with Lewis tomorrow night. You'll forgive me, won't you? It'll give you more room for the party.'

Katherine's face was open in disappointment.

'I hoped you would come,' she said.

'I should be in the way,' said Francis. 'It will definitely be much better if I disappear.'

Katherine recovered herself, and said:

'You are more or less expected to come, you know. Mr L. will say "If I am obliged to have the fellow residing in my house, I can't send him away while we make beasts of ourselves". He'll certainly expect you to come.'

'I don't think I should do you credit,' he said.

'You'll find points of interest, I promise you,' she said.

'I shouldn't know many of them, you see—'

'Look here,' said Katherine, 'do you want another Gentile to keep you company? I'm certain Lewis will oblige, won't you?'

She turned to me: as I heard that gibe of hers, I felt how fond she was of him.

Since Charles had spoken to me about Jewishness, so had she. It was no longer a forbidden subject. 'It was a bit hard,' Katherine had said, 'to be stopped riding one's scooter in the Park on Saturday because it was the Sabbath, and then on Sunday too. It seemed to me monstrously unjust.' She had gone on: 'But the point was, you were being treated differently from everyone else. You wouldn't have minded anything but that. As it was, you kept thinking about every single case.' Less proud than Charles, she had talked about her moments of shame: but she was still vulnerable. It was not till she teased Francis about being a Gentile that I heard her speak equably, as though it did not matter any more.

'It's a bit hard on him,' said Francis. He broke into a smile that, all of a sudden, narrowed his eyes, creased his cheeks, and made his whole expression warm: 'I'd better tell you, I'm feeling very shy.'

Charles broke in:

'It'll be slightly bizarre, but you must come. Even if it's only to oblige Lewis. I'm sure he can't resist the temptation. Incidentally, even if it weren't so tempting, he wouldn't be able to resist it.' Charles went on: 'Lewis is temperamentally incapable of refusing any invitation, whether he wants to go or not. Isn't that true?'

Katherine asked Mr March as soon as he entered the house. He came into the room and invited us both. I knew he felt it irregular; he did not want either of us at a family party; but his natural warmth prevailed.

'Eight o'clock sharp,' he said. 'And you must both dress suitably for once. For this occasion, I can't possibly let you off.'

I had never seen the house anything but empty before that Friday night. Cars were drawn up bonnet to stern in the square; from the hall one heard the clash of March voices; the drawing-room was full. There was already an orchestra-like effect of voices and laughs: this was the week's exchange of family news. Every day, the Marches told each other the latest pieces of family gossip; Mr March would meet his brother Philip at the club, Philip would tell his wife, she would ring up her children; but it was on Friday night that the stories were crystallised, argued over, and finally passed into the common stock.

Several of the characters in Mr March's sagas were that night present in the flesh. Sir Philip, a spare man, the furrows of whose face seemed engraved not by anxiety but by a stiff, caustic humour – he took for granted his position as head of the family and here, in his brother's house, he walked round the entire company, giving everyone a handshake and a switched-on truculent smile. Mr March's favourite sister Caroline, and her husband Lionel Hart, a brother of Charles's former master. Their son Robert, who, despite Mr March's pessimistic forecasts, had been for years successfully practising in company law. Florence Simon, the cousin who 'thought she wouldn't like it till she tried'. A large family of Herbert Marches, the children of the youngest brother. Mr March's eldest daughter Evelyn, plump and pleasant-looking in a different fashion from Katherine, much darker and brown-eyed. She had married the editor of a Jewish paper, who was not present. Charles and Katherine said she was happy, but Mr March sometimes referred to her marriage with gloom.

There were many unusual faces. Three or four looked, in the stereotyped sense, Jewish. Some of the older women were enormous. Both in face and figure, the party seemed the most unstandardised one could imagine. Beauty, grotesque oddity, gigantic fatness – the family went to all extremes. There was scarcely anyone there whom, for one reason or another, one would not look at twice.

Unfortunately for me, Mr March's eldest sister, Hannah, was not there. I wanted to see her, as she entered his narrative as a symbol of disapproval and the self-appointed leader of all oppositions. There was a legend of Mr March, on his way to his honeymoon at Mentone, putting his head out of the window at St Raphael and sniffing the sea: then he turned to his bride and said: 'The air is quite different here. Hannah would say it isn't, but it is.'

The dining-room was no more clearly lit than usual when we went in;
the table had been lengthened to contain the party. Mr March placed
Philip on his left hand, and Philip's wife on his right: then the brothers
and sisters in order of seniority: Charles at the far end of the table, and
the younger people near him. I sat a place or two from Charles between
Florence Simon and one of the Herbert March girls.

Voices rose and blared as, looking down the table, I saw faces coming
out of the shadows: I felt a glow because these Friday nights had gone on
for so long. It was the warm romantic glow, the feeling of past time: the
glow which made one of those dead and gone Friday nights become
more enchanted in our minds than it ever was to sit through. I felt exactly
as I sometimes did at dinner at the Inn, or when I was Francis's guest at
his High Table. That chain of lives – odd glimmers ran through my head,
the fragments of information which had come down about the first
English Marches sitting round their dinner-table in the City, just over
their bank. The two original March families dined together on the Friday
in the week they arrived in London from Deventer.

How they had first got established in Holland, where they had come
from before that, there was no record nor any tradition – not even of how
they derived their name. In Spain March could have been a Jewish name,
but there was no evidence that these Marches ever lived there. The first
mention of them in the archives was mid-seventeenth century: they were
already in Holland, already one of the leading families of the Ashkenazim
(the Northern group of Jews, as opposed to the Sephardim who lived in
Spain and round the Mediterranean coasts).

They were well-off when they left Deventer. During the last half of
the eighteenth century, Friday night by Friday night, these parties went
on, families walking to each other's houses across the narrow City
streets; their friends and relatives, the family of Levi Barend Cohen, the
Rothschilds, the Montefiores, the Henriques, lived close by.

The nineteenth century came in; all those families, like those of the
Gentile bankers, moved westward; and the Marches' dinners took place
now round Holborn. It was already the fourth generation since Deventer;
the children were no longer given Jewish first names. A honeymoon couple
travelled in postchaises along the French roads as soon as the war was
over, and Charlotte March wrote in 1816: 'it must be admitted that in the
arts of the toilette and the cuisine France excels our country: but we can
hearten ourselves as English people that in *everything* essential we are
infinitely superior to a country which shows so many profligacies that
it is charitable to attribute them to their infamous revolution.' This

though they stayed with their Rothschild uncle in Paris; that pair thought of themselves as English, differing as little from their acquaintances as the Roman Catholic families who, when Charlotte wrote, were still hoping to be emancipated.

Victoria's reign began. Round the dinner-table, the Marches were sometimes indignant at Jewish disabilities; David Salomons was not allowed to take his seat in Parliament. There was also talk, even in the forties, of liberalising themselves; one March became a Christian. Apart from him, no March had married 'out of the faith': nor indeed out of their own circle of Anglo-Jewish families. That was still true down to the people round this table; except for one defection, by a woman cousin of Mr March's, thirty years before.

The March bank flourished; many of the families moved to the neighbourhood of Bryanston Square; by the seventies, one of Mr March's uncles was holding Friday dinners at No. 17. The universities and Parliament became open, and Mr March's father went into the Commons. England was the least anti-Semitic of countries; when the news of the pogroms arrived from Russia in 1880, the Lord Mayor opened a fund for Jewish relief. Half the University of Oxford signed a protest. The outrages seemed an anachronistic horror to decent prosperous Englishmen. The Marches sent thousands of pounds to the Lord Mayor's fund. Yet that news was only a quiver, a remote quiver, in the distant world.

By then the Marches had reached their full prosperity; on Friday nights cabs made their way under the gaslight to the great town houses. The Marches were secure, they were part of the country, they lived almost exactly the lives of other wealthy men.

The century passed out: its last twenty years, and the next fourteen, were the best time for wealthy men to be alive. The Marches developed as prodigally as the other rich.

Those were the heroic days of Friday nights. A whole set of stories collected round them, most of which originated when Mr March was a young man. Of Uncle Henry March, who owned race-horses and was a friend of the Prince of Wales; how he regretted all his life his slowness in repartee, and after each Friday night used to wake his wife in bed so that she should jot down answers which had just occurred to him. Of his brother Justin, who, to celebrate a Harrow victory, rode to his house on one of the horses that drew the heavy roller at Lord's; and who, when only nine people attended one of his Friday nights, took hold of the tablecloth and pulled the whole dinner service to the ground. Of their cousin, Alfred March Hart, the balletomane who helped sponsor Diaghileff's first season in London: who as an old man, hearing someone at a Friday night during the war hope for a Lansdowne peace, rose to his feet and began: 'I am a very old man: and I hope the war will continue for many years after my death.'

They were the sort of stories which one finds in any family that has been prosperous for two hundred years. For me they evoked the imaginary land which exists just before one's childhood. Often as I heard them I felt something like homesick – homesick for a time before I was born, for a society which would have thought my father's home about as primitive as a Trobriand Islander's.

The dinner began. At the head of the table, Philip and Mr March were talking about expectations for the Budget. Mr March suggested that surtax would be applied at a lower limit.

'I don't believe it,' said Philip. 'That's on a par with your idea for the new trust, Leonard.'

Mr March chuckled:

'I should like to remind you that your last idea didn't bring in sufficient for your requirements. Also that you made an exhibition of yourself over that same trust. That was the time your husband wrote a letter so precipitately—' He turned to his sister-in-law and began to tell the story which I heard on my first visit to Bryanston Square.

'It's fantastic to imagine Winston doing anything of the kind,' Philip interrupted him. 'After what he said to the unfortunate George. I wouldn't believe it if George weren't much too incompetent to invent the story.'

The table quietened down. Philip gave the actual words. It was the first time I had heard behind-the-scenes gossip at that level: Philip endowed it with a special authority.

The elder Marches listened with satisfaction as Philip settled the question of surtax. Most of them were not only academically interested; there was a great deal of wealth in the room. Exactly how much, I should have liked very much to know, but about their fortunes they were more reticent than about anything else. None of the younger generation, at our end of the table, could do more than guess. Apparently no individual March had ever been enormously rich. There had probably never been a million pounds at any one man's disposal. So far as one could judge from wills, settlements, and their style of life, most of the fortunes at this dinner-table would be between £100,000 and £500,000.

Philip was talking about the next election:

'We've left it too late. We're a set of bunglers. Our fellows had better stick it out until they're bound to go.'

'What's going to happen?' said Caroline.

'We shall get the sack,' said Philip.

'Does that mean a socialist government?' asked Florence Simon of Charles.

'What else do you think it can mean?' Mr March exclaimed down the table. 'Now that your Aunt Winifred's wretched party has come to the end that they've always richly deserved.'

He was chuckling at Winifred, Herbert March's wife, who was the only Liberal of the older generation. The Marches had been Conservatives for a hundred years; when they stood for Parliament, it was as supporters of Salisbury, Balfour, Bonar Law; their political attitudes were those of other rich men.

At our end of the table, opinion moved a good way to the left. Herbert March's daughter Margaret, who had not long since graduated at Oxford, was working as secretary to a Labour member. She was the most practical of them, the only professional: Charles took her side in argument, was more radical than she was, and Katherine followed suit. Most of the others had undertaken to vote against Sir Philip's party. Of course, many other Marches had passed through a liberal phase in their youth – but to them that night, to me watching them, this seemed something harder, more likely to last.

Would it still seem so, I thought later, when this generation was being watched by their own children?

We had finished the pheasant. Philip and Mr March put politics aside, and began talking about one of their nieces by marriage, who was reported to be living apart from her husband. She had always possessed a reputation for good looks: 'the best-looking girl in the family, Herbert said, though I never knew why he was specially competent to judge,' said Mr March. She had stayed unmarried until she was over thirty.

She was said to have had a good many offers, 'but no one ever established where they came from,' said Mr March. 'The only reason I believed in them was that Hannah didn't.' And then, to everyone's surprise, she had married someone quite poor, unattractive and undistinguished. 'She married him,' Philip announced, 'because he was the only man who didn't look when she was getting over a stile.' His grin was caustic; but his dignity had broken for a moment, and there was a randy glitter in his eyes.

They were arguing about what had gone wrong with the marriage, when their sister Caroline, who was deaf, suddenly caught a word and said:

'Were you talking about Charles?' Mr March shook his head, but she went on:

'I hope he realises he's making an ass of himself. Albert Hart won't hear of his giving up the Bar.'

'It's all unsettled, there's nothing whatever to report,' said Mr March quickly.

Mr March had been compelled to speak loudly, even for a March, to make her understand. His voice silenced everyone else, and the entire table heard Caroline's next question.

'Why is it unsettled? Why has he taken to bees in his bonnet just when he might be becoming some use in the world?'

'The whole matter's being exaggerated,' said Mr March. 'Albert always was given to premature discussion—'

'What's this? What's this?' said Philip.

'I mentioned it to you. She's not made a discovery. I mentioned that my son Charles was going through a period of not being entirely satisfied with his progress at the Bar. Nothing has been concealed.'

Katherine was looking at Charles with a frown of distress.

'I expect he's got over it now. You're all serene, aren't you, Charles?' Philip asked down the table: his tone was dry but friendly.

'I'm quite happy, Uncle Philip.'

'You're getting down to it properly now, aren't you?'

'The whole matter's being grossly exaggerated,' Mr March broke in, rapidly, as though signalling to Charles.

'I expect I can take it that your father's right,' said Philip.

There was a pause.

'I'm sorry. I should like to agree. But you'd find out sooner or later. It's no use my pretending that I shall work at the Bar.'

'What's behind all this? They tell me you've made a good start. What's the matter with you?'

Charles hesitated again.

'You've got one nephew at the Bar, Uncle Philip.' Charles looked at Robert. 'Do you want all your nephews there too? Cutting each other's throats—'

He seemed to be passing it off casually, his tone was light; but Caroline, who was watching his face without hearing the words, broke out:

'I didn't mean to turn you into a board meeting. This comes of being so abominably deaf. Leonard, do you remember the day when Hannah thought I was deafer than I am?'

We went back to our pudding. Katherine had flushed: Charles smiled at her, but did not speak. He stopped the footman from filling his glass again. Most of us, after the questions ceased, had been glad of another drink, including Francis, who had been putting down his wine unobtrusively but steadily since dinner began.

The table became noisier than at any time that evening; the interruption seemed over; Charles's neighbours were laughing as he talked.

Florence Simon plucked at my sleeve. She was a woman of thirty, with abstracted brown eyes and a long sharp nose; all through dinner I had got nowhere with her; whatever I said, she had been vague and shy. Now her eyes were bright, she had thought of something to say.

'I wish you'd been at the dinner last Friday. It was much more interesting then.'

'Was it?' I said.

'Oh, we had some really good general conversation,' said Florence Simon. She relapsed into silence, giving me a kind, judicious and contented smile.

CHAPTER VII

TWO KINDS OF ANGER

By half-past eleven Katherine could speak to Charles at last. She had just said some goodbyes, and only Francis and I were left with them in the drawing-room.

'It was atrociously bad luck,' she burst out.

'I was glad it didn't go on any longer,' said Charles.

'It must have been intolerable,' she cried.

'Well,' said Charles, 'I was just coming to the state when I could hear my own voice getting rougher.'

'The family have never heard anyone put Uncle Philip off before.'

'I thought he was perfectly good-tempered,' Charles replied. He was being matter-of-fact in the face of the excitement. 'He's merely used to being told what he wants to know.'

'He's still talking to Mr L. in his study. There are several of them still there, you know,' she went on.

'Didn't you expect that?' Charles smiled at her.

'It's absolutely maddening,' she broke out again, 'this fluke happening just when Mr L. was ready to accept it.'

Charles was silent for a moment. Then he said:

'I'm not certain that he was.'

'You told me so,' said Katherine. 'But still – you're going to have a foul time. I wish to God I could help.'

She went on:

'He thinks the world of Uncle Philip, of course. Did you notice that he pretended to have told him? He'd obviously just muttered "my son Charles is mumpish" and was hoping that nobody would notice that you never appeared in court—'

'Is there anything I can do?' said Francis. His voice was a little thick. In his embarrassment at dinner, he had been drinking more than the rest of us; now, when he wanted to be useful and protective, he looked as though the light was dazzling him.

Charles shook his head and said no.

'You're sure?' said Francis, trying to speak with his usual crispness. Again Charles said no.

'In that case,' said Francis, 'it might be wiser if the rest of us left you to it.'

'I'd rather you didn't,' said Charles. 'I'd rather Mr L. found you all here.'

For a second it sounded as if he were trying to avoid a scene. Listening to his tone, I suddenly felt that that was the opposite of the truth.

He went on speaking to Francis. Katherine smiled at them anxiously, then turned to me.

'By the way, according to your theory, the mass of people at dinner must have sounded very forbidding,' she said. 'Did you find a few who made it tolerable? When you actually arrived?'

The question was incomprehensible, and yet she was clearly expecting me to understand. 'Your theory': I could not imagine what she meant.

'Don't you remember,' she said, 'saying that to me the first time we met? When I was being shunted off to the Jewish dance. I won't swear to the actual words, but I'm pretty certain they're nearly right. I thought over them a good many times afterwards, you see. I wondered whether you meant to take me down a peg or two for being too superior.'

It was the sort of attentive memory, the sort of extravagant thin-skinnedness, that I should have become accustomed to; but a new example still surprised me just as much.

'As a matter of fact,' said Katherine, 'I decided that you probably didn't mean that.'

Then Mr March entered. He went straight to Charles, paying no attention to anyone else: he stood in front of Charles's chair.

'Now you see what you're responsible for,' he said. Charles got up.

'You know how sorry I am that you're involved, Mr L.,' Charles said.

'I haven't time to speculate whether you're sorry or not. I've just been listening to my brothers telling me that you're making a fool of yourself. As though I wasn't perfectly aware of it already. I expressed exactly the same point of view myself but unfortunately I haven't succeeded in making much impression on you.'

'No one could have done more than you did.'

'A great many people could have done enormously more. Do you think my father listened to Herbert when he got up to his monkey tricks and wanted to study music? An astonishingly bad musician he would have made if you can judge by his singing in the drawing-room when we were children. Hannah said that he was only asked to sing because he was the youngest child. Anyone else would have done enormously more. In any case, I never gave my permission as you appear to have assumed. You may have thought the matter was closed, but that doesn't affect the issue.'

'It's no good reopening it, Mr L. I'm sorry.'

'Certainly it's some good reopening it. After tonight, I haven't any option.'

Charles suddenly broke out:

'You admit that tonight is making the difference?'

'I never allowed you to think that the matter was closed. But in addition to that, I don't propose to ignore—'

'The position is this: when we were left to ourselves, you disapproved of what I wanted and you brought up every fair argument there was. If it had been possible, you know that I should have given way. Now other people are taking a hand. I know what they mean to you, but I don't recognise their claim to interfere. Do you think I can possibly do for them what I wouldn't do for you alone?'

'You talk about them as if they were strangers. They're treated better by an outsider who's just married into us, like that abominable woman who married your cousin Alfred. They're your family—'

'They've no right to affect my life.'

'I won't have the family dismissed as strangers.'

'I should feel more justified in going against your wishes – now you've been influenced by them,' said Charles, 'than when you were speaking for yourself.' They were standing close together. There came a cough, and to my astonishment Francis began to speak.

'Will you forgive me for saying something, Mr March?'

His face was pallid under the sunburn; there was a film of sweat on his forehead. But he managed to make himself speak soberly: the words came out strained, uncomfortable, but positive.

Mr March, who had been totally indifferent to his presence or mine, did not notice anything unusual. With a mixture of irritableness and courtesy, Mr March said:

'My dear fellow, I'm always glad to hear your observations.'

'I assure you,' said Francis, uttering with care, 'that Charles would have gone further to meet your wishes than for any other reason. I completely agree with you that he's wrong to give up the Bar. I think it's sheer nonsense. I've told him so. I've argued with him since I first heard about it. But I haven't got him to change his mind. The only argument which would make him think twice was about the effect on yourself.'

Mr March regarded him with an expression that dubiously lightened; the frown of anger had become puzzled, and Mr March said, his voice more subdued than since he entered the room:

'That was civil of him, anyway.'

He went on:

'I don't know what's happening to the family. My generation weren't a patch on my father's. And as for yours, there's not one of you who'll get a couple of inches in the obituary column. My uncle Henry said that just before he died in '27, and all I could reply was "After all, you can say this for them. They don't drink, and they don't womanise."'

Mr March spoke straight to Charles:

'You might be the only chance of rescuing them from mediocrity. There's always been a consensus of opinion that you wouldn't disgrace yourself at the Bar. Ever since your preparatory schoolmaster said you had a legal head: though he was wrong in his prognostications about all your cousins. I don't know what I've done to deserve the most unsatisfactory children in the whole family. First your sister made her regrettable marriage. Of her there's nothing good to report. Then you choose to behave in this fashion. And neither you nor your sister Katherine have ever made any attempt to fit into the life of the people round you. You've always been utterly unsociable. You've never taken the part everyone wanted you to take. You've not had the slightest consideration for what the family thinks of me. You wouldn't cross the road to keep me in good repute. I've been more criticised about my children than anyone in the family since 1902, the time Justin's daughter married out of the faith. Justin had a worse time than anyone. He couldn't bear to inspect the wedding presents. It was always rumoured that he sent some secretly himself to cover up a few of the gaps. Since Justin, no one has been disapproved of as I have.'

Mr March sat down, in an armchair close to one of the side tables. For a second, I thought the quarrel was over. Then Charles said:

'I wish it weren't so, for your sake.'

Charles had spoken simply and with feeling: in reply, Mr March flushed to a depth of anger he had not reached that night. He clutched at the arm of his chair as he leant forward; in doing so, he swept off an ashtray from the little table. The rug was shot with cigarette-stubs and match-ends. Charles bent to clear them.

'Don't pick them up,' Mr March shouted. Charles replaced the ashtray, and put one or two stubs in it.

'Don't pick them up, I tell you,' Mr March cried with such an increase of rage that Charles hesitated.

'I refuse to have you perform duties for my sake. I refuse to listen to you expressing polite regrets for my sake. You appear to consider yourself completely separate from me in all respects. I am not prepared to tolerate that attitude.'

'What do you mean?' Charles's voice had become angry and hard.

'I am not prepared to tolerate your attitude that you can dissociate yourself from me in all your concerns. Even if I survive criticism from the family on your account, that isn't to admit that you've separated yourself from me.'

'I come to you for advice,' said Charles.

'Advice! You can go to the family lawyer for advice. Though I never knew why we've stood a fellow so long-winded as Morris for so long,' cried Mr March. 'I'm not prepared to be treated as a minor variety of family lawyer by my son. I shall have to consider taking actions that will make that clear.'

Charles broke out:

'Do you imagine for a moment that you can coerce me back to the law?'

Mr March said:

'I do not propose to let you abandon yourself to your own devices.'

Everyone was surprised by the calm, ambiguous answer and by Mr March's expression. As Charles's face darkened, Mr March's looked almost placid. He seemed something like triumphant, from the instant he evoked an outburst as angry as his own. He went on quietly:

'I want something for you. I wish I could know that you'll get something that I've always wanted for you.' He checked himself. Abruptly he broke off; he looked round at us as though there had been no disagreement whatever, and began an anecdote about a Friday night years before.

PART TWO

FATHER AND SON

CHAPTER VIII

THE COST OF HELP

FOR some time after the quarrel I did not get a clear account of Mr March's behaviour. According to Katherine, he was so depressed that he stopped grumbling; he listened to criticisms from his brothers and sisters, but even these he did not pass on. Weeks went by before he began to greet Charles at meals with: 'If you're determined to persist in your misguided notions, what alternative proposal have you to offer?' One afternoon, when I was in the drawing-room, Mr March burst in after his daily visit to the club and cried:

'I'm being persecuted on account of my son's fandango.'

That was all I heard directly. When I dined with them, there were times when he seemed melancholy, but his level of spirits was so high that I could not be sure. One day Charles mentioned to me that he thought Mr March had begun to worry about Katherine. I fancied that I could recall the signs.

As for Charles himself, none of his family had any idea what he was intending, or whether he was intending anything at all. He put on a front of cheerfulness and good temper in his father's presence. His days had become as lazy as Katherine's. He stayed in bed till midday, talked to her most afternoons, went dancing at night. Many of his acquaintances thought, just as he had predicted, that he was settling down to the life of a rich and idle young man.

They should have watched his manner as he set me going on my career.

By the early summer I still had had nothing like a serious case, and I was getting worn down with anxiety. Then Charles took charge of my affairs. He handled them with astuteness and nerve. He risked snubs, which he could not have done on his own behalf, and got me invited to the famous May party at the Holfords'. At the same time he approached Albert Hart and through him met the solicitors who sent Hart the majority of his work. One of them was glad to oblige Philip March's

595

nephew, and said he would like to meet me; another, one of the best-known Jewish solicitors in London, promised to be present at the Holfords' party. There were other skeins, concealed from me, in Charles's plans. They took up his entire attention. As he devoted himself to them, Charles was continuously angry with me.

A few minutes before the Holfords' party, where he planned for me to make a good impression, there was an edge to his voice. I was sitting in his bedroom at Bryanston Square while he knotted his white tie in front of the mirror. I mentioned a story of Charles's grandfather that Mr March had just told me – 'he must have been a very able man,' I said.

'Obviously he must have been,' said Charles. He was still looking into the mirror, smoothing down his thick, fair, wiry hair. 'But he didn't do so much after all. He was a rather successful banker. And acquired the position that a rather successful banker could in that period, if he happened to be a competent man. Don't you agree?'

I was referring to Mr March's account, but Charles interrupted: 'Oh, I know he'd got some human qualities. The point is, he didn't do so much. Look, don't you admit those jobs he spent his life on are really pretty frivolous? I mean, the traditional jobs of my sort of people. The Stock Exchange and banking and amateur politics when you've made enough money. Can you imagine taking them up if you had a free choice?'

'No,' I said.

Charles turned round.

'And if you had a free choice, can you imagine taking up – the profession you're anxious to be successful at?'

I did not answer.

'You can't imagine it. Don't you admit that you can't?' Charles said, with an angry, contemptuous smile.

'Not if I'd been given a completely free choice, perhaps.'

'Of course you can't. You don't want just money. You'll realise that if you make some. You don't want the sort of meaningless status that appeals to Herbert Getliffe. You'll realise that if you get it. Granted that you want to satisfy yourself instead, it's not a job a reasonable man would choose. Don't you agree?'

In my suspense that night, those 'ifs' were cruel: we each knew it. I was both hurt and angry. I could have told him that he was speaking out of bitter discontent. Did I admit to myself what kind of discontent it was? He was angry that I had direct ambitions and might satisfy them. I ought also to have known that he wanted to lead a useful life. He could not confide it or get rid of it, but he had a longing for the good. We faced each other, on the edge of quarrelling. He sounded arrogant, impatient, cruel; he was angry with me because we were different.

As he drove me to Belgrave Square through the May dusk, Charles suddenly turned as anxious as I was myself. He wanted me to be at ease; he wanted me to forget the doubts that he had raised by his own words five minutes before; he kept reiterating facts about the Holfords and their guests, and conversational gambits I could use with Albert Hart.

When we arrived in the crowded drawing-room, Charles took me to Hart's side as soon as my introduction to Lady Holford was over. He reminded Hart about me. He set us talking. Hart was an uneasy nervous man who broke into flashes of speech: he liked Charles, it was clear, and even more he liked having someone he knew at this party, so unfluctuating in its noise-level, so ornate. In a few minutes, we moved out through the great French windows, down the steps, into the sunken garden. A waiter brought us three balloon glasses and put into each a couple of inches of brandy.

'His lordship's compliments,' the waiter said to Charles, 'and he wishes to say that this is *not* Napoleon brandy. But it is reasonably old.'

As soon as the waiter turned to ascend the steps, Charles looked at Albert Hart and winked. Charles's face became gay, the more as he saw Hart and me beginning to make contact. Soon Charles left us to 'do his duty' in the house, and Hart and I enjoyed comparing the display round us to the subdued opulence of a March Friday night. He was supple, gossipy, devoted to his work and still, at the age of fifty or more, over-awed when he went into society. I felt his heart warm to me when I told him that this was the first time I had set foot in a London garden. He was shrewd, he was trying to find out whether there was anything in me: he also had a taste for sly jokes at the Holfords' expense, he was glad to have someone there to listen.

The garden was filling up. Hart was joined by his friend the solicitor, who at once asked me some leading questions about Herbert Getliffe. I had to try to be both forthcoming and discreet; but Hart was already friendly, and I thought the other man was ready to approve of me. The conversation returned to the Holfords: I began to feel happy as I watched the people round us, the lights at the bottom of the garden, the profound blue of the London evening sky.

Two women, mother and daughter, acquaintances of Hart and the Marches, joined us for a time. The girl was to be presented at Court the next month and the mention of royalty stimulated Albert Hart. He remembered a story of Holford, who was said, in the first heyday of his success, to have let drop at one of his parties: 'I suppose my daughter may as well be presented this year. It must be a bore for the monarchs, though, to see faces they know so well.'

That must have happened a few years before the Holfords' title finally submerged their name. They first appeared in England in 1860 and they were then called Samuel; they hyphenated themselves to Samuel-Ernly within ten years, and had dropped the Samuel by the end of the century. They had made a fortune out of cigarettes, and the man in whose garden we were standing could have bought up the entire March family. Their entertainments had been flamboyant thirty years before, and had grown steadily grander: although they boasted of their acquaintance with royalty, they genuinely had royal acquaintances to boast of. This 'little evening party in the garden' (in the largest garden within a mile of Hyde Park Corner) took place each year in May, just as a sign, so Albert Hart said, that they might do some less simple entertaining later in the year.

Though they had disguised their name and though nine out of ten of their guests were Gentiles, they had remained faithful Jews. And, though their success had been on a different scale, they still looked up to the Marches as one of the senior Jewish families in England, while they were newcomers. Invitations to their parties went to the Marches as a matter of right, but the Marches rarely attended. Charles would not have thought of coming that night, but for me: and yet, when he accepted the invitation and asked if he might bring a friend, the Holfords chose to forget his family's stiffness. They seemed to feel that Jewish society was still hierarchical, that rank still meant something. It was not by accident that Holford's message about the brandy had been sent to Charles.

It was curious to see two different social codes collide, I thought, taking my last sip of old, but not Napoleon, brandy. I felt satisfied with the evening. I felt so satisfied that when I caught sight of Charles again I did not care how much deference the Holfords gave him. He was standing at the top of the steps above the garden. A dark-haired girl was looking up at him. The light from an open window picked out the glass in his hand, the gardenia in his buttonhole, and threw his features into relief.

Then he came down the steps, and found our group. His eyes met mine, searching for how things had gone. It was not hard for him to see that I was pleased.

A moment afterwards, the lights round the garden suddenly went out. In the warm darkness we were left mystified; people asked each other what was happening. What was happening was soon known, as three gigantic Catherine wheels spurted out of the distance. Lord Holford was producing a fireworks display, extravagant, varied and, as we came to realise, inordinately long.

A case came to me not long after that party: not from the man I talked to there, but from another solicitor who sent a considerable amount of work to Hart and whom Charles had arranged for me to meet.

It was not such an important case as Charles's, but far better than anything I could reasonably expect. I had to prosecute in a libel action. It was not difficult, the case was fairly self-evident; but I had not much time, as someone else had thrown up the brief through illness, and with a case so good it would be disastrous not to win.

In fact, I did win, though I stumbled in the last stages. Charles had helped me prepare, and was present all through the hearing. I saw his face, clouded and frowning, as, with the case nearly won, I went off on a side-line that seemed tempting. A witness was obstinate, I knew that I might have done the case harm; but I was able to recover and make some pretence of passing it off.

When I got the verdict, I joined Charles. He congratulated me, and then, his eyes bright, said:

'I'm glad. But whatever possessed you to draw that absurd red herring?'

I defended myself. I said it had not been as bad as that.

'Oh, you did very well. Henriques [the solicitor] is satisfied with you; you're a good investment.'

His glance kept its glint. 'But still, you did lose sight of the point for five minutes, didn't you? It was a classical example of using two arguments where one would do, don't you agree?'

I felt let down. All in all I had done well: I wanted praise, not his kind of candour. He was fond of telling the truth, I thought with no detachment at all, especially when it was unpleasant.

Herbert Getliffe did just the opposite. He was fond of rejoicing with him who rejoices. Just as Charles recalled a disapproving voice from my childhood, so Getliffe was as chameleon-like as Jack Cotery – not specially reputable, but warm when one was warm oneself. Getliffe behaved as though he had won the case, instead of me, and immediately set about improvising a celebratory supper ('each man to pay for himself and partner. I always believe in Dutch treat,' he told me, with energy and sincerity). Over the telephone, at four hours' notice, he invited guests, most of whom were only acquaintances of mine. Charles could not come, and Getliffe whistled and clucked his tongue in disapprobation. 'He ought to have put everything else off, on a night like this! But you'll find, Eliot, that some people take one view of the responsibilities of friendship, and some take another.' He added, in his most reflective, earnest and affectionate tone: 'Of course some chaps in the position of young March would have done something for you in the way of introductions – instead of letting you sink or swim. I don't believe in flattering myself, Eliot, but I must say it was a providential thing that you came to my chambers, so that you had one well-wisher at any rate to look after you a bit –'

With genuine feeling he developed the theme. He was so sincere, so full of emotion, that he found it impossible to remember that he had done nothing for me whatsoever; listening, I found it nearly as impossible myself.

At the meal, I began by being jubilant and boastful, trying to impress my neighbour, a cool and handsome girl. Getting nowhere, I went on boasting, still exalted: yet I felt this party was becoming a joke against me, and as we stood about when we had finished eating I was smiling to myself.

It was then that I caught sight of a young woman watching me: she too was smiling, but with what looked like sympathy. All I knew about her was that her name was Ann Simon, and I had met her for the first time that night. I went across to her.

'You ought to be pleased, oughtn't you?' she said. Her tone was kind, a little shy, almost deferential. As I looked at her, I was struck by a contrast. Her face was open and intelligent, with bright-blue eyes folded at the inner corners; under her left eye was a mole. Against her thick dark hair, her temples seemed delicate and white. One could call her pretty, certainly good-looking, but at the first glance one was thinking of the character in her face. That was where the contrast came, for her figure was elegant, soft and supple, more carefully and expensively dressed, so I thought, than any woman in the room. Her manner was at the same time direct and shy, warm but not at all flirtatious. I found myself talking to her as an ally.

Yes, I ought to be pleased, I said, it had been an important day for me. But this celebration wasn't exactly what I might have imagined. The young woman I was fond of was not there, nor were any of my friends. On the other hand, Getliffe and some of his chums were having a remarkably good time.

'I suppose,' she said, 'you couldn't have arranged anything in advance, could you? I mean, you couldn't have got your friends to stand by?'

'I was touching wood too hard,' I replied.

She nodded her head in comprehension. It would have been easy to tell her about my love-affair. She asked about my friends: I mentioned Charles March, and asked if she knew the family. Yes, she did, and she had met him once. It was agreeable standing there talking to her, and I thought she felt so too. We were the same age; she was kind and clever and we were not making any demands on each other. Meeting her seemed a good end to that day.

I told Charles about her. He was not sure who she was, but he was interested in her effect on me. Just then we had sharper eyes for each other than for ourselves. He saw that I had fallen deeply in love too early, and that Sheila had already left a mark on my life: he saw also that, too much committed to Sheila as I was, I often felt disproportionate gratitude to women who gave me what she could not. Such as ordinary simple friendliness, which was what I had received from Ann Simon.

With him, I saw just as clearly that he wanted to find someone to love: or rather he wanted to lose himself in someone. It was the opposite of my experience. Why he had missed it, I could not imagine: but now that he was consciously looking for it, I thought his chances were getting less.

That summer he went on living his idle life. He spent days at Lord's and Wimbledon; took a season-ticket for the ballet; flirted with a young woman he met at a coming-out dance; arrived a good many times at Bryanston Square when the door was already unlocked for the morning.

The mantelpiece in his sitting-room was shining with invitations. Less than half came from Jewish houses. He was a highly eligibile match, and hostesses were anxious to secure him. That year, he was eager to accept. His car drove with the others to Grosvenor Square, Belgravia, Knightsbridge, the houses round the Park. It was a hot brilliant summer, and sometimes I used to walk past those houses, whose lights shone out while the sky was still bright. Dance-tunes sounded through the open windows, and girls' voices as they walked under the awning from the street.

Charles found someone to flirt with; but he did not find what he was looking for. Just before he went down to Mr March's country house for the summer, he was sharper-tempered than I had known him.

CHAPTER IX

WEEKEND IN THE COUNTRY

ONE afternoon in July, as I sat in the drawing-room at Bryanston Square, Mr March entered even more quickly than usual, said: 'I'm always glad to have your company. But I've a great many worries to occupy me now,' and went out again.

It sounded ominous: but I discovered that he was talking about the yearly move to Haslingfield, his country house in Hampshire. I also discovered that each year his move produced the same state of subdued commotion. Mr March sat in his study for hours every day for a fortnight 'seeing if it's possible to get anything safely down to that confounded house', but what he did no one knew. The elder servants became infected with the atmosphere of imminent catastrophe – all except the butler who, finding me alone on one of these occasions, suddenly said: 'I shouldn't take much notice of Mr March, sir. He'd die if he didn't worry. Believe me he would.'

I was asked down to Haslingfield for the last weekend in August. That year, for the first time, Katherine was acting as hostess, 'not entirely a job to look for,' she wrote. 'Mr L. may have intended it as a compliment, or as a sign that I'm getting on in years – but he still regards it as unlikely that any guests will receive or answer my invitations, or, if by any miracle they do come, that they'll ever go away. However, I've invited Ann Simon for the same weekend as you. Mr L. resisted having her, apparently on the grounds that she was a bit of a social come-down: actually her father's a highly successful doctor. Still, it's better to have Mr L. angry about her than about other topics. Anyway, she's coming. I thought you talked as though you were interested in her, when you met her after your first case. . . .'

Incidentally, that first case was now not my only one. Another small job had come my way in July, and at the end of the month the solicitor whom I met at the Holfords' sent me a case which any young man at my stage would have thought himself lucky to get. It was to be heard in the autumn, and through August I had been working at it obsessively hard.

Katherine had asked me to come down early, and so I took the train on the Friday afternoon, tired but encouraged. This case would get me known a bit; I had a foot in; the next year looked brighter. The Surrey fields passed by in the sunshine, the carriage cushions smelt stuffy in the heat, and I felt happy, sleepy and without any premonition at all.

Charles met me with his car at Farnham. He was sunburned, and his hair slightly bleached. For a second, I thought his face had aged in the last two years. Before I could ask him anything, he was talking – with the special insistence, I thought, of someone who wants to keep questions away.

'I've been doing absolutely nothing,' he said, 'except play tennis and read.'

As he drove through the lanes towards Hampshire, he let off a string of questions about the books he had just been reading. What did I think of the Sacco-Vanzetti case? What did the jury actually tell themselves when they were alone? How cynical can any of them have allowed themselves to be?

He had been reading the evidence: he drove with one hand, and used the other to draw diagrams in the air – the place where Sacco and Vanzetti were proved to stand and the street down which 'eye-witnesses' were later shown to have been travelling. 'Going at this pace,' said Charles, driving faster, 'identifying a man out of sight, roughly behind that clump of pines. Those seem to be the facts. How did the jury and those witnesses – most of them ordinary decent people, you must assume that – face what they were doing? Face it in their own minds, I mean?'

It was the kind of detective story in real life, full of concrete facts and edged with injustice, that he could not resist. Far more than me, he had a passionate personal interest in justice for its own sake.

That afternoon, though, he was using it to distract us both. 'Nothing's happening,' he said, when I asked him about himself. 'Nothing in the world.' Quickly, as though in self-defence, he pounced on me with another question about a book.

When I asked after Katherine, he glanced at me without expression. 'She's very well,' he said. 'She's very well indeed.'

'What do you mean?'

He shook his head. 'You'd better see for yourself.'

'Is she all right?'

'I think she's very happy.'

When I pressed him, he would not say any more. He returned to talk about literature, as he drove into a dark alley of trees; I noticed high banks, patches of sunshine, rabbit holes; I was listening, and at the same time trying to calculate the distance from the lodge. It turned out to be three miles to the house: 'the advantage being,' Charles said, 'that Mr L. can take his constitutional within his own territories.'

Mr March and Katherine were waiting in the courtyard.

'Glad to see you arrive safely in my son's car,' said Mr March. 'I wanted to send the chauffeur, but was overruled. I should have refused to answer for the consequences.'

He took me into the drawing-room, bigger and lighter than at Bryanston Square. A great bay of windows gave onto the terrace; below lay the tennis court, the shadow of a tree just beginning to touch one of the service lines. The view stretched, lush and wooded, to the blue Surrey hills; the English view, every square yard man-made, and yet with neither a house nor a path in sight.

Katherine poured out the tea. Mr March glanced at me.

'You're looking seedy,' he said. 'No! I'm prepared to believe that you can be allowed out of quarantine – if you admit that you've been living in a cellar.'

'I've been working hard, Mr L.,' I said.

'I'm very glad to hear it. It makes a great contrast to my deplorable family. I don't propose to make any observations upon my son. As for my daughter, I suppose she can hardly be expected to perform any serious function – but she can't even write foolproof letters to my guests. I detected her making a frightful ass of herself again on Tuesday: she admitted that she hadn't sent Charles's friend Francis Getliffe a list of the trains to Farnham.'

Mr March seemed in good spirits. Katherine said: 'For the fifth time, Mr L., I didn't send Francis the trains because he knows them as well as you do.' She smiled. 'And I object to being referred to as though I was feeble-minded. Why can't I be expected to perform any serious function?'

'Women can't,' said Mr March. 'Apart from any particular reflection on you as shown by these various incompetences.'

The evening flowed on. Dinner in the late summer half-twilight was just as at Bryanston Square, with Mr March dressed and no one else: the routine was not altered, we went in on the stroke of eight, Mr March declaimed the menu. He talked on, as though he had been compulsorily silent for some time. Sir Philip had just been made a Parliamentary Secretary. Mr March's astonishment and pride were each enormous. 'I never thought any son of my father would reach the heights of a Minister. Possibly they considered,' he added thoughtfully, 'that, as the Government is obviously about to go out in ignominy, it didn't matter much whom they put in. Still, my father would have been extremely gratified.' His reflections on Philip set him going on the main narrative-stream of his own journey round the world in the eighties, with subsidiary streams of, first, the attempt of Philip's wife, 'the biggest snob in the family', to invite the Queen to tea: second, the adventures of Hannah and the Belgian refugees, 'the only useful thing she ever tried to do, and of course she said it was a success; but no one else believed her': third, his morning walk with Katherine yesterday, and her ignorance of the difficulties of moving back to Bryanston Square (in time for the Jewish New Year in September).

Only the cricket scores were allowed to interrupt him when we moved back to the drawing-room. It was still very warm, and the butler brought in iced drinks after the coffee. We lay back, sipping them: but the heat did not quieten Mr March.

Then, at 10.40 exactly, he broke off and performed his evening ritual. The whole household was in for the night, and so he went round the house with the butler to examine all the doors, after giving Charles instructions about the drawing-room windows. At last we heard him go upstairs to bed.

Charles asked Katherine when the other two would arrive: he said (I did not catch the meaning for a moment): 'I still think you could have found a more ingenious excuse.' 'That's monstrous,' said Katherine. She smiled. Her hair was tousled over her forehead; she usually managed to become untidy, I thought, by this time of night. She appealed to me: 'I told you Mr L. is prepared to disapprove of Ann in advance, for reasons best known to himself. So I decided we wanted someone else to soothe him down – and Francis is the obvious choice, you can't deny it. It's a perfectly good excuse.' 'You only decided it was good,' Charles said, 'after concealing it from me for two days.'

'Privilege of hostess.' Katherine smiled again. 'Ah well – Lewis, don't you agree that Mr L. is getting more vigorous the older he becomes? I shall have to marry before he's exhausted me completely.'

She was laughing: but, as we listened to those words 'I shall have to marry . . .' and heard their caressing pleasure, we knew that she was in love.

Soon she went to bed herself.

'She liked being told that it was a bad excuse,' I said.

Charles said:

'She's only realised quite recently, I think.'

'When did you?'

'Shouldn't you say,' said Charles, 'that she's been getting fond of him for months?'

'He's very fond of her,' I said.

'Are you sure?'

I nodded. Charles broke out:

'I just can't tell whether he loves her, perhaps it's harder for me to tell than anyone.'

For a time we were silent. Then I asked, because the thought was in both our minds:

'How much has Mr L. noticed?'

'I've absolutely no idea.'

We were each thinking of her chances of being happy. Neither of us knew whether Francis wanted to marry her. If he did, I could not foresee what it would mean, her marrying a Gentile.

Nevertheless, as Charles spoke of her, there was a trace of envy in his voice. Partly because he might be losing her; but mainly, I thought that night, because she had been taken up by an overmastering emotion, because she had lost herself and been swept away.

We talked until late: of Katherine, Francis, Mr March, my work, and again of the books he had been reading. He had no news of his own.

CHAPTER X

A WALK WITH MR MARCH

At last we tiptoed up the broad slippery staircase, and went to our rooms. But in my case not to sleep, immediately at least; for the bedrooms at Haslingfield carried comfort to such a point that it was difficult to sleep at all.

There was a rack of books, picked by Charles, several of which were just out – a Huxley, the latest of the Scott-Moncrieff translations, the books we had talked about that afternoon. There was a plate of sandwiches, a plate of fruit, a plate of biscuits. A Thermos flask of tea and one of iced lemonade. A small bottle of brandy. After one had had a snack, read a book or two, and finished off the drinks, one could snatch a few hours' sleep – until, quite early in the morning, a footman began padding about the room, taking out clothes and drawing curtains. Which for me, who liked sleeping in the dark, finished the night for good.

There was nothing for it but to get up. Although I arrived in the breakfast-room early, one place at the table had already been occupied; Mr March had been and gone. As I chose my breakfast from the dishes on the sideboard, I was puzzled for a moment. There were several plates of fried tongue, none of bacon. For a visitor used to rich houses, that was the only unfamiliar thing at Bryanston Square and Haslingfield.

Katherine and Charles both came down late to breakfast. Twice, while I was sitting alone, Mr March entered rapidly, said 'Good morning' without stopping, and changed the newspaper he was holding out in front of him; first *The Times* for the *Daily Telegraph*, and then the *Daily Telegraph* for the *Manchester Guardian*.

It was another hot day. Katherine was complaining at the prospect of her five-mile walk with Mr March before lunch; why does he insist on a companion, she said, pretending that she was only complaining as a joke. I thought that, as she waited for Francis to arrive, she did not relish being alone with Mr March. So I volunteered; and at exactly half-past eleven we set off down the drive at Mr March's walking pace, which was not less than four miles an hour. He wore his deerstalker, and before we had walked four hundred yards took it off, saying: 'I must mop my bald pate.' Several times he groaned, without slowing down: 'I'm cracking up! I'm cracking up!'

Nothing interrupted his walking, he neither slackened nor quickened his pace. The only interruptions to his talking were those he made himself. His feats of total recall were as disconcerting as ever. For the first time I heard, out of the blue, the end of that gnomic story about his nephew Robert on the steps of the St James's, which had tantalised me on my first visit to Bryanston Square It appeared that Robert, tired of waiting for briefs, had taken to going to theatres, not just to pass the time or because of a disinterested passion for drama, but because he had conceived the idea of filling up his leisure by writing a play: all he was doing was study the technique. In Mr March's view, this procedure was ill-judged, since he regarded it as axiomatic that Robert did not possess a shred of talent.

We turned at the lodge gates and made off by a path among the trees. Mr March chuckled and pointed back to the lodge.

'My son Charles,' he said, 'got himself into an unfortunate predicament a fortnight ago last Saturday. I had Oliver Mendl staying with me for the weekend. Of course I knew that he obeyed the Lawgiver more strictly than I do myself. His father was just the same. When he visited us, I used to have to open his letters on Saturday morning. Though I noticed that he always read them quick enough if he thought they contained anything to his advantage. Oliver invited Charles to come for a stroll, and in the circumstances Charles couldn't very well refuse. It looked very threatening that morning. I said so as soon as I woke up: I was ten minutes later than usual, because my daughter Katherine had kept me awake by inconsiderately having a bath before she went to bed the previous night. She accuses me of shouting through the wall "You've done me in. I shall never get to sleep again, never again." I strongly advised them to take overcoats or at least umbrellas. However, they preferred their own opinion and they'd just reached the lodge when it started to rain with violence. The only drop of rain we've had since July 19: remember you're only allowed four inches in your bath. Charles showed more gumption than you might expect: he suggested ringing up from the lodge and asking Taylor to bring a car. It might have been a ridiculous suggestion, of course: you can't expect to get a car unless you make proper arrangements in advance. As it happened, Taylor was not occupied between 10.30 and 12 that morning. So Charles could have obtained his car, but unfortunately he didn't. Because Oliver begged him to order the car for himself, but depressed Charles by adding: "Of course I can't use it today, I shall have to walk." The Lawgiver forbade people of my religion to make journeys on the Sabbath: why, I've never been able to understand. Well, though I oughtn't to pay him compliments, my son Charles is a polite young man with people he doesn't know well. Hannah says he isn't, but she's only seen him when she's present herself. On this occasion he felt compelled to walk back with Oliver. We heard an infernal noise when they got back, and I went out and found him standing on a towel in the hall. He expressed himself angrily whenever I pointed out how he could have avoided disaster.'

Mr March was beaming with laughter. Then he added, quietly, and to my complete surprise:

'Of course, he's not bad-tempered as a rule. He wouldn't have minded so much if it hadn't been caused by the religion.'

He went on: 'Herbert was the same forty years ago. At the time when he was getting up to his monkey tricks about studying music. He didn't much like to be reminded that he belonged to our religion.'

Mr March added:

'Of course, Herbert found that troubles of that nature passed away as he got older. I am inclined to think that the thickening of one's skin is the only conceivable advantage of becoming old. If my son's trouble was entirely due to his thin skin, I should cease to have periods of worry about him. But it isn't so.'

Mr March talked no more on our walk home. We arrived at the house a few minutes before his standard time of 12.45, and found Katherine eating an early lunch before going out to meet Ann Simon.

CHAPTER XI

MR MARCH ENDS A REFLECTION

CHARLES and I were alone at lunch with Mr March, who was still half-saddened, half-anxious, as he had been on the way home. I was certain by now that he was innocent about Katherine. As he talked to Charles, he had no thought of trouble from her. His concern was all for his son; he did not imagine any other danger to his peace of mind.

He told some stories, but they were shot through with his affection for Charles. Because he was in that mood, he told us more than I had heard of his early life. At once one knew, more sharply than on the day he watched Charles's case, how much of himself he was re-creating in his son.

He described his own career. He talked, not as vivaciously as usual, but with his natural lack of pretence. 'I never made much progress,' he said.

His father and Philip's, the first Sir Philip, had been the most effective of all the Marches; he had controlled the March firm of foreign bankers and brokers when it was at its peak. 'And in my father's days,' said Mr March, 'they counted as more than a business house. Of course it would be different now. Everything's on too big a scale for a private firm. Look at the Rothschilds. They used to be the most influential family in Europe. And they've kept going after we finished, they've not done badly, and what are they now? Just merchant bankers in a fairly lucrative way of business.'

When his father died, Mr March, who would have preferred to go to the university, was brought in to fill a vacancy in the firm. 'It was a good opening,' he said to us, nearly fifty years after. 'I wasn't attracted specially to business, but I hadn't any particular inclinations. I hoped you would have,' he said to Charles.

It was not during his conversation, but previously, that I had the curiosity to ask him about the routine of foreign banking, when he first joined the firm. There had still been an air about it, so it seemed. Each morning, the letters came in from the Marches' correspondents: there had been two in Paris, and one in each of the other European capitals, including 'the very capable fellow at St Petersburg. We never believed he was a Russian.' Since the bank started, they had depended on their correspondents, a group of men very similar in gifts and outlook to the foreign-based journalists of the twentieth century. In 1880 the Marches were still better informed, over a whole area of acts where politics and economics fused, than any newspaper. The March correspondents acquired a curious mixture of cynicism and world-view. Just because their finding the truth could be measured in terms of money, they learned what the truth was. All through 1870 one of the Paris correspondents was predicting war, and war in which the French army would be outclassed: Mr March's father cleared some hundred thousand pounds. Right through the nineteenth century, up to the end of the bank in 1896, the foreign letters added sarcastic footnotes to history: they were unmoral, factual, hard-baked, much more hard-baked because they did not set out to be.

The secret correspondent declined in value as communications got faster. The Marches' telephone number was London 2; but they did not time their moves as certainly as when Mr March's father opened his despatches in the morning. Mr March gallantly telephoned in French to Paris and Brussels every day as the bourses opened; but as the nineties passed by, neither his uncles nor Philip, nor he above all, felt they were in touch, even as much in touch as ten years before.

Of course the scale of things was altering under their hands. Their loans of a million pounds or so to the Argentine or Brazil no longer went very far; they were coming near to a world of preposterous size – a world dangerous, mad, exciting beyond measure, and, as Mr March decided, no place for a financier of distinctly anxious temperament. It was about this time that the legend sprang up of his being only able to control his worry by balancing the firm's accounts each night.

They might have stayed in longer, but for a characteristic weakness against which Mr March struggled in vain. They would never take anyone outside the family into the firm. As Mr March argued and quarrelled with his uncles, he kept protesting that one man of a different sort from the Marches might vitalise them. But they were loyal to the family: the Marches had started the bank a hundred years before, they had controlled it ever since, they could not give power to a stranger. In fact, as they were good pickers of men, Mr March's policy would probably have made them richer; but, whatever happened, neither they nor any other 'merchant banker in a fairly lucrative way of business' would have stayed in usefully for long: the twentieth century needed, not single millions, but tens and hundreds of millions, and could only be financed by the joint stock banks.

So they ceased business in 1896. They had not made much money in the nineties, but each of the five partners retired with a comfortable fortune. Mr March was just thirty-two. As the three of us sat at lunch he was talking of that time.

'I was still a bachelor,' he said. 'I thought I possessed enough for my requirements. But it was a pity, a firm like ours terminating after a hundred years. I sometimes think we should have continued. But we hadn't improved our position noticeably since my father died. Of course if I had been like him, I should have carried on successfully. But I didn't do much. My temperament was quite unsuitable for business. I was too shy and anxious.'

He was accepting himself as always, but his eyes did not leave Charles and he was speaking with regret. Success, in the world of his father and uncles, meant multiplying one's fortune and adding to one's influence among solid men. Mr March, not valuing it as much as they did, knew nevertheless that he would have pursued it if his temperament had not let him down; he would have kept the firm going, or joined others, as his brother Philip had done. While in fact he had come to terms with himself and retired. He had been happier, he had followed his nature: but he made no excuses, and it meant admitting to himself that, compared with those others, he was not so good a man.

'I was too shy and anxious' – he had taken himself for granted and lived unrestrainedly according to his own comfort. Like many people who are obsessed by every detail in the world outside, he was driven to simplify his life. Business was unbearable with a real anxiety every day, and instead he let himself loose on anxieties such as locking the door at night. Like many people sensitised to others' feelings, he was driven to escape more and more from company – except of those he had known so long that they did not count. More than any other March, he came to live entirely inside the family. He retired from any competition (Charles had said the same of himself the night he announced he was abandoning the law), met few new faces, and enjoyed himself as he felt inclined.

His happiness grew as he lived at the centre of his family, and his own most extravagant stories began with his marriage. It was a good start, as he stood with his bride on Victoria Station, to arrange for a cab to meet their train on Monday afternoon exactly one month later. After they had been a week at Mentone, another thought occurred to him of a contingency left unprovided for. He walked alone to the post office and sent off a telegram, reserving for his wife a place next to himself in the Jewish Cemetery at Golders Green.

Thus he plunged among twenty-five years of marriage – not at all tranquil years, because he could not be tranquil anywhere, but full of the life he wanted and in which he breathed his native air. He was passionately fond of his wife, and he was occupied with plenty of excitements, major and minor; the major excitements about his children as they grew up, and the minor ones of his fortune, Bryanston Square, Haslingfield, the servants, the whole economico-personal system of which he was the core.

He had not been bored. He had enjoyed his life. He still enjoyed it. He would have taken it over again on the same terms, and gone through it with as much zest.

And yet, it was foreign to his nature not to be frank with himself, and he felt that he had paid a price. Underneath his life, which suited him, which soaked up the violence underneath and let him become luxuriantly himself, he knew that he had lost some self-respect. He had been happier than most men, but it meant that he chose to run away from the contest.

Even Mr March, the most realistic of men, could not always forgive himself for his own nature. He could not quite forget the illusion, which we all have, most strongly when we are young, that every kind of action is possible to us if only we use our will. He felt as we all do, when we have slowly come to terms with our temperament and no longer try to be different from ourselves; we may be happier now, but we cannot help looking back to the days when we struggled against the sight of our limitations, when, miserable and conflict-ridden perhaps, we still in flashes of hope held the whole world in our hands. For the loss, as we come to know ourselves, is that now we know what we can never do.

Mr March felt envious of himself as a young man, not yet reconciled, not yet abdicating from his hopes of success. There were times when he called himself a failure. It was then that he invested all those rejected hopes in Charles; for everything that he aspired to, and had to dismiss as he discovered his weakness, could be built up again in his son. Could be built up more extravagantly, as a matter of fact; because, even in youth, the frailities of his own temperament were always liable to bring him back to realism, while the frailities of his son's could be laughed off.

For a long time Mr March secretly expected a great deal from Charles's gifts, more than he expressed during any of their arguments when Charles gave up the law. I remembered the end of that evening, after their quarrel, when suddenly he said 'I have always wanted something for you' and broke off the conversation, as though he were ashamed.

This afternoon at Haslingfield he was speaking in the same tone, concerned, simple and with no trace of reproach. Months had passed. So far as he knew, Charles was still idle and ready to follow his own escape; Mr March could see his son also driven to waste himself. As he told us of his career at the bank, Mr March was speaking of his fears for Charles. When he let us see his own regret, he was desperately anxious that he and his son should not be too much alike. He looked at Charles as he told stories, in a voice more subdued than I had heard it. 'After all,' he said, '*I* didn't do much. *I* wasn't the man to make much of my opportunities.'

CHAPTER XII

FIRST AND SECOND SIGHT

AFTER lunch Mr March left us, and Charles and I went out to the deck-chairs in the garden. It was glaring and hot out of doors, by contrast with the shaded dining-room. Charles, affected by his father's self-description, sat by me without speaking.

I heard a car run up the drive. A quarter of an hour later, Ann and Katherine came down from the house towards us. I noticed that Ann's walk had the kind of stiff-legged grace one sometimes saw in actresses, as though it had been studied and controlled. By Katherine's side, it made her look a fashionable woman: she was wearing a yellow summer frock, and carrying a parasol: she was still too far off for us to see her face.

When they came up to us, and she was introduced to Charles, it was a surprise, just as it had been on the night of Getliffe's party, to see her smile, natural, direct and shy. In the same manner, both direct and shy, she said to him:

'We've met before, haven't we?'

Charles, standing up, her hand in his, said:

'I believe we have.'

He added:

'Yes, I remember the evening.'

She had spoken to him with friendliness. Although he was polite, I did not hear the same tone in his voice. He looked at Katherine. There was a glint in his eye I did not understand.

Ann lay back in her deck-chair, and for an instant closed her eyes, basking in the heat. With her face on one side, the line between dark hair and temple was sharp, the skin paper-white under the bright sun. She looked prettier than I had seen her. Charles was glancing at her: I could not tell whether he was attracted: the moment we began to talk, he was provoked.

Sitting up, she asked me a question about Herbert Getliffe, going back to our conversation at the party.

'I've heard a bit more about him since then,' she said.

'What have you heard?'

She hesitated; she seemed both interested and uneasy.

'I couldn't help wondering—'

'What about?'

'Well, why you ever chose to work with him.'

Charles interrupted:

'You'd better tell us why you think he shouldn't.'

'I warn you that you're going to meet his brother soon,' said Katherine.

'Look, I'm sorry,' Ann said to her, 'if Herbert Getliffe is a friend of yours.'

'No. I've never met the man,' said Katherine, who was nevertheless blushing.

'You've gone too far to back out, you know,' Charles broke in again. 'What have you really got against Herbert Getliffe?'

Ann looked straight at him.

'I don't want to overdo it,' she said uncomfortably and steadily. 'I can only go on what I've been told – but isn't he the worst lawyer who's ever earned £6,000 a year?'

'Where did you hear that?' asked Charles.

'I was told by a man I know.'

Charles's eyes were bright, he was ready (I found the irony agreeable) to defend Getliffe with spirit. 'I suppose,' he said, 'your friend isn't by any chance a less successful rival at the Bar?'

'His name is Ronald Porson. He happens to have been practising out in Singapore,' said Ann.

'He's really a very unsuccessful rival, isn't he?'

'He's a far more intelligent person than Getliffe,' she said. With Charles getting at her, her diffidence had become not greater, but much less. Just as his voice had an edge to it, so had hers.

'Even if that's so,' Charles teased her, 'for success, you know, intelligence isn't all it's cracked up to be.'

'I should like to know what you do claim for Getliffe.'

'He's got intuition,' said Charles.

'What do you really mean by that?'

'Why,' said Charles, with his sharpest smile, 'you must know what intuition is. At any rate, you must have read about it in books.'

Ann gazed at him without expression, her eyes clear blue. For a second it seemed that she was going to make it a quarrel. She shrugged her shoulders, laughed, and lay back again in the sun.

Soon Katherine asked her to play a game of tennis. Ann tried to get out of it, saying how bad she was. I imagined that it was her normal shyness, until we saw her play. Katherine, who had a useful forehand drive, banged the ball past her. By the end of the fourth game, we realised that Ann was not only outclassed but already tired.

'Are you sure that you ought to be doing this?' called Charles.

'It's all right.' She was panting.

'Are you sure that you're quite fit?'

'Not perfectly. But I want to go on.'

'We'd better stop,' said Katherine.

'If you do, I shall claim the game.' She was still short of breath, but her face was set in an obstinate, headstrong smile.

She served. They played another game. Charles was watching her with a frown. At the end of the set he went on to the court. She was giddy, and clutched his arm; he took her to her chair. Soon she was moving her head from side to side, as though making sure that the giddiness had passed. She smiled at Charles. He said in relief:

'Why didn't you behave reasonably?'

'This is ridiculous,' said Ann.

He scolded her:

'Why did you insist on playing on after you'd tired yourself out?'

'I was ill in the spring, you see.' She was explaining her collapse.

'Would it upset you,' said Charles, 'if I sent for a doctor?'

'I'd ask you to if I needed one, I promise you I would.'

'Just to relieve my own mind?'

'I'd ask you to, if there was the slightest need.'

'There really isn't any?'

'You'll only irritate one if you fetch him.'

'I don't mind that—'

'You haven't had a doctor as a father, have you?'

'You really don't think there's any need? You know enough about yourself to be sure?' Charles reiterated.

Their sparring had vanished. They were speaking with confidence in each other.

'You see,' said Ann, 'I used to have these bouts before. They're passing off now.'

Just then Mr March walked down after his afternoon sleep. Before he reached us, he was watching Ann and his son. Then he looked only at Ann, and his manner to her, from the moment Katherine introduced them, impressed us all.

'I am delighted to have you adorning my house,' said Mr March. 'It isn't often that my house has been so charmingly adorned.'

It was a speech of deliberate gallantry. It was so emphatic that Ann became flustered; she smiled back, but she could not make much of a reply.

Mr March went on:

'I hope my son has not been excessively negligent in entertaining you until I arrived.'

'Not at all,' said Ann, still at a loss.

'I am relieved to hear it,' said Mr March.

'But I didn't give Katherine much of a game at tennis,' she said over-brightly, casting round for words.

'You shouldn't let them inveigle you into action too soon after your arrival. I might remark that you're paler than you ought to be, no doubt as a result of their lack of consideration.'

'I've been looked after very nicely, Mr March—'

'It's extremely polite of you to say so,' he said.

'Really I have.' She was getting over the first impact, and she answered without constraint, smiling both at him and Charles.

Soon afterwards Francis arrived, and I watched Katherine's eyes as his plunging stride brought him through the drawing-room, over the terrace, down to the lawn. Tea was brought out to us, and we ate raspberries and cream in the sunshine.

After tea we played tennis; then, when Mr March went in to dress, Katherine took Francis for a walk round the rose-garden, and I left the other two together. I strolled down the drive before going to my room; the stocks were beginning to smell, now the heat of the day was passing, and the scent came to me as though to heighten, and at the same time to touch with languor, the emotions I had been living among that afternoon.

When I left Ann and Charles, their faces had been softened and glowing. No one would say that either was in love; but each was in the state when they knew at least that love was possible. They were still safe; they need not meet again; he could still choose not to ask her, she could still refuse; and yet, while they did not know each other, while they were still free, there was a promise of joy.

It seemed a long time since I had known that state, I thought, as the smell of the stocks set me indulging my own mood. It had gone too soon, and I had discovered other meanings in love. I wondered how long it would last for them.

Evening was falling, and as I turned back towards the house its upper windows shone like blazing shields in the last of the sunlight. Looking up, I felt a trace of worry about Francis and Katherine; I felt a trace of self-pity because Charles and Ann might be lucky; but really, walking back to the house through the warm air, I was enjoying being a spectator, I was excited about it all.

CHAPTER XIII

GAMBLE

At dinner Mr March was not subdued and acceptant, as he had been at that table a few hours before. Instead, he intervened in each conversation and produced some of his more unpredictable retorts. So far as I could notice, his glance did not stay too long on Katherine, whose face was fresh with happiness as she talked to Francis. He interrupted her, but only as he interrupted the rest of us, in order to stay the centre of attention. It was hard to be sure whether his high spirits were genuine or not.

Once or twice Mr March waited for a response from Ann, who sat, dressed all in black except for an aquamarine brooch on her breast, at his right hand. She was quiet, she was deferential, she laughed at his stories, but it was not until after dinner that Mr March forced her into an argument.

We had moved into the drawing-room, and Mr March sent for the footman to open more windows. There we sat, the lights on, the curtains undrawn and the windows open, while Mr March proceeded by way of the day's temperature to talk to Francis, who was going to Corsica for a month's holiday before the October term.

'I hope you will insist on ignoring any salad they may be misguided enough to offer you. My daughter last year failed to show competent discretion in that respect. Caroline made a similar frightful ass of herself just before the earthquake at Messina. The disaster might have been avoided if she had possessed the gumption to keep sufficiently suspicious of all foreigners—'

'If you mean me, Mr L.,' Katherine said, 'I've proved to you that being ill in Venice can't have had anything to do with what I ate abroad.'

'I refuse to accept your assurances,' said Mr March. 'I hope you too will refuse to accept my daughter's assurances,' he said to Francis. In each remark he made to Francis, Katherine was listening for an undertone: but she heard none, and protested loudly because she was relieved.

Mr March shouted her down, and went on talking to Francis: 'I should be sorry if my daughter's example lured you into risks that could possibly be fatal to your health.'

'As I've spent an hour before dinner trying to persuade him not to climb mountains without a guide,' said Katherine, 'I call that rather hard.'

'She definitely disapproves of the trip,' said Francis. 'She can't be blamed for not discouraging me enough.'

'I should advise you to ignore any of her suggestions for your welfare,' said Mr March.

It sounded no more than genial back-chat. Katherine kept showing her concern for Francis. She could not resist showing it: to do so was a delight. Yet Mr March gave no sign that he saw him as a menace.

Mr March left off talking to Francis, and addressed us all:

'My experience is that foreigners can always tempt one to abandon any sensible habit. I have never been able to understand why it is considered necessary to intrude oneself among them on the pretext of obtaining pleasure. Hannah always said that she came to life abroad, but I don't believe that she was competent to judge. Since I married my wife I have preferred to live in my own houses where foreigners are unlikely to penetrate. The more I am compelled to hear of foreign countries, the less I like them. I am sure that my charming guest will agree with me,' he said confidentially to Ann.

Ann was embarrassed. 'I don't think I should go quite as far as that, Mr March,' she said.

'You'll come to it in time, you'll come to it in time,' cried Mr March. 'Why, you must be too young to remember the catastrophe foreigners involved us in fifteen years ago.'

'I was nine,' she said.

'I am surprised to hear that you weren't even more of an infant. I should be prepared to guarantee that you will keep your present youth and beauty until you are superannuated. But still you can't conceivably remember the origins of that unfortunate catastrophe. You can't remember how we were bamboozled by foreigners and entangled in continental concerns that were no affair of ours—'

Mr March went on to develop a commentary, jingoistic and reactionary, on the circumstances of the 1914–18 war. He had the habit of pretending to be at the extreme limit of reaction, just because he knew that Charles's friends were nearly all of them on the left. But we did not argue with him:

when politics came up among the senior Marches, we usually avoided trouble and kept our mouths shut.

As she listened, Ann was frowning. She glanced at Charles, then at me, as though expecting us to contradict. When Mr March paused for a breathing space, she hesitated; she started to talk and checked herself. But the next time he stopped, she did not hesitate. In a tone timid, gentle but determined, she said:

'I'm sorry, Mr March, but I'm afraid I can't believe it.'

'I should be glad to be enlightened on what you do believe,' said Mr March, preserving his gallant manner.

Still quietly and uneasily, Ann told him, without any covering up, that she did not accept any of his views about the war, or nations, or the causes of politics.

'I suppose you're going to tell me next that we can't understand anything unless we take account of what those people call the class struggle.'

Mr March's voice had become loud; his face was heavy with anger.

Ann's tone was more subdued, but she continued without hesitation:

'I'm afraid I should have to say just that.'

'Economic poppycock,' Mr March burst out.

'It's a tenable theory, Mr L.,' Charles interrupted. 'You can't dispose of it by clamour.'

'My guest can't dispose of it by claptrap,' said Mr March. Then he suppressed his temper, and spoke to Ann in his most friendly and simple way:

'Obviously we take different views of the world. I presume that you think it will improve?'

'Yes,' said Ann.

'You are optimistic, as you should be at your age. I am inclined to consider that it will continue to get worse. I console myself that it will last my time.

'Yes,' Mr March added, as he glanced round the bright room, 'it will last my time.'

He had spoken in a tone matter-of-fact and yet elegiac. He did not want to argue with Ann any more. But then I saw that Ann was not ready to let it go. Her eyes were bright. For all her shyness, she was not prepared to be discreet, as I was. Perhaps she was contemptuous of that kind of discretion. I had an impression that she was gambling.

'I'm sure it won't last mine,' she said.

Mr March was taken aback, and she added:

'I'm also sure that it oughtn't to.'

'You anticipate that there will be a violent change within your lifetime?' said Mr March.

'Of course,' said Ann, with absolute conviction.

She had spoken with such force that we were all silent for an instant. Then Mr March said:

'You've no right to anticipate it.'

'Of course she has,' Charles broke in. 'She wants a good world. This is the only way in which she can see it happening.' He smiled at her. 'The only doubt is whether the world afterwards would be worth it.'

'I'm sure of that,' she said.

'You've no right to be sure,' said Mr March.

'Why don't you think I have?' she asked quietly.

'Because women would be better advised not to concern themselves with these matters.'

Mr March had spoken with acute irritability, but Ann broke suddenly into laughter. It was laughter so spontaneous, so unresentfully accepting the joke against herself, that Mr March was first taken at a loss and then reassured. He watched her eyes screw up, her self-control dissolve, as she abandoned herself to laughter. She looked very young.

Charles took the chance to smooth the party down. He acted as impresario for Mr March and led him on to his best stories. At first Mr March was still disturbed: but he was melted by his son's care, and by the warmth and well-being we could all feel that night in Charles.

Katherine joined in. Between them they poured all their attention on to Mr March, as though making up for the exhilaration of the last few hours.

They succeeded in getting Mr March on to the subject of Ann's family. He told her: 'Of course, you're not one of the real Simons,' and she proved that she was a distant cousin of the Florence Simon whom I had met at the family dinner at Bryanston Square and who even Mr March had to admit was 'real'. From then till 10.40 Mr March explored in what remote degree he and Ann were related; stories of fourth and fifth cousins 'making frightful asses of themselves' forty years ago became immersed in the timeless continuum in which Mr March, more extravagantly than on a normal night, let himself go.

When Mr March had rattled each door in the hall and gone upstairs, Katherine said to Ann:

'Well, I hope you're not too bothered after all that.' Ann shook her head.

'Did you want me to keep out?' she said to Charles. Charles was smiling. Francis asked:

'What would your own father have said if a strange young woman had started talking about the revolution?'

'Didn't you agree with me?' she said, quite sharply. She knew that Francis was on her side: he was as radical as his fellow scientists. Deferential as she often sounded, she was not to be browbeaten. Then she smiled too.

'I won't do it again,' she said. 'But tonight was a special occasion.'

Again I had the impression that she had been gambling. Whatever the gamble had been, it was over now, and she was relaxed.

Making it up with Francis, she said to him: 'As for my father, he wouldn't have had the spirit to argue. Even when I was growing up, he'd managed to tire himself out.'

One could guess from her tone that she loved him. One could guess too that she was not often relaxed enough to talk like this. She smiled again, almost as though her upper lip was twitching, and said:

'Can you remember the agony you went through when your father was first proved wrong?'

It was Katherine who answered her:

'I don't know,' she said. 'We were used to the whole family proving each other wrong, weren't we?'

'But I think I know what you mean,' Charles was saying to Ann.

'I've never forgotten,' said Ann. 'It was the day after my birthday – I was nine. Someone came in to dinner, a friend of mother's. He said to my father: "You call yourself a doctor. You remember how you swore last week that the sea was blue because of the salts that it dissolved? Well, I asked one of the men at school. He laughed and said it was a ridiculous idea." Then he gave the proper explanation. I never have been able to remember it to this day.' Ann went on: 'I've re-learned it several times, but it's no good. I told myself in bed that night that of course father was right. But I knew he wasn't. I knew people were laughing because he didn't know why the sea was blue. Every time I remembered that night for years, I wanted to shut my eyes.'

Charles said to Katherine:

'We know what that's like, don't we?' He turned back to Ann. 'But when I've felt like that, it wasn't over quite the same things.'

'Not over your father?'

Charles hesitated, and said:

'Not in the same way.'

'What was it about then?'

'Mostly about being a Jew,' said Charles.

'Curiously enough,' said Ann, 'I never felt that.'

'Which is no doubt why I met you,' said Charles, 'on my one and only appearance at the Jewish dance.'

He looked at me; this was the trick of fortune I had not recognised that afternoon. He was smiling at his own expense, and his expression, sarcastic and gay, brought back the first night I dined at Bryanston Square, when he talked 'with a furrowed brow' of Katherine being sent to the dance. Tonight he seemed free of that past.

'You were lucky to escape,' said Charles. 'There've been times when I've disliked other Jews – simply because I suffered through being one.'

'Yes,' said Katherine.

'I couldn't help it, but it was degrading to feel oneself doing it,' he said.

'Yes,' said Katherine again.

'I think you would have behaved better,' Charles said to Ann.

'No,' she said. 'I've hated my father sometimes because of the misery I've been through on his account.'

We all confided about our childhoods, but it was Charles and Ann, and sometimes Katherine, who spoke most about the moments of shame – not grief or sorrow, but shame. The kind of shame we all know, but which had been more vivid to them than to most of us: the kind of shame which, when one remembers it, makes one stop dead in one's tracks, and jam one's eyelids tight to shut it out.

They went on with those confidences until Ann went to bed. It was late, and Francis followed not long after. Katherine made an excuse and ran out, and from the drawing-room Charles and I heard her speak to Francis at the bottom of the stairs. For several minutes we heard their voices. Then Katherine rejoined us, and gave Charles a radiant smile. We opened the long windows, and walked on to the terrace. It was an August night of extreme beauty, the moon just about to rise over the hills. A meteor flashed among the many stars to the south.

No one spoke. Katherine threw her arm round Charles's shoulders, smiled at him, and sighed.

CHAPTER XIV

BORROWING A ROOM

EARLY in October, when the March household had returned to London, Katherine started gossip percolating through the family, just by having Francis Getliffe three or four times to dinner at Bryanston Square. We speculated often upon when the gossip would reach Mr March: we became more and more puzzled as to whether he was truly oblivious.

On an autumn night, warm and misty, with leaves sometimes spinning down in the windless air, Charles and I were walking through the square. He had not been talking much. Suddenly he said:

'I've got a favour to ask you.'

'What is it?'

He was speaking with diffidence, with unusual stiffness.

'I don't want you to say yes out of good-nature. It may be too much of an intrusion—'

'If you tell me what it is—'

'I don't want you to say yes on the spot.'

'What in God's name is it?'

At last he said:

'Well, we wondered whether you could bear it, if Ann and I met in your rooms—'

He produced timetables, which he had been thinking out, so I suspected, for days beforehand, of how they could fit in with my movements, of how they need not inconvenience me.

Up to that night he had said nothing about Ann. Hearing him forced to break his secretiveness open, I was both touched and amused. I was amused also to find him facing a problem that vexed me and my impoverished friends when I was younger – of 'somewhere to go' with a young woman. In our innocence we thought the problem would have solved itself if we had money. While in fact Charles, with all the March houses at his disposal, could get no privacy at all – less than we used to get in the dingy streets of the provincial town.

Walking with Charles that night, and other nights that autumn, I felt as one does with a friend in love – protective, superior, a little irritated, envious. His tongue was softened by happiness. He was full of hopes. Those hopes! He would not have dared to confess them. He would have blushed because they were so impossibly golden, romantic – and above all vague. They had no edge or limit, they were just a vista of grand, continuing and perfect rapture.

Charles was by nature both guarded and subtle. His imagination was a realistic one. If I had confessed any such hopes as uplifted him that autumn he would have riddled them with sarcasm. They would have sounded jejune by contrast to his own style. Yet now he fed on them for hours, they were part of the greatest happiness he had ever known.

As the autumn passed, I saw a good deal of Charles and Ann together. Inquisitive as I was, I did not know for certain what was happening to them. Then one evening when I returned to my flat they were still there. They were sitting by the fire; they greeted me; they did not tell me anything. Yet looking at them I felt jealous because they were so happy.

Ann said, gazing round the room as though she was noticing it for the first time:

'Why does Lewis make this place look like a station waiting-room?' Charles smiled at her, and she went on:

'We ought to take care of him for once, oughtn't we? Let's take care of him.'

She spoke with the absorbed kindness of the supremely happy: kindness which was not really directed towards me, but which was an overflow of her own joy.

I thought then that it had taken Ann longer than anyone else to recognise that she was in love: though from that afternoon at Haslingfield the barriers dropped away, and she gave him her trust. She had not known before that she could let the barriers fall like that; except with her father, she had not entrusted herself to another human being. To all of us round her, there seemed no doubt about it; each moment she was living through had become enhanced. Yet it was some time before she said to herself: 'I am in love.'

Of course, that conscious recognition to oneself – particularly in a character like Ann's – is a more important stage than we sometimes allow. Until it has happened, this present desire may still swim with others, there are plenty more we have never brought to light. But when once it is made conscious, there is no way of drawing back; the love must be lived out.

That moment, when Ann first thought 'I am in love' (to Charles it happened at once, during the weekend at Haslingfield), was more decisive for them than the dates which on the surface seemed to mark so much: of the first kiss, of when they first made love. Seeing them that night, when it was all settled, I guessed that it came later than the rest of us suspected:

and that, as soon as it came, there was no retreat. They knew – they told each other with the painful and extreme pleasure of surrender – that fate had caught them.

CHAPTER XV

BELIEVING ONE'S EARS

A DAY or two after I had watched Charles and Ann in my own sitting-room, she took me out to dinner alone. She took me out to a sumptuous dinner; shy as she could be, she was used to making her money work for her, and she led me to a corner table in Claridge's; more unashamed of riches than Charles, more lavish and generous, she persuaded me to eat an expensive meal and drink a bottle of wine to myself. Meanwhile she was getting me to talk about Charles.

For a time I was reticent. He was too secretive to tolerate being discussed, even with her, perhaps most of all with her.

Very gently she said:

'All I should like to know is what *you* think he really wants.' She did not mean about herself: that was taken for granted and not mentioned all night. There she was as delicate and proud as he was; she did not even suggest that they would get married. But about the rest of his life she was tender and not so delicate. She wanted anything she could learn about him which would help him. As she pressed me, her face open, her manner affectionate and submissive, I could realise the core of will within her.

What had he been like when I first knew him? What had he thought of doing with himself? What had he really felt when he gave up the Bar?

'He would always have hated it,' I said.' He was dead right to get out.'

'Of course he was,' said Ann.

'And yet,' I said, 'he's not so unambitious as he seems.'

'Aren't you reading yourself into him?' she said, suddenly sharp.

'Do you think he likes being idle?' I retorted.

'Don't you think' – she was gazing straight at me – 'there are other ways of not being idle?'

She took up the attack.

'Would you really say,' she went on, 'that he wants success on the terms that you want it, or most other men do?'

I hesitated.

'No,' I said. 'Perhaps not quite.'

'Not quite?' She was smiling. As she asked the question, I knew how tenacious and passionate she was.

'Not at all. Not in the ordinary sense,' I had to admit.

She smiled again, sitting relaxed in her corner. Once more she asked me in detail what he had done about giving up the Bar. She needed any-thing I could tell her about him; nothing was trivial; she was bringing her whole self to bear. When she had finished with me, she became silent. It was some time afterwards before she said:

'Have you got an idea of what he really wants?'

'Has he?'

She would not answer; but I was sure she thought he had. Alone with her, I knew for certain how single-minded her love was. She had no room for anyone but him. She liked me, she was friendly and comradely, she had good manners, she wanted to know how I was getting on: but really this was a business dinner. She was securing me as an ally, just because I was his intimate friend: she was picking my brains: that was all.

I was thinking, I had never seen her flirt. Only once had I seen her so much as give any meaning to another man's name: that was the first afternoon at Haslingfield, when Charles was baiting her and she replied by praising Ronald Porson. She had done it to defend herself, to provoke Charles. Apart from that, although she was admired by several other men, she had not let Charles worry about them.

Actually Porson was pressing her to marry him. She had talked to me once about him: he had meant little to her, but he had been infatuated with her for years: she felt a last shred of responsibility for him on that account. She found it hard to say the final no. From her description, he seemed to be an eccentric, violent character, and I thought that perhaps his oddity had found some niche in her imagination.

That night at Claridge's, I was on the point of asking her about him, when by chance I said something about politics. At once she was on to it; she was eager to discover whether I was an ally there also. In a few minutes I discovered that she was not playing. This was not just a rich young woman's fancy.

I had not been able to understand her outburst at Haslingfield; I was still puzzled by it, after this talk with her alone; but at least I respected her in a way that I had not reckoned on. Much of the radicalism of the younger Marches I could not take seriously, after being brought up in a different climate, the climate of those born poor. But Ann was different again.

As we argued that night, I could not help but see that there was nothing dilettante about her. This was real politics. She knew more than I did. She was more committed.

I respected her: on many things we agreed: it was a curious pleasure to agree on politics, to see her pretty face across the table, to feel that her warmth and force were on one's side. But, even then, it seemed a bit of a mystery. Much more so when I thought about it in cold blood. Why did politics mean so much to her? Why was she like this? What was she after?

I could not find any sort of answer. To another of that night's mysteries I did however get an answer – when, just before Christmas, I came back to my room late in the evening. As I got to the landing, I saw a crack of light under the door. When I went in, I had an impression they had waited for me. Ann was sitting in a chair by the fire, Charles on the rug at her feet. She was running her fingers through his hair. They went on talking as I laid down a brief. For an instant, I fancied I caught the words from Ann 'when you've finished at hospital'. I thought I must have misheard. But, as I came to sit down in the other armchair, she used the same phrase, unmistakably, again.

It seemed to me fantastic. It seemed so fantastic that I was just going to ask. But Ann then said:

'We're thinking that Charles might become a doctor.'

'That's going a bit far,' said Charles, who was in high spirits. But chiefly I noticed Ann's pleasure – soft, intense, youthful.

'Don't you think it would be a good idea?' she said.

Charles teased her for her enthusiasm, but she did not let it go. 'You wanted him to know, didn't you?' she said.

'It's only the barest possibility, you understand?' said Charles to me.

'But he wants to hear what you think.' Ann also was speaking to me.

Charles insisted that we keep secret even the most remote mention of the idea. As she promised, a smile flickered on Ann's happy face, and the sight of it made Charles, after an instant's lag and as though reluctantly, smile too.

CHAPTER XVI

CHOICE OF A PROFESSION

ONE afternoon in January, I went to tea at Bryanston Square and discovered that Charles had just confided in Katherine. I discovered it through their habit of repeating themselves. When I arrived, they were talking of a rumour that Aunt Caroline had been making enquiries about Francis Getliffe: how often did he go to Bryanston Square? How often did he go when Charles was otherwise engaged? Katherine was agitated and excited. There was another rumour that Caroline was considering whether she ought to speak to Mr March. Was it true? Then Katherine said, harking back to what they had been saying:

'I suppose he won't mind this idea of yours. Don't you agree that he won't mind it?'

'Can you give me a good reason why he should?'

'It will be a shock to him, you realise that?' she said. She looked at me, and went on: 'Does Lewis know anything about this, by the way?'

'He's had a bit of warning.' Charles then said to me: 'I've told Katherine this afternoon that I'm going to try to become a doctor.'

Since that hint in my room he had not asked my advice nor anyone else's. Only Ann had been inside his secret. He was presenting us, just as he had done when he gave up the law, with a resolution already made. By the time he told us, it was made once for all, and the rest of us could take it or leave it.

Katherine was frowning. 'I can't understand why you should do this.'

'It isn't as difficult as all that, is it?'

'You could do so many things.'

'I've evaded them so far with singular success,' said Charles.

'Is it the best scheme?' Katherine said. 'Don't you think he'll be wasted, Lewis?'

'It's exactly to prevent myself being wasted that I've thought of this.' Charles looked at her with a sarcastic, affectionate grin. 'I agree, I wouldn't like to feel that I had wasted my time altogether. The chief advantage of becoming a doctor is precisely that it might prevent me doing that. I shall still be some use in a dim way even if I turn out to be completely obscure. It's the only occupation I can find where you can be absolutely undistinguished and still flatter yourself a bit.'

'That's all very well for one of nature's saints,' said Katherine. 'But are you sure it's your line?'

Charles did not answer. He hesitated. He was embarrassed. Sharply, he went on to a new line:

'I've told you, there's a perfectly good practical reason. You both know, I'm hoping that Ann will marry me. We've got to look a reasonable way ahead. I suppose Mr L. will make me independent when I'm twenty-five, that is in April. He's always promised to do that, or when I marry, "whichever shall be the earlier", as he insists on saying. And I suppose I shall come into his money in time. But don't you see? I daren't count on any of this lasting many years. Too much may happen in the world. It's not exactly likely we shall be able to live on investments all our lives. Well, I think there's more security as a doctor than as anything else I could take up. Whatever happens to the world, it's rather unlikely that a doctor will starve.'

Those words sounded strange, in the drawing-room at Bryanston Square, from the heir to one of the March fortunes. But this was 1930, and we had already begun to speak in those terms. On this winter evening when Charles was talking, such an anxiety seemed, of course, remote, not quite real, not comparable for an instant with that which Katherine felt when she saw a letter from Aunt Caroline waiting for Mr March.

We were not to know it until we were middle-aged, but there was another kind of irony. In historical fact, the convulsion in Charles's world turned out to be not so great.

When Charles told Mr March a few days later, he gave the same justification – the desire to be some use, the need to be secure, though he did not mention Ann's name.

For some time, Charles's insight failed him; he did not understand how his father had responded. Mr March began by opposing: but that was nothing unusual, and Charles was not disturbed. Mr March's first remarks were on the plane of reason. He put forward entirely sensible arguments why Charles could not hope to become a doctor. He was nearly twenty-five. At best he would be well into the thirties before he was qualified. He had had no serious scientific education, and was, like all the Marches, clumsy with his hands. It would be an intolerable self-discipline to go through years of uncongenial study. 'You might begin it,' said Mr March, 'but you'd give it up after a few months. You've never shown the slightest disposition to persevere with anything when you're not interested. You've never shown the slightest disposition to persevere with anything at all. I refuse to believe that you're remotely capable of it.'

That was the end of the first discussion. Mr March's tone had become not quite so reasonable. As never before in all their quarrels over his career, Charles heard a gibe behind it. Mr March used to speak about his son's idleness with sympathy and regret. For the first time a gibe sprang out, harsh, almost triumphant.

Even so, Charles was slow to see what Mr March was feeling. The arguments went on, and became angrier. Mr March ceased to speak with caution; he was behaving not like a man troubled, or even sad and wounded, but one in a storm of savage distress. It seemed fantastic, but at last Charles had to admit that he had not seen his father in a state as dark as this before.

When Charles told me about it, he was enough upset to stay late in my room, retracing the arguments, trying to find a motive for Mr March's behaviour. Charles was having to guard his own temper. He was resentful because he had provoked a response like this – a response deeper, angrier and more ravaged than anyone in his senses could have expected.

It was no use my telling Charles that this was a torment of passion; he knew that as well and better than I did. He knew too that, as with so many of the torments of passion, Mr March's distress was bitter out of al' proportion to what appeared to have provoked it. It seemed just like love, I thought to myself, when a trivial neglect, such as not receiving a letter for a day or two, may suddenly make one seethe with anguish and hatred: the event, of course, being a trigger and not a cause. So Mr March heard Charles say that he was going to abandon a life of idleness and become a doctor, and was immediately shaken by passion such as no other action of his son had ever roused.

For day after day he got less controlled, not more. One night Charles was so worn down that I walked back with him, some time after one in the morning, to Bryanston Square. As we stood outside, he asked if I would mind coming in, he would like to go on talking. Before we had sat five minutes in the drawing-room, there was a heavy shuffle outside and Mr March pushed open the door.

Just by itself his appearance would have been bizarre. He was wearing red square-toed slippers and a bright-blue dressing-gown on which glittered rising-sun decorations, as though he was covered with the insignia of an unknown order. But the extraordinary thing about him was his face. For some reason difficult to understand, he had covered his eyelids, the skin under the eyes, in fact all the skin within the orbital area, with white ointment. He looked something like the end-man in an old-fashioned minstrel show.

He was scowling: his courtesy had been swept away, and he entered the room without any sign that I existed. He said to Charles: 'I've been considering the observations you insist on making—'

'Can't we leave it for tonight, Mr L.?' Charles's tone was tired, but even-tempered and respectful.

'We can only leave it if you abandon your ridiculous intentions. I should like to be assured that that is what you are now proposing.'

'I'm sorry.'

'In that case I want to inform you again that your intentions are nothing but a ridiculous fit of crankiness. I've listened to your maunderings about wanting your life to be useful. Herbert never maundered as crankily as that, to do him justice, which shows what you've come down to. I should like to know why you consider it's specially incumbent on you to decide in what particular fashion your life ought to be useful.'

'I've told you, I shouldn't be on terms with myself—'

'Stuff and nonsense. Why are you specially competent to decide that one man's life is useful and another's isn't? Was my father's life useful? Is my brother Philip's? Is John's [the butler's]? I suppose that I'm expected to believe that my brother Philip's life isn't as useful as any twopenny-ha'penny practitioner's.'

Charles stayed silent. Mr March flapped the arms of his dressing-gown and his eyes were furious in their white surround.

'Is that what I am expected to believe?' he cried.

'I don't expect you to believe it for yourself, Mr L.,' said Charles with restraint. 'I don't expect you to believe it for Uncle Philip. All I want you to accept is that it does happen to be true for me.'

'All I want you to accept,' shouted Mr March, 'is that it is a piece of pernicious cranky nonsense.'

The furore in the room made it hard to stay still. Yet it was true that Mr March could not credit that a balanced man should want to go to extravagant lengths to feel that his life was useful. He could not begin to understand the sense of social guilt, the sick conscience, which were real in Charles. To Mr March, who by temperament accepted life as it was, who was solid in the rich man's life of a former day, such a reason seemed just perverse. He could not believe that his son's temperament was at this point radically different from his own.

Without warning he began a new attack – from Charles's expression new to him, not only new but beyond comparison more offensive.

'I've been considering the origin of this pernicious nonsense,' said Mr March. His tone had suddenly dropped, not to a conversational level, but to something lower, like a hard whisper. It was a tone completely unexpected, coming from him, and the effect was jarring, almost sinister.

'I don't know what you mean,' said Charles.

'I refuse to be persuaded that you came to these ridiculous conclusions by yourself.'

'What do you mean to suggest?'

For the first time, Charles had raised his voice. Mr March kept his low.

'I have been considering how many of these conclusions can be attributed to another person.'

'Who would that be?' Charles burst out.

'My guest of last summer. Ann Simon.'

Mr March had not seen her since Haslingfield. Charles had told him nothing of their meetings: her name had been mentioned very seldom. Yet all of a sudden Mr March showed that he had been thinking of her with suspicion, with an elaborate, harsh, and jealous suspicion.

'Is she or is she not,' Mr March said, in a grating, obsessed tone, 'the daughter of a practitioner herself?'

'Of course she is.'

'Is she or is she not the kind of young woman who would encourage a man to go in for highfalutin nonsense?'

'Don't you think this had better stop straight away?' Charles said.

'Has she or has she not attempted to seduce you into adopting her own pestilential opinions?'

White with anger, Charles stood up, and went towards the door. For the first time that night, Mr March addressed a remark to me:

'Isn't this young woman set on making my son what she'd have the insolence to call a useful member of society?'

I did not reply, and in an instant Mr March was asking another obsessed question at Charles's back.

'How many times have you seen her since she visited my house?'

Charles turned round. Trying to command himself, he said, with dignity, with something like affection:

'It will be worse if we don't leave it, don't you see?'

'How many times,' cried Mr March, 'have you see her this last week?'

Charles looked at him, and to my astonishment Mr March said nothing more, did not wait for an answer, but rushed out of the room, his slippers scuffling.

The next day, however, Mr March repeated the questions again. Charles became enraged. At last his control broke down. He said curtly that there was no point in talking further. Without an explanation or excuse, he went out of the house.

When Charles had left, Mr March was subdued for a few hours. He did not know where his son had gone. His fury returned and he vented it on Katherine. 'Why hasn't Ann Simon been invited to my house?' he burst into the drawing-room shouting. 'I hold you responsible for not inviting her. If she had visited my house, I could have stopped this foolery before it showed signs of danger. I tell you, I insist on Ann Simon being invited here at once. I insist on seeing her before the weekend.'

Katherine invited her, but had to report to Mr March that Ann replied she was busy every day that week and could not come. Mr March did not say another angry word to Katherine. His silence was sombre and brooding.

CHAPTER XVII

A REASON FOR ESCAPE

FOR forty-eight hours after he left Bryanston Square, no one knew where Charles was. Katherine was distracted with anxiety; on the second afternoon, Ann rang me up and asked if I could tell her anything. There had not been a silence between them before.

He came to my rooms that night. I had taken a brief home from chambers and was still working on it at ten o'clock. I had not heard him on the stairs, and the first I knew was that he stood inside the room, the shoulders of his coat glistening from the rain.

'May I sleep on your sofa tonight?' he asked. He was tired, he wanted the question to be accepted as casually as he tried to ask it. In order to prevent any talk of himself, he asked what I was doing, picked up the brief and read it with his intense and penetrating attention. He had begun to read before he threw off his overcoat; he stood on the carpet where, only a month before, I had seen him sit at Ann's feet by the fire.

'What line are you taking?' he asked. 'Have you got anything written down?'

I gave him my sketch of the case. He read it, still with abnormal concentration. He looked at me, his eyes bright with a smile both contemptuous and resentful.

'Yes,' he said. 'You ought to win it that way. Unless you show more than usual incompetence when you get on your feet. But you oughtn't to be satisfied with the case you've made, don't you realise that? I should say you're doing it slightly better than the average young counsel at your stage. Do you think that's fair? I know you're cleverer than this attempt suggests. But I sometimes wonder whether you'll ever convey to the people who matter how clever you really are. You're missing the chance to make this case slightly more impressive than your previous ones, don't you admit it? If you just look here, you'll see—'

He set to work upon my draft. Impatiently, but with extreme thoroughness and accuracy, he reshaped it; he altered the form, pared down the argument in the middle, brought in the details so that the line of the case stood out from beginning to end. It was criticism that was more than criticism, it was a re-creation of the case. He did it so brutally that it was not easy to endure.

I tried to shut out pique and vanity. I thought how strange it was that, at this crisis of his conflict with his father, in which they were quarrelling over his new profession, he could immerse himself in the problems of the one he had deliberately thrown away. He would never go back; he was determined to find his own salvation; yet was there perhaps the residue of a wish that he could return to the time before the break was made?

'Well,' said Charles, 'that's slightly less meaningless. It's not specially elegant – but it will do you a bit less harm than your first draft would have done, don't you admit that?'

It was nearly midnight, and neither of us had eaten for a long time. I took him to a dingy café close by. Charles looked at the window, steamy in the cold wet night, smelt the frying onions, heard the rattle of dominoes in the inside room. 'Do you often come here?' he asked, but he saw, from the way the proprietor spoke to me, and the nods I exchanged, what the answer was. This was a side of my life he scarcely knew – the back streets, the cheap cafés, the ramshackle poverty, which I still took for granted.

We sat in an alcove, eating our plates of sausage and mash. Charles said:

'You haven't many ties, have you?'

'I've got those I make myself,' I said.

'They're not so intolerable,' said Charles. 'You're lucky. You've been so much more alone than I ever have. You've had such incomparably greater privacy. Most of the things you've done have affected no one but yourself. I tell you, Lewis, you're lucky.'

His eyes were gleaming.

'They think I'm irresponsible to have gone off like this. They're right. And they think I'm naturally not an irresponsible person. It might be better if I were. Can't they imagine how anyone comes to a point where he wants to throw off every scrap of responsibility – and just go where no one knows him? Can't they imagine how one's aching to hide somewhere where no one notices anything one does?

'That's why,' he said, 'you're lucky to have no ties.'

He could not break, he was telling me, from his: for a night or two he had escaped, behaved completely out of character, shown no consideration or feeling or even manners: but he was drawn back to the conflict of his home. For a night or two he had escaped from the attempts to confine him, not only his father's but also Ann's. He was drawn back. But, sitting in the alcove of the smoky cafe, his face pale against the tarnished purple plush, his eyes brilliant with lack of sleep, Charles talked little of his father or Ann. He was unassuageably angry with himself. Why had he behaved in this fashion? – without dignity, without courage, without warmth. He could not explain it. He felt, not only self-despising, but mystified.

He talked of himself, but he said nothing I had not heard before. He went over the arguments for the way he had chosen. He was exhausted, unhappy, nothing he said could satisfy him. We walked the streets in the cold rain, it was late before we went to bed, but he had not reached any kind of release.

In the morning, grey and dark, we sat over our breakfast. He had been dreaming, he said, and he looked absent, as though still preoccupied and weighed down by his dream. Suddenly he rose, went to my desk and took hold of the brief on which we had worked the night before. He turned to me, his lips pulled sideways in a smile, and said: 'I was unpleasant about this yesterday.' It was not an apology. 'You know what it is like. One hates it but goes on.'

At that moment we both knew, without another word, why he had escaped. He had not really escaped from the conflict: he had escaped from what he might do within it.

He knew – it was a link between us, for I also knew – what it was like to be cruel. To be impelled to be cruel, and to enjoy it. Other young men could let it ride, could take themselves for granted, but not he. He could not accept it as part of himself. It had to be watched and guarded against. With the force, freshness and hope of which he was capable, he longed to put it aside, to be kind and selfless as he believed he could be kind and selfless. When he spoke of wanting to lead a 'useful' life, he really meant something stronger; but he was still young enough, and so were the rest of us, to be inhibited and prudish about the words we used. He said 'useful'; but what he really meant was 'good'. When Ann fought shy of my questions about what he hoped for, we both had an idea: he wanted to lead a good life, that was all.

I sometimes thought it was those who were tempted to be cruel who most wanted to be good.

Charles wanted to dull his sadic edge. He knew the glitter which radiated from him in a fit of malice. He was willing to become dull, hum-drum, pedestrian, in order not to feel that special exhilaration of the nerves. For long periods he succeeded. By the time of that quarrel, he was gentler than when I first knew him. But he could not trust himself. To others the edge, the cruel glitter, might seem dead, but he had to live with his own nature.

So he was frightened of his conflict with his father. He must be free he must find his own way, he must fulfil his love for Ann; but he needed desperately that he should prevail without trouble, without the harsh excitement that he could feel latent within. Neither Ann nor his father must suffer through him.

In the grey bleak light of that winter morning, he stood, still heavy from his dream, and knew why he had run away. Yet he believed that he could keep them safe. Those fits of temptation seemed like a visitor to his true self. They faded before the steady warmth and strength which ran more richly in him than in most men. With all the reassurance of that warmth and strength, he believed that he could keep them safe.

'I shall go to stay with Francis for a few days,' he said. 'Then I'll come back to Mr L.'s. I'll let them know today, of course. It's monstrous to have given them this absurd piece of worry.'

CHAPTER XVIII

MR MARCH ASKS A QUESTION

As soon as Mr March heard from his son, he insisted once more that Katherine should invite Ann to the house. Again Ann refused. Katherine was frightened to bring the reply to Mr March, but he received it without expression.

Hearing what had happened, I met Ann and told her it was a mistake to have declined the invitation. We were sitting in a Soho pub. Her eyes were sparkling, as though she were laughing it off.

'Why shouldn't I?'

She spoke so lightly that I went on without concealing anything: I said that Mr March suspected her influence, and that for all their sakes she ought to calm him down.

Then I realised that I had completely misread her. It was anger that made her eyes bright; she was not only indignant, but outraged.

'I'm very glad that I didn't go,' she said.

'It will make things worse.'

'No,' she said with fierceness. 'He's got to see that Charles has decided for himself.'

'He'll never believe it,' I told her.

'I can't help that.'

'Can't you try?'

'No.' Her tone was dismissive and hard. 'I should have thought you knew that Charles had made his choice. I should have thought you knew that it was right for him.'

'I'm not asking you to make me realise it –' I began.

'Any sane father would realise it too. If Mr March insists on making a nuisance of himself, I can't help it.'

She added that she had rung up Charles to ask whether she might refuse the invitation – and he had said yes. The pleasure, the submissive pleasure, with which she spoke of asking Charles's permission glowed against the hardness she had just shown about Mr March.

She had been angry with me also, for telling her what she already knew. But she was tired by the conflict over Charles; she found it a relief to make it up with me and talk about him. She told me something, more than either of them had done before, about their plans for marriage. It was still not settled. Recently, there had been a reason for delay, with Charles deciding on his career; but Ann told me that, months before, he had been pressing her to marry him. I did not doubt her for a second, but it puzzled me. The delay had been on her side. Yet she returned his passion. That night, in the middle of trouble, she spoke like an adoring woman who might be abandoned by her lover.

'I wish it were all over,' she said to me. 'I wish he and I were together by ourselves.'

Her face was strained. It occurred to me that hers was the kind of strength which would snap rather than give way. To divert her, I arranged to take her to a concert the following night.

When I spoke to Katherine, in order to find out whether Mr March had taken any more steps, I mentioned that Ann was only putting a face on things by act of will.

Katherine said impatiently: 'I often wish Charles had found someone a bit more ordinary.'

As Ann and I walked to our seats at the Queen's Hall next evening, I noticed how many men's eyes were drawn to her. When the first piece had started and I was composing myself, because the music meant nothing to me, for two hours of day-dreaming, I looked at her: she was wearing a new red evening frock, the skin of her throat was white, she closed her eyes as she had done in the sun at Haslingfield.

In the interval, we moved down the aisle on our way out. Suddenly, with a start of astonishment and alarm, I saw Mr March coming towards us. Ann saw him at the same instant. Neither of us had any doubt that he had followed her there to force this meeting. All we could do was walk on. As I waited for the moment of meeting, I was thinking 'how did he learn we were here?' The question nagged at me, meaninglessly important, fretting with anxiety, 'how did he learn we were here?'

Mr March stood in our way. He looked at Ann, and said good evening to us both. Then, addressing himself entirely to Ann, he said without any explanation: 'I'm glad to see you here tonight. I haven't had the pleasure of your company since you graced my establishment in the country. My children, for some reason best known to themselves, have deprived me of the opportunity of renewing our acquaintance.'

'I'm sorry that I couldn't come this week, Mr March. Katherine asked me,' said Ann.

'It was at my special request that my daughter asked you. I see no reason why my house should not claim an occasional evening of your time,' said Mr March. From the first word his manner reminded me of his reception of her at Haslingfield: except that now he made more demands. 'I recall that shortly after our first acquaintance we had an unfortunate difference of opinion upon the future of the world. I should consider the views you expressed even more pernicious if they prevented you from coming to my house again.'

Ann made a polite mutter.

'I am expecting you to come tonight,' said Mr March. 'I expect you to give me the pleasure of your company when these performers have finished. I don't think you can refuse to call in at my house for an hour or so.'

Ann's expression stayed open and steady: but her eyes looked childishly young, just as I had seen others' at a sudden shock.

'I shall have the pleasure of escorting you,' said Mr March. For the first time, he turned to me: 'Lewis, I rely on you to see that when the performers have exhausted themselves you both find your way towards my car.'

Ann sat by my side through the rest of the concert without any restless tic at all, as though keeping herself deliberately still.

The drive to Bryanston Square was quiet. I sat in front and only once or twice heard any words pass between the two behind. Even when he did speak, Mr March's voice was unusually low. It was still not his full voice that he used in giving orders to the butler, as soon as we entered the house.

'Tell my daughter to join us in my study. See that something to eat and drink is provided for my guests. Tell Taylor he is to wait with the car to take Miss Simon home.' He took Ann's arm, eagerly, perhaps roughly, and led her across the hall.

His study was the darkest room in the house, the wallpaper a deep brown, the bookshelves full of leather-bound collections that came down from his ancestors, together with the *Encyclopaedia Britannica*, the *Jewish Encyclopaedia*, and rows of works of reference. A bright fire was blazing, though the room still seemed cavernous. A tray of sandwiches and glasses was brought in after us, and Katherine followed. At the sight of her face, I knew the answer to the nagging question 'how did he know where to find us?' She must have let fall, after my conversation with her, that I was taking Ann to the concert. I felt an instant of irrelevant satisfaction, as one does when a name one has forgotten suddenly clicks back to mind.

'I am not aware what refreshment you consider appropriate for this time of night,' said Mr March to Ann, as he sat down in his armchair on the opposite side of the fireplace. 'I hope you will ask for anything that may not be provided.'

It was at that moment that I thought it best to leave. What happened I heard later from Ann, who as I said goodbye was absently letting him give her a brandy-and-soda.

When I had gone, the first remark he made was this: 'I want to ask you why my son is contemplating a completely unsuitable career.'

CHAPTER XIX

FATHER AND SON

ANN did not possess precisely my own kind of memory, but from her account and Katherine's I tried to reconstruct that night.

'I want to ask you,' said Mr March, 'why my son is contemplating a completely unsuitable career.'

The firelight glowed on Ann's face. She did not show any change of expression. Politely she answered:

'I really don't know why you're asking me that.'

'I'm asking you,' said Mr March, 'because there is no one else qualified to give an opinion.'

'There is only one person who can give an opinion, you know,' said Ann.

'Who may that be?'

'Why, Charles himself.' She told me that she answered once more in a deferential tone, but Mr March's voice was growing harsh. He said:

'I do not consider that my son is responsible for his actions in this respect.'

'I wish you'd believe that he's entirely responsible.'

'I acknowledge your remark.' That was said furiously. 'I repeat that he is not responsible for this preposterous nonsense. You regard me as being considerably blinder than I am. From the moment I heard of it, I knew that he was committing it at your instigation. You have forced him into it for reasons of your own.'

'I assure you that isn't true,' said Ann. Mr March burst out again, but she went on, still 'trying to be respectful':

'Charles has discussed his future with me, I won't pretend he hasn't. I won't pretend that I haven't told him what I think. As a matter of fact I do believe that becoming a doctor is absolutely right for him. But the idea was entirely his own. Neither I nor anyone else has any influence over him when it comes to deciding his actions. As far as I'm concerned I shouldn't choose to have it otherwise.'

Mr March, she thought, had become maddened at not being able to upset her. He said:

'You are much too modest. You are aware that you are an exceedingly attractive woman. I have no doubt that you have tested your power of twisting men round your little finger. I have no doubt that you are testing it on my son now. I can imagine that he is enough in your power to be willing to throw away all I had hoped for him.'

'I can't think you know him,' said Ann.

'I know,' said Mr March, looking at her with an intense and bitter stare, 'that many men would do the same. They would do any nonsense you might want them to.'

'I shouldn't have any use for a man who did what I told him,' she said.

'Then you have no use for my son?' shouted Mr March. She believed that he sounded triumphant.

'He would never do what I told him.'

'What is your attitude towards him?'

'I love him,' she said.

Mr March groaned.

Ann had spoken straight out, she reported. Hearing her tell the story, I believed that she had been provoked. She might not have realised it at the time, but she could feel him torn by a double jealousy.

She was taking away his son, destroying all his hopes: this was the loss which kept biting into him. But there was another. He was jealous of his son for winning Ann. He too had been attracted to her. That had been evident under the gallantry he showed her at Haslingfield. There was nothing strange about it. Mr March was still a vigorous man. He could imagine by instinct what his son felt for her, down to the deep level where passion and emotion are one. He could imagine it because, with the slightest turn of opportunity, he could have felt it so himself.

Mr March's groan might have been the sound of a physical shock.

'If that is true,' he said, after Ann told him that she loved his son, 'I find it even more astonishing that you express approval of his absurd intention. Even though you refuse to accept responsibility for it, from what you have just said, I am more certain than ever that the responsibility is yours, and yours alone.'

'I was glad when he decided to become a doctor, of course I was. He knew I should be glad. That is all,' she said.

'Glad? Glad? What justification have you for feeling glad except that you are responsible for it yourself? Are you incapable of realising that he is ruining any reasonable prospects he might have had? Even if he goes through with this absurd intention –'

'He will go through with it.' For the first time she interrupted him.

'What then? You think my son ought to be satisfied to be a mediocre practitioner?'

'He'll be happier about himself,' said Ann.

There was a silence. A lull came over them. Katherine might have said something. Ann even talked of the music she had heard. Then Mr March began to start on his accusations again. A few minutes later, they heard a noise in the hall. As they listened, the clock on the mantelpiece struck midnight. The door opened, and Charles came into the room.

'I was given no warning to expect you back,' said Mr March.

'I only decided to come a couple of hours ago,' said Charles.

He looked at Katherine, and Ann guessed that she had let him know, as soon as she realised what her gaffe had meant.

Charles drew up a chair by the side of Ann's.

Mr March's expression had become sombre. He said:

'I met your friend Ann Simon being escorted by Lewis Eliot to the

Queen's Hall. A remarkably undistinguished evening the performers entertained us with, by the way. So I invited her here for refreshments, before Taylor transports her home.'

'I see,' said Charles.

Soon Mr March said:

'I have taken the opportunity to give Ann Simon my views on your present intentions. I have also asked her for an explanation as to why you have conceived such a ridiculous project.'

'I should have preferred you to do that in front of me,' said Charles.

'I refuse to listen to criticisms from my son upon my behaviour in my own house,' said Mr March.

'I shall make them,' said Charles, 'if you insist on intruding on my privacy. Don't you see that this is an intolerable intrusion, don't you see that?'

'Your privacy? Do you expect me to accept that your ruining your life is simply a private concern of your own?'

'Yes,' said Charles.

'I refuse to tolerate it in any circumstances,' Mr March said. 'Particularly when you're not acting as a free agent, and are simply letting this young woman gratify some of her misguided tastes.'

'You must leave her out of it.'

'I've told Mr March,' said Ann, 'that I'm very glad about your decision. But I've told him that I had nothing to do with your making it, and couldn't have had.'

'I shall leave her out of this matter when I have any reason to believe that she's not the source and origin of it all. If she enjoys wearing the trousers, she's got to be prepared to answer for the results.'

Up to that instant, Charles's manner had been stern without relief, Ann told me. Then he smiled as though, after Mr March's last remark, nothing could be so absurd again. The argument went on.

With their usual repetitiveness they went over the practical reasons time and time again: underneath one could have heard the assertion of Mr March's power, the claims of his affection, the anguish of his jealousies the passion of his hopes, and in Charles, his claustrophobic desire to be free, his longing for release in love with Ann, his search for the good, his untameable impulse to find his own way, whatever it cost to others and himself. Often Charles was on the point of an outburst, such as he had struggled against. He did not let it come to light; he had mastered himself enough for that.

It was getting on for two o'clock when Mr March made a last appeal.

'I have not alluded to the opinion of the family,' he said.

'You know they could not even begin to count,' said Charles.

'I must remind you that they will occupy a place in my regard as long as I live,' said Mr March. 'But I was aware you allowed yourself to entertain no feeling for them. You did not leave me any illusions on the point when you made known your intention not to continue for the time being at the Bar.

'You even had the civility to say,' Mr March went on, 'that you would pay considerably more attention to my wishes than to theirs. You expressed yourself as having some concern about me.'

'I meant it,' said Charles.

'You did not pretend that your actions had no effect on my happiness.'

'No.'

'I should like to inform you that, if you carry out your present intention, it will have a considerable effect on my happiness.'

'I wish it were not so,' said Charles. 'But I can't alter my mind.'

'You realise what it means for me?'

'I'm afraid I do,' said Charles.

Until that moment they might have been repeating their quarrel on the first Friday night I attended, the quarrel to which Mr March had just referred. All of a sudden it took a different turn. Immediately he heard Charles's answer, Mr March got up from his chair. He said:

'Then I must use my own means.'

He said goodbye to Ann, 'being extremely gallant again', all of them standing in the hall. He asked Katherine to see her into the car, and retired to his study with Charles. The door closed behind them.

Katherine waited in the cold, empty drawing-room. Once or twice she heard through the walls a voice raised in anger.

An hour passed before Charles entered. He asked her for a cigarette, and had almost smoked it through before he spoke again. Then he said, in a level, neutral tone: 'He's revoked his promise to make me independent.'

He went on:

'We've always known, haven't we, he was going to make over some money to me when I was twenty-five. He's just admitted that it has always been his intention.'

Mr March had repeated, Charles told her, that up to that night he had been arranging to transfer a substantial sum to Charles on his twenty-fifth birthday – something like £40,000. He had now altered his mind. He was prepared to continue paying Charles his allowance. But he was determined to make no irrevocable gift.

'I said that I might want to get married soon,' said Charles. 'He replied that he could not let that influence his judgment. He was not going to make me independent while I insisted on going in for misguided fooleries.'

'I can understand,' he said, 'that he wants me to lead the life he's imagined for me. I know I must be a desperate disappointment. You know, don't you, that for a long time I've tried to soften it as much as I possibly could? You do know that? But I tell you, I shan't find this easy to accept.'

Katherine said that she felt a sense of danger which she couldn't explain, even in retrospect. She couldn't even say which of them she was frightened for.

Charles asked her:

'Do you think he wants to stop me marrying?'

She hesitated.

'Do you think he wants to stop me marrying Ann?'

'He wouldn't have chosen her for you,' she said, after a pause. What she felt, she thought best left unspoken.

'What shall you do?' she said.

Suddenly he gave a smile.

'What do you think I shall do? Do you think I could stop now?'

PART THREE

THE MARRIAGES

CHAPTER XX

THE COMING-OUT DANCE

MR March did not have another talk in private with Charles that winter. In company they took on their old manner to each other, and no one outside guessed what had happened. Charles had begun to work for his first M.B., but the news was not allowed to leak out, any more than that of his assignations with Ann.

Meanwhile, tongues all over the March family had kept busy about Katherine and Francis Getliffe. Charles received a hint from Caroline's son, Robert; Katherine from someone at her club; Herbert Getliffe became inquisitive about his brother. For a long time, despite false alarms, the gossip seemed not to have been taken seriously by Mr March's brothers and sisters; certainly none of them had given him an official family warning.

When the invitations were issued for the coming-out dance of one of the Herbert March girls, we wondered again how far the gossip had spread. For that family scarcely knew Francis Getliffe; and yet he had been invited. Katherine threshed out with Charles what this could mean. Was it an innuendo? It looked like it. But invitations had gone out all over the place; the Holfords had been sent one, even Herbert Getliffe through the Hart connection, I myself. Francis's might have been sent in perfect innocence and good nature.

Katherine still remained suspicious. For days before the dance she and Charles re-examined each clue with their native subtlety, repetitiveness, realism and psychological gusto. One thing alone was certain, said Charles, grinning at his own expense: that for once his passion for secrecy had been successful, with the result that Ronald Porson had been invited, obviously as the appropriate partner for Ann.

This piece of consideration did not seem funny to Ann herself. Her pride rose at being labelled with the wrong man. It was her own fault.

Porson was still pressing her, begging her to marry him; she had not yet brought herself to send him away. Nevertheless, when the Herbert Marches picked him out as her partner, she was angry with them for making her face her own bad behaviour.

On the night itself, Herbert March's larger drawing-room had been converted into a ballroom. We stood round the floor waiting for the band to begin. The shoulders of young women gleamed, the jewels of old ones sparkled, under the bright lights: loud March voices were carried over the floor: the Holfords, the Harts, the Getliffes, formed a group round their host, while his sister Caroline, standing elephantine in their midst, pulled up her lorgnon and through it surveyed the room.

It was a room on the same scale as those at Bryanston Square, but brighter and more fashionable. The whole house was a little less massive, the decoration a little more modern, than Mr March's, and the company less exclusively family than anywhere else in the March circle. One remembered Mr March's stories about Herbert as the rebel of an older generation.

Standing in front of a pot of geraniums, Mr March himself was telling Sir Philip an anecdote with obscure glee. It was the obscure glee that usually possessed him when someone committed a *faux pas* against the Jewish faith. 'The new parson from the church round the corner paid me a visit the other day,' said Mr March. 'I thought it was uncommonly civil of him, but I was slightly surprised to have to entertain anyone of his persuasion. The last parson I was obliged to talk to descended from the ship at Honolulu when I was going round the world in '88. He was an extremely boring fellow. Well, as soon as I decently could, I asked this one why he had given me the pleasure of his company. And he had an unfortunate stammer, but gradually it emerged that he wanted a contribution for his Easter offering. So I said, I should like to be informed if you still pray on certain occasions for Jews, Turks and other infidels. He had to admit that he did. I replied that being a Jew I might be excused for finding the phrase a little invidious, and I couldn't make a donation for his present purposes. But I didn't want to embarrass him because he'd chosen an unfortunate occasion. So I said: "Come again at Christmas. We've got some common ground, you know. I'll give you something then."'

Just then Caroline's son Robert brought Ann to be introduced to Sir Philip. As usual, she was one of the smartest women in the room; as usual, she stayed quiet, let Sir Philip and Robert talk, got over her shyness just enough to put in a question. Mr March broke in:

'This is the first time I have seen you since you were good enough to come to my house after a concert, which you possibly remember.'

'Yes, Mr March,' said Ann.

'She is rather competed for, Uncle Leonard,' said Robert. He was a middle-aged man, bald, with a face more predatory than any other in the family – predatory but not clever. As soon as he spoke, Mr March resented his flirtatious air; and Mr March's own manner became more formidable and at the same time more intimate.

'I am well aware that it would be astonishing if she had time to spare for elderly acquaintances,' he said brusquely and, ignoring Robert, turned to Ann. 'I take it that my son Charles has been lucky enough to secure a certain fraction of your leisure.'

'I've seen him quite often,' she said.

'I assumed that must be so.'

Then the music started up. Robert took her on to the floor. I went to find a partner. As the first hour passed and I danced with various March cousins and visitors, I noticed that Charles and Ann had danced together only once. Whoever they had as partners, they were each followed by a good many sharp, attentive eyes. She was striking-looking in any company. And to some there, particularly among the women, he was the most interesting of the younger Marches.

Katherine and Francis, on the other hand, had decided that it was no use pretending to avoid each other. It seemed the sensible thing to take the polite average of dances together. As they did so, one could not fail to realise that some of the March aunts were watching them. Several times I saw Caroline's lorgnon flash, and even to me she shoved in an enquiry, when we happened to visit the refreshment table at the same time.

'How well do you know this young fellow Francis Getliffe?' she said.

I tried to pass it off, for she was too deaf to talk to quietly, and there were several people round us.

'I want to know,' said Caroline, 'whether he's engaged yet?'

'I don't think so,' I said.

'Why isn't he? He must be getting on for thirty. What has he been doing with himself?'

I smiled: it was easier than producing a noncommittal shout.

She went on with the interrogation. She had hoped that Francis might be entangled elsewhere. That hope extinguished, she was framing her plan of campaign.

When I returned to the drawing-room, Ann was dancing with Albert

Hart, and Charles with the cousin for whom the dance was being held, a good-looking, strapping girl. For the first time that night, I found Katherine free. She whispered at once, as we went on to the floor:

'It's slightly embarrassing being under inspection, isn't it? You would have expected Francis to mind tremendously, wouldn't you have expected him to? But he seems to be enjoying himself.'

She was so happy, despite her anxiety, despite the prying eyes, that it was obvious how well – when she and Francis were together – the night was going. She went on:

'You know, I wish Charles and Ann would decide what they want to happen. They've got to settle down some time, and it won't get any easier. It's preposterous that she should have this man Porson trailing after her tonight.'

She looked up at me. 'I think she enjoys it – am I being unfair? I expect I envy her, of course. Mind you, I know she's made a colossal difference to Charles.'

Then she glanced across the room, where Francis was talking to Mr March.

'But it is a superb party, don't you think?' she burst out. 'Francis dances abominably, but I forgive him even that. It means that I'm nothing like so jealous when I see him dancing with other women. I can always console myself with how disappointed they must be when they get a fairly nice-looking young man for a partner – at least I think he's fairly nice-looking – and he promptly insists on putting his foot on their toes.'

She was bubbling with happiness.

'It is a superb party, Lewis,' she said. She was silent for a moment, and I saw that she was smiling.

'What are you thinking?' I said.

She chuckled outright.

'I've remembered what I used to feel about the young men Charles brought to the house. I never believed that they could possibly want to see me. I thought they only came because they wanted to see Charles or needed a house to stay in when they were in London.'

I was sorry when the dance ended; at that time, as I watched others happy in love, I was sometimes envious – but not of Katherine. It was difficult to begrudge her any luck that came her way.

The next dance I watched by the side of Mr March and Sir Philip. Mr March was studying his dance programme before the band began.

'Though why they find it necessary to issue programmes to the super-annuated members of the party, I have never been able to understand,' he said to me. 'Possibly so that the superannuated can imbibe the names of these productions that your generation are accustomed to regard as tunes.'

The ban struck up, couples went on to the floor; Charles was dancing with Ann, Katherine with Francis. Mr March stopped talking; he let his programme swing by the pencil; he watched them. Katherine was smiling into Francis's face; Charles and Ann were dancing without speaking.

Philip also was watching.

'How many times,' he asked Mr March, 'has Katherine been to the regular dance this year?'

'She has missed occasionally.'

'How many times has she been?'

'I can't be expected to recollect particulars of her attendance,' said Mr March.

Philip went on asking; Mr March fidgeted with his programme and gave irascible replies. If he had been suppressing his knowledge about Katherine and Francis, he could do so no longer.

Philip's glance followed Katherine round the room. But even as he answered the questions, Mr March did not look in her direction. His expression was fixed and anxious: he had eyes for no one but his son.

'I should like you to meet Ronald Porson,' Ann said, as shortly afterwards I delivered a girl to her partner in the corner of the room. Ann, sitting with Porson close by, smiled at both him and me, making herself act as though this was a casual night out.

'I've heard about you,' said Porson. 'Don't you go about picking up the pieces after Getliffe? I suppose I oughtn't to speak to you about your boss—'

'Yes, I've been with him since I came to London,' I said.

'You have my blessing,' said Porson. 'And by God you'll need it.'

His voice was loud, his manner hearty and assertive, though tonight he was preoccupied. He kept looking at Ann, but his eyes flickered nervously away, if he caught hers. His appearance surprised me after what I had heard; he was a short, plethoric man with a ruddy face. His left cheek often broke into a twitch which, instead of putting one off, happened to make his expression companionable and humorous.

The room had cleared for an interval, and Charles was almost alone on the floor. Several times Ann's attention strayed to him, and then she said to Porson:

'Have you ever met Charles March, by any chance? He's the nephew of your host tonight. You've heard me talk about him. Perhaps you ought to be introduced.'

'I might as well,' said Porson.

He did not glance at Charles; I was sure that he had already identified him. Ann beckoned to Charles: Porson went on talking to me as he came up. It was not until they shook hands that Porson raised his eyes and looked into Charles's face.

'Are you enjoying this do tonight?' he said. 'Are you enjoying yourself?'

For a moment Charles did not answer. Before he spoke, Ann had turned to him. 'Ronald is thinking of starting a practice in London,' she said. 'I've been trying to persuade him that before he makes up his mind he really must get some up-to-date advice. He happens to know Getliffe, I mean Herbert Getliffe, quite well. He doesn't think much of him, but I don't see that ought to matter: he might be useful.'

'Getliffe's not gone far enough,' said Ronald. 'I dislike crawling unless it's worth while.'

'It can't do any harm.' Ann looked at Charles.

'It can't do any harm,' said Charles. 'Isn't that the point? I know it's an intolerable nuisance, going to people for this kind of purpose—'

'I dislike crawling in any case,' said Ronald. 'Particularly to men I don't care for and whose ability I despise.'

'He's climbing pretty fast, isn't he?' Ann was asking me.

'There are private reasons, which you know enough to guess,' Ronald said to her, 'which make it certain that, before I asked Getliffe for a favour, I'd sooner sweep the streets.'

I said:

'There are plenty of other people you could talk to, aren't there?'

'Albert Hart would give you a pretty sensible judgment,' said Charles. 'If ever you'd like me to introduce you—'

'I'm not prepared to go on my knees except for a very good reason.'

'I should feel exactly the same,' said Charles. 'But still, that never prevents one, does it, from pointing out that someone else is doing too much for honour.'

Ronald laughed. After his first remark, he seemed surprised that he was actually liking Charles's company.

'Ah well, my boy,' said Ronald, 'I might stretch a point some day. But I insist on tapping my own sources first—' Then he turned to Ann:

'I'm going to take you home soon, aren't I?'

'Yes,' said Ann.

'Are you ready to come now?'

'I think I'd like to wait half an hour,' said Ann.

'You'll be ready then? You'll remember, won't you?'

'Yes,' said Ann.

His masterfulness had dropped right away; suddenly he asserted himself by saying to me in a loud voice:

'Well, my lad, I'm going to take you away and give you some advice.'

We went to the study, where whisky bottles and glasses were laid out. Ronald said:

'Now you must develop a master plan too. Of course, you can't expect it to be on such a scale as mine, but I'm damned if we can't work out something for you. We must use some of my connections.'

He was at home, now he was giving help instead of taking it. His smile became domineering and good-natured; he could even put aside his obsession with Ann while he was giving me advice. Yet, though his connections were genuine enough, the advice was vague; his voice was throaty with worldly wisdom, but he was really an unworldly man. He was far more lost than Ann believed, I thought.

In time he left off advising me, took another drink, put an arm round my shoulders as we stood by the mantelpiece, told me a dirty story and confided his ambitions. 'It's incredible that they shouldn't recognise me soon,' he said in his masterful tone. Those ambitions, like the advice, turned out to be quite vague; he was getting on for forty, but he did not know what he wanted to do. When I enquired about details his manner was still overbearing, but he seemed to be longing for something as humble as a respectable status and a bare living at the Bar.

Soon he said, with a return of anxiety:

'We'd better be making our way back, old boy. Ann wants me to take her home tonight.'

When we returned to the dance-room, Ann and Charles were standing together. Ronald said to her:

'Do you feel you can tear yourself away yet?'

'I'd just like the next dance with Lewis,' said Ann.

Ronald gave an impersonation of nonchalance, heavy and painful.

'In that case I can use another drink,' he said.

He went away before the band began to play.

Neither Charles nor Ann spoke. When she looked at him, he gave her a smile which was intimate but not happy. Then Charles's gaze was diverted to the other end of the room, where his aunt Caroline had just buttonholed Mr March. He watched them walk up and down, Caroline protruding her great bosom like a shelf as she inclined her less deaf ear to catch Mr

March's replies. Charles had no doubt that she was catechising him about Katherine.

'I was afraid that they wouldn't leave him in peace,' he said.

As Ann and I were dancing, I asked her what Mr March would be forced to do. But she was scarcely attending: her mind was elsewhere: all she said was: 'Charles has too much trouble with his family, hasn't he?'

We danced round, the conversation ground to a stop. Then, to my surprise, she settled more softly in my arms, and said:

'I shan't be sorry when tonight is over.'

'What's the matter?'

She looked straight up at me, but slipped away from the question.

'I always used to dread meeting people till I got in the middle of them, didn't you?'

'Not much,' I said.

'Don't you really mind?'

'I'm nervous of lots of things you're not,' I said. 'But not of that.'

'Do you know,' said Ann, 'I used to make excuses to stay by myself. Not so long ago, either. As a matter of fact, last summer, I very nearly didn't go to Haslingfield.'

As we danced on, she said in a low voice:

'Yes. I very nearly didn't go. That would have altered things.'

I asked again:

'What's the matter?'

After a pause, she replied:

'You've seen Ronald now, haven't you?'

Then I guessed that all night she had been screwing herself up to make the final break. This was the night when she had to tell him that he had no hope.

I said that she should never have come with him at all.

'Perhaps,' said Ann. 'I'd better get it over.'

Then she softened again, and as she spoke of Charles she pressed my hand. 'I shall have to go off with Ronald now. I shan't be able to talk to Charles. Will you tell him that everything is well? You'll remember, won't you? I don't want him to go home alone without being told that.'

Ronald came to Ann as soon as we left the floor. She went to say good-bye to Herbert March's wife: Ronald and I walked into the hall, where we met Getliffe on the point of leaving. Before he saw us, he was trying to smooth down the nap of his old opera hat. He said to me: 'As soon as my wife comes, I depart from the shores of Canaan. But I must say they've done us pretty well.' Then he noticed Ronald. 'Why, I didn't realise it was you. It must be years since we met. Though I've always wanted to keep in touch with you. Everything satisfactory with the job?'

'It's been a complete success,' said Ronald. 'I've never regretted going out east for a minute.'

'I'm very glad to hear that,' said Getliffe earnestly. 'Look here, if you're not ashamed of your old friends, we ought to get together some time. Why, I've scarcely had a glass of water with you since we used to tune up the old Feathers – I don't believe you've forgotten the place.'

They fixed nothing, but Getliffe shook hands with both of us, though he was bound to see me the next morning, and said:

'The best of everything. Pleasant dreams.'

The Getliffes departed while Ronald and Ann were finishing their goodbyes. Charles and I waited with them in the hall while someone moved a car. At last they went out into the road, and Ann said to Charles: 'I shall see you soon.' Charles watched her climb into Ronald's car and draw her coat round her shoulders; she was talking to him as they drove away.

We went back to the dance for half an hour, and it was strange, after breathing the heavy air that descends sometimes on to any passion, to be making conversation to young girls – young girls pleased to find a partner, or else proud that they had not missed a dance all night.

One or two, as they noticed their cousin Charles dancing with Ann, must have wondered if they were in love: but they would have been surprised if they had known the pain and decision that had been going on under their noses in this house.

The dance was almost over when Charles and I began to walk the few hundred yards to Bryanston Square. It had been a wet day; the pavements were glistening, though now the rain had stopped. After the ballroom the air was cool on our cheeks.

Charles said that he was worried about Mr March and Katherine. He questioned me on what Caroline had said. But I saw that he was distracted, and he soon fell quiet.

When I gave him Ann's message, his face lit up.

'Life's very unfair.' He smiled. In a single instant he had become brilliantly cheerful. 'If I'd been capable of more civilised behaviour, she'd never have needed to think of me.'

'You made Porson feel flattered,' I said. 'I thought that was rather gallant.'

'No,' said Charles. 'I was behaving with the sort of excellence when I could almost see myself shine. And it's easy to take in everybody except oneself and the person to whom it matters most.'

Suddenly he said:

'It's ridiculous, you know, but I'm jealous of him. Though she's never loved him in the slightest. Still, I was jealous when I met him. Ann knew that from every word I said. That's why she sent me that message. She wanted to save me from a dismal night.'

He took my arm, and broke out with a warm, unexpected affection.

'I wish you'd been saved more, Lewis. You know so much more about that kind of suffering than I hope I ever shall.'

We had reached Bryanston Square. Mr March was long since home, and the house stood in darkness. Charles and I stayed under the lamp, just opposite the railings.

'It's curious,' said Charles, 'how the unexpected things catch one off one's guard. I went there tonight, knowing that I had to get him to talk and make him as comfortable as I could and so on. But there was one thing I hadn't reckoned with; it was the sight of them together in his car, just ready to drive away. For a second I felt that I had utterly lost her.'

CHAPTER XXI

WHISPERS IN THE EARLY MORNING

THE day after the coming-out dance, Katherine had to face a scene with her father.

'Your Aunt Caroline wants you to spend a month in her house,' Mr March said the moment she arrived at breakfast. 'There is a consensus of opinion that you don't meet enough people.'

'Shall I go?' said Katherine, so equably that Mr March became more angry.

'I naturally didn't consider your refusing.'

'Of course I'll go,' said Katherine.

Until she went to stay with Caroline, Mr March behaved as though Katherine's presence was irritating. Several of his relations had followed the lead of Caroline and Philip and advised him to 'keep an eye on Charles's friend Francis Getliffe'. The sight of Francis and Katherine together had impressed most of Mr March's brothers and sisters. With their own particular brand of worldliness, they decided that Leonard could not be too careful, the young fellow might think he had a chance of her money.

Katherine duly spent her month at Caroline's, and there, each night at dinner, was produced a selection of the eligible young men in the March world. It was all magnificent in its opulence and heavy-footedness. At the end of her stay Katherine returned with a collection of anecdotes to Bryanston Square. The anecdotes she had to keep for Charles. It struck everyone that Mr March did not enquire what had happened, and irascibly brushed aside any mention that Katherine made.

In July, on the customary date, Mr March moved his household to Haslingfield. I was invited there in August, and found, on the evening I arrived, that Katherine was still trying to imagine Charles's life as a doctor.

'I know you'll go through with it now,' she said. 'But I just can't see what it will be like, you know. It's too far-fetched for me.'

'You just want to purr away in comfort,' said Charles.

'You ought to be able to be happy, and get your dash of comfort into the bargain,' she said.

'I call that animal content,' said Charles.

'I only wish you could have it,' she said.

Beneath the backchat their voices showed their fondness and concern. Between them there flowed a current of intimacy – it was not only his future they were talking of. Katherine was at once apprehensive and happy, so happy that she had become maternally concerned for Charles. Two years earlier, she would have hero-worshipped him.

They told me nothing that evening. Mr March appeared to be in something like his old spirits; his manner to his son was not constrained, and he talked about a holiday abroad which Charles had spoken of, and then shelved, as 'my son's misguided expedition to gather energy for purposes which he was never able to justify. Like the time my Uncle Natty gave them all a fright by trying to go on the stage. But it was always rumoured that he had his eye on an actress. So he went to London University and they made him a knight.'

'It sounds rather easy, Mr L.,' said Charles.

'No! No!' said Mr March. 'He went to London University and became a professor and a member of their financial board. I always thought he was a superficial fellow. He went slightly off his head, of course, and they gave him his knighthood just before he died.'

Lying half-awake the next morning, after the footman had drawn the curtains, I heard the whisper of conversation in Charles's room next door. I could distinguish Charles's voice and Katherine's, hers raised and animated, and I caught one whole reply from Charles: 'I can easily ring him up at Cambridge.' When Katherine came down to breakfast I said:

'What conspiracy are you busy with now?'

She blushed. 'What do you mean?'

'Consultations before breakfast—'

'Lewis, you didn't hear? You can't possibly have heard, can you?'

Then Charles entered, and she said:

'Lewis pretends he overheard us this morning. He's probably bluffing, but I'm not quite sure.' She turned to me, smiling and excited: 'If you really do know, it's absolutely essential you shouldn't breathe a word.'

Charles said to Katherine:

'You're rather hoping he does know, aren't you? I mean, you wouldn't be entirely displeased to give yourself away.'

'You suggested telling him.' They were smiling at each other. Katherine burst out: 'Look here, I insist on being put out of my misery. Did you hear or didn't you?'

'No,' I said. 'I can see you're very cheerful, and it's about Francis. I couldn't very well help seeing that, could I? But I don't know exactly what's happening.'

'Is this a double bluff?' she said.

'You'd better tell him,' said Charles.

'Well,' said Katherine, 'it's important for me. You'll be discreet, won't you?'

I said yes.

'As a matter of fact,' she said, 'about a fortnight ago Francis asked me to marry him.'

I said how glad I was. Her delight seemed to become even greater as she shared the news. She had been forced to restrain herself for a good many days, except to Charles. 'When it came to the point,' said Katherine, smiling lazily, 'Francis was different from what any of you would expect.

'Now did you know?' she harped back.

'No.'

'But you see why I'm anxious that Charles shouldn't do anything more to upset Mr L. – till my marriage is settled. If Charles begins to talk about his career or his independence again, it will only make things more difficult. Of course, I shall be the chief affliction. If I'm to have the slightest hope of getting away with it, Mr L. mustn't feel there's anything else wrong with his family.'

Charles caught my glance.

'Don't you see, Lewis,' she said, 'I still have the worst time in front of me? Somehow I must break the news to Mr L.'

'How much does he know?'

She shook her head.

'It will be the biggest disaster he's ever had,' she said.

I said:

'Are you sure of that?'

Katherine said to Charles:

'Don't you agree? Don't you agree that I'm right?'

Charles did not answer.

Katherine said:

'I'm positive that I'm right. Lewis, you simply can't understand what this will mean to him.'

She spoke to Charles: 'You know, I feel gross asking you to think of the slightest point that might affect my chances. But, as things have turned out, I can't do anything else. I must have a clear field, mustn't I?'

'I've been telling you so for days,' Charles teased her.

'You see, Lewis,' said Katherine, 'I shall marry Francis whatever happens. I knew I should never have a minute's doubt – if ever he asked me. I'm not a self-sacrificing person, and however much it upsets Mr L. it's more important for me than for him. I'm worried about him, but I shan't feel that I've done wrong.'

'Yes,' I said.

'If the worst comes to the worst,' she said, 'we can live on what Francis earns. It won't exactly support me in the condition I've been accustomed to. But still—'

'Francis is pretty proud,' said Charles. 'He's not as sensible as he tries to appear. He'd like to have you without a penny.'

'He's always taken the gloomiest view and expected to keep me,' said Katherine. 'At any rate, that's settled. We shall be married by December. But it's obvious that I want to placate Mr L. as much as I humanly can. I'm prepared to be thrown out if there's no other way, but it would be an enormous horror for us both. I expect I should feel it even more than I think now.'

'Yes, you would,' said Charles.

'You know it, don't you?' She looked at him.

Then Katherine said:

'Whatever happens, Mr L. must be told soon.'

657

CHAPTER XXII

INVITATION

As soon as I got back to London after that weekend, Ann asked me to dine with her. Once more she took me out in luxury, this time to the Ritz. I took it for granted, going out with her, that the waiters would know her by name: I was not surprised when other diners bowed to her. As usual, she set herself out to buy me expensive food and wine.

Looking at her across the table, I had no idea what she wanted to talk to me about that night. Not Katherine's marriage, I was sure. Not Charles, at least directly, it soon seemed. No, the first person she began to mention was Ronald Porson. She wanted to tell me that he had given up trying to see her: that even he accepted that it was over and done with. As she told me, Ann was referring back to the coming-out dance three months before, when I blamed her for letting Ronald's attendance drag on: she wanted me to admit that she had been firm. Laughing at her, I saw the shyness wiped away from her face as though it had been make-up; and yet my piece of criticism rankled, she might have just been listening to it.

At the same time she was giving me something like a warning about Porson. She said that now he bore a grudge against the Marches, and that he was a man who could not stop his grudges breaking out; she talked about him with a kind of remorseful understanding, because she could not love him back.

She knew him well, she was fond of him, she was afraid of what he might do. Although he had got nowhere himself, she told me, he had some influence; his father had been an ambassador, he had his successful acquaintances.

'What can he do?' I said with scepticism.

'Would you like him as an enemy?' she replied.

But it was not really Porson she had got me there to talk about. Politics: the depression was deepening all over Europe: had I been following the German election? She was in earnest. All she said was business-like. She had a clear sight of what was coming. She was better informed than I was. It was not quite like the politics I used to talk with my friends in the provincial town; we had been born poor, we spoke with the edge of those who rubbed their noses against the shop windows and watched others comfortable within; she had known none of that. She was more generous than we were, but she hoped as much.

As we talked – we were not so much arguing as agreeing – I felt a curious excitement in the air. Her voice at the same time quickened and sank to something like a whisper; her blue eyes had gone wide open, were staring at me, or past me, with the kind of stare that one sees in someone who is obsessed by the thought of making love. In fact, it might have been the beginning of a love-affair.

Yet she was totally in love with Charles: I was just as single-minded in my love for Sheila: that was why Ann and I could keep up a friendship without trouble to either of us.

The excitement tightened, and I was completely at a loss.

She whispered:

'Look, Lewis. Isn't it time you came in with us?'

'What do you mean?'

'Isn't it time you came into the party?'

When at last I heard the question, I thought I had been a fool. Nevertheless, up to that evening she had been discreet, even with me; she had talked like someone on the left, but so did many of our friends, none of whom was a communist in theory, let alone a member of what she called 'the party'.

I looked at her. The strain had ended. She was brave, headstrong, and full of faith.

I owed her an honest answer. Trying to give it to her, I felt at a disadvantage just because she was brave and full of faith. I felt at a disadvantage, too, because I happened not to be well that summer. Giving her reasons why I could not come in I did not make either a good or an honest job of it. Yet I did manage to make the one point that mattered most to me. She wasn't as interested as I was, I told her, in the nature of power and those who held the power. The more I thought of it, the less I liked it. Any régime of her kind just had to give its bosses great power without any check. Granted that they were aiming at good things, it was still too dangerous. People with power began to get detached from anything but power itself. No one could be trusted with power for long.

For a time she argued back with the standard replies, which we both knew by heart, then she gave up.

'You're too cynical,' she said.

'I'm not in the least cynical.'

'You're too pessimistic.'

'I don't think so, in the long run.' But I wished that my hopes were as certain as hers.

She was disappointed with me, and put out, but she wasted no more time. This was what she had come for, and she had failed. She had a business-like gift of cutting her losses. She decided that, in my own fashion, I was as obstinate as she was.

She asked me to order more brandy: even after a disappointment, she liked giving me a good time. In a voice still lowered, but not excited by now, only brisk, she said:

'You'll keep this absolutely quiet, of course, won't you?'

She meant, about herself and the party. She spoke with trust. In the same tone I said:

'Of course.'

I went on:

'It's the sort of secret I'm not bad at keeping.'

She looked at me, her face open and gentle, and said:

'Nor am I.'

We both laughed. After the argument, we were glad to feel comradely again. She asked me (I thought it was a relief to her to be straightforward) whether I had suspected she was a member.

'No,' I said, and then suddenly a thought crossed my mind.

'You're pretty good at keeping your mouth shut, aren't you?' I said. 'But that first night at Haslingfield – why did you give everyone such a hint?'

Her reply did not come at once. At last she said:

'I think I knew already that Charles was going to be important to me.'

'And so—'

'And so I couldn't let them take me in on entirely false pretences, could I?'

I was pleased to think that, at the time, I had been somewhere near the truth. There was a streak of the gambler in her. She did not like being careful; even though she had to be, it seemed to her, more than to most of us, cowardly, impure, dishonourable. It was really part of her to tell the truth. That night at Haslingfield, a cardinal night for her, she had believed she could tell the truth and get away with it.

But there was no one outside the party, apart from Charles and me, who knew that she was in it – so she told me as we finished our last drinks at the Ritz. She had made clear to Charles exactly what she did, before their affair began. That I should have expected from her: what interested me was that she had made no attempt to invite him in. She had not tried to persuade him, even to the extent she had tried with me. It seemed that she did not want to influence him. She had taken care that he knew the exact truth about her. That done, she longed just to make him happy.

CHAPTER XXIII

KATHERINE TELLS MR MARCH

KATHERINE put off breaking the news to her father. It was the last week in October before she told him. The family were together at Bryanston Square, and Mr March, having written his usual hundred letters for the Jewish New Year, had been grumbling because others' greetings were so late. Katherine waited until the festival had passed by.

I had tea at Bryanston Square the day she finally brought herself to speak. We were alone. Francis had not long left for Cambridge, after staying the weekend in the house. She told me that she meant to face Mr March that night.

'I'm extremely embarrassed,' she said. 'No, I'm more than embarrassed, I'm definitely frightened. It's absurd to feel oneself being as frightened as this.'

She added: 'I can't shake off an absurd fear that when I do try to tell him, I shall find myself go absolutely dumb. I've been rehearsing some kind of an opening all day. To tell you the honest truth, I've been rehearsing it ever since Francis proposed. I never thought I should put it off as long.'

The next evening she and Charles came round to my rooms. She said at once: 'I've got it over. I think it's all right. But—'

'It's all right so far,' said Charles.

Mr March had been at moments extravagantly himself, and Katherine could laugh at some of his remarks: yet she was still shaken.

Immediately after dinner she had said to Mr March, falling back on the sentence she had rehearsed:

'I'm sorry, Mr L., but I've something to tell you that I'm afraid will make you rather unhappy.'

Mr March replied:

'I hope it isn't what I suppose it must be.'

They went into his study, and Katherine heard her own information sound blunt and cut-and-dried. It took only a minute or two, and then she said:

'Naturally, I'm tremendously happy about it myself. I'm not going to try and hide that from you, Mr L. I'm only sorry that it's going to make you slightly miserable.'

Mr March said:

'Of course, I wish you'd never been born.'

Katherine felt that he was saying simply and sincerely what he meant. She felt it again, when he said:

'My children have brought me nothing but disgrace.'

'I know I've given you a lot of trouble,' said Katherine.

'Nothing you've done matters by the side of what you are informing me of now.'

'I was afraid of that.'

'Afraid? Afraid? You knew that you were proposing something that I should never get over. You never gave a moment's thought to the fact that you'd make me a reproach for the rest of my life.'

'I've thought of nothing else for weeks, Mr L.,' she said.

'And you are determined to persevere?' he shouted.

'I can't do anything else.'

Mr March spoke in a calmer tone:

'I suppose I can't stop it. He can presumably maintain you in some sort of squalor. Not that I have any objection to his profession. It's all very well for men who are prepared to sacrifice all their material requirements. Though I can't understand how they venture to support their wives. How much does this fellow earn?'

'About eight hundred a year.'

'Twopence a week,' said Mr March. 'It's enough for you to contemplate existing on, unfortunately.' (It was at the time, though years later we had to do sums to calculate what money had been worth, a standard academic income.) 'I suppose I can't stop it. It was exactly the same when your Aunt Hetty insisted on marrying the painter. He took to drink before they'd been married three years.'

He broke off:

'I'm obliged to say, though I couldn't disapprove more strongly, that I've no particular objection to this fellow on personal grounds. He seems quiet, and he's surprisingly level-headed, apart from whatever proficiency he may have at his scientific pursuits. I realise that he exercises himself on mountains, but he doesn't look particularly strong.'

'He's as tough as I am,' said Katherine.

'The doctors said you were delicate when you were young,' said Mr March. 'They said the same about me in '79. If they had been right in either case, I might have been spared this intolerable state of affairs you're bringing on me. I say, I haven't any strong personal objection to the fellow. I could put up with his poverty, since he's pursuing a career which isn't discreditable. I should be willing to give you my approval apart from the fact that makes it impossible, as you must have known all along. It would be different if he were a member of our religion.'

'I realise that,' she said.

'What's the use of realising it?' said Mr March. 'When you come and tell me that you are determined to marry him. What's the use of realising it? When you're determined to do the thing that I shall never get over.'

Then he said:

'I know it's not so easy for a woman to refuse. If he'd satisfied the essential condition, I shouldn't have blamed you for accepting him on the spot. After all, you mightn't get a second chance.'

It was strange, Katherine felt as though she were noticing it for the first time, to see his distress suddenly streaked with domestic realism. Rather excessively so in this case, she grumbled to Charles and me, since she was not quite twenty-one, 'and not so completely repulsive as Mr L. seems to assume'. In the same realistic way, he appeared to be convinced that there was nothing for him to do. He cut the interview short, and neither Charles nor Katherine saw him again that night; Katherine took Charles off to the billiard-room, and they played for hours.

In the morning they arranged to come down to breakfast at the same time. As soon as they had sat down, Mr March came in, banging the door behind him.

'You never show the slightest consideration,' he said. 'You announce your intentions at night just before I'm going to bed. You might have known that it would keep me awake.'

Charles was reassured when he heard that first outburst. He tried to speak casually:

'What is the proper time to upset you, Mr L.? We should like an accurate answer for future reference.'

Mr March gave a reluctant chuckle.

'After dinner is the worst time of all,' said Mr March. 'If I must have an ungrateful family, the best thing they can do is not to interfere with my health. It was exactly the same when Evelyn contracted her lamentable marriage. She was thoughtless enough to tell me at half-past ten at night. So that I actually got to bed late in addition to finding it impossible to sleep.'

'I'm extremely sorry,' said Katherine.

'That's the least you should be,' said Mr March. He turned on her: 'You go on expressing your sorrow uselessly while you persist in making it intolerable for me to show myself in the streets.'

Charles had to intervene.

'This comes,' he said, 'of letting your children bring their disreputable friends to the house.'

'I've tried to consider where I'm to blame,' said Mr March. 'But no precautions that I might have been expected to take would have been certain to spare me from the present position."

That afternoon Charles said that Mr March would tolerate the marriage 'so long as no one else interferes'.

They argued about Mr March's state of mind. How deeply had he been wounded? None of us could be certain. They were surprised that he was not more crushed. True, he had a lively affection for Francis, and respect for his accomplishments. Possessive though he was, he was instinctively too healthy a man not to want to see his daughters married. But neither Charles nor Katherine could feel sure to what extent he had been afflicted, afflicted in himself apart from minding about other people's opinion, because Francis was not a Jew.

I did not have much doubt. I had so little doubt that to Katherine certainly, to Charles almost as much, I seemed right out of sympathy. Katherine told me flat that I could not understand. For I believed that Mr March was hurt a good deal less than by the first quarrel with Charles, at the time when he abandoned the law: and incomparably less than by the struggle over Ann and Charles's future. The suffering he felt now was on a different level, was on the level of self-respect and his external face to the world. It was not the deep organic suffering that he knew over his son, when he felt that a part of his own being was torn away.

Both on the first day and in the week after, he seemed far more pre-occupied with the family's criticism than with any distress of his own. He became irascible and hunted, and kept exploding about the esteem he would lose as soon as the news got out. In fact, Mr March tried to delay the news reaching outside the house. He did not object to seeing Francis and arranging the settlement; he greeted him with the cry: 'I've nothing against you personally. But I entirely disapprove.' Afterwards he said to Charles: 'The astonishing thing is, he knows something about business. He doesn't like imprudent methods any more than I do myself.'

But he invented excuses for delaying the announcement from day to day. He could not write to his relations for a few days, he said, since he had just written all round for the New Year. It might be better to wait for one of Herbert's daughters, whose engagement was just coming out, 'if the man doesn't fight shy, as I strongly suspect,' said Mr March. 'Hannah thought she'd hooked a man once. I never believed it was possible.' He would not put an announcement in *The Times* until he had let the family know: and he dreaded the thought of publication even more than anything Philip and Hannah and Caroline might say. For he knew himself how, after the first glance at the news, he read in order the deaths, the births and the forthcoming marriages. He could imagine too clearly how people throughout the Marches' world would do the same one morning and suddenly ask: 'Who's this Francis Getliffe that's going to marry Leonard March's daughter? Does it mean that she can be marrying "out"?'

A fortnight passed since Katherine broke the news, and then one day Mr March ordered the car in the afternoon. It was a breach in his daily timetable such as neither Charles nor Katherine could remember. His temper muttered volcanically at lunch, and he refused to say where he was going. At night they realised that he had at last confessed to his sister Caroline.

'She had furnished herself with an absurd ear-trumpet,' said Mr March. 'It was bad enough being obliged to divulge my family's disgrace without having to bawl it into this contraption of hers. Your mother made the same mistake when she bought a fur in Paris on the ridiculous assumption that it was cheaper than in London—'

'Sorry, Mr L.,' said Charles. 'What mistake?'

'Of not being able to resist articles in foreign shops, of course. My sister Caroline succumbed to the temptation when she was in Vienna recently. She caught sight of this apparatus in one of the latest shops. Women are unstable in these matters.'

'You are being a bit hard,' said Katherine. 'She probably gets on better—'

'Nonsense,' said Mr March. 'She found it exactly as difficult to comprehend what I was trying to say. Then she was polite enough to remark that I ought not to hold myself entirely to blame, and that these disappointments were bound to occur in the family, and that they'd all come round to it in time.'

Actually Caroline, just by being as tactless as usual, cheered him up; he had expected a far more violent outcry. He was so much relieved that he indulged in louder complaints.

'I can't dissociate myself from the responsibility according to her advice. I remember that she regarded it as my responsibility when she suggested that fishing trip for you at her house. Not that I ever had the slightest faith in her averting the disaster. I suppose I must have brought it on myself. Though I can't decide where I went wrong with my family. If I'd made you' – he said to Katherine – 'take your proper place at dances and other entertainments, I doubt whether it would have served any useful purpose.'

'I'm sure it wouldn't,' she said. 'Mr L., you mustn't blame yourself because your family is unsatisfactory. It's just original sin.'

I wondered, how long the Marches lived side-by-side with Christians before one of them used the Augustinian term.

'Everyone else's children have managed to avoid being a reproach,' said Mr March. 'Except Justin's daughter who did what you're doing in even more disastrous circumstances. The less said of her the better. I suppose I'm bound to accept responsibility for what you call original sin. Even though my wishes have never had the slightest effect on your lamentable progress.'

The next day, he told the news to Philip, who received it both robustly and sadly; that night, with great commotion and expressions of anger, Mr March drew up the announcement for *The Times*. He sat in his study with the door open, shouting 'Go away, don't you see I'm busy?' when Charles approached. 'I'm busy with an extremely distasteful operation.' Then, a moment afterwards, Mr March rushed into the drawing-room. 'Well, how does the fellow want to appear? I suppose he possesses some first names. . . .' Several times Mr March dashed into the drawing-room again: at last, standing by the open door, he read out his composition – '"A marriage has been arranged . . ." '

'That's done,' said Mr March, and, instead of leaving the letter for the butler to collect, he took it to the pillar-box himself.

Katherine was thinking of getting up the next morning when Mr March flung open the door.

'It's not my fault this has happened,' he said. 'It's your mother's fault. I never wanted another child. She made me.'

CHAPTER XXIV

A PIECE OF NEWS

FROM the morning of the announcement, Mr March was immersed in letters, notes, conversations and telephone calls. Since he had feared more than the worst, he became cheerful as he answered 'what they are civil enough to term "congratulations" '. Most of the March family wrote in a friendly way, though there were rumours that one cousin had threatened not to attend the wedding. Hannah was reported to have said:

'I never thought she'd find anyone at all. Even someone ineligible. Mind you, she's not married him yet.'

For several days Mr March did not receive any setback; Katherine thought she had been lucky.

Then Herbert Getliffe spoke to me one evening, in chambers, just before I went off to dine at Bryanston Square. He entered the room I worked in looking worried and abashed, and said:

'There's something I want to say to you, L.S.'

He had taken to calling me by my initials, though no one else did; as a rule, I was amused, but not that night, following him into his own room, for his alarm had already reached me. He sat at his desk: the smoke from his pipe whirled above the reading-lamp; his face was ominous, and the smell of the tobacco became ominous too.

'I want a bit of help, L.S.,' he said. 'They're getting at me. You've got to come along and clear up the mess. I may as well tell you at once that it can turn out badly for your friends.'

His misery was as immediate as a child's. It was hard to resist him when he asked for comfort.

'Your friend Mr Porson is trying to raise the dust,' said Getliffe. 'You know something about him, don't you? He was called at the same time as I was. But he didn't find this wicked city needed his services enough to keep him in liquor, so he went off to lay down the law in the colonies. Well, he's suddenly taken it into his head that I've been making more money than is good for me. He's decided that I've used some confidential knowledge to make a packet on the side. You remember the Whitehall people asked me for an opinion last year? You gave me a hand yourself. Remind me to settle up with you about that. The labourer is worthy of his hire. Well, Master Porson is trying to bully them into an inquiry about some of my investments. Involving me and other people who are too busy to want to go down to Whitehall to answer pointless questions. But I don't like it, L.S. I can't prevent these things worrying me. I ought to tell you that Porson is a man who can't forgive one for being successful. You'll find them yourself as you go up the ladder. But you'll also find that more people than not will lend half an ear to Porson and company when they start throwing darts. That's the world, and it's no use pretending it isn't. That's why I want you to help me out.'

He wanted support from someone. He quite forgot, he made me forget, that he was the older man.

He gave me his own version of what Porson had discovered. It was not altogether easy to follow. Getliffe gave as much trouble as any of the evasive clients about whom he had ever grumbled. All I learned for sure that night was that he had been asked an opinion by a government department eighteen months before; while giving it, he had guessed (Porson said he had been told as an official secret) a Cabinet decision about a new government contract; two of his brothers-in-law had bought large holdings in the firm of Howard & Hazlehurst; they had done well out of it.

After telling me this story, Getliffe said:

'Well, Mr Porson has just broken out in a new place. I've been told that he's trying to persuade some pundit to ask a question in the House. Porson's had the face to tell me so in as many words.'

'I warn you,' Getliffe went on, 'it's possible he may bring it off, L.S. I can talk to you frankly now you're going up the hill a bit. Of course, I don't worry much for myself. It may be a little difficult even for me, but it's a mistake to worry too much about the doings of people who would like to step into one's goloshes. I want you to believe that I'm thinking entirely of the effect on some of your friends. And particularly on my young brother. It's for their sakes that I want everyone to use their influence to calm Porson down.'

He knew that I had met Porson occasionally since the coming-out dance.

'If I can get the chance,' I said, 'I'll talk to him. Though it won't be easy. I don't know him well.'

'You mustn't get the impression that I'm exaggerating. Porson could make things awkward for your friends. You see, my name couldn't help but be brought in, whatever he did. That wouldn't be good for my brother. The Chosen People don't like public appearances. There are one or two members of the March family who would specially dislike this one. I give you fair warning. It's uncomfortable for all of us.'

He was speaking with a severe expression, almost as though I was responsible for the danger. When he wanted your help, he sometimes appealed, sometimes threatened you with his own anxiety: anything to get the weight from his shoulders to yours. Then he said:

'I can't make out why Porson has got into this state. I always thought he was unbalanced. I don't like to believe that he's trying to bring the place down on our heads simply because he hates me. After all, I've managed to get on with most of my fellow men. I don't like being hated, L.S. Even by that madman. It's a nasty sensation, and when people say they don't mind being hated they're just whistling to keep their spirits up. So I prefer to think something else may be moving Mr Porson. I shouldn't be altogether surprised. Didn't the young woman Ann Simon turn him down pretty flat not long ago? You may find that's got something to do with it.'

He warned me again not to think that he was exaggerating the trouble. In fact, I was uneasy. He was shrewd, despite (or partly because of) his excessively labile nature. He was not a man over-inclined to anxiety. I had often seen him badgered, I had often seen him inducing others to extricate him from troubles – but the troubles were real, the consequences of living his mercurial, tricky life.

When I left him, it was nearly eight o'clock, and I had to go to Bryanston Square by taxi. As I waited while the Oxford Street lights jostled by, rain throbbing against the windows, I was listening for the strike of eight. There was no chance of a word with Charles before dinner: I was greeted with genial shouts by Mr March: 'You've made a frightful ass of yourself. You're three minutes late. Anyone knows that you must allow five minutes extra on nights of this appalling nature.'

We went straight in to dinner. I was enough of a favourite of his not to be allowed to forget that I was late. Meanwhile I saw Charles several times, and Katherine once, looking in my direction: Charles at least knew that something was on my mind.

As luck would have it, Mr March was in more expansive form than for weeks past. Margaret March, whom I had met at my first Friday night, was there as well as Francis. After disposing temporarily of the topic of my incompetence, Mr March spent most of the night talking to Francis about buying a house.

The two of them were happy discussing plans and prices. Mr March occasionally burst out into accounts of his own struggles with Haslingfield and Bryanston Square. 'One trouble you won't have,' he said, 'since you are camping out in your Bohemian fashion, is that you won't surround yourself with a mass of ponderable material that you'll never extricate yourself from.' The internal furniture of Bryanston Square had been valued years before at £15,000; but Mr March was lamenting that he could not sell it for as many shillings.

Houses of this size were relics of another age, now that people 'camped out in a Bohemian fashion', as Mr March insisted on referring to the style in which Katherine and Francis proposed to live. So the solid furniture of the March houses had become almost worthless, and Mr March and his brothers spent considerable ingenuity in persuading one another to accept the bulky articles that they unwillingly received as legacies, as their older relations died off. Several of Mr March's stories on this night, told mainly for Francis to appreciate, finished up with the formula: 'I pointed out it was far more use to him than it was to me. And so I was willing to sacrifice it, provided he paid the cost of transport.'

When Mr March went to bed, Margaret settled down in her armchair. She was older than the rest of us, but still not married; she had a similar handsomeness to Charles's, and a similar hard, ruthless mind. Yet underneath, at the thought of any of our marriages, she was full of feeling. That night, she noticed the constraint in the air. Naturally she put it down to Mr March. So she said to Katherine:

'I'm sure he has come round now. I'm positive you haven't anything to fear.'

'I suppose not,' said Katherine.

Margaret had spoken warmly and protectively. She was surprised, a little put out, to feel us all still in suspense. She turned for confirmation to Charles:

'Don't you agree that she's safe enough?'

'She ought to be,' said Charles.

'I wouldn't have believed that Mr L. could come round so quickly.' Like her cousins, Margaret was not above plucking away at the same nerve. 'He's now drawn up your settlement good and proper, hasn't he?'

'Yes, he's gone as far as that,' Katherine replied.

Charles kept watching me, knowing I was not going to speak while Margaret was there. But Katherine was not so much on edge. At the mention of the settlement, she began to smile. 'I've actually got it here,' she said to Margaret.

She went to the writing-desk and brought out a sealed envelope. She broke the seal and looked over the document inside. It was printed, and ran into several pages.

'I still think this is extremely funny,' she said.

'You don't know what I shall become as I get older,' Francis said, and they laughed at each other.

'The point is,' Katherine went on, 'that really Mr L. has the greatest possible confidence in Francis. Apart from his not being a Jew. Actually, Francis would have been a far more suitable child for Mr L. than Charles. He wouldn't have rebelled anything like as much.'

'I should have managed,' said Francis. His cheeks were creased by a smile, but he meant it. He would have found his way to his science somehow; he would have been radical, but he would have kept quiet. That night his quixotic, fine-drawn expression was less evident than it used to be; he looked composed and well.

'Well,' said Katherine, 'it's obvious that Mr L. approves of the man.

But as soon as he drew up my settlement' – she pointed to the sheet in front of her – 'he at once acted on the assumption that I was an imbecile and Francis was a crook. He's taken every possible precaution to see that Francis never touches a penny. The settlement never gives him a chance. When I die, the money goes straight to our children. If Francis outlives me, he receives a small tip for watching his sons inherit their slice of their grandfather's estate.'

All the marriage settlements in the family followed the same pattern; no one but a March should handle March money. Katherine and Charles had been amused, but nevertheless they took for granted the whole apparatus as an ordinary part of a marriage: while in the propertyless world into which I had been born, no one would have known what a marriage settlement was.

I mentioned that I had never seen one. Katherine was just going to show me theirs, but Francis said: 'I think Mr L. would be shocked – even though it's Lewis.'

'You mean you'd be shocked yourself,' said Katherine, but slipped the papers into the envelope again.

It was nearly midnight, and Margaret rose to go.

As she said goodbye, she noticed that I was staying. Her bright eyes looked keenly, uncomfortably round, worried because there was something wrong, self-conscious because she had been in the way.

We heard the butler taking her across the hall.

'What's the matter?' said Charles, the moment the door clanged. 'What's the matter?'

'Is anything wrong with Sheila?' said Katherine.

'It's nothing like that,' I said. I told the story.

Katherine cried:

'Will he bring it out in the next three weeks? Before we're married?'

'No one knows,' I said. 'In any case, we may all be taking it too seriously—'

'I'm not sure,' said Charles. 'Herbert Getliffe is right, it's the sort of affair the family wouldn't like. You mustn't worry,' he said to Katherine. 'It ought to be possible to stop Porson yet.'

'That must be tried,' said Francis. 'There's plenty to do. We'll break the jobs down in a minute.'

Suddenly he had taken charge. He had the decision, the capacity for action, of a highly strung man who had been able to master his nerves. It was easy at that instant to understand the influence he had had on Charles when they were undergraduates, with Francis two years older.

He spoke straight to Katherine as though they were alone.

'The first thing is, we must prepare for the worst. We've got to assume that he'll act on it. It's better to assume that right away. If he does, we shan't let the family make any difference.'

'That's easier said than done,' said Katherine. 'But – no, we shan't.'

'Good work,' said Francis, and took her hand. 'Now let's get down to it. Lewis, tell us the practical steps Porson can take. If he wants to make as much fuss as possible. We want all the detail you can give us.'

Sharply he asked me: could Porson start anything more damaging than a parliamentary question? How long did it take to get a parliamentary question asked? Could it be delayed? Could we find out the moment it began to pass through the government department?

Francis arranged that on the next day I should try to see Porson. Charles would see Albert Hart, who might have an acquaintance in the department. Francis himself would speak to his brother.

That settled, Francis looked at Katherine, and said with a smile, tart and yet distressed:

'I'm sorry that my brother should be responsible for this. It isn't altogether his fault. Ever since I can remember, I've been listening to his latest manœuvre. He's got too much energy for one man. That's what has made him a success.'

He had just surprised me by being more effective than any of us. Now he surprised me again – by showing something he had never shown before, his true relation to his half-brother.

Occasionally he had not been able to disguise his shame and anger at one of Herbert's tricks: but he had usually spoken of him very much as Charles used to speak, with amusement at his exploits, with indifference, with humorous disapproval. His apology to Katherine had torn that cover aside. Now we saw the affection, the indulgent, irritated, and above all admiring affection, which a man like Herbert Getliffe so often inspires in his nearest circle; so that Herbert's children, for example, would come to worship him and make his extravaganzas into a romance. That was true even of Francis, so responsible and upright.

Francis soon controlled his smile, so that the distress was no longer visible. His expression became commanding and active.

'It's clear what must be done,' he said. 'I think it's all set. You'll do what you can with Porson, Lewis? I don't like to involve you in this business, but if it can be stopped it would be convenient.'

'It probably can be stopped,' said Charles. He was trying to reassure Katherine on a different plane from Francis's. 'I'll see Ann first thing tomorrow. She may know more about Porson. And there is something I might be able to say to the family myself.'

CHAPTER XXV

THE SMELL OF WET LEAVES IN THE SQUARE

FROM the night of Getliffe's warning, there were nineteen days before the wedding. On the first of them I could not find Ronald Porson, but within forty-eight hours of the news from Getliffe I had managed to have a long talk with him. I was able to assure Katherine that there did not seem much to fear.

Since we met at the coming-out dance, I had got on well with Porson. He was boastful, violent, uncontrolled; but he had the wild generosity one often finds in misfit lives, and I was the only one of his new circle who was still struggling. With me he could advise, help and patronise to his heart's content. And with me he could stick a flower in his button-hole, swing his stick, and lead the way to a shopgirl who had taken his fancy: he was a man at ease only with women beneath him in the social scale.

Ann had punctured his sexual vanity, as was so easy to do. He had talked to me about her with violent resentment and with love. He was more easily given to warm hate then anyone I knew.

So I did not dare tell him that he might be disturbing Katherine's marriage – and ask him to call off his attack on Getliffe on that account. He was capable of such inordinate good-nature that he might have agreed on the spot, even for a girl he scarcely knew; but on the other hand, because she was connected with Charles and Ann, he might have burst out against them all. Instead I felt it was safe to talk only of Herbert Getliffe and of what Porson was now planning.

To my surprise he was very little interested: he seemed to have given up the idea of a parliamentary question, if he had ever entertained it. He mentioned Ann affectionately, and I suspected she had gone to see him the day before. He was full of his scheme for going on to the Midland Circuit.

For some reason or other his anger had burned itself out. So I told Katherine, and Charles agreed that there seemed no danger from him. He had heard something more about Ronald, also reassuring, though exactly what I did not learn.

For a day or two there seemed nothing to worry over. Katherine had to show Francis off to some of her relations, and recaptured the fun of being engaged, which, since Mr March first came round, she had been revelling in.

Then, though Ronald Porson made no move, rumours spread through the Marches. One reached ·Charles; Katherine heard others hinted at. It was known that the Getliffe brothers had been discussed on the past Friday night, when Mr March happened to be away. No one was sure how the rumours started; but it became clear that Sir Philip knew more about Herbert Getliffe than anyone in the family did, and had described him with caustic contempt.

Both Charles and Katherine accepted that without question. Philip had his code of integrity. It was a worldly code, but a strict one. He did not forgive an offence against it. He was indignant that Herbert Getliffe should have laid himself open to suspicion, whether the suspicion was justified or not.

All the family were impressed by his indignation. Charles and Katherine were told by several of their cousins to expect him to visit Mr March. Katherine waited in anxiety. Night after night she could not get to sleep, and Charles played billiards with her at Bryanston Square. For three mornings running, Mr March grumbled at them; then he suddenly stopped, the day after Philip's visit.

Philip called at Bryanston Square on a Tuesday afternoon: the wedding was fixed for ten days ahead. He went into Mr March's study, and they were there alone for a couple of hours. On his way out, Philip looked into the drawing-room, said good afternoon to Charles and Katherine, but would not stay for tea and did not refer once to seeing her at her wedding.

When Philip left, they waited for Mr March; they expected him to break out immediately about what he proposed to do. But he did not come near them all the evening: the butler said that he was still in the study: at dinner he spoke little to them, though he made one remark about 'a visit from my brother about your regrettable connections'.

When Katherine tried to use the opening, he said bad-temperedly:

'I have been persecuted enough for one day. It is typical of my family that when they wish to make representations to me, they select the only relative whom I have ever respected.'

By the time I arrived for tea the next day, Charles had already heard, from various members of the family, versions of the scene between Mr March and Philip; the versions differed a good deal, but contained a similar core. They all agreed that Mr March had put up a resistance so strong that it surprised the family. He had made no attempt to challenge the facts about Herbert Getliffe, but protested, with extreme irritability, that 'though I refuse to defend my daughter's unfortunate choice, I have no intention of penalising the man because of the sharp practice of his half-brother'. According to one account, he had expressed his own liking and trust for Francis; and certainly, with his accustomed practicality, he had said that it was far too late to intervene now. 'If you had wanted me to refuse to recognise the marriage, you should have communicated your opinion in decent time.'

It sounded final. Charles, piecing together the stories, was relieved, but he was not quite reassured: even less so was Katherine. Mr March had brazened matters out, as though he were ready to defy the family. But his mood since had been sombre, not defiant; and they knew he was hurt, not so much by the family disapproval which Philip represented as by his feeling for Philip himself.

They knew the depth of his feeling. Warm-hearted as he was, yet with no intimate friends outside the family, this was the strongest of his human bonds, after his love for his children. When he had spoken the night before of 'the only relative whom I have ever respected', he was trying to mask, and at the same time relieve, his sadness. He made it sound like an outburst of ill-temper, an exaggerated phrase; but it was really a cry of pain.

So Charles and Katherine kept coming back to Philip's effect on Mr March. It was not till after tea that Charles said:

'It's possible that I may be able to help with Uncle Philip.' He asked me to take Katherine out for the evening: he would see Mr March, and persuade him to invite Philip for dinner.

Katherine looked puzzled as he made these plans. Charles said:

'It may help you. You see, Ann has promised to marry me. I think I ought to tell them at once.'

'Did you expect to be able to tell them this?' Katherine burst out. 'You said something – you remember – the night Lewis brought the news?'

Charles did not reply, but said:

'It may smooth things over with Uncle Philip.'

'Of course it will,' said Katherine, suddenly full of hope. 'It will put Mr L. right with the family. Your making a perfectly respectable marriage. And he ought to be glad about it himself.'

Charles looked across at me.

'Of course, he ought to be glad about it,' Katherine went on. 'I know he thinks she's got too much influence over you. But she's everything he could possibly wish, isn't she? He likes her, doesn't he?'

'Yes,' said Charles. 'Yes. In any case, he ought to be told at once.'

Then he got up from his chair, and added in a tone now vigorous and eager:

'I want to tell him tonight.'

Charles had become impatient. He scarcely had time to listen to our congratulations. He asked me again to take Katherine away for the evening, and before we were out of the house he had entered Mr March's study.

It was pouring with rain, and we went by taxi to our restaurant, and even then got wet as we crossed the pavement. But Katherine, without taking off her coat, went straight to the telephone to ring up Francis at Cambridge. In a few minutes she returned, her eyes shining, her hair still damp.

She was anxious, but her capacity for enjoyment was so great that it carried both of us along. In her bizarrely sheltered life, she had never dined out with a man alone, except Francis. She was interested in everything, the decoration of the restaurant, the relations between the pairs of people dining, my choice of food. It was her own sort of first-hand interest, as though no one had ever been out to dinner before.

With the same zest, she kept returning to the news Charles was at that moment telling Mr March. 'Lewis, when did he propose? It must have been what he hinted at that night, don't you agree? That was a week ago – don't you admit he's had it up his sleeve ever since?'

She chuckled fondly. Then she asked me:

'Lewis, do you think she'll make him happy?'

I told her what I thought: they would be happier together than either with anyone else. She was not satisfied. Did that mean I had my doubts? I said that Charles had been luckier than he ever expected. Katherine asked if Ann was not too complicated. I said that I guessed that in love she was quite simple.

Katherine broke off:

'If she makes him happy then everything is perfect. Lewis, you've just said that he never expected to be so lucky. What I am positive about is that he never expected a wife who would please the family. Don't you agree that's the astonishing part of it? That's why I'm fantastically hopeful tonight. I don't pretend that Mr L. and Uncle Philip will think she's a tremendous catch. She doesn't come from our group of families, and she's only moderately rich. But they'll have to admit that she passes. After all, most of Mr L.'s nephews have done worse for themselves. And

I don't think it will be counted against her that she's very pretty. She's been admired in the family already.'

I took her to a theatre, so that we should get back to Bryanston Square late enough for Charles to be waiting for us. On the way back her anxiety recurred, but Charles met us in the hall and his smile dispelled it.

'I'm pretty certain that all is well,' he said in a low voice.

She kissed him. He stopped her talking there, and we went into the drawing-room.

'I'm pretty certain all is well,' he repeated. 'You mustn't think it's due to me. It would have come out all right anyhow – don't you really believe that yourself?'

When she questioned him, he admitted that Philip had been pleased with the news. There had been considerable talk about the Getliffes and Porson. Mr March and Philip had parted on good terms.

We both noticed that Katherine suddenly looked very tired. Charles told her so; she was too much exhausted to deny it, and went obediently, first to the telephone and then to bed.

Charles's smile, as we heard the final tinkle of the call, and then her step upstairs, was tender towards her. His whole expression was open and happy: yet, despite the tender smile, it was not gentle. It was open and fiercely happy. He jumped up and went to the window. His movements were full of energy.

'Look,' he said, 'I think it has cleared up now. I'd very much like a stroll. Do you think you could bear it?'

It was just such a night as that on which we walked home after the coming-out dance. The rain had stopped: there was a smell of wet leaves from the garden in the square. The smell recalled to Charles the excitement, the misgivings, the promise of that night, as well as the essence of other nights, forgotten now. In an instant he was overcome by past emotion, and did not want to speak.

It was some time before I broke the silence.

'So you think Katherine is safe?' I said.

'Yes,' said Charles. 'It's quite true what I told her. I think the wedding would have come off without any more trouble – any more trouble in the open, anyway. But I'm glad I talked to them. Uncle Philip did seem to be placated. He was completely surprised about Ann. He said that I'd never been seen with her in public. He couldn't remember hearing anyone in the family couple our names together.'

Charles smiled. He broke off:

'By the way, he is very angry about this Getliffe business. I suppose he's sufficiently patriarchal to feel that all attachments to the family ought to come up to his standard of propriety. That must be the reason, don't you agree? It pleased him more than you'd think, when I said that Porson had probably got tired of his own indignation.'

Charles went on:

'And Uncle Philip was genuinely delighted about Ann. He decided that she would be a credit to us. He also said' – Charles laughed – 'that he did hear she was a bit of a crank, but he didn't take that seriously.'

'And Mr L.?'

Charles hesitated.

'He was not so pleased. Did you expect him to be?'

'What did he say?'

'Something rather strange. Something like – "I always knew it was inevitable. I have no objections to raise".'

In a moment, he said:

'Of course he was extremely glad that Uncle Philip is coming round. That is going to be the most important thing for him.'

Then Charles broke into his good-natured, malicious grin:

'It struck me as pleasing that I should be soothing the family. It struck me as even more pleasing that I should be doing it by announcing that I intended to marry in as orthodox a manner as my father did.' The malicious smile still flickered. 'There is also a certain beauty,' he reflected, 'in the fact that, after all the fuss I've made from time to time, I should be eager to tell my father so.

'Ah well,' he said, 'it's settled. It is superb to have it settled.'

Just as when he saw Ann at Haslingfield he smiled because he had first met her at the Jewish dance – so tonight he was amused that he of all men, who had once winced at the word 'Jew', should now be parading his engagement to a Jewess, should be insisting to his father that he was conforming as a Jewish son. It was a sarcastic touch of fate completely in his style; but it was more than that.

All of a sudden I realised why he had been so fiercely happy that day, why he had gained a release of energy, why as he walked with me he felt that his life was in his own hands. To him the day had been a special one – though all the rest of us had had our attention fixed on Katherine and her father, and had forgotten Charles except as a tactful influence in the background.

In Charles's own mind, the day marked the end of the obsession which had preyed on him since he was a child. It marked the death of a shame.

He felt absolutely free. Everything seemed open to him. He felt his whole nature to be fresh, simple, and at one.

We walked across Bayswater Road and into the Park. His stride was long and full of spring. He was talking eagerly, of his future with Ann, of what he hoped to do. He was more spontaneous, frank and trustful than I had ever known him. He had forgotten, or put aside for the night, any thought of his conflict with his father over Ann.

In the darkness I listened to his voice, lively, resonant, happy. I thought of this shame which had occupied so much of his conscious life. It had gone, so it seemed to him, because he had fallen in love with Ann, and that evening could tell his father, with unqualified happiness, that he was going to marry her – and, more than that, could use the fact that he was marrying a Jewess in order to ease the way for Katherine.

So Charles was talking with boyish spontaneity, completely off his guard, his secrecies thrown away. I felt a great affection for him. Perhaps the affection was greater because I did not see his state that night quite as he did himself. For me there was something unprotected about his openness and confidence.

I remembered his confession when he gave up the law. I had felt two things then, and I felt them more acutely now: that this shame had tormented him, and that at the same time he had used it as an excuse. Charles would always, I thought, have been prouder and more self-distrustful, harsher and more vulnerable to shame, than most of us. In his youth, he would in any case have gone through his torments. But even he, for all his insight, wanted to mollify and excuse them. Even he found it difficult to recognise his harshness, his self-distrust, above all his vulnerability, as part of his essential 'I'.

For years past, I had heard George Passant put the blame for the difference and violence of his character on to his humble origin. His vision of himself was more self-indulgent than Charles's. Yet Charles's insight did not prevent him from seizing at a similar excuse. He had felt passionately, as we have all felt, that everything would have been possible for him, life would have been utterly harmonious, he would have been successful and good 'if only it had not been for this accident'. Charles had felt often enough 'I should have been free, I should have had my fate in my hands – if only I had not been born a Jew'.

It was not true. It was an excuse. Even to himself it was an excuse which could not endure. For his vulnerability (unlike George Passant's) was of the kind that is mended by time; for years the winces of shame had become less sharp. It seemed to him that by telling his father and Philip he was marrying a Jewess he had conquered his obsession. I should have said that it was conquered by the passing of time itself and the flow of life. In any case, he could no longer believe in the excuse. That night for him signalised the moment of release, which really had been creeping on imperceptibly for years.

He was light with his sense of release. He felt that night that now he was truly free.

That was why I was stirred by a rush of affection for him. For he would be more unprotected in the future than he had been when the excuse still dominated him. In cold blood, when the light and warmth of release had died down, he would be left face to face with his own nature. Tonight he could feel fresh, simple, and at one; tomorrow he would begin to see again the contradictions within.

CHAPTER XXVI

MR MARCH CROSSES THE ROOM

Up till the day of the wedding, rumours still ran through the family, but I heard from Charles that Philip had sent an expensive present. I also heard on the wedding morning that Mr March was in low spirits but 'curiously relieved' to be getting ready to go to the register office.

When I arrived at Bryanston Square after the wedding, to which not even his brothers were invited, I thought Mr March was beginning to enjoy himself. Nearly all the family had come to the reception and, soon after being 'disgorged from obscurity' (his way of referring to the marriage in a register office) he seemed able to forget that this was different from any ordinary wedding.

In the drawing-room Mr March stood surrounded by his relatives. There were at least a hundred people there: the furniture had been removed and trestle-tables installed round two of the walls and under the windows, in order to carry the presents. The presents were packed tightly and arranged according to an order of precedence that had cost Katherine, in the middle of her suspense, considerable anxiety; for, having breathed in that atmosphere all her life, she could not help but know the heart-burnings that Aunt Caroline would feel if her Venetian glasses ('she hasn't done you very handsomely,' said Mr March, who made no pretence about what he considered an unsatisfactory present) were not placed near the magnificent Flemish tapestry from the Herbert Marches or Philip's gift of a Ming vase.

The tables glittered with silver and glass; it was an assembly of goods as elaborate, costly, ingenious and beautiful as London could show. At any rate, Mr March considered that the presents 'came up to expectations'. Hannah, so someone reported, had decided that they 'weren't up to much'; but, as that had been her verdict in all the March weddings that Mr March could remember, it merely reassured him that his daughter's was not continuously regarded as unique.

There were few of those absences of presents which had embarrassed the cousin whose daughter married a Gentile twenty years before. 'That appears to be ancient history,' said Mr March to Katherine, when presents had arrived from all his close relations and some of his fears proved groundless. The two or three lacunae among his cousins he received robustly: 'George is using his religious scruples to save his pocket. Not that he's saving much – judging from the knick-knack that he sent to Philip's daughter.' At the reception itself, he repeated the retort to Philip himself, and they both chuckled.

Philip had already gone out of his way to be affable. He had greeted Ann with special friendliness, and had even given a stiff smile towards Herbert Getliffe. He seemed set, in the midst of the family, on suppressing the rumours of the last fortnight.

Mr March responded at once to the signs of friendship. He began to refer with cheerfulness and affection to 'my son-in-law at Cambridge', meaning Francis, who was standing with Katherine a few feet away. A large knot of Mr March's brothers and sisters and their children had gathered round him, and he was drawn into higher spirits as the audience grew.

'I refuse to disclose my contribution,' he said, after Philip had been chaffing him about the absence of any present of his own. Everyone knew that Mr March had given them a house, but he had decided not to admit it. Philip was taking advantage of the old family legend that Leonard was peculiarly close with money.

'You might have produced half a dozen fish forks,' said Philip.

'I refuse to accept responsibility for their diet,' said Mr March. 'I gave Hetty some decanters for her wedding and she always blamed me for the regrettable events afterwards.'

'You could have bought them something for their house,' said Herbert.

'You could have passed on a piece of your surplus furniture,' said Philip. 'So long as Katherine's forgotten that you ever owned it.'

'There must have been something you could have bought for the house,' said Herbert's wife.

Mr March chuckled, and went off on a fugue. 'They insist on living in some residence in the provinces, owing to the nature of my son-in-law's occupation—'

Katherine interrupted: 'I wish you wouldn't make it sound like coal-mining, Mr L.' But he was going strongly:

'A month ago I went to inspect some of their possible places of abode. My son Charles told me the eleven-fifty went from King's Cross, and it goes from Liverpool Street, of course. However, I never had the slightest faith in his competence; naturally I had consulted the timetable before I asked him, and so arrived at the station in comfortable time. Incidentally, in twenty-five minutes my daughter and son-in-law will be compelled to leave to catch the boat train. On my honeymoon I had already left for the train at the corresponding time, allowing for the additional slowness of the cab as a means of conveyance. People always say Mentone is a particularly quiet resort, but I've never found it so. The first time I visited it was on my honeymoon with its general air of unrest. The second time my wife had some jewellery stolen and I was compelled to undergo some interviews with a detective. I never had any confidence in him, but the jewellery was returned several months later. The third time passed without incident. Having arrived despite Charles's attempt to make my journey impossible—'

'Where? When?' shouted several of his audience.

'At my daughter's future domicile in the provinces. On the occasion under discussion,' replied Mr March without losing way, 'I proceeded to inspect the three residences which were considered possibilities by the couple principally concerned—' Philip and the others threw in remarks, they gave Mr March the centre of the stage, and he was letting himself go.

Then, just after he had triumphantly ended that story and begun another, he looked across the room. Outside the large noisy crowd over which his own voice was prevailing, there were two or three knots of people, not so full of gusto – and Ann by the window, talking to Margaret March.

Mr March broke off his story, hesitated, and watched them. As Mr March stared at Ann, the room happened to become quiet. Mr March said loudly:

'I've scarcely spoken to my future daughter-in-law. I must go and have a word with her.'

Slightly flushed, he crossed the room, swinging his arms in his quick, awkward gait.

'Why haven't you talked to me, young woman? Why am I being deserted on this public occasion?'

He took her to the centre of the carpet, and there they stood.

Mr March showed no sign at all of the gallant, elaborately courteous manner which he had first used to her in company. He was speaking to her, here in public view, intimately, simply, brusquely.

'I shall have to see about your own wedding before long,' he said.

'Yes,' said Ann.

'The sooner the better,' said Mr March. 'Since we are to be related in this manner.'

Ann looked at him. His expression had become sad and resigned. His head was bent down in a posture unlike his normal one, a posture dejected, subdued.

'Now, whatever happens,' he said, 'we must bear with each other.'

Ann was still looking at him, and he took her hand. They went on talking, and some of us moved towards them. Katherine began teasing him about arranging another wedding in the middle of this. For a second he was silent, then he straightened himself and recovered his gaiety. Katherine was continuing to talk of weddings, funerals and Mr March's *Times* reading habits.

'You can't help paying attention to them,' he told her, 'when you reach my venerable years. I've attended a considerable number of both in my time. And I've also been informed of a great many births. Most of the results of which survived,' Mr March reflected. 'Even my cousin Oscar's child – even that lived long enough for me to give it the usual mug.'

CHAPTER XXVII

'MY FAVOURITE CHILD'

AFTER Katherine's wedding it seemed as though Mr March was groping round to heal the breach with his son. We had watched him cross the room to Ann at the wedding breakfast; he was acting not happily, not with an easy mind, but impelled to remove some of the weight that had for months, even through the excitement over Katherine, been pressing him down.

I intruded so far as to tell Charles that he ought to forget the night of the concert, and meet his father more than halfway. Charles himself was happy in the prospect of his marriage, which was fixed for three months ahead. He was also gratified that he could discipline himself enough to work patiently at his medicine; he had done it for a year, and he had no misgivings left. So that he was ready to listen to everything I said. His natural kindness, his deep feeling for his father now shone out. He wanted Mr March to be happy for the rest of his life. He would respond to any overture his father made. I tried to persuade him to go to his father, on his own initiative, and ask to be made independent. I did not need to give him reasons. Speaking to him, I had no sort of foresight. If I had been asked, I should just have said that if a man like Charles had to put up with domination, no good could come of it.

'Do it,' I pressed him, 'as though nothing had been said. As though the question hadn't ever been mentioned before. I believe that he will agree. He's in danger of losing more than you are, you know.'

Charles knew all that I meant. But he hesitated. As we talked his face became lined. If Mr March refused, the situation was worse than before. If Mr March refused, it would be even harder for Ann. They would know that all that was left was to put a civil face on things.

Nevertheless, I pressed him to go. He promised everything else but would not definitely promise that.

Then Mr March himself showed us the colour of his thoughts when he talked to Charles one Friday night in January.

It was Mr March's turn that night to give the family dinner party, and he invited me without any prompting, saying: 'You might oblige me by filling one of the gaps at my table.' He had never done so before; I felt the invitation on his own account marked a break with things Mr March had known.

The dinner party itself had changed since the first I went to. It was neither so lively nor so large. There were only eighteen people this time sitting round the great table at Bryanston Square. Some of the absences were caused by illness, as Mr March's generation was getting old; Herbert had just had a thrombosis. Florence Simon was married now, and living out of London. While Katherine's marriage not only kept her away, but at least two of Mr March's cousins.

Philip's glance went round the room, noticing those relatives who had attended his own house the week before but who had not come that night. He said nothing of it to Mr March, and instead chaffed him, as he had done at the wedding, with the dry, elder-brotherly friendliness that had been constant all their lives. But even Philip's sharp tongue did not make the party go; family gossip never began to flow at its usual rate; by a quarter to eleven the last car had driven away.

Mr March came into the drawing-room, where Charles and I were sitting. We were sitting as we had been on the night of Charles's quarrel with his father, after that different dinner party three years before. Mr March sat down and stretched out his hands to the fire.

'I never expected to see a Friday night in my own house finished in time for me to have only ten minutes less than my usual allowance,' he said.

'Mr L.,' said Charles, 'don't you remember saying they were nothing like they used to be, even in Uncle Philip's house? You said that months ago.'

'I appreciate your intention,' said Mr March, 'but I am unable to accept it entirely. I never expected to find myself in danger of being in Justin's position. After his daughter's marriage he did not venture to hold a Friday night until we were able to reassure him that there would be an adequate attendance. Which we were unable to do until a considerable number of years afterwards. I confess that I am surprised at not having a similar experience.'

'They respect you too much to treat you in the same way,' said Charles.

'It's not respect,' said Mr March. 'It's the family that has changed. It's curious to see the family changing in my own lifetime. I've already seen most things pass that we used to regard as completely permanent features of the world.'

He spoke with regret, in a matter-of-fact, acceptant, almost cheerful tone. He added:

'As for respect, the nearest I approach it is that at synagogue people are always ready to commiserate on the misfortunes which have happened to me through my children. Last Saturday one fellow insisted on keeping me talking in the rain. He said: "Mr March, I should like you to know I am as upset as you must be to see the Marches fall from their old position." I acknowledged his remark. The fellow was making it impossible for me to cover myself with my umbrella. He said: "We all feel the decline of our great houses." I said that it was very civil of him. He said: "Think of your family. Your father was a great man. And his brothers were known outside our community. But your generation, Mr March – I know you will excuse me for speaking frankly – you have just been living on the esteem of your father. What have any of you done compared with the old Marches?" I brought up the name of my brother Philip, but this man replied: "He was lucky enough to be the eldest son of your father. That's all. And you and your brothers weren't even that, again speaking frankly, Mr March." '

'Who was this man?' Charles asked.

'I refuse to disclose his name,' said Mr March, still reporting the conversation in such a matter-of-fact way that Charles had to copy him.

'Is he the man,' said Charles, 'who called you a radical reformer because you wanted to let women into the synagogue?'

'Of course not,' said Mr March. 'In any case, that was Hannah's fault. He proceeded to say: "You and your brothers did nothing to add to the family reputation. While among all your children and nephews and nieces, is there one who won't subtract something from the family name? Think of your own children. Your son's just an idler about town. One daughter married a man who lives by his pen. The other daughter has inflicted this great sorrow upon us. Whatever can happen to the next generation of Marches? What about your grandchildren?"'

'I must say,' said Charles, 'that he sounds a vaguely disagreeable companion.'

'He was just being frank,' said Mr March.

'If that's frankness,' said Charles, 'give me a bit of dissimulation.'

'It was possibly true,' said Mr March, 'though I thought it was rather pungently expressed. And I wished he had delivered himself before synagogue when it wasn't raining.

'I am inclined to think,' he added, 'that he represents what a number of my acquaintances are saying.'

'They're not worth considering.'

'No,' said Mr March. 'I can't help considering anything that is said about the family's position. These lamentations show how general opinion is preparing to dispose of the family. As I remarked previously, it's curious to see such changes occur in my own lifetime.'

Charles looked at him, astonished by the fortitude with which Mr March could see part of his world destroyed. He was realistic as ever, nostalgic also (for that was the other side of his realistic temperament) hankering after the world that was gone or going, but not pretending for a moment that it could be saved. His fortitude was stoical: but Charles knew there was nothing light about it. It came out in matter-of-fact terms, but it was only separated from melancholy because the pulse of his vitality was still throbbing deep and strong.

'You might blame me more than you do,' said Charles.

'I don't propose to,' said Mr March. 'I don't know how much either you or I can be held to blame. In any case, I should not consider the investigation profitable. We have arrived at the position we are now in. And I lay no claim to a philosophical turn of mind, but I have noticed one result of things changing outside. One has to fall back on those attachments tnat can't change so rapidly. After his daughter's marriage and its regrettable consequences, Justin always devoted himself entirely to his wife.'

Mr March gazed at his son, and added:

'Since I am deprived of other consolations, I find that I attach more value to your continued existence.'

For days afterwards, I kept trying to persuade Charles that now was the time to go to his father. Now if ever was the time. Sometimes he was nearly persuaded. Sometimes he advanced the old arguments. He was not obstinate, he was not resenting my intrusion. He was gripped by an indecision so deep that it seemed physical, not controllable by will. He said: 'I admit that he spoke with complete sincerity. He always does. He desperately wants everything to be right between us. But you notice that he didn't mention my marrying Ann? You noticed that, didn't you?'

Katherine joined in my efforts, warmly, anxiously, emphatically, when she came to Bryanston Square for a weekend in February. It was two months since her honeymoon, and there was a physical change in her face, as though some of the muscles had been relaxed. She was tranquil, happy, more positive than we had known her. When Charles had told Mr March of his engagement, she had shown less than her usual insight; she had even expected Mr March to be pleased. But now she saw the situation with clear eyes. It was worth the risk, she argued; it was the one step which could set them free with each other.

Once she grew angry with Charles, and told him that he would surely do it if only Ann were not holding him back. Her concern was so naked and intimate that he did not take offence. She continued to persuade him. For half an hour one night, I thought she had succeeded. Then, suddenly, his mood changed. In fatigue and resignation, he said, smiling at her with extreme affection:

'I'm sorry, my dear. I'd do anything else. But I can't do it.'

She knew that the decision was final. She called to see me the next evening in my rooms.

'Lewis,' she said, 'I've asked Charles if he minds my speaking to Mr L.'

'What did he say?'

'He welcomed it. Oh, it's wretched, don't you think it's wretched? He was within an inch of going himself, and yet he simply can't. I'm appallingly diffident about talking to Mr L. myself. But if I don't, I should feel cowardly for ever. Don't you agree?'

Katherine promised to return after she had talked to Mr March. I waited in a fret of apprehension, thinking time after time that it was her footsteps on the stairs. When she came at last, I knew that all had gone wrong.

She sat down heavily.

'He was absolutely unreasonable,' she said. 'He wouldn't even begin to listen to reason. His mind seemed absolutely shut.'

She had told him that he could not treat Charles like a child; he was a grown man; this attempt to keep him dependent was bound to make a gulf between them. Mr March replied that he did not propose to let such considerations influence his actions. She had told him that his actions were stupid as well as wrong. They could not even have the practical effect he wanted. Charles was committed to becoming a doctor now; and he would marry Ann in April, come what might. Mr March replied that he was aware of these facts; he did not propose to discontinue Charles's allowance, which might hinder his son's activities, but he refused, by making him independent, to give any sign of approval to either of his major follies. Katherine begged him to think of his own future relations with Ann. She was going to be his daughter-in-law. For the rest of his life he would meet her. Mr March said that he did not propose to consider the opinions of that young woman on the matter.

He was not angry, but utterly set in his purpose. He even told her that he needed his son's affection more than he had ever done; he said, quite naturally, that he had told Charles so. But, on the issue before them, he would not make the slightest concession.

'I do not believe,' Katherine burst out, 'that it would have made any difference if Charles had gone himself. I shall always console myself with that. I tell you, I'm sure it's true.'

She had finished by asking him to explain the contrast between his gentleness over her own marriage, and this obsessive harshness to Charles. Mr March had not answered for a long time. Then he said, in a sombre tone:

'He was always my favourite child.'

Katherine stayed with me for a long time, in order to put off breaking the news to Charles.

PART FOUR

THE DANGERS

CHAPTER XXVIII

SEVENTIETH BIRTHDAY

MR March's seventieth birthday was due in the May of 1936, and for weeks beforehand he had been calling on his younger relatives and friends, insisting that they keep the night of the twenty-second free. It was the only birthday he had celebrated since he was a child; usually he would not have the day so much as mentioned. But some caprice made him want everyone to realise that he was seventy. Many of the very young had not seen him as extravagant as this.

They had heard the family legends of Uncle Leonard, but they had not often been inside his house, except for the formal Friday nights. Since the marriages of Katherine and Charles five years before, he had given up entertaining the young.

For his seventieth birthday party, we were each invited, not only by a telephone call from Mr March in person, but also by a long letter in his own hand. Presents were prohibited with violence. None of us knew how large the dinner was to be until we arrived at Bryanston Square; the house was brighter than I ever remembered it, lights streaming onto the square, cocktails, which Mr March had not allowed there before, being drunk in the drawing-room. Mr March was moving from one young relative to another, his coat-tails flapping behind him. Wherever he went one heard noise and laughter.

As we waited for dinner, there were about fifty people standing in the room. None of Mr March's contemporaries was there; by another caprice of Mr March's, none of them had been invited. Perhaps, I thought, he did not want to be reminded that his generation of Marches was dying.

Since Charles married, Herbert and his wife had both died, and Caroline's husband. Hannah was still alive, but bed-ridden. Of Mr March's contemporaries, only Philip and Caroline were left at Friday nights.

At the birthday party, Margaret March and I seemed to be the oldest of the guests, and we were just over thirty. The majority of them were Mr March's youngest nephews and nieces and second cousins. To make up the number which he had set himself, Mr March had asked several to bring their young men and women.

Mr March walked among them, cordial to everyone, lingering once or twice appreciatively by the prettier girls. His spirits were not damped by Katherine's absence; she had had to cry off at a few hours' notice, since one of her children had measles. 'I should see no reason to anticipate serious consequences at this stage,' said Mr March, 'if it were not for the practitioners whom they insist on employing. They are reported to be competent, but I refuse to accept responsibility for their performances. I thought it wise to send my daughter an account of their careers, so far as I could discover them from the professional records, and draw special attention to those features I did not consider up to snuff.'

He added:

'I have to admit that I have not yet discovered a practitioner whose record appeared to me to be up to snuff in all respects.'

He returned to a knot of nephews and nieces in order to answer their chaff about presents. Why had he refused to allow us to give him any? Because the material objects offered on these occasions were always of singular uselessness. Books? All the books approved of by young persons of cultivated taste produce nothing but the deepest depression. Had he really received no presents from anyone? 'Well,' said Mr March, 'my second-cousin-once-removed Harry Stein didn't obey my instructions. He ignored the hint and sent me a box of cigars. If the fellow wants to be civil, I suppose I can't deprive him of the pleasure.'

Instead of receiving presents on his birthday, Mr March had decided to give some. Someone asked him whether this was true, and he said: 'I refuse either to deny or confirm.' Under pressure, he admitted that 'the juvenile members of the family had received a contribution towards their confectionery' that morning. But he became his most secretive when people wanted him to say exactly what he had given, and to how many. It came out later that each person under twenty-one in the March family, that is the March family in its widest sense, had found waiting for them at breakfast that morning a cheque for '*Seventy Pounds Exactly*'.

Mr March stood in his drawing-room, retorted to the questions of his nieces, sent the footmen hurrying about the bright room with trays of cocktails, sipped a glass of sherry. As I watched him, I thought how well preserved he still looked. His moustache had whitened in the last few years, the wings of hair above his ears were scantier and greyer, the veins on his temples stood out; but his step, his brusque, quick, clumsy movements, the resonance of his laughter, were still a robust man's.

He seemed gayer than I had seen him for a long time. Even the entrance of Ann did not seem to produce any strain. It was a long time since she had been inside his home. There had been no break, but since Mr March made his last unconceding answer to Charles before their marriage, she had without a word spoken slipped away. That night, as she went up to shake hands with Mr March, he greeted her in a curt, matter-of-fact fashion. His manner seemed to suggest, not that they met only on the most formal occasions within the March family life, but simply that there was no need of explanations between them. He asked Margaret March to introduce her to a group in the corner of the room, and despatched a footman after her.

He kept Charles by him a little longer, and teased him affectionately and without rancour. 'May I enquire about the vital statistics of Pimlico and similar unsalubrious neighbourhoods?'

'They're not much affected yet,' said Charles, also with good humour.

'I refuse to take responsibility for any deterioration,' said Mr March.

'Well, that will be bad for everyone's morale, won't it, Mr L.?' Charles replied.

Mr March chuckled. Just listening to them, no one would have guessed their story. Then Mr March moved off to meet Caroline's grandchildren.

For a second Charles was left alone, until two cousins joined him. He stood there, in the centre of his father's drawing-room, looking a little older than his age: his forehead had lined, but his expression was keen, healthy and settled: his face had taken on the shape it would wear until he was old.

His father's reference to 'Pimlico and similar unsalubrious neighbourhoods' meant that, not long after he graduated as a doctor, Charles had bought a partnership in a practice down by the river. Whether he bought it with Ann's money, none of us knew. It was certain that Mr March had made no contribution.

Charles himself was lighting a cigarette for a girl and as he straightened himself he looked at Ann. I followed his eyes. She had altered less than most of us; she had kept her open, youthful good looks. She was listening to a young man with the attention, gentle, friendly and positive, that I remembered so well. As he watched, there was a spark in Charles's eye. Their love had stayed not only strong but brilliant. For them both, except that they had still had no child, it had turned out the best of marriages.

There were two tables laid in the dining-room, and the butler went to Charles and told him that he and Ann were expected to preside at the smaller. Mr March was left free to have two bright, pert, pretty nieces sitting one on each hand. Between the two tables stood four standard lamps, brought in for the occasion; Mr March caused a commotion by demanding that two of them be removed, as soon as we had sat down. 'This room has been appallingly dark during my occupancy of thirty-eight years,' he said loudly. 'It was even darker in my uncle Horace's day. Now, the first time it's ever been properly lit, the confounded lights are arranged so as to obscure my view of half my guests.'

The lights were removed. Mr March surveyed the whole party with a satisfied, possessive and triumphant smile. There were fifty-seven people in the room. Mr March announced, and again over the fish, that he had reserved one and a half rows of the stalls at 'some theatre whose name you will be informed of in due course'.

Margaret teased him about this sudden burst of secrecy: she produced the theory that he refused to go to the sort of play admired by his children's 'intellectual friends', and so was luring us somewhere of his own choice.

'No! No!' said Mr March. Other members of the family joined in, shouting and laughing. Mr March's voice rose above them.

'No! No! My motives are being misinterpreted. But I will say this, if any of you want to be depressed tonight, you'd better stay in the house and read one of the books approved of by your literary friends. Not that I don't admire 'em –' he said to me, 'but now I'm getting old I find I don't want to be reminded of the unpleasant circumstances which afflicted me when I was young.'

'So that you find that you worry less than you used to, do you?' said one of the bright, pretty nieces.

Several people in the know were chuckling, for the night's celebration had been arranged with an expenditure of anxiety unusual even for Mr March.

'I worry dreadfully,' said Mr March complacently. 'I've never known anyone worry more dreadfully that I do.'

'Not so badly as you used to, though,' said Margaret.

'Worse. Much worse,' said Mr March. 'I've learnt to control myself, that's all.'

He chuckled, as loudly as anyone. 'I've also learned to avoid occasions that I dislike. The only advantage of getting old,' said Mr March, 'is that you're not faced by so many occasions that you're bound to dislike, if you're too shy and diffident a person.

'There are a corresponding number of disadvantages, of course,' Mr March went on. 'I shall shortly have to abandon my club because the people I know are dropping off one by one, and it's an unnecessary strain on the memory to burden yourself with new faces – a very ugly face, by the way, that fellow possesses that my brother Philip has just got into the club. It's an unnecessary strain to burden yourself with new faces for a period of time that can't be worth the effort. It's curious also how soon people are forgotten in the club when they're dead. When I die they'll discontinue my special brand of tea-buns next day.'

For a few moments the reflection sobered him. Before the end of the meal, he was enjoying himself again. On the way to the play, which turned out to be a revival of one of Lonsdale's, he enjoyed marshalling the cars, re-collecting the party on the steps of the theatre, taking the middle seat of the second row of the stalls. In the first interval he came out with Margaret March, and said with the utmost gratification: 'I call it a very mediocre play.'

Margaret protested, but Mr March overbore her in his most sincere and genial manner:

'It is extremely mediocre.' He turned to me thoughtfully. 'I believe you could write a play not much worse than that.'

While he was talking, Margaret noticed her Aunt Caroline coming down from the circle by herself. We saw the gleam of her lorgnon as she sighted her brother. She had become still fatter, and her flesh shook as she made her way down.

'I heard from a good many quarters,' she said to Mr March, 'that you were giving yourself a spree tonight. So I decided to come and inspect you.'

She could not resist the time-honoured joke about his meanness: was that why he had not invited the older Marches? Mr March grinned, but his manner was defensive.

She protruded a large silver ear-trumpet at him as he replied.

'Birthday parties have always been understood to come into a special category,' he said. 'I've never had any of you to my house on my birthday since I was married – except Hannah, and, needless to say, she invited herself.'

Just before we returned to our seats, Caroline said casually in her loud voice:

'By the way, I had dinner with Philip. The poor fellow would have been here with me, but he's afraid he's got his gout coming on. He gave me a message for you. He said that, in case I missed you, you'd find the same message waiting at your house.'

As she rummaged in her handbag for an envelope, she did not seem specially interested, nor Mr March specially concerned. But, as he read the note, his face darkened with anxiety, and he said to his sister:

'I shall need your company in the next interval.'

Mr March was on his feet in the stalls as the curtain came down at the end of the second act. He met his sister, and I watched them walk back and forth on the far side of the foyer. She walked slowly, with her ponderous tread, and her silver trumpet flew to and from her ear.

To my surprise, Mr March beckoned me to them. Their conversation had looked comic from a distance: at close quarters there was nothing comic in Mr March's expression.

'I wanted to ask you, Lewis, whether you have any recent knowledge of the activities of my daughter's brother-in-law? I mean the fellow Herbert Getliffe.'

The question was unexpected: Mr March asked it in a flat and heavy tone.

If he had not been so preoccupied, he would have known that the answer must be no. For Mr March was completely aware of the nature of my marriage: in a shy fashion he had been sympathetic about it, and sent invitations, as to this party, hoping that Sheila would be 'well enough' to come. He knew that, because of her, I had given up my practice at the Bar. Half my time nowadays I was spending in Cambridge, teaching law at Francis Getliffe's college. That again Mr March knew, and how his son-in-law had brought it about and helped give me some sort of comfort.

Nevertheless, he repeated his question about Herbert.

'No, I've not seen much of him lately,' I said. 'I dined with him a couple of years ago, that's all.'

'You can't give us any information upon how he can be affecting the position of my brother Philip?'

I was astonished. I said that I could not imagine it.

'So far as I can infer from the only information I possess,' said Mr March, 'this preposterous situation is connected with certain gossip which was circulating at the time of my daughter's marriage. You may remember that there was a certain amount of gossip at that time.'

I nodded. 'But that was five years ago.'

'I do not pretend to any greater enlightenment than you do. My brother has, however, sent a note asking for my advice, which is an entirely unprecedented occurrence. I have been trying to discover the reason for this occurrence from my sister, but she has not proved illuminating.'

Caroline caught this last sentence.

'I still think you're making a mountain out of a molehill,' she boomed.

'You said that twice about my son,' said Mr March. He was silent for a moment, then turned to me with a sad, friendly and trusting smile. 'I rely on you for the discretion and kindness you have always shown towards my family.'

The second bell sounded, and Mr March began to walk into the theatre. He said to me:

'I should be obliged if you would find my son's wife. I should like a word with her.'

I brought Ann to him in the aisle of the stalls. Without any explanation, he asked her:

'Do you still see Ronald Porson?'

'Do you know him?' she asked.

'Do you still see him?'

'Very occasionally.'

He began to ask her another question, something about Ronald Porson and Getliffe, in a voice which had become low but intensely angry. As he did so, the lights of the theatre were dimming, and Ann left to find her seat.

After the play was over, when we stood outside the theatre, Mr March was no calmer. He did not attempt to ask more questions, he just let his temper go. It was raining, the fleet of cars in which his party had arrived could not get round to the front of the theatre. Mr March watched car after car drive up to the pavement, and his temper grew worse.

'In former days,' he complained, 'there wasn't this congestion of owner-drivers from the suburbs. Owner-drivers are making the town intolerable for genuine inhabitants. A genuine inhabitant used to be able to reckon on returning to his house within a quarter of an hour of being disgorged from any suitable place of entertainment.'

The cars did not arrive: Mr March borrowed an umbrella from the commissionaire and went out into the middle of the road. The lights of taxis, golden bars on the wet asphalt, lit him up as he looked furiously round. Drivers honked at him as he stamped in front of them back to the theatre steps.

'It's intolerable,' he cried. 'They're taking my night's rest away from me now. They're changing everything under my feet, and I'm too old to change my ways. I suppose my existence has been prolonged unnecessarily already. Though Lionel Hart didn't think so, when he had a blood transfusion on his seventy-eighth birthday. They're changing everything under my feet.' He thudded the umbrella point against the pavement. 'I remarked at dinner-time, when I was under the illusion that I had completed seventy years without disaster, about not wanting to be reminded of the unpleasant circumstances which afflicted me when I was young. But when you're young you don't lose your sleep at night on account of your attachments. When you begin to do that, it makes you realise that you have lived too long.'

CHAPTER XXIX

REASSURANCE

THE morning after his birthday party, Mr March rang me up: would I be good enough to spare him an hour of my time, as soon as I could arrange it without prejudice to my duties? I went round to Bryanston Square immediately, and was taken into Mr March's study. I had not entered that room since the night he interrogated Ann.

'I appreciate your courtesy in visiting me without delay,' said Mr March. His eyes were bloodshot and the skin under them had darkened in the last few hours. 'I have to apologise, of course, for trespassing on your valuable time, but you are the only person whose opinion is of any appreciable value to me in the present regrettable circumstances. Owing to your acquaintance with the fellow Getliffe, and other factors which I need not specify.'

He had already been out to see Philip that morning; Philip was in bed and in pain, and had not been able to present all the facts. One thing, however, was clear to Mr March. Philip had now become certain about the nature of Herbert Getliffe's transactions, some time before Katherine's wedding. There was no doubt in Philip's mind that Getliffe had, while giving legal advice to a ministry, acquired knowledge in advance of a government contract. Getliffe had known that the contract was going to the firm of Howard & Hazlehurst; his relations had duly bought large holdings. That had happened. On the main points Porson had been right, though he had muddled some of the details.

That story would not by itself have worried Mr March. It was a piece of sharp practice by a rising barrister, but it was seven years old. By this time the Marches had completely accepted Francis Getliffe. There were, however, other stories which worried Mr March much more.

The first was that 'obnoxious propagandists', as Mr March kept referring to them, were passing the word round that a similar leakage had just occurred, and that Getliffe and his friends were again involved. According to Sir Philip, this news was going round the lobbies and clubs; it was still secret but there was a threat that it would soon break.

The second story was that not only Getliffe and his friends were involved, but so were several junior ministers. Philip had been taken back into the government the year before, into the same parliamentary secretaryship he had held for a few months in 1929. On Friday nights he had loved gossiping like a man in office, mentioning his colleagues' names. The 'obnoxious propagandists' were now mentioning some of those names, including that of Hawtin, one of the ablest youngish men in the government. They were being brought into the scandal. 'It's like another Marconi case,' said Mr March, harking back to a time when he felt more at home.

Philip had told him that among the names being mentioned was Philip's own.

Mr March was puzzled and distressed, more lost than angry. He would have liked to explode into rage, and dismiss the scandal as 'mischievous nonsense invented by agitators for their own purposes'. He had begun so, that morning: but stopped suddenly when he found Sir Philip fretted and impatient.

'I have never seen my brother Philip so much affected by any incident in his public life,' said Mr March. 'I was inclined at first to attribute his depressed state to his disease, but I was forced to realise that he is sick in mind apart from his physical discomfort. I had never realised that he was capable of being sick in mind. From the earliest time I can remember, I always envied him as not being vulnerable to the weaknesses that afflicted me.'

He was profoundly shaken at having to console Philip – Philip, whom throughout their lives he had thought self-sufficient. He went on:

'I do not profess to understand why he should take this criminal nonsense so much to heart. I did not need to be assured by my eldest brother that he had not taken advantage of his official position. But he was sufficiently over-wrought to insist on assuring me that he had completely given up any speculation of any kind whatsoever since he re-entered the government and that he had not made a single purchase of stock for the last twelve months.'

Philip had said that he did not know whether the stories of Herbert Getliffe's recent coups were true or not. Mr March was mystified by these stories, and so was I. Was there anything in them?

It was in both our minds how Philip had taken action against Getliffe at the time of Katherine's marriage.

I promised Mr March that I would try to find out what Getliffe had been up to. That morning, I did not need to remind him that it was not such an easy job for me as it would have been once. My name no longer appeared along with the others, at the foot of Getliffe's staircase. During my half-weeks in London, I was a consultant to an industrial firm.

I promised also that I would try to find out who was spreading the gossip, and why.

I began to realise that, of all Mr March's anxieties, that was the deepest. From all he had picked up, the gossip had originated with people who were familiar with Getliffe and his circle. Perhaps they were familiar with Sir Philip and his colleagues too: that did not seem so clear. It sounded like Ronald Porson: yet the scandal had, according to Philip, been started by the extreme left. It was not just malicious gossip, it was no more nor less than a piece of politics, he said. From what Mr March had heard of Porson, that ruled him out.

Mr March concealed his thoughts from me: but after a time I had no doubt – he was dark with a suspiciousness that seemed quite unrealistic, with a fear that seemed on the edge of paranoia – that he was thinking of Ann.

It was this fear, I was sure next day, that drove him to see Charles.

I had promised to make enquiries about Getliffe within twenty-four hours and return to Bryanston Square for dinner on the night following; when I arrived, I found Mr March and Charles alone in the drawing-room. There was a silence as though neither had spoken for some minutes. Mr March roused himself, and said: 'I asked my son to join us for dinner. As you see, he has found it possible to do so.'

Charles said:

'It happens to be a good night for me, Mr L. My partner is always at home on Wednesdays.'

Mr March did not reply. Charles looked at me with a frown, enquiring and concerned. It was clear that Mr March had not yet spoken.

We went into the dining-room with little conversation. Charles made an effort to get Mr March talking, and himself told a story of Katherine: Mr March sat absently at the head of the table.

Suddenly, Mr March said:

'Lewis, I should like to learn the results of your investigations.'

'I'm afraid they haven't got anywhere yet,' I said. 'Herbert Getliffe is out of London. He'll be back early next week, and I've arranged to see him then. I'm also trying to see Porson on the same day.'

Mr March inclined his head.

'I know that in the circumstances you will not permit any unnecessary delay.' He turned to Charles. 'You realise what I am referring to?'

'I haven't the slightest idea,' said Charles.

'It is desirable that I should enlighten you,' said Mr March. 'My brother Philip is being attacked by scurrilous gossip from various sources. This attack appears to be aimed at his personal honour and his public position. It is connected, in some way about which I am not in a position to give you precise details, with the speculations of my son-in-law Francis Getliffe's brother. Anyone in my family will recollect a previous occasion on which that subject exercised a certain importance. My brother Philip is being attacked for similar malpractices, though in his case they would be more reprehensible, since they would imply that he took advantage of his official position for these purposes.'

Mr March stopped, then asked in a loud harsh voice: 'I wish to ask you, what do you know of these attacks?'

'Nothing. Nothing whatever,' said Charles. His tone was unresentful, almost amused, and utterly candid. 'They sound very improbable.'

Mr March's relief was manifest and radiant. Then his face darkened again.

'I take it, your wife is still active politically?'

Charles looked surprised; it was years since they had argued over Ann's beliefs: in those days, Mr March had spoken as though her politics were academic. Nevertheless Charles replied at once:

'Yes, she is.'

'I am very sorry to hear it.'

Mr March was looking absent and sombre again.

Charles said, in a considerate, respectful but unyielding tone:

'I ought to say that I think she's doing good most of the time.'

By that year, men like Charles and Francis Getliffe and me had not much doubt about what was in store. It seemed to us that there was no choice except a war with Hitler – or rather that any other choice was going to be worse than the war. That conviction was separating us from our elders, even those we liked, such as Mr March and Sir Philip.

In the struggle, which was growing bitter, we felt that Ann and her party were on our side. While Sir Philip went confidently about Whitehall and talked to the family on Friday nights as though their world were invulnerable, placid, and permanent. Both he and Mr March were men of judgment: they were more detached and realistic than most of their class: they were Jews. But they could not believe what was coming. To us, they seemed often not to care.

Mr March did not reply to Charles, but asked abruptly:

'What does your wife know of these attacks?'

'I should think as little as I do.' Charles's tone was once more open and candid, so candid that Mr March was entirely reassured.

Charles asked for the full story, and Mr March told it him: as he spoke, Mr March's manner had become animated, but he finished:

'I must impress on you that my brother Philip takes this with the utmost seriousness. My first inclination was not to give it serious attention. But my brother's demeanour made me adopt a different attitude.'

'I don't understand him,' said Charles. 'It wouldn't be hard to make up a good many kinds of attack on Uncle Philip: but, if I'd been thinking of something improbable, I couldn't have invented anything as improbable as this.' He was speaking light-heartedly. He asked more questions about Getliffe, some of them sarcastic, so that Mr March chuckled. He went on: 'About Uncle Philip – aren't all people in public life absurdly sensitive to the slightest breath of criticism? Isn't that the explanation? Don't you really think that Uncle Philip sticks his press cuttings into an album every morning before he gets up? If you are as interested as that in your public personality, it must be uncomfortable when people are black-guarding you – even on singularly fantastic grounds. It's that kind of discomfort he's frightened of, don't you admit it?'

Mr March broke into laughter. He had become carefree in a way that made his black anxiety of a quarter of an hour before difficult to bring back to mind. He was, in fact, carefree as I had not seen him in his son's presence for years past. The last few minutes – after Charles showed his ignorance of the attacks – had seemed like the first days I saw them together. Mr March's cares were dispelled; he grinned at his son's teasing, he paid it back with teasing of his own. It was like old days. As we said good-night, Mr March remarked cheerfully to Charles: 'You're making a frightful ass of yourself, living in your unsalubrious abode by the river. I refuse to accept any responsibility for the effects on your health. But I'm always glad to see you in my house.'

CHAPTER XXX

A WALK FROM BRYANSTON SQUARE TO PIMLICO

It was a fine, warm night, and Charles and I decided to walk home. I had a house in Chelsea by this time, and so we could go the same way. As we crossed over to the park, Charles said:

'You'd heard all this commotion about Uncle Philip before?'

I told him that it had begun at the birthday party. 'It's a curious story,' he said.

He was not actively interested. He was sorry that Philip should be disturbed, but he did not feel himself involved. I thought of asking him to mention it to Ann, and considered that it was wiser not to. Soon he changed the subject.

The night air was soft, the park was spotted with couples lying mouth-to-mouth. We walked slowly, tired and comfortably relaxed. With the pleasure of an old intimacy, we talked as we had not done for years. Of our marriages, so different in all that had happened to us and yet both childless. 'Yes,' said Charles, with comradeship, 'it will be sad if neither of us leaves a son to follow him.'

We talked of our careers, and for the first time Charles told me how he felt about being a doctor. We had just left the park, and were waiting to cross the road near St George's. Cars were hooting by, and Charles had to pause until he could make himself heard.

'Often I've disliked it strongly, of course,' he said. 'More often I've found it extremely dull. You'd expect so, wouldn't you? There's a fair amount of human interest, of course, but one's got to be patient to get even that. A G.P. isn't dealing continually with crises of life and death, you know. Nine-tenths of his time he's seeing people with colds and nerves and indigestion and rheumatism. That's the basis of the job, and if you're looking for human interest, people exhibit slightly less of it when they've a bad cold than when they haven't.'

As we walked down Grosvenor Place, Charles went on:

'A doctor has his moments, but most of his time it can't be interesting. It just can't. The percentage of ordinary workaday tedium is bound to be high. And I suspect that's true of any job, isn't it? One always hears them described with their high moments heightened a bit; it's nice to hear, but it's quite different when you begin living them. Don't you agree? Don't you admit that's true? Look, Lewis, you possess a great capacity for getting interest out of what you're doing: I've never met anyone with a greater: but tell the truth, isn't your own job – aren't the various jobs you've tackled – mostly tedious when you come to live them?'

We argued for a time. Charles said:

'Anyway, doctoring is tedious for nine hours out of every ten. Anyone who tells you it isn't either doesn't know what excitement is or suffers from an overdose of romantic imagination. And for me it's also tedious in rather a different way. I don't think you'll sympathise much with this. But I mean that it doesn't give me anything hard to bite on mentally. I've got a taste for thinking: but I shouldn't be any worse a doctor if I were a much more stupid man.'

Since we began our walk, he had been talking without guard. He was not trying to protect or disguise himself, and at this point he did not attempt to conceal his intellectual arrogance, his certainty of his own intellectual power, his regret as he felt that power rusting.

'So you see,' Charles gave a smile, 'I'm resigned to being distinctly bored for the rest of my life.'

'But there are compensations,' I said.

'Yes,' said Charles, 'there are compensations.

'There are compensations,' he repeated. 'Each month I count up my earnings very carefully. Last month I made over eighty pounds – if they all pay me. You've no idea how pleasant it is to earn your own living. It's a pleasure you can only really appreciate if you've been supported in luxury ever since you were born.' He smiled broadly, and added:

'There are other compensations too. People show such confidence in one. It's nice to be able to justify that sometimes. Once or twice in the last few weeks I've felt some use.'

We had crossed in front of Victoria Station and came out into Wilton Road. I asked:

'Charles, if you had your time again, would you make the same choice?'

'Without any doubt,' he said.

I looked at him under the light of a street lamp. He had become older than any of us. He was carrying a mackintosh; he was stooping more than he used to. At that moment – while he was saying, his eyes glinting maliciously at his own expense: 'If I had my time again, I might not even take quite so long to make up my mind' – I was moved back to the evening in Regent Street long ago, when we argued about goodness. I felt the shock that assails one as one suddenly sees an intimate in a transfiguring light, the shock of utter familiarity and utter surprise. Here was Charles, whom I knew so well, whom I took for granted with the ease of a long friendship – and at the same time, I was thinking with incredulity, as though I had never met him before, what a curious choice he had made.

In Antrobus Street the light was glowing over the nightbell. We said good-night in front of his house, and I began to walk west along the Embankment. The night was so caressingly warm that I wanted to linger, looking at the river. There was an oily swell on the dark water, and on the swell the bands of reflected light slowly swayed. I could see the red and green eyes of lamps on the bridges up the river. I stayed there, watching the bands of light sway on the water, and, as I watched, among the day-dreams drifting through my mind were memories and thoughts about Charles.

The river smell was carried on a breath of air. Down towards Chelsea the water glistened and a red light flashed. Leaning on the Embankment, I thought that, in a different time, when the conscience of the rich was not so sick, Charles might not have sacrificed himself, at least not so completely. Some of his abnegation one could attribute to his time, just as some of his surface quirks, his outbursts of arrogance and diffidence, one could attribute to his being born a Jew.

But none of that seemed to me to matter very much, compared with what I thought I had seen in him, walking in the Wilton Road half an hour before.

I thought I had seen a nature which, at the deepest, was never sure of love. Never sure of receiving it: perhaps never sure of giving it: vulnerable and at the same time resenting any approach.

It was the kind of nature which could have broken his life – for men with that flaw at the root often spend their lives in pursuing unrequited love, or indulging their cruelty on others, or tormenting themselves with jealousy, or retiring into loneliness and spiritual pride. But in Charles this deepest self was housed in a temperament in all other respects strong, active, healthy, full of vigour. It was that blazing contrast which I had seen, or imagined that I had seen.

Perhaps it was that contrast which made him want to search for the good.

He had always been fascinated by the idea of goodness. Was it because he was living constantly with a part of himself which he hated? To know what goodness means, perhaps one needs to have laid awake at night, hating one's own nature. The sweet, the harmonious, the untempted, have no reason to hate their natures: it is the others, the guilty or the sadic – it seemed to me at that time most of all the sadic, though later I shouldn't have been too certain – who are driven to find what goodness is.

But men like Charles did not find it in themselves. It was not as easy as all that. He wanted to be good; so his active nature led him to want to' do good. He was living a useful life now – but that was all. No one felt that as a result he had reached a state of goodness: he never felt it for a moment himself. He knew that, with his insight and sarcastic honesty. He would have liked to feel goodness in himself – he would have liked to believe that others felt it. But he knew that in fact others often felt a sense of strain, because he was acting against part of his nature. They did not feel he was apt for a life of abnegation. They distrusted his conscience, and looked back with regret to the days before it dominated him – to the days, indeed, in which they remembered him as gay, malicious, idle, brilliant.

I looked down at the water, not wanting to drag myself away. I had never felt more fond of him, and into my thoughts there flickered and passed scenes in which he had taken part, the night of our examination years before, quarrels in Bryanston Square, a glimpse of him walking with his arm round Ann. I thought I had seen in him that night some of the goodness he admired. But not in the way he had searched for it. Instead, there was a sparkle of good in the irony with which he viewed his own efforts; in the disillusioned certainty with which he knew that he at least was right to be useful, that he could have chosen no other way, even if it now seemed prosaic, lacking in the radiance which others attained by chance.

Most of all there was a sparkle of good in the state to which his struggle with his own nature had brought him. He could still hate himself. Through that hatred, and not through his conscience, through the nights when he had lain awake darkened by remorse, he had taken into his blood the sarcastic astringent experience of life which shone out of him as he comforted another's self-approach and lack of self-forgiveness.

CHAPTER XXXI

A SUCCESS AND A FAILURE

I DID not see Mr March again before the day I had arranged to meet Herbert Getliffe, but I received an anxious note, saying that he hoped I would persevere with my enquiries and relieve his mind as soon as I had information. The lull of reassurance was over and his worry was nagging at him again. There were few states more infectious than anxiety, I thought, as I walked through the courts to Getliffe's chambers, with an edge to my own nerves.

There he was, sitting at his great desk, where I had sat beside him often enough. Four briefs were untied in front of him; on a side table stood perhaps thirty more, these neatly stacked and the pink ribbons tied. I caught sight of a lavish fee on the top one – it might not have been accidental that it was that fee a visitor could see.

For two or three minutes after I was shown in, Getliffe stared intently at the brief he was studying. His brow was furrowed, his neck stiff with concentration; he was the model of a man absorbed. This was a new mannerism altogether. At last he looked up.

'Heavens, you're here, are you, L.S.?' He said. 'I'm afraid I was so completely up to the eyes that I just didn't realise. Well, it's good to see you, L.S.'

I asked him how his practice was going since he took silk.

'I mustn't grumble,' said Getliffe, sweeping an arm towards the briefs on the side table. 'No, I mustn't grumble. It was a grave decision to take; I should like you to remember what a grave decision it was. I could have rubbed on for ever as a junior, and it would have kept me in shoe-leather' – his dignity cracked for a second – 'and the occasional nice new hat.' Then he settled himself even more impressively. 'But two considerations influenced me, L.S. I thought of the increased chances it would give one to help promising young men get a foot up on the ladder. One could be more useful to a lot more young men. Young men in the position you were, when you first came looking for a friendly eye. You remember how I told you, I thought of you personally, L.S., when I was making the decision. You know how much I like helping brilliant young men. Perhaps that was the most important consideration. The other was that one owes a duty to one's profession and if one can keep oneself alive as a counsel of His Majesty, one ought not to refuse the responsibility.'

No one could have enjoyed it more, I thought. No one could have more enjoyed throwing himself into this serious, senatorial part. He added: 'Of course, if one keeps one's head above water, one gets certain consolations for the responsibility. I'm thankful to say that has happened so far.' He chuckled. 'I haven't had to cut off my evening glass of beer. And it's fun to take my wife round the town and order a dollop of champagne without doing sums in the head.' He was in triumphant form. He felt he was going to arrive. He kept giving me heavy homilies, such as were due from a man of weight. He believed them, just as he believed in everything he said while he was saying it.

After a time I said:

'By the way, I came to ask you something.'

'If there is any help I can give you, L.S.,' said Getliffe, 'you have only to ask. Ask away.'

'You remember the trouble that happened just before your brother's wedding?'

'What trouble?'

'Rumours were going round about some investments in Howard & Hazlehurst.'

Getliffe looked at me sternly.

'Who are Howard & Hazlehurst?' he said.

He seemed to believe that he had forgotten. I reminded him of our conversation that evening in chambers, when he was frightened that Porson would expose the deal.

'I remember it vaguely,' said Getliffe. He went on reprovingly: 'I always thought that you exaggerated the danger. You're a bit too highly strung for the rough and tumble, you know. I think you were very wise to remove yourself most of your time to a place with ivy round the walls. One has to be very strong for this kind of life.' He paused. 'Yes, I remember it vaguely. I'm sorry to say that poor old Porson has gone right down the hill since then.'

'I wanted to ask you,' I said, 'if you'd heard that some similar rumours were going round now.'

'I have been told of some nonsense or other,' said Getliffe in a firm and confident tone. 'They appear to be saying that I used inside knowledge last year. I've ignored it so far: but if they go on I shall have to protect myself. One owes a duty to one's position.'

'Have they the slightest excuse to go on?'

'I shouldn't let everyone ask me that question, L.S.,' said Getliffe reproachfully. 'But we know each other well enough to pass it. You've seen me do things that I hope and believe I couldn't do nowadays. So I'll answer you. They haven't the slightest excuse, either in law or out of it. I've never had a cleaner sheet than I've had the last two years. And if I can prove these people are throwing mud, they'll find it a more expensive game than snooker.' He looked at me steadily with his brown, opaque eyes. He said:

'I can't answer for anyone else. I can't answer for March, Hawtin, or the ministerial bigwigs, but I'm glad to say that my own sheet is absolutely clean. A good deal cleaner, I might tell you, than some of our common acquaintances' about the time that you were dragging up just now. I suppose you know that old Sir Philip did himself remarkably well out of that Howard & Hazlehurst affair? He was much too slim to have anything to do with Howard & Hazlehurst, of course. No, he just bought a whole great wad in a rocky little company whose shares were down to twopence and a kiss from everyone on the board. Well, Howard & Hazlehurst took over that company six months later. They wanted it for their new contract. Those shares are now 41*s*. 6*d*. and as safe as your Aunt Fanny. Our friends in Israel must have made a packet.'

His manner became weighty again, as he went on:

'I must tell you that I strongly disapprove. I strongly disapproved when it happened, though I was a younger man then and I hadn't done as well as I have now. I don't believe anyone in an official position ought to have any dealings, that is, speculative dealings, on the Stock Exchange. And I should like to advise you against it, L.S. There must be times in your little consultancy when you gain a bit of inside knowledge that a not-too-scrupulous man could turn into money. I dare say you'd bring it off every now and then. But you'll be happier if you don't. I don't know what you collect from your little consultancy and that job of yours with the ivy round the walls. But I advise you to be content with it, whatever it is. I'm content with mine, I don't mind telling you.'

We went out for lunch. As usual, I paid. When I left him, on my way to find Porson, two thoughts were chasing each other through my mind. Getliffe was speaking the truth about his 'clean sheet' in recent years. His protests were for once innocent, not brazen; it was a luxury for him to have such a clear conscience. The rumours about him seemed to be quite false. That surprised me; but it did not surprise me anything like so much as his revelation about Sir Philip. I did not know how much to believe; remembering Mr March's report of his visit to Philip's bedside, I was sure there was something in it.

Porson had given me an address in Kensington. When I reached it, I was met by his landlady, who said that he had been called away that morning: he had left a message that he would write again and fix another rendezvous. The house was shabby-genteel, the landlady was suspicious of me, on guard for Porson; he was living in a flat up the third flight of shabby stairs.

I called on friends who might have heard the gossip – radical journalists, civil servants, barristers who knew Getliffe. Several of them had picked up the rumours, but no one told me anything new. Some were excited because there was scandal in the air. Even when one man said: 'I don't like the idea of a Dreyfus case started by the left,' his eyes were bright and glowing.

Then I told Mr March what I had found out. The rumours, I said, all referred to a leakage within the past year. I told him that Herbert Getliffe seemed not to be in any way responsible this time. If even one of these rumours was brought into the open, it looked entirely safe to sue straight away. But I also told Mr March that, though I could not see the relevance, he ought to hear Getliffe's story about Sir Philip.

Mr March listened in silence. At the end he said: 'I am deeply obliged to you for your friendly services.' His expression was not relieved, but he said: 'I may inform you that my brother Philip yesterday appeared to think that the affair was blowing over. I have always found that persons in public life become liable to a quite unwarranted optimism.' Mr March himself showed none.

I waited three weeks before I heard from Porson. Then a note came in his tall fluent hand, which said: 'I expect you have guessed what chase has kept me away from London. I will tell you about her when I meet you. I insist on going to the University match, and shall return in time for the first day. Do you feel like joining me, even though your respectable friends may see us there and count it against you?'

I found him on the first morning, sitting on the top of the stand at the Nursery end. I had not seen him for two years, and I was shocked by the change. Under his eyes, screwed up in the sunlight, the pouches were embossed, heavy, purplish-brown. His colour was higher and more plethoric than ever, and the twitch convulsed his face every time he spoke. His suit was old, shiny at the cuffs, but he was wearing a carnation in his buttonhole and an Authentic tie. He welcomed me with a hearty aggressive show of pleasure. 'Ah well, my boy, I'm glad you haven't boycotted me. I need some company, the way these people are patting about.' His face twitched as he looked irascibly out to the pitch. 'It's going to be bloody dull. I hope it won't mean your being crossed off many visiting lists if some of your friends notice you're here with me. Anyway, it's bloody good to see you.'

We sat there in the sun most of that day. In his loud, resonant, angry voice Porson told me of his misfortunes. Three years before, he had lost the Passant case, with Herbert Getliffe leading for the other side. He had never worked up a steady practice. But he persuaded himself that, until that time, he was just on the point of success. Even now he could not admit that he had mismanaged the case. It was intolerable for him to remember that he had been out-manœuvred by Getliffe, on the one occasion they had been on opposite sides in court. But he could not help admitting that for three years past the solicitors had fought shy of him. He went out of his way to admit it, pressing on the aching tooth, in a loud, rancorous tone that rang round the top of the stand at Lord's.

Often his discontent vented itself on the batsmen. A young man was playing a useful, elegant innings. It was pretty cricket, but Porson was not appeased. 'What does he think he's playing at?' he demanded. 'What does he think he's doing? I insist these boys ought to be taught to hit the bloody ball.'

At the close of play we walked down to Baker Street, and Porson became quieter in the hot, calm evening, in the light which softened the faces in the streets. He confided the reason he had been away from London. A girl half his age had fallen in love with him, and they had been staying together by the sea. 'The way it began was the most wonderful thing that has ever happened to me,' he said. 'She was old ——'s secretary, and I used to borrow her sometimes. Not that I need a secretary nowadays. Ah well, she came in one morning, and I hadn't the least idea, my boy. She just threw her arms round my neck and said she loved me. I couldn't believe it, I told her that she wanted a nice young man who'd make her a decent husband. She said she wanted me. She thought that I was so clever and so masterful and so kind. And she was sure I ought to have been happy if some woman hadn't treated me badly. She thought she could make it up for me.' He looked at me with an expression humble, bewildered, incredulous. 'I tell you, my boy, I do believe she loved me a little. I've chased a few women, but I don't think that's ever happened to me before. I've been glad if they've liked me. I've been prepared to pay for my fun and when they got tired I've sent them away with a bit of jewellery and a smack on the behind.'

We walked on a few steps. He said:

'I hope I haven't done the girl any harm. She wasn't really my cup of tea. Ah well, she's not losing much. It can't matter much to anyone, losing me.'

He insisted on taking me to the Savoy and giving me a lavish dinner. I could not refuse, for fear of reminding him that now I was comfortably off and that he was living on his capital. He exulted in being generous; it gave him an overbearing pleasure to press food and drink on me. 'You can use another drink,' he kept on saying. 'And so can I. By God, we'll have another bottle of champagne.'

Soon he became drunk, vehemently drunk. He abandoned himself to hates and wishes. He boasted of the things he could still do; there was still time to gain triumphs at the Bar and, he said, 'show them how wrong they are. Show them just where their bloody intrigues and prejudices

709

have led them. Just because I'm not a pansy or a Jew they've preferred to ignore me. I tell you, my lad, you've got to be a pansy or a Jew to get a chance in this bloody country.' Drunkenly he saw lurid, romantic conspiracies directed at himself; drunkenly he talked politics. It was the crudest kind of reactionary politics, inflamed by drink, hate and failure. He talked of women: he boasted of his conquests now, instead of speaking as he had done on the way to Baker Street. Boastfully he talked of nights in the past. Yet his tongue was far less coarse than when he talked politics, less coarse than most men's when talking sex. He was a man whom people disliked for being aggressive, boastful, rancorous and vulgar; he was all those things; but, when he thought of women, he became delicate, diffident and naïf.

Throughout the day, I had not mentioned why I had written to him. Partly because I had an affection for him, and wanted him to feel I was with him for his own sake: partly because I thought it was not safe to talk while he was in a resentful mood. At last I risked asking when he had last seen Ann. He answered, gently enough, in the spring: he remembered the exact date. I went on to ask whether he knew what she was doing politically nowadays.

He stared at me with an over-intent, over-steady gaze, as though if I moved my head he might fall down. He said: 'If you want to talk about her, you'd better come to my blasted flat. It's only a temporary place, of course. I shall insist on somewhere better soon.'

As we got into the taxi, he repeated, with drunken fury:

'I shall insist on somewhere better soon. It's not the sort of place most of your friends are living in.' He went on: 'I can't talk about her until I've cooled down.'

After we had climbed the shabby stairs I looked at his little sitting-room. It was crowded with furniture. There was a glass-fronted book-case, another glass-fronted case full of china, two tables, a desk, a divan. Yet each piece was dusted and shining: I suddenly realised that he must be obsessively tidy. It might have been the room of a finicky old maid.

On the table by the divan stood a photograph of Ann. She did not photograph well. Her face looked flat, undistinguished, lifeless; there was no sign of the moulding of her cheekbones. Anyone who knew her only from this photograph would not have thought her so much as good-looking. As I turned away, I saw Porson's face. He was still looking at the picture with eyes clouded and bloodshot with drink, and his expression was rapt.

'You loved her very much, didn't you?' I said.

He did not reply immediately. Then he said:

'I still do.'

He added:

'I think I always shall.'

A little later, he said:

'I should like to tell you something. It may sound incredible to you, but I should like to tell you. I believe she'll come to me some day. She can't be happy with her husband. She's loyal, she's told me that she is happy, but I've never credited it. Anyway, she knows that I'm waiting for her if ever she wants to come. She knows that I'd do anything for her. By God, she knows that will always be true.'

He wanted us both to start drinking again, but I dissuaded him.

We sat on the divan and I led him back to my question about Ann's political actions. His face became sullen and pained.

'I never liked them, of course. But I attribute them entirely to her blasted husband. If she were really happy with him, she would have given them up. It stands to reason. If she had married me, I believe I should have made her happy, and these things wouldn't have interested her any more. I insist on attributing them to that blasted March.' He told me many facts about her, most of which I knew.

Then he told me something which I did not know – that she was one of the group that produced the *Note*. The *Note* was a private news-sheet, cyclostyled like an old-fashioned school magazine, distributed through the post, on the model of one or two others of that time. It was run by an acquaintance of mine called Humphrey Seymour; he was a communist, but he had been born into the ruling world and still moved within it. In fact, the charm of the *Note* (it was subscribed to by many who had no idea of its politics) was that its news seemed to come from right inside the ruling world. Some of the news, so Porson told me, was provided by ˙ ⁀n.

'Of course she can go anywhere,' he said. 'She was brought up in the right places, and she's got the entrée wherever she wants. And I don't put that down to the Jews, I might tell you. It's just because she makes herself liked wherever she goes.'

Ronald Porson was still doing the detective work of love; he followed her track from dinner-party to dinner-party; often he could see where she had picked up a piece of information for use in the *Note*.

'That's why I had to refuse her something for the first time in my life,' he said.

'Why?' It did not seem likely to be interesting: the heavy drunken sentiment was wearing me down.

'She's an honourable person, isn't she?'

I nodded, but he came back at me fiercely.

'I don't want to be humoured,' he shouted. 'Despite her blasted politics, isn't she the soul of honour, yes or no?'

I thought, and gave a serious answer.

'Yes.'

'And I am too, aren't I? Damn you, am I an honourable man, yes or no?'

'Yes.' Again, in a curious sense, it was dead true.

'Well then. The last time I saw her, I told you it was in the spring, she wanted to see me at short notice. That's what she'll do when she comes back to me. And she reminded me that I once found out some pretty stories about that shyster Getliffe – I found out how he'd played the markets and laughed at decent people who respect positions of trust and got away with the whole blasted shoot. Well, Ann wanted all the details. She told me – that's where her honour comes in, that's where she'd never think of going behind my back – is that true, yes or no?'

After I had answered, his voice quietened, and he said: 'She asked me for the details. She told me that she might want to use them.'

He was by this time speaking in a throbbing whisper, but it seemed loud.

'I couldn't give her them,' said Ronald Porson. He wiped trickles of sweat from his cheeks. 'I've not refused her anything before, but I couldn't do that. I didn't like refusing, but it stuck in my gullet to help that blasted group of reds. I insist they've got at her, of course. She's always had a good heart and they've taken advantage of it. I insist on putting the blame on to them and her blasted husband. And I refuse to help them impose on her. I've never said no to anything she's asked me before, but I couldn't stomach helping those reds in their blasted games. I've no use for Getliffe, he's a bloody charlatan and a bloody crook, and the sooner he's exposed the better. But I insist that the reds aren't the people to do it.' He paused. 'I was tempted when she asked me. I don't want to say no to her again. Ah well! I expect she understands.'

CHAPTER XXXII

TWO KINDS OF SELF-CONTROL

THE next morning I rang up Ann and asked if I could see her at once. The same evening I arrived at Antrobus Street at half-past six, in the middle of Charles's surgery hour. She was waiting for me in her drawing-room; outside the house was dingy, but the room struck bright. It was her own taste, I thought, as I glanced at the Dufys on the cream-papered walls. She herself looked both calm and pretty. Her first words were: 'We know what you've come for, don't we?' She gazed at me with steady blue eyes, without expression. I said:

'Do you? It will be easier if you do.'

'It can't be very easy, can it?'

'How in God's name,' I said, 'did you come to get into this mess?'

'No.' She sounded more equable and business-like than I did; she was not going to begin on those terms. 'It isn't as simple as that.'

I settled myself to wait for her.

'I suppose,' I said, 'you haven't decided what to do?'

'We're not certain yet.'

She was saying 'we' again. Business-like as she sounded, she was making it clear that Charles knew everything. She was glad to bring him in. It was the only sign of emotion she had shown so far.

'Of course,' she said, 'you've come about the Getliffe affair?'

I nodded.

'We knew it.'

'You've been mixed up in that, haven't you?' I asked.

'Oh yes.'

'Didn't you see what it was going to mean?'

She was unmoved. 'Not everything, no,' she said.

'I can't understand what you were trying to do.'

'I'm not sure,' she said, 'how much I can tell you.'

'I don't even understand what the line is,' I said.

Deliberately I was using a bit of her own jargon. She looked at me, knowing that I was not unsophisticated politically, knowing that I had an idea how 'the party' went about its work.

She began to explain, keeping back little, so far as I could judge, though some of the manœuvres still puzzled me. The 'line', she said, I ought to know: it was to get rid of this government and rally all the anti-fascists to do so, whoever they were, Churchillites, middle-of-the-roaders,

Labour people, intellectuals. Unless we did just that, this government would sell the pass altogether, she said. Unless we got rid of it, Hitler and his fascists would have power on a scale no one had had before: that meant the end of us all, liberals and men of good will, Gentiles and Jews.

'Jews first,' said Ann in a neutral tone. 'Mr March and his friends might remember that.'

She looked at me and said:

'The point is, we've got to get people acting now. You can't disagree about that, can you?'

'No,' I said. I was speaking out of conviction. 'I can't disagree with that.'

'There isn't much time,' she said.

That was where the *Note* got its orders. Its job was to damage personal credit: it was to chase any scandal anywhere near the government, or even the chance of any scandal. It was not to run straight into libels, but it would take risks that an ordinary newspaper would not. Oddly enough, it was better placed than an ordinary newspaper to collect some kinds of scandal: Ann and another colleague and Seymour himself most of all had acquaintances deep in official society, at nearly all levels except at the very top.

Yet, I began to ask her, what were they hoping for? Sending out the cyclostyled sheets – what was the circulation of the paper?

'Nineteen thousand,' she said.

'A bit of scandal going to a few thousand people – what was the use of that?'

'It helps,' she said. Once more she spoke without expression, with the absence of outward emotion which had surprised, and indeed harassed me, since I arrived. Nevertheless I felt within her a kind of satisfaction which those who only look on at politics never reach. It was a satisfaction made up of a sense of action, of love for action, and of humility. It did not occur to her to argue that the *Note*'s significance was greater than it seemed, that its public was an influential one, that what it said in its messy sheets got round. No: this was the job she had been set, and she was devoted to it. It was as humble as that.

Early in the year, she told me, someone had collected a piece of gossip about Hawtin, the man Mr March had mentioned. Hawtin, like Sir Philip, was a parliamentary secretary: but, unlike Sir Philip, he was not an old man occupying his last post, but a young one on the rise. He also happened to be a focus of detestation for the left. The gossip was that he had made money because he knew where an armaments contract was to be placed. But Seymour and his friends, Ann said, could not prove it. They could not get at him; they tried all their usual sources, but found nothing to go on. I gathered that one or two of their sources were shady, and some not so much shady as irregular in a most unexpected way: I was almost sure they had an informant in the civil service. When they were at a loss, someone discovered that Hawtin, who was a lawyer by profession, had once had business dealings with Herbert Getliffe. It was then that Ann recalled what she had heard against Getliffe years before. At once she told the stories inside the *Note* office: this had been a real scandal, she could track it down and get it tied and labelled.

'Why didn't you remember?' I said.

'What was there to remember?'

'Didn't you think how Philip March's name kept coming in, when we were all worried before Katherine's wedding?'

'I didn't give it a thought,' she replied.

'Why not?'

'I had plenty of things against him, but I could never have imagined he'd have got mixed up in a wretched business like this, could you have done?'

I took her at her word. I asked her:

'But you must have imagined that if you dug up the Getliffe affair—'

'What do you mean?'

'If you did that, it was coming close to home.'

I meant that it would damage Katherine through her husband: Ann knew what I meant, and did not pretend.

'I thought of that, of course I did. But we wanted the exact dope on Getliffe just as a lead-in to the job. It was a good time ago, I didn't think we should need to use it.'

'Did you think there was a risk?'

She looked straight at me.

'Yes, I thought there was a risk. I didn't think it was very real.'

'Are you going to use it?' I asked.

'I don't know. It's possible.'

'How possible?'

'It's just about as likely as not.'

All the time I had been with her, I had had a feeling that I scarcely knew her at all. It was not her politics that struck so strange: I expected all that. I expected her sense of duty. It was not that she had been unfriendly or ambiguous. On the contrary, she had been precise, direct, completely in command of herself. It had been I who was showing the temper and wear-and-tear. What made her seem so strange was just that control. Her voice had not even a quiver of strain. Her head had stayed erect, unnaturally still, as though the muscles of her neck were stiff.

To my astonishment, she did not know the exact position about the original Getliffe scandal. Porson had refused to tell her the details, and she had not discovered them from anyone else: when she failed, the *Note* had set another person on the same search. It was characteristic of them that she had not been told whom he had been talking to, or whether he had got all the facts. I asked again if the *Note* were going to use the story. She gave the same answer as before.

'Can it be stopped?' I broke out.

'I could go to Humphrey Seymour—'

'You'd better not waste any time.'

'I don't want to go unless it's necessary.'

She meant: this was her work, these people were her allies, it was bitter to get in their way.

'It's irresponsible,' I said, 'not to go to him at once.'

'We have different ideas of responsibility, haven't we?'

'Not so completely different,' I said. 'If your people really begin splashing Philip March's name about, you know what it will mean.'

'I haven't any special concern for Philip,' she said. 'He's a reactionary old man. If he has had his fingers in this business, then he deserves what comes to him.'

'I wasn't thinking so much of him,' I paused. 'But Mr March?'

She replied:

'You know what happened between us. Since then I haven't felt that he had any claim on me.'

I paused again. Then I said:

'Have you thought what it would mean for Charles?'

Her eyes stayed steady, looking into mine. For a second I totally misread her face. She had spoken of Mr March in a reasonable tone, but one hardened, I thought, with resentment, the memory of an injustice still fresh. Her eyes were sparkling; she seemed just about to smile. Instead her throat and cheeks reddened: her brow went smooth with anger. At last her control had broken, and she said:

'I won't tolerate any interference between Charles and me. Go and make your own wife love you as much as I love Charles. If she's capable of recognising who you are. Then I might listen to anything you say about my marriage.'

I did not speak.

Ann said: 'I'm sorry. That was an unforgivable thing to say.'

Slowly – I was not thinking of her or Charles – I replied:

'You wouldn't have said it unless—' I stopped, my own thoughts ran away with me. I made another effort: 'Unless you were afraid of what you might do to Charles.'

We both sat silent. I was leaning forward, my chin in my hands. I scarcely noticed that she had crossed the room until I felt her arm round my shoulders.

'I'm desperately sorry,' she said.

I tried to talk to her again.

'I still think,' I said, 'that you ought to speak to Seymour pretty soon.'

'It's not easy. Don't you see it's not easy?'

I told her that she would have to do it. She pressed my hand and went back to her chair. We sat opposite each other, not speaking again, until Charles came in.

She sprang up. He took her in his arms and kissed her. She asked how the surgery had gone. He told her something about a case, his arms still round her, and asked about herself. They were absorbed in each other. No one could have seen them that night without being moved by the depth and freshness of their love.

Over his shoulder Charles glanced at me, sitting in the pool of light from the reading-lamp.

'Hallo,' he said. 'You're looking pale.'

'It's nothing.'

'Are you sure?'

'I tell you, it's nothing. No, I've been talking to Ann about this Getliffe business.'

He glanced at Ann. 'I expected that was it,' he said.

They sat side by side on the sofa. Without waiting for any kind of preliminaries, I said:

'I've been telling Ann she ought to go straight to Seymour.'

To my astonishment, Charles began to smile.

'Why is that funny?' I was on edge.

'Did you know he was at school with me? It's strange, I shouldn't have guessed that he'd crop up again—'

He was still smiling at what seemed to be a memory.

'I'm quite sure,' I said, 'that Ann ought to go round to the *Note* tomorrow.'

'That's getting a bit frantic, isn't it?' Charles said, in a friendly tone.

I could not help overstating my case. 'Tomorrow,' I repeated, getting more emphatic because I could not find a reason.

'You don't want to go along unless it's the last resort, do you?' said Charles to Ann, and their eyes met in trust.

The curious thing was, Charles did not seem much worried. Ann was so torn that she had said something I should not be able to forget. That apart, I was acutely anxious. Yet Charles, who was himself given to anxiety, who had much more foresight than most men, seemed almost immune from what was affecting us. True, he was much further from politics than Ann was, a good deal further than I was myself. Nevertheless, it was strange to see him so unruffled, giving us the drinks which, in the grip of the argument, Ann had not thought of. With a kind of temperate irritation, he said:

'I must say, the thing which I really dislike is that we misled Mr L. Quite unintentionally, of course, but it's the sort of thing any of us would dislike, wouldn't they?'

He meant, when Mr March told him of the rumours about Sir Philip and he had said that neither he nor Ann had any knowledge of them. It had been true then: at the time, Ann was trying to find out about Getliffe and no one but Getliffe. But it would not have been true a week or two later.

'I've explained the position to him now, of course,' he said.

'Did he accept it?' I asked.

'As much as he could accept anything,' said Charles.

'When did you talk to him?'

Charles gave me the date. I had seen Mr March since, but he had not mentioned a word about it.

'I also explained Ann's connection with the *Note*,' said Charles. 'I thought it was right to do that.'

For a few seconds it was all quiet. Then Ann said to him: 'Look, if you think Lewis is right and I ought to tell the *Note* about it—'

'It means making a private plea, doesn't it? And you wouldn't want to unless it's really dangerous?'

'Of course I shouldn't want to.' She added, talking to him as though I was not there: 'I'll do it tomorrow if you think I ought to.'

Suddenly I felt that she wanted him to tell her to. He was hesitating. He could have settled it for her, but he seemed reluctant or disinclined.

He knew, of course, better than I did, how much political action, the paper itself, meant to her. But it was not only consideration and empathy which held him back. Nearly all the Marches, seeing his hesitation, would have had no doubt about it: he was under her influence, she was the stronger, he did what she told him.

The truth was just the opposite. Often he behaved to her, as now, with what seemed to many people an exaggerated consideration, a kind of chivalry which made one uncomfortable. But the reason was not that he was her slave, but that she was his. She adored him: at the heart of their marriage she was completely in his power. It was out of a special gratitude, it was to make a kind of amend, that he was driven to consider her so, in things which mattered less.

To understand his hesitation just then, one needed to have been present that night when Mr March accused her of 'wearing the trousers' – and Charles's smile, unpredictable as forked lightning, lit up the room.

'If you think I ought to,' she said.

'You mustn't decide anything now,' he said, with deliberation, with careful sense. 'But there might be a time when you'll have to, mightn't there?'

CHAPTER XXXIII

SUMMER NIGHT

AFTER that night I did not hear whether Ann had made her explanations to the *Note*. On my way down to Haslingfield, a fortnight later, I took with me a file of the paper: I wanted to know what legal risks they ran.

It was on a Saturday afternoon that I arrived at Haslingfield. I found Mr March occupied with Katherine's children, telling me that he had had no fresh news from Philip and at the same time rolling a ball along the floor for his grandson to run after. It was a wet, warm summer day and the windows of the drawing-room stood open. The little boy was aged four, and his fair hair glistened as he scampered after the ball. His sister, aged two, was crawling round Mr March's legs. Mr March rolled the ball again, and told them they were 'making frightful asses of themselves'.

Gazing at them, Mr March said to Katherine and me:

'I must say they look remarkably Anglo-Saxon.'

Each of the children had the March eyes, and Mr March seemed to be hoping that they would stay blond.

Mr March went on:

'They look remarkably unlike the uglier members of our family.

Hannah says that everyone in the family is more presentable when young, but I told her that she must have forgotten Caroline's children in their infancy.'

Katherine chuckled. She and her father were not only becoming fonder of each other, but the bond of sympathy between them seemed to grow stronger each time I saw them. She was pregnant again, and he had insisted that she came to Haslingfield during July, 'on the firm undertaking', as he wrote to her, 'that you attempt to run the household, though I have never concealed my lack of faith in your abilities in that direction, until a date when your attention is distracted by other developments'.

Actually, she ran the household so that it was more comfortable than I remembered: since her marriage, she had cultivated a talent for comfort. Not even Mr March kept a closer eye on one's physical whims, frailties, likes and dislikes.

That evening, as we waited before dinner for Mr March, I was presented with a Moselle which she had noticed me enjoy on my first visit to Haslingfield, when Charles and Ann were within a few hours of meeting.

Katherine said: 'You remember that night, don't you, Lewis? I was tremendously excited because Francis was coming next day. And you made a remark which might have meant that you guessed I was in love. I lay awake a bit that night wondering whether you really intended it. Francis says that was probably the only sleep he's ever cost me. But I remind him that it was only for about an hour.'

She was content. Her third child was due in early August; with Mr March-like precision, she announced the probable day with a margin of error plus or minus. Also like Mr March, she harried her doctors, wanted to know the reasons for their actions, and would not be put off by bedside patter. Francis had told me some stories about her which were very much in her father's line, full of the same physical curiosity and the same assumption that a doctor is someone whose time you pay for, and whose advice you consider rather as you would an electrician's when he brings a new type of bulb. 'I don't believe you treat doctors in her fashion,' Francis had said, 'unless you have been born scandalously rich.'

Katherine denied it. But as a rule she was content to follow his lead. Just as she had once accepted her brother's opinions, now she accepted her husband's. She had resisted everyone's attempts to educate her: first Charles's, and then Francis's, with some irregular incursions of my own.

Yet I often felt that she had matured faster than any of us. In a way singularly like her father's after he retired from business, she had become at twenty-seven completely, solidly, and happily herself.

Her anxieties now were all about her children. Her self-conscious moments were so mild that she laughed at them. After one of her dinner parties she would keep Francis awake wondering if a remark of hers had been misunderstood, and why a pair of guests left at a quarter past ten; she worked round and round her speculations with the family persistence; the habit remained but the edge had gone.

On this night at Haslingfield, though she kept saying every ten minutes: 'Charles promised to ring up about coming down tomorrow. I'm getting into a state. It will be intolerable if he forgets,' it was nothing but the residue of the old habit.

At last the telephone bell rang in the hall, and the butler told her that Mr Charles was asking for her. Having seen her run to the telephone so many times, I found it strange to wait while she walked upright, slow, eight months gone.

Katherine returned and said that Charles was hoping to come down for dinner on the following night, but would have to get back to London to sleep. 'Whether that's because of his practice or Ann I couldn't tell,' she said. 'I should think it's because of Ann, shouldn't you?' Her face became thoughtful and hard. For a moment she looked set, determined, middle-aged. 'That takes me back again to the first time you came here. You realise that I invited Ann specially for you, don't you? I definitely hoped you'd make a match of it. I thought she might be attractive enough to distract you from Sheila. I never thought of her for Charles at all.' She looked at me intently. 'Well, Lewis, my dear, I believe my scheme might have been better for everyone. I know I oughtn't to talk about Sheila, but you must realise that your friends hate to see her eating your life away. And on the other hand, if you had married Ann, you would have kept her in order. She wouldn't have tried to make a different man of you as she's tried with Charles. Yes, it would have been better if my scheme had come off.'

The warm, wet wind lashed round the house all Sunday, and I spent the whole day indoors. In the morning I talked for an hour with Mr March alone. He said that Philip was now convinced that the gossip had blown itself out, and accordingly did not consider it worth while to discuss 'ancient history' in the shape of the Howard & Hazlehurst dealings in 1929. Mr March was left apprehensive. I wished I could have told him that Ann and Charles had settled his worries. But I did say that there might be good news for him soon.

After lunch I sat in the library reading the file of the *Note* which I had brought down. The issues ran from the middle of 1935 to the week before; I read with attention, forgetting the beat of rain against the windows and the howl of the wind. I found nothing in the way of a financial accusation, except one tentative hint. But there was a series of facts, bits of personal information, quoted sayings, about people in the circles where Sir Philip moved, the circles of junior ministers, permanent secretaries, chairmen of large firms. Some of the facts I recognised, and I had heard some of the sayings: I knew them to be accurate.

I had tea brought up to the library, and went on reading. In some numbers it was not hard to guess which pieces of information Ann had brought in. Occasionally I thought I could see the hands of other acquaintances. I was making notes, for I thought there was no harm in being prepared, when Katherine came in with Charles. 'He's just driven down through this wretched rain,' she said. 'I told him you'd been appallingly unsociable all afternoon.'

Charles came over to my chair and saw what I was reading. 'I didn't know he had such a passion for political information, did you?' he said to Katherine.

He seemed quite untroubled.

'Have you noticed,' he asked me, 'how many of their predictions actually come off?'

'Too many,' I said.

He turned to Katherine. 'Ann does a good deal for it, did you realise that?' He spoke casually, but with affection and pride.

'I take the rag,' said Katherine, 'but I hadn't the slightest idea.'

'I don't suppose you read it,' Charles teased her. 'Do you make Francis read it aloud in bed? Don't you agree that's the only way you ever hear anything at all?'

Mr March had come into the room behind them.

'I assume that your meditations have been completely disturbed by my family,' he said to me. 'I suggest that it would be considerably less sepulchral in the drawing-room. I don't remember such a July since Hannah came to stay in 1912. She said that she wouldn't have noticed the weather so much in her own house, but that didn't prevent her from outstaying her invitation.'

There were only a few minutes before dinner when I could talk to Charles alone. No, he said, Ann had not yet appealed to Seymour. No, so far as Ann knew, the *Note* had not found any usable facts about Getliffe or anyone else. Yes, she would call the *Note* off for good and all; she was seeing Seymour next week; there was nothing to worry about.

All evening the talk was gay and friendly. Charles showed how glad he was to meet Katherine; he was demonstratively glad, more so than she. His manner to his father was easy, as though they had come together again after all that had happened – come together, not as closely as in the past, but on a new friendly footing where neither of them was making much demand. It was Charles's wish that they should stay like this.

Mr March responded at dinner, more brilliantly even than when I last saw him and Charles together. It was the suspicious and realistic, I thought, who were most easy to reassure. It was the same in love: the extravagantly jealous sometimes needed only a single word to be transported into absolute trust.

Keeping up his liveliness Mr March told a story of someone called Julian Baring, 'a man I like very much if I am not under the obligation of meeting him'. Then I discovered at last the secret of Mr March's Sunday night attire. The first time I went to Haslingfield, I had noticed with astonishment that on the Sunday night he wore a dinner jacket over his morning trousers and waistcoat. I had stayed there on a good many Sundays since, and I found this to be his invariable custom. Somehow I had never been able to enquire why, but this evening I did, and learned, through Mr March's protestations, shouts, stories, and retorts to his children, that it was his way of lessening the servants' Sunday work. The servants, as I knew, were always Gentiles. Mr March thought it proper that they should go to church on Sunday evening: and he felt that they would get there quicker if they had to put out only his jacket instead of a whole suit.

We went on talking of the March servants. All of them, like Mr March's, were Gentiles. They moved from house to house within the family (for instance, Mr March's butler had started as a footman in Sir Philip's house). They seemed to become more snobbish about the family reputation than the Marches themselves. When Katherine married Francis some of them protested to her maid – what a comedown it was! To them it was shameful that she had not made a brilliant match. They thought back with regret to the days when the March households had been full of opulent, successful guests. Mr March's servants in particular could not forgive Charles and Katherine for bringing to Bryanston Square and Haslingfield no one but young men like Francis and myself, without connections, without wardrobes, instead of the titles, the money, the clothes, which brought a thrill into their lives and which they felt in a position to expect.

Most of these accounts came through Katherine's maid. Mr March guffawed as he heard them, but with a nostalgia of his own.

We listened, as we could not help doing that month, to the nine o'clock news. When the items about the Spanish war had finished, Charles switched off the wireless and both he and I were silent. Mr March looked at us, becoming irascible as he saw our concern. He said loudly:

'I say, a plague on both your houses.'

'You don't really say that,' said Charles. 'It wouldn't be quite so dangerous if you did.'

'I repeat,' retorted Mr March, 'it's six of one and half a dozen of the other.'

'It's as clear an issue,' said Charles, 'as we shall have in our time.'

'You're only indulging in this propaganda,' cried Mr March, 'because of the influence of your connections.'

'No,' I put in. 'I should say exactly the same. I'm afraid I should say more, Mr L. I believe this is only the beginning. The next ten or twenty years aren't going to be pretty.'

'You're all succumbing to a bad attack of nerves,' said Mr March.

Charles said with a grin:

'I don't think so. But remember I've got some reason to be nervous. If it does come to the barricades, Ann will insist, of course, on fighting herself. But she'll also insist on making me fight too.'

Katherine and I laughed, but Mr March merely smiled with his lips. He was preoccupied; his voice, instead of being animated, went flat, as though the mind behind it was being dragged away, dragged from question to question. Charles rose to go. He said goodbye affectionately to his father, and very warmly to Katherine, whom he did not expect to see until her child was born; I went down with him to his car. It was still raining, and a wild night. Charles was in a hurry to get back home by midnight, as he had promised Ann. I mentioned that I wanted to have another word with her, and he said, casually and in entire friendliness, how much she would like that. Then he drove off. I stood for some moments watching the tail-lamp of his car dwindling down the drive.

The next day passed quietly until the late evening. The afternoon was a fine interval among the storms, and I walked in the grounds. When I returned for tea, I found a professional letter had just arrived, which occupied me for a couple of hours. I noticed, without giving it a second thought, that the same post had brought Katherine one or two letters, as well as her daily one from Francis.

After dinner, when we moved into the drawing-room, Katherine rested on a sofa. Mr March was talking to her about her children. Both of them gained satisfaction from providing against unlikely contingencies in the years ahead. The curtains were not drawn yet, the sky was still bright at ten o'clock. It was pleasant to bask there, listening to Mr March, while the short summer night began to fall.

Then Katherine remembered her afternoon mail.

'The only letter I've opened is my husband's,' she said comfortably. 'Being in this state makes me even more lazy than I usually am. Lewis, will you pander to my condition and fetch in the others?'

As I gave them to her, I saw that one was a long foolscap envelope, with her address in green typescript, and I realised that it was her weekly copy of the *Note*.

She read it last. I felt a flicker of uneasiness, nothing more, as she opened the sheets, and went on chatting to Mr March. Suddenly we heard Katherine's voice, loud and harsh.

'I think you ought to listen to this, Mr L.'

She read, angrily and deliberately:

' "*Armaments and Shares*. As foreshadowed in *Note* (Mar. 24 '36) certain personages close to Government appear interested in armaments programme in more ways than one. Hush-husk talk in Century (exclusive City luncheon club, HQ 22 Farringdon St.), Jewish candidates quietly blackballed, president George Wyatt, co-director of Sir Horace (Cartel-spokesman) Timberlake – (see *Note*, Nov. 17 '35, Feb. 2 '36, Apr. 15 '36), that heavy killings made through inside knowledge (official) armaments contracts, both '35 (Abyssinian phony scare) and '29. E.g. '29 Herbert Getliffe KC employed Jan. 2–June 6, advice WO contract Howard & Hazlehurst: £10,000 worth H & H bought name of G. L. Paul, May 30, £15,000 worth H & H F. E. Paul, June 2. G. L. and F. E. Paul brothers H. Getliffe's wife. Usual linkman technique (see *Note*, Feb. 9 '36). Have junior ministers, names canvassed in Century, also used linkmen? Allow for Century's anti-Semitism. But *Note* satisfied background hush-hush scandal. Story, transactions, dates, ministers, later." '

The room was quiet. Then Mr March cried out:

'My son has done this.'

Katherine said: 'It's an outrage. It must be Ann. Don't you agree that it must be Ann? Charles told me that she wrote for them—'

Mr March said: 'He must have known her intentions and he is responsible for it all. He is responsible for it all.'

I broke in:

'I'm sure that is not true. God knows this is bad enough. But I'm sure neither of them knew it was coming. Charles knew nothing last night. Unless he's read this thing today, he still knows nothing now.'

'How can you speak for my son?' Mr March shouted.

I said: 'If he had done this he would have told you. He couldn't have made himself speak to you as he did last night, if he knew this was on the way. It's not in his nature.'

I had spoken with insistence, and Mr March sat silent, huddled in his chair, his chin sunk in his breast.

I had to go on speaking. I tried to explain, without making excuses for Ann, what had happened. I said that she was on the point of going to the *Note* and asking them to keep the story out. After the threat at the end of this piece, it was imperative to say nothing which might make it harder for her.

Mr March gave a sullen nod of acquiescence, but he was looking at me as though I were an enemy, not a friend.

He said: 'I shall judge my son by his actions now. That is all that I can do.'

Katherine said: 'This is her fault. She's not content with crippling Charles. Now she's trying to damage the rest of us. I wish to God she'd never set foot in this house.'

Mr March said quietly:

'I wished that the first moment I saw her. I have never been able to forgive him for marrying her.'

CHAPTER XXXIV

ANSWER TO AN APPEAL

As soon as I arrived back in London, I telephoned to Ann. She had already seen the issue, she said, and spoken to Seymour. He had guaranteed that nothing more would be published on the story for four weeks: he was himself going to Paris for a fortnight, picking up news, but he would be ready to discuss the problem with her as soon as he returned, and with Charles also if he liked to come along.

'You'll do it,' I said, 'the minute he gets back?'

'Of course.'

'He's not putting you off while he slips something in?'

'He wouldn't do that to me.' Her reply sounded constrained, on the defensive: she did not like my being so suspicious: she could feel that I suspected something else. I thought it more likely than not that Seymour had already got the first piece in without giving her a chance to see it. She resented any such thought: when she gave her trust, as she did to Seymour, she gave it without reserve. Yet she went on to ask me a favour: when she and Charles arranged the meeting with Seymour, would I come too? I was puzzled: what use could I be, I said. She stuck to it. She said, as was true, that I had given Seymour legal advice once or twice; on some things, she went on, he might listen to me.

When Seymour got back, he raised no objection. On the contrary, he rang up on the day they had fixed for the talk, and invited me himself, in his high-spirited, easy, patrician voice. I might even call for him after dinner at the *Note* office, he suggested.

So I duly climbed the five flights of stairs, in the murk and the smell of shavings and mildew. The *Note* office was at the top of a house just off the Charing Cross Road: on the other floors were offices of art photographers, dingy solicitors, something calling itself a trading company: on the fifth landing, in two rooms, was produced – not only edited but set up, duplicated, and distributed – the *Note*. In one of the rooms a light was burning, as Seymour's secretary was still working there, at half-past eight. She was working for nothing, as I knew, a prettyish girl with a restless smile. Humphrey (she enjoyed being in the swim, calling him by his Christian name) had been called away, she said, but he was expecting us all at his flat in Dolphin Square.

When at last I got there, he was alone. He was a short, cocky, confident man, nearly bald, although he was no older than Charles; he was singularly ugly, with a mouth so wide that it gave him a touch of the grotesque. His manner was warm and amiable. He put a drink into my hand and led me outside on to the terrace; his flat was high up in the building, and from the terrace one could look down over all western London, the roofs shining in the sunset. But Seymour did not look down: he did not refer to why I was there: he just launched, with a kind of obsessive insistence mixed with his habitual jauntiness, into what he had been hearing in Paris, whom he had seen, what he had been learning about the Spanish war. When I made a remark, he kept up a sighing noise which indicated that he had more to say.

At last I managed to get in my own preoccupation. He was an easy man to be off-hand with, because he was so off-hand and confident himself. I said:

'What about the campaign?'

'What campaign?'

'The one that Ann March and Charles are coming about.'

'Oh that.' He gave a gnome-like grin.

'Why did you start on Philip March at all?'

'Do you think we're really interested in him?' said Seymour with cheerful contempt. 'He's never been more than a city figurehead. No, the chaps we're really interested in are Hawtin and his pals. I think we might be able to put them on the spot, don't you?'

I asked him – what facts had he really got hold of? About Philip March? About Hawtin? What facts were there, besides those about the Getliffe dealings?

Seymour grinned again, but did not answer. Instead he said:

'Should you say old March cut any ice among that gang?' ('That gang' meant the people who had the real power, the rulers, the authorities: Seymour, like other communists I knew, had a habit of breaking into a curious kind of slang: from him, in his cultivated tone, it sounded odd.)

'That's the sort of thing *you* know,' I said.

'Hawtin's quite a different cup of tea,' said Seymour. 'Now he does cut some ice, and if we get his blood the rest of the gang will feel it, won't they now?'

I asked again, what facts had he collected about Hawtin? And when was the next instalment due to appear? To the second question, he gave a straight answer. Not for some weeks. They were not ready yet. If they had to delay for months rather than weeks, he might repeat what he had already printed – 'just to remind some of our friends that we're still thinking about them'.

It was the same answer as he had given to Ann: so there was time, I thought. Meanwhile, as we waited for Ann and Charles, Seymour went on talking, dismissing the 'Hawtin racket', elated and obsessed by 'stories' which, to him, mattered out of comparison more.

Below us, the haze of London was changing from blue to grey as night fell, and through the haze the lights were starting out. From second to second a new light quivered through, now in the Pimlico streets beneath us, now on the skyline. Soon there was a galaxy of lights. It made me think of the press of human lives, their struggles, and their peace.

The bell of Seymour's flat rang, and on his way to open the door he switched on his own lights. Outside in the passage were standing Ann and Charles. Seymour grinned up at Charles.

'Tardy book,' he said. It was a recognition-symbol, a token of their days at school: I had heard Seymour use it before as a kind of upper-class password.

As we sat down, all of us except Seymour were unrelaxed: but he, just as confidently as he had done with me, started talking: his trip, the 'lowdown' which he had collected, he went on just as with me. It took Ann an effort to say:

'Look, Humphrey, do you mind if we get this over!'

Her voice was tight. I could feel how much she respected him. On his side, he was at once polite and considerate. 'Of course, we'd better if you want to,' he said with a kind, friendly, encouraging smile.

'I think I've got to bring up this Philip March story,' she said.

'Right,' said Seymour.

Though she looked strained, she began her appeal with extreme lucidity. It was agreed by everyone, wasn't it, she said, that Philip March had had nothing whatever to do with any recent dealings? Seymour nodded his head. Philip March was absolutely in the clear, she said; last year's rumours had nothing to do with him? Seymour nodded. If she herself hadn't brought in the name of Herbert Getliffe, and an almost forgotten piece of gossip, no one would have remotely considered any smear against Philip March?

'Absolutely true,' said Seymour. 'I was just telling Lewis, he never seriously counted, with all due respect to your family, Charles.'

He was sitting back with one leg crossed over the other. For all his cockiness and the tincture of the grotesque, he was a man in whom one could feel authority. It was an authority that did not come merely from his commitment, from his position in the party: it was the authority of his nature. Even Charles, leaning forward on the sofa, watching him with hard eyes, paid attention to it. Certainly Ann, more given than Charles to admit authority in others, recognised it. She sat with her backbone straight as a guardsman's by Charles's side, and said: 'Well then, I shouldn't ask for anything impossible. I shouldn't ask to call off anything that was important. But it isn't important, is it? I didn't even know that anyone would think it worth while to revive the Getliffe business. I should have thought it was too long ago to count. I should have thought whatever Philip March did or didn't do at that time, it was too long ago to count. And anyway it's more obscure than the Getliffe business, we couldn't get it cut and dried. I think there would be pretty strong arguments for leaving him alone, in any case. But of course we want him left alone because it's bound to affect my husband's family. It's not often that one can ask for special treatment, is it? I think I can, this time.'

Seymour smiled at her, and said:

'There isn't any such thing as private news, is there?'

She repeated 'I think I can, this time', because his tone was so light that it did not sink in. It took her seconds to realise that he had refused her. Without a qualm.

Charles had realised at once. In a harsh and angry voice he said:

'You admit that you've got no foundation at all for any scandal last year – as far as my uncle is concerned. You admit the same about Herbert Getliffe, don't you? Is there any foundation for the scandal at all, even about this man Hawtin? Or are you just wishing that it happened?'

'I don't know,' said Seymour.

'What do you mean, you don't know?'

'Precisely what I say.'

Bitterly Charles went on with his questions. About 1935 there was nothing proved or provable at all: it seemed most likely that there was nothing in the rumour. But, as Seymour said jauntily, the 1929 dealings were on the record – the transactions of Getliffe's brothers-in-law and, as he hoped to demonstrate, those of Philip March.

'You're proposing to use those, in fact,' said Charles, 'to give a bit of credibility to a sheer lie?'

'That's putting it rather more strongly than I should myself. If there was jiggery-pokery some years ago, there's no reason why there shouldn't have been some last year.'

'But you're really pretty certain that there wasn't?'

Seymour twitched his shoulders.

'I must say,' said Charles, 'it's more dishonest even than I thought.'

'I shan't have time for your moral sensitivity,' said Seymour, his voice suddenly as passionate as Charles's, 'until we've beaten the fascists and got a decent world.'

In the angry silence I put in:

'If you're seriously proposing to print rumours without even a scrap of evidence, the paper isn't going to last very long, is it?'

'Why in God's name not?'

'What's going to stop a crop of libel actions?'

'The trouble with you lawyers,' said Seymour, jaunty once more, 'is that you never know when a fact is a fact, and you never see an inch beyond your noses. I am prepared to bet any of you, or all three if you like, an even hundred pounds that no one, *no one*, brings an action against us over this business. Trust old Father Mouse and bob's your uncle.'

He went on, enjoying himself:

'While I'm about it, I'm prepared to bet you that the paper never runs into a libel action. You trust old Father Mouse. I'm nothing like as wild and woolly as I seem. No, the only thing that could ever finish the paper is that we might come up against the Official Secrets Act. That's the menace, and if we had bad luck that would be the end. I don't suppose I'm telling any of you anything you don't know. Anyway, Ann's seen how we collect some of our stuff and she must have enough documents in her own desk to finish the poor old paper off in a couple of hours.'

It sounded like an indiscretion, like a piece of his cocksureness. Listening, I believed it was the opposite. He had done it deliberately. He was not the man to underestimate just how competent and ruthless other people could be. He took it for granted that Ann and Charles knew that she had it in her power to kill the paper; he took it for granted too, that after his refusal, having no other conceivable way to protect Charles's family, they would consider it.

He knew her well. It would have been stupid to hide anything, it was good tactics to bring the temptation into the open, brandish it in front of her and defy her with it. He knew, of course, that she was as much committed to the party as he was himself. Outside her marriage, it was her one devotion. It was so much a devotion – only a religious person could know something similar in kind, perhaps – that she had not been shocked when Seymour admitted that he was fabricating a set of scandals. To Charles, it was a moral outrage. To her, so upright in her own dealings, it was not. Any more, oddly enough, than it was to Seymour himself. Both she and Seymour were believers by nature. At times it gave them a purity and innocence that men like Charles never knew: at times it gave Seymour, and perhaps even Ann, a capacity to do things from which Charles, answering to his own conscience, would have been repelled.

As Seymour told Ann that she could ruin the paper next day, I watched her glance at Charles. Their faces were set, but their eyes met with recognition, with understanding.

They left soon after. I stayed behind, so that they could talk alone the minute they got outside.

Seymour did not say another word about them, or the paper. He had the knack of turning off his attention with a click, as though he had pressed a switch. He did not make a comment. Instead, cheerful and unflagging, he insisted on driving me to White's for a night-cap. There, just for once, his cocksureness let him down. A member whom I faintly knew brought in a guest of distinguished appearance. I asked Seymour who he was.

'Oh, that's Lord Kilmainham,' he said, with supreme confidence.

It was not. Enquiring a little later in the lavatory, I found that the guest was an income-tax accountant.

CHAPTER XXXV

THE FUTURE OF TWO OLD MEN

SINCE the first instalment in the *Note*, Charles and Mr March had not met nor spoken to each other. Charles had, however, telephoned to Katherine after the visit to Seymour. He had told her, so I gathered, that Ann had done her best to call the paper off. Whether either Katherine or Mr March believed this, I had no means of judging. But they knew I had been present. Within a few days I received a letter from Mr March, telling me that he would once more be grateful for my 'friendly assistance': would I lunch with him at his club, so that we could go together to Sir Philip's office afterwards?

The club servants were surprised to see Mr March there in the month of August, having become used to the clockwork regularity of his life; he had not left Haslingfield during his summer stay for twenty years. Just as, though he went to the club for tea each day he was in London, he had not lunched there since Charles was a child. He did not know where or how to write his order, and had to be helped by the servants. They teased him for it: he, usually so uncondescending, was gruff with them.

He said little at the meal. We had a table to ourselves, but those round us were soon filled. I saw one or two faces I knew, all of civil servants from the departments close by. I felt that Mr March, unable to talk of the bitter anxiety in his mind, was also depressed because he recognised so few. There were only two men he nodded to, and they were very old.

In Pall Mall, on our way to Sir Philip's ministry, he tried to rouse himself from his gloom. We turned into St James's Park towards White-hall, and Mr March looked over the trees at the domes of the Admiralty, the turrets and towers, all soft and opal grey in the moist sunlight.

'I must say,' he remarked, 'that it looks comparatively presentable. But I have never been able to understand the fascination which makes my brother Philip and others wish to spend their entire lives in this neighbour-hood. I once said as much to Hannah, and she replied that it was sour grapes on my part. No doubt I was envious on account of my failure to cut any kind of figure in the world. Nevertheless, Lewis, if I hadn't been a failure, and had been given my choice of where to have a reasonable success, I should not have chosen this particular neighbourhood.'

His face darkened in a scowl of misery and anger. 'But my brother Philip did. I cannot endure the thought that, because of these happenings, he may find it harder to continue here.'

In the ministry we were led down the corridors to the office of Sir Philip's secretary, who was a youngish man called Williams, smooth-faced, spectacled, dressed for his job in black coat and striped trousers, and full of self-importance in it. 'I will go and find out when the Parliamentary Secretary will be free,' he said, enjoying the chance to bring out his master's appellation. He came back promptly and announced: 'The Parliamentary Secretary will be glad to see you at once.'

We went through the inside door, and Sir Philip came across his room to meet us. He shook hands with Mr March, then said 'How do you do?' to me with his stiff, furrowed smile. As he sat down at his desk by the window which overlooked the park, I saw that his skin had taken on a yellowness, a matt texture, such as one sometimes sees in ageing men. He was seventy-three, only three years older than Mr March, but in the bright summer light the difference looked much greater.

'I expect you're dying of drought as usual at Haslingfield,' Sir Philip began their ritual of brotherly baiting. 'The country is under water everywhere else.'

'I regard the rainfall as having been reasonable for once,' said Mr March. 'And I am pleased to report that I have sufficient water for my requirements.'

These exchanges went on for a few moments. They had made them for so many years, and Sir Philip at least could not let go of them now: Mr March's replies were forced and mechanical. Sir Philip was, as the afternoon began, by far the less perturbed of the two. Soon he said:

'I suppose we must get down to business. I should like to say, Eliot, that I am obliged to you for giving me your time. I should be glad to regard it as a professional service, of course, but my brother informs me that you are certain to prefer it otherwise. I appreciate your feelings and, as I say, I am obliged to you. I think you know some of the facts of this affair. In May there was gossip about myself and some of my colleagues. We were alleged to have used our official knowledge during the past twelve months to buy holdings in companies where government contracts were soon going to be laid. This gossip also included some names outside the government, one of them being that fellow Getliffe. It has now been published, or at least a first instalment has. I believe you've seen it?'

I nodded.

'I can answer for myself and my colleagues,' Sir Philip went on. 'So far as we are concerned, there's not a word of truth in it. When I came back into the government last year, I decided to spend the rest of my life being as useful to the country as I could, if they wanted me. It was a sacrifice, but I believe that some of us have to accept responsibility. These aren't easy years to hold responsibility: I needn't tell you that.'

Even Sir Philip, I was thinking, could not avoid the expressions of convention, talked about 'sacrifice', perhaps used the word to himself – even Sir Philip, who was not a humbug but a hard and realistic man, who loved office and what he thought of as power and knew that he loved it.

'I was prepared to make the sacrifice,' Sir Philip went on. 'I had to resign my directorships when I became a minister, naturally. I also decided to finish with all speculation. I've already told Leonard this.' He glanced at Mr March.

'I acknowledged your assurance,' said Mr March, 'on hearing it at your bedside during your period of incapacity owing to gout.'

'I finished with it,' said Sir Philip. 'I am not a rich man, of course, but I can get along. I have not taken part in any single transaction since I entered the government last autumn. I cannot make such a categorical statement for my colleagues, whose names have been bandied about, but I'm completely satisfied that they are clear.'

'You mentioned people outside the government,' I broke in. 'I'm also satisfied in the same way about Getliffe.'

'You mean he's bought nothing in the last twelve months?'

'Nothing that could be thought suspicious.'

'What evidence are you going on?'

'Nothing as definite as yours,' I said. 'But I've talked to him on this actual point, and I know him well.'

'I reported Lewis Eliot's observations on this matter,' said Mr March.

Sir Philip's eyes were bright and alert. 'You're convinced about this fellow Getliffe?'

'Quite convinced,' I said.

'I accept that,' said Sir Philip. 'And it makes me certain that the whole campaign is a put-up job and there's no backing to it at all.'

Mr March, who had been listening with painful attention, showed no relief as he heard these words. He looked at his brother, with an expression stupefied, harassed, distressed.

'That being so,' I said, 'your solicitors are telling you to go ahead with a libel action, aren't they?'

'It's not quite so easy,' Sir Philip replied without hesitation, in a tone as authoritative as before. I admired his hard competence. Professionally, I thought, he would have been an ideal client. 'They've tied up this affair with certain other transactions. The other transactions are supposed to have happened when I was in the government in 1929. You will notice that, in the case of Getliffe, they have taken care to tie these two allegations together. It is clever of them. I detest their politics, I've no use for their general attitude, and if I can put them in their place, I shall – but we mustn't imagine that we are dealing with fools.'

'I have never thought so,' said Mr March.

'If they go ahead with these allegations about last year, I should win a libel action, shouldn't I?' Sir Philip asked me.

'Without the slightest doubt,' I said.

'I should also do myself more harm than good,' he went on.

I was thinking how precisely Seymour had calculated the risk.

'There happens to be some substance in what they say about 1929,' said Sir Philip.

We waited for him to go on.

'I may say at once that I've done nothing which men of decent judgment could think improper. But one step I took in good faith which these people might twist against me. I am very much to blame for giving them such a handle. I've always thought it was not only essential to be honest: it was also essential to seem honest. I take all the blame for not watching out for snakes in the grass. That is the only blame I am disposed to take.'

He paused, and gave a sardonic chuckle.

'I should like to distinguish my actions from Getliffe's quite sharply. In 1929 Getliffe made a disgraceful use of information he had acquired professionally. In my judgment, there is no question of it. He knew the government were giving a contract to Howard & Hazlehurst. He used catspaws to buy a fair-sized block of shares. He must have done very well out of it. Howard & Hazlehurst were down to 9s in 1929: they stand at 36s today.'

'Thirty-six and sixpence,' said Mr March, as though by sheer habit.

'Getliffe is as crooked as a cork-screw and I shouldn't have the faintest compunction about going ahead with a libel action if it only meant involving him. If he were disbarred, I should simply consider that he had brought it on himself. He's downright dishonest, and I was sorry that you' – he turned to Mr March – 'permitted Katherine to marry into the fellow's family. Though I've always liked Francis from the little I've seen of him.'

Mr March burst out, in violent and excessive anger:

'I refuse to accept that criticism at the present juncture. My son-in-law has made an excellent husband for my daughter Katherine in all respects.

I refused at the time to penalise them on account of his regrettable connections, and I still refuse, despite the fact that Herbert Getliffe's name is linked with yours in these deplorable circumstances. I refuse to accept this preposterous criticism. If other marriages in my family had been as sound as my daughter's, we should not be troubled with the discussion on which we are supposed to be engaged.'

Sir Philip seemed to understand his brother's rage.

'Yes, Leonard,' he said, with an awkward, constrained affection. 'But you can appreciate that Getliffe isn't my favourite character just at present, can't you?' His tone became once more efficient, organised, businesslike. 'My own activities were considerably different from that fellow's. I only spent a few months in the government in 1929, you may remember, but of course I knew of the Howard & Hazlehurst contract, and of course I knew of the trend of policy about armaments. Naturally I thought over the implications, which appeared to suggest that, even at the height of disarmament, certain types of weapon would still have to be developed. So certain firms connected with those types of weapon would flourish for the next few years. That wasn't a foolish piece of reasoning, and I felt entitled to act on it. If one struck lucky, one had a good buy. I looked round at various firms. I found one which was in fairly low water, and I backed my guess. The shares were down somewhere that didn't matter, and I put in a fairish sum of money. My guess came off, but I should have preferred it otherwise. For this firm was bought by Howard & Hazlehurst three months after I had put my money in. I had no conceivable foreknowledge of that transaction. I did very well out of it, from the nature of the case. So did one or two of my colleagues, who sometimes follow my guidance in financial matters. It's apparent that an ugly construction could be put on our actions – and these people are putting it. The facts are as I have stated them.'

He looked at Mr March and me in turn.

'I know there are silly persons who, without imputing motives, would still think that what Getliffe and I did were very much the same. I find those silly persons both tiresome and stupid. The point is that Getliffe acted in a way which the rules don't permit, while I kept strictly inside them. That is the only point. There are no absolute principles in these matters. There are simply rules on which all financial dealings depend. If you upset them, you upset the whole structure. If the rules go, then confidence and stability go. That is why I should show no mercy to anyone who breaks them. I should be sorry to see Getliffe escape scotfree.'

He added:

'It would not have occurred to me to break the rules. I blame myself for giving the appearance of having done so. I have had a long life in these matters, and I have never taken part in a transaction of which I am ashamed. The only thing left is to stop this business before it goes further. I want to ask you whether that is in our power.'

His conscience was clear, his self-respect untouched. Mr March had reported, after visiting him when ill, that his brother was 'sick in mind'; but it was not through any inner conflict. He was certain of his integrity. Yet he was desperately taxed. He was an old man, threatened with humiliation. In his hard, simple, strong-willed fashion he had coiled himself up to meet the danger. Throughout the afternoon he had kept his authority. But as he asked 'whether that is in our power' his face was shrunken: he still controlled his tone, but he looked imploring.

I saw that Mr March was stricken by this change. All through the afternoon, he had been torn by a sorrow his brother did not know; but even without that, he would still have flinched from the sight of Philip turning to him for pity and help. It had been painful to him to see the first traces of Philip's anxiety, when he was ill: it was worse now. For Philip had been the hero of his childhood, the brother who did all that he would have liked to do, the brother who had none of his timidities, who was self-sufficient, undiffident, effective: it was intolerable to see him weak. It filled Mr March with revulsion, even with anger against Philip.

Mr March said in a low voice to his brother:

'As I've already told you, whether it is in our power or not depends on my son's wife.'

'I still don't believe it,' said Sir Philip.

'Will you tell my brother whether she's responsible for this, or not?' said Mr March to me.

'How much do you know about this?' Sir Philip asked me.

'Have you told Sir Philip,' I asked Mr March, 'that she's tried to set it right?'

'I remain to be convinced of that,' said Mr March.

'I assure you.'

'All I can do,' said Mr March, 'is acknowledge your remark.'

'Why are you making it worse than it need be?' I broke out. I explained as much as I was free to do of her share in the story, and of how she had made her plea to Seymour and been refused. As I was speaking, Sir Philip's face was lighter, more ready to accept what I said, than his brother's, which was set in an obstinate, incredulous frown. Yet at last Mr March said, as though reluctantly:

'Apparently she has expressed some concern.'

I repeated part of what I had said. All of a sudden he shouted:

'Do you deny that if she wished she could still stop this abomination?'

I hesitated. Yes, she could inform against the *Note*. She could finish it for good. The loyalties that she would have to betray went through my mind, inhibiting my answer. The hesitation made me seem less straightforward than I was really being. Mr March shouted:

'Do you deny it?'

'It's possible, but—'

'Lewis Eliot knows very well,' Mr March said to Sir Philip, 'that it's more than possible.'

'No,' I said. 'It's only possible by a way that no one would like to use. I don't think many people could do it.'

'Can you explain yourself?' said Sir Philip.

I had to shake my head.

'I should be breaking a confidence,' I said.

'At any rate,' said Sir Philip, 'I can take it that this is all part and parcel of her cranky behaviour?'

'In a sense, yes.' I said I could not add to that answer.

Sir Philip became brisk, almost relieved. 'Well,' he said, 'that is the best news I've heard today. Charles must bring her to heel. I've always thought it was scandalous for him to let her indulge in this nonsense. Particularly a young woman as good-looking as she is. He ought to keep her busier himself.' Into the yellowing parchment face there came a smile, appreciative and salacious. It might have been a flicker of himself as a younger man, the Philip who had an eye for the women, the Philip who, so the family gossip said, had kept a string of mistresses.

'I cannot let you delude yourself,' said Mr March.

'What do you mean?'

'You are inclined to think the position is less dangerous because my son's wife is responsible for it.'

The weight of Mr March's words told on Sir Philip.

He replied irritably:

'I don't understand what you're getting at. I've always heard that the young woman is devoted to Charles.'

'I have no reason to believe the contrary.'

'Then she'll do what he tells her, in the end.'

There was a silence. Mr March cried:

'I cannot answer for what my son will tell her.'

'You're not being reasonable.' Sir Philip's tone was harassed and sharp.

'Charles has always had decent feelings as far as I am concerned, hasn't he? You've only got to let him know that this is serious for me. If they go on far enough, they may make it impossible for me to stay in public life. Well then. Be as considerate as you can, and tell him none of us would interfere with his wife's activities as a general rule, though he might as well remember that she should have something better to do with her time. But tell him this is too important for me and the family for us to be delicate. We must ask him to assert himself.'

'You don't know how much you're asking,' I said.

'If the thing's possible, it's got to be done,' said Sir Philip.

'I will make those representations,' said Mr March. 'But I cannot answer for the consequences.'

'If you prefer it,' said Sir Philip, 'I am quite prepared to speak to Charles.'

'No, Philip,' Mr March said. 'I must do it myself.'

Sir Philip stared at him, and then said:

'I'm not willing to leave anything to chance. I expect Charles to act immediately.'

He looked at his brother for agreement, but Mr March barely moved his head in acquiescence.

'I shouldn't like to go out under a cloud,' said Sir Philip. 'Of course, we've all got to go some time, but no one likes being forced out.' Suddenly his tone altered, and he said quickly:

'Mind you, I'm not ready to admit that my usefulness is over yet. I've some pieces of work in this department I want to carry through, and after that—'

Inexplicably his mood had changed, and he began to talk of his expectations. He hoped to keep in office for six months, until there was a reshuffle in the government; he speculated on the reshuffle name by name, knowing this kind of politics just as he knew the March family. If one combination came off, he might still get a minor ministry for himself, for that he was hoping.

It was strange to hear him that afternoon. It was stranger still to hear Mr March, after a time, join in. Preoccupied, with occasional silences, he nevertheless joined in, and they forecast the chances of Sir Philip's acquaintances, among them Holford's son. Lord Holford – to whose party Charles had taken me years before – had a son whom he was trying to manœuvre into a political success. Both Sir Philip and Mr March were anxious to secure that he did not get so much as a parliamentary private secretaryship.

It was strange to listen to them. No one (so it seemed to me, observing them when I myself was young) had the power continuously to feel old. There were moments, many of them, when a man as realistic as Mr March was menaced by the grave – as in the club that afternoon, when he saw that his contemporaries were decrepit men. But those moments did not last. There were others, as now, when Sir Philip and Mr March could fear, could hope, just as they would have feared and hoped thirty years before. They were making plans at that moment: Sir Philip at seventy-three was still hoping for a ministry. There was no incongruity to himself: he hoped for it exactly as a young man would. The griefs and hopes of Mr March or Sir Philip might seem to an outsider softened and pathetic, because of the man's age: but to the man himself, age did not matter, they were simply the griefs and hopes of his own timeless self.

CHAPTER XXXVI

EITHER/OR

AFTER the talk with Sir Philip, Mr March went straight back to Hasling-field. He made no attempt that afternoon to get into touch with Charles; it was several days before he wrote to him. I heard from Katherine that a letter had at last been sent – a noncommittal letter, she gathered, just asking Charles down. We were struck by the procrastination.

Meanwhile, Ann and Charles, in a state when they wished to see no one but each other, did not know what she should do. It was either/or, and whichever she did there was not a tolerable way out.

She did not need to tell Charles what it would be like to betray all she believed in. In fact, I got an impression that they did not talk much about what each feared more, they were too close for that. When I was with them, the discussion was oddly matter-of-fact. If she should decide that the less detestable course was to get the paper stopped, what was the quickest way of doing it? She asked the question without expression. It was not difficult to give practical answers. She possessed, as Seymour had said in his defiant bluff, documents which would do the job: she had only to pass them to someone like Ronald Porson, and an injunction would be out within a few hours.

Charles went down to Haslingfield with nothing settled between them, but resolved to speak intimately and affectionately to his father. None of us knew precisely what was said at that meeting, but it did not go like that. All the news I had came from Katherine, who was, without any qualification at all, on Mr March's side. She felt nothing but hostility to Ann: she had only a residue of sympathy, the faintest residue from the past, for Charles. Yet even she admitted that Mr March had made it more bitter for himself and his son with each word he said. He had never shown less control or less understanding of Charles. He seemed to have exemplified the law of nature according to which, when a human relation has gone profoundly wrong, one is driven to do anything that can make it worse.

Mr March, having delayed for so many days in seeing his son at all, received him with a storm of accusations. He insisted that Charles had deliberately dissimulated, had professed ignorance, had given lying reassurances, whenever Mr March had asked. Charles was outraged. He had gone to see his father with a feeling of guilt: he was in one of those situations where one is half-guilty and half-innocent, or rather guilty at one level and innocent at another. He deserved reproaches, he was forming them against himself – but he was maddened at being accused of behaviour he could never have committed.

Katherine believed that there had been the bitterest words about Ann. It seemed, very strangely, that Mr March had spoken of her as though she were just a slave of Charles's, not an independent human being. What had really been said no one knew but themselves.

They parted in anger, Mr March's wildly possessing him, Charles's hard and strained. But as he went without a goodbye, Charles, still not knowing where to turn in spite of his harsh replies, offered to see Mr March again when he returned to Bryanston Square. It was an attempt to keep a card of re-entry, such as one makes when one is not prepared to face an end. Violently and ungraciously, Mr March accepted it.

The second reference in the *Note* was published before the end of August. It went just as Seymour had told me; in itself, it was innocuous. It produced no more facts, hinted at Hawtin as the chief figure in the case, contained nothing which pointed specifically at Sir Philip, and ended by promising to publish the whole story in 'three-four weeks'.

There were no consequences, at any rate none in the open. I heard some gossip, went to a political dinner party and listened to the hostess moving pieces about the chessboard. Did this mean that Alex Hawtin would soon find himself on the back-benches? Would there be a reshuffle in the government before long? Would they take the opportunity to put one or two men 'out'? But I was used to that kind of gossip, in which reputations rose and fell in a week: however informed the gossips were, however shrewd, their judgments had a knack of reversing themselves when one was not looking, and next month they would, with equal excitement, malice, and human gusto, be deciding that Alex Hawtin was safely 'in' and that someone else had 'blotted his copybook'.

In the March family, nothing happened for some days: except that Mr March closed Haslingfield and, breaking his seasonal ritual by a fortnight, which had not happened since he took the house forty years before, was back in Bryanston Square by the first week in September. It was known that he had seen the second article, but he said nothing and made no attempt to have another private talk with Charles. In fact, the only action he took as soon as he returned to Bryanston Square was a singular one: he invited Charles and Ann, his niece Margaret March and several others, including me, to dine with him, on the pretext that he wished to celebrate the birth of Katherine's child.

The child, her second son, had been born a week before Mr March moved back to London. With all his physical exuberance he rejoiced in a birth. He was pleased that, of the child's two first names, one was to be his own. But no one believed that this was the true reason for his invitation. Margaret March, who knew most of the facts, thought he was making the opportunity for a scene with Ann: she was nervous at having to be a spectator, although her sympathies were mainly with Mr March.

Others of his relations believed much the same. They knew that a disaster hung over Mr March and Charles, and they felt that Mr March could not endure it much longer. Several of them were apprehensive enough to make excuses not to go. Most of them had learned something of the situation, pitied Mr March and took his side; this was the case even with the younger generation. They did not begin to understand Charles's position, though he attracted a kind of baffled sympathy from some, simply because he was liked and respected. Ann got no sympathy at all.

Ann herself had no doubt of the reason behind Mr March's invitation. I called at Antrobus Street on my way home one night, just after we had all received the letters asking us to dine; I found Ann alone. For the first time in the years I had known her, her courage would not answer her. She was trying to screw up her will, but she was frightened.

I tried to hearten her. I said that it was possible Mr March had invited us for a much simpler reason. He might want to prove that he had not yet broken with his son. When Charles left Haslingfield, he had shown his card of re-entry, and now perhaps Mr March was playing to it.

It did not sound likely. When Charles came in, I saw that she was not only frightened, but torn, just as Charles himself was torn. With her he was tender and protective. It was clear that he had not made her choice for her about the *Note*, and that he was not prepared to.

Nevertheless, that night I believed that, however much he kept from forcing her, however much he respected her choice, she would do as he wanted. I believed it more positively when she mentioned Mr March's invitation, and said that she did not want to go.

'When did it arrive?' said Charles quietly.

'This morning. It's too much of an ordeal, and it couldn't do any good. Even if I did go, it couldn't do any good.'

Charles paused and said:

'I'm afraid that I want you to.'

'Why do you?' Her face was open, but hurt and clouded.

'You must see why. He's made an approach, and I can't refuse him. I'm afraid that I want you to go.'

'Must I?' said Ann.

'Yes,' said Charles.

CHAPTER XXXVII

'WE'RE VERY SIMILAR PEOPLE'

ANN asked me to call for her on the night of Mr March's dinner party. She had been away from home for some nights, and had not seen Charles since she got back; he had an engagement at his old hospital, and would have to go to Bryanston Square direct.

As soon as I caught sight of her I was troubled. She was dressed for the party, as though she had determined to look her best that night. But it was not her dress that took my eye. Her cheeks were flushed; on her forehead there was a frown of strain. At first I took it for granted that these were signs of anxiety because of the evening ahead; then I asked if she were well.

'I've got a cold, I think,' said Ann. 'I felt it coming on a day or two ago. It's nothing much.'

'Any temperature?'

'Perhaps a little,' said Ann.

'Does Charles know?'

'No. I told you, I've not seen him since I went away.'

'Wouldn't it be wiser if you didn't come?'

'Do you think,' Ann said, 'that I could possibly not come now? I've told Mr March that I shall be there, haven't I?'

Suddenly I was reminded of her making herself play on at tennis, her first afternoon at Haslingfield.

'I must make sure that no one takes any notice, though,' she said. 'I'll see if anything can be done about it.' She went upstairs, and was some time away. At last she came into the room, halted in front of me, and said 'How will that do?'

She had gone over her make-up, hiding the flush on her cheeks, over-painting her lips. One thing alone she could not wipe away, and that was the constricted, strained expression round her eyes.

'You look very pretty,' I said. In our long, comradely acquaintance-ship, I had scarcely paid her a compliment before.

She smiled with pleasure. She was vainer than one thought, she dis-trusted her looks more. She studied herself in the looking-glass over the fireplace. She gave another smile, faint, approving, edged with self-regard.

'I think it will do,' she said.

Again I tried to make her stay at home, but she would not listen.

The September night was fresh, and Ann shivered in the taxi. As we stood on the steps in Bryanston Square just before eight o'clock, the smell of fallen leaves in the garden was blown on the sharp wind. Even for myself, I wished that the evening was over.

In the drawing-room, Margaret March and a cousin whom I scarcely knew were sitting by the fire. Ann began to talk to the cousin, who was a shy, gauche youth of twenty. Margaret said to me quietly: 'I don't think anyone else is coming. And I accepted before I heard what was happen-ing. Otherwise I think I should have got out of it. Perhaps it would have been behaving grossly, but still—'

Then Charles entered, and she became silent. Before any of us had spoken again, Mr March followed his son into the room.

He felt the silence. He looked at Charles, at Ann, and then at the rest of us. At last he shook hands with Ann in a stiff, constrained manner, and said: 'I'm glad to have your company on this occasion. I'm glad that you were not prevented from attending.'

Through dinner, he went on as though trying not to disappoint us. He showed no sign of working up to a scene.

He knew he was expected to show pleasure at the birth, and he tried to act it. He talked of Katherine's children and Katherine herself. He made an attempt, as it were mechanically, to recall the times when 'my daughter had previously made a frightful ass of herself'.

Everyone at the table knew what he was doing. It was no relief to laugh at the jokes. I could not keep from looking at Charles, whose own glance came back time and again to his father. And I could not keep from looking at Ann; once I noticed Charles anxiously watching her. Glancing often from one to the other, I had to maintain more than my share of the conversation, replying to Mr March's mechanical chaff.

Margaret March helped, but the cousin was too shy to speak. In that way we got through dinner, though there was one incident, quite trivial, which chilled us all. Mr March's knife slipped as he was cutting his meat; as he righted himself he knocked his claret glass over. We heard the tinkle, watched the stain seep over the cloth, expecting at any instant that Mr March's usual extravagant stream-of-consciousness grumbling would begin. But he said nothing. He stared at the cloth while the butler dried it up. He did not make a single complaint to save his face.

In the drawing-room, Mr March again attempted to behave as though this were nothing but a celebration. He told Margaret a story at my expense; as he developed it, he became less preoccupied. Then Margaret March made a tactless remark. For she talked about Katherine's children, and said, casually but wistfully:

'If I married, I wonder if I should dare to have a child. I don't suppose I shall have the chance now, worse luck: but I wonder if I should.'

She was getting on into the mid-thirties. I looked at her handsome face, fair and clean-cut.

She added quietly:

'Of course, I know that really I should do the same as Katherine. I should want children, I should start a family. But it would worry me. I'm not sure that it would be wise.'

'Yes,' said Ann, breaking from her silence with feverish intensity. 'Of course you'd have children, of course you would.'

Mr March stared at her. Then he turned away to Margaret March.

'I am not certain that I understand your suggestion,' he said.

She hesitated: 'I mean – when you think of what the world may be.'

Mr March shouted: 'You need not try to respect my feelings. I am not accustomed to having my feelings respected in more important matters. I suppose you mean the world may not be a tolerable place for people of our religion?'

Margaret March nodded.

Mr March cried out:

'I wish the *Jews* would stop being *news*!'

It was a shout of protest: but somehow he said it as a jingle, and as though the Jews were doing it on purpose. Even that night there were lips being compelled not to smile. Mr March could feel the ripple round him. He scowled and went on:

'You need not respect my feelings about such matters. I admit I never expected to see my religion getting this deplorable publicity. I never expected to spend my declining years watching people degraded because they belong to the same religion as myself. But I do not consider that these events should compel any of my relations to cripple their lives. I refuse to believe that they can be affected. And if they should be affected, which I repeat is not possible, they would be better off in the company of their children. If their children turn out to be a consolation, and not a source of grief.'

At that moment, Charles started to talk to his father. That last cry sounded in Charles's ears. The lines of his face became deeper. Across the table he saw the wife whom he adored. He saw her looking strained and ill. With her face before him, he had to speak to his father.

As we listened, nearly everyone there thought there was going to be a reconciliation. It sounded as though he knew which choice must be made. Each word he spoke was affectionate, subtle, concerned. He seemed at first to be talking casually to his father about Haslingfield and Bryanston Square. Yet the words were charged with his feeling for his father, with his family pride, so long concealed, with his longing for privacy and ease with those he loved.

Gradually Charles got Mr March to talk, not in his old vein, but with some show of ease. He soon began to expand on the weather. 'It's been remarkable weather this summer,' said Mr March. 'Only exceeded in wretchedness in my experience by the summer of 1912, which I always blamed for the regrettable misadventure of the third housemaid. It is the first summer since 1929 when there has been no danger of drought at my house in the country. It is the first summer since 1929 that I have not been compelled to make my guests ration the amount of water in their baths.' He turned to me, '1929 was, of course, singularly difficult. I remember that, on your first visit to my house in the country, I was compelled to allow you a maximum of four inches in your bath. The time I issued those instructions to you was immediately followed by the appearance of Ann Simon after luncheon.'

He did not look at Ann.

The name came as a shock. There was a silence.

Charles recovered himself, and said:

'It wasn't a direct consequence, Mr L.'

'No! No! I've always presumed that she was invited through the ordinary channels.'

Mr March was quiet.

'You're not certain that anyone has ever been properly invited to any house of yours, are you?' said Charles.

From his tone, so much more intimate than teasing, I knew that he would not stop trying to persuade Mr March of what he felt.

'You've never been able to trust your children to behave with reasonable decorum, have you?' Charles went on.

'That is so,' said Mr March. 'As I remarked recently, I ought to have been born in a different epoch.'

'I think perhaps I ought to have been too,' said Charles.

'You're better prepared to endure unpleasantnesses than I am,' said Mr March. 'Whereas I only require to pass my declining years in peace.'

'I'm not as well prepared as you are, Mr L.,' Charles said. 'And I don't like the prospect of the future much more than you do.'

'I never liked the prospect of any unpleasantness,' said Mr March. 'But that's my temperament, I've told you before. I'm a diffident and retiring person.'

'Don't you see that our temperaments are very much alike?' said Charles. His tone suddenly turned urgent and anxious. 'Even though we seem to do different things. I may do things you wouldn't have done, but we're much more alike that most fathers and sons. I wish you'd believe it. At bottom, we're very similar people. Father, don't you know that we are?'

A smile forced itself, as though with difficulty, through to Mr March's face, a smile that became delighted, open and naïf.

While some of us felt a wave of relief, thought it was all over, felt a sense of relief overwhelming, tired and at the same time sparklingly gay, Mr March seemed half-incredulous, half-happy.

He said, in a rapid mutter, that he would like to have a 'consultation' with Charles and Ann 'not later than the end of the present week'.

Charles said yes.

Mr March deliberately changed the conversation, and talked happily to the rest of us, about subjects in which he and we were equally un-uninterested.

As Charles rose to say goodbye, Ann gave a gasp. As soon as I looked at her, I knew it was a gasp of pain. Charles went to her, asking with extreme anxiety what was the matter.

'I'm not particularly well,' she said.

'You've not been well all night,' he said. He put a hand on her forehead and felt her pulse.

'Why haven't you told me?' he said, in a tone so distressed that it sounded harsh and scolding. He turned to his father. 'I must get her home at once. Lewis, will you ring my partner and tell him that I shall want him to attend to her?'

Mr March stood up and went to him.

'Is she ill?' he said.

'Yes,' said Charles.

'Is it undesirable to move her?'

Charles hesitated, and before he replied Mr March said in a loud voice:

'I insist that she stays in my house. I refuse to accept responsibility if you subject her to unnecessary movement.'

'She would rather be at home,' said Charles.

'I cannot regard her inclinations as decisive. I believe that you would make her stay if it were not for previous circumstances. I cannot accept your recent assurances if you find it necessary to remove her from my house now.'

They looked into each other's eyes. Their faces were transformed from what they had been half an hour before, when Charles made his 'assurances' to his father. They were heavy, frowning, distressed.

'I think I had better stay,' said Ann, who was lying back below them in her chair.

'You're sure?'

'Yes.'

'Will you tell them to be quick? She ought to be in bed at once,' said Charles curtly to his father.

Mr March rang for the butler, and said to Charles:

'If you have no strong objection, I should prefer to send for my practitioner. He is competent as those fellows go, and he can be available without so much delay.'

Before Charles replied, Ann said:

'Yes, let him come.'

The servants worked at speed. Within five minutes Ann and Charles were out of the room; within ten the car of Mr March's doctor drew up outside. The rest of us stayed there. We talked perfunctorily. Once or twice Mr March startled us by speaking with animation: then he relapsed into his thoughts.

It was a long time before Charles came back. His face was drained of colour, and he spoke straight to his father. His voice was quiet and hard:

'It may be a pneumonia. She's ill.'

A look of recognition passed between them. Mr March did not speak.

CHAPTER XXXVIII

DESIRES BY A BEDSIDE

I CALLED to ask after her on each of the next two afternoons. On the first day I found Mr March alone, distracted and restless, telling me it was beyond doubt pneumonia, inventing one service after another that he might do for Ann. His car shuttled between Bryanston Square and Pimlico, fetching her belongings; he kept questioning the doctors and nurses; he went out himself to buy her flowers.

On the second afternoon Mr March and Charles both came to see me in the drawing-room. Mr March was still fretting for things that he could do. He behaved as though any action was a relief to his mind: but, when he asked Charles three times in ten minutes what else was needed, he got cold replies. Those replies did not spring simply from suspense. They were cold because of the tension present in the room between them.

In a short time Mr March went out. At once Charles's whole expression changed; his face became at once less hard and more ravaged. He spoke without any pretence.

'It will be days before we know that she's safe. Orange – Mr March's doctor – says that he wouldn't have expected it to take hold of her like this.' He cried out: 'Lewis, I wish I had her courage.'

'I've often wished that,' I said.

'It's the sort of courage I just can't compete with,' Charles said. 'She won't stop thinking about this affair of the *Note*. She told me that it was on that account she must know exactly how ill she is. She wouldn't ask me, but she did ask Orange. She just said that her father and her husband were both doctors, and she wanted to be discussed as though she were a case in front of the class. Mind you,' he said, with an automatic smile, 'intelligent people often ask one to do that. It doesn't prevent one from lying to them.' He went on: 'But so far as a human being can, she meant it.'

749

'Did he tell her?'

'He told her that she was dangerously ill.'

He had mentioned 'this affair of the *Note*' almost with indifference. I wondered, didn't he think of connecting it with her illness? She could not have fallen ill at a more critical time; if she had been a stranger, wouldn't he have said that perhaps it was not entirely a coincidence?

Yet he spoke of 'this affair of the *Note*' as though it did not matter: even when he went on to say:

'He told her that she was dangerously ill. When she knew that, she asked to see you before tonight. She wants to tell you something in private – it must be the same business. She wants to see you very much, Lewis. Do you mind going in? Can you spare the time? Are you sure it won't make you late?'

The strain sharpened his courtesy and for an instant he was genuinely worrying about my comfort. On the stairs, going towards Ann's room, he said:

'Do what she asks. Do what she asks – whatever it is.'

As he opened the bedroom door he forced his manner to change.

'Here is Lewis,' he said. 'You mustn't speak for very long. You can let him have his share of the conversation, can't you?'

Mr March's wife had once occupied this bedroom, the largest in the house. The bed itself was wide and high, and was overhung by a canopy; it drew my eyes across the great room, to the figure lying still under the clothes.

She was lying on her right side. Her face was flushed and her eyes bright, and her expression was constricted with strain. She gave a short dry cough, which made her give a painful frown. Her breathing was quick and heavy. There was sweat on her upper lip, and what looked to me like a faint rash.

She muttered a greeting to me, and said to Charles:

'Darling. Will you leave him here a bit?'

'If you want me to,' said Charles, standing by her, looking down at her, unwilling to go.

No one spoke for a moment. There was no noise but the gasp of her breathing. Then she said:

'Please.'

Charles glanced at me, and went out.

When the door closed, she said:

'Lewis, this isn't so good for Charles to go through. He's been here all night. It wasn't a good night for him. We talked about some things. When

I was lucid more or less. It's the worst thing – Lewis – feeling that you are soon not going to be lucid.' She had to stop. After a pause she went on:

'They think there's a chance I may die, don't they?'

'I don't know.'

'Be honest.'

'I suppose there's a chance.'

She stared at me.

'Somehow I don't think I shall,' she said.

She broke out:

'But there's one thing I must get settled. I shall feel easier if I get it settled.'

She coughed and paused again.

'There's one thing I haven't talked out with Charles. I can't rely on thinking it out properly now, can I?' she said. 'I mean the showdown over the paper.'

She went on:

'Some people wouldn't be sorry if I were finished with.'

Her voice was faint and husky. Suddenly her will shone out, undefeated.

'I'm not going to back out now,' she whispered. 'If I get over this, then I'll have plenty of time to talk to Charles again. If I don't, will you give him a message? He'll understand that I wasn't ready to back out – the last thing I did—' She was not quite coherent, but I knew that by 'backing out' she meant ruining the *Note*, reneging on the cause. 'But tell him, now he must settle it. He can do whatever he likes. The letters are in my steel filing cabinet under H. He'll find the key in my bag. If Charles decides to stop the paper, he's only got to send them to Ronald or the chap in the Home Office. The letters are mixed up with some others, they'll need a bit of organising. I couldn't do that now.'

The effort tired her out. She fell asleep, although her body moved without resting. Sometimes she spoke. Once she said, quite clearly, as though continuing the conversation: 'Charles would have to marry again. Someone who wouldn't make trouble. And could give him children, of course.' At other times she called on her father, cried out Charles's name. Most of the time in her sleep she seemed – although when conscious she had spoken so coolly – tormented by anxiety or sheer fear. Her cries sounded as though she were in a nightmare.

Sitting there – through the window the trees of the square shone green and gold in the sunlight – I could imagine what Charles's night by the bedside must have been like. As I watched her, fears seemed to be piling upon her like faces in a nightmare. She woke for a few minutes, lucid and controlled again: she said without fuss that she was afraid of dying. But, when she lost consciousness, quite different fears broke out of her. She cried about the hate that others felt for her. She was terrified of them, terrified that they were persecuting her, terrified that she was at their mercy. She tossed about the bed, calling out names, some of which I had never heard, but among them several times that of Mr March; she called out his name in fright, she was trying to get away from an enemy. Then she seemed to be making a speech.

I went down to the drawing-room, where the afternoon sun was streaming in. Mr March and Charles sat there, but neither spoke.

'How did you leave her, Lewis?' said Mr March at last.

'She was asleep,' I said.

'How did you think she seemed?' he went on.

I did not know how to reply.

'I've not seen enough illness to tell,' I said.

Mr March was fretted with anxiety. His eyes were sombre; he was more restless than Charles.

'I should like to be reassured that everything within human power is being done. I should like to insist that my practitioner is instructed to obtain further advice apart from the fellow he brought in yesterday.'

Charles did not reply to his father. He said to me:

'Did she tell you what she wanted to?'

'Yes,' I said.

'I'm glad of that,' said Charles.

'I shall not be easy,' said Mr March again, 'until I am convinced that everything within human power is being done.'

Charles looked at him and said:

'Leave it to me, that's all I ask of you.'

PART FIVE

ALONE

CHAPTER XXXIX

WAITING IN THE DRAWING-ROOM

THROUGH each of those days when no one knew whether Ann would live, the sun shone into the great bedroom at Bryanston Square.

It was a warm and glowing autumn, and she lay in the mellow sunshine, not conscious for many minutes together. But I suspected that, while she was conscious, she had made a request to Charles. All of a sudden he gave orders that no one but the nurses was to visit her room, unless he specially asked them. He told his father so, giving no reason. Mr March knew that it was he himself who had to be kept from her sight.

Charles spent most of each night by her bed. After the fourth night, he rang me up and said she had had a long lucid interval, in which she was worried that she had not made herself clear to me. 'She's worrying about everything that occurs to her. If I can satisfy her about one thing, there's another on her mind before she's stopped thanking me. This *Note* affair is the worst.' As he mentioned it, his voice became harsher. 'I should be grateful if you'd tell her that you understood exactly what she meant.'

When I went into her room that afternoon, however, she scarcely recognised me. Her breathing seemed faster and her skin very hot. The rash on her lip was now full out, and her face was angrily flushed. She coughed and muttered. I waited for some time in the hope she would know me, but, though once she said something, her eyes stared at me unseeing and opaque.

I joined Mr March in the drawing-room. During those days, he could not bring himself to go to the club; he was deserted, with no one to speak to. He spoke little to me, but we had tea together. He was listening for any movement of the nurses on the stairs so that he could rush outside and ask for the latest news. Occasionally he talked to me, and appeared glad of my presence.

He wanted her to die. He wanted her to die for a practical reason. He believed – he had not discovered the precise situation – that, if she were out of the way, it would not take long to stop the *Note*. He believed, quite correctly, that the means of stopping it would pass to Charles. His family would be left in peace. He took it for granted that there would be a temporary breach with his son. But nothing would come out. In the end they would be reconciled, and he would be left in peace for the rest of his life.

He knew that he wanted it. He was not an introspective man, but he was a completely candid one. Only a man much more dishonest with himself than Mr March could have resisted realising what his feelings meant. As soon as he knew she was ill, he imagined what the benefit would be if she were dead. He could no more pretend the desire had not risen within him than he could deny a dream from which he had just awakened. It was there.

He was too realistic to cover it with self-deceptions. He could not console himself that he was not the first man to watch a sickbed and find his longings uncomfortable to face. He did not think – how many of us have wished, not even for good or tragic reasons, but simply to make our own lives easier, that someone else, someone whom we may be fond of, should just be blotted out? Mr March would not console himself. He wanted Ann to die, whom his son passionately loved, whom he had himself once come near to loving.

It was on this account that he fretted so continuously. He could not suppress his thoughts: but anything he could do to help her he did with as much intensity as if her life had been precious to him. He had, on the second day, made his 'practitioners' bring in the consultant of whom Charles thought most highly; he had sent for the most expensive nurses; he could not have exerted himself more, if this had been Charles ill as a child.

He followed the illness minute by minute. Each time he could get a word with a nurse, he pressed her for the news. They were all astonished, as were the whole March family, by how violently he felt.

Meanwhile, Mr March thought often about death. He thought of her death and his own. He hated the thought of his death with all his robust, turbulent, healthy vigour.

Realistic as he was, he could not face it starkly in himself. On the outside, he could appear stoical, he could refer to the fact that in the nature of things his death must come before long. But, left alone, he did not think of it so.

Death to him meant the silence and the dark. It meant that he, who had been so much alive, would have been annihilated. Other lives would go on, busy, violent and content, ecstatic and anguished, comfortable and full of anxiety, and utterly indifferent to what he had been. Other people would eat in this house, talk in this room, love and get married and have their children, walk through the square, quarrel and come together; and he would be gone from it for ever. Any life, he cried to himself, any life, however stricken with pain, racked by conflict, beaten in all its hopes, is better than the nothingness. It would be better to be a shadow in the darkness, to be able to watch without taking part, than to be struck into that state for which all images are more consoling than the truth – just this world of human beings living out their lives, and oneself not there.

Those thoughts visited him as he waited day by day for news of Ann, never seeing her, forbidden by his son to see her. One afternoon I found him reading the current issue of the *Note*. He read it word by word. 'Pernicious nonsense,' he said. 'But there is naturally nothing further about my brother Philip.'

Reports of Ann's illness went round the March family, and the telephone in Bryanston Square rang many times a day. Sir Philip enquired each morning: I wondered whether he too faced his thoughts. There were whispers, rumours, hopes and alarms. So far as I knew, Katherine put through only one call. But Porson rang me up nightly in my own house. 'How is she?' his voice came, booming, assertive, drunken, distressed. 'I insist that she's always wanted someone to look after her. How is she? You're not keeping anything from me?' Each day he sent flowers, more lavish even than Mr March's. One evening, after I had called at the Marches' and was going home, I thought I saw him watching in the square: but, if it were he, he did not want to be seen, and hurried away out of sight.

Charles paid no attention to any of these incidents. He spoke very little to anyone in the house, and scarcely at all to his father. He was grey with fatigue, so tired that once in the drawing-room he went to sleep in his chair. He was entirely concentrated in Ann. Her sickroom was the only place where he seemed alive.

On the seventh day of her illness, the crisis came. Charles was in the house all that day; his partner had taken charge of his cases for the last forty-eight hours. Charles's voice over the telephone was hard, un-inflected:

'She would like to see you again. I must warn you, she is looking much better. You'll probably think the danger has gone. That isn't true.'

Despite his warning, when I saw her I could not help thinking she was better. She was weak, she could not talk much; but her breathing was quiet now, the fever had gone, and she spoke almost in her ordinary voice.

'You've got it clear, have you? I don't want to force Charles's hand. I've been worrying whether I made that clear. If anything happens to me, he must make a free choice.'

'I've got it clear,' I replied.

'Thank you,' she said. She gave a friendly matter-of-fact smile and said faintly: 'I hope it won't be necessary.'

Charles returned to take me away. He stood by the bedside, looking down at Ann; he made an attempt to smile at her.

With the clumsiness of fatigue, she interleaved her fingers into those of the hand he had rested on her pillow.

'I've been giving Lewis instructions about the *Note*,' she whispered. 'That isn't finished, you know. Had you forgotten it?'

'Not quite,' said Charles. 'Not quite.'

For two days after, Charles was ravaged by a suspense and apprehension greater than he had yet known. The consultant had been called in again. They thought she had no resilience left. Mr March's doctor told Charles that no one now could be certain of the end. Then she seemed to be infused by a faint glow of vitality, when they thought it had all gone.

In the afternoon of the ninth day, a warm and cloudless autumn afternoon, she had been a long time asleep. Mr March and Charles were sitting opposite to each other in the drawing-room, Charles could not forget, so he told me later, the clock ticking on the mantelpiece; each quarter of an hour there came its chime, sweet, monotonous and maddening. It was beyond either of them to go outside into the sunshine. It would have seemed like tempting fate.

As they sat together, Mr March once, with a grinding effort, broke the silence:

'I believe that this sleep may be a good sign. They informed me before luncheon that they had considerably more hope.'

Charles could not reply.

At last, it was well after four o'clock, they heard footsteps down the stairs, and a tap on the door. A nurse entered and beckoned Charles. He was out of the room at once. The nurse's manner had not been specially grave, and Mr March was left alone. The quarters chimed – half-past, a quarter to. Later that day, Charles discovered that the clock had been stopped at a quarter past five – presumably by Mr March.

At last, he must have heard a noise on the stairs, and the sound of a loud, unmuted, orotund voice: 'I think she'll do, March. If we look after her properly, I think she'll do.'

Charles came into the room. He spoke directly to his father for the first time for many hours.

'Did you hear that?' he cried triumphantly. 'Did you hear that?'

CHAPTER XL

BY HIMSELF

ANN'S convalescence was a slow one, and she could not be moved from Mr March's house. I ceased calling when the danger was past, but heard of her each day from Charles. She had asked Mr March to visit her in her room; it seemed that she had apologised for the inconvenience she had caused him by falling ill; she promised to go as soon as the doctors would let her. From what she told Charles, it had been an interview formal and cool on the surface. After it, Mr March had not spoken to Charles about her.

One afternoon soon after, Charles rang me up.

'You remember when Ann was ill? She gave you a message for me?'

I said yes.

'She said this morning that I could ask you about it. She'd rather you told me than tell me herself.'

I was taken aback, so much so that I did not want to speak over the telephone. I arranged to call at his house. As I walked there along the reach from Chelsea, the river oily in the misty sunshine, the chimneys quivering in the languid Indian summer, I was seized by a sense of strangeness. This new wish of Ann's – for she had, while in danger, said that if she recovered she would tell Charles herself – this wish to have her message given him at second hand seemed bizarre. But it was not really that wish which struck so strange. It was the comfort of the senses, the warmth of the air and the smell of the autumn trees, assuring one that life might be undisturbed.

Charles was in his surgery. He was not pleased to see me. He did not want to be reminded of what I had come to tell him. He was looking better than when I had last seen him: he had made up sleep, the colour had come back to his face. But he was not rested. In a tone brittle and harsh, he began:

'I'd better hear what she said. I suppose it's about this wretched paper, isn't it? I'd better hear it.'

I was sure that, since she got better, he had not been able to put the choice out of his mind. I gave him her message, as I should have been obliged to if she had died.

'So she left it to me,' Charles said.

He did not ask for any explanation at all. With a deliberate effort – it was the habit I had got used to when he was a younger man – he talked of things which prevented me saying any more.

'I've been writing a letter,' he said. 'Would you like to read it? Do you think you would?'

I did not know what to expect. In was, in fact, a letter to the *Lancet*. In August, just before Ann's illness, one of Charles's cases had been a child of three ill with a form of diphtheria, in such a way that the ordinary feeding-tube could not be used: Charles had improvised a kind of two-way tube which had worked well. In the last fortnight, since he knew Ann would recover, he had discovered another case in a hospital, and persuaded them to use the same technique. It had worked again, and now he thought it worth while to publish the method.

'You see, no one has ever been worse with his hands than I am,' said Charles. 'So if I can use this trick, anyone else certainly can. I can't understand why some practical man hasn't thought of it long ago. Still, it's remarkably satisfying. You can believe that, can't you?'

He put the letter on his desk, ready to be typed.

'It's all very odd,' he said. 'When I was very young, I used to think that I might write something. I imagined I might write something on a simply enormous scale. I should have been extremely surprised to be told that my first published work would be a note on a minor device to make life slightly more comfortable for very small children suffering from a rather uncommon disease.'

He was talking to keep me at a distance: but the sarcasm pleased him. He was genuinely gratified by what he had done. It was good to have aroused a bit of professional envy, to receive a bit of professional praise. It was good to have something definite to one's credit. Concentrated and undiffuse as he was, he had been distracted for a few hours, even at this time, by getting a result.

But I was frightened, because he would not talk about the *Note*. I tried to get him to.

We had been intimate so long: not thinking it out as a technique to soften him, but just because I did not want to leave him quite alone, I confided something about my own marriage – something I had not told him before, nor anyone else. His eyes became sharp with insight, he gave me that support with which he had never failed me. But I did not get any other response.

At last I said:

'Charles, will you let me ask you about something else?'

'What is it?'

'I don't want to add to your trouble. You know that.'

'I know that,' he said.

'Can you tell me what you propose to do? About stopping this paper?'

There was a silence.

'No,' he said. His eyes were steady. He went on:

'I don't know. It's no use talking about it.'

The words were slow, dragged out. Looking at him, I believed he had spoken the precise truth. What his decision would be, he just did not know. But he was by himself, and nothing that anyone said could affect it now.

We went on talking. We even talked politics. I knew by his tone, what I already knew, that whatever he chose, politics would not move him either way.

As I sat with him, I believed that, whatever he chose, he was asking himself – I remembered, with a trace of superstition, the story of the night in Bryanston Square after I had taken Ann to the concert – how much he could bear to dominate another. He had gone through too much in order to be free himself: it was harder for him to choose that she should not be.

Late that night I happened to see him again. I had been dining in Dolphin Square, and was walking home along the Embankment in the moonlight. I saw Charles coming very slowly towards me on the opposite side of the road. His head was bent, he was wearing no overcoat or hat; he might have been out at a case. As he came nearer, he did not look up. Soon I could see his face in the bright moonlight: I did not cross the road, I did not say good-night.

CHAPTER XLI

FAMILY GATHERING

THREE days later, I was surprised to be rung up by Charles. He told me that Katherine, her children and Francis had arrived the evening before at Bryanston Square. I was surprised again; it was only a month since the baby was born; then I realised from Charles's tone that they had come for a purpose.

They were pressing him to go to Bryanston Square for tea that afternoon: would I pick him up and go with him?

As soon as I saw him, I thought he looked transformed. He was still pale and tired: he was tired but not restless, tired but easy, as though he had just finished playing a game.

At once he asked me, in a relaxed, affectionate voice:

'I'm sorry to be a nuisance, but just tell me again exactly what Ann said to you, will you, Lewis?'

At that moment, I knew he had made up his mind.

When I had finished, he was quiet for a few seconds. Then he said, almost as though he were making fun of her:

'I suppose she is much braver than you or me, isn't she? I've always thought she was, haven't you? Yet she didn't want to tell it me herself. She was glad to get out of that.'

He smiled.

'She's been incomparably nearer to me than any other human being ever has, or could be again,' he said. 'She thinks I know her. But I was astonished when she wanted to get out of telling me. Sometimes I think that I don't know her at all.'

On the way to Bryanston Square he asked me if I had ever felt the same, if I had ever felt that someone I knew and loved had for the moment become a stranger – utterly mysterious, utterly unknown. It was like the talks we used to have when we were younger.

Katherine and Francis were waiting in the drawing-room. Charles embraced his sister, held her in his arms, asked about the child. She told him how the delivery had been quick and easy. Charles showed a doctor's interest as he questioned her. She replied with zest; she was physically happier, and more unreticent, than anyone there. She looked blooming with health, radiant as though she had just come from a holiday. The next hour was preying on her mind, she was heavy-hearted, but still she gave out happiness. It set her apart from Charles, or even from her husband, in whom one could see already the signs of strain.

Charles said:

'I must run up and see Ann for five minutes.'

'I suppose,' said Francis, 'that she can't come down for tea?'

'It wouldn't be a good idea,' said Charles. 'Don't you admit that it wouldn't be a good idea?'

There was a sarcastic edge to his tone, and Francis flushed. When Charles had gone, Francis said to me:

'This is intolerable whatever happens.'

He had become more than ever used to getting his own way: but his feelings had stayed delicate. He was still colouring from Charles's snub. He would go through with what he had come to say, just as he went through with any job he set himself. But it cost him an effort which would have deterred a good many of us.

Katherine wanted to begin talking of Charles and Ann, but he stopped her. 'We shall have enough of it soon,' he said. I asked about his work; he was trying a major problem, but had struck a snag. We exchanged some college gossip. Full term was starting in a couple of days. The Master seemed a shade peaky, unusual for him.

We were beginning tea when Charles came down.

'How is Ann now?' said Francis, with a difficult friendliness.

'She'll be able to leave here next week,' said Charles.

'Good work,' said Francis.

There was a pause. A spoon tinkled in a saucer.

'As a matter of fact,' said Francis, 'it was about her, of course, that we wanted to talk.'

'Yes,' said Charles. His eyes gleamed.

'I think we're bound to ask you,' Francis went on, 'what the present position is about the *Note*. Has Ann stopped that affair?'

Charles answered:

'I shouldn't think so for a minute.'

'What is the position then?' said Katherine.

'I imagine it's exactly the same as when she fell ill,' Charles said.

'You mean, everything's coming down on our heads, that's what you mean, don't you?' she cried.

Francis asked:

'I take it we're right to gather that the only certain way of stopping this business is to get the *Note* suppressed?'

'You're quite right,' said Charles.

'And we're right to gather that it's in Ann's power to do it?'

'You're quite right,' said Charles.

'She could do it if you told her?'

'Certainly.'

'Have you tried?'

For the first time, Charles did not answer immediately. He might have been considering telling them that by now the choice was his. At last he just said:

'No.'

'We must ask you to.' Francis's temper was rising. 'You ought to know that I dislike interfering, but this is too serious to let go by. We must ask you to tell her.'

'I absolutely agree with Francis,' said Katherine loudly. 'It would be gross to interfere between you and Ann, but this is an occasion which we simply can't shut our eyes to, surely you admit that? We must ask you to tell her.'

Charles's voice was quiet, level, self-possessed after theirs.

'I haven't the slightest intention of doing so.'

He looked from one set face to the other. Unexpectedly he smiled.

'I'm sorry,' he said. 'You know how fond I am of both of you. Nothing will affect that, so far as I am concerned, don't you know that? I would do anything for you both.'

'Then for God's sake do this,' cried Katherine.

Charles shook his head. 'I gave you my answer more unpleasantly than I ought to have done. But it's still my answer.'

Francis tried to control himself, to subdue his tone in response to Charles's. 'Look,' he said, 'we can't leave it there. You know, Charles, I feel responsible to some extent. If it hadn't been for my brother Herbert, we might never have got into this mess. He seems to have covered his tracks somehow—'

'You needn't worry about Herbert,' I said.

'Are you sure?' said Francis.

'Quite sure,' I said. 'He's still got a chance of finishing up as a judge.'

'I shouldn't be surprised by anything he did. Not even that,' said Francis. He turned to Charles again. 'Well,' he said, 'you understand that we can't leave it there.'

'I know it's difficult for you. And I'm sorry.'

Francis went on:

'I want to make one point clear. Before I go on. We're not prejudiced by Ann's political motives: you know that, but I want to tell you. I think she over-simplifies it all: but if it comes to a fight, we're with her, of course we are. So far as that goes, we're all together. I'm also prepared to admit that the *Note* has its uses. By and large it's making a contribution. I should just say that it's not such a major contribution – it's not such a major contribution that she's justified in driving on whoever is getting hurt. It is certainly not worth disgracing your family and breaking up Mr L.'

'You must agree with that,' said Katherine. Her voice was angry and menacing: unlike Francis, she was making no attempt to conciliate Charles. 'Anyone in their senses must agree with that.'

'I agree with you politically much more than I do with Ann,' said Charles to Francis. 'In fact, I've always been less committed than you, don't you realise that?'

It was true. Of us in that room, Francis was the furthest to the left. 'I'm much more sceptical than you, I suspect,' said Charles, 'about what Ann and her friends can possibly achieve. You think this paper of theirs has some value. I must say I doubt it. It's different for her. She doesn't doubt it in the slightest. If you're going to lead that kind of life, you must believe from the start that every little action is important—'

Katherine was frowning, but Francis nodded his head.

'For myself,' said Charles, 'I don't think any of that matters.'

'What does matter?' said Katherine.

'Simply that this is something Ann believes in. The suggestion is that I should force her to betray it.'

'You must be mad,' said Katherine. 'You can't give us a better reason than that for getting Uncle Philip into the newspapers?'

'What reason would you like me to give?'

'It's not good enough,' said Francis.

'It won't do her any harm to be forced,' said Katherine. 'If you'd done more of it earlier, this would never have happened. Don't you see that you've been wrong since the day you met her?'

'No,' said Charles. 'I don't see that.'

'We mustn't criticise your marriage,' said Francis.

Katherine interrupted him:

'If your marriage is worth anything at all, this can't make any difference. Don't you see that you can't afford to be too considerate? And we can't afford to let you be. Could anyone in the world think the reason you've given is enough excuse for ruining Mr L.'s peace of mind for the rest of his life?'

Charles said:

'There was a time when you were prepared to take a risk like that.' Katherine looked at him. Her bitter indignation lessened, for he had spoken, for the first time that afternoon, with sadness.

'There was a time,' he repeated, 'when you were prepared to take a risk like that. And that time I was on your side, you know.'

'It was the easy side for you.' Her tone was stern and accusing again.

'I should have taken your side whether it was easy or hard,' said Charles. 'I've always loved you, don't you know that?'

Katherine was near to tears. He had spoken with a warmth and freedom such as she had scarcely heard. She said:

'I can't take your side now. I can't take your side.'

She burst out:

'Don't you see that I can't? Do you think that I don't know you at all? You've never forgiven Mr L. for being in power over you. You've never forgiven him for trying to stop your marriage. And he was absolutely right. Since you married this woman, you've never cared for the rest of us. You've been ready to destroy everything in the family because of her. You're not sorry now, are you? You're not sorry for anything you've done? I believe you're glad.'

Charles had stood up. He leant by the fireplace and spoke with a fierce release of energy:

'I repeat, you were ready to do all these things to marry Francis. I would have done anything on earth to help you. I would still.'

'You won't say this one word which would cost you nothing,' Katherine cried furiously. 'You won't stop your wife finishing off a piece of wickedness she should never have thought of. I know you won't think twice about what this means for Mr L. You've always been capable of being cruel. But is it possible for you to think twice of what it means to us?'

'Yes,' said Francis. 'Can you bring yourself to do that?'

Charles replied:

'You have said some hard things of me. Many of them are true. You have said hard things of Ann. Those you should have kept to yourselves. I won't trouble to tell you how untrue they are. Are you sure that in all this concern of yours you're not thinking of your own convenience? Are you sure that your motives are as pure as you seem to think? It will be a nuisance for you to have a scandal in the family. Aren't you both so comfortable that you'd like to prevent that – whatever else is lost in the process?'

Francis and Katherine sat silent, looking up at him as he stood. Francis, who in much of the quarrel had shown sympathy, was dark with anger. Katherine said, as a last resort:

'You won't trust us. Perhaps you'll trust Lewis. He's got nothing at stake. Lewis, will you tell him what you think?'

They all waited for me.

I said: 'I've already said what I think – to Ann.'

'What did you say?' cried Katherine.

'I said she ought to go to Charles and tell him she wanted to call it off.'

I spoke directly to Charles:

'I should like to ask you something. Will you and Ann talk the whole matter over for the last time?'

He smiled at me and said, without hesitation:

'No, Lewis.' He added, for my benefit alone: 'She did that through you.'

Katherine and Francis exchanged a glance. Francis said:

'There it is. It's no use going on. But we must say this. If Ann doesn't stop this business, we shan't be able to meet her. Obviously, we shan't want to create any embarrassment. If we meet socially, we shall put a decent face on it. But we shall not be able to meet her in private.'

'You know that must include me,' said Charles.

'I was afraid you would take it that way,' said Francis.

Charles said:

'There's no other way to take it.'

'No,' said Francis.

'I think you are being just,' Charles said in a level and passionless voice. 'All I can say is this: from you both I hoped for something different from justice. Once, if I had been in your place, I should have done as you are doing. I think perhaps I shouldn't now.'

He added:

'It is hard to lose you. It always will be.'

His energy had ebbed away for a moment.

He sat down. We made some kind of conversation. Ten minutes passed before Mr March came in.

'I should be obliged,' he said, 'if I could have a word with my daughter.'

'I'm afraid that I've given her my answer,' said Charles.

CHAPTER XLII

AN ANSWER

'I ASSUMED that you knew what she was asking me,' said Charles. 'I'm afraid that I've given her my answer.'

He had risen as Mr March came in, and they stood face to face by the window, away from the fireplace and the small tea-table, round which the rest of us were still sitting. They stood face to face, Charles some inches taller than his father, his hair catching the sunlight as it had done years before in the examination hall. Against him his father stood, his head less erect, his whole bearing in some way unprepared.

'I don't want to hear it,' said Mr March.

'You'll hear it from Katherine as soon as I've gone. Don't you admit that you will? Isn't it better for me to tell you myself?'

'I refuse to hear anything further until your wife has completely recovered,' said Mr March. 'I don't regard you as in a fit state to make a decision.'

'I should make the same decision whether she's ill or well,' said Charles. 'I shan't change my mind.'

'What is it?' said Mr March, in despair.

'You don't want me to say much, do you? Katherine has heard it all. All I need say is that, now she's heard it, she and Francis don't wish to meet me again.'

'I knew it,' said Mr March. They looked at each other.

'You can endure being lonely?' Mr March said at last, still in a sub-dued voice.

'I can endure that kind of loneliness.'

'Then it's useless to ask you to consider mine.'

Charles did not reply at once, and Mr March for the first time raised his voice.

'It's useless to ask you to consider my loneliness. I suppose I had better be prepared to take the only steps which are open to me.'

'I'm afraid that is for you to decide.'

'You know,' cried Mr March, 'I'm not telling you anything original. You know the position you are placing me in. You're forcing me to deprive myself of my son.'

We each knew that this quarrel was different from those in the past. Always before Mr March had a power over his son. Now it had gone. Mr March knew: he could not admit it, and his anger rose at random, wildly, without aim.

'You're forcing me,' he shouted, 'to deprive myself of my son. If this outrage happens' – he was clinging to a last vestige of hope – 'if this outrage happens, I shall be compelled to take a step which you will recognise.'

'It won't matter to me, don't you realise that?'

'Nothing that I possess will come to you. You will be compelled to recognise what you've done after my death,' said Mr March.

'I'm sorry, but that doesn't matter.'

Suddenly Katherine cried out:

'Father, why ever didn't you make him independent? When he wanted to marry? I told you at the time it wouldn't be the same between you. Do you remember?'

Mr March turned towards the fireplace, and rounded on her with fury:

'I only consider it necessary to remind you of what my Uncle Justin said to his daughter.' For a second all his anger was diverted to her. 'I reproach myself that I allowed you to make representations between myself and my son.'

'She did her best,' said Charles. 'She tried to bring us together. She tried her best to keep me in your will.'

'Charles!' Katherine cried. He had spoken with indifference: but she cried out as though he had been brutal. Mr March ignored her, and returned to face Charles.

'I should never have spoken of money,' he said, 'if I could have relied on your affection.'

For the first time, as they stood there, Charles's face softened.

'My affection was greater than you were ever ready to admit,' he said. 'Did you hear me speak to you, the night Ann was taken ill? That was true.'

Mr March's voice rang in our ears:

'There's only one thing you can say that I'm prepared to hear.'

Charles had not recovered himself. He said:

'That's impossible for me.'

'Do you consider it more impossible than destroying my family? And showing your utter ingratitude as a son? And condemning yourself to squalor now and after I am dead? And leaving me with nothing to live for in the last years of my life?'

Charles did not answer. Mr March went on: 'Do you consider it is more impossible than what you're bringing about?'

'I'm afraid it is,' said Charles.

The tone of that reply affected Mr March. Since he appealed to Charles's affection, he had reached his son. As though interpreting Charles's reply, which was loaded with remorse, Mr March spoke of Ann.

'If you hadn't married your wife,' Mr March said, 'you would have given a different answer. She is responsible for your unnatural attitude.'

Immediately Charles's manner reverted to that in which he had begun: be became hard again, passionate, almost gay.

'I am responsible for everything I've done,' he said. 'You know that. Don't you know that?'

'I refuse to accept your assurance.'

'You know that it's true,' said Charles.

'If she hadn't begun this outrage, you would never have believed it possible,' Mr March exclaimed. 'If she had desisted, you would have been relieved and—'

'If she had died, you mean. If she had died.' The word crashed out. 'That's what you mean.'

Mr March's head was sunk down.

'You were wrong. You've never been so wrong,' said Charles. 'I tell you this. If she had died, I wouldn't have raised a finger to save you trouble. I should have let it happen.'

The sound died away. The room rested in silence. Charles turned from his father, and glanced indifferently, slackly, across the room, as though he were exhausted by his outburst, as though it had left him without anger or interest.

As Charles turned away, Mr March walked from the window towards us by the fireplace. His face looked suddenly without feeling or expression.

He settled in an armchair; as he did so, his foot touched the tea-table, and I noticed the tinker-bell reflections, set dancing on the far wall.

Mr March said, in a low voice:

'Why was it necessary to act as you have done? You seem to have been compelled to break every connection with the family.'

Charles, still standing by the window, did not move or speak.

'You seem to have been compelled to break away at my expense. It was different with Herbert and my father. But you've had to cut yourself off through me.'

Mr March was speaking as though the pain was too recent to feel; he did not know all that had happened to him, he was light-headed with bereavement and defeat. He spoke like a man baffled, in doubt, still unaware of what he was going to feel, groping and mystified. He forgot Ann, and asked Charles why this conflict must come between them, just because they were themselves. A little time before, he had spoken as though he believed that, without Ann, he and his son would have been at peace. It was inconsistent in terms of logic, but it carried the sense of a father's excessive love, of a love which, in the phrase that the old Japanese used to describe the love of parents for their children, was a darkness of the heart.

'Yes,' said Mr March, 'you found it necessary to act against me. I never expected to have my son needing to act against me. I never contemplated living without my son.'

'Believe what I said to you at that last party,' said Charles quietly. 'I want you to believe that. As well as what I've said today.'

Mr March asked, not angrily, but as though he could not believe what had happened:

'You've counted the cost of this intention of yours? You've asked people what it's like to be penniless?'

'Yes,' said Charles.

'You're ready to put yourself in the shameful position of living on your wife's money?'

Charles had been answering listlessly. He gave a faint smile.

'I may even earn a little myself.'

'Pocket-money. I disregard that,' said Mr March. 'You're prepared to live on your wife?'

'Yes.'

'You're not deterred by my disgrace in seeing you in such a position?'

'No,' said Charles.

'You're not deterred by the disgrace your wife's action will inflict upon my brother and my family?'

'I thought I'd made myself clear,' said Charles, with a revival of energy.

'You're not deterred by the misery you're bringing upon me?'

'I don't want to repeat what I've said.'

Without looking at Charles again, Mr March said:

'So, if this calamity happens, you're requiring me to decide on my own actions?'

Even now he was hoping. He could still ask a question about the future.

'Yes,' said Charles.

Charles came into the middle of the room, and said:

'I might as well go now. I told Ann I would see her before I left.'

We heard him run upstairs. Katherine spoke to her father: 'It's no use. I wish I could say something, Mr L., but it's no use. There's nothing to do.' Her mouth was trembling. She added:

'I've never seen him like that before.'

Though she was supporting her father, there was something else in her voice. It dwelt more gently on Charles than any word she had said while he was there. She had made her choice; she could not help but take her father's side. But that remark was brimming with regret, with admiration, with the idolatrous love she bore Charles when she was a girl.

CHAPTER XLIII

RED BOX ON THE TABLE

DURING most of October there was no news. I saw Francis regularly in Cambridge, but he and Katherine knew no more than I. Charles had already cut himself away from them. We heard a number of rumours – that Sir Philip had seen Charles and threatened a libel action whatever the consequences, that Mr March had visited Ann, convalescing by the sea, that Ronald Porson had visited her, that Charles would not have her back unless she broke with the *Note*.

There were many more rumours, most of them fantasies; but it was true that Sir Philip had seen Charles. Charles mentioned it himself, when I was dining with him on one of my nights in London. He mentioned it with indifference, as though it were a perfectly ordinary occurrence, as though his concerns were as pedestrian as anyone else's. He wanted to regard them as settled; he did not want to see that there was a part of his nature, even yet, after all he had said and done, waiting in trepidation, just as the rest of us were waiting.

The final article in the *Note* was published in the fourth week of October. I did not subscribe to the *Note*, but a colleague of mine used to send it round to me; it was brought to my rooms in college by the messenger, on his last delivery, at ten o'clock on a Friday night. For two Fridays past I had raced my eyes over it, before looking at the mail. On this Friday night I did the same; and, as soon as I had unfolded the sheet, I knew this was it. Though I was prepared, I felt the prick of sweat at my temples.

It was the second item on the first page (the first was a three-line report of a meeting between Edward VIII and the Prime Minister), and it read:

Armament Share Scandal

Note can now give final dope about scandal of Ministers, Ministers' stooges, linkmen in Whitehall, Inns of Court, official circles, making profits from prior knowledge of armaments programme. Back references (*Note* May 26, August 10, August 24, for background, see also . . .). In '29 Tory Government laid contract of £3,000,000, engine development, with Howard & Hazlehurst (Chairman Sir Horace (Cartelspokesman) Timberlake; on board of Howard & Hazlehurst is Viscount Talland, cousin of Alex Hawtin). Alex (Britain First) Hawtin, Under-

Secretary of ..., rising hope Tory party, groomed for cabinet in immediate future, bought £20,000 – approx. – Enlibar shares. Enlibar subsidiary of Howard & Hazlehurst. Sir Philip March, Parliamentary Secretary, Ministry of ..., ex-banker, ex-director 17 companies, ex-President Jewish Board of Guardians, bought £15,000 Enlibar shares. Shares in parent firm – quantities not known to nearest pound but over £10,000 – bought by G. L. and F. E. Paul, brothers-in-law of Herbert Getliffe, K.C., legal consultant Hawtin's ministry. Shares also bought by S ..., H ... Profits on these transactions (approx.):

Hawtin	£35,000
March	£46,000*
G. L. and	
F. E. Paul	£11,000
S ...	£5,000
H ...	£3,000

'35, aircraft programme, same story, contract laid with aircraft firms. ... Details of investments not to hand, but Hawtin and March repeated gambit. G. L. and F. E. Paul not concerned this round – Getliffe no longer consultant to ministry. S ..., H ... took a rake-off, possibly catspaws for bigger players, but *Note* not in position to confirm this. Hawtin, March still in Government. Hawtin due for promotion. 'Friend of Franco' speech, Oct. 16, Liverpool; 'Franco is at any rate a Christian' speech, Oct. 23, Birmingham.

* March, old city hand, held on longer.

That was all.

The effects did not come at once. Mr March referred to it in his weekly letter to Katherine, but briefly and without comment. She went to comfort him, but on her return reported that he was composed, strangely passive, almost glad that the words were down on paper; there was nothing to imagine now. He showed no sign at all of taking action. He seemed to have feared that, the instant the words appeared, he would be surrounded by violence and disgrace: but no one except Sir Philip spoke to him about the article for several days. In that time-lag, he had a last hope, strong and comforting, that it would all be forgotten: if he stayed in his house, hid away from gossip, this would pass over, as everything else had done.

We had, in fact, all expected that there would be a blaze of publicity from the beginning. That did not happen; partly because there was another scandal going round the clubs, and people were not to be distracted from Mrs Simpson and the King. The *Note* attack had gone off half-cock. A member of the extreme left asked a question in the House, and demanded a select committee. A few eccentric Liberals and malcontents of various kinds (including a Conservative antisemite) occupied a committee room for some hours, but could not agree on a plan of action. There was a leader, so stately and stuffed that it was incomprehensible unless one knew the story, in one of the Conservative papers.

Some of the column writers made references. One or two weekly papers, on the extreme right as well as the left, let themselves go. It did not seem to amount to much.

About three weeks after the article came out, however, there were rumours of changes in the government. The political correspondents began tipping their fancies. No one suggested that the changes had anything to do with the *Note*'s article; it was not even explicitly denied. In private the gossips were speculating whether Hawtin would be 'out' or whether he would lose his promotion. He was disliked, he was cold and self-righteous; but to put him out now, after his stand on Spain, would look like a concession to the left. As for Sir Philip, his name was not canvassed much. He had never been a figure in politics; he was old and had no future. The only flicker of interest in him, apart from the scandal, was because he was a Jew.

Meanwhile, Herbert Getliffe was showing the resource and pertinacity that most people missed unless they knew him well. He had a streak of revengefulness, and he was determined that his enemies should pay. He knew that neither Hawtin nor Philip March would bring an action; nor could the Pauls without more damage to himself. So Getliffe concentrated on the minor figures, S . . ., H . . . He worked out that there was a good chance of one of them bringing an action which need involve no one else.

He wrote to Sir Philip, suggesting that they should promote an action in H . . .'s name. Sir Philip replied curtly that the less said or done the better. Despite the rebuff, Getliffe approached Mr March, to persuade him to influence his brother; and, leaving nothing to chance, he sent me the outline of the case.

Mr March and Sir Philip each snubbed him again. Getliffe, suggestible as he was when one met him face to face, was utterly impervious when on the make. He wrote to them in detail; he added that I should be familiar with the legal side, if they wanted an opinion; he wrote to me twice, begging me to do my best.

The March brothers were not weak characters, but, like most men, they could be hypnotised by persistence. Ill-temperedly Mr March arranged for me to meet him one morning at Sir Philip's office – 'to discuss the proposals which Getliffe is misguidedly advancing and which are, in my view, profoundly to be regretted at the present juncture.'

That morning when I was due to meet them, a drizzling November day, I opened *The Times* and saw, above a column in the centre page, 'Changes in the Government'. Sir Philip's name was not among them. Hawtin was promoted to full cabinet rank; to make room for him, someone was sent to the Lords. A Parliamentary Secretary and an Under-Secretary were shelved, in favour of two backbenchers. It was difficult to read any meaning into the changes. Hawtin's promotion might be a brushing-off of the scandal, a gesture of confidence, or a move to the right. The other appointments were neutral. At the end of the official statement, there was a comment that more changes would be announced shortly.

I arrived at the room of Sir Philip's secretary a little before my time. He was pretending to work, as I sat looking out at the park. The rain seeped gently down; after the brilliant autumn, the leaves had not yet fallen and shone dazzlingly out of the grey, mournful, misty morning. I heard the rain seep down, and the nervous, restless movements of the young man behind me. He was on edge with nerves: Sir Philip's fate did not matter to him, but he had become infected by the tension. He was expecting a telephone call from Downing Street. Soon he stopped work, and in his formal, throaty, sententious voice (the voice of a man who was going to enjoy every bit of pomp and circumstance in his official life) asked me whether I had studied the government changes, and what significance I gave them. He was earnest, ambitious, self-important: yet each time the telephone rang his face was screwed up with excitement, like that of a boy who is being let into an adult's secret. As each call turned out to be a routine enquiry, his voice went flat with anti-climax. As soon as Mr March came in, Williams showed us into Sir Philip's room. Before we entered, Mr March had time only to shake hands and say that he was obliged to me for coming – but even in that time I could see his face painful with hope, his resignation broken, every hope and desire for happiness evoked again by the news that Hawtin was safe. Sir Philip's first words were, after greeting us both:

'I suppose you saw in the papers that Hawtin's still in? They've given him a leg-up.'

'I was considering what effect it would have on your prospects,' said Mr March.

'It won't be long before I know. This means they're not going to execute us, anyway,' said Sir Philip, with a cackle which did not conceal that he too felt relief, felt active hope. 'As for Alex Hawtin, he's doing better for himself than he deserves. Still, he can't be worse than old . . .' Sir Philip broke off, and looked at us across his desk. He had dressed with special care that day, and with a new morning suit was wearing a light-blue, flowing silk tie. It was incongruous, against the aged yellow skin. Yet, even about his face, there was something jaunty still.

'Well,' he said, 'I wanted to consult you about this fellow Getliffe. He's got hold of someone called Huff or Hough – who must be a shady lot himself, judging from the book of words – and they want to bring a libel action if they can get financial support – I needn't go over the ground again. You've seen it for yourselves, I gather.'

'I received another effusion from Herbert Getliffe yesterday,' said Mr March, 'which I regret to say I have omitted to bring. It did not add anything substantial to his previous lucubrations.'

'And you're familiar with it, Eliot?'

'Yes,' I said.

Sir Philip suddenly snapped:

'I don't want to have anything to do with the fellow. No good can come of it. I won't touch anything he's concerned with.'

Anxiety and hope had made his temper less equable.

'I concur in your judgment,' said Mr March. 'The fellow is a pestilential nuisance.'

'I want to stop his damned suggestions,' said Sir Philip. 'Where are they? Why isn't the file here?'

He pushed the button on his desk, and the secretary entered. Sir Philip was just asking for the Getliffe file when in the outer office the telephone rang. 'Will you excuse me while I answer it, sir?' said Williams officiously, once more excited. After he went away, we could hear his voice through the open door. 'Yes, this is Sir Philip March's secretary. . . . Yes . . . Yes, I will give him that message. . . . Yes, he will be ready to receive the letter.'

Williams came in, and said with formality: 'It was a message from the Prime Minister's principal private secretary, sir. It was to say that a letter from the Prime Minister is on its way.'

Sir Philip nodded. 'Do you wish me to stay, sir?' said Williams hopefully.

'No,' said Sir Philip in an absent tone. 'Leave the Getliffe file. I'll ring if I need you.'

As soon as the door was closed, Mr March cried:

'What does it mean? What does it mean?'

'It may mean the sack,' said Sir Philip. 'Or it may mean they're offering me another job.'

At that instant Mr March lost the last particle of hope.

Sir Philip, meeting his brother's despairing gaze, went on stubbornly:

'If he is offering me another job, I shall have to decide whether to turn it down or not. I should like a rest, of course, but after this brouhaha I should probably consider it my duty to accept it. I should want your advice, Leonard, before I let him have his answer.'

Mr March uttered a sound, half-assent, half-groan.

The morning had grown darker, and Sir Philip switched on the reading lamp above his desk. The minutes passed; he looked at the clock and talked in agitation; Mr March was possessed by his thoughts. Sir Philip looked at the clock again, and said irritably:

'Whatever happens to me, I won't have this fellow Getliffe putting a foot in. I won't find a penny for his wretched case and I want to warn him off the business altogether.'

Mr March, as though he had scarcely heard, said yes. Knowing Getliffe better than they did, I said the only method was to prove to him that any conceivable case had a finite risk of involving the Pauls, and in the end himself. I thought that that was so, and that I could convince Getliffe of it. Sir Philip at once gave me the file, and Mr March asked me to go home with him shortly and pick up the recent letter. They were tired of trouble. They forgot this last nuisance as soon as the file was in my hands.

The minutes ticked on. Sir Philip complained:

'It can't take a fellow all this time to walk round from Downing Street. These messengers have been slackers ever since I've known them.'

At length we heard a shuffle, a mutter of voices, in the secretary's room. A tap on the door, and Williams came in, carrying a red oblong dispatch box.

'This has just come from the Prime Minister, sir.'

He placed it on the table in front of Sir Philip. The red lid glowed under the lamp.

Sir Philip said sharply:

'Well, well, where is the key?'

'Surely you have it, sir?'

'I remember giving it to you the last time a box arrived. After I opened it, I remember giving it to you perfectly well.'

'I'm certain that I remember your keeping the key after you opened that box, sir. I'm almost certain you put it on your key ring—'

'I tell you I've never had the key in my possession for a single moment.

You've been in charge of it ever since you've been in that office. I want you to find it now—'

Williams had blushed to his neck and ears. For him that was the intolerable moment of the morning. He went out. Sir Philip and Mr March were left to look at the red box glowing under the light. Sir Philip swore bitterly.

It was some minutes before Williams returned. 'I've borrowed this' – he said, giving a small key to Sir Philip – 'from Sir ——' (the Cabinet Minister).

'Very well, very well. Now you'd better go and find yours.'

Williams left before Sir Philip had opened the box and the envelope inside. As soon as he began to read, his expression gave the answer.

'It's the sack, of course,' he said.

He spoke slowly:

'He's pretty civil to me. He says that I shan't mind giving up my job to a younger man.'

He added:

'I didn't bank on going out like this.'

Mr March said:

'Nor did I ever think you would.'

Then Sir Philip spoke as though he were recalling his old, resilient tone. 'Well,' he said, 'I've got a good deal to clear up today. I want to leave things shipshape. You'll look after that fellow Getliffe, Eliot? We don't want any more talk. This will be in the papers tonight. After that they'll forget about me soon enough.'

In the middle of his new active response, he seemed to feel back to his brother's remark. He said to Mr March with brotherly, almost protective kindness:

'Don't take it too much to heart, Leonard. It might be worse.'

'I'm grateful for your consideration,' cried Mr March. 'But it would never have happened but for my connections.'

'That's as may be,' said Sir Philip. 'That's as may be.'

He spoke again to his brother, stiffly but kindly:

'I know you feel responsible because of Charles's wife. That young woman's dangerous, and we shan't be able to see much of her in the family after this. But I shouldn't like you to do anything about Charles on my account. It can't be any use.'

Mr March said:

'Nothing can be any use now.'

Sir Philip said:

'Well then. Leave it alone.'

Mr March replied, in a voice firm, resonant and strong:

'No. I must do what I have to do.'

CHAPTER XLIV

COMPENSATION

As soon as we left the office, Mr March reminded me that I was to come home with him to get Getliffe's last letter. He was quick and energetic in his movements; the slowness of despair seemed to have left him; outside in the street, he called for a taxi at the top of his voice, and set off in chase of it like a young man.

We drove down Whitehall. Mr March remarked:

'I presume this is the last occasion when I shall go inside those particular mausoleums. I cannot pretend that will be a hardship for me personally. Though for anyone like my brother Philip, who had ambitions in this direction, it must be an unpleasant wrench to leave.'

I was amazed at his matter-of-fact tone, at the infusion of cheerfulness and heartiness which I had not heard in him for many weeks. He had spoken of his brother with his old mixture of admiration, envy, sense of unworthiness and detached incredulity, incredulity that a man should choose such a life. He had spoken as he might have done in untroubled days. It was hard to remember his silent anguish an hour before in Sir Philip's room. He said:

'I shall want to speak to my son Charles this morning.'

His tone was still matter-of-fact. He said that he would ring Charles up as soon as he got home. Then he talked of other things, all the way to Bryanston Square. The end had come and he was released. He was flooded by a rush of power. He could go through with it, he knew. He could act as though of his own free will. It set him speaking cheerfully and heartily.

He took me into his study. He gave me Getliffe's letter and said casually: 'I hope you will be able to settle the fellow for us.' Then he asked:

'Are you sufficiently familiar with my son's efforts as a practitioner to know where he is to be found at this time in the morning?' It was ten past twelve.

'He's usually back from his rounds about half-past,' I said.

'I will telephone him shortly,' said Mr March. 'I shall require to see him before luncheon.'

He asked me to excuse him, and rang up, not Charles, but the family solicitor. Mr March said that he needed to transact some business in the early afternoon. The solicitor tried to put off the appointment until later in the day, but Mr March insisted that it must be at half-past two. 'I shall be having luncheon alone,' he said on the telephone. 'I propose to come directly afterwards to your office. My business may occupy a considerable portion of the afternoon.'

When that was settled, Mr March talked to me for a few minutes. He enquired, with his usual consideration, about my career, but for the most part he wanted to talk of Charles. What would his future be? What society was he intending to move in? Would he make any headway as a practitioner? I told him about the letter to the *Lancet*. Even at that moment, he was full of pride. 'Not that I expect for a minute it is of any value,' he said. 'But nevertheless it shows that he may not be prepared to vegetate.' He sat and considered, on his lips a sad but genuine smile, with no trace of rancour.

'It would be a singular circumstance,' said Mr March, 'if he contributed something after all.'

It was time for him to ring up Charles. When he got an answer, his expression suddenly became fixed. I guessed that he was hearing Ann's voice. 'This is Leonard March,' he said, not greeting her. 'I wish urgently to speak to my son.' There was a pause before he spoke to Charles. 'If it is not inconvenient for you, I should like you to come here without delay.' Mr March did not say any more to Charles. To me he said:

'No doubt it is inconvenient for him, my requiring his presence in this manner.' He paused. 'But I shall make no further demands upon his time.'

Mr March stood up, shook my hand, and said:

'I hope you will forgive me, Lewis, for not inviting you to stay for luncheon. I shall have certain matters to attend to for the remainder of the day.'

He added:

'If you wish to stay in order to see my son, I hope you will not be deterred from doing so. I think you are familiar enough with my house to make yourself at home. I should be sorry if you ceased to be familiar with my house. I shall be obliged if you find it possible to visit me occasionally.'

CHAPTER XLV

'I SUPPOSE I DON'T KNOW YET'

I WENT into the drawing-room, affected by the other times I had waited there. I sat by the fire, picked up a biography, and tried to read. The soft rain fell in the square outside. The light of the wet autumn day was diffuse and gentle, and the fire burned high in the chimney. I heard Charles's car drive up, and the sound of the butler's voice greeting him in the hall.

Again I tried to read. But, within a few minutes, far sooner that I expected, Charles joined me. He said:

'Mr L. told me that I should find you here.'

He sat down, and looked at me with a tired, composed smile.

He said:

'He did it with great dignity.'

He said no more of their last meeting.

He began to talk, practically, about his financial condition. Ann's income would go down now that her father had retired. Charles himself was earning about £900 a year from his practice. 'It ought to mount up in the next two or three years,' he said. 'But I shall be lucky if I work it up to £1500. Altogether, it will be slightly different from the scale of life I was brought up to expect.'

He smiled. 'I suppose it doesn't matter much,' he said. 'It may be a nuisance sometimes not to have a private income – you used to say what a difference it made, didn't you? I don't mean for luxuries. I mean there are times when it's valuable for a doctor to be independent of his job. He can do things and say things that otherwise he wouldn't dare. Some of us ought to be able to say things without being frightened for our livelihood, don't you agree? Well, I shan't be able to. I don't know how much difference it will make.'

He was showing the kind of realistic worry which I had seen in him so often. It was genuine; for most of his life he had expected that when Mr March died he would become a rich man; he had always lived in comfort, even since his marriage.

He did not restrain his worry. He was not in a hurry to leave his father's house. He spoke about Mr March with a concern so strong and steady that one could not miss it.

'He mustn't be left alone more than anyone can help,' said Charles. 'I've done this, so of course I'm no use to him now. But everyone else must see that he's got plenty to catch his interest. He finds it hard to be desperately unhappy when there are people round him, you know that, don't you? Even though—' Charles paused. 'Even though he's lost something. He can't be swallowed up by unhappiness while there are people round him. He has to expend himself on them.'

His face was tired, kind. He went on: 'I know it's a different story when he is alone at night.'

He reiterated his concern:

'They mustn't be frightened to intrude on him. When he's unhappy, I mean. It's easy to be too delicate. Sometimes it's right. I assure you it isn't right with Mr L. I think Katherine will know that by instinct. If she doesn't, you must tell her, Lewis. Will you promise to tell her?

'I'm cut off from them,' he added. 'I can't tell them what to do. But I think I know him better than they do.'

Behind his worry, behind his concern, he was thinking of what he had done.

'I've done this,' he said, repeating the phrase he had used as he gave me messages about his father. 'I've done this. Sometimes I can't believe it. It sounds ridiculous, but I feel I've done nothing.' He gave a smile, completely open, unguarded, and candid. I had never seen his face so brilliant and innocent.

'At other times,' he said, 'I feel remorse.'

The words weighed down. I said:

'I know what you mean. I've told you, once I did something more unforgivable than you've done. I know what you mean.'

Charles said eagerly:

'Sometimes it seems the most natural thing in the world to do what one did, isn't that true? It seems so – ordinary, doesn't it? Didn't you feel that? And sometimes you felt you wouldn't forget it, you wouldn't be free of the memory, for the rest of your life?'

'I'm not free yet,' I said.

We smiled. There was great intimacy between us.

'Did yours seem like mine? Did it seem you were bound to make a choice? Did it seem you had to hurt one person or another whatever you did?'

'I hadn't any justification at all,' I said.

'With me,' said Charles, 'it seemed to be wrapped up with everything in my life.'

He waited for some time before he spoke again. His expression was heavy, but not harassed. 'Until it happened, I didn't know what I should have to live with. Live with in myself, I mean: you must have faced that too, haven't you?' He looked. at me with simplicity, with a kind of brotherly directness. He said: 'I suppose I don't know yet.'

Did it make nonsense of what he had tried to do with his life? More than any of us, I was thinking, he had searched into his own nature, and had distrusted it more. Did this make nonsense of what he had tried to do? To him the answer would sometimes, and perhaps often, be yes.

Sitting with him in the drawing-room, I could not feel it so. Not that I was trying to judge him: all I had was a sense of expectancy, curiously irrelevant, but reassuring as though the heart were beating strongly, about what the future held.

CHAPTER XLVI

HIS OWN COMPANY

SOME weeks later, in January, I went to dinner at Bryanston Square. As I heard from Katherine, Mr March was inventing excuses to keep his house full; that night he had chosen to celebrate what he regarded as a success of mine. The 'success' was nothing but a formality: I had just been confirmed in my college job and now, if I wanted, could stay there until retiring age. For Mr March it was a pretext for a party; as he greeted me it seemed to be something more.

When the butler showed me into the drawing-room, comforting after the cold night outside, Mr March had already come down, and was standing among Francis and Katherine and a dozen or more of our contemporaries. It was the biggest party I had seen there since his seventieth birthday. He came across to me, swinging his arm, and the instant he shook hands, said without any introduction:. 'I always viewed your intention to support yourself by legal practice as misguided.'

It sounded brusque. It sounded unemollient. Taken aback, Katherine said:

'He was doing well in it, after all, Mr L.'

'No! No!' He brushed her aside, and spoke straight to me: 'I didn't regard legal practice as a suitable career for someone with other burdens.'

He spoke with understanding. He knew what my marriage meant: this was his way of telling me so. How much time – he broke off shyly – did I intend to devote to my London job? Three days a week, as before, I told him: and I could feel him thinking that that was the amount of time

781

I spent with my wife in the Chelsea house. 'Oh well,' he remarked, 'so long as that brings in sufficient for your requirements.'

As for Francis, so for me, Mr March ignored any earnings from academic life. His tone had not altered; apart from the burst of sympathy, which no one else in the room recognised, he was talking as he used to do. At dinner he went on addressing us round the table, just as he had done on my earliest visits there. The only difference that I should have noticed, if I had not known what had happened, was a curious one: the food, which had always been good, was now luxurious. Mr March, living alone in Bryanston Square, was doing himself better than ever in the past.

He spread himself on anecdotes: his talent for total recall was in good working order: there was plenty of laughter. I looked at Francis. It happened that just as that time there was a disagreement between us: we were beginning to be divided by a piece of college politics. But still, as our glances met, we had a fellow-feeling. In that sumptuous dinner party, we should have been hard put to it to say why we were so uncomfortable, when Mr March himself was not. Perhaps we had counted on giving him support, which he would not take.

Towards the end of dinner, Mr March drank my health, and, still holding his glass, got into spate:

'On the occasion of Lewis Eliot first giving me the pleasure of his company in this house, I observed to my daughter Katherine that no proper preparations had been taken for the eventuality that he might prove to be a teetotaller. I failed to observe to my daughter Katherine on the identical anniversary that no proper precautions had been taken for the eventuality that Leonard might not be disposed to welcome a four-foot-high teddy-bear.'

'Who mightn't like a teddy-bear?' someone cried, apparently nervous in case Mr March was talking of himself.

'My grandson Leonard, of course,' shouted Mr March. 'The anniversary of whose birth, which took place last week, coincides as to day and month, but not however as to year, with that of the first visit of Lewis Eliot to my house. Of course, the opposite mistake used to be made with even more distressing consequences, though naturally not by my daughter Katherine.'

'What mistake?'

'Of teetotallers not making adequate provision for non-teetotallers, as opposed to the hypothetical reception of Lewis Eliot, as previously mentioned. On accepting hospitality from my second cousin Archibald Waley I constantly found myself in an intolerable dilemma. Not owing to his extraordinary habit of gnashing his teeth, which was owing to a physiological peculiarity and unconnected with any defects of temperament which he nevertheless possessed, and demonstrated by his lamentable behaviour over his expulsion from Albert Hart's club during a certain disagreement. My intolerable dilemma was of a different nature. I used to present myself at his house – Philip used to say that it was the most inconvenient house in Kensington – and we used to make our entrance into the dining-room in a perfectly orthodox manner that I could see no reason for objecting to. Then, however, we were confronted as we sat down in our places with a printed card which I have always regarded as the height of bad form, and which did not improve the situation by informing us that we were required to assimilate nine courses. It is perhaps common fairness to point out that at the relevant period it was customary to provide more elaborate refreshments than the fork-suppers we've all taken to fobbing off on our guests.'

'Was this a fork supper, Mr L. ?' asked a niece, waving at the plates.

'I don't know what else you'd call it,' said Mr March. 'The over-ostentation of the provender was nevertheless not the main point at issue. One could possibly have contemplated nine courses until one was discouraged by hearing the footman ask "What would you like to drink, sir ?" One then inquired for possible alternatives and was given the choice "Orangeade, lemonade, lemon squash, lime juice, ginger beer, ginger ale, barley water. . . ." It was always said that when Herbert dined there he put a flask of brandy in his trouser pocket and made an excuse to go to the lavatory at least twice during the proceedings.' Mr March raised his voice above questions, comments, grins:

'The presumed discomfort to Lewis Eliot as a teetotaller entering this, a non-teetotal house, was in my judgment less than that experienced by myself at Archibald Waley's.' He added:

'In practice, Lewis Eliot turned out not to be a teetotaller at all. As could have been ascertained from the person instrumental in giving me the pleasure of his company. That person being my son Charles.'

No one said anything. Mr March went on:

'At that time there was nothing to prevent me communicating with my son Charles. However, I did not, at least not upon the point under discussion.'

He said it with absolute stoicism. It was a stoicism which stopped any of us taking up the reference to Charles, or mentioning him again.

I left early, before any of the others. In the square it was cold enough to take one's breath, and in the wind the stars flashed and quivered above the tossing trees. Trying to find a taxi, I walked along the pavement, across the end of the square, as I had walked with Charles after my first visit to the house, listening to him talk about his father. I was not thinking of them, though: my thoughts had gone to my own house. Just for a random instant, I recalled our housekeeper running down the local doctors, and then admitting, in a querulous, patronising fashion, that some people in Pimlico spoke of Charles March as a good doctor, and seemed to trust him now. That thought did not last: it drifted into others of our housekeeper, my own home.

Standing at the corner, I stamped my feet, waiting for a taxi. Through the bare trees of the garden, I could see a beam of light, as the door of Mr March's house opened, letting out some more of his guests. Soon the party would be over. He would test the latches and switch off the lights: then he would be left in his own company.

The Light and the Dark

1935–43

The Light and the Dark

CONTENTS

PART ONE. WALKS AT NIGHT

PART TWO. THE GLIMMER OF HOPE

Contents

PART THREE. THE LAST ATTEMPT

PART FOUR. CLARITY

The Light and the Dark

WALKS AT NIGHT

CHAPTER I

A SPRING AFTERNOON

I SMELT blossom everywhere as I walked through the town that afternoon. The sky was bright, cloudless and pale, and the wind cut coldly down the narrow Cambridge streets. Round Fenner's the trees flared out in bloom, and the scent was sweet, heady and charged with one's desires.

I had been walking all the afternoon weighed down by a trouble. It was a trouble I was used to, there was no help for it, it could only be endured. It gnawed acutely that day, and so I had tried to comfort myself, walking alone; but I should have said nothing, if Roy Calvert had not asked me direct.

I had turned towards the college, and was still engrossed in my thoughts; it was not until he called out that I saw him moving towards me with his light, quick stride. He was over middle height, slightly built but strong; and each physical action was so full of ease and grace that he had only to enter a room for eyes to follow him.

'You look extremely statesman-like, Lewis,' he said, mimicking an acquaintance's favourite word of praise. His eyes were glinting a clear transparent hazel yellow, and his whole expression was mischievous and gay. It was often otherwise. In repose, as I had noticed when he was fifteen and I first met him, his face became sad and grave, and in a moment the brilliant high spirits could be swept away and he would look years older, more handsome, more finely shaped. And once or twice already I had seen his face, not sad, but stricken and haunted by a wild melancholy, inexplicably stricken it seemed for so young a man.

Now he was cheerful, gay and mocking. 'Do you need to address your colleagues? Do you need to make something clear to unperceptive persons?'

I said no, and at the sound of my voice he glanced at me sharply. He walked at my side under the trees by the edge of Parker's Piece. When he next spoke, his tone had changed.

'Lewis, why are you unhappy?'

'There's nothing the matter.'

'Why are you unhappy?'

'It's nothing.'

'Not true,' he said.

To put him off, I asked about a predicament of his own which I had heard about, week by week, for some time past. Roy shook his head and smiled. 'No,' he said. 'You mustn't escape by talking about me. It's very like you. It's the way you protect yourself, old boy. You mustn't. You need to talk.'

I was twenty-eight, and Roy five years younger. I was fond of him in a casual, protective fashion, and I expected to be told of his adventures and have him seek me out when he was despondent. I knew a good deal of his life, and he very little of mine. This was the habit I had formed, not only with him but with most people that I cared for. And so I was not used to Roy's insistence, clear, intimate, direct. With another I should have passed it off for ever, but about his affection there was something at the same time disarming and piercing. It seemed quite free from self. To my own surprise, I found myself beginning to talk.

We walked along the back streets to Maid's Causeway, over Midsummer Common to the river, came back to Christ's Piece and then, still intent, retraced our steps. It was bitterly cold in the shade, but we walked slowly: the dense snow-white masses of the chestnuts gleamed in the sunshine: there was a first hint of lilac in the wind. Once, after I had fallen silent and Roy had said 'just so' and was waiting for me to start again, I heard a series of college clocks clanging out the hour, very faintly, for the wind took the sound away.

The story I told Roy was about my marriage to Sheila. No one else knew all I told him, though one or two must have guessed something near the truth. I had been desperately in love with her when I was a very young man; when at twenty-six I married her, I still loved her, and I married her knowing that she did not love me and that her temperament was unstable. This was over two years before. I went into it thinking I might have to look after her: it had turned out worse than I feared.

'Just so,' said Roy. 'You can't leave her now, can you? You couldn't if you tried. You need to go on looking after her. You need to go on looking after her always.'

'Yes,' I said.

'You know,' he said, 'you're not the one I pity. Should you be? I'm extremely sorry, things must be made as easy for you as they can. But you're interested in life, you've got tremendous spirits, you can bear anything. No, it's she whom I pity desperately. I don't see what she has to hope for.'

He was utterly right. I knew it too well. Again we walked under the fragrant trees. 'You mustn't lose too much,' said Roy. I had forgotten by now how young he was, and he was talking as though we had each been through the same darkness.

'As you've just said,' I replied, 'there's nothing to be done. One has to go on, that's all.'

'Just so,' said Roy. 'Life's very unfair. Why should this happen to you?'

Yet I felt he liked me more because it had happened.

Now that I had said so much, I thought I might as well explain why I had taken a job in Cambridge at all. As he knew, I had been born poor. Through a mixture of good luck and good management, I had done well in the Bar examinations. By the time I married, I was making a fair living at the Bar. But I was overstrained, I confessed to him, my inner life racked me more after marriage than before, I wanted to rest a little. Some of my influential friends made enquiries, and soon Francis Getliffe told me there might be an opening in his college for an academic lawyer. At last the offer was officially made: I accepted it, and was elected late in 1933, a few months before this talk with Roy. The college did not object to my keeping on a consultant's job with an industrial firm, and I spent some days each week in London, where my wife was still living in our Chelsea house. I usually stayed in Cambridge from Thursday to Monday, and slept in my college rooms on those nights, as though I had been a bachelor fellow.

It was since I came to live so much in college that Roy began to call on me. I had met him once when he was a boy, and occasionally in his undergraduate days not only during the Passant trial. I knew he was a member of the college when Francis first approached me and I had heard several conflicting rumours about him – that he was drinking himself to death, spending all his nights with women, becoming an accomplished oriental scholar. But it was a coincidence that his rooms should be on the next staircase to mine, and that we should be waited on by the same servant. The first weekend I spent in college he ran up to see me, and since then it was unusual if I did not hear his step on my stairs once or twice a day.

I had come to the end of what I could tell him: we stood under the trees in the bright sunshine; Roy said 'just so' again to lead me further, but the clear light reedy voice died away without reply from me, for I had finished. He smiled because he felt I was less careworn, and took me to his rooms for tea.

They were a curious set of rooms, in a turret over the kitchen, right in the middle of the college. From a window on the staircase one could look out over the first court to the front gate, and his sitting-room window gave onto the palladian building in the second court and the high trees in the garden beyond. It was for strictly nepotic reasons that Roy was allowed to live there. He had ceased to be an undergraduate nearly three years before; he would normally have gone out of college then. He was well off, and it would have been easy for him to live in comfort anywhere in the town. But he was a favourite pupil of the Master's and of Arthur Brown's, the tutor who arranged about rooms: and they decided that it would be good for his researches if he stayed where he was.

The sitting-room itself struck oddly and brightly on the eye. There were all kinds of desks in a glazed and shining white – an upright one, at which he could work standing and read a manuscript against an opalescent screen, several for sitting at, one with three arms like a Greek pi, one curved like a horseshoe, and one very low which he could use by lying on cushions on the floor. For the rumours about him had a knack of containing a scrap of truth, and the one which to many of his acquaintances sounded the most fantastic was less extraordinary than the fact. He had already put a mass of original scholarship behind him; most days he worked in this room for seven or eight hours without a break, and he had struck a field where each day's work meant a discovery both new and certain.

The whole room was full of gadgets for his work, most of which he had designed. There were holders for his manuscripts, lights to inspect them by, a small X-ray apparatus which he had learned to work, card indexes which stood up and could be used with one hand. Everything glistened in its dazzling white, except for some van Goghs on the walls, a rich russet carpet all over the floor, and a sofa and armchair by the fire.

A kitchen porter brought us a big tray wrapped in green baize; underneath stood a robust silver teapot, a plate of toast, a dish of mulberry jam, a bowl of thick cream.

Roy patted the shining silver.

'You deserve some tea,' he said. 'Reward for interesting conversation.'

He gave a smile, intimate and kind. He knew now that he had helped bring me somewhere near a normal state. He was sure enough to laugh at me. As I spread jam and cream on a piece of toast and tasted the tart mulberry flavour through cream, butter, burned bread, I saw he had a mocking glint in his eyes.

'Well?' I said.

'I was only thinking.'

'What of?'

'Women.'

'Well?' I said again.

'Each to his métier,' said Roy. 'You'd better leave them to me in future. You take them too seriously.'

In fact, he attracted much love. He had been sought after by women since he was a boy: and he enjoyed making love, and threw it lightly away.

Five o'clock struck, and Roy sprang from his chair. 'Not much time,' he said. 'We must be off. I need you. I need to buy some books.'

'What is it?' I asked, but he smiled demurely and secretively.

'You'll know quite soon,' he said.

He led the way to the nearest bookshop. 'Quick,' he said as I followed through the press of people on the narrow pavement. 'We need to get through them all in half-an-hour.'

He was playing a trick, but there was nothing to worry about. He was enjoying himself. When we arrived at the shop, he stared round with an expression serious, eager, keenly anxious. Then he moved over to the shelf of theological works, and said with intensity:

'There are still some here. We're not too late.' He had taken hold of three copies of a thin volume. The dust cover carried a small cross and the words: *The Middle Period of Richard Heppenstall* by Ralph Udal. 'Who in God's name was Richard Heppenstall?' I asked.

'Seventeenth-century clergyman,' Roy whispered. 'Somewhat old-brandy, but very good.' Then in a loud clear voice he greeted the manager of the shop, who was coming to attend to him.

'I see I've just got here in time. How many have you sold?'

'None as far as I know, Mr Calvert. It's only come in today—'

'That's extremely odd,' said Roy.

'Is it a good book, Mr Calvert?'

'It's a very remarkable book,' said Roy. 'You must read it yourself. Promise me you will, and tell me what you think of it. But you need to buy some more. We shall have to take these three. I'm extremely sorry, but you'll have to wait before you read it. I want one myself *urgently* tonight. I need to send one at once to Mr Despard-Smith. And of course Lord Boscastle needs one too. You'd better put that one down to Mr

Lewis Eliot—' he walked the manager away from me, whispering confidentially, the manager responding by wise and knowing nods. I never learned for certain what he said; but for the rest of my time in Cambridge, the manager, and the whole of the staff of his shop, treated me with uneasy deference, as though, instead of being an ordinary law don, I might turn out to be a peer incognito.

I was half-ruffled, half-amused, when Roy rushed me away to another shop.

'I'm buying these books,' he said before I could protest. 'Just lend me your name. I'll settle tonight. Talking of names, Lord B. is staying at the Lodge tomorrow' (for Lord Boscastle was a real person, and his sister, Lady Muriel, was the Master's wife).

We hurried from bookshop to bookshop, buying every copy of Udal's book before half-past five. Roy sent them as presents, had them put down to my account, asked me to enquire for them myself.

As we left the last shop, Roy grinned.

'Well, that was quite a rush,' he said.

He insisted on paying three pounds for the books that had been put down to me – and, to tell the truth, I did not feel like stopping him.

'I suppose I'm right in thinking that Udal is a friend of yours?' I said.

Roy smiled.

On our way back to the college, he asked:

'Tell me, Lewis, are you extremely tired?'

'Not specially.'

'Nor am I. We need some nets. Let's have some.'

We changed, and he drove me down to Fenner's in the cold April evening. The freshman's match was being played, and we watched the last overs of the day; then Roy bought a new ball in the pavilion, we went over to the nets, and I began to bowl to him. Precisely how good he was I found it difficult to be sure. He had a style of extreme elegance and ease; he seemed to need no practice at all, and the day after a journey abroad or a sleepless night would play the first over with an eye as sure as if he had been batting all the summer. When he first came up, people had thought he might get into the university team, but he used to make beautiful twenties and thirties against first-class bowling, and then carelessly give his wicket away.

He was fond of the game, and batted on this cold evening with a sleek lazy physical content. Given the new ball, I was just good enough a bowler to make him play. My best ball, which went away a little off the seam, he met with a back stroke from the top of his height, strong, watchful, leisurely and controlled. He hit the ball very hard – but, when one watched him at the wicket, his strength was not so surprising as if one had only seen him upright and slender in a fashionable suit.

I bowled to him for half-an-hour, but my only success was to get one ball through and rap him on the pads.

'Promising,' said Roy.

Then we had a few minutes during which I batted and he bowled, but at that point the evening lost its decorum, for Roy suddenly ceased to be either graceful or competent when he ran up to bowl.

The ground was empty now, the light was going, chimes from the Catholic church rang out clearly in the quiet. We stopped to listen; it was the hour, it was seven o'clock. We walked across the ground and under the trees in the road outside. The night was turning colder still, and our breath formed clouds in the twilight air. But we were hot with exercise, and Roy did not put on his sweater, but knotted the sleeves under the chin. A few white petals fell on his shoulders on our way towards the car. His eyes were lit up as though he were smiling at my expense, and his face was at rest.

'At any rate,' he said, 'you should be able to sleep tonight.'

CHAPTER II

INSPECTION AT DINNER

THE next morning, as I was going out of the college, I met the Master in the court.

'I was wanting to catch you, Eliot,' he said. 'I tried to get you by telephone last night, but had no luck.'

He was a man of sixty, but his figure was well preserved, the skin of his cheeks fresh, rosy and unlined. He was continuously and excessively busy, yet his manner stayed brisk and cheerful; he complained sometimes of the books he had left unwritten or had still to write, but he was happier in committees, meetings, selection boards than in any other place. He was a profoundly humble man, and had no faith in anything original of his own. But he felt complete confidence in the middle of any society or piece of business; he went briskly about, cheerful and unaffected, indulging in familiar intimate whispers; he had never quite conquered his tongue, and if he was inspired by a malicious thought he often was impelled to share it. He asked me to the Lodge for dinner the following night, in order to meet the Boscastles. 'My wife's note will follow, naturally, but I was anxious not to miss you.' It was clear that I was being invited to fill a gap, and the Master, whose manners were warm as well as good, wanted to make up for it.

'We've already asked young Calvert,' he went on, and dropped into his intimate whisper: 'Between ourselves, my brother-in-law never has considered this was the state of life his sister was born to. I fancy she wants to present him with someone who might pass muster. It's a very singular coincidence that we should possess a remarkably talented scholar who also cuts his hair. It's much more than we could reasonably expect.'

I chuckled.

'Yes,' said the Master, 'our young friend is distinctly presentable. Which is another strong reason for electing him, Eliot. The standard of our colleagues needs raising in that respect.'

I was left in no doubt that Roy had been invited to the original party, and that I was a reserve. The Master could not explain or apologise more, for, indiscreetly as he talked about fellows of the college, he was completely loyal to his wife. Yet it could not have escaped him that she was a formidable and grandiose snob. She was much else besides, she was a woman of character and power, but she was unquestionably a snob. I wondered if it surprised the Master as much as it did me, when I first noticed it. For he, the son of a Scottish lawyer, had not married Lady Muriel until he was middle-aged; he must have come strange to the Boscastles, and with some preconceptions about the aristocracy. In my turn, they were the first high and genuine aristocrats I had met; they were Bevills and the family had been solidly noble since the sixteenth century (which is a long time for a genuine descent); I had expected them to be less interested in social niceties than the middle classes were. I had not found it so. Nothing could be further from the truth. They did it on a grander scale, that was all.

On the night of the dinner party, I was the first guest to arrive, and the Master, Lady Muriel, and their daughter Joan were alone in the great drawing-room when I was announced.

'Good evening, Mr Eliot,' said Lady Muriel. 'It is very good of you to come to see us at such short notice.'

I was slightly amused: that sounded like rubbing it in.

I was not allowed to chat; she had discovered that I had an interest in world affairs, and every time I set foot in the Lodge she began by cross-questioning me about the 'latest trends'. She was a stiffly built heavy woman, her body seeming cylindrical in a black evening dress; she looked up at me with bold full tawny eyes, and did not let her gaze falter. Yet I had felt, from the first time I met her and she looked at me so, that there was something baffled about her, a hidden yearning to be liked – as though she was a little girl, aggressive and heavy among children smaller than herself, unable to understand why they did not love her.

Seeing her in her own family, one felt most of all that yearning and the strain it caused. In the long drawing-room that night, I looked across at her husband and her daughter. The Master was standing beside one of the lofty fire screens, his hand on a Queen Anne chair, trim and erect in his tails like a much younger man. He and Lady Muriel exchanged some words: there was loyalty between them, but no ease. And Joan, the eldest of the Royces' children, a girl of eighteen, stood beside him, silent and constrained. Her face at the moment seemed intelligent, strong and sulky. When she answered a direct question from her mother, the friction sounded in each syllable. Lady Muriel sturdily asked another question in a more insistent voice.

The butler called out 'Mr Calvert', and Roy came quickly up the long room, past the small tables, towards the group of us standing by the fire. Lady Muriel's face lightened, and she cried out: 'Good evening, Roy. I almost thought you were going to be late.'

'I'm never late, Lady Muriel,' said Roy. 'You should know that, shouldn't you? I am never late, unless it's somewhere I don't want to go. Then I usually appear on the wrong day.'

'You're quite absurd,' said Lady Muriel, who did not use a hostess's opening topic with Roy. 'I wonder why I allow you in the house.'

'Because you know I like to come,' said Roy.

'You've learned to flatter too young,' she said with a happy crow of laughter.

'You're suspicious of every nice thing you hear, Lady Muriel. Particularly when it's true,' said Roy. 'Now aren't you?'

'I refuse to argue with you.' She laughed happily. Roy turned to Joan, and began teasing her about what she should do at the university next year: but he did not disarm her as easily as her mother.

Just then the Boscastles entered from one of the inner doors. They were an incongruous pair, but they had great presence and none of us could help watching them. Lord Boscastle was both massive and fat; there was muscular reserve underneath his ample, portly walk, and he was still light on his feet. His face did not match his comfortable body: a great beak of a nose stood out above a jutting jaw, with a stiff grey moustache between them. By his side, by the side of Lady Muriel and

Joan, who were both strong women, his wife looked so delicate and frail that it seemed she ought to be carried. She was fragile, thin with an invalid's thinness, and she helped herself along with a stick. In the other hand she carried a lorgnette, and, while she was limping slowly along, she was studying us all with eyes that, even at a distance, shone a brilliant porcelain blue. She had aged through illness, her skin was puckered and brown, she looked at moments like a distinguished monkey; but it was easy to believe that she had once been noted for her beauty.

I watched her as I was being presented to her, and as Roy's turn came. He smiled at her: as though by instinct, she gave a coquettish flick with the lorgnette. I was sure he felt, as I had felt myself, that she had always been courted, that she still, on meeting a strange man at a party, heard the echoes of gallant words.

Lord Boscastle greeted us with impersonal cordiality, and settled down to his sherry. The last guest came, Mrs Seymour, a cousin of Lady Muriel's who lived in Cambridge, and soon we set out to walk to the dining-room. This took some time, for the Lodge had been built, reconstructed, patched up and rebuilt for five hundred years, and we had to make our way along narrow passages, down draughty stairs, across landings: Lady Boscastle's stick tapped away in front, and I talked to Mrs Seymour, who seemed gentle, inane, vague and given to enthusiasms. She was exactly like Lady Muriel's concept of a suitable dinner partner for one of the younger fellows, I thought. In addition, Lady Muriel, to whom disapproval came as a natural response to most situations, disapproved with particular strength of my leaving my wife in London. She was not going to let me get any advantages through bad conduct, so far as she could help it.

Curiously enough, the first real excitement of the dinner arrived through Mrs Seymour. We sat round the table in the candlelight, admired the table which had come from the family house at Boscastle – 'from our house,' said Lady Muriel with some superbity – admired the Bevill silver, and enjoyed ourselves with the food and wine. Both were excellent, for Lady Muriel had healthy appetites herself, and also was not prepared to let her dinners be outclassed by anything the college could do. She sat at the end of the table, stiff-backed, bold-eyed, satisfied that all was well with her side of the evening, inspecting her guests as though she were weighing their more obvious shortcomings.

She began by taking charge of the conversation herself. 'Mr Eliot was putting forward an interesting point of view before dinner,' she said in an authoritative voice, and then puzzled us all by describing my opinions on Kirkwood. It seemed that I had a high opinion of his profundity. Joan questioned her fiercely, Roy soothed them both, but it was some time before we realised that she meant Kierkegaard. It was a kind of intellectual malapropism such as she frequently made. I thought, not for the first time, that she was at heart uninterested in all this talk of ideas and books – but she did it because it was due to her position, and nothing would have deterred her. Not in the slightest abashed, she repeated 'Kierkegaard' firmly twice and was going ahead when Mrs Seymour broke in:

'Oh, I'd forgotten. I meant to tell you straightaway, but that comes of being late. I've always said that they ought to put an extra light on your dressing-table. Particularly in strange bedrooms—'

'Yes, Doris?' Lady Muriel's voice rang out.

'I haven't told you, have I?'

'You have certainly told us nothing since you arrived.'

'I thought I'd forgotten. Tom's girl is engaged. It will be in *The Times* this week.'

The Boscastles and the Royces all knew the genealogy of 'Tom's girl'. For Mrs Seymour might be scatterbrained, but her breeding was the Boscastles' own; she had married a Seymour, who was not much of a catch but was eminently 'someone one had heard of', and Tom was her husband's brother. Though I did not know it that night, another brother, Humphrey, was to enter my life before long, and later on a good many other relatives. Tom's girl was taken seriously, even though Lord Boscastle had never met her, and Lady Muriel only once. She was part of the preserve. Abandoning in a hurry all abstract conversation, Lady Muriel plunged in with her whole weight. She sat more upright then ever and called out:

'Who is the man?'

'He's a man called Houston Eggar.'

Lord Boscastle filled the chair on his sister's right. He finished a sip of hock, put down the glass, and asked:

'Who?'

'Houston Eggar.'

Lady Muriel and Lord Boscastle looked at each other. In a faint, tired, disconsolate tone Lord Boscastle said:

'I'm afraid I don't know the fellow.'

'I can help,' said the Master briskly from the other end of the table. 'He's a brother-in-law of the Dean of this college. He's dined in hall once or twice.'

'I'm afraid,' said Lord Boscastle, 'that I don't know who he is.'

There was a moment's silence, and I looked at the faces round the table. Lord Boscastle was holding his glass up to the candlelight and staring unconcernedly through it. Roy watched with an expression solemn, inquiring: but I caught his eye for a second, and saw a gleam of pure glee: each word was passing into his mimic's ear. By his side, Joan was gazing down fixedly at the table, the poise of her neck and strong shoulders full of anger, scorn and the passionate rebellion of youth. Mrs Seymour seemed vaguely troubled, as though she had mislaid her bag; she patted her hair, trying to get a strand into place. On my right Lady Boscastle had mounted her lorgnette and focused the others one by one.

It was she who asked the next question.

'Could you tell us a little about this Dean of yours, Vernon?' she said to the Master, in a high, delicate, amused voice.

'He's quite a good Dean,' said the Master. 'He's very useful on the financial side. Colleges need their Marthas, you know. The unfortunate thing is that one can never keep the Marthas in their place. Before you can look round, you find they're running the college and regarding you as a frivolous and irresponsible person.'

'What's the Dean's name?' said Lord Boscastle, getting back to the point.

'Chrystal.'

'It sounds Scotch,' said Lord Boscastle dubiously.

'I believe, Lord Boscastle,' Roy put in, seeming tentative and diffident, 'that he comes from Bedford.'

Lord Boscastle shook his head.

'I know his wife, of course,' said Lady Muriel. 'Naturally I have to know the wives of the fellows. She's a nice quiet little thing. But there's nothing special about her. She's an Eggar, whoever they may be.'

'She's the sister of this man you're telling us about,' Lord Boscastle remarked, half to himself. 'I should have said he was nothing out of the ordinary, shouldn't you have said so?'

His social judgments became more circuitous the nearer they came to anyone the company knew: Lady Muriel, more direct and unperceptive than her brother, had never quite picked up the labyrinthine phrases with which he finally placed an acquaintance of someone in the room; but in effect she and he said the same thing.

Mrs Seymour, who was still looking faintly distressed, suddenly clapped her hands.

'Of course, I'd forgotten to tell you. I've just remembered about the post office place—'

'Yes, Doris?' said Lady Muriel inexorably.

'Houston's a brilliant young man. He's in the Foreign Office. They said he was first secretary' – Mrs Seymour gabbled rapidly in case she should forget – 'at that place which looks after the post, the place in Switzerland, I forget—'

'Berne,' Roy whispered.

'Berne.' She smiled at him gratefully.

'How old is your Houston?' asked Lady Boscastle.

'About forty, I should say. And I think that's a very nice and sensible age,' said Mrs Seymour with unexpected firmness. 'I always wished my husband had been older—'

'If he's only a first secretary at forty, I shouldn't think he was going so terribly far.' Lady Boscastle directed her lorgnette at her husband. 'I remember one years younger. We were in Warsaw. Yes, he was clever.' A sarcastic smile crossed her face. Lord Boscastle smiled back – was I imagining it, or was there something humble, unconfident, about that smile?

At any rate, he began to address the table again.

'I shouldn't have thought that the Foreign Office was specially distinguished nowadays. Though I've actually known one or two people who went in since the war,' he added as though he were straining our credulity.

While he thought no one was looking, Roy could not repress a smile of delight. He could no longer resist it: his face composed again, he was just beginning to ask Lord Boscastle a question, when Lady Muriel cut across him.

'Of course,' she said, 'it's not what it used to be. But someone's obliged to do these things.'

'Someone's obliged to become civil servants and look after the drains,' said Lord Boscastle with good-natured scorn.

Roy started again.

'Should you have said, Lord Boscastle,' (the words, the tone, sounded suspiciously like Lord Boscastle's own) 'that the Foreign Office was becoming slightly *common?*'

Lord Boscastle regarded him, and paused. He was not without suspicion He said:

'Perhaps that would be going rather far, Calvert.'

'Oh, it must be wonderful to make treaties and go about in secret—'

cried Mrs Seymour, girlish with enthusiasm, her voice trailing off.

'Make treaties!' Lord Boscastle remarked. 'All they do is clerk away in offices and get one out of trouble if one goes abroad. They've really become superior post offices, you know.'

'So you wouldn't like your son to enter, Lord Boscastle?' Roy asked.

'I must say, I hope he'll choose something slightly more out of the ordinary.'

Lord Boscastle wore a fixed smile. Roy looked more than ever solemn.

'Of course,' said Roy, 'he might pick up an unfortunate accent from one of those people. One needs to be careful. Do you think,' he asked earnestly, 'that is the reason why some of them are so anxious to learn foreign languages? Do you think they hope it will cover up their own?'

'Mr Calvert!' Lady Boscastle's voice sounded high and gentle. Roy met the gaze behind the lorgnette.

'Mr Calvert, have you been inside an embassy?'

'Only once, Lady Boscastle.'

'I think I must take you to some more. You'll find they're quite nice people. And really not inelegant. They talk quite nicely too. I'm just a little surprised you didn't know that already, Mr Calvert.'

Roy burst into a happy, unguarded laugh: a blush mounted his cheeks. I had not seen him blush before. It was not often people played him at his own game. Usually they did not know what to make of him, they felt befogged, they left him still enquiring, straight-faced, bright-eyed.

The whole table was laughing – suddenly I noticed Joan's face quite transformed. She had given way completely to her laughter, the sullenness was dissolved; it was the richest of laughs, and hearing it one knew that some day she would love with her whole nature.

Lord Boscastle himself was smiling. He was not a slow-witted man, he had known from the beginning that he was being baited. I got the impression that he was grateful for his wife's support. But his response to being baited was to stick more obstinately to his own line. So now he said, as though summing up: 'It's a pity about Tom Seymour's girl. She ought to have fished up something better for herself.'

'You'll all come round to him,' said Mrs Seymour. 'I know he'll do.'

'It's a pity,' said Lord Boscastle with finality, 'that one doesn't know who he is.'

Joan, melted by her laughter, still half-laughing and half-furious, broke out:

'Uncle, you mean that you don't know who his grandfather is.'

'Joan!' Lady Muriel boomed, but, with an indulgent nod, Lord

Boscastle went on to discuss in what circumstances Tom's girl had a claim to be invited to the family house. Boscastle was a great mansion: 'my house' as Lord Boscastle called it with an air of *grand seigneur*, 'our house' said Lady Muriel with splendour: but the splendour and the air of *grand seigneur* disappeared at moments, for they both had a knack of calling the house 'Bossy'. Lady Boscastle never did: but to her husband and his sister there seemed nothing incongruous in the nickname.

After port, as soon as I got inside the drawing-room, Lady Boscastle called out: 'Mr Eliot! I want you to talk to me, please.' I sat with her in a corner by the fire, and she examined me about my hopes and prospects; she was very shrewd, used to having her own way, accustomed to find pleasure in men's confidences. We should have gone on, if it had not been that Lord Boscastle, on the largest sofa a few feet away, was asking Roy to describe his work. It was a perfectly serious question, and Roy treated it so. He explained how he had to begin unravelling a language which was two-thirds unknown. Then he passed on to manuscripts in that language – manuscripts battered, often with half the page missing, so faded that much could not be read at all, sometimes copied by incompetent and careless hands. Out of all this medley he was trying to restore the text.

'Tell me, how long will it take you?' said Lord Boscastle.

'Eight years,' said Roy at once.

Lord Boscastle reflected.

'I can imagine starting it,' he said. 'I can see it must be rather fun. But I really can't imagine myself having the patience to go through with it.'

'I think you might,' said Roy simply. 'I think you might have enjoyed having something definite to do.'

'Do you think I could have managed it?'

'I'm sure,' said Roy.

'Perhaps I might,' said Lord Boscastle with a trace of regret.

The drawing-room was left with no one speaking. Then Lady Muriel firmly suggested that her brother ought to see Roy's manuscripts. It was arranged (Lady Muriel pushing from behind) that the Boscastles should lunch with Roy next day.

A few minutes later, though it was only half-past ten, Roy made his apologies to Lady Muriel and left. She watched him walk the length of the room: then we heard his feet running down the stairs.

'He was a little naughty with you at dinner, Hugh,' she said to her brother, 'but you must admit that he has real style.'

'Young men ought to get up to monkey tricks,' said Lord Boscastle. 'One grows old soon enough. Yes, he's an agreeable young fellow.'

He paused, drank some whisky, enquired as though compelled to: 'Who is his father?'

'A man called Calvert,' said the Master.

'I know that,' said Lord Boscastle irritably.

'He's distinctly rich and lives in the midlands.'

'I'm afraid I've never heard of him.'

'No, you wouldn't have, Hugh,' said the Master, with a fresh smile.

'But I must say,' Lord Boscastle went on, 'that if I'd met Calvert anywhere I should really have expected to know who he was.'

This implied, I thought, a curious back-handed social acceptance. But it was not necessary, for the Master said:

'He's got everything in front of him. He's going to be one of the great orientalists of the day. Between ourselves, I believe that's putting it mildly.'

'I can believe you,' said Lord Boscastle. 'I hope he enjoys himself. We must keep an eye on him.'

That meant definite acceptance. It was not, I thought, that Roy had 'real style', had been to Lord Boscastle's school, could pass as a gentleman through any tests except Lord Boscastle's own; it was not only that Roy had struck a human want in him, by making him think of how he might have spent his life. He might have received Roy even if he had liked him less: for Lord Boscastle had a genuine, respectful tenderness for learning and the arts. His snobbery was a passion, more devouring as he got older, more triumphant as he found reasons for proving that almost no one came inside his own preserve; nevertheless, he continued to have a special entrance which let in his brother-in-law, which let in Roy, which let in some of the rest of us; and he welcomed us more as his snobbery outside grew more colossal and baroque.

Lady Boscastle was trying to resume our conversation, but the others were still talking of Roy. Mrs Seymour was rapt with vague enthusiasm.

'He's so handsome,' she said.

'Interesting-looking, I think I should say,' commented Lady Boscastle.

'He's not handsome at all,' said Joan. 'His nose is much too long.'

'Don't you like him?' cried Mrs Seymour.

'I can never get him to talk seriously,' the girl replied.

'He's very lucky.' Mrs Seymour's enthusiasm grew. 'It must be wonderful to be A1 at everything.'

No one could be freer from irony than Mrs Seymour; and yet, even on that night, those words rang through me with a harsh ironic note.

The Master was saying:

'One thing is certain. We must elect the young man to a fellowship here before long.'

'I should have thought you would jump at him,' said Lord Boscastle.

'No society of men is very fond of brilliance, Hugh,' said the Master. 'We needs must choose the dullest when we see it. However, I hope this time my colleagues will agree with me without undue pressure.'

He smiled confidentially at me.

'Between ourselves, Eliot,' he went on, 'when I reflect on the modest accomplishments of some of our colleagues, I think perhaps even undue pressure might not be out of place.'

CHAPTER III

TWO RESOLVES

I WOKE because of a soft voice above my bed – 'beg pardon, sir, beg pardon, sir, beg pardon, sir'. In the half-light I could see Bidwell's face, round, ruddy, simultaneously deferential and goodfellow-like, wide open and cunning.

'I don't know whether I'm doing right, sir. I know I oughtn't to disturb you, and' – he inclined his head in the direction of the college clock – 'that's got twenty minutes to go to nine o'clock. But it's a young lady. I think it's a young lady of Mr Calvert's, sir. She seemed what you might call anxious to see you.'

I let him pull up the blind, and the narrow cell-like room seemed bleaker than ever in the bright cold morning sunlight. I had drunk enough at the Lodge the night before to prefer to get up slowly. As I washed in warmish water from a jug, I was too moiled and irritated to wonder much who this visitor might be.

I recognised her, though, as soon as I saw her sitting in an armchair by my sitting-room fire. I had met her several times before. She was an acquaintance of my wife's and knew her family. She was Roy's own age, and her name was Rosalind Wykes. She came across the room to meet me, and looked up contritely with clear brown eyes.

'I'm frightfully sorry to disturb you,' she said. 'I know it's very wicked of me. But I thought you might be going out to give a lecture. Sit down and I'll get your breakfast for you.'

Breakfast was strewn about the hearth, in plates with metal covers on top. Rosalind took off the covers, dusted the rim of the plates, dusted a cup, poured out my tea.

'I must say they don't look after you too well,' she said. 'Get on with your breakfast. You won't feel so much like wringing my neck then, will you?'

She was nervous; there was a dying fall in her voice which sometimes made her seem pathetic. She had an oval face, a longish nose, a big humorous mouth with down just visible on her upper lip. She was dressed in the mode, and it showed how slender she was, though she was wider across the hips than one observed at a first glance. She was often nervous: sometimes she seemed restless and reckless: yet underneath one felt she was tough and healthy and made for a happy physical life. Her hair was dark, and she had done it up from the back, which was unusual at that time: with her oval face, brown eyes, small head, that tier of hair made her seem like a portrait of the First Empire – and in fact to me she frequently brought a flavour of that period, modish, parvenu, proper outside and raffish within, materialistic and yet touching.

I drank two cups of tea. 'Better,' I said.

'You look a bit morning afterish, I must say,' said Rosalind. At that time she was very prim in speech, much more so than most of the people among whom she moved: yet she had a singular gift for investing the most harmless remark with an amorous aura. My state that breakfast-time was due to nothing more disreputable than a number of glasses of claret at dinner and some whiskies afterwards with the Master and Lord Boscastle; but, when Rosalind mentioned it, it might have been incurred through an exhausting night of love.

I began eating some breakfast, and said:

'Well, I shall revive soon. What did you get me out of bed for, Rosalind?'

She shook her head. 'Nothing very special. I only arrived yesterday and I'm going back tonight, and I shouldn't have liked to miss you altogether.'

I looked at her. The clear eyes were guileless. She glanced round the room.

'I wish you'd let me do this place up for you,' she said. 'It would look lovely with just a bit of care. I could make you so comfortable you wouldn't credit it, you know.'

I was prepared to believe that she was right. The bedroom was a monk's cell, but this sitting-room was a large and splendid medieval chamber. I knew that, given a week and a cheque-book, she would transform it. She was kind and active, she took pleasure from making one comfortable. But I did not think that she had come that morning to tell me so.

While I went on eating, she stood by the wall and examined the panelling. She asked how old it was, and I told her sixteenth century. Then, over her shoulder, she said:

'Did you notice that Roy left the dinner party early last night?'

I said yes.

'Did you know what for?'

I said no.

Still over her shoulder, in a tone with a dying fall, she said:

'I'm afraid it was to come and see me.'

It was suggestive, shameless and boasting. I burst into laughter, and she turned and looked at me with a lurking, satisfied smile.

In a moment Bidwell came in, quiet footed, to clear up. When he had left again, she said:

'Your servant has got a very sweet face, hasn't he?'

'I'm rather fond of him.'

'I'm sure you are.' Her eyes were shrewd. 'I must say, I wish you and Roy didn't leave so much to him. I hope you don't let him do your ordering.'

I did not mind Bidwell taking a percentage, I said, if it avoided fuss. She frowned, she did not want to let it pass: but there was still something on her mind. It was not only to confess or boast that she had come to see me.

'Did you know,' she said, 'that Roy is having Lord and Lady Boscastle to lunch?'

'I heard him invite them.'

'I'm making him have me too. I'm terrified. Are they dreadfully frightening?'

'What did Roy say about that?'

'He said that Lord Boscastle's bark was worse than his bite. And that Lady Boscastle was the stronger of the two.'

'I think that's true,' I said.

'But what am I going to say to them?' she said. She was genuinely nervous. 'I've never met people like that before. I haven't any idea what to say.'

'Don't worry. And make love to Lord B. as lavishly as you like,' I said.

It was sound advice, for Lord Boscastle's social standards were drastically reduced in the presence of attractive young women who seemed to enjoy his company.

She smiled absently for a second, then cried again:

'I don't know anything about people like that. I don't even know what to call an earl. Lewis, what do I call them?'

I told her. I believed this was a reason for her visit. She would rather ask that question of me than of Roy.

'I'm glad I remembered to ask you,' she said disingenuously, her eyes open and clear. 'It's a relief. But I am terrified,' she added.

'Why did you work it then?' I said.

'I was dreadfully silly,' she said. 'I thought I should like to see a bit of high life.'

That may have been true, but I was sure there was another purpose behind it. She could live as though each day were sufficient to itself: so she had thrown herself at Roy, took what she could get, put up with what she called his 'moods', went to bed with him when she could, schemed no more than a month or two ahead.

But, deep in her fibres, there was another realism. She was set on marrying him. It did not need thought or calculation, it just took all of herself – though on the way to her end she would think and calculate with every scrap of wits she had. She was nervous, kind, sensitive in her fashion, tender with the good nature of one who is happy with instinctive life: she was also hard, ruthless, determined, singleminded and un-scrupulous: or rather she could act as though scruples did not exist. She meant to marry him.

So she knew that she must get on with the Boscastles. Roy was not a snob, no man was less so: but he gave himself to everyone who took his fancy, whether they came from the ill-fated and lost, or from the lucky. Usually (and here for me there fell the shadow of Sheila) they were the world's derelicts. I often grumbled that he treated badly any acquaintance who might be of practical use: but if by chance he liked someone eminent, then he was theirs as deeply as though they were humble. He felt no barriers except what his affections told him. Rosalind knew this, and knew that she must acquire the same ease. Hence she had driven herself, despite her diffidence, into this luncheon party.

Hence too, I was nearly certain, she decided she must know me well. So far as anyone had influence over Roy, I had. She must make me into an ally if she could. She must see that I was friendly, she must take a part in my life, even if it only meant decorating my rooms. She had come that morning to ask me how to address an earl: but she would have found another reason, if that had not existed. I strongly suspected that she had bribed Bidwell to wake me up before my time.

Roy brought Rosalind back to my rooms after lunch.

'I hear you met this morning,' said Roy.

'Can you bear the sight of me again?' Rosalind said.

'He'll pretend to,' said Roy. 'He's famous for his self-control.'

She made a face at him, half-plaintive, half-comic, and said:

'I couldn't stay and see Roy's tables all littered with plates. I should want to do something about it.' She was talkative and elated, like someone released from strain.

'How did it go?' I said.

'I tried to find a corner to hide in. But it's not very easy when there are only four.'

'You get a small prize,' Roy said to her. 'Not the first prize. Only the second. You did very nicely.'

I guessed that she had been diffident, had not taken much part. But it was not as bad as she feared, and with her indomitable resolve she would try again. Roy was smiling at her, amused, stirred to tenderness because she made such heavy weather of what would, at any age, have been his own native air.

He said to me:

'By the way, old boy, you've made a great hit with Lady B. I'm extremely jealous.'

'She wanted to know all about you,' said Rosalind.

'I think she likes very weighty men.' Roy chuckled. 'Old Lewis is remarkably good at persuading them that he's extremely weighty.'

He went on to tease Rosalind about Lord Boscastle's compliments. I noticed that Roy and Rosalind were very easy with each other, light with the innocence that may visit a happy physical love.

The telephone bell rang: it was for Roy, and as he answered he exclaimed with enthusiasm – 'excellent', 'of course', 'I'm sure he would' 'I'll answer for him', 'come straight up'.

'You see, you've got to be civil now,' said Roy. 'It's Ralph Udal. He's just back from Italy. It's time you met him.'

Roy added, with a secret smile: 'Now, I wonder what he wants.'

Udal himself came in as Roy finished speaking. I had found out something about him since the episode of the bookshops: now I saw him in the flesh, I was surprised. I had not expected that he should have such natural and pleasant manners. For the stories I had heard were somewhat odd. He was an exact contemporary of Roy's at the college, and they had known each other well, though they were not intimate friends. Udal came from a professional family, but he was a poor man, and he and Roy moved in different circles. They had known each other as academic rivals, for Udal had had a brilliant undergraduate career. Then his life became very strange. He spent a year among the seedy figures of Soho – not to indulge himself, not to do good works, but just to 'let the wind of God blow through him'. Then he had served another year in a church settlement in Poplar. Afterwards, he had, passively so it seemed, become ordained. But he had not taken a curacy or any kind of job; he had written his little book on Heppenstall, and had gone off to Italy for six months.

He was a big man, tall, loose-framed, dark-haired, and dark-skinned. He looked older than his age; his face was mature, adult and decided. As he greeted us, there was great warmth in his large, dark, handsome eyes. He was dressed in old flannels and a thin calico coat, but he talked to Rosalind as though he also had been to a smart lunch, and he settled down between her and me without any sign that this was a first meeting.

'How's the book going?' asked Roy.

'It's very gratifying,' said Udal. 'There doesn't seem to be a copy left in Cambridge.'

'Excellent,' said Roy, without blinking, without a quiver on his solemn face.

Udal had arrived back from Italy the day before.

'Didn't you adore Italy? Were the women lovely? What were you doing there?' asked Rosalind.

'Visiting churches,' said Udal amiably. Rosalind had just remembered that he was a clergyman. She looked uncomfortable, but Udal was prepared to talk about anything she wanted. He thought the women were beautiful in the Veneto and Friulia, but not in the South. He suggested that one required a dash of nordic blood to produce anything more than youthful comeliness. He had gone about with his eyes open, and spoke without inhibition. Rosalind was discomfited.

She was discomfited again when, with the same ease, he began talking of his practical requirements.

'Roy,' he said, 'it's time I found a job.'

'Just so,' said Roy.

'You don't mind me talking about myself?' Udal said affably to Rosalind and me. 'But I wanted to see Roy about my best moves. I'm not much good at these things.

'I've been thinking,' he said to Roy. 'A country living would suit me down to the ground. I can make do on three hundred a year. And it would mean plenty of leisure. I shouldn't get so much leisure in any other way.'

'That's true,' said Roy.

'How do I set about getting one?'

'Difficult,' said Roy. 'I don't think you can straightaway.'

They talked about tactics. Udal knew exactly what he wanted; but he was oddly unrealistic about the means. He seemed to think it would be easy to persuade the college to give him a living. Roy, on the other hand, was completely practical. He scolded Udal for indulging in make-believe, and told him what to do; he must take some other job at once, presumably a curacy; then he must 'nurse' the college livings committee, he must become popular with them, he must unobtrusively keep his existence before them. He must also cultivate any bishop either he or Roy could get to know.

Udal took it well. He was not proud; he accepted the fact that Roy was more worldly and acute.

'I'll talk to people, I'll spy out the land,' said Roy. He smiled. 'I may even make old Lewis get himself put on the livings committee.'

'Do what you can,' said Udal.

Rosalind was upset. She could not understand. She could not help asking Udal:

'Doesn't it worry you?'

'Doesn't what worry me?'

'Having – to work it all out,' she said.

'I manage to bear it. Would it worry you?'

'No, of course not. But I thought someone in your position—'

'You mean that I'm supposed to be a religious man,' said Udal. 'But religious people are still ordinary humans, you know.'

'Does it seem all right to you?'

'Oh, I don't know about that,' he said.

'I'm afraid I still think it's peculiar.' She appealed to Roy. 'Roy, don't you think so?'

'No,' he said. 'Not in the least.'

His tone was clear and final. Suddenly I realised she was making a mistake in pressing Udal. She was exposing a rift between herself and Roy. In other things she would have felt him getting further away: but here she was obtuse.

'I'm not able to speak from the inside,' said Roy. 'But I believe religion can include anything. It can even include,' his face, which had been grave, suddenly broke into a brilliant, malicious smile, 'the fact that Ralph hasn't just called on me – for valuable advice.'

'That's not fair,' said Udal. For a moment he was put out.

'You need someone to unbelt. I'm sure you do.'

'I am short of money,' said Udal.

'Just so,' said Roy.

Udal had recovered his composure. He turned to Rosalind.

'You expect too much of us, you know. You expect us to be perfect – and then you think the rest of the world just go about sleeping with each other.'

Rosalind blushed. Earthy as she was, she liked a decent veil: while he had the casual matter-of-fact touch that one sometimes finds in those who have not gone into the world, or have withdrawn from it.

'You're not correct either way, if you'll forgive me,' Udal went on. 'Roy here wouldn't let me call him a religious man yet: but do you think he's done nothing so far but what they call "enjoy himself"? He's already done much odder things than that, you know. And I'm inclined to think he will again. I'm just waiting.'

He spoke lightly, but with immense confidence. Then he smiled to himself.

'This is the right life for me, anyway,' he said. 'It will give me all I want.'

'Will it?' said Rosalind sharply.

He was relaxed, strong in his passiveness.

But she opposed her own strength, that of someone who had gone into the world and could imagine no other life. It was not a strength to be despised. Udal looked at her, and his face was no more settled than hers.

Roy watched them with a glance that was penetrating, acute, and, it suddenly seemed to me, envious of each of them.

CHAPTER IV

A NATURE MARKED OUT BY FATE?

From the afternoon when he forced me to confide, my relation with Roy became changed. Before, he had seemed a gifted and interesting young man whose temperament interested me, whom I liked seeing when I had the time. Now he had reached out to me. He had put self aside, risked snubs, pierced all the defence I could throw in his way. He had made me accept him as an intimate on even terms. Insensibly, perhaps before I knew it, my friendship with him became in some senses the deepest of my life.

That would have surprised me, if it had been foretold when I first met him. I could still remember cross-questioning him when he was fifteen, and had embarrassed us all by falling in love with Jack Cotery. His speech had even then been curiously precise, and one heard the echoes of that precision years later: as an affirmative when we questioned him, he used a clear 'just so'.

Roy himself was not embarrassed by the incident either then or later. I sometimes thought, in fact, that it gave him an added and gentler sympathy. He was not the man to respect any conventions but his own. With his first-hand knowledge of life, he knew that any profound friendship must contain a little of the magic of love. And he was always as physically spontaneous as an Italian. He liked physical contact and endearing words. He would slip his arm into a friend's on the way to hall or as the team went out to field: if anyone had recalled that scandal of the past, he would only have met Roy's most mischievous and mocking grin.

After that encounter in his boyhood, I did not see him again until he went to Cambridge. It was only by chance that his outburst had affected my circle, and, in the large town where we were both born, our paths were not likely to cross. His father had made a considerable fortune and moved among such society as the town could give. His career and way of life were, as a matter of fact, fairly typical of the rich manufacturers of that day. His father, Roy's grandfather, had risen from the artisan class, and made enough money out of boots to send his son to a minor public school: then Roy's father, a man of obstinate inarticulate ability with an obsessional passion for detail, expanded the business and took his chance in the 1914–18 war. He became really rich, more so than many of my London friends who were thought wealthy and lived in greater style: by 1934 he cannot have been worth less than £300,000. He did very little with it, except buy a local newspaper and a large house on the outskirts of the town, and take every opportunity of spending money on his only son. He idolised Roy, in an embarrassed, puzzled fashion; he sent him to fashionable preparatory and public schools (it was only by a personal accident that he came to the college, which was not at all fashionable; his house master, whom Roy liked, happened to be a loyal old member); from the time Roy was twenty-one, his father allowed him £1500 a year, and settled a substantial sum on him as well.

When I ran across him in his undergraduate days, he was more outwardly eccentric than he later seemed – not in dress, for he was always elegant, but in actions which at the time I thought were only a very young man's whims. I found him one night sleeping on a seat on the Embankment. He did not explain himself, although he was, as usual, polite, easy-mannered, affectionate and direct. He went in for bouts of hard drinking which seemed more abandoned than an undergraduate's blinds, more deliberately an attempt to escape. And he started his love affairs quite early. Yet each examination was a triumph for him, and he was one of the outstanding classics of his year.

After taking his degree, he was at a loss. He felt vaguely drawn to some kind of scholarly research, but he did not make any determined start. He drank more and felt a despondency overcome him of which previously he had only known the shadow's edge. This was the first time that he was forced, without any help or protection, to know the burden of self.

In a few weeks that darkness left him, and he tried to forget it. The Master, whose subject was comparative religion, suggested that he should apply himself to oriental languages. To help himself forget the period of melancholy not long past, Roy threw all his attention into Syriac and Aramaic: and then, partly by sheer chance, came the offer of the research which was to occupy so much of his working life.

It was an odd story, how this ever reached him.

Of all the Christian heresies, one spread the furthest, touched imaginations most deeply, and had the richest meaning. Perhaps it should have been called a new religion. It was the heresy of Mani. It began towards the end of the third century A.D. in the pleasure city of Antioch and the decadent luxurious towns of Syria; it swept through them as a new religion might sweep through California today.

It was a new religion, but it drew its strength from something as old and deep as human feeling; for, just as the sexual impulse is ineluctably strong, so can the hate of it be; the flesh is seductive, beyond one's power to resist – and one hates the flesh as an enemy, one prays that it will leave one in peace. The religion of the Manichees tried to give men peace against the flesh. In its cosmology, the whole of creation is a battle of the light against the dark. Man's spirit is part of the light, and his flesh of the dark. The battle sways from side to side, and men are taking part in it, here and now. The religion was the most subtle and complex representation of sexual guilt.

Such a subtle and complex religion must have drawn its believers from the comfortable classes. There was none of the quick simple appeal that helped Christianity to spark from man to man, perhaps even more woman to woman, among the hopeless dispossessed of the Roman slums. Manichæism must have been chiefly the religion of those with time to think – and probably of a comfortable leisured class in a dying society, a class with little to do except pursue its sensual pleasures and be tormented by their guilt.

Anyway, through the third and fourth centuries the religion spread. The Manichæan missionaries followed the trade routes, into Egypt, the African coastal fringe, Persia; churches were founded, psalm books and liturgies and statements of faith were translated from their original Syriac. And very soon the Manichees were being systematically and ruthlessly persecuted. For some reason, this subtle and gentle faith, or anything resembling it, like that of the Albigenses in Provence or the Bogomils in Bulgaria, always excited the hatred of the orthodox. Before long the Manichæan congregations had been exterminated in the Levant and round the Mediterranean; others were driven out of Persia and found a home for a while in what is now Chinese Turkestan. Then they too were finished off by the Moslems.

It is an error, of course, to think that persecution is never successful. More often than not, it has been extremely so. For hundreds of years, this religion, which once had rich churches in the most civilised towns in the world, which attracted to its membership such men as Saint Augustine (for whom Roy had a personal veneration), would not have been known to exist except for the writings of its enemies. It was as though communism had been extirpated in Europe in the nineteen twenties, and was only known through what is said of it in *Mein Kampf*. No words of the Manichees themselves were left to be read.

During the twentieth century, however, the technique and scale of archaeological expeditions were each developed, and there were one or two Manichæan finds. A psalm book and a hymnal, translated into a Coptic dialect, were discovered in upper Egypt; and one of the expeditions to Turkestan brought back what was recognised to be a complete liturgy. But it was written in an unknown variety of Middle Persian called Early Soghdian; and for a year the liturgy stayed unread.

The committee who had charge of it intended to ask an Oxford scholar to make an edition but, just as that time, he fell ill. Quite by accident, Sir Oulstone Lyall and Colonel Foulkes happened to be consulting the Master about other business. He mentioned Roy to them and introduced him. They thought he was intelligent, they knew that he had picked up Syriac at high speed; it was possible that Colonel Foulkes's devotion to cricket disposed him to take a favourable view of Roy's character. There was an amateur flavour about all this esoteric scholarship – anyway, they asked if he would like to try.

Only a man of means could have risked it. If he did not get the language out, he had wasted critical years. Something caught in Roy's imagination, perhaps the religion itself, and he said yes.

That was over two years before, in the January of 1932. Within eighteen months he had worked out the language, so precisely that no one need touch it again. His Soghdian grammar and lexicon were just in proof, and were to be published during 1934. He had already transcribed part of the liturgy, and he was working faster than ever. It was a remarkable record, unbelievable to those who knew a little of his life, the loves, the drinking, the games and parties. But to me, who saw more of him, the miracle disappeared like a conjuring trick which is explained. I knew how, even in the blackest melancholy, he could throw himself with clear precise attention into his work for seven or eight hours a day. I had seen him drink himself into stupor, sleep it off, recover over breakfast, and be back at work by nine o'clock.

His own attitude to his work was one of the most matter-of-fact things about him. His preoccupation was in the words themselves and what they meant; the slightest hitch in the text, and he was absorbed, with all his imagination and powers in play. He was intent on knowing precisely what the words of that liturgy meant, to the priests who translated it, to the scribe who copied it somewhere in a Central Asian town in the sixth century.

Outside the text his imagination, so active upon the words themselves, so lively in his everyday life, seemed not to be much engaged. His mind was not elastic, and did not stretch wide. He gave only a passing thought to the societies where this religion grew or to the people in the congregations which used his liturgy. There was something in such speculations which offended his taste – 'romantic' he called them, as a term of abuse. 'Romantic,' said Roy scornfully, who himself was often described in that one word.

Yet, right from the beginning, there were times when his work seemed nothing but a drug. He had thrown himself into it, in revulsion from his first knowledge of despair. Despair: the black night of melancholy: he had already felt the weight of inexplicable misery. I thought that too often his work was a charm against the dark. He did not seem to revel in success, to get any pleasure apart from a mild sense of skill. I watched him when he finished his Soghdian grammar. He knew it was a nice job – 'I am rather clever,' he said with a mocking smile. But when others praised him, he became irritated and angry, genuinely, morbidly angry, took to a fit of drinking and then worked such immoderate hours at the liturgy that I was afraid for his health, tough as he was.

At the dinner party Mrs Seymour had cried out how much he was to be envied. She was a silly woman, but she said only what everyone round him thought. Some people resented him because he had so much. Many saw the gaiety and felt that he could not have a worry in the world. None of them saw the weight that crushed him down.

Even Roy himself did not see it. In his boyhood and youth, he had been buoyed up by the animal spirits of the young. His spirits at twenty, like those of any vigorous man, were strong enough to defy fate or death; they drew their strength from the body, and for a time could drive away any affliction that was lying in wait. Now he was a little older he had passed through hours and days of utter blackness, in which his one feeling was self-hatred and his one longing to escape himself. But those hours and days passed off, and he still had the boundless hope of a young man. He hoped he could escape – perhaps in love (though he never counted much on that), perhaps in work, perhaps in a belief in which he could lose himself. He hoped he could escape at last, and come to peace and rest.

At that time, I could not resist believing that he had the special melancholy which belongs to some chosen natures. It did not come through suffering, though it caused him to suffer much. It came by the same fate as endowed him with his gifts.

Looking back, I thought that I ought to have been less resigned. My own life had gone wrong. I had not yet had a chance to reshape it, or to see how others could reshape theirs. I was too willing to accept his despair: the despair which drove him into something like manic fugues.

It would have been wrong to think that it was just a chance of his upbringing: that was the hygienic fallacy. I believed that he was born with this melancholy. It was a case of fate, like a hereditary disease. Even if that was right, I believed it too completely.

Yet, looking back once more, I realised that I did not continuously believe it. Often I wished him more commonplace and selfish. If only he could cease to be so shadowed. But he exhilarated me with his gaiety, and deepened what I knew of life. So that I too forgot what in the black moments I thought that fate had done to him, and I hoped that he would be happy.

CHAPTER V

LESSON IN POLITICS

THE Master's campaign to get Roy elected did not make much progress. All decisions in the college had to be taken by a vote of the fellows, who in 1934 numbered thirteen, including the Master himself: and most formal steps, such as electing a fellow, needed a clear majority of the society, that is seven votes.

For various reasons, the Master was not finding it easy to collect seven votes for Roy. First, one old man was ill and could not come to college meetings. Second, the Master was not such a power in the college as in the university; his intimate sarcasms had a habit of passing round, and he had made several irreconcilable enemies, chief among them the Bursar, Winslow, a bitter disappointed man, acid-tongued in a fashion of his own. Third, the Master, fairminded in most ways, could not conceal his dislike and contempt for scientists, and had recently remarked of one deserving candidate 'What rude mechanical are we asked to consider now?' The comment had duly reached the three scientific fellows and did not dispose them in favour of the Master's protege.

As a result, the political situation in the college was more than usually fluid. For most questions there existed – though no one spoke of it – a kind of rudimentary party system, with a government party which supported the Master and an opposition whose leader was Winslow. When I first arrived, the government party generally managed to find a small majority, by attracting the two or three floating votes. In all personal choices, particularly in elections to fellowships, the parties were not to be relied on, although there were nearly always two opposing cores: the remainder of the college dissolved into a vigorous, talkative, solemn anarchy. It was an interesting lesson in personal politics, which I sometimes thought, and continued to think long afterwards, should be studied by anyone who wanted to take a part in high affairs.

Through the last half of 1934 Winslow and his allies devoted themselves with some ingenuity to obstruction, for which the college statutes and customs gave considerable opportunity. Could the college afford another fellow? If so, ought it not to discuss whether the first need was not for an official rather than a research fellowship? If a research fellowship, was not the first step to decide in which subject it should be offered? Did the college really need another fellow in an out-of-the-way subject? Could it really afford such luxuries, when it did not possess an engineer?

'Fellowships' occurred on the agenda for meeting after meeting in 1934. By the end of the year, the debate had scarcely reached Roy by name. This did not mean that gossip was not circulating against him at high table or in the combination room. But even in private, arguments were phrased in the same comfortable language: 'could the college afford . . .?' 'is it in the man's own best interests. . . .?' It was the public face, it was the way things were done.

Meanwhile, nothing decisive was showing itself in Roy's life. The months went by; the grammar was published, highly thought of by a handful of scholars; he tired himself each day at the liturgy. He saw Rosalind sometimes in Cambridge, oftener in London; she persuaded him to take her to Pallanza in September, but she had got no nearer marrying him. There were other affairs, light come, light go.

He became a greater favourite with Lady Muriel as the months passed, was more often at the Lodge, and had spent a weekend at Boscastle.

He knew this roused some rancour in the college, and I told him that it was not improving his chances of election. He grinned. Even if he had not been amused by Lady Muriel and fond of her, the thought of solemn head-shaking would have driven him into her company.

Yet he wanted to be elected. He was not anxious about it, for anxiety in the ordinary sense he scarcely knew: any excitement, anything at stake, merely gave him a heightened sense of living. At times, though, he seemed curiously excited when his fortunes in this election rose or fell. It surprised me, for he lacked his proper share of vanity. Perhaps he wanted the status, I thought, if only to gratify his father: perhaps he wanted, like other rich men, to feel that he could earn a living.

At any rate, it mattered to him, and so I was relieved when Arthur Brown took control. The first I heard of the new manœuvres was when Brown invited me to his rooms on a January evening. It was wet and cold, and I was sitting huddled by my fire when Brown looked in.

'I suppose,' he said, 'that you don't by any chance feel like joining me in a glass of wine? I might be able to find something a bit special. I can't help feeling that it would be rather cheering on a night like this.'

I went across to his rooms, which were on the next staircase. Though he lived in domestic comfort with his wife and family, those rooms in college were always warm, always welcoming: that night a fire was blazing in the open grate, electric fires were glowing in the corners of the room, the curtains were drawn, the armchairs were wide and deep. The fire crackled, and on the windows behind the curtains sounded the tap of rain. Brown brought out glasses and a bottle.

'I hope you like marsala on a cold night,' he said. 'I'm rather given to it myself as a change. I find it rather fortifying.'

He was a broad plump well-covered man, with a broad smooth pink face. He wore spectacles, and behind them his eyes were small, acute, dark, watchful and very bright. He was the junior of the two tutors, a man of forty-four, though most of the college, lulled by his avuncular kindness, thought of him as older.

He was a man easy to under-estimate, and his colleagues often did so. He was hospitable, comfort-loving, modestly self-indulgent. He disliked quarrels, and was happy when he could compose one among his colleagues. But he was also a born politician. He loved getting his own way, 'running things', manipulating people, particularly if they never knew.

He was content to leave the appearance of power to others. Some of us, who had benefited through his skill, called him 'Uncle Arthur': 'the worthy Brown,' said Winslow contemptuously. Brown did not mind. In his own way, deliberate, never moving a step faster than he wanted, talking blandly, comfortably, and often sententiously, he set about his aims. He was by far the ablest manager among the Master's party. He was a cunning and realistic, as well as a very warm-hearted, man. And in the long run, deep below the good fellowship, he possessed great obstinacy and fortitude.

We drank our wine, seated opposite each other across the fire-place.

'It is rather consoling, don't you think?' said Brown amiably, as he took a sip. He went on to talk about some pupils, for most of the young men I supervised came into his tutorial side.

He was watching me with his intent, shrewd eyes and quite casually, as though it were part of the previous conversation, he slipped in the question:

'You see something of our young friend Calvert, don't you? I suppose you don't feel that perhaps we ought to push ahead a bit with getting him considered?'

I said that I did.

Brown shook his head.

'It's no use trying to rush things, Eliot. You can't take these places by storm. I expect you're inclined to think that it could have been better handled. I'm not prepared to go as far as that. The Master's in a very difficult situation, running a candidate in what people regard as his own subject. No, I don't think we should be right to feel impatient.' He gave a cautious smile. 'But I think we should be perfectly justified, and we can't do any harm, if we push a little from our side.'

'I'm ready to do anything,' I said. 'But I'm so relatively new to the college, I didn't think it was wise to take much part.'

'That shows very good judgment,' said Brown approvingly. 'Put it another way: it'll be a year or two before you'll carry as much weight here as some of us would like. But I believe you can dig in an oar about Calvert, if we set about it in the right way. Mind you, we've got to feel our steps. It may be prudent to draw back before we've gone too far.'

Brown filled our glasses again.

'I'm inclined to think, Eliot,' he went on, 'that our young friend could have been elected last term if there weren't some rather unfortunate personal considerations in the background. He's done quite enough to satisfy anyone, even if they don't believe he's as good as the Master says. They'd have taken him if they wanted to, but somehow or other they don't like the idea. There's a good deal of personal animosity somehow. These things shouldn't happen, of course, but men are as God made them.'

'Some of them dislike the Master, of course,' I said.

'I'm afraid that's so,' said Brown. 'And some of them dislike what they've heard of our young friend Calvert.'

'Yes.'

'Has that come your way?' His glance was very sharp.

'A little.'

'It would probably be more likely to come to me. Why, Chrystal' – (the Dean, usually Brown's inseparable comrade in college politics) – 'isn't completely happy about what he hears. Of course,' said Brown steadily, 'Calvert doesn't make things too easy for his friends. But once again men are as God made them, and it would be a damned scandal if the college didn't take him. I'm a mild man, but I should feel inclined to speak out.'

'What do you think we should do?'

'I've been turning it over in my mind,' said Brown. 'I can't help feeling this might be an occasion to take the bull by the horns. It occurs to me that some of our friends won't be very easy about their reasons for trying to keep him out. It might be useful to force them into the open. I have known that kind of method take the edge off certain persons' opposition in a very surprising way. And I think you can be very useful there. You're not so committed to the Master's personal way of looking at things as some of us are supposed to be – and also you know Francis Getliffe better than any of us.'

Under his stately, unhurried deliberations Brown had been getting down to detail – as he would say himself, he had been 'counting heads'.

'I suggest those might be our tactics for the time being,' said Brown. 'We can wait for a convenient night, when some of the others who don't see eye to eye with us are dining. Then we'll have a bottle of wine and see just how unreasonable they're prepared to be. We shall have to be careful about tackling them. I think it would be safer if you let me make the pace.'

Brown smiled: 'I fancy there's a decent chance we shall get the young man in, Eliot.' Then he warned me, as was his habit at the faintest sign of optimism: 'Mind you, I shan't feel justified in cheering until we hear the Master reading out the statute of admission.'

Brown studied the dining list each day, but had to wait, with imperturbable patience, some weeks before the right set of people were dining. At last the names turned up – Despard-Smith, Winslow, Getliffe, and no others. Brown put himself down to dine, and told the kitchen that I should be doing the same.

It was a Saturday night towards the end of term. As we sat in hall, nothing significant was said: from the head of the table, Despard-Smith let fall some solemn comments on the fortunes of the college boats in the Lent races. He was a clergyman of nearly seventy, but he had never left the college since he came up as an undergraduate. He had been Bursar for thirty years, Winslow's predecessor in the office. His face was mournful, harassed and depressed, and across his bald head were trained a few grey hairs. He was limited, competent, absolutely certain of his judgment, solemn, self-important and self-assured. He could make any platitude sound like a moral condemnation. And, when we went into the combination room after hall, he won a battle of wills upon whether we should drink claret or port that night.

Brown had been at his most emollient in hall, and had not given any hint of his intention. As soon as we arrived in the combination room, he asked permission to present a bottle, 'port or claret, according to the wishes of the company'.

Brown himself had a taste in claret, and only drank port to be clubbable. Francis Getliffe and I preferred claret, but were ready to drink port. But none of the three of us had any say.

We had seated ourselves at the end of the long, polished, oval table; glasses were already laid, sparkling in the light, reflected in the polished surface of the wood; the fire was high.

'Well, gentlemen,' said Despard-Smith solemnly, 'our c-colleague has kindly offered to present a bottle. I suppose it had better be a bottle of port.'

'Port?' said Winslow. 'Correct me if I am wrong, Mr President, but I'm not entirely certain that is the general feeling.'

His mouth had sunk in over his jaw, and his nose came down near his upper lip. His eyes were heavy-lidded, his face was hollowed with ill-temper and strain; but his skin was healthy, his long body free and active for a man of nearly sixty. There was a sarcastic twitch to his lips as he spoke: as usual he was caustically polite, even when his rude savage humour was in charge. His manners were formal, he had his own perverse sense of style.

Most of the college disliked him, yet all felt he had a kind of personal distinction. He had done nothing, had not published a book, was not even such a good Bursar as Despard-Smith had been, though he worked long hours in his office. He was a very clever man who had wasted his gifts.

'I've always considered,' said Despard-Smith, 'that claret is not strong enough for a dessert wine.'

'That's very remarkable,' said Winslow. 'I've always considered that port is too sweet for any purpose whatsoever.'

'You would s-seriously choose claret, Bursar?'

'If you please, Mr President. If you please.'

Despard-Smith looked round the table lugubriously.

'I suppose no one follows the Bursar in pressing for claret. No. I think' – he said triumphantly to the butler – 'we must have a bottle of port.'

Francis Getliffe grinned at me, the pleasant grim smile which I was used to, since I first met him in Mr March's London house. It had been through Francis, as I explained, that I came to the college at all. At this time we had not become intimates as his brother-in-law Charles March and I were. But our friendship was steady, and as it happened was to continue for a long time. We thought alike in most arguments and usually found ourselves at one, without any need to talk it over, over any college question. He was a physicist, with an important series of researches on the upper atmosphere already published. As I knew well enough already, he was a just, thin-skinned, strong-willed, and strenuously ambitious man.

The port went round, Despard-Smith gravely proposed Brown's health; Brown himself asked one or two quiet, encouraging questions about Winslow's son – for Winslow was a devoted father, and his son, who had entered the college the previous October, roused in him extravagant hopes: hopes that seemed dangerously extravagant, when one heard his blistering disparagement of others.

Then Brown, methodically twirling his wineglass, went on to ask:

'I suppose none of you happen to have thought any more about the matter of electing R. C. E. Calvert, have you? We shall have to decide one way or the other some time. It isn't fair to the man to leave him hanging in mid-air for ever.'

Winslow looked at him under hooded eyes.

'I take it you've gathered, my dear Tutor, that the proposal isn't greeted with unqualified enthusiasm?'

'I did feel,' said Brown, 'that one or two people weren't altogether convinced. And I've been trying to imagine why. On general grounds, I should have expected you to find him a very desirable candidate. Myself, I rather fancy him.'

'I had the impression you were not altogether opposed,' said Winslow.

Brown smiled, completely good-natured, completely undisturbed. 'Winslow, I should like to take a point with you. I think you'll admit that everything we've had on paper about Calvert is in his favour. Put it another way: he's been as well spoken of as anyone can be at that age. What do you feel is the case against him?'

'A great deal of the speaking in his favour,' said Winslow, 'has been done by our respected Master. I have considerable faith in the Master as an after-dinner speaker, but distinctly less in his judgment of men. I still remember his foisting O'Brien on us—' It was thirty years since Royce supported O'Brien, and there had been two Masters in between; but O'Brien had been a continual nuisance, and colleges had long memories. I felt all Winslow's opposition to Roy lived in his antagonism to the Master. He scarcely gave a thought to Roy as a human being, he was just a counter in the game.

'Several other people have written nearly as highly of Calvert,' said Brown. 'I know that in a rather obscure subject it's difficult to amass quite as much opinion as we should all like—'

'That's just it, Brown,' said Francis Getliffe. 'He's clearly pretty good. But he's in a field which no one knows about. How can you compare him with a lad like Luke, who's competing against some of the ablest men in the world? I'm not certain we ought to take anyone in these eccentric lines unless they're really extraordinarily good.'

'I should go a long way towards agreeing with you,' said Brown. 'Before I came down in favour of Calvert, I satisfied myself that he was extraordinarily good.'

'I'm not convinced by the evidence,' said Francis Getliffe.

Despard-Smith intervened, in a tone solemn, authoritative and damning:

'I can't be satisfied that it's in the man's own best interests to be elected here. I can't be satisfied that he's suited to collegiate life.'

'I don't quite understand, Despard,' said Brown. 'He'd be an asset to any society. He was extremely popular as an undergraduate.'

'That only makes it worse,' said Despard-Smith. 'I can't consider that our fellowships ought to be f-filled by young men of fashion. I'm by no means happy about Calvert's influence on the undergraduates, if we took the very serious risk of electing him to our society.'

'I can't possibly take that view,' said Brown. 'I believe he'd be like a breath of fresh air.'

'You can't take Despard's view, can you?' I asked Francis Getliffe across the table.

'I shouldn't mind what he was like, within reason,' said Francis, 'so long as he was good enough at his stuff.'

'But you've met him several times,' I said. 'What did you think of him?'

'Oh, he's good company. But I should like to know what he really values. Or what he really wants to do.'

I realised with a shock, what I should have seen before, that there was no understanding or contact between them. There was an impatient dismissal in Francis's tone: but suddenly, as though by a deliberate effort of fair-mindedness and responsibility, he turned to Despard-Smith.

'I ought to say,' he remarked sharply, 'that I should think it wrong to vote against him on personal grounds. If he's good enough, we ought to take him. But I want that proved.'

'I cannot think that he'd be an acquisition,' said Despard-Smith. 'When he was an undergraduate, I soon decided that he had no sense of humour. He used to come up to me and ask most extraordinary questions. Quite recently he sent me a ridiculous book by an unsatisfactory young man called Udal.'

'I expect he was just showing his respect,' said Brown.

'In that case,' said Despard-Smith, 'he should do it in a more sensible fashion. No, I think he would have a l-lamentable effect on the undergraduates. It's impossible to have a fellow who might attract undesirable notice. He still has women to visit him in his rooms. I can't think that it would be in his own interests to elect him.'

This was sheer intuitive hostility. Some obscure sense warned the old clergyman that Roy was dangerous. Nothing we could say would touch him. Brown, always realistic and never willing to argue without a purpose, gave him up at once.

'Well, Despard,' he said, 'we must agree to differ. But I should like to make a point or two with you others.'

'If you please, my dear Tutor,' said Winslow. 'I find it more congenial hearing it from you than from our respected Master. Even though you spend a little longer over it.'

Patiently, steadily, never ruffled, Brown went over the ground with them. Neither had shifted by the end of the evening: afterwards, Brown and I agreed that Winslow could be moved only if Roy ceased to be the Master's protégé, but that Francis Getliffe was fighting a prejudice and was not irretrievably opposed. We also agreed that it was going to be a very tight thing: we needed seven votes, we could see our way to five or six, but it was not certain where the others were coming from.

Through most of the Easter term, Arthur Brown was busy with talks, deliberate arguments, discussions on tactics, and bargains. It became clear that he could count on five votes for certain (the Master, Brown and myself; the senior fellow, who was a very old man; and the Senior Tutor, Jago). Another elderly fellow could almost certainly be relied upon, but he would be abroad all the summer, and votes had to be given in person. In order to get a majority at all, Brown needed either his friend Chrystal or mine, Getliffe; in order to force an issue during the summer, he needed both. There were talks in all our rooms, late into summer nights. Chrystal might come in, reluctantly and ill-temperedly, as a sign of personal and party loyalty: I could not use those ties with Francis Getliffe, who prided himself on his fairness and required objective proof.

Brown would not be hurried. 'More haste, less speed,' he said comfortably. 'If we have a misfire now, we can't bring our young friend up again for a couple of years.' He did not propose to take an official step until he could 'see his votes'. By statute, a fellowship had to be declared vacant before there could be any election. Brown could have collected a majority to vote for a vacancy: but it was not sensible to do so, until he was certain it could not be filled by anyone but Roy.

These dignified, broad-bottomed, middle-aged talks went on, seemingly enjoyed by most of those engaged. For they loved this kind of power politics, it was rich with its own kind of solid human life. It was strange to hear them at work, and then see the subject of it all walk lightly through the college. There was a curious incongruity that he of all men should be

debated on in those comfortable, traditional, respectable, guarded words:
I felt it often when I looked at him, his white working coat over a handsome suit, reading a manuscript leaf at his upright desk: or watched
him leave in his car, driving off to his London flat to meet Rosalind or
another: or saw his smile, as I told him Arthur Brown's latest move –
'extremely statesman-like, extremely statesman-like,' mimicked Roy, for
it was Brown himself who liked to use the word.

As a research student and ex-scholar, Roy was invited to the college's
summer feast. This took place near the first of June and was not such a
great occasion as the two great feasts of the year, the audit and the com-
memoration of benefactors. The foundation plate was not brought out;
nevertheless, on the tables in the hall silver and gold glittered in the
candlelight. Well above the zone of candlelight, high towards the roof of
the hall, the windows glowed with the light of the summer evening all
the time we sat there and ate and drank. The vintages were not the
college's finest, but they were good enough; the food was lavish; as the
high windows slowly darkened and the candles flickered down, the faces
round one shone out, flushed and bright-eyed.

It was to this feast that the college invited a quota of old members each
year, selected at random from the college lists. As junior fellow, I was
sitting at the bottom of one of the two lower tables, with an old member
on each hand: Roy came next to one of these old members, with a fellow
of another college on his left. It seemed that he decided early that the
fellow was capable of looking after himself; from the first courses he
devoted himself to making the old member happy, so that I could concentrate on the one on my right. With half an ear I kept listening to Roy's
success. His old member was a secondary schoolmaster of fifty, with a
sensitive, unprepossessing face. One felt that he had wanted much and
got almost nothing. There was a streak of plain silliness in him, and failure
had made him aggressive and opinionated. I tried, but he put me off
before I could get close: in a few moments, he was giving advice to Roy,
as an experienced man to a younger, and there was brilliance in the air.
Roy teased him simply, directly, like a brother. It was all spontaneous.
Roy had found someone who was naked to life. Before the end of dinner
Roy was promising to visit the school, and I knew he would.

The feast ended, and slowly the hall cleared as men rose and went by
twos and threes into the combination room. At my table we were still
sitting. Roy looked at his happiest.

'It's a pity we need to move,' he said.

On our way out, we passed the high table on the dais, where a small group was sitting over cigars and a last glass of port. Roy was whispering to me, when Chrystal called out:

'Eliot! I want you to meet our guest.'

He noticed Roy, and added: 'You too, Calvert! I want you all to meet our guest.'

Chrystal, the Dean, was a bald, beaky, commanding man, and 'our guest' had been brought here specially that evening. He was an eminent surgeon to whom the university was giving an honorary degree in two days' time. He sat by Chrystal's side, red-complexioned, opulent, with protruding eyes that glanced round whenever he spoke to make sure that all were listening. He nodded imperially to Roy and me, and went on talking.

'As I was saying, Dean,' he remarked loudly, 'I feel strongly that a man owes certain duties to himself.'

Roy was just sitting down, after throwing his gown over the back of a chair. I caught a glint in his eyes. That remark, the whole atmosphere of Anstruther-Barratt, was a temptation to him.

'And those are?' said Chrystal respectfully, who worshipped success in any form.

'I believe strongly,' said Anstruther-Barratt, 'that one ought to accept all the recognition that comes to one. One owes it to oneself.'

He surveyed us all.

'And yet, you wouldn't believe it,' he said resonantly, 'but I am quite nervous about Friday's performance. I don't feel I know all there is to be known about your academic things.'

'Oh, I think I should believe it,' said Roy in a clear voice. His expression was dangerously solemn.

'Should you?' Anstruther-Barratt looked at him in a puzzled fashion.

'Certainly,' said Roy. 'I expect this is the first time you've tried it—'

Roy had a grave, friendly look, and spoke as though Anstruther-Barratt was taking an elementary examination.

It was just possible that he did not know that Anstruther-Barratt was receiving an honorary degree. Chrystal must have thought it possible, for, looking on in consternation, he tried to break in.

'Calvert, I suppose you know—'

'Is it the first time?' Roy fixed the bold protruding eyes with a gaze from which they seemed unable to escape.

'Of course it is. One doesn't—'

'Just so. It's natural for you to be nervous,' said Roy. 'Everyone's nervous when they're trying something for the first time. But you know, you're lucky, being a medical – I hope I'm right in thinking you are a medical?'

'Yes.'

'It doesn't matter so much, does it? There's nothing so fatal about it.'

Anstruther-Barratt looked badgered and bewildered. This young man appeared to think that he was a medical student up for an examination. He burst out:

'Don't you think I look a bit old to be—'

'Oh no,' said Roy. 'It makes you much more nervous. You need to look after yourself more than you would have done twenty years ago. You oughtn't to do any work between now and Friday, you know. It's never worth while, looking at books at the last minute.'

'I wish you'd understand that I haven't looked at books for years, young man.'

'Calvert,' Chrystal began again.

'You've done much more than you think,' said Roy soothingly. 'Everyone feels as you do when it comes to the last day.'

'Nonsense. I tell you—'

'You must believe me. It's not nonsense. We've all been through it.' Roy gave him a gentle, serious smile. 'You ought to spend the day on the river tomorrow. And don't worry too much. Then go in and win on Friday. We'll look out for your name in the *Reporter*.'

CHAPTER VI

THE BEGINNING OF A SLEEPLESS NIGHT

Roy's antic at the end of the feast meant more delay for Brown. He had listened to an indignant outburst from his old ally Chrystal, who was, like so many people, mystified by Roy's manner. 'I don't know,' Chrystal snapped. 'He may have thought Barratt was an old man who was trying to get qualified. In that case he's a born bloody fool. Or it may be his idea of a joke. But I don't want that sort of joke made by a fellow of this college. I tell you, Barratt was right up in the air about it. He earns £20,000 a year if he earns a penny, and he's not used to being made an exhibition of.'

It did not seem as though anything could make Chrystal vote for Roy now, and Brown had to change his tactics. 'It's an infernal nuisance,' he said. 'I should almost feel justified in washing my hands of the whole business. I wish you'd keep Calvert in order, the damned ass.'

But, though Brown was annoyed because his particular craft was being interfered with, he was secretly amused; and, like the politician he was, he did not waste time thinking of opportunity lost. He was committed to getting Calvert in. He believed he was backing a great talent, he had a stubborn and unshakeable affection for Roy (behind Brown's comfortable flesh there was a deep sympathy with the wild), and with all the obstinacy of his nature he started on a new plan. Wait for the absentee to return in October: then invite down to the college the only two men in England who were authorities on Roy's work. 'It's a risk,' said Brown in a minatory voice. 'Some people may feel we're using unfair influence. It's one thing to write for opinions, it's quite another to produce the old gentlemen themselves. But I'm anxious to give Getliffe something to think about. Our friends mustn't be allowed to flatter themselves that we've shot our bolt.'

So, in the first week of the Michaelmas term, one of the customary college notes went out: 'Those fellows who are interested in Mr R. C. E. Calvert's candidature may like to know that Sir Oulstone Lyall and Colonel E. St G. Foulkes, the chief authorities on Mr Calvert's subject, will be my guests in hall on Sunday night. A.B.'

The Master, after talking to Brown, thought it politic not to dine in hall that Sunday night; none of the old men came, though it was by now certain that the two seniors would vote for Roy; Despard-Smith had said, in a solemn grating voice the night before, that he had ordered cold supper for himself in his rooms. Winslow was the next in seniority, and he presided with his own cultivated rudeness.

'It's a most remarkable occasion that we should have you two distinguished visitors,' he said as soon as dinner began. 'We appear to owe this remarkable occasion to the initiative of our worthy Mr Brown.'

'Yes,' said Colonel Foulkes undiplomatically. 'We've come to talk about Calvert.'

He was in his sixties, but neither his black hair nor his thick, down-curling, ginger moustache showed any grey at all. His cheeks were rubicund, his eyes a bright and startled brown. He always answered at extreme speed, as though the questions were reflected instantaneously off the front of his head. Action came more easily than reflection, one felt as soon as one heard him – and hot-tempered explosions a good deal more easily than comfortable argument. Yet he was fond of explaining the profound difference Yoga had meant in giving him peace beyond this world, since his time in the Indian Army. India had also led him to the study of the early Persian languages, as well as to Yoga – and everyone agreed that he was a fine scholar. He held a great many cranky interests at once, and at heart was fervent and very simple.

'Indeed,' said Winslow. 'Yes, I remember that we were promised the benefit of your judgment. I had a faint feeling, though, that we had already seen your opinion on paper about this young man. I may be stupid, I'm very ignorant about these things. But I seem to recall that the Master circulated what some of my colleagues would probably call a "dossier".'

'Does no harm to say it twice,' said Colonel Foulkes at once. 'You can't do better.'

'If you please?'

'You can't do better than Calvert. Impossible to get a better man.'

'It's most interesting,' said Winslow, 'to hear such a favourable opinion.'

'Not just my opinion,' said Colonel Foulkes. 'Everyone agrees who's competent to give one. Listen to Lyall.'

Sir Oulstone Lyall inclined his high, bald, domed head towards Winslow. He wore an impersonal, official, ambassadorial smile. He was used to being the spokesman for Central Asian history. He did it with a lofty gratification and self-esteem.

'I must begin by covering myself under a warning, Mr President,' said Sir Oulstone in measured tones. 'We all try to keep our sense of perspective, but it's straining humanity not to exaggerate the importance of the subject to which one has devoted one's small abilities for most of one's life.'

Heads were nodded. The table was used to this kind of public approach. They could stand more pomp than most bodies of men.

'I must make that qualification,' said Sir Oulstone without any sign of hurry. 'I may have a certain partiality for the studies with which I have associated for longer than I sometimes care to think. But, if you will kindly allow for that partiality, I may be able to assist you about Mr Calvert.' He paused. 'I think I can say, with a full sense of responsibility, that among the younger workers Mr Calvert is the chief hope that our studies now possess.'

It never occurred to Sir Oulstone that the college might dispute his judgment. For a time, his confidence had a hypnotic effect on all there, and on Brown's face there grew a comfortable, appreciative smile. Even Winslow did not produce a caustic remark, and it was left for Francis

Getliffe to cross-examine Sir Oulstone about his detailed knowledge of Roy's work. Francis knew that all Roy's published work was linguistic – and he was right in thinking that Sir Oulstone was a historian, not a linguist at all. But Sir Oulstone was quite unperturbed by the questions: he turned to Foulkes, with the manner of one whistling up a technical assistant, and said with unshaken confidence: 'Foulkes, I should like you to deal with that interesting point.' And Foulkes was off the mark at once.

Colonel Foulkes was off the mark even more rapidly when someone made a remark about Roy's character.

'Splendid fellow. Everything you could wish for,' said Foulkes.

'I have heard reports,' said Winslow, 'that the young man finds time for some night life. In the intervals of making his contribution to your subject, Sir Oulstone,' he added caustically, but I fancied that he was reluctant to bring in scandal. He had not done it before, and it was not his line.

'Nonsense,' said Colonel Foulkes instantaneously. 'Fine clean-living fellow. He's got his books and games, he doesn't want anything else.'

Someone said a word, and Foulkes became incensed. 'Listening to women's gossip.' He glared round with hot, brown eyes. 'Utterly unthinkable to anyone who knows Calvert as well as I do.'

Sir Oulstone intervened.

'I cannot pretend to have very intimate knowledge of Mr Calvert personally,' he said. 'Though I may say that I've formed a very favourable impression. He does not thrust himself forward in the presence of his elders. But my friend Colonel Foulkes has been in constant touch with him—'

'The army teaches you to see the seamy side,' said Foulkes, still irate but simmering down. 'Perhaps living in sheltered places makes you see things that aren't there. Afraid I can't leave this thing in its present state. I must correct this impression. Absolute nonsense. You couldn't have a finer specimen of a young man.'

Immediately after we rose from hall, Foulkes went away without going into the combination room. He would not let a minute pass before he 'corrected the impression', and he had gone off, without thinking twice, to see the Master. Sir Oulstone blandly continued his praise of Roy for an hour in the combination room: for all his blandness, for all his impenetrable pomposity, he had a real desire to see his subject grow. As we broke up, I could not decide what had been the effect of this curious evening.

Later that night, I called on Roy. He was alone, the opalescent viewing screen was still lighted at the top of his tall desk, but he was sunk into an armchair. At the little table by his side, books had been pushed out of order, so as to make room for a bottle of brandy and a glass.

'Tired?' I asked.

'Not tired enough.'

He did not smile, he scarcely looked at me, his face was drawn and fixed with sadness.

'Have a drink, Lewis.'

'No.'

'You don't mind me?' he said with a sad ironic courtesy, poured himself another glass, and took a gulp.

'There's nothing special the matter, is there?' I asked, but I knew that it was not so.

'How could there be?'

He seemed to struggle from a depth far away, as he asked:

'What have you been doing?'

'I've been in hall.'

'A good place, hall.'

'We were talking of you.'

'You should have something better to do,' he cried.

'It must happen just now, you know.' I tried to soothe him.

'They should forget me.'

'I told you, Oulstone Lyall was coming down—'

'He's a dreadful man.'

'He's pretty pompous,' I said. 'But he was doing you very proud—'

'He should be told to stop,' said Roy with a grimace, sombre and frowning. 'He's a dreadful man. He's stuffed. He's never doubted himself for a minute in his life.'

In any mood, Roy was provoked by the Lyalls, by the self-satisfied, protected, and content. But now he was inflamed.

'He never even doubted himself when he pinched Erzberger's work,' cried Roy.

Roy drank another brandy, and wildly told me of a scandal of thirty years before.

'It's true,' said Roy. 'You don't believe it, but it's true.'

'Tell me the whole story some time.'

'You don't need to humour me. That dreadful man oughtn't to be talking nonsense about me. I need to stop him.'

I had never seen Roy so overwhelmed by despondency as this. I did not know what to expect, or what to fear next. I was appalled that night by the wild active gleam that kept striking out of the darkness. He did not submit to the despair, but struggled for anything that gave release.

All I could do, I thought, was try to prevent any action that might damage himself. I said that stretches of unhappiness had to be lived through; somehow one emerged from them; they were bad enough in themselves, it was worse if they left consequences when one was calm once again.

Roy listened, his eyes bright, bloodshot. He replied more gently than he had spoken that night.

'Dear old boy, you know what it is to be miserable, don't you? But you think it ought to be kept in separate compartments, don't you? You don't believe that it ought to interfere with really serious things. Such as getting fellowships.'

'It's better if it doesn't,' I said.

'I wish I were as stoical as you,' he said. 'Yet you've been hopeless, haven't you?'

'Yes.'

'Just so. I'll try, I'll try. I can't promise much.'

He was quiet for a time, and did not take another drink until Ralph Udal came in. Since I first met him, he had borrowed a considerable sum of money from Roy. He had followed Roy's advice, and had taken a London curacy. He kept coming up to see Roy, so as to plan support within the college; but I knew he was also watching for Roy to be converted. His watch was patient, effortless, almost sinister. However, he was not so patient about obtaining his country living. Despite Roy's instructions, he had been trying to hurry things that weekend. He had been calling on the Master, Despard-Smith, the Senior Tutor, Brown, in order to sound them about the next vacancy; he was being much more open than Roy thought wise.

'Wonderful!' shouted Roy as Udal entered. 'Old Lewis won't drink, but you will, won't you?'

Udal took a sip of brandy, and looked at Roy with passive good-nature. 'Haven't you had enough?' he said.

'Probably,' said Roy, drinking again. 'Well, what did they say to you?'

Udal shrugged his shoulders. He seemed irritated and chagrined.

'They don't seem anxious to let me retire.'

'The devils,' said Roy.

'They think I'm too young to settle down in comfort. I've always had a faint objection,' said Udal, 'to people who find it necessary to make one do unpleasant things for the good of one's soul. Why do they take it on themselves?'

'Why do they, Lewis? You should know,' cried Roy.

I shook my head, and caught his eye. The gleam had come again; but, as he saw my look, he still seemed enough in command to quieten himself.

'At any rate,' he added in a level tone, 'you're spared having a man like old Lyall talking nonsense about you.'

'Who is Lyall?' said Udal.

'You wouldn't like him. He's stuffed.' Again Roy told the scandal of Lyall and Erzberger's work, but this time in a sad, contemptuous voice.

'Yours must be a curious trade,' said Udal.

'It doesn't signify,' said Roy. 'All men are the same, aren't they?'

He went on drinking, though neither of us kept him company. It was getting late, and soon after midnight Udal and I both wanted to go. Roy begged us to stay a little longer. At last we got up, although he implored us not to leave him.

'You two may sleep, but I shan't. So why should you go?' There was a trace of a smile. 'Please don't go. What's the use of going to bed if you can't sleep? And if you do sleep, you only dream. Dreams are horrible.'

'You'll sleep now, if you go to bed,' I said.

'You don't know,' said Roy. 'I shan't sleep tonight. I'll do anything you like. Let's do anything. Let's play cards. Three-handed bezique. Please stay and play bezique with me. Good game, three-handed bezique. It's a wonderful game. Please stay and play. Please stay with me.'

CHAPTER VII

WALK IN THE MOONLIGHT

DAY after day, Roy was left with the darkness on his mind. He read his manuscripts until he was faint, but no relief came to him. He had never been through melancholy that was as dark, that lasted so long. He could not sleep, and his nights were worse than his days.

It was heart-rending to watch, now I saw his affliction clear for the first time. At least once I was cowardly enough to make an excuse not to see him at night.

And I was frightened. I was lost. I had never before felt my way among this kind of darkness. I had known Sheila's, but that was different in kind. I could read of experiences which here and there resembled his, but books are empty when one is helpless beside the fact. Nothing I found to read, nothing I had learned myself, could tell me what was likely to come next. Often I was frightened over quite practical things: would he collapse? would he break out in some single irreparable act? I was never afraid that he might kill himself: from a distance, it might have seemed a danger, but in his presence I did not give it a thought. But I imagined most other kinds of disaster.

The melancholy, which fell on him the week-end that Lyall and Foulkes arrived, did not stay uniform like one pitch-black and unchanging night. Occasionally, it was broken by a wild, lurid elation that seemed like a caricature of his natural gaiety. The high spirits with which he took me round the bookshops or baited the surgeon at the feast – those spirits seemed suddenly distorted into a frenzy. I feared such moments most: they happened very seldom. I was waiting for them, but I did not know whether sympathy or love could help him then. Sometimes the melancholy lifted for a time much more gradually, for a day or a night, and he became himself at once, though sadder, more tired and more gentle. 'I must be an awful bore,' he said. 'You'd better spend your time with Arthur Brown. You'll find it less exhausting.'

All through, in melancholy or false elation, his intelligence was as lucid as ever: in fact, I sometimes thought that he was more lucid and penetrating than I had known him. He was given none of the comfort of illusion. He worked with the same precision and resource; some of his best emendations came during a phase of melancholy. And once or twice, struggling away from his own thoughts, he talked to me about myself as no one else could have done.

Whenever he could lose himself in another, I thought one night, he gained a little ease. It was a night not long after Lyall's visit, and Roy and I were dining in the Lodge. The Master was in Oxford, and Lady Muriel had asked us to dine *en famille* with herself and Joan. After I had dressed, I went up to Roy's room, and found him in shirtsleeves and black waistcoat studying his image in the mirror.

'If I keep out of the light, I may just pass.' He smiled at me ruefully. 'I don't look very bright for Lady Mu.'

Nights of insomnia had left stains under his eyes and taken the colour from his cheeks. There were shadows under his cheekbones, and his face, except when he smiled, was tired and drawn.

'I'll have to do my best for her,' he said. He gazed again at his reflection.

'It's bad to look like death. It makes them worry, doesn't it?' He turned away. 'I'm also going bald, but that's quite another thing.'

For once, Lady Muriel had not asked Mrs Seymour as the inevitable partner for me. There were only the four of us, and I was invited just as an excuse for having Roy: for Lady Muriel intended to enjoy his presence without being distracted at all.

She sat straightbacked at the end of the table, but if one had only heard her voice one would have known that Roy was there.

'Why have I been neglected, Roy?' she said.

'That is extremely simple,' said Roy.

'What do you mean, you impertinent young man?' she cried in delight.

'I've not been asked, Lady Mu,' he said, using her nickname to her face, which no one else would have dared.

He was using the tone, feline, affectionate, gently rough, which pleased her most. He was trying to hide his wretchedness, he acted a light-hearted mood in order to draw out her crowing laugh.

He smiled as he watched her face, suddenly undignified and unformidable, wrinkled, hearty, joyous as she laughed.

She recovered herself for a moment, however, when she talked of the Christmas vacation. Lord Boscastle had taken a villa outside Monte Carlo, and the Royces were going down 'as soon as the Master (as Lady Muriel always called him) has finished the scholarship examination'.

I mentioned that I was arranging to spend a week in Monte Carlo myself.

'How very strange, Mr Eliot,' said Lady Muriel, with recognition rather than enthusiasm. 'How very strange indeed.'

I said that I often went to the Mediterranean.

'Indeed,' said Lady Muriel firmly. 'I hope we may see something of you there.'

'I hope so, Lady Muriel.'

'And I hope,' she looked at me fixedly, 'we may have the pleasure of seeing your wife.'

'I want to take her,' I said. 'She may not be well enough to travel, though.'

It was nearly true, but Lady Muriel gave an ominous: 'I see, Mr Eliot.'

Lady Muriel still expressed surprise that I should be going to Monte Carlo. She had all the incredulity of the rich that anyone should share their pleasures. Rather as though she expected me to answer with the name of an obscure *pension*, she asked:

'May I ask where you are staying?'

'The Hermitage,' I said.

'Really, Mr Eliot,' she said. 'Don't you think that you will find it very expensive?'

During this conversation, I had noticed that Joan's glance had remained on Roy. Her own face was intent. It was still too young to show the line of her cheekbones. Her eyes were bright blue, and her hair brown and straight. It struck me that she had small, beautiful ears. But her face was open and harassed; I could guess too easily what had fascinated her: I looked across for a second, away from Lady Muriel, and saw Roy, stricken and remote. Usually he would have hung on to each word of the exchange, and parodied it later at my expense: now he was not listening. It seemed by an unnatural effort that he spoke again. Lady Muriel was remarking, in order to reprove my extravagance: 'My brother considers it quite impossibly expensive to live in Monte itself. We find it much more practical to take this place outside.'

'How terrible it must be to be poor, Lady Mu,' broke in Roy's voice. Joan started as he spoke: it made what she had seen appear ghostly. He was smiling now, he teased Lady Muriel, just as she wanted. She had noticed nothing, and was very happy. She crowed as he made fun of the Boscastle finances – which amused him, for he was enough his father's son to have a lively interest in money. And she was delighted when he threatened not to be left out of the party at Christmas, but to join me at the hotel. She even regarded me with a kind of second-hand favour.

Her response to Roy was very simple, I thought. Life had never set her free, but underneath the armour she was healthy, vital and coarse-fibred. She had borne three daughters, but no sons. Roy was the son she had never had. And he was an attractive young man, utterly unimpressed by her magnificence. She could never find a way to tell people she liked them, but that did not matter with this young man, who could hear what she was really saying behind the gruff, clumsy words.

And Roy? She was a continual pleasure to him in being exactly what she was, splendid in her unperceptive courage, her heavy-footedness, her snobbery, her stiff and monumental gusto. But there was much more. He came into immediate touch with her. He knew how she craved to be liked, how she could never confess her longing for affection, fun and love. It was his nature to give it. He was moved deeply, moved to a mixture of pity and love, by the unexpectedly vulnerable, just as he was by the tormented, the failures, and the strays. So he could not resist being fond of Lady Muriel; and even that night, when left to himself he would have known only despair, he was forced to make sure that she enjoyed her party.

Roy and I had not long left the Lodge and were sitting in his rooms, when we heard a woman's footsteps on the stairs.

'What's this?' said Roy wearily.

It was Joan. She hesitated when she saw me, but then spoke direct to Roy.

'I'm sorry. But I had to come. At dinner you looked so – ill.'

'It's nice of you, Joan,' he said, but I felt he was put out. 'I'm pretty well.'

She looked at him with steady, intelligent, dark blue eyes.

'In all ways?'

'Oh yes.'

'I don't believe it,' said Joan.

Roy made a grimace, and leant back.

'Look,' she said, 'you don't think I like intruding, do you? But I want to ask something. Is it this wretched fellowship? We're bound to hear things we shouldn't, you must know that.'

'It would be extremely surprising if you didn't,' said Roy.

'We do,' said Joan, transformed by her rich laugh. 'Well, I've heard about this wretched business. Is it that?'

'Of course not,' said Roy.

'I should like to ask Lewis Eliot,' she said, and turned to me. 'Has that business got on his nerves?'

'I don't think so,' I said. 'It would be better if it were settled, of course.' I was actually anxious that his election should come through quickly, so as to divert his mind (Brown had been satisfied with the results of Lyall's and Foulkes's visit, so much so that he was pressing to have a vacancy declared at the next college meeting).

'Are you sure?' Joan looked stubborn and doubtful. She spoke to Roy again: 'You must see that it doesn't matter. Whatever they do, it can't really matter to you.'

'Just so,' said Roy. 'You need to tell your father that. It would please him if I got in.'

'He worries too much about these people,' said Joan, speaking of her father with scorn and love. 'You say you don't. I hope it's true.'

She gazed at him.

'Yes?' he said.

'I was trying to imagine why you were looking as you did.'

'I can't suggest anything,' said Roy. He had been restless all the time she was questioning him: had he not noticed the physical nervousness which had made her tremble as she entered, the utter diffidence which lay behind her fierce direct attack?

'I'm not so young as you think,' said Joan, and a blush climbed up her strong neck, reddened her cheeks, left her bright-eyed, ashamed, angry and defenceless.

I went away from Roy's rooms as the clocks were chiming midnight, and was in the depth of sleep when softly, persistently, a hand on my shoulder pulled me half-awake.

'Do you mind very much?' Roy was speaking. 'I need to talk to you.'

'Put the light on,' I said crossly.

His face was haggard, and my ill-temper could not survive.

'It's nothing original,' he said. 'I can't sleep, that's all. It must be a very useful accomplishment, being able to sleep.'

He had not been to bed, he was still wearing his dinner jacket.

'What do you want to do?'

He shook his head. Then suddenly, almost eagerly, he said:

'I think I need to go for a walk. Will you come?' He caught at anything which would pass the night. 'Let's go for a walk,' he said.

I got up and dressed. It was just after three when we walked through the silent courts towards the back gate of the college. The roofs gleamed like silver under the harvest moon, and the shadows were dense, black, and sharply edged.

A light shone in an attic window; we knew the room, it was a scholar working late.

'Poor fool,' Roy whispered, as I was unlocking the small back door. 'He doesn't realise where that may lead.'

'Where?'

'It might even keep him here,' said Roy with a faint smile. 'If he does too well. So that he's woken up in the middle of the night and taken out for walks.'

We walked along Regent Street and Hills Road, straight out of the town. It was all quiet under the moon. It was brilliantly quiet. The road spread wide in the moonlight, dominating the houses as on a bright day; the houses stood blank-faced. Roy walked by my side with quick, light, easy steps. He was soothed by the sheer activity, by being able to move without thought, by the beautiful night. He talked, with a trace of his good-natured malice, about some of our friends. We had a good many in common, both men and women, and we talked scandal and Roy mimicked them as we made our way along the gleaming, empty road.

But when we turned left at the Strangeways and crossed the fields, he fell more silent. For a quarter of a mile along the Roman road neither of us spoke. Then Roy said, quietly and clearly:

'I need some rest.'

'Yes,' I said. He did not mean sleep or bodily rest.

'Shall I ever get it?'

I could not answer that.

'Sometimes,' he said, 'I think I was born out of my time. I should have been happier when it was easier to believe. Wouldn't you have been happier? Wouldn't you?'

He wanted me to agree. I was tempted to fall in, to muffle my answer, to give him a little comfort. Yet he was speaking with absolute nakedness. I could not escape the moment in which we stood.

I hesitated. Then I told the truth.

'I don't think so.'

He walked on a few yards in silence, then looked me in the face.

'Lewis, have you never longed to believe in God?'

'No,' I said. I added:

'Not in any sense which has much meaning. Not in any sense which would mean anything to you.'

'You don't long to believe in God?' he insisted.

'No.'

'Yet you're not stuffed.' He paused. 'No man is less stuffed. In spite of your business manner. You even feel a good deal, don't you? Not only about love. That's the trouble with all those others' – he was dismissing some of our contemporaries – 'they can only feel about love. They're hollow, aren't they? But I can't accuse you of that. Yet you don't long to believe—'

His eyes searched me. He had been mystified about it since he first knew me well. So much of our sense of life we felt in common: he could not easily or willingly accept that it led me to different fulfilments, even to different despairs. Most of all, he could not accept that I could get along, with fairly even spirits.

He was quiet again. Then he said:

'Lewis, I've prayed that I might believe in God.'

He looked away from me, down from the ridge; there was a veil of mist on the lower fields.

'I knew,' I said.

'It's no good,' he said, as though off-handedly. 'One can't make oneself believe. One can't believe to order.'

'That must be so,' I said.

'Either it comes or it doesn't. For me it doesn't. For some – it is as easy as breathing. How lucky they are,' he said. 'Think of the Master. He's not a very good scholar, you know, but he's an extremely clever man. But he believes exactly as he did when he was a child. After reading about all the religions in the world. He's very lucky.'

He was still looking over the fields.

'Then there's Ralph Udal.' Suddenly he gave me a glance acute and piercing. 'By the way, why do you dislike him so much?'

'I don't dislike him—'

'Come off it.' Roy smiled. 'I've not seen you do it with anyone else – but when you meet him you bristle like a cat.'

I had not wanted to recognise it, but it was true. I could not explain it.

'Anyway,' said Roy, 'he's not an empty man. You'd give him that, wouldn't you? And he believes without a moment's trouble.'

Slowly we began to walk back along the path. Roy was still thinking of those who did not need to struggle in order to believe in God. He spoke of old Martineau, whose story had caught his imagination. By this time, after a spell as a tramp preacher, he had become a pavement artist on the streets of Leeds, drawing pictures with a religious message. I had seen him fairly recently: he was very happy, and surprisingly unchanged.

'He must have been certain of God,' said Roy.

'I'm not at all sure,' I said. 'He was never able to explain what he really believed. That was always the hardest thing to understand.'

'Well, I hope he's certain now,' said Roy. 'If anyone deserves to be, he does.'

Then he spoke with intense feeling:

'I can't think what it's like to be certain. I'm afraid that it's impossible for me. There isn't a place for me.'

His voice was full of passion. As he went on, it became louder, louder than the voice I was used to, but still very clear:

'Listen, Lewis. I could believe in all the rest. I could believe in the catholic church. I could believe in miracles. I could believe in the inquisition. I could believe in eternal damnation. If only I could believe in God.'

'And yet you can't.'

'I can't begin to,' he said, his tone quiet once more. 'I can't get as far as "help Thou mine unbelief".'

We left the ridge of the Roman road, and began to cross the shining fields.

'The nearest I've got is this,' he said. 'It has happened twice. It's completely clear – and terrible. Each time it has been on a night when I couldn't sleep. I've had the absolute conviction – it's much more real than anything one can see or touch – that God and His world exist. And everyone can enter and find their rest. Except me. I'm infinitely far away for ever. I am alone and apart and infinitesimally small – and I can't come near.'

I looked at his face in the moonlight. It was pale, but less haunted, and seemed to be relaxed into a kind of exhausted peace. Soon he began to sing, very quietly, in a light, true, reedy voice. Quiet though it was, it became the only sound under the sky. There was a slight ironic smile on his face; for he was singing a child's prayer to be guarded while asleep.

CHAPTER VIII

ELECTION OF A FELLOW

FOR once in his life, Arthur Brown considered that he had been guilty of 'premature action'. After the visit of Lyall and Foulkes, he had considered Roy as good as elected, although as a matter of form he warned me against excessive optimism. Francis had told him, in his honest fashion, that he had been impressed by the expert evidence. Even Winslow had remarked that, though the case for Calvert rested mainly on nepotism, there did appear to be a trace of merit there. Brown went steadily ahead, persuaded the college to create a vacancy and to perform the statutory rites so that there could be an election on the first Monday in November.

So far, so good. But it happened that young Luke, a scientist two years Roy's junior, finished a research sooner than anyone expected. Francis Getliffe came in with the news one night. The work was completely sound and definite, he said, though some loose ends needed tying up; it was an important advance in nuclear physics. Francis had been intending to bring Luke's name up the following year, but now he wanted him discussed at the fellowship meeting.

'That puts everything back in the melting pot,' said Arthur Brown. 'I don't wish Luke any harm, but it's a pity his confounded apparatus didn't blow up a fortnight ago. Just to give us time to squeeze our young friend in. I dare say Luke is pretty good, I know Getliffe has always thought the world of him. But there's plenty of time to give him a run next year. Well, Eliot, it's a great lesson to me never to count my chickens before they're hatched. I shan't take anything for granted next time I'm backing someone until I actually see him admitted in the Chapel. I don't mind telling you that I shall be relieved if we ever see Calvert there. Well, we've got to make as good a showing as we can. I'm rather inclined to think this is the time to dig in our heels.'

Brown's reflection did not prevent him from letting Francis Getliffe know that his 'present intention' would be to support Luke next year. I did the same. Francis was not the man who would 'do a deal', but he was practical and sensible. He would get Luke in anyway, if he waited a few months: we made sure he knew it, before he went to extravagant lengths to fight an election now.

That was all we could do. Roy was still depressed, though not so acutely as on the night of our walk. About his election, I was far more anxious than he.

The day of the election was damp and dark, with low clouds, and a drizzle of rain. In the courts, red and copper leaves of creepers slithered underfoot; umbrellas glistened in the streets as they passed the lighted shops. The meeting was called for the traditional hour of half-past four, with tea beforehand; to quieten my nerves, I spent the middle of the afternoon walking in the town, looking at bookshops, greeting acquaintances; the streets were busy, the window lights shone under the dark sky. There was the wistful smell of the Cambridge autumn, and in the tailors' shops gleamed the little handbills, blue letters on white with the names of the week's university teams.

At four o'clock I entered the college by the great gate. The bell was tolling for the meeting, the curtains of the combination room were already drawn. Through the curtains, the lights of the room glowed orange and drew my eyes from the dark court; like any lighted room on a dusky evening, it tempted me with domestic comfort, even though I was wishing that the meeting were all over or that I need not go.

As soon as I got inside, I knew so much of it by heart – the burnished table reflecting, not wineglasses and decanters, but inkpots and neat piles of paper in front of each of our chairs – old Gay, the senior fellow, in his seventies, tucking with shameless greed and gusto into an enormous tea, and congratulating everyone on its excellence – the great silver teapots, the muffin covers, the solid fruit cakes, the pastries – the little groups of two or three colloguing in corners, with sometimes a word, louder than the rest of their conversation, causing others to frown and wonder.

It did not vary meeting by meeting. Nor indeed did the business itself, when the half-hour struck, and the Master, brisk, polite, called us to our places, asked for the minutes, said his opening word about the day's proceedings. For by tradition the day's proceedings had to begin first with any questions of college livings and second with financial business. That afternoon there was only a report that someone was considering a call to the one vacant living ('he'll take it,' said Despard-Smith bleakly): but when the Master, so used to these affairs that his courtesy was first nature, his impatience long since dulled, asked: 'Bursar, have you any business for us?' Winslow replied: 'If you please, Master. If you please.' We listened to a long account of the difficulty of collecting rents from some of the college farms. We then heard the problem of the lease of one of the Cambridge shops, and discussed how to buy a house owned by another college, which was desirable in order to rectify a strategic frontier. It was routine, it was quite unselfconscious, it was what we were used to: it only happened that I could have dispensed with it that afternoon, that was all.

As usual, the financial business tailed away about half-past five. The Master, completely fresh, looked round the table. It was a gift of his to seem formal, and yet natural and relaxed.

'That seems to bring us to our main business, gentlemen,' he said. 'As will be familiar to you, we have appointed today for the election of a fellow. I suggest we follow the custom that is becoming habitual – though it wasn't so when I was a junior fellow' – he smiled at some of the older men, as though there was a story to be told later – 'and have a straw vote first, to see if we can reach a majority for any candidate. After that, we will proceed to a formal vote, in which we have been known to put on a somewhat greater appearance of agreement.'

There were a few suppressed smiles.

'Well,' said the Master, 'the college is well aware of my own position. I thought it right and proper – in fact I felt obliged – to bring up the name of Mr R. C. E. Calvert for consideration. I have told the college, no doubt at excessive length, that in my own view Mr Calvert is our strongest candidate for years past. The college will be familiar with the written reports on his work, and I understand that some fellows had the opportunity of meeting Sir Oulstone Lyall and Colonel Foulkes in person, who probably expressed to them, as they have expressed to me, their opinions upon Mr Calvert.' For a second a slight smile crossed the Master's face. 'The whole case has been explored, if I may say so, with praiseworthy thoroughness. I seem to recall certain discussions in this room and elsewhere. I do not know whether the college now feels that it has heard enough to vote straightaway, or whether there are some fellows who would prefer to examine the question further.'

'If you please, Master,' began Winslow. 'I am afraid that I should consider it rushing things,' said Despard-Smith, at the same moment.

'You wish for a discussion, Bursar?' said the Master, his colour a shade higher, but still courteous.

'*Seniores priores*,' Winslow said, inclining his head to Despard-Smith.

'Mr Despard-Smith?' said the Master.

'Master,' Despard-Smith gazed down the table with gloom, 'I am afraid that I must impress upon the college the d-disastrous consequences of a risky election. The consequences may be worse than disastrous, they may be positively catastrophic. I must tell the college that my doubts about Mr Calvert are very far from being removed. With great respect, Master, I am compelled to say that nothing I have yet heard has even begun to remove my doubts. I need not tell the college that nothing would please me more than being able conscientiously to support Mr Calvert. But, as I am at present s-situated, I should be forsaking my duty if I did not raise my doubts at this critical juncture.'

'We should all be grateful,' said the Master formally.

'It is a thankless task,' said Despard-Smith, with sombre relish, 'but I feel it is in the man's own best interests. First of all, I am compelled to ask whether any of Mr Calvert's sponsors can reassure me on this point: if he were to be elected, would he take his share of the' – Despard-Smith stuttered, and then produced one of his descents into funereal anticlimax – 'the bread-and-butter work of the college? I cannot see Mr Calvert doing his honest share of the bread-and-butter work, and a college of this size cannot carry passengers.'

'Perhaps I might answer that, Master?' said Arthur Brown, bland, vigilant, his tone conciliatory, stubbornly prepared to argue all through the night.

The Master was glad to hear him.

'Anyone who knows Mr Calvert,' said Brown roundly, 'could feel no shadow of doubt about his willingness to undertake any duties the college put upon him. Put it another way: he would never let us down, whatever we asked him to do. But I must reply to Mr Despard-Smith that I myself, and I feel sure I am speaking for several fellows, would feel very dubious about the wisdom of our asking Mr Calvert to undertake these bread-and-butter duties. If he is as good at his research work as some of us are inclined to think, he should not be encumbered with more pedestrian activities. We can always find willing horses among ourselves to carry out the more pedestrian activities. As for Mr Calvert, I should be inclined to say that I don't expect a nightingale to crack nuts.'

Despard-Smith shook his head. He went on:

'Many of us have had to sacrifice our own interests for the college. I do not see why this young man should be an exception. I am also compelled to ask a second question, to which I attach even more serious importance. Is Mr Calvert sound enough in character to measure up to his responsibilities? We demand from our fellows a high standard of character. It will be scandalous if we ever cease to. It will be the beginning of the end. Speaking from many years' judgment of men, I cannot conceal grave doubts as to whether Mr Calvert's character has developed sufficiently to come up to our high standard.'

It was as open as the conventions allowed. All his life Despard-Smith had been used to damning people at this table by the solemn unspoken doubt. And the debate stayed at that level, full of anger, misunderstandings, personal imperialisms, often echoes of echoes that biased men for or against Roy, that made it urgent for them to vote him in or out that afternoon. For an instant, through my fret and anxiety, I thought this was how all humans judged each other. Lightweight, said one. Dilettante, said another (which I said was the least true comment I could imagine). Charming and modest, said one of the old men, who liked his looks. 'At any rate, he's not prosaic,' declared Jago, the Senior Tutor, the dramatic and brilliant, the most striking figure in the college. Chrystal, out of loyalty to Brown, did not discuss the incident at the feast, but said he intended to reserve judgment. Conceited and standoffish, said someone. Brown met all the opinions imperturbably, softened them when he could, gave a picture of Roy – quiet, devoted to his work, anxious to become a don in the old style. The Master's politeness did not leave him, though it was strained as he heard some of the criticisms; he stayed quick and alert in the chair, and repressed all his sarcasms until the name of Luke came up.

But, when it came, his sarcasm was unfortunate. After the exchange of opinions about Roy's personality, it became clear that we could not lose that afternoon. There were twelve men present (one was still ill). Of the twelve, six had now declared themselves as immovably determined to vote for Roy in this election – the Master, Brown, Jago, myself and the two senior fellows. There were four votes against for certain, with Chrystal and Getliffe still on the fence. At this point, Winslow, who had so far only interposed a few rude comments, took over the opposition from Despard-Smith. He talked of the needs of the college, gibed at the Master by speaking contemptuously of the 'somewhat exotic appeal of esoteric subjects', and finished by saying that he would like Getliffe to 'ventilate' the question of Luke. Brown greeted them both with the blandest of encouragement: it was always his tactic to be most reasonable and amiable when things were going well.

In his taut crisp fashion Francis described Luke's career in research. He was the son of a dockyard riveter – had won a scholarship from his secondary school, taken high firsts in his triposes ['there's no difference between him and Calvert there,' said Francis], begun research in the Cavendish two years before. 'He's just finished that first bit of work,' said Francis Getliffe. 'He's said the last word on the subject.'

'Isn't that just the trouble with some of your scientific colleagues, Dr Getliffe?' said the Master in a cheerful whisper. 'They're always saying the last word, but they never seem to say the first.'

There was laughter, but not from the scientists. Francis flushed. He was never self-forgetful on public occasions.

I was maddened. It was innocent, it carried no meaning except that the Master liked to feel the witticism on his tongue: it was incredible that after all his years of intimate affairs he could not resist a moment's score. Francis would not forgive him.

But Arthur Brown was on watch.

'I think I should like it known, Master,' he said in his rich, deliberate, fat man's voice, 'that I for one, and I rather fancy several others, are very much interested in Mr Luke's candidature. If it weren't for what in our judgment are the absolutely overwhelming claims of Mr Calvert, it would seem to me very difficult not to vote for the other young man today. He hasn't had the advantages that most of our undergraduates have, and I consider his performance is perfectly splendid. Unfortunately I do feel myself obliged to vote for Mr Calvert this evening, but if Dr Getliffe brings up the other name next term, I rather fancy we can promise him a very sympathetic hearing.'

Brown gave Francis Getliffe, all down the length of the table, his broadest and most affable smile. After a moment, Francis's cheeks creased with a good-natured grin. Brown was watching him with eyes that, behind the broad smile, did not miss the shadow of an expression: as soon as he saw Francis's face relax, he spoke, still richly but very quick to get in first.

'I don't know,' said Brown, 'how far Dr Getliffe intends to press us about Luke this afternoon – in all the circumstances and considering what has just been said?'

Francis hesitated, and then said:

'No, I won't go any further. I take the strongest exception, Master, to any suggestion that Luke's work is not original. It's as original as any work can be. And I shall propose him at the first opportunity next year. I hope the college doesn't let him slip. He's quite first class. But I'm satisfied that Calvert has done distinguished work, and looks like going on with it. I'm ready to vote for him this afternoon.'

There was a hum, a rustle, a shuffle of papers. I glanced at Winslow: he pulled down his mouth in a grimace that was twisted, self-depreciating, not unpleasant. Arthur Brown was writing with great care on a quarter sheet of paper, and did not look up. The Master gave Francis a fresh, intimate, lively smile, and said:

'I withdraw completely. Don't take it amiss.'

Brown folded up his note, and wrote a name on it. It was passed round to me. Inside it read, simply: WE MIGHT HAVE LOST.

The straw vote followed soon after. There were seven votes for Roy, four against. Chrystal did not vote.

Before we made the statutory promises and gave our formal vote in writing, Despard-Smith got in a bleak speech in which he regretted that he could not vote for Calvert even for the sake of a gesture of unanimity. Winslow said that, for his part, he was prepared to give anyone the satisfaction of meaningless concord. At last, Roy was formally elected by ten votes to two, Despard-Smith and another, a man called Nightingale, sticking it out to the last.

The Master smiled. It was nearly seven o'clock, he was no more stale than when we began.

'I should like to congratulate everyone,' he said, 'on having done a good day's work for the college.'

I went out of the room to send the butler in search of Roy. When I returned, the college was indefatigably considering the decoration of the hall, a subject which came on each list of agenda, roused the sharpest animosities, and was never settled. The old fellows took a more dominant part than in the election. Some of them had been arguing over college aesthetics for over fifty years, and they still disagreed with much acerbity. They were vigorously at it when the butler opened the door and announced that Mr Calvert was waiting. According to custom, the Master at once adjourned the meeting, and eyes turned towards the door.

Roy come in, lightfooted, his head high. Under his gown, he was wearing a new dark grey suit. Everyone watched him. His face was pale and grave. No one's eyes could leave him, neither his friends' nor those who had been decrying him half an hour before.

He stood at the table, on the opposite side to the Master. The Master himself stood up, and said:

'Mr Calvert, it is my pleasant duty to tell you that you have this day been elected into our society.'

Roy inclined his head.

'If it is agreeable to you,' the Master went on briskly, 'I propose to admit you at once.'

'Yes, Master.' They were Roy's first words.

'Then we will go into chapel this moment,' said the Master. 'Those fellows who are free will perhaps follow us.'

The Master and Roy walked together, both slender and upright, out of the combination room into the first court, dark in the November night. We followed them, two by two, along the wet shining path. We carried some wisps of fog in with us, as we passed through the chapel door, and a haze hung over the painted panels. We crowded into the fellows' stalls, where few of us now attended, except for formal duties such as this – that night Winslow and Francis Getliffe, the doctrinaire unbelievers, did not come.

Roy knelt in the Master's stall, his palms together, the Master's hands pressing his. The clear light voice could be heard all over the chapel, as he took the oath. The Master said the final words, and began shaking Roy's hand. As we moved forward to congratulate him, Brown nudged me and whispered:

'Now I really do believe that fate can't touch us.'

CHAPTER IX

BIRTHDAY CELEBRATION

LADY Muriel gave an intimate dinner party in the Lodge: Arthur Brown presented three bottles on the night of the election, and some more in the week that followed: the Master went round, excelling himself in cheerful, familiar whispers: Bidwell greeted Roy with his sly, open, peasant smile, and said: 'We're all very glad about that, sir. Of course we knew something was going on. We like to keep our eye on things in our own way. I'm very glad myself, if you don't mind me saying so.'

With all of them Roy pretended to be light-hearted: their pleasure would be spoilt unless he were himself delighted. He could not take joy away from those he liked. He even simulated cheerfulness with me, for

854

he knew that I was pleased. But it was no good. The melancholy would not let him go. It was heavier than it had ever been.

He increased his hours of work. Bottles of brandy kept coming into his room, and he began drinking whenever he had to leave his manuscripts. There were evenings when he worked with a tumbler of spirits beside him on the upright desk.

One night I found him in an overall, with pots of paint scattered on the floor.

'What are you doing?' I asked.

'Brightening things up,' he said. His mockery did not leave him for long, even in this state. 'I need things bright round me. Otherwise I might get depressed.'

For days he painted the room from the ceiling to the floor. In the end, the walls gleamed in pink, green and terra cotta. The desks, once a shining white, he painted also, the platforms pink and the legs green. It picked out their strange shapes. From then on, the whole room was bright with colour, was covered with the vivid desks in their bizarre lines. It took visitors aback, when they called to inspect his manuscripts.

I felt helpless and utterly useless, though he seemed to like having me with him. I was afraid, with a growing dread, of the lightning flashes of elation. I told myself that perhaps this state would pass, and meanwhile tried to prevent him dining in hall or being seen much in the college. I did not want him to do himself harm there – and also I had the selfish and practical reason that I did not want him to do harm to myself or Arthur Brown. I dined with him in the town, we went to see friends in their colleges and houses, I persuaded him to spend several nights in his London flat. Rosalind, who had written to me often during the past eighteen months and who kept sending me presents, needed only a word by telephone: she followed him there, and for the first day or two gave him release – temporary, perhaps, thoughtless, certainly, not the release he himself looked for, but still release.

It was, of course, noticed by the college that he had not dined often in hall since his election. But they concluded that he was indulging in a round of celebration. They minded very little; by the custom of their class, and of this particular academic society, they did not take much notice of drinking. They nodded in a matter-of-fact and cheerful way. The Master met him once in the court when his eyes were bright with drink, and said to me next day:

'Roy Calvert seems to be going about with vineleaves in his hair. I suppose it's only natural.'

I wished it were as natural as that.

I paid very little attention when Roy asked me to the meeting in honour of Lyall. It was on one of my usual evenings in London, during Roy's stay. I had gone round from my house in Chelsea to his flat in Connaught Street, just behind the Bayswater Road. Rosalind let me in. She was busy trying the effect of some new boxes with bright, painted, porcelain lids.

Roy had taken the flat while he was an undergraduate, but Rosalind was the only woman who had left her stamp on it. Soon after she first stayed there, she set about making it into something more ornate, lush, comfortable, and mondaine.

'How do you like them?' she said, viewing the boxes.

'A bit boudoir-ish,' I said.

'Oh dear.' Superficially she was easy to discourage. She and I got on very well in an unexacting fashion.

'How is Roy?'

'The old thing's dressing. I don't think there's much the matter with him.'

'Is he cheerful?'

'He's as cheerful as you bright people usually manage to be. I don't take too much notice of his moods, Lewis. I've been keeping him in bed. There's plenty of life in the old thing still,' she said with a dying fall. One of her uses to him, I thought suddenly, was that she treated him as though he were a perfectly ordinary man. She loved what to her meant romance, the pink lamp-shades in the restaurant car, the Italian sky, great restaurants, all the world of chic and style: at a distance Roy was romantic because he gave her those: in the flesh, though she loved him dearly, he was a man like other men, who had better be pampered though 'there was not much wrong with him'.

Roy entered in a dressing-gown, shaved and fresh.

'You here?' he said to me in mock surprise. And to Rosalind: 'What may you be doing, dear?'

'Flirting with Lewis,' she said immediately.

He smacked her lightly, and they discussed where they should go for dinner, so that he might know what clothes to wear. 'We're not taking you, old boy,' said Roy over her shoulder: he gave her just the choice that made her eyes rounder, Claridge's, the Savoy, Monseigneur's. He seemed far less depressed than when I last saw him, and I was nothing but amused when he asked me to the Lyall celebration.

'We shan't take you tonight,' he said. 'I'm simply jealous of you with

Rosalind. But I'll take you somewhere else on Thursday. You need to come and hear us honour old Lyall.'

'Oulstone Lyall?'

'Just so. I need you to come. You'll find it funny. He'll be remarkably stuffed.'

I soon had reason to try to remember that invitation exactly, for I was compelled to learn this state of his right through; but I was almost certain that there was nothing dionysiac about him at all that evening, no lightning flash of unnatural gaiety. It was probable that his ease and pleasure with Rosalind made his spirits appear higher than they were. In reality, he was still borne down, though he could appear carefree as he entertained Rosalind or laughed at me.

Sir Oulstone Lyall was seventy years of age that autumn, and scholars in all the oriental subjects had arranged this meeting as a compliment. It was arranged for the Thursday afternoon in the rooms of the British Academy. There were to be accounts of the contemporary position in various fields of scholarship – with the intention of bringing out, in a gentlemanly fashion, the effect and influence of Lyall's own work. It was a custom borrowed from German scholars, and the old-fashioned did not like it. Nevertheless, most of the orientalists in the country came to the meeting.

The Master travelled up from Cambridge that morning and lunched with Roy and me. Away from the Lodge, he was in his most lively form, and it was he who first made a light remark about Sir Oulstone.

'Between ourselves,' said the Master, 'it's a vulgar error to suppose that distinguished scholars are modest souls who shrink from the glory. Knighthoods and addresses on vellum – that's the way to please distinguished scholars. I advise you to study the modesty of our venerable friend this afternoon.'

Roy laughed very loudly. There was something wild in the sound; at once I was worried. I wished I could get him alone.

'And if you want to observe human nature in the raw,' said the Master, jumping into his favourite topic, 'it's a very interesting point whether you ought to go out and find a pogrom or just watch some of our scientific colleagues competing for honours.'

'How did Lyall get there?' said Roy, in a piercing insistent tone.

'Between ourselves,' the Master replied, 'I've always felt that he was rather an old humbug.'

'I've heard a story about Erzberger. Master, do you remember anything?' said Roy.

The Master did remember. He was himself modest and humble, his professional life was blameless. But he was always ready to indulge in a detached, abstract and cheerful cynicism. He did not notice that Roy's glance was preternaturally attentive – or perhaps he was stimulated by it.

For the rest of our lunch until it was time to walk up to Piccadilly, he told Roy what he knew of Lyall and Erzberger. The Master had actually met Erzberger when they were both young men.

'He was an astonishingly ugly Jew. I thought he was rather pushful and aggressive. He once asked me – "What does an outsider like me have to do to get a fellowship?" ' But, so we gathered from the Master, he was brilliantly clever, and had a rarer gift than cleverness, a profound sense of reality. He went to work with Lyall, and they published several papers together on the medieval trade routes in Central Asia. 'It was generally thought that the real views were Erzberger's.' Then there was an interval of several years, in which Erzberger told a good many people that he was preparing a major work. 'He did not believe in under-rating himself.' He had never been healthy, and he died in his thirties of consumption. No unfinished work was ever published, but two years after his death Lyall produced his own *magnum opus*, the foundation of his fame, on the subject on which they had worked together. In the preface he acknowledged his gratitude to his lamented friend Erzberger for some fruitful suggestions, and regretted his untimely death.

'Just so,' said Roy. 'Just so.'

It was a dark, foggy afternoon as we walked up Piccadilly. Cars' head-lights were making swathes in the mist, and Roy's voice sounded more than ever clear as he talked to the Master all the way to Burlington House. He was intensely, brilliantly excited. A laugh kept ringing out. On the Master's other side, I walked silent and apprehensive in the murk. Could I calm him down, could anyone? Was it sensible or wise to try now? I was tied by doubt and ignorance. I knew he was suffering, but I did not know how justified my apprehensions were.

As we took off our coats, and the Master left us for a moment, I made one attempt.

'Are you desperately anxious to attend this pantomime?' I said.

'Why do you ask?' said Roy sharply.

'There are other things which might amuse us—'

'Oh no,' said Roy. 'I need to be here.' Then he smiled at me. 'Don't you stay. It was stupid of me to drag you here. You're certain to be bored. Let's meet later.'

I hesitated, and said:

'No. I may as well come in.'

The Academy room was quite small and cosy; the lights were thrown back from the fog-darkened windows. There were half a dozen men on the dais, among them Lyall and Colonel Foulkes. The Master was placed among minor dignitaries in the front row beneath. Perhaps sixty or seventy men were sitting in the room, and it struck me that nearly all of them were old. Bald heads shone, white hair gleamed, under the lights. As the world grew more precarious, rich young men did not take to these eccentric subjects with such confidence: amateurs flourished most, as those old men had flourished, in a tranquil and secure age.

Roy found me a chair, and then suddenly went off by himself to sit under the window. My concern flared up: but in a moment the meeting began.

The chairman made a short speech, explaining that we had come to mark Sir Oulstone's seventieth birthday and express our gratitude for his work. As the speech went on, Sir Oulstone's head inclined slowly, weightily, with dignity and satisfaction, at each mention of his own name.

Then came three accounts of Central Asian studies. The first, given by an Oxford professor with a high, fluting voice, struck me as straightforward old-fashioned history – the various conquering races that had swept across the plateau, the rise and fall of dynasties, and so on. The second, by Foulkes, dealt with the deciphering of the linguistic records. Foulkes was a rapid, hopping, almost incomprehensible speaker, and much of the content was technical and would have been, even if I could have heard what he said, unintelligible to me: yet one could feel that he was a master of his subject. He paid a gabbling, incoherent and enthusiastic compliment to Roy's work on Soghdian.

The third account I found quite fascinating. It was delivered in broken English by a refugee, and it described how the history of Central Asia between 500 B.C. and A.D. 1000 had been studied by applying the methods of archaeology and not relying so much on documentary evidence – by measuring areas of towns at different periods, studying the tools men used and their industrial techniques. It was the history of common men in their workaday lives, and it made sense of some of the glittering, burbling, dynastic records. The pioneer work had been done over forty years before, said the speaker vigorously, in the original articles of Lyall and Erzberger: then the real great step forward had been taken by Lyall himself, in his famous and classical book.

There was steady clapping. Sir Oulstone inclined his head very slowly. The speaker bowed to him, and Sir Oulstone inclined his head again.

The speech came to an end. It had been a masterpiece of exposition, and the room stirred with applause. There followed a few perfunctory questions, more congratulations to Sir Oulstone from elderly scholars in the front row, one or two more questions. The meeting was warm with congratulation and self-congratulation, feet were just beginning to get restless, it was nearly time to go.

Then I heard Roy's voice, very clear.

'Mr Chairman, may I ask a question?'

He was standing by the window, with vacant chairs round him. Light fell directly on his face, so that it looked smooth and young. He was smiling, his eyes were shining with exaltation.

'Of course, Mr—'

'Calvert,' said Roy.

'Ah yes, Mr Calvert,' said the chairman. Sir Oulstone smiled and bowed.

'We've listened to this conspectus of Asian social history,' said Roy precisely. 'I should like to ask – how much credit for the present position should be given to the late Dr Erzberger?'

No one seemed to feel danger. The chairman smiled at the lecturer, who replied that Erzberger deserved every credit for his share in the original publications.

'Thank you,' said Roy. 'But it does not quite meet my point. This subject has made great progress. Is it possible for no one to say how much we need to thank Dr Erzberger for?'

The chairman looked puzzled. There was a tension growing in the room. But Sir Oulstone felt nothing of it as he rose heavily and said:

'Perhaps I can help Mr Calvert, sir.'

'Thank you,' said the chairman.

'Thank you, Sir Oulstone,' came Roy's voice.

'I am grateful to my young friend, Mr Calvert,' said Sir Oulstone, suspecting nothing, 'for bringing up the name of my old and respected collaborator. It is altogether appropriate that on this occasion, when you are praising me beyond my deserts, my old helper should not be forgotten. Some of you will remember, though it was well before Mr Calvert's time,' Sir Oulstone smiled, 'that poor Erzberger, after helping me in my first efforts, was cut off in his prime. That was a tragedy for our subject. It can be said of him, as Newton said of Cotes, that if he had lived we should have learned something.'

'Just so,' said Roy. 'So he published nothing except the articles with you, Sir Oulstone?'

'I am afraid that is the fact.'

Roy said, quietly, with extreme sharpness:

'Could you tell us what he was working on before he died?'

By now many in the room had remembered the old scandal. Faces were frowning, intent, distressed, curious. But Sir Oulstone was still impervious. He still looked at Roy as though he were a young disciple. Sir Oulstone acted as though he had never heard of the scandal: if there were no basis for it, if he were quite innocent, that could have been true.

As Roy waited for the answer, his glance rested on me. For a second I looked full at him, begging him to stop. Fiercely, impatiently, he shook his head. He was utterly possessed.

'Alas,' said Sir Oulstone, 'we have no trace of his last years of work.'

'Did he not work – on the subject of your own book?'

'There was no trace, I say.' Suddenly Sir Oulstone's voice was cracked and angry.

'Did no one publish his manuscripts?'

'We could find no manuscripts when he died.'

'You could find no result of years of work?' cried Roy.

'He left nothing behind him.'

'*Remarkable.*' The single word dropped into the hushed room. It plucked all nerves with its violence, scorn, and extreme abandon.

Sir Oulstone had turned bitterly angry.

'I do not consider this is very profitable. Perhaps, as Mr Calvert is a newcomer to our subject, I had better refer to my obituaries of Erzberger in the two journals. I regard these questions as most unnecessary, sir.'

He sat down. Roy was still on his feet.

'Thank you, Mr Chairman,' he said in his normal tone. 'I am so sorry to have taken the time of the meeting.'

He bowed to the chair, and went out alone.

CHAPTER X

A MOMENT OF GRACE

THE meeting broke up, and the Master took me off to tea at the Athenæum. On the way down St James's Street, the windows of the clubs glowing comfortably warm through the deepening fog, the Master said:

'Roy Calvert seems a little upset, Eliot. I suppose it's a phase we all go through.'

'Yes.'

'He's been overstrained, of course. Between you and me, our judicious colleagues have something to answer for. It was imbecile to make him wait so long for his fellowship.'

For once the Master was in a thoroughly bad temper. Over the toasted teacakes in the long club morning-room, he broke out:

'It's nothing to worry about, Eliot. I did silly things when I was a young man. I suppose he hasn't got his feet on the earth quite as firmly as I had, but he's not so different as all that. We must just make sure that all turns out well.'

In his irritation, he let me see something of what he felt for Roy. The Master believed that Roy was far more gifted than himself: he knew that Roy was capable of the scholarly success he could never have managed – for Roy had the devotion, the almost obsessional devotion, which a scholar needs, as well as the touch of supreme confidence. The Master, who found it easier to go about from meeting to meeting using his quick wits, who in his heart felt diffident and uncreative, admired those gifts which he had never had. But also he felt an attraction of like for like. Roy's elegance and style – with those the Master could compete. Often among his colleagues he had the illusion that he was just playing at being an ordinary man. At times, in daydreams, he had seen himself like Roy.

I noticed too that, as though by instinct, he pretended that nothing much was wrong. Often it seemed to him wiser to soften the truth. The worst did not always happen. Before I left, he said, almost in his cheerful whisper:

'I don't think our colleagues need to be worried by any news of this afternoon's entertainment, do you, Eliot? We know how easily worried they are, and I shouldn't like to feel that the Bursar was losing sleep because one of the younger fellows has been overworking.'

The club was filling with men who had been present at the meeting, and the Master went across to them, pleasant-mannered, fresh-faced, not over-troubled.

I went to see Roy, but found Rosalind alone in the flat. She said he had gone out to buy some wine; they were to dine at home that night.

'It will be very nice, having the old thing to myself for once,' she said, and I could not help smiling, though this was not the most suitable time for her brand of realism.

She had seen him since the meeting. 'He's nice and relaxed,' she said. 'He's sweet when there's nothing on his mind. I wish he weren't so elusive sometimes.' She added: 'I don't know what's taken the weight off his mind. He did say that he'd made a frightful ass of himself some-where.'

The phrase meant nothing to her, but it was a private joke of his and mine, borrowed from Mr March.

I saw Roy for an instant just before I went away. One glance reassured me. He was himself, composed, gentle, at ease.

'How are you?' I asked.

'Very much all right,' he said.

As I walked into the foggy street, I heard his voice call cheerfully from the window:

'Shan't be in Cambridge till next week. Come back before then. Need to talk to you.'

In college I was watching for any sign of the story coming through: I was ready to laugh it off, to explain Roy's action in terms designed to make it seem matter-of-fact, uninteresting, a mixture of a joke and an academic controversy. It was only to Arthur Brown that I confided there had been a scene; and even with him, stout-hearted, utterly dependable, capable of accepting anything in his friends, I was not quite frank – for by that time in my life I was already broken in to keeping secrets, often more so than was good for me or others. I paled down both Roy's des-pondency and his outburst. Arthur Brown said: 'We shall have to be very careful about our young friend.' Then, the politician never far away, he wondered what effect the news would have upon the college, and how we could conceal it.

Curiously enough, very little news arrived, and that we were able to smother. Colonel Foulkes came to Cambridge for a meeting of electors to a professorship, and I discovered that he thought nothing specially unusual had happened. Whether this was because Roy could do no wrong in his eyes, or because he really did not like Lyall, or because he was abnormally blank to human atmosphere, I could not decide. He said: 'Very interesting point, Calvert's. Perhaps not the best time to bring it up. These scholars aren't men of the world, you know. They don't learn tact. Don't have the corners rubbed off as you do in the army.'

He was so simple that I was completely at a loss, but I took him into hall, and he talked casually about the Lyall celebratory meeting and enthusiastically about Roy. The most subtle acting would not have been so effective. Some rumour about Roy had reached Despard-Smith, and he began to produce it, with solemn gratification, the next night: but Winslow, fresh from hearing Foulkes, endowed with nothing like the persistence in rancour that vitalised the old clergyman, said: 'If you please, Despard. Shall we wait until the young man starts throwing knives about in hall? In point of fact, he seems to have pleasant table manners, which I must say is more than one is accustomed to expect.'

Within three days of the meeting, the Master was able to forget his first impression and to treat the whole affair as though it had been a piece of combination-room baiting, like teasing the doctor after the feast. I seemed the only person who could not domesticate it so.

Even Roy, when I saw him at his flat the following week, was free from any cloud.

'What have you been doing these days in Cambridge?' he asked.

'Nothing much.'

'Covering up tracks?'

'A little.'

He gave me a curiously protective smile.

'When you took me on,' he said, 'you took all this on yourself.'

'How are you now?' I said, but there was no need for me to ask. He was entirely tranquil.

'Better than I've been for weeks and months,' he said.

He added:

'How are you? You're looking worse than I did. Too much worry. Too much drink. Above all,' his eyes flashed, 'above all, not enough sleep.'

I grinned. It was hard to resist his spirits, it was hard to retain my fears.

'We'll get you better at "Monty".' Roy, precise in his speech, isolated the word to remind me of Lady Muriel; for she and Lord Boscastle, after calling the family mansion "Bossy", took to nicknames of places with the utmost naturalness.

'Meanwhile,' said Roy, 'I need to give you some fresh air. I need to take you a walk in the park.'

We left the flat empty, for Rosalind had returned home: Roy was going to Cambridge next day. We entered the park by the Albion gate. A gusty wind was blowing from the west, the trees soughed, the last leaves were spinning under the lamps in the street. The clouds were low, it was dark early; through the trees one could see the lights of the tall houses in Bayswater Road. The wind blew in our faces as we walked down to the Serpentine. It was fresh as a night by the sea.

'It's wonderful not to be wretched,' cried Roy. 'It's all gone! It's wonderful to be free!'

He looked at me in the twilight.

'You're glum, Lewis. You've been pitying me for being wretched, haven't you? You can pity me for the gloom. That was frightful. Don't pity me for the time when I broke out. It was very exciting. For a few minutes I was let out of prison. Everything was rosy-edged.'

'It might be a slightly expensive excitement,' I said.

He smiled.

'It won't do me any good with Oulstone, will it?'

There was a trace of satisfaction in his tone. 'Oh, never mind. I wasn't cut out to be stuffed. I'll go on doing my work. But I don't want anything in return that those people can give me. I need them to leave me alone, that's all. I'll go on with the work. It's become a habit. But it isn't going to settle me. Once I hoped it might. Now I know it can't. I need to search elsewhere. I shall get there in the end.'

The wind blew, his voice was clear and happy. He said earnestly:

'Pity me for the gloom. But it made me see things – that otherwise I never could have seen. Don't think that all I told you was nonsense. Don't think I've forgotten what I saw.'

'I believe that,' I said.

He stopped suddenly, and held my arm.

'Lewis, why are you so sombre? What is hurting you?'

I did not reply.

'Are you thinking that this will happen to me *again*?'

'It may,' I said, half-miserably, half-intoxicated by his hope. 'Anyway, you ought to be ready. You won't always be so happy, will you?'

'You think it may come back. It may,' Roy repeated. 'It may. I need to take it if it comes.' He had spoken evenly, then his voice rose: 'It's something to know the worst.' He was smiling in the dark, with no cover and no reserve: it seemed as though for a second he were deliberately challenging fate.

The next time he spoke, it was very quietly and intimately. We were getting near the water, as he said:

'I shall be all right if I can only find somewhere to rest.'

He added:

'I shall find my way there. It may not be the way you'd choose for me. But that doesn't matter so much to you, does it?'

We walked along the bank, the gale grew louder, the little waves lapped at our feet. He passed from his hopes to mine, selflessly sarcastic, selflessly protective. For a while, in the exhilaration of his spirits and the winter night, I could almost believe as he believed, hope as he hoped, and be as happy.

If it could be so, I thought. I did not want to make any forecast of his chances. This was a moment of grace.

PART TWO

THE GLIMMER OF HOPE

CHAPTER XI

SERENE NIGHT BY THE SEA

ROY returned to college for the rest of the Michaelmas term. His reading lamp was alight all day; his window in the turret gleamed above the court through the dark afternoons and the December evenings. He dined regularly at high table; and no one meeting him there could have guessed what he had just passed through. Though I had seen it, I often forgot. His step on my stairs at night now meant ease, and well-being. He was quite unstrained, as though he had only to wait for good things to happen.

After he had talked to them at dinner, some of his opponents felt he had been misjudged. He sat by Winslow's side for several nights running. He had a respect for the cross-grained, formidable, unsuccessful man, and he happened to know his son. It was generally thought that Dick Winslow was nothing but a stupid waster, but Roy both liked him and felt his father's vulnerable, unassuageable love. So they talked about Dick – Winslow pretending to be realistic and detached. Roy was very gentle, both at the time and afterwards, when he said to me: 'It must be dreadful, never being able to give yourself away. He needs to stop keeping his lips so tight, doesn't he?'

Roy did not, however, make the slightest progress towards melting Despard-Smith. He began by making a genuine attempt, for Ralph Udal's sake: Despard-Smith was the most influential member of the livings committee, and, if Udal were to have a chance of a college living, the old man had to be placated. But Roy met with a signal failure. He suppressed the glint in his eye that usually visited him in the presence of the self-satisfied and self-important. Deferentially he discussed the Church of England, college finance, and early heresies. Despard-Smith replied bleakly and with certainty, looking at Roy with uncompromising suspicion. Roy led up to the question of a living for Udal. 'I can't speak for my colleagues, Calvert,' said Despard-Smith, meaning that he could. 'But I should personally regard it as nothing short of scandalous to let a man of Udal's age eat the bread of idleness. It certainly would not be in the man's own best interests. When he has got down to the c-collar for twenty or thirty years, then perhaps he might come up for consideration.'

'He wants peace to think,' said Roy.

'The time to get peace, as some of us know,' said Despard-Smith, 'is when one has borne the heat and burden of the day.'

Roy knew it was no good. But his next question was innocent enough. He asked who would get the vacant living, which was the second best in the college's gift.

'I've told you, I can't speak for my colleagues,' said Despard-Smith reprovingly. 'But I should personally regard Anderson as a very suitable choice. He was slightly junior to me here, so he is no longer in his first youth. But he is a very worthy man.'

'Should you say he was witty?' said Roy, no longer able to repress himself or deciding it was not worth while.

'I don't know what you mean, Calvert.'

'Worthy people are not witty,' said Roy. 'That's how we can tell they're worthy.'

He looked at Despard-Smith with steady, solemn eyes.

'Isn't that so, Despard?'

Despard-Smith looked back with mystification, anger and disapproval.

From that time on, Roy selected Despard-Smith for his most preposterous questions – partly because the old man incited him, and partly because, knowing of Despard-Smith's speeches over the election, Roy had a frail and unsaintly desire for revenge. Whenever he could catch Despard-Smith in the court or the combination room, Roy advanced on him with a shimmering net of requests for information. Despard-Smith became badgered. He was never sure whether Roy might not be in earnest, at least part of the time. 'What an extraordinary young man Calvert is,' he used to grumble in a creaking, angry voice. 'He's just made a most extraordinary remark to me—'

The Boscastles had gone down to the villa at Roquebrune late in November, and the Master and his family followed them a few days before Christmas. Roy spent Christmas with his family, and I with my wife in Chelsea. She asked me to stay a little longer, and so I arrived at Monte Carlo the day after Roy.

I had lain awake all night in the train, and went to bed in the afternoon. When I woke it was early evening, and from my window I could see lights springing out along the coast. Roy was not in his room, was not in the hotel. He had already told me that we were dining that night out at the Boscastles'. It was not time to dress, and I took a walk away from the sea, through the hilly streets at the back of the town.

I was thinking of nothing, it was pleasant to smell the wood smoke and garlic in the narrow streets: then I heard two voices taking an amorous farewell. A woman's said something in Italian, was saying goodbye: then another, light, reedy, very clear in the crisp, cold air. 'Ciaō,' he called back to her, and I saw in the light from a window a girl disappearing into the house. 'Ciaō,' she called, when I could no longer see her: her voice was rough but young. 'Ciaō,' Roy replied again, softly, and then he saw me.

He was disconcerted, and I extremely amused. I knew as well as he about his minor escapades: some woman would catch his fancy, in a shop, in a theatre, behind the desk in an hotel, and he would pursue her with total concentration for a day. He sometimes told me of his rebuffs, but never of his conquests; and he did not like being caught at the end of one.

'Remarkable Italian they speak here,' he said with a somewhat precarious dignity, as we descended into the clean, bright, shop-lined streets. He gave me a pedantic lecture on the Italian of Liguria contrasted with Provencal; it was no doubt correct, his linguistic skill was beyond question, but I was grinning.

We came to the square; the flowers stood out brilliantly under the lights; as though unwillingly, Roy grinned too.

'It's just my luck,' he said. 'Why need you come that way?'

A motor car drove in to take us to the Villa Prabaous.

'The Boscastles have hired three cars for all the time they're here,' said Roy. 'Plus two which they need occasionally for visitors. There's nothing like economy. They sweep in and out all day.'

On our way, along the edge of the calm sea, he was speculating with interest, with amusement, over the Boscastle fortune. 'Poor as church mice', 'they haven't two sixpences to rub together', 'it's really heroic of them to keep up the house' – we had both heard those descriptions from Lady Muriel and her friends. Yet, with occasional economies, such as taking a villa at Roquebrune, the Boscastles lived more grandly than any of the rich people we knew. The problem was complicated by the fact that the estate had, as a device through which they paid less taxes, been made into a company. The long necklace of lights twinkled through the pines on Cap Martin: Roy had just satisfied himself that, if Lord Boscastle died next day, his will would not be proved at less than £600,000.

The Villa Prabaous was rambling, large, very ugly, and, like many houses on the north side of the Mediterranean, seemed designed for a climate much hotter than where it found itself. That night an enormous log fire sputtered and smoked in the big dining-room, and we were all cold, except Lady Muriel. For Lady Muriel it provided an excellent opportunity to compare the degree of discomfort with that of several mansions she had visited in her childhood, and to advise her sister-in-law how, if one's experience were great enough, these privations could be overcome. Lady Muriel was not a passive guest.

It was exactly the same party as when Roy was first presented to the Boscastles. Mrs Seymour was staying at the villa; I had escaped her for some time past, but now found myself sitting next to her at dinner.

'It must be wonderful to see heaps and heaps of counters being pushed towards you,' she said.

'It must,' I said.

'Yes, Doris?' said Lady Muriel loudly. 'Have you been playing today?'

Mrs Seymour giggled, and was coy. I was surprised and irritated (uncharitably, but she annoyed me more than was reasonable) to meet her there. One reason, I thought, was that Lord Boscastle should never miss his evening bridge; Mrs Seymour, like Lady Muriel and Joan, was a player of good class.

Sure of his game that night, out of which I had managed to disentangle myself, Lord Boscastle wished to spend dinner talking of Saint-Simon's memoirs, which he had just been reading. I would willingly have listened, but Roy distracted him by asking his opinion of various fashionable persons staying in Monte Carlo and the villas near. Lord Boscastle, as I now knew for certain, took a perverse pleasure in acting in character. He was always ready, in fact, to caricature himself. And so, as Roy produced name after name with a flicker in his eye, Lord Boscastle was prompt with his comment. 'I don't know him, of course, but I shouldn't have thought he was anything out of the ordinary, should you have thought so?' 'I don't know whether any of you have met her, but I shouldn't have expected her to be specially distinguished.'

The Master chuckled. It was hard to guess precisely what he thought of his brother-in-law's turns; but it was patent that he was delighted to see Roy so manifestly happy and composed. The Master smiled at me with camaraderie, but rather as though I had always exaggerated the fuss. Yet I was sure that he had not shared our knowledge with anyone in the villa that night, certainly not with his wife.

Lady Muriel herself, not perceiving any secrets round her, had been led to mention acquaintances of hers who were wintering in the town. She finished by saying:

'Doris tells me the Houston Eggars have arrived. No doubt for a very short holiday. They are not staying at your hotel, I think?'

'No,' said Roy.

'Doris! Where are they staying?'

Mrs Seymour opened her eyes vaguely, then gave the name of an hotel slightly more modest than the Hermitage.

'I'm glad to hear it.' Lady Muriel looked at me accusingly. 'I should think it is very suitable to their income.'

After dinner, just before the bridge four broke away, I saw Joan take Roy aside. She was wearing a blue dress, and I thought how much prettier she was becoming. She asked him straight out:

'Why do you lead my uncle on? Why don't you make him talk about something worth while?'

'Too stupid,' said Roy.

'He's not too stupid.'

'Of course he's not. I am.'

'You're impossible.' She had begun to laugh, as she could not help doing whenever the solemn expression came over him. Then she turned fierce again, stayed by him, and went on quarrelling as Lord Boscastle led off Lady Muriel, Mrs Seymour and the Master for their bridge. Meanwhile Lady Boscastle was commanding: 'Lewis, bring your chair here, please. I am going to scold you a little.'

She glanced at me through her lorgnette.

'Yes,' she said, as I came beside her, arranged her table, filled her glass, 'I think I must scold you a little.'

'What have I done now?' I said.

'I notice that you are wearing a soft shirt tonight. It looks quite a nice shirt, my dear Lewis, but this is not quite the right time. What have you to say for yourself?'

'I loathe stiff shirts,' I said. 'This is very much more comfortable.'

'My dear boy, I should call that excuse rather – untravelled.' It was her final word of blame. 'The chief aim of civilised society is not comfort, as you know very well. Otherwise you would not be sitting in a draughty room listening to an old woman—'

She was an invalid, her temples were sunk in, her skin minutely wrinkled; yet she could make me feel that she was twenty years younger, she could still draw out the protests of admiration. And, when I made them, she could still hear them with pleasure.

'Quite nicely said.' She smiled as she spoke. 'Perhaps you would always have found some compensations in civilised society. Though we did our best to make you obey the rules.'

She flicked her lorgnette, and then went on:

'But it's not only soft shirts, my dear Lewis. Will you listen to your old friend?'

'To anything you like to tell me.'

'I want you to be a success. You have qualities that can take you anywhere you choose to go.'

'What are they?'

'Come! I've heard you called the least vain of men.'

'Not if you're going to praise me,' I said.

She smiled again.

'I needn't tell you that you're intelligent,' she said. 'You're also very obstinate. And for a man of – what is it, my dear?'

'Thirty.'

'For a man of thirty, you know something of the human heart.'

She went on quickly:

'Believe me about those things. I have spent my life among successful men. You can compete with them. But they conformed more than you do, Lewis. I want you to conform a little more.'

'I don't parade my opinions—'

'We shouldn't mind if you did. I have seen that you are a radical. No one minds what a man of distinction thinks. But there are other things. Sometimes I wish you would take some lessons from your friend Roy. He couldn't do anything untravelled if he tried. I wish you would go to his tailor. I think you should certainly go to his barber. Your English accent will pass. Your French is deplorable. You need some different hats.'

I laughed.

'But these things are important,' said Lady Boscastle. 'You can't imagine your friend Roy not attending to them.'

'He's a good-looking and elegant man,' I said.

'That's no reason for your being too humble. You can do many things that he can't. Believe me, Lewis. If you took care, you could look quite impressive.'

Then she focused her lorgnette on me. Her porcelain eyes were glittering with indulgence and satire. 'Perhaps Roy is really much more humble than you are. I think you are very arrogant at heart. You just don't care. You have the sort of carelessness, my dear boy, that I have heard people call "aristocratic". I do not remember knowing any aristocrats who possessed it.'

Just as the car drew up outside to take Roy and me back to Monte Carlo, the Boscastles' son returned from a dinner party. He was only eighteen and still at school; he had been born to them when Lady Boscastle was nearly forty and they had given up hope of a child. I had not met him before, and caught just a glimpse before we left. He was slender, asthenic, with a wild, feminine face.

It was after midnight when our car dropped us at the hotel, and, like other pairs of friends in sight of the casino, we had a disagreement. One of us was addicted to gambling, and the other hated it. Some might have expected Roy to play lavishly the night through; but the facts were otherwise. It was I who spent the next two hours at baccarat; it was Roy who stood behind me, smoking cigarette after cigarette, who walked irritably round the square, who entered again hoping that I should have finished.

'Excellent,' he said, when at last I had had enough.

'Why didn't you come in?' I said, as we took a walk in the casino gardens.

'I've something better to do with my money,' said Roy, as though he were the guardian of all the prudent virtues.

I had won forty pounds, but that did not placate him.

'It'll only lead you on,' he said. 'I wish you'd lost.'

'It will pay for my holiday,' I said.

'You'll lose it all tomorrow. And a lot more.'

It was a brilliant frosty night, utterly calm on the sea. The two lights of the harbour shone, one green, one red, and their reflection lay still upon the water. The stars were bright in the moonless sky, and below the lights of the coast road blazed out.

'Extremely serene,' said Roy. 'Now I shall go and sleep.'

We were tired and contented. A few moments later, the porter at the hotel said that there was a telegram for Mr Calvert. As he read it, Roy made a grimace.

'Not quite so serene,' he said, and gave it to me. It was from Rosalind, the English words curiously distorted on the way. It must have been written as something like:

ARRIVE IN CANNES TOMORROW TWENTYNINTH PROPOSE STAY MONTE CARLO UNLESS INCONVENIENT FOR YOU SHALL APPEAR THIRTYFIRST UNLESS YOU SEND MESSAGE TO AMBASSADEURS SAYING NO.

CHAPTER XII

SOME WOMEN

WE discovered that, several days before, Rosalind had reserved a room, not at the Hermitage but at the Hôtel de Paris. Whether this was to save Roy's face or simply to show off, no one could be sure. Rosalind's origins were similar to mine, though less poverty-stricken: she still lived in our native town, where she earned a large income for a young woman: she had a flair for bold dramatic design and, applying her usual blend of childish plaintiveness and business-like determination, took £600 a year from an advertising company. She lived simply at home and spent her money on extravagant presents and holidays at the most expensive hotels, which she examined with shrewd business-like eyes and basked in with a hearty provincial gusto.

When he realised that she was coming not on a sudden caprice but by plan, Roy was amused, irritated, pleased, hunted, and somewhat at a loss. He knew he could not keep her unobserved while the Boscastle party spent its days in Monte Carlo; he knew that Rosalind would see that did not happen. But he was too fond of her to forbid her to come.

He decided that he must brazen it out. Lady Muriel and Joan lunched with us at the hotel, and half-way through Roy said, less unselfconsciously than usual:

'By the way, Lady Mu, a friend of mine is coming down on Thursday.'

'Who may that be, Roy?'

'A girl called Rosalind Wykes. I brought her in for tea one day, do you remember? I only knew she was coming this morning.'

'Indeed.' Lady Muriel looked at him. 'Roy, is this young woman staying here *alone*?'

'I should think so.'

'Indeed.'

Lady Muriel said no more. But when I arrived at the Café de Paris for tea, I found the four women of the Boscastle party engrossed in a meeting of disapproval and indignation. There were shades of differences about their disapproval, but even Lady Boscastle, the fastidious and detached, agreed on the two main issues: Roy was to be pitied, and Rosalind was not fit for human company.

'Good afternoon, Mr Eliot. I am glad you were able to join us,' said Lady Muriel, and got back to the topic in hand. 'I cannot understand how any woman has the shamelessness to throw herself at a man's head.'

'I can't help admiring her courage,' said Joan. 'But—'

'Joan! I will not listen to anything you say in her favour. She is a mercenary and designing woman.'

'I've said already,' said Joan, 'that I think she's absolutely unsuitable for him. And if she thinks this is the way to get him, she's even stupider than I thought. Of course, she's appallingly stupid.'

'I should have called her rather – uninformed,' said Lady Boscastle. 'I think our mothers would have thought her a little forward.'

'I don't know how any man ever allows himself to get married,' said Mrs Seymour, 'the way some women behave.'

'She's a Clytemnestra,' said Lady Muriel surprisingly. We all looked puzzled, until Lady Boscastle observed in a gentle tone: 'I think you mean Messalina, Muriel.'

'She's a Messalina,' said Lady Muriel with passion and violence. 'Of course, she's not a lady. No lady could do what this woman is doing.'

Lady Boscastle raised her lorgnette.

'I'm not quite sure, Muriel. I think this girl's behaviour is rather unbecoming – but haven't you and I known cases—?'

'It was not the same,' said Lady Muriel grandly. 'If a lady did it, she would do it in a different way.'

Soon afterwards Roy came in. When he apologised for being late, Lady Muriel was banteringly, clumsily affectionate, as though she wanted to say that he was still in favour. Then Lady Boscastle began to talk about her party on New Year's Eve.

'I have at last succeeded in persuading my husband to enter the Sporting Club. It has taken some time,' she said. 'We are dining at ten o'clock. I am counting on you two to make up the party. Will you come, Lewis?'

I said that I should love to.

Roy hesitated.

'I don't know whether Lady Muriel has told you, Lady Boscastle,' he said, 'but a friend of mine is arriving that day.'

'I had heard,' said Lady Boscastle.

'I think I need to look after her.'

His tone was light but firm. He looked at Lady Boscastle. For a second her eyes wavered to Lady Muriel, and then came back to him. In a few moments, I knew that she would not invite Rosalind, and that he would not give way.

'I'm so sorry,' said Roy, as though there had been no challenge. 'It's a shame to miss you all on New Year's Eve. I should have enjoyed it so much.'

I was shocked that Lady Boscastle could be rude in this fashion. She was acting, so it seemed to me that afternoon, not as herself but as part of the clan. These were not her manners, but the manners of the whole Boscastle circle. Which were often, under their formal politeness, not designed to give pleasure. For instance, it was not politeness of the heart when Lady Muriel, seeing Roy and me constantly together, called him by his Christian name and me 'Mr Eliot', year in, year out, without softening or change. She was intensely fond of him, of course, and neutral to me, but some codes of manners would have concealed those feelings.

On the afternoon of the thirty-first, I was told that Rosalind had come, but I did not see her. Roy and she were together, I assumed, but they avoided the normal meeting-places of the Boscastle party. So I had tea with the Master and Lady Muriel, dressed early, and put in some hours at the tables before dinner. Mrs Seymour, who was becoming an insatiable gambler, was also in the casino, but I managed to pass her undetected. That was too good to last; and at dinner at the Sporting Club her place was inevitably on my right. Full of excitement, she described to me how she had been invited to a French house at five o'clock that afternoon and offered an aperitif.

'I don't like *wine* for *tea*,' said Mrs Seymour. For once her vagueness, even her enthusiasm vanished, and she felt like the voice of England.

Lord Boscastle's table was in an alcove which commanded the whole room. Lights shone, shoulders gleamed, jewellery flashed, expensive dresses rustled, expensive scent touched the air: champagne buckets were being carried everywhere: there were at least a dozen faces in the room whom I recognised from photographs. Lord Boscastle viewed the spectacle with disfavour.

'I don't know any of these people,' he said. He looked at his sister who, despite his approval of scholarly pursuits, he sometimes affected to think moved in a different circle of existence.

'Muriel!' he called out. 'I suppose you know who these people are?'

'Certainly I do not,' said Lady Muriel indignantly.

To her profound annoyance, an elderly man bowed to her.

'Who is that fellow?' asked Lord Boscastle.

'Lord Craycombe,' said Mrs Seymour.

'That family are nothing but nineteenth-century *arrivistes*,' said Lord

Boscastle. 'Not a very distinguished acquaintance, my dear Muriel, I should have thought—?'

He was on the rampage. This was his revenge for being dragged into society.

'Talking of *arrivistes*,' he said, 'I noticed one or two over-luxurious yachts in the harbour. I didn't think they were in specially good taste. But it's obvious that people whom one simply wouldn't have known some time ago have managed to do remarkably well for themselves.'

Which noble families was he disposing of now? I wished that Roy had been there.

The party contained eight people. Houston Eggar had been asked to fill Roy's place; his wife ('Tom Seymour's girl') had already left for Rome, where they had been posted for a year past. Lord Boscastle proceeded to interrogate Eggar upon the Abyssinian war. The Boscastles had lived years in Italy; he had a passion for the country; though he called himself a whig, the squabble about a colonial war seemed to him hypocritical nonsense. Eggar tried hard to be both familiar and discreet, but I got the impression that in private he agreed. With one criticism of Lord Boscastle's he did not agree, however; and I could not help feeling that this particular criticism would have seemed unfamiliar to my left-wing friends. For Lord Boscastle appeared to regard the mishandling of British policy towards Italy as due to the increasingly middle-class constitution of the Foreign Office.

Joan argued stormily with her uncle. She thought he was clever but misguided, and never gave up hope of converting him. Eggar she dismissed as set in his ways. Actually, Eggar put on a tough assertive manner, as though he were anxious to talk to Lord Boscastle as man to man. Underneath the assertiveness he was deferential and eager to please. He was powerfully built, dark, young-looking for a man in early middle age; he was kindly, vulgar, inordinately ambitious, and not at all subtle.

It was eleven, and the room was full. Suddenly Joan said: 'There's Roy.'

Our table fell into silence as we watched. Across the floor, up an aisle between the tables, Roy walked, quite slowly with Rosalind on his arm. They attracted many glances. Roy looked more than ever spruce, with a white gardenia in his buttonhole; but Rosalind took attention away from him. She was not a beauty, in the sense that several women in this room were beauties; she had none of the remoteness that beauty needs. But her face was mobile, pathetic, humorous and living, and she had dressed to make sure that she would not be overlooked.

The aisle ran only one row of tables away from ours. As they came near, Rosalind, who was on the far side, kept talking to Roy; but he turned half-round and gave us a brilliant smile. It did not look a smile of defiance or triumph; it was fresh, cheerful, alight with high spirits.

I caught Lady Boscastle's eye. She must have seen a glint of satisfaction in mine, for she shrugged her shoulders and her mouth twitched. She had too much humour, too much sense of style, not to be amused. Yet she was stubborn in the arguments which followed.

'She's a very personable young woman,' said Lord Boscastle, approvingly. 'We'd better have them over here, Helen.'

'I don't think that would be at all suitable,' said Lady Muriel.

'Why not? I remember meeting her. Young Calvert's got an eye for a pretty woman.'

'She is rather untravelled perhaps for tonight, my dear Hugh,' said Lady Boscastle.

'Have you just discovered that? I got on perfectly well with her,' said Lord Boscastle. He was annoyed. 'And I regard Calvert as someone I know.'

Lady Boscastle, with heavy support from Lady Muriel, maintained her opposition. Lord Boscastle became nettled. One could feel the crystalline strength of Lady Boscastle's will. In that marriage, I thought, she had had the upper hand all the way through. He had been jealous, she had gone her own way, she had never sacrificed that unscratchable diamond-hard will. Yet Lord Boscastle was accustomed to being the social arbiter. In the long run, even Lady Muriel deferred to his judgment on what could and could not be done. That night he was unusually persistent. Mainly because he did not mean to be deprived of a pretty girl's company – but also he had a masculine sympathy with Roy.

In the end, they agreed on a compromise rather in his favour. Roy and Rosalind were to be left to have dinner alone, but were to be invited to visit our table afterwards. Lady Boscastle wrote a note: it was like her that it should be delicately phrased. 'My dear Roy, It is so nice, and such a pleasant surprise, to see you here tonight. Will you give us the pleasure of bringing your friend Miss Wykes to this table when you have finished your dinner? We are all anxious to wish you a happy new year.'

They came. Rosalind was overawed until she was monopolised for half-an-hour by Lord Boscastle. Afterwards I heard her talking clothes with Mrs Seymour. As the night went on, her eyes became brighter, more victorious, more resolved. She talked to everyone but Lady Muriel. She did not want the glorious night to end.

Roy did not show, perhaps he did not feel, a glimmer of triumph. He exerted himself to be his most gentle, teasing and affectionate with the other women, particularly with Lady Muriel.

Within a few hours of the party, I heard the rumour that Roy and Rosalind were engaged. It came first from Mrs Seymour, who had been driven in alone and marked me down across the square.

'I think it's perfectly certain,' she said.

'Why do you think so?'

'I seem to remember something,' she said vaguely. 'I seem to remember that young woman giving me to understand –'

Joan came in with her father later that morning, and asked me point-blank if I knew anything.

'Nothing at all,' I said.

'Are you being honest?' she said. She was suspicious, and yet as soon as I answered her face was lightened with relief.

'Yes.'

'Do you think it's likely?'

'I should have thought not.'

She looked at me with a troubled and hopeful smile.

Another member of the New Year's party found it necessary to talk to me that morning, but on quite a different subject. Houston Eggar took me for a walk in the gardens, and there in the bright sunlight told me of an embarrassment about that day's honours list. 'You won't have seen it yet, of course,' he said. 'But they happen to have given me a little recognition. If these things come, they come.' But what had come, he felt, needed some knowledgeable explanation. Before he was appointed to Rome, he had been seconded for two years to another ministry. He considered, as an aside, that this had temporarily slowed down his promotion in the Foreign Office, but he assured me that it ought to pay in the long run. As a reward for his work, he was now being given a C.B.E.: whereas anyone of his seniority in the Foreign Office would expect, in the ordinary course of things, to be getting near a C.M.G. – 'which has more cachet, needless to say,' said Houston Eggar. 'You see, Eliot,' he went on earnestly, 'to anyone who doesn't know the background, this C of mine might seem like a slap in the face. Instead of being a nice little compliment. I'd be very much obliged if you'd explain the situation to the Boscastles. Don't go out of your way, but if you get a chance you might just remove any misconceptions. I'll do the same for you some day.'

Several more rumours about the engagement reached me during the next twenty-four hours, and I knew that Roy had heard what was bubbling round him. But I scarcely saw him; he did not eat a meal in our hotel; it was from someone else I learned that Rosalind had been invited out to the villa on the third of January – but only for tea, apparently as another compromise between Lord and Lady Boscastle.

It was the day before, the second, when Lady Muriel announced that she would make 'tactful enquiries' of Roy himself. 'I shall not embarrass him,' she said. 'I shall merely use a little finesse.'

Lady Boscastle said nothing. We had met for tea at our usual place in the window of the Café de Paris; we were a little early, and Roy was expected. *The Times* of the day before had been delivered after lunch; Lady Muriel had studied it and made comments on the honours list, which Mrs Seymour was now reading through.

'Muriel,' she cried excitedly, 'did you see that Houston has got a C.B.E.?'

'No, Doris,' said Lady Muriel with finality. 'I never read as low in the list as that.'

Roy joined us and made a hearty tea.

'I must say, Roy,' said Lady Muriel in due course, with heavy-footed casualness, 'that you're looking very well.'

It happened to be true. Roy smiled at her.

'So are you, Lady Mu,' he said demurely.

'Am I?' Lady Muriel was thrown out of her stride.

'I have never seen you look better,' Roy assured her. 'Coming back to the scene of your conquests, isn't it?'

'You're a very naughty young man.' Lady Muriel gave her crowing laugh. Then she remembered her duty, and stiffened. 'You're looking very well, Roy,' she began again. 'Have you by chance had any good news?'

'Any good news, Lady Mu?'

'Anything really exciting?'

Roy reflected.

'One of my investments has gone up three points since Christmas,' he said. 'I wonder if it could be that?'

Lady Muriel plunged.

'I suppose none of our friends are getting engaged just now, are they?'

'I expect they are,' said Roy. 'But I haven't seen *The Times*. There's always a batch on New Year's Day, isn't there? I wonder why? Could I borrow *The Times*, Mrs Seymour?'

Under Lady Muriel's baffled eyes, Roy worked down a column and a half of engagements. He took his time over it. There were nearly fifty couples in the paper; and the party at tea knew at least a third of them by name, and half-a-dozen personally.

'There you are, Lady Mu,' said Roy at last. 'I've put a cross against two or three. Those are the ones you need to write to.'

Lady Muriel gave up.

'By the way,' Roy asked, 'is anyone going to the ballet tonight?'

We all said no.

'I think we will go,' said Roy. 'I think I should take Rosalind.'

CHAPTER XIII

A COMPLAINT OF ELUSIVENESS

Roy did not, however, find it pleasant to fend off the Master. Lady Muriel made her 'tactful enquiries' on the Saturday afternoon; next morning, the Master, Roy and I went for a walk along the hill road. The Master used no finesse; he asked no questions with a double meaning: he walked briskly between us, upright and active as a young man, breathing confidential whispers about Cambridge acquaintances, but he let it be seen that he felt Roy's silence was a denial of affection.

Roy was in a difficult position. For he was not cherishing a secret. He had not proposed to Rosalind. Yet it was awkward to contradict the rumour. For he guessed, as I had, that Rosalind had set it going herself.

He was not willing to put her to shame. He knew she was determined to marry him, and would, if she thought it useful, lie and cheat and steal until she brought it off. He did not think the worse of her. Nor did he think the worse of Lady Muriel because, if she could lie in ambush in the dark and cease to be a great lady, she would with relish have pulled Rosalind's hair out by the roots. He was fond of them all. But for Rosalind he felt the special animal tenderness that comes from physical delight, and he would not consent to see her humiliated among those who hated her.

So there was nothing for it but to take her round Monte Carlo, dine with her each night, ignore all hints and questions, and go on as though the rumour did not exist.

But I did not believe for a minute that Rosalind would win: she had miscalculated completely if she thought those were the tactics. Probably she knew that, whatever happened, he would not give her away before the Royces and the Boscastles. Down to a certain level, she understood him well. But below that, I thought, she must be living with a stranger, if she imagined that she could take him by storm.

We turned back down the hill. In the distance, down below the white patches of houses, the sea shone like a polished shield. I made an excuse and stayed behind, taking off a shoe, so that they would have a word together. I watched their faces turn to each other, their profiles sharp against the cloudless sky. The Master was talking, Roy listening, they were near together, their faces were softened by seriousness and intimacy. In profile Roy's nose ran too long for beauty: the Master looked more regularly handsome, with trim clear lines of forehead, chin and mouth; his skin had been tinged a little by the January sun, and he seemed as healthy as Roy, and almost as young.

After we had seen his car drive away in the direction of Roquebrune, I said to Roy:

'What did he ask you?'

'He didn't ask me anything. But he told me something.'

'What?'

'He told me that, if ever I thought of getting married, I was to consider nothing but my own feelings. It was the only occasion in life when one needed to be absolutely selfish in one's choice. Otherwise one brings misery to others as well as to oneself.'

Roy looked at me.

'It cost him an effort to say that,' he said. 'It was brave of him.'

He added, as though off-handedly:

'You know, old boy, if he had let himself go he could have had a high old time with the women. It's almost not too late for him to start.'

Roy's relation with the Master had nothing of the strain that comes between a protégé and his patron – where all emotion is ambivalent, unless both parties are magnanimous beyond the human limits: if they are ordinary humans, there is the demand for gratitude on one side, resentment on the other, and those forces must drive them further apart. Roy's feeling was different in kind. It was deep, it had nothing to do with their positions. It was more like a successful younger brother's for an elder who has had a bad time. And underneath there was a strong current of loving envy; for, whatever had happened to the Master, his essential self had been untouched. He might regret that he had done little, he might be painfully lonely, but in himself there was repose. He was cynical in his speech, sceptical in his human reflections, observant and disinterested: how had he kept his faith?

The Boscastle cars were busy that day, carrying out guests for lunch, bringing them back; and one called in the afternoon for Roy, Rosalind and me. Rosalind was spectacular in black and white.

'I've worn ten different outfits in four days,' she said. 'Do you think this will get by?'

She was excited, full of zest, apprehensive but not too much so to enjoy herself. She exclaimed rapturously as we drove round the stretch of coast. It did not matter to her that it had been praised before. She thought it was romantically beautiful; she said so, and gasped with pleasure.

Both the dress and Rosalind 'got by' with Lord Boscastle. Lady Boscastle was polite, Lady Muriel gave what she regarded as a civil greeting; but Lord Boscastle was an obstinate man, and here was a decorative young woman asking only to sit at his feet and be impressed. He was happy to oblige. Her taste in dress might be bold, but she was incomparably better turned out than any of the women of his party, except his own wife. And each time he met her, he felt her admiration lapping round him like warm milk. He felt, as other men felt in her presence, a size larger than life.

He placed her in the chair next to his. Tea was brought in.

'I'm afraid I'm not much good at tea,' said Lord Boscastle to Rosalind, as though it were a very difficult game. 'But I expect you are, aren't you?' He pressed her to take some strawberry jam. 'From my house,' he said. 'We grow a few little things at my house, you know.'

Roy, sitting between Lady Muriel and Joan, was watching with the purest glee. It did not need his prompting that afternoon to send Lord Boscastle through his hoops.

'We have always grown a few things at my house,' said Lord Boscastle.

'Have you, Lord Boscastle?' said Rosalind.

They discussed the horticultural triumphs of the house for the past two hundred years, Lord Boscastle taking all the credit, Rosalind giving him all the applause.

Then he remembered a displeasing fact. 'The trouble is,' he said to her, 'that one never knows who is coming to live near one's house nowadays. I heard from my steward only today that someone is going to squat himself down ten miles away. His name appears to be' – Lord Boscastle reached for a letter and held it at arm's length – 'Woolston. A certain Sir Arthur Woolston.'

He pronounced the name with such painful emphasis that Lady Muriel and the rest of us waited for his next words.

'I'm afraid I don't know the fellow,' he said. 'I think,' he added, in a tone of tired dismissal, 'I think he must be some baronet or other.'

He stared across at his sister, and said:

'I suppose you probably know him, Muriel.'

'I have never heard of him,' Lady Muriel replied in dudgeon. Then, using the same technique, she turned on her sister-in-law: 'Or is he some sort of lawyer? Would your father have known him, Helen?'

'I scarcely think so,' said Lady Boscastle.

'Don't I remember one of your father's cases having something to do with the name of Woolston?'

'Perhaps you do, Muriel,' said Lady Boscastle. 'In that case you remember more than I.'

A moment later, Lady Boscastle said to me:

'It is such a beautiful sunset, Lewis. I should like to take a little walk in the garden. Will you come with me, my dear?'

She rang for her maid, who brought her coat and wraps and dressed her. She took my arm, leaned on me, and her stick tapped slowly along the terrace. It was a magnificent evening. The sun had already set behind the hills, but the sky above was a startling luminous green, which darkened to velvet blue and indigo as one looked over the sea towards Italy. The lights of Mentone sparkled across the water (did that bring back thoughts of being alone there, and ill?) and the first stars had come out.

'Had I told you that my father was a barrister, Lewis?' said Lady Boscastle.

'No, never,' I said.

'It may have made me more interested in you, my dear boy,' she said.

She told me his name; he had been an eminent chancery lawyer, some of whose cases I had studied for my Bar examinations. It came as a surprise to me. Rather oddly – so it seemed to me later – I had never enquired about her history. Somehow I had assumed that she was born in the Boscastle circle. She had acclimatised herself so completely, she was so much more fine-grained than they, so much more cultivated, so much more sophisticated. No one could be more exquisite and 'travelled'; she told me of the sweetness of life which she and her friends had known, and, far more than Lord Boscastle or Lady Muriel, made me feel its graces; she had been famous in Edwardian society, she had been loved in the last days of the old pre-war world.

But she had not been born in that society. She had been born in a comfortable place, but not there. When I knew, I could understand how she and Lady Muriel scored off each other. For Lady Boscastle, detached as she was, was enough child of her world not to be able to dismiss Lady Muriel's one advantage; she knew she was far cleverer than Lady Muriel, more attractive to men, more certain of herself; but still she remembered, with a slight sarcastic grimace, that Lady Muriel was a great aristocrat and she was born middle-class.

We retraced our steps along the terrace, her stick tapping. The curtains had not been drawn, and we could see the whole party in the bright drawing-room. Rosalind was listening to Lord Boscastle with an expression of pathetic, worshipping wonder.

'That young woman,' said Lady Boscastle, 'is having a *succès fou*. Lewis, have you a penchant for extremely stupid women?'

'Not at all,' I said.

'That is very sensible,' Lady Boscastle approved.

'By the way,' I said, 'Rosalind is far from stupid.'

'Perhaps you are right,' she said indifferently. 'She is a little effusive for my taste. Perhaps I am not fair.' She added, with a hint of pleasure: 'I shall be surprised if she catches your friend Roy. In spite of the bush telegraph.'

'So shall I.'

She glanced into the drawing-room. She did not need her lorgnette, her long-sighted blue eyes could see a clear tableau of Roy, Joan, and Lady Muriel: Lady Muriel had turned away, as if to hide a smile, Joan was beginning her lusty, delightful laugh, Roy was sitting solemn-faced between them.

'I shall also be surprised,' said Lady Boscastle, 'if my niece Joan succeeds in catching him.'

'She's very young,' I said.

'Do you think she realises that she is getting excessively fond of him?' Lady Boscastle asked. 'Which is why she quarrels with him at sight. Young women with advanced ideas and strong characters often seem quite remarkably obtuse.'

'Under it all,' I said, 'she's got great capacity for love.'

I felt Lady Boscastle twitch her shoulders as we slowly made our way.

'She will never capture anyone like your friend Roy,' she said coolly. 'Our dear Joan is rather – unadorned.'

She began to laugh, and turned up her face in the brilliant twilight.

'I am sure that her mother will never notice that Joan is getting fond of him,' said Lady Boscastle. 'Muriel has never been known to notice anything of the kind in her life. It was sometimes convenient that she didn't, my dear Lewis. Perhaps it was as well.'

In the small hours of the next morning, I was having my usual game of baccarat. I heard Rosalind's dying fall behind me.

'I thought I should find you here. Shall I join in?'

But she did not know the rules. Sooner than explain them, it was easier for me to take her across to a roulette table.

'Don't tell Roy that I've been here,' she said. 'Or else I shall get into trouble.'

She gambled with the utmost method. She had decided to invest exactly ten pounds. If she made it twenty, she would stop: if she lost it, she would also stop. She sat there, looking modish, plaintive, and open-eyed: in fact, I thought, if it came to a deal she was more than a match for the violet-powdered, predatory faces round her. That night the numbers ran against her, and in half-an-hour she had lost her quota.

'That's that,' said Rosalind. 'Please can I have a drink?'

She liked money, but she threw away sums which to her were not negligible. In presents, in loans, in inventing and paying for treats, she was the most generous of women. The ten pounds had gone, and she did not give it a thought.

We sat in two of the big armchairs by the bar.

'Where's Roy?' I asked.

'In bed, of course. And fast asleep. He sleeps like a child, bless him.'

'Always?'

'Oh, I've known him have a bout of insomnia. You knew that, did you? But as a rule he just goes to sleep as soon as his head touches the pillow.' She smiled. 'He's rather a dear old thing.'

She looked with clear open eyes into mine. 'Lewis,' she said, 'is there any reason why I shouldn't do?'

'What do you mean?'

'You know what I mean. Does he want more from a woman than I manage to give him? He seems to like me when we're alone—' she gave her prudish, reminiscent, amorous smile. 'Is there anything more he wants?'

'You ought to know.'

'I don't know,' she said, almost ill-temperedly. 'I haven't the faintest idea. I give him all the chances to speak I can think of, but he never takes them. He says nice things at the proper time, of course' — again she gave a smile – 'but that is neither here nor there. He never tells me his plans. I never know where I am with him. He's frightfully elusive. Sometimes I think I don't matter to him a scrap.'

'You do, of course.'

'Do I? Are you sure?'

'You've given him some peace.'

'That's not enough,' she said. 'I want something to take hold of. I want to be certain I mean something to him.'

She added:

'Do you think he wants to marry me?'

'I don't know.'

'Do you think he ought to marry me?'

I hesitated, for a fraction of time. Very quickly Rosalind cried, not plaintively but with all her force:

'Why shouldn't I make him a passable wife?'

CHAPTER XIV

ONE WAY TO KNOWLEDGE

AFTER that talk with Rosalind, I thought again that she was living with a stranger. She knew him with her hands and lips; yet she did not know any more than his dinner partners that January in Monte Carlo, two things about him.

First, he was sometimes removed from her, removed from any human company, by an acute and paralysing fear. It was the fear that, unless he found his rest in time, he might be overcome by melancholy again. In the moment of grace when we walked by the Serpentine, that fear was far away – and so it was during most of the mystifying holiday. But once or twice, as he talked, made love, and invented jokes, he felt what to another man would have been only an hour's sadness or fatigue. Roy was at once gripped, forced to watch his own mood.

It was like someone who has had an attack of a disease; he feels what may be a first symptom, which another would not notice or would laugh away: he cannot ignore it, he can attend to nothing else, he can only think '*is it beginning again?*'

Sometimes Rosalind thought he was elusive: he was distant from her because he had to attend to something else – is it beginning again? Those occasions were very rare in the winter after his outburst. The period of near-grace, of almost perfect safety, lasted right through the weeks on the Mediterranean, the months of the Cambridge spring. Rosalind came often to Cambridge, and spent weekends in the flat in Connaught Street. She was pressing, persuading, bullying him into marrying her – with tears, pathos, storms, scenes of all kinds. But she did not know of those moments of fear.

She did not know also of his brilliant, insatiable hopes. Those he tried to tell her of; she listened indulgently, they were part of the meaningless discontent with which so many men fretted themselves. If she had been as lucky as Roy, if she had what he had, she would have been ineffably happy. God? If she had been born in a religious time, she would have enjoyed the ceremonies, she would have assumed that she believed in God. As it was, she disbelieved just as cheerfully. There was no gap in her life; it was full and it would always have been full; she was made for the bright and pagan world, and whatever the appearances she would always have found it.

So she dismissed, tenderly, half-contemptuously, half-admiringly, all that she heard of Roy's hopes. She thus failed to understand the second reason why he was 'elusive'. For her, love was an engrossing occupation. She had not been chaste when she met Roy, she was physically tolerant, she could have loved many men with happiness; but, loving Roy, she could make do without any other human relation, either in love or outside it. She liked her friends in a good-natured casual way, she had a worldly-wise gossipy interest in those round her, she liked to talk clothes and scandal to her women confidantes, she liked to show off her knowledge of books and art to men – but, if Roy had suddenly taken her to the Pacific, she would have missed nothing that she left behind.

She could not begin to realise how profoundly different it was with him. He lived in others more than any man I knew. It was through others that he drew much of his passionate knowledge of life. It was through others, such as the Master and Ralph Udal, that he tried to find one way to belief in God. Into anything human he could project himself and learn and feel. In the stories people told him, he found not only kinship with them, but magic and a sense of the unseen.

By contrast, he often seemed curiously uninterested and insensitive about non-human things. Places meant little to him except for the human beings they contained, and nature almost nothing at all. It was like him to talk of the Boscastle finances as we drove that night along the beautiful coast. He had very little feeling for traditional Cambridge, though no one had as many friends in the living town. He was amused by my interest in the past of the college: 'romantic', he called it scornfully: even when I produced sharp, clear facts about people in the past, he was only faintly stirred; they were not real beside the people that he knew.

Because he lived so much in others, his affections had some of the warmth, strength, glamour and imagination of love. His friendship with me did not become important to either of us until we were both grown men, but the quality he brought to it transformed it: it was different from any other of my friendships, more brilliant than anything I expected when I was no longer very young. He made others feel the same. They were the strangest variety, those to whom he brought this radiance: Lady Muriel – the 'little dancer' (who was a consumptive woman in Berlin) – Winslow, who soon looked for Roy to sit next to him in hall – Mrs Seymour – the Master. There were many others, in all sorts of places from Boscastle to the tenements of Berlin, and the number grew each year.

In nearly all those affections he gave himself without thinking twice, though his parodic interest went along with his love. He had no scrap of desire to alter or 'improve' those he was fond of. He was delighted by Lady Boscastle's determination to reform me, but he was himself quite devoid of any trace of reforming zeal.

There were only one or two in all his human relations where there seemed the friction and strain of self. He liked Ralph Udal, but he was never so utterly untroubled and unselfconscious with Udal as with ten or twenty people who mattered to him less, as with, say, Mrs Seymour or Lord Boscastle. It puzzled me for a long time – until I saw that with Udal Roy for once wanted something for himself. He wanted to know how to find the peace of God.

There were others too, besides Udal, whom Roy marked down as having spiritual knowledge denied to him. He felt they could be of use to him; he tracked them down, got to know them; he had a sharp eye for anyone who could be of this special use, as sharp an eye as a man develops who is out to borrow money or is on the make. They were always youngish men, as though he felt no old man's experience could help him. Yet he was never easy with them. He gave each of them up, as soon as he felt sure they had not known his own experience. Udal was the only one for whom he had a strong personal feeling. Rosalind did not realise that, through Udal, through some of those others, Roy was living an intent and desperate search. She did realise, as she had shown with the Boscastles and with me, that Roy's friends captured his imagination and that she must know them. That was all she could see; it was a move in her plan to marry him. His hopes, his sense of life through others, his search – they would go, he would cease to be elusive, once she had him safely in the marriage bed.

It was in the early summer that he told her he could not marry her

Rosalind let herself go. She had been crying, reproaching him, imploring him, for some days when I first heard what had happened. I went round to Connaught Street one night, and found Roy lying on the sofa, his face pale and tired. Rosalind was sitting in an armchair; the skin under her eyes was heavily powdered, but even so one could see that she had not long since been in tears.

They were in silence when I entered.

'Hallo, old boy,' said Roy. He was relieved to see me.

'I'd better tell Lewis,' said Rosalind.

'You needn't,' said Roy. 'It would be better if you didn't.'

'You'll only tell him yourself the minute you've got rid of me,' she said.

Roy turned his face away. She faced me with open, brimming eyes.

'He's got tired of me,' she said.

'Not true,' said Roy, without turning round.

'He won't marry me. He's told me that he won't marry me.' She spoke to Roy. 'You can't deny that you've told me that, can you?'

Roy did not reply.

'I'm no good to him,' said Rosalind. She took out a crumpled handkerchief and began to cry, very quietly.

In time she said to me:

'What do you think of it, Lewis? I expect you think it's right.'

'I'm very sorry: that's all one can ever say.'

'You think he'll be better off without me, don't you?' she cried.

I shook my head. 'It's for you two only,' I said.

She made a pretence of smiling.

'You're a nice old thing, Lewis. If you don't think he will be better off without me, everyone else will. All the people who think I'm a little bitch – they'll all feel I've got what I deserve. Oh, what do I care what they all think? They don't matter, now he's turning me out.'

'I'm not turning you out.'

Roy's voice was flat and exhausted, and Rosalind found it easier to talk to him through me. She looked at his back and said:

'I've told him that I've got to get married some time. I can't wait for ever. And someone quite nice is rather anxious to marry me.'

Whether it was an invention or not, I could not guess. In any case, she had thrust it in front of him. She had first mentioned it three days before, and since then she had been blackmailing and begging. She had not reckoned that he would be so firm.

At this point Roy broke in:

'I can only say it again. If you need to marry, you might marry him.'

It was very harsh. But it was harsh through a cause I had not expected. He was jealous. He was resolved not to marry her, yet he was jealous that she should marry another.

'I don't know whether I could bear it.'

'I expect he will make you happier than I ever could.'

'You're horrible,' said Rosalind, and sobbed again.

She did not move him, either then or later. He stayed firm, though he became more gentle when the first shock wore off. He wanted to go on living with her, but he would not marry her. Rosalind still kept coming to see him, though more fitfully. I heard nothing more about her engagement to the other man.

The scene left Roy quiet and saddened. For some days I dreaded that he was being overcome by another wave of depression. But it fell away. It was good to see him light-hearted with relief. Yet I thought, as the summer passed, that he was never as carefree after the scene with Rosalind; even at his liveliest he never reached the irresponsible, timeless content of Monte Carlo. He became more active, impatient, eager, more set on his own search. He spent much more time with Ralph Udal in Lewisham. He persuaded me to try to trace old Martineau for him: but Martineau had moved from the Leeds pavement, no one knew where.

One afternoon in August I saw something which surprised me and set me thinking. I was being driven over the Vauxhall bridge, when through the car window I saw Rosalind and Ralph Udal walking together. Neither was speaking, and they were walking slowly to the north side of the river. What was she doing now, I thought? Did she think that he had become the most powerful influence on Roy? Was she playing the same game that she had once played with me?

The first part of the liturgy was published in the summer. In due course, often after months of delay, there followed respectful reviews in three or four scholarly periodicals. Colonel Foulkes, as usual putting in his word without a pause, got in first with his review in the *Journal of Theological Studies*; he wrote that the complete edition of the liturgy looked like being the most authoritative piece of oriental scholarship for a generation. But apart from him English scholars did not go out of their way to express enthusiasm. The reviews were good enough, but there was none of the under-current of gossipy personal praise. I had no doubt that, if Roy had kept quiet at the December meeting, he would have had different luck; Sir Oulstone would have paid a state visit to the college, all Sir Oulstone's friends would have been saying that Roy had once for all 'arrived'. But none of those things happened. Sir Oulstone and his school were silent.

The Master was painfully disappointed. Arthur Brown said to me with sturdy resignation: 'I want to tell them, Eliot, that our young friend is the best scholar this college has had since the war. But it looks as though I shall have to wait for a few years.' He gave me one of his warnings: 'It's never wise to claim more than we can put on the table. People remember that you've inflated the currency, and they hold it against you next time.'

We were downcast and angry. Roy's own response was singular. He was amused, he treated it as a good joke as his own expense – and also at ours, who wanted him to be famous. 'It's a flop, old boy,' he said cheerfully in his room one afternoon. He developed the habit of referring to his work as though he were a popular writer. 'It's a flop. I shan't be able to live on the royalties. I'm really very worried about the sales.'

I wanted him to make his peace with Lyall, but he smiled.

'Too late. Too late. Unsuccessful author, that's what I shall be. I shall need to work harder to make ends meet.' He jumped to his feet, and went towards the upright reading desk. He was busy with a difficult psalm. 'Can't stay talking,' he said. 'That won't buy Auntie a new frock.'

He was gaining a perverse satisfaction. I realised at last that he did not want the fame we wanted for him. He would do the work – that was a need, a drug, an attempt at escape – but if he could choose he would prefer to be left obscure.

Most men, I thought, are content to stay clamped within the bonds of their conscious personality. They may break out a little – in their daydreams, their play, sometimes in their prayers and their thoughts of love. But in their work they stay safely in the main stream of living. They want success on the ordinary terms, they scheme for recognition, titles, position, the esteem of solid men. They want to go up step by step within their own framework. Among such men one finds the steadily and persistently ambitious – the Lyalls and the Houston Eggars.

Roy always shied from them. He thought of them as 'stuffed'. It had been obtuse of us to imagine he would seek a career as they might seek it. Arthur Brown and I were more ordinary men than he was. We were trying to impose on him the desires we should have had, if we had been as gifted. But one could not separate his gifts from the man he was.

No one was less willing, less able, to stay clamped within the bonds of self. Often he wished that he could: he cried out in envy of the comfortable. But he was driven. He was driven to his work by the same kind of compulsion that drives an artist. It gave him the obsessed, the morbid concentration that none of the ordinary healthy ambitious scholars could achieve; it did not give him the peace he hoped, although he knew he would be lost without it; above all it did not give him the matter-of-fact ambition that everyone round him took for granted. In his place, they would all have longed to be distinguished savants, men of weight, Fellows of the British Academy, recipients of honorary degrees – and in time they would have got there. Yet, at the prospect Roy felt imprisoned.

Perhaps it had been wrong of Arthur Brown and me to see that he became a fellow. He seemed to want it – but perhaps even then we were reading our desires into him. Was his outburst a shriek of protest against being hemmed in?

Yet I had my own minor amusement. Roy's enemies in the college had heard the Master prophesy an overwhelming triumph; the book came out, and with gratification Despard-Smith and others slowly sensed that there was an absence of acclaim.

Despard-Smith said one night:

'I have always been compelled to doubt whether Calvert's work will s-stand the test of time. I wish I could believe otherwise. But it will be a scandal for the college if his work turns out to be a flash in the pan.'

Roy was not dining, but I told him afterwards. He was no more consistent than other men, and he became extremely angry.

'What does he know about it?' said Roy in fury while I laughed at him. 'He's never written a line in his life, except asking some wretched farmer to pay the rent. Why should some tenth-rate mathematician be allowed to speak about my work? I need to talk to him.'

Roy spoke to Despard-Smith the next night.

'I hear that you've become an oriental scholar, Despard?'

'I don't know what you mean, Calvert.'

'I hear that you doubt the soundness of my edition. I suppose that you needed to study it first?'

Roy was still angry, and his subtle, mystifying, hypnotic approach had deserted him. Despard-Smith felt at home, and a gleam of triumph shone in his eye.

'No, Calvert, that wasn't necessary. I relied on my judgment from what I picked up round me. Exactly as one has to do – in electing a fellow. One has to rely on one's judgment. I don't pretend to be clever, Calvert, but I do congratulate myself on my judgment. I might tell you that some people never acquire it.'

Roy had no reply. I was very much amused, but it was a joke that he did not see.

It was not long before the Master and Arthur Brown were able to score a success for Roy within the college. Roy's reputation had been high with

German scholars since he brought out his grammar, and the liturgy they praised as soon as it was published. The Professor of Oriental Religions at Berlin and a colleague came to London for a conference in October, and wrote to the Master asking if he could present them to Roy. They stayed in the Lodge for a weekend and met Roy at dinner. The Professor was a stocky round-faced roguish-looking man called Ammatter. When Roy was introduced to him, he clowned and pretended not to believe it.

The Master translated his remark with victorious zest. 'Professor Ammatter says,' the Master addressed himself to Despard-Smith, 'that it is impossible anyone so young should have done such work. He says that we must be foisting an impostor upon them.'

Despard-Smith made a creaking acknowledgment, and sat as far down the table as he could. The Master and Roy each spoke good German; Ammatter was tricky, fluid, entertaining, comic and ecstatic; the wine went round fast in the combination room, the Master drinking glass for glass with Ammatter, Roy and the other German. Old Despard-Smith glowered as they laughed at jokes he did not understand. The Master, cheerful, familiar, dignified though a little drunk, broke off their conversation several times in order to translate; he chose each occasion when they were paying a compliment to Roy. The Master spoke a little more loudly than usual, so that the compliments carried all over the room. It was one of his happiest evenings, and before the end Roy had arranged to spend the next three months in Berlin.

CHAPTER XV

TEA IN THE DRAWING-ROOM

I RECEIVED some high-spirited letters from Germany, in which there were references to acquaintances all over Berlin, from high party officials to the outcasts and those in danger; but I did not see Roy again until early January, after we had heard bad news.

The Master had been taken ill just before Christmas; he had not been in his briskest form all through the autumn, but in his spare, unpampered fashion he thought little of it. He got worse over Christmas, vomited often and could not eat. In the first week of January he was taken to hospital and examined. They gave him a gastroscopy, and sent him back to the Lodge the same night. They had found the answer. He had an inoperable cancer. There was no hope at all. He would die within a few months.

The day after the examination, all the college knew, but the doctors and Lady Muriel agreed that the Master should not be told. They assured him that nothing was seriously the matter, only a trivial duodenal ulcer. He was to lie still, and would recover in a few weeks. I was allowed to see him very soon after they had talked to him; I knew the truth, and heard him talk cheerfully of what he would do in two years' time, of how he was looking forward to Roy's complete edition. He looked almost as fresh and smooth-faced as the year before in the hills above Monte Carlo. He was cordial, sharp-tongued and indiscreet. His anxiety had been taken away, and so powerful was the psychological effect that he felt well. He spoke of Roy with intimacy and affection.

'He always did insist on behaving like a gilded dilettante. I wonder if he'll ever get over it. Why will he insist on going about with vineleaves in his hair?'

He looked up at the ceiling of the great bedroom, and said quietly:

'I think I know the answer to that question.'

'What do you think?'

'I think you know it too. He's not a trifler.' He paused. He did not know that he was exhausted.

He said simply: 'No, he's searching for God.'

I was too much distressed to find what he knew of Roy's search. Did he really understand, or was it just a phrase?

Most people in the college thought it was a mistake to lie to the Master. Round the table in the combination room there were arguments whether he should or should not have been told the truth. The day I went to the Lodge, I heard Joan disagree violently with her mother.

But Lady Muriel, even if all thought her wrong, had taken her decision. When he was demonstrably worse, when he could no longer think he would get better, he would have to be told. Meanwhile he would get a few weeks of hope and peace. It would be the last comfort he would enjoy while he was alive. Whatever they said, she would give it to him. Her daughter passionately protested. If he could choose, cried Joan, there was no doubt what he would say.

'I am positive that we are doing right,' said Lady Muriel. Her voice was firm and unyielding. There was grandeur in her bold eyes, her erect head, her stiff back.

Roy returned from Berlin a couple of days later. He had heard the news before he ran up my stairs, but he was looking well and composed. It was too late to see the Master that night, but he arranged to visit him the next afternoon, and for us both to have tea with Lady Muriel.

So next day I went over to the Lodge alone, and was shown into the empty drawing-room. I stood by the window. Snow had lain on the court for days, and, though it was thawing, the ground still gleamed white against the sombre dusk. The sky was heavy with dense grey clouds. The court was empty, it was still the depth of the vacation, no lights shone from the windows. In the drawing-room there was no light yet except the roaring fire.

Roy joined me there. His face was stricken. 'This is dreadful,' he said. 'What did he talk about?'

'The little book on the heresies which we're to work at in a year or two. After my liturgy is safely out.'

'I know,' I said.

'There was a time,' said Roy, 'when I should have jumped at any excuse for getting out of that little book.'

'You invented several good reasons.'

'Just so. Now I shall do it in memory of him.'

I doubted whether I should be able to dissuade him. He would do it very well, but not superbly; it would not suit him; as a scholar his gifts were, as the mathematicians say, deep, sharp, and narrow; this kind of broad commentary was not at all in his line. People would suspect that he was losing his scholar's judgment.

'I'd expected a good deal,' said Roy. 'But it is dreadful. Much worse than anyone could guess.'

Lady Muriel threw open the door and switched on the lights.

'Good afternoon, Roy,' she said. 'I'm very glad you've come to see us. It's so long since you were here. Good afternoon, Mr Eliot.'

Roy went to her, took her hand in his. 'I've been talking to the Master, you know,' he said. 'It's dreadful to have to pretend, isn't it? I wish you'd been spared that, Lady Mu. No one could have known what to do.'

He alone could have spoken to her so. He alone would take it for granted that she was puzzled and dismayed.

'It was not easy, but—'

'No one could help you. And you'd have liked help, wouldn't you? Everyone would.'

Her eyes filled with tears.

She was embarrassed, flustered, choked like one unused to crying: soon Roy got her sitting beside him on the sofa, and helped her to tea. She smiled at him, her bold eyes misted and bloodshot.

'I should be filling your cup. In my own drawing-room.'

Roy smiled. 'You may, the next time I come.'

She gripped hold of her drawing-room manner – for my benefit, perhaps. Her neck straightened, she made a brave attempt to talk of Roy's journey from Berlin. He told her that he had had to sleep sitting up in a crowded carriage.

'How could you?' cried Lady Muriel. 'I couldn't bear the thought of being watched when I was asleep.'

'Why not, Lady Mu?'

'One wouldn't know how one was looking before strangers. One couldn't control oneself.'

He glanced at her: in a second, her face broke, and she smiled back.

Soon afterwards Joan came into the room. She walked in with her determined, gawky stride: then she saw Roy, and her whole bearing changed. She seemed to shiver. For an instant she went stiff. She came towards him, and he jumped up and welcomed her. He said a word about her father; she looked at him steadily, shook her head, deliberately put it aside and went on to argue with him over living in Germany.

'Don't you feel pressed down? You must feel that it's a relief to get to the frontier. I felt it very strongly—'

'The Dutch porters have no necks,' said Roy. He disliked arguments, particularly among intellectual persons.

'Seriously—'

'Seriously—' he mimicked her exactly. She flushed, and then gave her unexpected laugh.

'You can't get away with it by parlour tricks,' she said. 'In a police state you're bound to feel a constant friction, anyone is. And—'

'In any sort of state,' he said, 'most lives of most people are much the same.'

'I deny that,' said Joan.

'They've got their married lives, they've got their children, they've got their hobbies. They've got their work.'

'*Your* work wouldn't be affected.' She seized the chance to talk about Roy himself. 'But you're an unusual man. Your work could go on just the same – in the moon. Imagine that you were a writer, or a civil servant, or a parson, or a lawyer, in Berlin now. Do you deny that the police state would make a difference? You must agree.'

'Just so,' said Roy, giving in to evade the argument. 'Just so.'

Both women smiled at him tenderly. They were always amused by the odd affirmative, which seemed so out of keeping. Joan's tenderness was full of a love deep and clear-eyed for so young a woman.

Roy returned to bantering with Lady Muriel. He was out to give them some relief. He told her of some Junker acquaintances in Berlin, the von Heims. 'They reminded me of you so much, Lady Mu.'

'Why ever was that?'

'The Gräfin spent most of her time reading Gotha,' said Roy, sparkling with affectionate malice. 'Just like you, Lady Mu, idly turning over the pages of *Debrett*.'

She gave her loud crowing laugh, and slapped his hand. Then she said seriously:

'Of course, no one has ever called me snobbish.'

She laughed again at Roy. Joan, who knew her mother well and also knew that no one could treat her as Roy did, was melted in a smile of envy, incredulity, and love.

It was a dark rainy night when Roy and I walked out of the Lodge. On the grass in the court there were left a few patches of melting snow, dim in the gloom. The rain pelted down. Roy wanted to go shopping, and soon the rain had soaked his hair and was running down beside his ears.

I said something about Joan being in love with him, but he would not talk of her. It was rare for him to want to talk of love, rarer still of the love he himself received.

That night he was sad over the Master, but otherwise serene. He had come back with his spirits even and tranquil. Despite the shock of the afternoon, he was enjoying our walk in the rain.

He asked me for the latest gossip, he asked gently after my concerns. The rain swirled and gurgled in the gutters, came down like a screen between us and the bright shop windows. Roy took me from shop to shop, water dripping from us on to the floors, in order to buy a set of presents. On the way he told me whom he wanted them for – the strange collection of the shady, the shabbily respectable, the misfits who lived in the same house in the Knesebeckstrasse. Roy would go back there, though his flat was uncomfortable, whenever he went to Berlin; for the rest, the 'little dancer' and the others, had already come to be lost without him. Some thought he was an unworldly professor, a rich simple Englishman, easy to fleece.

'Poor goops.' Roy smiled. 'If I were going to make a living as a shark, I should do it well, shouldn't you? We should make a pretty dangerous pair, old boy. I must try to instruct them some time.'

Nevertheless, he took the greatest pains about their presents.

CHAPTER XVI

'I HATE THE STARS'

ON those winter nights the light in the Master's bedroom dominated the college. The weeks passed: he had still not been told; we paid our visits, came away with shamefaced relief. We came away into a different, busy, bustling, intriguing life; for, as soon as it was known that the Master must die, the college was set struggling as to who should be his successor. That struggle was exciting and full of human passion. It engrossed Arthur Brown completely, me in part, and Roy a little. We were all on the same side, and Winslow on the other. It was the sharpest and most protracted personal conflict that the college went through in my time. It taught me a good deal, perhaps most of what I came to know, about what one might call closed politics.

So much so that I shall tell it in its own right, separated from the story of Roy Calvert. This means that several incidents will have to be told twice, for they were significant both to the election and to Roy. When I recalled them, though, they came back with a different stress. Years after, as I tried to recapture what had happened to Roy, I reconstructed conversations with him and about him. In the process I didn't pay so much attention to other words spoken on the identical occasion: though those words might have had their relevance in the political context, have been examined intently some day between me and Arthur Brown, and have to be resurrected in the account of the election. Such conversations had of course their own objective existence: and I have had to take from them what I need for each of my two purposes.

Meanwhile, Roy spent more time in the Lodge than the rest of us put together. He sat for whole afternoons with the Master, planning their book on the heresies, and he became Lady Muriel's only support. In the Lodge he forgot himself entirely. He devoted himself, everything he was, to each of the three of them. Outside he remembered what he was watching there. It filled him with dread. At times he waited for the first sign of melancholy to take hold of him. I was waiting too. I watched him turn to his work with savage absorption: and there came nights when he drank for relief.

It was harrowing for anyone to watch, even for those far tougher-minded than Roy. We saw the Master getting a little more tired each time we visited him; and each time he was more surprised that his appetite and strength were not coming back. For a few days after he had been told that all was well, the decline seemed to stop. He even ate with relish. Then slowly, imperceptibly to himself, the false recovery left him. By February he was so much thinner that one could see the smooth cheeks beginning to sag. He no longer protested about not being allowed up. The deterioration was so visible that we wondered when he would suspect, or whether he had already done so. Yet there was not a sign of it. He complained once or twice that 'this wretched ulcer is taking a lot of getting rid of', but his spirits stayed high and he confided his sarcastic indiscretions with the utmost vivacity. It was astonishing to see, as he grew worse under our eyes, what faith and hope could do.

Everyone knew that he would have to be told soon. The disease appeared to be progressing very fast, and Lady Muriel told Roy that he must be given time to settle his affairs. She was dreading her duty, dreading it perhaps more than an imaginative person would have done; we knew that she would not shirk it for an hour once she decided that the time had come.

One February afternoon, I met Joan in the court. I asked first about her mother. She looked at me with her direct, candid gaze: then her face, which had been heavy with sadness, lost it all as she laughed.

'That's just like Roy,' she said.

'What do you mean?'

'Asking the unexpected question. Particularly when it's right. Of course, she's going through more than he is at present. She will, until she's told him. After that, I don't know, Lewis. I haven't seen enough of death to be sure. It may still be worse for her.' She spoke gravely, with a strange authority, as though she were certain of her reserves of emotional power. Then she smiled, but looked at me like an enemy. She said:

'Has Roy learned some of his tricks from you?'

'I have learned some from him,' I said. She did not believe it. She resented me, I knew. She resented the times he agreed with me; she thought I over-persuaded him. She envied the casual intimacy between us which I took for granted, for which she would have given so much. She would have given so much to have, as I did, the liberty of his rooms. Think of seeing him whenever she wanted! She loved him from the depth of her warm and powerful nature. Her love was already romantic, sacrificial, dedicated. Yet she longed too for the dear prosaic domestic nearnesses of everyday.

It was a Sunday when I spoke to Joan; the Wednesday after Roy's name was on the dining list for hall, but he did not come. Late at night, long after the porter's last round at ten o'clock, he entered my room without knocking and stood on the hearth-rug looking down at me. His face was drawn and set.

'Where have you been?' I said.

'In the Lodge. Looking after Lady Mu.'

'She told him this afternoon,' he added, in a flat, exhausted voice. 'She needed someone to look after her. She wouldn't have been able to cope.'

'Joan?'

'Joan was extremely good. She's very strong.'

He paused, and said quietly:

'I'll tell you later, old boy. I need to do something now. Let's go out. I'd like to drive over to ——' – the town where we had both lived – 'and have a blind with old George. I can't. They may want me tomorrow. Let's go to King's. There's bound to be a party in King's. I need to get out of the college.'

We found a party in King's, or at least some friends to talk and drink with. Roy drank very little, but he seemed the highest-spirited person there. I was watching for the particular glitter of which I was afraid. But it did not come. He quietened down, and young men clustered round to ask him to next week's parties. He was gentle to the shy ones, and by the time we set off home was resigned, quiet and composed.

We let ourselves into college by the side door, and walked through the court. When we came in sight of the Lodge windows, one light was still shining.

'I wonder,' said Roy, 'if he can sleep tonight.'

It was a fine clear night, not very cold. We stood together gazing at the lighted window.

Roy said quietly:

'I've never seen such human misery and loneliness as I did today.'

I glanced up at the stars, innumerable, brilliant, inhumanly calm. Roy's eyes followed mine, and he spoke with desolating sadness.

'I hate the stars,' he said.

We went to his rooms in silence, and he made tea. He began to talk, in a subdued and matter-of-fact tone, about the Master and Lady Muriel. They had never got on. It had not been a happy marriage. They had never known each other. Both Roy and I had guessed that for a long time past, and Joan knew it. I had once heard Joan talk of it to Roy. And he, who knew so much of sexual love, accepted the judgment of this girl, who was technically 'innocent'. 'I don't believe,' said Joan, direct and uncompromising, 'that they ever hit it off physically.'

Yet, as Roy said that night, they had lived together for twenty-five years. They had had children. They had had some kind of life together. They had not been happy, but each was the other's only intimate. Perhaps they felt more intimate in the supreme crisis just because of the unhappiness they had known in each other. It was not always those who were flesh of each other's flesh who were most tied together.

So, with that life behind them, she had to tell him. She screwed up her resolve, 'and if I know Lady Mu at all, poor dear,' said Roy, 'she rushed in and blurted it out. She hated it too much to be able to tell him gently. Poor dear, how much she would have liked to be tender.'

Her husband did not reproach her for not having told him before, he did not hate her, he scarcely seemed aware of her presence. He just said: 'This alters things. There's no future then. It's hard to think without a future.'

He had had no suspicion, but he did not mind being fooled. He did not say a word about it. He was thinking of his death.

She could not reach him to comfort him. No one could reach him. She might as well not be there.

That was what hurt her most, said Roy, and he added, with a sad and bitter protest, 'we're all egotists and self-regarding to the last, aren't we? She didn't like not mattering. And yet when she left him, it was intolerable to see a human being as unhappy as she was. I told you before, I've never seen such misery and loneliness. How could I comfort her? I tried, but whatever could I do? She's not been much good to him. She feels that more than anyone thinks. Now, at the end, all she can do is to tell him this news. And he didn't seem to mind what she said.'

Roy was speaking very quietly.

Silently, we sat by the dying fire. At last Roy said:

'We're all alone, aren't we? Each one of us. Quite alone.' He asked: 'Lewis – how does one reach another human being?'

'Sometimes one thinks one can in love.'

'Just so,' he said. After a time, he added:

'Yet, sometimes after I've made love, I've lain with someone in my arms and felt lonelier than ever in my life.'

He broke out:

'If she was miserable and lonely today, what was it like to be him? Can anyone imagine what it's like to know your death is *fixed*?'

After she left him, Lady Muriel had gone to his room once again, to enquire about his meals. Joan had visited him for a few minutes. He had asked to be left alone for the evening. That was all Roy knew of his state.

'Can you imagine what he's gone through tonight? Is he lying awake now? Do you think his dreams are cheating him?'

Roy added:

'I don't believe he's escaped the thought of death tonight. It must be dreadful to face your death. I wonder how ours will come.'

CHAPTER XVII

STRUGGLE THROUGH SUMMER NIGHTS

WHEN he knew the truth, it was a long time before the Master asked to see any of his friends. He told Roy, who alone was allowed to visit him, that he wished to 'get used to the idea'.

He talked to Roy almost every day. Throughout those weeks, he saw no one else, except his family and his doctor. He no longer mentioned the book on the heresies. He said much less than he used to. He was often absent-minded, as though he were trying to become familiar with his fate.

Then there came a time, Roy told me, as his own spirits darkened, when the Master seemed to have thought enough of his condition. He seemed to have got bored – it was Roy's phrase, and it was not said lightly – with the prospect of death. He had faced it so far as he could. For a time he wanted to forget. And he became extraordinarily considerate.

That was at the end of term, and he invited us to call on him one by one – not for his sake, but for ours. In his detached and extreme consideration, he knew that each of us wanted to feel of some help to him. He felt, with a touch of his old sarcasm, that he could give us that last comfort.

Everyone who talked to him was impressed and moved by his kindness. Yet I was appalled to receive so much consideration from him, to be asked about my affairs with wise detached curiosity – and then face the eyes of a dying man. His cheeks were hollow and yellow, and his skin had a waxy texture; his clothes hung on him in folds, on him who had been the best preserved of men, and as well groomed as Roy. There was one macabre feature of his appearance, which I learned afterwards had upset him for a time. He had always been slender, he was now emaciated – but under his waistcoat swelled the round pseudo-paunch of his disease.

He had never been so kind, and I went out of the room with dread. It struck me with more distress than anyone, even Roy. For Roy, each hour in the Master's bedroom had been an agony; he had seen too much of suffering, too much of the inescapable human loneliness; yet this state of detached sub-ironic sympathy, to which the Master had now come, seemed to Roy a triumph of the spirit as the body died. He was moved to admiration and love; I was moved too, in the same way; but I also felt a personality dissolving in front of my eyes, a human being already passing into the eternal dark and cold.

At the beginning of the summer, the disease seemed to slow down. The doctors had guessed that he would be at the point of death by May or June: they admitted now that they had calculated wrong. He sat up a little each day in his bedroom above the sunny court. He was slightly more exhausted, still disinterestedly kind, still curious about each of us. It was clear that he might live for several months yet.

This lengthening of the Master's life had several effects upon those round him. The tension in the college about the next Master had been growing; everyone had reckoned that the election would be settled by the summer. Now the uncertainty was going to be indefinitely prolonged – and the news did not relax the tension, but increased it. The hostility between the two main parties, the talks at night, the attempts to cajole the three or four wavering votes – they all grew more urgent. And so did the campaign of propaganda and scandal. There were all kinds of currents of emotion in that election – men were moved, not only by personal feelings in the intimate sense, but also by their prejudices in subjects, in social origins, in political belief. At least two men, Francis Getliffe and old Pilbow, were much influenced by the candidates' attitude to the Spanish war, the critical test in external politics. And there was a great deal of rancour set free. On the side which Winslow led, there was a determined attempt to label us others as rackety and disreputable. Winslow himself did not take part, although he was too much committed to the struggle to control his own party. He was set on getting his candidate in. Old Despard-Smith did some sombre calumny, and one or two others became virulent.

It was inevitable that much of this virulence should direct itself at Roy. Some of the men who had opposed his election, though not Winslow, envied and hated him still. By now they knew more about him. They had had him under their eyes for nearly two years. They knew a little, they suspected much more. In such an intimate society, small hints passed into circulation; often the facts were wildly askew but the total picture preserved a sort of libellous verisimilitude. With a self-righteous satisfaction, Roy's enemies acquired a sense, groping but not everywhere false, of a wild and dissipated life. They knew something of drunken parties, of young women, of a separate existence in London. They knew something of Joan's love for him.

The slander became more venomous, as though in a last desperate campaign. One heard Roy attacked night after night in hall and the combination room and in private gossip. Very often women's names were mentioned: as the summer term went on, Joan's was the most frequent of all.

It was a curious technique, attacking our candidate through his friends and supporters. But it was not altogether ineffective. It cost us a good deal of anxiety. We tried hard to conceal these particular slanders from Roy himself, but in the end they reached him.

If he had been untroubled, he would have laughed them away. No one cared less for what others thought. He might have amused himself in executing some outrageous reprisal. But in fact he had no resilience left. He did not laugh when he heard he was being maligned. He took it darkly. It was a weight upon him. He went from the Master's bedroom to face his own thoughts, and harsh, jeering voices came to him as he lay lucidly and despairingly awake. For what he had been waiting for had happened. The melancholy had gripped him again. He made less fight this time. He was both more frightened and more resigned.

It did not stop him spending all his spare time at the Lodge. He worked as hard as ever, he was drinking alone at night; but, whenever they wanted him, he was there. Perhaps it was because of them that he did not make his old frantic attempts to escape from his affliction. He did not see Udal at all, he scarcely left Cambridge for a day, he had not spent a night with Rosalind for months. He was living more chastely than at any time since I knew him. He did not talk to me about his wretchedness or hopes; he seemed resigned to being alone, lost, terrified.

I knew, though he said nothing, that thoughts pressed in on him with merciless clarity as he lay staring into the long bright summer dawns. In the Lodge he had seen the approach of death, the extreme of loneliness, faith, despair, the helpless cries of human beings as they try to give each other help. He had seen it, and now saw himself in this torment of his own melancholy. I believed later that in those nights he learned about despair.

He was looking harrowed and ill. Depriving himself of his minor pleasures, he played no cricket that summer; he was mewed up all the daytime with his manuscripts, or inside the Lodge, and for the first time one saw his face with no sunburn at all. There was no colour in his face, except for the skin under his eyes.

I had to submit myself again to watch him suffer so. Much of the time I lived in apprehension. Some things I feared less than the first time, some more. I knew roughly now the course of these attacks. They differed a little among themselves; this was quieter, more despondent, more rooted in human grief; but even so I had already seen the occasional darts of elation. I had not to worry so much about the unknown. I expected that, after the melancholy had deranged and played with him, in another outburst it would end. All I could do was take such precautions as I could that this outburst would not hurt him or his friends.

But I feared something much more terrible, which last time I had not feared at all. I wanted to turn my mind away from what he must bear – not because of his present misery, but because it had overcome him *again*. He must have faced it often. He must have seen it, in different lights and shades of recognition. All were intolerable. Sometimes – *this was a doom he was born with. He was as much condemned as the Master. There was no more he could do.* He would be swept like this all through his life; at times, as now, he would be driven without will; he could not have the appearance of will which gives life dignity, meaning and self-respect.

The Master still had will, facing his death. *He was more condemned.* He must be ready to suffer aimlessly, for no reason, whenever this affliction came. He would always be helpless.

Sometimes – *he could still escape. But why were the doors closed?* If he could escape, why was it so preposterously harder than for others? He had to struggle, to push back the sense of doom, and still the doors would not open, and misery came upon him again. He should have escaped before this attack, and yet he was caught. It was worse to feel that he could escape, and yet be caught. It was harder to endure, if there was a way out which he could not find.

I remembered that winter evening by the Serpentine, and I was wrung by pain and by acute fear. There were nights when I too lay awake.

It was during May that Joan first told Roy that she loved him. The reprieve to her father seemed to act as a trigger to her love. It had begun long since, in the days when as an awkward girl she used to decry Roy in company and quarrel with him whenever she could make the opportunity. It had accumulated through those harsh winter days in the Lodge, when they all depended on him. Now it was set loose and pouring out.

I knew it, because she talked to me about his unhappiness. Unlike

Rosalind, she could not take it as a matter of course. She was forced to discover what had stricken him. She was the proudest of young women, and yet she humbled herself to ask me – even though she thought I was her enemy, even though she felt she alone should possess his secrets. Whatever it cost her, she must learn him through and through. I was touched both by her humility and her pride. So she watched him in those weeks of affliction. But she was spared the climax.

I was nervous about him almost to the end of Arthur Brown's claret party. Brown gave this party to his wine-drinking colleagues each year at the beginning of June.

That summer he arranged it for the second night of May week. As a rule this would have been the night of the college ball, but, though the Master asked that all should continue normally, it was not being held this year. The undergraduates took their young women to balls at other colleges: Roy had danced with Joan at Trinity the previous night. Now he turned up at Brown's party, heavy-eyed for lack of sleep, and deceived all the others into believing that his sparkle was the true sparkle of a joyous week.

All through the evening, I could not keep my eyes away from him for long. Time after time, I was compelled to look at him, to confirm what I dreaded. For this was the sparkle I had seen before. I wished I could take him out of danger.

Six of us sat in Brown's rooms on that warm June night, and the decanters stood in a shapely row on the table. Brown was giving us the best clarets of 1920 and 1924.

'I must say, Tutor,' said Winslow, 'that you're doing us remarkably proud.'

'I thought,' said Brown comfortably, 'that it was rather an opportunity for a little comparative research.'

Although it was late evening, the sun had scarcely set, and over the roofs opposite the sky glowed brilliantly. From the court there drifted the scent of acacia, sweet and piercing. We settled down to some luxurious drinking.

Roy had begun the evening with some of his malicious imitations, which rubbed away the first stiffness of the party. Winslow, who had once more come to see him in the glare of propaganda, was soon melted.

Since then Roy had been drinking faster than any of us. The mood was on him.

He talked with acute intensity. Somehow – to the others it sounded harmless enough – he brought in the phrase 'psychological insight'. One of the party said that he had never considered that kind of insight to be a special gift.

'It's time you did, you know,' said Roy.

'I don't believe in it. It's mumbo-jumbo,' said Winslow.

'You think it's white man's magic?' Roy teased him, but the wild glint had come into his eyes.

'My dear young man, I've been watching people since long before you were born,' said Winslow, with his hubristic and caustic air. 'And I know there's only one conclusion. It's impossible for a man to see into anyone else's mind.'

Roy began again, the glint brighter than ever.

Suddenly I broke in, with a phrase he recognised, with a question about Winslow's son.

Roy smiled at me. He was half-drunk, he was almost overcome by desperate elation – but he could still control it that night when he heard my signal. Instead of the frantic taunt I had been waiting for, he said:

'You'll see, Winslow. The kind of insight that one or two odd fish possess. It may be white man's magic, but it's quite real. Too real.'

He fell quiet as Winslow talked, for the second time that evening, about his son. Soon after he entered, Brown asked about his son's examination, which had just finished. Winslow had been rude in his own style, professing ignorance of how the boy was likely to have got on. Now, in the middle of the party, he gave a different answer.

'My dear Brown,' he said, 'I don't know what kind of a fool of himself the stupid child has really made. He thinks he has done reasonably well. But his judgment is entirely worthless. I shall be relieved if the examiners let him through.'

'Oh, they'll let him through,' said Brown amiably.

'I don't know what will happen to him if they don't,' said Winslow. 'He's a stupid child. But I believe there's something in him. He's a very nice person. If they give him a chance now, I honestly believe he may surprise you all in ten years' time.'

I had never heard Winslow speak with so little guard. He gazed at Brown from under his heavy lids, and recovered his caustic tone:

'My dear Tutor, you've had the singular misfortunate to teach the foolish creature. I drink to you in commiseration.'

'I drink to his success,' said Brown.

After the party, Roy and I walked in the garden. It was a warm and balmy night, with a full moon lemon-yellow in the velvet sky. The smell of acacia was very strong. On the great trees the leaves lay absolutely still.

'I shall sleep tonight,' said Roy, after we had walked round once in silence. His face was pale, his eyes filmed and bloodshot, but the dionysiac look had gone. 'I shall sleep tonight,' he said, with tired relief.

He had not been to bed for forty-eight hours, he was more than a little drunk, yet he needed to reassure himself that he would sleep.

The smell of acacia hung over us.

'I think I'll go to bed,' he said. 'I shall be able to sleep tonight. You know, I've been getting out of practice.'

CHAPTER XVIII

OUTBURST

THE last college meeting of the academic year took place a fortnight after Brown's claret party. By tradition, it was called for a Saturday morning, to distinguish it from all other meetings of the year. For this was the one at which examination results were considered; the last of the results were published that morning, and Brown and I studied them together, a couple of hours before the bell was due to ring. There were several things to interest us – but the chief was that we could not find Dick Winslow's name. Brown thought it might be a clerical mistake, and rang up the examiners to make sure. There was no mistake. He had done worse than one could have believed.

The meeting began at half-past eleven. As the room filled up, whispers about young Winslow were passing round the table; Winslow himself had not yet come. In the whispers one could hear excitement, sometimes pity, sometimes pleasure, sometimes pity and pleasure mixed. At last Winslow entered and strode to his place, looking at no one there.

An old man, who had not picked up the news, said a cheerful good morning.

'Good morning to you,' said Winslow in a flat leaden desolate voice. He was remote, absent-minded in his misery.

There were some minor courtesies before the meeting. Winslow was asked a question. He sat mute. He could not rouse himself to a tart reply. His head had sunk down, bent towards the table.

Despard-Smith, who had taken the chair since the Master fell ill, at last opened the business. The sacramental order was followed, even at this special examination meeting. There was only one trivial matter connected with livings: then came the financial items, when as a rule Winslow did most of the talking and entertained us in his own style. He could usually be relied on to keep us for at least half-an-hour – just as he had done at Roy's election. That morning, when Despard-Smith asked:

'Bursar, will you take us through your business?'

Winslow replied in defeat and dejection:

'I don't think it's necessary. It explains itself.'

He said nothing more. He sat there, the object of curious, pitying, triumphant glances. There were some who remembered his arrogance, his cutting words. An opponent made several financial proposals: Winslow had not the strength even to object.

Then Jago, our candidate in the election, the Senior Tutor (who had been an enemy of Winslow's for years past) went through the examination results name by name. There were startling successes: there was a man who had a great academic future; there were failures of the hardworking and dense, there were failures among the gilded youth. There was one failure owing to a singular personal story. The Senior Tutor went through from subject to subject, until at last he came to history, which young Winslow had studied. The table was very quiet. I looked at Roy, and his expression filled me with alarm. Roy's eyes were fixed on Winslow, eyes full of angry pity, sad and wild. Since the claret party he had been unendurably depressed, and much of the time he had shut himself up alone.

The Senior Tutor congratulated Brown on the performance of one pupil. He exuded enthusiasm over another. Then he looked at his list and paused. He said: 'I think there's nothing else to report,' and hurried on to the next subject.

It had been meant as sympathy, I believed. How Winslow felt it, no one could know. He sat silent, eyes fixed on the table, as though he had not heard.

We had not quite finished the business by one o'clock, but broke off for lunch. Lunch was laid in an inner room; it was cold, but on the same profuse scale as the tea before the usual meetings. There were piles of sandwiches, pâtés, jellies, meringues, pastries, savouries, jugs of beer, decanters of hock, claret, burgundy: the sight of the meal drew approving cries from some of the old men.

Most of the society ate their lunch with zest. Winslow stood apart, staring out of the window, taking one single sandwich. Roy watched him; he looked at no one but Winslow, he said nothing, his eyes sharpened. I noticed him push the wine away, and I was temporarily relieved. Someone spoke to him, and received a sharp uncivil answer, unlike Roy even at his darkest.

There were only a few speeches after lunch, and then the meeting closed. Men filed out, and I waited for Roy. Then I noticed Winslow still sitting at the table, the bursarial documents, order-book and files in front of him: he stayed in his place, too lost and dejected to move. Roy's eyes were on him. The three of us were left alone in the room. Without glancing at me or speaking, Roy sat down by Winslow's side.

'I am dreadfully sorry about Dick,' he said.

'That's nice of you.'

'And I am dreadfully sorry you've had to sit here today. When one's unhappy, it's intolerable to have people talking about one. It's intolerable to be watched.'

He was speaking with extreme and morbid fervour, and Winslow looked up from the table.

'You don't care what they say,' Roy cried, his eyes alight, 'but you want them to leave you alone. But none of us are capable of that much decency. I haven't much use for human beings. Have you, Winslow, have you? You know what people are feeling now, don't you? They're feeling that you've been taken down a peg or two. They're thinking of the times you've snubbed them. They're saying complacently how arrogant and rude you've been. But they don't matter. None of us matter.'

His tone was not loud but very clear, throbbing with an anguished and passionate elation.

Winslow looked at him.

'There is something in what they say, young man,' he said with resignation.

'Of course there is. There's something in most things they say about anyone.' Roy laughed. It was a frightening sound. 'They say I'm a waster and seduce women. There's something in that too.'

I moved round the table, and put a hand on his shoulder. Frantically he shook it off.

'Would you like to know how much there is in it?' he cried. 'We're both miserable. It may relieve you just a bit. Would you like to know how many loving invitations I've coaxed for myself – out of women connected with this college?'

Winslow was roused out of his wretchedness.

'Don't trouble yourself, Calvert. It's no concern of mine.'

'That's why I shall do it.' Roy took a sheet of blank paper, began to write fast in his fluent scholar's hand. I seized his arm, and his pen made a line across the paper.

He swore with frenzied glee. 'Go away, Lewis,' he said. At that moment the elation had reached its height. 'Go away. You're no use. This is only for Winslow and me. I need to finish it now.'

He wrote a few more words, dashed off his signature, gave the sheet to Winslow. 'This has been a frightful day for you,' Roy cried. 'Keep this to remind you that people don't matter.'

He smiled, said good afternoon, went with quick strides out of the room. There was a silence.

'This is distressing,' said Winslow.

'He'll calm down soon.' I was alert, ready to explain, ready to guard secrets once more.

'I never had any idea that Calvert was capable of making an exhibition of himself. Is this the first time it has happened?'

I evaded and lied. I had never seen Roy lose control until this afternoon, I said. It was a shock to me, as it was to Winslow. Of course, Roy was sensitive, highly strung, easily affected by the sorrows of his friends. He was profoundly upset over the Master, and it was wearing his nerves to see so much suffering. I tried to keep as near the truth as I safely could. In addition, I said, taking a risk, Roy was very fond of Winslow's son.

Winslow was recalled to his own wretchedness. He looked away from me, absently, and it was some time before he asked, in a flat tone:

'I'm very ignorant of these matters. Should you say that Calvert was seriously unstable?'

I did not tell Winslow any of the truth. He was a very clever man, but devoid of insight; and I gave him the sort of explanation which most people find more palatable than the strokes of fate. I said that Roy was physically not at his best. His blood pressure was low, which helped to make him despondent. I explained how he had been overworking for years, how his long solitary researches had affected his health and depressed his spirits.

'He's a considerable scholar, from all they say,' said Winslow indifferently. 'I had my doubts about him once, but I've found him an engaging young man.'

'There's nothing whatever to worry about.'

'You know him well,' said Winslow. 'I expect you're right. I think you should persuade him to take a good long holiday.'

Winslow looked down at the sheet of paper. It was some time before he spoke. Then he said:

'So there is something in the stories that have been going round?'

'I don't know what he has written there,' I said. 'I've no doubt that the stories are more highly painted than the facts. Remember they've been told you by people who envy him.'

'Maybe,' said Winslow. 'Maybe. If those people have this communication,' he tapped the paper, 'I don't see how Master Calvert is going to continue in this college. The place will be too hot to hold him.'

'Do you want to see that happen?' I was keyed up to throw my resolve against his. Winslow was thinking of his enemies in the college, how a scandal about Roy would confute them, how he could use it in the present struggle. He stared at me, and told me so without any adornment.

'You can't do it,' I said, with all the power I could call on.

'Why not?'

'You can't do it. You know some of the reasons that brought Calvert to the state he was in this afternoon. They're enough to stop you absolutely, by themselves.'

'If you'd bring it to a point—'

'I'll bring it to a point. We both know that Calvert lost control of himself. He got into a state pretty near despair. And he wouldn't have got into that unless he'd seen that you were unhappy and others were pleased at your expense. Who else had any feeling for you?'

'It doesn't matter to me one way or the other,' said Winslow.

Then I asked:

'Who else had any feeling for your son Dick? You know that Calvert was upset about him. Who else had any feeling for your son?'

Winslow looked lost, bewildered, utterly without arrogance or strength. He looked sadly away from me. He did not speak for some moments. At last in a tired, dejected, completely uninterested tone, he said, the words coming out slowly:

'What shall I do with this?' He pointed to the sheet of paper.

'I don't mind,' I said, knowing that it was safe.

'Perhaps you'd better have it.'

Winslow pushed it towards me, but did not give another glance as I walked to the fireplace, and put a match to it over the empty grate.

CHAPTER XIX

THE COST OF KNOWLEDGE

I WENT up to Roy's room. He was lying on his sofa, stretched out and relaxed. He jumped up and greeted me with a contrite smile.

'Have I dished everything?' he said.

He was quite equable now, affectionate, and happy because the shadow had passed over.

'Have I dished everything?' he said.

'I think I've settled it,' I said, in tiredness and strain. I could let myself go at last. I felt overwhelmed by responsibility. 'But you'll do something one day that I can't settle.'

'I'm frightened of that too,' said Roy.

'I shan't always be there to pick up the pieces,' I said.

'You look pretty worn. I need to order you some strawberries for tea,' he said. He went into his bedroom to telephone, and talked to the kitchens in the voice of the senior fellow, ludicrously like the life. I could not help but smile, despite fatigue and worry and unreasonable anger. He came back and stood looking down at me.

'It's very hard on you,' he said, suddenly but very quietly. 'Having me to look after as well as poor Sheila. There's nothing I can say, is there? You know as much about it as I do. Or at least, if you don't now, you never will, you know.'

'Never mind,' I said.

'Of course,' said Roy, 'just at this minute I feel that I shall never be depressed again.'

In the next few days he spent much of his time with me. He was inventive and entertaining, as though to show me that I need not worry. He was quite composed and even-spirited, but not as carefree as after the first outburst. The innocence, the rapture, the hope, did not flood him and uplift him. He put on his sparkle for my benefit, but underneath he was working something out. What it was I could not guess. I caught him looking at me several times with a strange expression. There was something left unsaid.

On a night early in July, he invited me out to dinner in the town. It was strange for us to dine together in a restaurant in Cambridge: we had not done so since he became a fellow. It was stranger still for Roy to be forcing the conversation, to be unspontaneous, anxious to make a confidence and yet held back. He was specially anxious to look after me; he had brought a bottle of my favourite wine, and had chosen the dinner in advance out of dishes that I liked. He told me some gleeful anecdotes of people round us. But we came to the end of the meal and left the restaurant: he had still not managed to speak.

It was a fine and glowing evening, and I suggested that we should walk through one of the colleges down to the river. Roy shook his head.

'We're bound to meet someone if we do,' he said. 'They'll catch us. Some devils will catch us.' He was smiling, mocking himself. 'I don't want to be caught. I need to say something to you. It's not easy.'

So we walked to Garret Hostel Bridge. There was no one standing there, though some young men and girls on bicycles came riding over. Roy looked down into the water. It was burnished in the bright evening light, and the willows and bridges seemed to be painted beneath the surface, leaf by leaf and line by line: it was the time, just as the sun was dying, when all colours gained a moment of enhancement, and the reflections of the trees were brilliant.

'Well?' I said.

'I suppose I need to talk,' said Roy.

In a moment he said:

'I know what you think. About my nature. About the way I'm made.'

'Then you know more than I do,' I said, trying to distract him, but he turned on me in a flash with a sad, teasing, acute smile.

'That's what you say when you want someone to think you're nice and kind and a bit of an old buffer. I've heard you do it too often. It's quite untrue. You mustn't do it now.'

He looked into the water again.

'I know enough to be going on with,' he said. 'I know you reasonably well, old boy. I have seen what you believe about me.'

I did not answer. It was no use pretending.

'You believe I've got my sentence, don't you? I may get time off for good conduct – but you don't believe that I can get out altogether. A bit of luck can make a difference on the surface. And I need to struggle, because that can make a little difference too. But really, whatever happens to me, I can never change. I'm always sentenced to be myself. Isn't that what you believe? Please tell me.'

I did not reply for a moment. Then I said:

'I can't alter what you say – enough to matter.'

'Just so,' he said.

He cried:

'It's too stark for me. I can't believe it.'

He said quietly:

'I can't believe as you do, Lewis. It would make life pointless. My life isn't all that important, but I know it better than anyone else's. And I know that I've been through misery that I wouldn't inflict on a living soul. No one could deserve it. I couldn't deserve it, whatever I've done or whatever I shall do. You know that—'

'Yes, I know that,' I said.

'If you're right, I've gone through that quite pointlessly. And I shall again. I can't leave it behind. If you're right, it could happen to others. There must be others who go through the same. Without reason, according to you. Just as a pointless joke.'

'It must happen to a few,' I said. 'To a few unusual men.'

'I can't accept a joke like that,' he said. 'It would be like living in a prison governed by an imbecile.'

He was speaking with passion and with resentment I had never heard. Now I could feel what the terrible nights had done to him. Yet they had not left him broken, limp, or resigned. He was still choosing the active way. His whole body, as he leaned over the bridge, was vigorous with determination and purpose.

Neither of us spoke for some time. I too looked down. The brilliant colours had left the sky and water, and the reflections of the willows were dark by now.

'There's something else,' said Roy. His tone was sad and gentle.

He added, after a pause:

'I don't know how I'm going to say it. I've needed to say it all night. I don't know how I can.'

He was still gazing down into the water.

'Lewis,' he said, 'you believe something that I'm not strong enough to believe. There might come a time – there might come a time when I was held back – because of what you believe.'

I muttered.

'I've got a chance,' he said. 'But it will be a near thing. I need to have nothing hold me back. You can see that, can't you?'

'I can see that,' I said.

'You believe in predestination,' he said. 'It doesn't prevent you battling on. It would prevent me, you know. You're much more robust than I am. If I believed as you believe, I couldn't go on.'

He went on:

'I think you're wrong. I need to act as though you're wrong. It may weaken me if I know what you're thinking. There may be times when I shall not want to be understood. I can't risk being weakened. Sooner than be weakened, I should have to lose everything else. Even you.'

A punt passed under the bridge and broke the reflections. The water had ceased swirling before he spoke again.

'I shan't lose you,' he said. 'I don't think I could. You won't get rid of me. I've never felt what intimacy means, except with you. And you—'

'It is the same with me.'

'Just so,' said Roy.

He added very quietly:

'I wouldn't alter anything if I could help it. But there may come a time when I get out of your sight. There may come a time when I need to keep things from you.'

'Has that time come?' I asked.

He did not speak for a long time.

'Yes,' he said.

He was relieved to have it over. As soon as it was done, he wanted to assure me that nearly everything would be unchanged. On the way back to the college, he arranged to see me in London with an anxiety, a punctiliousness, that he never used to show. Our meetings had always been casual, accidental, comradely: now he was telling me that they would go on unchanged, our comradeship would not be touched; the only difference was that some of his inner life might be concealed.

It was the only rift that had come between us. During the time we had known each other, his life had been wild and mine disordered, but our relation had been profoundly smooth, beyond anything in my experience. We had not had a quarrel, scarcely an irritable word.

It made his rejection of intimacy hard for me to bear. I was hurt, sharply, sickly and bitterly hurt. I had the same sense of deprivation as if I had been much younger. Perhaps the sense of deprivation was stronger now; for, while as a younger man my vanity would have been wounded, on the other hand I should still have looked forward to intimacies more transfiguring even than this of ours; now I had seen enough to know that such an intimacy was rare, and that it was unlikely I should take part in one again.

Yet he could do no other than draw apart from me. If he were to keep his remnant of hope, he could do nothing else. For I could not hope on his terms: he had seen into me, and that was all.

It had been bitter to watch him suffer and know I could not help. That was a bitterness we all taste, one of the first facts we learn of the human condition. It was far more bitter to know that my own presence might keep him from peace of mind. It was the harshest of ironies: for he was he, and I was I, as Montaigne said, and so we knew each other: just because of that mutual knowledge, I stood in his way.

CHAPTER XX

A YOUNG WOMAN IN LOVE

ROY and Joan became lovers during that summer. I wondered who had taken the initiative – but it was a question without meaning. Roy was ardent, fond of women, inclined to let them see that he desired them, and then wait for the next move: in his self-accusation to Winslow, he said that he 'coaxed invitations' from women, and that was no more than the truth. At the same time, Joan was a warm-blooded young woman, direct and canalised in all she felt and did. She was not easily attracted to men; she was fastidious, diffident, desperately afraid that she would lack physical charm to those she loved. But she had been attracted to Roy right back in the days when she thought he was frivolous and criticised his long nose. She had not known quite what it meant, but gradually he came to be surrounded by a haze of enchantment; of all men he was the first she longed to touch. She stayed at her window to watch him walk through the court. She thought of excuses to take a message to his rooms.

She told herself that this was her first knowledge of lust. She had a taste for the coarse and brutal words, the most direct and uncompromising picture of the facts. This was lust, she thought, and longed for him. She saw him with Rosalind and others, women who were elegant, smart, alluring, and she envied them ferociously, contemptuously and with self-abasement. She thought they were fools; she thought none of them could understand him as she could; and she could not believe that he would ever look at her twice.

She found, incredulously, that he liked her. She heard him make playful love to her, and she repeated the words, like a charm, before she went to sleep at night. At once her longing for him grew into dedicated love, love undeviating, wholehearted, romantic and passionate. And that love became deeper, richer, pervaded all her thoughts, during the months her father lay dying and Roy sat with them in the Lodge.

For she was not blinded by the pulse of her blood. Some things about him she did not see, for no girl of twenty could. But others she saw more vividly, with more strength of fellow-feeling, even with more compassion, than any woman he had known. She could throw aside his caprices and whims, for she had seen him comfort her mother with patience, simplicity and strength. She had seen him suffer with them. She had heard him speak from the depth of feeling, not about her, but about her father's state and human loneliness: after his voice, she thought, all others would seem dull, orotund and complacent. She had watched his face stricken, or as she put it, 'possessed by devils' that she did not understand. She wanted to spend her life in comforting him.

So her love filled her and drove her on. I thought it would be like her if, despite her shrinking diffidence, she finally asked to become his mistress. It was too easy to imagine her, with no confidence at all, talking to him as though fiercely and choosing the forthright words. But that did not really mean that she had taken the initiative. Their natures played on each other. Somehow it would have happened. There was no other end.

From the beginning, Roy felt a deeper concern for her than for anyone he loved. She was, like her mother, strong and defenceless. Stronger and abler than her mother, and even less certain of love. Roy was often irresponsible in love, with women who took it as lightly as he did. But Joan was dependent on him from the first time he kissed her. He could not pretend otherwise. Perhaps he did not wish it otherwise, for he was profoundly fond of her. He was amused by her sulkiness and fierceness, he liked to be able to wipe them away. He had gone through them to the welling depths of emotion, where she was warm, tempestuous, violent and tender.

Like her, he too had been affected by their vigil in the Lodge. It had surrounded her, and all that passed between them, with its own kind of radiance – the radiance of grief, suffering, intense feeling, and ineluctable death. In that radiance, they had talked of other things than love. He had told her more than he had told any woman of his despair, his search, his hope. He was moved to admiration by her strength, which never turned cold, never wilted, stayed steady through the harsh months in the Lodge. There were times when he rested on that strength himself. He came to look upon her as an ally, as someone who might take his hand and lead him out of the dark.

It was not that she had any obvious escape to offer him. She was not a happy young woman, except when she caught light from his presence. She had left her father's faith, and in her beliefs and disbeliefs she was typical of her time. Like me, she was radical in politics and sceptical in religion. But Roy felt with her, as he had done with me, that deep down he could find a common language sometimes. She was unusually clever, but it was not her intellect that he valued. He had spent too much time with clever men; of all of us, he was the most indifferent to the intellect; he was often contemptuous of it. It was not Joan's intellect he valued, but her sense of life. He thought she might help him, and he turned to her with hope.

Meanwhile, the Master's state seemed to change very little. Over the months Joan told us that she could see the slow decline. Gradually he ate less, was sick more often, spent more of his time in bed; he had had little pain throughout the illness, and was free of it now; the curve dipped very slowly, and it was often hard for her and her mother to realise that he was dying. He was so mellow and understanding that it humbled everyone round him, and they spoke of him with magnified affection. They spoke of him in quiet tones, full of something like hero worship. Lady Muriel, so Joan said, was gentler than anyone had ever known her.

I thought of that comment when I next saw her. Throughout the year, at the Master's request, she had stoically continued some of her ordinary entertaining, and the official Lodge lunches had gone on without check. She had, however, asked no guests at night. It was Joan's idea that Roy and I should call in after dinner one night in July, and treat her to a four at bridge. Like Lord Boscastle, Lady Muriel liked a game of bridge more than most things in the world; she had deprived herself of the indulgence since the Master fell ill.

Roy and I entered the drawing-room that night as though we had been invited by Joan, and Lady Muriel was still enough herself to treat me so.

'I am always glad for my daughter to have her friends in the house, Mr Eliot,' she said. 'I am only sorry that I have not been able to see as much of the fellows recently as I used to set myself.'

She sat in her armchair, stiff and formal. She looked a little older; her eyelids had become heavier, and her cheeks were pinched. But, as she spoke to me, her back was as poker-like as ever, and her voice just as unyielding. She said:

'How is your wife, Mr Eliot? I do not remember seeing her for a considerable time.'

'She's rather better, Lady Muriel.'

'I am very glad to hear it. I am still hoping that you will find a suitable house in Cambridge, so that you will not be separated so often. I believe there are suitable houses in Grantchester Meadows.'

She looked at me suspiciously, and then at her daughter, as though she were signalling my married state. It seemed incredible that she should think me a danger when she could see Joan in Roy's presence. For Joan was one of those women who are physically transmuted by the nearness of their lover, as it seemed by the bodily memory of the act of love. Her face was softer for hours together, the muscles relaxed, the lines of her mouth altered as she looked at him. Even her strong coltish gawky gait became loosened, when he was there.

Roy had been deputed to propose bridge. Lady Muriel was gratified, but at once objected:

'I couldn't, Roy. I have not touched a card for months.'

'We need you to,' said Roy. 'Do play with us.'

'I think it would be better if I left you three to yourselves,' she said.

'You don't think you ought, do you, Lady Mu?' Roy asked quietly. She looked confused.

'Perhaps it isn't the most appropriate time—'

'Need you go without the little things?' said Roy. 'I'm sure the Master would tell you not to.'

'Perhaps he would,' said Lady Muriel, suddenly weak.

We played some bizarre rubbers. Roy arranged for stakes of sixpence a hundred, explaining, out of pure devilry, that 'poor old Lewis can't afford more. If he's going to save up for a suitable house.' (Lady Muriel's idea of a 'suitable house' for me was something like the house of a superior college servant: and Roy had listened with delight.) Even at those stakes, Lady Muriel took several pounds from both Roy and me. It gave her great pleasure, for she had an appetite for money as well as for victory. The night passed, Lady Muriel's winnings mounted; Joan was flushed and joyful with Roy at the same table; Lady Muriel dealt with her square, masterful hands and played with gusto. Yet she was very quiet. Once the room would have rung with her indignant rebukes – 'I am surprised you had such diamonds, Mr Eliot'. But now, though she was pleased to be playing, though she enjoyed her own skill, she had not the heart to dominate the table. After Roy's word about the Master, she was subdued.

It was a long time before she seemed to notice the heterogeneous play. For it was the oddest four. Lady Muriel herself was an excellent player, quick, dashing, with a fine card memory. Joan was very good. I was distinctly poor, and Roy hopelessly bad; I might have been adequate with practice, but he could never have been. He was quite uninterested, had no card sense, disliked gambling, and had little idea of the nature of odds. It was curious to see him frowning over his hand, thinking three times as long as anyone at the table: then he would slap down the one card for which there was no conceivable justification. It was hard to guess what could be going on in his mind.

Joan was smiling lovingly. For he had entered into it out of good nature, but she knew that he was irritated. He chose to do things expertly, or not at all.

At last Lady Muriel said:

'Do you like playing bridge, Roy?'

He smiled.

'I like playing with you, Lady Mu.'

She was just ready to deal, but held the pack in her hand.

'Do you like the game?'

'Of course I do.'

'Do you really like the game, Roy?' Her tone was not her usual firm one, but insistent. Roy looked at her, and gave her an affectionate smile.

'No, not very much, Lady Mu,' he said.

'It's good of you to give up your evening,' she said. She added, in a low, almost inaudible murmur: 'I wonder if the Master ever liked the game. I don't remember asking him. I'm afraid he may have felt the same as you.'

She still did not deal. Suddenly we saw the reason. A tear rolled down her face.

She felt ashamed, she tried to imagine now things which had not troubled her for thirty years. It was almost incredible, as Roy said to me late that night in the garden, that she could have played with her husband night after night and never have known if he enjoyed the game. She was broken down by his heightened understanding, as he came near to death. Her imagination was quickened; she wanted to make up for all her obtuseness had cost him. She felt unworthy. If his illness had made him more selfish, had worn her out with trouble, she would have undergone less pain.

I was asked myself to call on the Master towards the end of August. Roy had been obliged to return to Berlin in order to give a course of lectures, and it was Joan who gave me the message. She had heard from Roy the day before, and could not help telling me so. 'He doesn't keep me waiting for letters,' she said, happily and humbly. 'I never expected he'd write so often.' She longed to confess how much she loved him, she longed to throw away her self-respect.

By this time the Master did not often leave his bed, and I looked at him as he lay there. His face had become that of a very old man; it was difficult to remember him in the days when he seemed so well preserved. The skin was dried up, waxy-yellow, lined and pouched. His eyes had sunk deeply in their orbits, and the lids were very dark. Yet he managed to keep his voice enough like its former self not to upset those who listened to him.

He spoke to me with the same kind, detached curiosity that had become his habit. He asked after my affairs as though nothing else interested him. Suddenly he saw that he was distressing me.

'Tell me, Eliot,' he said gently, 'would it embarrass you less if I talk of what it's like to be in this condition?'

'Much less,' I said.

'I believe you mean that,' he said. 'You're a strange man.'

'Well,' he went on, 'stop me if I ramble. I've got something I particularly want to say to you, before you go. I can think quite clearly. Sometimes I fancy I think more clearly that I ever did in my life. But then the ideas start running away from me, and I get tired. Remember, this disease is something like being slowly starved.'

He was choosing the tone which would distress me least. He went on to discuss the election of his successor; he asked about the parties and intrigues, and talked with his old sarcastic humour, with extraordinary detachment, as though he were an observer from another world – watching the human scene with irony, and the kind of pity which hides on the other side of cynicism. He made one or two good jokes. Then he asked whether the college had expected to get the election over before now. I said yes. He smiled.

'It can't be long,' he said. 'There are days even with this disease when you feel a little better. And you *hope*. It's ridiculous, but you hope. It seems impossible that your will should count for nothing. Then you realise that it's *certain* that you must die in six months. And you think it is too horrifying to bear. People will tell you, Eliot, that uncertainty is the worst thing. Don't believe them. Certainty is the worst thing.'

He was very tired, and closed his eyes. I thought how he was facing death with stoicism and with faith. Yet even he would have prayed: take this from me at least. Do not let me be certain of the time of my death. His faith assured him that he would pass into another existence. But that was a comfort far away from the animal fact. Just like the other comfort that I should one day have to use myself: they tell me that, when I am dead, I shall not know. Those consolations of faith or intellect could not take away the fear of the animal fact. (At least mine seemed a consolation of the intellect. There was to be a time when it recoiled on me.)

He began to talk again, but now he seemed light-headed, his words flew like the associations of a dream. I had to remind him:

'You said you had something important to tell me, before I go.'

He made an effort to concentrate. The ideas set off in flight again, but he frowned and gathered up his will. He found a clue, and said:

'What is happening about Roy Calvert?'

'He's in Berlin. The proofs of the new part of the liturgy are just coming in.'

'Berlin. . . . I heard some talk about him. Didn't he take my daughter to a ball?'

'Yes.'

He was quiet. I wondered what he was thinking.

Again he frowned with concentration.

'Eliot,' he said. 'I want you to do me a favour. Look after Roy Calvert. He's the great man of the future in my field. I like to think that he won't forget all about my work. Look after him. He'll need it. People like him don't come twice in a generation. I want you to do me a favour. Look after Roy Calvert.'

That cry came partly from the altruistic kindness in which he was ending his life. I was moved and shaken as I gave him my promise.

But it was not only self-forgetting kindness that brought out that cry; it was also a flicker of his own life; it was a last assertion of his desire not to be forgotten. He had not been a distinguished scholar, and he was a modest man who ranked himself lower than he deserved. But he still did not like to leave this mortal company without something to mark his place. For him, as for others I had sat by in their old age, as for Mr March, it was abhorrent to imagine the world in which he had lived going on as though he had never been. It was a support, bare but not illusory, to know that he would leave a great scholar behind him, whom he could trust to say: 'You will find that point in one of old Royce's books. He made it completely clear.' A shadow of himself would linger as Roy became illustrious. His name would be repeated among his own kind. It was his defiance of the dark.

I thought by his bedside, and again a few minutes later when I met Joan, how tough the core of our selves can be. The Master's vanities had been burned away, he was detached and unselfish as he came towards his death, and yet the desire to be remembered was intact. And Joan was waiting for me in the drawing-room, and her first question was:

'What did he say about Roy?'

She knew that the Master had wished to tell me something. It was necessary for her to know any fact which affected Roy.

I told her that the Master had asked me to do what I could for him.

'Is that all?'

'Yes.'

'There was nothing else?'

I repeated one or two of the Master's observations, looking at us from a long way off.

'I mean, there was nothing else about Roy?'

She was deeply attached to her father, she had suffered by his side – but it counted for nothing beside her love for Roy. She was tough in her need for him. All her power was concentrated into feeling about him. Human beings in the grip of passion are more isolated than ever, I thought. She was alone with her love. Perhaps, in order to be as healthy and strong as she was, one had to be as tough.

The Master had asked me to look after Roy. As I listened to that girl, I felt that she would take on the task, even if she knew as much as I did. She would welcome the dangers that she did not know. She cross-examined me with single-minded attention. She made me hope.

CHAPTER XXI

TOWARDS THE FUNERAL

Roy came back from Berlin in October, and I watched contrasts in Joan as sharp as I had seen them in any woman. Often she was a girl, fascinated by a lover whom she found enchanting, seeing him hazily, adoringly, through the calm and glorious Indian summer. The college shimmered in the tranquil air, and Joan wanted to boast of him, to show off the necklace he had brought her. She loved being teased, having her sulkiness devastated, feeling mesmerised in front of his peculiar mischief. She was too much a girl not to let his extravagant presents be seen by accident; she liked her contemporaries to think she was an abandoned woman, pursued by a wicked, distinguished, desirable and extremely lavish lover. Once or twice, in incredulous delight, she had to betray her own secret.

She confided it to Francis Getliffe and his wife, and Francis talked to me. He liked and understood her, and he could not believe that Roy would bring her anything but unhappiness. Francis had never believed that

Roy was a serious character; now he believed it less than ever, for Roy had come back from Berlin, apparently cheerful and composed, but ambiguous in his political attitude. This had already made me anxious, and I had told him so. For Francis it was just a source of irritation. Like many scientists of his age, he was a straightforward progressive, with technical backing behind his opinions and no nonsense or frills.

He was angered by Roy's new suggestions, which were subtle, complex and seemed to Francis utterly irresponsible. He was angered almost as much by Roy's inconsistency; for Roy, despite his friends in high places in the Third Reich, had just smuggled into England a Jewish writer and his wife. It was said that Roy had taken some risks to do it; I knew for certain that he was spending a third of his income on them. Francis heard this news with grudging approval, and was then maddened when Roy approached him with a solemn face and asked whether, in order to ease relations with Germany, the university could not decree that Jewish scholars were 'Welsh by statute'.

'He'll be no good to her,' said Francis.

'She's very happy now.'

'She's happy because he's good at making love,' said Francis. 'It won't last. She wants someone who'll marry her and make her a decent husband. Do you think he will?'

Francis was right about Joan. She needed marriage more than most women, because she had so often felt diffident and unlike others. It was more essential to her than to someone like Rosalind, who had never tormented herself with thoughts of whether men would pass her by. Joan recognised that it was essential to her, if ever she were to become whole. She thought now, like any other girl, of marrying Roy, sometimes hoped, sometimes feared: but she was much too proud to give him a sign. She was so proud that she told herself they had gone into this love affair as equals; she had done it with her eyes open, and she must not let herself forget it.

So she behaved like a girl in love, sometimes like a proud and unusual girl, sometimes like anyone who has just known what rapture is. But I saw her when she was no longer rapturous, no longer proud, no longer exalted by the wonder of her own feelings, but instead compassionate, troubled, puzzled by what was wrong with him, set upon helping him. For she had seen him haunted in the summer, and she would not let herself rest.

She was diffident about attracting him: but she had her own kind of arrogance, and she believed that she alone could understand him. And she was too healthy a woman, too optimistic in her flesh and bone, not to feel certain that there was a solution; she did not believe in defeat.

It was not made easy for her – for, though he wanted her help, he did not tell her all the truth. He shut out parts of his nature from her: shut them out, because he did not want to recognise them himself. She knew that he was visited by desperate melancholy, but he told her as though it came from a definite cause. She knew he was frightened at any premonition that he was going to be attacked again: she believed, as he wanted to, that they could find a charm which kept him in the light.

The Master lay overlooking the court through that sunny, tranquil autumn. Joan tried to learn what faith would mean to Roy.

She found it unfamiliar, foreign to her preconceptions of him, foreign to her own temperament. One thing did not put her off, as it did Francis Getliffe and so many others; since she loved him, she was not deceived by some of his fooling; she believed that underneath his thought was grave. But the thought itself she found strange, and often forbidding.

He was searching for God. Like me, she had heard her father's phrase. But she discovered that the search was not as she imagined. She had expected that he was longing to be at one with the unseen, to know the immediate presence of God. Instead, he seemed to be seeking the authority of God. He seemed to want to surrender his will, to be annihilated as a person. He wanted to lose himself eternally in God's being.

Joan knew well enough the joy of submission to her lover; but she was puzzled, almost dismayed, that this should be his vision of faith. She loved him for his wildness, his recklessness, his devil-may-care; he took anyone alive as his equal; why should he think that faith meant that he must throw himself away? 'Will is a burden. Men are freest when they get rid of will.' She rebelled at his paradox, with all her sturdy protestant nature. She hated it when he told her that men might be happiest under the authority of the state – 'apart from counter-suggestible people like you, Joan.' But she hated most his vision, narrow and intense, of the authority of God.

In his search for religion, he did not give a thought to doing good. She knew that many people thought of him as 'good', she often did herself – and yet any suggestion that one should interfere with another's actions offended him. 'Pecksniffery', he called it. He was for once angry with her when she told him that he was good himself. 'Good people don't do good,' he said later, perversely. In fact, the religious people he admired were nearly all of them contemplative. Ralph Udal sponged on him shamelessly, wanted to avoid any work he did not like, prodded Roy year in, year out to get him a comfortable living, and was, very surprisingly, as tolerant of others as of himself. None of this detracted from Roy's envy of his knowledge of God. And old Martineau, since he took to the religious life, had been quite useless. To Roy it was self-evident that Martineau knew more of God than all the virtuous, active, and morally useful men.

Joan could not value the Martineaus and Udals so (nor could I, and even less in retrospect), and she argued with him. But she did not argue about his experience. He told her, as he told me that night we walked on the Roman road, about his hallucination that he was lost, thrown out of God's world, condemned to opposition while all others were at rest. That sense had visited him once again, for the third time, during the blackness of the summer.

Joan had never met anything like it, but she knew it was a passionate experience. It was a portent that nothing could exorcise or soften. While the remembrance haunted him, he could not believe.

She called on all she knew to save him from it. She pressed love upon him, surrounded him with love (too much, I sometimes thought, for she did not understand the claustrophobia of being loved). She asked others about the torments of doubt and faith – loyally and unconvincingly keeping out Roy's name. She talked to me: it cost her an effort, for, though she had with difficulty come to believe that I admired her and wished her well, she was never at ease with me as Rosalind was. Rosalind had confided in me when she was miserable over Roy – but it had been simple nature to her to flatter me, to make me feel that in happier days she might not have been indifferent to me. With Joan, there was not a ray of flirtatiousness, not the faintest aura of love to spare. Except as a source of information, I did not exist. Each heart beat served him, and him alone.

She came to a decision which took her right outside herself. Wise or unwise, it showed how she was spending her imagination in his life. Herself, she stayed in her solid twentieth-century radical unbelief: but him she tried to persuade to act as though he had found faith, in the hope that faith would come.

It was bold and devoted of her. And there were a few weeks, unknown at the time to anyone but themselves, when he took her guidance. He acted to her as though his search was over. He went through the gestures of belief, not in ritual but in his own mind. He struggled to hypnotise himself.

He could not keep it up. Sadness attacked him, and he was afraid that the melancholy was returning. Even so, he knew that his acts of faith were false; he felt hollow and gave them up. Inexplicably, his spirits rose. The attempt was at an end.

Joan did not know what to do next. The failure left its mark on her. She was seized with an increased, an unrestrainable passion to marry him. Even her pride could not prevent her giving signs.

It became obvious as one saw them together in the late autumn. Often she was happy, flushing at his teasing, breaking out into her charming laugh, which was richer now that she had been loved. But more than once I saw them in a party, when she thought herself unobserved: she looked at him with a glance that was heavy with her need to be sure of him.

I was anxious for her, for about that time I got the impression that something had broken. She did not seem to know, except that she was becoming more hungry for marriage; but I felt sure that for him the light had gone out. Why, I could not tell or even guess. It did not show itself in any word he spoke to her, for he was loving, attentive, insistent on giving her some respite from the Lodge, always ready to sit with her there in the last weeks of her father's life.

He was good at dissimulating, though he did it seldom; yet I was certain that I was right, for lack of ease in a love affair is one of the hardest things to conceal.

I was puzzled. One night in late November I heard him make a remark which sounded entirely strange, coming from him. It was said in fun, but I felt that it was forced out, endowed with an emotion he could not control. The occasion was quite trivial. The three of us had been to a theatre, and Roy had mislaid the tickets for our coats. It took us some time, and a little explanation, to redeem them. Joan scolded him as we walked to the college along the narrow street.

'I didn't do it on purpose,' he said.

'You're quite absurd,' said Joan. 'It was very careless.'

Then Roy said:

'Think as well of me as you can.' He was smiling, and so was she, but his voice rang out clear. 'Think as well of me as you can.'

I had never before heard him, either in play or earnest, show that kind of concern. It was a playful cry, and she hugged his arm and laughed. Yet it came back to my ears, clear and thrilling, long after outbursts of open feeling had gone dead.

Through November the Master became weaker and more drowsy. He was eating very little, he was always near the borderline of sleep. Joan said that she thought he was now dying. The end came suddenly. On the second of December the doctor told Lady Muriel and Joan that he had pneumonia, and that it would soon be over. Two days later, just as we were going into hall for dinner, the news came that the Master had died.

After hall, I went to see Roy, who had not been dining. I found him alone in his rooms, sitting at a low desk with a page of proofs. He had already heard the news.

He spoke of Joan and her mother. He said that he would complete the 'little book' on heresies as soon as he was clear of the liturgy. He would bring it out as a joint publication by Royce and himself. 'Would that have pleased him?' said Roy. 'Perhaps it would please them a little.'

A woman's footsteps sounded on the stairs, and Joan came in. She looked at me, upset to see me there. Without a word, Roy took her in his arms and kissed her. For a moment she rested with her head against his shoulder, but she heard me get up to go.

'Don't bother, Lewis,' she said. She was quite dry-eyed. 'I've come to take Roy away, if he will. Won't you come to mother?' she asked him, her eyes candid with love. 'You're the only person who can be any use to her tonight.'

'I was coming anyway,' said Roy.

'You're very tired yourself,' I said to Joan. 'Hadn't you better take a rest?'

'Let me do what's got to be done before I think about it,' she said.

She was staunch right through. Roy went to eat and sleep in the Lodge until after the funeral. Joan made no claims on him; she asked him to look after her mother, who needed him more.

Lady Muriel was inarticulately glad of his presence. She could not say that she was grateful, she could not speak of loss or grief or any regret. She could not even cry. She sat up until dawn each night before the funeral, with Roy beside her. And each night, as she went at last to bed, she visited the room where lay her husband's body.

At the funeral service in the chapel, she and Joan sat in the stalls nearest the altar. Their faces were white but tearless, their backs rigid, their heads erect.

And, after we had returned from the cemetery to the college, word came that Lady Muriel wished to see all the fellows in the Lodge. The blinds of the drawing-room were drawn back now; we filed in and stood about while Lady Muriel shook hands with us one by one. Her neck was still unbent, her eyes pitiably bold. She spoke to each of us in her firm, uncompromising voice, and her formula varied little. She said to me: 'I should like to thank you for joining us on this sad occasion. I appreciate your sign of respect to my husband's memory. I am personally grateful for your kindness during his illness. My daughter and I are going to my brother, and our present intention is to stay there in our house. We may be paying a visit to Cambridge next year, and I hope you will be able to visit us.'

Roy and I walked away together.

'Poor thing,' he said.

He went back to the Lodge to see them through another night. At last Lady Muriel broke down. 'I shall never see him again,' she cried. 'I shall never see him again.' In the drawing-room, where she had bidden us goodbye so formally, that wild, animal cry burst out; and then she wept passionately in Roy's arms, until she was worn out.

For hours Joan left them together. Her own fortitude still kept her from being another drag on Roy. She remained staunch, trying to help him with her mother. Yet that night words were trembling on her lips; she came to the edge of begging him to love her for ever, of telling him how she hungered for him to marry her. She did not speak.

CHAPTER XXII

STRAIN IN A GREAT HOUSE

ROY was working all through the spring in the Vatican Library, and then moved on to Berlin. I only saw him for a few hours on his way through London, but I heard that he was meeting Joan. He had not mentioned her in his letters to me, which were shorter and more stylised than they used to be, though often lit up by stories of his acquaintances in Rome. When I met him, he was affectionate, but neither high-spirited nor revealing. I did not see him again until he returned to England for the summer: as soon as he got back, we were both asked down to Boscastle.

I had twice visited Boscastle by myself, though not since Lady Muriel and Joan had gone to live there. Lady Boscastle had invited me so that she could indulge in two pleasures – tell stories of love affairs, and nag me into being successful as quickly as might be. She had an adamantine will for success, and among the Boscastles she had found no chance to use it. So I came in for it all. She was the first person, albeit then closest to me, to whom I confided my hidden intuition. Yes, I should write books: in the midst of troubles, I had already begun. She half-approved, but was anxious that I might be leaving it too late. She counted on me to carve out something realisable within the next three years. She was sarcastic, flattering, insidious and shrewd. She even invited publishers, whom she had known through her father, down to Boscastle so that I could talk to them.

Since the Royces arrived at the house, I had had no word from her or them. It was June when she wrote to say that Roy was going straight there: she added, the claws just perceptible beneath the velvet, 'I hope this will be acceptable to our dear Joan. It is pleasant to think that it will be almost a family party.'

I arrived in Camelford on a hot midsummer afternoon. A Boscastle car met me, and we drove down the valley. From the lower road, as it came round by the sea, one got a dramatic view of the house, 'our house', 'Bossy' itself.

It stood on the hill, a great pilastered classical front, with stepped terraces leading up from the lawns. When I first went, I was a little surprised that not a stone had been put there earlier than the eighteenth century: but the story explained it all.

Like good whig aristocrats with an eye to the main chance, the Boscastles had taken a step up after 1688. They had been barons for the last two centuries: now they managed to become earls. At the same time – it may not have been a coincidence – they captured a great heiress by marriage. Suitably equipped with an earldom and with money, it was time to think about the house. And so they indulged in the eighteenth-century passion for palatial building.

The previous house, the Tudor Boscastle, had lurked in the valley. The domestic engineers could now supply them with water if they built on the hill. With a firm eighteenth-century confidence that what was modern was best, they tore the Tudor house down to its foundations. They had not the slightest feeling for the past – like most people in a vigorous, expanding age. They were determined to have the latest thing. And they did it in the most extravagant manner, like a good many other Georgian grandees. They built a palace, big enough for the head of one of the small European states. They furnished it in the high eighteenth-century manner. They had ceilings painted by Kent. They had the whole scheme, inside and out, vetted by Lord Burlington, the arbiter of architectural taste.

They impoverished the family for generations: but they had a certain reward. It was a grand and handsome house, far finer than the Tudor one they had destroyed. It impressed one still as being on the loftiest scale. It also impressed one, I thought as I went from my bedroom to a bathroom after tea, as being grandiosely uncomfortable. There were thirty yards of corridors before I got to my bathroom: and the bathroom itself, which had been installed in the nineteenth century, was of preposterous size and struck cold as a vault. There were also great stretches of corridor between the kitchens and the dining-rooms, and no dish ever arrived quite warm.

I discovered one piece of news before I had been in the house an hour. Lord Boscastle had in his gift several of the livings round the countryside; one of these had recently fallen vacant, and Roy had persuaded him to give it to Ralph Udal. So far as I could gather, Roy had sent letter after letter to Lord Boscastle, offered to return from Berlin to describe Udal, invoked both Joan and her mother to speak for him. He was always importunate when begging a favour for someone else. Lord Boscastle had given way, saying that these fellows were much of a muchness, and Udal was now vicar of a small parish, which included the house of Boscastle itself. His church and vicarage were a mile or two along the coast.

I walked there before dinner, thinking that I might find Roy; but Udal was alone in the vicarage, although Roy had called that morning. Udal brought me a glass of sherry on to the lawn. It was a long time since we had last met, but he greeted me with cordiality and with his easy, unprickly, almost impersonal good nature. He had altered very little in appearance; the hair was turning grey over his ears, but since he was twenty-five he had looked a man in a tranquil and indefinite middle age. He was in shirtsleeves, and looked powerful, sunburnt and healthy. He drank his sherry, and smiled at me, with his eyes narrowed by interest and content.

'How do you think Roy is?' he said, going back to my question about Roy's visit.

'How do you?'

'You see much more of him than I do,' said Udal.

'Not since he's been abroad,' I said.

'Well,' said Udal, after a pause, 'I don't think he is to be envied.'

He looked at me with his lazy kindness. 'To tell you the truth, Eliot, I didn't think he was to be envied the first time I set eyes on him. It was the scholarship examination. I saw him outside the hall. I said to myself "that lad will be too good for you. But he's going to have a rough time." '

He smiled, and added: 'It seems to me that I wasn't far wrong.'

He asked me about Roy's professional future. I said that everything must come to him; the university could not help creating a special readership or chair for him within three or four years.

Udal nodded his head.

'He's very talented,' he said. 'Yet you know, Eliot, sometimes I think it would have been better – if he had chosen a different life.'

'Such as?'

'He might have done better to join my trade. He might have found things easier if he'd become a priest.' Suddenly Udal smiled at me. 'You've always disliked my hanging round, in case he was going to surrender, haven't you? I thought it was the least I could do for him, just wait in the slips, so to speak.'

I asked him how much Roy had talked to him about faith. He said, with calm honesty, very little: was there really much to say? Roy had not been looking for an argument. Whichever side he emerged, he had to live his way towards it.

Udal went on:

'Sometimes I wonder whether he would have found it easier – if he'd actually lived a different life. I mean with women.'

'It would have been harder without them,' I said.

'I wonder,' said Udal. 'There's much nonsense talked on these matters, you know. I'm trying to be guided by what I've seen. And some of the calmest and happiest people I've seen, Eliot, have led completely "frustrated" lives. And some of the people I've seen who always seem sexually starved – they're people who spend their whole time hopping in and out of bed. Life is very odd.'

We talked about some acquaintances, then about Roy again. Udal said:

'Well, we shall never know.' Then he smiled. 'But I can give him one bit of relief, anyhow. Now I've got this job, I don't see any particular reason why I should have to borrow any more money from him. It will save him quite a bit.'

I laughed, but I was put off. I tried to examine why. From anyone else, I should have found that shameless candour endearing. I did not mind, in fact I admired, his confidence in his own first-hand experience. I did not mind his pleasure, quite obvious although he was so settled, in an hour of scabrous gossip. They were all parts of an unusual man, who had gone a different way from most of our acquaintances.

Yet I was on edge in his company. Roy had once accused me of disliking him. As we talked that afternoon, I felt that was not precisely true. I did not dislike him, I found him interesting – but I should be glad to leave him, I found his presence a strain. I could not define it further. Was it that he took everything that happened to him too much as his by right? He had slid through life comfortably, without pain, without much self-questioning: did I feel he ought to be more thankful for his luck? Did he accept his own nature too acquiescently? His idleness, his lack of conscience, his amiable borrowing – he took them realistically, without protest, with what seemed to me an over-indulgent pleasure. He looked at himself and was not dissatisfied.

It was strange. Though I was not comfortable with him, he seemed perfectly so with me. He told me of how he proposed to adjust his life, now that at last he had arrived at a decent stopping place.

He intended to devote Sunday and one other day a week to his parish: three days a week to his own brand of biographical scholarship: one day to sheer physical relaxation, mowing his lawn, ambling round the hills, sitting by the sea: which would leave one day 'for serious purposes'. I was curious about the 'serious purposes', and Udal smiled. But he was neither diffident nor coy. He meant to spend this one day a week in preparing himself for the mystical contemplation. One day a week for spiritual knowledge: it sounded fantastically business-like. I said as much, and Udal smiled indifferently.

'I told Roy about it,' he said. 'It's the only time I've ever shocked him.'

It struck me as so odd that I spoke to Roy when we met in the inner drawing-room before dinner. I said that I had heard Udal's timetable.

'It's dreadful,' said Roy. 'It makes everything nice and hygienic, doesn't it?' He shrugged his shoulders, and said:

'Oh, he may as well be left to it.'

Just then Lady Muriel entered and caught the phrase. She gave me a formal, perfunctory greeting: then she turned to Roy and demanded to know whom he was discussing. Her solid arms were folded over her black dress, as I had seen them in the Lodge: my last glimpse of her after the funeral, when she kept erect only by courage and training, was swept aside: she was formidable again. Yet I felt she depended more on Roy than ever.

Roy put his preoccupations behind him, and talked lightly of Udal. 'You must remember him, Lady Mu. You'll like him.' He added: 'You'll approve of him too. He doesn't stay at expensive hotels.'

Lady Muriel did not take the reference, but she continued to talk of Udal as we sat at dinner in the 'painted room'. The table was a vast circle, under the painted Italianate ceiling, and there were only six of us spread round it, the Boscastles, Lady Muriel and Joan, Roy and I.

Lady Muriel's boom seemed the natural way to speak across such spaces.

'I consider,' she told her brother, 'that you should support the new vicar.'

Lord Boscastle was drinking his soup. The butler was experimenting with some device for reheating it in the actual dining-room, but it was still rather cold.

'What are you trying to get me to do now, Muriel?' he said crossly.

'I consider that you should attend service occasionally.' She looked at her sister-in-law. 'I have always regarded going to service as one of the responsibilities of our position. I am sorry to see that it has not been kept up.'

'I refuse to be jockeyed into doing anything of the kind,' said Lord Boscastle with irritation. I guessed that, as Lady Muriel recovered her energies, he was not being left undisturbed. 'I did not object to putting this fellow in to oblige Roy. But I strongly object if Muriel uses the fellow to jockey me with. I don't propose to attend ceremonies with which I haven't the slightest sympathy. I don't see what good it does me or anyone else.'

'It was different for you in college, Muriel,' said Lady Boscastle gently. 'You had to consider other people's opinions, didn't you?'

'I regarded it as the proper thing to do,' said Lady Muriel, her neck stiff with fury. She could think of no retort punishing enough for her sister-in-law, and so pounded on at Lord Boscastle. 'I should like to remind you, Hugh, that the Budes have never missed a Sunday service since they came into the title.'

The Budes were the nearest aristocratic neighbours, whom even Lord Boscastle could not pretend were social inferiors. But that night, pleased by his wife's counter-attack, he reverted to his manner of judicial consideration, elaborate, apparently tentative and tired, in reality full of triumphant contempt.

'Ah yes, the Budes. I forgot you knew them, Muriel. I suppose you must have done before you went off to your various new circles. Yes, the Budes.' His voice trailed tiredly away. 'I should have thought they were somewhat rustic, shouldn't you have thought?'

Revived, Lord Boscastle proceeded to dispose of Udal.

'I wish someone would tell him,' he said in his dismissive tone, 'not to give the appearance of blessing me from such an enormous height.'

'He's a very big man,' said Roy, defending Udal out of habit.

'I'm a rather short one,' said Lord Boscastle. 'And I strongly object to being condescended to from an enormous height.'

But, despite the familiar repartees, there was tension through the party that night.

One source was Joan: for she sat, speaking very little, sometimes, when the rest of us were talking, letting her gaze rest broodingly on Roy. There was violence, reproach, a secret between them. Roy was subdued, as the Boscastles had never seen him, although he put in a word when Lady Muriel was causing too much friction.

Even if Roy and Joan had been in harmony, however, there would still have been frayed nerves that night. For the other source of tension was political. At Boscastle, when I first stayed there, people differed about political things without much heat. But it was now the summer of 1938, and on both sides we were feeling with the force of a personal emotion. The divisions were sharp: the half-tones were vanishing: in college it was 8–6 for Chamberlain and appeasement; here it was 3–3. On the Chamberlain side were Lord Boscastle, Lady Muriel, and Roy. On the other side (which in college were called 'warmongers', 'Churchill men', or 'Bolsheviks') were Lady Boscastle, Joan and I.

Roy's long ambivalence had ended, and he and I were in opposite camps.

Bitterness fired up in a second. Lady Muriel favoured a temporary censorship of the press. I disagreed with her. In those days I did not find it easy to hold my tongue.

'Really, Mr Eliot,' she said, 'I am only anxious to remove the causes of war.'

'I'm anxious,' I said, 'not to lose every friend we have in the world. And then stagger into a war which we shall duly lose.'

'I'm afraid I think that's a dangerous attitude,' said Lord Boscastle.

'It's an attitude which appears to be prevalent among professional people. Mr Eliot's attitude is fairly common among professional people, isn't it, Helen?' Lady Muriel was half-angry, half-exultant at having taken her revenge.

'I should think it very likely,' said Lady Boscastle. 'I think I should expect it to be fairly common among thinking people.' She raised her lorgnette. 'But it's easy to exaggerate the influence of thinking people, shouldn't you agree, Hugh?'

Lord Boscastle did not rise. He was out of humour, I was less welcome than I used to be, but he was never confident in arguing with his wife. And Roy broke in:

'Do you like thinking people, Lady Boscastle?'

He was making peace, but they often struck sparks from each other, and Lady Boscastle replied in her high sarcastic voice:

'My dear Roy, I am too old to acquire this modern passion for dumb oxen.'

'They're sometimes very wise,' said Roy.

'I remember dancing with a number of brainless young men with cauliflower ears,' said Lady Boscastle. 'I found them rather unenlightening. A modicum of brains really does add to a man's charm, you know. Hasn't that occurred to you?'

She was a match for him. Of all the women we knew, he found her the hardest to get round. That night, with Joan silent at the table, he could not persevere; he gave Lady Boscastle the game.

But the rift was covered over, and Lady Muriel began asking energetically what we should do the following day. We were still at dinner, time hung over the great dining-room. No one had any ideas: it seemed as though Lady Muriel asked that question each night, and each night there was a waste of empty time ahead.

'I consider,' said Lady Muriel, 'that we should have a picnic.'

'Why should we have a picnic?' said Lord Boscastle.

'We always used to,' said Lady Muriel.

'I don't remember enjoying one,' he said.

'I always did,' said Lady Muriel with finality.

Lord Boscastle looked to his wife for aid, but she gave a slight smile.

'I can't see any compelling reason why we shouldn't have a picnic, Hugh,' she said, as though she also did not see any compelling reason why we should. 'Apparently you must have had a regular technique. Perhaps Muriel—'

'Certainly,' said Lady Muriel, and shouted to the butler, who was a few feet away. 'You remember the picnics we used to have, don't you, Jonah?' The butler's name was Jones. He had a refined but lugubrious face. 'Yes, my lady,' he said, and I thought I caught a note of resignation. Lady Muriel made a series of executive decisions, like a staff major moving a battalion. Hope sounded in the butler's voice only when he suggested that it might rain.

Lord Boscastle was having a bad evening. We did not stay long over port, for Roy only took one glass and was so quiet that it left all the work to me. When we went into the biggest of the drawing-rooms (called simply the 'sitting-room'; it was a hundred feet long) Lord Boscastle received another blow. His wife never played bridge, and he was relying on Joan to give him his rubber. He asked whether she was ready for a game, with an eager expectant air: at last he was in sight of a little fun.

'I'm sorry, Uncle, I can't,' said Joan. 'I've promised to go for a walk with Roy.'

She said it flatly, unhappily but without concession.

Lord Boscastle sulked: there was no other word for it. He stayed in the room for a few minutes, complaining that it did not seem much to ask, a game of cards after dinner. People were willing to arrange picnics, which he detested, but no one ever exerted themselves to produce a four at bridge. He supposed that he would be reduced to inviting the doctor next.

That was the limit of degradation he imagined that night. In a few minutes, he took a volume from his collection of eighteenth-century memoirs and went off sulkily to bed.

Roy and Joan went out immediately afterwards, and Lady Boscastle, Lady Muriel and I were left alone in the 'sitting-room'. It was clear that Lady Boscastle wanted to talk to me. She made it limpidly clear: but Lady Muriel did not notice. Instead, she brought out a series of improvements which Lady Boscastle should adopt in her regime for the house.

Lady Boscastle could not move up to her own suite, for that meant calling her maid to help her. In all this gigantic mansion, she could not speak a word to me in private. It seemed very comic.

At last she insinuated some doubts about the orders for the next day's picnic. Lady Muriel rebuffed them, but was shaken enough to agree that she should confer with the butler. 'In your study, my dear,' said Lady Boscastle. 'You see, you will have plenty of paper there.'

Lady Muriel walked out, business-like and erect.

'Our dear Muriel's stamina used to be perfectly inexhaustible.' Lady Boscastle's eyes were very bright. 'She has changed remarkably little.'

She went on:

'Lewis, my dear boy, I wanted to talk to you a little about Humphrey. I think I should like your advice.'

Humphrey was the Boscastles' son, whom I had met at Monte Carlo; he was a wild effeminate lad, clever, violent-tempered, restlessly looking for gifted people to respect.

'All his friends,' said Lady Boscastle, 'seem to be singularly precious. I'm not specially concerned about that. I've known plenty of precious young men who become extremely satisfactory afterwards.' She smiled. 'But I should be relieved if he showed any sign of a vocation.'

She talked with cool detachment about her son. It was better for him to do something: he would dissipate himself away, if he just settled down to succeed his father. Their days were over. Lord Boscastle was not willing to accept it, preferred that his son should wait about as he himself haq done; but Lord Boscastle's response to any change was to become more obstinate. Instead of taking a hand in business, he plunged himself into his gorgeous and proliferating snobbery. There was imagination and self-expression in his arrogance. It was his art – but his son would never be able to copy him.

Lady Boscastle asked me to take up Humphrey.

'He will do the talking if you sit about,' she said. 'That is one of your qualities, my dear boy. Do what you can, won't you? I shouldn't like him to go off the rails too far. He would always have his own distinction, you know, whatever he did. But it would distress his father so much. There are very strong bonds between them. These Bevill men are really very unrestrained.'

Lady Boscastle gave a delicate and malicious smile. She had an indulgent amused contempt for men whose emotions enslaved them. There was a cat-like solitariness about her. That night, while everyone else in the party was bored or strained, she was bright-eyed, mocking, cynically enjoying herself. Her concern about her son did not depress her. She waved it away, and talked instead of Roy and Joan; for now, in her invalid years, observing love affairs was what gave her most delight.

She had, of course, no doubt of their relation. Her eyes were too experienced to miss anything so patent. In fact, she was offended because Joan made it too patent. Lady Boscastle had a fastidious sense of proper reserve. 'Of course, my dear boy, it is a great pleasure to brandish a lover, isn't it? Particularly when one has been rather uncompeted for.' Otherwise it seemed to her only what one would expect. She was not used to passing judgments, except on points of etiquette and taste. And she conceded that Roy 'would pass'. She had never herself found him profoundly *sympathique*. I thought that night that I could see the reason. She was suspicious that much of his emotional life had nothing to do with love. She divined that, if she had been young, he would have smiled and made love – but there were depths she could not have touched. She would have resented it then, and she resented it now. She wanted men whose whole emotional resources, all of whose power and imagination, could be thrown into gallantry, and the challenge and interplay of love.

She would have kept him at a distance: but she admitted that other women would have chased him. Her niece was showing reasonable taste. As for her niece, Lady Boscastle had a pitying affection.

She speculated on what was happening that night. 'There's thunder in the air,' she said. She looked at me.

'I know nothing,' I said.

'Of course, he's breaking away,' said Lady Boscastle. 'That jumps to the eye. And it's making her more infatuated every minute. No doubt she feels obliged to put all her cards on the table. Poor Joan, she would do that. She's rather unoblique.'

Lady Boscastle went on:

'And he feels insanely irritable, naturally. It's very odd, my dear Lewis, how being loved brings out the worst in comparatively amiable people. One sees these worthy creatures lying at one's feet and protesting their supreme devotion. And it's a great strain to treat them with even moderate civility. I doubt whether anyone is nice enough to receive absolutely defenceless love.'

'Love affairs,' said Lady Boscastle, 'are not intriguing unless both of you have a second string. Never go lovemaking, my dear boy, unless you have someone to fall back upon in case of accidents. I remember – ah! I've told you already.' She smiled with a reminiscence, sub-acid and amused. 'But our dear Joan would never equip herself with a reserve. She'll never be *rusee*. She's rather undevious for this pastime.'

'It's a pity,' I said.

'Poor Joan. Of course it's she who's taken him out tonight. It's she who wants to get things straight. You saw that, of course. She has insisted on meeting him after dinner tonight. I suppose she's making a scene at this minute. She couldn't wait another day before having it out. I expect that is how she welcomed Master Roy this morning. Poor Joan. She ought to know it's fatal. If a love affair has come to the point when one needs to get things straight, then' – she smiled at me – ''it's time to think a little about the next.'

CHAPTER XXIII

A CRY IN THE EVENING

THE next day was fine, and the rooms of Boscastle stood lofty and deserted in the sunshine. I had breakfast alone, in the parlour, which was the mirror-image of the 'painted room' on the south side of the house, away from the sea. The Boscastles breakfasted in their rooms, and there was no sign of Joan or Roy. Lady Muriel had been up two hours before, and was – so I gathered from whispered messages which a footman kept bringing to the butler – issuing her final orders for the picnic.

The papers had not yet arrived, and I drank my tea watching the motes dance in a beam of sunshine. It was a warm, hushed, shimmering morning.

The butler came and spoke to me. His tone was hushed, but not at all sleepy. He looked harassed and overburdened.

'Her ladyship sends her compliments, sir, and asks you to make your own way to the picnic site during the morning.'

'I haven't any idea where the site is,' I said.

'I think I can show you, sir, from the front entrance. It is just inside the grounds, where the wall goes nearest to the sea.'

'Inside the grounds? We're having this picnic inside the grounds?'

'Yes, sir. Her ladyship's picnics have always been inside the grounds. It makes it impossible for the party to be observed.'

I walked into the village to buy some cigarettes. At the shop I overheard some gossip about the new vicar. Apparently a young lady had arrived the night before at one of the hotels. She had gone to the vicarage that morning.

On my way to the site I wondered casually to myself who it might be. The thought of Rosalind crossed my mind, and then I dismissed it. I went into the grounds, through the side gates which opened on to the cliff road, down through the valley by the brook. It was not hard to find the site, for it was marked by a large flag. Lady Muriel was already sitting beside it on a shooting stick, looking as isolated as Amundsen at the South Pole. The ground beside her was arrayed with plates, glasses, dishes, siphons, bottles of wine. She called out to me with unexpected geniality.

'Good morning. You're the first. I'm glad to see someone put in an appearance. We couldn't have been luckier in the weather, could we?'

From the site there was no view, except for the brook and trees and wall, unless one looked north: there one got a magnificent sight of the house of Boscastle: the classical front, about a mile away, took in the whole foreground. It was a crowning stroke, I thought, to have chosen a site with that particular view.

But Lady Muriel was on holiday.

'I consider that all the arrangements are in hand,' she said. 'Perhaps you would like me to show you some things?'

She led me up some steps in the wall, which brought us to a small plateau. From the plateau we clambered down across the road over to a headland. Below the headland the sea was slumberously rolling against the cliffs. There was a milky spume fringing the dark rocks: and further out the water lay a translucent green in the warm, misty morning.

'We used to have picnics here in the old days,' said Lady Muriel. 'Before I decided it was unnecessary to go outside our grounds.'

She looked towards the mansion on its hill. It moved her to see it reposing there, the lawns bright, the house with the sun behind it. She was as inarticulate as ever.

'We're lucky to have such an excellent day.' Then she did manage to say: 'I have always been fond of our house.'

She tried to trace the coastline for me, but it was hidden in the mist.

'Well,' she said briskly, in a moment, 'we must be getting back to our picnic. All the arrangements are in order, of course. I have never found it difficult to make arrangements. I did not find them irksome in the Lodge. I have found it strange not to have to make them – since my husband's death.'

She missed them, of course, and she was happy that morning.

We had begun to leave the headland, with Lady Muriel telling me of how she used to climb the rocks when she was a girl. Then, in the distance along the road, I saw a woman walking. I thought I recognised the walk. It was not stately, it was not poised, it was hurried, quick-footed and loose. As she came nearer, I saw that I was right. It was Rosalind. She was wearing a very smart tweed suit, much too smart by the Boscastles' standards. And she was twirling a stick.

I hoped that she might not notice us. But she looked up, started, broke into a smile open-eyed, ill-used, pathetic and brazen. She gave a cheerful, defiant wave. I waved back. Lady Muriel did not stir a muscle.

When we saw Rosalind's back, Lady Muriel inquired, in an ominous tone:

'Is that the young woman who used to throw her cap so abominably at Roy?'

'Yes,' I said.

'What is she doing here?'

'She is a friend of Ralph Udal's,' I said. 'She must be visiting him.' To myself I could think of no other explanation. So far as I knew, she had given up the pursuit of Roy. In any case, she could not have known that he was staying at Boscastle that week. It was a singular coincidence.

'Really,' said Lady Muriel. Her indignation mounted. She was no longer genial to me. 'So now she sees herself as a clergyman's wife, does she? Mr Eliot, I understand that the lower classes are very lax with their children. If that young woman had been my daughter, she would have been thrashed.'

She continued to fume as we made our way back to the site. It was too far from the house for Lady Boscastle to walk; she had been driven as far as the path would take a car, and supported the rest of the way by her maid. Lord Boscastle was sitting there disconsolately, and complaining to Roy. Roy listened, his face grave. It was the first time I had seen him that day, and I knew no more than the night before.

Lady Muriel could not contain her disgust. She gave a virulent description of Rosalind's latest outrage.

'You didn't know she was coming, Roy, I assume?'

'No. She hasn't written to me for a year,' said Roy.

'I'm very glad to hear it,' said Lady Muriel, and burst out into fury at the picture of Rosalind walking 'insolently' past the walls of Boscastle.

Roy said nothing. I fancied there was a glint – was it admiration? – in his eye.

'I hope this fellow Udal isn't going to be a nuisance,' said Lord Boscastle. 'There's a great deal to be said for the celibacy of the clergy. But I don't see why the young woman shouldn't look him up. I always felt you were hard on her, Muriel.'

'Hard on her?' cried Lady Muriel. 'Why, she's nothing more nor less than a trollop.'

Soon after, Joan came walking by the brook. Her dress was white and flowered, and glimmered in the sunshine. As she called out to us, in an even voice, I was watching her closely. She was very pale. She had schooled herself not to do more than glance at Roy. She made conversation with her uncle. She was carrying herself with a hard control. She had all her mother's inflexible sense of decorum. In public, one must go on as though nothing had happened.

A file of servants came down from the house with hampers, looking like the porters on de Saussure's ascent of Mont Blanc. Cold chickens were brought out, tongues, patties: Lady Muriel jollied us in vigorous tones to get to our lunch. Meanwhile Lady Boscastle's glance was directed for a moment at Joan, and then at Roy.

'I don't for the life of me see,' said Lord Boscastle, gazing wistfully at the house, 'why I should be dragged out here. When I might be eating in perfect comfort in my house.'

It sounded a reasonable lament. It sounded more reasonable than it was. For in the house we should in fact have been eating a tepid and indifferent lunch, instead of this delectable cold one. Lady Muriel had bludgeoned the kitchen into efficiency, which Lady Boscastle did not exert herself to do. It was the best meal I remembered at Boscastle.

We ended with strawberries and moselle. Lady Boscastle, who was eating less each month, got through her portion.

'It's a fine taste, my dear Muriel,' she said. 'I recall vividly the first time someone gave it me—'

I recognised that tone by now. It meant that she was thinking of some admirer in the past. I did not know how much Joan was listening to her aunt: but she made herself put a decent face on it.

After lunch, Lady Muriel was not ready to let us rest.

'Archery,' she said inexorably. Another file of servants came down with targets, quivers, cases of bows. The targets were set up and we shot through the sleepy afternoon. Lord Boscastle was fairly practised, and it was the kind of game to which Roy and I applied ourselves. I noticed Lady Boscastle watching the play of muscle underneath Roy's shirt. She kept an interest in masculine grace. I thought she was surprised to see how strong he was.

Joan shot with us for a time. She and Roy spoke to each other only about the game, though once, when he misfired, she said: 'It must have bounced off that joint. Didn't you feel it?' She was speaking of the first finger of his left hand; the top joint had grown askew. She was not looking at his hand. She knew it by heart.

Lady Boscastle was assisted to the car before tea. For the rest of us, tea was brought down from the house, though Lady Muriel maintained the al fresco spirit by boiling our own water over a spirit stove. Lord Boscastle said, as though aggrieved: 'You ought to know by now, Muriel, that I'm no good at tea.' He drank a cup, and felt that he had served his sentence for the day. So he too went towards the house, having taken the precaution of booking Joan for bridge that night.

Some time after, the four of us started to follow him. Lady Muriel had uprooted the flag, and was carrying it home; all the paraphernalia of the meals was left for the servants. The site looked overcrowded with crockery: we had left it behind when Roy suddenly challenged me to a last round with the bow.

'Just two more shots, Lady Mu,' he said. 'We'll catch you up.'

Joan hesitated, as if she were pulled back to watch. Then she walked away with her mother.

Roy and I shot our arrows. As we went towards the target to retrieve them, Roy said:

'It's over with Joan and me.'

'I was afraid so.'

'If she comes to you, try and help. She may not come. She's dreadfully proud. But if she does, please try and help.' His face was dark. 'She has so little confidence. Try everything you know.'

I said that I would.

'Tell her I'm useless,' he said. 'Tell her I can't stand anyone for long unless they're as useless as I am. Tell her I'm mad.'

He plucked an arrow from the target, and said:

'There's one thing she mustn't believe. She mustn't think she's not attractive. It matters to her – intolerably. Tell her anything you like about me – so long as she doesn't think that.'

He was torn and overcome. He was unusually reticent about his love affairs: even in our greatest intimacy, he had told me little. But that afternoon, as we walked up the valley, he spoke with a bitter abandon. Physical passion meant much to Joan, more than to any woman he had known. Unless she found it again, she could not stop herself becoming harsh and twisted. We were getting close behind Joan and her mother, and he could not say more. But before we caught them up, he said: 'There's not much left.'

It was some days before I spoke to Joan. She was not a woman on whom one could intrude sympathy. The party stretched on through empty days. Roy took long walks with Lady Muriel, and I spent much time by Lady Boscastle's chair. She had diagnosed the state of her niece's affair, and had lost interest in it. 'My dear boy, the grand climaxes of all love affairs are too much the same. Now the overtures have a little more variety.' At dinner the political quarrels became rougher: we tried to shut them out, but the news would not let us. There was only one improvement as the days dragged by: Roy and I became steadily more accurate with the long bow.

One night towards the end of the week I went for a walk alone after dinner. I climbed out of the grounds and up to the headland, so as to watch the sun set over the sea. It was a cloudless night: the western sky was blazing and the horizon clear as a knife-edge.

As I stood there, I heard steps on the grass. Joan had also come alone. She gazed at me, her expression heavy and yet open in the bright light.

'Lewis,' she said. So much feeling welled up in the one word that I took a chance.

'Joan,' I said, 'I've wanted to say something to you. Twelve months ago Roy told me I made things harder for him. You ought to know the reason. It was because I understood a little about him.'

'Why are you telling me this?' she cried.

'It is the same with you.'

'Are you trying to comfort me?'

She burst out:

'I wonder if it's true. I don't know. I don't know anything now. I've given up trying to understand.'

I put my arm round her, and at the touch she began to speak.

'I can't give him up,' she said. 'Sometimes I think I only exist so far as I exist in his mind. If he doesn't think of me, then I fall to pieces. There's nothing of me any more.'

'Would it be better,' I said, 'if he went away?'

'No,' she cried, in an access of fear. 'You're to tell him nothing. You're not to tell him to go. He must stay here. My mother needs him. You know how much she needs him.'

It was true, but it was a pretext by which Joan saved her pride. For still she could not bear to let him out of her sight.

Perhaps she knew that she had given herself away, for suddenly her tone changed. She became angry with a violence that I could feel shaking her body.

'He'll stay because she needs him,' she said with ferocity. 'He'll consider anything she wants. He's nice and considerate with her. So he is with everyone – except me. He's treated me abominably. He's behaved like a cad. He's treated me worse than anyone I could have picked up off the streets. He's wonderful with everyone – and he's treated me like a cad.'

She was trembling, and her voice shook.

'I don't know how I stood it,' she cried. 'I asked less than anyone in the world would have asked. And all I get is this.'

Then she caught my hand. The anger left her as quickly as it had risen. She had flared from hunger into ferocity, and now both fell away from her.

'You know, Lewis,' she said, 'I can't think of him like that. It's perfectly true, he's treated me abominably, yet I can't help thinking that he's really good. I see him with other people, and I think I am right to love him. I know he's done wicked things. I know he's done wicked things to me. But they seem someone else's fault.'

The sun had dipped now to the edge of the sea. Her eyes glistened in the radiance; for the first time that night, they were filmed with tears. Her voice was even.

'I wish I could believe,' she said, 'that he'll be better off without me. I might be able to console myself if I believed it. But I don't. How does he expect to manage? I'm sure he's unhappier than any human soul. I can look after him. How does he expect to manage, if he throws it away?'

She cried out:

'I don't think he knows what will become of him.'

PART THREE

THE LAST ATTEMPT

CHAPTER XXIV

TWO DISMISSALS

AFTER Boscastle I saw little of Roy for months. He altered his plans, and returned to Germany for the summer and autumn; I heard rumours that he was behaving more wildly than ever in his life, but the difference between us was at its deepest. We met one day in September, when he flew back at the time of Munich. It was a strange and painful afternoon. We knew each other so well; at a glance we knew what the other was feeling. We were on opposite sides. There was something like distrust between us. We were each guarding our words: once or twice a harsh note sounded.

I talked about myself, on the chance of drawing a confidence from him. But he was mute. He was mute by intention, I knew. He was keeping from me some inner resolve and a vestige of hope. He was secretive, hard, and restless.

I thought for the first time that the years were touching him. His smile was still brilliant, and made him look very young. But the dark nights had at last begun to leave their mark. The skin under his eyes was prematurely rough and stained, and the corners of his mouth were tight. His face was lined less than most men's at twenty-eight – but it showed the wear of sadness. If one met him now as a stranger, one would have guessed that he had been unhappy.

There was another change which, as I noticed with amusement, sometimes ruffled him. It ruffled him the morning of our discoveries about Bidwell.

Roy had come back to the college in November and was working in Cambridge until the new year. One December morning, Bidwell woke me in the grey twilight with his habitual phrase: 'That's nine o'clock, sir.' He pattered soft-footed about my bedroom and said, in his quiet soothing bedside voice: 'Mr Calvert sends his compliments, sir. And he wonders if you would be kind enough to step up after breakfast. He says he has something to show you, sir.'

The message brought back more joyous days, when Roy 'sent his compliments' two or three mornings a week – usually with some invitation or piece of advice attached, which Bidwell delivered, as honest-faced, as solemn, as sly-eyed, as a French mayor presiding over a wedding.

I went up to Roy's rooms immediately after breakfast. His sitting-room was empty: the desks glinted pink and green and terra cotta in the crepuscular morning light. Roy called from his bedroom:

'Bidwell is a devil. We need to stop him.'

He was standing in front of his mirror, brushing his hair. It was then I noticed that he was taking some care about it. His hair was going back quickly at the temples, more quickly than I had realised, since he managed to disguise it.

'Still vain,' I jeered. 'Aren't you getting too old for vanity?' I was oddly comforted to see him at it. The face in the mirror was sad and grave; yet somehow it brought him to earth, took the edge from my forebodings, to watch him seriously preoccupied about going bald.

'Nothing will stop it,' said Roy. 'The women will soon be saying – "Roy, you're bald." And I shall have to point a bit lower down and tell them – "Yes, but don't you realise that I've got nice intelligent eyes?" '

Then he turned round.

'But it's Bidwell we need to talk about. He's a devil.'

Roy had now been back in his rooms for a fortnight. During that time, he had made a list of objects which, so far as he remembered, had disappeared during his months abroad. The list was long and variegated. It included two gowns, several bottles of spirits, a pair of silver candlesticks, most of his handkerchiefs and several of his smartest ties.

I was amused. Our relations with Bidwell had been curious for a long while past. We had known that he was mildly dishonest. There was a line between what a college servant could regard by tradition as his perquisites and what his fingers should not touch. We had known for years that Bidwell crossed that line. Any food left over from parties, half-empty bottles – those were legitimate 'perks'. But Bidwell did not content himself with them. He took a kind of tithe on most of the food and drink we ordered. Neither of us had minded much. I shut my eyes to it through sheer negligence and disinclination to be bothered: Roy was nothing like so careless, and had made one sharp protest. But we were neither of us made to persist in continuous nagging.

We happened to be very fond of Bidwell. He was a character, sly, peasant-wise, aphoristic. He had a vivid picture of himself as a confidential gentlemen's servant, and acted up to it. He loved putting on his dress suit and waiting at our big dinner parties. He loved waking us up with extreme care after he had found the glasses of a heavy night. He loved being discreet and concealing our movements. 'I hope I haven't done wrong, sir,' he used to say with a knowing look. We did not mind his being lazy, we were prepared to put up with some dishonesty: we felt he liked us too much to go beyond a decent friendly limit.

Roy worked him harder than I did, but we were both indulgent and tipped him lavishly. Each of us had a suppressed belief that he was Bidwell's favourite. Our guests at dinner parties, seeing that wise, rubicund, officiating face, told us how much they envied our luck in Bidwell. All in all, we thought ourselves that we were lucky.

I was half-shocked, half-amused, to hear of his depredations at Roy's expense. I was still confident that he would not treat me anything like as badly: we had always been on specially amiable terms.

'You haven't much for him to pinch,' said Roy. 'He doesn't seem to like books.'

Then suddenly a thought occurred to Roy.

'Do you look at your buttery bills?' he said.

'I just cast an eye over them,' I said guiltily.

'Untrue,' said Roy. 'I bet you don't. I once caught the old scoundrel monkeying with a bill. Lewis, I want to look at yours.'

I had not kept any, but Roy found copies in the steward's office. Soon he glanced at me.

'You drink too much,' he said. 'Alone, I suppose. I never knew.'

He made me study the bills. I used to order in writing one bottle of whisky a fortnight; on my account, time after time, I was put down for four bottles. I asked for the latest order, which, like the rest, had been taken to the office by Bidwell. The figure 1 had been neatly changed into a 4. As I looked at other items, I saw some other unpleasant facts. I felt peculiarly silly.

'He must have cost you quite a bit,' said Roy, who was doing sums on a piece of paper. 'Haven't you let him "bring things away" from your tailor's?'

'I'll bring it away from the shop' was a favourite phrase of Bidwell's.

'Yes,' I said helplessly.

'You're dished, old boy,' said Roy. 'We're both dished, but you're absolutely done.' He added: 'I think we need to speak to Bidwell.'

Neither of us wanted to, but Roy took the lead. He sent another servant to find Bidwell, and we waited for him in Roy's room.

Bidwell came in and stood just inside the door, his face benign and attentive.

'They said you were asking for me, sir?'

'Yes, Bidwell,' said Roy. 'Too many things have gone from these rooms.'

'I'm very sorry to hear that, sir.'

'Where have they gone?'

'What might the old things be, sir?' Bidwell was wary. In the past he had diverted Roy by his use of the word 'old', but now Roy had fixed him with a hard and piercing glance. He did not wilt, his manner was perfectly possessed.

Roy ran through the list.

'That's a terrible lot to lose, I must say.' Bidwell frowned. 'If you don't mind my saying so, sir, I never did like the steward using this as a guest room when you were away. We had men up for examinations' – Bidwell shook his head – 'and I know I'm doing wrong in speaking, sir, but it's the class of men we have here nowadays. It's the class of men we get here today. Things aren't what they used to be.'

Bidwell was not an ordinary man in any company, but he ran true to his trade in being a snob, open, nostalgic and unashamed.

Roy looked at me. I said:

'I've been going through my buttery bills, Bidwell.'

'Yes, sir?'

'I've never ordered four bottles of whisky at a go since I came here.'

'Of course not, sir. You've never been one for whisky, have you? I spotted that as soon as you came on my staircase. It was different with an old gentleman I used to have before your time, sir. When I had you instead of him, it made a big old difference to my life.'

'I gave you an order for one bottle last week. The buttery say that when you handed it in, that order was for four bottles.'

Bidwell's face darkened, and instantaneously cleared.

'I meant to tell you about that, sir. I may have done wrong. You must tell me if I have. But I heard the stock was running low, and I took it on myself to bring away what you might call a reserve—'

'Come off it, Bidwell,' said Roy. 'We know you've been cheating us. And you know we know.'

'I don't like to hear you saying that, sir—'

'Look here,' said Roy, 'we like you. We hope you like us. Do you want to spoil it all?'

Bidwell ceased to be impassive.

'It would break my heart, Mr Calvert, if either of you went away.'

'Why have you done this?'

'I'm glad you've both spoken to me,' said Bidwell. 'It's been hurting me – here.' He pressed his hand to his heart. 'I know I oughtn't to have done what I have done. But I've got short of cash now and again. I don't mind telling this to you two gentlemen – I've always said that everyone has a right to his fancy. But it's made me do things I shouldn't have done. I haven't treated you right, I know I haven't.'

His mouth was twitching, his eyes were tearful, we were all raw and distressed.

'Just so,' said Roy quietly. 'Well, Bidwell, I'm ready to forget it. So is Mr Eliot. On one—'

'You've always been every inch a gentleman, sir. Both of you.'

'On one condition,' said Roy. 'Listen. I mean this. If anything else goes from these rooms, I go straight to the steward. And you'll be sacked out of hand.'

'It won't happen again, sir.'

'Wait a minute. Listen again. I shall go through Mr Eliot's bill myself each week. You can trust me to do it, can't you?'

'Yes, sir. Mr Eliot can never be bothered with his old bills, sir.'

'I can,' said Roy. 'You've got it clear? If you take another penny from either of us, I shan't stop to ask Mr Eliot. I shall get you sacked.'

'Yes, sir. I'm very much obliged to both of you gentlemen.'

Bidwell went out, his face once more rubicund, open, benign and composed. Both Roy and I were puzzled. His emotion was genuine: yet he had pulled it out with cunning. How had he played on that particular note, which was certain to affect us both? Was there a touch of triumph about his exit? As with Arthur Brown, Bidwell's was a nature that became deeper and tougher when once one was past the affable fat man's façade.

Roy teased me because I – 'the great realist', as he called me – was upset at Bidwell's duplicity. He told me that I bore major treacheries better than domestic ones. For my part, I was thinking how final his own manner had become. In giving his ultimatum to Bidwell, his voice was keen, as though it were a relief to take this action, to take any kind of action. He was restless, he seemed driven to do things once for all.

I heard him speak with finality again before that term ended.

The college chaplain had just resigned, as some friendly bishop had given him preferment. As soon as he heard the news, Arthur Brown set unhurriedly to work: the chaplaincy did not carry a fellowship, it had no political importance in the college, but Brown's instinct for patronage was too strong for him: he was obliged to keep his hand in. So he went round 'getting the feeling of a few people', as he explained to Roy and me. The upshot was that, before he spoke to us, he had invited Udal to spend a night in college. 'I'm not committing anyone, naturally,' said Arthur Brown. 'But I thought it might be profitable to explore the ground a little. I'm afraid I've rather taken it for granted that you wouldn't object to the idea, Calvert, if we get as far as mentioning his name. I remember that you backed him strongly at several meetings.'

Roy gave a slight smile – I wondered if it was at his own expense.

'I don't know how you'd feel about it, Eliot? I'm inclined to think myself that Udal would be rather an addition to the combination room.'

'If you all want him,' I said, 'I'm ready to fall in.' I looked at Roy: he smiled again, but the mention of Udal had disturbed him.

Udal arrived in time for dinner, and Arthur Brown brought him into hall. It was one of the few occasions that I had seen him wearing a dog-collar. He towered above the rest of us in the combination room, impassively at ease. If he wanted the job, I thought in hall, he was doing pretty well. Perhaps he was a little too casual; most societies liked a touch of nervousness when a man was under inspection – not too much, but just a fitting touch. Udal would have been slightly too natural in any interview.

After we had drunk port in the combination room, we moved on to Brown's rooms – Brown and Udal, Roy and I. The room was warm, the fire bright as usual: and as usual Brown went straight to unlock his cupboard.

'I don't know what the company would say to a sip of brandy,' he remarked. 'Myself, I find it rather gratifying at this time of night.'

We sat round the fire with our glasses in our hands, and Brown began to speak with luxurious caution.

'Well, Udal,' he said, 'we were a bit rushed before dinner, but I tried to give you the lie of the land. We mustn't promise more than we can perform. The chaplain is elected by the college, and the college is capable of doing some very curious things. Put it another way: I never feel certain that we've got a man in until I see it written down in black and white in the order book. I shouldn't be treating you fairly if I gave you the impression that we could offer you the chaplaincy tonight. But I don't think I'm going further than I should if I say this – let me see' – Brown picked out his words – 'if you see your way to letting your name go forward, I regard it as distinctly possible that we should be able to pull it off. I can go as far as that. I've spoken to one or two people, and I'm fairly satisfied that I'm not being over-optimistic.'

This meant that Arthur Brown had a majority assured for Udal, if he decided to stand. There would be opposition from Despard-Smith, but the old man was losing his power, even on clerical matters. Step by step Arthur Brown had become the most influential person in the college.

'It's very nice of you to think of me,' said Udal. 'In many ways there's nothing I should like better. Of course, there's a good deal to weigh up. There's quite a lot to be thought of for and against.'

'Of course there must be,' said Arthur Brown, who had a horror of premature decisions. 'I should have thought you ought to sleep on it, before you even give us an indication of which way you're going to come down. I don't mean to suggest' – Brown added – 'that you can possibly give us an answer tomorrow. But you might be able to produce one or two first impressions.'

I was certain that Udal would not take the job, and so was Roy. I did not know about Brown. He was so shrewd and observant that he must have caught the intonation of refusal: but it was part of his habit to proceed with negotiations for a decent customary period, even when it was clear that the other had made up his mind. Brown's intuitions were quick, but he disliked appearing to act on them. He preferred all the panoply of reasonable discussion. He knew as well as any man that most decisions are made on the spot and without thought; but it was proper to behave as though men were as rational and deliberate as they pretended to be. So, with every appearance of enjoyment, he answered Udal's questions about the chaplaincy, the duties, stipend, possibilities of a fellowship: he met objections, raised some of his own, compared prospects, examined the details of Udal's living. He even said:

'If, as I very much hope, we finally manage to get you here, Udal, there is just one slightly delicate matter I might take this opportunity of raising. I take it that you wouldn't find it absolutely necessary to introduce observances that some of us might think were rather too high?'

'I think I could promise that,' said Udal with a cheerful smile.

'I'm rather relieved to hear you say so,' Brown replied. 'I shouldn't like to interfere between any man and his religion. Some of the Catholics we've had here are as good chaps as you're ever likely to meet. But I do take the view rather strongly that the public services of the college ought to keep a steady middle course. I shouldn't like to see them moving too near the Holy Joes.'

'Someone once said,' Roy put in, 'that the truth lies at both extremes. But never in the middle. You don't believe that, Brown, do you?'

'I do not,' said Brown. 'I should consider it was a very cranky and absurd remark.'

At last Udal said that he thought he could soon give a reply. Brown stopped him short.

'I'm not prepared to listen to a word tonight,' he said. 'I'm not prepared to listen until you've slept on it. I've always regretted the occasions when I've spoken too soon. I don't presume to offer advice to people like Eliot and Calvert here, but I've even sometimes suggested to them that they ought to sleep on it.'

Brown departed for his home in the town, and the rest of us went from his room to mine. It was dark, bare, inhospitable after Brown's; we drew the armchairs round the fire.

Roy said to Udal:

'You're not taking this job, are you?'

'No,' said Udal. 'I don't think I shall.'

'Less money. Much more work.'

'It's not quite as simple as that,' said Udal, slightly nettled.

'No?' Roy's smile was bright.

'No,' said Udal. 'I don't specialise in bogus reasons, as you know. But there are genuine ones why I should like to come. It would be pleasant' – he said with easy affection – 'to be near you.'

'What for?' said Roy sharply.

'It doesn't need much explanation.'

'It may,' said Roy. 'You used to hope that you'd catch me for your faith. Isn't that true?'

'I did hope so,' said Udal.

'If you were here, you think it might be more likely. Isn't that true as well?'

'It had crossed my mind,' said Udal.

'You can forget it,' said Roy. 'It will never happen now. It's too late.'

'It's not too late.'

'Listen, Ralph. I know now. I've known for some time.' Roy was speaking with absolute finality. I was reminded of that scene with Bidwell. It was as though he were cutting ties which had once been precious. Bidwell's was a minor one; now he was marking the end of something from which he had hoped so much. He said clearly:

'I shall not come your way now. I shall not believe. It's not for me.'

Udal could not mistake the tone. He did not dissent. He said, with compassion and warmth:

'I'm more sorry than I can say.'

For the first time, I saw Udal uncertain of himself, guilty, hesitating. He added:

'I can't help feeling some of this is my fault. I feel that I've failed you.'

Roy did not speak.

'Have I failed you?' said Udal.

Roy could have answered yes. For a second, I thought he was going to. It was at Boscastle that Roy knew without the slightest particle of doubt that Udal was no use to him – when he heard him plan his days, allow one day's exercises for the integral knowledge of God. It was a little thing, but to Roy it meant much. It turned him away without hope from Udal's experience, that seemed now so revoltingly 'hygienic', so facile. He had once thought that Udal, never mind his frailties, had discovered how to throw away the chains of self. Now it seemed to Roy that he was unbelievably self-absorbed, content to be self-absorbed.

Roy answered:

'No one could have made any difference. I should never have found it.'

'I hope you're speaking the truth,' said Udal.

'I think I am,' said Roy.

'I haven't failed you,' said Udal, 'because of Rosalind?'

'Of course not.' Roy was utterly surprised: had she been on Udal's mind all the time?

'You see,' Udal went on, 'I'm thinking of marrying her.'

'Good luck to you,' said Roy. He was taken aback, he gave a bewildered smile, full of amusement, memory, chagrin and shock. 'Give her my love.'

'It isn't certain,' said Udal.

Udal was lying back in his chair, and I watched his face, heavy featured and tranquil. It was a complete surprise to me. I wondered if he could be as confident as he seemed. I wondered about Rosalind, and why she had done it.

Then Roy leaned forward, so that his eyes gleamed in the firelight. He did not speak again about Rosalind. Instead, he said:

'Could there be a world, Ralph, in which God existed – but with some people in it who were never allowed to believe?'

'It would be a tragic world,' said Udal.

'Why shouldn't it be tragic?' Roy cried. 'Why shouldn't there be some who are rejected by God from the beginning?'

957

'It isn't my picture of the world,' said Udal.

Suddenly Roy's face, which had been sombre, set and haunted, lit up in his most lively smile.

'No,' he said, 'yours is really a very nice domestic place, isn't it? Tragic things don't happen, do they? You're an optimistic old creature in the long run, aren't you?'

Udal could not cope with that lightning change of mood. Roy baited him, as though everything that night had passed in fun. It was in the same light, teasing tone that Roy said a last word to Udal before we went to bed.

'I expect you think I ought to have tried harder to believe, don't you? If one tries hard enough, things happen, if you're an optimistic old creature, don't they? I did try a bit, Ralph. I even pretended to myself that I did believe. It didn't come off, you know. I could have gone on pretending, of course. I could have pretended well enough to take you in. I've done that before now. I could even have taken old Lewis in. I could have taken everyone in – except myself and God. And there wouldn't have been much point in that, would there?'

We walked with Udal through the courts towards the guest-room. On the way back, I stumbled over a grass verge: there was no moon, the lamps in the court had been put out at midnight, and I could not see in the thick darkness. Roy took my arm, so that he could steer me.

'I shouldn't like to lose you just yet,' he said.

I knew that he was smiling. I also knew that he was near to confiding, within a word of it. There had been horror behind what he had said a few minutes before – and yet there was still hope. It was not easy just at that moment to reject our intimacy.

The moment passed. He took me to the foot of my staircase.

'Good night. Sleep well.'

'Shall you?' I said.

There I could see him smile.

'I might,' he said. 'You never know. I did, last Tuesday.'

CHAPTER XXV

A NEST OF PEOPLE

ROY went back to Berlin just after Christmas. I did not hear from him, but one morning in February I received a letter with the Boscastle crest.

It was from Joan, saying that she urgently wanted to talk to me about Roy – 'don't misunderstand me,' she wrote with her bleak and painful honesty. 'There is nothing to say about him and me. I want your advice on something much more important, which concerns him alone.'

She suggested that she should give me dinner at her London club, but I made her come to the Berkeley. As she sat on the other side of the table, I thought her face was becoming better looking as she grew older; she had lost the radiance of happy love, but the handsome structure of her cheekbones was beginning to give her distinction; it was a face in which character was showing through the flesh.

She went straight to it.

'I'm very worried about Roy,' she said, and told me her news. Houston Eggar had recently got a promotion, after steady and resolute pushing; he had left Rome and been sent to Berlin as an extra counsellor. Late in January, he had written out of the blue to Lord Boscastle about Roy. He said that he was presuming upon his wife's relationship to Lord Boscastle's family; he knew that Roy was a friend of theirs, and the whole matter needed to be approached with the utmost discretion. I thought as I listened that Eggar was in part doing his duty, in part showing his natural human kindness, and in part – and probably a very large part – seizing an opportunity of getting into what he might have called Lord Boscastle's good books. If Lord Boscastle exerted himself, he could be valuable to Eggar's career. But thoughts of Eggar soon vanished as Joan described his report. It sounded factual, and we both believed it.

Roy, so Eggar said, was being a great social success in Berlin. He was being too great a social success. He was repeatedly invited to official and party functions. He was friendly with several of the younger party leaders. With some of them he had more influence than any Englishman in Berlin. 'I wish I could be satisfied,' ran Eggar's letter, which Joan gave to me, 'that he was using his influence in a manner calculated to help us through this difficult period. It is very important that Englishmen with contacts in the right quarters should give the authorities here the impression that they are behind the policy of H.M.G. Calvert has gone too far in the direction of encouraging the German authorities that they have the sympathy and understanding of Englishmen like himself. I can give you chapter and verse for several unfortunate remarks.'

Eggar had done so. They had the tone of Roy. Some of them might have been jokes, uttered with his mystifying solemnity. One or two had the touch which Joan and I had heard him use when he was most in earnest. And Eggar also quoted a remark in 'very embarrassing circumstances' about the Jewish policy: at an august official dinner, Roy had denounced it. 'You're a wonderful people. You're grave. You're gifted. You might begin a new civilisation. I wish you would. I'm speaking as a friend, you see. But don't you think you're slightly mad? Your treatment of the Jews – why need you do it? It's unnecessary. It gets you nowhere. It's insane. Sometimes I think that, whatever else you do, it will be enough to condemn you.'

It had been said in German, and I did not recognise the phrases as typically Roy's. But the occasion was exactly in his style. It had given offence to 'important persons', and Eggar seemed as concerned about that as about the indiscretions in the other direction. All his reporting seemed objective, and Joan and I were frightened.

We were not simply perturbed, as Eggar was, that he might commit a gaffe at an awkward time. Eggar obviously thought that he was a frivolous and irresponsible young man, who was flirting with a new creed. Eggar was used to Englishmen with social connections who for a few months thought they had discovered in Rome or Berlin a new way of life, and in the process made things even more difficult for a hard-working professional like himself. To him, Roy was just such another.

Across the table, Joan and I stared at each other, and wished that it were so. But we knew him too well. We were each harrowed because of him and for him.

Because of him – since we were living in a time of crisis, and it was bitter to find an enemy in someone we loved. Both Joan and I believed that it hung upon the toss of a coin whether or not the world would be tolerable to live in. And Roy was now wishing that we should lose. I felt bitter, and worse than bitter, against him.

Yet we were harrowed for him. We could only guess what he was going through, and where this would lead him. He was without fear, he was without elementary caution. He had none of the cushions of self-preservation which guard most men; he did not want success, he cared nothing for others' opinion, he had no respect for any society, he was alone. There was nothing to keep him safe, if the mood came on him.

'Ought I to go and see him?' said Joan.

I hesitated. She was distracted for him, with a devotion that was unselfish and compassionate – and also she wanted any excuse to meet him again, in case the miracle might happen. Her love was tenacious, it was stronger than pride, she could not let him go.

'He might still listen to me,' Joan insisted. 'It will be difficult, but I feel I've got to try.'

Nothing would put her off. That was the advice she had come to get. Whether she got it or not, she was determined to go in search of him.

I heard another, and a very different, account of Roy a few days later. It came from Colonel Foulkes, whom I ran into by chance when I was lunching as a guest at the Athenaeum. Oulstone Lyall had died suddenly at the end of 1938 (I was interested to see in one of the obituaries a hint of the Erzberger scandal: it seemed now that the truth would never be known) and Foulkes had become the senior figure in Asian studies.

'Splendid accounts of Calvert,' he said without any preliminaries, as we washed our hands side by side. The Oriental faculty at Berlin University had decided, Foulkes went on, that Roy was the finest foreign scholar who had worked there since the 1914–18 war. 'They're thinking of doing something for him,' Foulkes rapped out. 'Only right. Only right. Subject's cluttered up with old has-beens. Such as me. Get rid of us. Get rid of us. That's what they ought to do.'

He had also heard that Roy was sympathetic to the régime, but it did not cause him the slightest concern. 'Great deal to be said for it, I expect,' said Foulkes, briskly towelling his hands. 'Great deal to be said for most things. People ought to be receptive to new ideas. Only way to keep young. Glad to see Calvert is.'

He had himself, it then appeared, just become absorbed in theosophy. It had its advantages, I thought, being able to over-trump any eccentricity. He remained curiously simple, positive and unimaginative, and he took it for granted that Roy was the same.

I had a letter from Roy himself early in March. He invited me to spend a few days of the vacation, longer if I could get away from home, with him in Berlin. He seemed acutely desirous that I should go, but the letter was not an intimate one. It was stylised, almost awkward, almost remote – usually he wrote with liquid ease, but this invitation was stiff. I suspected a purpose that he wished to hold back.

I arrived at the Zoo station in Berlin on a snowy afternoon in March. I looked for Roy up and down the platform, but did not see him. I was cold, a little apprehensive; I spoke very little German, and I stood there with my bags, in a fit of indecision.

Then a young woman spoke to me:

'You are Mr Eliot, please?'

She was spectacularly thin. Beneath her fur coat, her legs were like stalks. But she had bright clever grey eyes, and as I said yes she suddenly and disconcertingly burst into laughter.

'What is the joke?' I asked.

'Please. I did not quite understand you.' She spoke English slowly, but her ear was accurate and her intonation good.

'Why do you laugh?'

'I am sorry.' She could not straighten her face. 'Mr Calvert has said that you look more like a professor than he. But he said you are really less like.'

She added:

'He has also said that you will have something wrong with your clothes. Such as shoelace undone. Or other things.' She was shaken with laughter as she pointed to the collar of my overcoat, which I had put up against the cold and which had somehow got twisted. She thought it was an extraordinarily good joke. 'It is so. It is so.'

It was one way of being recognised, I thought. I asked why Roy was not there.

'He is ill,' she said. 'Not much. He works too hard and does not think of himself. He must stay in bed today.'

As we got into a taxi, she told me that her name was Mecke, Ursula Mecke. I had already identified her as the 'little dancer': and she told me: 'I am tänzerin.' I liked her at sight. She was ill, hysterical and highly strung; but she was also warm-hearted. She was quick and business-like with the taxi driver; but when she talked about her earnings on the stage, I felt sure she was hopelessly impractical in running her life. I did not think she had been a love of Roy's. She spoke of him with a mixture of comradeship and touching veneration. 'He is so good,' she said. 'It is not only money, Mr Eliot. That is easy. But Mr Calvert thinks for us. That is not easy.' She told me how that winter her mother had fallen ill in Aachen. The little dancer could not afford to go; she was always in debt, and her salary, after she had paid taxes and the party contributions, came to about thirty shillings a week. But within a few hours she found in her room a return ticket, a hamper of food for the journey, an advance on her salary, and a bottle of Lanvin scent. 'He denies it, naturally,' said Ursula Mecke. 'He says that he has not given me these things. He says that I have an admirer. Who else has given me them, Mr Eliot?' Her grammar then got confused in her excitement: but she meant who else, in those circumstances, would have remembered that she would enjoy some scent.

The Knesebeckstrasse lay in the heart of the west end, between the Kurfürstendamm and the Kantstrasse. No. 32 was near the Kantstrasse end of the street; like all the other houses, it was six-storeyed, grey-faced, and had once been fashionable. Now it was sub-let like a complex honeycomb. Roy had the whole suite of five rooms on the ground floor, but the storeys above were divided into flats of three rooms or two or one: the tänzerin had a single attic right at the top.

All Roy's rooms were high, dark, and panelled in pine which had been painted a deep chocolate brown; they were much more sparsely furnished and stark than anywhere else he had lived, although he had added to them sofas, armchairs, and his usual assortment of desks. The family of von Haltsdorff must have lived there in austere poverty; now that Roy had leased the flat from them they had gone to live in dignified poverty on their estate on the Baltic. They had permitted themselves one decoration in the dining-room; on the barn-like expanse of wall there stood out a large painted chart. It was the family genealogy. It began well before the Great Elector. It came down through a succession of von Haltsdorffs, all of whom had been officers in the Prussian Army. They had intermarried with other Prussian families. None had apparently had much success. The chart ended with the present head, who was a retired colonel.

We had to pass through the dining-room on the way to Roy. I glanced at the chart, and wondered what Lord Boscastle would have said.

Roy's bed was placed in the middle of another high, spacious room: the bed itself had four high wooden posts. Roy was lying underneath a great pillow-like German eiderdown.

'How are you?' I said.

'Slightly dead,' said Roy.

But he did not look or sound ill. He was unshaven and somewhat bedraggled. I gathered that he had had a mild influenza; his friends in the house, Ursula Mecke and the rest, had rushed round fetching him a doctor, nursing him, expressing great distress when he wanted to get up. He could not laugh it off without hurting them.

That night I sat at his bedside while he held a kind of levée. A dozen people looked in to enquire after him as soon as they arrived home from work. Several of them stayed talking, went away for their supper, and returned after Roy had eaten his own meal. There was a clerk, a school teacher, a telephone girl, a cashier from a big shop, a librarian, a barber's assistant, a draughtsman.

Some of them were nervous of me, but they were used to calling on Roy, and he talked to them like a brother. It mystified them just as much. His German sounded as fluent as theirs, and after supper, when I was alone with Ursula, I asked how good it was. She said that she might not have known he was a foreigner, but she would have wondered which part of Germany he came from. I envied him, when I found the fog of language cutting me off from his friends.

Faces told one something, though. The lined forehead of the librarian, with the opaque pallor one often sees in anxious people: he had a kind, gentle, terrified expression, frightened of something he might have left undone. The hare eyes and bulbous nose of the elderly woman school teacher, who had strong opinions on everything, not much sense of reality, and an unquenchable longing for adventure: at the age of fifty-eight, she had nearly saved up enough money for a holiday abroad. The hot glare, swelling neck and smooth unlined cheeks of the clerk, who was a man of forty: he had got religion and sex inextricably mixed up. It was he who was keeping the barber's assistant, Willy Romantowski; though some of the rooms in the house were very cheap, like Ursula's, none of them would have come within that boy's means.

I wished I could talk to them as Roy did. Of them all, I found the little dancer the most sympathetic. I did not much like young Romantowski, but he was the oddest and perhaps the ablest of them. He had the kind of bony features one sometimes meets in effeminate men: so that really his face, and his whole physique, were strong and masculine, and his mincing smile and postures seemed more than ever bizarre. His manner was strident, he insisted on getting our attention, he was petulant, vain, selfish and extremely shrewd. He was not going to be content with a two-room flat in the Knesebeckstrasse for long. He was about twenty-two, very fair and pale: Roy called him the 'white avised', by contrast with his patron, who was the 'black avised' and who doted on him.

When they had all gone, I asked Roy their stories; he lay smoking a cigarette, and we speculated together about their lives. What would happen to the little dancer? Was there any way of getting her into a sanatorium? Might she find a husband? How long would Romantowski stay with his patron? Would the school teacher be disappointed in her holiday, if ever she achieved it?

Roy was fond of them in his own characteristic fashion – unsentimental, half-malicious, attentive to those secret kindnesses which appeared like elaborate practical jokes.

Perhaps he had a special tenderness for some of them, for they were riff-raff and outcasts: and often it was among such that he felt most at home.

But I had a curious feeling as we talked about those friends of his. He was interested, scurrilous, tender – but he was cross that I had seen them. He was impatient that I had become caught up, just as it might have been in Pimlico, in a tangle of human lives. Whatever he had invited me for, it was not for that.

CHAPTER XXVI

LOSS OF A TEMPER

ALTHOUGH Roy got up the day after I arrived, it was too cold for him to leave the house. Through the afternoon and evening, we sat in the great uncomfortable drawing-room, and for a long time we were left alone.

All the time, I knew that Roy did not want us to be left alone. He was listening for steps in the hall, a knock on the door – not for any particular person, just anyone who would disturb us.

I was at a loss. He was affectionate, for that was his first nature. He was even amusing, as he made the minutes pass by mimicking some of our colleagues: but he would have done the same to an acquaintance in the combination room I felt he was sad, but he did not utter a word about it: once he had been spontaneous in his sadness, but not now.

There was one interruption, when for a few minutes he behaved as in the old days. By the afternoon post he received a letter with a German stamp on; I saw him study the postmark and the handwriting with a frown. As he read the note, which was on a single piece of paper, the frown became fixed and guilty.

'She's run me down,' he said. Joan had arrived in Berlin, and was staying with the Eggars. Roy looked at me, as he used to when he was out-manœuvred by a woman from whom he was trying to escape. For Joan he had a special feeling; yet there were times when she seemed just another mistress, and when he felt he was going through the accustomed moves.

He was confused. Clean breaks did not come easy to him. He would have liked to spend that night with Joan. If it had been someone who minded less, like Rosalind, he would have rung her up on the spot. But he could not behave carelessly with Joan. He had done so once, and it was a burden he could not shift.

So he sat, irresolute, rueful, badgered. There was something extremely comic about the winning end of a love affair, I thought. It needed Lady Boscastle's touch. For she never had much sympathy with the agony of the loser, the one who loved the more, the one who ate out her heart for a lover who was becoming more indifferent. Lady Boscastle had not suffered much in that fashion. She had been the winner in too many love affairs – and so she was superlatively acid about the comic dilemmas of love.

At last Roy decided. There was no help for it: he must meet Joan; it was better to meet her in public. He started to arrange a party, before he spoke to her. From his first call, it was clear the party would be an eccentric one. For he rang up Schäder, his most influential friend in the German government. From Roy's end of the conversation, I gathered that Schäder was free for a very late dinner the following night and that he insisted on being the host. When Roy had put down the telephone, he looked at me with acute, defiant eyes.

'Excellent. I needed you to meet him. He is an interesting man.'

I asked what exactly his job was. Roy said that he was the equivalent of a Minister in England, the kind of Minister who is just on the fringe of the cabinet.

'He's quite young,' said Roy. 'About your age. You must forget your preconceived ideas. He's not a bit stuffed.'

They had arranged that Roy should invite the party. He found one German friend was already booked, but got hold of Ammatter, the orientalist whom I had met in Cambridge. Then he rang up Joan. She was demanding to see him at once, that afternoon, that night: Roy nearly weakened, but held firm. At last she acquiesced. I could imagine the resignation with which she turned away. She was to bring Eggar 'if he does not think it will set him back a peg or two'. Roy also invited Eggar's wife, but she was expecting a child in the next fortnight. 'It looks like being Joan and five men,' he said. He was smiling as he must have done when they were in love.

'That's her idea of a social evening. A well-balanced little party. She likes feeling frivolous, you know. Because it's not her line.' He sighed. 'Oh – there's no one like her, is there?'

The next morning, he was well enough to take me for a walk through the Berlin streets. It was still freezingly cold, and the sky was steely. The weather had not changed since the German army marched into Prague, a few days before I set out. Outside Roy's house, the pavement rang with our footsteps in the cold: the street was empty under the bitter sky. Roy was wearing earcaps, as though he were just going to plunge into a scrum.

He took me on a tour under the great grey buildings; lights twinkled behind the office windows; the shops and cafés were full, people jostled us on the pavements, the air was frosty and electric; an aeroplane zoomed invisibly overhead, above the even pall of cloud. We walked past the offices of the Friedrichstrasse and the Wilhelmstrasse; the rooms were a blaze of light. Roy showed me Schäder's ministry, a heavy nineteenth-century mansion. Official motor cars went hurtling by, their horns playing an excited tune.

We came to the Linden. The trees were bare, but the road was alive with cars and the pavements crammed with men and women hurrying past. Roy stopped for a moment and looked down the street. He broke his silence.

'It has great power,' he said. 'Don't you feel that it has great power?'

He spoke with extreme force. As he spoke, I knew for sure what I had already suspected: he had brought me to Berlin to convert me.

For the rest of that morning we argued, walking under the steely sky through the harsh, busy streets. We had never had an argument before – now it was painful, passionate, often bitter. We knew each other's language, each of us knew all the experience the other could command, it was incomparably more piercing than arguing with a stranger.

When once we began, we could not leave it all day; on and off we came back to the difference between us. Most of the passion and bitterness was on my side. I was not reasonable that day, either as we walked the streets or sat in his high cold rooms. I kept breaking out with incredulity and rancour. We were still talking violently, when it was ten o'clock and time to leave for the Adlon.

He seemed to be using his gifts for a purpose that I detested. He had not wanted me to become absorbed in the ragtag and bobtail of the Knesebeckstrasse. He loved them, but it was not that part of Germany he wanted me to see. They did not talk politics, except to grumble passively at laws and taxes which impinged on them; the only political remarks on the night I arrived were a few diatribes against the régime by the school teacher, who was as usual opinionated, hot-headed and somewhat half-baked. Roy warned her to be careful outside the house. There was an asinine endearingness about her.

Roy wanted me to see what he called – in the face of my scorn – the revolution. That day he made his case for it, in a temper that was better than mine, though even his was sometimes sharp. He had set out to convince me that the Nazis had history on their side.

The future would be in German hands. There would be great suffering on the way, they might end in a society as dreadful as the worst of this present one: but there was a chance – perhaps a better chance than any other – that in time, perhaps in our lifetime, they would create a brilliant civilisation.

'If they succeed,' said Roy, 'everyone will forget the black spots. In history success is the only virtue.'

He knew how to use the assumptions that all our political friends made at that period. He had not lived in the climate of 'fellow travellers' for nothing. Francis Getliffe, like many other scientists, had at that period moved near to the communist line: my brother Martin, now a research student at our college, was not far away. We had all been affected by that climate of thought. Men needed to plan on a superhuman scale, said Roy with a hint of the devil quoting scripture; Europe must be one, so that men could plan wide and deep enough; soon the world must be one. How could it become one except by force? Who had both the force and the will? No price was too high to pay, to see the world made one. 'It won't be made one by reason. Men never give up jobs and power unless they must.'

Only the Germans or Russians could do it. They had both got energy set free, through a new set of men seizing power. 'They've got the energy of a revolution. It comes from very deep.' They had both done dreadful things with it, for men in power always did dreadful things. But the Promethean force might do something wonderful. 'Either of them might. I've told you before, the truth lies at both extremes,' said Roy. 'But I'll back these people. They're slightly crazy, of course. All revolutionaries are slightly crazy. That's why they are revolutionaries. A good solid well-adjusted man like Arthur Brown just couldn't be one. I'm not sure that you could. But I could, Lewis. If I'd been born here, I should have been.'

Not many people had the nature to be revolutionaries, said Roy. And those who had felt dished when they had won their revolution and then could not keep their own jobs. Like the old Bolsheviks. Like Röhm. The Nazis had collected an astonishing crowd of bosses – some horrible, some intensely able, some intellectuals who had seen their chance, some fanatics. 'That's why something may come of them,' said Roy. 'They may be crazy, but they're not commonplace men. You won't believe it, but one or two of them are good. *Good*, I tell you.'

It was that fantastic human mixture that had taken hold of him. They were men of flesh and bone. They were human. He said one needed to choose between them and the Russians. He had made his choice. Communism was the most dry and sterile of human creeds – 'no illustrations, no capital letters. Life is more mixed that that. Life is richer than that. It's darker than the communists think. They're optimistic children. Life is darker than they think, but it's also richer. You know it is. Think of their books. They're the most sterile and thinnest you've ever seen.' Roy talked of our communist friends. 'They're shallow. They can't feel anything except moral indignation. They're not human. Lewis, I can't get on with them any more.'

Inflamed by anxiety and anger, I accused him of being perverse and self-destructive: of being intoxicated by the Wagnerian passion for death; of losing all his sense through meeting, for the first time, men surgent with a common purpose: of being seduced by his liking for Germany, by the ordinary human liking for people one has lived among for long. He was deceiving himself. Like other rich men, I said, he was blinding himself to the horrors, pretending that though this was evil it was evil out of which good might come, and incidentally saving his money.

'This isn't the time to fool yourself,' I cried. 'If ever there was a time to keep your head—'

'Are you keeping yours?' said Roy quietly. He pointed to the mirror behind us. His face was sombre, mine was white with anger. I had lost my temper altogether. I accused him of being overwhelmed by his success in Berlin, by the flattery and attentions.

'Not fair,' said Roy. 'You've forgotten that you used to know me. Haven't you?'

Out of doors, as we walked to the Adlon, the night was sullen. The mercury-vapour lamps shone livid on the streets and on the lowering clouds. We made our way beneath them, and I recovered myself a little. Partly from policy: it was not good to let a man like Schäder see us shaken. But much more because of that remark of Roy's: 'You used to know me'. He had said it without a trace of reproach. Walking in the frosty night, I felt a pang of sorrow.

At the hotel, we were shown into a private room, warm, glowing, soft-carpeted, the table glittering with linen, silver, and glass. Houston Eggar had decided that the party would not harm his prospects; he gave us his tough, cheerful greeting, and talked to us and Joan in a manner that was masculine, assertive, anxious to make an impression, both on the niece of Lord Boscastle and on a comely woman. He had also noted me down as potentially useful – not useful enough to make him fix a lunch during my remaining days in Berlin, but quite worth his trouble to say with matey heartiness that we must 'get together soon'. I had a soft spot for Eggar. There was something very simple and humble about his matter-of-fact ambitiousness. Incidentally, he was only a counsellor at forty-five: he had still to make up for lost time.

Joan said to Roy:

'Are you better? You look very tired.'

'Just so,' said Roy. 'Through listening to Lewis. He gets more eloquent.'

'You shouldn't have got up. It's stupid of you.'

'He could talk to me in bed.'

Joan laughed. His solemn expression had always melted her. For the moment, she was happy to be near him, on any terms.

Servants flung open the door, and Schäder and Ammatter came in. Roy introduced each of us: Schäder spoke good English, though his accent was strange: in an efficient and courteous fashion, he discovered exactly how much German we each possessed.

'We shall speak English then,' said Schäder. 'Perhaps we find difficulties. Then Roy shall translate and help us.'

This left Ammatter out of the conversation for most of the dinner. But he accepted the position in a flood of what appeared to be voluble and deferential compliments. It was interesting to notice his excessive deference to Schäder. Ammatter was, as I had seen in Cambridge, a tricky, cunning, fluid-natured man, very much on the make. But I was familiar with academic persons on the make, and I thought that, even allowing for his temperament, his obsequiousness before official power marked a real difference in tradition. At the college, Roy and I were used to eminent politicians and civil servants coming down for the week-end; the connection in England between colleges such as ours and the official world was very close; perhaps because it was so close, the visitors did not receive elaborate respect, but instead were liable to be snubbed caustically by old Winslow.

Ammatter made up unashamedly to Schäder, who took very little notice of him. Schäder said that it was late, asked us whether, as soon as we had finished a first drink, we would not like to begin dinner. He took Joan to the table, and I watched him stoop over her chair.

He was, as Roy had said, in the early thirties. His face was lined and mature, but he still looked young. His forehead was square, furrowed and massive, and there was nearly a straight line from temple to chin, so that the whole of his face made up a triangle. His hair was curly, untidy in a youthful fashion; he seemed tough and muscular. It was the kind of physical make-up one does not often find in 'intellectual' people, though I knew one or two businessmen who gave the same impression of vigour, alertness and activity.

As he presided over the dinner, his manners were pleasant, sometimes rather over-elaborate. He was the son of a bank clerk and in his rush to power he had, as it were, invented a form of manners for himself. And he showed one aching cavity of a man who had worked unremittingly hard, who had attained great responsibility early, who had never had time to play. He was getting married in a month, and he talked about it with the naïve exaggerated trenchancy of a very young man. He was a little afraid.

I thought that he knew nothing of women. It flashed out once that he envied Roy his loves. As a rule, his attitude to Roy was half-contemptuous, half-admiring. He had a kind of amused wonder that Roy showed no taste for place or glory. With pressing friendliness, he wanted Roy to cut a figure in the limelight. If nowhere else, then he should get all the academic honours – and Schäder asked Ammatter sharply when the university would do something for Roy.

Dinner went on. Schäder passed some elaborate compliments to Joan: he was interested, hotly interested like a young man, in her feeling for Roy. Then he called himself back to duty, and addressed me:

'Roy has told me, Mr Eliot, that you are what we call a social democrat?'

'Yes.'

Schäder was regarding me intently with large eyes in which there showed abnormally little white: they were eyes dominating, pertinacious, astute. He grinned.

'We found here that the social democrats gave us little trouble. We thought they were nice harmless people.'

'Yes,' I said. 'We noticed that.'

Roy spoke to Schäder.

'I am sure,' said Schäder with firm politeness, 'that I shall find much in common with Mr Eliot.'

It was clear that I had to do the talking. Eggar was too cautious to enter the contest; he made an attempt to steer us away to placid subjects, such as the Davis Cup. Roy gave him a smile of extreme diablerie, as though whispering the letters 'C.M.G.'. It was left to me to stand against Schäder, and in fact I was glad to. It was a relief after the day with Roy. I was completely in control of my temper now. Joan was an ally, backing me up at each turn of the conflict. I had never felt her approve of me before.

First Schäder tried me out by reflecting on the machinery of government. What did I think about the way governments must develop – not morally, that should not enter between us, said Schäder, but technically? Did I realise the difference that organised science must mean? Two hundred years ago determined citizens with muskets were almost as good as the King's armies. Now the apparatus was so much more complex. A central government which could rely on its armed forces was able to stay in power for ever. 'So far as I can see, Mr Eliot, revolution is impossible from now on – unless it starts among those who hold the power. Will you tell me if I am wrong?'

I thought he was right, appallingly right: it was one of the sinister facts of the twentieth-century scene. He went on to tell me his views about what the central government could and must control, and how it must operate. He knew it inside out; there was no more sign of the young man unaccustomed to society, timid with women. Although he was a Minister, he did much work that in England would have been done by his Permanent Secretary: as a matter of fact, he seemed to do a considerable amount of actual executive work, which in an English department would never have reached the higher civil servants, let alone the Minister. He ran his department rather as an acquaintance of mine, Paul Lufkin, a gifted English industrialist, ran his business. It was the general practice of the régime; sometimes it made for confusion, particularly (as Schäder straightforwardly admitted) when the party officials he had introduced as his own staff got across the old, regular, German civil service. He made another admission: they were finding it hard to collect enough men who could be trained into administrators, high or low. 'That may set a limit to the work a government can do, Mr Eliot. And we are an efficient race. If you plan your society, you will find this difficulty much greater – for you educate such a small fraction of your population. Also, forgive me, I do not think you are very efficient.'

'We're not so stupid as we look,' I said.

Schäder looked at me, and laughed. He went on questioning me, stating his experience on the technique of government – the mechanical technique, the paper work, the files, the use of men.

He was being patient in coming to his point. At last he knew enough about me. He said:

'Tell me, Mr Eliot, what is to cause war between your country and mine? You are not the man to give me hypocritical reasons. Do you think you will fight for the balance of power?'

I waited for a second.

'I think we should,' I said.

He narrowed his eyes.

'That is interesting. You cannot keep the balance of power for ever. Why should you trouble—'

'No one is fit to be trusted with power,' I said. I was replying to Roy, as well as to him. 'No one. I should not like to see your party in charge of Europe, Dr Schäder. I should not like to see any group of men in charge – not me or my friends or anyone else. Any man who has lived at all knows the follies and wickedness he's capable of. If he does not know it, he is not fit to govern others. And if he does know it, he knows also that neither he nor any man ought to be allowed to decide a single human fate. I am not speaking of you specially, you understand: I should say exactly the same of myself.'

Our eyes met. I was certain, as one can be certain in a duel across the table, that for the first time he took me seriously.

'You do not think highly of men, Mr Eliot.'

'I am one,' I said.

He shrugged. He got back to his own ground, telling me that he did not suppose my countrymen shared my rather 'unusual reasons' for believing in the balance of power. I was taking up the attack now, and replied that men's instincts were often wiser than their words.

'So you think, if we become too powerful, you will go to war with us?'

I could see nothing at that table but Roy's face, grave and stricken. During this debate he had been silent. He sat there before my eyes, listening for what I was bound to say.

'I think we shall,' I said.

'You are not a united country, Mr Eliot. Many people in England would not agree with you?'

He was accurate, but I did not answer. I said:

'They hope it will not be necessary.'

'Yes,' said Roy. 'They hope that.'

Joan was staring at him with love and horror, praying that he would not say too much.

'We all hope that,' she said, in a voice that was deep with yearning for him. 'But you've not been in England much lately. Opinion is changing. I must tell you about it – perhaps on the way home?'

'You must,' said Roy with a spark of irony. But he had responded to her; for a moment she had reached him.

'Will they not do more than hope?' said Schäder.

'It depends on you,' said Joan.

'Will they not do more than hope?' Schäder repeated to Roy.

'Some will,' said Roy clearly.

Joan was still staring at him, as though she were guarding him from danger.

Eggar intervened, in a companionable tone:

'There is all the good will in the world —'

'Let us suppose,' said Schäder, ignoring him, 'that it comes to war. Let us suppose that we decide it is necessary to become powerful. To

973

become more powerful than you and your friends believe to be desirable, Mr Eliot—'

'Believe to be safe,' I said.

'Let us suppose we have to extend our frontiers, Mr Eliot. Which some of your friends appear to dislike. You go to war. Then what happens?'

'We have been to war before,' I said.

'I am not interested in history. I am interested in this year and the next. You go to war. Can you fight a war?'

'We must try.'

'You will not be a united people. There will be many who do not wish for war. There will be many who like us. They see our faults, but they like us. If there is a war, they will not wish to conquer us. What will they do?'

He expected Roy to answer. So did Joan and I. But Roy sat gazing at the table. Was he considering either of us?

Schäder looked at him curiously. Not getting an answer, Schäder paused, and then went on:

'How can you fight a war?'

In a few moments the conversation lagged, and Joan said, quite easily:

'I really think I ought to get Roy to his house, Dr Schäder. This is his first day out of bed, you know. He looks awfully tired.'

Roy said without protest:

'I should go, perhaps.' He gave a slight smile. 'Eliot can stay and talk about war, Reinhold. You two need to talk about war.'

Schäder said, with the comradely physical concern that one often meets in aggressive, tough, powerful men: 'Of course you must go if you are tired. You must take care, Roy. Please look after him, Miss Royce. He has many friends who wish to see him well.'

He showed them out with elaborate kindness, and then returned to Eggar and me. Eggar had realised that he must let Joan have Roy to herself, and he stayed listening while Schäder and I talked until late. I told Schäder – much more confidently than I felt at the time – that he must not exaggerate the effect of disunity in England. He must not underestimate the organised working class. He wasn't hearing representative voices. As for those he did hear, it was easy to alter opinions very quickly in the modern world. We had a long discussion on the effectiveness of propaganda. In the long run, said Schäder, it is utterly effective. 'If we entertained you here for a few years, Mr Eliot, you would accept things that now you find incredible. In the long run, people believe what they hear – if they hear nothing else.'

He was a formidable man, I thought, as I walked home with Houston Eggar. I was troubled by his confidence: it was not the confidence of the stupid. He was lucky in his time, for he fitted it exactly. He was born for this kind of world.

'Calvert is not as discreet as he ought to be,' said Eggar, as we walked down the deserted street.

'No.' All my anxiety returned.

'It does *not* make our job easier. I wish you'd tell him. I know it's just thoughtlessness.'

'I will if I get the chance,' I said.

'Between ourselves,' said Houston Eggar, 'this is a pretty thankless job, Eliot. I suppose I can't grumble. It's a good jumping-off ground. It ought to turn out useful, but sometimes one doesn't know what to do for the best. Everyone likes to have something to show for their trouble.'

A clock was striking two when I let myself in at Roy's front door. I had been anxious ever since he left the dinner. Now I was shaken by a sudden, unreasonable access of anxiety, such as I had felt so often on going home after a week away.

I tip-toed in, across the great cold rooms. Then, worried and tense, I meant to satisfy myself that he was no worse. I went to his bedroom door. I stopped outside. Through the oak I could hear voices, speaking very quietly. One was a woman's.

I lay awake, thinking of them both. Could Joan calm him, even yet? I wished I could believe it. It was much later, it must have been four o'clock, before I heard the click of a door opening. By that time I was drowsing fitfully, and at the sound I jumped up with dread. Another door clicked outside: Joan had left: I found it hard to go to sleep again.

CHAPTER XXVII

UNDER THE MERCURY-VAPOUR LAMPS

ROY did not refer to Joan's visit. She stayed with the Eggars a day or two longer, and then moved on to some friends of the Boscastles in Stockholm. I saw her with Roy only once. She seemed precariously hopeful, and he gentle.

For the rest of my week in Berlin, he was quiet and subdued, though he seemed to be fighting off the true melancholy. He took time from his work to entertain me; he arranged our days so that, like tourists, we could occupy ourselves by talking about the sights.

We slippered our way round Sans Souci, stood in the Garrison Church at Potsdam, sailed along the lakes in the harsh weather, walked through the Brandenburg villages. We had travelled in Europe together before, but this was the first time we had searched for things to see: it was also the first time we had said so little.

I did not meet Schäder again, nor any of his official friends. But I saw a good deal of Ammatter and the university people, in circumstances of fairly high-class farce. Months before, Ammatter had interpreted Schäder's interest in Roy to mean that the university should give him some honour. Ammatter promptly set about it. And, academic dignitaries having certain characteristics in common everywhere, his colleagues behaved much as our college would have done.

They suspected that Ammatter was trying to suck up to high authorities; they suspected he had an eye on some other job; they could not have been righter. The prospect of someone else getting a job moved them to strong moral indignation. They duly took up positions for a stately disapproving minuet. What opinions of Roy's work besides Ammatter's had been offered? Ammatter diligently canvassed the oriental faculty in Berlin, Tübingen, Stuttgart, Breslau, Marburg, Bonn: there seemed to be no doubt, the senate reluctantly admitted, that this Englishman was a scholar of extreme distinction.

That step had taken months. The next step was according to pattern. Though everyone would like to recognise his distinction (which was the positive equivalent of 'in his own best interests'), surely they were prevented by their code of procedure? It was impossible to give an honorary degree to a man of twenty-nine; it would open the door to premature proposals of all kinds; if they departed from custom for this one orientalist, they would be flooded with demands from all the other faculties. It was even more impossible to make him a Corresponding Member of the Academy: the orientalists were already above their quota: it would mean asking for a special dispensation: it was unthinkable to ask for a special dispensation, when one was breaking with precedent in putting forward a candidate so young.

Those delays had satisfactorily taken care of several more months. I thought that the resources of obstruction were well up to our native standard – though I would have backed Arthur Brown against any of them as an individual performer.

That was the position at the time of our dinner with Schäder. Ammatter had taken Schäder's question as a rebuke and an instruction to deliver a suitable answer in quick time. So, during that week, he conferred with the Rector. If they abandoned the hope of honorary degrees and corresponding memberships, could they not introduce the American title of visiting professor? It would recognise a fine achievement: it would cost them nothing: it would do the university good. No doubt, I thought when I heard the story, there was a spirited and enjoyable exchange of sentiments about how the university could in no way whatsoever be affected by political influences. No doubt they agreed that, in a case like this, which was crystal-pure upon its own merits, it would do no harm to retain a Minister's benevolent interest.

The upshot of it all was that Roy found himself invited to address a seminar at very short notice. At the seminar the Rector and several of the senate would be present: Roy was to describe his recent researches. Afterwards Ammatter planned that the Rector would make the new proposal his own; it would require 'handling', as Arthur Brown would say, to slip an unknown title into the university; it was essential that the Rector should speak from first-hand knowledge. Apparently the Rector was convinced that it would be wise to act.

I heard some of the conferences between Ammatter and Roy, without understanding much of them. It was when we were alone that Roy told me the entire history. His spirits did not often rise nowadays to their old brilliance: but he had not been able to resist giving Ammatter the impression that he needed recognition from the University of Berlin more than anything on earth. This impression had made Ammatter increasingly agitated; for he took it for granted that Roy told Schäder so, and that his, Ammatter's, fortunes hung on the event. Ammatter took to ringing up Roy late at night on the days before the seminar: another member of the senate was attending: all would come well. Roy protested extreme nervousness about his address, and Ammatter fussed over the telephone and came round early in the morning to reassure him.

I begged to be allowed to come to the seminar. With a solemn face, Roy said that he would take me. With the same solemn face, he answered Ammatter on the telephone the evening before: I could hear groans and cries from the instrument as Ammatter assured, encouraged, cajoled, reviled. Roy put down the receiver with his most earnest, mystifying expression.

'I've told him that I must put up a good show tomorrow,' he said. 'But

I was obliged to tell him that too much depends on it. I may get stage fright.'

Roy dressed with exquisite care the next morning. He put on his most fashionable suit, a silk shirt, a pair of suede shoes. 'Must look well,' he said. 'Can't take any risks.' In fact, as he sat on the Rector's right hand in the oriental lecture room at the university, he looked as though he had strayed in by mistake. The Rector was a bald fat man with rimless spectacles and a stout pepper-coloured suit; he sat stiffly between Roy and Ammatter, down at the lecturer's desk. The theatre ran up in tiers, and there sat thirty or forty men in the three bottom rows. Most of them were homely, academic, middle-aged, dressed in sensible reach-me-downs. In front of their eyes sat Roy, wooden-faced, slight, elegant, young, like a *flâneur* at a society lunch.

It was an oriental seminar, and so Ammatter was in the chair. He made a speech to welcome Roy; I did not understand it, but it was obviously jocular, flattering, the speech of an impresario who, after much stress, knows that he has pulled it off. Roy stood up, straight and solemn. There was some clapping. Roy began to speak *in English*. I saw Ammatter's face cloud with astonishment, used as he was to hear Roy speak German as well as a foreigner could. Other faces began to look slightly glazed, for German scholars were no better linguists than English ones, and not more than half a dozen people there could follow spoken English comfortably. But many more had to pretend to understand; they did not like to seem baffled; very soon heads were nodding wisely when the lecturer appeared to be establishing a point.

Actually Roy had begun with excessive formality to explain that his subject was of great intricacy, and he found it necessary to use his own language, which of course they would understand. His esteemed master and colleague, his esteemed professor Ammatter, had said that the lecture would describe recent advances in Manichaean studies. 'I think that would be *much* too broad a subject to attempt in one afternoon. It would be extremely rash to make such an attempt,' said Roy, and uncomprehending heads began to shake in sympathy. 'I should regard it as coming dangerously near *journalism* to offer my learned colleagues a kind of popular précis. So with your permission I have chosen a topic where I can be definite enough not to offend you. I hope to examine to your satisfaction five points in Soghdian lexicography.'

He lectured for an hour and twenty minutes. His face was imperturbably solemn – except that twice he made a grotesque donnish pun, and gave a shy smile. At that sign, the whole room rocked with laughter, as though he had revealed a ray of humour of the most divine subtlety. When he frowned, they shook their heads. When he sounded triumphant, they nodded in unison.

Even those who could understand his English must have been very little the wiser. For he was analysing some esoteric problems about words which he had just discovered; they were in a dialect of Soghdian which he was the only man in the world to have unravelled. To add a final touch of fantasy, he quoted long passages of Soghdian: so that much of the lecture seemed to be taking place in Soghdian itself.

He recited from memory sentence after sentence in this language, completely incomprehensible to anyone but himself. The strange sounds finished up as though he had asked a question. Roy proceeded to answer it himself.

'Just so,' he said firmly, and then went on in Soghdian to what appeared to be the negative view. That passage came to an end, and Roy at once commented on it in a stern tone. 'Not a bit of it,' he said.

It was the most elaborate of all his tricks. He knew that, if one had an air of wooden certainty and a mesmerising eye, they would never dare to say that it was too difficult for them. None of these learned men would dare to say that he had not understood a word.

An hour went by. I wondered when he was going to end. But he had set himself five words to discuss, and even when he arrived at the fifth he was not going to leave his linguistic speculations unsaid. He finished strongly in a wave of Soghdian, swelled by remarks in the later forms of the language, with illustrations from all over the Middle East. Then he said, modestly and unassumingly:

'I expect you may think that I have been too bold and slapdash in some of my conclusions. I have not had time to give you all the evidence, but I think I can present it. I very much hope that if any of my colleagues can show me where I have been too superficial, he will please do so now.'

Roy slid quietly into his seat. There was a little stupefied applause, which became louder and clearer. The clapping went on.

Ammatter got up and asked for contributions and questions. There was a long stupefied silence. Then someone rose. He was an eminent philologist, possibly the only person present who had profited by the lecture. He spoke in halting, correct English:

'These pieces of analysis are most deep and convincing, if I may say so. I have one thing to suggest about your word—'

He made his suggestion which was complex and technical and sounded ingenious. At once Roy jumped up to reply – and replied at length *in*

German. In fluent German. Then I heard the one complaint of the afternoon. Two faces in the row in front of me turned to each other. One asked why he had not lectured in German. The other could not understand.

Roy's discussion with the philologist went on. It was not a controversy; they were agreeing over a new possibility, which Roy promised to investigate (it appeared later as a paragraph in one of his books). The Rector made a speech to thank Roy for his lecture. Ammatter supported him. There was more applause, and Roy thanked the meeting in a few demure and solemn words.

Before we left the lecture theatre, Ammatter went up to Roy in order to shake hands before parting for the day. He was smiling knowingly, but as he gazed at Roy I caught an expression of sheer, bemused, complete bewilderment.

Roy and I went out into the Linden. It was late afternoon.

'Well,' said Roy, 'I thought the house was a bit cold towards the middle. But I got a good hand at the end, didn't I?'

I had nothing to say. I took him to the nearest café and stood him a drink.

That afternoon brought back the past. I hoped that it might buoy him up, but soon he was quiet again and stayed so till we said goodbye at the railway station.

He was quiet even at Romantowski's party. This happened the night before I left, and many people in the house were invited, as well as friends from outside. Romantowski and his patron lived in two rooms at the top of the house, just under the little dancer's attic. It was getting late, the party was noisy, when Roy and I climbed up.

The rooms were poor, there was linoleum on the floor, the guests were drinking out of cups. Somehow Romantowski's patron had managed to buy several bottles of spirits. How he had afforded it, Roy could not guess. Presumably he was being madly extravagant in order to please the young man. Poor devil, I said to Roy. For it looked as though Romantowski had demanded the party in order to hook a different fish. There were several youngish men round him.

I asked what Schäder and his colleagues would think of this sight. 'Schäder would be shocked,' said Roy. 'He's a bit of a prude. But he needn't mind. Most of these people will fight – they'll fight better than respectable men.'

That reminded him of war, and his face darkened. We were standing by the window over the street: we looked inwards to the shouting, rackety crowd.

'If there is a war,' said Roy, 'what can I do?'

He was seared by the thought. He said:

'There doesn't seem to be a place for me, does there?'

The little dancer joined us, lapping up her drink, cheerful, lively, bright-eyed.

'How are you, Ursula?' said Roy.

'I think I am better,' she said, with her unquenchable hope. 'Soon it will be good weather.'

'Really better?' said Roy. He had still not contrived a plan for sending her to the mountains: he did not dare talk to her direct.

'In the summer I shall be well.'

She laughed at him, she laughed at both of us, she had a bright cheeky wit.

Then Romantowski came mincing up. He offered me a cigarette, but I said I did not smoke. 'Poor you!' said Willy Romantowski, using his only English phrase, picked up heaven knows how. He spoke to Roy in his brisk Berlin twang, of which I could scarcely make out a word. I noticed Roy mimic him as he replied. Romantowski gave a pert grin. Again he asked something. Roy nodded, and the young man went away.

'Roy, you should not!' cried Ursula. 'You should not give him money! He treats poor Hans' (Hans was the clerk, the 'black avised') 'so badly. He is cruel to poor Hans. He will take your money and buy clothes – so as to interest these little gentlemen.' She nodded towards the knot in the middle of the room. 'It is not sensible to give him money.'

'Too old to be sensible.' Roy smiled at her. 'Ursula, if I don't give him money, he will take it from poor Hans. Poor Hans will have to find it from somewhere. He is spending too much money. I'm frightened that we shall have Hans in trouble.'

'It is so,' said Ursula.

Roy went on to say that we could not save Willy for Hans, but we might still save Hans from another disaster. Both Roy and the little dancer were afraid that he was embezzling money, to squander it on Willy. Ursula sighed.

'It is bad,' she said, 'to have to buy love.'

'It can be frightful,' said Roy.

'It is bad to have to run after love.'

'Have you seen him today?' said Roy.

'No. He was too busy.' 'He' was an elderly producer in a ramshackle theatre. Ursula's eyes were full of tears.

'I'm sorry, my dear.'

'Perhaps I shall see him tomorrow. Perhaps he will be free.'

She smiled, lips quivering at Roy, and he took her hand.

'I wish I could help,' he said.

'You do help. You are so kind and gentle.' Suddenly she gazed at him. 'Roy, why are you unhappy? When you have so many who love you. Have you not all of us who love you?'

He kissed her. It was entirely innocent. Theirs was a strange tenderness. The little dancer wiped her eyes, plucked up her hope and courage, and went off to find another drink.

The air was whirling with smoke, and was growing hot. Roy flung open the window, and leaned out into the cold air. Over the houses at the bottom of the road there hung a livid greenish haze: it was light diffused from the mercury-vapour lamps of the Berlin streets.

'I like those lamps,' said Roy.

He added:

'I've walked under them so often in the winter. I felt I was absolutely – anonymous. I don't think I've ever been so free. I used to put up my coat collar and walk through the streets under those lamps, and I was sure that no one knew me.'

CHAPTER XXVIII

SELF-HATRED

In Cambridge that May, the days were cold and bright. Roy played cricket for the first time since the old Master's death; I watched him one afternoon, and was surprised to see that his eye was in. His beautiful off-drive curled through the covers, he was hooking anything short with instants to spare, he played a shot of his own, off the back foot past point; yet I knew, though he did not wake me nowadays, that his nights were haunted. He was working as he used in the blackest times; I believed he was drinking alone, and one or twice I had heard in his voice the undertone of frantic gaiety. Usually he sat grave and silent in hall, though he still bestirred himself to cheer up a visitor whom everyone else was ignoring. Several nights, he scandalised some of our friends by his remarks on Germany.

Towards the end of May, he had a letter from Rosalind, in which she said that she would soon be announcing her engagement to Ralph Udal. When he told me, I wondered for an instant whether she was playing a last card.

He smiled at the news. Yet I thought he was not quite indifferent. He had been wretched when the letter came, and he smiled with a kind of scathing fondness. But Rosalind had been able to rouse his jealousy, as no other woman could. In their time together, she had often behaved like a bitch and he like a frail and ordinary lover. Even now, in the midst of the most frightening griefs, he was moved by the thought of losing her for good. He wrote to Ralph and to her. Somehow, the fact that she should have chosen Ralph added to Roy's feeling of loss and loneliness, added to an entirely unheroic pique. He said that he had told Rosalind to call on him some time. 'I expect she'll come with her husband,' said Roy with irritated sadness. 'It will be extremely awkward for everyone. I've never talked to her politely. It's absurd.'

The announcement was duly published in *The Times*. Roy read it in the combination room, and Arthur Brown asked him inquisitively:

'I see your friend Udal is getting married, Roy. I rather fancied that I remembered the name of the young woman. Isn't it someone you introduced me to in your rooms quite a while ago?'

'Just so,' said Roy.

'From what I remember of her,' said Brown, 'of course it was only a glimpse, I shouldn't have regarded her as particularly anxious to settle down as a parson's wife in a nice quiet country living.'

'No?' said Roy. He did not like the sight of their names in print: he was not going to be drawn.

But, annoyed though he was at the news, he could not help chuckling with laughter at a letter from Lady Muriel. It was the only time in those weeks that I saw him unshadowed. He had written several times to Lady Muriel about that time; for the Boscastles were visiting Cambridge in June, to mark the end of Humphrey's last term at Magdalene, and Roy had been persuading Lady Muriel to come with them. So far as I knew, he had not asked Joan – I was not certain what had happened between them, but I was afraid that it was the irreparable break.

Roy showed me Lady Muriel's letter. She was delighted that he was pressing her to come to Cambridge; since she left the Lodge, she had been curiously diffident about appearing in the town. Perhaps it was because, after domineering in the Lodge, she could not bear taking a dimmer place. But she was willing to accompany the Boscastles, now that Roy had invited her. She went on:

'You will have seen this extraordinary action on the part of our vicar. I am compelled to take very strong exception to it. Unfortunate is too mild a word. I know this young woman used to be a friend of yours, but that was a different matter. You may sometimes have thought I was old-fashioned, but I realise men have their temptations. That cannot, however, be regarded as any excuse for a *clergyman*. He is in a special position, and I have never for a single moment contemplated such an outrage from any vicar of our own church. I do not know what explanations to give to our tenants, and I find Helen no help in this, and very remiss in performing her proper duties. I have found it necessary to remind her of her obligations (though naturally I am always very careful about keeping myself in the background). I consider our vicar has put me in an impossible position. I do not see how I can receive this woman in our house. Hugh says it is your fault for bullying him into giving the living to our present vicar – but I defend you, and tell him that it takes a woman to understand women, and that I knew this woman was a designing hussy from the first moment I set eyes on her. Men are defenceless against such creatures. I have noticed it all my life, or certainly since Hugh got married. I shall be most surprised,' Lady Muriel finished in magnificent rage, 'if this woman does not turn out to be *barren*.'

'Now just why has Lady Mu decided that?' cried Roy.

It gave him an hour's respite. But the days were dragging by in black searing fears and ravaged nights, in anguish from the moment when, after he had lain awake through the white hours of the early morning, he roused himself exhaustedly to open the daily paper. The news glared at him – for his melancholy was the melancholy of his nature, but it had drawn into him the horror of war.

Most of the college were uncomfortable and strained about the prospect of war; only one or two of the very old escaped. Several men were torn, though not so deeply as Roy. They were solid conservatives, men of property, used to the traditional way of life; they were not fools, they knew a war must destroy many of their comforts and perhaps much else; they had hated communism for twenty years, in secret they still hated it more than national socialism; yet, with the obstinate patriotic sense of their class and race, they were slowly coming to feel that they might have to fight Germany. They felt it with extreme reluctance. Even now, they were chary of the prospect of letting 'that man Churchill' into the cabinet. There might still be time for a compromise. In May, that was the position which Arthur Brown took up. He was just as stubborn as he was in college politics: he was appreciably more anti-German than most of the college right. Some were much more willing to appease at almost any cost.

They had all gathered rumours about Roy's sympathies, they had heard some of his comments in hall. Ironically, his name was flaunted about, this time as an authority, by old Despard-Smith. The old man had been virulently pro-Munich, was bitterly in favour of any other accommodation. He kept quoting Roy: 'Calvert has just come back from Germany and he says. . . .' 'Calvert told someone yesterday. . . .' Roy smiled, to find himself approved of at last in that quarter.

But Francis Getliffe did not smile at all. He was away from Cambridge many days in that summer term; we knew he was busy on Air Ministry experiments, but it was only much later that we realised he had been occupied with the first installations of radar. He came back and dined in hall one night, looking as tired as Roy – looking in fact more worn, though not so hag-ridden. It happened to be a night when most of the left were not dining. Nor was Winslow, who was an old-fashioned liberal but spoke on Getliffe's side – he had quarrelled acidly with the older men over Munich.

That night Despard-Smith and others were saying that war was quite unnecessary. Francis Getliffe, short-tempered with fatigue, told them that they would soon present Hitler with the whole game. 'Calvert says,' began Despard-Smith. Getliffe interrupted him: 'Unless you all keep your nerve, the devils have got us. It's our last chance. I'm tired of this nonsense.'

The high table was truculent and quarrelsome in its own fashion, but it was not used to words so openly harsh. With some dignity, old Despard-Smith announced that he did not propose to drink port that night: 'I have been a fellow for fifty years next February, and it is too late to begin having my head bitten off in this hall.'

Arthur Brown, Roy, Francis Getliffe and I were by ourselves in the combination room, and Brown ordered a bottle of claret.

'It's rather sensible to drink an occasional bottle,' said Brown, looking shrewdly at the others. 'We never know whether it will be so accessible in the near future.'

'I'm sorry, Brown,' said Francis Getliffe. 'I oughtn't to have cursed the old man.'

'It's all right, old chap,' said Arthur Brown. 'Everyone wants to address a few well-chosen remarks to Despard on some subject or other. How are you yourself?' He smiled at Francis, for Arthur Brown, whatever his hopes of a compromise, believed, as he said himself, in keeping his powder dry: and hence scientists wearing themselves out in military preparations had to be cherished.

'In good order,' said Francis. But it was false: he seemed as though he should be put to bed for a fortnight. He was painfully frayed, thinking of his experiments, thinking of how he could flog himself on, thinking of how many months were left. He turned to Roy:

'Calvert, you're doing harm.'

'Harm to what?'

'To our chances of winning this war.'

'The war hasn't come.'

'It will. You know as well as I do that it will.'

'I'm frightened that it will,' said Roy.

'The only thing to be frightened about,' said Francis, 'is that we shall slide out of it. That's what I'm frightened of. If we get out of it this time, we're finished. The fascists have won.'

'I suppose you mean the Germans,' said Arthur Brown, who never accepted anything which he suspected was a left-wing formula. 'I don't think I can go all the way with you, Getliffe. It might suit our book to have another breathing space.'

'No,' said Francis. 'Our morale will weaken. Theirs will get tougher.'

'Yes,' said Roy, 'theirs will get tougher.'

'You like the idea, don't you?' Francis cried.

'They are remarkable people.'

'Good God.' Francis's face was flushed with passion. 'You like authority wherever it rears its head.'

'That may be so. I haven't been very clever at finding it, have I?'

Roy had spoken with the lightness that deceived, and Francis did not realise that he had struck much deeper than he knew. Neither Arthur Brown nor I could take our eyes from Roy's face.

'I don't know what you've found,' said Francis. 'I should have thought you might be content among your fascist friends.'

'If so,' said Roy, 'I might have stayed there.'

'I don't see why not.'

'No,' said Roy, 'you wouldn't see why not.'

'You'd be less dangerous there than you are here,' shouted Francis.

'I dare say. I'm not so concerned about that as you are.'

'Then you've got to be,' Francis said, and the quarrel became fiercer. Arthur Brown tried to steady them, offered to present another bottle, but they were too far gone. Brown listened with a frown of puzzlement and concern. He admired Francis Getliffe, but his whole outlook, even his idioms, were foreign to Brown. Francis took it for granted, in the way in which he and I and many of our generation had been brought up, that there were two sides in the world, and that the battle between them was joined, and that no decent man could hesitate an instant. 'My Manichaeans had the same idea,' said Roy, which made Francis more angry.

To Francis, to all men like him and many less incisive, it all seemed starkly plain in black and white. Issues have to seem so at the fighting-points of history. At that moment, Francis was saying, everything must be sacrificed to win: this was the great crisis, and until it was over we could not afford free art, disinterested speculation, the pleasure of detachment, the vagaries of the lonely human soul. They were luxuries. This was no time for luxuries. Our society was dying, and we could not rest until we had the new one safe.

Roy replied, sometimes with his clarity, sometimes with the kind of gibe that infuriated Francis most. 'Do you believe everything that's written in Cyrillic letters?' asked Roy. 'I must learn Russian. I'm sure you'd be upset if I translated *Pravda* to you every night.' He told Francis that communism (or Francis's approach to it, for Francis was not a member of the party) was a 'romantic' creed, for all its dryness. 'It's realistic about the past. Entirely so. But it's wildly romantic about the future. Why, it believes it's quite easy to make men good. It's far more optimistic than Christianity. You need to read Saint Augustine, you know. Or Pascal. Or Hügel. But then they knew something of life.'

Once or twice Brown chuckled, but he was uneasy. He was deeply fond of Roy; much of what Roy said came far nearer to him than anything of Francis's.

But Brown was cautious and realistic. He believed Roy was utterly reckless – and every word he said on Germany filled Brown with alarm. Brown was ready to anticipate that his protégés would get into trouble. Roy's folly might be the most painful of all.

As for me, I was watching for the terrible elation. His wretchedness had weighed him down for weeks; it was melancholy at its deepest, and it was beginning to break into the lightning flashes.

I was expecting an outburst, and this time I was terrified where it would end.

It was that sign I was listening for, not anything else in their quarrel. But Roy's last words that night were quite calm.

'You think I'm dangerous, don't you?' he said. 'Believe this: you and your friends are much more so. You know you're right, don't you? It has never crossed your mind that you might be wrong. And that doesn't seem to you – dreadful.'

For a few days nothing seemed to change. Roy did not often dine in hall, but I listened for each rumour about him: when I saw Arthur Brown walking towards me in the court, intending to carry me off for a confidential talk, I wanted to shy away – but it was only to consider whether the time had come to 'ventilate' the question of a new fellow. Wars might be near us, but Arthur Brown took it for granted that the college government must be carried on. I asked Bidwell each morning how Mr Calvert was. 'He's not getting his sleep, sir,' said Bidwell. 'No, he's not getting his sleep. As I see it, sir – I know it's not my place to say it – but it's all on account of his old books. He's overtaxed his brain. That's how I see it, sir.'

Then, as a complete surprise, I received a note from Lady Muriel. She was staying at the University Arms: would I excuse the short notice, and go to the hotel for tea? I knew that she had arrived, I knew that Roy had given her dinner the night before: but I was astonished to be summoned. I had never been exactly a favourite of hers. I felt a vague malaise: I was becoming morbidly anxious.

Lady Muriel had taken a private sitting-room, looking out upon Parker's Piece. She greeted me as she used to in the Lodge; she seemed almost to fancy that she was still there.

'Good afternoon, Mr Eliot. I am glad that you were able to come.' Her neck was stiff, her back erect as ever; but it took more effort than it used. Trouble was telling, even on her. 'I will ring at once for tea.'

She asked about my work, my pupils and – inexorably – my wife. It all sounded like the rubric of days past. She poured out my cup of Indian tea; it was like her, I thought, to remember that I disliked China, to disapprove of my taste and attribute it to my lowly upbringing, and yet still to feel that a hostess was obliged to provide for it. She put her cup down, and regarded me with her bold innocent eyes.

'Mr Eliot, I wish to ask you a personal question.'

'Lady Muriel?'

'I do not wish to pry. But I must ask this question. Have you noticed anything wrong with Roy?'

I was taken aback.

'He's desperately overstrained,' I said.

'I considered that you might have noticed something,' said Lady Muriel. 'But I believe it is worse. I believe he has some worry on his mind.'

She stared at me.

'Do you know what this worry is, Mr Eliot?'

'He's very sad,' I began. 'But—'

'Mr Eliot,' Lady Muriel announced, 'I am a great believer in woman's intuition. Men are more gifted than we are intellectually. I should never have presumed to disagree with the Master on a purely intellectual matter. But it takes a woman to see that a man is hiding some private worry. Roy has always been so wonderfully carefree. I saw the difference at once.'

She sighed.

'Is it because of some woman?' she said.

'No.'

'Are you certain of that?'

'Absolutely.'

'We must put our finger on it,' said Lady Muriel. She was baffled, distressed, unhappy; her voice was firm and decided, but only by habit; 'Surely he knows we want to help him. Does he know that I would do anything to help him?'

'I am quite sure he does.'

'I am very glad to hear you say that. I should like to have told him. But there are things one always finds it impossible to say.'

She turned her head away from me. She was looking out of the window, when she said:

'I tried to get him to confide this worry last night.'

'What did you do?'

'I used a little finesse. Then I asked him straight out.'

She burst out:

'He put me off. I know men like to keep their secrets. But there are times when it is better for them to talk. If only they would see it. It is so difficult to make them. And one feels that one is only an intruder.'

She faced me again. Then I knew why she had averted her eyes. She was fighting back the tears.

'There is one thing I can do, Mr Eliot. I shall ring up my daughter Joan. She knows Roy better than I do. Perhaps she will be able to discover what is wrong. Then between us we could assist him.'

I used all my efforts to dissuade her. I argued, persuaded, told her that it was unwise. But the only real reason I could not give: and Lady Muriel stayed invincibly ignorant.

'Mr Eliot, you must allow me to judge when to talk to my daughter about a common friend.' She added superbly: 'My family have been brought up to face trouble.'

On the spot, she telephoned Joan, who was in London. There could be only one answer, the answer I had been scheming to avoid. It came, of course, Joan would catch the next train and see Roy that evening.

Lady Muriel said goodbye to me.

'My daughter and I will do our best, Mr Eliot. Thank you for giving my your advice.'

I went straight from the hotel to Roy's rooms. It was necessary that he should be warned at once. His outer door was not locked, as it was most evenings now – but he himself was lying limp in an armchair. There was no bottle or glass in sight; there was no manuscript under his viewing lamp, and no book open; it was as though he had lain there, inert, for hours.

'Hullo,' he said, from a far distance.

'I think you should know,' I said. 'Joan will be here in an hour or two.'

'Who?'

I repeated my message. It was like waking him from sleep.

At last he spoke, but still darkly, wearily.

'I don't want to see her.'

Some time afterwards he repeated:

'I don't want to see her. I saw her in Berlin. It made things worse. I've done her enough harm.'

'Roy,' I said, 'I'm afraid you must.'

His answer came after a long interval.

'I won't see her. It will be worse for her. It will be worse for both of us. I'm not fit to see anyone.'

'You can't just turn her away,' I said. 'She's trying to care for you. You must be good to her.'

Another long interval.

'I'm not fit to see anyone.'

'You must,' I said. 'You've meant too much to her, you know.'

Up to then I had had very little hope. In a moment I should have given up. But then I saw an astonishing thing. With a prodigious strain, as though he were calling frantically on every reserve of body and mind, Roy seemed to bring himself back into the world. He did not want to leave his stupor: there he had escaped, perhaps for hours: but somehow he forced himself. The strain lined him with grief and suffering. Yet he was himself, normal in speech, quiet, sad, able to smile, very gentle.

'I need to put a face on it,' he said. 'Poor dear. I shouldn't have brought her to this.'

He glanced at me:

'Am I fit to be seen now?'

'I think so.'

'I've got to look pretty reasonable when Joan comes. It's important,

Lewis. She mustn't think I'm ill.' He added, with a smile: 'She mustn't think I'm – mad.'

'It will be all right.'

'If she thinks I'm really off it,' again he smiled, 'she will want to look after me. And I might want her to. That mustn't happen, Lewis. I owe her more than the others. I can't inflict myself upon her now.'

He went on:

'She will try to persuade me. But it would do us both in. I was never free with her. And I should get worse. I don't know why it is.'

Nor did I. Of all women, she was most his equal. Yet she was the only one with whom he was not spontaneous. Somehow she had invaded him, she had not let him lose himself; by the very strength of her devotion, by her knowledge of him, by her share in his struggle, she had brought him back to the self he craved to throw away.

'Poor dear,' he said. 'I shall never find anyone like her. I must make her believe that I'm all right without her. If there's no other way, I must tell her I'm better without her. That's why I've got to look reasonable, Lewis. I've done her enough harm. She must get free of me now. It doesn't matter what she thinks of me.'

Then he spoke in a tone that was matter-of-fact, quiet, and utterly and intolerably unguarded.

'I hate myself,' said Roy. 'I've brought unhappiness to everyone I've known. It would have been better if I'd never lived. I should be wiped out so that everyone could forget me.'

I could not go through the pretence of consoling him, I could not reply until he spoke again.

'You would have been much happier if I'd never lived, Lewis. You can't deny it. This isn't the time to be hearty, is it?'

'Never mind about happiness,' I said. 'It can cut one off from too much. My life would have been different without you. I prefer it as it is.'

For a second, his face lit up.

'You've done all you could,' he said. 'I needed to tell you that – before it's too late. You've done more than anyone. You've done more even than she did. Now I must send her away. There will only be you whom I've ever talked to.'

I went back to my rooms, and from the window seat watched Joan enter the court. The undergraduates were in hall, she was alone on the path, walking with her gawky, sturdy step. She passed out of sight on her way to Roy's staircase. I sat there gazing down; I had missed dinner myself, I could not face high table that night; the court gleamed in the summer evening. The silence was broken as men came out of hall; they shouted to each other, sat on the edge of the grass; then they went away. Lights came on in some of the lower windows, though it was not yet sunset and bright in the court. Beside one light I could see a young man reading: the examinations were not yet finished, and the college was quiet for nine o'clock on a summer night.

I turned my thoughts away from Roy and Joan, and then they tormented me again. Would she see that he was acting?

At last I saw her pass under my window again. She was alone. Her face was pallid, heavy and set, and her feet were dragging.

CHAPTER XXIX

REALISM AT A CRICKET MATCH

LADY Muriel's observations on Roy might once have amused me. I should like to have told him that, for the first occasion since we met her, she had noticed something she had not been told; and he would have laughed lovingly at her obtuseness, the pent-in power of her stumbling, hobbled feelings.

In fact, that afternoon she had made me more alarmed. Roy must be visibly worse than I imagined. Living by his side day after day, I had become acclimatised to much; if one lives in the hourly presence of any kind of suffering, one grows hardened to it in time. I knew that too well, through Sheila. It is those who are closest and dearest who see a fatal transformation last of all.

I reassured myself a little. Apart from Arthur Brown, no one in the college seemed to have detected anything unusual in Roy's state that summer. He dined in hall two or three nights a week, and, except for his views on Germany, passed under others' eyes without evoking any special interest. He stayed preternaturally silent when he dined (I once taxed him with it, and he whispered 'lanthanine is the word for me'), but nevertheless it was curious they should observe so little. They were, of course, more used than most men to occasional displays of extreme eccentricity; most of our society, like any other college at this period, were solid middle-aged men but they had learned to put up with one or two who had grown grotesquely askew. It was part of the secure, confident air.

After Lady Muriel talked to me, I was preparing myself for a disaster. I tried to steady myself by facing it: this will be indescribably worse than what has happened before, this will be sheer disaster. I might have to accept any horror. What I feared and expected most was an outburst about Germany and the war – a speech in public, a letter to the press, a public avowal of his feeling for the Reich. I feared it most for selfish reasons – at that period, such an outburst I could not bear myself.

After he sent Joan away, he was sunk in the abyss of depression. But he did nothing. The day that the Boscastles arrived, he even sustained with Lord Boscastle a level, realistic and sober conversation about the coming war.

The Boscastles had invited us to lunch, and Lady Muriel and Humphrey were there as well.

Through the beginning of the meal Lord Boscastle and Roy did all the talking. They found themselves in a strong and sudden sympathy about the prospect of war. They could see no way out, and they were full of revulsion. Lady Muriel looked startled that men should talk so frankly about the miseries of war: but she knew that her brother had been decorated in the last war, and it would never even have occurred to her that men would not fight bravely if it was their duty.

'It will be frightful,' said Roy. Throughout he had spoken moderately and sensibly; he had said no more than many men were saying; he had remarked that he did not know his own courage – it might be adequate, he could not tell.

'It will be frightful.' Lord Boscastle echoed the phrase. And I saw his eyes leave Roy and turn with clouded, passionate anxiety upon his son. Humphrey Bevill was still good-looking in his frail, girlish way; his skin was pink, smooth and clear; he had his father's beaky nose, which somehow did not detract from his delicacy. His eyes were bright china blue, like his mother's. He had led a disreputable life in Cambridge. He had genuine artistic feeling without, so far as I could discover, a trace of talent.

Lord Boscastle stared at his son with anxiety and longing; for him war meant nothing more nor less than danger to his son.

I watched Lady Boscastle mount her lorgnette and regard them both, with a faint, charming, contemptuous, coolly affectionate quiver on her lips.

Then Lord Boscastle took refuge in his own peculiar brand of stoicism. He asked Humphrey to show him again the photograph of that year's Athenaeum. This bore no relation to the Athenaeum where I had tea with the old Master, the London club of successful professional men. The Cambridge Athenaeum was the ultra-fashionable élite of a fashionable club; it was limited to twenty, and on the photograph of twenty youthful, and mainly titled, faces Lord Boscastle cast a scornful and dismissive eye.

At any rate, he appeared to feel, there was still time to reject these absurd pretensions to be classed among their betters. Several of them had names much more illustrious than that of Bevill; but it took more than centuries of distinction to escape Lord Boscastle's jehovianic strictures that afternoon. 'Who is this boy, Humphrey? I'm afraid I can't for the life of me remember his name.' He was told 'Lord Arthur ——' 'Oh, perhaps that accounts for it, should you have thought? They have never really quite managed to recover from their obscurity, should you think they have?' He pointed with elaborate distaste to another youth. 'Incorrigibly parvenu, I should have said. With a certain primitive cunning in financial matters. Such as they showed when they fleeced my great-grandfather.'

Lord Boscastle placed the photograph a long way off along the table, as though he might get a less displeasing view.

'Not a very distinguished collection, I'm afraid, Humphrey. I suppose it was quite necessary for you to join them? I know it's always easier to take the course of least resistance. I confess that I made concessions most of my life, but I think it's probably a mistake for us to do so, shouldn't you have thought?'

The Boscastles, Lady Muriel and I were all dining with Roy the following night. I did not see any more of him for the rest of that day, and next morning Bidwell brought me no news. Bidwell was, however, full of the preparations for the dinner. 'Yes, sir. Yes, sir. It will be a bit like the old times. Mr Calvert is the only gentleman who makes me think back to the old times, sir, if you don't mind me saying so. It will be a pleasure to wait on you tonight, I don't mind telling you, sir.'

So far as I could tell, Roy was keeping to his rooms all day. I hesitated about intruding on him; in the end, I went down to Fenner's for a few hours' escape. It was the Free Foresters' match. Though it was pleasant to chat and sit in the sunshine, there was nothing noteworthy about the play. Two vigorous ex-blues, neither of them batsmen of real class, were clumping the ball hard to extra cover. If one knew the game, one could immerse oneself in points of detail. There could not have been a more peaceful afternoon.

Then I felt a hand on my shoulder.

'They told me I should find you here, but I didn't really think I should.' The voice had a dying fall; I looked round and saw the smile on Rosalind's face. I apologised to my companion, and walked with Rosalind round the ground.

'I wonder if I could beg a cup of tea?' she said.

I gave her tea in the pavilion; with the hearty appetite that I remembered, she munched several of the cricketers' buns. She talked about herself and me, not yet of Roy. Her manner was still humorously plaintive, as though she were ill-used, but she had become more insistent and certain of herself. Her determination was not so far below the surface now. She had been successful in her job, and had schemed effectively for a better one. Her eyes were not round enough, her voice not enough diminuendo, to conceal as effectively as they used that she was a shrewd and able woman. And there was another development, minor but strange. She was still prudish in her speech, still prudish when her eyes gave a shameless hint of fornication – but she had become remarkably profane.

She looked round the pavilion, and said:

'We can't very well talk here, can we?'

Which, since several of the Free Foresters' team were almost touching us, seemed clear. I took her to a couple of seats in the corner of the ground: on the way, Rosalind said:

'I know I oughtn't to have interrupted you, really. But it is a long time since I saw you, Lewis, isn't it? Did you realise it, I very nearly tracked you down that day at Boscastle?'

'It's a good job you didn't,' I said. 'Lady Muriel was just about ready to take a stick to you.'

Rosalind swore cheerfully and grinned.

'She's in Cambridge now, by the way,' I said.

'I knew that.'

'You'd better be careful. If you mean to marry Ralph Udal.'

'Of course I mean to marry him. Why ever do you say such horrid things?' She opened her eyes wide.

'Come off it,' I said, copying Roy's phrase. It was years since I had been her confidant, but at a stroke we had gone back to the old terms.

'No, I shall marry Ralph, really I shall. Mind you, I'm not really in love with him. I don't think I shall ever really fall in love again. I'm not sure that I want to. It's pretty bloody, being too much in love, isn't it? No, I shall settle down with Ralph all right. You just won't know me as the vicar's wife.'

'That's true,' I said, and Rosalind looked ill-used.

We had just sat down under one of the chestnut trees.

'I shall settle down so that you wouldn't believe it,' said Rosalind. 'But I'm not going to fool myself. After old Roy, other men seem just a tiny little bit dull. It stands to sense that I should want to see the old thing now and again.'

'It's dangerous,' I said.

'I'm not so bad at covering up my traces when I want to,' said Rosalind, who was willing only to think of practical dangers.

She asked, with a glow of triumph:

'Do you think I oughtn't to have come? He asked me to look him up. When he wrote about me and Ralph. And he did seem rather pleased to see me last night. I really think he was a bit pleased to see me.'

She laid her hand on my arm, and said, half-guiltily, half-provocatively:

'Anyway, he asked me to go to a ball with him tonight.'

'Are you going?'

'What do you think? It's all right, I'll see that the old gorgon doesn't find out. I'm not going to have her exploding down in Boscastle. I won't have Ralph upset. After all,' she said, 'a husband in the hand is worth two in the bush.'

She and Roy had arranged to go to a ball at one of the smaller colleges, where none of us had close friends. I warned her that it was still a risk.

She pursed her lips. 'Why do you want to stop us?' she said. 'You know it might take the old thing out of himself. He's going through one of his bad patches, isn't he? It will do him good to have a night on the tiles.'

I could not prevent myself laughing. Under the chestnut, an expensive lingering scent pervaded the hot afternoon. There was a bead of moisture on her upper lip, but her hair was swept up in a new, a rakish, a startling Empire coiffure. I asked when she had had time to equip herself like the Queen of the May.

'When do you think?' said Rosalind with lurking satisfaction. 'I went up to town first thing this morning and told my hairdresser that she'd got to do her damnedest. The idiot knows me, of course, and when she'd finished she said with a soppy smile that she hoped my fiancé would like it. I nearly asked her why she thought I should care what my fiancé thinks of it. It's what my young man thinks of it that I'm interested in.'

What was going through her head, I wondered, as I walked back across Parker's Piece? She was reckless, but she was also practical. If need be, she would marry Ralph Udal without much heartbreak and without repining. But need it be? I was ready to bet that, in the last few hours, she had asked herself that question. I should be surprised if she was in a hurry to fix the date of her wedding.

As I was dressing for dinner, Roy threw open my bedroom door. His white tie was accurately tied, his hair smooth, but I was thrown into alarm at the sight of him. His eyes were lit up.

I was frightened, but in a few minutes I discovered that this had been only a minor outrage. It came as a respite. I even smiled from relief when I found how he had broken out. But I felt that he was on the edge of catastrophe. It could not be far away: perhaps only a few hours. His smile was brilliant, but frantic and bitter; his voice was louder than usual, and a laugh rang out with reedy harshness.

Yet his actions that afternoon were like hitting out at random, and would not do much harm. They had been set off by an unexpected provocation. The little book on the heresies, by Vernon Royce and R. C. E. Calvert, had been published at last, early in the summer. Since Lyall's death, Roy's reputation had increased sharply in English academic circles, owing to the indefatigable herald-like praise by Colonel Foulkes, who was now quite unhampered. But the heresy book had been received with bleakness; most of the academic critics seemed to relish dismissing Royce now that he was dead. That morning Roy had read a few sentences about the book in the *Journal of Theological Studies*: '. . . Mr Calvert is becoming recognised as a scholar of great power and penetration. But there is little sign of those qualities in this book's treatment of a subject which requires the most profound knowledge of the sources and origins of religious belief and its perversions. From internal evidence, it is not over-difficult to attribute most of the insufficiently thought out chapters to the late Mr Royce, who, in all his writings on comparative religion, never revealed the necessary imagination to picture the religious experience of others nor the patient and detailed scholarship which might have given value to his work in the absence of the imaginative gifts. . . .'

Roy was savagely and fantastically angry. He had sent off letters of which he showed me copies. They were in the Housmanish language of scholarly controversy – one to the editor asking why he permitted a man 'ignorant, unteachable, stupid, and corrupt' to write in his journal, and one to the reviewer himself. The reviewer was a professor at Oxford, and to him Roy had written: 'I have before me your witty review. You are either too old to read: or too venal to see honestly. You attribute some chapters to my collaborator and you have the effrontery to impugn the accuracy of that work, and so malign the reputation of a better man than yourself. I wrote those chapters; I am a scholar; that you failed to see the chapters were precise is enough to unfit you for such tasks as reading proofs. If you are not yet steeped in your love of damaging others you will be so abashed that you will not write scurrilities about Royce again. You should state publicly that you were wrong, and that you stand guilty of incompetence, self-righteousness and malice.'

Roy was maddened that they should still decry Royce. With the clarity which visited him in his worst hours, he saw them gloating comfortably, solidly, stuffed with their own rectitude, feeling a warm comfortable self-important satisfaction that Royce had never come off, could not even come off after his death: he saw them saying in public what a pity it was that Royce was not more gifted, how they wanted so earnestly to praise him, how only duty and conscience obliged them so reluctantly to tell the truth. He saw the gloating on solid good-natured faces.

As we walked through the court to his dinner party, he broke out in a clear, passionate tone:

'All men are swine.'

He added, but still without acceptance, charity, or rest:

'The only wonder is, the decent things they manage to do now and then. They show a dash of something better, once or twice in their lives. I don't know how they do it – when I see what we are really like.'

CHAPTER XXX

WAITING AT NIGHT

THE desks in Roy's sitting-room had been pushed round the wall, where one noticed afresh their strange shapes and colours. In the middle, the table had been laid for eight – laid with five glasses at each place and a tremendous bowl of orchids in the middle. It was not often Roy indulged in the apolaustic; he used to chuckle even at the subdued display of Arthur Brown's claret parties; extravagant meals were not in Roy's style, they contained for him something irresistibly comic, a hint of Trimalchio. But that night he was giving one himself. Decanters of burgundy and claret stood chambering in a corner of the room; the cork of a champagne bottle protruded from a bucket; on a small table were spread out plates of fruit, marrons glacés, petits fours, cold savouries for aperitifs and after-tastes.

The person who enjoyed it all most was undoubtedly Bidwell. He took it upon himself to announce the guests; the first we knew of this new act was when Bidwell threw open the door, decorous and rubicund, the

perfect servant, and proclaimed with quiet but ringing satisfaction:
  'The Lady Muriel Royce!'

And then, slightly less vigorously (for Bidwell needed a title to move him to his most sonorous):
  'Mrs Seymour!'
  'Mrs Houston Eggar!'

Since Lady Muriel left the Lodge, I had escaped my old dinner-long conversations with Mrs Seymour; in the midst of despondency, Roy had been able to think out that joke; it was time to see that she pestered me again. Before they came in, he had been talking to me with his fierce, frightening excitement. As he greeted her, he was enough himself to give me a glance.

I attached myself to Mrs Eggar, whom I had only met once before. Eggar had sent her back from Berlin with her baby, and she was staying with Mrs Seymour for the summer. She was a pretty young woman with a beautiful skin and eyes easily amused, but a thin, tight, pinched-in mouth. She had considerable poise, and often seemed to be laughing to herself. I found her rather attractive, somewhat to my annoyance, for she was obstinate, self-satisfied, far less amiable than her pushing, humble, masterful husband.

Bidwell came to the door again and got our attention. Then he called out in triumph:
  'Right Honourable The Earl and Countess of Boscastle!'

It was a moment for Bidwell to cherish.

His next call, and the last, was an anticlimax. It was simply:
  'Mr Winslow!'

I was surprised; I had not known till then who was making up the party. It seemed a curious choice. Roy had not been seeing much of the old man. He was not even active in the college any longer, for he had resigned the bursarship in pride and rage over a year before. Yet in one way he was well fitted for the party. He had been an enemy of the old Master's, Lady Muriel had never liked him – but still he had been the only fellow whom she treated as some approximation to a social equal. Winslow was fond of saying that he owed his comfortable fortune to the drapery trade, and in fact his grandfather had owned a large shop in St Paul's Churchyard; but his grandfather nevertheless had been a younger son of an old county family, a family which had remained in an unusually static position for several hundred years. They had been solid and fairly prosperous country gentlemen in the seventeenth century: in the twentieth, they were still solid country gentlemen, slightly more prosperous. Winslow referred to his ancestors with acid sarcasm, but it did not occur to Lady Muriel, nor apparently to Lord Boscastle, to enquire who they were.

With Roy in the state I knew, I was on edge for the evening to end. (I was strung up enough to suspect that he might have invited Winslow through a self-destructive impulse. Winslow had watched one outburst, and might as well have the chance to see another.) In any other condition, I should have revelled in it. To begin with, Winslow was patently happy to be there, and there was something affecting about his pleasure. He was, as we knew, cross-grained, rude, bitter with himself and others for being such a failure; yet his pleasure at being asked to dinner was simple and fresh. He did not produce any of the devastating snubs he used on guests in hall; but he was not at all overborne by Lord Boscastle, either socially or as a man. They got on pretty well. Soon they were exchanging memories of Italy (meanwhile Mrs Seymour, who was, of course, seated next to me, confided her latest enthusiasm in an ecstatic breathless whisper. It was for Hitler – which did not make it easier to be patient. 'It must be wonderful,' she said raptly, 'to know that everyone is obliged to listen to you. Imagine seeing all those faces down below. . . . And no one can tell you to stop.')

The dinner was elaborate and grand. Roy had set out to beat the apolaustic at their own game. And he had contrived that each person there should take special delight in at least one course – there were oysters for Lady Muriel, whitebait for me, quails for Lady Boscastle. Most of the party, even Lady Boscastle, ate with gusto. I should have been as enthusiastic as any of them, but I was anxious only that the courses should follow more quickly, that we could see the party break up in peace. Roy was not eating and drinking much; I told myself that he had a ball to attend when this was over. But I should have been more reassured to see him drink. His eyes were brighter and fuller than normal, and his voice had changed. It was louder, and without the inflections, the variety, the shades of different tone as he turned from one person to another. Usually his voice played round one. That night it was forced out.

He spoke little. He attended to his guests. He mimicked one or two people for Winslow's benefit: it affected me that the imitations were nothing like as exact as usual. The courses dragged by; at last there was a chocolate mousse, to be followed by an ice. Both Lord Boscastle and Winslow, who had strongly masculine tastes, refused the sweet. Lady Muriel felt they should not be left unreproved.

'I am sorry to see that you're missing this excellent pudding, Hugh,' she said.

'You ought to know by now, Muriel,' said Lord Boscastle, 'that I'm not much good at puddings.'

'It has always been considered a college speciality,' said Lady Muriel, clinching the argument. 'I remember telling the Master that it should become recognised as the regular sweet at the Audit feast.'

'I'm very forgetful of these matters,' said Winslow, 'but I should be slightly surprised if that happened, Lady Muriel. To the best of my belief, this admirable concoction has never appeared at a feast at all.'

He could not resist the gibe: for it was not a function of the Master to prescribe the menus for feasts, much less of Lady Muriel.

'Indeed,' said Lady Muriel. 'I am astonished to hear it, Mr Winslow. I think you must be wrong. Let me see, when is the next audit?'

'November.'

'I hope you will pay particular attention.'

'If you please, Lady Muriel. If you please.'

'I think you will find I am right.'

They went on discussing feasts and college celebrations as though they were certain to happen, as though nothing could disturb them. There was a major college anniversary in 1941, two years ahead.

'I hope the college will begin its preparations in good time,' said Lady Muriel. 'Two years is not long. You must be ready in two years' time.'

Suddenly Roy laughed. They were all silent. They had heard that laugh. They did not understand it, but it was discomforting. 'Two years' time,' he cried. He laughed again.

The laugh struck into the quiet air. Across the table, across the sumptuous dinner, Lady Boscastle looked at me: I was just going to try. But it was Lady Muriel who awkwardly, hesitatingly, did not shirk her duty.

'I know what you are feeling, Roy,' she said. 'We all feel exactly as you do. But it is no use anticipating. One has to go on the trust that things will get better.'

Roy smiled at her.

'Just so, Lady Mu,' he said.

Perhaps it was best that she had spoken. Her sheer ineptness had gone through him. He became calmer, though his eyes remained fiercely bright.

With relief, even though it meant only a postponement, I saw the port go round, the sky darken through the open windows. We heard the faint sound of music from the college ball.

Mrs Eggar had to leave early because of her child. Roy escorted her and Mrs Seymour to their taxi and then came back. He was master of himself quite enough to seem unhurried; no one would have thought that he was waiting to go to a young woman. It was between eleven and twelve. Lord Boscastle and Winslow decided to stroll together in the direction of Winslow's house. Lady Boscastle wished to stop in my rooms for a little; so Roy was free to take Lady Muriel to the hotel.

I helped Lady Boscastle into an armchair beside my fireplace.

'I haven't had the chance to tell you before, my dear boy,' she said, 'but you look almost respectable tonight.'

But she had not settled down into badinage before Bidwell, who was on duty at the ball, tapped softly at the door and entered. 'Lord Bevill is asking whether he can see Lady Boscastle, sir.' I nodded, and Bidwell showed Humphrey Bevill into the room.

Humphrey had been acting in an undergraduate performance, and there were still traces of paint on his face. He was exhilarated and a little drunk. 'I didn't really want to see you, Lewis,' he said. 'I've been trying to discover where my mother is hiding.' He went across to Lady Boscastle. 'They've kept you from me ever since you arrived, Mummy. I won't let you disappear without saying goodnight.'

He adored her; he would have liked to stay, to have thrown a cushion on the floor and sat at her feet.

'This is very charming of you, Humphrey.' She smiled at him with her usual cool, amused indulgence. 'I thought I had invited myself to tea in your rooms tomorrow – *tête-à-tête*?'

'You'll come, won't you, Mummy?'

'How could I miss it?' Then she asked: 'By the way, have you seen your father tonight?'

'No.'

'He'd like to see you, you know. He has probably got back to the hotel by now.'

'Must I?'

'I really think you should. He will like it so much.'

Humphrey went obediently away. Lady Boscastle sighed.

'The young are exceptionally tedious, Lewis, my dear. They are so preposterously uninformed. They never realise it, of course. They are very shocked if one tells them that they seem rather – unrewarding.'

She smiled.

'Poor Humphrey,' she said.

'He's very young,' I said.

'Some men,' said Lady Boscastle, 'stay innocent whatever happens to them. I have known some quite well-accredited rakes who were innocent all through their lives. They never knew what this world is like.'

'That can be true of women too,' I said.

'Most women are too stupid to count,' said Lady Boscastle indifferently. 'No, Lewis, I'm afraid that Humphrey will always be innocent. He's like his father. They're quite unfit to cope with what will happen to them.'

'What will happen to them?'

'You know as well as I do. Their day is done. It will finish this time – if it didn't in 1914, which I'm sometimes inclined to think. It will take someone much stronger than they are to live as they've been bred to live. It takes a very strong man nowadays to live according to his own pleasure. Hugh tried, but he hadn't really the temperament, you see. I doubt whether he's known much happiness.'

'And you?'

'Oh, I could always manage, my dear. Didn't you once tell me that I was like a cat?'

She was scrutinising her husband and her son with an anthropologist's detachment. She was far more detached than the rest of them about the fate of their world. She liked it; it suited her; it had given her luxury, distinction and renown; now it was passing for ever, and she didn't care. 'I thought,' she said, 'that your friend Roy was rather *égaré* tonight.'

'Yes.'

'What is the matter? Is my niece still refusing to let him go? Or am I out of date?'

She was not much worried or interested. If Roy had been exhibiting some new phase of a love affair, she would have been the first to observe, identify and dissect. As it was, her perception stopped short, and she was ready to ignore him.

She leaned back against the head-rest of the chair. Under the reading-lamp, her face was monkey-like and yet oddly beautiful. The flesh was wizened, but the architecture of the bones could never be anything but exquisite.

'Lewis!' she asked. 'Do you feel that you are doing things for the last time?'

I was too much engrossed in trouble to have speculated much.

'I do,' said Lady Boscastle. 'Quite strongly. I suppose the chances are that we shall not dine here again. It tends to give such occasions a certain poignancy.'

She smiled.

'It didn't happen so last time, you know. It all came from a clear sky. A very clear sky, my dear boy. Have I ever told you? I think I was happier in 1914 than I ever was before or since. I had always thought people were being absurdly extravagant when they talked of being happy. Yet I had to admit it. I was ecstatically happy myself. It was almost humiliating, my dear Lewis. And distinctly unforeseen.'

I had heard something of it before. Of all her conquests, this was the one to which she returned with a hoarding, secretive, astonished pleasure. She would not tell me who he was. 'He has made his own little reputation since. I am not quite ungallant enough to boast.' I believed that it was someone I knew, either in person or by name.

The whirr and clang and chimes of midnight broke into a pause. Reluctantly Lady Boscastle felt that she must go. I was just ringing for a taxi, when she stopped me.

'No, my dear,' she said. 'I have an *envie* for you to take me back tonight.'

Very slowly, for she had become more frail since I first met her, she walked on my arm down St Andrew's Street. The sky had clouded, there was no moon or stars, but the touch of the night air was warm and solacing. Her stick stayed for an interval on the pavement at each step; I had to support her; she smiled and went on talking, as we passed Emmanuel, decked out for a ball. Fairy lights glimmered through the gate, and a tune found its way out. A party of young men and women, in tails and evening frocks and cloaks, made room for us on the pavement and went in to dance. They did not imagine, I thought, that they had just met a great beauty recalling her most cherished lover.

Lord Boscastle was waiting up for her in their sitting-room at the hotel.

'How very nice of you, Hugh,' she said lightly, much as she spoke to her son. 'I have been keeping Lewis up. Do you mind if I leave you both now? I think I will go straight to my room. Good night, Hugh, my dear. Good night, Lewis, my dear boy.'

Lord Boscastle did not seem inclined to let me go. He poured out a whisky for me and for himself, and, when I had drunk mine, gave me some more. He was impelled to find out what his wife and I had been saying to each other; he could not ask directly, he shied away from any question, and yet he went too far for either of us to be easy. There was a curious tone about those enquiries, so specific that I was certain I ought to recognise it – but for a time I could not. Then, vividly, it struck me. To think that he was jealous of his wife's affection for me was, of course, ridiculous. To think he was still consumed by the passionate and possessive love for her which had (as I now knew) darkened much of his manhood – that was ridiculous too. But he was behaving as though the habit of that consuming passion survived, when everything else had died. In his youth he had waited up for her; it was easy to imagine him striding up and down the opulent rooms of Edwardian hotels. In his youth he had been forced to question other men as he had just questioned me; he was forced under the compulsion of rivalry, he was driven to those intimate duels. At long last the hot and turbulent passion had died, as all passions must; but it had trained his nerves to habits he could not break.

His was a nature too ardent to have come through lightly; I thought it again when he confronted me with Roy's demeanour that night.

'I was afraid the man was going to make an exhibition of himself,' he said.

I had no excuse to make.

'He'll have to learn that he mustn't embarrass his guests. We've all sat through dinners wanting to throw every scrap of crockery on to the floor. But we've had to hide it. Damn it, I shall wake up in the night wondering what's wrong with the young man.'

He added severely:

'One will have to think twice about accepting invitations – if there's a risk of being made miserable. One will just have to refuse.'

It sounded heartless. In a sense, it came from too much heart. It was the cool, like Lady Boscastle, who could bear to look at others' wretchedness. Her husband became hurt, troubled, angry – angry with the person whose wretchedness embarrassed him so much.

When I went out into the street, I stood undecided, unable to make up my mind. Should I look in at the ball where Roy was dancing – to ease my mind, to see if he was there? Sometimes any action seemed soothing: it was better than waiting passively to hear bad news. It was difficult to check myself; I began to walk to the ball. Then, quite involuntarily, the mood turned within me. I retraced my steps, I went down the empty street towards my rooms.

CHAPTER XXXI

ABSOLUTE CALM

I SLEPT fitfully, heard the last dance from the college hall, and then woke late. Bidwell did not wake me at nine o'clock; when he drew up the blind, he told me that he had let me sleep on after last night's party. He also told me that he had not seen Roy that morning: Roy had not been to bed nor come in to breakfast.

I got up with a veil of dread in front of the bright morning. I ate a little breakfast, read the newspaper without taking it in, read one or two letters. Then Roy himself entered. He was still wearing his dress suit: he was not smiling, but he was absolutely calm. I had never seen him more calm.

'I've been waiting about outside,' he said. 'Until you'd finished breakfast. Just like a pupil who daren't disturb you.'

'*What have you done?*' I cried.

'Nothing,' said Roy.

I did not believe him.

'You have finished now, haven't you? I didn't want to hurry you, Lewis.' He looked at me. 'If you're ready – will you come into the garden?'

Without a word between us, we walked through the courts. Young men were sitting on the window sills, some of them still in evening clothes; through an open window, we heard a breakfast party teasing each other, the women's voices excited and high.

Roy unlocked the garden gate. The trees and lawns opened to us; no sight had ever seemed so peaceful. The palladian building stood tranquil under a cloudless summer sky.

'*What have you done?*' I cried again.

'Nothing,' said Roy.

His face was grave, quite without strain, absolutely calm. He said:

'I've done nothing. You expected me to break out, didn't you? No, it left me all of a sudden. I've done nothing.'

Then I believed him. I had an instant of exhausted ease. But Roy said:

'It's not so good, you know. I've done nothing. But I've seen it all. Now I know what I need to expect.'

His words were matter-of-fact. Suddenly they pierced me. No frantic act could have damaged him like this. Somehow his melancholy had vanished in an instant; during the night it had broken, but not into violence. At last he had given up struggling.

'It's not easy to take,' said Roy.

He looked at me, and said:

'You've always known that I should realise it in the end.'

'I was afraid so,' I said.

'That's why I hid things from you.' He paused, and then went on:

'I don't see it as you do. But I see that I can't change myself. One must be very fond of oneself not to want to change. I can't believe that anyone would willingly stay as I am. Well, I suppose I must try to get used to the prospect.'

He did not smile. There was a humorous flick to the words, but the humour was jet-black.

'Shall I go mad?' he asked.

I said: 'I don't know enough.'

'Somehow I don't think so,' said Roy with utter naturalness. 'I believe that I shall go through the old hoops. I shall have these stretches of abject misery. And I shall have fits when I feel larger than life and can't help bursting out. And the rest of the time—'

'For the rest of the time you'll get more out of life than anyone. Just as you always have done. You've got the vitality of three men.'

'Except when—'

I interrupted him again.

'That's the price you've got to pay. You've felt more deeply than any of us. For all that – you've got to pay a price.'

'Just so,' said Roy, who did not want to argue. 'But no one would choose to live such a life.'

'There is no choice,' I said.

'I've told you before, you're more robust than I am. You were made to endure.'

'So will you endure.'

He gazed at me. He did not reply for a moment. Then he said, as though casually:

'I shall always think it might have been different. I shall think it might have been different – if I could have believed in God. Or even if I could throw myself into a revolution. Even the one that you don't like. Our friends don't like it much either.'

The thought diverted him, and he said in a light tone:

'If I told them all I'd done – some of our friends would have some remarkable points to make. Fancy telling Francis Getliffe the whole story. He would look like a judge and say I must have manic-depressive tendencies.'

For the first time that morning, Roy gave a smile.

'Very wise,' he said. 'I could have told him that when I was at school. If that were all.'

He talked, concealing nothing, about how the realisation had come. It had been in the middle of the night. Rosalind was dancing with an acquaintance. Roy was smoking a cigarette outside the ballroom.

'It had been breaking through for a long time. Some of my escapes were pretty – unconvincing. You would have seen that if I hadn't kept you away. Perhaps you did. But in the end it seemed to come quite sharply. It was as sharp as when I have to lash out. But it wasn't such fun. Everything became terribly lucid. It was the most lucid moment I've ever had. It was dreadful.'

'Yes,' I said.

'I shall be lucky if I forget it. It was like one of the dreams of God. But I knew that I could not get over this. I had seen how things must come.

'Lewis,' he said, 'if someone gave me a mirror in which I could see myself in ten years' time – I should not be able to look.'

We had been sitting down; now, without asking each other, we walked round the garden. The scent of syringa was overmastering in that corner of the garden, and it was only close to the bush that one could pick up the perfume of the roses.

'It's not over,' said Roy. 'We've got some way to go, haven't we?'

His step was light and poised on the springy turf. After dancing all night, he was not tired.

He said: 'I hope you can bear it. You won't need to look after me now. There will be nothing to look after.'

He was speaking with extreme conviction. He took it for granted that I should understand and believe. He said: 'I should like to make things easier for you. I need to make up for lost time.'

PART FOUR

CLARITY

CHAPTER XXXII

A NOISY WINTER EVENING

I HAD thought, at the dinner party in the Adlon, how in England it was still natural for men like Roy and me to have our introductions to those in power. I thought it again, at the beginning of the war; for, within a few days, Roy had been asked for by a branch of intelligence, Francis Getliffe had become assistant superintendent of one of the first radar establishments, I was a civil servant in Whitehall. And so with my brother Martin and a good many of our Cambridge friends. It was taken for granted. The links between the universities and 'government' were very strong. They happened, of course, as a residue of privilege, the official world in England was still relatively small and compact; when in difficulties it asked who was a useful man, and brought him in.

Of all our friends, I was much the luckiest. Francis Getliffe's job was more important, Roy's was more difficult, but mine was the most interesting by far. My luck in practical matters had never deserted me, and I landed on my feet, right in the middle of affairs. I was attached to a small ministry which had, on paper, no particular charge; in fact, it was used as a convenient ground for all kinds of special investigations, interdepartmental committees, secret meetings. These had to be held somewhere, and came to us simply because of the personality of our Minister. It was his peculiar talent to be this kind of handyman. I became assistant to his Permanent Secretary, and so, by sheer chance, gained an insight into government such as I had no right to hope for. In normal times it could not have come my way, since one can only live one life. It was a constant refreshment during the long dark shut-in years.

At times it was the only refreshment. For I went through much trouble at that period. My wife died in the winter of 1939. Everyone but Roy thought it must be a relief and an emancipation, but they did not know the truth. They also did not know, as he did, how she had died. That was a private misery which I kept to myself, but there were others.

Sometimes I could forget them, in the Whitehall meetings or the Minister's office. There he sat, handing out horrible biscuits, which he called 'bikkies', unassuming, imperturbably discreet, realistic, resilient, and eupeptically optimistic. But away from the office I could not sustain that kind of optimism.

For the first three years of the war, until the autumn of 1942, I carried a weight of fear. I was frightened that we should lose. It was a straightforward fear, instinctive and direct. The summer of 1940 was an agony for me: I envied – and at times resented – the cheerful thoughtless invincible spirits of people round me, but I thought to myself that the betting was 5–1 against us. I felt that, as long as I lived, I should remember walking along Whitehall in the pitiless and taunting sun.

I also knew a different fear, one of which I was more ashamed, a fear of being killed. When the bombs began to fall on London, I suspected that I was less brave than the average of men. I was humiliated to find it so. I could just put some sort of face on it, but I dreaded the evening coming, could not sleep, was glad of an excuse to spend a night out of the town. It was not always easy to accept one's nature. And most of my friends were brave beyond the common, which made me feel worse. Francis Getliffe was a man of cool and disciplined courage. Lady Muriel was unthinkingly gallant, and Joan as staunch in physical danger as in unhappy love. Roy had always been extremely brave.

He noticed, of course, that I was frightened. He did not take it as seriously as I did. Like many men who possess courage, he did not value it much. Without my knowing, he took a flat for me in Dolphin Square, the great steel-and-concrete block on the Embankment, about a mile from my old house. He told me, sensibly, that it was important I should be able to sleep. He also told me that he had consulted Francis Getliffe upon the safest place in the safest type of building. London was emptying, and it was easy to have one's pick. He had incidentally given Francis the impression that he was inquiring for his own sake. He made it seem that he was abnormally preoccupied about his own skin. It was the kind of trick that he could not resist bringing out for Francis. Francis replied with scientific competence – 'between the third and seventh floor in a steel frame' – and thought worse of Roy than ever. Roy grinned.

For himself, Roy did not pay any attention to such dangers. He gave most acquaintances the impression that he did not care at all. They thought the war had not touched him.

He worked unenthusiastically in a comfortable government job. He stayed at the office late, as we all did, but he did not tire himself with the obsessed devotion that he had once spent on his manuscripts. At night he went out into the dark London streets in search of adventure. He found a lot of trivial love affairs, or rather, sexual bouts. He gave parties in the flat in Connaught Street, he went all over the town in chase of women, and often, just as I used to find so strange when he was a younger man, he went to bed with someone for a single night and then forgot her altogether. Rosalind often came to see him, but, when the air-raids started, she tried to persuade him to meet her out of London. He would not go.

It was an existence which people blamed as irresponsible, out of keeping with the time. He attracted a mass of disapproval, heavier than in the past. Even Lady Muriel wondered how he could bear to be out of uniform. I told her that, having once been forced into this particular job, he would never get permission to leave. But she was only partially appeased. All her young relations were fighting. Even Humphrey was being trained as an officer in motor torpedo boats. She was too loyal to condemn Roy, but she did not know what to think.

I saw more of him that I had done since my early days in Cambridge. Our intimacy had returned, more unquestioning because of the time we had been kept at a distance. We knew each other all through now, and we depended on each other more than we had ever done. For these were times when only the deepest intimacy was any comfort. Casual friends could not help; they were more a tax than strangers. We were each in distress; in our different ways we were hiding it. We had both aged; I had become guarded, more patient, more suspicious; he was lighter in speech than ever, not serious now even though it hurt others not to be serious, dissipated, purposeless and without hope. He was still kind by nature, perhaps more kind than when he thought he would come through; he was often lonely; but he could see no meaning in his life.

I knew that he was suffering more than I. It was not the war, though it had become tied up with that – for many states of unhappiness are like a vacuum which fills itself with whatever substance comes to hand. The vacuum would remain, if whatever was now filling it were taken away. So with Roy: the cause lay elsewhere. War or no war, he would have been tormented. If there had been no war, the vacuum would have filled itself with a different trouble. For the wound could not heal: he could see nothing to look forward to.

I could not forget the darkness of his face that morning in the college garden. For him it had been the starkest and bitterest of hours. He could not recover from it. Though for the next year or more he did not undergo the profoundest depression again, he never entered that calm beautiful high-spirited state in which his company made all other men seem leaden; with me he was usually subdued, affectionately anxious to help me on, controlled and sensible. His cries of distress only burst out in disguise, when he talked about the war.

So he watched me through the bright and terrible summer of 1940 with protective sympathy, with a feeling more detached and darker than mine. And, as the news got a little better in my eyes, as it became clear through the winter that the war would not end in sudden disaster, I had to accept that he could not share my pleasure and relief. For me the news might turn better; for him all news about the war was black, and brought to his mind only the desert waste to come.

It was an evening in the early spring of 1941, and already so dark that I had to pick my way from the bus stop to Dolphin Square. It had become a habit to arrive home late, in the dark, tired and claustrophobic. I had to pull my curtains and tamper with a fitting, before I could switch on the light. I lay on my sofa, trying to rouse myself to go down to the restaurant for dinner, when Roy came in. He usually called in at night, if he was not entertaining one of his young women.

Although our flats were two miles apart, he visited me as often as when we lived on neighbouring staircases. His face had changed little in the last years, but he was finding it harder to pretend that his hair still grew down to his temples. That night he seemed secretly amused.

'Just had a letter,' he said. 'I must say, a slightly remarkable letter.'

'Who from?'

'You should have said where from. Actually, it comes from Basel.'

'Whom do you know in Basel?'

'I used to be rather successful with the Swiss. They laughed when I made a joke. Very flattering,' said Roy.

'It must be some adoring girl,' I said.

'I can't think of any description which would please him less,' said Roy. 'No, I really can't. It's an old acquaintance of yours. It's Willy Romantowski.'

I said a word or two about Willy, and then exclaimed how odd it was.

'It's extremely odd,' said Roy. 'It's even odder when you see the letter. You won't be able to read it, though. You're not good at German holograph, are you? Also Willy uses very curious words. Sometimes of a slightly *slangy* nature.' Roy began to translate.

It was a puzzling letter.

'Dear Roy,' so his translation went, 'Since you left Berlin I have not had a very good time. They made me go into the army which made me sick. So I got tired of wasting my time in the army, and decided to come here.'

'He makes it sound simple,' I interjected.

'I have arrived here,' Roy went on, 'and like it much better. But I have no money, and the Swiss people do not let me earn any. That is why I am writing you this letter, Roy. I remember how kind you were to us all at No. 32. You were always very kind to me, weren't you? So I am hoping that you will be able to help me now I am in difficult circumstances. I expect you have a Swiss publisher. Could you please ask him to give me some money? Or perhaps you could bring me some yourself? I expect you could get to Switzerland somehow. I know you will not let me starve. Your friend Romantowski (Willy).' And he had added: 'There were some changes at No. 32 after you left, but I have not heard much since I went into the army.'

The letter was written in pencil, in (so Roy said) somewhat illiterate German. He had never seen Willy's handwriting, so he had nothing to compare it with. It gave an address in a street in Basel, and the postmark was Swiss. The letter had been opened and censored in several different countries, but had taken only about a month to arrive.

It was a singular event. We could not decide how genuine the letter was. As stated, Willy's story sounded highly implausible. From the beginning Roy was suspicious.

'It's a plant,' he said. 'They're trying to hook me.'

'Who?'

'I don't know. Perhaps Reinhold Schäder. They think I might be useful. They're very thorough people.'

I could believe that easily enough. But I could not understand why, if Schäder or Roy's other high-placed friends were behind the move, they should use this extraordinary method. It seemed ridiculous, and I said so.

'They sometimes do queer things. They're not as rational as we are.' Then he smiled. 'Or of course they may have mistaken my tastes.'

He considered.

'That shouldn't be likely. Perhaps Willy was the only one who'd volunteer to do it. You can't imagine the little dancer trying to get hold of me for them, can you? But Willy wasn't a particularly scrupulous young man. Or do you think I'm misjudging him?'

I asked him what he was going to do about it.

'You're not going to reply?' I asked.

'Not safe,' said Roy. I had half-expected a different reply, but he was curiously prudent and restrained at that time. 'I need to stop them getting me into trouble. It might look shady. I'm not keen on getting into trouble. Particularly if they're trying to hook me.'

He had, in fact, already behaved with sense and judgment. The letter had arrived the day before. Roy had at once reported it to his departmental chief, and written a note to Houston Eggar, who was back at the Foreign Office handling some of the German work. Roy had told them (as Eggar already knew) that he had many friends in Berlin, and that this was a disreputable acquaintance. He added that one or two of the younger German ministers had reason to believe that he was well disposed to them and to Germany.

He was far more cautious than he used to be, I thought. His chief and Eggar had both told him not to worry; it was obviously none of his doing; Eggar had gone on to say that the Foreign Office might want to follow the letter up, since they had so little contact with anyone who had recently been inside Germany.

Outside, the sirens ululated. They were late that night. In a few minutes, down the estuary we heard the first hollow thud of gunfire. The rumble came louder and sharper. It was strangely warming to be sitting there, in that safe room, as the noise grew. It was like lying in front of the fire as a child, while the wind moaned and the rain thrashed against the windows. It gave just the same pulse of rich, exalted comfort.

We turned off the light and drew aside the curtains. Searchlights were weaving on the clouds: there was an incandescent star as a shell burst short, but most were exploding above the cloud shelf. There were only a few aircraft, flying high. The night was too stormy for a heavy raid. Two small fires were rising, pink, rosy, out to the east. The searchlights crossed their beams in a beautiful three-dimensional design.

The aircraft were unseen, undetected, untouched. We heard their engines throbbing smoothly and without a break. They flew west and then south; the gunfire became distant again, and died away.

We looked out into the dark night; one searchlight still smeared itself upon the clouds.

'They won't find it so easy soon,' I said.

'Who'll stop them? Getliffe and his gang?'

'They'll help,' I said. 'It won't be any fun to fly.'

'You're sure, old boy?' said Roy very clearly, in the dark room.

'I'm pretty sure,' I said. I had always had a minor interest in military history: since the war, with the opportunities of my job, it had become more informed. 'It was the most dangerous job in the last war. It's bound to become so again.'

'On both sides?'

'Yes.'

'What do you mean – the most dangerous job?'

I defined what I meant. I said that élite troops on land, like commandos, might take greater risks than the average fighting airman; but that the whole fighting strength of the air force would suffer heavier casualties than any similar number of men on land or sea.

'They'll take very heavy losses,' I said, staring at the night sky.

'And we shall too?'

'Quite certainly,' I said. 'I don't know how many fighting airmen will survive the war. It won't be a very large percentage.'

'Just so.' I heard his voice behind me.

Two mornings later, Houston Eggar rang me up at my office. He was excessively mysterious. In him discretion was becoming both a passion and an art; both he and I had scrambled telephones, but he thought it safest not to speak. It would be wiser to meet, he said zestfully, revelling in his discretion. He could not give me an inkling of the reason. Would I mind going round to the Foreign Office?

I was annoyed. I did not believe that he was as busy as I was. I knew that he enjoyed all the shades of secrecy. Irritated, I went past guards, sandbags, into the dingy entrance of the Foreign Office, followed a limping messenger down corridors and up stairs.

Eggar was occupying a tiny ramshackle room, marked off by a paste-board partition. The building was overcrowded, and, somewhat to his chagrin, he could not be accommodated according to his rank. One window had been blown out, and was not yet boarded over. It was a cold morning, and bitter draughts kept sweeping in. Eggar sat there in his black coat and striped trousers, vigorous and cheerful. He did not mind the cold. He worked like an engine, and he would be sitting in that arctic room until late at night, plodding through the day's stack of files.

He greeted me with his effusive cordiality, man-to-man, eyes looking straight into eyes.

'Between ourselves,' he said, 'I think I've got a job for you.'

'I'm pretty well booked,' I said.

'I know you're not disponible. I know you're getting well-thought-of round here. I hear your Minister thinks the world of you.' Eggar was genuinely pleased that I should get some praise. Also he was thinking of one of his own simple, cunning, pushful moves. 'But I want you for something important. I think we may be able to extract you for a week or two.'

'I do rather doubt it,' I said. 'What do you want me for?'

'You've kept in touch with young Calvert, have you?'

The question surprised me.

'Yes.'

'Well, this is strictly in confidence – we're particularly anxious that it shouldn't get round, for reasons that I'm obliged to keep to myself. Strictly in confidence, young Calvert has received a letter from a German friend of his. I don't want to give you a wrong impression. There's nothing to blame Calvert for. He has behaved perfectly correctly.' Eggar told me the story of Romantowski's letter over again; he produced a copy of the original, and I listened to another translation.

'Very curious,' I said.

'It may be useful,' said Eggar. 'We're finding out whether this chap Romantowski is really living at that address. If so, we want to chase it up.' He explained, as he had done to Roy, that they were uncomfortably short of news from inside Germany. 'We think it might be worth the trouble of sending Calvert to talk to him.'

I nodded.

'Yes, we shall probably send Calvert out,' said Eggar.

He looked at me, and added:

'If we do, we should like you to go with him.'

'Why?'

Then Eggar took me completely aback.

'Between ourselves, Eliot, you ought to know. You ought to remember that two or three years ago Calvert was inclined to see some good points in the German set-up. I don't count it against him: a lot of people did the same. I'm not saying for a minute that today he isn't a hundred per cent behind the war. But we can't afford to take chances. I should be more comfortable if you went and helped him out in Switzerland. I expect he would be more comfortable too.'

It was informal, rough-and-ready, fixed up like an arrangement between friends. It was the way things got done. I felt a new respect for Eggar's competence.

I could not escape being persuaded. If they wanted news badly enough to send Roy, it was as well that I went with him. Eggar beamed at me. He would not have got me ordered there against my will, but now all was clear, he said, for him to call upon my Minister. It was quite unnecessary, for the Minister was the least ceremonious of men; I could have explained it to him in five minutes.

But he was also a uniquely influential man, and Eggar was determined to know him. On its own merits, it was a good idea to despatch me to look after Roy, Eggar could always keep one eye on the ball. But the other eye was fixed elsewhere. From the moment he had thought of sending me, Eggar had been determined to make the most of the opportunity. It was an admirable excuse to introduce himself to the Minister; he was out to create the best of impressions. He would not have a finer chance.

CHAPTER XXXIII

JOURNEY INTO THE LIGHT

'WE'LL get you there somehow,' said Houston Eggar heartily, when I asked about our route. The more I thought of it, the more my apprehensions emerged. In fact, it was so difficult to arrange the journey that it was cancelled twice. Each time I felt reprieved. But Eggar was determined that we should go, and at last he managed it.

The Foreign Office had been able to trickle a few people in since the fall of France, and Eggar used the same method for us: but even so, and getting us the highest priority, he took weeks to produce our papers complete. The delay was almost entirely caused by the French, for we needed a visa through Vichy France.

Though I viewed the journey with trepidation, I could not help being amused at the technique. For we were to fly to Lisbon in the ordinary way; there was nothing comic about that, but then the unexpected began; we were instructed to catch a German plane from Lisbon to Madrid, and another on the standard Lufthansa route from Madrid up north through Europe. We were to get off at Lyons, though the plane went on to Stuttgart. It had been done several times before by visitors on important missions, said Eggar: like them, we should carry Red Cross papers, and he expected all would be well. The French at last gave way. Eggar told us as though he had done all the difficult part, and ours was trivial; but, as a matter of fact, he was beginning to feel responsible.

He became slightly too genial, and stood us a dinner the night before we left.

We flew from Bristol on a halcyon spring afternoon. But we saw nothing of it, for the windows of the aircraft were covered over, and let in only a dim, tawny, subfusc light. The dimness made my plan for getting through the journey a little more difficult; I had to reckon on three hours' fright before we landed at Lisbon, and to help myself through I read quotas of fifty pages at a go before letting myself look at my watch. I had taken the *Tale of Genji* with me. Subtle and lovely though it was, I wished it had more narrative power. I could not keep myself from listening for unpleasant sounds. I envied Roy.

He was exhilarated, much as he had been in the most joyous days. He had been exhilarated ever since he was asked to make the journey. He seemed glad that I was going; he had not shown the slightest suspicion or resentment; he had not asked a single question why I should be there. Yet I felt he was too incurious. He could not accept it as naturally as he seemed to. He was much too astute not to guess. Still, his face lit up at the news of our journey, just as it used before any travel. He had always been excited by the thought, not of anything vague like the skies of Europe, but of the unexpected things which he might hear and see: I remembered the post-cards that used to arrive as he went from library to library: 'Palermo. The post office here has pillars fifty-six feet high, painted red, white and blue.' 'Nice. Yesterday a Romanian poetess described her country and France as the two bulwarks of Latin civilisation.' 'Berlin. The best cricketer of German nationality is called Maus. (All German cricketers appear to have very short names.) He is slightly worse than I am, slightly better than you.'

He was excited again in just that fashion, as we got into the aircraft. He was stimulated through the faint tang of danger. I envied him, reading my book with forced concentration, hearing him chat to a Portuguese businessman. He knew that I should be frightened, that I should prefer to be left sullenly alone. His imagination was at least as active as mine, but it produced a different result: the thought of danger made him keen, braced, active, like a first-class batsman who requires just enough of the needle, just enough tingle of the nerves, to be brought to the top of his form. Portuguese was a language Roy had never had reason to look at, but he was asking his acquaintance to pronounce some words: Roy was mimicking the squashed vowel sounds, apparently with accuracy, to judge from the admiring cries.

My first quota of pages dragged by, then in time another, then another. I had to read a good many pages again, to draw any meaning from them; not that they were obscure (they were about lords and ladies of the Japanese court in the year 1000, making an expedition to view the beauty of the autumn flowers), but I was listening too intently for noises outside. I wondered for an instant how the Genji circle would have faced times like ours. They happened to live in an interval of extreme tranquillity, though their civilisation was destroyed a couple of generations later. The Victorians too – they lived in an interval of tranquillity, though they did not feel it so. How would they have got on, if they had been born, like Roy and me and our friends, into one of the most violent times? About the same as we did, I thought. Not better. They would have endured it, for human beings are so made that they struggle on.

The plane began to lose height earlier than I calculated. I was alarmed, but Roy had picked up a word, and smiled across at me with an eyebrow lifted:

'We're here, old boy, Lisbon.'

It was comforting to feel the bumps beneath the wheels, comforting to walk with Roy across the airfield.

'Five o'clock,' said Roy. 'In time for tea. You need some tea. Also some cakes.'

We were staying that night in Lisbon, and we strolled through the brilliant streets in the warm and perfumed air. For five minutes, it was a release after the darkness of England. The lights streamed from the shops and one felt free, confined no longer. But almost at once, one forgot the darkness, we were walking in lighted streets as we had done before. Roy went from shop to shop, sending off presents; except that the presents were mostly parcels of food, it might have been a night in Cambridge in days past.

We caught the German aircraft next day. It seemed a little bizarre, but not so much as when I first heard that this was the most practical way. The lap was a short one, Lisbon to Madrid; the windows were not darkened, I looked down on the tawny plains of Estremadura and Castille; we were all polite, everything went according to plan. I had been in Madrid just before the beginning of the civil war; it was strange to sit in a café there again, to read newspapers prophesying England's imminent defeat, to remember the passions that earlier war had stirred in England. It had been the great plane of cleavage between left and right; we could recall Arthur Brown, the most sensible and solid of conservatives, so far ceasing to be his clubbable self as to talk about 'those thieves and murderers whom Getliffe and Eliot are so fond of'.

Roy mimicked Arthur Brown making that reproachful statement, and one saw again the rubicund but frowning face by the fire in the combination room. 'I regard a glass of port as rather encouraging on a cold night,' Roy went on mimicking. We were sometimes nostalgic for those autumn nights.

The Lufthansa plane, on the run Madrid-Barcelona-Lyons-Stuttgart, was full of German officials, businessmen and officers. They knew we were English; but most of them were civil. One youngish businessman pressed sandwiches on us.

So, in that odd company, I had my first glimpse of the Mediterranean for three years, as we flew over the Catalan coast. Since we landed at Lisbon, I was not so timid about physical danger; but I had two other cares on my mind. I was not sure whether it was a convenience for both sides to let Englishmen travel under this deception of ours. If not, it was always possible that someone here would report our names when he got to Germany: Roy was well enough known in Berlin for it to be a finite risk. I did not believe that the German intelligence would be taken in for a moment by our Red Cross status – and we were due to return on this same route.

For the same reason, I was nervous about the weather. If it did not let us touch down at Lyons, we should be taken on to Stuttgart. Could we possibly get away with it? Roy would have to do most of the talking: could I trust him to throw himself into whole-hearted lying? This time I was more afraid for him: of all men, he was the least fit to stand prison. I watched the clouds rolling up to the east.

We made our proper landing. Our German acquaintances inside the aeroplane said goodbye, and I felt that now we had put the last obstacle behind us. It turned out otherwise. The French officials were not willing to let us disembark; they held the aircraft, the German officers getting first bleakly, then bitterly angry, while we were questioned. Our papers were in order; they could not find anything irregular; they remained sharp, unsatisfied. Both Roy and I lost our tempers. Though I was too angry to note it then, I had never seen him abandoned to rage before. He thumped on the table in the control-room; he was insolently furious; he demanded that they put us in touch that instant with the protecting power; he treated them like petty officials; he loved riffraff and outcasts and those who were born to be powerless – but that afternoon, when he was crossed, he assumed that authority must be on his side.

Suddenly, with a good many acid comments, they let us through. They had no formal case against us – but they might have persisted longer if we had kept our tempers and continued with rational argument. As we walked into the town to the railway station (there was no car and they would not help us to find any sort of vehicle) it occurred to me that we were angry because of their suspicions: we were the more angry because the suspicions happened to be entirely justified. It was curious, the genuine moral outrage one felt at being accused of a sin of which one was guilty. I told Roy.

'Just so,' he said, with a smile that was a little sour.

The train was crowded up to the frontier, with people standing in each carriage. It arrived hours late at Annemas, and there we had another scene. At last we sat in a Swiss train, clean and empty.

'Now you can relax,' said Roy. His smile vanished, as the excitement and thrill of the journey dropped from him. He looked out of the window as the train moved towards Geneva.

He had become by this time in his life sad without much intermission. It was not like an overmastering bout of melancholy; I wondered if that was creeping on him now. It was hard to tell, when so much of his time he was burdened – burdened without much up and down, as though this were a steady, final state.

He turned away from the window, and found my eyes upon him. His own gaze met mine. I noticed his eyes as though it were the first time. They were brilliant, penetrating: most people found them hard to escape: they had often helped him in his elaborate solemn dialogues, in the days when he played his tricks upon the 'stuffed'.

'Anxious?' he said.

'Yes.'

'About me?'

'Yes.'

'You needn't worry, Lewis,' he said. 'I shan't disgrace you. I shan't do anything unorthodox.'

He looked at me with a faint smile.

'There's no need to worry. I promise you.'

He spoke as he had come to speak so often – quietly, sensibly, kindly, without fancy. I accepted the reassurance implicitly. I knew I had nothing to fear at the end of this journey. It was a relief. Whatever happened now, I could cease to worry at the level of practical politics at the level where Houston Eggar would be concerned.

Yet, in those quiet, intimate words, there was an undercurrent of something more profound. Perhaps I did not hear it at its sharpest. I was not then attuned.

We arrived at Basel late at night, and went at once to Willy Romantowski's address. We were met by an anticlimax. Yes, he was living there. No, he was not in. He had been staying with some friends for a night or two. He was expected back tomorrow or the next day.

'Willy must have found someone very, very nice,' said Roy with a grin, as we left the house. 'Really, I'm surprised at the Swiss. Very remarkable.'

I grinned too, though I was more frustrated than he by the delay. I wanted to get it over, return safely to England, clear off the work that was waiting for me. Roy was indifferent, quite ready to spend some time in this town.

He remarked that Willy was not doing himself too badly. It was midnight, and difficult to get an impression of a strange street. But it was clearly not a slum. The street seemed to be full of old middle-class houses, turned into flats – not unlike the Knesebeckstrasse, except that the houses were less gaunt, more freshly painted and spick-and-span. Willy was living in a room under the eaves.

'His standard of living is going up,' said Roy. 'Why? Just two guesses.'

Willy did not get in touch with us the next day, and we spent the time walking round Basel: I was still restless, and Roy set out to entertain me. If one did not walk too far, one saw only red roofs, jutting eaves, the narrow bustling old streets, the golden ball of the Spalenthor above the roofs, gleaming in the spring sunlight. It took one back immediately to childhood, like the smell of class-room paint; it was as though one had slept as a child in one of those tiny bedrooms, and been wakened by the church bells.

We used an introduction to some of the people at the university. They took us out and gave us a gigantic dinner, but they regarded us with pity, as one might look at someone mortally ill. For they took it for granted that England had already lost the war. They were cross with us for making them feel such painful pity – just as Lord Boscastle sounded callous at having his heart wrung by Roy's sorrow. I found myself perversely expressing a stubborn, tough, blimpish optimism which I by no means felt. They became angry, pointing out how unrealistic I was, how like all Englishmen I had an over-developed character and very little intelligence.

Roy took no part in the argument. He was occupying himself, with the professional interest that had not left him, in learning some oddities of Swiss-German.

Roy had left a note for Willy, and we called again at his lodging house. At last he came to our hotel, on our second afternoon there. His mincing mannerisms were not flaunted quite so much; he was wearing a pin-stripe suit in the English style, his cheeks were fatter, he looked healthy and well fed. He was patently upset to find me with Roy. Roy said that he was sure Willy would be glad to see another old friend, and asked him to have some tea.

Willy would love to. He explained that he had become very fond of tea. He had also become, I thought, excessively genteel.

Roy began by asking him about the people at No. 32. Willy said that he had not seen them for eighteen months (both Roy and I thought this was untrue). But the little dancer had unexpectedly and suddenly married a schoolmaster, back in her native town; she had had a child and was said to be very happy. We sent for a bottle of wine, and drank to her. For a few moments, we were light-hearted.

Roy questioned Willy up to dinner, through the meal, through the first part of the night. Roy mentioned the clerk, Willy's old patron, the 'black avised' – Willy shrugged his shoulders: 'I do not know where he is. He was tiresome. I left him. I do not know him any more.' Roy scolded him: 'It is hard to be kind to those who love you, Willy. But you need to try. It is shameful not to try.' It was strange that he took the trouble to rebuke Willy, who had always seemed to me inescapably hard, petty and vain. Perhaps Roy was rebuking something else. Perhaps he remembered that he himself had sometimes behaved unforgivably to those who loved him.

From the black avised, he switched to Willy's own adventures. Here we became inextricably entangled for a long time: it was difficult to pick out exactly where he was lying. His first, as it were official, story was this: he had been called up in the summer of 1939, had gone with an infantry division into Poland, had spent the winter with the army of occupation, had been transferred to the western front in the spring of 1940. His division had been sitting opposite Verdun, and had done no fighting; in the winter, they were moved across Europe again. It was then that Willy 'got tired of it'. He had deserted, on the way through Germany, and smuggled himself over the Swiss frontier. Since then he had been living in Basel. 'How are you keeping alive?' asked Roy. 'Thanks to friends,' said Willy, turning his eyes aside modestly – but added in a hurry: 'I am poor. Will you please help me, Roy?'

Most of those statements were lies. That was quite clear. It was also quite clear that, if he wanted to make a proposition to Roy, he would have to admit they were lies. So we examined him, tripped him up on inconsistencies, just to give him a chance to come down to the real business. Meanwhile I was hoping, in the exchange, to collect a few useful facts.

We drank a good deal before and during dinner. We hoped to get him drunk, for we were both, of course, accustomed to wine. But he turned out to have, despite his youth, an abnormally strong head. Roy said to me in English, over dinner: 'We shall be dished, old boy – if he sees us under the table.'

However, after dinner Willy made some pointed hints that I should leave him and Roy alone. I did not budge. Willy pouted. He might be acquiring great gentility, I thought, but he still had some way to go. His patience was not lasting – all of a sudden he began commiserating with Roy on the dangers of life in England. 'You too will be destroyed. It is stupid to stay in England. Why do you not come to Germany? It can be arranged. We will have everything nice for you.'

So that was it. I glanced at Roy. It was certain now that he would get more from Willy if I went away. He nodded. I made an excuse. 'Don't be too late,' said Roy. 'He won't have gone when you come back.' Willy regarded me with an absence of warmth.

I sat at a cafe in the Petergraben, not far away. The night was warm enough for all the windows to be open; lusty young men and girls went by on the narrow pavement. It was all cheerful, jolly with bodily life. It was different from anything we should know for long enough.

I bought a paper, ordered a large glass of beer, and thought about this affair of Willy Romantowski. It was grotesque. I was not worrying; I had faith that Roy would behave like the rest of us. Yet it was grotesque. Who had suggested it? What lay behind it? Maybe the motives were quite commonplace. In the middle of bizarre events, it was hard to remember that they might be simply explained. Yet I doubted whether we should ever know the complete truth behind Willy's invitation.

I was sure of one minor point – that Willy himself was a singularly unheroic character. He was terrified of the war and determined to avoid it. It seemed to me distinctly possible that he had volunteered to fetch Roy in order to establish a claim on a good safe job back in Berlin. I remembered Roy's judgment on how gallant these epicene young men would be; this was a joke against him.

I returned to the Spalenbrunnen. From outside, I could see Roy and Willy still sitting at the dinner-table. When I joined them, I noticed with a shock that Willy was in tears.

'Nearly finished, Lewis,' said Roy to me. 'I've been telling Willy that I can't go back with him. I've asked him to tell my friends that I love them. And that I love Germany.'

'I only came for your good,' said Willy.

'You must not pretend, Willy,' said Roy gently. 'It is not so.'

Willy gulped with distress – perhaps through disappointment at not bringing off his coup, perhaps through a stab of feeling. He shook hands with Roy: then, though he hated me to perdition, he remembered his manners and shook hands with me. Without another word he went out of the room.

'Very remarkable,' said Roy. He looked tired and pale.

I took him out of the smoky room, and we sauntered along the street. Roy had packed a black hat for the journey, and he pulled it down low over his forehead. The lights were uneven in the gothic lanes, and his face was shadowed, a little sinister. I laughed at him. 'Special hat,' he said. Whatever else left him, the mockery stayed. 'Suitable for spying. I chose it on purpose.'

He was now certain that the first move had come from Schäder, though Willy did not have much idea. Someone from the 'government' (no doubt an official in Schäder's ministry) had gone to the Knesebeckstrasse to discover whether anyone knew Roy. Willy had been there, and had been only too anxious to please.

That was intelligible. But why had he been despatched to Basel, long before they had the slightest indication that Roy would come? That was one of the puzzling features of the whole story. Roy brought out the theory that Willy was given other work to do in Switzerland. This was only one of his jobs. He was the kind of low-grade agent that the Germans used for their petty inquiries, just as all governments did. He had a nose for private facts, particularly when they were unpleasant. Probably he mixed pleasure with business, and put in a little blackmail on the side.

But Roy had not been able to make him confess. It was no more than a guess. About the connection with Schäder, however (whom Willy had hardly heard of, any more than a bright cockney of the same class would have heard of a junior cabinet minister), Roy was able to convince me. For Willy had produced, parrot-like, several messages which he could not have invented. The most entertaining ran thus: a few days before the war began, the university had resolved that Roy's work during his stay in Berlin 'had been of such eminence as to justify the title of visiting professor, and this title could probably be bestowed upon him, if he did similar work at a later period'. That is, the opposition had stone-walled until they got a compromise which must have irritated everybody.

Why had Schäder taken this trouble to lure Roy? It was true that Roy knew things that would be of use – but how had they discovered that? was it in any case sufficient reason? I suggested that it might be, in part, friendly concern.

'They must be absolutely confident that they've got it won,' I said. 'It must be easy to sit back and do a good turn for a friend.'

'I wonder if they are so confident,' said Roy. 'I bet they still think sometimes of defeat and death.'

He knew them so much better than I did. He went on:

'Reinhold Schäder is a bit like you, old boy. But he's very different when it comes to the point. He's a public man. He never forgets it. He might think of doing something disinterested. Such as fetching me out for the good of my health. But he wouldn't do it. Unless he could see a move ahead. No, they must think I could be some use. It's very nice of them, isn't it?'

Then there was the final puzzle. Schäder, or his subordinates, must have thought it out. Roy said that there were complete arrangements for passing him into Germany. How likely had they reckoned the chance of getting him? Did Schäder really think that Roy would go over?

Roy shook his head.

'Too difficult,' he said.

Then he said:

'Did you think I should go?'

I replied, just as directly:

'Not this time.'

'You came to watch over me, of course,' said Roy, not as a question, but as a matter of fact.

'Yes.'

'You needn't have done,' said Roy. His tone was casual, even, sad, as though he were speaking with great certainty from the depth of self-knowledge. It was a tone that I was used to hearing, more and more. Suddenly it was broken with humour. 'If I'd wanted to go, what would you have done? What could you have done? I wish you'd tell me. It interests me, you know.'

I would not play that game. We walked silently out by the old town gate, and Roy said, again in that even tone:

'It wouldn't be easy to be a traitor.'

He added:

'One would need to believe in a cause – right to the end. If our country went to war with Russia – would our communist friends find it easy to be traitors?'

I considered for a second.

'Some of them,' I said, 'would be terribly torn.'

'Just so,' said Roy. He went on:

'I may be old-fashioned. But I couldn't manage it.'

So we walked through the old streets of Basel, talking about political motives, the way our friends would act, the future so far as we could see it. Roy said that he had never quite been able to accept the Reich. It was a feeble simulacrum of his search for God. Yet he knew what it was like to believe in such a cause. 'If they had been just a little different, they would have been the last hope.' I said that was unrealistic: by the nature of things, they could not have been different. But he turned on me:

'It's as realistic as what you hope for. Even if they lose, the future isn't going the way you think. Lewis, this is where your imagination doesn't seem to work. But you'll live to see it. It will be dreadful.'

He spoke with extreme conviction, almost as though he had the gift of foresight.

We turned back, each of us heavy with his thoughts. Then Roy said:

'I used to be sorry that I hurt you. When I tried to fall in on the opposite side.'

Between the gabled houses, the shadows were dramatic; Roy's face was pale, brilliantly lit on one cheek, the features unnaturally sharp.

'I was clutching at anything, of course,' he said.

'Yes.'

'It was my last grab.' He smiled. 'It left me with nothing, didn't it? Or with myself.'

The clocks struck from all round us. He said:

'I'm keeping you up. I mustn't. High officials need to become respectable. It's time you did, you know. Part of your duties.'

CHAPTER XXXIV

SURRENDER AND RELIEF

SHORTLY after we returned from Basel, Roy's department was moved out of London, and I did not see him for some months. But I heard of him – just once, but in a whisper that one believes as soon as one hears, one seems to have known it before. I heard of him in a committee meeting: it was Houston Eggar who told me, in a moment's pause between two items on the agenda.

We used to meet in the Old Treasury, in a room which overlooked Whitehall itself. It was a committee at under-secretary level, which was set up to share out various kinds of supplies; there were several different claimants – Greece, when she was still in the war, partisan groups which were just springing up by the end of the summer of 1941, when this meeting took place, and neutrals such as Turkey.

The committee behaved (as I often thought, with frantic irritation or human pleasure, according to the news or my own inner weather) remarkably like a college meeting. Each of the members was representing a ministry, and so was speaking to instructions. Sometimes he was at one with his instructions, and so expressed them with energy and weight; Houston Eggar, for instance, could nearly always feel as the Foreign Office felt. Sometimes a member did not like what he was obliged to say; sometimes a strong character was etching out a line for himself, and one saw policy shaped under one's eyes by a series of small decisions. (In fact, it was rare for policy to be clearly thought out, though some romantics or worshippers of 'great men' liked to think so. Usually it built itself from a thousand small arrangements, ideas, compromises, bits of give-and-take. There was not much which was decisively changed by a human will.) Sometimes one of the committee was over-anxious to ingratiate himself or was completely distracted by some private grief.

As in a college meeting, the reasons given were not always close to the true reasons. As in a college meeting, there was a public language – much of which was common to both. That minatory phrase 'in his own best interests' floated only too sonorously round Whitehall. The standard of competence and relevance was much higher than in a college meeting, the standard of luxurious untrammelled personality perceptibly lower. Like most visitors from outside, I had formed a marked respect for the administrative class of the civil service. I had lived among various kinds of able men, but I thought that, as a group, these were distinctly the ablest. And they loved their own kind of power.

Houston Eggar loved his own kind of power. He loved to think that a note signed by him affected thousands of people. He loved to speak in the name of the Foreign Office: '*my* department', said Houston Eggar with possessive gusto. It was all inseparable as flesh and blood from his passion for getting on, his appetite for success – which, as it happened, still did not look certain to be gratified. It had become a race with the end of the war. He was forty-eight in 1941, and unless the war ended in five or six years he stood no chance of becoming an ambassador. However, he was a man who got much pleasure from small prizes; his C.M.G. had come through in the last honours list, which encouraged him; he plunged into the committee that afternoon, put forward his argument with his usual earnestness and vigour, and thoroughly enjoyed himself.

He was effective in committee; he was not particularly clever, but he spoke with clarity, enthusiasm, pertinacity and above all weight. Even among sophisticated men, weight counted immeasurably more than subtlety or finesse.

Accordingly he secured a little more than the Foreign Office could reasonably expect. It was a hot afternoon, and he leaned back in his chair, mopping his forehead. He always got hot in the ardour of putting his case. He beamed. He was happy to have won a concession.

I was due to speak on the next business, but the chairman was looking through his papers. I was sitting next to Eggar; he pushed an elbow along the table, and leant towards me. He said in a low voice, casual and confidential:

'So Calvert is getting his release.'

'What?'

'He has got his own way. Good luck to him. I told his chief there's no use trying to keep a man who is determined to go.'

'Where is he going?'

Eggar looked incredulous, as though I must know.

'Where is he going?' I said.

'Oh, he wants to fly, of course. It's quite natural.'

I had known nothing of it, not a word, not a hint. I heard the chairman's voice, a little impatient:

'Isn't this a matter for you, Eliot?'

'I'm sorry, Mr Chairman,' I said, and mechanically began to explain a new piece of government machinery. I could hear my own words, faint and toneless like words in a dream – yet they came out in a shape fluent, practised, articulate. It was too hard to break the official habit. One was clamped inside one's visor.

Eggar left before the end of the meeting; and so I could not get another word with him. I put through a call to Roy's office, but he was out. I gave a message for him: would he telephone me at my flat, without fail, after eleven that night?

I went straight from Whitehall to have dinner with Lady Muriel and Joan. They had come to London in the first week of the war, and were living in the Boscastles' town house in Charles Street. They were extravagantly uncomfortable. The house was not large, judged by the magnificent criterion of Boscastle (Lord Boscastle's grandfather had sold the original town mansion); but it was a good deal too large for two women, both working at full-time jobs. It was also ramshackle and perilously unsafe. Nothing would persuade Lady Muriel to forsake it. A service flat seemed in her eyes common beyond expression – as for danger, she dismissed us all as a crowd of 'jitterbugs', getting the idiom wrong. 'This disturbance is much exaggerated,' she said, and slept with a soundness that infuriated many of us and put us to shame.

Her sense of duty would not permit her to employ any servants who could possibly do other work. In fact, they had two women who had been with the family all their lives, both well over seventy and infirm. Lady Muriel did all the cooking herself when she gave a dinner party, but made them both wait at table. It was a quixotic parody of nights in the Lodge and Boscastle.

She and Joan were sitting together in the drawing-room. The pictures had been taken away for safety, and the walls were bare.

'Good evening, Mr – Lewis,' said Lady Muriel. 'It is good of you to come and see us.'

Nowadays, she used my Christian name when she remembered. The explanation was a little complicated. It did not mean for an instant that she thought the time had come to relax her social standards. As a matter of fact, the exact opposite was the case. She might officiate at a refugee centre each day and every day – which she did inexorably. She submitted to being slapped on the back by cheery women helpers: it was part of her job. But at night, in the privacy of Charles Street, where she had lived as a girl, she became so magniloquently snobbish that her days in the Lodge came to seem like slumming. Lord Boscastle responded in just the same fashion – not with accommodation, not trying to fit in, but with an exaggerated, a considered, a monumental arrogance. They were both dropping most of their old acquaintances.

No, when Lady Muriel called me by my Christian name it did not imply that she accepted me in any social sense. Perhaps she liked me a little more; with her, getting used to people and liking them tended to run together. But really her softening came from quite a different cause: it was a gesture of respect towards the government and those who organised the war. She was passionately determined that her country should win; and it made her respectful to anyone who seemed to be in control. She had decided that I was far more important than in fact I was; she had also decided that I knew every conceivable military secret. Nothing would remove these misconceptions; a flat denial merely strengthened her faith in my astuteness and responsibility. Then someone told her that I was doing well, and that finished it. She listened open-mouthed to every word I said about the war, like a girl student with a venerated teacher; she drew inferences when I was silent; and, with a certain effort, she brought herself after all those years to use my Christian name.

I smiled at Joan. Despite her exertions, thick and heavy as she was, Lady Muriel was well preserved at fifty-five. But Joan no longer looked a girl. She had worked in the Treasury from the first winter, and her face had changed through success as well as unhappiness. She had shown how able she was; it was just the outlet for her tough, strong nature; and it had stamped its mark on her, for on the surface she was a little more formidable a little more decisive, ruthless and blunt.

Though everyone praised her, though she knew that she could go high if she wanted, she recoiled. She liked it and hated it. In protest, she lived at night the gayest life she could snatch. She went out with every man who asked her. I saw her often in public-houses and smart bars and restaurants. She was searching for a substitute for Roy, I knew – and yet also she longed for the glitter and the lights more than many giggling thoughtless women.

I did not want to hurt her, but I was driven to ask at once about Roy. I could not begin to make conversation. I had to ask: did they know anything of him?

To my consternation, Joan smiled.

'You must have heard.' She told me the same news as Eggar.

'I've heard nothing.'

'I should have thought he would have told you,' said Joan. 'He let me know.'

'It was only to be expected,' said Lady Muriel, 'that he should let us know.'

I gathered that he had written to Lady Muriel. Joan was glad that she had heard the secret, and I had not; even now her love would not let her go, searched for the slightest sign, found an instant of dazzling hope in a letter to her mother. His friend had not been told; was this letter a signal to her?

'He seems content,' said Joan. 'I hope it's right for him. I think perhaps it is.'

'It is certainly right for him,' said Lady Muriel.

'He's such a strange man,' said Joan. 'I hope it is.'

'I've always known that he's been uncomfortable since the war began. A woman feels these things,' said Lady Muriel. 'I can rely on my intuition.'

'What has it told you, Mother?' said Joan, as though she had picked up a spark of mischief from Roy.

'He could not bear being kept back while others fought. I consider that he would never have been happy until he fought.'

Joan smiled at her. Now that Joan had been battered by her own experience, she was much fonder of her mother, much kinder to her, more able to see the rich nature behind the absurd, forbidding armour.

They took the news of Roy quite differently, and yet with one point in common. For Lady Muriel, all was now clear and well. When she gave her trust, she gave it naïvely and absolutely, like a little girl; white was white, and she admired with her whole heart; and there was no one whom she admired more than Roy. She tried to get used to a war in which young men had safe jobs, did not want to leave them; but she could not manage it. She could not reconcile herself to Roy inert and indecisive. Now her trust was justified. She could worship again, in her simple, loyal, unqualified fashion. 'I always knew it would happen,' said Lady Muriel, forgetting that she had ever been troubled, forgetting it just as completely as she forgot she had once herself opposed the war.

Joan's feelings were far less simple. Although she had not spoken to him for two years, she could divine some of the reasons that had impelled him. She knew how reckless he was and how self-destructive. Yet she had loved him partly because of that dark side. She was frail enough to rejoice that he did not find his life sweeter after he had deserted her. She was both *relieved* and proud.

She and her mother had one point in common. They did not give much thought to his danger. It was the first thing that had struck me: in the committee room, I was thinking of that only: he stood about an even chance of coming through alive. Yet Lady Muriel and Joan took it without a blench. Partly, of course, they were ignorant of the statistics, Lady Muriel entirely so; they did not realise how dangerous it was; they had not been, as I had, behind the scenes in the bitter disputes about the bombing 'master plan'. But, even if they had, it would not have made much difference. They were stout-hearted themselves, and they assumed the same courage in their men. They were bred to a tradition of courage. They had very strong nerves.

In fact, Lady Muriel found a certain bellicose relish in having her beloved Roy to set against Humphrey Bevill. It had been galling to her to hear first that her nephew Humphrey had shown unexpected skill in charge of a small boat – and then, that he was taking risks in the Channel skirmishes with a wild, berserk bravery. He had just been cited for a D.S.C. It might have pleased Lady Muriel to see credit come to the family name; perhaps it did a little. But much more, it brought back a grief. Lady Muriel had craved for a son, and she was taunted by having daughters. It had taunted her again when her sister-in-law, after being childless so long, bore a son. It had seemed just to Lady Muriel that the boy should turn out worthless, dissipated, bohemian, effeminate. Now he was suddenly talked about as the bravest young man in their whole circle. Lady Muriel was not good at disguising her rancour. I had always known that she both envied and despised Lady Boscastle: now I saw that she detested her.

I got back to my flat before eleven, in time for the telephone call; I found Roy there himself. He was sitting in a dressing-gown, clean from a bath but heavy-eyed.

'Just going to bed,' he said. 'Night duty last night. I'm extremely tired.'

He was still working in his civilian office. He had received my message, and taken the first train to London.

'I hear the news is true,' I said.

'It's true,' said Roy.

'Why didn't you tell me?'

'It was the one thing I couldn't tell you.' He looked at me with a troubled gaze, as though I and he each knew the reason. Yet nothing came home to me; I was angry and mystified. Quickly, he went on:

'I've nothing to keep from you now. You see? I've come tonight to tell you something no one else knows. I'm going to get married.'

'Who to?'

'Rosalind, of course.'

Roy was smiling.

'You're not to speak of it,' he said. 'I haven't asked her yet. I don't know whether she'll have me. I hope she will.'

'I think she might.'

'Excellent,' said Roy, taking my sarcasm equably. 'You've always had a weakness for her yourself, old boy. Remember: I shall be a jealous husband. I need a child.'

He went on:

'I couldn't ask her, of course, until the other thing was settled. It will be nice to have everything settled.'

Then he said that he could not keep his eyes open, and must go to bed. I fetched him a book, in case he wanted to read in the morning: he was asleep before I went out of the room.

I could not think of sleep myself. I turned off the lights, pulled back the curtains, and gazed out of the window for a long time. The night was very still. There was no moon; the river glistened in the starlight; there was neither light nor sound down there, except for a moment when an engine chugged across to the southern bank. All over the sky, the stars were brilliant. 'I hate the stars.' I heard that cry again.

So he had no hope left at all. I could see no other meaning. I could understand Joan's relief. I shared it, and knew it was selfish at the root. If he must be driven so – I had felt more than once that night – then I was glad he could make this choice: I was glad he could choose a way which those round him could accept and approve. It might have been far otherwise. Somehow he had kept within society, which a man like George Passant couldn't. It was a help to Joan and me, who cared for society more than Roy did.

Yet that was a trivial relief, by the side of his surrender. For he had given up now. For years he had struggled with his nature. Now he was tired of it, and he had given up. Active as he was, still eager with the pulse of life, he had done it in the most active way. He was going into battle, he wanted a wife and child. But he had no hope left.

I looked at the brilliant stars: There was no comfort there.

CHAPTER XXXV

CONSEQUENCES OF A MARRIAGE

ROY's marriage caused more stir than his other choice. The wedding took place in the autumn, three weeks before he sailed across to America for his flying training. I was held in London and could not attend it. One of the features of those years was the geographical constraint under which we had to live; a few years earlier, we had had more leisure than most people in the world; now I could not get out of my office even for the day of Roy's wedding. In fact, I had only seen him for an hour or two since that night he made the special visit to tell me his news. We were all confined, as it were in prison. Many friends I had not seen since the beginning of the war.

But sitting in London, dining now and then with the Royces, I heard enough furore about the marriage. Lady Muriel was at first incredulous; then, contrary to all expectations, she became unusually indulgent. 'I refuse to blame him,' she said. 'I've seen other men make marriages almost as impossible as this before they went to fight. When a man goes off to fight, he feels a basic need to find a – *squaw*. I consider this young woman is simply his squaw. As for the future,' she said in a grand, gnomic fashion, 'I prefer not to speak.'

Joan suffered afresh from all the different wounds of humiliated and unrequited love. She could feel her confidence and self-respect seeping away; she ached with the hunger of her fibres; she was lost. She had been able to adjust herself to loss before, while she could believe that he was weighted down with misery, that neither she nor any woman could reach or console him. But now he had married a stupid, scheming, ordinary woman, as though he were an ordinary domestic man!

Joan was not only desolated, but bitterly angry. And the anger was good for her. It burned away some of her self-distrust. Anything was better than that she should be frightened off love for good. Her formidable temper blazed out. I was glad to see it. I was glad to see her defiantly going from party to party on the arm of another man.

From two sources I heard that Ralph Udal had also taken it bitterly. Apparently Rosalind had not considered it necessary to break her engagement to him until she was simultaneously engaged to Roy. Had he suspected nothing? Was he so self-sufficient that he convinced himself all was well? I had not met Lady Boscastle since that final end-of-the-world week in Cambridge, but this was a subject peculiarly suited to her talents. She wrote me several feline letters about the 'emotional misadventures of our unfortunate vicar'.

Udal was really unhappy. He showed it by one clear sign. He could not bear to stay in Boscastle where Rosalind had so often visited him. He begged Arthur Brown to find him a living, any kind of living, 'even one', Arthur Brown reported over the telephone with a rotund wily chuckle, 'even one with slightly less amenities.' Arthur Brown had exerted himself with his usual experienced kindliness; he managed to find Udal a slightly better living in Beccles.

Before Ralph Udal left the vicarage at Boscastle, Roy stayed with him for a week-end. It happened while Roy was on embarkation leave, and I did not see him afterwards. I would have given much to know what they said to each other; I was beginning to realise that Udal was a more singular man that I had at first detected.

During the autumn, Rosalind came to see me. It was her first visit to London since Roy married her, and she was living in state at the Dorchester. As soon as she arrived in my flat, she busied herself tidying it up.

'I must find someone to look after you. It's time you married again,' she scolded me. 'I must say, it depresses me to think of you coming back here – and nothing ready for you.'

Then she sat down with a smile.

'I'd better be careful,' she said. 'It's a bit of a drag for the first few months, so they tell me.' It was her way of telling me that she was pregnant. 'We didn't waste much time, did we?' Again she gave her mock-modest, surreptitious grin. 'Of course, there wasn't much time to waste. We only had three weeks, and that isn't very long, is it?'

I laughed.

'It did mean we had to rush things rather,' said Rosalind. She gave an affectionate, earthy frown, and went on:

'It's all Roy's fault. I've got no patience with him. I could kick him. The bloody old fool. If only he'd had the sense to marry me years ago, when I wanted to, we should have had a wonderful time. I ought to have dragged him to church by the scruff of his neck. Why didn't he ask me then, the blasted fool? Our eldest child would be six now. That's how it ought to be. You know, Lewis, I do wish I'd worked on him.'

She was serene, blissfully happy, but matter-of-fact in her triumph. I almost reminded her that she had no cause to reproach herself: she had done her damnedest. But well as I knew her, shameless and realistic as she was, I held my tongue. Curiously, it would have hurt her. She had the kind of realism that buried schemes as soon as they were no longer necessary. She would have stopped at nothing to marry Roy; but, having brought it off, she conveniently shelved all memory of plans, lies, stratagems, tears, pride abandoned. If she were confronted with it, she would look and feel ill-used.

She basked in her well-being.

'He is a nice old thing, though, isn't he?' she said. 'Do you know, Lewis, I enjoy looking at him when he's reading. He *has* got a nice face. Don't you think it's lucky for a woman when she likes a man for something different' – she dropped her eyes – 'and then finds she enjoys just looking at his face? I've never thought he was handsome – but it is a nice face.'

As the evening went on, I was unkind enough to remind her of Ralph Udal. She showed a faint, sisterly desire that he should find a wife. As for herself, she would never have done, she said, contentedly. It was much better for him that she had broken it off: 'in his own best interests', I thought to myself, and made a note to tease Roy with it some time.

Her only worry was where to have the child. Roy would not have returned before it was born. His father was ill, and she could not (and for some reason was violently disinclined to) stay in the Calverts' house. I suspected that she had not been well received; the Calverts knew her family, since her grandfather and Roy's had started in the same factory. In any case, Rosalind was determined not to live near her home. After marrying Roy, she did not intend to spend any time at all in the provincial town. She had thrown up her job; her skill and reputation meant nothing to her, she was happy not to earn another penny. Roy would not be rich until his father died, but they were comfortably off. Rosalind meant to spread herself.

She would have liked to live in London; but though the nights were quiet then, the autumn of 1941, war-time London was not a good place to beat a child. And Rosalind said without any shame that she was a coward; she would come to London at the end of the war. Meanwhile, she hesitated. Suddenly she had her mind made up for her in an unlooked-for manner. Lady Muriel took charge.

Lady Muriel heard that Rosalind was with child; how I did not know, but I suspected that Rosalind had flaunted the news. She was kind and careless, but she liked revenge; the Royces used to snub her, Joan had taken away Roy for years, even in her triumph Rosalind was obscurely jealous of her. It was shameful to exult over her, but Rosalind was not likely to be deterred, when it was so sweet. I ought to have foreseen it, and have warned her not to gloat.

Anyway, Lady Muriel knew, and was strongly affected. Since her husband died, she had invested all her suppressed warmth in Roy. She felt responsible and possessive about anything of his. Most of all a child. His child must be cared for. Her feeling for her own babies had been outwardly gruff, in truth healthy and animal: and she was moved at the thought of one of Roy's. It must be cared for.

Lady Muriel had no doubt forgotten that she once pronounced Rosalind barren. Here was Rosalind in the flesh, in the luxurious, triumphant, pregnant flesh. If Lady Muriel were to help with Roy's child, she had to accept that 'impossible young woman'.

Lady Muriel gave way. She was humbled by love. She did not see much of Rosalind; that was too bitter; she wrote her suggestions (which soon became orders) in letters which began 'Dear Mrs Calvert'. Sometimes, I thought to myself, she behaved remarkably as though the child were illegitimate. It had to be cherished for the father's sake – meanwhile one made as few concessions as possible to the sinful mother.

Yet, like it or not, Lady Muriel had to become interested in Rosalind's plans. Soon she became more than interested, she became the planner. For Lady Muriel decided that the baby should be born at Boscastle.

She would not listen to arguments against. Was there not plenty of room there? Would they not be reasonably waited on – despite her sister-in-law's unworthy management? Was it not as safe, as far from the war, as anywhere in England? Did not the estate grow its own food, which was important nowadays? Could not Lady Muriel guarantee the competence of the family doctor?

But, of course, she wanted it for her own sake. It would give her a claim on the child.

Rosalind effaced herself. She was prepared to put up with insults, high-handedness, Lady Muriel's habit of disregarding her, anything that came, if only this could happen. The idea entranced her. It was like a gorgeous, unexpected present. Like most realistic people, Rosalind was not above being a snob.

A correspondence took place between Lady Muriel and Lady Boscastle – firm, hortatory, morally righteous on Lady Muriel's side, sarcastic and amused on Lady Boscastle's. At first Lady Boscastle did not take the proposal seriously. Then she saw that it was being inexorably advanced. She objected. She was not a particular friend of Roy's, she found Rosalind tiresome, she was bored by the war, she saw no reason why she should be inconvenienced; unlike Lady Muriel, she was not buoyed up by sheer vigour of the body, by the impulse of good crude health; Lady Boscastle often felt old, neglected, uninterested now, and she did not see why she should put herself out.

Lady Muriel quoted passages from her sister-in-law's letters with burning indignation. Lady Boscastle, with cynical ingenuity, raised the question of the tenants' peace of mind; they knew of Rosalind's engagement to the late vicar; what would they be likely to think now? Usually, Lady Muriel was only too preoccupied with the tenants' moral welfare; but she had not room for two concerns at once, and she brushed that point aside as though they were Tasmanian aborigines.

On paper, Lady Boscastle had the better of the argument; but, as usual when there was a difference about the family house, Lady Muriel had the greater staying-power, and harangued the others until she prevailed. Lord Boscastle appeared to turn into an ally; and in the end Lady Boscastle sent Rosalind an invitation. Lady Boscastle knew when she was beaten, and her letter was far more friendly than any Lady Muriel wrote to Rosalind (Lady Muriel still began 'Dear Mrs Calvert'): Rosalind showed it to me with delight: I thought I could detect just one malicious flick, put in for the writer's own benefit.

Rosalind accepted by return, and went to Boscastle in time for Christmas. In February, I had a letter myself from Lady Boscastle, in that fine, elegant, upright hand.

'This is really quite ridiculous,' she wrote. 'God appears to have a misplaced sense of humour, which he reserves for those who haven't paid him enough attention. There is no question, he scores in the end. Lewis, my dear boy, I once was pursued with singular pertinacity by a young gentleman of literary pretensions. He was remarkably, in fact embarrassingly faithful, and had a curious knack of turning up in unexpected places. I did not find him a particularly agreeable young man, but he added an element of interest by indulging in throaty prophecies about my future. He used to quote "Quand tu seras bien vieille" in impassioned but distinctly imperfect French. He produced so many pictures of my old age that I was prepared for one of them to turn out right. (I should remark that he appeared to find them deeply moving: he was, as you would expect, a little too fervent for my taste.)

'But now I am *bien vieille* – pity me, for it is the only tragedy, as you will discover, my dear. Now I am *bien vieille*, and none of that young man's absurd prognostications were anything like so undecorated as the truth. Really I did not expect this. It is a little much. I attribute it entirely to poor Muriel's unappreciated virtue.

'Imagine me listening to the opinions, confessions, and simple aspirations of your friend Rosalind. It seems to me the most improbable occupation for my declining years. Except when I am immobilised and kept in bed (which, I have a feeling, will happen more often in the next few months), I do little else. Your friend Rosalind appears to think that I am a sympathetic listener. I have pointed out the opposite, but she laughs indulgently and feels it is just my little way.

'I have never been an admirer of my own sex. Listening to this young woman, I reflect on such interesting themes as why men are so obtuse as to be taken in. Feminine delicacy? Refinement? Frailty? Fineness of feeling? I reflect also on poor Muriel and poor Joan. I have to grant them certain estimable but slightly unlovable qualities: should one, under the eye of eternity, really prefer them to this companion of mine? [Should one, I thought much later, have preferred Lady Boscastle herself? How should I have regarded her if I had met her when I was less susceptible to glamour?] To which of them does one give the prize for womanhood? I have never been a confidante of your Roy, but I admit I should like his answer to that question.

'I have met very few people, even very few women, who are as singularly unmoral as this young woman. I have known many whose interest in morality was slightly detached: but this one scarcely seems to have heard of such a subject. I must admit that I find it engaging when she assumes the same of me. It has not taken her long to regard herself and me as sisters.

'By the way, it also did not take her long to become unimpressed by the battlements and other noble accessories. Including my poor Hugh. She rapidly recognised that she could reduce him to a state of gibbering admiration. They both get a good deal of innocent pleasure from their weekly bridge with the new vicar and his wife. I suspect they are happier because my less enthusiastic eye is removed. Possibly I am becoming slightly maudlin about the ironies of time; but I do feel it is unfitting that nowadays Hugh should be reduced to this one high event each week. He fidgets intolerably each Thursday evening, as we wait for the vicar and his wife. No one could call the vicar a deep thinker, and he has large red ears.'

All through that winter and spring, I was attending committees, preparing notes for the Minister, reading memoranda, talking to Francis Getliffe and his scientific friends; for decisions were being taken about the bombing campaign, and we were all ranged for or against. In fact, all the people I knew best were dead against. My Minister was one of the chief opponents in the government; through Francis, I had met nearly all the younger scientists, and they were as usual positive, definite, and scathing. They had learned a good deal about the effect of bombing, from the German raids; they worked out what would be the results, if we persisted in the plan of bombing at night. I read the most thorough of these 'appreciations'. I could not follow the statistical arguments, but the conclusions were given as proved beyond reasonable doubt: we should destroy a great many houses, but do no other serious damage; the number of German civilians killed would be relatively small; our losses in aircrew would be a large proportion of all engaged; in terms of material effect, the campaign could have little military significance. The Minister shook his head; he had seen too many follies; he was a sensible man, but he did not believe in the victory of sense; and he knew that too many in power had a passionate, almost mystical faith in bombing. They were going to bomb, come what may; and naturally human instruments arose who could fit in. Against the scientific arguments, the advocates of bombing fell back on morale. There was something the scientists could not speak about nor measure. The others said, as though with inner knowledge, that the enemy would break under the campaign.

I went to a committee where Francis Getliffe made one of the last attempts to put the scientific case. Like most of his colleagues, Francis had left the invention of weapons and took to something like the politics of scientific war. He was direct, ruthless, and master of his job; he had good military sense; he had not found any circumstances which gave him more scope, and he became powerful in a very short time. But now he was risking his influence in this war. Opponents of bombing were not in fashion. Bombing was the orthodoxy of the day. As I observed it, it occurred to me that you can get men to accept any orthodoxy, religious, political, even this technical one, the last and oddest of the English orthodoxies; the men who stood outside were rare, and would always be so.

But Francis's integrity was absolute. He was pliable enough to bend over little things; this was a very big thing. Someone ought to oppose it to the end; he was the obvious person; he took it on himself to do it.

He was much the same that afternoon as he used to be at college meetings – courteous, formal, clear, unshakeably firm. He was high-strung among those solid steady official men, but his confidence had increased, and he was more certain of his case than they were. He was skilful at using his technical mastery.

He was setting out to prove the uneconomic bargain if we threw our resources into bombing. The amount of industrial effort invested in bombers was about twice what those same bombers would destroy. Bombing crews were first-class troops, said Francis Getliffe. Their training was very long, their physical and mental standard higher than any other body of troops. For every member of an aircrew killed, we might hope to kill three or four civilians. 'That's not business,' said Francis. 'It's not war. It doesn't begin to make sense.' He described what was then known of the German radar defences. Most of us round that table were ignorant of technical things. He made the principles of the German ground control limpidly clear. He analysed other factors in the probable rate of loss.

It was a convincing exposition. He was putting forward a purely military case. He was engrossed in the war. He was out to win at any cost. He would not have minded bombing Germans, if it helped us to win. He would not have minded losing any number of aircrews, if we gained an advantage from their loss.

For me, his words struck cold. Roy would be back in this country by August. He would be flying in operations before the new year.

I had to fend off the chill. Someone had just admitted that the German defences were a 'pretty bit of work'. I listened to the fierce argument in the smoky air; I was in attendance on the Minister, and could not take part myself. The Minister did his best, but his own stock was going down. As was inevitable, Francis Getliffe lost: he could not even get a few equipments diverted to the submarine war.

We went away together to have a drink.

'I'm on the way out,' said Francis Getliffe. 'This is the best test of judgment there's ever been. Anyone who believes in this bloody nonsense will believe anything.'

From that day, the department in which I worked had to accept the decision. We did other things: but about a fifth of our time was spent on the bombing campaign. I found it irksome.

All that spring I was imprisoned in work, living in committee rooms, under the artificial light. I saw less still of my friends. I had an occasional lunch with Joan, and letters came from Boscastle. When I dined with Lady Muriel, she pronounced that the course of the pregnancy was satisfactory.

The child was born at midsummer. It was a girl, and was christened Muriel. That fact moved Lady Boscastle to write to me, at her most characteristic. I chuckled, but thought it wise to burn the letter.

During those months, I heard a few times from Roy. He was not being a great success on his pilot's course. He was having to struggle to be allowed through; it irritated him, who liked to do things expertly, and I could not help smiling at that touch of vanity. He thought he would have done better ten years earlier; at thirty-two one did not learn so easily. In the end, he managed to pass, and landed in England in September.

After a week with Rosalind, he spent a night in my flat. He was sun-burned and healthy; in uniform, his figure was less deceptive, one could have guessed that he was strong; at last his face was carrying the first lines, but he looked tranquil. His spirits were not so intoxicatingly high as in his days of exaltation, but he laughed at me, talked about our friends, mimicked them with his features plastic, so that one saw a shadow of Lord Boscastle, of Arthur Brown, of Houston Eggar. Since he had to return next day, we sat up most of the night. He seemed no longer driven.

He did not say much of his future – except that he would now be sent to his training in heavy aircraft. There was not much for either of us to say. But he talked of his daughter with extreme pleasure.

'It's good to have a child,' he said. 'It's a shame you haven't some. You'd like it, wouldn't you?'

'Of course.'

'You must soon. It's very important.'

His pleasure was simple, natural, radiant.

'She'll be pretty,' he said happily. 'Very pretty. Excellent.'

A month later, I received an unexpected telephone call from his wife. I knew she was coming to London, for Lady Muriel had announced that her godchild was staying with her for a week-end and had invited me to dine; it was only during the course of the invitation that Lady Muriel reluctantly mentioned 'Roy's wife'. Rosalind's voice always sounded faint, falling-away, on the telephone, but that morning she seemed worried and urgent. 'I must see you at lunch time. No, it can't wait till tonight. I can't tell you in front of Lady Battleship.'

I put off an appointment and met her for lunch.

'I want you to help me, Lewis,' she said. 'Roy mustn't hear a word about it.'

She was dressed in the height of style, her shoulders padded, her hat tilted over one eye; but her expression was neither gamine nor mock-decorous, but tired, strained, intent. I jumped to a conclusion.

'What is wrong with him?'

'Nothing,' said Rosalind impatiently, as though I did not understand. 'He's very well and very happy. Didn't you think I should make him happy? The old thing has never been so comfortable in his life. He's got a bit of peace.'

She stared at me with hurt brown eyes, pleading and determined.

'Lewis, I want you to help me get him out of flying.'

'Does he want it?'

'Do you think he'd ever say so? Men never dare to confess that they're frightened. God's truth, I've got no patience with you all.'

I said:

'My dear, I think it would be impossible.'

'You'd rather let things happen than try,' she flared out like a cat.

'No. Remember he left an important job. He made a nuisance of himself to get out. It would be very hard to persuade the Air Ministry to leave go now.'

'Wouldn't he be more useful on the ground? How many people in the world speak all the languages he speaks?'

'That's true,' I said.

'Then we must get to work.'

'I'm afraid,' I said, 'that they won't leave go of a single man. They've been given complete priority.'

'Why are they so keen to keep them?' she cried. 'Because they're going to lose so many?'

'Yes.'

'They won't throw him away if I can help it.' Her face was dark and twisted, as if she were in physical pain. 'Let me tell you something. The other night I got him to talk a bit. I know he doesn't talk to me as he does to you. He says you're the only person who knows everything about him. But I got him to talk. It was in the middle of the night. He hasn't been sleeping too well this last week. It's not as bad as it used to be, but I know that he's been lying awake. Somehow I can't sleep if I think he's lying there with his eyes open.'

She paused.

'The other night I knew he was awake. I hadn't been to sleep either.

In the middle of the night I asked him if anything was the matter. He said no. I asked him if he was happy with me. He said yes. Then I got into his bed and cried till he promised to talk to me. He said it was a long story and that no one understood it all but you. You know how he speaks when he's being serious, Lewis? As though he was laughing and didn't give a damn. It makes my blasted heart turn over. Anyway he said that he'd been miserable for years. It was worse than being mad, he said. He hoped he'd get out of it. He'd struggled like a rat in a trap. But he couldn't escape. So he couldn't see any point in things. He might as well be eliminated. That was why he chose to fly.'

She stared at me.

'Then he kissed me, and laughed a bit. He said that nowadays it didn't always seem such a good idea. He was caught again. But he needn't worry this time, because there was nothing he could do.'

I exclaimed.

'You know, Lewis,' Rosalind went on, 'he must have got it all worked out when he decided to fly. He said that he was looking round for the easiest way to disappear. He didn't want to give too much trouble. So he found out from someone reliable what was the most dangerous thing to do.'

She cried out sharply:

'What's the matter, Lewis? Why are you looking so terrible?'

'Nothing,' I said, trying to speak in an even tone. 'I just thought of something else.'

Rosalind watched me.

'I hope you're all right,' she said. 'I want you to help me today.'

CHAPTER XXXVI

THE END OF A REPROACH

ROSALIND had two lines of attack ready planned. She was cunning, she had not been successful at her business for nothing; she knew it was worse than useless for a move to come from Roy's friends. The only hope was to get hold of people of influence. She wanted two different kinds of plea: first, by the leading orientalists, to say that as a scholar he was irreplaceable; second, by officials, to say that he was needed for a special job. She was cunning, but she did not know her way about this world; she needed me to tell her where to try.

She had no luck that afternoon. I sent her to old Foulkes, who was back in uniform again, a brigadier at the War Office. He had worked there seven days a week since the beginning of the war. I took her to the door in the side street, and waited on the pavement. It was an hour before she came out. She was angry and downcast. 'I don't believe the old idiot has ever seen a woman before. Oh, I suppose he's rather sweet, but it's just my luck to find someone who's not susceptible.' Foulkes had told her that her husband had a European reputation. 'Tell anyone so. Often do. Only man to keep our end up.' Rosalind parodied Foulkes ill-temperedly. But Foulkes would not say a word that would stand in the way of a man who wanted to fight. He had heard his colleagues wonder why Calvert had thrown up a safe job. 'I've told them,' Foulkes had said, with his usual vigour. 'No mystery. No mystery at all. He just wants to fight for his country. Proud of him. So ought you to be,' he had finished at great speed.

There was no other scholar in reach that day; and the officials who might be useful had all gone home for the week-end. Rosalind was frustrated, aching for something to do; but I persuaded her there was nothing, at least for the moment, and she returned to Charles Street for tea. When I saw her next, as I arrived there for dinner that same night, I noticed at once that she was more restless.

I was surprised to see the table laid for four. I had expected that Joan would spare herself; but she had decided with tough, masochistic endurance, to stick it out, and meet Roy's wife and child. Both Joan and Lady Muriel agreed that it was a beautiful baby. I watched Joan nurse it with an envious satisfaction, a satisfaction that to my astonishment seemed stronger than envy. Her voice, like her mother's, was warm and loving when she spoke to it.

At dinner she was far more at her ease than Rosalind, who sat silent, dark-faced, going over her plans. Joan tried to cheer her up. I was not prepared for such magnanimity. And I was not prepared to hear Rosalind suddenly tell them that she intended to go to any lengths to get Roy out.

'Behind his back?' Lady Muriel inquired.

'It's the only way,' said Rosalind.

'I should consider that quite unsuitable, Mrs Calvert,' said Lady Muriel.

'You can't, Rosalind,' cried Joan. 'You can't do such a thing.'

'I may want you to introduce me to people,' said Rosalind to Lady Muriel.

'I couldn't think of it without Roy's permission,' said Lady Muriel.

'I know he would not consider giving it. It would be unforgivable to go behind his back.'

Rosalind had not expected such opposition. She had wanted Lady Muriel as an ally.

'If you were his wife,' she said, 'you wouldn't be so ready to do nothing.'

Joan put in:

'I know how you feel. We should all feel like that. It's awful to do nothing. But you've got to think of him.'

'I'm thinking of nothing else—'

'I mean in another way. He has made his choice. It wasn't an easy choice, surely you must know. It came out of all he's gone through. He hasn't had an easy life. You must leave him free. You can't presume to interfere with him. There are some parts of anyone's life – however much you love them – that you have to force yourself to leave alone.'

She was consumed with feeling. She leaned forward and asked Rosalind:

'Do you deny for a moment that Roy would say the same?'

'Of course he'd say the same,' said Rosalind. 'He'd have to. He's too proud to do anything else. But—'

'He's not proud,' cried Joan. 'No one could possibly be less proud. This is so much deeper, it's part of him, surely you must see.' She hesitated, and then spoke sternly, almost harshly:

'Perhaps this will make you understand. You know that I loved him?'

'Yes.'

'I would go to him now if he called me. Well, if he had been mine – I should have done what I'm telling you to do. It would have been agony – it is agony enough now, don't you see? – but I should have left him alone.'

For a moment Rosalind was overawed by the passion of the other woman. Then Rosalind said:

'I've got to keep him alive.'

They looked at each other with dislike and misunderstanding. They would never understand each other. They knew him quite differently, I thought. Joan knew the struggle of his spirit, his melancholy, his tragic experience, better than any woman. Rosalind did not seem to know those at all. She paid no attention to the features which distinguished him among men. She knew him where he was like all other men – she took it for granted that, like all other men, he was frail, frightened, a liar to himself and her. She took him for granted as a creature of flesh and bone; whatever he said, whatever the dark moods, he longed to live.

Was that why he had married her?

I caught sight of Lady Muriel, heavy-footedly leading the conversation away. She was horrified. Perhaps until that moment she had not let herself recognise her daughter's love for Roy. Now it had been proclaimed in public: that was the final horror. Her sense of propriety was ravaged. It plucked away the screen behind which she had been trained to live. She gazed at her daughter with dismay, indignation – and an inarticulate pity.

Rosalind left London next day, and she did not confide her plan to me again. However, she sent me a note, saying that Roy had discovered what she was up to, and had stopped her. It was probably true, I thought, that he had found out. But I very much doubted whether it would stop her: she would merely take more care about her secrecy.

Yet she did not bring it off. I was certain that she was not deterred by Roy's order. Probably she was only stopped by a more remote, abstract obstacle: it was next thing to impossible to extract a trained pilot. I talked the whole affair over with the Minister. He was the most adept of men at knowing when a door would give. He shook his head, and said it was too late.

After listening to Rosalind, I had to speak to Roy alone. He had borrowed a house in Cambridge for her and the baby; he was training on an East Anglian airfield, and it was long odds that he would be stationed on one the following spring; he could get back to Cambridge often. I wrote that I must see him; I would take an evening off: could he arrange to dine in hall one night?

When I arrived at the college, it was just before dinner time. Roy was waiting for me at the porter's lodge. He was wearing one of his old elegant suits, and had a gown thrown over his shoulder.

He called out my name.

We walked through the court. It was half-past seven on an October night, and already dark. The lights at the foot of the staircase were very dim, and one could scarcely see the list of names. Mine was still there, the white paint very faded; when we passed Roy's old staircase, we saw a new name where his had been.

'On the shelf,' said Roy.

The bell began to clang. Roy mentioned, as we went towards the combination room, that he had not dined in college since he returned. I asked him why not; he was frequently in Cambridge and still a fellow.

'Too much changed,' said Roy.

'It's not much changed,' I said.

'Of course it's not,' said Roy. 'I have, though.'

Sherry in the combination room: dinner in hall; they happened as they used to. It was a small party. Arthur Brown had discovered that Roy and I were dining, had put himself down at short notice, and had asked Winslow to come in. Otherwise there was only Despard-Smith, gloomily presiding.

Much of the college was unchanged. Francis Getliffe, Roy and I were away, as well as the new Master and the two most junior fellows; the others were all in residence. There had been a few of the secular changes which everyone reckoned on, as college officers came to the end of their span; Arthur Brown, for instance, was now Senior Tutor. Some of the old men were visibly older, and one noticed the process more acutely if one saw them, as I did, at longish intervals. Winslow was not yet seventy, but he was ageing fast. His mouth had sunken deeply since I last met him the year before; his polished rudeness was going also, and he was altogether less conspicuous. His son had inflicted another disappointment on him, though not a dramatic one. Dick Winslow had not been able to get through his officer's training course, and had been returned to his unit; he was now a corporal in the Ordnance Corps, fixed there for the rest of the war. I should have liked a crack or two of old Winslow's blistering sarcasm. It was hard to see him resigned and defeated at last.

Despard-Smith showed no effects of time at all. He was seventy-six now, still spare, solemn, completely self-confident, self-righteous, expecting to get his own way by moral right. He was actually more certain of his command than we remembered him. Partly because it was harder to get spirits, which at one time he drank heavily, alone in his dark rooms: partly because the young men had gone away, and there was a good deal of executive work about the college for anyone who volunteered. Despard-Smith had taken on some of the steward's work, which Francis Getliffe had left. It was a new lease of power. The servants were grumbling, but the old man issued pernickety instructions, went into nagging detail, just as in his prime: he was able to complain with a croaking, gloating satisfaction, that he had 'to bear the heat and burden of the day'.

He greeted Roy and me with his usual bleak courtesy. Winslow's face lit up as he shook hands with Roy: 'Good evening to you, young man. May I sit next to you?'

Not much had changed, except through the passage of time. But the conversation in hall was distinctly odd. Arthur Brown had developed a passion for military detail. In his solid conservative fashion, he was as engrossed in the war as Francis Getliffe. He believed – with a passion that surprised those who took him at his face value – in 'killing Germans'. With bellicose interest, he wanted to hear about Roy's training.

Roy was going through his first practice flights at night. He said simply that he hated it.

'Why?' said Arthur Brown.

'It's dreadful, flying at night. Dark. Cold. Lonely. And you lose your way.'

It was the last phrase which made Arthur Brown frown. He interrupted Roy. He just could not believe it. Hadn't our aeroplanes got to learn to attack individual factories? Roy replied, that up to six months ago they had done well to get to the right country. Brown was angry: what was all this he had heard about factories going up in sheets of flame? And all this about pin-pointing targets? He regarded all those reports as too well established to doubt. I joined in on Roy's side. Arthur Brown was discomfited, out of humour with both of us, still not convinced. For a man so shrewd in his own world, he was singularly credulous about official news. (I remembered Schäder's remarks on how propaganda convinced everybody in time.) Here were Roy and I, his protégés and close friends: he loved us and trusted us: he realised that we both knew the facts, Roy in the flesh, I on paper: yet he found it hard to believe us, against the official news of *The Times* and the B.B.C.

But he smiled again, benignly, enjoying the treat he had prepared for us, as soon as we went into the combination room. Two decanters stood ready on the table, one of port, one of claret. In front of them was a basket of silver wicker work, full of walnuts.

'They're a bit special,' said Arthur Brown, as he confided in a discreet whisper what the two wines were. 'I'm going to ask for the pleasure of presenting them. I thought they'd be rather bracing on a foggy night. It's splendid to have the two of you back at once.'

We filled our glasses. The crack of the nuts was a cheerful noise. It was a night in that room such as we had often known in other autumns. There were wisps of mist in the courts, and the leaves were falling from the walls. Here it was warm; the rich curtains glowed placidly, the glasses gleamed; even though one liked claret better than port, perhaps one could do no better than drink port with the nuts.

Arthur Brown smiled at Roy. Despard-Smith expressed thanks in a grating voice, cracked more nuts than any of us, rang the bell and asked why salt had not been served. He finished his first glass of port before the decanter had come round to him again.

We talked as we had talked in other autumns. The Master of another college had died suddenly; whom would they elect? We produced some names in turn. Despard-Smith rejected all of ours solemnly and disapprovingly. One: 'I have heard things against him.' Another: 'That would be catastrophic, Eliot. The man's no better than a bolshevik.' A third (whose wife had deserted him twenty years before): 'I should not think his college would be easy about his private life. They ought not to take the risk of electing someone unstable. It might bring the place down round their ears.'

Then he made his own suggestion.

'Isn't he extremely stuffed?' said Roy.

Despard-Smith looked puzzled, deaf, and condemnatory.

'*Stuffed*,' Roy repeated.

'I'm afraid I don't know what you mean, Calvert. He's a very sound man. He's not a showman, but he'd sacrifice himself for his college.'

Once, I thought, Roy would have followed up with mystifying questions. But he sat back, smiled, drank his wine, and played no trick. By now Despard-Smith had got into his stride. He was, in the Master's absence, acting as chairman of the livings committee. It happened that the college's best living was still vacant. The last incumbent had gone off to become an archdeacon. The committee, which for the moment meant Despard-Smith, could not make up its mind. In reality, the old man could not bear to bestow so desirable a prize. Most of the college livings were worth four or five hundred a year, since they had not risen as the value of money fell; but this one was nearly two thousand. In the nineteenth century it had meant riches, and there had been some resolute jockeying on the part of fellows to secure it in time for their marriage. It was then, and still remained, one of the richer livings of the Church of England. Even now, it would give some clergyman a comfortable middle-class life.

'It's a heavy responsibility,' said Despard-Smith. He began to run through all the old members of the college who were in orders. He disapproved of all of them, except one or two who, for different reasons, could not be offered this living. One man had the month before taken one at three hundred and fifty a year. 'It would be no kindness to him,' said Despard-Smith, 'to go so far as mention this vacancy. He is a man of conscience, and he would not want to leave a charge he has just undertaken.'

Brown pleaded this man's cause. 'It's wretched luck,' he said. 'Can't we find a way round? I should regard it as legitimate to put in someone for a decent interval, say a year or two—'

'I'm afraid that would be a scandalous dereliction of duty,' said Despard-Smith.

Winslow drank another glass of claret, and took no part. He used, in his style as a nineteenth-century unbeliever, to make caustic interjections on 'appointments in this mysterious profession'. He used to point out vinegarishly that he had not once attended chapel. Now he had not the heart for satire.

Despard-Smith gazed at Roy with gloomy satisfaction.

'I seem to remember that Udal was a friend of yours, Calvert. He was your exact contemporary, if I'm not mistaken.'

'Just so,' said Roy.

'I needn't say that we have carefully considered whether we could invite him to take Melton. He is a man of higher intellectual quality than we are accustomed to get in the Church in its present disastrous condition. We have given Udal's name the most careful consideration, Calvert. I am very sorry to say that we don't feel able to approach him. It would only do him harm to give him exceptional promotion at his age. I was very sorry, but naturally we were thinking entirely of the man himself.'

Roy was looking at him.

'You must not say that, Despard,' said Roy, in a clear and deliberate tone. 'It is not so.'

'What do you mean, Calvert?' said Despard-Smith, with grating anger.

'I mean that you've not thought of Udal at all. You don't know him. He is a very difficult man to know. You have no idea what is best for him. And you do not care. You must not say these things.'

'I'm not prepared to listen,' Despard-Smith was choking. 'Scandalous to think that my responsibility—'

Roy's eyes were fixed on the old clergyman's, which were bleared, full, inflamed.

'You like your responsibility,' said Roy. 'You like power very much. You must not disguise things so much, Despard. You must not pretend.'

Roy had spoken throughout calmly, simply, and with extreme authority. It was exactly – I suddenly remembered – as he had spoken to Willy Romantowski; he had even used the same words. I had seen him with many kinds of human beings, in many circumstances: those two, the old clergyman and the young blackmailing spy, were the only ones I had ever heard him judge.

Arthur Brown hurriedly filled Despard-Smith's glass. I thought there was a faint appreciative twinkle under Winslow's hooded lids. The party got back to ordinary small talk. That room was used to hard words. The convention was strong that, after a quarrel, the room made an attempt at superficial peace.

So, for a few minutes, we did now. Then we broke up, and Arthur Brown took Roy and me to his rooms. He finished off his treat for us by giving us glasses of his best brandy.

Then he settled himself down to give a warning.

'I must say,' he scolded Roy, 'that I wish you hadn't gone for old Despard. I know he's irritating. But he'll stick about in this college for a long time yet, you know, and he still might be able to put a spoke in your wheel. There's no point in making an unnecessary enemy. I wish you'd wait till you've absolutely arrived.'

'No.' Roy smiled. 'We wait too long, you know. There isn't so much time.'

'I expect you think I'm a cautious old woman,' said Arthur Brown, 'but I'm only anxious to see you getting all the honours this place can give you. I am anxious to have that happiness before I die.'

'I know,' said Roy. 'But I shall need to say a word now and then.'

He said it with affection and gratitude, to the man who had guarded his career with such unselfishness and so much worldly skill. But he meant more than he said. He meant that his pupilage was quite over. He was mature now. He had learned from his life. For the rest of his time, he would know what mattered to him, whom and what to take risks for, and when to speak.

Roy took another brandy, and set Arthur Brown talking about his water colours. Roy was in no hurry to be left alone with me; he had sensed what I had come to ask, and was avoiding it. Brown liked staying with us, and it was reluctantly that he pressed our hands, said how splendid it would be when we both returned for good, promised to save 'something special' to celebrate the occasion.

Roy and I went up to my sitting-room. It struck dank through being empty for so long; there was a low smouldering fire, built up of slack.

'The old devil,' said Roy, grinning at the thought of Bidwell: since I went away, my rooms were being slowly and methodically stripped of their smaller objects.

I pulled down the old iron draught-screen to its lowest socket. Soon the flames began to roar. Roy pushed the sofa in front of the fireplace, and lay with his legs crossed, his hands behind his head.

I sat in my armchair. Those had been our habitual places in that room. I looked at him, and said:

'I want to talk a little.'

'Better leave it,' he said. 'Much better to leave it,' he repeated.

'No,' I said. 'I must know.'

'Just so,' said Roy.

'I didn't say much when you chose to—'

I hesitated, and Roy said, in a light, quiet tone:

'Try to get myself killed.'

'It was too clear,' I said.

'I got tired of struggling,' he said. 'I thought it was time for me to resign.'

'I knew that,' I said. 'I hadn't the heart to speak.'

'I told you once, you'd done all you could. Believe me. No one on earth could have done as much.'

I shook my head.

'I was no use to you in the end,' I said.

'Everyone is alone. Dreadfully alone,' said Roy. 'You've thought that often enough, haven't you? One hates it. But it's true.'

'Sometimes,' I said, in pain, 'it does not seem so true.'

'Often,' Roy repeated, 'it does not seem so true.'

Suddenly he smiled. 'I'm not as tough as you. Sometimes it wasn't true. I've not been alone always. You may have been – but I've not.'

I could not smile back.

'I hadn't the heart to speak,' I said slowly. 'It was too clear what had happened to you. But I didn't understand one thing. Why did you make that particular choice? Why did you decide to go and fly?'

With one quick move he sat upright. His eyes met mine, but they were troubled, distraught, almost – shifty.

He was for once not ready with a word.

'Was it,' I asked, 'because of that night in Dolphin Square? When you asked me what was the most dangerous thing to do?'

'Oh God,' said Roy, 'that was why I kept it from you. I was afraid you'd guess. I didn't want you to learn from other people. But if I'd told you myself what I was doing, I should have given it away. You'd have remembered that night.'

'I remember it now.'

'It was only a chance,' he said violently. 'We happened to be talking. If I hadn't seen you that night, I should have asked someone else. We happened to be talking, that was all.'

'What I said – decided you?'

'Yes.'

'You might have spared me that,' I cried.

We looked at each other; quite suddenly, reproach, remorse, guilt, all died away; the moment could hold them no more. There was no room for anything but the understanding which had sustained us for so long. We had the comfort of absolute acceptance.

In a tone that was simple and natural, Roy said:

'I wasn't mad when I decided to resign, you know. I couldn't struggle any more, but I wasn't a bit mad. Did you think I should be?'

'I wasn't sure,' I said, just as easily.

'I thought you might feel that I did it when I was lashing out. As I did with poor old Winslow once. No, it wasn't so. I haven't had one of those fits for quite a long time. But I'd been depressed for years. Until I threw in my hand. I was sad enough when you saw me, wasn't I? I was much worse when you weren't there. It was dreadful, Lewis.'

'I knew,' I said.

'Of course you did. I was quite lucid, though. All the time. Just like that night in May week. When I threw in my hand, I was frightfully lucid. Perhaps if everyone were as lucid as that, they would throw in their hand too.' He smiled at me. 'I've always felt you covered your eyes at the last minute. Otherwise why should you go on?'

It was half-envious, half-ironic: it was so intimate that it lit our faces.

'You'll always have a bit of idiot hope, won't you?' said Roy. 'I'm glad that you always will.'

'Sometimes I think you have,' I said. 'Deeper than any of your thoughts.'

Roy smiled.

'It's inconvenient – if I have it now.'

He went on:

'What would have happened to me, Lewis, if there hadn't been a war? I don't know. I believe it wouldn't have made much difference. I should have come to a bad end.'

He smiled again, and said:

'It makes things a bit sharper, that's all. One can't change one's mind. It holds one to it. That's all.'

The fire had flared up now, and his face was rosy in the glow. The shadows exaggerated his smile.

He had once said, just before the only flaw in our intimacy, that I believed in predestination. It was not true in full, and it would have been less true later in my life. I believed that neither he nor any of us could alter the essence of our nature, with which we had been born. I believed that he would not have been able to escape for good from the melancholy, the depth of despondency, the uncontrollable flashes and the brilliant calm, the light and dark of his nature. That was his endowment. Despite his courage, the efforts of his will, his passionate vitality, he could not get rid of that burden. He was born to struggle, to pursue false hopes, to know despair – to know what, for one of his nature, was an intolerable despair. For, with the darkness on his mind, he could not avoid seeing himself as he was, with all hope and pretence gone.

So far, I believed in what he called 'predestination'. I believed that some parts of our endowment are too heavy to shift. The essence of our nature lay within us, untouchable by our own hands or any other's, by any chance of things or persons, from the cradle to the grave. But what it drove us to in action, the actual events of our lives – those were affected by a million things, by sheer chance, by the interaction of others, by the choice of our own will. So between essence and chance and will, Roy had, like the rest of us, had to live his life.

It was the interplay of those three that had brought him to that moment in my room, smiling, talking of his 'bad end'. They had brought him to his present situation.

It could have happened otherwise. In any case, perhaps, he would have known despair so black that he would have been driven to 'throw in his hand', he would have felt it was time to 'resign'. That was what he meant by a 'bad end'. If we had been born in a different time, when the outside world was not so violent, it was easy to imagine ways along which he might have gone. He might not have been driven into physical danger: he might have tried to lose himself in exile or the lower depths.

But that was not his luck. He had had to make his choice in the middle of a war. And war, as he said, 'held one to it'. It made his choice one of life and death. It was irrevocable. It gave no time for the hope of the fibres, which underlay even his dark vision of the mortal state, to collect itself, steady him, and help him to struggle on.

And I felt that hope was gathering in him now. Through his marriage, through his child, perhaps ironically through the very fact that he had 'resigned' and needed to trouble no more, he had come out of the dark. Perhaps he had married Rosalind because he did not trouble any more; it was good for him not to care. He was more content than he had been since his youth. Hope was pulsing within him, the hope which is close to the body and part of the body's life, the hope that one possesses just because one is alive.

He was going into great danger. He said that it was 'inconvenient' to hope now. The mood in which he had made his choice should have lasted, But he was not to be spared that final trick of fate. He was to go into danger: but his love of life was not so low; it was mounting with each day that passed.

He was smiling, happy that we should be enjoying this evening together by my fire. Each second, each sound, seemed extraordinarily distinct. I did not want to see, I wished my eyes were closed, I could not bear the brightness of the room.

CHAPTER XXXVII

MIST IN THE PARK

Roy began to fly on bombing raids in the January of 1943. From that time, he came to see me regularly once a fortnight; it was his device for trying to ease my mind. He could come to London to visit me more easily than I could get away. He had far more leisure, which seemed a joke at my expense. His life had become strangely free; mine was confined; I did not so much as see a bombing airfield through the whole length of the war.

When we met, Roy kept nothing from me. Sometimes I thought of the days, long before, when we sat by the bedside of the old Master. He had known he must soon die for certain; the end was fixed; and, for me at least, it was more terrible because he talked only of his visitors' concerns – he, who lay there having learnt the date of his death.

Roy knew me too well to do the same. He was more natural and spontaneous than the Master; he took it for granted that I was strained, that he was strained himself; he left it to instinct to make it bearable for us both. And, of course, there was one profound difference between his condition and the Master's; Roy did not know for certain whether he would live or die.

As a rule, he called at my office in the afternoon and stayed with me until he caught a train at night. In that office he looked down into Whitehall, and told me simply that he was getting more frightened. He told me of his different kinds of fear: of how one wanted to stop short, throw the bombs away, and run for home.

'It's peculiarly indecent for me to bomb Stuttgart, isn't it? Me of all men.' (He had worked in the library there.)

I nodded.

'They'll want me to bomb Berlin soon. Think of that.'

Then he said:

'But you don't believe in bombing anyway, do you?'

'No,' I said.

'You don't think it's any use? It won't win the war?'

'I don't believe so.'

'You're pretty sure?'

'Reasonably.'

'What does he think?' Roy pointed to the door which led through to the Minister's room.

'The same.'

'Just so,' said Roy. 'He's a wise old bird. So are you, aren't you?'

He said:

'There's never been a place for me, has there?'

On those afternoons I heard something about his crew. He had become interested in them, realistically, affectionately, with amusement, just as with everyone he met, just as with the inmates of No. 32 Knesebeckstrasse. They were nearly all boys, and the oldest was twenty-six, seven years younger than himself. 'I'm getting too old for this game,' said Roy. There was a Canadian among them. Most of them were abnormally inarticulate, and Roy mimicked them to me. Some were extremely brave. 'Too brave for me,' he said.

I often speculated about what they thought of him. So far as I could gather, they did not consider him academic, donnish, or learned; it had always surprised people to discover his occupation. But also they did not think him intelligent or amusing. They liked him, they respected him as a pilot, and thought he was a kind, slightly eccentric old thing. I suspected he had gone in for some deliberate dissimulation – partly to stay anonymous, partly to shield them from what he was really like. For instance, they certainly did not know that he was a notorious lover of women. They just placed him as an uxorious married man, devoted to his daughter and inclined to show them photographs of his wife and baby.

He told me that with a smile. It was often, I reflected, odd enough to send a shiver down the spine, when one heard a friend described by other people.

It was as though each of us went about speaking a private language which no one else could understand; yet everyone caught a few words, uttered a cheerful, confident, dismissive judgment, and passed on. It reminded me of the fellows discussing Roy before he was elected.

Actually, the opinions formed by Roy's crew were quite explicable. He was devoted to the child, with a strength of feeling that at times astonished me. And he was content and comfortable with Rosalind.

During one of his visits to my office, both he and I were set to write letters that were difficult to put together. For I had heard from Joan the day before that Humphrey Bevill had just died in hospital. He had been decorated again for one of the small boat actions; then, a week or so past, his boat had been sunk and he had spent some hours in the water. His inordinate courage was a courage of the nerves, and he was as frail as he looked. He had died from exposure and loss of blood, when a normally tough young man would have recovered.

'Poor boy,' said Roy. 'It must have been dreadful to go out and fight – and then come back in an hour or two. Everything clean and normal. It makes it much harder.'

He said that he felt it acutely himself. In the daytime he would be at home in peace, all tranquil. At night they would be flying out in fear. Next morning he came back home again. It would have been easier if all his life were abnormal, disturbed, spent nearer the dark and cold. It would have been easier in trenches in a foreign country. Here the hours of danger were placed side by side with days of clean sheets, in familiar rooms with one's child, one's wife and friends.

'Poor boy,' said Roy. 'He wouldn't have had a happy life, would he?'

We each wrote separate letters to Lord and Lady Boscastle.

'It's hard to write,' said Roy. 'It will break up Lord B. It's a mistake to be fond of people. One suffers too much.'

We had no doubt that Lord Boscastle would be afflicted, but even so we were amazed by the manner of his grief. I heard of it from Lady Boscastle, who wrote in reply to my letter of condolence. Herself, she was taking bereavement with her immaculate stoicism – but she seemed overborne, almost stunned, by her husband's passion of inconsolable misery. He shut himself up in Boscastle, would acknowledge no letters, not even from his family, would see no one except his servant. He had only spoken once to his wife since he heard of Humphrey's death. It was a rage of misery, misery that was like madness, that made him in sheer ferocity of pain shut himself away from every human touch.

Lady Boscastle would have liked to help him; yet, for once in her life, she felt ignorant and inept. She had never been possessed as he was now; for all her adventures, she had never been overmastered by an emotion; she had never abandoned herself to love, as her husband did, with all the wildness of his nature, first in love for her and then for his son. She could not meet such a passion on equal terms.

When Roy next came to see me, it was a warm, sunny day at the end of February; the other side of Whitehall was gilded by the soft, misty, golden light.

I told Roy about Lady Boscastle's letter.

'She's too cold,' he said. He had never liked her, though he felt a kind of reluctant, sparring admiration. 'She'll survive. But he'll live with the dead.'

Roy looked at me, and spoke with extreme gentleness and authority: 'You mustn't live with the dead too much. You could.'

He had seen me live on after my wife's death; he was the only person who had seen me close to. He knew that I had the chance of marrying again.

'If you lose me as well,' said Roy, 'you mustn't mourn too long. You mustn't let it haunt you. You must go on.'

He was pale and quiet that afternoon. He and his crew had moved a few days before to another airfield. 'They don't want us to see our losses. They need to keep us cheerful,' he said.

He went on:

'If we started with thirty aeroplanes' (he never used the current terms, but always with great precision brought out the outmoded ones, such as 'aeroplanes') 'and we notice that two don't come back each night, they think we mightn't like it much. Because we've got to make thirty trips before they give us a rest. Even if the losses are only five per cent – we might start working out our chances. They're not good, are they?'

It was such a beautiful afternoon that we went for a walk in St James's Park. The sky was a light, radiant blue; but, although it was only early afternoon, a mist was creeping on to the brilliant grass.

'Excellent,' said Roy. 'I like to see that.'

I misunderstood him.

'It is a lovely day,' I said.

'No so aesthetic,' said Roy. 'I meant – as long as this weather lasts, we shan't have to fly.'

He walked by my side, over the soft winter turf.

'Some nights,' he said in a moment, 'I'm pretty certain that I'm not coming back. I want to ask them to let me stay at home. I need to be safe. I feel like saying that I can't go through it once again. Those nights, I feel certain that I'm going to die.'

He added:

'Somehow I've come back, though.'

We walked along through the calm, warm, fragrant air. Roy turned to me, his face quite open.

'I am afraid, you know,' he said. 'I am afraid of my death.'

CHAPTER XXXVIII

AN EVENING WITHOUT INCIDENT

ON Roy's next visit, nothing of importance happened; he said nothing which struck me at the time; it was a placid evening, but I came to remember it in detail.

He was shown into my office about half-past two on a Saturday afternoon. I should not normally have been there, even in wartime, but I was preparing a draft for the Minister. Roy saw that I was writing, cocked an eyebrow, and with exaggerated punctiliousness would not come round my side of the desk.

'Too secret,' he said.

'No. Just a speech.'

Roy was light-hearted, and his mood infected me. He had the next four days free, and when he left me that evening was going on to Cambridge. He was so calm and light that I could not stay in a grey, ordinary, work-aday mood. I had nearly finished the speech, but I recalled that the Minister had one or two idioms which he always got wrong: 'they can't pull the wool over my ears,' he used to say with great shrewdness. I was fond of him: it occurred to me that those idioms should be inserted in the speech. I told Roy what I was doing.

'I thought you'd become much too responsible.' He smiled with cheerful malice. 'Remarkable occupation for a high civil servant. You should model yourself on Houston Eggar. I'm afraid you'll never catch him up.'

When we went down into the street, Roy said that he needed some books for the next four days. So we took a bus, cut down Charles II Street, and reached the London Library before it closed. Roy bent over a rack of recent books; his nose looked inquisitively long, since the peak of his cap cut off his forehead. He talked about one or two of the books. Then suddenly, with an expression serious and concerned, he pointed to a title. He was pointing to a single word – FISH. 'Lewis,' he said, in a clear, audible tone, 'I'm losing my grip. I've forgotten the Soghdian for fish.'

He looked up, and saw a member, fat, stately, in black hat and fur-lined overcoat, walking out with books under his arm. 'I wonder if he knows,' said Roy. 'I need to ask him.'

Roy stepped in front of the fat man, and gave him a smart salute.

'Excuse me, sir,' he said, 'but I have forgotten the Soghdian for fish. Can you help me?'

'The what?'

'Soghdian.'

'I'm afraid not.'

'One ought to keep one's languages up,' said Roy: his gaze was solemn, reproving, understanding. 'It's terrible how one forgets them. Isn't it?'

Hypnotised, the member agreed that it was. Roy let him go.

On the bus to Dolphin Square, the word returned to Roy. He professed extreme relief. The bus racketed and swayed round the corner at Victoria. Roy said:

'If I live, I shall go back to the Soghdian, you know. I may as well.'

'I think you should,' I said.

'I shall become extremely eminent. And remarkably rude.'

'I wish you'd study that whole Central Asian civilisation. It must be very interesting – how did it keep alive? and why did it die?'

'You always wanted me to turn into a journalist,' said Roy. 'I'm too old to change now. I shall stick to something nice and sharp.'

In my flat, we made a kind of high tea, since Roy was catching a train just after seven. But it was a high tea composed of things we had not eaten for a long time. I had a small hoard of foods that once we ate and did not know how good they were – butter, strawberry jam, a few eggs. We had bought a loaf of bread on our way; we boiled a couple of eggs each, and finished with several rounds of bread and butter and jam.

'Excellent,' said Roy. 'This is good stuff.'

Afterwards, we made another pot of tea; Roy lay on the sofa, smoked a cigarette, asked me about my love affair.

For I had fallen in love in the middle of the war. It had given me days of supernatural brilliance among the pain, anxiety and darkness.

'You should let me vet them,' said Roy. 'I still don't like the sound of her.'

'She wouldn't do for you,' I said.

'You like women who wouldn't do for anyone, old boy. Such as Lady B.'

'Life wouldn't have been dull,' I said, 'with Lady B.'

Roy smiled mockingly.

'You've not tired yourself out, have you?' he said. 'So much has happened to you – and yet you still don't need life to be dull.'

He gave me advice, made me promise to arrange a dinner with both him and the young woman. Once I turned and caught him watching me, a half-smile on his lips, his eyes intent.

Then he said:

'We haven't had a walk for a long time, have we? Walk with me to the station.'

It was several miles, but I was glad to. We were both active that day. As soon as we got into the open air, we felt the prick of a Scotch mist, almost a drizzle. I asked if he minded about his buttons.

'Never mind them,' he said. 'Rosalind will clean them tomorrow. She likes to.'

The drizzle persisted, but the moon was getting up behind the clouds, and the last of the daylight had not quite faded. Along the Embankment to Westminster it was not oppressively dark; the derelict houses of Millbank stood blacker than the sky, and on our right there was a sheen upon the water. The tide was running full, and brought a smell from the sea.

'It's a good night,' said Roy.

We left the river at Westminster, strolled down Whitehall, and then went back to the Embankment as far as Blackfriars Bridge. Trams clanked past us, sparks flashing in the dusk. Now and then a torch shone a beam on the wet road. Roy recalled jokes against us both, predicaments we had run into when we were younger, the various attempts to domesticate us.

'They got me at last,' he said. 'They got me at last.'

He talked fondly of his daughter.

'I wonder what she'll be like,' he said. 'She won't be stupid, will she?'

I smiled.

'I hope not,' said Roy. 'I've got a feeling she'll be anxious to please. If so, there'll be trouble for someone.'

He took my arm, and went on:

'They mustn't teach her too much. They mustn't teach her to hold herself in. I'd like her to be easy. She's my daughter. She'll find the dark things for herself.'

Arm-in-arm, we went up Ludgate Hill towards St Paul's. Roy was talking with affection about one who 'held herself in' – Lady Muriel. She must not be let loose on her godchild; he teased me about all her efforts to make me respectable in a way fitting to my station.

'Yet you dote on her,' I said.

'Ah, she needs so much love.'

'And Joan?'

He never laughed much about Joan. Of all the people we knew intimately, she was the only one he never mimicked. Even that evening, when he was so free, when his feelings flowed like quicksilver, he paused.

'And Joan?' I repeated.

'She needs more still,' said Roy.

We passed the cathedral; the rain was pattering down, but by now the invisible moon was high enough to lighten the sky, so that we could see the waste land close by; we stopped on the city side, near what used to be Bread Street, and gazed at the empty expanse under the gentle rain.

'Not pretty,' said Roy.

'No,' I said.

Then we discovered that we had cut it fine, if he were to catch his train. We walked fast the rest of the way to Liverpool Street. 'Good for you,' said Roy, as he made the pace.

He was smiling as we entered the station. 'I'll send you a book,' he said, with a flick in his voice, as though he were playing an obscure joke.

He had only two minutes to spare. The train was at the platform, the carriage-doors were being shut, men were standing in the corridors. Roy ran towards it, waving back at me. He was the most graceful of men – but I thought then, as I used when he ran up to bowl, how he suddenly ceased to be so as he ran. His running stride was springy and loose but had a curious, comic, rabbit-like lollop. He got a place in the corridor and waved again: I was smiling at the picture of him on the run.

CHAPTER XXXIX

GRIEF

The following Friday afternoon, I was in my office reading through a file. The telephone bell rang: it was a trunk call. There were mutters, faint sounds at the other end – then Arthur Brown's rich, steady, measured voice.

'Is that you, Lewis?'

'Yes.'

'I have bad news for you, old chap.'

'Yes.'

It did not need saying, but the deliberate voice went on:

'Roy Calvert is missing from last night. His wife has just been in. I'll see that she is properly looked after. She's taking it very sturdily.'

'Thank you, Arthur.'

'I'm more sorry than I can say. I suppose there is a little hope, but I cannot hold it out to you.'

I did not reply.

'If he is dead,' Arthur Brown's voice came firmly, 'we have lost someone who will never be replaced.'

For nights I could not sleep – or when I did, awoke from nightmares that tormented me as Roy's had once tormented him. I thought of his nightmares, to get away for a second from my own. For mine, in those first nights, were intolerable with the physical imagination of his death. Sleeping or waking, I was lapped by waves of horror. A word would bring him back – 'stuffed' or 'Welsh' or often one that was not his special use – and I could not shut out the terrifying pictures of the imagination: the darkness, the face in the fire, the moments of unendurable anguish and fear, the face in the fire, the intolerable agony of such a death.

Nothing could guard me from that horror.

While that physical dread swept over me night and day, I could not bear to see anyone who wanted to give me hope. I could not bear to see anyone who knew him. I got through my committees somehow. I did my work. For the rest, I went about alone, or searched for company. Any company that would not bring him back.

This was the second time I had known intense grief through death. I could understand well enough the mad, frantic, obsessed concentration on his grief into which Lord Boscastle threw himself after the death of his son. I could understand well enough how some in grief squandered themselves in orgies.

After a fortnight of those days and nights, the first shock lessened. I had still spoken to no one about him, though I had managed to write a note to Rosalind. I found myself searching for recollections of him. Time after time, I went over each detail of that last evening: it had seemed so light and casual when it happened, far less significant than a hundred other times we had talked together. Now I knew it off by heart. I kept asking myself questions to which there could never be an answer: just because of that they were sharp as a wound. What was the book that I should never receive? When he talked of his daughter, was he giving me instructions? Did he fear that this was his last chance to do so? Had he been fey that evening? Was he acting so lightly, to give me peace?

Then came the final news that he was dead. It was not an added shock. It meant only that I could indulge myself no longer. It was time to see others who were stricken. I should have avoided it if there had been a way: there was nothing for it but to go among them, and listen.

I sat through a night in Charles Street with Lady Muriel and Joan. Joan was prostrate and speechless, her face brooding, white, so still that it seemed the muscles were frozen. Of those who loved him, perhaps she suffered most. Lady Muriel was like a rock. In the first shriek of pain, her daughter had told her everything about her love for Roy. Lady Muriel had forgotten propriety, had forgotten control, and had tried to comfort her. Lady Muriel had never been able to speak from her own heart; she had never seen into another's; but when Joan came to her in agony, she lavished all her dumb, clumsy, overpowering affection. It was better for Joan than any subtler sympathy. For the first time since her childhood, she depended on her mother. She gained a deep, primitive consolation. Like all of us, she had laughed at Lady Muriel; she had produced for Roy's benefit some of the absurdities, the grotesque snobberies, the feats of misunderstanding, which Lady Muriel incorrigibly perpetrated; but after Joan was driven to tell Lady Muriel how she suffered, she felt again that her mother was her one support.

I thought that, of the two, Lady Muriel would be more crippled. For Joan was very strong; she had not a happy nature, but underneath there was a fierce, tough vitality as unquenchable as her mother's; and she was still young. She would never be quite the same through knowing Roy – but I believed she was resilient enough to love again with all her power.

It would not be so for Lady Muriel. It had taken an unusual man to tease her, to see that she was not formidable, to make her crow with delight. To find a friend like Roy – so clear-sighted, so utterly undeceived by exterior harshness – was a chance which would not come again. With age, disaster and loss, she was becoming on the outside more gruff and unbending. She would put everyone off, more completely than in the past. It would only be Joan who came close to her. Yet that night, her neck was stiff, her head upright, as she said goodbye in the old formula.

'Good evening, Mr – Lewis. It was good of you to come and see us.'

I went to see Rosalind in Cambridge. She had hoped right up to the end. She had seemed callous and thoughtless to many people; but I noticed that, in a few weeks, the hair on her temples had gone grey. I mentioned it.

'It doesn't matter,' she cried. 'He won't see it, will he?'

She sobbed most of the time I was with her. She was trying to recapture every physical memory of him. She wanted to think of him, feature, skin and muscle, until she could recreate him in the flesh.

It was pagan. It was what I had felt when Sheila died. It was what all human beings felt, I thought, when someone dies whom they have loved in the body. Above all with sexual love – but also with the love one bears a son or anyone who is physically dear. If one has been truly bereaved, all resignation is driven away. Whatever one's mind says, one craves that they may live again. One cannot help but crave for resurrection and a life to come. But it would all be meaningless, a ghastly joke, without the resurrection of the body. One craves for that above all. Anything else would be a parody of the life we cry out to have restored. Rosalind did not believe in an afterlife, did not believe in resurrection, either of the body or anything else; she believed that Roy had gone into annihilation. Yet with every atom of her whole existence, she begged that he might come to her again in the flesh.

We all found a kind of comfort in anything to do with his memory: as though by putting ourselves out, by being busy, by talking of him and making arrangements, we were prolonging his life. So Arthur Brown spent days organising the memorial service; and I occupied myself with the obituaries. It seemed to push back the emptiness – and I became obsessed, beyond any realism, beyond any importance that they could possibly carry, that the notices should praise his work and should not lie. I wanted them to say that he was a great scholar, and try to explain his achievement. For the rest, let them say as little as could be. It was hard to tell the truth about any man; the conventional phrases, the habits of thought which came so glibly, masked all that men were like. For Roy to be written about in the 'stuffed' terms which he had spent so much of his life mocking – that I found painful out of proportion. He had spoken of himself with nothing but candour: with none of the alleviating lies which helped the rest of us to fancy ourselves at times: with a candour that was clear, light, naked and terrible. It would be too much of an irony to have that tone silenced, and hear the public voices boom out about his virtues and his sacrifice.

I broke my silence about my own feelings in order to get Arthur Brown's help. He saw the point; he saw also that I was obsessively moved, and exerted himself for my sake as well as Roy's. The chief obituaries finally appeared as curiously technical, bare, and devoid of human touches; they puzzled and disappointed many people.

Perhaps because I was silent about Roy's death, I did not receive much sympathy myself. One or two near to me were able to intrude. Otherwise, I would rather have things as they were, and hear nothing.

Lady Boscastle wrote to me delicately and gracefully. And, to my astonishment, I had a note from her husband. It was short:

'My dear Eliot, They tell me that Roy Calvert is dead too. When last I saw you, those young men were alive. I had my son, and you your friend. I have no comfort to offer you. It is only left for us to throw away the fooleries of consolation, and curse into the silly face of fate until our own time comes. B.'

I was given one other unexpected sign of feeling. One night I was sitting in my office; the memorial service was taking place next morning, and I was just above to leave for Cambridge. The attendant opened the door, and Francis Getliffe came in.

'I'm very sorry about Calvert,' he said without any introduction, curtly and with embarrassment.

'Thank you, Francis,' I said.

'The memorial service is tomorrow, isn't it?'

I was surprised at the question, for Francis was rigid in never going inside the chapel. He and Winslow were the only unbelievers in the college who made it a matter of principle.

'Yes.'

'I'd come,' he said. 'But I've got this meeting. I daren't leave it.'

Francis had been found unimportant jobs, had been kept off committees, since he opposed the bombing campaign. He was just forcing his way back.

'No, you mustn't,' I said. 'It's good of you to tell me, though.'

'I didn't understand him,' said Francis. 'I'm sorry we didn't get on.'

He looked at me with a frown of distress.

'He must have been a very brave man,' he went on. He added, with difficult, friendly concern: 'I'm sorry for you personally, Lewis.'

CHAPTER XL

MEMORIAL SERVICE

I was lying awake the next morning when Bidwell pulled up the blind. The room filled with the bright June sunlight; above the college roofs, the sky was a milky blue.

'It's a sad old day, sir,' said Bidwell.

I muttered.

'I wish I was bringing you his compliments, sir, and one of his messages.'

Bidwell came to the side of the bed, and gazed down at me. His small cunning eyes were round and open with trouble.

'Why did he do it, sir? I know you've got ways of thinking it out that we haven't. But I've been thinking it out my own way, and I don't feel right about it now. He'd got everything he could wish for, hadn't he, sir? He wasn't what you'd call properly happy, though he'd always got a joke for any of us. I don't see why he did it. There's something wrong about it. I don't claim to know where. It won't be the same place for me now, sir. Though he did give me a lot of trouble sometimes. He was a very particular gentleman, was Mr Calvert. But I should feel a bit easy if I knew why he did it.'

When I went out into the court, the smell of wistaria – with pitiless intensity – brought back other mornings in summer. The servants were walking about with brushes and pans; one or two young men were sitting in their windows. For a second, I felt it incredible that Roy should be dead; it was so incredible that I felt a mirage-like relief.

Then in reaction I was gripped by savage resentment – resentment that these people were walking heedlessly through the court, resentment that all was going on as before. Their lives were unchanged, they carried no mark, they were calling casually to each other. I felt, with a sudden chill, the irrevocability of death.

The bell began to toll at a quarter to eleven. Soon the paths in the court were busy with groups of people moving to the chapel. From my window, I saw the senior fellow, Gay, who was in his eighties, hobbling his way there with minute steps. Lady Muriel and Joan followed him, both in black; as at the old Master's funeral, they walked with their backs stiff and their mouths firm.

I took my place in the fellows' stall. The chapel was full, as full as it had been for the funeral of Vernon Royce. Roy had been a figure in the town, and there were many visitors from other colleges. There was also Foulkes, in uniform, and a knot of other orientalists, sitting together. All the fellows had come except Getliffe, Luke (who was at his reasearch establishment) – and old Winslow. Stubborn to the last, he had decided he would not set foot in the chapel – even to honour the memory of a young man he liked. It was like his old proud, cross-grained self.

There were many women in the chapel. Rosalind was given a stall by the Master's; she was veiled and weeping. Lady Muriel and Joan sat just under her. Mrs Seymour was placed near the undergraduates. There were other, younger women, some of whom I knew slightly or had heard of from Roy. One or two I did not know at all – one struck me in particular, for she was beautiful.

'There seems to be several widows,' I heard someone in front of me whisper. He came from another college. I did not mind. I was ready for them to know him as he was.

For days past there had been a hidden bitter dispute in the college about who should officiate at the service. By all tradition, convention, and precedent, Despard-Smith had an unshakeable claim. He was the only fellow in orders; he had taken every memorial service for the last thirty years; he assumed that as of right he would preside at this one, as he had done at the old Master's.

But Arthur Brown did not like it. He remembered Despard-Smith's oration about Royce. That had been bad enough. What was worse, Brown had heard that last conflict between the old man and Roy. He knew, and so did most of the fellows, that Despard-Smith had been an enemy of Roy's, throughout his time there. Brown also knew that Despard-Smith was one of the few people alive who did not come within Roy's charity.

Brown was the last man in the college to make an unnecessary disturbance; he was willing to put up with a great many nuisances for the sake of a decent and clubbable life; and no one had more respect for precedent. But he could not let this pass. It was not fitting for Despard-Smith to speak in memory of Roy. Brown used all his expertness, all his experience of managing awkward situations, all his ability to get hints dropped and friendly representations made: but nothing came of it. Despard-Smith took it for granted that he would celebate the service. Brown caused it to be suggested by other fellows that Calvert had intimate friends, such as Udal, in the Church. It would give great pleasure if one of those officiated. Despard-Smith said that it would be reprehensible on his part to forsake his duty.

At last Brown fell back on the extreme obstinacy which he always held in reserve. He decided to 'have it out' with the old man. For Brown, who disliked any unpleasant scene, it was an ordeal. But I had no doubt that he spoke his mind with absolute firmness. Even when Despard-Smith would not give way. He could not abrogate his moral responsibility, he said. If his taking the service gave too much offence, then there should be no service at all.

All that Brown could secure was a compromise about the actual oration. Despard-Smith was willing to be guided by Calvert's friends upon what should be said. He would not pledge himself to use any specific form of words. But, if Brown gave him the notes for an address, he would use them so far as he felt justified.

So that morning Despard-Smith took the service. He looked younger than usual, buoyed up like other old men when a young one died – as though re-invigorated because he was living on.

He did his office with dignity. Despite his age he was still spare, bleak, and erect. He viewed the crowded chapel severely: his voice had not lost its resonance. Some of the women cried as he spoke of Roy. Lady Muriel and Joan were dry-eyed, just as they had been at the old Master's funeral. Just as at that service, Despard-Smith got through his work. Brown frowned, heavy-faced, his high colour darkened, throughout the address.

I was glad when it was over. The old clergyman told us, as he had told us before at other memorial services, that there was no sorrow in death for him who had passed over. 'He has gone in great joy to meet his God. There should be no sorrow for the sake of our dear colleague. It is we who loved him who feel the sorrow. It is our lives which are darker, not his. We must try to conquer our deprivation in the thought of his exceeding joy.'

That was common form. So was much of what he said about Roy's life in college – 'very quiet in all his good actions, never seeking power or fame or worldly pleasures, never entertaining an unkind thought, never saying an unkind word.'

He had said almost exactly the same of Vernon Royce: I remembered catching a flash in Roy's eye as he heard that last astonishing encomium.

Then Despard-Smith put in something new.

'Our dear colleague was young. Perhaps he had not yet come to his full wisdom. If he had a fault, perhaps it was to be impatient of the experience that the years bring to us. Perhaps he had not yet learned all that the years must tell us of the tears of things. *Lachrymae rerum*. The tears of things. But how fortunate he was, our dear colleague, to pass over in the glory of his youth, before he tasted the tears of things. There is no sorrow in such a death. To have known only the glory and happiness of youth, and then to cast away life for one's country. "Dulce et decorum est pro patria mori".'

The old man realised he had departed from his brief. He was a man who stuck to his contract; he adjusted his spectacles, fumbled with his notes, and began to read Arthur Brown's version. It was clear and simple. Despard-Smith read it monotonously, without much meaning or inflection until the end. Brown had put down Roy's great successes. And he had written: 'He could have stayed in safety. But he chose otherwise. The heart knows its own bitterness.' Brown meant it as a comment on Roy's whole experience, but Despard-Smith read it as mechanically as the rest.

The service ended. The fellows filed out first. Arthur Brown pressed my hand without a word. I wanted to escape before the others came into the court. I went across quickly to my rooms in the bright sunlight. The cold wind was getting up.

I had a few last things to do. Our belongings in college had been mixed up together. I happened to have a safe in my room, and there he had stored some of his manuscripts. I unlocked it, took out one or two of his papers, read through them, considered how they should be disposed of. Then I went down to the college cellar, under the kitchen. For years we had shared a section of the cellar together; we did not buy much wine, but there were a few dozen bottles of mine on the top racks, a rather less number of his below. His racks were labelled in his own hand.

Inexplicably, that sight wounded me more than anything at the service. I had been prepared for much: but to this I had no defence. I could not bear to stay there. Without any plan or intention, I went up into the court, began walking through the streets.

It was dark in the sunshine, and difficult to see.